The Norton Anthology of World Literature

SHORTER SECOND EDITION

VOLUME 2

The Norton Anthology
of World Literature

SHORTER SECOND EDITION

VOLUME 2

W • W • NORTON & COMPANY • *New York* • *London*

W. W. Norton & Company has been independent since its founding in 1923, when William Warder Norton and Mary D. Herter Norton first published lectures delivered at the People's Institute, the adult education division of New York City's Cooper Union. The firm soon expanded its program beyond the Institute, publishing books by celebrated academics from America and abroad. By mid-century, the two major pillars of Norton's publishing program— trade books and college texts—were firmly established. In the 1950s, the Norton family transferred control of the company to its employees, and today—with a staff of four hundred and a comparable number of trade, college, and professional titles published each year—W. W. Norton & Company stands as the largest and oldest publishing house owned wholly by its employees.

Editor: Peter Simon
Assistant Editor: Conor Sullivan
Marketing Associate: Katie Hannah
Electronic Media Editor: Eileen Connell
Permissions Management: Margaret Gorenstein, Nancy J. Rodwan
Book Design: Antonina Krass
Production Manager: Jane Searle
Managing Editor, College: Marian Johnson

The text of this book is composed in Fairfield Medium with the display set in Bernhard Modern. Composition by Binghamton Valley Composition. Manufacturing by RR Donnelley & Sons.

ISBN 978-0-393-93303-1 (pbk.)

W. W. Norton & Company, Inc. 500 Fifth Avenue, New York NY 10110
wwnorton.com

W. W. Norton & Company Ltd. Castle House, 75/76 Wells Street, London W1T 3QT

1 2 3 4 5 6 7 8 9 0

Contents

The Enlightenment in Europe 91

The Rise of Popular Arts in Premodern Japan 249

The Nineteenth Century: Romanticism 281

The Nineteenth Century: Realism and Symbolism

Preface

The Norton Anthology of World Literature, Shorter Second Edition, offers many new works from around the world and a fresh new format that responds to contemporary needs. The global reach of this anthology encompasses important works from Asia and Africa, central Asia and India, the Near East, Europe, and North and South America—all presented in the light of their own literary traditions, as a shared heritage of generations of readers in many countries and as part of a network of cultural and literary relationships whose scope is still being discovered. With this edition, we institute a shift in title that reflects the way the anthology has grown. In altering the current title to *The Norton Anthology of World Literature,* we do not abandon the anthology's focus on major works of literature or a belief that these works especially repay close study. It is their consummate artistry, their ability to express complex signifying structures that give access to multiple dimensions of meaning, meanings that are always rooted in a specific setting and cultural tradition but that further constitute, upon comparison, a thought-provoking set of perspectives on the varieties of human experience. Readers familiar with the anthology's one-volume predecessor, whose size reflected the abundance of material contained within it, will welcome the new boxed format, which divides the anthology's contents into two portable and attractive volumes.

For pedagogical reasons, our structure is guided by the broad continuities of different cultural traditions and the literary or artistic periods they recognize for themselves. This means that chronology advises but does not dictate the order in which works appear. If Western tradition names a certain time slot "the Renaissance" or "the Enlightenment" (each term implying a shared set of beliefs), that designation has little relevance in other parts of the globe; similarly, "vernacular literature" does not have the same literary-historical status in all traditions; and "classical" periods come at different times in India, China, and western Europe. We find that it is more useful to start from a tradition's own sense of itself and the specific shape it gives to the community memory embodied as art. Occasionally there are displacements of absolute chronology: Petrarch, for example, belongs chronologically with Boccaccio and Chaucer, and Rousseau is a contemporary of Voltaire. Each can be read as a new and dissonant voice within his own century, a foil and balance for accepted ideas, or he can be considered as part of a powerful new consciousness, along with those indebted to his thought and example. In the first and last sections of the anthology, for different pedagogical purposes, we have chosen to present diverse cultural traditions together. The first section, "The Invention of Writing and the Earliest Literatures," introduces students to the study of world literature with works from three different cultural traditions—Babylonian, Egyptian, Judaic—each among the oldest works that have come down to us in written form, each in its origins reaching well back into a preliterate past, yet directly accessible as an image of human experience and still provocative at the beginning of the twenty-first century. The last section, "The Twentieth Century," reminds us that separation in the modern world is no longer a possibility. Works in the twentieth century are demonstrably part of a new global consciousness, itself fostered by advances in communications, that experiences reality in terms of interrelationships, of boundaries asserted or transgressed, and of the creation of personal and social identity from the interplay of sameness and difference. We have tried to structure an anthology that is usable, accessible, and engaging in the classroom—that clarifies patterns and relationships for your students, while leaving you free to organize selections from this wealth of material into the themes, genres, topics, and special emphases that best fit your needs.

In renewing this edition, we have taken several routes: introducing new authors, choosing an alternate work by the same author when it resonates with material in other sections or speaks strongly to current concerns, and adding small sections to existing larger pieces to fill out a theme or narrative line or to suggest connections with other texts. What follows is an overview of these changes.

Volume 1

Four new pieces, including Akhenaten's "Hymn to the Sun," have been added to our selection of Egyptian poetry. *The Epic of Gilgamesh* is now offered in Benjamin Foster's recent verse translation. The passages from Genesis and Exodus in the Hebrew Bible are newly translated by Robert Alter and now include the stories of Abraham and Sarah and of Moses receiving the Law. Job is newly translated by Raymond Scheindlin. (The familiar and influential cadence of the King James version is retained in our selections from the Psalms and the Song of Songs.) Selections from Homer's *Iliad*—in a dynamic recent translation by Stanley Lombardo—are newly added to the anthology, joining *The Odyssey*, which is now offered in Robert Fagles's widely praised translation. An expanded selection of Sappho's lyrics are now translated by Anne Carson, and Plato's *Apology*, by C. D. Reeve. The selections from the Chinese "Classic of Poetry" are now translated by Stephen Owen. The *Rāmāyaṇa of Vālmīki* is now offered in an increased selection and a new and exceptionally accessible translation by Swami Venkatesananda. Our selection from Barbara Stoler Miller's translation of *The Bhaghavad-Gītā* is also increased. The selections from both Catullus and Ovid have been augmented, and both are newly offered in translations by Charles Martin. Richmond Lattimore translates the selections from the New Testament. The section "India's Classical Age,"—previously consisting of only the Sanskrit drama *Sakuntala*—now contains selections from Viṣṇuśarman's *Pañcatantra*, Bhartṛhari's *Śatakatrayam*, Amaru's *Amaruśataka*, and Somadeva's *Kathāsaritsāgara*, thus providing a more wide-ranging and teachable introduction to this cultural moment. The surah "Jonah" has been added to an already extensive selection from the Koran, and the poet-mystic Jalâloddin Rumi, is newly added to this edition. One of the anthology's new complete texts is *Beowulf*, in Seamas Heaney's celebrated new translation. Marie de France is now represented by two lais—"Lanval" and "Laüstic"—in a translation by Glyn S. Burgess and Keith Busby. Dante's *Inferno* is now offered in Mark Musa's translation, and a new illustration provides students with a "map" of Dante's hell. Boccaccio's *Decameron* is now represented by three newly selected tales: the first tale of the first day (Ser Cepperello), the eighth story of the fifth day (Nastagio), and the tenth story of the tenth day (Griselda), and the entire selection is newly offered in G. H. McWilliams's translation. *Nō* drama is now represented by two plays by the great theorist of *Nō*, Zeami Motokiyo: *Atsumori* and *Haku Rakuten*. Montaigne's essay, "Of the Powers of the Imagination" has been newly added, as have a few famous episodes (and the important "Prologue" to Part II) from Cervantes's *Don Quixote*.

Volume 2

Our collection of Chinese vernacular literature adds a selection from Wu Ch'eng-en's *Monkey*. Rousseau's *Confessions* is offered in an expanded selection and in a new translation by J. M. Cohen. We are especially pleased to offer Goethe's *Faust*, Part I in Martin Greenberg's remarkable translation. Newly included lyric poets from the nineteenth century are Friedrich Hölderlin, John Keats, Heinrich Heine, Giacomo Leopardi, Victor Hugo, and Arthur Rimbaud. Our selection of Walt Whitman now adds "Out of the Cradle Endlessly Rocking." Henrik Ibsen's *Hedda Gabler* is now offered in a new translation by Rick Davis and Brian Johnston. The twentieth-century selection begins with another new complete work, Joseph Conrad's *Heart of Darkness*. The poets William Butler Yeats and Federico García Lorca are newly included. Virginia Woolf is now represented by chapters two and three of *A Room of Her Own*. Franz Kafka's *Metamorphosis* is offered in a new translation by Michael Hoffman. Closing out our selection, in addition to Chinua Achebe's *Things Fall Apart*, still offered in its entirety, are newly included short stories by Albert Camus, Tadeusz Borowski, Mahasweta Devi, Gabriel García Márquez, Nawal el Saadawi, and Leslie Marmon Silko.

The Shorter Second Edition contains all of the pedagogical support to which our users are accustomed: maps, time lines, pronunciation glossaries, and, of course, the informative introductions and notes. The thirty-two color plates new to this edition are captioned and broadly coordinated with each period. In addition, *The Norton Anthology of World Literature* now provides free access to Norton Literature Online, Norton's extensive online resource for students of literature. Each section of *The Norton Anthology of World Literature* has added new material to old favorites, allowing the teacher to keep tried-and-true works and also to experiment with different contexts and combinations. Some links are suggested by the organization of the table of contents, but there is no prescribed way of using the anthology, and we are confident that the materials presented here offer a wealth of viable options to support customized syllabi geared to specific student needs. A separate *Instructor's Guide*, with further suggestions and helpful guidance for new and experienced instructors alike, is available from the publisher on request.

Acknowledgments

Among our many critics, advisers, and friends, the following were of special help in providing suggestions and corrections: Joseph Barbarese (Rutgers University); Carol Clover (University of California, Berkeley); Patrick J. Cook (George Washington University); Janine Gerzanics (University of Southern California); Matthew Giancarlo (Yale University); Kevis Goodman (University of California at Berkeley); Roland Greene (University of Oregon); Dmitri Gutas (Yale University); John H. Hayes (Emory University); H. Mack Horton (University of California at Berkeley); Suzanne Keen (Washington and Lee University); Charles S. Kraszewski (King's College); Gregory F. Kuntz; Michelle Latiolais (University of California at Irvine); Sharon L. James (Bryn Mawr College; Ivan Marcus (Yale University); Timothy Martin (Rutgers University, Camden); William Naff, University of Massachusetts; Stanley Radosh Our Lady of the Elms College); Fred C. Robinson (Yale University); John Rogers (Yale University); Robert Rothstein (University of Massachusetts); Lawrence Senelick (Boston University); Jack Shreve (Alleghany Community College); Frank Stringfellow (University of Miami); Nancy Vickers (Bryn Mawr College); and Jack Welch (Abilene Christian University).

We would also like to thank the following people who contributed to the planning of the Second Edition: Charles Adams, University of Arkansas; Dorothy S. Anderson, Salem State College; Roy Anker, Calvin College; John Apwah, County College of Morris; Doris Bargen, University of Massachusetts; Carol Barrett, Austin Community College, Northridge Campus; Michael Beard, University of North Dakota; Lysbeth Em Berkert, Northern State University; Marilyn Booth, University of Illinois; George Byers, Fairmont State College; Shirley Carnahan, University of Colorado; Ngwarsungu Chiwengo, Creighton University; Stephen Cooper, Troy State University; Bonita Cox, San Jose State University; Richard A. Cox, Abilene Christian University; Dorothy Deering, Purdue University; Donald Dickson, Texas A&M University; Alexander Dunlop, Auburn University; Janet Eber, County College of Morris; Angela Esterhammer, University of Western Ontario; Walter Evans, Augusta State University; Fidel Fajardo-Acosta, Creighton University; John C. Freeman, El Paso Community College, Valle Verde Campus; Barbara Gluck, Baruch College; Michael Grimwood, North Carolina State University; Rafey Habib, Rutgers University, Camden; John E. Hallwas, Western Illinois College; Jim Hauser, William Patterson College; Jack Hussey, Fairmont State College; Dane Johnson, San Francisco State University; Andrew Kelley, Jackson State Community College; Jane Kinney, Valdosta State University; Candace Knudson, Truman State University; Jameela Lares, University of Southern Mississippi; Thomas L. Long, Thomas Nelson Community College; Sara MacDonald, Sterling College; Linda Macri, University of Maryland; Rita Mayer, San

Antonio College; Christopher Morris, Norwich University; Deborah Nestor, Fairmont State College; John Netland, Calvin College; Kevin O'Brien, Chapman University; Mariannina Olcott, San Jose State University; Charles W. Pollard, Calvin College; Pilar Rotella, Chapman University; Rhonda Sandford, Fairmont State College; Daniel Schenker, University of Alabama at Huntsville; Robert Scotto, Baruch College; Carl Seiple, Kutztown University; Glenn Simshaw, Chemeketa Community College; Evan Lansing Smith, Midwestern State University; William H. Smith, Piedmont College; Floyd C. Stuart, Norwich University; Cathleen Tarp, Fairmont State College; Diane Thompson, Northern Virginia Community College; Sally Wheeler, Georgia Perimeter College; Jean Wilson, McMaster University; Susan Wood, University of Nevada, Las Vegas; Tom Wymer, Bowling Green State University.

Phonetic Equivalents

For use with the Pronouncing Glossaries preceding most selections in this volume.

a as in *cat*
ah as in *father*
ai as in *light*
aw as in *raw*
ay as in *day*
e as in *pet*
ee as in *street*
ehr as in *air*
er as in *bird*
eu as in *lurk*
g as in *good*
i as in *sit*
j as in *joke*
nh a nasal sound (as in French *vin, vẽ*)
o as in *pot*
oh as in *no*
oo as in *boot*
or as in *bore*
ow as in *now*
oy as in *toy*
s as in *mess*
ts as in *ants*
u as in *us*
zh as in *vision*

The Norton Anthology of World Literature

SHORTER SECOND EDITION

VOLUME 2

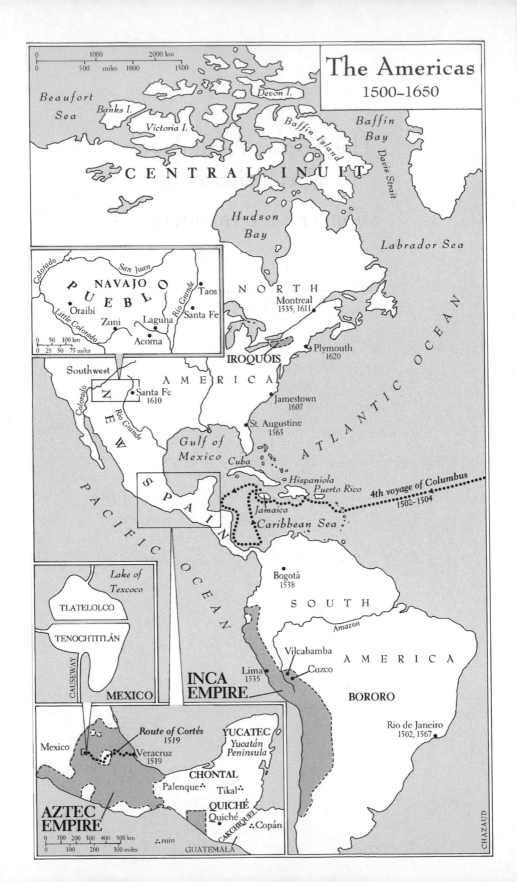

The Americas
1500–1650

Beaufort Sea

Banks I.

Victoria I.

Devon I.

Baffin Island

Baffin Bay

Davis Strait

CENTRAL INUIT

Hudson Bay

Labrador Sea

Colorado

San Juan

NAVAJO

PUEBLO

Oraibi

Little Colorado

Zuni

Laguna

Acoma

Rio Grande

Taos

Santa Fe

0   50   100 km
0 25 50 75 miles

Southwest

N   E   W

Santa Fe
1610

NORTH

AMERICA

Montreal
1535, 1611

Montreal

Plymouth
1620

IROQUOIS

Jamestown
1607

St. Augustine
1565

ATLANTIC OCEAN

Colorado

Rio Grande

Gulf of Mexico

Cuba

Hispaniola

Puerto Rico

4th voyage of Columbus
1502–1504

S   P   A   I   N

Jamaica

Caribbean Sea

PACIFIC OCEAN

Lake of Texcoco

TLATELOLCO

TENOCHTITLÁN

CAUSEWAY

MEXICO

INCA
EMPIRE

Bogotá
1538

SOUTH

Amazon

AMERICA

Vilcabamba

Lima
1535

Cuzco

BORORO

Rio de Janeiro
1502, 1567

Mexico

Route of Cortés
1519

Veracruz
1519

YUCATEC

Yucatán
Peninsula

CHONTAL

Palenque

Tikal

AZTEC
EMPIRE

QUICHÉ

Quiché

Copán

CAKCHIQUEL

0 100 200 300 400 500 km
0   100   200   300 miles

ruin

GUATEMALA

0   1000   2000 km
0   500   1000   1500 miles

CHAZAUD

Native America
and Europe
in the New World

The definitive meeting between alien cultures, an event unmatched in world history, took place the morning of November 8, 1519, as the conquistador Hernán Cortés with his band of four hundred soldiers entered the Aztec capital of Tenochtitlán. To be sure, there had been earlier expeditions, Columbus's among them, that had brought Europeans into contact with native Americans—but none that could produce the far-reaching shock of Cortés' introduction to the Aztec emperor Moteuczoma (better known in the English-speaking world as Montezuma).

The encounter provided one of the rare moments in history when life seems to imitate art. Surrounded by the dazzling architecture of a city larger than Rome, the newly arrived Spaniards compared the scene before them to the fantasies of which they had read in *Amadis of Gaul* (one of the chivalric romances to be satirized a century later in Cervantes' *Don Quixote*). In the words of the soldier-chronicler Bernal Díaz del Castillo: "We said it seemed like the things of enchantment told in the book of Amadis" and wondered aloud "if this were a dream."

As for the reluctant hosts, forewarned by couriers from the Gulf Coast, a decision had already been made that the newcomers were spirits stepped out of the pages of the Quetzalcoatl (Plumed Serpent) cycle, a body of narrative chronicling the deeds of a hero god who had fled eastward in deep disgrace but had promised to return. The interview itself was conducted in Nahuatl, the language of the Aztecs, with Cortés assisted by a pair of interpreters to get him from Spanish to Chontal (a Gulf Coast language) and from Chontal to Nahuatl. According to native records, the proceeding began with these phrases:

> CORTÉS: *Cuix ahmo teh? Cuix ahmo yeh teh? Yeh toh in tiMoteuczomah?* (Is it not you? Are you not he? Are you Montezuma?)
> MONTEZUMA: *Ca quemahca, ca nehhuatl. Toteucyoe!* (Yes, it is I. O Our Lord [i.e., Quetzalcoatl]!)

The sequence of events that preceded and followed this meeting, leading to the conquest of 1521, would be painstakingly re-created in Spanish chronicles, in the celebrated letters of Cortés, in the native-language Florentine Codex, and, for readers of English, in William H. Prescott's *History of the Conquest of Mexico* (1843), a constellation of works that would come to be esteemed for their literary as well as their historical value.

The immediate consequence of the fall of Tenochtitlán was the dismantling of an empire that had stretched from the Gulf Coast to the Pacific and from what is now the state of San Luis Potosí in central Mexico eastward to just within the present boundary of Guatemala. In due course, Tenochtitlán, or Tenochtitlán Mexico (now Mexico City), became the base from which further conquests were launched, reaching to the upper Rio Grande Valley and deep into Central America. Cortés' example inspired a generation of opportunistic intruders, notably Francisco Pizarro, whose conquest of the Inca empire of Peru was completed in 1533. Exploration by other European nations, including Britain and Portugal, had begun even before Cortés, and within a hundred years European outposts would be implanted all along the eastern rim of the Americas.

Devastating to native people and permanently disruptive to long-established cultures, the conquests nevertheless prepared the way for exchange. Wheat, livestock, horses, and firearms entered the so-called New World. From the Americas came tomatoes, chocolate, chilies, avocados (the names are all from the Nahuatl: *tomatl, xocolatl, chilli, ahuacatl*), not to mention tobacco, corn, potatoes, and the near-legendary gold and silver that heated the economy of Europe through the sixteenth century.

There were intellectual exchanges as well. In Aztec territory Spaniards, especially members of the clergy, learned Nahuatl, while native people became proficient in Spanish. Founded in 1536, the Royal College of Santa Cruz in the borough of Tlatelolco (part of Mexico City) taught young Aztec men to read and write Spanish and Nahuatl and even Latin. This Franciscan-run academy proved to be the principal training ground for what in retrospect would be recognized as the great era of Nahuatl letters, extending to about 1650. During this period Aesop's Fables, the Life of Saint Francis, portions of the Bible, and writings by Saint Augustine, Calderón de la Barca, Lope de Vega, and other authors were translated into Nahuatl.

At the same time works of Aztec verbal art were recorded for posterity in the alphabetic script of western Europe and, in some cases at least, translated into Spanish. Among the most noteworthy of these are the creation epic known as Legend of the Suns, the massive Florentine Codex (including traditional narratives, oratory, and the history of the Spanish Conquest), and the song compilation called Cantares Mexicanos. Owing to censorship and the fear of encouraging native religion, however, none of these works, whether in the native language or in translation, could be published in its own time.

The native literary materials were prepared in manuscript and stored in libraries on both sides of the Atlantic. In some cases missionary-scholars served as the recorders, writing from the dictation of a knowledgeable elder. In other cases native scribes took the lead, either writing from live recitals or transcribing, so to speak, from the old pictorial books. These often magnificent volumes were bark-paper screen-folds that opened to form a lengthy streamer, crowded with illustrations typically read from right to left. Although the pictures contained a few phonetic features, they were essentially mnemonic, intended to call forth a text that had been learned orally.

On a somewhat smaller scale, literary activity of the same sort was initiated in Maya territory in the mid-1500s. There was no academy of Maya-Spanish-Latin learning on the level of the College of Santa Cruz. But in local monasteries and in church schools gifted Maya quickly learned the new script and began preparing native-language documents for their own use. Transcriptions in the full sense of the word might have been possible using the old bark-paper books, because Maya writing—in many communities at least—had been fully phonetic.

Though the Mayan languages are entirely different from Nahuatl and make up a linguistic family in themselves (including Chontal, spoken in the Mexican state of Tabasco; Quiché, one of many Mayan languages of the Guatemalan highlands; and the widespread Yucatec Maya of the Yucatán peninsula), both cultures developed in the Mexican-Central American region known to modern anthropologists as Mesoamerica. Both show such distinguishing traits as stepped pyramids, floating gardens, specialized markets, an eighteen-month calendar, and screen-fold books. And in their verbal arts both have themes and genres in common, in particular a sacred book, or world history, in which the creation of the earth and the deeds of gods and kings are narrated in chronological sequence. The Popol Vuh of the Quiché Maya is the best-known work of this type.

The pattern of literary preservation set by the Aztec example and matched in sixteenth- and seventeenth-century Maya communities was to be repeated over the centuries and throughout the hemisphere. Again and again, after contact with Europeans, one or a few exceptional individuals would cooperate with outsiders to make a permanent record of historical narratives, prayers, song texts, or other matter. In many cases native intellectuals took a leading role or even worked on their own, independent of a missionary's or an anthropologist's agenda. The result of this activity is a vast and still growing native literature, preserved in the western European, or Latin, script and generally available to the world through translations into European languages, especially English and Spanish but also German, French, Portuguese, and Italian. (It is fascinating to contemplate what might have been the outcome had the Americas joined the Old World through contact with Asia or Africa instead of Europe.)

In view of the written record, one may speak of native American *literature* in the strict sense of the term. The works have become texts. Still it should be kept in mind that the language arts of the Maya, Zuni, Navajo, and other American cultures have continued to live in oral tradition, and even those works that have been written down and published must be regarded as mere variants, possibly to be contradicted, perhaps improved, by later recordings. Therefore, the term *oral literature,* suggesting change and spontaneous creation, is often used by students of native American speech arts, even if particular renderings may be singled out as masterworks.

The texts themselves are intimately linked to the languages from which they spring, and it is essential to recognize the uniqueness of each linguistic tradition. Estimates have placed the number of American languages spoken at the beginning of the sixteenth century at approximately two thousand, of which several hundred are still in use. Moreover, these languages have served a variety of cultures, ranging from small nomadic bands and village communities to complex, stratified societies like the Aztec, Maya, and Inca, which formerly gave rise to city-states and empires.

But in spite of differing cultures, native peoples have not lived in isolation. They have been accomplished linguists and traders and have borrowed freely across cultural boundaries, disseminating literary themes and genres and even figures of speech. As a starting point toward grasping the unity of native literature, the anthropologist Donald Bahr has proposed three basic genres: song, narrative, and oratory.

Song tends to be the most perfectly memorized of the genres, with texts sometimes varying not at all from one performer to the next. Divorced from music, as is seldom or never the case in native performance, the texts by themselves do not exhibit meter or rhyme. But the interjection of vocables, or song syllables, create patterns, and stanzas are often paired.

Narrative, by contrast, is improvised by the performer, who, while following a prescribed plot line, adds details at will. The English terms *myth* and *folktale* reflect a division recognized in many native cultures, where a more serious, more sacred, or more "ancient" kind of story is contrasted with less serious narratives felt to be "new" or "false" (that is, fictional).

Oratory, a genre more significant in native American (and African) than in European lore, encompasses prayer, educational monologues, ceremonial colloquy, and the magical prose poems, or formulas, calculated to bring about a desired result by coercion. Composed of set phrases, whose sequence may be varied considerably, oratory falls between the strictness of song and the freedom of narrative.

Obviously the most expansive of the genres is narrative, the principal vehicle for relating the deeds of deities and heroes (more rarely heroines). In many cases the hero is a trickster or has tricksterlike attributes, which means that he is gullible, clownish, ribald, conniving, or a combination of all four. Often the tale tells of twin heroes, who either aid or antagonize one another. Human in their foibles (like the Greek Olympians), these figures may also be the divine creators of the universe and of social institutions.

Mixed genres are not uncommon. Often a narrative will be punctuated by short songs. The Aztec story of Quetzalcoatl, noted earlier, tells how the ill-fated king and all his pages were tricked by sorcerers, who not only caused the priestly ruler to become drunk but steered him toward an incestuous embrace with his sister, necessitating his flight from the brilliant palace appointed with red shell and decorated with the plumage of such brilliant birds as the quetzal and the troupial:

> When the sorcerers had gotten them completely drunk, they said to Quetzalcoatl, "My child, may it please you to sing, and here's a song for you to recite." Then Ihuimecatl [one of the sorcerers] recited it for him.
>
>> I must leave my
>> house of quetzal, of quetzal,
>> my house of troupial,
>> my house of redshell.
>
> When he had gotten into a happy mood, he said, "Go get my sister Quetzalpetlatl. Let the two of us be drunk together."

Narratives interlaced with song are especially typical of Mexico and the North American Southwest. In a variation of the mixed-genre style, narratives may be punctuated by oratory. In many if not most native traditions, the stories are joined in lengthy sequences to form what may be called epics. Finally, the epic as a whole may be condensed into song or oratory for ritualized performance at winter solstice gatherings, at funerals, or on other ceremonial occasions.

In approaching this literature, the question of cultural barriers comes to the fore. Is it possible for outsiders to make meaningful contact with traditions so far removed from their own? Without doubt, the challenge is there, but so is the opportunity. The planet holds no other land mass that could have given rise to cultures (and literatures) both so varied and so completely isolated from the sphere of Europe, Africa, and Asia that has come to dominate world thinking. For the student of literature, native America reintroduces—in ways that are distinctly fresh—the role of supernatural power, the problem of humanity versus nature, and the great themes centering on social obligation and the development of the individual.

Despite its reliance on symbolism and imagery, native American literature may be regarded as essentially technological, or functional, rather than aesthetic. For the individual its function is medicinal—to facilitate safe progress toward old age and to weaken destructive powers, especially those of disease and death. For society it functions to reinforce mores drawn from the timeless realm of deities; it also reorders the natural world so as to assign the human community its proper place, at the same time preserving a link to untamed nature as the source of livelihood and power. Such considerations may be suspended as native audiences submit to the charms of music or enjoy the antics of the trickster or the deeds of the monster slayer. Close juxtaposition of the divine and the irreverent, the awe-inspiring and the comic, is one of the hallmarks of native traditions. The important point is that this literature in its own setting is not an afterthought or an amenity; it is a necessary component of individual and social well-being.

PRONOUNCING GLOSSARY

The following list uses common English syllables and stress accents to provide rough equivalents of selected words whose pronunciation may be unfamiliar to the general reader.

Cantares Mexicanos: *kahn-tah'-rays may-hee-kah'-nohs*

Cortés: *kohr-tays'*

Ihuimecatl: *ee-wee-may'-kahtl*

matasanos: *mah-tah-sáh-nohs*

Mexico: *may-shee'-koh* (in English: *meks'-ee-koh*)

Moteuczoma: *moh-tayk-soo'-mah*

Nahuatl: *nah'-wahtl*

Popol vuh: *poh-pohl' woo* (in English: *poh'-puhl voo*)

Quetzalcoatl: *kay-tzahl-koh'-ahtl*

Quetzalpetlatl: *kay-tzahl-pay'-tlahtl*

Quiché: *kee-chay'*

Tenochtitlán: *tay-nohch-tee-tlahn'*

Tlatelolco: *tlah-tel-ohl'-koh*

TIME LINE

TEXTS	CONTEXTS
	1500 Pedro Álvares Cabral sights the coast of Brazil and claims it for Portugal
	1502 Montezuma II ascends the throne of Tenochtitlán • Maya trading canoe contacted in Bay of Honduras during fourth voyage of Columbus
1508 Rodríguez de Montalvo, *Amadis of Gaul,* a chivalric romance that inspired the future conquistadors of Mexico	
1519–26 Hernán Cortés, six letters to Charles I of Spain on the conquest of Mexico, with descriptions of Aztec warfare, statecraft, and daily life	**1519–22** Voyage of Ferdinand Magellan around the world
	1521 Fall of Tenochtitlán, conquered for Spain by Hernán Cortés
	1524 Fall of Quiché, conquered for Spain by Pedro de Alvarado
	1525 Execution of Cuauhtémoc, last Aztec emperor, hanged by order of Cortés
1528 *Annals of Tlatelolco,* earliest Latin-script chronicle in the Aztec language	**1528** Beginning of civil war between Huascar and Atahualpa, rivals for the Inca throne
	1533 Fall of the Inca empire, conquered for Spain by Francisco Pizarro
1547–79 **Florentine Codex,** the encyclopedic compilation of Aztec lore and literature	
1550–81 **Cantares Mexicanos,** principal source of Aztec poetry	
1554–58 **Popol Vuh,** sacred book of the Quiché Maya of Guatemala	
1556– Books of Chilam Balam, native compilations of Maya lore, including histories, prayers, and prophecies, still in use in the Yucatán	
1558 *Legend of the Suns,* history of the world according to the Aztecs, written in the Aztec language by an anonymous scribe	

Boldface titles indicate works in the anthology.

TIME LINE

TEXTS	CONTEXTS
	1572 Fall of Vilcabamba, last outpost of the Inca empire
	1588 England defeats the Spanish Armada
1590s? Aesop's Fables translated into Aztec	**1598** Beginning of Spanish settlement in New Mexico
	1607 Founding of Jamestown, first permanent English settlement in North America
1609–17 Garcilaso de la Vega, El Inca, *Royal Commentaries of the Incas,* history of pre-Conquest Peru by an author who was himself a son of the Incas	
1611 Shakespeare, *The Tempest,* inspired in part by Silvester Jourdain's *A Discovery of the Bermudas* and thus the first major European work of imaginative literature to touch on a New World theme	
	1619 Beginning of African slavery in North America
	1620 Arrival of the *Mayflower* at Plymouth (Massachusetts), bringing English Puritans
	1630s League of the Iroquois, in existence since the 1400s, enters recorded history
1632 Bernal Díaz del Castillo, *True History of the Conquest of New Spain*	
1640 Plays by Calderón de la Barca and Lope de Vega translated into Aztec	
1649 Luis Lasso de la Vega, *Huei Tlamahuiçoltica . . .* (By means of a great miracle . . .), legend of the Virgin of Guadalupe, a cornerstone of Mexican nationalism, published in the Aztec language, Mexico City	

FLORENTINE CODEX
1547–1579

Compiled over three decades, the encyclopedic Florentine Codex represents the joint effort of the Franciscan missionary-ethnographer Bernardino de Sahagún and the knowledgeable Aztec elders and scribes who labored with him to produce a permanent record of Aztec culture. There had never been a document quite like this, and there have been few since. In view of its linguistic precision, its scope, and its objectivity, it emerges as the first work of modern anthropology.

The name Florentine Codex, it should be pointed out, is merely a latter-day scholar's designation for the most finished version of a corpus properly known as *General History of the Things of New Spain*. Several versions of the *History* have survived. But the manuscript now at the Laurentian Library in Florence, although it lacks some texts preserved in the so-called Madrid codices, is the copy that best deserves to be called complete.

Written in paired columns, with Aztec (that is, Nahuatl) on the left and a Spanish paraphrase on the right, the codex's twelve books begin with descriptions of the pre-Conquest gods and ceremonies, followed by detailed expositions of native astronomy, botany, zoology, commerce, industry, medicine, time counting, prophecy, and other topics. The final book is devoted to a native history of the Spanish Conquest.

Of particular interest for the study of literature is book 6, containing what Sahagún called "rhetoric." Voluminous and varied, it is the single richest body of Native American oratory ever assembled. Here, in native text, are the speeches used by kings on state occasions, the great prayer to the rain god Tlaloc, the admonitions addressed by fathers to their sons and by mothers to their daughters, the marriage counsels, the prayers for schoolchildren—and the remarkable sequence of midwifery orations, from which selections have been printed here.

According to the texts on midwifery, which include not only the orations but the associated customs, the midwife is chosen by the married couple's parents during the woman's seventh or eighth month of pregnancy. Shortly thereafter a party of kinswomen visit the candidate, flattering her with set speeches, calling her "artisan" and "expert," begging her to accept the contract. In response she protests, she is unworthy, others are more skilled. After seeming to disqualify herself, she abruptly relents, announcing, "Let the water be boiled."

From that moment on the expectant woman is in the care of the midwife, who now represents Night Midwife, the tutelary spirit of her profession. Similarly, the patient becomes identified with the deity Cihuacoatl Quilaztli, progenitor of the human race. Such titles are frequently invoked in the orations used as the midwife assumes her duties and prepares the "flower house," or birthing room. When the time arrives she exhorts the expectant woman, urging her to emulate Cihuacoatl Quilaztli.

If the fetus should die in the womb, the midwife removes it surgically, using an extreme form of curettage. Should the woman herself die in labor, the midwife addresses her in one of the most eloquent of the orations, initiating her into the company of the celestial soldiers and thereby conferring the highest honor of which Aztec society can conceive. The woman in labor is imagined as a warrior, seeking to bring a live captive into the world—just as the male warrior in battle seeks not to kill but to bring home a prisoner (who will be ceremonially sacrificed to the gods). Should the male lose his life in battle he joins the company of slain warriors in the eastern sky who greet the sun each morning and conduct it to the zenith; at the zenith it is handed over to the women who have died in childbirth, and it is they who lead the sun downward to the western horizon. Thus the male and female roles are mirror images of one another.

Should the woman deliver successfully, the midwife addresses her as one would greet a victorious warrior. But again, as elsewhere in the orations (and in Aztec deportment generally), humility is the watchword. The new mother must not be "boastful" of the child, respecting the will of the Creator, the supreme spirit, who both gives and takes away.

PRONOUNCING GLOSSARY

The following list uses common English syllables and stress accents to provide rough equivalents of selected words whose pronunciation may be unfamiliar to the general reader.

Cihuacoatl Quilaztli: *see-wah-koh'-aht kee-lahs'-tlee*

Nahuatl: *nah'-waht*

Sahagún: *sah-ah-goon'*

Tlaloc: *tlahl'-ohk*

Tloque Nahuaque: *tloh'-kay nah-wah'-kay*

FROM FLORENTINE CODEX

[The Midwife Addresses the Woman Who Has Died in Childbirth][1]

The woman who dies in childbirth, of whom it is said she stands up as a woman, when she dies they say she becomes a god. Then the midwife calls to her, greets her, prays to her, while she is still lying there, while she is still stretched out, saying:

Precious feather, child,
Eagle woman, dear one,
Dove, darling daughter,[2]
You have labored, you have toiled,
Your task is finished.   5
You came to the aid of your Mother, the noble lady, Cihuacoatl
    Quilaztli.[3]
You received, raised up, and held the shield, the little buckler that she
    laid in your hands: she your Mother, the noble lady, Cihuacoatl
    Quilaztli.

Now wake! Rise! Stand up!
Comes the daylight, the daybreak:
Dawn's house has risen crimson, it comes up standing.   10
The crimson swifts, the crimson swallows, sing,
And all the crimson swans[4] are calling.
Get up, stand up! Dress yourself!
Go! Go seek the good place, the perfect place, the home of your Mother,
    your Father, the Sun,[5]
The place of happiness, joy,   15

---

1. Translated by John Bierhorst. 2. Terms of endearment. "Eagle woman": implies valor. 3. Cihuacoatl (Woman Serpent) and Quilaztli (untranslatable) are names for the principle female deity. 4. Male warriors slain in battle, now in the eastern sky with the sun. 5. The sun is both mother and father.

Delight, rejoicing.

Go! Go follow your Mother, your Father, the Sun.

May his elder sisters bring you to him: they the exalted, the celestial
    women,[6] who always and forever know happiness, joy, delight, and
    rejoicing, in the company and in the presence of our Mother, our
    Father, the Sun; who make him happy with their shouting.

My child, darling daughter, lady,

You spent yourself, you labored manfully: 20

You made yourself a victor, a warrior for Our Lord, though not without
    consuming all your strength; you sacrificed yourself.

Yet you earned a compensation, a reward: a good, perfect, precious death.

By no means did you die in vain.

And are you truly dead? You have made a sacrifice. Yet how else could you
    have become worthy of what you now deserve?

You will live forever, you will be happy, you will rejoice in the company
    and in the presence of our holy ones, the exalted women. Farewell,
    my daughter, my child. Go be with them, join them. Let them hold
    you and take you in.   25

May you join them as they cheer him and shout to him: our Mother, our
    Father, the Sun;

And may you be with them always, wherever they go in their rejoicing.

But my little child, my daughter, my lady,

You went away and left us, you deserted us, and we are but old men and
    old women.

You have cast aside your mother and your father.   30

Was this your wish? No, you were summoned, you were called.

Yet without you, how can we survive?

How painful will it be, this hard old age?

Down what alleys or in what doorways will we perish?

Dear lady, do not forget us! Remember the hardships that we see, that we
    suffer, here on earth: 35

The heat of the sun presses against us; also the wind, icy and cold:

This flesh, this clay of ours, is starved and trembling. And we, poor
    prisoners of our stomachs! There is nothing we can do.

Remember us, my precious daughter, O eagle woman, O lady!

You lie beyond in happiness. In the good place, the perfect place,

You live.   40

In the company and in the presence of our lord,

You live.

You as living flesh can see him, you as living flesh can call to him.

Pray to him for us!

Call to him for us!   45

This is the end,

We leave the rest to you.

---

6. Women who have died in childbirth, now in the western sky.

[The Midwife Addresses the Newly Delivered Woman][1]

O my daughter, O valiant woman, you worked, you toiled.
You soared like an eagle, you sprang like a jaguar,
you put all your strength behind the shield, behind the buckler;
    you endured.
You went forth into battle, you emulated Our Mother,
    Cihuacoatl Quilaztli,
and now our lord has seated you on the Eagle Mat, the Jaguar
    Mat.[2]   5
You have spent yourself, O my daughter, now be tranquil.
What does our lord Tloque Nahuaque[3] will?
Shall he bestow his favors upon each of you separately, in separate
    places?
Perhaps you shall go off and leave behind the child that has arrived.
Perhaps, small as he is the Creator will summon him, will call out
    to him,   10
or perhaps he shall come to take you.
Do not be boastful of [the child].
Do not consider yourself worthy of it.
Call out humbly to our lord, Tloque Nahuaque.

1. Translated by Thelma Sullivan.   2. Warriors' seat of honor.   3. Ever Present, Ever Near, the supreme spirit.

CANTARES MEXICANOS
1550–1581

Taken from the lips of singers by native scribes during the second half of the six-teenth century, the Cantares Mexicanos ("songs of the Aztecs") is the principal sur-viving source of Aztec poetry and one of the monuments of native American literature. Voluminous and fascinating, if difficult to decipher, it has attracted a mod-ern following of scholars and poets determined to distill its essence and make fresh versions for new audiences. It is one of those bodies of work that for itself alone prompts the dedicated to study a difficult language.

The songs are composed in grammatical Nahuatl, or Aztec. But they are not imme-diately accessible, even to fluent speakers. Replete with tropes and word distortions, the Cantares diction, though some of its imagery is shared by oratory, belongs to a special genre called *netotiliztli* (freely, "dance associated with worldly entertain-ment"). Interspersed song syllables, coupled metaphors, and kennings comparable to those in Norse and Old English verse abound. And yet, even if textually obscure, the *netotiliztli* as performed in sixteenth-century Mexico were well calculated to chill the blood of European eavesdroppers. As correctly noted by the Spanish academician Francisco Cervantes de Salazar, drawing on observations made in the 1550s and 1560s, "In these songs they speak of conspiracy against ourselves."

A native document, prepared without missionary interference, the Cantares, nev-ertheless, is more than native. A better term is *nativistic*, implying work that aggres-sively reasserts—and to an extent reformulates—the values of a people under stress.

In fact some of the songs defiantly rehearse the Spanish Conquest of 1521 in ways that hint at native retribution; others introduce Christian themes overlaid by Aztec interpretations that were deeply disturbing to missionaries. No doubt a number of the pieces in the repertory had been used before the Conquest, possibly to intimidate enemy ambassadors or to inspire martial ardor or, in the case of the many satirical pieces, simply to entertain. Thus the genre has deep roots, even if reshaped by mid-sixteenth-century concerns.

War, the taking of captives, the immortalizing of slain warriors by means of song, the nature of song itself, the valor of dead kings, and the taunting of enemies and laggard soldiers are the pervasive themes. For all its hyperaesthetic imagery devoted to birds and flowers, this is an intensely masculine, militarist poetry, from which women, either as composers or performers, were apparently excluded. (It may come as no surprise to the psychoanalytically minded that the corpus includes a homosex-ual song and several pieces in which the male monologuist assumes female, even les-bian, roles.)

The two selections printed here are among the least taxing interpretively yet pro-vide a full-blown taste of the sensuous imagery for which the genre is renowned. In the first, a singer reveals his version of the Aztec theory—also expounded in surviving narratives—by which music is a sky world phenomenon reproduced on earth. The related theme of musical intoxication, much treated in the Cantares, is also intro-duced. In the second selection, a singer exhorts the fainthearted, inspiring them to emulate slain comrades now enjoying immortality in the sky. In both pieces the supreme spirit is identified as Tloque Nahuaque (Ever Present, Ever Near), a name often associated with the great god Tezcatlipoca in unacculturated lore. In the Cantares, however, the "ever present" is identified with *Dios* (God), permitting one to say, albeit with understatement, that the two songs express a modified Christianity.

In performance such texts were accompanied by the *huehuetl,* or upright skin drum (played with bare hands), and the horizontal two-toned *teponaztli,* or slit drum (played with mallets). Gongs, flutes, whistles, and other instruments might also be present, as the singer intones his phrases, punctuated by the cries of dancers in mil-itary attire. Although the program for any particular song text cannot be recon-structed, contemporary descriptions allow one to imagine a lively scene, staged as an outdoor theatrical complete with its ominous drumming and the sight of glistening unsheathed weapons.

PRONOUNCING GLOSSARY

The following list uses common English syllables and stress accents to provide rough equiva-lents of selected words whose pronunciation may be unfamiliar to the general reader.

Cantares Mexicanos: *kahn-tah'-rays may-hee-kah'-nohs*

Ce Olintzin: *say oh-leen'-tzeen*

huehuetl: *way'-wayt*

Nahuatl: *nah'-waht*

netotiliztli: *nay-toh-tee-lees'-tlee*

Otomi: *oh-doh-mee'*

teponaztli: *tay-poh-nahs'-tlee*

Tezcatlipoca: *tays-kahtl-ee-poh'-kah*

Tloque Nahuaque: *tloh'-kay nah-wah'-kay*

CANTARES MEXICANOS[1]

Song IV

Mexican Otomi[2] Song

Burnishing them as sunshot jades, mounting them as trogon feathers, I
recall the root songs, I, the singer, composing good songs as troupials:[3]
I've scattered them as precious jades, producing a flower brilliance to
entertain the Ever Present, the Ever Near.[4]

As precious troupial feathers, as trogons, as roseate swans, I design my
songs. Gold jingles are my songs. I, a parrot corn-tassel bird,[5] I sing, and
they resound. In this place of scattering flowers I lift them up before the
Ever Present, the Ever Near.

Delicious are the root songs, as I, the parrot corn-tassel bird, lift them
through a conch of gold, the sky songs passing through my lips: like sunshot jades I make the good songs glow, lifting fumes of flower fire, a singer
making fragrance before the Ever Present, the Ever Near.

The spirit swans[6] are echoing me as I sing, shrilling like bells from the Place
of Good Song. As jewel mats, shot with jade and emerald sunray, the
Green Place[7] flower songs are radiating green. A flower incense, flaming
all around, spreads sky aroma, filled with sunshot mist, *as* I, the singer, in
this gentle rain of flowers sing *before the Ever Present, the Ever Near.*[8]

As colors I devise them. I strew them as flowers in the Place of Good Song.
*As jewel mats, shot with jade and emerald sunray, the Green Place flower
songs are radiating green. A flower incense, flaming all around, spreads sky
aroma, filled with sunshot mist, as I, the singer, in this gentle rain of flowers
sing before the Ever Present, the Ever Near.*

I exalt him, rejoice him with heart-pleasing flowers in this place of song.
With narcotic fumes my heart is pleasured. I soften my heart, inhaling
them. My soul grows dizzy with the fragrance, inhaling good flowers in
this place of enjoyment. My soul is drunk with flowers.

Song XII

Song for Admonishing Those Who Seek No Honor in War

Clever with a song, I beat my drum to wake our friends, rousing them to
arrow deeds, whose never dawning hearts know nothing, whose hearts lie
dead asleep in war, who praise themselves in shadows, in darkness. Not in
vain do I say, "They are poor." Let them come and hear the flower dawn
songs drizzling down incessantly beside the drum.

---

1. Translated by John Bierhorst. 2. Here an Aztec warrior class distinguished by superior achievement;
usually the name of a non-Aztec ethnic group. 3. Tropical orioles. "Trogon": a brilliant tropical bird.
4. Tezcatlipoca, the all-powerful Aztec deity. 5. A tiny yellow songbird not otherwise identified; here
joined with the parrot, implying that the singer resembles either or both. "Roseate swans": roseate spoon-
bills or their feathers. 6. Gorgeous birds of the sky world, formerly warriors on earth. 7. Evidently
the sky world, but terms such as "Good Song" and "Green Place" may also designate the singer's earthly
locale, beautified by music, war deeds, or both. 8. Passages in italics indicate the translator is filling out
an "et cetera" in the text.

Sacred flowers of the dawn are blooming in the rainy place of flowers that belongs to him the Ever Present, the Ever Near. The heart pleasers are laden with sunstruck dew. Come and see them: they blossom uselessly for those who are disdainful. Doesn't anybody crave them? O friends, not useless flowers are the life-colored honey flowers.

They that intoxicate one's soul with life lie only there, they blossom only there, within the city of the eagles, inside the circle, in the middle of the field, where flood and blaze are spreading, where the spirit eagle shines, the jaguar growls, and all the precious bracelet stones[1] are scattered, all the precious noble lords dismembered, where the princes lie broken, lie shattered.

These princes are the ones who greatly crave the dawn flowers. So that all will enter in, he causes them to be desirous, he who lies within the sky, he, Ce Olintzin,[2] ah the noble one, who makes them drizzle down, giving a gift of flower brilliance to the eagle-jaguar princes, making them drunk with the flower dew of life.

If, my friend, you think the flowers are useless that you crave here on earth, how will you acquire them, how will you create them, you that are poor, you that gaze on the princes at their flowers, at their songs? Come look: do they rouse themselves to arrow deeds for nothing? There beyond, the princes, all of them, are troupials, spirit swans, trogons, roseate swans: they live in beauty, they that know the middle of the field.

With shield flowers, with eagle-trophy flowers, the princes are rejoicing in their bravery, adorned with necklaces of pine flowers. Songs of beauty, flowers of beauty, glorify their blood-and-shoulder toil. They who have accepted flood and blaze become our Black Mountain friends, with whom we rise warlike on the great road.[3] Offer your shield, stand up, you eagle jaguar!

---

1. "Eagle," "jaguar," and "bracelet stones" denote the noble warrior. "City of the eagles" and "the circle" signify the battlefield.   2. One Movement, a calendrical sign, or the tutelary spirit of that sign; that is, Tezcatlipoca.   3. Here the sun's road to the sky. Black Mountain represents, perhaps, paradise. The ordinary meaning is: Our comrades with whom we march down the causeway ("great road") that leads from the Mexican capital (which was surrounded by water) to Black Mountain (a town traditionally at war with Mexico).

POPOL VUH
1554–1558

A compendium of stories cherished by the ancient, the colonial, and even the modern Maya, the Popol Vuh of the sixteenth-century Quiché people of Guatemala has been compared with the *Odyssey* of the Greeks and the *Mahābhārata* of India. Such omnibus compositions, repeatedly mined by the artist and the moralist, serve as cultural touchstones; they dramatize the life of a nation and help bind it together. In the case of the Popol Vuh, as with similar works, the stories have been woven together to form an epic, with threads of continuity that may be called novelistic. On account of this seemingly modern feature, rare in New World literatures, the Quiché book strikes nonnative observers as the single most significant work of Native American verbal art. Viewed from yet another perspective, focusing on its lofty account of world creation and tribal origins, it has been called America's Bible.

But if the Popol Vuh is comparable, it is also different. By Western standards it might be judged too formal—and at the same time too earthy. Derived from a fascination with numbers, its formalism is expressed stylistically in the pairing, tripling, and quadrupling of phrases. Major characters, likewise, are paired, acting almost as duplicates of one another; deities also are paired, occasionally tripled, with a strong suggestion that they are the same. The structure of the work itself is reiterative, fitted to a traditional pattern of four successive worlds, or creations: the first three are said to have ended in failure, our own is the fourth. Yet against this stately patterning, the hero-gods appear as light-hearted boys, even as tricksters. Their adventures—from which ribaldry is not excluded—have a playful, anecdotal quality. For the uninitiated reader willing to accept this juxtaposition of the sacred and the profane, the high and the low, an experience both rewarding and unusual lies in wait.

Despite the best efforts of scholarship, the author of the Popol Vuh remains anonymous. It has been generally assumed that he is a man—because known scribes of the period are male—and, with less agreement, that he is a lone composer who uses the authorial *we* (some have conjectured a team of authors). Evidently, he is a native of the town variously called Utatlán, Rotten Cane, or Quiché, political center of the pre-Columbian confederacy that controlled most of the Guatemalan highlands.

Inevitably, following the conquest of Mexico in 1521, Spanish imperialism cast its eye toward Guatemala, and in 1524, after a brief struggle, Quiché fell to Spanish and Mexican troops under the command of the red-haired conquistador Pedro de Alvarado (called "the sun" by native people). By the 1530s, Quiché scribes, presumably including the Popol Vuh author, were being trained to use alphabetic writing. From internal evidence in the manuscript, coordinated with other records, the date of the Popol Vuh has been tentatively fixed at 1554–58.

In the text itself the author hints at the existence of a certain "council book" (*popol vuh*), presumably a pre-Columbian screen-fold that served him as a source. The sixteenth-century Quiché were well acquainted with books of this sort, some dating from the classic period of Maya culture (100–900 C.E.), which saw the rise of such imposing centers as Tikal, Copán, and Palenque. By the time of European contact those important sites, abandoned in the mysterious collapse of Maya civilization ca. 900 C.E., lay in ruins. But Maya learning survived along the rim of the now-depopulated central area, notably in southern Guatemala among the Quiché and their neighbors, also in the northern part of the Yucatán peninsula. As Mayanists have recently demonstrated, the old books do contain phonetic writing. But judging from the few examples that have been preserved, it is likely that even during the classic period extended narratives were transmitted orally, with the picture-filled books acting only as prompts. The conclusion usually drawn is that the Popol Vuh is by no means a transcription of ancient screen-folds; yet it no doubt borrows from them.

Though not so indicated in the manuscript, the Popol Vuh falls naturally into four parts, as most translators have recognized. The first three attempts at creation—that is, the creation of humans—are compressed into Part 1, saving the climactic dawning of the sun, preceded by the fourth, successful creation of humans, for the opening passages of Part 4.

The first sunrise, typically, is the defining event in Mesoamerican chronology. Before it, the world is in darkness or is lit by mere substitute suns. The earth's surface, moreover, is said to be soft and moist; it does not harden until the sun finally comes up. During the dark, or soft, time all things are possible. Thus Parts 1, 2, and 3 of the Popol Vuh relate the events of a formative age. History, it may be said, begins with Part 4. In the version printed here the translator has chosen to set off the concluding passages of Part 4, labeling the most recent phase of history "Part 5." The selections printed here were chosen to represent each of these five parts.

As the author plainly states in the preamble that begins Part 1, "We shall write about this now amid the preaching of God, in Christendom now." Admittedly, then, the Popol Vuh is a latter-day work. But the question of missionary influence is not easy to settle. Most critics have assumed that the account of the earth's creation that immediately follows the preamble owes something to the book of Genesis. If so, the material has been thoroughly assimilated to the Maya pantheon and to the Native American concept of primordial water. Comparisons with Aztec accounts, in which a company of gods (including the deity Plumed Serpent, named also in the Quiché text) deliberates, then places the earth on the surface of a preexisting sea, are just as applicable as comparisons with Genesis.

Part 1 continues with a description of the first three efforts at creating humans, in line with a widespread pattern shared by Aztec and other Mesoamerican traditions. As Part 1 ends, the narrative changes gears, moving directly into the exploits of the divine heroes Hunahpu and Xbalanque. The work of these two heroes may be said to prepare the world for society and for the well-being of individuals within society. Thus Part 2 deals with the problem of human arrogance; Part 3 confronts the scourge of death.

The cycle of trickster tales that makes up Part 2 appears to be purely Central American, not shared by Aztec lore. In Part 2, the twin heroes bring low the overproud Seven Macaw and, in further adventures not included here, defeat his two "self-magnifying" sons, Zipacna and Earthquake.

In the cycle of tales that makes up Part 3, the most celebrated portion of the Popol Vuh, Hunahpu and Xbalanque vanquish the lords of the Maya underworld, called Xibalba (a term of obscure etymology, provisionally translated "place of fright"). This material, likewise, is Central American—and quintessentially Mayan. Scenes from the story are preserved on painted vases of the classic period, recovered by archaeologists from Maya burial chambers. Evidently, the sequence of events, in which the heroes' twin fathers, One Hunahpu and Seven Hunahpu, are undone by Xibalba and are ultimately avenged by their two sons, served as a paradigm for the dying and the dead, promising them victory over the powers of the afterworld. From the archaeological evidence, the story told in Part 3 of the Popol Vuh must have aided the Maya in their journey through the realms of death somewhat as the *Book of the Dead* comforted the ancient Egyptians. Indeed, the vase paintings as a whole, with their depictions of underworld lords and the trials of the twin heroes, have lately called the "Maya Book of the Dead."

Parts 4 and 5 complete the vast epic, relating the connected stories of the origin of humans, the discovery of corn, the birth of the sun, and the history of the Quiché tribes and their royal lineages down to the time of the Spanish Conquest and, subsequently, to the 1550s.

Old as the stories are, they are also new. Narratives of the origin and destruction of early humans can still be heard in traditional Maya storytelling sessions. The traditional account of the discovery of corn continues to be widely told; and tales of the trickster Zipacna and of exploits identical to those of the hero twins also persist, even if much abbreviated and without the grand continuity of the Popol Vuh.

Beyond the native community, knowledge of the Popol Vuh among Central Americans is not only widespread but taken for granted. When the Nicaraguan poet Pablo Antonio Cuadra writes (in *The Calabash Tree,* 1978), "A hero struggled against the lords of the House of Bats, / against the lords of the House of Darkness," his readers understand that although he refers to a contemporary revolutionary figure he is also alluding to the ordeal of Hunahpu and Xbalanque. For the Salvadoran novelist Manlio Argueta (*Cuzcatlán,* 1986) the story of the origin of humans from corn as told in the Popol Vuh is a reminder, in Argueta's words, that "the species will not perish"—a theme equally detectable (and inspired by the same source) in the title of the 1949 novel *Men of Maize* by the Guatemalan Nobel laureate Miguel Angel Asturias.

In the translation printed here, wherever the text solidifies into a string of three or more couplets the passage is set apart as though it were a poem. This is a device of the translator. It is not meant to imply that the lines were chanted but rather to show off the more pronounced moments of formalism in a prose that borders on oratory.

PRONOUNCING GLOSSARY

The following list uses common English syllables and stress accents to provide rough equivalents of selected words whose pronunciation may be unfamiliar to the general reader.

anonas: *ah-noh'-nahs*

Auilix: *ah-wee-leesh'*

Cauiztan Copal: *kah-weez-tahn' koh-pahl'*

Chimalmat: *chee-mahl-maht'*

Hacauitz: *hah-kah-weets'*

Hunahpu: *hoo-nah-poo'*

jocotes: *hoh-koh'-tays*

matasanos: *mah-tah-sah'-nohs*

Mixtam Copal: *meesh-tahm' koh-pahl'*

nance: *nahn'-say*

naual: *nah'-wahl*

Palenque: *puh-leng'-kay*

pataxte: *pah-tahsh'-tay*

Popol Vuh: *poh-pohl' woo* (in English: *poh'-puhl voo*)

Quiché: *kee-chay'*

Quitze: *kee-tsay'*

Tikal: *tee-kahl'*

Tohil: *toh-heel'*

Xbalanque: *shbah-lahn-kay'*

Xibalba: *shee-bahl-bah'*

Xmucane: *shmoo-kah-nay'*

Xpiyacoc: *shpee-yah-kok'*

zapotes: *sah-poh'-tays*

Zipacna: *see-pahk-nah'*

Popol Vuh[1]

FROM PART 1

[Prologue, Creation]

This is the beginning of the ancient word, here in this place called Quiché. Here we shall inscribe, we shall implant the Ancient Word, the potential and source for everything done in the citadel of Quiché, in the nation of Quiché people.

And here we shall take up the demonstration, revelation, and account of how things were put in shadow and brought to light by

1. Translated by Dennis Tedlock.

the Maker, Modeler,
named Bearer, Begetter,
Hunahpu Possum, Hunahpu Coyote,
Great White Peccary,
Sovereign Plumed Serpent,
Heart of the Lake, Heart of the Sea,
plate shaper,
bowl shaper,[2] as they are called,
also named, also described as
the midwife, matchmaker
named Xpiyacoc, Xmucane,
defender, protector,[3]
twice a midwife, twice a matchmaker,

as is said in the words of Quiché. They accounted for everything—and did it, too—as enlightened beings, in enlightened words. We shall write about this now amid the preaching of God, in Christendom now. We shall bring it out because there is no longer

a place to see it, a Council Book,
a place to see "The Light That Came from
    Beside the Sea,"
the account of "Our Place in the Shadows,"
a place to see "The Dawn of Life,"

as it is called. There is the original book and ancient writing, but the one who reads and assesses it has a hidden identity.[4] It takes a long performance and account to complete the lighting of all the sky-earth:

the fourfold siding, fourfold cornering,
measuring, fourfold staking,
halving the cord, stretching the cord
in the sky, on the earth,
the four sides, the four corners,[5]
by the Maker, Modeler,
mother-father of life, of humankind,
giver of breath, giver of heart,
bearer, upbringer in the light that lasts
of those born in the light, begotten in the light;
worrier, knower of everything, whatever there is:
sky-earth, lake-sea.

This is the account, here it is:
    Now it still ripples, now it still murmurs, ripples, it still sighs, still hums, and it is empty under the sky.
    Here follow the first words, the first eloquence:

---

2. All thirteen names refer to the Creator or to a company of creators, a designation applicable clearly to the first four names and "Sovereign Plumed Serpent." "Heart of the Lake" and "Heart of the Sea" also apply because the creators will later be described as "in the water," and somewhat obscurely, so does the last pair of names (*plate* and *bowl* may be read as "earth" and "sky," respectively). "Hunahpu Possum," "Hunahpu Coyote," "Great White Peccary," and "Coati" refer specifically to the grandparents of the gods, usually called Xpiyacoc and Xmucane.   3. Four names for Xpiyacoc and Xmucane.   4. The hieroglyphic source ("Council Book") was suppressed by missionaries; it was said to have been brought to Quiché in ancient times from the far side of a lagoon ("Sea"). The reader hides his identity to avoid the missionaries.   5. As though a farmer were measuring and staking a cornfield.

There is not yet one person, one animal, bird, fish, crab, tree, rock, hollow, canyon, meadow, forest. Only the sky alone is there; the face of the earth is not clear. Only the sea alone is pooled under all the sky; there is nothing whatever gathered together. It is at rest; not a single thing stirs. It is held back, kept at rest under the sky.

Whatever there is that might be is simply not there: only the pooled water, only the calm sea, only it alone is pooled.

Whatever might be is simply not there: only murmurs, ripples, in the dark, in the night. Only the Maker, Modeler alone, Sovereign Plumed Serpent, the Bearers, Begetters are in the water, a glittering light. They are there, they are enclosed in quetzal feathers, in blue-green.

Thus the name, "Plumed Serpent." They are great knowers, great thinkers in their very being.

And of course there is the sky, and there is also the Heart of Sky. This is the name of the god, as it is spoken.

And then came his word, he came here to the Sovereign Plumed Serpent, here in the blackness, in the early dawn. He spoke with the Sovereign Plumed Serpent, and they talked, then they thought, then they worried. They agreed with each other, they joined their words, their thoughts. Then it was clear, then they reached accord in the light, and then humanity was clear, when they conceived the growth, the generation of trees, of bushes, and the growth of life, of humankind, in the blackness, in the early dawn, all because of the Heart of Sky, named Hurricane. Thunderbolt Hurricane comes first, the second is Newborn Thunderbolt, and the third is Sudden Thunderbolt.[6]

So there were three of them, as Heart of Sky, who came to the Sovereign Plumed Serpent, when the dawn of life was conceived:

"How should the sowing be, and the dawning? Who is to be the provider, nurturer?"[7]

"Let it be this way, think about it: this water should be removed, emptied out for the formation of the earth's own plate and platform, then should come the sowing, the dawning of the sky-earth. But there will be no high days and no bright praise for our work, our design, until the rise of the human work, the human design," they said.

And then the earth arose because of them, it was simply their word that brought it forth. For the forming of the earth they said "Earth." It arose suddenly, just like a cloud, like a mist, now forming, unfolding. Then the mountains were separated from the water, all at once the great mountains came forth. By their genius alone, by their cutting edge[8] alone they carried out the conception of the mountain-plain, whose face grew instant groves of cypress and pine.

And the Plumed Serpent was pleased with this:

"It was good that you came, Heart of Sky, Hurricane, and Newborn Thunderbolt, Sudden Thunderbolt. Our work, our design will turn out well," they said.

6. Alternate names for Heart of Sky, the deity who cooperates with Sovereign Plumed Serpent. The triple naming adapts the Christian trinity to native theology, perhaps more in the spirit of defiant preemption than of conciliation.   7. That is, humanity, which alone is capable of nurturing the gods with sacrifices.
8. * * * Refers to the cutting of flesh with a knife. * * * In the present context, it implies that "the mountains were separated from the water" through an act resembling the extraction of the heart (or other organs) from a sacrifice [translator's note].

And the earth was formed first, the mountain-plain. The channels of water were separated; their branches wound their ways among the mountains. The waters were divided when the great mountains appeared.

Such was the formation of the earth when it was brought forth by the Heart of Sky, Heart of Earth, as they are called, since they were the first to think of it. The sky was set apart, and the earth was set apart in the midst of the waters.

Such was their plan when they thought, when they worried about the completion of their work.[9]

FROM PART 2

[The Twins Defeat Seven Macaw]

Here is the beginning of the defeat and destruction of the day of seven macaw by the two boys, the first named Hunahpu and the second named Xbalanque.[1] Being gods, the two of them saw evil in his attempt at self-magnification before the Heart of Sky.

* * *

This is the great tree of Seven Macaw, a nance,[2] and this is the food of Seven Macaw. In order to eat the fruit of the nance he goes up the tree every day. Since Hunahpu and Xbalanque have seen where he feeds, they are now hiding beneath the tree of Seven Macaw, they are keeping quiet here, the two boys are in the leaves of the tree.

And when Seven Macaw arrived, perching over his meal, the nance, it was then that he was shot by Hunahpu. The blowgun shot went right to his jaw, breaking his mouth. Then he went up over the tree and fell flat on the ground. Suddenly Hunahpu appeared, running. He set out to grab him, but actually it was the arm of Hunahpu that was seized by Seven Macaw. He yanked it straight back, he bent it back at the shoulder. Then Seven Macaw tore it right out of Hunahpu. Even so, the boys did well: the first round was not their defeat by Seven Macaw.

And when Seven Macaw had taken the arm of Hunahpu, he went home. Holding his jaw very carefully, he arrived:

"What have you got there?" said Chimalmat, the wife of Seven Macaw.

"What is it but those two tricksters! They've shot me, they've dislocated my jaw.[3] All my teeth are just loose, now they ache. But once what I've got is over the fire—hanging there, dangling over the fire—then they can just come and get it. They're real tricksters!" said Seven Macaw, then he hung up the arm of Hunahpu.

Meanwhile Hunahpu and Xbalanque were thinking. And then they invoked a grandfather, a truly white-haired grandfather, and a grandmother, a truly humble grandmother—just bent-over, elderly people. Great White

---

9. That is, the creation of humans; an account of the first three, unsuccessful, attempts at creating humans occupies the remainder of Part 1.   1. First mention of the twin hero gods (their origin is recounted in Part 3). Here they confront the false god Seven Macaw, who has arisen during the time of primordial darkness, boasting, "My eyes are of metal; my teeth just glitter with jewels, and turquoise as well. . . . I am like the sun and the moon." Note that all the characters in Parts 1, 2, and 3 are supernatural; humans are not created until Part 4.   2. A pickle tree (*Byrsonima crassifolia*).   3. This is the origin of the way a macaw's beak looks, with a huge upper mandible and a small, retreating lower one [translator's note].

Peccary is the name of the grandfather, and Great White Coati is the name of the grandmother.[4] The boys said to the grandmother and grandfather:

"Please travel with us when we go to get our arm from Seven Macaw; we'll just follow right behind you. You'll tell him:

'Do forgive us our grandchildren, who travel with us. Their mother and father are dead, and so they follow along there, behind us. Perhaps we should give them away, since all we do is pull worms out of teeth.' So we'll seem like children to Seven Macaw, even though *we're* giving *you* the instructions," the two boys told them.

"Very well," they replied.

After that they approached the place where Seven Macaw was in front of his home. When the grandmother and grandfather passed by, the two boys were romping along behind them. When they passed below the lord's house, Seven Macaw was yelling his mouth off because of his teeth. And when Seven Macaw saw the grandfather and grandmother traveling with them:

"Where are you headed, our grandfather?" said the lord.

"We're just making our living, your lordship," they replied.

"Why are you working for a living? Aren't those your children traveling with you?"

"No, they're not, your lordship. They're our grandchildren, our descendants, but it is nevertheless *we* who take pity on *them*. The bit of food they get is the portion we give them, your lordship," replied the grandmother and grandfather. Since the lord is getting done in by the pain in his teeth, it is only with great effort that he speaks again:

"I implore you, please take pity on me! What sweets can you make, what poisons[5] can you cure?" said the lord.

"We just pull the worms out of teeth, and we just cure eyes. We just set bones, your lordship," they replied.

"Very well, please cure my teeth. They really ache, every day. It's insufferable! I get no sleep because of them—and my eyes. They just shot me, those two tricksters! Ever since it started I haven't eaten because of it. Therefore take pity on me! Perhaps it's because my teeth are loose now."

"Very well, your lordship. It's a worm, gnawing at the bone.[6] It's merely a matter of putting in a replacement and taking the teeth out, sir."

"But perhaps it's not good for my teeth to come out—since I am, after all, a lord. My finery is in my teeth—and my eyes."

"But then we'll put in a replacement. Ground bone will be put back in." And this is the "ground bone": it's only white corn.

"Very well. Yank them out! Give me some help here!" he replied.

And when the teeth of Seven Macaw came out, it was only white corn that went in as a replacement for his teeth—just a coating shining white, that corn in his mouth. His face fell at once, he no longer looked like a lord. The last of his teeth came out, the jewels that had stood out blue from his mouth.

And when the eyes of Seven Macaw were cured, he was plucked around the eyes, the last of his metal came off.[7] Still he felt no pain; he just looked

---

4. Animal names of the divine grandparents, Xpiyacoc and Xmucane, who are also the twins' genealogical grandparents.   5. Play on words as *qui* is translated as both "sweet" and "poison."   6. The present-day Quiché retain the notion that a toothache is caused by a worm gnawing at the bone [translator's note]. 7. This is clearly meant to be the origin of the large white and completely featherless eye patches and very small eyes of the scarlet macaw [translator's note].

on while the last of his greatness left him. It was just as Hunahpu and Xbalanque had intended.

And when Seven Macaw died, Hunahpu got back his arm. And Chimalmat, the wife of Seven Macaw, also died.

Such was the loss of the riches of Seven Macaw: only the doctors got the jewels and gems that had made him arrogant, here on the face of the earth. The genius of the grandmother, the genius of the grandfather did its work when they took back their arm: it was implanted and the break got well again. Just as they had wished the death of Seven Macaw, so they brought it about. They had seen evil in his self-magnification.

After this the two boys went on again. What they did was simply the word of the Heart of Sky.

FROM PART 3

[*Victory over the Underworld*]

And now we shall name the name of the father of Hunahpu and Xbalanque. Let's drink to him, and let's just drink to the telling and accounting of the begetting of Hunahpu and Xbalanque. We shall tell just half of it, just a part of the account of their father. Here follows the account.

These are the names: One Hunahpu and Seven Hunahpu,[8] as they are called.

*   *   *

And One and Seven Hunahpu went inside Dark House.[9]

And then their torch was brought, only one torch, already lit, sent by One and Seven Death, along with a cigar for each of them, also already lit, sent by the lords. When these were brought to One and Seven Hunahpu they were cowering, here in the dark. When the bearer of their torch and cigars arrived, the torch was bright as it entered; their torch and both of their cigars were burning. The bearer spoke:

" 'They must be sure to return them in the morning—not finished, but just as they look now. They must return them intact,' the lords say to you," they were told, and they were defeated. They finished the torch and they finished the cigars that had been brought to them.

And Xibalba is packed with tests, heaps and piles of tests.

This is the first one: the Dark House, with darkness alone inside.

And the second is named Rattling House, heavy with cold inside, whistling with drafts, clattering with hail. A deep chill comes inside here.

And the third is named Jaguar House, with jaguars alone inside, jostling one another, crowding together, with gnashing teeth. They're scratching around; these jaguars are shut inside the house.

Bat House is the name of the fourth test, with bats alone inside the house,

---

8. Twin sons of Xpiyacoc and Xmucane; the elder of these twins, One Hunahpu, will become the father of Hunahpu and Xbalanque. "As for Seven Hunahpu," according to the text, "he has no wife. He's just a partner and just secondary; he just remains a boy."   9. The first of the "test" houses in Xibalba (the underworld) to which One and Seven Hunahpu, avid ballplayers, have been lured by the underworld lords, One and Seven Death; the lords have promised them a challenging ball game. The Mesoamerican ball game, remotely comparable to both basketball and soccer, was played on a rectangular court, using a ball of native rubber.

squeaking, shrieking, darting through the house. The bats are shut inside; they can't get out.

And the fifth is named Razor House, with blades alone inside. The blades are moving back and forth, ripping, slashing through the house.

These are the first tests of Xibalba, but One and Seven Hunahpu never entered into them, except for the one named earlier, the specified test house.

And when One and Seven Hunahpu went back before One and Seven Death, they were asked:

"Where are my cigars? What of my torch? They were brought to you last night!"

"We finished them, your lordship."

"Very well. This very day, your day is finished, you will die, you will disappear, and we shall break you off. Here you will hide your faces: you are to be sacrificed!" said One and Seven Death.

And then they were sacrificed and buried. They were buried at the Place of Ball Game Sacrifice,[1] as it is called. The head of One Hunahpu was cut off; only his body was buried with his younger brother.

"Put his head in the fork of the tree that stands by the road," said One and Seven Death.

And when his head was put in the fork of the tree, the tree bore fruit. It would not have had any fruit, had not the head of One Hunahpu been put in the fork of the tree.

This is the calabash tree, as we call it today, or "the skull of One Hunahpu," as it is said.

And then One and Seven Death were amazed at the fruit of the tree. The fruit grows out everywhere, and it isn't clear where the head of One Hunahpu is; now it looks just the way the calabashes look. All the Xibalbans see this, when they come to look.

The state of the tree loomed large in their thoughts, because it came about at the same time the head of One Hunahpu was put in the fork. The Xibalbans said among themselves:

"No one is to pick the fruit, nor is anyone to go beneath the tree," they said. They restricted themselves; all of Xibalba held back.

It isn't clear which is the head of One Hunahpu; now it's exactly the same as the fruit of the tree. Calabash came to be its name, and much was said about it. A maiden heard about it, and here we shall tell of her arrival.

And here is the account of a maiden, the daughter of a lord named Blood Gatherer.[2]

And this is when a maiden heard of it, the daughter of a lord. Blood Gatherer is the name of her father, and Blood Moon is the name of the maiden.

And when he heard the account of the fruit of the tree, her father retold it. And she was amazed at the account:

"I'm not acquainted with that tree they talk about. '"Its fruit is truly sweet!" they say,' I hear," she said.

Next, she went all alone and arrived where the tree stood. It stood at the Place of Ball Game Sacrifice:

---

1. Probably not a place name, but rather a name for the altar where losing ball players were sacrificed [translator's note].   2. Fourth-ranking lord of Xibalba, whose commission is to draw blood from people.

"What? Well! What's the fruit of this tree? Shouldn't this tree bear something sweet? They shouldn't die, they shouldn't be wasted. Should I pick one?" said the maiden.

And then the bone spoke; it was here in the fork of the tree:

"Why do you want a mere bone, a round thing in the branches of a tree?" said the head of One Hunahpu when it spoke to the maiden. "You don't want it," she was told.

"I do want it," said the maiden.

"Very well. Stretch out your right hand here, so I can see it," said the bone.

"Yes," said the maiden. She stretched out her right hand, up there in front of the bone.

And then the bone spit out its saliva, which landed squarely in the hand of the maiden.

And then she looked in her hand, she inspected it right away, but the bone's saliva wasn't in her hand.

"It is just a sign I have given you, my saliva, my spittle. This, my head, has nothing on it—just bone, nothing of meat. It's just the same with the head of a great lord: it's just the flesh that makes his face look good. And when he dies, people get frightened by his bones. After that, his son is like his saliva, his spittle, in his being, whether it be the son of a lord or the son of a craftsman, an orator. The father does not disappear, but goes on being fulfilled. Neither dimmed nor destroyed is the face of a lord, a warrior, craftsman, orator. Rather, he will leave his daughters and sons. So it is that I have done likewise through you. Now go up there on the face of the earth; you will not die. Keep the word. So be it," said the head of One and Seven Hunahpu—they were of one mind when they did it.

This was the word Hurricane, Newborn Thunderbolt, Sudden Thunderbolt had given them. In the same way, by the time the maiden returned to her home, she had been given many instructions. Right away something was generated in her belly, from the saliva alone, and this was the generation of Hunahpu and Xbalanque.

And when the maiden got home and six months had passed, she was found out by her father. Blood Gatherer is the name of her father.

* * *

And they came to the lords.[3] Feigning great humility, they bowed their heads all the way to the ground when they arrived. They brought themselves low, doubled over, flattened out, down to the rags, to the tatters. They really looked like vagabonds when they arrived.

So then they were asked what their mountain[4] and tribe were, and they were also asked about their mother and father:

"Where do you come from?" they were asked.

"We've never known, lord. We don't know the identity of our mother and father. We must've been small when they died," was all they said. They didn't give any names.

---

3. Forced to flee the underworld the maiden (Blood Moon) finds refuge on earth with Xmucane. There she gives birth to the twins, who, like their father and uncle, become ballplayers and are enticed to the underworld. Surviving the Dark House and other tests, they disguise themselves as vagabonds and earn a reputation as clever entertainers among the denizens of Xibalba; as such they are summoned to entertain the high lords.   4. A metonym for almost any settlement, but especially a fortified town or citadel, located on a defensible elevation [translator's note].

"Very well. Please entertain us, then. What do you want us to give you in payment?" they were asked.

"Well, we don't want anything. To tell the truth, we're afraid," they told the lord.

"Don't be afraid. Don't be ashamed. Just dance this way: first you'll dance to sacrifice yourselves, you'll set fire to my house after that, you'll act out all the things you know. We want to be entertained. This is our heart's desire, the reason you had to be sent for, dear vagabonds. We'll give you payment," they were told.

So then they began their songs and dances, and then all the Xibalbans arrived, the spectators crowded the floor, and they danced everything: they danced the Weasel, they danced the Poorwill,[5] they danced the Armadillo. Then the lord said to them:

"Sacrifice my dog, then bring him back to life again," they were told.

"Yes," they said.

> When they sacrificed the dog
> he then came back to life.
> And that dog was really happy
> when he came back to life.
> Back and forth he wagged his tail
> when he came back to life.

And the lord said to them:

"Well, you have yet to set my home on fire," they were told next, so then they set fire to the home of the lord. The house was packed with all the lords, but they were not burned. They quickly fixed it back again, lest the house of One Death be consumed all at once, and all the lords were amazed, and they went on dancing this way. They were overjoyed.

And then they were asked by the lord:

"You have yet to kill a person! Make a sacrifice without death!" they were told.

"Very well," they said.

And then they took hold of a human sacrifice.

And they held up a human heart on high.

And they showed its roundness to the lords.

And now One and Seven Death admired it, and now that person was brought right back to life. His heart was overjoyed when he came back to life, and the lords were amazed:

"Sacrifice yet again, even do it to yourselves! Let's see it! At heart, that's the dance we really want from you," the lords said now.

"Very well, lord," they replied, and then they sacrificed themselves.

And this is the sacrifice of Hunahpu by Xbalanque. One by one his legs, his arms were spread wide. His head came off, rolled far away outside. His heart, dug out, was smothered in a leaf,[6] and all the Xibalbans went crazy at the sight.

So now, only one of them was dancing there: Xbalanque.

---

5. The goatsucker. The dances apparently were imitations of these animals and birds.   6. As a tamale is wrapped. In the typical Mesoamerican heart sacrifice, the victim's arms and legs were stretched wide and the heart was excised and offered to a deity.

"Get up!" he said, and Hunahpu came back to life. The two of them were overjoyed at this—and likewise the lords rejoiced, as if they were doing it themselves. One and Seven Death were as glad at heart as if they themselves were actually doing the dance.

And then the hearts of the lords were filled with longing, with yearning for the dance of little Hunahpu and Xbalanque, so then came these words from One and Seven Death:

"Do it to us! Sacrifice us!" they said. "Sacrifice both of us!" said One and Seven Death to Hunahpu and Xbalanque.

"Very well. You ought to come back to life. What is death to you?[7] And aren't we making you happy, along with the vassals of your domain?" they told the lords.

And this one was the first to be sacrificed: the lord at the very top, the one whose name is One Death, the ruler of Xibalba.

And with One Death dead, the next to be taken was Seven Death. They did not come back to life.

And then the Xibalbans were getting up to leave, those who had seen the lords die. They underwent heart sacrifice there, and the heart sacrifice was performed on the two lords only for the purpose of destroying them.

As soon as they had killed the one lord without bringing him back to life, the other lord had been meek and tearful before the dancers. He didn't consent, he didn't accept it:

"Take pity on me!" he said when he realized. All their vassals took the road to the great canyon, in one single mass they filled up the deep abyss. So they piled up there and gathered together, countless ants, tumbling down into the canyon, as if they were being herded there. And when they arrived, they all bent low in surrender, they arrived meek and tearful.

Such was the defeat of the rulers of Xibalba. The boys accomplished it only through wonders, only through self-transformation.

☼   ☼   ☼

Such was the beginning of their disappearance and the denial of their worship.

> Their ancient day was not a great one,
> these ancient people only wanted conflict,
> their ancient names are not really divine,
> but fearful is the ancient evil of their faces.
>
> They are makers of enemies, users of owls,[8]
> they are inciters to wrongs and violence,
> they are masters of hidden intentions as well,
> they are black and white,[9]
> masters of stupidity, masters of perplexity,

as it is said. By putting on appearances they cause dismay.

Such was the loss of their greatness and brilliance. Their domain did not return to greatness. This was accomplished by little Hunahpu and Xbalanque.

---

7. Evident sarcasm.   8. The lords had used owls as messengers to lure the ballplayers to Xibalba. 9. Contradictory, duplicitous.

FROM PART 4

[*Origin of Humanity, First Dawn*]

And here is the beginning of the conception of humans, and of the search for the ingredients of the human body. So they spoke, the Bearer, Begetter, the Makers, Modelers named Sovereign Plumed Serpent:

"The dawn has approached, preparations have been made, and morning has come for the provider, nurturer, born in the light, begotten in the light. Morning has come for humankind, for the people of the face of the earth," they said. It all came together as they went on thinking in the darkness, in the night, as they searched and they sifted, they thought and they wondered.

And here their thoughts came out in clear light. They sought and discovered what was needed for human flesh. It was only a short while before the sun, moon, and stars were to appear above the Makers and Modelers. Split Place, Bitter Water Place is the name: the yellow corn, white corn came from there.

And these are the names of the animals who brought the food: fox, coyote, parrot, crow. There were four animals who brought the news of the ears of yellow corn and white corn. They were coming from over there at Split Place, they showed the way to the split.[1]

And this was when they found the staple foods.

And these were the ingredients for the flesh of the human work, the human design, and the water was for the blood. It became human blood, and corn was also used by the Bearer, Begetter.

And so they were happy over the provisions of the good mountain, filled with sweet things, thick with yellow corn, white corn, and thick with pataxte and cacao, countless zapotes, anonas, jocotes, nances, matasanos,[2] sweets— the rich foods filling up the citadel named Split Place, Bitter Water Place. All the edible fruits were there: small staples, great staples, small plants, great plants. The way was shown by the animals.

And then the yellow corn and white corn were ground, and Xmucane did the grinding nine times. Corn was used, along with the water she rinsed her hands with, for the creation of grease; it became human fat when it was worked by the Bearer, Begetter, Sovereign Plumed Serpent, as they are called.

After that, they put it into words:

> the making, the modeling of our first mother-father,
> with yellow corn, white corn alone for the flesh,
> food alone for the human legs and arms,
> for our first fathers, the four human works.

It was staples alone that made up their flesh.
These are the names of the first people who were made and modeled.

---

1. In the widespread Mesoamerican story of the discovery of corn, one or more animals reveal that corn and other foods are hidden within a rock or a mountain, accessible through a cleft; in some versions the mountain is split apart by lightning.   2. Quincelike fruits of the tree *Casimiroa edulis*. "Pataxte": a species of cacao (*Theobroma bicolor*) that is inferior to cacao proper (*T. cacao*). "Zapotes": fruits of the sapota tree (*Lucuma mammosa*). "Anonas": custard apples (genus *Anona*). "Jocotes": yellow plumlike fruits of the tree *Spondias purpurea*.

> This is the first person: Jaguar Quitze.
> And now the second: Jaguar Night.
> And now the third: Not Right Now.
> And the fourth: Dark Jaguar.[3]

And these are the names of our first mother-fathers.[4] They were simply made and modeled, it is said; they had no mother and no father. We have named the men by themselves. No woman gave birth to them, nor were they begotten by the builder, sculptor, Bearer, Begetter. By sacrifice alone, by genius alone they were made, they were modeled by the Maker, Modeler, Bearer, Begetter, Sovereign Plumed Serpent. And when they came to fruition, they came out human:

They talked and they made words.

They looked and they listened.

They walked, they worked.

They were good people, handsome, with looks of the male kind. Thoughts came into existence and they gazed; their vision came all at once. Perfectly they saw, perfectly they knew everything under the sky, whenever they looked. The moment they turned around and looked around in the sky, on the earth, everything was seen without any obstruction. They didn't have to walk around before they could see what was under the sky; they just stayed where they were.

As they looked, their knowledge became intense. Their sight passed through trees, through rocks, through lakes, through seas, through mountains, through plains. Jaguar Quitze, Jaguar Night, Not Right Now, and Dark Jaguar were truly gifted people.

And then they were asked by the builder and mason:

"What do you know about your being? Don't you look, don't you listen? Isn't your speech good, and your walk? So you must look, to see out under the sky. Don't you see the mountain-plain clearly? So try it," they were told.

And then they saw everything under the sky perfectly. After that, they thanked the Maker, Modeler:

> "Truly now,
> double thanks, triple thanks
> that we've been formed, we've been given
> our mouths, our faces,
> we speak, we listen,
> we wonder, we move,
> our knowledge is good, we've understood
> what is far and near,
> and we've seen what is great and small
> under the sky, on the earth.
> Thanks to you we've been formed,
> we've come to be made and modeled,
> our grandmother, our grandfather,"

they said when they gave thanks for having been made and modeled. They understood everything perfectly, they sighted the four sides, the four corners in the sky, on the earth, and this didn't sound good to the builder and sculptor:

---

3. The four original Quiché males.　　4. That is, parents, although only the first three founded lineages; Dark Jaguar had no son.

"What our works and designs have said is no good:

'We have understood everything, great and small,' they say." And so the Bearer, Begetter took back their knowledge:

"What should we do with them now? Their vision should at least reach nearby, they should see at least a small part of the face of the earth, but what they're saying isn't good. Aren't they merely 'works' and 'designs' in their very names? Yet they'll become as great as gods, unless they procreate, proliferate at the sowing, the dawning, unless they increase."

"Let it be this way: now we'll take them apart just a little, that's what we need. What we've found out isn't good. Their deeds would become equal to ours, just because their knowledge reaches so far. They see everything," so said

the Heart of Sky, Hurricane,
Newborn Thunderbolt, Sudden Thunderbolt,
Sovereign Plumed Serpent,
Bearer, Begetter,
Xpiyacoc, Xmucane,
Maker, Modeler,

as they are called. And when they changed the nature of their works, their designs, it was enough that the eyes be marred by the Heart of Sky. They were blinded as the face of a mirror is breathed upon. Their vision flickered. Now it was only from close up that they could see what was there with any clarity.

And such was the loss of the means of understanding, along with the means of knowing everything, by the four humans. The root was implanted.

And such was the making, modeling of our first grandfather, our father, by the Heart of Sky, Heart of Earth.

And then their wives and women came into being. Again, the same gods thought of it. It was as if they were asleep when they received them, truly beautiful women were there with Jaguar Quitze, Jaguar Night, Not Right Now, and Dark Jaguar. With their women there they really came alive. Right away they were happy at heart again, because of their wives.

Red Sea Turtle is the name of the wife of Jaguar Quitze.

Prawn House is the name of the wife of Jaguar Night.

Water Hummingbird is the name of the wife of Not Right Now.

Macaw House is the name of the wife of Dark Jaguar.

So these are the names of their wives, who became ladies of rank, giving birth to the people of the tribes, small and great.

* * *

And here is the dawning and showing of the sun, moon, and stars. And Jaguar Quitze, Jaguar Night, Not Right Now, and Dark Jaguar were overjoyed when they saw the sun carrier.[5] It came up first. It looked brilliant when it came up, since it was ahead of the sun.

After that they unwrapped their copal[6] incense, which came from the east, and there was triumph in their hearts when they unwrapped it. They gave their heartfelt thanks with three kinds at once:

---

5. The morning star. 6. Resin used as incense.

Mixtam Copal is the name of the copal brought by Jaguar Quitze.

Cauiztan Copal, next, is the name of the copal brought by Jaguar Night.

Godly Copal, as the next one is called, was brought by Not Right Now.

The three of them had their copal, and this is what they burned as they incensed the direction of the rising sun. They were crying sweetly as they shook their burning copal,[7] the precious copal.

After that they cried because they had yet to see and yet to witness the birth of the sun.

And then, when the sun came up, the animals, small and great, were happy. They all came up from the rivers and canyons; they waited on all the mountain peaks. Together they looked toward the place where the sun came out.

So then the puma and jaguar cried out, but the first to cry out was a bird, the parrot by name. All the animals were truly happy. The eagle, the white vulture, small birds, great birds spread their wings, and the penitents and sacrificers knelt down.

FROM PART 5

[Prayer for Future Generations]

And this is the cry of their hearts, here it is:

> "Wait! On this blessed day,
> thou Hurricane, thou Heart of the Sky-Earth,
> thou giver of ripeness and freshness,
> and thou giver of daughters and sons,
> spread thy stain, spill thy drops
> of green and yellow;[8]
> give life and beginning
> to those I bear and beget,
> that they might multiply and grow,
> nurturing and providing for thee,
> calling to thee along the roads and paths,
> on rivers, in canyons,
> beneath the trees and bushes;
> give them their daughters and sons.
>
> "May there be no blame, obstacle, want or misery;
> let no deceiver come behind or before them,
> may they neither be snared nor wounded,
> nor seduced, nor burned,
> nor diverted below the road nor above it;
> may they neither fall over backward nor stumble;
> keep them on the Green Road, the Green Path.
>
> "May there be no blame or barrier for them
> through any secrets or sorcery of thine;
> may thy nurturers and providers be good
> before thy mouth and thy face,
> thou, Heart of Sky; thou, Heart of Earth;

---

7. Note that the Mesoamerican pottery censer must be shaken or swayed back and forth to keep the incense burning.   8. The imagery, denoting human offspring, alludes to semen and plant growth.

thou, Bundle of Flames;[9]
and thou, Tohil, Auilix, Hacauitz,[1]
under the sky, on the earth,
the four sides, the four corners;
may there be only light, only continuity within,
before thy mouth and thy face, thou god."

9. A sacred relic left to the Quiché lords by Jaguar Quitze; like the sacred bundles of the North American peoples, a cloth-wrapped ark with mysterious contents [translator's note]. 1. Patron deities of the Quiché lineages.

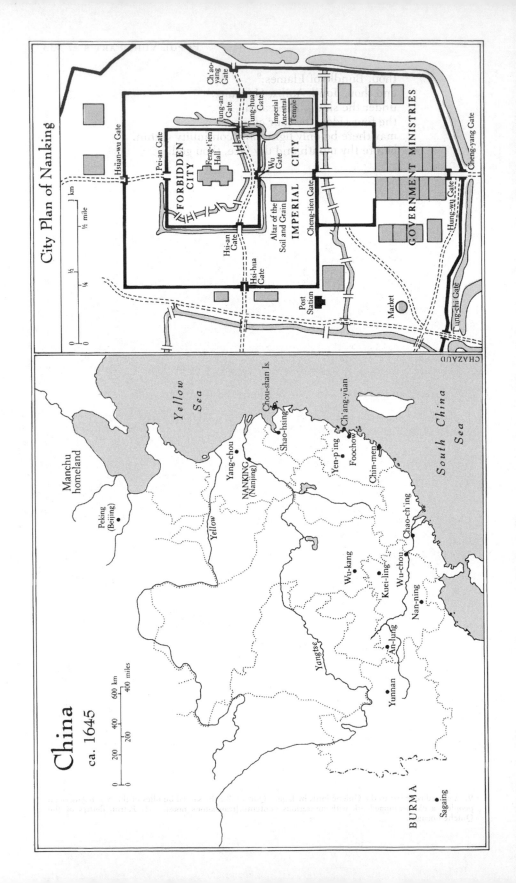

City Plan of Nanking

Ch'ao-yang Gate
Tung-an Gate
Tung-hua Gate
Imperial Ancestral Temple
Hsüan-wu Gate
Pei-an Gate
Feng-t'ien Hall
FORBIDDEN CITY
Wu Gate
IMPERIAL CITY
Cheng-yang Gate
Hsi-an Gate
Hsi-hua Gate
Altar of the Soil and Grain
Cheng-tien Gate
GOVERNMENT MINISTRIES
Hung-wu Gate
T'ung-chi Gate
Post Station
Market

km
½
¼
½ mile
0
0

China
ca. 1645

Manchu homeland
Peking (Beijing)

Yellow Sea

Chou-shan Is.
Yang-chou
NANKING (Nanjing)
Shao-hsing
Yen-p'ing
Ch'ang-yüan
Foochow
Chin-men
Wu-kang
Kuei-ling
Wu-chou
Chao-ch'ing
Nan-ning
An-lung
Yunnan

Yellow
Yangtse

South China Sea

BURMA
Sagaing

0   200   400   600 km
0   200   400 miles

Vernacular Literature in China

Several decades after completing the conquest of north China, Mongol armies crossed the Yangtse River and conquered the Southern Sung Dynasty in 1279. At the time their empire stretched across all of Asia, but as a Chinese dynasty the Mongols were known as the Yüan. Although they assumed a Chinese dynastic title and some of the trappings of Chinese imperial government, the Mongols did not base their state on Confucian principles, for which they had the greatest contempt. To the ever-lasting shock of Chinese intellectuals, the Mongols suspended the examination system, by which members of the educated elite were recruited for government service. The long-established links among classical literature (poetry and nonfiction prose), an education in the Confucian classics, and service in the government were temporarily broken. Even after the civil service examinations were reestablished later in the dynasty, classical literature never regained its place as the core around which public, social, and private life was organized. Through the rest of the imperial period, classical literature remained an important part of the life of intellectuals, but its general role had been diminished to something like that of literature in Western civilization, an important adjunct of social life but not at its core.

As classical literature lost its importance, literature in vernacular Chinese (plays, verse romances, and prose fiction) began to be published. The steady rise of the bourgeoisie in the great cities and the spread of literacy in urban areas created a market for written versions of literary forms that already flourished in performance. In Europe and Great Britain the authority of classical drama could be used to defend the validity of Renaissance drama in the vernacular tongues. Greek and Latin prose romance, though with lesser prestige than drama, likewise informed the development of vernacular narrative prose. In China, by contrast, there was no ancient drama, and classical prose fiction was generally considered pure entertainment.

In the cities of China, however, rich traditions of theater, oral verse romance, and storytelling flourished. The thirteenth and fourteenth centuries produced the first published versions of these forms, with each written form carefully preserving the ambience of performance. Some intellectuals were fascinated by this urban popular literature, and what survives of it is the result of their efforts. Such literature grew steadily in volume and importance through the Ming Dynasty (1368–1644).

Although Yüan and Ming vernacular literature lacked the subtlety of classical literature, much that had been repressed in classical literature burst forth in the vernacular: sex, violence, satire, and humor. Plays, verse romances, and prose stories were often elaborations of some source in the classical language, spinning out a few pages into thirty or a thousand. This was a literature whose strength lay not in inventing plots but in filling in details and saying what had been omitted. In that strength, it became something different in kind from classical literature, with new virtues and new failings.

Chinese popular literature is largely a vast tissue of interrelated stories. The illiterate and semiliterate population had learned history from storytellers, who took a time period and elaborated it in the spoken tongue, including poems and songs. A dramatist might take one incident from a story cycle and develop it into a play. A fiction writer might cover an entire story cycle in a novel. A number of these historical romances survive, the most famous being *The Romance of the Three Kingdoms* (*San-kuo chih yen-yi*)—attributed to Lo Kuan-chung (earliest printed version 1522)—an elaboration of the official history of the period in which the Han Dynasty disintegrated, around the turn of the third century C.E. In *The Romance of the Three Kingdoms*, the somewhat dry historical account was transformed into a dazzling saga of battles and clever stratagems.

Popular literature worked with other materials as well. Murder mysteries, often based on recent cases, circulated, in which the wise magistrate, "Judge Pao," played a role equivalent to that of the modern detective. Stories of a famous group of twelfth-century bandits, like Robin Hood representing justice against corrupt authority, developed into the novel *Water Margin* (*Shui-hu chuan*, early 1500s). One small incident in *Water Margin* was elaborated into the saga of a corrupt sensualist whose greed and sexual escapades give a vivid if skewed portrait of urban life in Ming China; this is *Golden Lotus* (*Chin P'ing Mei*, 1617). And the story of the Buddhist monk Hsuan Tsang who went west to India to get scriptures, guarded by a band of fantastic creatures headed by a wily monkey possessed of supernatural powers, became the novel *Monkey* (*Hsi-yu chi*, 1592).

As literature lost its role in public life, the vital link between literature and Confucian intellectual culture also gave way. High culture favored neo-Confucianism, at best prim and at worst dogmatic. Neo-Confucianism was an attempt to discover the philosophical grounds of the Confucian classics, and it developed into a system of private and social ethics that was to guide all aspects of life. Its rigid strictures on self-cultivation and ethical behavior failed in basic ways to address the complexities of human nature and the pressures of living in an increasingly complex world. Except among a very few committed thinkers, it was a philosophical position that invited gross hypocrisy. Vernacular literature, on the other hand, celebrated liberty, violent energy, and passion. Though such works often contained elements of neo-Confucian ethics and were later given pious neo-Confucian interpretations, by and large they either voiced qualities that neo-Confucianism sought to repress or savagely attacked society as a world of false appearances and secret evils.

In 1644 Manchu armies from the northeast descended into China and established a new dynasty, the Ch'ing, which would rule China until the revolution in 1911. Once again under non-Chinese rule and forced to wear the Manchu queue, a long ponytail, as a mark of submission, many Chinese harbored strong anti-Manchu sentiments. The Manchus, for their part, became very sensitive to native opposition. Censors set to survey current writings for hostility to the regime continually discovered slights, both real and imagined, against the dynasty. The late seventeenth and eighteenth centuries, known as the "literary inquisition," had a chilling effect on writing, especially in classical Chinese.

Such political realities may strongly affect, but do not entirely determine the intellectual and literary climate of an era. Ch'ing intellectual culture was a strong reaction against the radical individualism of the last part of the Ming, when personal freedom was celebrated at the expense of social responsibility. Early Ch'ing intellectuals held this late Ming ethos responsible for the decline of the Ming Dynasty. In the latter part of the seventeenth century and into the eighteenth century intellectuals turned away from Ming "subjectivism," the belief that each individual contained within himself or herself the grounds to make moral decisions and to interpret the authoritative texts of the tradition. The reaction saw not only a conservative public morality but also a new historical and philological rigor in the interpretation of early texts. This was closely analogous to the contemporary Western conflict in biblical studies between subjectivist "liberty of interpretation" and the development of historical philology—that is, the understanding of early texts by close study of how words were used at the time when the text was written. The new emphasis on historical scholarship had profound consequences for both China and the West, each of which had depended to some degree on the authority of received texts. This historical and philological approach to early texts was a form of empiricism, basing judgments on evidence and proof rather than tradition or private inclination. In China, as in the West at the same time, such empiricism in scholarship became linked to other forms of empiricism, such as interest in the natural sciences.

Ming subjectivist thought had found its strongest literary manifestation in a fascination with dreams, a world of illusion that was both a prominent theme in and a metaphor for the theater. And like Shakespeare, Chinese dramatists also observed that "all the world's a stage" and thus also a dream, as did the Spanish dramatist Pedro Calderón, author of *Life Is a Dream*. Drama, far more than prose fiction, dominated the literary world, both in the theater and in published texts. Social rituals and ceremonies had been one of the pillars of Confucian society, and these came increasingly to be represented in terms of theatrical performance. What had been norms of behavior became "roles," strongly suggesting awareness of their unreality and the presence of an individual who was only "playing" a role.

The eighteenth century was the last period of glory and self-confidence for traditional Chinese civilization. Although China had been in continuous contact with Europe since the sixteenth century, in the early nineteenth century European colonial powers began to make major inroads on Chinese autonomy. The opium trade, dominated by British merchants, drained away silver while producing a major social problem. In their campaign to stop the drug trade, the Chinese fired on a ship flying the British flag. From this followed the Opium War (1840–42), in which Great Britain inflicted a series of humiliating defeats on Chinese forces. In the treaty that followed, Hong Kong was ceded to Great Britain and five so-called treaty ports were established, subject to British law and control. Other European powers rushed to carve out their own enclaves. Christian missionaries, protected by treaty, spread throughout the country. One consequence was the T'ai-p'ing T'ien-kuo, the "Heavenly Kingdom of Great Peace," a political movement and religious sect that mingled Christianity and native Chinese beliefs. The T'ai-p'ing T'ien-kuo rose in rebellion against the Ch'ing government and between 1850 and 1864 carried out a war that left central China in desolation.

Humiliated and exhausted, the Ch'ing government found itself unable to adapt, either culturally or technologically, to the world that had been thrust on it. Through the latter half of the nineteenth century and first decade of the twentieth, the Ch'ing Dynasty slowly disintegrated, until it was overthrown with remarkable ease in 1911, when the Republic of China was established.

TIME LINE

TEXTS	CONTEXTS
1300–1350 Earliest printed versions of vernacular drama	
ca. 1350 Earliest publication of vernacular short stories	
	1368 Ming Dynasty is established with the capital at Nanking
	1405–21 Ming admiral Cheng Ho explores southeast Asia, Sri Lanka, and the coast of Africa
	1421 The capital is moved to Peking
early 16th century Earliest edition of *Water Margin*, an episodic novel about a band of outlaws	
1522 Earliest edition of *Romance of the Three Kingdoms*, a long historical novel about the fall of the Han Dynasty	
1550–1617 T'ang Hsien-tsu, a major dramatist who developed the long *ch'uan-ch'i* play into a literary form	
1574–1646 Feng Meng-lung, collector and author of vernacular stories and popular songs, important in raising the status of vernacular literature	**1580–1644** Late Ming, a period of radical subjectivism and questioning of authority of tradition
	1583–1610 Matteo Ricci, Jesuit missionary, serves in China
1592 Earliest extant edition of *Monkey* (*Journey to the West*)	
1611–80 Li Yü, comic dramatist, story writer, and champion of vernacular literature	
1617 Earliest edition of *Chin P'ing Mei* (*Golden Lotus*), a satirical novel of manners about a corrupt sensualist	
	1644–45 Manchus conquer China • Ch'ing Dynasty is established • All Chinese males are forced to cut their hair and wear the queue

Boldface titles indicate works in the anthology.

TIME LINE

TEXTS	CONTEXTS
1648–1718 K'ung Shang-jen, author of *The Peach Blossom Fan* (1699) **1715–63** Cao Xueqin, author of **The Story of the Stone** (1740–50)	
	1736–1794 "Literary inquisition": earlier works are censored and many writers imprisoned for suspected critical references to the Ch'ing Dynasty
ca. 1750 *Ju-lin wai-shih* (*The Scholars*), a satirical novel; first extant edition 1803 **1788** The completion of the *Ssu-k'u ch'üan-shu,* a massive collection of all important earlier literature	

WU CH'ENG-EN
ca. 1506–1581

The prose romance *Monkey* (properly, "Journey to the West," *Hsi-yu chi*) was not the work of a single person. First published in 1592, it represents a cumulative retelling and elaboration of materials that evolved over many centuries. Yet the final form of these stories in a vast, sprawling novel of one hundred chapters, often attributed to Wu Ch'eng-en, transformed the traditional material into a work of genius. The core of the story had a historical basis in the journey of the T'ang Buddhist monk Hsüan Tsang, or Tripitaka (596–664), from China to India in search of Buddhist scriptures. On his return, Hsüan Tsang left a short account of his experiences. The contents of this account had virtually nothing to do with the novel, but they may have served as the early basis from which the story began to be retold. Pilgrimages to India were by no means unique among Chinese monks of this era, but Tripitaka's journey somehow captured the popular imagination; it was retold in stories and plays, until it finally emerged as *Monkey*.

As Hsüan Tsang's journey was retold, the most important addition was his acquisition of a wondrous disciple Sun Wu-k'ung, Monkey Aware-of-Vacuity. Monkey had already made his appearance in a thirteenth-century version of the story and came to so dominate the full novel version that Arthur Waley named his condensation of the novel after this character.

It has long been debated whether *Monkey* is a work of exuberant play, celebrating Monkey's free spirit and turbulent ingenuity, or a serious allegory of Monkey and Tripitaka's journey toward Buddhist enlightenment. The novel is certainly something of both. An argument can be made, from a Buddhist point of view, that Tripitaka, however inept and timorous, is the novel's true hero. But for most readers, Chinese and Western, Monkey's splendid vitality and boundless humor remain the center of interest. Monkey's guardianship over Tripitaka is seconded by the ever-hungry and lustful Pigsy, a straightforward and predictable emblem of human sensual appetites, who becomes increasingly unsympathetic as the journey progresses. Tripitaka's third disciple and protector is the gentle dragon Sandy, a former marshal of the hosts of Heaven who was sent to the bottom of a river to expiate the sin of having broken the Jade Emperor's (a Taoist divinity) crystal cup.

Above the four travelers is a divine machinery built of a synthesis of benign boddhisattvas (potential buddhas who linger in this world to help suffering humanity) and a Taoist pantheon of unruly and sometimes dangerous deities. On the earthly plane the pilgrims move through a landscape of strange kingdoms and monsters, stopping sometimes to help those in need or to protect themselves from harm. Some of the earthly monsters belong to the places where the pilgrims find them, but many of the demons and temptresses that the travelers encounter either are exiles and escapees from the heavenly realm or are sent on purpose to test the pilgrims.

Surrounded by three guardian disciples whose characters at the very least verge on the allegorical, Tripitaka is not only human but all too human. He is easily frightened, sometimes petulant, and never knows what to do. He is not so much driven on the pilgrimage by determined resolve as merely carried along by it. Yet he alone is the character destined for full buddhahood at the end, and his apparent lack of concern for the quest and for his disciples has been interpreted as the true manifestation of Buddhist detachment. Although Monkey grows increasingly devoted to his master through the course of the novel, Tripitaka never fully trusts him, however much he depends on him; and if there is a difficult Buddhist lesson in the novel, it is to grasp how Tripitaka, the ordinary man as saint, can be the novel's true hero. He is the empty center of the group, kept alive and carried forward by his more powerful and active disciples, both willing and unwilling. Yet he remains the master, and without him the pilgrimage would not exist.

During the course of the pilgrimage, Monkey becomes increasingly bound both to his master and to the quest itself, without ever losing his energy and humor. Despite occasional outbursts of his former mischief making, the quest becomes for Monkey a structured series of challenges by which he can focus and discipline his rambunctious intellect. The journey is driven forward by Monkey alone, with Tripitaka ever willing to give up in despair. Monkey understands the world with a comic detachment that is in some ways akin to Buddhist detachment, and this detachment makes him always more resourceful and often wiser than Tripitaka. Yet in his fierce energy and sheer joy in the use of his mind, Monkey falls short of the Buddhist ideal of true tranquility, while remaining the hero for unenlightened mortals.

The short selections from this very long novel printed here treat Monkey's birth and his release by Tripitaka from imprisonment under the mountain. After a long series of fantastical adventures, the pilgrims finally reach India and acquire the scriptures. In the last chapters all the pilgrims are whisked back to China by divine winds and are rewarded according to their merits.

PRONOUNCING GLOSSARY

The following list uses common English syllables to provide rough equivalents of selected words whose pronunciation may be unfamiliar to the general reader.

Amitabha: *ah-mee-tahb-ha*

Ao-lai: *au–lai*

Chang Liang: *jahng lyahng*

Erh-lang: *ur–lahng*

Hsiao Ho: *shyau huh*

hsing: *shing*

Huang Shih Kung: *hwahng shir goong*

Hsüan Tsang: *shooahn dzahng*

Hui-yen: *hway–yen*

Jambudvīpa: *jahm-bood-vee-pah*

Kao Ts'ai: *gau tsai*

Kuan-yin: *gwahn–yin*

Lao Tzu: *lau dzuh*

Li Shih-min: *lee shir–min*

Lu Chia: *loo jyah*

Manjúsrī: *mahn-joosh-ree*

Sākyamuni: *shahk-yah-moo-nee*

śramana: *shrah-mah-nah*

Subodhi: *soo-bod-hee*

Sun Wu-k'ung: *swun woo-koong*

Trayaśimstra: *trah-ya-sheem-strah*

Wu Ch'eng-en: *woo chung-uhn*

Wu-ssu: *woo–suh*

Yü: *yoo*

From Monkey[1]

CHAPTER I

There was a rock that since the creation of the world had been worked upon by the pure essences of Heaven and the fine savours of Earth, the vigour of sunshine and the grace of moonlight, till at last it became magically pregnant and one day split open, giving birth to a stone egg, about as big as a playing ball. Fructified by the wind it developed into a stone monkey, complete with every organ and limb. At once this monkey learned to climb

1. Translated by and with notes adapted from Arthur Waley.

and run; but its first act was to make a bow towards each of the four quarters. As it did so, a steely light darted from this monkey's eyes and flashed as far as the Palace of the Pole Star. This shaft of light astonished the Jade Emperor[2] as he sat in the Cloud Palace of the Golden Gates, in the Treasure Hall of the Holy Mists, surrounded by his fairy Ministers. Seeing this strange light flashing, he ordered Thousand-league Eye and Down-the-wind Ears[3] to open the gate of the Southern Heaven and look out. At his bidding these two captains went out to the gate and looked so sharply and listened so well that presently they were able to report, "This steely light comes from the borders of the small country of Ao-lai, that lies to the east of the Holy Continent, from the Mountain of Flowers and Fruit. On this mountain is a magic rock, which gave birth to an egg. This egg changed into a stone monkey, and when he made his bow to the four quarters a steely light flashed from his eyes with a beam that reached the Palace of the Pole Star. But now he is taking a drink, and the light is growing dim."

The Jade Emperor condescended to take an indulgent view. "These creatures in the world below," he said, "were compounded of the essence of heaven and earth, and nothing that goes on there should surprise us." That monkey walked, ran, leapt and bounded over the hills, feeding on grasses and shrubs, drinking from streams and springs, gathering the mountain flowers, looking for fruits. Wolf, panther and tiger were his companions, the deer and civet were his friends, gibbons and baboons his kindred. At night he lodged under cliffs of rock, by day he wandered among the peaks and caves. One very hot morning, after playing in the shade of some pine-trees, he and the other monkeys went to bathe in a mountain stream. See how those waters bounce and tumble like rolling melons!

There is an old saying, "Birds have their bird language, beasts have their beast talk." The monkeys said, "We none of us know where this stream comes from. As we have nothing to do this morning, wouldn't it be fun to follow it up to its source?" With a whoop of joy, dragging their sons and carrying their daughters, calling out to younger brother and to elder brother, the whole troupe rushed along the streamside and scrambled up the steep places, till they reached the source of the stream. They found themselves standing before the curtain of a great waterfall.

All the monkeys clapped their hands and cried aloud, "Lovely water, lovely water! To think that it starts far off in some cavern below the base of the mountain, and flows all the way to the Great Sea! If any of us were bold enough to pierce that curtain, get to where the water comes from and return unharmed, we would make him our king!" Three times the call went out, when suddenly one of them leapt from among the throng and answered the challenge in a loud voice. It was the Stone Monkey. "I will go," he cried, "I will go!" Look at him! He screws up his eyes and crouches; then at one bound he jumps straight through the waterfall. When he opened his eyes and looked about him, he found that where he had landed there was no water. A great bridge stretched in front of him, shining and glinting. When he looked closely at it, he saw that it was made all of burnished iron. The water under it flowed through a hole in the rock, filling in all the space

---

2. The chief deity in the Taoist pantheon.   3. Here and throughout *Monkey* there are fantastic deities and places invented by the author.

under the arch. Monkey climbed up on to the bridge and, spying as he went, saw something that looked just like a house. There were stone seats and stone couches, and tables with stone bowls and cups. He skipped back to the hum of the bridge and saw that on the cliff there was an inscription in large square writing which said, "This cave of the Water Curtain in the blessed land of the Mountain of Flowers and Fruit leads to Heaven." Monkey was beside himself with delight. He rushed back and again crouched, shut his eyes and jumped through the curtain of water.

"A great stroke of luck," he cried, "A great stroke of luck." "What is it like on the other side?" asked the monkeys, crowding round him. "Is the water very deep?" "There is no water," said the Stone Monkey. "There is an iron bridge, and at the side of it a heaven-sent place to live in." "What made you think it would do to live in?" asked the monkeys. "The water," said the Stone Monkey, "flows out of a hole in the rock, filling in the space under the bridge. At the side of the bridge are flowers and trees, and there is a chamber of stone. Inside are stone tables, stone cups, stone dishes, stone couches, stone seats. We could really be very comfortable there. There is plenty of room for hundreds and thousands of us, young and old. Let us all go and live there; we shall be splendidly sheltered in every weather." "You go first and show us how!" cried the monkeys, in great delight. Once more he closed his eyes and was through at one bound. "Come along, all of you!" he cried. The bolder of them jumped at once; the more timid stretched out their heads and then drew them back, scratched their ears, rubbed their cheeks, and then with a great shout the whole mob leapt forward. Soon they were all seizing dishes and snatching cups, scrambling to the hearth or fighting for the beds, dragging things along or shifting them about, behaving indeed as monkeys with their mischievous nature might be expected to do, never quiet for an instant, till at last they were thoroughly worn out. The Stone Monkey took his seat at the head of them and said, "Gentlemen! 'With one whose word cannot be trusted there is nothing to be done!'[4] You promised that any of us who managed to get through the waterfall and back again, should be your king. I have not only come and gone and come again, but also found you a comfortable place to sleep, put you in the enviable position of being householders. Why do you not bow down to me as your king?"

Thus reminded, the monkeys all pressed together the palms of their hands and prostrated themselves, drawn up in a line according to age and standing, and bowing humbly they cried, "Great king, a thousand years!" After this the Stone Monkey discarded his old name and became king, with the title "Handsome Monkey King." He appointed various monkeys, gibbons and baboons to be his ministers and officers. By day they wandered about the Mountain of Flowers and Fruit; at night they slept in the Cave of the Water Curtain. They lived in perfect sympathy and accord, not mingling with bird or beast, in perfect independence and entire happiness.

The Monkey King had enjoyed this artless existence for several hundred years when one day, at a feast in which all the monkeys took part, the king suddenly felt very sad and burst into tears. His subjects at once ranged themselves in front of him and bowed down, saying, "Why is your Majesty so sad?" "At present," said the king, "I have no cause for unhappiness. But I

4. From Confucius's *Analects* II.22.

have a misgiving about the future, which troubles me sorely." "Your Majesty is very hard to please," said the monkeys, laughing. "Every day we have happy meetings on fairy mountains, in blessed spots, in ancient caves, on holy islands. We are not subject to the Unicorn or Phoenix, nor to the restraints of any human king. Such freedom is an immeasurable blessing. What can it be that causes you this sad misgiving?" "It is true," said the Monkey King, "that to-day I am not answerable to the law of any human king, nor need I fear the menace of any beast or bird. But the time will come when I shall grow old and weak. Yama, King of Death, is secretly waiting to destroy me. Is there no way by which, instead of being born again on earth, I might live forever among the people of the sky?"

When the monkeys heard this they covered their faces with their hands and wept, each thinking of his own mortality. But look! From among the ranks there springs out one monkey commoner, who cries in a loud voice "If that is what troubles your Majesty, it shows that religion has taken hold upon your heart. There are indeed, among all creatures, three kinds that are not subject to Yama, King of Death." "And do you know which they are?" asked the Monkey King. "Buddhas, Immortals and Sages,"[5] he said. "These three are exempt from the Turning of the Wheel, from birth and destruction. They are eternal as Heaven and Earth, as the hills and streams." "Where are they to be found?" asked the Monkey King. "Here on the common earth," said the monkey, "in ancient caves among enchanted hills."

The king was delighted with this news. "To-morrow," he said, "I shall say good-bye to you, go down the mountain, wander like a cloud to the corners of the sea, far away to the end of the world, till I have found these three kinds of Immortal. From them I will learn how to be young forever and escape the doom of death." This determination it was that led him to leap clear of the toils of Re-incarnation and turned him at last into the Great Monkey Sage, equal of Heaven. The monkeys clapped their hands and cried aloud, "Splendid! Splendid! To-morrow we will scour the hills for fruits and berries and hold a great farewell banquet in honour of our king."

Next day they duly went to gather peaches and rare fruits, mountain herbs, yellow-sperm,[6] tubers, orchids, strange plants and flowers of every sort, and set out the stone tables and benches, laid out fairy meats and drinks. They put the Monkey King at the head of the table, and ranged themselves according to their age and rank. The pledge-cup[7] passed from hand to hand; they made their offerings to him of flowers and fruit. All day long they drank, and next day their king rose early and said, "Little ones, cut some pine-wood for me and make me a raft; then find a tall bamboo for pole, and put together a few fruits and such like. I am going to start." He got on to the raft all alone and pushed off with all his might, speeding away and away, straight out to sea, till favoured by a following wind he arrived at the borders of the Southern World. Fate indeed had favoured him; for days on end, ever since he set foot on the raft, a strong southeast wind blew and carried him at last to the north-western bank, which is indeed the frontier of the Southern World. He tested the water with his pole and found that it was shallow; so he left the raft and climbed ashore. On the beach were people

5. The highest stages of religious perfection in Buddhism, Taoism, and Confucianism, respectively.
6. Unidentified plant.   7. A cup used for offering toasts.

fishing, shooting wild geese, scooping oysters, draining salt. He ran up to them and for fun began to perform queer antics which frightened them so much that they dropped their baskets and nets and ran for their lives. One of them, who stood his ground, Monkey caught hold of, and ripping off his clothes, found out how to wear them himself, and so dressed up went prancing through towns and cities, in market and bazaar, imitating the people's manners and talk. All the while his heart was set only on finding the Immortals and learning from them the secret of eternal youth. But he found the men of the world all engrossed in the quest of profit or fame; there was not one who had any care for the end that was in store for him. So Monkey went looking for the way of Immortality, but found no chance of meeting it. For eight or nine years he went from city to city and town to town till suddenly he came to the Western Ocean. He was sure that beyond this ocean there would certainly be Immortals, and he made for himself a raft like the one he had before. He floated on over the Western Ocean till he came to the Western Continent, where he went ashore, and when he had looked about for some time, he suddenly saw a very high and beautiful mountain, thickly wooded at the base. He had no fear of wolves, tigers or panthers, and made his way up to the very top. He was looking about him when he suddenly heard a man's voice coming from deep amid the woods. He hurried towards the spot and listened intently. It was some one singing, and these were the words that he caught:

> I hatch no plot, I scheme no scheme;
> Fame and shame are one to me,
> A simple life prolongs my days.
> Those I meet upon my way
> Are Immortals, one and all,
> Who from their quiet seats expound
> The Scriptures of the Yellow Court.[8]

When Monkey heard these words he was very pleased. "There must then be Immortals somewhere hereabouts," he said. He sprang deep into the forest and looking carefully saw that the singer was a woodman, who was cutting brushwood. "Reverend Immortal," said Monkey, coming forward, "your disciple raises his hands." The woodman was so astonished that he dropped his axe. "You have made a mistake," he said, turning and answering the salutation, "I am only a shabby, hungry woodcutter. What makes you address me as an 'Immortal'?" "If you are not an Immortal," said Monkey, "why did you talk of yourself as though you were one?" "What did I say," asked the woodcutter, "that sounded as though I were an Immortal?" "When I came to the edge of the wood," said Monkey, "I heard you singing 'Those I meet upon my way are Immortals, one and all, who from their quiet seats expound the Scriptures of the Yellow Court.' Those scriptures are secret, Taoist texts. What can you be but an Immortal?" "I won't deceive you," said the woodcutter. "That song was indeed taught to me by an Immortal, who lives not very far from my hut. He saw that I have to work hard for my living and have a lot of troubles; so he told me when I was worried by anything to say to myself the words of that song. This, he said, would comfort me and get me out of

8. Texts of esoteric knowledge, containing secrets of immortality.

my difficulties. Just now I was upset about something and so I was singing that song. I had no idea that you were listening."

"If the Immortal lives close by," said Monkey, "how is it that you have not become his disciple? Wouldn't it have been as well to learn from him how never to grow old?" "I have a hard life of it," said the woodcutter. "When I was eight or nine I lost my father. I had no brothers and sisters, and it fell upon me alone to support my widowed mother. There was nothing for it but to work hard early and late. Now my mother is old and I dare not leave her. The garden is neglected, we have not enough either to eat or wear. The most I can do is to cut two bundles of firewood, carry them to market and with the penny or two that I get buy a few handfuls of rice which I cook myself and serve to my aged mother. I have no time to go and learn magic." "From what you tell me," said Monkey, "I can see that you are a good and devoted son, and your piety will certainly be rewarded. All I ask of you is that you will show me where the Immortal lives; for I should very much like to visit him."

"It is quite close," said the woodcutter. "This mountain is called the Holy Terrace Mountain, and on it is a cave called the Cave of the Slanting Moon and Three Stars. In that cave lives an Immortal called the Patriarch Subodhi. In his time he has had innumerable disciples, and at this moment there are some thirty or forty of them studying with him. You have only to follow that small path southwards for eight or nine leagues,[9] and you will come to his home." "Honoured brother," said Monkey, drawing the woodcutter towards him, "come with me, and if I profit by the visit I will not forget that you guided me." "It takes a lot to make some people understand," said the woodcutter. "I've just been telling you why I can't go. If I went with you, what would become of my work? Who would give my old mother her food? I must go on cutting my wood, and you must find your way alone."

When Monkey heard this, he saw nothing for it but to say good-bye. He left the wood, found the path, went uphill for some seven or eight leagues and sure enough found a cave-dwelling. But the door was locked. All was quiet, and there was no sign of anyone being about. Suddenly he turned his head and saw on top of the cliff a stone slab about thirty feet high and eight feet wide. On it was an inscription in large letters saying, "Cave of the Slanting Moon and Three Stars on the Mountain of the Holy Terrace." "People here," said Monkey, "are certainly very truthful. There really is such a mountain, and such a cave!" He looked about for a while, but did not venture to knock at the door. Instead he jumped up into a pine-tree and began eating the pine-seed and playing among the branches. After a time he heard someone call; the door of the cave opened and a fairy boy of great beauty came out, in appearance utterly unlike the common lads that he had seen till now. The boy shouted, "Who is making a disturbance out there?" Monkey leapt down from his tree, and coming forward said with a bow, "Fairy boy, I am a pupil who has come to study Immortality. I should not dream of making a disturbance." "*You* a pupil!" said the boy laughing. "To be sure," said Monkey. "My master is lecturing," said the boy. "But before he gave out his theme he told me to go to the door and if anyone came asking for instruction, I was to look after him. I suppose he meant you." "Of course he meant me," said

9. One league was equal to 360 steps.

Monkey. "Follow me this way," said the boy. Monkey tidied himself and followed the boy into the cave. Huge chambers opened out before them, they went on from room to room, through lofty halls and innumerable cloisters and retreats, till they came to a platform of green jade, upon which was seated the Patriarch Subodhi, with thirty lesser Immortals assembled before him. Monkey at once prostrated himself and bumped his head three times upon the ground, murmuring, "Master, master! As pupil to teacher I pay you my humble respects." "Where do you come from?" asked the Patriarch. "First tell me your country and name, and then pay your respects again." "I am from the Water Curtain Cave," said Monkey, "on the Mountain of Fruit and Flowers in the country of Ao-lai." "Go away!" shouted the Patriarch. "I know the people there. They're a tricky, humbugging set. It's no good one of them supposing he's going to achieve Enlightenment." Monkey, kowtowing violently, hastened to say, "There's no trickery about this; it's just the plain truth I'm telling you." "If you claim that you're telling the truth," said the Patriarch, "how is it that you say you came from Ao-lai? Between there and here there are two oceans and the whole of the Southern Continent. How did you get here?" "I floated over the oceans and wandered over the lands for ten years and more," said Monkey, "till at last I reached here." "Oh well," said the Patriarch, "I suppose if you came by easy stages, it's not altogether impossible. But tell me, what is your *hsing*?"[1] "I never show *hsing*," said Monkey. "If I am abused, I am not at all annoyed. If I am hit, I am not angry; but on the contrary, twice more polite than before. All my life I have never shown *hsing*."

"I don't mean that kind of *hsing*," said the Patriarch. "I mean what was your family, what surname had they?" "I had no family," said Monkey, "neither father nor mother." "Oh indeed!" said the Patriarch. "Perhaps you grew on a tree!" "Not exactly," said Monkey. "I came out of a stone. There was a magic stone on the Mountain of Flowers and Fruit. When its time came, it burst open and I came out."

"We shall have to see about giving you a school-name,"[2] said the Patriarch. "We have twelve words that we use in these names, according to the grade of the pupil. You are in the tenth grade." "What are the twelve words?" asked Monkey. "They are Wide, Big, Wise, Clever, True, Conforming, Nature, Ocean, Lively, Aware, Perfect and Illumined. As you belong to the tenth grade, the word Aware must come in your name. How about Aware-of-Vacuity?" "Splendid!" said Monkey, laughing. "From now onwards let me be called Aware-of-Vacuity."

So that was his name in religion. * * *

* * *

CHAPTER XIV

The hunter and Tripitaka were still wondering who had spoken, when again they heard the voice saying, "The Master has come." The hunter's servants said, "That is the voice of the old monkey who is shut up in the stone casket of the mountain side." "Why, to be sure it is!" said the hunter. "What

---

1. This is a pun. *Hsing* can mean "surname" or "temper."   2. A religious name assumed by a disciple.

old monkey is that?" asked Tripitaka. "This mountain," said the hunter, "was once called the Mountain of the Five Elements. But after our great T'ang Dynasty had carried out its campaigns to the West, its name was changed to Mountain of the Two Frontiers. Years ago a very old man told me that at the time when Wang Mang overthrew the First Han Dynasty, Heaven dropped this mountain in order to imprison a magic monkey under it. He has local spirits as his gaolers, who, when he is hungry give him iron pills to eat, and when he is thirsty give him copper-juice to drink, so that despite cold and short commons[3] he is still alive. That cry certainly comes from him. You need not be uneasy. We'll go down and have a look."

After going downhill for some way they came to the stone box, in which there was really a monkey. Only his head was visible, and one paw, which he waved violently through the opening, saying, "Welcome, Master! Welcome! Get me out of here, and I will protect you on your journey to the West." The hunter stepped boldly up, and removing the grasses from Monkey's hair and brushing away the grit from under his chin, "What have you got to say for yourself?" he asked. "To you, nothing," said Monkey. "But I have something to ask of that priest. Tell him to come here." "What do you want to ask me?" said Tripitaka. "Were you sent by the Emperor of T'ang to look for Scriptures in India?" asked Monkey. "I was," said Tripitaka. "And what of that?" "I am the Great Sage Equal of Heaven," said Monkey. "Five hundred years ago I made trouble in the Halls of Heaven, and Buddha clamped me down in this place. Not long ago the Bodhisattva Kuan-yin,[4] whom Buddha had ordered to look around for someone to fetch Scriptures from India, came here and promised me that if I would amend my ways and faithfully protect the pilgrim on his way, I was to be released, and afterwards would find salvation. Ever since then I have been waiting impatiently night and day for you to come and let me out. I will protect you while you are going to get Scriptures and follow you as your disciple."

Tripitaka was delighted. "The only trouble is," he said, "that I have no axe or chisel, so how am I to get you out?" "There is no need for axe or chisel," said Monkey. "You have only to want me to be out, and I shall be out." "How can that be?" asked Tripitaka. "On the top of the mountain," said Monkey, "is a seal stamped with golden letters by Buddha himself. Take it away, and I shall be out." Tripitaka was for doing so at once, but the hunter took him aside and said there was no telling whether one could believe the monkey or not. "It's true, it's true!" screamed Monkey from inside the casket. At last the hunter was prevailed upon to come with him and, scrambling back again to the very top, they did indeed see innumerable beams of golden light streaming from a great square slab of rock, on which was imprinted in golden letters the inscription OM MANI PADME HUM.[5]

Tripitaka knelt down and did reverence to the inscription, saying, "If this monkey is indeed worthy to be a disciple, may this imprint be removed and may the monkey be released and accompany me to the seat of Buddha. But if he is not fit to be a disciple, but an unruly monster who would discredit my undertaking, may the imprint of this seal remain where it is." At once

---

3. Daily provisions.   4. Associated with mercy and compassion. "Bodhisattva": a potential buddha who remains in the world to help others achieve salvation.   5. A magic spell (in Sanskrit) that keeps Monkey imprisoned.

there came a gust of fragrant wind that carried the six letters[6] of the inscription up into the air, and a voice was heard saying, "I am the Great Sage's gaoler. To-day the time of his penance is ended and I am going to ask Buddha to let him loose." Having bowed reverently in the direction from which the voice came, Tripitaka and the hunter went back to the stone casket and said to Monkey, "The inscription is removed. You can come out." "You must go to a little distance," said Monkey. "I don't want to frighten you." They withdrew a little way, but heard Monkey calling to them "Further, further!" They did as they were bid, and presently heard a tremendous crushing and rending. They were all in great consternation, expecting the mountain to come hurtling on top of them, when suddenly the noise subsided, and Monkey appeared, kneeling in front of Tripitaka's horse, crying, "Master, I am out!" Then he sprang up and called to the hunter, "Brother, I'll trouble you to dust the grass-wisps from my cheek." Then he put together the packs and hoisted them on to the horse, which on seeing him became at once completely obedient. For Monkey had been a groom in Heaven, and it was natural that an ordinary horse should hold him in great awe.

Tripitaka, seeing that he knew how to make himself useful and looked as though he would make a pretty tolerable śramana,[7] said to him, "Disciple, we must give you a name in religion." "No need for that," said Monkey, "I have one already. My name in religion is 'Aware-of-Vacuity.'" "Excellent!" said Tripitaka. "That fits in very well with the names of my other disciples. You shall be Monkey Aware-of-Vacuity."

The hunter, seeing that Monkey had got everything ready, said to Tripitaka, "I am very glad you have been fortunate enough to pick up this excellent disciple. As you are so well provided for, I will bid you good-bye and turn back." "I have brought you a long way from home," said Tripitaka, "and cannot thank you enough. Please also apologize to your mother and wife for all the trouble I gave, and tell them I will thank them in person on my return."

Tripitaka had not been long on the road with Monkey and had only just got clear of the Mountain of the Two Frontiers, when a tiger suddenly appeared, roaring savagely and lashing its tail. Tripitaka was terrified, but Monkey seemed delighted. "Don't be frightened, Master," he said. "He has only come to supply me with an apron."[8] So saying, he took a needle from behind his ear and, turning his face to the wind, made a few magic passes, and instantly it became a huge iron cudgel.[9] "It is five hundred years since I last used this precious thing," he said, "and to-day it is going to furnish me with a little much-needed clothing."

Look at him! He strides forward, crying, "Cursed creature, stand your ground!" The tiger crouched in the dust and dared not budge. Down came the cudgel on its head. The earth was spattered with its blood. Tripitaka rolled off his horse as best he could, crying with an awe-struck voice, "Heavens! When the hunter killed that stripy tiger yesterday, he struggled with it for hours on end. But this disciple of mine walked straight up to the tiger and struck it dead. True indeed is the saying 'Strong though he be, there is always a stronger.'" "Sit down a while," said Monkey, "and wait while I

6. The inscription consists of six letters in devanagari, the script in which Sanskrit is written.   7. A Buddhist monk.   8. That is, Monkey will kill the tiger and take the tiger skin to wear around his waist.
9. A club.

undress him; then when I am dressed, we'll go on." "How can you undress him?" said Tripitaka. "He hasn't got any clothes." "Don't worry about me," said Monkey. "I know what I am about." Dear Monkey! He took a hair from his tail, blew on it with magic breath, and it became a sharp little knife, with which he slit the tiger's skin straight down and ripped it off in one piece. Then he cut off the paws and head, and trimmed the skin into one big square. Holding it out, he measured it with his eye, and said, "A bit too wide. I must divide it in two." He cut it in half, put one half aside and the other round his waist, making it fast with some rattan that he pulled up from the roadside. "Now we can go," he said, "and when we get to the next house, I'll borrow a needle and thread and sew it up properly."

"What has become of your cudgel?" asked Tripitaka, when they were on their way again. "I must explain to you," said Monkey. "This cudgel is a piece of magic iron that I got in the Dragon King's palace, and it was with it that I made havoc in Heaven. I can make it as large or as small as I please. Just now I made it the size of an embroidery needle and put it away behind my ear, where it is always at hand in case I need it." "And why," asked Tripitaka, "did that tiger, as soon as it saw you, crouch down motionless and allow you to strike it just as you chose?" "The fact is," said Monkey, "that not only tigers but dragons too dare not do anything against me. But that is not all. I have such arts as can make rivers turn back in their course, and can raise tempests on the sea. Small wonder, then, that I can filch a tiger's skin. When we get into real difficulties you will see what I am really capable of."

"Master," said Monkey presently, "it is getting late. Over there is a clump of trees, and I think there must be a house. We had better see if we can spend the night there." Tripitaka whipped his horse, and soon they did indeed come to a farm, outside the gates of which he dismounted. Monkey cried "Open the door!" and presently there appeared a very old man, leaning on a staff. Muttering to himself, he began to push open the door, but when he saw Monkey, looking (with the tiger skin at his waist) for all the world like a thunder demon, he was terrified out of his wits and could only murmur "There's a devil at the door, sure enough there's a devil!" Tripitaka came up to him just in time to prevent him hobbling away. "Old patron," he said, "you need not be afraid. This is not a devil; it is my disciple." Seeing that Tripitaka at any rate was a clean-built, comely man, he took comfort a little and said, "I don't know what temple you come from, but you have no right to bring such an evil-looking fellow to my house." "I come from the Court of T'ang," said Tripitaka, "and I am going to India to get Scriptures. As my way brought me near your house, I have come here in the hope that you would consent to give me a night's lodging. I shall be starting off again tomorrow before daybreak." "You may be a man of T'ang," said the old man, "but I'll warrant that villainous fellow is no man of T'ang!" "Have you no eyes in your head," shouted Monkey. "The man of T'ang is my master. I am his disciple, and no man of T'ang or sugar-man[1] or honey-man either. I am the Great Sage Equal to Heaven. You people here know me well enough, and I have seen you before." "Where have you seen me?" he asked. "Didn't you when you were small cut the brushwood from in front of my face and gather the

1. *Tang* can mean "sugar."

herbs that grew on my cheek?" "The stone monkey in the stone casket!" gasped the old man. "I see that you are a little like him. But how did you get out?" Monkey told the whole story, and the old man at once bowed before him, and asked them both to step inside. "Great Sage, how old are you?" the old man asked, when they were seated. "Let us first hear your age," said Monkey. "A hundred and thirty," said the old man. "Then you are young enough to be my great-great-grandson at least," said Monkey. "I have no idea when I was born. But I was under that mountain for five hundred years." "True enough," said the old man. "I remember my grandfather telling me that this mountain was dropped from Heaven in order to trap a monkey divinity, and you say that you have only just got out. When I used to see you in my childhood, there was grass growing out of your head and mud on your cheeks. I was not at all afraid of you then. Now there is no mud on your cheeks and no grass on your head. You look thinner, and with that tiger-skin at your waist, who would know that you weren't a devil?" "I don't want to give you all a lot of trouble," said Monkey presently, "but it is five hundred years since I last washed. Could you let us have a little hot water? I am sure my Master would be glad to wash too."

When they had both washed, they sat down in front of the lamp. "One more request," said Monkey. "Could you lend me a needle and thread?" "By all means, by all means," said the old man, and he told his old wife to bring them. Just then Monkey caught sight of a white shirt that Tripitaka had taken off when he washed and not put on again. He snatched it up and put it on. Then he wriggled out of the tiger-skin, sewed it up in one piece, made a "horse-face fold"[2] and put it round his waist again, fastening the rattan belt. Presenting himself to Tripitaka he said, "How do you like me in this garb? Is it an improvement?" "Splendid!" said Tripitaka. "Now you really do look like a pilgrim." "Disciple," added Tripitaka, "if you don't mind accepting an off-cast, you can have that shirt for your own."

They rose early next day, and the old man brought them washing-water and breakfast. Then they set out again on their way, lodging late and starting early for many days. One morning they suddenly heard a cry and six men rushed out at them from the roadside, all armed with pikes and swords. "Halt, priest!" they cried. "We want your horse and your packs, and quickly too, or you will not escape with your life."

Tripitaka, in great alarm, slid down from his horse and stood there speechless. "Don't worry," said Monkey. "This only means more clothes and travelling-money for us." "Monkey, are you deaf?" said Tripitaka. "They ordered us to surrender the horse and luggage, and you talk of getting clothes and money from them!" "You keep an eye on the packs and the horse," said Monkey, "while I settle matters with them! You'll soon see what I mean." "They are very strong men and there are six of them," said Tripitaka. "How can a little fellow like you hope to stand up against them single-handed?"

Monkey did not stop to argue, but strode forward and, folding his arms across his chest, bowed to the robbers and said, "Sirs, for what reason do you stop poor priests from going on their way?" "We are robber kings," they said, "mountain lords among the Benevolent.[3] Everyone knows us. How

2. Unclear; the modern edition reads "sewed it into a skirt."   3. The thieves' slang for "bandit."

comes it that you are so ignorant? Hand over your things at once, and we will let you pass. But if half the word 'no' leaves your lips, we shall hack you to pieces and grind your bones to powder." "I, too," said Monkey, "am a great hereditary king, and lord of a mountain for hundreds of years; yet I have never heard your names." "In that case, let us tell you," they said. "The first of us is called Eye that Sees and Delights; the second, Ear that Hears and is Angry; the third, Nose that Smells and Covets; the fourth, Tongue that Tastes and Desires; the fifth, Mind that Conceives and Lusts; the sixth, Body that Supports and Suffers." "You're nothing but six hairy ruffians," said Monkey, laughing. "We priests, I would have you know, are your lords and masters, yet you dare block our path. Bring out all the stolen goods you have about you and divide them into seven parts. Then, if you leave me one part, I will spare your lives."

The robbers were so taken aback that they did not know whether to be angry or amused. "You must be mad," they said. "You've just lost all you possess, and you talk of sharing our booty with us!" Brandishing their spears and flourishing their swords they all rushed forward and began to rain blows upon Monkey's head. But he stood stock still and betrayed not the slightest concern. "Priest, your head must be very hard!" they cried. "That's all right," said Monkey, "I'm not in a hurry. But when your arms are tired, I'll take out my needle and do my turn." "What does he mean?" they said. "Perhaps he's a doctor turned priest. But we are none of us ill, so why should he talk about using the needle?"

Monkey took his needle from behind his ear, recited a spell which changed it into a huge cudgel, and cried, "Hold your ground and let old Monkey try his hand upon you!" The robbers fled in confusion, but in an instant he was among them and striking right and left he slew them all, stripped off their clothing and seized their baggage. Then he came back to Tripitaka and said laughing, "Master, we can start now; I have killed them all." "I am very sorry to hear it," said Tripitaka. "One has no right to kill robbers, however violent and wicked they may be. The most one may do is to bring them before a magistrate. It would have been quite enough in this case if you had driven them away. Why kill them? You have behaved with a cruelty that ill becomes one of your sacred calling." "If I had not killed them," said Monkey, "they would have killed you." "A priest," said Tripitaka, "should be ready to die rather than commit acts of violence." "I don't mind telling you," said Monkey, "that five hundred years ago, when I was a king, I killed a pretty fair number of people, and if I had held your view I should certainly never have become the Great Sage Equal of Heaven." "It was because of your unfortunate performances in Heaven," said Tripitaka, "that you had to do penance for five hundred years. If now that you have repented and become a priest you go on behaving as in old days, you can't come with me to India. You've made a very bad start." The one thing Monkey had never been able to bear was to be scolded, and when Tripitaka began to lecture him like this, he flared up at once and cried, "All right! I'll give up being a priest, and won't go with you to India. You needn't go on at me any more. I'm off!" Tripitaka did not answer. His silence enraged Monkey even further. He shook himself and with a last "I'm off!" he bounded away. When Tripitaka looked up, he had completely disappeared. "It's no use trying to teach people like that," said Tripitaka to himself gloomily. "I only said a word or two, and off he goes. Very well then. Evidently it is not my fate to have a disciple; so I must get on as best I can without one."

He collected the luggage, hoisted it on to the horse's back and set out on foot, leading the horse with one hand and carrying his priest's staff with the other, in very low spirits. He had not gone far, when he saw an old woman carrying a brocaded coat and embroidered cap. As she came near, Tripitaka drew his horse to the side of the road to let her pass. "Where are you off to all alone?" she asked. "The Emperor of China has sent me to India to fetch Scriptures," said Tripitaka. "The Temple of the Great Thunder Clap where Buddha lives," said she, "is a hundred and one thousand leagues away. You surely don't expect to get there with only one horse and no disciple to wait upon you?" "I picked up a disciple a few days ago," said Tripitaka, "but he behaved badly and I was obliged to speak rather severely to him; whereupon he went off in a huff, and I have not seen him since." "I've got a brocade coat and a cap with a metal band," said the old woman. "They belonged to my son. He entered a monastery, but when he had been a monk for three days, he died. I went and fetched them from the monastery to keep in memory of him. If you had a disciple, I should be very glad to let you have them." "That is very kind of you," said Tripitaka, "but my disciple has run away, so I cannot accept them." "Which way did he go?" asked the old woman. "The last time I heard his voice, it came from the east," said Tripitaka. "That's the way that my house lies," said the old woman. "I expect he'll turn up there. I've got a spell here which I'll let you learn, if you promise not to teach it to anybody. I'll go and look for him and send him back to you. Make him wear this cap and coat. If he disobeys you, say the spell, and he'll give no more trouble and never dare to leave you." Suddenly the old woman changed into a shaft of golden light, which disappeared towards the east. Tripitaka at once guessed that she was the Bodhisattva Kuan-yin in disguise. He bowed and burned incense towards the east. Then having stored away the cap and coat he sat at the roadside, practising the spell.

After Monkey left the Master, he somersaulted through the clouds and landed right in the palace of the Dragon King of the Eastern Ocean. "I heard recently that your penance was over," said the dragon, "and made sure you would have gone back to be king in your fairy cave." "That's what I am doing," said Monkey. "But to start with I became a priest." "A priest?" said the dragon. "How did that happen?" "Kuan-yin persuaded me to accompany a priest of T'ang," said Monkey, "who is going to India to get Scriptures; so I was admitted to the Order." "That's certainly a step in the right direction," said the dragon. "I am sure I congratulate you. But in that case, what are you doing here in the east?" "It comes of my master being so unpractical," said Monkey. "We met some brigands, and naturally I killed them. Then he started scolding me. You may imagine I wasn't going to stand that. So I left him at once, and am going back to my kingdom. But I thought I would look you up on the way, and see if you could give me a cup of tea."

When he had been given his cup of tea, he looked round the room, and saw on the wall a picture of Chang Liang[4] offering the slipper. Monkey asked what it was about. "You were in Heaven at the time," said the dragon, "and naturally would not know about it. The immortal in the picture is

4. A general who helped found the Han Dynasty; he was supposed to have had magical skills.

Huang Shih Kung, and the other figure is Chang Liang. Once when Shih Kung was sitting on a bridge, his shoe came off and fell under the bridge. He called to Chang Liang to pick it up and bring it to him. Chang Liang did so, whereupon the Immortal at once let it fall again, and Chang Liang again fetched it. This happened three times, without Chang Liang showing the slightest sign of impatience. Huang Shih Kung then gave him a magic treatise, by means of which he defeated all the enemies of the House of Han, and became the greatest hero of the Han dynasty. In his old age he became a disciple of the Immortal Red Pine Seed and achieved Tao.[5] Great Sage, you must learn to have a little more patience, if you hope to accompany the pilgrim to India and gain the Fruits of Illumination." Monkey looked thoughtful. "Great Sage," said the dragon, "you must learn to control yourself and submit to the will of others, if you are not to spoil all your chances." "Not another word!" said Monkey, "I'll go back at once."

On the way he met the Bodhisattva Kuan-yin. "What are you doing here?" she asked. "The seal was removed and I got out," said Monkey, "and became Tripitaka's disciple. But he said I didn't know how to behave, and I gave him the slip. But now I am going back to look after him." "Go as fast as you can," said the Bodhisattva, "and try to do better this time." "Master," said Monkey, when he came back and found Tripitaka sitting dejectedly by the roadside, "what are you doing still sitting here?" "And where have you been?" asked Tripitaka. "I hadn't the heart to go on, and was just sitting here waiting for you." "I only went to the dragon of the eastern ocean," said Monkey, "to drink a cup of tea." "Now Monkey," said Tripitaka, "priests must always be careful to tell the truth. You know quite well that the dragon king lives far away in the east, and you have only been gone an hour." "That's easily explained," said Monkey. "I have the art of somersaulting through the clouds. One bound takes me a hundred and eight thousand leagues." "It seemed to me that you went off in a huff," said Tripitaka, "because I had to speak rather sharply to you. It's all very well for you to go off and get tea like that, if you are able to. But I think you might remember that I can't go with you. Doesn't it occur to you that I may be thirsty and hungry too?" "If you are," said Monkey, "I'll take a bowl and go and beg for you." "There isn't any need to do that," said Tripitaka. "There are some dried provisions in the pack." When Monkey opened the pack, his eye was caught by something bright. "Did you bring this coat and cap with you from the east?" he asked. "I used to wear them when I was young," replied Tripitaka, saying the first thing that came into his head. "Anyone who wears this cap can recite scriptures without having to learn them. Anyone who wears this coat can perform ceremonies without having practised them." "Dear Master," said Monkey, "let me put them on." "By all means," said Tripitaka. Monkey put on the coat and cap, and Tripitaka, pretending to be eating the dried provisions, silently mumbled the spell. "My head is hurting!" screamed Monkey. Tripitaka went on reciting, and Monkey rolled over on the ground, frantically trying to break the metal fillet of the cap. Fearing that he would succeed, Tripitaka stopped for a moment. Instantly the pain stopped. Monkey felt his head. The cap seemed to have taken root upon it. He took out his needle and tried

---

5. That is, immortality.

to lever it up; but all in vain. Fearing once more that he would break the band, Tripitaka began to recite again. Monkey was soon writhing and turning somersaults. He grew purple in the face and his eyes bulged out of his head. Tripitaka, unable to bear the sight of such agony, stopped reciting, and at once Monkey's head stopped hurting.

"You've been putting a spell upon me," he said. "Nothing of the kind," said Tripitaka. "I've only been reciting the Scripture of the Tight Fillet."[6] "Start reciting again," said Monkey. When he did so, the pain began at once. "Stop, stop!" screamed Monkey. "Directly you begin, the pain starts; you can't pretend it's not you that are causing it." "In future, will you attend to what I say?" asked Tripitaka. "Indeed I will," said Monkey. "And never be troublesome again?" said Tripitaka. "I shouldn't dare," said Monkey. So he said, but in his heart there was still lurking a very evil intent. He took out his cudgel and rushed at Tripitaka, fully intending to strike. Much alarmed, the Master began to recite again, and Monkey fell writhing upon the ground; the cudgel dropped from his hand. "I give in, I give in!" he cried. "Is it possible," said Tripitaka, "that you were going to be so wicked as to strike me?" "I shouldn't dare, I shouldn't dare," groaned Monkey. "Master, how did you come by this spell?" "It was taught me by an old woman whom I met just now," said Tripitaka. "Not another word!" said Monkey. "I know well enough who she was. It was the Bodhisattva Kuan-yin. How dare she plot against me like that? Just wait a minute while I go to the Southern Ocean and give her a taste of my stick." "As it was she who taught me the spell," said Tripitaka, "she can presumably use it herself. What will become of you then?" Monkey saw the logic of this, and kneeling down he said contritely, "Master, this spell is too much for me. Let me go with you to India. You won't need to be always saying this spell. I will protect you faithfully to the end." "Very well then," said Tripitaka. "Help me on to my horse." Very crestfallen, Monkey put the luggage together, and they started off again towards the west.

* * *

6. A "fillet" is usually a strip of cloth—but here a band of metal—worn around the head. By reciting the scripture like a spell, Tripitaka can make the fillet tighten.

CAO XUEQIN (TS'AO HSÜEH-CH'IN)
1715–1763

Of all the world's novels perhaps only *Don Quixote* rivals *The Story of the Stone* as the embodiment of a nation's cultural identity in recent times, much as the epic once embodied cultural identity in the ancient world. For Chinese readers of the past two centuries *The Story of the Stone* (also known as the *Dream of the Red Chamber*) has come to represent the best and worst of traditional China in its final phase. It is the story of an extended family, centered around its women, and of the relationships within the family. Even after nearly a century of war, revolution, and social experiment, a century that has seen the dissolution of the traditional extended family and explosive economic growth, *The Story of the Stone* has retained its hold on the Chinese imagination.

As the title tells us, the novel is also, on a basic level, the story of a magical and conscious stone, the one block left over when the goddess Nü-wa repaired the damaged vault of the sky in the mythic past. Transported into the mortal world by a pair of priests, one Buddhist and one Taoist, Stone is destined to find enlightenment by suffering the pains of love, loss, and disillusion as a human being. In his incarnation, Stone is born as the sole legitimate male heir of a wealthy and powerful household, the Jias, which is about to pass from the height of prosperity into decline. Miraculously, the baby is born with an inscribed piece of jade in his mouth, from which he is given his name Bao-yu (Precious Jade) and which he wears always.

The novel itself has a peculiar genesis. The first eighty chapters are the work of Cao Xueqin, himself the scion of a once-wealthy family fallen on hard times. It is believed that he wrote the novel, in at least five drafts, between 1740 and 1750. There is another figure in the process of the novel's composition, someone who used the pseudonym "Red Inkstone" (or more properly "He of Red Inkstone Studio") and who added commentary and made corrections to the manuscript versions. He was obviously a close friend or relative of Cao Xueqin and acted the role of virtual collaborator. His comments suggest that the characters in the main portion of the novel are based on real people.

The novel was left unfinished and probably was never intended for publication, but it did circulate widely in Peking in manuscript copies, whose many variations show a complex process of revision. One version of the manuscript came into the hands of the writer Gao E (ca. 1740–ca. 1815), who completed the story by adding another 40 chapters, publishing the full 120-chapter version in 1791, about a half century after Cao Xueqin began to write. The transformations of the novel in its manuscript versions, the role of the mysterious Red Inkstone (and of another early commentator who calls himself "Odd Tablet"), and the relation of the characters to Cao's life are questions that continue to engage professional and amateur scholars.

Chinese novels are, as a rule, very long, and *The Story of the Stone* is longer than most, taking up five substantial volumes in its complete English translation. The narrative is impossible to summarize and difficult to excerpt. It has a huge cast of characters, both major and minor, who appear and disappear in intricately interwoven incidents. But, in part because of its very magnitude, the novel gradually draws its readers into the details of everyday life and the complexities of human relationships, occasionally punctuated by reminders that the intense emotions and the values given to things are all illusory. That sense of illusion is underscored by the family name Jia, a real Chinese surname that happens to be homophonous with another character meaning "false" or "feigned."

In addition to Bao-yu, the human metamorphosis of Stone, one other central character originates in the supernatural frame story and its fanciful landscape. This is Crimson Pearl Flower, a semidivine plant that grew near the Rock of Rebirth. In the opening chapter, while Stone is serving at the court of the goddess Disenchantment, he takes a fancy to this flower and waters it with sweet dew. This eventually brings the flower to life in the form of a fairy girl, who is obsessed with repaying the kindness of Stone, and for his gift of sweet dew she owes him the "debt of tears." This character is born as Bao-yu's cousin, the delicate and high-strung Lin Dai-yu (*Dai-yu* means "Black Jade").

The early chapters are devoted to the supernatural frame story and to bringing the characters together. In chapters seventeen and eighteen, Bao-yu's elder sister, an imperial concubine, has been permitted to pay a visit to her home. The women of the emperor's harem were usually confined to the palace; in permitting her to return, the emperor is displaying his favor to her and to her family. In her honor a huge garden (Prospect Garden) is constructed on the grounds of the family compound. After the imperial concubine's departure, the adolescent girls of the extended family are allowed to take up residence in the various buildings in the garden, and by special permission Bao-yu is also permitted to live there with his maids. The world of the garden is one of adolescent love in full flower, though we never forget the violent and ugly world outside, a world that often creeps into the garden world.

The adolescent love between Bao-yu and Dai-yu forms the core of the novel. Each is intensely sensitive to the other, and neither can express what he or she feels. Communication between them often depends on subtle gestures with implicit meanings, meanings that are inevitably misunderstood. Both, and particularly Dai-yu, believe in a perfect understanding of hearts; but even in the charmed world of the garden, closeness eludes them. The novel often juxtaposes brutish characters (usually male) with those possessed of a finer sensibility; but in the case of Dai-yu, sensibility is carried to the extreme. Dai-yu's relation to Bao-yu is balanced by that of another distant relation, Xue Bao-chai, whose plump good looks and gentle common sense are the very opposite of Dai-yu's frailty and histrionic morbidity. Bao-chai ("Precious Hairpin") has a golden locket with an inscription that matches Bao-yu's jade, and the marriage of "jade and gold" is a possibility seriously considered by older members of the family. Eventually, in Gao E's ending for the novel, as Dai-yu is dying of consumption, Bao-yu will be tricked into marrying Bao-chai. Bao-yu will finally carry out his obligation to continue the family line and at last renounce the world to become a Buddhist monk.

Although the triangle of Bao-yu, Dai-yu, and Bao-chai stands at the center of the novel, scores of subplots involve characters of all types. *The Story of the Stone* is, as noted, a novel about family, its internal relationships and its place in the larger social world. The reader easily becomes absorbed in the intensity of the family's internal relationships, always to be reminded how those relationships touch and are touched by the world outside. Because this family has social power, the actions taken by family members to serve its interests and loyalties can also be seen as corruption. In some cases the corruption is obvious, but in a far subtler way the reader comes to identify with the family and takes many acts of power and privilege for granted. At the same time, the outside world has the capacity to impinge on the protected space of the family, and the reader sees these forces from the point of view of the insider, as intrusions. It is a world of concentric circles of proximity, both of kinship and affinity. Petty details and private loves and hates grow larger and larger as they approach the center. And above this is the Buddhist and Taoist lesson about the illusion of care, of a world driven by blind but powerful emotions that at last cause only suffering, both to self and others.

The reader will find much unfamiliar about the Jia household, a vast establishment of close and distant family members, personal maids, and servants, each with his or her own level of status. Although the personal maids had some responsibilities, it will be obvious that the number of maids attached to each family member was primarily a mark of status. For a girl from a poor family, the position of personal maid was very desirable, providing room, board, and income to send to her own family. Bao-yu often flirts with his maids, but he has sexual relations only with his chief maid, Aroma.

The selection printed here includes part of the opening frame story and a series of chapters on Bao-yu and his female relations in Prospect Garden, with the blossoming of the love between him and Dai-yu.

The following list uses common English syllables to provide rough equivalents of selected words whose pronunciation may be unfamiliar to the general reader.

Cao Xueqin: *tsao shueh-chin*

Feng-shi: *fuhng–shir*

Feng Zi-ying: *fuhng dzuh–ying*

Gao E: *gau uh*

Jia Yu-cun: *jyah yow–tswuhn*

Jia Zheng: *jyah juhng*

Kong Mei-xi: *koong may–shee*

qiang: *chyahng*

Shi Xiang-yun: *shir shyahng–yoon*

Wang Ji-ren: *wahng jee–ruhn*

Wu Yu-feng: *woo yow–fuhng*

Xi-feng: *shee–fuhng*

Xue Bao-chai: *shooeh bau–chai*

Ying-lian: *ying–lyen*

Zhao: *jau*

Zhen Shi-yin: *juhn shir–yin*

Zhi-xiao: *juhr–shyau*

From The Story of the Stone[1]

From *Volume 1*

FROM CHAPTER 1

Zhen Shi-yin makes the Stone's acquaintance in a dream
And Jia Yu-cun finds that poverty is not incompatible with romantic
feelings

Gentle Reader,

What, you may ask, was the origin of this book?

Though the answer to this question may at first seem to border on the absurd, reflection will show that there is a good deal more in it than meets the eye.

Long ago, when the goddess Nü-wa was repairing the sky, she melted down a great quantity of rock and, on the Incredible Crags of the Great Fable Mountains, moulded the amalgam into thirty-six thousand, five hundred and one large building blocks, each measuring seventy-two feet by a hundred and forty-four feet square. She used thirty-six thousand five hundred of these blocks in the course of her building operations, leaving a single odd block unused, which lay, all on its own, at the foot of Greensickness Peak in the aforementioned mountains.

Now this block of stone, having undergone the melting and moulding of a goddess, possessed magic powers. It could move about at will and could grow or shrink to any size it wanted. Observing that all the other blocks had been used for celestial repairs and that it was the only one to have been rejected as unworthy, it became filled with shame and resentment and passed its days in sorrow and lamentation.

One day, in the midst of its lamentings, it saw a monk and a Taoist approaching from a great distance, each of them remarkable for certain eccentricities of manner and appearance. When they arrived at the foot of

1. Translated by David Hawkes. Note that Hawkes used the pinyin system of spelling (whereas this volume usually uses the Wade-Giles system).

Greensickness Peak, they sat down on the ground and began to talk. The monk, catching sight of a lustrous, translucent stone—it was in fact the rejected building block which had now shrunk itself to the size of a fan-pendant[2] and looked very attractive in its new shape—took it up on the palm of his hand and addressed it with a smile:

"Ha, I see you have magical properties! But nothing to recommend you. I shall have to cut a few words on you so that anyone seeing you will know at once that you are something special. After that I shall take you to a certain

> brilliant
> successful
> poetical
> cultivated
> aristocratic
> elegant
> delectable
> luxurious
> opulent
> locality on a little trip."

The stone was delighted.

"What words will you cut? Where is this place you will take me to? I beg to be enlightened."

"Do not ask," replied the monk with a laugh. "You will know soon enough when the time comes."

And with that he slipped the stone into his sleeve and set off at a great pace with the Taoist. But where they both went to I have no idea.

Countless aeons went by and a certain Taoist called Vanitas in quest of the secret of immortality chanced to be passing below that same Greensickness Peak in the Incredible Crags of the Great Fable Mountains when he caught sight of a large stone standing there, on which the characters of a long inscription were clearly discernible.

Vanitas read the inscription through from beginning to end and learned that this was a once lifeless stone block which had been found unworthy to repair the sky, but which had magically transformed its shape and been taken down by the Buddhist mahāsattva[3] Impervioso and the Taoist illuminate Mysterioso into the world of mortals, where it had lived out the life of a man before finally attaining nirvana and returning to the other shore.[4] The inscription named the country where it had been born, and went into considerable detail about its domestic life, youthful amours, and even the verses, mottoes and riddles it had written. All it lacked was the authentication of a dynasty and date. On the back of the stone was inscribed the following quatrain:

> Found unfit to repair the azure sky
> Long years a foolish mortal man was I.
> My life in both worlds on this stone is writ:
> Pray who will copy out and publish it?

---

2. Jade decoration strung from the bottom of a fan.   3. Wise man.   4. That is, achieving enlightenment and passing beyond the cycles of rebirth.

From his reading of the inscription Vanitas realized that this was a stone of some consequence. Accordingly he addressed himself to it in the following manner:

"Brother Stone, according to what you yourself seem to imply in these verses, this story of yours contains matter of sufficient interest to merit publication and has been carved here with that end in view. But as far as I can see (a) it has no discoverable dynastic period, and (b) it contains no examples of moral grandeur among its characters—no statesmanship, no social message of any kind. All I can find in it, in fact, are a number of females, conspicuous, if at all, only for their passion or folly or for some trifling talent or insignificant virtue. Even if I were to copy all this out, I cannot see that it would make a very remarkable book."

"Come, your reverence," said the stone (for Vanitas had been correct in assuming that it could speak), "must you be so obtuse? All the romances ever written have an artificial period setting—Han or Tang for the most part. In refusing to make use of that stale old convention and telling my *Story of the Stone* exactly as it occurred, it seems to me that, far from *depriving* it of anything, I have given it a freshness these other books do not have.

"Your so-called 'historical romances,' consisting, as they do, of scandalous anecdotes about statesmen and emperors of bygone days and scabrous attacks on the reputations of long-dead gentlewomen, contain more wickedness and immorality than I care to mention. Still worse is the 'erotic novel,' by whose filthy obscenities our young folk are all too easily corrupted. And the 'boudoir romances,' those dreary stereotypes with their volume after volume all pitched on the same note and their different characters undistinguishable except by name (all those ideally beautiful young ladies and ideally eligible young bachelors)—even they seem unable to avoid descending sooner or later into indecency.

"The trouble with this last kind of romance is that it only gets written in the first place because the author requires a framework in which to show off his love-poems. He goes about constructing this framework quite mechanically, beginning with the names of his pair of young lovers and invariably adding a third character, a servant or the like, to make mischief between them, like the *chou*[5] in a comedy.

"What makes these romances even more detestable is the stilted, bombastic language—inanities dressed in pompous rhetoric, remote alike from nature and common sense and teeming with the grossest absurdities.

"Surely my 'number of females,' whom I spent half a lifetime studying with my own eyes and ears, are preferable to this kind of stuff? I do not claim that they are better people than the ones who appear in books written before my time; I am only saying that the contemplation of their actions and motives may prove a more effective antidote to boredom and melancholy. And even the inelegant verses with which my story is interlarded could serve to entertain and amuse on those convivial occasions when rhymes and riddles are in demand.

"All that my story narrates, the meetings and partings, the joys and sorrows, the ups and downs of fortune, are recorded exactly as they happened.

---

5. The stock role of the clown in a play.

I have not dared to add the tiniest bit of touching-up, for fear of losing the true picture.

"My only wish is that men in the world below may sometimes pick up this tale when they are recovering from sleep or drunkenness, or when they wish to escape from business worries or a fit of the dumps, and in doing so find not only mental refreshment but even perhaps, if they will heed its lesson and abandon their vain and frivolous pursuits, some small arrest in the deterioration of their vital forces. What does your reverence say to that?"

For a long time Vanitas stood lost in thought, pondering this speech. He then subjected *The Story of the Stone* to a careful second reading. He could see that its main theme was love; that it consisted quite simply of a true record of real events; and that it was entirely free from any tendency to deprave and corrupt. He therefore copied it all out from beginning to end and took it back with him to look for a publisher.

As a consequence of all this, Vanitas, starting off in the Void (which is Truth) came to the contemplation of Form (which is Illusion); and from Form engendered Passion; and by communicating Passion, entered again into Form; and from Form awoke to the Void (which is Truth). He therefore changed his name from Vanitas to Brother Amor, or the Passionate Monk, (because he had approached Truth by way of Passion), and changed the title of the book from *The Story of the Stone* to *The Tale of Brother Amor.*

Old Kong Mei-xi from the homeland of Confucius called the book *A Mirror for the Romantic.* Wu Yu-feng called it *A Dream of Golden Days.* Cao Xueqin in his Nostalgia Studio worked on it for ten years, in the course of which he rewrote it no less than five times, dividing it into chapters, composing chapter headings, renaming it *The Twelve Beauties of Jinling,* and adding an introductory quatrain. Red Inkstone restored the original title when he recopied the book and added his second set of annotations to it.

This, then, is a true account of how *The Story of the Stone* came to be written.

> Pages full of idle words
> Penned with hot and bitter tears:
> All men call the author fool;
> None his secret message hears.

The origin of *The Story of the Stone* has now been made clear. The same cannot, however, be said of the characters and events which it recorded. Gentle reader, have patience! This is how the inscription began:

Long, long ago the world was tilted downwards towards the south-east; and in that lower-lying south-easterly part of the earth there is a city called Soochow; and in Soochow the district around the Chang-men Gate is reckoned one of the two or three wealthiest and most fashionable quarters in the world of men. Outside the Chang-men Gate is a wide thoroughfare called Worldly Way; and somewhere off Worldly Way is an area called Carnal Lane. There is an old temple in the Carnal Lane area which, because of the way it is bottled up inside a narrow *cul-de-sac,* is referred to locally as Bottle-gourd Temple. Next door to Bottle-gourd Temple lived a gentleman of private means called Zhen Shi-yin and his wife Feng-shi, a kind, good woman with a profound sense of decency and decorum. The household was not a particularly wealthy one, but they were nevertheless looked up to by all and sundry as the leading family in the neighbourhood.

Zhen Shi-yin himself was by nature a quiet and totally unambitious person. He devoted his time to his garden and to the pleasures of wine and poetry. Except for a single flaw, his existence could, indeed, have been described as an idyllic one. The flaw was that, although already past fifty, he had no son, only a little girl, just two years old, whose name was Ying-lian.

Once, during the tedium of a burning summer's day, Shi-yin was sitting idly in his study. The book had slipped from his nerveless grasp and his head had nodded down onto the desk in a doze. While in this drowsy state he seemed to drift off to some place he could not identify, where he became aware of a monk and a Taoist walking along and talking as they went.

"Where do you intend to take that thing you are carrying?" the Taoist was asking.

"Don't you worry about him!" replied the monk with a laugh. "There is a batch of lovesick souls awaiting incarnation in the world below whose fate is due to be decided this very day. I intend to take advantage of this opportunity to slip our little friend in amongst them and let him have a taste of human life along with the rest."

"Well, well, so another lot of these amorous wretches is about to enter the vale of tears," said the Taoist. "How did all this begin? And where are the souls to be reborn?"

"You will laugh when I tell you," said the monk. "When this stone was left unused by the goddess, he found himself at a loose end and took to wandering about all over the place for want of better to do, until one day his wanderings took him to the place where the fairy Disenchantment lives.

"Now Disenchantment could tell that there was something unusual about this stone, so she kept him there in her Sunset Glow Palace and gave him the honorary title of Divine Luminescent Stone-in-Waiting in the Court of Sunset Glow.

"But most of his time he spent west of Sunset Glow exploring the banks of the Magic River. There, by the Rock of Rebirth, he found the beautiful Crimson Pearl Flower, for which he conceived such a fancy that he took to watering her every day with sweet dew, thereby conferring on her the gift of life.

"Crimson Pearl's substance was composed of the purest cosmic essences, so she was already half-divine; and now, thanks to the vitalizing effect of the sweet dew, she was able to shed her vegetable shape and assume the form of a girl.

"This fairy girl wandered about outside the Realm of Separation, eating the Secret Passion Fruit when she was hungry and drinking from the Pool of Sadness when she was thirsty. The consciousness that she owed the stone something for his kindness in watering her began to prey on her mind and ended by becoming an obsession.

"'I have no sweet dew here that I can repay him with,' she would say to herself. 'The only way in which I could perhaps repay him would be with the tears shed during the whole of a mortal lifetime if he and I were ever to be reborn as humans in the world below.'

"Because of this strange affair, Disenchantment has got together a group of amorous young souls, of which Crimson Pearl is one, and intends to send them down into the world to take part in the great illusion of human life. And as today happens to be the day on which this stone is fated to go into the world too, I am taking him with me to Disenchantment's tribunal for the purpose of getting him registered and sent down to earth with the rest of these romantic creatures."

"How very amusing!" said the Taoist. "I have certainly never heard of a debt of tears before. Why shouldn't the two of us take advantage of this opportunity to go down into the world ourselves and save a few souls? It would be a work of merit."

"That is exactly what I was thinking," said the monk. "Come with me to Disenchantment's palace to get this absurd creature cleared. Then, when this last batch of romantic idiots goes down, you and I can go down with them. At present about half have already been born. They await this last batch to make up the number."

"Very good, I will go with you then," said the Taoist. Shi-yin heard all this conversation quite clearly, and curiosity impelled him to go forward and greet the two reverend gentlemen. They returned his greeting and asked him what he wanted.

"It is not often that one has the opportunity of listening to a discussion of the operations of *karma*[6] such as the one I have just been privileged to over-hear," said Shi-yin. "Unfortunately I am a man of very limited understanding and have not been able to derive the full benefit from your conversation. If you would have the very great kindness to enlighten my benighted under-standing with a somewhat fuller account of what you were discussing, I can promise you the most devout attention. I feel sure that your teaching would have a salutary effect on me and—who knows—might save me from the pains of hell."

The reverend gentlemen laughed. "These are heavenly mysteries and may not be divulged. But if you wish to escape from the fiery pit, you have only to remember us when the time comes, and all will be well."

Shi-yin saw that it would be useless to press them. "Heavenly mysteries must not, of course, be revealed. But might one perhaps inquire what the 'absurd creature' is that you were talking about? Is it possible that I might be allowed to see it?"

"Oh, as for that," said the monk: "I think it is on the cards for you to have a look at *him*," and he took the object from his sleeve and handed it to Shi-yin.

Shi-yin took the object from him and saw that it was a clear, beautiful jade on one side of which were carved the words "Magic Jade." There were sev-eral columns of smaller characters on the back, which Shi-yin was just going to examine more closely when the monk, with a cry of "Here we are, at the frontier of Illusion," snatched the stone from him and disappeared, with the Taoist, through a big stone archway above which

THE LAND OF ILLUSION

was written in large characters. A couplet in smaller characters was inscribed vertically on either side of the arch:

6. The accumulation of good and bad deeds that determines a soul's future lives.

Truth becomes fiction when the fiction's true;
Real becomes not-real where the unreal's real.

Shi-yin was on the point of following them through the archway when suddenly a great clap of thunder seemed to shake the earth to its very foundations, making him cry out in alarm.

And there he was sitting in his study, the contents of his dream already half forgotten, with the sun still blazing on the ever-rustling plantains outside, and the wet-nurse at the door with his little daughter Ying-lian in her arms. Her delicate little pink-and-white face seemed dearer to him than ever at that moment, and he stretched out his arms to take her and hugged her to him.

* * *

Chapters 1–25 Summary

After waking from his dream in the middle of the first chapter, Zhen Shi-yin meets the monk and the Taoist in the flesh, and they seek to take his daughter Ying-lian from him, informing him that otherwise she will be involved in misfortune. Zhen Shi-yin refuses and subsequently, in a series of misadventures, the baby is stolen from her nurse and will reappear in chapter 4 as "Caltrop," raised by kidnappers and eventually sold to be the concubine of Xue Pan in the Jia household.

In chapter 3 the scene shifts to the Jia household, which has made a home for the young Lin Dai-yu after her mother's death and for the Xue family, including Xue Pan and his sister Xue Bao-chai. The Xues had been a powerful family in Nanjing; but in acquiring Caltrop as his concubine, Xue Pan had another suitor beaten to death, and after Xue Pan had bribed his way out of a murder charge, the family thought it prudent to move to the capital to stay with their powerful relatives, the Jias.

The Jia household is dominated by Grandmother Jia, whose favorite is the adolescent Bao-yu, the only surviving son of Jia Zheng and his wife Lady Wang. Bao-yu, born with a piece of jade in his mouth, is the metamorphosis of Stone. Jia Zheng has another son, Jia Huan, by his concubine, known as Aunt Zhao. Note that concubinage was commonly practiced in large households, though normally only the sons of the legitimate wife could inherit.

In chapter 17 Prospect Garden is constructed to receive the visit of the imperial concubine, one of Lady Wang's daughters and Bao-yu's sister. After the visit, all the young girls of the household are given lodgings in the various buildings in the garden; Bao-yu, who is very close to his sisters and cousins and prefers the company of girls to boys, is also allowed to take up residence in the garden.

As we pick up the story in chapter 26, Jia Huan has spilled hot wax on his half brother Bao-yu's face in a fit of jealousy. Lady Wang rebukes Aunt Zhao for the behavior of her son, and Aunt Zhao, in a rage, pays a sorceress to cast a spell on Bao-yu. Bao-yu is ill for a while, but recovers.

CHAPTER 26

*A conversation on Wasp Waist Bridge is a cover for
communication of a different kind
And a soliloquy overheard in the Naiad's House reveals
unsuspected depths of feeling.*

By the time the thirty-three days' convalescence had ended, not only were Bao-yu's health and strength completely restored, but even the burn-marks on his face had vanished, and he was allowed to move back into the Garden.

It may be recalled that when Bao-yu's sickness was at its height, it had been found necessary to call in Jia Yun[7] with a number of pages under his command to take turns in watching over him. Crimson[8] was there too at that time, having been brought in with the other maids from his apartment. During those few days she and Jia Yun therefore had ample opportunity of seeing each other, and a certain familiarity began to grow up between them.

Crimson noticed that Jia Yun was often to be seen sporting a handkerchief very much like the one she had lost. She nearly asked him about it, but in the end was too shy. Then, after the monk's visit, the presence of the men-folk was no longer required and Jia Yun went back to his tree-planting. Though Crimson could still not dismiss the matter entirely from her mind, she did not ask anyone about it for fear of arousing their suspicions.

A day or two after their return to Green Delights,[9] Crimson was sitting in her room, still brooding over this handkerchief business, when a voice out-side the window inquired whether she was in. Peeping through an eyelet in the casement she recognized Melilot,[1] a little maid who belonged to the same apartment as herself.

"Yes, I'm in," she said. "Come inside!"

Little Melilot came bounding in and sat down on the bed with a giggle.

"I'm in luck!" she said. "I was washing some things in the yard when Bao-yu asked for some tea to be taken round to Miss Lin's for him and Miss Aroma[2] gave *me* the job of taking it. When I got there, Miss Lin had just been given some money by Her Old Ladyship[3] and was sharing it out among her maids; so when she saw me she just said 'Here you are!' and gave me two big handfuls of it. I've no idea how much it is. Will you look after it for me, please?"

She undid her handkerchief and poured out a shower of coins. Crimson carefully counted them for her and put them away in a safe place.

"What's been the matter with you lately?" said Melilot. "If you ask me, I think you ought to go home for a day or two and call in a doctor. I expect you need some medicine."

"Silly!" said Crimson. "I'm perfectly all right. What should I want to go home for?"

"I know what, then," said Melilot. "Miss Lin's very weakly. She's always taking medicine. Why don't you ask her to give you some of hers? It would probably do just as well."

"Oh, nonsense!" said Crimson. "You can't take other people's medicines just like that!"

"Well, you can't go on in this way," said Melilot, "never eating or drinking properly. What will become of you?"

"Who *cares*?" said Crimson. "The sooner I'm dead the better!"

"You shouldn't say such things," said Melilot. "It isn't right."

"Why not?" said Crimson. "How do you know what is on my mind?"

Melilot shook her head sympathetically.

"I can't say I really blame you," she said. "Things *are* very difficult here at times. Take yesterday, for example. Her Old Ladyship said that as Bao-yu

---

7. A poor relation of the Jias employed in the household.   8. One of Bao-yu's maids.   9. Bao-yu's res-idence in the garden.   1. One of Bao-yu's maids.   2. Bao-yu's chief maid. Miss Lin is Lin Dai-yu.
3. Bao-yu's grandmother.

was better now and there was to be a thanksgiving for his recovery, all those who had the trouble of nursing him during his illness were to be rewarded according to their grades. Well now, I can understand the very young ones like me not being included, but why should they leave *you* out? I felt really sorry for you when I heard that they'd left you out. Aroma, of course, you'd expect to get more than anyone else. I don't blame *her* at all. In fact, I think it's owing to her. Let's be honest: none of us can compare with Aroma. I mean, even if she didn't always take so much trouble over everything, no one would want to quarrel about *her* having a bigger share. What makes me so angry is that people like Skybright and Mackerel should count as top grade when everyone knows they're only put there to curry favour with Bao-yu. Doesn't it make you angry?"

"I don't see much point in getting angry," said Crimson. "You know what they said about the mile-wide marquee: 'Even the longest party must have an end'? Well, none of us is here for ever, you know. Another four or five years from now when we've each gone our different ways it won't *matter* any longer what all the rest of us are doing."

Little Melilot found this talk of parting and impermanence vaguely affecting and a slight moisture was to be observed about her eyes. She thought shame to cry without good cause, however, and masked her emotion with a smile:

"That's perfectly true. Only yesterday Bao-yu was going on about all the things he's going to do to his rooms and the clothes he's going to have made and everything, just as if he had a hundred or two years ahead of him with nothing to do but kill time in."

Crimson laughed scornfully, though whether at Melilot's simplicity or at Bao-yu's improvidence is unclear, since just as she was about to comment, a little maid came running in, so young that her hair was still done up in two little girl's horns. She was carrying some patterns and sheets of paper.

"You're to copy out these two patterns."

She threw them in Crimson's direction and straightway darted out again. Crimson shouted after her:

"Who are they for, then? You might at least finish your message before rushing off. What are you in such a tearing hurry about? Is someone steaming wheatcakes for you and you're afraid they'll get cold?"

"They're for Mackerel." The little maid paused long enough to bawl an answer through the window, then picking up her heels, went pounding off, *plim-plam, plim-plam, plim-plam,* as fast as she had come.

Crimson threw the patterns crossly to one side and went to hunt in her drawer for a brush to trace them with. After rummaging for several minutes she had only succeeded in finding a few worn-out ones, too moulted for use.

"Funny!" she said. "I could have sworn I put a new one in there the other day . . ."

She thought a bit, then laughed at herself as she remembered:

"Of course. Oriole[4] took it, the evening before last." She turned to Melilot. "Would you go and get it for me, then?"

"I'm afraid I can't," said Melilot. "Miss Aroma's waiting for me to fetch some boxes for her. You'll have to get it yourself."

---

4. One of Bao-chai's maids.

"If Aroma's waiting for you, why have you been sitting here gossiping all this time?" said Crimson. "If I hadn't asked you to go and get it, she wouldn't have been waiting, would she? Lazy little beast!"

She left the room and walked out of the gate of Green Delights and in the direction of Bao-chai's courtyard. She was just passing by Drenched Blossoms Pavilion when she caught sight of Bao-yu's old wet-nurse, Nannie Li, coming from the opposite direction and stood respectfully aside to wait for her.

"Where have you been, Mrs. Li?" she asked her. "I didn't expect to see you here."

Nannie Li made a flapping gesture with her hand:

"What do you think, my dear: His Nibs has taken a fancy to the young fellow who does the tree-planting—'Yin' or 'Yun' or whatever his name is—so Nannie has to go and ask him in. Let's hope Their Ladyships don't find out about it. There'll be trouble if they do."

"Are you really going to ask him in?"

"Yes. Why?"

Crimson laughed:

"If your Mr. Yun knows what's good for him, he won't agree to come."

"He's no fool," said Nannie Li. "Why shouldn't he?"

"Anyway, if he *does* come in," said Crimson, ignoring her question, "you can't just bring him in and then leave him, Mrs. Li. You'll have to take him back again yourself afterwards. You don't want him wandering off on his own. There's no knowing *who* he might bump into."

(Crimson herself, was the secret hope.)

"Gracious me! I haven't got *that* much spare time," said Nannie Li. "All I've done is just to tell him that he's got to come. I'll send someone else to fetch him in when I get back presently—one of the girls, or one of the older women, maybe."

She hobbled off on her stick, leaving Crimson standing there in a muse, her mission to fetch the tracing-brush momentarily forgotten. She was still standing there a minute or two later when a little maid came along, who, seeing that it was Crimson, asked her what she was doing there. Crimson looked up. It was Trinket, another of the maids from Green Delights.

"Where are you going?" Crimson asked her.

"I've been sent to fetch Mr. Yun," said Trinket. "I have to bring him inside to meet Master Bao."

She ran off on her way.

At the gate to Wasp Waist Bridge Crimson ran into Trinket again, this time with Jia Yun in tow. His eyes sought Crimson's; and hers, as she made pretence of conversing with Trinket, sought his. Their two pairs of eyes met and briefly skirmished; then Crimson felt herself blushing, and turning away abruptly, she made off for Allspice Court.

Our narrative now follows Jia Yun and Trinket along the winding pathway to the House of Green Delights. Soon they were at the courtyard gate and Jia Yun waited outside while she went in to announce his arrival. She returned presently to lead him inside.

There were a few scattered rocks in the courtyard and some clumps of jade-green plantain. Two storks stood in the shadow of a pine-tree, preening themselves with their long bills. The gallery surrounding the courtyard was hung with cages of unusual design in which perched or fluttered a wide variety of birds, some of them gay-plumaged exotic ones. Above the steps was a little five-frame[5] penthouse building with a glimpse of delicately-carved partitions visible through the open doorway, above which a horizontal board hung, inscribed with the words

CRIMSON JOYS AND GREEN DELIGHTS

"So that's why it's called 'The House of Green Delights,'" Jia Yun told himself. "The name is taken from the inscription."

A laughing voice addressed him from behind one of the silk gauze casements:

"Come on in! It must be two or three months since I first forgot our appointment!"

Jia Yun recognized the voice as Bao-yu's and hurried up the steps inside. He looked about him, dazzled by the brilliance of gold and semi-precious inlay-work and the richness of the ornaments and furnishings, but unable to see Bao-yu in the midst of it all. To the left of him was a full-length mirror from behind which two girls now emerged, both about fifteen or sixteen years old and of much the same build and height. They addressed him by name and asked him to come inside. Slightly overawed, he muttered something in reply and hurried after them, not daring to take more than a furtive glance at them from the corner of his eye. They ushered him into a tent-like summer "cabinet" of green net, whose principal furniture was a tiny lacquered bed with crimson hangings heavily patterned in gold. On this Bao-yu, wearing everyday clothes and a pair of bedroom slippers, was reclining, book in hand. He threw the book down as Jia Yun entered and rose to his feet with a welcoming smile. Jia Yun swiftly dropped knee and hand to floor in greeting. Bidden to sit, he modestly placed himself on a bedside chair.

"After I invited you round to my study that day," said Bao-yu, "a whole lot of things seemed to happen one after the other, and I'm afraid I quite forgot about your visit."[6]

Jia Yun returned his smile:

"Let's just say that it wasn't my luck to see you then. But you have been ill since then, Uncle Bao. Are you quite better now?"

"Quite better, thank you. I hear you've been very busy these last few days."

"That's as it should be,' said Jia Yun. "But I'm glad you are better, Uncle. That's a piece of good fortune for *all* of us."

As they chatted, a maid came in with some tea. Jia Yun was talking to Bao-yu as she approached, but his eyes were on her. She was tall and rather thin with a long oval face, and she was wearing a rose-pink dress over a closely pleated white satin skirt and a black satin sleeveless jacket over the dress.

In the course of his brief sojourn among them in the early days of Bao-yu's illness, Jia Yun had got by heart the names of most of the principal females of Bao-yu's establishment. He knew at a glance that the maid now serving him tea was Aroma. He was also aware that she was in some way more important than the other maids and that to be waited on by her in the seated

5. A unit for measuring space in a building. A "five-frame" building is relatively small.   6. Earlier, Jia Yun had been invited to pay a visit on Bao-yu.

presence of her master was an honour. Jumping hastily to his feet he addressed her with a modest smile:

"You shouldn't pour tea for *me*, Miss! I'm not like a visitor here. You should let me pour for myself!"

"Oh *do* sit down!" said Bao-yu. "You don't have to be like that in front of the *maids!*"

"I know," said Jia Yun. "But a body-servant![7] I don't like to presume."

He sat down, nevertheless, and sipped his tea while Bao-yu made conversation on a number of unimportant topics. He told him which household kept the best troupe of players, which had the finest gardens, whose maids were the prettiest, who gave the best parties, and who had the best collection of curiosities or the strangest pets. Jia Yun did his best to keep up with him. After a while Bao-yu showed signs of flagging, and when Jia Yun, observing what appeared to be fatigue, rose to take his leave, he did not very strongly press him to stay.

"You must come again when you can spare the time," said Bao-yu, and ordered Trinket to see him out of the Garden.

Once outside the gateway of Green Delights, Jia Yun looked around him on all sides, and having ascertained that there was no one else about, slowed down to a more dawdling pace so that he could ask Trinket a few questions. Indeed, the little maid was subjected to quite a catechism: How old was she? What was her name? What did her father and mother do? How many years had she been working for his Uncle Bao? How much pay did she get a month? How many girls were there working for him altogether? Trinket seemed to have no objection, however, and answered each question as it came.

"That girl you were talking to on the way in," he said, "isn't her name 'Crimson'?"

Trinket laughed:

"Yes. Why do you ask?"

"I heard her asking you about a handkerchief. Only it just so happens that I picked one up."

Trinket showed interest.

"She's asked me about that handkerchief of hers a number of times. I told her, I've got better things to do with my time than go looking for people's handkerchiefs. But when she asked me about it again today, she said that if I could find it for her, she'd give me a reward. Come to think of it, you were there when she said that, weren't you? It was when we were outside the gate of Allspice Court. So you can bear me out. Oh Mr. Jia, please let me have it if you've picked it up and I'll be able to see what she will give me for it!"

Jia Yun had picked up a silk handkerchief a month previously at the time when his tree-planting activities had just started. He knew that it must have been dropped by one or another of the female inmates of the Garden, but not knowing which, had not so far ventured to do anything about his discovery. When earlier on he had heard Crimson question Trinket about her loss, he had realized, with a thrill of pleasure, that the handkerchief he had picked up must have been hers. Trinket's request now gave him just the

7. A personal servant of higher status than maids.

opening he required. He drew a handkerchief of his own from inside his sleeve and held it up in front of her with a smile:

"I'll give it to you on one condition. If she lets you have this reward you were speaking of, you've *got* to let me know. No cheating, mind!"

Trinket received the handkerchief with eager assurances that he would be informed of the outcome, and having seen him out of the Garden, went back again to look for Crimson.

Our narrative returns now to Bao-yu.

After disposing of Jia Yun, Bao-yu continued to feel extremely lethargic and lay back on the bed with every appearance of being about to doze off to sleep. Aroma hurried over to him and, sitting on the edge of the bed, roused him with a shake:

"Come on! Surely you are not going to sleep *again*? You need some fresh air. Why don't you go outside and walk around for a bit?"

Bao-yu took her by the hand and smiled at her.

"I'd like to go," he said, "but I don't want to leave you."

"Silly!" said Aroma with a laugh. "Don't say what you don't mean!"

She hoicked[8] him to his feet.

"Well, where am I going to go then?" said Bao-yu. "I just feel so *bored*."

"Never mind where, just go out!" said Aroma. "If you stay moping indoors like this, you'll get even more bored."

Bao-yu followed her advice, albeit half-heartedly, and went out into the courtyard. After visiting the cages in the gallery and playing for a bit with the birds, he ambled out of the courtyard into the Garden and along the bank of Drenched Blossoms Stream, pausing for a while to look at the goldfish in the water. As he did so, a pair of fawns came running like the wind from the hillside opposite. Bao-yu was puzzled. There seemed to be no reason for their mysterious terror. But just then little Jia Lan came running down the same slope after them, a tiny bow clutched in his hand. Seeing his uncle ahead of him, he stood politely to attention and greeted him cheerfully:

"Hello, Uncle. I didn't know you were at home. I thought you'd gone out."

"Mischievous little blighter, aren't you?" said Bao-yu. "What do you want to go shooting them for, poor little things?"

"I've got no reading to do today," said Jia Lan, "and I don't like to hang about doing nothing, so I thought I'd practise my archery and equitation."[9]

"Goodness! You'd better not waste time jawing, then," said Bao-yu, and left the young toxophilite[1] to his pursuits.

Moving on, without much thinking where he was going, he came presently to the gate of a courtyard.

> Denser than feathers on the phoenix' tail
> The stirred leaves murmured with a pent dragon's moan.

The multitudinous bamboos and the board above the gate confirmed that his feet had, without conscious direction, carried him to the Naiad's House. Of their own accord they now carried him through the gateway and into the courtyard.

---

8. Yanked.   9. Horseback riding.   1. Archer.

The House seemed silent and deserted, its bamboo door-blind hanging unrolled to the ground; but as he approached the window, he detected a faint sweetness in the air, traceable to a thin curl of incense smoke which drifted out through the green gauze of the casement. He pressed his face to the gauze; but before his eyes could distinguish anything, his ear became aware of a long, languorous sigh and the sound of a voice speaking:

"Each day in a drowsy waking dream of love."

Bao-yu felt a sudden yearning for the speaker. He could see her now. It was Dai-yu, of course, lying on her bed, stretching herself and yawning luxuriously.

He laughed:

"Why 'each day in a drowsy waking dream of love'?" he asked through the window (the words were from his beloved *Western Chamber*[2]); then going to the doorway he lifted up the door-blind and walked into the room.

Dai-yu realized that she had been caught off her guard. She covered her burning face with her sleeve, and turning over towards the wall, pretended to be asleep. Bao-yu went over intending to turn her back again, but just at that moment Dai-yu's old wet-nurse came hurrying in with two other old women at her heels:

"Miss Lin's asleep, sir. Would you mind coming back again after she's woken up?"

Dai-yu at once turned over and sat up with a laugh:

"Who's asleep?"

The three old women laughed apologetically.

"Sorry, miss. We thought you were asleep. Nightingale! Come inside now! Your mistress is awake."

Having shouted for Nightingale, the three guardians of morality retired.

"What do you mean by coming into people's rooms when they're asleep?" said Dai-yu, smiling up at Bao-yu as she sat on the bed's edge patting her hair into shape.

At the sight of those soft cheeks so adorably flushed and the starry eyes a little misted with sleep a wave of emotion passed over him. He sank into a chair and smiled back at her:

"What was that you were saying just now before I came in?"

"I didn't say anything," said Dai-yu.

Bao-yu laughed and snapped his fingers at her:

"Put that on your tongue, girl! I heard you say it."

While they were talking to one another, Nightingale came in.

"Nightingale," said Bao-yu, "what about a cup of that excellent tea of yours?"

"Excellent tea?" said Nightingale. "There's nothing very special about the tea we drink here. If nothing but the best will do, you'd better wait for Aroma to come."

"Never mind about *him!*" said Dai-yu. "First go and get me some water!"

"He *is* our guest," said Nightingale. "I can't fetch you any water until I've given him his tea." And she went to pour him a cup.

"Good girl!" said Bao-yu.

2. A 13th-century romantic play.

> "If with your amorous mistress I should wed,
> 'Tis you, sweet maid, must make our bridal bed."

The words, like Dai-yu's languorous line, were from *Western Chamber,* but in somewhat dubious taste. Dai-yu was dreadfully offended by them. In an instant the smile had vanished from her face.

"*What* was that you said?"

He laughed:

"I didn't say anything."

Dai-yu began to cry.

"This is your latest amusement, I suppose. Every time you hear some coarse expression outside or read some crude, disgusting book, you have to come back here and give me the benefit of it. I am to become a source of entertainment for the *menfolk* now, it seems."

She rose, weeping, from the bed and went outside. Bao-yu followed her in alarm.

"Dearest coz, it was very wrong of me to say that, but it just slipped out without thinking. Please don't go and tell! I promise never to say anything like that again. May my mouth rot and my tongue decay if I do!"

Just at that moment Aroma came hurrying up:

"Quick!" she said. "You must come back and change. The Master[3] wants to see you."

The descent of this thunderbolt drove all else from his mind and he rushed off in a panic. As soon as he had changed, he hurried out of the Garden. Tealeaf[4] was waiting for him outside the inner gate.

"I suppose you don't know what he wants to see me about?" Bao-yu asked him.

"I should hurry up, if I were you," said Tealeaf. "All I know is that he wants to see you. You'll find out why soon enough when you get there."

He hustled him along as he spoke.

They had passed round the main hall, Bao-yu still in a state of fluttering apprehensiveness, when there was a loud guffaw from a corner of the wall. It was Xue Pan,[5] clapping his hands and stamping his feet in mirth.

"Ho! Ho! Ho! You'd never have come this quickly if you hadn't been told that Uncle wanted you!"

Tealeaf, also laughing, fell on his knees. Bao-yu stood there looking puzzled. It was some moments before it dawned on him that he had been hoaxed. Xue Pan was by this time being apologetic—bowing repeatedly and pumping his hands to show how sorry he was:

"Don't blame the lad!" he said. "It wasn't his fault. I talked him into it."

Bao-yu saw that he could do nothing, and might as well accept with a good grace.

"I don't mind being made a fool of," he said, "but I think it was going a bit far to bring my father into it. I think perhaps I'd better tell Aunt Xue and see what *she* thinks about it all."

"Now look here, old chap," said Xue Pan, getting agitated, "it was only because I wanted to fetch you out a bit quicker. I admit it was very wrong of

---

3. Jia Sheng, Bao-yu's father.   4. One of Bao-yu's male pages.   5. A troublemaker, Xue Bao-chai's brother.

me to make free with your Parent, but after all, you've only got to mention *my* father next time you want to fool *me* and we'll be quits!"

"Aiyo!" said Bao-yu. "Worse and worse!" He turned to Tealeaf: "Treacherous little beast! What are you still kneeling for?"

Tealeaf kotowed and rose to his feet.

"Look," said Xue Pan. "I wouldn't have troubled you otherwise, only it's my birthday on the third of next month and old Hu and old Cheng and a couple of the others, I don't know where they got them from but they've given me:

> a piece of fresh lotus root, ever so crisp and crunchy, as thick as that, look, and as long as that;
> a huge great melon, look, as big as that;
> a freshly-caught sturgeon as big as that;
> and a cypress-smoked Siamese sucking-pig as big as that that came in the tribute from Siam.

Don't you think it was clever of them to get me those things? Maybe not so much the sturgeon and the sucking-pig. They're just expensive. But where would you go to get a piece of lotus root or a melon like that? However did they get them to *grow* so big? I've given some of the stuff to Mother, and while I was about it I sent some round to your grandmother and Auntie Wang, but I've still got a lot left over. I can't eat it all myself; it would be unlucky. But apart from me, the only person I can think of who is *worthy* to eat a present like this is you. That's why I came over specially to invite you. And we're lucky, because we've got a little chap who sings coming-round as well. So you and I will be able to sit down and make a day of it, eh? Really enjoy ourselves."

Xue Pan, still talking, conducted Bao-yu to his "study," where Zhan Guang, Cheng Ri-xing, Hu Si-lai and Dan Ping-ren (the four donors of the feast) and the young singer he had mentioned were already waiting. They rose to welcome Bao-yu as he entered. When the bowings and courtesies were over and tea had been taken, Xue Pan called for his servants to lay.[6] A tremendous bustle ensued, which seemed to go on for quite a long time before everything was finally ready and the diners were able to take their places at the table.

Bao-yu noticed sliced melon and lotus root among the dishes, both of unusual quality and size.

"It seems wrong to be sharing your presents with you before I have given you anything myself," he said jokingly.

"Yes," said Xue Pan. "What are you planning to give me for my birthday next month? Something new and out of the ordinary, I hope."

"I haven't really *got* anything much to give you," said Bao-yu. "Things like money and food and clothing I don't want for, but they're not really mine to give. The only way I could give you something that would *really* be mine would be by doing some calligraphy or painting a picture for you."

"Talking of pictures," said Xue Pan genially, "that's reminded me. I saw a set of dirty pictures in someone's house the other day. They were real beauties. There was a lot of writing on top that I didn't pay much attention to, but I did notice the signature. I think it was 'Geng Huang,' the man who painted them. They were really good!"

---

6. That is, to set the table.

Bao-yu was puzzled. His knowledge of the masters of painting and callig-raphy both past and present was not inconsiderable, but he had never in all his experience come across a "Geng Huang." After racking his brains for some moments he suddenly began to chuckle and called for a writing-brush. A writing-brush having been produced by one of the servants, he wrote two characters with it in the palm of his hand.

"Are you quite *sure* the signature you saw was 'Geng Huang'?" he asked Xue Pan.

"What do you mean?" said Xue Pan. "Of course I'm sure."

Bao-yu opened his hand and held it up for Xue Pan to see:

"You sure it wasn't these two characters? They *are* quite similar."

The others crowded round to look. They all laughed when they saw what he had written:

"Yes, it must have been 'Tang Yin.'[7] Mr. Xue couldn't have been seeing straight that day. Ha! Ha! Ha!"

Xue Pan realized that he had made a fool of himself, but passed it off with an embarrassed laugh:

"Oh, Tankin' or wankin'," he said, "what difference does it make, anyway?"

Just then "Mr. Feng" was announced by one of the servants, which Bao-yu knew could only mean General Feng Tang's son, Feng Zi-ying. Xue Pan and the rest told the boy to bring him in immediately, but Feng Zi-ying was already striding in, talking and laughing as he went. The others hurriedly rose and invited him to take a seat.

"Ha!" said Feng Zi-ying. "No need to go out then. Enjoyin' yourselves at home, eh? Very nice too!"

"It's a long time since we've seen you around," said Bao-yu. "How's the General?"

"Fahver's in good health, thank you very much," said Feng Zi-ying, "but Muvver hasn't been too well lately. Caught a chill or somethin'."

Observing with glee that Feng Zi-ying was sporting a black eye, Xue Pan asked him how he had come by it:

"Been having a dust-up, then? Who was it this time? Looks as if he left his signature!"

Feng Zi-ying laughed:

"Don't use the mitts any more nowadays—not since that time I laid into Colonel Chou's son and did him an injury. That was a lesson to me. I've learned to keep my temper since then. No, this happened the other day durin' a huntin' expedition in the Iron Net Mountains. I got flicked by a goshawk's wing."

"When was this?" Bao-yu asked him.

"We left on the twenty-eighth of last month," said Feng Zi-ying. "Didn't get back till a few days ago."

"Ah, that explains why I didn't see you at Shen's party earlier this month," said Bao-yu. "I meant at the time to ask why you weren't there, but I forgot. Did you go alone on this expedition or was the General there with you?"

---

7. This joke shows Xue Pan's ignorance: he has misread the Chinese characters for one of the most famous of all Ming painters.

"Fahver most certainly *was* there," said Feng Zi-ying. "I was practically dragged along in tow. Do you think I'm mad enough to go rushin' off in pursuit of hideous hardships when I could be sittin' comfortably at home eatin' good food and drinkin' good wine and listenin' to the odd song or two? Still, some good came of it. It was a lucky accident."

As he had now finished his tea, Xue Pan urged him to join them at table and tell them his story at leisure, but Feng Zi-ying rose to his feet again and declined.

"I ought by rights to stay and drink a few cups with you," he said, "but there's somethin' very important I've got to see Fahver about now, so I'm afraid I really must refuse."

But Xue Pan, Bao-yu and the rest were by no means content to let him get away with this excuse and propelled him insistently towards the table.

"Now look here, this is too bad!" Feng Zi-ying good-humouredly protested. "All the years we've been knockin' around togevver we've never before insisted that a fellow should have to stay if he don't want to. The fact is, I really *can't*. Oh well, if I *must* have a drink, fetch some decent-sized cups and I'll just put down a couple of quick ones!"

This was clearly the most he would concede and the others perforce acquiesced. Two sconce-cups were brought and ceremoniously filled, Bao-yu holding the cups and Xue Pan pouring from the wine-kettle.[8] Feng Zi-ying drank them standing, one after the other, each in a single breath.

"Now come on," said Bao-yu, "let's hear about this 'lucky accident' before you go!"

Feng Zi-ying laughed:

"Couldn't tell it properly just now," he said. "It's somethin' that needs a special party all to itself. I'll invite you all round to my place another day and you shall have the details then. There's a favour I want to ask too, by the bye, so we'll be able to talk about that then as well."

He made a determined movement towards the door.

"Now you've got us all peeing ourselves with curiosity!" said Xue Pan. "You might at least tell us when this party is going to be, to put us out of our suspense."

"Not more than ten days' time and not less than eight," said Feng Zi-ying; and going out into the courtyard, he jumped on his horse and clattered away.

Having seen him off, the others went in again, reseated themselves at table, and resumed their potations. When the party finally broke up, Bao-yu returned to the Garden in a state of cheerful inebriation. Aroma, who had had no idea what the summons from Jia Zheng might portend and was still wondering anxiously what had become of him, at once demanded to know the cause of his condition. He gave her a full account of what had happened.

"Well really!" said Aroma. "Here were we practically beside ourselves with anxiety, and all the time you were there enjoying yourself! You might at least have sent word to let us know you were all right."

"I was going to send word," said Bao-yu. "Of course I was. But then old Feng arrived and it put it out of my mind."

8. Chinese wine was heated before it was drunk. "Sconce-cups": large wine cups.

At that moment Bao-chai walked in, all smiles.

"I hear you've made a start on the famous present," she said.

"But surely you and your family must have had some already?" said Bao-yu. Bao-chai shook her head:

"Pan was very pressing that I should have some, but I refused. I told him to save it for other people. I know I'm not really the right sort of person for such superior delicacies. If *I* were to eat any, I should be afraid of some frightful nemesis overtaking me."

A maid poured tea for her as she spoke, and conversation of a desultory kind proceeded between sips.

Our narrative returns now to Dai-yu.

Having been present when Bao-yu received his summons, Dai-yu, too, was greatly worried about him—the more so as the day advanced and he had still not returned. Then in the evening, some time after dinner, she heard that he had just got back and resolved to go over and ask him exactly what had happened. She was sauntering along on the way there when she caught sight of Bao-chai some distance ahead of her, just entering Bao-yu's courtyard. Continuing to amble on, she came presently to Drenched Blossoms Bridge, from which a large number of different kinds of fish were to be seen swimming about in the water below. Dai-yu did not know what kinds of fish they were, but they were so beautiful that she had to stop and admire them, and by the time she reached the House of Green Delights, the courtyard gate had been shut for the night and she was obliged to knock for admittance.

Now it so happened that Skybright had just been having a quarrel with Emerald, and being thoroughly out of temper, was venting some of her ill-humour on the lately arrived Bao-chai, complaining *sotto voce* behind her back about "people who were always inventing excuses to come dropping in and who kept other people staying up half the night when they would like to be in bed." A knock at the gate coming in the midst of these resentful mutterings was enough to make her really angry.

"They've all gone to bed," she shouted, not even bothering to inquire who the caller was. "Come again tomorrow!"

Dai-yu was aware that Bao-yu's maids often played tricks on one another, and it occurred to her that the girl in the courtyard, not recognizing her voice, might have mistaken her for another maid and be keeping her locked out for a joke. She therefore called out again, this time somewhat louder than before:

"Come on! Open up, please! It's me."

Unfortunately Skybright had still not recognized the voice.

"I don't care who you are," she replied bad-temperedly. "Master Bao's orders are that I'm not to let *anyone* in."

Dumbfounded by her insolence, Dai-yu stood outside the gate in silence. She could not, however much she felt like it, give vent to her anger in noisy expostulation. "Although they are always telling me to treat my Uncle's house as my own," she reflected, "I am still really an outsider. And now that Mother and Father are both dead and I am on my own, to make a fuss about a thing like this when I am living in someone else's house could only lead to further unpleasantness."

A big tear coursed, unregarded, down her cheek.

She was still standing there irresolute, unable to decide whether to go or stay, when a sudden volley of talk and laughter reached her from inside. It resolved itself, as she listened attentively, into the voices of Bao-yu and Bao-chai. An even bitterer sense of chagrin took possession of her. Suddenly, as she hunted in her mind for some possible reason for her exclusion, she remembered the events of the morning and concluded that Bao-yu must think she had told on him to his parents and was punishing her for her betrayal.

"But I would never betray you!" she expostulated with him in her mind. "Why couldn't you have asked first, before letting your resentment carry you to such lengths? If you won't see me today, does that mean that from now on we are going to stop seeing each other altogether?"

The more she thought about it the more distressed she became.

> Chill was the green moss pearled with dew
> And chill was the wind in the avenue;

but Dai-yu, all unmindful of the unwholesome damp, had withdrawn into the shadow of a flowering fruit-tree by the corner of the wall, and grieving now in real earnest, began to cry as though her heart would break. And as if Nature herself were affected by the grief of so beautiful a creature, the crows who had been roosting in the trees round about flew up with a great commotion and removed themselves to another part of the Garden, unable to endure the sorrow of her weeping.

> Tears filled each flower and grief their hearts perturbed,
> And silly birds were from their nests disturbed.

The author of the preceding couplet has given us a quatrain in much the same vein:

> Few in this world fair Frowner's looks surpassed,
> None matched her store of sweetness unexpressed.
> The first sob scarcely from her lips had passed
> When blossoms fell and birds flew off distressed.

As Dai-yu continued weeping there alone, the courtyard door suddenly opened with a loud creak and someone came out.

But in order to find out who it was, you will have to wait for the next chapter.

From *Volume 2*

CHAPTER 27

*Beauty Perspiring sports with butterflies
by the Raindrop Pavilion
And Beauty Suspiring weeps for fallen blossoms
by the Flowers' Grave*

As Dai-yu stood there weeping, there was a sudden creak of the courtyard gate and Bao-chai walked out, accompanied by Bao-yu with Aroma and a bevy of other maids who had come out to see her off. Dai-yu was on the point of stepping forward to question Bao-yu, but shrank from embarrassing him in front of so many people. Instead she slipped back into the shadows to let Bao-chai pass, emerging only when Bao-yu and the rest were back inside and the gate was once more barred. She stood for a while facing it, and shed a few silent tears; then, realizing that it was pointless to remain standing there, she turned and went back to her room and began, in a listless, mechanical manner, to take off her ornaments and prepare herself for the night.

Nightingale and Snowgoose had long since become habituated to Dai-yu's moody temperament; they were used to her unaccountable fits of depression, when she would sit, the picture of misery, in gloomy silence broken only by an occasional gusty sigh, and to her mysterious, perpetual weeping, that was occasioned by no observable cause. At first they had tried to reason with her, or, imagining that she must be grieving for her parents or that she was feeling homesick or had been upset by some unkindness, they would do their best to comfort her. But as the months lengthened into years and she still continued exactly the same as before, they gradually became accustomed and no longer sought reasons for her behaviour. That was why they ignored her on this occasion and left her alone to her misery, remaining where they were in the outer room and continuing to occupy themselves with their own affairs.

She sat, motionless as a statue, leaning against the back of the bed, her hands clasped about her knees, her eyes full of tears. It had already been dark for some hours when she finally lay down to sleep.

Our story passes over the rest of that night in silence.

Next day was the twenty-sixth of the fourth month, the day on which, this year, the festival of Grain in Ear was due to fall. To be precise, the festival's official commencement was on the twenty-sixth day of the fourth month at two o'clock in the afternoon. It has been the custom from time immemorial to make offerings to the flower fairies on this day. For Grain in Ear marks the beginning of summer; it is about this time that the blossom begins to fall; and tradition has it that the flowerspirits, their work now completed, go away on this day and do not return until the following year. The offerings are therefore thought of as a sort of farewell party for the flowers.

This charming custom of "speeding the fairies" is a special favourite with the fair sex, and in Prospect Garden all the girls were up betimes on this day making little coaches and palanquins[1] out of willow-twigs and flowers and little banners and pennants from scraps of brocade and any other pretty material they could find, which they fastened with threads of coloured silk to the tops of flowering trees and shrubs. Soon every plant and tree was decorated and the whole garden had become a shimmering sea of nodding blossoms and fluttering coloured streamers. Moving about in the midst of it all, the girls in their brilliant summer dresses, beside which the most vivid hues of plant and plumage became faint with envy, added the final touch of brightness to a scene of indescribable gaiety and colour.

---

1. Sedan chairs, carried on poles by bearers.

All the young people—Bao-chai, Ying-chun, Tan-chun, Xi-chun, Li Wan, Xi-feng[2] and her little girl and Caltrop, and all the maids from all the different apartments—were outside in the Garden enjoying themselves—all, that is, except Dai-yu, whose absence, beginning to be noticed, was first commented on by Ying-chun:

"What's happened to Cousin Lin? Lazy girl! Surely she can't *still* be in bed at this hour?"

Bao-chai volunteered to go and fetch her:

"The rest of you wait here; I'll go and rout her out for you," she said; and breaking away from the others, she made off in the direction of the Naiad's House.

While she was on her way, she caught sight of Élégante and the eleven other little actresses, evidently on their way to join in the fun. They came up and greeted her, and for a while she stood and chatted with them. As she was leaving them, she turned back and pointed in the direction from which she had just come:

"You'll find the others somewhere over there," she said. "I'm on my way to get Miss Lin. I'll join the rest of you presently."

She continued, by the circuitous route that the garden's contours obliged her to take, on her way to the Naiad's House. Raising her eyes as she approached it, she suddenly became aware that the figure ahead of her just disappearing inside it was Bao-yu. She stopped and lowered her eyes pensively again to the ground.

"Bao-yu and Dai-yu have known each other since they were little," she reflected. "They are used to behaving uninhibitedly when they are alone together. They don't seem to care what they say to one another; and one is never quite sure what sort of mood one is going to find them in. And Dai-yu, at the best of times, is always so touchy and suspicious. If I go in now after him, *he* is sure to feel embarrassed and *she* is sure to start imagining things. It would be better to go back without seeing her."

Her mind made up, she turned round and began to retrace her steps, intending to go back to the other girls; but just at that moment she noticed two enormous turquoise-coloured butterflies a little way ahead of her, each as large as a child's fan, fluttering and dancing on the breeze. She watched them fascinated and thought she would like to play a game with them. Taking a fan from inside her sleeve and holding it outspread in front of her, she followed them off the path and into the grass.

To and fro fluttered the pair of butterflies, sometimes alighting for a moment, but always flying off again before she could reach them. Once they seemed on the point of flying across the little river that flowed through the midst of the garden and Bao-chai had to stalk them with bated breath for fear of startling them out on to the water. By the time she had reached the Raindrop Pavilion she was perspiring freely and her interest in the butterflies was beginning to evaporate. She was about to turn back when she became aware of a low murmur of voices coming from inside the pavilion.

Raindrop Pavilion was built in such a way that it projected into the middle of the pool into which the little watercourse widened out at this point, so that on three of its sides it looked out on to the water. It was surrounded by

2. The wife of Bao-yu's uncle; she manages the household.

a verandah, whose railing followed the many angles formed by the bays and projections of the base. In each of its wooden walls there was a large paper-covered casement of elegantly patterned latticework.

Hearing voices inside the pavilion, Bao-chai halted and inclined her ear to listen.

"Are you *sure* this is your handkerchief?" one of the voices was saying. "If it is, take it; but if it isn't, I must return it to Mr. Yun."

"Of course it's mine," said the second voice. "Come on, let me have it!"

"Are you going to give me a reward? I hope I haven't taken all this trouble for nothing."

"I promised you I would give you a reward, and so I shall. Surely you don't think I was deceiving you?"

"All right, I get a reward for bringing it to you. But what about the person who picked it up? Doesn't *he* get anything?"

"Don't talk nonsense," said the second voice. "He's one of the masters. A master picking up something belonging to one of us should give it back as a matter of course. How can there be any question of *rewarding* him?"

"If you don't intend to reward him, what am I supposed to tell him when I see him? He was most insistent that I wasn't to give you the handkerchief unless you gave him a reward."

There was a long pause, after which the second voice replied:

"Oh, all right. Let him have this other handkerchief of mine then. That will have to do as his reward—But you must swear a solemn oath not to tell anyone else about this."

"May my mouth rot and may I die a horrible death if I ever tell anyone else about this, amen!" said the first voice.

"Goodness!" said the second voice again. "Here we are talking away, and all the time someone could be creeping up outside and listening to every word we say. We had better open these casements;[3] then even if anyone outside sees us, they'll think we are having an ordinary conversation; and *we* shall be able to see *them* and know in time when to stop."

Bao-chai, listening outside, gave a start.

"No wonder they say 'venery and thievery sharpen the wits,'" she thought. "If they open those windows and see me here, they are going to feel terribly embarrassed. And one of those voices sounds like that proud, peculiar girl Crimson who works in Bao-yu's room. If a girl like that knows that I have overheard her doing something she shouldn't be doing, it will be a case of 'the desperate dog will jump a wall, the desperate man will hazard all': there'll be a great deal of trouble and *I* shall be involved in it. There isn't time to hide. I shall have to do as the cicada does when he jumps out of his skin: give them something to put them off the scent—"

There was a loud creak as the casement yielded. Bao-chai advanced with deliberately noisy tread.

"Frowner!" she called out gaily. "*I* know where you're hiding."

Inside the pavilion Crimson and Trinket, who heard her say this and saw her advancing towards them just as they were opening the casement, were speechless with amazement; but Bao-chai ignored their confusion and addressed them genially:

3. That is, casement windows.

"Have you two got Miss Lin hidden away in there?"

"I haven't *seen* Miss Lin," said Trinket.

"I saw her just now from the river-bank," said Bao-chai. "She was squatting down over here playing with something in the water. I was going to creep up and surprise her, but she spotted me before I could get up to her and disappeared round this corner. Are you *sure* she's not hiding in there?"

She made a point of going inside the pavilion and searching; then, coming out again, she said in a voice loud enough for them to hear:

"If she's not in the pavilion, she must have crept into that grotto. Oh well, if she's not afraid of being bitten by a snake—!"

As she walked away she laughed inwardly at the ease with which she had extricated herself from a difficult situation.

"I think I'm fairly safely out of *that* one," she thought. "I wonder what those two will make of it."

What indeed! Crimson believed every word that Bao-chai had said, and as soon as the latter was at a distance, she seized hold of Trinket in alarm:

"Oh, how terrible! If Miss Lin was squatting there, she must have heard what we said before she went away."

Her companion was silent.

"Oh dear! What do you think she'll *do*?" said Crimson.

"Well, suppose she *did* hear," said Trinket, "it's not *her* backache. If we mind our business and she minds hers, there's no reason why anything should come of it."

"If it were Miss Bao that had heard us, I don't suppose anything *would*," said Crimson; "but Miss Lin is so critical and so intolerant. If *she* heard it and it gets about—oh dear!"

*   *   *

We now return to Dai-yu, who, having slept so little the night before, was very late getting up on the morning of the festival. Hearing that the other girls were all out in the garden "speeding the fairies" and fearing to be teased by them for her lazy habits, she hurried over her toilet and went out as soon as it was completed. A smiling Bao-yu appeared in the gateway as she was stepping down into the courtyard.

"Well, coz," he said, "I hope you *didn't* tell on me yesterday. You had me worrying about it all last night."

Dai-yu turned back, ignoring him, to address Nightingale inside:

"When you do the room, leave one of the casements open so that the parent swallows can get in. And put the lion doorstop on the bottom of the blind to stop it flapping. And don't forget to put the cover back on the burner after you've lighted the incense."

She made her way across the courtyard, still ignoring him.

Bao-yu, who knew nothing of the little drama that had taken place outside his gate the night before, assumed that she was still angry about his unfortunate lapse earlier on that same day, when he had offended her susceptibilities with a somewhat risqué quotation from *The Western Chamber*. He offered her now, with energetic bowing and hand-pumping, the apologies that the previous day's emergency had caused him to neglect. But Dai-yu walked straight past him and out of the gate, not deigning so much as a glance in his direction, and stalked off in search of the others.

Bao-yu was nonplussed. He began to suspect that something more than he had first imagined must be wrong.

"Surely it can't only be because of yesterday lunchtime that she's carrying on in this fashion? There must be something else. On the other hand, I didn't get back until late and I didn't see her again last night, so how *could* I have offended her?"

Preoccupied with these reflections, he followed her at some distance behind.

Not far ahead Bao-chai and Tan-chun were watching the ungainly courtship dance of some storks. When they saw Dai-yu coming, they invited her to join them, and the three girls stood together and chatted. Then Bao-yu arrived. Tan-chun greeted him with sisterly concern:

"How have you been keeping, Bao? It's three whole days since I saw you last."

Bao-yu smiled back at her.

"How have *you* been keeping, sis? I was asking Cousin Wan about you the day before yesterday."

"Come over here a minute," said Tan-chun. "I want to talk to you."

He followed her into the shade of a pomegranate tree a little way apart from the other two.

"Has Father asked to see you at all during this last day or two?" Tan-chun began.

"No."

"I thought I heard someone say yesterday that he had been asking for you."

"No," said Bao-yu, smiling at her concern. "Whoever it was was mistaken. He certainly hasn't asked for *me*."

Tan-chun smiled and changed the subject.

"During the past few months," she said, "I've managed to save up another ten strings or so of cash.[4] I'd like you to take it again like you did last time, and next time you go out, if you see a nice painting or calligraphic scroll or some amusing little thing that would do for my room, I'd like you to buy it for me."

"Well, I don't know," said Bao-yu. "In the trips I make to bazaars and temple fairs, whether it's inside the city or round about, I can't say that I ever see anything *really* nice or out of the ordinary. It's all bronzes and jades and porcelain and that sort of stuff. Apart from that it's mostly dress-making materials and clothes and things to eat."

"Now what would I want things like that for?" said Tan-chun. "No, I mean something like that little wickerwork basket you bought me last time, or the little box carved out of bamboo root, or the little clay burner. I thought they were sweet. Unfortunately the others took such a fancy to them that they carried them off as loot and wouldn't give them back to me again."

"Oh, if *those* are the sort of things you want," said Bao-yu laughing, "it's very simple. Just give a few strings of cash to one of the boys and he'll bring you back a whole cartload of them."

"What do the boys know about it?" said Tan-chun. "I need someone who can pick out the interesting things and the ones that are in good taste. You get me lots of nice little things, and I'll embroider a pair of slippers for you

4. Chinese copper coins had holes in the center and thus could be strung together.

like the ones I made for you last time—only this time I'll do them more carefully."

"Talking of those slippers reminds me," said Bao-yu. "I happened to run
into Father once when I was wearing them. He was Most Displeased. When
he asked me who made them, I naturally didn't dare to tell him that *you* had,
so I said that Aunt Wang had given them to me as a birthday present a few
days before. There wasn't much he could do about it when he heard that
they came from Aunt Wang; so after a very long pause he just said, 'What a
pointless waste of human effort and valuable material, to produce things
like that!' I told this to Aroma when I got back, and she said, 'Oh, that's
nothing! You should have heard your Aunt Zhao complaining about those
slippers. She was *furious* when she heard about them: "Her own natural
brother so down at heel he scarcely dares show his face to people, and she
spends her time making things like that!" '"

Tan-chun's smile had vanished:

"How *can* she talk such nonsense? Why should *I* be the one to make shoes
for him? Huan[5] gets a clothing allowance, doesn't he? He gets his clothing
and footwear provided for the same as all the rest of us. And fancy saying a
thing like that in front of a roomful of servants! For whose benefit was this
remark made, I wonder? I make an occasional pair of slippers just for something to do in my spare time; and if I give a pair to someone I particularly
like, that's my own affair. Surely no one else has any business to start telling
me who I should give them to? Oh, she's so *petty*!"

Bao-yu shook his head:

"Perhaps you're being a bit hard on her. She's probably got her reasons."

This made Tan-chun really angry. Her chin went up defiantly:

"Now you're being as stupid as her. Of *course* she's got her reasons; but
they are ignorant, stupid reasons. But she can think what she likes: as far
as *I* am concerned, Sir Jia is my father and Lady Wang is my mother, and who
was born in whose room doesn't interest me—the way I choose my friends
inside the family has nothing to do with that. Oh, I know I shouldn't talk
about her like this; but she is *so* idiotic about these things. As a matter of fact
I can give you an even better example than your story of the slippers. That
last time I gave you my savings to get something for me, she saw me a few
days afterwards and started telling me how short of money she was and how
difficult things were for her. I took no notice, of course. But later, when the
maids were out of the room, she began attacking me for giving the money
I'd saved to other people instead of giving it to Huan. Really! I didn't know
whether to laugh or get angry with her. In the end I just walked out of the
room and went round to see Mother."

There was an amused interruption at this point from Bao-chai, who was
still standing where they had left her a few minutes before:

"Do finish your talking and come back soon! It's easy to see that you two
are brother and sister. As soon as you see each other, you get into a huddle
and start talking about family secrets. Would it *really* be such a disaster if
anything you are saying were to be overheard?"

Tan-chun and Bao-yu rejoined her, laughing.

---

5. Jia Huan, Bao-yu's half-brother, born to his father and the concubine Aunt Zhao.

Not seeing Dai-yu, Bao-yu realized that she must have slipped off elsewhere while he was talking.

"Better leave it a day or two," he told himself on reflection. "Wait until her anger has calmed down a bit."

While he was looking downwards and meditating, he noticed that the ground where they were standing was carpeted with a bright profusion of wind-blown flowers—pomegranate and balsam for the most part.

"You can see she's upset," he thought ruefully. "She's neglecting her flowers. I'll bury this lot for her and remind her about it next time I see her."

He became aware that Bao-chai was arranging for him and Tan-chun to go with her outside.

"I'll join you two presently," he said, and waited until they were a little way off before stooping down to gather the fallen blossoms into the skirt of his gown. It was quite a way from where he was to the place where Dai-yu had buried the peach-blossom on that previous occasion,[6] but he made his way towards it, over rocks and bridges and through plantations of trees and flowers. When he had almost reached his destination and there was only the spur of a miniature "mountain" between him and the burial-place of the flowers, he heard the sound of a voice, coming from the other side of the rock, whose continuous, gentle chiding was occasionally broken by the most pitiable and heart-rending sobs.

"It must be a maid from one of the apartments," thought Bao-yu. "Someone has been ill-treating her, and she has run here to cry on her own."

He stood still and endeavoured to catch what the weeping girl was saying. She appeared to be reciting something:

> The blossoms fade and falling fill the air,
> Of fragrance and bright hues bereft and bare.
> Floss drifts and flutters round the Maiden's bower,
> Or softly strikes against her curtained door.
>
> The Maid, grieved by these signs of spring's decease,
> Seeking some means her sorrow to express,
> Has rake in hand into the garden gone,
> Before the fallen flowers are trampled on.
>
> Elm-pods and willow-floss are fragrant too;
> Why care, Maid, where the fallen flowers blew?
> Next year, when peach and plum-tree bloom again,
> Which of your sweet companions will remain?
>
> This spring the heartless swallow built his nest
> Beneath the eaves of mud with flowers compressed.
> Next year the flowers will blossom as before,
> But swallow, nest, and Maid will be no more.
>
> Three hundred and three-score the year's full tale:
> From swords of frost and from the slaughtering gale
> How can the lovely flowers long stay intact,
> Or, once loosed, from their drifting fate draw back?

---

6. A reference to an incident in chap. 23. Dai-yu explains that she is burying the blossoms to return them to the earth, rather than letting them be simply swept away. Because beautiful women were commonly compared to flowers, this foreshadows her own death.

Blooming so steadfast, fallen so hard to find!
Beside the flowers' grave, with sorrowing mind,
The solitary Maid sheds many a tear,
Which on the boughs as bloody drops appear.

At twilight, when the cuckoo sings no more,
The Maiden with her rake goes in at door
And lays her down between the lamplit walls,
While a chill rain against the window falls.

I know not why my heart's so strangely sad,
Half grieving for the spring and yet half glad:
Glad that it came, grieved it so soon was spent.
So soft it came, so silently it went!

Last night, outside, a mournful sound was heard:
The spirits of the flowers and of the bird.
But neither bird nor flowers would long delay,
Bird lacking speech, and flowers too shy to stay.

And then I wished that I had wings to fly
After the drifting flowers across the sky:
Across the sky to the world's farthest end,
The flowers' last fragrant resting-place to find.

But better their remains in silk to lay
And bury underneath the wholesome clay,
Pure substances the pure earth to enrich,
Than leave to soak and stink in some foul ditch.

Can I, that these flowers' obsequies attend,
Divine how soon or late *my* life will end?
Let others laugh flower-burial to see:
Another year who will be burying me?

As petals drop and spring begins to fail,
The bloom of youth, too, sickens and turns pale.
One day, when spring has gone and youth has fled,
The Maiden and the flowers will both be dead.

All this was uttered in a voice half-choked with sobs; for the words recited seemed only to inflame the grief of the reciter—indeed, Bao-yu, listening on the other side of the rock, was so overcome by them that he had already flung himself weeping upon the ground.

But the sequel to this painful scene will be told in the following chapter.

CHAPTER 28

A crimson cummerbund becomes a pledge of friendship
And a chaplet of medicine-beads becomes a source of
embarrassment

On the night before the festival, it may be remembered, Lin Dai-yu had mistakenly supposed Bao-yu responsible for Skybright's refusal to open the gate for her. The ceremonial farewell to the flowers of the following morning had transformed her pent-up and still smouldering resentment into a more generalized and seasonable sorrow. This had finally found its expression in a violent outburst of grief as she was burying the latest collection of fallen blossoms in her flower-grave. Meditation on the fate of flowers had led her to a contemplation of her own sad and orphaned lot; she had burst into tears, and soon after had begun a recitation of the poem whose words we recorded in the preceding chapter.

Unknown to her, Bao-yu was listening to this recitation from the slope of the near-by rockery. At first he merely nodded and sighed sympathetically; but when he heard the words

> "Can I, that these flowers' obsequies attend,
> Divine how soon or late *my* life will end?"

and, a little later,

> "One day when spring has gone and youth has fled,
> The Maiden and the flowers will both be dead."

he flung himself on the ground in a fit of weeping, scattering the earth all about him with the flowers he had been carrying in the skirt of his gown.

Lin Dai-yu dead! A world from which that delicate, flower-like countenance had irrevocably departed! It was unutterable anguish to think of it. Yet his sensitized imagination *did* now consider it—went on, indeed, to consider a world from which the others, too—Bao-chai, Caltrop, Aroma and the rest—had also irrevocably departed. Where would *he* be then? What would have become of him? And what of the Garden, the rocks, the flowers, the trees? To whom would they belong when he and the girls were no longer there to enjoy them? Passing from loss to loss in his imagination, he plunged deeper and deeper into a grief that seemed inconsolable. As the poet says:

> Flowers in my eyes and bird-song in my ears
> Augment my loss and mock my bitter tears.

Dai-yu, then, as she stood plunged in her own private sorrowing, suddenly heard the sound of another person crying bitterly on the rocks above her.

"The others are always telling me I'm a 'case,'" she thought. "Surely there can't be another 'case' up there?"

But on looking up she saw that it was Bao-yu.

"Pshaw!" she said crossly to herself. "I thought it was another girl, but all the time it was that cruel, hate—"

"Hateful" she had been going to say, but clapped her mouth shut before uttering it. She sighed instead and began to walk away.

By the time Bao-yu's weeping was over, Dai-yu was no longer there. He realized that she must have seen him and have gone away in order to avoid him. Feeling suddenly rather foolish, he rose to his feet and brushed the earth from his clothes. Then he descended from the rockery and began to retrace his steps in the direction of Green Delights. Quite by coincidence Dai-yu was walking along the same path a little way ahead.

"Stop a minute!" he cried, hurrying forward to catch up with her. "I know you are not taking any notice of me, but I only want to ask you one simple question, and then you need never have anything more to do with me."

Dai-yu had turned back to see who it was. When she saw that it was Bao-yu still, she was going to ignore him again; but hearing him say that he only wanted to ask her one question, she told him that he might do so.

Bao-yu could not resist teasing her a little.

"How about *two* questions? Would you wait for two?"

Dai-yu set her face forwards and began walking on again.

Bao-yu sighed.

"If it has to be like this now," he said, as if to himself, "it's a pity it was ever like it was in the beginning."

Dai-yu's curiosity got the better of her. She stopped walking and turned once more towards him.

"Like *what* in the beginning?" she asked. "And like what now?"

"Oh, the *beginning!*" said Bao-yu. "In the *beginning,* when you first came here, I was your faithful companion in all your games. Anything I had, even the thing most dear to me, was yours for the asking. If there was something to eat that I specially liked, I had only to hear that you were fond of it too and I would religiously hoard it away to share with you when you got back, not daring even to touch it until you came. We ate at the same table. We slept in the same bed. I used to think that because we were so close then, there would be something special about our relationship when we grew up— that even if we weren't particularly affectionate, we should at least have more understanding and forbearance for each other than the rest. But how wrong I was! Now that you *have* grown up, you seem only to have grown more touchy. You don't seem to care about *me* any more at all. You spend all your time brooding about outsiders like Feng and Chai. I haven't got any *real* brothers and sisters left here now. There are Huan and Tan, of course; but as you know, they're only my half-brother and half-sister: they aren't my mother's children. I'm on my own, like you. I should have thought we had so much in common—But what's the use? I try and try, but it gets me nowhere; and nobody knows or cares."

At this point—in spite of himself—he burst into tears.

The palpable evidence of her own eyes and ears had by now wrought a considerable softening on Dai-yu's heart. A sympathetic tear stole down her own cheek, and she hung her head and said nothing. Bao-yu could see that he had moved her.

"I know I'm not much use nowadays," he continued, "but however bad you may think me, I would never wittingly do anything in your presence to offend you. If I *do* ever slip up in some way, you ought to tell me off about it and warn me not to do it again, or shout at me—hit me, even, if you feel like it; I shouldn't mind. But you don't do that. You just ignore me. You leave me utterly at a loss to know what I'm supposed to have done wrong, so that I'm driven half frantic wondering what I ought to do to make up for it. If I were to die now, I should die with a grievance, and all the masses and exorcisms in the world wouldn't lay my ghost. Only when you explained what your reason was for ignoring me should I cease from haunting you and be reborn into another life."

Dai-yu's resentment for the gate incident had by now completely evaporated. She merely said:

"Oh well, in that case why did you tell your maids not to let me in when I came to call on you?"

"I honestly don't know what you are referring to," said Bao-yu in surprise. "Strike me dead if I ever did any such thing!"

"Hush!" said Dai-yu. "Talking about death at this time of the morning! You should be more careful what you say. If you did, you did. If you didn't, you didn't. There's no need for these horrible oaths."

"I really and truly didn't know you had called," said Bao-yu. "Cousin Bao came and sat with me a few minutes last night and then went away again. That's the only call I know about."

Dai-yu reflected for a moment or two, then smiled.

"Yes, it must have been the maids being lazy. Certainly they can be very disagreeable at such times."

"Yes, I'm sure that's what it was," said Bao-yu. "When I get back, I'll find out who it was and give her a good talking-to."

"I think some of your young ladies could *do* with a good talking-to," said Dai-yu, "—though it's not really for me to say so. It's a good job it was only me they were rude to. If Miss Bao or Miss Cow were to call and they behaved like that to *her,* that would be really serious."

She giggled mischievously. Bao-yu didn't know whether to laugh with her or grind his teeth. But just at that moment a maid came up to ask them both to lunch and the two of them went together out of the Garden and through into the front part of the mansion, calling in at Lady Wang's[7] on the way.

* * *

7. Bao-yu's mother.

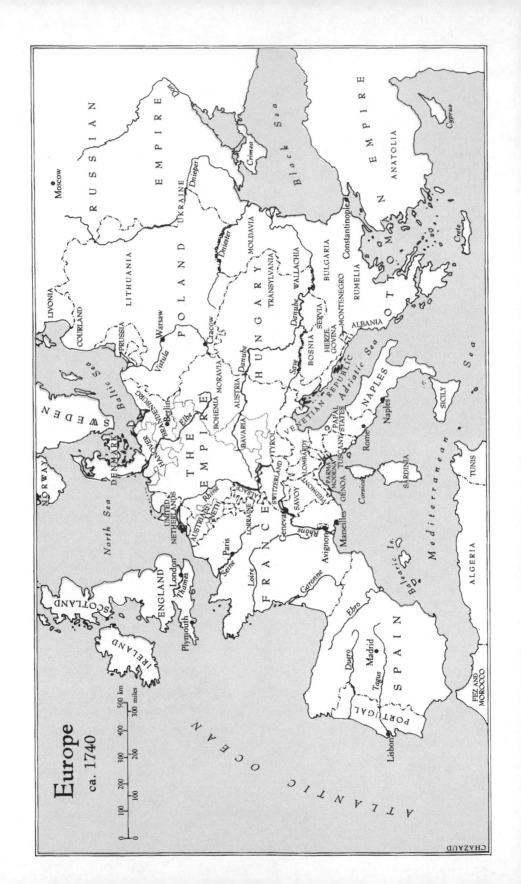

Europe
ca. 1740

CHAZAUD

The Enlightenment in Europe

"I wonder if it is not better to try to correct and moderate men's passions than to try to suppress them altogether." The sentence, from Jean-Baptiste Molière's 1669 preface to his biting comedy about religious hypocrisy, *Tartuffe,* captures something of the anxiety and the optimism of a period for which subsequent generations have found no adequate single designation. "The Neo-Classic Period," "The Age of Reason," "The Enlightenment": such labels suggest, accurately enough, that thinkers between (roughly) 1660 and 1770 emphasized the powers of the mind and turned to the Roman past for models. But these terms do not convey the awareness of limitation expressed in Molière's sentence, an awareness as typical of the historical period to which the sentence belongs as is the expressed aspiration toward correctness and moderation. The effort to correct and moderate the passions might prove less foolhardy than the effort to suppress them, but both endeavors would involve human nature's struggle with itself, a struggle necessarily perpetual. "On life's vast ocean diversely we sail, / Reason the card, but Passion is the gale," Alexander Pope's *Essay on Man* (1733) pointed out. One could hope to steer with reason as guide only by remembering the omnipresence of passion as impetus. Eighteenth-century thinkers analyzed, and eighteenth-century imaginative writers dramatized, intricate interchanges and conflicts between these aspects of our selves.

The drama of reason and passion played itself out in society, the system of association human beings had devised partly to control passion and institutionalize reason. Structured on the basis of a rigid class system, the traditional social order began to face incipient challenges in the eighteenth century as new commerce generated new wealth, whose possessors felt entitled to claim their own share of social power. The threat to established hierarchies extended even to kings. Thomas Hobbes, in *Leviathan* (1651), had argued for the secular origins of the social contract. Kings arise, he said, not by divine ordinance but out of human need; they exist to prevent what would otherwise be a war of all on all. Monarchs still presided over European nations in the eighteenth century, but with less security than before. The English had executed their ruler in 1649; the French would perform another royal decapitation before the end of the eighteenth century. The mortality of kings had become a political fact, a fact implying the conceivable instability of the social order over which kings presided.

A sense of the contingencies of the human condition impinged on many minds in a world where men and women no longer automatically assumed God's benign supervision of human affairs or the primacy of their own Christian obligations. The fierce strife between Protestants and Catholics lapsed into relative quiescence by the end of the seventeenth century, but the Protestant English deposed their king in 1688 because of his marriage to a Catholic princess and their fear of a Catholic dynasty; and in France Louis XIV in 1685 revoked the Edict of Nantes, which had granted religious toleration to Protestants. The overt English struggle of Cavaliers and Puritans ended with the restoration of Charles II to the throne in 1660. Religious differences now became translated into divisions of social class and of political conviction—divisions no less powerful for lacking the claim of supernatural authority. To England, the eighteenth century brought two unsuccessful but bitterly divisive rebellions on behalf of the deposed Stuart succession, as well as the cataclysmic American Revolution. In France, the century ended in revolution. Throughout the eighteenth century, wars erupted over succession to European thrones and over nationalistic claims, although no fighting took place on such a scale as that of the devastating Thirty Years' War (1618–48). On the whole, divisions *within* nations (in France and England) assumed greater importance than those between nations.

Philosophers now turned their attention to defining the possibilities and limitations of the human position in the material universe. "I think, therefore I am," René Descartes pronounced, declaring the mind the source of individual being. But this idea proved less reassuring than it initially seemed. Subsequent philosophers, exploring the concept's implications, realized the possibility of the mind's isolation in its own constructions. Perhaps, Wilhelm Leibniz suggested, no real communication can take place between one consciousness and another. Possibly, according to David Hume, the idea of individual identity itself derives from the mind's efforts to manufacture continuity out of discontinuous memories. Philosophers pointed out the impossibility of knowing for sure even the reality of the external world: the only certainty is that we think it exists. If contemplating the nature of human reason thus led philosophic skeptics to restrict severely the area of what we can know with certainty, other contemplations induced other thinkers to insist on the existence, beyond ourselves, of an entirely rational physical and moral universe. Isaac Newton's demonstrations of the order of natural law greatly encouraged this line of thought. The fullness and complexity of the perceived physical world testified, as many wrote, to the sublime rationality of a divine plan. The Planner, however, did not necessarily supervise the day-to-day operations of His arrangements; He might rather, as a popular analogy had it, resemble the watchmaker who winds the watch and leaves it running.

Deism, evoking a depersonalized deity, insisted on the logicality of the universe and encouraged the separation of ethics from religion. Ethics, too, could be understood as a matter of reason. "He that thinks reasonably must think morally," Samuel Johnson observed. But such statements expressed wish more than perception. Awareness of the passions continued to haunt thinkers yearning for rationality.

Although the social, economic, and political organizations in which the thinkers of this period participated hardly resemble our own, the questions they raised about the human condition have plagued the Western mind ever since. If we no longer locate the solution to all problems in an unattainable ideal of "reason," we too struggle to find the limits of certainty, experience problems of identity and isolation, and recognize the impossibility of altogether controlling internal forces now identified as "the unconscious" rather than "the passions." But we confront such issues largely from the position of isolated individuals. In the late seventeenth and early eighteenth centuries, in England and on the Continent, the sense of obligation to society had far more power than it possesses today. Society provided the standards and the instruments of control that might help to counter the tumult of individual impulse.

SOCIETY

Society, in this period, designates both a powerful idea and an omnipresent fact of experience. Prerevolutionary French society, like English society of the same period, depended on clear hierarchical structures. The literature of both countries issued from a small cultural elite, writing for others of their kind and assuming the rightness of their own knowledge of how people should feel and behave.

For the English and French upper classes, as for the ancient Romans they admired, public life mattered more than private. At one level, the "public" designated the realms of government and diplomacy: occupations allowing and encouraging oratory, frequent travel, negotiation, the exercise of political and economic power. In this sense, the public world belonged entirely to men, who determined the course of government, defined the limits of the important, enforced their sense of the fitness of things. By another definition, "public" might refer to the life of formal social intercourse. In France, such social life took place often in "salons," gatherings to engage in intellectual, as well as frivolous, conversation. Women typically presided over these salons, thus declaring both their intellectual authority and their capacity to combine high thought with high style.

Both the larger and the more limited public spheres depended on well-defined codes of behavior. The discrepancy between the forms of self-presentation dictated by these codes and the operations such forms might disguise—a specific form of the reason-versus-passion conflict—provides one of the insistent themes of European literature in the century beginning around 1660. Molière, examining religious sham, for example, or Voltaire, sending a naive fictional protagonist to encounter the world's inconsistencies of profession and practice—such writers call attention to the deceptiveness and the possible misuses of social norms, as well as to their necessity. None suggests that the codes themselves are at fault. If people lived up to what they profess, the world would be a better place; ideally, they would modify not their standards of behavior but their tendency to hide behind them.

In general, women fill subordinate roles in the harsh social environments evoked by these satiric works. As the evoked social scene widens, erotic love plays a less important part and the position of women becomes increasingly insignificant: women's sphere is the home, and home life matters less than does public life. It is perhaps not irrelevant to note that no work in this section describes or evokes children. Only in adulthood do people assume social responsibility; only then do they provide interesting substance for social commentary.

We in the twenty-first century have become accustomed to the notion of the sacredness of the individual, encouraged to believe in the high value of expressiveness, originality, specialness. Eighteenth-century writers, on the other hand, assumed the superior importance of the social group and of shared opinion. "Expressiveness," in their view, should provide an instrument for articulating the will of the community, not the eccentric desires of individuals. Society implies subordination: not only class hierarchy but individual submission to the good of the group.

NATURE

Society establishes one locus of reality for eighteenth-century thinkers, although they understand it as a human construct. Nature makes up another assumed measure of the real. The meanings of the word *nature* vary greatly in eighteenth-century usage, but two large senses are most relevant to the works here included: nature as the inherent order of things, including the physical universe, hence evidence of the deity's plan; and nature meaning specifically *human* nature.

Despite their pervasive awareness of natural contingency (vividly dramatized by Voltaire among others, in his account of the disastrous Lisbon earthquake), writers of this period locate their sense of permanence particularly in the idea of nature. Contemplation of nature can both humble and exalt its practitioner, teaching the insufficiency of human powers in comparison with divine but also reminding human beings that they inhabit a wondrous universe in which all functions precisely as it should.

The notion of a permanent, divinely ordained natural order offers a good deal of comfort to those aware of flaws in actual social arrangements. It embodies an ideal of harmony, of order in variety, which, although it cannot be fully grasped by human intelligence, can yet provide a model for social complexities. It posits a *system*, a structure of relationships that at some theoretical level necessarily makes sense; thus it provides an assumed substructure of rationality for all experience of irrationality. It supplies a means of valuing all appearances of the natural world: every flower, every minnow, has meaning beyond itself, as part of the great pattern. The ardency with which the period's thinkers cling to belief in such a pattern suggests once more a pervasive anxiety about what human reason could not do. Human beings create a vision of something at once sublimely reasonable and beyond reason's grasp to reassure themselves that the limits of the rational need not coincide with the limits of the human.

The permanence of the conceptual natural order corresponds to that of human nature, as conceived in the eighteenth century. Human nature, it was generally believed, remains in all times and places the same. Thinkers of the Enlightenment emphasized the common aspects of humanity far more than they considered cultural divergencies. Readers and writers alike could draw on this conviction about universality. It provided a test of excellence: if an author's imagining of character failed to conform to what eighteenth-century readers understood as human nature, a work might be securely judged inadequate. Conversely, the idea of a constant human nature held out the hope of longevity for writers who successfully evoked it. Moral philosophers could define human obligation and possibility in the conviction that they too wrote for all time; ethical standards would never change. Like the vision of order in the physical universe, the notion of constancy in human nature provided bedrock for an increasingly secularized society.

CONVENTION AND AUTHORITY

Eighteenth-century society, like all societies, operated, and its literary figures wrote, on the basis of established conventions. Manners are social conventions: agreed-on systems of behavior declared appropriate for specific situations. Guides to manners proliferated in the eighteenth century, expressing a widespread sense that commitment to decorum helped preserve society's important standards. Literary conventions—agreed-on systems of verbal behavior—served comparable purposes in another sphere. Like established codes of manners, such conventions declare continuity between present and past.

The literary conventions of the past, like outmoded manners or styles of dress, may strike the twenty-first-century reader as antiquated and artificial. A woman who curtseyed in a modern living room, a man who appeared in a wig, would seem to us ridiculous, even insane; but, of course, a young woman in jeans would strike our predecessors as equally perverse. The plaintive lyrics of current country music, like the extravagances of rap, operate within restrictive conventions that affect their hearers as "natural" only because they are familiar. Eighteenth-century writers had at their disposal an established set of conventions for every traditional literary genre. As the repetitive rhythms of the country ballad tell listeners what to expect, these literary conventions provided readers with clues about the kind of experience they could anticipate in a given poem or play.

Underlying all specific conventions was the classical assumption that literature existed to delight and to instruct its readers. The various genres represented in this period embody such belief in literature's dual function. Stage comedy and tragedy, the early novel, satire in prose and verse, didactic poetry, the philosophic tale: each form developed its own set of devices for involving audiences and readers in situations requiring moral choice, as well as for creating pleasure.

One dominant convention of twenty-first-century poetry and prose is something we call "realism." In fiction, verse, and drama, writers often attempt to convey the literal feel of experience, the shape in which events actually occur in the world, the way people really talk. European writers during the Enlightenment pursued no such goal. Despite their concern with permanent patterns of thought and feeling, they employed deliberate and obvious forms of artifice as modes of emphasis and of indirection. Artistic transformation of life, the period's writers believed, involves the imposition of formal order on the endless flux of event and feeling. The formalities of this literature constitute part of its meaning: its statement that what experience shows as unstable, art makes stable.

Reliance on convention as a mode of control expressed an aspect of the period's constant effort toward elusive stability. The classical past, for many, provided an emblem of that stability, a standard of permanence. But some felt a problem inherent in the high valuing of the past, a problem dramatized by the so-called quarrel of Ancients and Moderns in England and in France. At stake in this controversy was the value of permanence as against the value of change. Proponents of the Ancients believed that the giants of Greece and Rome had not only established standards applicable to all subsequent accomplishment but provided models of achievement never to be excelled. Homer wrote the first great epics; subsequent endeavors in the same genre could only imitate him. Innovation came when it came by making the old new. Moderns who valued originality for its own sake, who multiplied worthless publications, who claimed significance for what time had not tested thereby testified to their own inadequacies and their foolish pride.

Those proud to be Moderns, on the other hand, held that men (possibly even women) standing on the shoulders of the Ancients could see farther than their predecessors. The new conceivably exceeded in value the old; one might discover flaws even in revered figures of the classic past. Not everything had yet been accomplished; fresh possibilities remained always possible. This view, of course, corresponds to one widely current since the eighteenth century, but it did not triumph easily: many powerful thinkers of the late seventeenth and early eighteenth century adhered to the more conservative position.

Also at issue in this debate was the question of authority. What position should one assume who hoped to write and be read? Did authority reside only in tradition? If so, one must write in classical forms, rely on classical allusions. Until late in the eighteenth century, virtually all important writers attempted to ally themselves with the authority of tradition, declaring themselves part of a community extending through time as well as space. The problems of authority became particularly important in connection with satire, a popular Enlightenment form. To establish the right to criticize fellow men and women, the satirist must establish a rhetorical ascendancy such as the pulpit gives the priest—an ascendancy most readily obtained by at least implicit alliance with literary and moral tradition. The satirist, like the moral philosopher, cannot afford to seem idiosyncratic when prescribing and condemning the behavior of others. The fact that satire flourished so richly in this period suggests another version of the central conflict between reason and passion, the forces of stability and of instability. In its heightened description of the world, satire calls attention to the powerful presence of the irrational, opposing to that presence the clarity of the satirist's own claim to reason and tradition. As it chastises human beings for their eruptions of passion, urging resistance and control, satire reminds its readers of the universality of the irrational as well as of opposition to it. The effort "to correct and moderate men's [and women's] passions," that great theme of the Enlightenment, can equally generate hope or despair: opposed moods richly expressed throughout this period.

TIME LINE

TEXTS	CONTEXTS
1664 Jean-Baptiste Poquelin Molière, **Tartuffe**	**1660** Civil War in England ends with Charles II's ascension to the throne (the "Restoration")
1665 François de La Rochefoucauld, *Reflections*	
	1666 Isaac Newton uncovers laws of gravitation • London, already stricken by plague, is destroyed in the Great Fire and subsequently rebuilt in more orderly fashion
1667 Publication of John Milton's *Paradise Lost*	
1677 Jean Racine, *Phaedra*	**1670** The London-based Hudson's Bay Company is incorporated by royal charter to trade in North America
1678 Marie de la Vergne de La Fayette, *The Princess of Clèves*	
1690 John Locke, *Essay Concerning Human Understanding*	
1691 Sor Juana Inés de la Cruz, **Reply to Sor Filotea de la Cruz**	**1694** Bank of England is chartered, forerunner of modern national banks and treasury systems; London stock exchange follows in 1698
	1697 Russian czar Peter the Great visits western Europe and England, resolves to Westernize Russia
	1707 United Kingdom of Great Britain formed by union of England and Scotland
1710 First British copyright law, transferring rights of property in a published work from publisher to author	**1709** Up to 100,000 slaves a year cross the Atlantic, 20,000 to Britain's Caribbean colonies alone
1717 Alexander Pope, *The Rape of the Lock*	
1719 Daniel Defoe publishes *Robinson Crusoe*, often called the first true novel in English	
1726 Jonathan Swift, *Gulliver's Travels*	**1721** J. S. Bach, *The Brandenburg Concertos*

Boldface titles indicate works in the anthology.

TIME LINE

TEXTS	CONTEXTS
1729 Swift, *A Modest Proposal*	
1733–34 Alexander Pope, *An Essay on Man*	
1751 First edition of French *Encyclopédie,* edited by Denis Diderot	
	1753 British Museum founded
1755 Samuel Johnson publishes the *Dictionary of the English Language,* the first comprehensive English dictionary on historical principles	**1756–63** Seven Years' War, involving nine European powers; Britain acquires Canada and Florida, Spain gets Cuba and the Philippines, France wins colonies in India and Africa as well as Guadeloupe and Martinique
1759 François-Marie Arouet de Voltaire, *Candide* • Samuel Johnson, *The History of Rasselas, Prince of Abissinia*	
	1765 James Watt, a Scott, invents the steam engine, first in a series of mechanical innovations ushering in the industrial revolution
1771 First publication of *Encyclopaedia Britannica* and complete French *Encyclopédie* testify to characteristic "Enlightenment" impulse to organize knowledge	**1775–83** American War of Independence; Declaration of Independence, 1776 • Constitution of the United States, 1787, the year of Mozart's opera *Don Giovanni*
1792 Mary Wollstonecraft, *Vindication of the Rights of Woman,* makes feminist case for female equality	**1789** French Revolution begins; French National Assembly adopts the Declaration of the Rights of Man
	1799 After successful conquests throughout Europe, Napoleon Bonaparte becomes first consul—in effect, dictator—of France • Ludwig van Beethoven writes his first symphony (1799–1800)

JEAN-BAPTISTE POQUELIN ("MOLIÈRE")
1622–1673

Son of a prosperous Paris merchant, Jean-Baptiste Poquelin (known by his stage name, Molière) devoted his entire adult life to the creation of stage illusion, as playwright and as actor. At about the age of twenty-five, he joined a company of traveling players established by the Béjart family; with them he toured the provinces for about twelve years. In 1658 the company was ordered to perform for Louis XIV in Paris; a year later, Molière's first great success, The High-Brow Ladies (Les Précieuses ridicules), was produced. The theatrical company to which he belonged, patronized by the king, became increasingly successful, developing finally (1680) into the Comédie-Française. In 1662, Molière married Armande Béjart. He died a few hours after performing the lead role in his own play The Imaginary Invalid.

Molière wrote both broad farce and comedies of character, in which he caricatured some form of vice or folly by embodying it in a single figure. His targets included the miser, the aspiring but vulgar middle class, female would-be intellectuals, the hypochondriac, and, in Tartuffe, the religious hypocrite.

In Tartuffe (1664), as in his other plays, Molière employs classic comic devices of plot and character—here, a foolish, stubborn father blocking the course of young love; an impudent servant commenting on her superiors' actions; a happy ending involving a marriage facilitated by implausible means. He often uses such devices, however, to comment on his own immediate social scene, imagining how universal patterns play themselves out in a specific historical context. Tartuffe had contemporary relevance so transparent that the Catholic Church forced the king to ban it, although Molière managed to have it published and produced once more by 1669.

The play's emotional energy derives not from the simple discrepancy of man and mask in Tartuffe ("Is not a face quite different from a mask?" inquires the normative character Cléante, who has no trouble making such distinctions), but from the struggle for erotic, psychic, and economic power in which people employ their masks. One can readily imagine modern equivalents for the stresses and strains within Orgon's family. Orgon, an aging man with grown children, seeks ways to preserve control. His mother, Madame Pernelle, encourages his efforts, thus fostering her illusion that she still runs things. Orgon identifies his own interests with those of the hypocritical Tartuffe, toward whom he plays a benevolent role. Because Tartuffe fulsomely hails him as benefactor, Orgon feels utterly powerful in relation to his fawning dependent. When he orders his passive daughter Mariane to marry Tartuffe, he reveals his vision of complete domestic autocracy. Tartuffe's lust, one of those passions forever eluding human mastery, disturbs Orgon's arrangements; in the end, the will of the offstage king orders everything, as though a benevolent god had intervened.

To make Tartuffe a specifically religious hypocrite is an act of inventive daring. Orgon, like his mother, conceals from himself his will to power by verbally subordinating himself to that divinity which Tartuffe, too, invokes. Although one may easily accept Molière's defense of his intentions (not to mock faith but to attack its misuse), it is not hard to see why the play might trouble religious authorities. Molière suggests how readily religious faith lends itself to misuse, how high-sounding pieties allow men and women to evade self-examination and immediate responsibilities. Tartuffe deceives others by his grandiosities of mortification ("Hang up my hair shirt") and charity; he encourages his victims in their own grandiosities. Orgon can indulge a fantasy of self-subordination (remarking of Tartuffe, "He guides our lives") at the same time that he furthers his more hidden desire for power. Religion offers ready justification for a course manifestly destructive as well as self-seeking.

Cléante, before he meets Tartuffe, claims (accurately) to understand him by his effects on others. Throughout the play, Cléante speaks in the voice of wisdom, counseling moderation, common sense, and self-control, calling attention to folly. More important, he emphasizes how the issues Molière examines in this comedy relate to dominant late seventeenth-century themes:

> Ah, Brother, man's a strangely fashioned creature
> Who seldom is content to follow Nature,
> But recklessly pursues his inclination
> Beyond the narrow bounds of moderation,
> And often, by transgressing Reason's laws,
> Perverts a lofty aim or noble cause.

To follow Nature means to act appropriately to the human situation in the created universe. Humankind occupies a middle position, between beasts and angels; such aspirations as Orgon's desire to control his daughter completely or his apparent wish to submit himself absolutely to Tartuffe's claim of heavenly wisdom imply a hope to surpass limitations inherent in the human condition. As Cléante's observations suggest, "to follow Nature," given the rationality of the universe, implies adherence to "Reason's laws." All transgression involves failure to submit to reason's dictates. Molière, with his stylized comic plot, makes that point as insistently as does Racine, who depicts grand passions and cataclysmic effects from them.

Although Cléante understands and can enunciate the principles of proper conduct, his wisdom has no direct effect on the play's action. Although the comedy suggests a social world in which women exist in utter subordination to fathers and husbands, in the plot, two women bring about the clarifications that unmask the villain. The virtuous wife, Elmire, object of Tartuffe's lust, and the articulate servant girl, Dorine, confront the immediate situation with pragmatic inventiveness. Dorine goads others to response; Elmire encourages Tartuffe to play out his sexual fantasies before a hidden audience. Both women have a clear sense of right and wrong, although they express it in less resounding terms than does Cléante. Their concrete insistence on facing what is really going on, cutting through all obfuscation, rescues the men from entanglement in their own abstract formulations.

The women's clarifications, however, do not resolve the comedy's dilemmas. Suddenly the context shifts: economic terms replace erotic ones. It is as though Tartuffe were only playing in his attempt to seduce Elmire; now we get to what really matters: money. For all his claims of disinterestedness, Tartuffe has managed to get control of his dupe's property. Control of property, the action gradually reveals, amounts to power over life itself: prison threatens Orgon, and the prospect of expulsion from their home menaces him and his family alike. Only the convenient and ostentatious artifice of royal intervention rescues the victims and punishes their betrayer.

Comedies conventionally end in the restoration of order, declaring that good inevitably triumphs; rationality renews itself despite the temporary deviations of the foolish and vicious. At the end of *Tartuffe*, Orgon and his mother have been chastened by revelation of their favorite's depravity, Mariane has been allowed to marry her lover, Tartuffe has been judged, and the king's power and justice have reasserted themselves and been acknowledged. In the organization of family and nation (metaphorically a larger family), order reassumes dominion. Yet the arbitrary intervention of the king leaves a disturbing emotional residue. The play has demonstrated that Tartuffe's corrupt will to power (as opposed to Orgon's merely foolish will) can ruthlessly aggrandize itself. Money speaks, in Orgon's society as in ours; possession of wealth implies total control over others. Only a kind of miracle can save Orgon. The miracle occurs, given the benign world of comedy, but the play reminds its readers of the extreme precariousness with which reason finally triumphs, even given the presence of such reasonable people as Cléante and Elmire. Tartuffe's monstrous lust, for women, money, power, genuinely endangers the social structure. *Tartuffe* enforces recognition of the constant threats to rationality, of how much we have at stake in trying to use reason as principle of action.

PRONOUNCING GLOSSARY

The following list uses common English syllables and stress accents to provide rough equivalents of selected words whose pronunciation may be unfamiliar to the general reader.

Cléante: *clay-ahnt'*

Damis: *dah-meece'*

Dorine: *do-reen'*

Elmire: *el-meer'*

Flipote: *flee-pot'*

Laurent: *lor-awnh'*

Loyal: *lwah-yal'*

Molière: *moh-lyehr'*

Orante: *oh-rahnt'*

Orgon: *or-gohnh'*

Pernelle: *payr-nel'*

Tartuffe: *tahr-tewf'*

Valère: *vah-lehr'*

Vincennes: *vanh-sen'*

Tartuffe[1]

Preface

Here is a comedy that has excited a good deal of discussion and that has been under attack for a long time; and the persons who are mocked by it have made it plain that they are more powerful in France than all whom my plays have satirized up to this time. Noblemen, ladies of fashion, cuckolds, and doctors all kindly consented to their presentation, which they themselves seemed to enjoy along with everyone else; but hypocrites do not understand banter: they became angry at once, and found it strange that I was bold enough to represent their actions and to care to describe a profession shared by so many good men. This is a crime for which they cannot forgive me, and they have taken up arms against my comedy in a terrible rage. They were careful not to attack it at the point that had wounded them: they are too crafty for that and too clever to reveal their true character. In keeping with their lofty custom, they have used the cause of God to mask their private interests; and *Tartuffe,* they say, is a play that offends piety: it is filled with abominations from beginning to end, and nowhere is there a line that does not deserve to be burned. Every syllable is wicked, the very gestures are criminal, and the slightest glance, turn of the head, or step from right to left conceals mysteries that they are able to explain to my disadvantage. In vain did I submit the play to the criticism of my friends and the scrutiny of the public: all the corrections I could make, the judgment of the king and queen[2] who saw the play, the approval of great princes and ministers of state who honored it with their presence, the opinion of good men who found it worthwhile, all this did not help. They will not let go of their prey, and every day of the week they have pious zealots abusing me in public and damning me out of charity.

I would care very little about all they might say except that their devices make enemies of men whom I respect and gain the support of genuinely good men, whose faith they know and who, because of the warmth of their

---

1. Translated by Richard Wilbur. The first version of *Tartuffe* was performed in 1664 and the second in 1667. When a second edition of the third version was printed in June 1669, Molière added his three petitions to Louis XIV; they follow the Preface. 2. Louis XIV was married to Marie-Thérèse of Austria.

piety, readily accept the impressions that others present to them. And it is this which forces me to defend myself. Especially to the truly devout do I wish to vindicate my play, and I beg of them with all my heart not to condemn it before seeing it, to rid themselves of preconceptions, and not aid the cause of men dishonored by their actions.

If one takes the trouble to examine my comedy in good faith, he will surely see that my intentions are innocent throughout, and tend in no way to make fun of what men revere; that I have presented the subject with all the precautions that its delicacy imposes; and that I have used all the art and skill that I could to distinguish clearly the character of the hypocrite from that of the truly devout man. For that purpose I used two whole acts to prepare the appearance of my scoundrel. Never is there a moment's doubt about his character; he is known at once from the qualities I have given him; and from one end of the play to the other, he does not say a word, he does not perform an action which does not depict to the audience the character of a wicked man, and which does not bring out in sharp relief the character of the truly good man which I oppose to it.

I know full well that by way of reply, these gentlemen try to insinuate that it is not the role of the theater to speak of these matters; but with their permission, I ask them on what do they base this fine doctrine. It is a proposition they advance as no more than a supposition, for which they offer not a shred of proof; and surely it would not be difficult to show them that comedy, for the ancients, had its origin in religion and constituted a part of its ceremonies; that our neighbors, the Spaniards, have hardly a single holiday celebration in which a comedy is not a part; and that even here in France, it owes its birth to the efforts of a religious brotherhood who still own the Hôtel de Bourgogne, where the most important mystery plays of our faith were presented;[3] that you can still find comedies printed in gothic letters under the name of a learned doctor[4] of the Sorbonne; and without going so far, in our own day the religious dramas of Pierre Corneille[5] have been performed to the admiration of all France.

If the function of comedy is to correct men's vices, I do not see why any should be exempt. Such a condition in our society would be much more dangerous than the thing itself; and we have seen that the theater is admirably suited to provide correction. The most forceful lines of a serious moral statement are usually less powerful than those of satire; and nothing will reform most men better than the depiction of their faults. It is a vigorous blow to vices to expose them to public laughter. Criticism is taken lightly, but men will not tolerate satire. They are quite willing to be mean, but they never like to be ridiculed.

I have been attacked for having placed words of piety in the mouth of my impostor. Could I avoid doing so in order to represent properly the character of a hypocrite? It seemed to me sufficient to reveal the criminal motives which make him speak as he does, and I have eliminated all ceremonial phrases, which nonetheless he would not have been found using incorrectly.

---

3. A reference to the *Confrérie de la Passion et Résurrection de Notre-Seigneur* (Fraternity of the passion and resurrection of our Savior), founded in 1402. The Hôtel de Bourgogne was a theater in rivalry with Molière's.   4. Probably Maître Jehán Michel, a medical doctor who wrote mystery plays.   5. Corneille (1606–1684) and Racine were France's two greatest writers of classic tragedy. The two dramas Molière doubtless had in mind were *Polyeucte* (1643) and *Théodore, vierge et martyre* (1645).

Yet some say that in the fourth act he sets forth a vicious morality; but is not this a morality which everyone has heard again and again? Does my comedy say anything new here? And is there any fear that ideas so thoroughly detested by everyone can make an impression on men's minds; that I make them dangerous by presenting them in the theater; that they acquire authority from the lips of a scoundrel? There is not the slightest suggestion of any of this; and one must either approve the comedy of *Tartuffe* or condemn all comedies in general.

This has indeed been done in a furious way for some time now, and never was the theater so much abused.[6] I cannot deny that there were Church Fathers who condemned comedy; but neither will it be denied me that there were some who looked on it somewhat more favorably. Thus authority, on which censure is supposed to depend, is destroyed by this disagreement; and the only conclusion that can be drawn from this difference of opinion among men enlightened by the same wisdom is that they viewed comedy in different ways, and that some considered it in its purity, while others regarded it in its corruption and confused it with all those wretched performances which have been rightly called performances of filth.

And in fact, since we should talk about things rather than words, and since most misunderstanding comes from including contrary notions in the same word, we need only to remove the veil of ambiguity and look at comedy in itself to see if it warrants condemnation. It will surely be recognized that as it is nothing more than a clever poem which corrects men's faults by means of agreeable lessons, it cannot be condemned without injustice. And if we listened to the voice of ancient times on this matter, it would tell us that its most famous philosophers have praised comedy—they who professed so austere a wisdom and who ceaselessly denounced the vices of their times. It would tell us that Aristotle spent his evenings at the theater[7] and took the trouble to reduce the art of making comedies to rules. It would tell us that some of its greatest and most honored men took pride in writing comedies themselves;[8] and that others did not disdain to recite them in public; that Greece expressed its admiration for this art by means of handsome prizes and magnificent theaters to honor it; and finally, that in Rome this same art also received extraordinary honors; I do not speak of Rome run riot under the license of the emperors, but of disciplined Rome, governed by the wisdom of the consuls, and in the age of the full vigor of Roman dignity.

I admit that there have been times when comedy became corrupt. And what do men not corrupt every day? There is nothing so innocent that men cannot turn it to crime; nothing so beneficial that its values cannot be reversed; nothing so good in itself that it cannot be put to bad uses. Medical knowledge benefits mankind and is revered as one of our most wonderful possessions; and yet there was a time when it fell into discredit, and was often used to poison men. Philosophy is a gift of Heaven; it has been given to us to bring us to the knowledge of a God by contemplating the wonders

---

6. Molière had in mind Pierre Nicole's two attacks on the theater: *Visionnaires* (1666) and *Traité de la Comédie* (1667), as well as the prince de Conti's *Traité de la Comédie* (1666).   7. A reference to Aristotle's *Poetics* (composed between 335 and 322 B.C.E., the year of his death).   8. Scipio Africanus Minor (ca. 185–129 B.C.E.), the Roman consul and general responsible for the final destruction of Carthage in 146 B.C.E., collaborated with Terence (Publius Terentius Afer, ca. 195 or 185–ca. 159 B.C.E.), a writer of comedies.

of nature; and yet we know that often it has been turned away from its function and has been used openly in support of impiety. Even the holiest of things are not immune from human corruption, and every day we see scoundrels who use and abuse piety, and wickedly make it serve the greatest of crimes. But this does not prevent one from making the necessary distinctions. We do not confuse in the same false inference the goodness of things that are corrupted with the wickedness of the corrupt. The function of an art is always distinguished from its misuse; and as medicine is not forbidden because it was banned in Rome, nor philosophy because it was publicly condemned in Athens,[9] we should not suppress comedy simply because it has been condemned at certain times. This censure was justified then for reasons which no longer apply today; it was limited to what was then seen; and we should not seize on these limits, apply them more rigidly than is necessary, and include in our condemnation the innocent along with the guilty. The comedy that this censure attacked is in no way the comedy that we want to defend. We must be careful not to confuse the one with the other. There may be two persons whose morals may be completely different. They may have no resemblance to one another except in their names, and it would be a terrible injustice to want to condemn Olympia, who is a good woman, because there is also an Olympia who is lewd. Such procedures would make for great confusion everywhere. Everything under the sun would be condemned; now since this rigor is not applied to the countless instances of abuse we see every day, the same should hold for comedy, and those plays should be approved in which instruction and virtue reign supreme.

I know there are some so delicate that they cannot tolerate a comedy, who say that the most decent are the most dangerous, that the passions they present are all the more moving because they are virtuous, and that men's feelings are stirred by these presentations. I do not see what great crime it is to be affected by the sight of a generous passion; and this utter insensitivity to which they would lead us is indeed a high degree of virtue! I wonder if so great a perfection resides within the strength of human nature, and I wonder if it is not better to try to correct and moderate men's passions than to try to suppress them altogether. I grant that there are places better to visit than the theater; and if we want to condemn every single thing that does not bear directly on God and our salvation, it is right that comedy be included, and I should willingly grant that it be condemned along with everything else. But if we admit, as is in fact true, that the exercise of piety will permit interruptions, and that men need amusement, I maintain that there is none more innocent than comedy. I have dwelled too long on this matter. Let me finish with the words of a great prince on the comedy, *Tartuffe*.[1]

Eight days after it had been banned, a play called *Scaramouche the Hermit*[2] was performed before the court; and the king, on his way out, said to this great prince: "I should really like to know why the persons who make so much noise about Molière's comedy do not say a word about *Scaramouche*."

---

9. An allusion to Socrates' condemnation to death. Pliny the Elder says that the Romans expelled their doctors at the same time that the Greeks did theirs.   1. One of Molière's benefactors who liked the play was the prince de Condé; de Condé had *Tartuffe* read to him and also privately performed for him.   2. A troupe of Italian comedians had just performed the licentious farce, in which a hermit dressed as a monk makes love to a married woman, announcing that *questo e per mortificar la carne* (this is to mortify the flesh).

To which the prince replied, "It is because the comedy of *Scaramouche* makes fun of Heaven and religion, which these gentlemen do not care about at all, but that of Molière makes fun of *them,* and that is what they cannot bear."

THE AUTHOR

FIRST PETITION[3]

(Presented to the King on the Comedy of Tartuffe)

Sire,

As the duty of comedy is to correct men by amusing them, I believed that in my occupation I could do nothing better than attack the vices of my age by making them ridiculous; and as hypocrisy is undoubtedly one of the most common, most improper, and most dangerous, I thought, Sire, that I would perform a service for all good men of your kingdom if I wrote a comedy which denounced hypocrites and placed in proper view all of the contrived poses of these incredibly virtuous men, all of the concealed villainies of these counterfeit believers who would trap others with a fraudulent piety and a pretended virtue.

I have written this comedy, Sire, with all the care and caution that the delicacy of the subject demands; and so as to maintain all the more properly the admiration and respect due to truly devout men, I have delineated my character as sharply as I could; I have left no room for doubt; I have removed all that might confuse good with evil, and have used for this painting only the specific colors and essential lines that make one instantly recognize a true and brazen hypocrite.

Nevertheless, all my precautions have been to no avail. Others have taken advantage of the delicacy of your feelings on religious matters, and they have been able to deceive you on the only side of your character which lies open to deception: your respect for holy things. By underhanded means, the Tartuffes have skillfully gained Your Majesty's favor, and the models have succeeded in eliminating the copy, no matter how innocent it may have been and no matter what resemblance was found between them.

Although the suppression of this work was a serious blow for me, my misfortune was nonetheless softened by the way in which Your Majesty explained his attitude on the matter; and I believed, Sire, that Your Majesty removed any cause I had for complaint, as you were kind enough to declare that you found nothing in this comedy that you would forbid me to present in public.

Yet, despite this glorious declaration of the greatest and most enlightened king in the world, despite the approval of the Papal Legate[4] and of most of our churchmen, all of whom, at private readings of my work, agreed with the views of Your Majesty, despite all this, a book has appeared by a certain

---

3. The first of the three *petitions* or *placets* to Louis XIV concerning the play. On May 12, 1664, *Tartuffe*—or at least the first three acts roughly as they now stand—was performed at Versailles. A cabal unfavorable to Molière, including the archbishop of Paris, Hardouin de Péréfixe, Queen Mother Anne of Austria, certain influential courtiers, and the Brotherhood or Company of the Holy Sacrament (formed in 1627 to enforce morality), arranged that the play be banned and Molière censured.   4. Cardinal Legate Chigi, nephew to Pope Alexander VII, heard a reading of *Tartuffe* at Fontainebleau on August 4, 1664.

priest[5] which boldly contradicts all of these noble judgments. Your Majesty expressed himself in vain, and the Papal Legate and churchmen gave their opinion to no avail: sight unseen, my comedy is diabolical, and so is my brain; I am a devil garbed in flesh and disguised as a man,[6] a libertine, a disbeliever who deserves a punishment that will set an example. It is not enough that fire expiate my crime in public, for that would be letting me off too easily: the generous piety of this good man will not stop there; he will not allow me to find any mercy in the sight of God; he demands that I be damned, and that will settle the matter.

This book, Sire, was presented to Your Majesty; and I am sure that you see for yourself how unpleasant it is for me to be exposed daily to the insults of these gentlemen, what harm these abuses will do my reputation if they must be tolerated, and finally, how important it is for me to clear myself of these false charges and let the public know that my comedy is nothing more than what they want it to be. I will not ask, Sire, for what I need for the sake of my reputation and the innocence of my work: enlightened kings such as you do not need to be told what is wished of them; like God, they see what we need and know better than we what they should give us. It is enough for me to place my interests in Your Majesty's hands, and I respectfully await whatever you may care to command.

(*August, 1664*)

SECOND PETITION[7]

(Presented to the King in His Camp Before the City of Lille, in Flanders)

Sire,

It is bold indeed for me to ask a favor of a great monarch in the midst of his glorious victories; but in my present situation, Sire, where will I find protection anywhere but where I seek it, and to whom can I appeal against the authority of the power[8] that crushes me, if not to the source of power and authority, the just dispenser of absolute law, the sovereign judge and master of all?

My comedy, Sire, has not enjoyed the kindnesses of Your Majesty. All to no avail, I produced it under the title of *The Hypocrite* and disguised the principal character as a man of the world; in vain I gave him a little hat, long hair, a wide collar, a sword, and lace clothing,[9] softened the action and carefully eliminated all that I thought might provide even the shadow of grounds for discontent on the part of the famous models of the portrait I wished to present; nothing did any good. The conspiracy of opposition revived even at mere conjecture of what the play would be like. They found a way of persuading those who in all other matters plainly insist that they are not to be

---

5. Pierre Roullé, the curate of St. Barthélemy, who wrote a scathing attack on the play and sent his book to the king.   6. Molière took some of these phrases from Roullé.   7. On August 5, 1667, *Tartuffe* was performed at the Palais-Royal. The opposition—headed by the first president of parliament—brought in the police, and the play was stopped. Because Louis was campaigning in Flanders, friends of Molière brought the second *placet* to Lille. Louis had always been favorable toward the playwright; in August 1665 Molière's company, the *Troupe de Monsieur* (nominally sponsored by Louis's brother Philippe, duc d'Orléans), had become the *Troupe du Roi.*   8. President of Lanvignon, in charge of the Paris police.   9. There is evidence that in 1664 Tartuffe played his role dressed in a cassock, thus allying him more directly to the clergy.

deceived. No sooner did my comedy appear than it was struck down by the very power which should impose respect; and all that I could do to save myself from the fury of this tempest was to say that Your Majesty had given me permission to present the play and I did not think it was necessary to ask this permission of others, since only Your Majesty could have refused it.

I have no doubt, Sire, that the men whom I depict in my comedy will employ every means possible to influence Your Majesty, and will use, as they have used already, those truly good men who are all the more easily deceived because they judge of others by themselves.[1] They know how to display all of their aims in the most favorable light; yet, no matter how pious they may seem, it is surely not the interests of God which stir them; they have proven this often enough in the comedies they have allowed to be performed hundreds of times without making the least objection. Those plays attacked only piety and religion, for which they care very little; but this play attacks and makes fun of them, and that is what they cannot bear. They will never forgive me for unmasking their hypocrisy in the eyes of everyone. And I am sure that they will not neglect to tell Your Majesty that people are shocked by my comedy. But the simple truth, Sire, is that all Paris is shocked only by its ban, that the most scrupulous persons have found its presentation worthwhile, and men are astounded that individuals of such known integrity should show so great a deference to people whom everyone should abominate and who are so clearly opposed to the true piety which they profess.

I respectfully await the judgment that Your Majesty will deign to pronounce: but it's certain, Sire, that I need not think of writing comedies if the Tartuffes are triumphant, if they thereby seize the right to persecute me more than ever, and find fault with even the most innocent lines that flow from my pen.

Let your goodness, Sire, give me protection against their envenomed rage, and allow me, at your return from so glorious a campaign, to relieve Your Majesty from the fatigue of his conquests, give him innocent pleasures after such noble accomplishments, and make the monarch laugh who makes all Europe tremble!

(*August, 1667*)

THIRD PETITION

(*Presented to the King*)

Sire,

A very honest doctor[2] whose patient I have the honor to be, promises and will legally contract to make me live another thirty years if I can obtain a favor for him from Your Majesty. I told him of his promise that I do not deserve so much, and that I should be glad to help him if he will merely agree not to kill me. This favor, Sire, is a post of canon at your royal chapel of Vincennes, made vacant by death.

May I dare to ask for this favor from Your Majesty on the very day of the glorious resurrection of *Tartuffe*, brought back to life by your goodness? By

---

1. Molière apparently did not know that de Lanvignon had been affiliated with the Company of the Holy Sacrament for the previous ten years.   2. A physician friend, M. de Mauvillain, who helped Molière with some of the medical details of *Le Malade imaginaire*.

this first favor I have been reconciled with the devout, and the second will reconcile me with the doctors.[3] Undoubtedly this would be too much grace for me at one time, but perhaps it would not be too much for Your Majesty, and I await your answer to my petition with respectful hope.

(February, 1669)

CHARACTERS

MADAME PERNELLE, *Organ's mother*
ORGON, *Elmire's husband*
ELMIRE, *Organ's wife*
DAMIS, *Organ's son, Elmire's stepson*
MARIANE, *Organ's daughter, Elmire's stepdaughter, in love with Valère*

VALÈRE, *in love with Mariane*
CLÉANTE, *Organ's brother-in-law*
TARTUFFE,[4] *a hypocrite*
DORINE,[5] *Mariane's lady's-maid*
M. LOYAL, *a bailiff*
A POLICE OFFICER
FLIPOTE, *Mme Pernelle's maid*

The SCENE *throughout:* ORGON's *house in Paris.*

Act I

SCENE 1[6]

MADAME PERNELLE *and* FLIPOTE, *her maid,* ELMIRE,
MARIANE, DORINE, DAMIS, CLÉANTE

MADAME PERNELLE   Come, come, Flipote; it's time I left this place.
ELMIRE   I can't keep up, you walk at such a pace.
MADAME PERNELLE   Don't trouble, child; no need to show me out.
　It's not your manners I'm concerned about.
ELMIRE   We merely pay you the respect we owe.　　　　　　　　　　　　5
　But, Mother, why this hurry? Must you go?
MADAME PERNELLE   I must. This house appals me. No one in it
　Will pay attention for a single minute.
　I offer good advice, but you won't hear it.
　Children, I take my leave much vexed in spirit.　　　　　　　　　　10
　You all break in and chatter on and on.
　It's like a madhouse with the keeper gone.
DORINE   If . . .
MADAME PERNELLE
　　　　　Girl, you talk too much, and I'm afraid
　You're far too saucy for a lady's-maid.
　You push in everywhere and have your say.　　　　　　　　　　　15
DAMIS   But . . .

---

3. Doctors are ridiculed to varying degrees in earlier plays of Molière: *Dom Juan, L'Amour médecin,* and *Le Médecin malgré lui.*　　4. The name *Tartuffe* has been traced back to an older word associated with liar or charlatan: *truffer,* "to deceive" or "to cheat." Then there was also the Italian actor Tartufo, physically deformed and truffle-shaped. Most of the other names are typical of this genre of court comedy and possess rather elegant connotations of pastoral and *bergerie.*　　5. She is a *demoiselle de compagne* and not a mere maid, that is, a female companion to Mariane of roughly the same social status. This in part accounts for the liberties she takes in conversation with Orgon, Madame Pernelle, and others. Her name is short for Théodorine.　　6. In French drama, the scene changes every time a character enters or exits.

MADAME PERNELLE
        You, boy, grow more foolish every day.
  To think my grandson should be such a dunce!
  I've said a hundred times, if I've said it once,
  That if you keep the course on which you've started,
  You'll leave your worthy father broken-hearted.   20
MARIANE   I think . . .
MADAME PERNELLE   And you, his sister, seem so pure,
  So shy, so innocent, and so demure.
  But you know what they say about still waters.
  I pity parents with secretive daughters.
ELMIRE   Now, Mother . . .
MADAME PERNELLE   And as for you, child, let me add   25
  That your behavior is extremely bad,
  And a poor example for these children, too.
  Their dear, dead mother did far better than you.
  You're much too free with money, and I'm distressed
  To see you so elaborately dressed.   30
  When it's one's husband that one aims to please,
  One has no need of costly fripperies.
CLÉANTE   Oh, Madam, really . . .
MADAME PERNELLE   You are her brother, Sir,
  And I respect and love you; yet if I were
  My son, this lady's good and pious spouse,   35
  I wouldn't make you welcome in my house.
  You're full of worldly counsels which, I fear,
  Aren't suitable for decent folk to hear.
  I've spoken bluntly, Sir; but it behooves us
  Not to mince words when righteous fervor moves us.   40
DAMIS   Your man Tartuffe is full of holy speeches . . .
MADAME PERNELLE   And practises precisely what he preaches.
  He's a fine man, and should be listened to.
  I will not hear him mocked by fools like you.
DAMIS   Good God! Do you expect me to submit   45
  To the tyranny of that carping hypocrite?
  Must we forgo all joys and satisfactions
  Because that bigot censures all our actions?
DORINE   To hear him talk—and he talks all the time—
  There's nothing one can do that's not a crime.   50
  He rails at everything, your dear Tartuffe.
MADAME PERNELLE   Whatever he reproves deserves reproof.
  He's out to save your souls, and all of you
  Must love him, as my son would have you do.
DAMIS   Ah no, Grandmother, I could never take   55
  To such a rascal, even for my father's sake.
  That's how I feel, and I shall not dissemble.
  His every action makes me seethe and tremble
  With helpless anger, and I have no doubt
  That he and I will shortly have it out.   60
DORINE   Surely it is a shame and a disgrace

To see this man usurp the master's place—
To see this beggar who, when first he came,
Had not a shoe or shoestring to his name
So far forget himself that he behaves   65
As if the house were his, and we his slaves.
MADAME PERNELLE   Well, mark my words, your souls would fare far better
   If you obeyed his precepts to the letter.
DORINE   You see him as a saint. I'm far less awed;
   In fact, I see right through him. He's a fraud.   70
MADAME PERNELLE   Nonsense!
DORINE   His man Laurent's the same, or worse;
   I'd not trust either with a penny purse.
MADAME PERNELLE   I can't say what his servant's morals may be;
   His own great goodness I can guarantee.
   You all regard him with distaste and fear   75
   Because he tells you what you're loath to hear,
   Condemns your sins, points out your moral flaws,
   And humbly strives to further Heaven's cause.
DORINE   If sin is all that bothers him, why is it
   He's so upset when folk drop in to visit?   80
   Is Heaven so outraged by a social call
   That he must prophesy against us all?
   I'll tell you what I think: if you ask me,
   He's jealous of my mistress' company.
MADAME PERNELLE   Rubbish!
   [To ELMIRE.]
                              He's not alone, child, in complaining   85
   Of all of your promiscuous entertaining.
   Why, the whole neighborhood's upset, I know,
   By all these carriages that come and go,
   With crowds of guests parading in and out
   And noisy servants loitering about.   90
   In all of this, I'm sure there's nothing vicious;
   But why give people cause to be suspicious?
CLÉANTE   They need no cause; they'll talk in any case.
   Madam, this world would be a joyless place
   If, fearing what malicious tongues might say,   95
   We locked our doors and turned our friends away.
   And even if one did so dreary a thing,
   D' you think those tongues would cease their chattering?
   One can't fight slander; it's a losing battle;
   Let us instead ignore their tittle-tattle.   100
   Let's strive to live by conscience' clear decrees,
   And let the gossips gossip as they please.
DORINE   If there is talk against us, I know the source:
   It's Daphne and her little husband, of course.
   Those who have greatest cause for guilt and shame   105
   Are quickest to besmirch a neighbor's name.
   When there's a chance for libel, they never miss it;
   When something can be made to seem illicit

They're off at once to spread the joyous news,
Adding to fact what fantasies they choose.   110
By talking up their neighbor's indiscretions
They seek to camouflage their own transgressions,
Hoping that others' innocent affairs
Will lend a hue of innocence to theirs,
Or that their own black guilt will come to seem   115
Part of a general shady color-scheme.

MADAME PERNELLE   All this is quite irrelevant. I doubt
That anyone's more virtuous and devout
Than dear Orante; and I'm informed that she
Condemns your mode of life most vehemently.   120

DORINE   Oh, yes, she's strict, devout, and has no taint
Of worldliness; in short, she seems a saint.
But it was time which taught her that disguise;
She's thus because she can't be otherwise.
So long as her attractions could enthrall,   125
She flounced and flirted and enjoyed it all,
But now that they're no longer what they were
She quits a world which fast is quitting her,
And wears a veil of virtue to conceal
Her bankrupt beauty and her lost appeal.   130
That's what becomes of old coquettes today:
Distressed when all their lovers fall away,
They see no recourse but to play the prude,
And so confer a style on solitude.
Thereafter, they're severe with everyone,   135
Condemning all our actions, pardoning none,
And claiming to be pure, austere, and zealous
When, if the truth were known, they're merely jealous,
And cannot bear to see another know
The pleasures time has forced them to forgo.   140

MADAME PERNELLE [*Initially to* ELMIRE.]
That sort of talk[7] is what you like to hear;
Therefore you'd have us all keep still, my dear,
While Madam rattles on the livelong day.
Nevertheless, I mean to have my say.
I tell you that you're blest to have Tartuffe   145
Dwelling, as my son's guest, beneath this roof;
That Heaven has sent him to forestall its wrath
By leading you, once more, to the true path;
That all he reprehends is reprehensible,
And that you'd better heed him, and be sensible.   150
These visits, balls, and parties in which you revel
Are nothing but inventions of the Devil.
One never hears a word that's edifying:
Nothing but chaff and foolishness and lying,

---

7. In the original, a reference to a collection of novels about chivalry found in *La Bibliothèque bleue* (The blue library), written for children.

As well as vicious gossip in which one's neighbor 155
Is cut to bits with épée, foil, and saber.
People of sense are driven half-insane
At such affairs, where noise and folly reign
And reputations perish thick and fast.
As a wise preacher said on Sunday last, 160
Parties are Towers of Babylon,[8] because
The guests all babble on with never a pause;
And then he told a story which, I think . . .
[*To* CLÉANTE.] I heard that laugh, Sir, and I saw that wink!
Go find your silly friends and laugh some more! 165
Enough; I'm going; don't show me to the door.
I leave this household much dismayed and vexed;
I cannot say when I shall see you next.
     [*Slapping* FLIPOTE.]
Wake up, don't stand there gaping into space!
I'll slap some sense into that stupid face. 170
Move, move, you slut.

SCENE 2

CLÉANTE, DORINE

CLÉANTE   I think I'll stay behind;
I want no further pieces of her mind.
How that old lady . . .
DORINE   Oh, what wouldn't she say
If she could hear you speak of her that way!
She'd thank you for the *lady*, but I'm sure 5
She'd find the *old* a little premature.
CLÉANTE   My, what a scene she made, and what a din!
And how this man Tartuffe has taken her in!
DORINE   Yes, but her son is even worse deceived;
His folly must be seen to be believed. 10
In the late troubles,[9] he played an able part
And served his king with wise and loyal heart,
But he's quite lost his senses since he fell
Beneath Tartuffe's infatuating spell.
He calls him brother, and loves him as his life, 15
Preferring him to mother, child, or wife.
In him and him alone will he confide;
He's made him his confessor and his guide;
He pets and pampers him with love more tender
Than any pretty maiden could engender, 20
Gives him the place of honor when they dine,
Delights to see him gorging like a swine,

---

8. Tower of Babel. Madame Pernelle's malapropism is the cause of Cléante's laughter.   9. A series of political disturbances during the minority of Louis XIV. Specifically, these consisted of the *Fronde* ("opposition") of the Parlement (1648–49) and the *Fronde* of the Princes (1650–53). Orgon is depicted as supporting Louis XIV in these outbreaks and their resolution.

Stuffs him with dainties till his guts distend,
And when he belches, cries "God bless you, friend!"
In short, he's mad; he worships him; he dotes;   25
His deeds he marvels at, his words, he quotes,
Thinking each act a miracle, each word
Oracular as those that Moses heard.
Tartuffe, much pleased to find so easy a victim,
Has in a hundred ways beguiled and tricked him,   30
Milked him of money, and with his permission
Established here a sort of Inquisition.
Even Laurent, his lackey, dares to give
Us arrogant advice on how to live;
He sermonizes us in thundering tones   35
And confiscates our ribbons and colognes.
Last week he tore a kerchief into pieces
Because he found it pressed in a *Life of Jesus:*
He said it was a sin to juxtapose
Unholy vanities and holy prose.   40

SCENE 3

ELMIRE, MARIANE, DAMIS, CLÉANTE, DORINE

ELMIRE [*To* CLÉANTE.]   You did well not to follow; she stood in the door
And said *verbatim* all she'd said before.
I saw my husband coming. I think I'd best
Go upstairs now, and take a little rest.
CLÉANTE   I'll wait and greet him here; then I must go.   5
I've really only time to say hello.
DAMIS   Sound him about my sister's wedding, please.
I think Tartuffe's against it, and that he's
Been urging Father to withdraw his blessing.
As you well know, I'd find that most distressing.   10
Unless my sister and Valère can marry,
My hopes to wed *his* sister will miscarry.
And I'm determined . . .
DORINE   He's coming.

SCENE 4

ORGON, CLÉANTE, DORINE

ORGON   Ah, Brother, good-day.
CLÉANTE   Well, welcome back, I'm sorry I can't stay.
How was the country? Blooming, I trust, and green?
ORGON   Excuse me, Brother; just one moment.
[*To* DORINE.]   Dorine . . .
[*To* CLÉANTE.] To put my mind at rest, I always learn   5
The household news the moment I return.
[*To* DORINE.] Has all been well, these two days I've been gone?
How are the family? What's been going on?

DORINE   Your wife, two days ago, had a bad fever,
  And a fierce headache which refused to leave her.   10
ORGON   Ah. And Tartuffe?
DORINE   Tartuffe? Why, he's round and red.
  Bursting with health, and excellently fed.
ORGON   Poor fellow!
DORINE   That night, the mistress was unable
  To take a single bite at the dinner-table.
  Her headache-pains, she said, were simply hellish.   15
ORGON   Ah. And Tartuffe?
DORINE   He ate his meal with relish,
  And zealously devoured in her presence
  A leg of mutton and a brace of pheasants.
ORGON   Poor fellow!
DORINE   Well, the pains continued strong,
  And so she tossed and tossed the whole night long,   20
  Now icy-cold, now burning like a flame.
  We sat beside her bed till morning came.
ORGON   Ah. And Tartuffe?
DORINE   Why, having eaten, he rose
  And sought his room, already in a doze,
  Got into his warm bed, and snored away   25
  In perfect peace until the break of day.
ORGON   Poor fellow!
DORINE   After much ado, we talked her
  Into dispatching someone for the doctor.
  He bled her, and the fever quickly fell.
ORGON   Ah. And Tartuffe?
DORINE   He bore it very well.   30
  To keep his cheerfulness at any cost,
  And make up for the blood Madame had lost,
  He drank, at lunch, four beakers full of port.
ORGON   Poor fellow.
DORINE   Both are doing well, in short.
  I'll go and tell Madame that you've expressed   35
  Keen sympathy and anxious interest.

SCENE 5

ORGON, CLÉANTE

CLÉANTE   That girl was laughing in your face, and though
  I've no wish to offend you, even so
  I'm bound to say that she had some excuse.
  How can you possibly be such a goose?
  Are you so dazed by this man's hocus-pocus   5
  That all the world, save him, is out of focus?
  You've given him clothing, shelter, food, and care;
  Why must you also . . .
ORGON   Brother, stop right there.

You do not know the man of whom you speak.
CLÉANTE   I grant you that. But my judgment's not so weak   10
    That I can't tell, by his effect on others . . .
ORGAN   Ah, when you meet him, you two will be like brothers!
    There's been no loftier soul since time began.
    He is a man who . . . a man who . . . an excellent man.
    To keep his precepts is to be reborn,   15
    And view this dunghill of a world with scorn.
    Yes, thanks to him I'm a changed man indeed.
    Under his tutelage my soul's been freed
    From earthly loves, and every human tie:
    My mother, children, brother, and wife could die,   20
    And I'd not feel a single moment's pain.
CLÉANTE   That's a fine sentiment, Brother; most humane.
ORGAN   Oh, had you seen Tartuffe as I first knew him,
    Your heart, like mine, would have surrendered to him.
    He used to come into our church each day   25
    And humbly kneel nearby, and start to pray.
    He'd draw the eyes of everybody there
    By the deep fervor of his heartfelt prayer;
    He'd sigh and weep, and sometimes with a sound
    Of rapture he would bend and kiss the ground;   30
    And when I rose to go, he'd run before
    To offer me holy-water at the door.
    His serving-man, no less devout than he,
    Informed me of his master's poverty;
    I gave him gifts, but in his humbleness   35
    He'd beg me every time to give him less.
    "Oh, that's too much," he'd cry, "too much by twice!
    I don't deserve it. The half, Sir, would suffice."
    And when I wouldn't take it back, he'd share
    Half of it with the poor, right then and there.   40
    At length, Heaven prompted me to take him in
    To dwell with us, and free our souls from sin.
    He guides our lives, and to protect my honor
    Stays by my wife, and keeps an eye upon her;
    He tells me whom she sees, and all she does,   45
    And seems more jealous than I ever was!
    And how austere he is! Why, he can detect
    A moral sin where you would least suspect;
    In smallest trifles, he's extremely strict.
    Last week, his conscience was severely pricked   50
    Because, while praying, he had caught a flea
    And killed it, so he felt, too wrathfully.[1]
CLÉANTE   Good God, man! Have you lost your common sense—
    Or is this all some joke at my expense?
    How can you stand there and in all sobriety . . .   55

1. In the *Golden Legend* (*Legenda Sanctorum*), a popular collection of the lives of the saints written in the 13th century, it is said of St. Macarius the Elder (died 390) that he dwelt naked in the desert for six months, a penance he felt appropriate for having killed a flea.

ORGON   Brother, your language savors of impiety.
    Too much free-thinking's made your faith unsteady,
    And as I've warned you many times already,
    'Twill get you into trouble before you're through.
CLÉANTE   So I've been told before by dupes like you: 60
    Being blind, you'd have all others blind as well;
    The clear-eyed man you call an infidel,
    And he who sees through humbug and pretense
    Is charged, by you, with want of reverence.
    Spare me your warnings, Brother; I have no fear   65
    Of speaking out, for you and Heaven to hear,
    Against affected zeal and pious knavery.
    There's true and false in piety, as in bravery,
    And just as those whose courage shines the most
    In battle, are the least inclined to boast,   70
    So those whose hearts are truly pure and lowly
    Don't make a flashy show of being holy.
    There's a vast difference, so it seems to me,
    Between true piety and hypocrisy:
    How do you fail to see it, may I ask?   75
    Is not a face quite different from a mask?
    Cannot sincerity and cunning art,
    Reality and semblance, be told apart?
    Are scarecrows just like men, and do you hold
    That a false coin is just as good as gold?   80
    Ah, Brother, man's a strangely fashioned creature
    Who seldom is content to follow Nature,
    But recklessly pursues his inclination
    Beyond the narrow bounds of moderation,
    And often, by transgressing Reason's laws,   85
    Perverts a lofty aim or noble cause.
    A passing observation, but it applies.
ORGON   I see, dear Brother, that you're profoundly wise;
    You harbor all the insight of the age.
    You are our one clear mind, our only sage,   90
    The era's oracle, its Cato[2] too,
    And all mankind are fools compared to you.
CLÉANTE   Brother, I don't pretend to be a sage,
    Nor have I all the wisdom of the age.
    There's just one insight I would dare to claim: 95
    I know that true and false are not the same;
    And just as there is nothing I more revere
    Than a soul whose faith is steadfast and sincere,
    Nothing that I more cherish and admire
    Than honest zeal and true religious fire,   100
    So there is nothing that I find more base
    Than specious piety's dishonest face—
    Than these bold mountebanks, these histrios

---

2. Roman statesman (95–46 B.C.E.) with an enduring reputation for honesty and incorruptibility.

Whose impious mummeries and hollow shows
Exploit our love of Heaven, and make a jest   105
Of all that men think holiest and best;
These calculating souls who offer prayers
Not to their Maker, but as public wares,
And seek to buy respect and reputation
With lifted eyes and sighs of exaltation;   110
These charlatans, I say, whose pilgrim souls
Proceed, by way of Heaven, toward earthly goals,
Who weep and pray and swindle and extort,
Who preach the monkish life, but haunt the court,
Who make their zeal the partner of their vice—   115
Such men are vengeful, sly, and cold as ice,
And when there is an enemy to defame
They cloak their spite in fair religion's name,
Their private spleen and malice being made
To seem a high and virtuous crusade,   120
Until, to mankind's reverent applause,
They crucify their foe in Heaven's cause.
Such knaves are all too common; yet, for the wise,
True piety isn't hard to recognize,
And, happily, these present times provide us   125
With bright examples to instruct and guide us.
Consider Ariston and Périandre;
Look at Oronte, Alcidamas, Clitandre;[3]
Their virtue is acknowledged; who could doubt it?
But you won't hear them beat the drum about it.   130
They're never ostentatious, never vain,
And their religion's moderate and humane;
It's not their way to criticize and chide:
They think censoriousness a mark of pride,
And therefore, letting others preach and rave,   135
They show, by deeds, how Christians should behave.
They think no evil of their fellow man,
But judge of him as kindly as they can.
They don't intrigue and wangle and conspire;
To lead a good life is their one desire;   140
The sinner wakes no rancorous hate in them;
It is the sin alone which they condemn;
Nor do they try to show a fiercer zeal
For Heaven's cause than Heaven itself could feel.
These men I honor, these men I advocate   145
As models for us all to emulate.
Your man is not their sort at all, I fear:
And, while your praise of him is quite sincere,
I think that you've been dreadfully deluded.
ORGON   Now then, dear Brother, is your speech concluded?   150

---

3. Vaguely Greek and Roman names derived from the elegant literature of the day.

CLÉANTE   Why, yes.
ORGON   Your servant, Sir.
    [*He turns to go.*]
CLÉANTE   No, Brother; wait.
    There's one more matter. You agreed of late
    That young Valère might have your daughter's hand.
ORGON   I did.
CLÉANTE   And set the date, I understand.
ORGON   Quite so.
CLÉANTE   You've now postponed it; is that true?   155
ORGON   No doubt.
CLÉANTE   The match no longer pleases you?
ORGON   Who knows?
CLÉANTE   D'you mean to go back on your word?
ORGON   I won't say that.
CLÉANTE   Has anything occurred
    Which might entitle you to break your pledge?
ORGON   Perhaps.
CLÉANTE   Why must you hem, and haw, and hedge?   160
    The boy asked me to sound you in this affair . . .
ORGON   It's been a pleasure.
CLÉANTE   But what shall I tell Valère?
ORGON   Whatever you like.
CLÉANTE   But what have you decided?
    What are your plans?
ORGON   I plan, Sir, to be guided
    By Heaven's will.
CLÉANTE   Come, Brother, don't talk rot.   165
    You've given Valère your word; will you keep it, or not?
ORGON   Good day.
CLÉANTE   This looks like poor Valère's undoing;
    I'll go and warn him that there's trouble brewing.

Act II

SCENE 1

ORGON, MARIANE

ORGON   Mariane.
MARIANE   Yes, Father?
ORGON   A word with you; come here.
MARIANE   What are you looking for?
ORGON [*Peering into a small closet.*]   Eavesdroppers, dear.
    I'm making sure we shan't be overheard.
    Someone in there could catch our every word.
    Ah, good, we're safe. Now, Mariane, my child,   5
    You're a sweet girl who's tractable and mild,
    Whom I hold dear, and think most highly of.
MARIANE   I'm deeply grateful, Father, for your love.

ORGON   That's well said, Daughter; and you can repay me
   If, in all things, you'll cheerfully obey me.   10
MARIANE   To please you, Sir, is what delights me best.
ORGON   Good, good. Now, what d'you think of Tartuffe, our guest?
MARIANE   I, Sir?
ORGON   Yes. Weigh your answer; think it through.
MARIANE   Oh, dear. I'll say whatever you wish me to.
ORGON   That's wisely said, my Daughter. Say of him, then,   15
   That he's the very worthiest of men,
   And that you're fond of him, and would rejoice
   In being his wife, if that should be my choice.
   Well?
MARIANE   What?
ORGON   What's that?
MARIANE   I . . .
ORGON   Well?
MARIANE   Forgive me, pray.
ORGON   Did you not hear me?
MARIANE   Of *whom*, Sir, must I say   20
   That I am fond of him, and would rejoice
   In being his wife, if that should be your choice?
ORGON   Why, of Tartuffe.
MARIANE   But, Father, that's false, you know.
   Why would you have me say what isn't so?
ORGON   Because I am resolved it shall be true.   25
   That it's my wish should be enough for you.
MARIANE   You can't mean, Father . . .
ORGON   Yes, Tartuffe shall be
   Allied by marriage[4] to this family,
   And he's to be your husband, is that clear?
   It's a father's privilege . . .   30

SCENE 2

DORINE, ORGON, MARIANE

ORGON [*To* DORINE.]   What are you doing in here?
   Is curiosity so fierce a passion
   With you, that you must eavesdrop in this fashion?
DORINE   There's lately been a rumor going about—
   Based on some hunch or chance remark, no doubt—   5
   That you mean Mariane to wed Tartuffe.
   I've laughed it off, of course, as just a spoof.
ORGON   You find it so incredible?
DORINE   Yes, I do.
   I won't accept that story, even from you.

---

4. This assertion is important and more than a mere device in the plot of the day. The second *placet*, or petition, insists that Tartuffe be costumed as a layman, and Orgon's plan for him to marry again asserts Tartuffe's position in the laity. In the 1664 version of the play Tartuffe had been dressed in a cassock, suggesting the priesthood, and Molière was now anxious to avoid any suggestion of this kind.

ORGON   Well, you'll believe it when the thing is done.   10

DORINE   Yes, yes, of course. Go on and have your fun.

ORGON   I've never been more serious in my life.

DORINE   Ha!

ORGON   Daughter, I mean it; you're to be his wife.

DORINE   No, don't believe your father; it's all a hoax.

ORGON   See here, young woman . . .

DORINE   Come, Sir, no more jokes;   15
  You can't fool us.

ORGON   How dare you talk that way?

DORINE   All right, then: we believe you, sad to say.
  But how a man like you, who looks so wise
  And wears a moustache of such splendid size,
  Can be so foolish as to . . .

ORGON   Silence, please!   20
  My girl, you take too many liberties.
  I'm master here, as you must not forget.

DORINE   Do let's discuss this calmly; don't be upset.
  You can't be serious, Sir, about this plan.
  What should that bigot want with Mariane?   25
  Praying and fasting ought to keep him busy.
  And then, in terms of wealth and rank, what is he?
  Why should a man of property like you
  Pick out a beggar son-in-law?

ORGON   That will do.
  Speak of his poverty with reverence.   30
  His is a pure and saintly indigence
  Which far transcends all worldly pride and pelf.
  He lost his fortune, as he says himself,
  Because he cared for Heaven alone, and so
  Was careless of his interests here below.   35
  I mean to get him out of his present straits
  And help him to recover his estates—
  Which, in his part of the world, have no small fame.
  Poor though he is, he's a gentleman just the same.

DORINE   Yes, so he tells us; and, Sir, it seems to me   40
  Such pride goes very ill with piety.
  A man whose spirit spurns this dungy earth
  Ought not to brag of lands and noble birth;
  Such worldly arrogance will hardly square
  With meek devotion and the life of prayer.   45
  . . . But this approach, I see, has drawn a blank;
  Let's speak, then, of his person, not his rank.
  Doesn't it seem to you a trifle grim
  To give a girl like her to a man like him?
  When two are so ill-suited, can't you see   50
  What the sad consequence is bound to be?
  A young girl's virtue is imperilled, Sir,
  When such a marriage is imposed on her;
  For if one's bridegroom isn't to one's taste,

It's hardly an inducement to be chaste,   55
And many a man with horns upon his brow
Has made his wife the thing that she is now.
It's hard to be a faithful wife, in short,
To certain husbands of a certain sort,
And he who gives his daughter to a man she hates   60
Must answer for her sins at Heaven's gates.
Think, Sir, before you play so risky a role.
ORGON   This servant-girl presumes to save my soul!
DORINE   You would do well to ponder what I've said.
ORGON   Daughter, we'll disregard this dunderhead.   65
Just trust your father's judgment. Oh, I'm aware
That I once promised you to young Valère;
But now I hear he gambles, which greatly shocks me;
What's more, I've doubts about his orthodoxy.
His visits to church, I note, are very few.   70
DORINE   Would you have him go at the same hours as you,
And kneel nearby, to be sure of being seen?
ORGON   I can dispense with such remarks, Dorine.
[*To* MARIANE.] Tartuffe, however, is sure of Heaven's blessing.
And that's the only treasure worth possessing.   75
This match will bring you joys beyond all measure;
Your cup will overflow with every pleasure;
You two will interchange your faithful loves
Like two sweet cherubs, or two turtle-doves.
No harsh word shall be heard, no frown be seen,   80
And he shall make you happy as a queen.
DORINE   And she'll make him a cuckold, just wait and see.
ORGON   What language!
DORINE   Oh, he's a man of destiny;
He's *made* for horns, and what the stars demand
Your daughter's virtue surely can't withstand.   85
ORGON   Don't interrupt me further. Why can't you learn
That certain things are none of your concern?
DORINE   It's for your own sake that I interfere.
[*She repeatedly interrupts* ORGON *just as he is turning to speak to his daughter.*]
ORGON   Most kind of you. Now, hold your tongue, d'you hear?
DORINE   If I didn't love you . . .
ORGON   Spare me your affection.   90
DORINE   I'll love you, Sir, in spite of your objection.
ORGON   Blast!
DORINE   I can't bear, Sir, for your honor's sake,
To let you make this ludicrous mistake.
ORGON   You mean to go on talking?
DORINE   If I didn't protest
This sinful marriage, my conscience couldn't rest.   95
ORGON   If you don't hold your tongue, you little shrew . . .
DORINE   What, lost your temper? A pious man like you?
ORGON   Yes! Yes! You talk and talk. I'm maddened by it.

Once and for all, I tell you to be quiet.
DORINE   Well, I'll be quiet. But I'll be thinking hard.   100
ORGON   Think all you like, but you had better guard
That saucy tongue of yours, or I'll . . .
[*Turning back to* MARIANE.]   Now, child,
I've weighed this matter fully.
DORINE [*Aside.*]   It drives me wild
That I can't speak.
        [ORGON *turns his head, and she is silent.*]
ORGON   Tartuffe is no young dandy,
But, still, his person . . .
DORINE [*Aside.*]   Is as sweet as candy.   105
ORGON   Is such that, even if you shouldn't care
For his other merits . . .
        [*He turns and stands facing* DORINE, *arms crossed.*]
DORINE [*Aside.*]   They'll make a lovely pair.
If I were she, no man would marry me
Against my inclination, and go scot-free.
He'd learn, before the wedding-day was over,   110
How readily a wife can find a lover.
ORGON [*To* DORINE.]   It seems you treat my orders as a joke.
DORINE   Why, what's the matter? 'Twas not to you I spoke.
ORGON   What *were* you doing?
DORINE   Talking to myself, that's all.
ORGON   Ah! [*Aside.*] One more bit of impudence and gall,   115
And I shall give her a good slap in the face.
        [*He puts himself in position to slap her;* DORINE, *whenever he glances at her, stands immobile and silent.*]
Daughter, you shall accept, and with good grace,
The husband I've selected . . . Your wedding-day . . .
[*To* DORINE.] Why don't you talk to yourself?
DORINE   I've nothing to say.
ORGON   Come, just one word.
DORINE   No thank you, Sir. I pass.   120
ORGON   Come, speak; I'm waiting.
DORINE   I'd not be such an ass.
ORGON [*Turning to* MARIANE.]
In short, dear Daughter, I mean to be obeyed,
And you must bow to the sound choice I've made.
DORINE [*Moving away.*] I'd not wed such a monster, even in jest.
        [ORGON *attempts to slap her, but misses.*]
ORGON   Daughter, that maid of yours is a thorough pest;   125
She makes me sinfully annoyed and nettled.
I can't speak further; my nerves are too unsettled.
She's so upset me by her insolent talk,
I'll calm myself by going for a walk.

SCENE 3

DORINE, MARIANE

DORINE [*Returning.*]   Well, have you lost your tongue, girl? Must I play
　Your part, and say the lines you ought to say?
　Faced with a fate so hideous and absurd,
　Can you not utter one dissenting word?
MARIANE   What good would it do? A father's power is great.　　　　　5
DORINE   Resist him now, or it will be too late.
MARIANE   But . . .
DORINE　　　　　　　　Tell him one cannot love at a father's whim;
　That you shall marry for yourself, not him;
　That since it's you who are to be the bride,
　It's you, not he, who must be satisfied;　　　　　　　　　　　10
　And that if his Tartuffe is so sublime,
　He's free to marry him at any time.
MARIANE   I've bowed so long to Father's strict control,
　I couldn't oppose him now, to save my soul.
DORINE   Come, come, Mariane. Do listen to reason, won't you?　　15
　Valère has asked your hand. Do you love him, or don't you?
MARIANE   Oh, how unjust of you! What can you mean
　By asking such a question, dear Dorine?
　You know the depth of my affection for him;
　I've told you a hundred times how I adore him.　　　　　　20
DORINE   I don't believe in everything I hear;
　Who knows if your professions were sincere?
MARIANE   They were, Dorine, and you do me wrong to doubt it;
　Heaven knows that I've been all too frank about it.
DORINE   You love him, then?
MARIANE　　　　　　　　Oh, more than I can express.　　　　25
DORINE   And he, I take it, cares for you no less?
MARIANE   I think so.
DORINE　　　　　　And you both, with equal fire,
　Burn to be married?
MARIANE　　　　　　That is our one desire.
DORINE   What of Tartuffe, then? What of your father's plan?
MARIANE   I'll kill myself, if I'm forced to wed that man.　　　30
DORINE   I hadn't thought of that recourse. How splendid!
　Just die, and all your troubles will be ended!
　A fine solution. Oh, it maddens me
　To hear you talk in that self-pitying key.
MARIANE   Dorine, how harsh you are! It's most unfair.　　　　35
　You have no sympathy for my despair.
DORINE   I've none at all for people who talk drivel
　And, faced with difficulties, whine and snivel.
MARIANE   No doubt I'm timid, but it would be wrong . . .
DORINE   True love requires a heart that's firm and strong.　　40
MARIANE   I'm strong in my affection for Valère,
　But coping with my father is his affair.

DORINE   But if your father's brain has grown so cracked
  Over his dear Tartuffe that he can retract
  His blessing, though your wedding-day was named,   45
  It's surely not Valère who's to be blamed.
MARIANE   If I defied my father, as you suggest,
  Would it not seem unmaidenly, at best?
  Shall I defend my love at the expense
  Of brazenness and disobedience?   50
  Shall I parade my heart's desires, and flaunt . . .
DORINE   No, I ask nothing of you. Clearly you want
  To be Madame Tartuffe, and I feel bound
  Not to oppose a wish so very sound.
  What right have I to criticize the match?   55
  Indeed, my dear, the man's a brilliant catch.
  Monsieur Tartuffe! Now, there's a man of weight!
  Yes, yes, Monsieur Tartuffe, I'm bound to state,
  Is quite a person; that's not to be denied;
  'Twill be no little thing to be his bride.   60
  The world already rings with his renown;
  He's a great noble—in his native town;
  His ears are red, he has a pink complexion,
  And all in all, he'll suit you to perfection.
MARIANE   Dear God!
DORINE   Oh, how triumphant you will feel   65
  At having caught a husband so ideal!
MARIANE   Oh, do stop teasing, and use your cleverness
  To get me out of this appalling mess.
  Advise me, and I'll do whatever you say.
DORINE   Ah, no, a dutiful daughter must obey   70
  Her father, even if he weds her to an ape.
  You've a bright future; why struggle to escape?
  Tartuffe will take you back where his family lives,
  To a small town aswarm with relatives—
  Uncles and cousins whom you'll be charmed to meet.   75
  You'll be received at once by the elite,
  Calling upon the bailiff's[5] wife, no less—
  Even, perhaps, upon the mayoress,[6]
  Who'll sit you down in the *best* kitchen chair.[7]
  Then, once a year, you'll dance at the village fair   80
  To the drone of bagpipes—two of them, in fact—
  And see a puppet-show, or an animal act.[8]
  Your husband . . .
MARIANE   Oh, you turn my blood to ice!
  Stop torturing me, and give me your advice.

---

5. A high-ranking official in the judiciary, not simply a sheriff's deputy as today.   **6.** The wife of a tax collector (*élue*), an important official controlling imports, elected by the Estates General.   **7.** In elegant society of Molière's day, there was a hierarchy of seats, and the use of each was determined by rank. The seats descended from *fauteuils* to *chaises, perroquets, tabourets,* and *pliants.* Thus Mariane would get the lowest seat in the room.   **8.** In the original, *fagotin,* literally "a monkey dressed up in a man's clothing."

DORINE [*Threatening to go.*]
   Your servant, Madam.
MARIANE.   Dorine, I beg of you . . .   85
DORINE   No, you deserve it; this marriage must go through.
MARIANE   Dorine!
DORINE   No.
MARIANE   Not Tartuffe! You know I think him . . .
DORINE   Tartuffe's your cup of tea, and you shall drink him.
MARIANE   I've always told you everything, and relied . . .
DORINE   No. You deserve to be tartuffified.   90
MARIANE   Well, since you mock me and refuse to care,
   I'll henceforth seek my solace in despair:
   Despair shall be my counsellor and friend,
   And help me bring my sorrows to an end. [*She starts to leave.*]
DORINE   There now, come back; my anger has subsided.   95
   You do deserve some pity, I've decided.
MARIANE   Dorine, if Father makes me undergo
   This dreadful martyrdom, I'll die, I know.
DORINE   Don't fret; it won't be difficult to discover
   Some plan of action . . . But here's Valère, your lover.   100

SCENE 4

VALÈRE, MARIANE, DORINE

VALÈRE   Madam, I've just received some wondrous news
   Regarding which I'd like to hear your views.
MARIANE   What news?
VALÈRE   You're marrying Tartuffe.
MARIANE   I find
   That Father does have such a match in mind.
VALÈRE   Your father, Madam . . .
MARIANE   . . . has just this minute said   5
   That it's Tartuffe he wishes me to wed.
VALÈRE   Can he be serious?
MARIANE   Oh, indeed he can;
   He's clearly set his heart upon the plan.
VALÈRE   And what position do you propose to take,
   Madam?
MARIANE   Why—I don't know.
VALÈRE   For heaven's sake—   10
   You don't know?
MARIANE   No.
VALÈRE   Well, well!
MARIANE   Advise me, do.
VALÈRE   Marry the man. That's my advice to you.
MARIANE   That's your advice?
VALÈRE   Yes.
MARIANE   Truly?
VALÈRE   Oh, absolutely.
   You couldn't choose more wisely, more astutely.

MARIANE   Thanks for this counsel; I'll follow it, of course.   15
VALÈRE   Do, do; I'm sure 'twill cost you no remorse.
MARIANE   To give it didn't cause your heart to break.
VALÈRE   I gave it, Madam, only for your sake.
MARIANE   And it's for your sake that I take it, Sir.
DORINE   [*Withdrawing to the rear of the stage.*]
   Let's see which fool will prove the stubborner.   20
VALÈRE   So! I am nothing to you, and it was flat
   Deception when you . . .
MARIANE   Please, enough of that.
   You've told me plainly that I should agree
   To wed the man my father's chosen for me,
   And since you've deigned to counsel me so wisely,   25
   I promise, Sir, to do as you advise me.
VALÈRE   Ah, no, 'twas not by me that you were swayed.
   No, your decision was already made;
   Though now, to save appearances, you protest
   That you're betraying me at my behest.   30
MARIANE   Just as you say.
VALÈRE   Quite so. And I now see
   That you were never truly in love with me.
MARIANE   Alas, you're free to think so if you choose.
VALÈRE   I choose to think so, and here's a bit of news:
   You've spurned my hand, but I know where to turn   35
   For kinder treatment, as you shall quickly learn.
MARIANE   I'm sure you do. Your noble qualities
   Inspire affection . . .
VALÈRE   Forget my qualities, please.
   They don't inspire you overmuch, I find.
   But there's another lady I have in mind   40
   Whose sweet and generous nature will not scorn
   To compensate me for the loss I've borne.
MARIANE   I'm no great loss, and I'm sure that you'll transfer
   Your heart quite painlessly from me to her.
VALÈRE   I'll do my best to take it in my stride.   45
   The pain I feel at being cast aside
   Time and forgetfulness may put an end to.
   Or if I can't forget, I shall pretend to.
   No self-respecting person is expected
   To go on loving once he's been rejected.   50
MARIANE   Now, that's a fine, high-minded sentiment.
VALÈRE   One to which any sane man would assent.
   Would you prefer it if I pined away
   In hopeless passion till my dying day?
   Am I to yield you to a rival's arms   55
   And not console myself with other charms?
MARIANE   Go then; console yourself; don't hesitate.
   I wish you to; indeed, I cannot wait.
VALÈRE   You wish me to?
MARIANE   Yes.

VALÈRE   That's the final straw.
    Madam, farewell. Your wish shall be my law.   60
       [*He starts to leave, and then returns: this repeatedly.*]
MARIANE   Splendid.
VALÈRE [*Coming back again.*]
               This breach, remember, is of your making;
    It's you who've driven me to the step I'm taking.
MARIANE   Of course.
VALÈRE [*Coming back again.*]
              Remember, too, that I am merely
    Following your example.
MARIANE   I see that clearly.
VALÈRE   Enough. I'll go and do your bidding, then.   65
MARIANE   Good.
VALÈRE [*Coming back again.*]
           You shall never see my face again.
MARIANE   Excellent.
VALÈRE [*Walking to the door, then turning about.*]
         Yes?
MARIANE   What?
VALÈRE   What's that? What did you say?
MARIANE   Nothing. You're dreaming.
VALÈRE   Ah. Well, I'm on my way.
    Farewell, Madame.
       [*He moves slowly away.*]
MARIANE   Farewell.
DORINE [*To* MARIANE.]   If you ask me,
    Both of you are as mad as mad can be.   70
    Do stop this nonsense, now. I've only let you
    Squabble so long to see where it would get you.
    Whoa there, Monsieur Valère!
       [*She goes and seizes* VALÈRE *by the arm; he makes a great show*
       of resistance.]
VALÈRE   What's this, Dorine?
DORINE   Come here.
VALÈRE   No, no, my heart's too full of spleen.
    Don't hold me back; her wish must be obeyed.   75
DORINE   Stop!
VALÈRE   It's too late now; my decision's made.
DORINE   Oh, pooh!
MARIANE [*Aside.*]   He hates the sight of me, that's plain.
    I'll go, and so deliver him from pain.
DORINE [*Leaving* VALÈRE, *running after* MARIANE.]
    And now *you* run away! Come back.
MARIANE   No, no
    Nothing you say will keep me here. Let go!   80
VALÈRE [*Aside.*]   She cannot bear my presence, I perceive.
    To spare her further torment, I shall leave.
DORINE [*Leaving* MARIANE, *running after* VALÈRE.]
    Again! You'll not escape, Sir; don't you try it.
    Come here, you two. Stop fussing and be quiet.

     [*She takes* VALÈRE *by the hand, then* MARIANE,
       and draws them together.]
VALÈRE [*To* DORINE.]   What do you want of me?   85
MARIANE [*To* DORINE.] What is the point of this?
DORINE We're going to have a little armistice.
  [*To* VALÈRE.] Now, weren't you silly to get so overheated?
VALÈRE Didn't you see how badly I was treated?
DORINE [*To* MARIANE.]   Aren't you a simpleton, to have lost your head? 90
MARIANE Didn't you hear the hateful things he said?
DORINE [*To* VALÈRE.]   You're both great fools. Her sole desire, Valère,
  Is to be yours in marriage. To that I'll swear.
  [*To* MARIANE.] He loves you only, and he wants no wife
  But you, Mariane. On that I'll stake my life.   95
MARIANE [*To* VALÈRE.]   Then why you advised me so, I cannot see.
VALÈRE [*To* MARIANE.]   On such a question, why ask advice of *me?*
DORINE Oh, you're impossible. Give me your hands, you two.
  [*To* VALÈRE.] Yours first.
VALÈRE [*Giving* DORINE *his hand.*]
                But why?
DORINE [*To* MARIANE.]   And now a hand from you.
MARIANE [*Also giving* DORINE *her hand.*]
  What are you doing?
DORINE   There: a perfect fit.   100
  You suit each other better than you'll admit.
     [VALÈRE *and* MARIANE *hold hands for some time without*
     looking at each other.]
VALÈRE [*Turning toward* MARIANE.]
  Ah, come, don't be so haughty. Give a man
  A look of kindness, won't you, Mariane?
     [MARIANE *turns toward* VALÈRE *and smiles.*]
DORINE I tell you, lovers are completely mad!
VALÈRE [*To* MARIANE.]   Now come, confess that you were very bad 105
  To hurt my feelings as you did just now.
  I have a just complaint, you must allow.
MARIANE *You* must allow that you were most unpleasant . . .
DORINE Let's table that discussion for the present;
  Your father has a plan which must be stopped.   110
MARIANE Advise us, then; what means must we adopt?
DORINE We'll use all manner of means, and all at once.
  [*To* MARIANE.] Your father's addled; he's acting like a dunce.
  Therefore you'd better humor the old fossil.
  Pretend to yield to him, be sweet and docile,   115
  And then postpone, as often as necessary,
  The day on which you have agreed to marry.
  You'll thus gain time, and time will turn the trick.
  Sometimes, for instance, you'll be taken sick,
  And that will seem good reason for delay;   120
  Or some bad omen will make you change the day—
  You'll dream of muddy water, or you'll pass
  A dead man's hearse, or break a looking-glass.
  If all else fails, no man can marry you

Unless you take his ring and say "I do."   125
But now, let's separate. If they should find
Us talking here, our plot might be divined.
[*To* VALÈRE.] Go to your friends, and tell them what's occurred,
And have them urge her father to keep his word.
Meanwhile, we'll stir her brother into action,   130
And get Elmire,[9] as well, to join our faction.
Good-bye.
VALÈRE [*To* MARIANE.]
      Though each of us will do his best,
It's your true heart on which my hopes shall rest.
MARIANE [*To* VALÈRE.]   Regardless of what Father may decide,
None but Valère shall claim me as his bride.   135
VALÈRE Oh, how those words content me! Come what will . . .
DORINE Oh, lovers, lovers! Their tongues are never still.
Be off, now.
VALÈRE [*Turning to go, then turning back.*]
      One last word . . .
DORINE   No time to chat:
You leave by this door; and *you* leave by that.
    [DORINE *pushes them, by the shoulders, toward opposing doors.*]

Act III

SCENE I

DAMIS, DORINE

DAMIS May lightning strike me even as I speak,
May all men call me cowardly and weak,
If any fear or scruple holds me back
From settling things, at once, with that great quack!
DORINE Now, don't give way to violent emotion.   5
Your father's merely talked about this notion,
And words and deeds are far from being one.
Much that is talked about is never done.
DAMIS No, I must stop that scoundrel's machinations;
I'll go and tell him off; I'm out of patience.   10
DORINE Do calm down and be practical. I had rather
My mistress dealt with him—and with your father.
She has some influence with Tartuffe, I've noted.
He hangs upon her words, seems most devoted,
And may, indeed, be smitten by her charm.   15
Pray Heaven it's true! 'Twould do our cause no harm.
She sent for him, just now, to sound him out
On this affair you're so incensed about;
She'll find out where he stands, and tell him, too,
What dreadful strife and trouble will ensue   20
If he lends countenance to your father's plan.

---

9. Orgon's second wife.

I couldn't get in to see him, but his man
Says that he's almost finished with his prayers.
Go, now. I'll catch him when he comes downstairs.
DAMIS   I want to hear this conference, and I will.   25
DORINE   No, they must be alone.
DAMIS   Oh, I'll keep still.
DORINE   Not you. I know your temper. You'd start a brawl,
And shout and stamp your foot and spoil it all.
Go on.
DAMIS   I won't; I have a perfect right . . .
DORINE   Lord, you're a nuisance! He's coming; get out of sight.   30
   [DAMIS *conceals himself in a closet at the rear of the stage.*]

SCENE 2

TARTUFFE, DORINE

TARTUFFE [*Observing* DORINE, *and calling to his manservant off-stage.*]
Hang up my hair-shirt, put my scourge in place,
And pray, Laurent, for Heaven's perpetual grace.
I'm going to the prison now, to share
My last few coins with the poor wretches there.
DORINE [*Aside.*] Dear God, what affectation! What a fake!   5
TARTUFFE   You wished to see me?
DORINE   Yes . . .
TARTUFFE [*Taking a handkerchief from his pocket.*]
                              For mercy's sake,
Please take this handkerchief, before you speak.
DORINE   What?
TARTUFFE   Cover that bosom,[1] girl. The flesh is weak.
And unclean thoughts are difficult to control.
Such sights as that can undermine the soul.   10
DORINE   Your soul, it seems, has very poor defenses,
And flesh makes quite an impact on your senses.
It's strange that you're so easily excited;
My own desires are not so soon ignited,
And if I saw you naked as a beast,   15
Not all your hide would tempt me in the least.
TARTUFFE   Girl, speak more modestly; unless you do,
I shall be forced to take my leave of you.
DORINE   Oh, no, it's I who must be on my way;
I've just one little message to convey.   20
Madame is coming down, and begs you, Sir,
To wait and have a word or two with her.
TARTUFFE   Gladly.
DORINE [*Aside.*]   *That* had a softening effect!
I think my guess about him was correct.
TARTUFFE   Will she be long?

---

1. The Brotherhood of the Holy Sacrament practiced alms giving to prisoners and kept a careful, censorious check on women's clothing if they deemed it lascivious. Thus Molière's audience would have identified Tartuffe as sympathetic—hypocritically—to the aims of the organization.

DORINE   No: that's her step I hear.   25
　　Ah, here she is, and I shall disappear.

SCENE 3

ELMIRE, TARTUFFE

TARTUFFE　　May Heaven, whose infinite goodness we adore,
　　Preserve your body and soul forevermore,
　　And bless your days, and answer thus the plea
　　Of one who is its humblest votary.
ELMIRE　　I thank you for that pious wish. But please,   5
　　Do take a chair and let's be more at ease.
　　　　[*They sit down.*]
TARTUFFE　　I trust that you are once more well and strong?
ELMIRE　　Oh, yes: the fever didn't last for long.
TARTUFFE　　My prayers are too unworthy, I am sure,
　　To have gained from Heaven this most gracious cure;   10
　　But lately, Madam, my every supplication
　　Has had for object your recuperation.
ELMIRE　　You shouldn't have troubled so. I don't deserve it.
TARTUFFE　　Your health is priceless, Madam, and to preserve it
　　I'd gladly give my own, in all sincerity.   15
ELMIRE　　Sir, you outdo us all in Christian charity.
　　You've been most kind. I count myself your debtor.
TARTUFFE　　'Twas nothing, Madam. I long to serve you better.
ELMIRE　　There's a private matter I'm anxious to discuss.
　　I'm glad there's no one here to hinder us.   20
TARTUFFE　　I too am glad; it floods my heart with bliss
　　To find myself alone with you like this.
　　For just this chance I've prayed with all my power—
　　But prayed in vain, until this happy hour.
ELMIRE　　This won't take long, Sir, and I hope you'll be   25
　　Entirely frank and unconstrained with me.
TARTUFFE　　Indeed, there's nothing I had rather do
　　Than bare my inmost heart and soul to you.
　　First, let me say that what remarks I've made
　　About the constant visits you are paid   30
　　Were prompted not by any mean emotion,
　　But rather by a pure and deep devotion,
　　A fervent zeal . . .
ELMIRE   No need for explanation.
　　Your sole concern, I'm sure, was my salvation.
TARTUFFE [*Taking* ELMIRE's *hand and pressing her fingertips.*]
　　Quite so; and such great fervor do I feel . . .   35
ELMIRE　　Ooh! Please! You're pinching!
TARTUFFE   'Twas from excess of zeal.
　　I never meant to cause you pain, I swear.
　　I'd rather . . .
　　　　[*He places his hand on* ELMIRE's *knee.*]
ELMIRE   What can your hand be doing there?

TARTUFFE   Feeling your gown: what soft, fine-woven stuff!

ELMIRE   Please, I'm extremely ticklish. That's enough.   40

    [*She draws her chair away;* TARTUFFE *pulls his after her.*]

TARTUFFE [*Fondling the lace collar of her gown.*]

  My, my, what lovely lacework on your dress!

  The workmanship's miraculous, no less.

  I've not seen anything to equal it.

ELMIRE   Yes, quite. But let's talk business for a bit.

  They say my husband means to break his word   45

  And give his daughter to you, Sir. Had you heard?

TARTUFFE   He did once mention it. But I confess

  I dream of quite a different happiness.

  It's elsewhere, Madam, that my eyes discern

  The promise of that bliss for which I yearn.   50

ELMIRE   I see: you care for nothing here below.

TARTUFFE   Ah, well—my heart's not made of stone, you know.

ELMIRE   All your desires mount heavenward, I'm sure,

  In scorn of all that's earthly and impure.

TARTUFFE   A love of heavenly beauty does not preclude   55

  A proper love for earthly pulchritude;

  Our senses are quite rightly captivated

  By perfect works our Maker has created.

  Some glory clings to all that Heaven has made;

  In you, all Heaven's marvels are displayed.   60

  On that fair face, such beauties have been lavished,

  The eyes are dazzled and the heart is ravished;

  How could I look on you, O flawless creature,

  And not adore the Author of all Nature,

  Feeling a love both passionate and pure   65

  For you, his triumph of self-portraiture?

  At first, I trembled lest that love should be

  A subtle snare that Hell had laid for me;

  I vowed to flee the sight of you, eschewing

  A rapture that might prove my soul's undoing;   70

  But soon, fair being, I became aware

  That my deep passion could be made to square

  With rectitude, and with my bounden duty,

  I thereupon surrendered to your beauty.

  It is, I know, presumptuous on my part   75

  To bring you this poor offering of my heart,

  And it is not my merit, Heaven knows,

  But your compassion on which my hopes repose.

  You are my peace, my solace, my salvation;

  On you depends my bliss—or desolation;   80

  I bide your judgment and, as you think best,

  I shall be either miserable or blest.

ELMIRE   Your declaration is most gallant, Sir,

  But don't you think it's out of character?

  You'd have done better to restrain your passion   85

  And think before you spoke in such a fashion.

It ill becomes a pious man like you . . .

TARTUFFE   I may be pious, but I'm human too:
　　With your celestial charms before his eyes,
　　A man has not the power to be wise.　　　　　　　　　90
　　I know such words sound strangely, coming from me,
　　But I'm no angel, nor was meant to be,
　　And if you blame my passion, you must needs
　　Reproach as well the charms on which it feeds.
　　Your loveliness I had no sooner seen　　　　　　　　95
　　Than you became my soul's unrivalled queen;
　　Before your seraph glance, divinely sweet,
　　My heart's defenses crumbled in defeat,
　　And nothing fasting, prayer, or tears might do
　　Could stay my spirit from adoring you.　　　　　　　100
　　My eyes, my sighs have told you in the past
　　What now my lips make bold to say at last,
　　And if, in your great goodness, you will deign
　　To look upon your slave, and ease his pain,—
　　If, in compassion for my soul's distress,　　　　　　105
　　You'll stoop to comfort my unworthiness,
　　I'll raise to you, in thanks for that sweet manna,
　　An endless hymn, an infinite hosanna.
　　With me, of course, there need be no anxiety,
　　No fear of scandal or of notoriety.　　　　　　　　　110
　　These young court gallants, whom all the ladies fancy,
　　Are vain in speech, in action rash and chancy;
　　When they succeed in love, the world soon knows it;
　　No favor's granted them but they disclose it
　　And by the looseness of their tongues profane　　　　115
　　The very altar where their hearts have lain.
　　Men of my sort, however, love discreetly,
　　And one may trust our reticence completely.
　　My keen concern for my good name insures
　　The absolute security of yours;　　　　　　　　　　120
　　In short, I offer you, my dear Elmire,
　　Love without scandal, pleasure without fear.

ELMIRE   I've heard your well-turned speeches to the end,
　　And what you urge I clearly apprehend.
　　Aren't you afraid that I may take a notion　　　　　125
　　To tell my husband of your warm devotion,
　　And that, supposing he were duly told,
　　His feelings toward you might grow rather cold?

TARTUFFE   I know, dear lady, that your exceeding charity
　　Will lead your heart to pardon my temerity;　　　　130
　　That you'll excuse my violent affection
　　As human weakness, human imperfection;
　　And that—O fairest!—you will bear in mind
　　That I'm but flesh and blood, and am not blind.

ELMIRE   Some women might do otherwise, perhaps,　　135
　　But I shall be discreet about your lapse;

I'll tell my husband nothing of what's occurred
If, in return, you'll give your solemn word
To advocate as forcefully as you can
The marriage of Valère and Mariane,   140
Renouncing all desire to dispossess
Another of his rightful happiness,
And . . .

SCENE 4

DAMIS, ELMIRE, TARTUFFE

DAMIS [*Emerging from the closet where he has been hiding.*]
       No! We'll not hush up this vile affair;
I heard it all inside that closet there,
Where Heaven, in order to confound the pride
Of this great rascal, prompted me to hide.
Ah, now I have my long-awaited chance   5
To punish his deceit and arrogance,
And give my father clear and shocking proof
Of the black character of his dear Tartuffe.
ELMIRE   Ah no, Damis; I'll be content if he
Will study to deserve my leniency.   10
I've promised silence—don't make me break my word;
To make a scandal would be too absurd.
Good wives laugh off such trifles, and forget them;
Why should they tell their husbands, and upset them?
DAMIS   You have your reasons for taking such a course,   15
And I have reasons, too, of equal force.
To spare him now would be insanely wrong.
I've swallowed my just wrath for far too long
And watched this insolent bigot bringing strife
And bitterness into our family life.   20
Too long he's meddled in my father's affairs,
Thwarting my marriage-hopes, and poor Valère's.
It's high time that my father was undeceived,
And now I've proof that can't be disbelieved—
Proof that was furnished me by Heaven above.   25
It's too good not to take advantage of.
This is my chance, and I deserve to lose it
If, for one moment, I hesitate to use it.
ELMIRE   Damis . . .
DAMIS   No, I must do what I think right.
Madam, my heart is bursting with delight,   30
And, say whatever you will, I'll not consent
To lose the sweet revenge on which I'm bent.
I'll settle matters without more ado;
And here, most opportunely, is my cue.[2]

---

2. In the original stage directions, Tartuffe now reads silently from his breviary—in the Roman Catholic Church, the book containing the Divine Office for each day, which those in holy orders are required to recite.

SCENE 5

ORGON, DAMIS, TARTUFFE, ELMIRE

DAMIS   Father, I'm glad you've joined us. Let us advise you
   Of some fresh news which doubtless will surprise you.
   You've just now been repaid with interest
   For all your loving-kindness to our guest.
   He's proved his warm and grateful feelings toward you;   5
   It's with a pair of horns he would reward you.
   Yes, I surprised him with your wife, and heard
   His whole adulterous offer, every word.
   She, with her all too gentle disposition,
   Would not have told you of his proposition;   10
   But I shall not make terms with brazen lechery,
   And feel that not to tell you would be treachery.
ELMIRE   And I hold that one's husband's peace of mind
   Should not be spoilt by tattle of this kind.
   One's honor doesn't require it: to be proficient   15
   In keeping men at bay is quite sufficient.
   These are my sentiments, and I wish, Damis,
   That you had heeded me and held your peace.

SCENE 6

ORGON, DAMIS, TARTUFFE

ORGON   Can it be true, this dreadful thing I hear?
TARTUFFE   Yes, Brother, I'm a wicked man, I fear:
   A wretched sinner, all depraved and twisted,
   The greatest villain that has ever existed.
   My life's one heap of crimes, which grows each minute;   5
   There's naught but foulness and corruption in it;
   And I perceive that Heaven, outraged by me,
   Has chosen this occasion to mortify me.
   Charge me with any deed you wish to name;
   I'll not defend myself, but take the blame.   10
   Believe what you are told, and drive Tartuffe
   Like some base criminal from beneath your roof;
   Yes, drive me hence, and with a parting curse:
   I shan't protest, for I deserve far worse.
ORGON [To DAMIS.] Ah, you deceitful boy, how dare you try   15
   To stain his purity with so foul a lie?
DAMIS   What! Are you taken in by such a fluff?
   Did you not hear . . . ?
ORGON   Enough, you rogue, enough!
TARTUFFE   Ah, Brother, let him speak: you're being unjust.
   Believe his story; the boy deserves your trust.   20
   Why, after all, should you have faith in me?
   How can you know what I might do, or be?
   Is it on my good actions that you base
   Your favor? Do you trust my pious face?

Ah, no, don't be deceived by hollow shows;   25
I'm far, alas, from being what men suppose;
Though the world takes me for a man of worth,
I'm truly the most worthless man on earth.
[*To* DAMIS] Yes, my dear son, speak out now: call me the chief
Of sinners, a wretch, a murderer, a thief;   30
Load me with all the names men most abhor;
I'll not complain; I've earned them all, and more;
I'll kneel here while you pour them on my head
As a just punishment for the life I've led.
ORGON [*To* TARTUFFE.]
   This is too much, dear Brother.
   [*To* DAMIS.]   Have you no heart?   35
DAMIS   Are you so hoodwinked by this rascal's art . . . ?
ORGON   Be still, you monster.
   [*To* TARTUFFE.]   Brother, I pray you, rise.
   [*To* DAMIS.] Villain!
DAMIS   But . . .
ORGON   Silence!
DAMIS   Can't you realize . . . ?
ORGON   Just one word more, and I'll tear you limb from limb.
TARTUFFE   In God's name, Brother, don't be harsh with him.   40
   I'd rather far be tortured at the stake
   Than see him bear one scratch for my poor sake.
ORGON [*To* DAMIS.] Ingrate!
TARTUFFE   If I must beg you, on bended knee,
   To pardon him . . .
ORGON [*Falling to his knees, addressing* TARTUFFE.]
          Such goodness cannot be!
   [*To* DAMIS.] Now, *there's* true charity!
DAMIS   What, you . . . ?
ORGON   Villain, be still!   45
   I know your motives; I know you wish him ill:
   Yes, all of you—wife, children, servants, all—
   Conspire against him and desire his fall,
   Employing every shameful trick you can
   To alienate me from this saintly man.   50
   Ah, but the more you seek to drive him away,
   The more I'll do to keep him. Without delay,
   I'll spite this household and confound its pride
   By giving him my daughter as his bride.
DAMIS   You're going to force her to accept his hand?   55
ORGON   Yes, and this very night, d'you understand?
   I shall defy you all, and make it clear
   That I'm the one who gives the orders here.
   Come, wretch, kneel down and clasp his blessed feet,
   And ask his pardon for your black deceit.   60
DAMIS   I ask that swindler's pardon? Why, I'd rather . . .
ORGON   So! You insult him, and defy your father!
   A stick! A stick! [*To* TARTUFFE.] No, no—release me, do.

[*To* DAMIS.] Out of my house this minute! Be off with you,
And never dare set foot in it again.   65
DAMIS   Well, I shall go, but . . .
ORGON   Well, go quickly, then.
I disinherit you; an empty purse
Is all you'll get from me—except my curse!

SCENE 7

ORGON, TARTUFFE

ORGON   How he blasphemed your goodness! What a son!
TARTUFFE   Forgive him, Lord, as I've already done.
[*To* ORGON.] You can't know how it hurts when someone tries
To blacken me in my dear brother's eyes.
ORGON   Ahh!
TARTUFFE   The mere thought of such ingratitude   5
Plunges my soul into so dark a mood . . .
Such horror grips my heart . . . I gasp for breath,
And cannot speak, and feel myself near death.
ORGON [*He runs, in tears, to the door through which he has
      just driven his son.*]
You blackguard! Why did I spare you? Why did I not
Break you in little pieces on the spot?   10
Compose yourself, and don't be hurt, dear friend.
TARTUFFE   These scenes, these dreadful quarrels, have got to end.
I've much upset your household, and I perceive
That the best thing will be for me to leave.
ORGON   What are you saying!
TARTUFFE   They're all against me here;   15
They'd have you think me false and insincere.
ORGON   Ah, what of that? Have I ceased believing in you?
TARTUFFE   Their adverse talk will certainly continue,
And charges which you now repudiate
You may find credible at a later date.   20
ORGON   No, Brother, never.
TARTUFFE   Brother, a wife can sway
Her husband's mind in many a subtle way.
ORGON   No, no.
TARTUFFE   To leave at once is the solution;
Thus only can I end their persecution.
ORGON   No, no, I'll not allow it; you shall remain.   25
TARTUFFE   Ah, well; 'twill mean much martyrdom and pain,
But if you wish it . . .
ORGON   Ah!
TARTUFFE   Enough; so be it.
But one thing must be settled, as I see it.
For your dear honor, and for our friendship's sake,
There's one precaution I feel bound to take.   30
I shall avoid your wife, and keep away . . .
ORGON   No, you shall not, whatever they may say.

It pleases me to vex them, and for spite
I'd have them see you with her day and night.
What's more, I'm going to drive them to despair   35
By making you my only son and heir;
This very day, I'll give to you alone
Clear deed and title to everything I own.
A dear, good friend and son-in-law-to-be
Is more than wife, or child, or kin to me.   40
Will you accept my offer, dearest son?
TARTUFFE   In all things, let the will of Heaven be done.
ORGON   Poor fellow! Come, we'll go draw up the deed.
Then let them burst with disappointed greed!

Act IV

SCENE 1

CLÉANTE, TARTUFFE

CLÉANTE   Yes, all the town's discussing it, and truly,
Their comments do not flatter you unduly.
I'm glad we've met, Sir, and I'll give my view
Of this sad matter in a word or two.
As for who's guilty, that I shan't discuss;   5
Let's say it was Damis who caused the fuss;
Assuming, then, that you have been ill-used
By young Damis, and groundlessly accused,
Ought not a Christian to forgive, and ought
He not to stifle every vengeful thought?   10
Should you stand by and watch a father make
His only son an exile for your sake?
Again I tell you frankly, be advised:
The whole town, high and low, is scandalized;
This quarrel must be mended, and my advice is   15
Not to push matters to a further crisis.
No, sacrifice your wrath to God above,
And help Damis regain his father's love.
TARTUFFE   Alas, for my part I should take great joy
In doing so. I've nothing against the boy.   20
I pardon all, I harbor no resentment;
To serve him would afford me much contentment.
But Heaven's interest will not have it so:
If he comes back, then I shall have to go.
After his conduct—so extreme, so vicious—   25
Our further intercourse would look suspicious.
God knows what people would think! Why, they'd describe
My goodness to him as a sort of bribe;
They'd say that out of guilt I made pretense
Of loving-kindness and benevolence—   30
That, fearing my accuser's tongue, I strove
To buy his silence with a show of love.

CLÉANTE   Your reasoning is badly warped and stretched,
　　And these excuses, Sir, are most far-fetched.
　　Why put yourself in charge of Heaven's cause?   35
　　Does Heaven need our help to enforce its laws?
　　Leave vengeance to the Lord, Sir; while we live,
　　Our duty's not to punish, but forgive;
　　And what the Lord commands, we should obey
　　Without regard to what the world may say.   40
　　What! Shall the fear of being misunderstood
　　Prevent our doing what is right and good?
　　No, no: let's simply do what Heaven ordains,
　　And let no other thoughts perplex our brains.
TARTUFFE   Again, Sir, let me say that I've forgiven   45
　　Damis, and thus obeyed the laws of Heaven;
　　But I am not commanded by the Bible
　　To live with one who smears my name with libel.
CLÉANTE   Were you commanded, Sir, to indulge the whim
　　Of poor Orgon, and to encourage him   50
　　In suddenly transferring to your name
　　A large estate to which you have no claim?
TARTUFFE   'Twould never occur to those who know me best
　　To think I acted from self-interest.
　　The treasures of this world I quite despise;   55
　　Their specious glitter does not charm my eyes;
　　And if I have resigned myself to taking
　　The gift which my dear Brother insists on making,
　　I do so only, as he well understands,
　　Lest so much wealth fall into wicked hands,   60
　　Lest those to whom it might descend in time
　　Turn it to purposes of sin and crime,
　　And not, as I shall do, make use of it
　　For Heaven's glory and mankind's benefit.
CLÉANTE   Forget these trumped-up fears. Your argument   65
　　Is one the rightful heir might well resent;
　　It is a moral burden to inherit
　　Such wealth, but give Damis a chance to bear it.
　　And would it not be worse to be accused
　　Of swindling, than to see that wealth misused?   70
　　I'm shocked that you allowed Orgon to broach
　　This matter, and that you feel no self-reproach;
　　Does true religion teach that lawful heirs
　　May freely be deprived of what is theirs?
　　And if the Lord has told you in your heart   75
　　That you and young Damis must dwell apart,
　　Would it not be the decent thing to beat
　　A generous and honorable retreat,
　　Rather than let the son of the house be sent,
　　For your convenience, into banishment?   80
　　Sir, if you wish to prove the honesty
　　Of your intentions . . .

TARTUFFE Sir, it is a half past three.
  I've certain pious duties to attend to,
  And hope my prompt departure won't offend you.
CLÉANTE [*Alone.*] Damn. 85

SCENE 2

ELMIRE, MARIANE, CLÉANTE, DORINE

DORINE Stay, Sir, and help Mariane, for Heaven's sake!
  She's suffering so, I fear her heart will break.
  Her father's plan to marry her off tonight
  Has put the poor child in a desperate plight.
  I hear him coming. Let's stand together, now, 5
  And see if we can't change his mind, somehow,
  About this match we all deplore and fear.

SCENE 3

ORGON, ELMIRE, MARIANE, CLÉANTE, DORINE

ORGON Hah! Glad to find you all assembled here.
  [*To* MARIANE.] This contract, child, contains your happiness,
  And what it says I think your heart can guess.
MARIANE [*Falling to her knees.*]
  Sir, by that Heaven which sees me here distressed,
  And by whatever else can move your breast, 5
  Do not employ a father's power, I pray you,
  To crush my heart and force it to obey you,
  Nor by your harsh commands oppress me so
  That I'll begrudge the duty which I owe—
  And do not so embitter and enslave me 10
  That I shall hate the very life you gave me.
  If my sweet hopes must perish, if you refuse
  To give me to the one I've dared to choose,
  Spare me at least—I beg you, I implore—
  The pain of wedding one whom I abhor; 15
  And do not, by a heartless use of force,
  Drive me to contemplate some desperate course.
ORGON [*Feeling himself touched by her.*]
  Be firm, my soul. No human weakness, now.
MARIANE I don't resent your love for him. Allow
  Your heart free rein, Sir; give him your property, 20
  And if that's not enough, take mine from me;
  He's welcome to my money; take it, do,
  But don't, I pray, include my person too.
  Spare me, I beg you; and let me end the tale
  Of my sad days behind a convent veil. 25
ORGON A convent! Hah! When crossed in their amours,
  All lovesick girls have the same thought as yours.
  Get up! The more you loathe the man, and dread him,
  The more ennobling it will be to wed him.

Marry Tartuffe, and mortify your flesh!   30
Enough; don't start that whimpering afresh.
DORINE   But why . . . ?
ORGON   Be still, there. Speak when you're spoken to.
Not one more bit of impudence out of you.
CLÉANTE   If I may offer a word of counsel here . . .
ORGON   Brother, in counselling you have no peer;   35
All your advice is forceful, sound, and clever;
I don't propose to follow it, however.
ELMIRE [To ORGON.]   I am amazed, and don't know what to say;
Your blindness simply takes my breath away.
You are indeed bewitched, to take no warning   40
From our account of what occurred this morning.
ORGON   Madam, I know a few plain facts, and one
Is that you're partial to my rascal son;
Hence, when he sought to make Tartuffe the victim
Of a base lie, you dared not contradict him.   45
Ah, but you underplayed your part, my pet;
You should have looked more angry, more upset.
ELMIRE   When men make overtures, must we reply
With righteous anger and a battle-cry?
Must we turn back their amorous advances   50
With sharp reproaches and with fiery glances?
Myself, I find such offers merely amusing,
And make no scenes and fusses in refusing;
My taste is for good-natured rectitude,
And I dislike the savage sort of prude   55
Who guards her virtue with her teeth and claws,
And tears men's eyes out for the slightest cause:
The Lord preserve me from such honor as that,
Which bites and scratches like an alley-cat!
I've found that a polite and cool rebuff   60
Discourages a lover quite enough.
ORGON   I know the facts, and I shall not be shaken.
ELMIRE   I marvel at your power to be mistaken.
Would it, I wonder, carry weight with you
If I could *show* you that our tale was true?   65
ORGON   Show me?
ELMIRE   Yes.
ORGON   Rot.
ELMIRE   Come, what if I found a way
To make you see the facts as plain as day?
ORGON   Nonsense.
ELMIRE   Do answer me; don't be absurd.
I'm not now asking you to trust our word.
Suppose that from some hiding-place in here   70
You learned the whole sad truth by eye and ear—
What would you say of your good friend, after that?
ORGON   Why, I'd say . . . nothing, by Jehoshaphat!

It can't be true.
ELMIRE   You've been too long deceived,
I'm quite tired of being disbelieved.   75
Come now: let's put my statements to the test,
And you shall see the truth made manifest.
ORGON   I'll take that challenge. Now do your uttermost.
We'll see how you make good your empty boast.
ELMIRE [*To* DORINE.]   Send him to me.
DORINE   He's crafty; it may be hard   80
To catch the cunning scoundrel off his guard.
ELMIRE   No, amorous men are gullible. Their conceit
So blinds them that they're never hard to cheat.
Have him come down.
[*To* CLÉANTE *and* MARIANE.]
Please leave us, for a bit.

SCENE 4

ELMIRE, ORGON

ELMIRE   Pull up this table, and get under it.
ORGON   What?
ELMIRE   It's essential that you be well-hidden.
ORGON   Why there?
ELMIRE   Oh, Heavens! Just do as you are bidden.
I have my plans; we'll soon see how they fare.
Under the table, now; and once you're there,   5
Take care that you are neither seen nor heard.
ORGON   Well, I'll indulge you, since I gave my word
To see you through this infantile charade.
ELMIRE   Once it is over, you'll be glad we played.
[*To her husband, who is now under the table.*]
I'm going to act quite strangely, now, and you   10
Must not be shocked at anything I do.
Whatever I may say, you must excuse
As part of that deceit I'm forced to use.
I shall employ sweet speeches in the task
Of making that impostor drop his mask;   15
I'll give encouragement to his bold desires,
And furnish fuel to his amorous fires.
Since it's for your sake, and for his destruction,
That I shall seem to yield to his seduction,
I'll gladly stop whenever you decide   20
That all your doubts are fully satisfied.
I'll count on you, as soon as you have seen
What sort of man he is, to intervene,
And not expose me to his odious lust
One moment longer than you feel you must.   25
Remember: you're to save me from my plight
Whenever . . . He's coming! Hush! Keep out of sight!

SCENE 5

TARTUFFE, ELMIRE, ORGON

TARTUFFE   You wish to have a word with me, I'm told.

ELMIRE   Yes, I've a little secret to unfold.
  Before I speak, however, it would be wise
  To close that door, and look about for spies.
    [TARTUFFE *goes to the door, closes it, and returns.*]
  The very last thing that must happen now   5
  Is a repetition of this morning's row.
  I've never been so badly caught off guard.
  Oh, how I feared for you! You saw how hard
  I tried to make that troublesome Damis
  Control his dreadful temper, and hold his peace.   10
  In my confusion, I didn't have the sense
  Simply to contradict his evidence;
  But as it happened, that was for the best,
  And all has worked out in our interest.
  This storm has only bettered your position;   15
  My husband doesn't have the least suspicion,
  And now, in mockery of those who do,
  He bids me be continually with you.
  And that is why, quite fearless of reproof,
  I now can be alone with my Tartuffe,   20
  And why my heart—perhaps too quick to yield—
  Feels free to let its passion be revealed.

TARTUFFE   Madam, your words confuse me. Not long ago,
  You spoke in quite a different style, you know.

ELMIRE   Ah, Sir, if that refusal made you smart,   25
  It's little that you know of woman's heart,
  Or what that heart is trying to convey
  When it resists in such a feeble way!
  Always, at first, our modesty prevents
  The frank avowal of tender sentiments: 30
  However high the passion which inflames us,
  Still, to confess its power somehow shames us.
  Thus we reluct, at first, yet in a tone
  Which tells you that our heart is overthrown,
  That what our lips deny, our pulse confesses,   35
  And that, in time, all noes will turn to yesses.
  I fear my words are all too frank and free,
  And a poor proof of woman's modesty;
  But since I'm started, tell me, if you will—
  Would I have tried to make Damis be still,   40
  Would I have listened, calm and unoffended,
  Until your lengthy offer of love was ended,
  And been so very mild in my reaction,
  Had your sweet words not given me satisfaction?
  And when I tried to force you to undo   45
  The marriage-plans my husband has in view,

What did my urgent pleading signify
If not that I admired you, and that I
Deplored the thought that someone else might own
Part of a heart I wished for mine alone?   50
TARTUFFE   Madam, no happiness is so complete
As when, from lips we love, come words so sweet;
Their nectar floods my every sense, and drains
In honeyed rivulets through all my veins.
To please you is my joy, my only goal;   55
Your love is the restorer of my soul;
And yet I must beg leave, now, to confess
Some lingering doubts as to my happiness.
Might this not be a trick? Might not the catch
Be that you wish me to break off the match   60
With Mariane, and so have feigned to love me?
I shan't quite trust your fond opinion of me
Until the feelings you've expressed so sweetly
Are demonstrated somewhat more concretely,
And you have shown, by certain kind concessions,   65
That I may put my faith in your professions
ELMIRE   [*She coughs, to warn her husband.*]
Why be in such a hurry? Must my heart
Exhaust its bounty at the very start?
To make that sweet admission cost me dear,
But you'll not be content, it would appear,   70
Unless my store of favors is disbursed
To the last farthing, and at the very first.
TARTUFFE   The less we merit, the less we dare to hope,
And with our doubts, mere words can never cope.
We trust no promised bliss till we receive it;   75
Not till a joy is ours can we believe it.
I, who so little merit your esteem,
Can't credit this fulfillment of my dream,
And shan't believe it, Madam, until I savor
Some palpable assurance of your favor.   80
ELMIRE   My, how tyrannical your love can be,
And how it flusters and perplexes me!
How furiously you take one's heart in hand,
And make your every wish a fierce command!
Come, must you hound and harry me to death?   85
Will you not give me time to catch my breath?
Can it be right to press me with such force,
Give me no quarter, show me no remorse,
And take advantage, by your stern insistence,
Of the fond feelings which weaken my resistance?   90
TARTUFFE   Well, if you look with favor upon my love,
Why, then, begrudge me some clear proof thereof?
ELMIRE   But how can I consent without offense
To Heaven, toward which you feel such reverence?
TARTUFFE   If Heaven is all that holds you back, don't worry.   95

I can remove that hindrance in a hurry.
Nothing of that sort need obstruct our path.
ELMIRE Must one not be afraid of Heaven's wrath?
TARTUFFE Madam, forget such fears, and be my pupil,
　And I shall teach you how to conquer scruple.　　　　　　　100
　Some joys, it's true, are wrong in Heaven's eyes;
　Yet Heaven is not averse to compromise;
　There is a science, lately formulated,
　Whereby one's conscience may be liberated,[3]
　And any wrongful act you care to mention　　　　　　　　105
　May be redeemed by purity of intention.
　I'll teach you, Madam, the secrets of that science;
　Meanwhile, just place on me your full reliance.
　Assuage my keen desires, and feel no dread:
　The sin, if any, shall be on my head.　　　　　　　　　　110
　　　　　[ELMIRE *coughs, this time more loudly.*]
　You've a bad cough.
ELMIRE　　　　　　　　Yes, yes, It's bad indeed.
TARTUFFE [*Producing a little paper bag.*]
　A bit of licorice may be what you need.
ELMIRE No, I've a stubborn cold, it seems. I'm sure it
　Will take much more than licorice to cure it.
TARTUFFE How aggravating.
ELMIRE　　　　　　　　　　Oh, more than I can say.　　　　115
TARTUFFE If you're still troubled, think of things this way:
　No one shall know our joys, save us alone,
　And there's no evil till the act is known;
　It's scandal, Madam, which makes it an offense,
　And it's no sin to sin in confidence.　　　　　　　　　　120
ELMIRE [*Having coughed once more.*]
　Well, clearly I must do as you require,
　And yield to your importunate desire.
　It is apparent, now, that nothing less
　Will satisfy you, and so I acquiesce.
　To go so far is much against my will;　　　　　　　　　125
　I'm vexed that it should come to this; but still,
　Since you are so determined on it, since you
　Will not allow mere language to convince you,
　And since you ask for concrete evidence, I
　See nothing for it, now, but to comply.　　　　　　　　130
　If this is sinful, if I'm wrong to do it,
　So much the worse for him who drove me to it.
　The fault can surely not be charged to me.
TARTUFFE Madam, the fault is mine, if fault there be,
　And . . .
ELMIRE Open the door a little, and peek out;　　　　　　135
　I wouldn't want my husband poking about.
TARTUFFE Why worry about the man? Each day he grows

---

3. Molière created his own footnote to this line: "It is a scoundrel who speaks."

More gullible; one can lead him by the nose.
To find us here would fill him with delight,
And if he saw the worst, he'd doubt his sight.   140
ELMIRE   Nevertheless, do step out for a minute
Into the hall, and see that no one's in it.

SCENE 6

ORGON, ELMIRE

ORGON [*Coming out from under the table.*]
That man's a perfect monster, I must admit!
I'm simply stunned. I can't get over it.
ELMIRE   What, coming out so soon? How premature!
Get back in hiding, and wait until you're sure.
Stay till the end, and be convinced completely;   5
We mustn't stop till things are proved concretely.
ORGON   Hell never harbored anything so vicious!
ELMIRE   Tut, don't be hasty. Try to be judicious.
Wait, and be certain that there's no mistake.
No jumping to conclusions, for Heaven's sake!   10
   [*She places* ORGON *behind her, as* TARTUFFE *re-enters.*]

SCENE 7

TARTUFFE, ELMIRE, ORGON

TARTUFFE [*Not seeing* ORGON.]
Madam, all things have worked out to perfection;
I've given the neighboring rooms a full inspection;
No one's about; and now I may at last . . .
ORGON [*Intercepting him.*]   Hold on, my passionate fellow, not so fast!
I should advise a little more restraint.   5
Well, so you thought you'd fool me, my dear saint!
How soon you wearied of the saintly life—
Wedding my daughter, and coveting my wife!
I've long suspected you, and had a feeling
That soon I'd catch you at your double-dealing.   10
Just now, you've given me evidence galore;
It's quite enough; I have no wish for more.
ELMIRE [*To* TARTUFFE.]   I'm sorry to have treated you so slyly,
But circumstances forced me to be wily.
TARTUFFE   Brother, you can't think . . .
ORGON   No more talk from you;   15
Just leave this household, without more ado.
TARTUFFE   What I intended . . .
ORGON   That seems fairly clear.
Spare me your falsehoods and get out of here.
TARTUFFE   No, I'm the master, and you're the one to go!
This house belongs to me, I'll have you know,   20
And I shall show you that you can't hurt *me*
By this contemptible conspiracy,

That those who cross me know not what they do,
And that I've means to expose and punish you,
Avenge offended Heaven, and make you grieve   25
That ever you dared order me to leave.

SCENE 8

ELMIRE, ORGON

ELMIRE   What was the point of all that angry chatter?
ORGON   Dear God, I'm worried. This is no laughing matter.
ELMIRE   How so?
ORGON   I fear I understood his drift.
I'm much disturbed about that deed of gift.
ELMIRE   You gave him . . . ?
ORGON   Yes, it's all been drawn and signed.   5
But one thing more is weighing on my mind.
ELMIRE   What's that?
ORGON   I'll tell you; but first let's see if there's
A certain strong-box in his room upstairs.

Act V

SCENE 1

ORGON, CLÉANTE

CLÉANTE   Where are you going so fast?
ORGON   God knows!
CLÉANTE   Then wait;
Let's have a conference, and deliberate
On how this situation's to be met.
ORGON   That strong-box has me utterly upset;
This is the worst of many, many shocks.   5
CLÉANTE   Is there some fearful mystery in that box?
ORGON   My poor friend Argas brought that box to me
With his own hands, in utmost secrecy;
'Twas on the very morning of his flight.
It's full of papers which, if they came to light,   10
Would ruin him—or such is my impression.
CLÉANTE   Then why did you let it out of your possession?
ORGON   Those papers vexed my conscience, and it seemed best
To ask the counsel of my pious guest.
The cunning scoundrel got me to agree   15
To leave the strong-box in his custody,
So that, in case of an investigation,
I could employ a slight equivocation
And swear I didn't have it, and thereby,
At no expense to conscience, tell a lie.   20
CLÉANTE   It looks to me as if you're out on a limb.
Trusting him with that box, and offering him
That deed of gift, were actions of a kind

Which scarcely indicate a prudent mind.
With two such weapons, he has the upper hand,   25
And since you're vulnerable, as matters stand,
You erred once more in bringing him to bay.
You should have acted in some subtler way.

ORGON   Just think of it: behind that fervent face,
A heart so wicked, and a soul so base!   30
I took him in, a hungry beggar, and then . . .
Enough, by God! I'm through with pious men:
Henceforth I'll hate the whole false brotherhood,
And persecute them worse than Satan could.

CLÉANTE   Ah, there you go—extravagant as ever!   35
Why can you not be rational? You never
Manage to take the middle course, it seems,
But jump, instead, between absurd extremes.
You've recognized your recent grave mistake
In falling victim to a pious fake;   40
Now, to correct that error, must you embrace
An even greater error in its place,
And judge our worthy neighbors as a whole
By what you've learned of one corrupted soul?
Come, just because one rascal made you swallow   45
A show of zeal which turned out to be hollow,
Shall you conclude that all men are deceivers,
And that, today, there are no true believers?
Let atheists make that foolish inference;
Learn to distinguish virtue from pretense,   50
Be cautious in bestowing admiration,
And cultivate a sober moderation.
Don't humor fraud, but also don't asperse
True piety; the latter fault is worse,
And it is best to err, if err one must,   55
As you have done, upon the side of trust.

SCENE 2

DAMIS, ORGON, CLÉANTE

DAMIS   Father, I hear that scoundrel's uttered threats
Against you; that he pridefully forgets
How, in his need, he was befriended by you,
And means to use your gifts to crucify you.

ORGON   It's true, my boy. I'm too distressed for tears.   5

DAMIS   Leave it to me, Sir; let me trim his ears.
Faced with such insolence, we must not waver.
I shall rejoice in doing you the favor
Of cutting short his life, and your distress.

CLÉANTE   What a display of young hotheadedness!   10
Do learn to moderate your fits of rage.
In this just kingdom, this enlightened age,
One does not settle things by violence.

SCENE 3

MADAME PERNELLE, MARIANE, ELMIRE, DORINE, DAMIS, ORGON, CLÉANTE

MADAME PERNELLE   I hear strange tales of very strange events.
ORGON   Yes, strange events which these two eyes beheld.
  The man's ingratitude is unparalleled.
  I save a wretched pauper from starvation,
  House him, and treat him like a blood relation,   5
  Shower him every day with my largesse,
  Give him my daughter, and all that I possess;
  And meanwhile the unconscionable knave
  Tries to induce my wife to misbehave;
  And not content with such extreme rascality,   10
  Now threatens me with my own liberality,
  And aims, by taking base advantage of
  The gifts I gave him out of Christian love,
  To drive me from my house, a ruined man,
  And make me end a pauper, as he began.   15
DORINE   Poor fellow!
MADAME PERNELLE   No, my son, I'll never bring
  Myself to think him guilty of such a thing.
ORGON   How's that?
MADAME PERNELLE   The righteous always were maligned.
ORGON   Speak clearly, Mother. Say what's on your mind.
MADAME PERNELLE   I mean that I can smell a rat, my dear.   20
  You know how everybody hates him, here.
ORGON   That has no bearing on the case at all.
MADAME PERNELLE   I told you a hundred times, when you were small,
  That virtue in this world is hated ever;
  Malicious men may die, but malice never.   25
ORGON   No doubt that's true, but how does it apply?
MADAME PERNELLE   They've turned you against him by a clever lie.
ORGON   I've told you, I was there and saw it done.
MADAME PERNELLE   Ah, slanderers will stop at nothing, Son.
ORGON   Mother, I'll lose my temper . . . For the last time,   30
  I tell you I was witness to the crime.
MADAME PERNELLE   The tongues of spite are busy night and noon,
  And to their venom no man is immune.
ORGON   You're talking nonsense. Can't you realize
  I saw it; saw it; saw it with my eyes?   35
  Saw, do you understand me? Must I shout it
  Into your ears before you'll cease to doubt it?
MADAME PERNELLE   Appearances can deceive, my son. Dear me,
  We cannot always judge by what we see.
ORGON   Drat! Drat!
MADAME PERNELLE   One often interprets things awry;   40
  Good can seem evil to a suspicious eye.
ORGON   Was I to see his pawing at Elmire
  As an act of charity?
MADAME PERNELLE   Till his guilt is clear,

A man deserves the benefit of the doubt.
You should have waited, to see how things turned out.   45
ORGON   Great God in Heaven, what more proof did I need?
Was I to sit there, watching, until he'd . . .
You drive me to the brink of impropriety.
MADAME PERNELLE   No, no, a man of such surpassing piety
Could not do such a thing. You cannot shake me.   50
I don't believe it, and you shall not make me.
ORGON   You vex me so that, if you weren't my mother,
I'd say to you . . . some dreadful thing or other.
DORINE   It's your turn now, Sir, not to be listened to;
You'd not trust us, and now she won't trust you.   55
CLÉANTE   My friends, we're wasting time which should be spent
In facing up to our predicament.
I fear that scoundrel's threats weren't made in sport.
DAMIS   Do you think he'd have the nerve to go to court?
ELMIRE   I'm sure he won't: they'd find it all too crude   60
A case of swindling and ingratitude.
CLÉANTE   Don't be too sure. He won't be at a loss
To give his claims a high and righteous gloss;
And clever rogues with far less valid cause
Have trapped their victims in a web of laws.   65
I say again that to antagonize
A man so strongly armed was most unwise.
ORGON   I know it; but the man's appalling cheek
Outraged me so, I couldn't control my pique.
CLÉANTE   I wish to Heaven that we could devise   70
Some truce between you, or some compromise.
ELMIRE   If I had known what cards he held, I'd not
Have roused his anger by my little plot.
ORGON [*To* DORINE, *as* M. LOYAL *enters.*]
What is that fellow looking for? Who is he?
Go talk to him—and tell him that I'm busy.   75

SCENE 5

MONSIEUR LOYAL, MADAME PERNELLE, ORGON, DAMIS, MARIANE,
DORINE, ELMIRE, CLÉANTE

MONSIEUR LOYAL   Good day, dear sister. Kindly let me see
Your master.
DORINE   He's involved with company,
And cannot be disturbed just now, I fear.
MONSIEUR LOYAL   I hate to intrude; but what has brought me here
Will not disturb your master, in any event.   5
Indeed, my news will make him most content.
DORINE   Your name?
MONSIEUR LOYAL   Just say that I bring greetings from
Monsieur Tartuffe, on whose behalf I've come.
DORINE [*To* ORGON.]   Sir, he's a very gracious man, and bears
A message from Tartuffe, which, he declares,   10

Will make you most content.

CLÉANTE   Upon my word,
I think this man had best be seen, and heard.

ORGON   Perhaps he has some settlement to suggest.
How shall I treat him? What manner would be best?

CLÉANTE   Control your anger, and if he should mention   15
Some fair adjustment, give him your full attention.

MONSIEUR LOYAL   Good health to you, good Sir. May Heaven confound
Your enemies, and may your joys abound.

ORGON [*Aside, to* CLÉANTE.]   A gentle salutation: it confirms
My guess that he is here to offer terms.   20

MONSIEUR LOYAL   I've always held your family most dear;
I served your father, Sir, for many a year.

ORGON   Sir, I must ask your pardon; to my shame,
I cannot now recall your face or name.

MONSIEUR LOYAL   Loyal's my name; I come from Normandy,   25
And I'm a bailiff, in all modesty.
For forty years, praise God, it's been my boast
To serve with honor in that vital post,
And I am here, Sir, if you will permit
The liberty, to serve you with this writ . . .   30

ORGON   To—*what?*

MONSIEUR LOYAL   Now, please, Sir, let us have no friction:
It's nothing but an order of eviction.
You are to move your goods and family out
And make way for new occupants, without
Deferment or delay, and give the keys . . .   35

ORGON   I? Leave this house?

MONSIEUR LOYAL   Why yes, Sir, if you please.
This house, Sir, from the cellar to the roof,
Belongs now to the good Monsieur Tartuffe,
And he is lord and master of your estate
By virtue of a deed of present date,   40
Drawn in due form, with clearest legal phrasing . . .

DAMIS   Your insolence is utterly amazing!

MONSIEUR LOYAL   Young man, my business here is not with you
But with your wise and temperate father, who,
Like every worthy citizen, stands in awe   45
Of justice, and would never obstruct the law.

ORGON   But . . .

MONSIEUR LOYAL   Not for a million, Sir, would you rebel
Against authority; I know that well.
You'll not make trouble, Sir, or interfere
With the execution of my duties here.   50

DAMIS   Someone may execute a smart tattoo
On that black jacket[4] of yours, before you're through.

MONSIEUR LOYAL   Sir, bid your son be silent. I'd much regret

---

4. In the original, *justaucorps à longues basques,* a close-fitting, long black coat with skirts, the customary
dress of a bailiff.

Having to mention such a nasty threat
Of violence, in writing my report.   55
DORINE [*Aside.*]   This man Loyal's a most disloyal sort!
MONSIEUR LOYAL   I love all men of upright character,
And when I agreed to serve these papers, Sir,
It was your feelings that I had in mind.
I couldn't bear to see the case assigned   60
To someone else, who might esteem you less
And so subject you to unpleasantness.
ORGON   What's more unpleasant than telling a man to leave
His house and home?
MONSIEUR LOYAL   You'd like a short reprieve?
If you desire it, Sir, I shall not press you,   65
But wait until tomorrow to dispossess you.
Splendid. I'll come and spend the night here, then,
Most quietly, with half a score of men.
For form's sake, you might bring me, just before
You go to bed, the keys to the front door.   70
My men, I promise, will be on their best
Behavior, and will not disturb your rest.
But bright and early, Sir, you must be quick
And move out all your furniture, every stick:
The men I've chosen are both young and strong,   75
And with their help it shouldn't take you long.
In short, I'll make things pleasant and convenient,
And since I'm being so extremely lenient,
Please show me, Sir, a like consideration,
And give me your entire cooperation.   80
ORGON [*Aside.*]   I may be all but bankrupt, but I vow
I'd give a hundred louis, here and now,
Just for the pleasure of landing one good clout
Right on the end of that complacent snout.
CLÉANTE   Careful; don't make things worse.
DAMIS   My bootsole itches   85
To give that beggar a good kick in the breeches.
DORINE   Monsieur Loyal, I'd love to hear the whack
Of a stout stick across your fine broad back.
MONSIEUR LOYAL   Take care: a woman too may go to jail if
She uses threatening language to a bailiff.   90
CLÉANTE   Enough, enough, Sir. This must not go on.
Give me that paper, please, and then begone.
MONSIEUR LOYAL   Well, *au revoir.* God give you all good cheer!
ORGON   May God confound you, and him who sent you here!

SCENE 5

ORGON, CLÉANTE, MARIANE, ELMIRE, MADAME PERNELLE, DORINE, DAMIS

ORGON   Now, Mother, was I right or not? This writ
Should change your notion of Tartuffe a bit.
Do you perceive his villainy at last?

MADAME PERNELLE   I'm thunderstruck. I'm utterly aghast.
DORINE   Oh, come, be fair. You mustn't take offense   5
　At this new proof of his benevolence.
　He's acting out of selfless love, I know.
　Material things enslave the soul, and so
　He kindly has arranged your liberation
　From all that might endanger your salvation.   10
ORGON   Will you not ever hold your tongue, you dunce?
CLÉANTE   Come, you must take some action, and at once.
ELMIRE   Go tell the world of the low trick he's tried.
　The deed of gift is surely nullified
　By such behavior, and public rage will not   15
　Permit the wretch to carry out his plot.

SCENE 6

VALÈRE, ORGON, CLÉANTE, ELMIRE, MARIANE,
MADAME PERNELLE, DAMIS, DORINE

VALÈRE   Sir, though I hate to bring you more bad news,
　Such is the danger that I cannot choose.
　A friend who is extremely close to me
　And knows my interest in your family
　Has, for my sake, presumed to violate   5
　The secrecy that's due to things of state,
　And sends me word that you are in a plight
　From which your one salvation lies in flight.
　That scoundrel who's imposed upon you so
　Denounced you to the King an hour ago   10
　And, as supporting evidence, displayed
　The strong-box of a certain renegade
　Whose secret papers, so he testified,
　You had disloyally agreed to hide.
　I don't know just what charges may be pressed,   15
　But there's a warrant out for your arrest;
　Tartuffe has been instructed, furthermore,
　To guide the arresting officer to your door.
CLÉANTE   He's clearly done this to facilitate
　His seizure of your house and your estate.   20
ORGON   That man, I must say, is a vicious beast!
VALÈRE   You can't afford to delay, Sir, in the least.
　My carriage is outside, to take you hence;
　This thousand louis should cover all expense.
　Let's lose no time, or you shall be undone;   25
　The sole defense, in this case, is to run.
　I shall go with you all the way, and place you
　In a safe refuge to which they'll never trace you.
ORGON   Alas, dear boy, I wish that I could show you
　My gratitude for everything I owe you.   30
　But now is not the time; I pray the Lord
　That I may live to give you your reward.
　Farewell, my dears; be careful . . .

CLÉANTE   Brother, hurry.
We shall take care of things; you needn't worry.

SCENE 7

The OFFICER, TARTUFFE, VALÈRE, ORGON, ELMIRE, MARIANE,
MADAME PERNELLE, DORINE, CLÉANTE, DAMIS

TARTUFFE   Gently, Sir, gently; stay right where you are.
  No need for haste; your lodging isn't far.
  You're off to prison, by order of the Prince.
ORGON   This is the crowning blow, you wretch; and since
  It means my total ruin and defeat,   5
  Your villainy is now at last complete.
TARTUFFE   You needn't try to provoke me; it's no use.
  Those who serve Heaven must expect abuse.
CLÉANTE   You are indeed most patient, sweet, and blameless.
DORINE   How he exploits the name of Heaven! It's shameless.   10
TARTUFFE   Your taunts and mockeries are all for naught;
  To do my duty is my only thought.
MARIANE   Your love of duty is most meritorious,
  And what you've done is little short of glorious.
TARTUFFE   All deeds are glorious, Madam, which obey   15
  The sovereign prince who sent me here today.
ORGON   I rescued you when you were destitute;
  Have you forgotten that, you thankless brute?
TARTUFFE   No, no, I well remember everything;
  But my first duty is to serve my King.   20
  That obligation is so paramount
  That other claims, beside it, do not count;
  And for it I would sacrifice my wife,
  My family, my friend, or my own life.
ELMIRE   Hypocrite!
DORINE   All that we most revere, he uses   25
  To cloak his plots and camouflage his ruses.
CLÉANTE   If it is true that you are animated
  By pure and loyal zeal, as you have stated,
  Why was this zeal not roused until you'd sought
  To make Orgon a cuckold, and been caught?   30
  Why weren't you moved to give your evidence
  Until your outraged host had driven you hence?
  I shan't say that the gift of all his treasure
  Ought to have damped your zeal in any measure;
  But if he is a traitor, as you declare,   35
  How could you condescend to be his heir?
TARTUFFE [*To the* OFFICER.]
  Sir, spare me all this clamor; it's growing shrill.
  Please carry out your orders, if you will.
OFFICER[5] Yes, I've delayed too long, Sir. Thank you kindly.

---

5. In the original, *un exempt*. He would actually have been a gentleman from the king's personal body-
guard with the rank of lieutenant colonel or "master of the camp."

You're just the proper person to remind me.   40
Come, you are off to join the other boarders
In the King's prison, according to his orders.
TARTUFFE   Who? I, Sir?
OFFICER   Yes.
TARTUFFE   To prison? This can't be true!
OFFICER   I owe an explanation, but not to you.
[*To* ORGON.] Sir, all is well; rest easy, and be grateful.   45
We serve a Prince to whom all sham is hateful,
A Prince who sees into our inmost hearts,
And can't be fooled by any trickster's arts.
His royal soul, though generous and human,
Views all things with discernment and acumen;   50
His sovereign reason is not lightly swayed,
And all his judgments are discreetly weighed.
He honors righteous men of every kind,
And yet his zeal for virtue is not blind,
Nor does his love of piety numb his wits   55
And make him tolerant of hypocrites.
'Twas hardly likely that this man could cozen
A King who's foiled such liars by the dozen.
With one keen glance, the King perceived the whole
Perverseness and corruption of his soul,   60
And thus high Heaven's justice was displayed:
Betraying you, the rogue stood self-betrayed.
The King soon recognized Tartuffe as one
Notorious by another name, who'd done
So many vicious crimes that one could fill   65
Ten volumes with them, and be writing still.
But to be brief: our sovereign was appalled
By this man's treachery toward you, which he called
The last, worst villainy of a vile career,
And bade me follow the impostor here   70
To see how gross his impudence could be,
And force him to restore your property.
Your private papers, by the King's command,
I hereby seize and give into your hand.
The King, by royal order, invalidates   75
The deed which gave this rascal your estates,
And pardons, furthermore, your grave offense
In harboring an exile's documents.
By these decrees, our Prince rewards you for
Your loyal deeds in the late civil war,[6]   80
And shows how heartfelt is his satisfaction
In recompensing any worthy action,
How much he prizes merit, and how he makes
More of men's virtues than of their mistakes.
DORINE   Heaven be praised!

---

6. A reference to Orgon's role in supporting the king during the *Frondes*.

MADAME PERNELLE.   I breathe again, at last.   85
ELMIRE   We're safe.
MARIANE   I can't believe the danger's past.
ORGON [To TARTUFFE.]   Well, traitor, now you see . . .
CLÉANTE   Ah, brother, please
    Let's not descend to such indignities.
    Leave the poor wretch to his unhappy fate,
    And don't say anything to aggravate   90
    His present woes; but rather hope that he
    Will soon embrace an honest piety,
    And mend his ways, and by a true repentance
    Move our just King to moderate his sentence.
    Meanwhile, go kneel before your sovereign's throne   95
    And thank him for the mercies he has shown.
ORGON   Well said: let's go at once and, gladly kneeling,
    Express the gratitude which all are feeling.
    Then, when that first great duty has been done,
    We'll turn with pleasure to a second one,   .   100
    And give Valère, whose love has proven so true,
    The wedded happiness which is his due.

SOR JUANA INÉS DE LA CRUZ
1648–1695

One hardly expects to find a spirited defense of women's intellectual rights issuing from the pen of a seventeenth-century Mexican nun, but *Reply to Sor Filotea de la Cruz,* by Sister Juana Inés de la Cruz, is exactly that. In the guise of declaring her humility and her religious subordination, this nun manages to advance claims for her sex more far-reaching and profound than any previously offered.

Born into an upper-class family, Sister Juana in her teens served as lady-in-waiting at the Viceregal court. She soon took the veil, however; her *Reply* suggests as a reason her desire for a safe environment in which to pursue her intellectual interests. Religious vocation did not prevent her from writing in secular forms: lyric poetry and drama. Indeed, she achieved an important literary reputation, later coming to be known throughout the Spanish-speaking world as the "Tenth Muse." Because her religious superiors intermittently rebuked her for her worldly interests, however, she appears to have developed a powerful sense of guilt. It is said that the natural disturbances and disasters—a solar eclipse, storms, and famine—plaguing Mexico City in the 1690s may have intensified her guilt; in 1694, she reaffirmed her faith, signing the statement in her own blood with the words "I, Sister Juana Inés de la Cruz, the worst in the world." She died after nursing the sick in an epidemic.

The *Reply* stems directly from Sister Juana's venture into theological polemic. In 1690 she wrote a commentary on a sermon delivered forty years earlier by the Portuguese Jesuit Antonio Vieira, a sermon in which he disputed with Saint Augustine and Saint Thomas about the nature of Christ's greatest expression of love at His life's end. Her commentary, in the form of a letter, was published, without her consent, by the bishop of Puebla. The bishop provided the title *Athenagoric Letter,* or "letter worthy of the wisdom of Athena," but he also prefixed his own letter to Sister Juana, signed with the pseudonym "Filotea de la Cruz." Here he advised the nun to focus her attention and her talents more on religious matters. In her *Reply* (1691), she nominally accepted the bishop's rebuke; the smooth surface of her elegant prose, however, conceals both rage and determination to assert her right—and that of other women—to a fully realized life of the mind.

The artistry of this piece of self-defense demonstrates Sister Juana's powers and thus constitutes part of her justification. Systematically refusing to make any overt claims for herself, she declares her desire to do whatever her associates wish or demand of her. While asserting her own unimportance, she illustrates the range of her knowledge and of her rhetorical skill. The sheer abundance of her biblical allusions and of her quotations from theological texts, for instance, proves that she has mastered a large body of religious material and that she has not sacrificed religious to secular study. Her elaborate protestations of deference, her vocabulary of insignificance, her narrative of subservience: all show the verbal dexterity that enables her to achieve her own rhetorical ends even as she denies her commitment to purely personal goals.

If she acknowledges no self-seeking, she nevertheless declares and demonstrates her ungovernable passion for the life of the mind. She tells of how she joined the convent despite fears that the community "would intrude upon the peaceful silence of my books." "Certain learned persons," however, explained to her that her desire for solitary intellectual experience constituted "temptation." She, therefore, entered the religious life, believing, she says, "that I was fleeing from myself, but—wretch that I am!—I brought with me my worst enemy, my inclination, which I do not know whether to consider a gift or a punishment from Heaven; for once dimmed and encumbered by the many activities common to Religion, that inclination exploded in me like gunpowder." Although this sentence explicitly labels her intellectual inclinations her worst enemy and suggests that they might be considered divine punishment, the same sentence dramatizes the uncontrollable, explosive force of those inclinations and hints at the negative potential of religious experience, which dims and encumbers the mind. No matter how often Sister Juana admits that her longings amount to a form of "vice," she embodies in her prose the energy and the vividness that they generate and makes her audience feel their positive weight.

The autobiographical aspects of Sister Juana's self-defense give it special immediacy for modern readers, who may recognize a version of their own dilemmas in her narrative of difficulties. Of course, girls no longer have to trick their way into learning or plead for permission to dress in boy's clothes to go to a university. But even twenty-first-century young women have been known to experience the kind of hostility Sister Juana reports as the response to her remarkable achievement. Yet more recognizable as a frequent form of female anxiety is the nun's concern to praclaim her responsiveness to others, her "tender and affable nature," which causes the other nuns, she says, to hold her "in great affection." She insists that she fills all the responsibilities of a woman as well as displays the kind of capacity more generally associated with men, and she performs her womanly and her religious duties *first*, reserving her scholarly pursuits for leisure hours.

But, of course, her larger argument depends on her utter denial that intelligence or a thirst for knowledge should be conidered a sex-limited characteristic. She draws on history for evidence of female intellectual power; one may feel the irony of the fact that her list of female worthies requires so much annotation today. The names of these notable women have hardly become household words. Still, these names, these histories, do exist, providing powerful support for Sister Juana's position. Even more forceful is the testimony of her own experience: her account of how, deprived of books, she finds matter for intellectual inquiry everywhere—in the yolk of an egg, the spinning of a top, the reading of the Bible. This is, the reader comes to believe, a woman born to think. If she arouses uneasiness when she implicitly equates herself, as object of persecution, with Christ, she also makes one feel directly the horror of women's official exclusion, in the past, from intellectual pursuits.

PRONOUNCING GLOSSARY

The following list uses common English syllables and stress accents to provide rough equivalents of selected words whose pronunciation may be unfamiliar to the general reader.

Albertus Magnus: *ahl-bayrl'-tus mahg'*
   -noos

Arete: *ah-reh-tay'*

Atenagórica: *ah-tay-nah-goh'-ree-kah*

Duquesa of Abeyro: *doo-kay'-zah of*
   ah-bay'-roh

Machiavelli: *mah-kee-ah-vel'-ee*

señora: *sen-yoh'rah*

sueño: *swayn'-yoh*

Reply to Sor Filotea de la Cruz[1]

My most illustrious *señora*, dear lady. It has not been my will, my poor health, or my justifiable apprehension that for so many days delayed my response. How could I write, considering that at my very first step my clumsy pen encountered two obstructions in its path? The first (and, for me, the most uncompromising) is to know how to reply to your most learned, most prudent, most holy, and most loving letter. For I recall that when Saint Thomas, the Angelic Doctor of Scholasticism, was asked about his silence regarding his teacher Albertus Magnus,[2] he replied that he had not spoken because he knew no words worthy of Albertus. With so much greater reason, must not I too be silent? Not, like the Saint, out of humility, but because in reality I know nothing I can say that is worthy of you. The second obstruction is to know how to express my appreciation for a favor as unexpected as extreme, for having my scribblings printed, a gift so immeasurable as to surpass my most ambitious aspiration, my most fervent desire, which even as an entity of reason never entered my thoughts. Yours was a kindness, finally, of such magnitude that words cannot express my gratitude, a kindness exceeding the bounds of appreciation, as great as it was unexpected—which is as Quintilian said: *aspirations engender minor glory; benefices,[3] major.* To such a degree as to impose silence on the receiver.

When the blessedly sterile—that she might miraculously become fecund—Mother of John the Baptist saw in her house such an extraordinary visitor as the Mother of the Word, her reason became clouded and her speech deserted her; and thus, in the place of thanks, she burst out with doubts and questions: *And whence is to me [that the mother of my Lord*

---

1. The Spanish text for this 17th-century declaration of women's intellectual freedom was discovered by Gabriel North Seymour during her Fulbright Scholarship in Mexico in 1980, following graduation from Princeton University. The English language translation by Margaret Sayers Peden was commissioned by Lime Rock Press, Inc., a small independent press in Connecticut, and was originally published in 1982 in a limited edition that included Seymour's black-and-white photographs of Sor Juana sites, under the title "A Woman of Genius: The Intellectual Autobiography of Sor Juana Inés dé la Crúz." The publication was honored at a special convocation of Mexican and American scholars at the Library of Congress. 2. Saint Albert the Great (1193?–1280), scholastic philosopher, called the Universal Doctor; he exercised great influence on his student Thomas Aquinas. 3. That is, good works. Marcus Fabius Quintilianus (ca. 35–100 C.E.), born in Spain, became a famous Roman orator and wrote on rhetoric.

should come to me?]⁴ And whence cometh such a thing to *me*? And so also it fell to Saul when he found himself the chosen, the anointed, King of Israel: *Am I not a son of Jemini, of the least tribe of Israel, and my kindred the last among all the families of the tribe of Benjamin? Why then hast thou spoken this word to me?*⁵ And thus say I, most honorable lady. Why do I receive such favor? By chance, am I other than an humble nun, the lowliest creature of the world, the most unworthy to occupy your attention? "Wherefore then speakest thou so to me?" "And whence is this to me?" Nor to the first obstruction do I have any response other than I am little worthy of your eyes; nor to the second, other than wonder, in the stead of thanks, saying that I am not capable of thanking you for the smallest part of that which I owe you. This is not pretended modesty, lady, but the simplest truth issuing from the depths of my heart, that when the letter which with propriety you called *Atenagórica*⁶ reached my hands, in print, I burst into tears of confusion (withal, that tears do not come easily to me) because it seemed to me that your favor was but a remonstrance God made against the wrong I have committed, and that in the same way He corrects others with punishment He wishes to subject me with benefices, with this special favor for which I know myself to be myself to be His debtor, as for an infinitude of others from His boundless kindness. I looked upon this favor as a particular way to shame and confound me, it being the most exquisite means of castigation, that of causing me, by my own intellect, to be the judge who pronounces sentence and who denounces my ingratitude. And thus, when here in my solitude I think on these things, I am wont to say: Blessed art Thou, oh Lord, for Thou hast not chosen to place in the hands of others my judgment, nor yet in mine, but hast reserved that to Thy own, and freed me from myself, and from the necessity to sit in judgment on myself, which judgment, forced from my own intellect, could be no less than condemnation, but Thou hast reserved me to Thy mercy, because Thou lovest me more than I can love myself.

I beg you, lady, to forgive this digression to which I was drawn by the power of truth, and, if I am to confess all the truth, I shall confess that I cast about for some manner by which I might flee the difficulty of a reply, and was sorely tempted to take refuge in silence. But as silence is a negative thing, though it explains a great deal through the very stress of not explaining, we must assign some meaning to it that we may understand what the silence is intended to say, for if not, silence will say nothing, as that is its very office: *to say nothing.* The holy Chosen Vessel, Saint Paul, having been caught up into paradise, and having heard the arcane secrets of God, *heard secret words, which it is not granted to man to utter.*⁷ He does not say what he heard; he says that he cannot say it. So that of things one cannot say, it is needful to say at least that they cannot be said, so that it may be understood that not speaking is not the same as having nothing to say, but rather being unable to express the many things there are to say. Saint John says that if all the marvels our Redeemer wrought "were written every one, the world itself, I think, would not be able to contain the books that should be written."⁸ And Vieyra says on this point that in this single phrase the Evangelist said more

---

4. Luke 1.43.   5. 1 Samuel 9.21.   6. Sister Juana's letter criticizing Father Vieira's sermon was retitled by the bishop *Carta Atenagórica* (Letter worthy of Athena). Athena was the Greek goddess of wisdom.   7. 2 Corinthians 12.4.   8. John 21.25.

than in all else he wrote; and this same Lusitanian[9] Phoenix speaks well (but when does he not speak well, even when he does not speak well of others?) because in those words Saint John said everything left unsaid and expressed all that was left to be expressed. And thus I, lady, shall respond only that I do not know how to respond; I shall thank you in saying only that I am incapable of thanking you; and I shall say, through the indication of what I leave to silence, that it is only with the confidence of one who is favored and with the protection of one who is honorable that I presume to address your magnificence, and if this be folly, be forgiving of it, for folly may be good fortune, and in this manner I shall provide further occasion for your benignity and you will better shape my intellect.

Because he was halting of speech, Moses thought himself unworthy to speak with Pharaoh, but after he found himself highly favored of God, and thus inspired, he not only spoke with God Almighty but dared ask the impossible: *shew me thy face.*[1] In this same manner, lady, and in view of how you favor me, I no longer see as impossible the obstructions I posed in the beginning: for who was it who had my letter printed unbeknownst to me? Who entitled it, who bore the cost, who honored it, it being so unworthy in itself, and in its author? What will such a person not do, not pardon? What would he fail to do, or fail to pardon? And thus, based on the supposition that I speak under the safe-conduct of your favor, and with the assurance of your benignity, and with the knowledge that like a second Ahasuerus[2] you have offered to me to kiss the top of the golden scepter of your affection as a sign of conceding to me your benevolent license to speak and offer judgments in your exalted presence, I say to you that I have taken to heart your most holy admonition that I apply myself to the study of the Sacred Books, which, though it comes in the guise of counsel, will have for me the authority of a precept, but with the not insignificant consolation that even before your counsel I was disposed to obey your pastoral suggestion as your direction, which may be inferred from the premise and argument of my Letter. For I know well that your most sensible warning is not directed against it, but rather against those worldly matters of which I have written.[3] And thus I had hoped with the Letter to make amends for any lack of application you may (with great reason) have inferred from others of my writings; and, speaking more particularly, I confess to you with all the candor of which you are deserving, and with the truth and clarity which are the natural custom in me, that my not having written often of sacred matters was not caused by disaffection or by want of application, but by the abundant fear and reverence due those Sacred Letters, knowing myself incapable of their comprehension and unworthy of their employment. Always resounding in my ears, with no little horror, I hear God's threat and prohibition to sinners like myself. *Why dost thou declare my justices, and take my covenant in thy mouth?*[4] This question, as well as the knowledge that even learned men are forbidden to read the Canticle of Canticles[5] until they have passed thirty

---

9. Roman name for Portugal. Antonio Vieira (1608–1697), author of the sermon that Sister Juana had earlier criticized, was a Portuguese ecclesiastic whose most important work was converting the Indians of Brazil.   1. Exodus 33.13.   2. King of Persia, who stretched out his gold scepter to his queen, Esther, and said he would grant her whatever she wished (Esther 5.2–3).   3. Sister Juana had published secular poetry and drama.   4. Psalm 50.16.   5. The Song of Solomon (also called Song of Songs), which employs erotic imagery.

years of age, or even Genesis—the latter for its obscurity; the former in order that the sweetness of those epithalamia not serve as occasion for imprudent youth to transmute their meaning into carnal emotion, as borne out by my exalted Father Saint Jerome,[6] who ordered that these be the last verses to be studied, and for the same reason: *And finally, one may read without peril the Song of Songs, for if it is read one may suffer harm through not understanding those Epithalamia of the spiritual wedding which is expressed in carnal terms.* And Seneca[7] says: *In the early years the faith is dim.* For how then would I have dared take in my unworthy hands these verses, defying gender, age, and, above all, custom? And thus I confess that many times this fear has plucked my pen from my hand and has turned my thoughts back toward the very same reason from which they had wished to be born: which obstacle did not impinge upon profane matters, for a heresy against art is not punished by the Holy Office but by the judicious with derision, and by critics with censure, and censure, *just or unjust, is not to be feared,* as it does not forbid the taking of communion or hearing of mass, and offers me little or no cause for anxiety, because in the opinion of those who defame my art, I have neither the obligation to know nor the aptitude to triumph. If, then, I err, I suffer neither blame nor discredit: I suffer no blame, as I have no obligation; no discredit, as I have no possibility of triumphing—*and no one is obliged to do the impossible.* And, in truth, I have written nothing except when compelled and constrained, and then only to give pleasure to others; not alone without pleasure of my own, but with absolute repugnance, for I have never deemed myself one who has any worth in letters or the wit necessity demands of one who would write; and thus my customary response to those who press me, above all in sacred matters, is, what capacity of reason have I? what application? what resources? what rudimentary knowledge of such matters beyond that of the most superficial scholarly degrees? Leave these matters to those who understand them; I wish no quarrel with the Holy Office, for I am ignorant, and I tremble that I may express some proposition that will cause offense or twist the true meaning of some scripture. I do not study to write, even less to teach—which in one like myself were unseemly pride—but only to the end that if I study, I will be ignorant of less. This is my response, and these are my feelings.

I have never written of my own choice, but at the urging of others, to whom with reason I might say, *You have compelled me.*[8] But one truth I shall not deny (first, because it is well-known to all, and second, because although it has not worked in my favor, God has granted me the mercy of loving truth above all else), which is that from the moment I was first illuminated by the light of reason, my inclination toward letters has been so vehement, so overpowering, that not even the admonitions of others—and I have suffered many—nor my own meditations—and they have not been few—have been sufficient to cause me to forswear this natural impulse that God placed in me: the Lord God knows why, and for what purpose. And He knows that I have prayed that He dim the light of my reason, leaving only that which is

---

6. Eusebius Sophronius Hieronymus (ca. 342–420), ascetic and scholar, most learned of the Latin Church fathers, a prolific author of treatises and commentaries. Sister Juana belonged to a Jeronymite convent; Jerome had founded the order.   7. Lucius Annaeus Seneca (ca. 3 B.C.E.–63 C.E.), Roman philosopher and orator.   8. 2 Corinthians 12.11.

needed to keep His Law, for there are those who would say that all else is unwanted in a woman, and there are even those who would hold that such knowledge does injury. And my Holy Father knows too that as I have been unable to achieve this (my prayer has not been answered), I have sought to veil the light of my reason—along with my name—and to offer it up only to Him who bestowed it upon me, and He knows that none other was the cause of my entering into Religion, notwithstanding that the spiritual exercises and company of a community were repugnant to the freedom and quiet I desired for my studious endeavors. And later, in that community, the Lord God knows—and, in the world, only the one who must know[9]—how diligently I sought to obscure my name, and how this was not permitted, saying it was temptation: and so it would have been. If it were in my power, lady, to repay you in some part what I owe you, it might be done by telling you this thing which has never before passed my lips, except to be spoken to the one who should hear it. It is my hope that by having opened wide to you the doors of my heart, by having made patent to you its most deeply-hidden secrets, you will deem my confidence not unworthy of the debt I owe to your most august person and to your most uncommon favors.

Continuing the narrations of my inclinations, of which I wish to give you a thorough account, I will tell you that I was not yet three years old when my mother determined to send one of my elder sisters to learn to read at a school for girls we call the *Amigas*. Affection, and mischief, caused me to follow her, and when I observed how she was being taught her lessons I was so inflamed with the desire to know how to read, that deceiving—for so I knew it to be—the mistress, I told her that my mother had meant for me to have lessons too. She did not believe it, as it was little to be believed, but, to humour me, she acceded. I continued to go there, and she continued to teach me, but now, as experience had disabused her, with all seriousness; and I learned so quickly that before my mother knew of it I could already read, for my teacher had kept it from her in order to reveal the surprise and reap the reward at one and the same time. And I, you may be sure, kept the secret, fearing that I would be whipped for having acted without permission. The woman who taught me, may God bless and keep her, is still alive and can bear witness to all I say. I also remember that in those days, my tastes being those common to that age, I abstained from eating cheese because I had heard that it made one slow of wits, for in me the desire for learning was stronger than the desire for eating—as powerful as that is in children. When later, being six or seven, and having learned how to read and write, along with all the other skills of needlework and household arts that girls learn, it came to my attention that in Mexico City there were Schools, and a University, in which one studied the sciences. The moment I heard this, I began to plague my mother with insistent and importunate pleas: she should dress me in boy's clothing and send me to Mexico City to live with relatives, to study and be tutored at the University. She would not permit it, and she was wise, but I assuaged my disappointment by reading the many and varied books belonging to my grandfather, and there were not enough punishments, nor reprimands, to prevent me from reading: so that when I came to the city

---

9. Presumably her confessor, Father Antonio Núñez.

many marveled, not so much at my natural wit, as at my memory, and at the amount of learning I had mastered at an age when many have scarcely learned to speak well.

I began to study Latin grammar—in all, I believe, I had no more than twenty lessons—and so intense was my concern that though among women (especially a woman in the flower of her youth) the natural adornment of one's hair is held in such high esteem, I cut off mine to the breadth of some four to six fingers, measuring the place it had reached, and imposing upon myself the condition that if by the time it had again grown to that length I had not learned such and such a thing I had set for myself to learn while my hair was growing, I would again cut it off as punishment for being so slow-witted. And it did happen that my hair grew out and still I had not learned what I had set for myself—because my hair grew quickly and I learned slowly—and in fact I did cut it in punishment for such stupidity: for there seemed to me no cause for a head to be adorned with hair and naked of learning—which was the more desired embellishment. And so I entered the religious order, knowing that life there entailed certain conditions (I refer to superficial, and not fundamental, regards) most repugnant to my nature; but given the total antipathy I felt for marriage, I deemed convent life the least unsuitable and the most honorable I could elect if I were to insure my salvation. Working against that end, first (as, finally, the most important) was the matter of all the trivial aspects of my nature which nourished my pride, such as wishing to live alone, and wishing to have no obligatory occupation that would inhibit the freedom of my studies, nor the sounds of a community that would intrude upon the peaceful silence of my books. These desires caused me to falter some while in my decision, until certain learned persons enlightened me, explaining that they were temptation, and, with divine favor, I overcame them, and took upon myself the state which now so unworthily I hold. I believed that I was fleeing from myself, but—wretch that I am!—I brought with me my worst enemy, my inclination, which I do not know whether to consider a gift or a punishment from Heaven, for once dimmed and encumbered by the many activities common to Religion, that inclination exploded in me like gunpowder, proving how *privation is the source of appetite.*

I turned again (which is badly put, for I never ceased), I continued, then, in my studious endeavour (which for me was respite during those moments not occupied by my duties) of reading and more reading, of study and more study, with no teachers but my books. Thus I learned how difficult it is to study those soulless letters, lacking a human voice or the explication of a teacher. But I suffered this labor happily for my love of learning. Oh, had it only been for love of God, which were proper, how worthwhile it would have been! I strove mightily to elevate these studies, to dedicate them to His service, as the goal to which I aspired was to study Theology—it seeming to me debilitating for a Catholic not to know everything in this life of the Divine Mysteries that can be learned through natural means—and, being a nun and not a layperson, it was seemly that I profess my vows to learning through ecclesiastical channels; and especially, being a daughter of a Saint Jerome and a Saint Paula,[1] it was essential that such erudite parents not be shamed

---

1. A Roman woman (died 404), who converted to Christianity after her daughter's death, founded a nunnery next to Saint Jerome's monastery at Bethlehem, and helped Jerome in his studies.

by a witless daughter. This is the argument I proposed to myself, and it seemed to me well-reasoned. It was, however (and this cannot be denied) merely glorification and approbation of my inclination, and enjoyment of it offered as justification. And so I continued, as I have said, directing the course of my studies toward the peak of Sacred Theology, it seeming necessary to me, in order to scale those heights, to climb the steps of the human sciences and arts; for how could one undertake the study of the Queen of Sciences if first one had not come to know her servants?

How, without Logic, could I be apprised of the general and specific way in which the Holy Scripture is written? How, without Rhetoric, could I understand its figures, its tropes, its locutions? How, without Physics,[2] so many innate questions concerning the nature of animals, their sacrifices, wherein exist so many symbols, many already declared, many still to be discovered? How should I know whether Saul's being refreshed by the sound of David's harp was due to the virtue and natural power of Music, or to a transcendent power God wished to place in David? How, without Arithmetic, could one understand the computations of the years, days, months, hours, those mysterious weeks communicated by Gabriel to Daniel,[3] and others for whose understanding one must know the nature, concordance, and properties of numbers? How, without Geometry, could one measure the Holy Ark of the Covenant and the Holy City of Jerusalem, whose mysterious measures are foursquare in their dimensions, as well as the miraculous proportions of all their parts? How, without Architecture, could one know the great Temple of Solomon, of which God Himself was the Author who conceived the disposition and the design, and the Wise King but the overseer who executed it, of which temple there was no foundation without mystery, no column without symbolism, no cornice without allusion, no architrave without significance; and similarly others of its parts, of which the least fillet was never intended solely for the service and complement of Art, but as symbol of greater things? How, without great knowledge of the laws and parts of which History is comprised, could one understand historical Books? Or those recapitulations in which many times what happened first is seen in the narrated account to have happened later? How, without great learning in Canon and Civil Law, could one understand Legal Books? How, without great erudition, could one apprehend the secular histories of which the Holy Scripture makes mention, such as the many customs of the Gentiles, their many rites, their many ways of speaking? How without the abundant laws and lessons of the Holy Fathers could one understand the obscure lesson of the Prophets? And without being expert in Music, how could one understand the exquisite precision of the musical proportions that grace so many Scriptures, particularly those in which Abraham beseeches God in defense of the Cities,[4] asking whether He would spare the place were there but fifty just men therein; and then Abraham reduced that number to five less than fifty, forty-five, which is a ninth, and is as Mi to Re; then to forty, which is a tone, and is as Re to Mi; from forty to thirty, which is a diatessaron, the interval of the perfect fourth; from thirty to twenty, which is the perfect fifth; and from twenty

2. That is, physic, or medicine.   3. While Daniel was praying, Gabriel came to him to interpret, in great chronological detail, a vision Daniel had previously had (Daniel 9.21–27).   4. Abraham beseeches God to save Sodom for the sake of its just inhabitants (Genesis 18.23–33).

to ten, which is the octave, the diapason; and as there are no further harmonic proportions, made no further reductions. How might one understand this without Music? And there in the Book of Job, God says to Job: *Shalt thou be able to join together the shining stars the Pleiades, or canst thou stop the turning about of Arcturus? Canst thou bring forth the day star in its time, and make the evening star to rise upon the children of the earth?*[5] Which message, without knowledge of Astrology, would be impossible to apprehend. And not only these noble sciences; there is no applied art that is not mentioned. And, finally, in consideration of the Book that comprises all books, and the Science in which all sciences are embraced, and for whose comprehension all sciences serve, and even after knowing them all (which we now see is not easy, nor even possible), there is one condition that takes precedence over all the rest, which is uninterrupted prayer and purity of life, that one may entreat of God that purgation of spirit and illumination of mind necessary for the understanding of such elevated matters: and if that be lacking, none of the aforesaid will have been of any purpose.

Of the Angelic Doctor Saint Thomas[6] the Church affirms: *When reading the most difficult passages of the Holy Scripture, he joined fast with prayer. And he was wont to say to his companion Brother Reginald that all he knew derived not so much from study or his own labor as from the grace of God.* How then should I—so lacking in virtue and so poorly read—find courage to write? But as I had acquired the rudiments of learning, I continued to study ceaselessly divers subjects, having for none any particular inclination, but for all in general; and having studied some more than others was not owing to preference, but to the chance that more books on certain subjects had fallen into my hands, causing the election of them through no discretion of my own. And as I was not directed by preference, nor, forced by the need to fulfill certain scholarly requirements, constrained by time in the pursuit of any subject, I found myself free to study numerous topics at the same time, or to leave some for others; although in this scheme some order was observed, for some I deigned[7] study and others diversion, and in the latter I found respite from the former. From which it follows that though I have studied many things I know nothing, as some have inhibited the learning of others. I speak specifically of the practical aspect of those arts that allow practice, because it is clear that when the pen moves the compass must lie idle, and while the harp is played the organ is stilled, *et sic de caeteris.*[8] And because much practice is required of one who would acquire facility, none who divides his interest among various exercises may reach perfection. Whereas in the formal and theoretical arts the contrary is true, and I would hope to persuade all with my experience, which is that one need not inhibit the other, but, in fact, each may illuminate and open the way to others, by nature of their variations and their hidden links, which were placed in this universal chain by the wisdom of their Author in such a way that they conform and are joined together with admirable unity and harmony. This is the very chain the ancients believed did issue from the mouth of Jupiter, from which were suspended all things linked one with another, as is demon-

5. Job 38.31–32.   **6.** Thomas Aquinas (ca. 1225–1274), Dominican theologian, author of *Summa Theologica* (ca. 1266), and for centuries the most important authority on church doctrine.   **7.** Deemed, considered.   **8.** And so for other things (Latin).

strated by the Reverend Father Athanasius Kircher[9] in his curious book, *De Magnate*. All things issue from God, Who is at once the center and the circumference from which and in which all lines begin and end.

I myself can affirm that what I have not understood in an author in one branch of knowledge I may understand in a second in a branch that seems remote from the first. And authors, in their elucidation, may suggest metaphorical examples in other arts: as when logicians say that to prove whether parts are equal, the means is to the extremes as a determined measure to two equidistant bodies; or in stating how the argument of the logician moves, in the manner of a straight line, along the shortest route, while that of the rhetorician moves as a curve, by the longest, but that both finally arrive at the same point. And similarly, as it is when they say that the Exegetes are like an open hand, and the Scholastics like a closed fist.[1] And thus it is no apology, nor do I offer it as such, to say that I have studied many subjects, seeing that each augments the other; but that I have not profited is the fault of my own ineptitude and the inadequacy of my intelligence, not the fault of the variety. But what may be offered as exoneration is that I undertook this great task without benefit of teacher, or fellow students with whom to confer and discuss, having for a master no other than a mute book, and for a colleague, an insentient inkwell; and in the stead of explication and exercise, many obstructions, not merely those of my religious obligations (for it is already known how useful and advantageous is the time employed in them), rather, all the attendant details of living in a community: how I might be reading, and those in the adjoining cell would wish to play their instruments, and sing; how I might be studying, and two servants who had quarreled would select me to judge their dispute; or how I might be writing, and a friend come to visit me, doing me no favor but with the best of will, at which time one must not only accept the inconvenience, but be grateful for the hurt. And such occurrences are the normal state of affairs, for as the times I set apart for study are those remaining after the ordinary duties of the community are fulfilled, they are the same moments available to my sisters, in which they may come to interrupt my labor; and only those who have experience of such a community will know how true this is, and how it is only the strength of my vocation that allows me happiness; that, and the great love existing between me and my beloved sisters, for as love is union, it knows no extremes of distance.

With this I confess how interminable has been my labor; and how I am unable to say what I have with envy heard others state—that they have not been plagued by the thirst for knowledge: blessed are they. For me, not the knowing (for still I do not know), merely the desiring to know, has been such torment that I can say, as has my Father Saint Jerome (although not with his accomplishment) . . . *my conscience is witness to what effort I have expended, what difficulties I have suffered, how many times I have despaired, how often I have ceased my labors and turned to them again, driven by the hunger for knowledge; my conscience is witness, and that of those who have lived beside me.* With the exception of the companions and witnesses (for I have been denied even this consolation), I can attest to the truth of these words. And

9. German Jesuit scientist (1601?–1680), author of *Magnes sive de arte magnetica* (The magnet; or, of the magnetic science). 1. The Exegetes emphasized interpretation; the Scholastics, logic.

to the fact that even so, my black inclination has been so great that it has conquered all else!

It has been my fortune that, among other benefices,[2] I owe to God a most tender and affable nature, and because of it my sisters (who being good women do not take note of my faults) hold me in great affection, and take pleasure in my company; and knowing this, and moved by the great love I hold for them—having greater reason than they—I enjoy even more *their* company. Thus I was wont in our rare idle moments to visit among them, offering them consolation and entertaining myself in their conversation. I could not help but note, however, that in these times I was neglecting my study, and I made a vow not to enter any cell unless obliged by obedience or charity; for without such a compelling constraint—the constraint of mere intention not being sufficient—my love would be more powerful than my will. I would (knowing well my frailty) make this vow for the period of a few weeks, or a month; and when that time had expired, I would allow myself a brief respite of a day or two before renewing it, using that time not so much for rest (for *not* studying has never been restful for me) as to assure that I not be deemed cold, remote, or ungrateful in the little-deserved affection of my dearest sisters.

In this practice one may recognize the strength of my inclination. I give thanks to God, Who willed that such an ungovernable force be turned toward letters and not to some other vice. From this it may also be inferred how obdurately against the current my poor studies have sailed (more accurately, have foundered). For still to be related is the most arduous of my difficulties—those mentioned until now, either compulsory or fortuitous, being merely tangential—and still unreported the more directly aimed slings and arrows that have acted to impede and prevent the exercise of my study. Who would have doubted, having witnessed such general approbation, that I sailed before the wind across calm seas, amid the laurels of widespread acclaim. But our Lord God knows that it has not been so; He knows how from amongst the blossoms of this very acclaim emerged such a number of aroused vipers, hissing their emulation and their persecution, that one could not count them. But the most noxious, those who most deeply wounded me, have not been those who persecuted me with open loathing and malice, but rather those who in loving me and desiring my well-being (and who are deserving of God's blessing for their good intent) have mortified and tormented me more than those others with their abhorrence. "Such studies are not in conformity with sacred innocence; surely she will be lost; surely she will, by cause of her very perspicacity and acuity, grow heady at such exalted heights." How was I to endure? An uncommon sort of martyrdom in which I was both martyr and executioner. And for my (in me, twice hapless) facility in making verses, even though they be sacred verses, what sorrows have I not suffered? What sorrows not ceased to suffer? Be assured, lady, it is often that I have meditated on how one who distinguishes himself—or one on whom God chooses to confer distinction, for it is only He who may do so— is received as a common enemy, because it seems to some that he usurps the applause they deserve, or that he dams up the admiration to which they aspired, and so they persecute that person.

---

2. Benefits or kindnesses.

That politically barbaric law of Athens by which any person who excelled by cause of his natural gifts and virtues was exiled from his Republic in order that he not threaten the public freedom still endures, is still observed in our day, although not for the reasons held by the Athenians. Those reasons have been replaced by another, no less efficient though not as well founded, seeming, rather, a maxim more appropriate to that impious Machiavelli[3]—which is to abhor one who excels, because he deprives others of regard. And thus it happens, and thus it has always happened.

For if not, what was the cause of the rage and loathing the Pharisees[4] directed against Christ, there being so many reasons to love Him? If we behold His presence, what is more to be loved than that Divine beauty? What more powerful to stir one's heart? For if ordinary human beauty holds sway over strength of will, and is able to subdue it with tender and enticing vehemence, what power would Divine beauty exert, with all its prerogatives and sovereign endowments? What might move, what effect, what not move and not effect, such incomprehensible beauty, that beauteous face through which, as through a polished crystal, were diffused the rays of Divinity? What would not be moved by that semblance which beyond incomparable human perfections revealed Divine illuminations? If the visage of Moses, merely from conversation with God, caused men to fear to come near him,[5] how much finer must be the face of God-made-flesh? And among other virtues, what more to be loved than that celestial modesty? That sweetness and kindness disseminating mercy in every movement? That profound humility and gentleness? Those words of eternal life and eternal wisdom? How therefore is it possible that such beauty did not stir their souls, that they did not follow after Him, enamored and enlightened?

The Holy Mother, my Mother Teresa,[6] says that when she beheld the beauty of Christ never again was she inclined toward any human creature, for she saw nothing that was not ugliness compared to such beauty. How was it then that in men it engendered such contrary reactions? For although they were uncouth and vile and had no knowledge or appreciation of His perfections, not even as they might profit from them, how was it they were not moved by the many advantages of such benefices as He performed for them, healing the sick, resurrecting the dead, restoring those possessed of the devil? How was it they did not love Him? But God is witness that it was for these very acts they did not love Him, that they despised Him. As they themselves testified.

They gather together in their council and say: *What do we? for this man doth many miracles.*[7] Can this be cause? If they had said: here is an evildoer, a transgressor of the law, a rabble-rouser who with deceit stirs up the populace, they would have lied—as they did indeed lie when they spoke these things. But there were more apposite reasons for effecting what they desired, which was to take His life; and to give as reason that he had performed wondrous deeds seems not befitting learned men, for such were the Pharisees. Thus it is that in the heat of passion learned men erupt with such

3. Niccolò Machiavelli (1469–1527), Italian statesman whose writings (notably *The Prince*) advocated political unscrupulousness.   4. Members of a strict Jewish sect that emphasized conformity to the law who were, according to the New Testament of the Bible, prominent in plotting the death of Jesus (Mark 3.6, John 11.47–57).   5. Exodus 34.30.   6. Saint Teresa de Ávila (1515–1582), a mystical writer, responsible for a great awakening of religious fervor.   7. John 11.47.

irrelevancies; for we know it as truth that only for this reason was it determined that Christ should die. Oh, men, if men you may be called, being so like to brutes, what is the cause of so cruel a determination? Their only response is that "this man doth many miracles." May God forgive them. Then is performing signal deeds cause enough that one should die? This "he doth many miracles" evokes *the root of Jesse, who standeth for an ensign of the people*,[8] and that *and for a sign which shall be contradicted.*[9] He is a sign? Then He shall die. He excels? Then He shall suffer, for that is the reward for one who excels.

Often on the crest of temples are placed as adornment figures of the winds and of fame, and to defend them from the birds, they are covered with iron barbs; this appears to be in defense, but is in truth obligatory propriety: the figure thus elevated cannot survive without the very barbs that prick it; there on high is found the animosity of the air, on high the ferocity of the elements, on high is unleashed the anger of the thunderbolt, on high stands the target for slings and arrows. Oh unhappy eminence, exposed to such uncounted perils. Oh sign, become the target of envy and the butt of contradiction. Whatever eminence, whether that of dignity, nobility, riches, beauty, or science, must suffer this burden; but the eminence that undergoes the most severe attack is that of reason. First, because it is the most defenseless, for riches and power strike out against those who dare attack them; but not so reason, for while it is the greater it is more modest and long-suffering, and defends itself less. Second, as Gracian[1] stated so eruditely, *favors in man's reason are favors in his nature.*

For no other cause except that the angel is superior in reason is the angel above man; for no other cause does man stand above the beast but by his reason; and thus, as no one wishes to be lower than another, neither does he confess that another is superior in reason, as reason is a consequence of being superior. One will abide, and will confess that another is nobler than he, that another is richer, more handsome, and even that he is more learned, but that another is richer in reason scarcely any will confess: *Rare is he who will concede genius.* That is why the assault against this virtue works to such profit.

When the soldiers mocked, made entertainment and diversion of our Lord Jesus Christ, they brought Him a worn purple garment and a hollow reed, and a crown of thorns to crown Him King of Fools.[2] But though the reed and the purple were an affront, they did not cause suffering. Why does only the crown give pain? Is it not enough that like the other emblems the crown was a symbol of ridicule and ignominy, as that was its intent? No. Because the sacred head of Christ and His divine intellect were the depository of wisdom, and the world is not satisfied for wisdom to be the object of mere ridicule, it must also be done injury and harm. A head that is a storehouse of wisdom can expect nothing but a crown of thorns. What garland may human wisdom expect when it is known what was bestowed on that divine wisdom? Roman pride crowned the many achievements of their Captains with many crowns: he who defended the city received the civic crown; he who fought his way into the hostile camp received the camp crown; he who

---

8. Isaiah 11.10.   9. Luke 2.34.   1. Baltasar Gracián (1601–1658), Spanish Jesuit philosopher.
2. Matthew 27.28–31.

scaled the wall, the mural;[3] he who liberated a beseiged city, or any army besieged either in the field or in the enemy camp, received the obsidional, the siege, crown; other feats were crowned with naval, ovation, or triumphal crowns, as described by Pliny and Aulus Gellius.[4] Observing so many and varied crowns, I debated as to which Christ's crown must have been, and determined that it was the siege crown, for (as well you know, lady) that was the most honored crown and was called obsidional after *obsidio*, which means siege; which crown was made not from gold, or silver, but from the leaves and grasses flourishing on the field where the feat was achieved. And as the heroic feat of Christ was to break the siege of the Prince of Darkness, who had laid siege to all the earth, as is told in the Book of Job, quoting Satan: *I have gone round about the earth, and walked through it,*[5] and as St. Peter says: *As a roaring lion, goeth about seeking whom he may devour.*[6] And our Master came and caused him to lift the siege: *Now shall the prince of this world be cast out.*[7] So the soldiers crowned Him not with gold or silver but with the natural fruit of the world, which was the field of battle—and which, after the curse *Thorns also and thistles shall it bring forth to thee,*[8] produced only thorns—and thus it was a most fitting crown for the courageous and wise Conqueror, with which His mother Synagogue crowned Him. And the daughters of Zion, weeping, came out to witness the sorrowful triumph,[9] as they had come rejoicing for the triumph of Solomon,[1] because the triumph of the wise is earned with sorrow and celebrated with weeping, which is the manner of the triumph of wisdom; and as Christ is the King of wisdom, He was the first to wear that crown; and as it was sanctified on His brow, it removed all fear and dread from those who are wise, for they know they need aspire to no other honor.

The Living Word, Life, wished to restore life to Lazarus, who was dead. His disciples did not know His purpose and they said to Him: *Rabbi, the Jews but now sought to stone thee; and goest thou thither again?* And the Redeemer calmed their fear: *Are there not twelve hours of the day?*[2] It seems they feared because there had been those who wished to stone Him when He rebuked them, calling them thieves and not shepherds of sheep.[3] And thus the disciples feared that if He returned to the same place—for even though rebukes be just, they are often badly received—He would be risking his life. But once having been disabused and having realized that He was setting forth to raise up Lazarus from the dead, what was it that caused Thomas, like Peter in the Garden, to say *Let us also go, that we may die with him?*[4] What say you, Sainted Apostle? The Lord does not go out to die; whence your misgiving? For Christ goes not to rebuke, but to work an act of mercy, and therefore they will do Him no harm. These same Jews could have assured you, for when He reproved those who wished to stone Him, *Many good works I have shewed you from my Father; for which of those works do you stone me?* they replied: *For a good work we stone thee not; but for blasphemy.*[5] And as they say they will not stone Him for doing good

---

3. Pertaining to walls; the word *crown* is understood.   4. Latin writer (2nd century c.e.), author of *Noctes Atticae,* valuable for its quotations from lost works. Pliny the Younger (62?–ca. 113), Roman orator and statesman and author of well-known letters about Roman life.   5. Job 1.7.   6. 1 Peter 5.8.   7. John 12.31.   8. The curse on Adam and Eve after the Fall (Genesis 3.18).   9. Luke 23.27–28.   1. Song of Solomon 3.11.   2. John 11.8–9.   3. John 10.1–31.   4. John 11.16.   5. John 10.32–33.

works, and now He goes to do a work so great as to raise up Lazarus from the dead, whence your misgiving? Why do you fear? Were it not better to say: let us go to gather the fruits of appreciation for the good work our Master is about to do; to see him lauded and applauded for His benefice; to see men marvel at His miracle. Why speak words seemingly so alien to the circumstance as *Let us also go?* Ah, woe, the Saint feared as a prudent man and spoke as an Apostle. Does Christ not go to work a miracle? Why, what *greater* peril? It is less to be suffered that pride endure rebukes than envy witness miracles. In all the above, most honored lady, I do not wish to say (nor is such folly to be found in me) that I have been persecuted for my wisdom, but merely for my love of wisdom and letters, having achieved neither one nor the other.

At one time even the Prince of the Apostles was very far from wisdom, as is emphasized in that *But Peter followed afar off*.[6] Very distant from the laurels of a learned man is one so little in his judgment that he was *Not knowing what he said*.[7] And being questioned on his mastery of wisdom, he himself was witness that he had not achieved the first measure: *But he denied him, saying: Woman, I know him not*.[8] And what becomes of him? We find that having this reputation of ignorance, he did not enjoy its good fortune, but, rather, the affliction of being taken for wise. And why? There was no other motive but: *This man also was with him*[9] He was fond of wisdom, it filled His heart, He followed after it, He prided himself as a pursuer and lover of wisdom; and although He followed from so *afar off* that He neither understood nor achieved it, His love for it was sufficient that He incur its torments. And there was present that soldier to cause Him distress, and a certain maid-servant to cause Him grief. I confess that I find myself very distant from the goals of wisdom, for all that I have desired to follow it, even from *afar off*. But in this I have been brought closer to the fire of persecution, to the crucible of torment, and to such lengths that they have asked that study be forbidden to me.

At one time this was achieved through the offices of a very saintly and ingenuous Abbess who believed that study was a thing of the Inquisition, who commanded me not to study. I obeyed her (the three some[1] months her power to command endured) in that I did not take up a book; but that I study not at all is not within my power to achieve, and this I could not obey, for though I did not study in books, I studied all the things that God had wrought, reading in them, as in writing and in books, all the workings of the universe. I looked on nothing without reflection; I heard nothing without meditation, even in the most minute and imperfect things; because as there is no creature, however lowly, in which one cannot recognize that *God made me,* there is none that does not astound reason, if properly meditated on. Thus, I reiterate, I saw and admired all things; so that even the very persons with whom I spoke, and the things they said, were cause for a thousand meditations. Whence the variety of genius and wit, being all of a single species? Which the temperaments and hidden qualities that occasioned such variety? If I saw a figure, I was forever combining the proportion of its lines and measuring it with my reason and reducing it to new proportions. Occasionally as

---

6. Luke 22.54.   7. Refers to Peter (Luke 9.33).   8. Luke 22.57.   9. A serving maid says this of Peter, who thereupon denies knowing Jesus (Luke 22.56).   1. That is, "the three or so."

I walked along the far wall of one of our dormitories (which is a most capacious room) I observed that though the lines of the two sides were parallel and the ceiling perfectly level, in my sight they were distorted, the lines seeming to incline toward one another, the ceiling seeming lower in the distance than in proximity: from which I inferred that *visual* lines run straight but not parallel, forming a pyramidal figure. I pondered whether this might not be the reason that caused the ancients to question whether the world were spherical. Because, although it so seems, this could be a deception of vision, suggesting concavities where possibly none existed.

This manner of reflection has always been my habit, and is quite beyond my will to control; on the contrary, I am wont to become vexed that my intellect makes me weary; and I believed that it was so with everyone, as well as making verses, until experience taught me otherwise; and it is so strong in me this nature, or custom, that I look at nothing without giving it further examination. Once in my presence two young girls were spinning a top and scarcely had I seen the motion and the figure described, when I began, out of this madness of mine, to meditate on the effortless *motus*[2] of the spherical form, and how the impulse persisted even when free and independent of its cause—for the top continued to dance even at some distance from the child's hand, which was the causal force. And not content with this, I had flour brought and sprinkled about, so that as the top danced one might learn whether these were perfect circles it described with its movement; and I found that they were not, but, rather, spiral lines that lost their circularity as the impetus declined. Other girls sat playing at spillikins[3] (surely the most frivolous game that children play); I walked closer to observe the figures they formed, and seeing that by chance three lay in a triangle, I set to joining one with another, recalling that this was said to be the form of the mysterious ring of Solomon,[4] in which he was able to see the distant splendor and images of the Holy Trinity, by virtue of which the ring worked such prodigies and marvels. And the same shape was said to form David's harp, and that is why Saul was refreshed at its sound; and harps today largely conserve that shape.

And what shall I tell you, lady, of the natural secrets I have discovered while cooking? I see that an egg holds together and fries in butter or in oil, but, on the contrary, in syrup shrivels into shreds; observe that to keep sugar in a liquid state one need only add a drop or two of water in which a quince or other bitter fruit has been soaked; observe that the yolk and the white of one egg are so dissimilar that each with sugar produces a result not obtainable with both together. I do not wish to weary you with such inconsequential matters, and make mention of them only to give you full notice of my nature, for I believe they will be occasion for laughter. But, lady, as women, what wisdom may be ours if not the philosophies of the kitchen? Lupercio Leonardo[5] spoke well when he said: how well one may philosophize when preparing dinner. And I often say, when observing these trivial details: had Aristotle prepared victuals, he would have written more. And pursuing the manner of my cogitations, I tell you that this process is so continuous in me that I have no need for books. And

---

2. Motion.   3. Jackstraws, or pickup sticks.   4. It may, like Solomon's seal, have contained the image of the Star of David, composed of triangles.   5. Lupercio Leonardo de Argensola (1559–1639), poet, playwright, and historian.

on one occasion, when because of a grave upset of the stomach the physicians forbade me to study, I passed thus some days, but then I proposed that it would be less harmful if they allowed me books, because so vigorous and vehement were my cogitations that my spirit was consumed more greatly in a quarter of an hour than in four days' studying books. And thus they were persuaded to allow me to read. And moreover, lady, not even have my dreams been excluded from this ceaseless agitation of my imagination; indeed, in dreams it is wont to work more freely and less encumbered, collating with greater clarity and calm the gleanings of the day, arguing and making verses, of which I could offer you an extended catalogue, as well as of some arguments and inventions that I have better achieved sleeping than awake. I relinquish this subject in order not to tire you, for the above is sufficient to allow your discretion and acuity to penetrate perfectly and perceive my nature, as well as the beginnings, the methods, and the present state of my studies.

Even, lady, were these merits (and I see them celebrated as such in men), they would not have been so in me, for I cannot but study. If they are faults, then, for the same reasons, I believe I have none. Nevertheless, I live always with so little confidence in myself that neither in my study, nor in any other thing, do I trust my judgment; and thus I remit the decision to your sovereign genius, submitting myself to whatever sentence you may bestow, without controversy, without reluctance, for I have wished here only to present you with a simple narration of my inclination toward letters.

I confess, too, that though it is true, as I have stated, that I had no need of books, it is nonetheless also true that they have been no little inspiration, in divine as in human letters. Because I find a Debbora[6] administering the law, both military and political, and governing a people among whom there were many learned men. I find a most wise Queen of Saba,[7] so learned that she dares to challenge with hard questions the wisdom of the greatest of all wise men, without being reprimanded for doing so, but, rather, as a consequence, to judge unbelievers. I see many and illustrious women; some blessed with the gift of prophecy, like Abigail, others of persuasion, like Esther; others with pity, like Rehab; others with perseverance, like Anna,[8] the mother of Samuel; and an infinite number of others, with divers gifts and virtues.

If I again turn to the Gentiles, the first I encounter are the Sibyls,[9] those women chosen by God to prophesy the principal mysteries of our Faith, and with learned and elegant verses that surpass admiration. I see adored as a goddess of the sciences a woman like Minerva,[1] the daughter of the first Jupiter and mistress over all the wisdom of Athens. I see a Polla Argentaria, who helped Lucan, her husband, write his epic *Pharsalia*.[2] I see the daughter of the divine Tiresias,[3] more learned than her father. I see a Zenobia,[4]

---

6. Or Deborah, a prophetess who judged the Israelites (Judges 4.4–14).   7. Or Sheba, who tested King Solomon with questions (1 Kings 10.1–3).   8. Or Hannah, who after years of childlessness received the answer to her prayers in the birth of Samuel (1 Samuel 1.1–20). Abigail was the wife of a surly husband, Nabal. After Nabal insulted King David, she went to the king with presents and prophesied his future triumphs, thus saving her husband's life (1 Samuel 25.2–35). Esther persuaded her husband, King Ahasuerus, to protect the Jews (Esther 5–9). Rehab, or Rahab, was a harlot who protected two Israelites from the King of Jericho (Joshua 2.1–7).   9. Female prophets of the ancient world.   1. Or Athena, goddess of wisdom.
2. Epic poem on the civil war between Caesar and Pompey, properly called *Bellum Civile* (ca. 62–65 C.E.).
3. A legendary blind Theban seer. His daughter was Manto, known for her skill in divination by fire.
4. The learned widow of Odenathus, declared her independence from Rome and expanded the Middle-Eastern territory under her rule, naming herself Augusta, empress of Rome. She was finally defeated and captured in 272.

Queen of the Palmyrans, as wise as she was valiant. An Arete, most learned daughter of Aristippus.[5] A Nicostrate,[6] framer of Latin verses and most erudite in Greek. An Aspasia Milesia, who taught philosophy and rhetoric, and who was a teacher of the philosopher Pericles. An Hypatia, who taught astrology, and studied many years in Alexandria. A Leontium, a Greek woman, who questioned the philosopher Theophrastus, and convinced him. A Julia, a Corinna, a Cornelia;[7] and, finally, a great throng of women deserving to be named, some as Greeks, some as muses, some as seers; for all were nothing more than learned women, held, and celebrated—and venerated as well—as such by antiquity. Without mentioning an infinity of other women whose names fill books. For example, I find the Egyptian Catherine,[8] studying and influencing the wisdom of all the wise men of Egypt. I see a Gertrudis[9] studying, writing, and teaching. And not to overlook examples close to home, I see my most holy mother Paula, learned in Hebrew, Greek, and Latin, and most able in interpreting the Scriptures. And what greater praise than, having as her chronicler a Jeronimus Maximus,[1] that Saint scarcely found himself competent for his task, and says, with that weighty deliberation and energetic precision with which he so well expressed himself: "If all the members of my body were tongues, they still would not be sufficient to proclaim the wisdom and virtue of Paula." Similarly praiseworthy was the widow Blesilla; also, the illustrious virgin Eustochium,[2] both daughters of this same saint; especially the second, who, for her knowledge, was called the Prodigy of the World. The Roman Fabiola[3] was most well-versed in the Holy Scripture. Proba Falconia, a Roman woman, wrote elegant centos,[4] containing verses from Virgil, about the mysteries of Our Holy Faith. It is well-known by all that Queen Isabel,[5] wife of the tenth Alfonso, wrote about astrology. Many others I do not list, out of the desire not merely to transcribe what others have said (a vice I have always abominated); and many are flourishing today, as witness Christina Alexandra, Queen of Sweden,[6] as learned as she is valiant and magnanimous, and the Most Honorable Ladies, the Duquesa of Abeyro and the Condesa of Villaumbrosa.

The venerable Doctor Arce[7] (by his virtue and learning a worthy teacher of the Scriptures) in his scholarly *Bibliorum* raises this question: *Is it permissible for women to dedicate themselves to the study of the Holy Scriptures, and to their interpretation?* and he offers as negative arguments the opinions of many saints, especially that of the Apostle: *Let women keep silence in the churches; for it is not permitted them to speak,* etc.[8] He later cites other opinions and, from the same Apostle, verses from his letter to Titus: *The aged women in like manner, in holy attire . . . teaching well,*[9] with interpretations by the Holy Fathers. Finally he resolves, with all prudence, that teaching

---

5. Greek philosopher (ca. 435–ca. 360 B.C.E.).   6. Or Carmentis, legendary daughter of Pallas, king of Arcadia, and (in legend) inventor of the Roman alphabet.   7. Noted for her devotion to her children's education after her husband's death (2nd century B.C.E.); she was the second daughter of Scipio Africanus and wife of Tiberius Sempronius Gracchus. Julia Domna (2nd century C.E.), wife of the Roman emperor Septimius Severus, known for her learning as Julia the Philosopher. Corinna (ca. 500? B.C.E.), a lyric poet of Tanagra who wrote for a group of women.   8. Saint Catherine (4th century?), allegedly so wise she could refute fifty philosophers at once.   9. Saint Gertrude (died 1302), Benedictine nun and visionary, an important mystic.   1. Saint Jerome.   2. Blesilla and Eustochium were daughters of Saint Paula and, like her, were taught by Saint Jerome.   3. One of Jerome's disciples.   4. Compositions made up of verses from other authors.   5. Of Spain, wife of Alfonso X, Alfonso the Wise (1221–1284).   6. She attracted many scholars and artists to her court (1626–1689).   7. Juan Díaz de Arce (1594–1653), author of theological books.   8. 1 Corinthians 14.34.   9. Titus 2.3–5.

publicly from a University chair, or preaching from the pulpit, is not permissible for women; but that to study, write, and teach privately not only is permissible, but most advantageous and useful. It is evident that this is not to be the case with all women, but with those to whom God may have granted special virtue and prudence, and who may be well advanced in learning, and having the essential talent and requisites for such a sacred calling. This view is indeed just, so much so that not only women, who are held to be so inept, but also men, who merely for being men believe they are wise, should be prohibited from interpreting the Sacred Word if they are not learned and virtuous and of gentle and well-inclined natures; that this is not so has been, I believe, at the root of so much sectarianism and so many heresies. For there are many who study but are ignorant, especially those who are in spirit arrogant, troubled, and proud, so eager for new interpretations of the Word (which itself rejects new interpretations) that merely for the sake of saying what no one else has said they speak a heresy, and even then are not content. Of these the Holy Spirit says: *For wisdom will not enter into a malicious soul.*[1] To such as these more harm results from knowing than from ignorance. A wise man has said: he who does not know Latin is not a complete fool; but he who knows it is well qualified to be.[2] And I would add that a fool may reach perfection (if ignorance may tolerate perfection) by having studied his tittle of philosophy and theology and by having some learning of tongues, by which he may be a fool in many sciences and languages: a great fool cannot be contained solely in his mother tongue.

For such as these, I reiterate, study is harmful, because it is as if to place a sword in the hands of a madman; which, though a most noble instrument for defense, is in his hands his own death and that of many others. So were the Divine Scriptures in the possession of the evil Pelagius and the intractable Arius, of the evil Luther, and the other heresiarchs like our own Doctor (who was neither ours nor a doctor) Cazalla.[3] To these men, wisdom was harmful, although it is the greatest nourishment and the life of the soul; in the same way that in a stomach of sickly constitution and adulterated complexion, the finer the nourishment it receives, the more arid, fermented, and perverse are the humors it produces; thus these evil men: the more they study, the worse opinions they engender, their reason being obstructed with the very substance meant to nourish it, and they study much and digest little, exceeding the limits of the vessel of their reason. Of which the Apostle says: *For I say, by the grace that is given me, to all that are among you, not to be more wise than it behoveth to be wise, but to be wise unto sobriety, and according as God hath divided to every one the measure of faith.*[4] And in truth, the Apostle did not direct these words to women, but to men; and that *keep silence* is intended not only for women, but for *all* incompetents. If I desire to know as much, or more, than Aristotle or Saint Augustine, and if I have not the aptitude of Saint Augustine or Aristotle, though I study more

---

1. Book of Wisdom 1.4 (in the Apocrypha).   2. Alludes to the Spanish proverb "A fool, unless he knows Latin, is never a great fool."   3. Augustino Cazallo (1510–1559), Spanish Protestant executed by the Inquisition for promulgating Lutheran doctrine. Pelagius was a heretical monk (ca. 355–ca. 425) who taught that people do not need divine grace because they have a natural tendency to seek the good. Arius was a Libyan theologian (ca. 256–336), founder of the Arian heresy that declared that Christ was neither eternal nor equal with God. Martin Luther (1483–1546), was the German leader of the Protestant Reformation and, from Sister Juana's point of view, another heretic.   4. Romans 12.3.

than either, not only will I not achieve learning, but I will weaken and dull the workings of my feeble reason with the disproportionateness of the goal.

Oh, that each of us—I, being ignorant, the first—should take the measure of our talents before we study, or, more importantly, write, with the covetous ambition to equal and even surpass others, how little spirit we should have for it, and how many errors we should avoid, and how many tortured intellects of which we have experience, we should have had no experience! And I place my own ignorance in the forefront of all these, for if I knew all I should, I would not write. And I protest that I do so only to obey you; and with such apprehension that you owe me more that I have taken up my pen in fear than you would have owed had I presented you more perfect works. But it is well that they go to your correction. Cross them out, tear them up, reprove me, and I shall appreciate that more than all the vain applause others may offer. *That just men shall correct me in mercy, and shall reprove me; but let not the oil of the sinner fatten my head.*[5] And returning again to our Arce, I say that in affirmation of his opinion he cites the words of my father, Saint Jerome: *To Leta, Upon the Education of Her Daughter.* Where he says: *Accustom her tongue, still young, to the sweetness of the Psalms. Even the names through which little by little she will become accustomed to form her phrases should not be chosen by chance, but selected and repeated with care; the prophets must be included, of course, and the apostles, as well, and all the Patriarchs beginning with Adam and down to Matthew and Luke, so that as she practices other things she will be readying her memory for the future. Let your daily task be taken from the flower of the Scriptures.* And if this Saint desired that a young girl scarcely beginning to talk be educated in this fashion, what would he desire for his nuns and his spiritual daughters? These beliefs are illustrated in the examples of the previously mentioned Eustochium and Fabiola, and Marcella, her sister, and Pacatula, and others whom the Saint honors in his epistles, exhorting them to this sacred exercise, as they are recognized in the epistle I cited, *Let your daily task . . .* which is affirmation of and agreement with the *aged women . . . teaching well* of Saint Paul. My illustrious Father's *Let your daily task . . .* makes clear that the teacher of the child is to be Leta herself, the child's mother.

Oh, how much injury might have been avoided in our land if our aged women had been learned, as was Leta, and had they known how to instruct as directed by Saint Paul and by my Father, Saint Jerome. And failing this, and because of the considerable idleness to which our poor women have been relegated, if a father desires to provide his daughters with more than ordinary learning, he is forced by necessity, and by the absence of wise elder women, to bring men to teach the skills of reading, writing, counting, the playing of musical instruments, and other accomplishments, from which no little harm results, as is experienced every day in doleful examples of perilous association, because through the immediacy of contact and the intimacy born from the passage of time, what one may never have thought possible is easily accomplished. For which reason many prefer to leave their daughters unpolished and uncultured rather than to expose them to such notorious peril as that of familiarity with men, which quandary could be prevented if there were learned elder women, as Saint Paul wished to see,

5. Psalm 141.5.

and if the teaching were handed down from one to another, as is the custom with domestic crafts and all other traditional skills.

For what objection can there be that an older woman, learned in letters and in sacred conversation and customs, have in her charge the education of young girls? This would prevent these girls being lost either for lack of instruction or for hesitating to offer instruction through such dangerous means as male teachers, for even when there is no greater risk of indecency than to seat beside a modest woman (who still may blush when her own father looks directly at her) a strange man who treats her as if he were a member of the household and with the authority of an intimate, the modesty demanded in interchange with men, and in conversation with them, is sufficient reason that such an arrangement not be permitted. For I do not find that the custom of men teaching women is without its peril, lest it be in the severe tribunal of the confessional, or from the remote decency of the pulpit, or in the distant learning of books—never in the personal contact of immediacy. And the world knows this is true; and, notwithstanding, it is permitted solely from the want of learned elder women. Then is it not detrimental, the lack of such women? This question should be addressed by those who, bound to that *Let women keep silence in the church,* say that it is blasphemy for women to learn and teach, as if it were not the Apostle himself who said: *The aged women . . . teaching well.* As well as the fact that this prohibition touches upon historical fact as reported by Eusebium:[6] which is that in the early Church, women were charged with teaching the doctrine to one another in the temples and the sound of this teaching caused confusion as the Apostles were preaching and this is the reason they were ordered to be silent; and even today, while the homilist is preaching, one does not pray aloud.

Who will argue that for the comprehension of many Scriptures one must be familiar with the history, customs, ceremonies, proverbs, and even the manners of speaking of those times in which they were written, if one is to apprehend the references and allusions of more than a few passages of the Holy Word. *And rend your heart and not your garments.*[7] Is this not a reference to the ceremony in which Hebrews rent their garments as a sign of grief, as did the evil pontiff when he said that Christ had blasphemed? In many scriptures the Apostle writes of succour for widows; did they not refer to the customs of those times? Does not the example of the valiant woman, *Her husband is honourable in the gates,*[8] allude to the fact that the tribunals of the judges were at the gates of the cities? That *Dare terram Deo,* give of your land to God, did that not mean to make some votive offering? And did they not call the public sinners *hiemantes,* those who endure the winter, because they made their penance in the open air instead of at a town gate as others did? And Christ's plaint to that Pharisee who had neither kissed him nor given him water for his feet,[9] was that not because it was the Jews' usual custom to offer these acts of hospitality? And we find an infinite number of additional instances not only in the Divine Letters, but human, as well, such as *adorate purpuram,* venerate the purple, which meant obey the King; *manumittere eum,* manumit them, alluding to the custom and ceremony of striking the slave with one's hand to signify his freedom. That *intonuit coelum,*

---

6. Probably Eusebius of Caesaria (ca. 263–339?), an early church historian.   7. Joel 2.13.
8. Proverbs 31.23.   9. Luke 7.44–45.

heaven thundered, in Virgil, which alludes to the augury of thunder from the west, which was held to be good.[1] Martial's *tu nunquam leporem edisti,*[2] you never ate hare, has not only the wit of ambiguity in its *leporem,*[3] but, as well, the allusion to the reputed propensity of hares [to bless with beauty those who dine on them]. That proverb, *maleam legens, que sunt domi obliviscere,* to sail along the shore of Malia is to forget what one has at home, alludes to the great peril of the promontory of Laconia.[4] That chaste matron's response to the unwanted suit of her pretender: "the hinge-pins shall not be oiled for my sake, nor shall the torches blaze," meaning that she did not want to marry, alluded to the ceremony of anointing the doorways with oils and lighting the nuptial torches in the wedding ceremony, as if now we would say, they shall not prepare the thirteen coins for my dowry, nor shall the priest invoke the blessing. And thus it is with many comments of Virgil and Homer and all the poets and orators. In addition, how many are the difficulties found even in the grammar of the Holy Scripture, such as writing a plural for a singular, or changing from the second to third persons, as in the Psalms, *Let him kiss me with the kiss of his mouth, for thy breasts are better than wine.*[5] Or placing adjectives in the genitive instead of the accusative, as in *Calicem salutaris accipiam,* I will take the chalice of salvation.[6] Or to replace the feminine with the masculine, and, in contrast, to call any sin adultery.

All this demands more investigation than some believe, who strictly as grammarians, or, at most, employing the four principles of applied logic, attempt to interpret the Scriptures while clinging to that *Let the women keep silence in the church,* not knowing how it is to be interpreted. As well as that other verse, *Let the women learn in silence.*[7] For this latter scripture works more to women's favor than their disfavor, as it commands them to learn; and it is only natural that they must maintain silence while they learn. And it is also written, *Hear, oh Israel, and be silent.*[8] Which addresses the entire congregation of men and women, commanding all to silence, because if one is to hear and learn, it is with good reason that he attend and be silent. And if it is not so, I would want these interpreters and expositors of Saint Paul to explain to me how they interpret that scripture, *Let the women keep silence in the church.* For either they must understand it to refer to the material church, that is the church of pulpits and cathedras,[9] or to the spiritual, the community of the faithful, which is the Church. If they understand it to be the former, which, in my opinion, is its true interpretation, then we see that if in fact it is not permitted of women to read publicly in church, nor preach, why do they censure those who study privately? And if they understand the latter, and wish that the prohibition of the Apostle be applied transcendentally—that not even in private are women to be permitted to write or study—how are we to view the fact that the Church permitted a Gertrudis, a Santa Teresa, a Saint Birgitta, the Nun of Agreda,[1] and so

---

1. Sister Juana possibly misremembers *Aeneid* 2.693: "thunder on the left."   2. Marcus Valerius Martialis (ca. 40–ca. 104), Roman epigrammatic poet; "Edisti numquam, Gellia, tu leporem" (*Epigrams* 5.29).
3. *Leporem* can also mean "charm, grace, attractiveness."   4. The site of ancient Sparta, conquered by Macedonia in the 4th century B.C.E.   5. Song of Solomon 1.2.   6. Psalm 116.13.   7. I Timothy 2.11.   8. Not a biblical quotation.   9. A cathedra is the throne of the bishop in his church.
1. Maria de Agreda (1602–1635), Spanish Franciscan nun, author of *The Mystic City of God* (1670), a work allegedly divinely inspired. Birgitta, or Bridget (1303–1373), of Sweden.

many others, to write? And if they say to me that these women were saints, they speak the truth; but this poses no obstacle to my argument. First, because Saint Paul's proposition is absolute, and encompasses all women not excepting saints, as Martha and Mary, Marcella, Mary, mother of Jacob, and Salome,[2] all were in their time, and many other zealous women of the early church. But we see, too, that the Church allows women who are not saints to write, for the Nun of Agreda and Sor María de la Antigua[3] are not canonized, yet their writings are circulated. And when Santa Teresa and the others were writing, they were not as yet canonized. In which case, Saint Paul's prohibition was directed solely to the public office of the pulpit, for if the Apostle had forbidden women to write, the Church would not have allowed it. Now I do not make so bold as to teach—which in me would be excessively presumptuous—and as for writing, that requires a greater talent than mine, and serious reflection. As Saint Cyprian[4] says: *The things we write require most conscientious consideration.* I have desired to study that I might be ignorant of less; for (according to Saint Augustine[5]) some things are learned to be enacted and others only to be known: *We learn some things to know them, others, to do them.* Then, where is the offense to be found if even what is licit to women—which is to teach by writing—I do not perform, as I know that I am lacking in means, following the counsel of Quintilian: *Let each person learn not only from the precepts of others, but also let him reap counsel from his own nature.*

If the offense is to be found in the *Atenagórica* letter, was that letter anything other than the simple expression of my feeling, written with the implicit permission of our Holy Mother Church? For if the Church, in her most sacred authority, does not forbid it, why must others do so? That I proffered an opinion contrary to that of de Vieyra was audacious, but, as a Father, was it not audacious that he speak against the three Holy Fathers of the Church? My reason, such as it is, is it not as unfettered as his, as both issue from the same source? Is his opinion to be considered as a revelation, as a principle of the Holy Faith, that we must accept blindly? Furthermore, I maintained at all times the respect due such a virtuous man, a respect in which his defender was sadly wanting, ignoring the phrase of Titus Lucius:[6] *Respect is companion to the arts.* I did not touch a thread of the robes of the Society of Jesus; nor did I write for other than the consideration of the person who suggested that I write. And, according to Pliny, *how different the condition of one who writes from that of one who merely speaks.* Had I believed the letter was to be published I would not have been so inattentive. If, as the censor says, the letter is heretical, why does he not denounce it? And with that he would be avenged, and I content, for, which is only seemly, I esteem more highly my reputation as a Catholic and obedient daughter of the Holy Mother Church than all the approbation due a learned woman. If the letter is rash, and he does well to criticize it, then laugh, even if with the

---

2. In the King James Bible, Mary, the mother of James (or Jacob), and Salome came to the empty sepulcher to anoint Jesus' body (Mark 16.1). Martha and Mary were sisters. Mary anointed Jesus' feet (John 12.3). Martha was preoccupied with household tasks (Luke 10.40–42). Marcella was one of the women taught by Jerome. 3. Spanish nun (1544–1617). 4. Thascius Caecilius Cyprianus (ca. 200–258), one of the church fathers, known for his efforts to enforce church discipline. 5. Aurelius Augustinus (354–430), baptized by Saint Ambrose in 387, author of *De Civitate Dei*, a vindication of the church that long possessed great authority. 6. Better known as Saturantius Apuleius (2nd century C.E.), greatly celebrated in his time for eloquence.

laugh of the rabbit, for I have not asked that he approve; as I was free to dissent from de Vieyra, so will anyone be free to oppose my opinion.

But how I have strayed, lady. None of this pertains here, nor is it intended for your ears, but as I was discussing my accusers I remembered the words of one that recently have appeared, and, though my intent was to speak in general, my pen, unbidden, slipped, and began to respond in particular. And so, returning to our Arce, he says that he knew in this city two nuns: one in the Convent of the Regina, who had so thoroughly committed the Breviary to memory that with the greatest promptitude and propriety she applied in her conversation its verses, psalms, and maxims of saintly homilies. The other, in the Convent of the Conception, was so accustomed to reading the Epistles of my Father Saint Jerome, and the Locutions of this Saint, that Arce says, *It seemed I was listening to Saint Jerome himself, speaking in Spanish*. And of this latter woman he says that after her death he learned that she had translated these Epistles into the Spanish language. What pity that such talents could not have been employed in major studies with scientific principles. He does not give the name of either, although he offers these women as confirmation of his opinion, which is that not only is it licit, but most useful and essential for women to study the Holy Word, and even more essential for nuns; and that study is the very thing to which your wisdom exhorts me, and in which so many arguments concur.

Then if I turn my eyes to the oft-chastized faculty of making verses—which is in me so natural that I must discipline myself that even this letter not be written in that form—I might cite those lines, *All I wished to express took the form of verse*.[7] And seeing that so many condemn and criticize this ability, I have conscientiously sought to find what harm may be in it, and I have not found it, but, rather, I see verse acclaimed in the mouths of the Sibyls; sanctified in the pens of the Prophets, especially King David, of whom the exalted Expositor my beloved Father[8] says (explicating the measure of his meters): *in the manner of Horace and Pindar, now it hurries along in iambs, now it rings in alcaic, now swells in sapphic, then arrives in broken feet*. The greater part of the Holy Books are in meter, as is the Book of Moses; and those of Job (as Saint Isidore[9] states in his *Etymologiae*) are in heroic verse. Solomon wrote the Canticle of Canticles in verse; and Jeremias, his *Lamentations*. And so, says Cassiodorus:[1] *All poetic expression had as its source the Holy Scriptures*. For not only does our Catholic Church not disdain verse, it employs verse in its hymns, and recites the lines of Saint Ambrose,[2] Saint Thomas, Saint Isidore, and others. Saint Bonaventure[3] was so taken with verse that he writes scarcely a page where it does not appear. It is readily apparent that Saint Paul had studied verse, for he quotes and translates verses of Aratus: *For in him we live, and move, and are*.[4] And he quotes also that verse of Parmenides: *The Cretians are always liars, evil beasts, slothful bellies*.[5] Saint Gregory Nazianzen[6] argues in elegant verses

---

7. Ovid's *Tristia* 4.10.25ff. 8. Jerome. 9. Spanish archbishop (ca. 560–636), who helped organize the church in Spain. 1. Flavius Magnus Aurelius Cassiodorus (ca. 485–ca. 580), Roman monk and author of *Institutiones*, a course of studies for monks. 2. Bishop of Milan (339–397), who had an important share in the conversion of Saint Augustine. 3. Franciscan bishop and cardinal (1221–1274), who preached the importance of study. 4. Acts 17.28. 5. Titus 1.12. 6. Gregorius Nazianzenus, bishop of Constantinople and associate of Jerome. The allusion is to the first of his forty moral poems, 732 lines eulogizing virginity.

the questions of matrimony and virginity. And, how should I tire? The Queen of Wisdom, Our Lady, with Her sacred lips, intoned the Canticle of the Magnificat;[7] and having brought forth this example, it would be offensive to add others that were profane, even those of the most serious and learned men, for this alone is more than sufficient confirmation; and even though Hebrew elegance could not be compressed into Latin measure, for which reason, although the sacred translator, more attentive to the importance of the meaning, omitted the verse, the Psalms retain the number and divisions of verses, and what harm is to be found in them? For misuse is not the blame of art, but rather of the evil teacher who perverts the arts, making of them the snare of the devil; and this occurs in all the arts and sciences.

And if the evil is attributed to the fact that a woman employs them, we have seen how many have done so in praiseworthy fashion; what then is the evil in my being a woman? I confess openly my own baseness and meanness; but I judge that no couplet of mine has been deemed indecent. Furthermore, I have never written of my own will, but under the pleas and injunctions of others; to such a degree that the only piece I remember having written for my own pleasure was a little trifle they called El sueño.[8] That letter, lady, which you so greatly honored, I wrote more with repugnance than any other emotion; both by reason of the fact that it treated sacred matters, for which (as I have stated) I hold such reverent awe, and because it seems to wish to impugn, a practice for which I have natural aversion; and I believe that had I foreseen the blessed destiny to which it was fated—for like a second Moses I had set it adrift, naked, on the waters of the Nile of silence, where you, a princess, found and cherished it[9]—I believe, I reiterate, that had I known, the very hands of which it was born would have drowned it, out of the fear that these clumsy scribblings from my ignorance appear before the light of your great wisdom; by which one knows the munificence of your kindness, for your goodwill applauds precisely what your reason must wish to reject. For as fate cast it before your doors, so exposed, so orphaned, that it fell to you even to give it a name, I must lament that among other deformities it also bears the blemish of haste; both because of the unrelenting ill-health I suffer, and for the profusion of duties imposed on me by obedience, as well as the want of anyone to guide me in my writing and the need that it all come from my hand, and, finally, because the writing went against my nature and I wished only to keep my promise to one whom I could not disobey, I could not find the time to finish properly, and thus I failed to include whole treatises and many arguments that presented themselves to me, but which I omitted in order to put an end to the writing—many, that had I known the letter was to be printed, I would not have excluded, even if merely to satisfy some objections that have since arisen and which could have been refuted. But I shall not be so ill-mannered as to place such indecent objects before the purity of your eyes, for it is enough that my ignorance be an offense in your sight, without need of entrusting to it the effronteries of others. If they should wing your way (and they are of such little weight

---

7. Luke 1.46–55. 8. *The Dream,* one of Sister Juana's best-known poems, which tells of the flight of her soul toward learning. 9. Because Pharaoh had ordered all male Hebrew infants killed, Moses' mother placed him in a basket by the Nile, where he was found and rescued by Pharaoh's daughter (Exodus 2.1–10).

that this will happen), then you will command what I am to do; for, if it does not run contrary to your will, my defense shall be not to take up my pen, for I deem that one affront need not occasion another, if one recognizes the error in the very place it lies concealed. As my Father Saint Jerome says, *good discourse seeks not things,* and Saint Ambrose, *it is the nature of a guilty conscience to lie concealed.* Nor do I consider that I have been impugned, for one statute of the Law states: *An accusation will not endure unless nurtured by the person who brought it forth.* What *is* a matter to be weighed is the effort spent in copying the accusation. A strange madness, to expend more effort in denying acclaim than in earning it! I, lady, have chosen not to respond (although others did so without my knowledge); it suffices that I have seen certain treatises, among them one so learned I send it to you so that reading it will compensate in part for the time you squandered on my writing. If, lady, you wish that I act contrary to what I have proposed here for your judgment and opinion, the merest indication of your desire will, as is seemly, countermand my inclination, which, as I have told you, is to be silent, for although Saint John Chrysostom says, *those who slander must be refuted, and those who question, taught,* I know also that Saint Gregory[1] says, *It is no less a victory to tolerate enemies than to overcome them.* And that patience conquers by tolerating and triumphs by suffering. And if among the Roman Gentiles it was the custom when their captains were at the highest peak of glory—when returning triumphant from other nations, robed in purple and wreathed with laurel, crowned-but-conquered kings pulling their carriages in the stead of beasts, accompanied by the spoils of the riches of all the world, the conquering troops adorned with the insignia of their heroic feats, hearing the plaudits of the people who showered them with titles of honor and renown such as Fathers of the Nation, Columns of the Empire, Walls of Rome, Shelter of the Republic, and other glorious names— a soldier went before these captains in this moment of the supreme apogee of glory and human happiness crying out in a loud voice to the conqueror (by his consent and order of the Senate): Behold how you are mortal; behold how you have this or that defect, not excepting the most shameful, as happened in the triumph of Caesar, when the vilest soldiers clamored in his ear: *Beware, Romans, for we bring you the bald adulterer.* Which was done so that in the midst of such honor the conquerers not be swelled up with pride, and that the ballast of these insults act as counterweight to the bellying sails of such approbation, and that the ship of good judgment not founder amidst the winds of acclamation. If this, I say, was the practice among Gentiles, who knew only the light of Natural Law, how much might we Catholics, under the injunction to love our enemies, achieve by tolerating them? And in my own behalf I can attest that calumny has often mortified me, but never harmed me, being that I hold as a great fool one who having occasion to receive credit suffers the difficulty and loses the credit, as it is with those who do not resign themselves to death, but, in the end, die anyway, their resistance not having prevented death, but merely deprived them of the credit of resignation and caused them to die badly when they might have died well.

---

1. Gregory the Great (ca. 540–604), pope from 590, deeply concerned with the reformation of the church. Chrysostom (ca. 347–407), a Syrian prelate known as the greatest orator of the church, author of many homilies and treatises.

And thus, lady, I believe these experiences do more good than harm, and I hold as greater the jeopardy of applause to human weakness, as we are wont to appropriate praise that is not our own, and must be ever watchful, and carry graven on our hearts those words of the Apostle: *Or what hast thou that thou hast not received? And if thou hast received, why doest thou glory as if thou hadst not received it?*[2] so that these words serve as a shield to fend off the sharp barbs of commendations, which are as spears which when not attributed to God (whose they are), claim our lives and cause us to be thieves of God's honor and usurpers of the talents He bestowed on us and the gifts that He lent to us, for which we must give the most strict accounting. And thus, lady, I fear applause more than calumny, because the latter, with but the simple act of patience becomes gain, while the former requires many acts of reflection and humility and proper recognition so that it not become harm. And I know and recognize that it is by special favor of God that I know this, as it enables me in either instance to act in accord with the words of Saint Augustine: *One must believe neither the friend who praises nor the enemy who detracts.* Although most often I squander God's favor, or vitiate with such defects and imperfections that I spoil what, being His, was good. And thus in what little of mine that has been printed, neither the use of my name, nor even consent for the printing, was given by my own counsel, but by the license of another who lies outside my domain, as was also true with the printing of the *Atenagórica* letter, and only a few *Exercises of the Incarnation* and *Offerings of the Sorrow* were printed for public devotions with my pleasure, but without my name; of which I am sending some few copies that (if you so desire) you may distribute them among our sisters, the nuns of that holy community, as well as in that city. I send but one copy of the *Sorrows* because the others have been exhausted and I could find no other copy. I wrote them long ago, solely for the devotions of my sisters, and later they were spread abroad; and their contents are disproportionate as regards my unworthiness and my ignorance, and they profited that they touched on matters of our exalted Queen; for I cannot explain what it is that inflames the coldest heart when one refers to the Most Holy Mary. It is my only desire, esteemed lady, to remit to you works worthy of your virtue and wisdom; as the poet said: *Though strength may falter, good will must be praised. In this, I believe, the gods will be content.*

If ever I write again, my scribbling will always find its way to the haven of your holy feet and the certainty of your correction, for I have no other jewel with which to pay you, and, in the lament of Seneca, he who has once bestowed benefices has committed himself to continue; and so you must be repaid out of your own munificence, for only in this way shall I with dignity be freed from debt and avoid that the words of that same Seneca come to pass: *It is contemptible to be surpassed in benefices.*[3] For in his gallantry the generous creditor gives to the poor debtor the means to satisfy his debt. So God gave his gift to a world unable to repay Him: He gave his son that He be offered a recompense worthy of Him.

If, most venerable lady, the tone of this letter may not have seemed right and proper, I ask forgiveness for its homely familiarity, and the less than seemly respect in which by treating you as a nun, one of my sisters, I have

2. Corinthians 11.4.   3. *On Benefits* 5.2.1.

lost sight of the remoteness of your most illustrious person; which, had I seen you without your veil, would never have occurred; but you in all your prudence and mercy will supplement or amend the language, and if you find unsuitable the *Vos* of the address I have employed, believing that for the reverence I owe you, Your Reverence seemed little reverent, modify it in whatever manner seems appropriate to your due, for I have not dared exceed the limits of your custom, nor transgress the boundary of your modesty.

And hold me in your grace, and entreat for me divine grace, of which the Lord God grant you large measure, and keep you, as I pray Him, and am needful. From this convent of our Father Saint Jerome in Mexico City, the first day of the month of March of sixteen hundred and ninety-one. Allow me to kiss your hand, your most favored

JUANA INÉS DE LA CRUZ

FRANÇOIS-MARIE AROUET DE VOLTAIRE
1694–1778

Voltaire's *Candide* (1759) brings to near perfection the art of black comedy. It subjects its characters to an accumulation of horrors so bizarre that they provoke a bewildered response of laughter as self-protection—even while they demand that the reader pay attention to the serious implications of such extravagance.

Voltaire had prepared himself to write such a work by varied experience—including that of political imprisonment. He was born François-Marie Arouet, son of a minor treasury official in Paris. After attending a Jesuit school, he took up the study of law, which, however, he soon abandoned. In his early twenties (1717–18), he spent eleven months in the Bastille for writing satiric verses about the aristocracy. His incarceration did not dissuade him from a literary career; by 1718 he was using the name Voltaire and beginning to acquire literary and social reputation—as well as some wealth (his speculations in the Compagnie des Indes made him rich by 1726). Money, however, did not protect him from spending more time in the Bastille during that year; after his release, he passed three years in exile, mainly in England. From 1734 to 1749, he studied widely, living with Madame du Châtelet on her estate at Cirey. For the next three years he stayed with Frederick the Great of Prussia at his Potsdam court; after that arrangement collapsed, Voltaire bought property in Switzerland and in adjacent France, settling first at his own château, Les Delices, outside Geneva, and later at nearby Ferney, in France. His international reputation as writer and social critic steadily increased; in the year of his death, he returned triumphantly to Paris.

Like his English contemporary Samuel Johnson, Voltaire wrote in many important genres: tragedy, epic, history, philosophy, fiction. His *Philosophical Dictionary* (1764), with its witty and penetrating definitions, typifies his range and acumen and his participation in his period's effort to take control of experience by intellect. While still a young man, Voltaire wrote a *History of Charles XII* of Sweden, a work unusual for its time in its novelistic technique and its assumption that "history" includes the personal lives of powerful individuals and has nothing to do with divine intervention. Before *Candide* he had published another philosophic tale, *Zadig* (1748), following the pattern of Asian narrative. Like Candide, Zadig goes through an experiential education; it teaches him inconclusive lessons about life's unforeseeable contingencies.

Candide mocks both the artificial order of fiction (through its ludicrously multiplied recognition scenes and its symmetrical division of the protagonist's travels into three equal parts) and what Voltaire suggests is the equally artificial order posited by philosophic optimists. The view of the universe suggested by Pope's *Essay on Man,* for instance, insists on the rationality of a pattern ungraspable by human reason. *Candide* implicitly argues, however, that it does so only by attending to the abstract and undemonstrable and ignoring the omnipresent pain of immediate experience. Gottfried Leibniz, the German philosopher, provides Voltaire's most specific target in *Candide,* with the complexities of his version of optimism reduced for satiric purposes to the facile formula "Everything is for the best in this best of all possible worlds." The formulation is, of course, unfair to Leibniz, whose philosophic optimism, like Pope's, implies belief in an unknowable universal order—roughly equivalent to Christian Providence—but no lack of awareness about the actual misery and depravity human beings experience.

The exuberance and extravagance of Voltaire's imagination force us to laugh at what we may feel embarrassed to laugh at: the plight of the woman whose buttock has been cut off to make rump steak for her hungry companions, the weeping of two girls whose monkey-lovers have been killed, the situation of six exiled, poverty-stricken kings. Like Swift, Voltaire keeps his readers off balance. Raped, cut to pieces, hanged, stabbed in the belly, the central characters of *Candide* keep coming back to life at opportune moments, as though no disaster could have permanent or ultimately destructive effects. Such reassuring fantasy suggests that we don't need to worry, it is all a joke, an outpouring of fertile fancy designed to ridicule an outmoded philosophic system with no particular relevance to us. On the other hand, historical reality keeps intruding. Those six hungry kings are real, actual figures, actually dispossessed. Candide sees Admiral Byng executed: an admiral who really lived and really died by firing squad for not engaging an enemy with sufficient ferocity. The Lisbon earthquake actually occurred; thirty to forty thousand people lost their lives in it. The extravagances of reality equal those of the storyteller; Voltaire demands that the reader imaginatively confront and somehow come to terms with horrors that surround us still.

The real problem, *Candide* suggests, is not natural or human disaster so much as human complacency. When Candide sees Admiral Byng shot, he comments on the injustice of the execution. "That's perfectly true, came the answer; but in this country it is useful from time to time to kill one admiral in order to encourage the others." Early in the nineteenth century, William Wordsworth wrote, "much it grieved my heart to think / What man has made of man." His tone and perspective differ dramatically from Voltaire's, but his point is the same: human beings use their faculties to increase corruption. Failure to take seriously any human death is a form of moral corruption; failure to acknowledge the intolerability of war, in all its concrete detail of rape and butchery, epitomizes such corruption at its worst.

In a late chapter of *Candide,* the central character, less naive than he once was, inquires about whether people have always massacred one another. Have they, he asks, "always been liars, traitors, ingrates, thieves, weaklings, sneaks, cowards, backbiters, gluttons, drunkards, misers, climbers, killers, calumniators, sensualists, fanatics, hypocrites, and fools?" His interlocutor, Martin, responds that, just as hawks have always devoured pigeons, human beings have always manifested the same vices. This ironic variation on the period's conviction of the universality and continuity of human nature epitomizes Voltaire's sense of outrage. Voltaire shows how the claim of a rational universal order avoids the hard problems of living in a world where human beings have become liars, traitors, and so on; his catalog of vice and folly expresses the moral insufficiency and perversity of humankind. Martin's cynical assumption that people are naturally corrupt, as hawks naturally eat smaller birds, constitutes another form of avoidance. The assumed inevitability of vice, like belief that all is for the best, justifies passivity. Nothing *can* be done, nothing *should* be done, or nothing *matters* (the view of Lord Pococurante, another figure Candide encounters). So the characters of this fiction, including Candide himself, mainly pursue self-gratification. Even this course they do not follow judiciously: when Candide and Cacambo find themselves in the earthly paradise of Eldorado, "the two happy men resolved to be so no longer," driven by fantasies of improving their condition. And yet, they acquire wisdom at last, learning to withstand "three great evils, boredom, vice, and poverty," by working hard at what comes to hand and avoiding futile theorizing about the nature of the universe.

Although Voltaire's picture of the human condition reveals fierce indignation, he allows at least conditional hope for moderate satisfaction in this life. Candide's beloved Cunégonde loses all her beauty, but she becomes an accomplished pastry cook; Candide possesses a garden he can cultivate. Greed, malice, and lust do not make up the total possibility for humankind. If Voltaire's tone sometimes expresses outrage, at other times it verges on the playful. When, for example, he mocks the improbabilities of romance by his characters' miraculous resuscitations or parodies the restrictions of classical form by sending Candide and his friends on an epic journey, one can feel his amused awareness of our human need to make order and our human desire to comfort ourselves by fictions. But as he insists that much of the order we claim to perceive itself a comforting fiction, as he uses satire's energies to challenge our complacencies, he reveals once more the underside of the Enlightenment ideal of reason. That we human beings have reason, Voltaire tells us, is no ground on which to flatter ourselves; rightly used, it exposes our insufficiencies.

PRONOUNCING GLOSSARY

The following list uses common English syllables and stress accents to provide rough equivalents of selected words whose pronunciation may be unfamiliar to the general reader.

Abare: *a-bahr'*

Cacambo: *ka-kahm'-bo*

Candide: *kahn-deed'*

Cunégonde: *kew-nay-gohnd'*

Giroflée: *zhee-roh-flay'*

Issachar: *ee-sah-shahr'*

Pangloss: *pan-glaws'*

Paquette: *pah-ket'*

Pococurante: *poh-koh-ku-rahnt'*

Thunder-Ten-Tronckh: *tun-dayr'–ten–trawnk*

Candide, or Optimism[1]

translated from the German of Doctor Ralph with the additions which were found in the Doctor's pocket when he died at Minden in the Year of Our Lord 1759

CHAPTER 1

How Candide Was Brought up in a Fine Castle and How He Was Driven Therefrom

There lived in Westphalia,[2] in the castle of the Baron of Thunder-Ten-Tronckh, a young man on whom nature had bestowed the perfection of

---

1. Translated and with notes by Robert M. Adams.   2. A province of western Germany, near Holland and the lower Rhineland. Flat, boggy, and drab, it is noted chiefly for its excellent ham. In a letter to his niece, written during his German expedition of 1750, Voltaire described the "vast, sad, sterile, detestable countryside of Westphalia."

gentle manners. His features admirably expressed his soul; he combined an honest mind with great simplicity of heart; and I think it was for this reason that they called him Candide. The old servants of the house suspected that he was the son of the Baron's sister by a respectable, honest gentleman of the neighborhood, whom she had refused to marry because he could prove only seventy-one quarterings,[3] the rest of his family tree having been lost in the passage of time.

The Baron was one of the most mighty lords of Westphalia, for his castle had a door and windows. His great hall was even hung with a tapestry. The dogs of his courtyard made up a hunting pack on occasion, with the stable-boys as huntsmen; the village priest was his grand almoner. They all called him "My Lord," and laughed at his stories.

The Baroness, who weighed in the neighborhood of three hundred and fifty pounds, was greatly respected for that reason, and did the honors of the house with a dignity which rendered her even more imposing. Her daughter Cunégonde,[4] aged seventeen, was a ruddy-cheeked girl, fresh, plump, and desirable. The Baron's son seemed in every way worthy of his father. The tutor Pangloss was the oracle of the household, and little Candide listened to his lectures with all the good faith of his age and character.

Pangloss gave instruction in metaphysico-theologico-cosmoloonigology.[5] He proved admirably that there cannot possibly be an effect without a cause and that in this best of all possible worlds the Baron's castle was the best of all castles and his wife the best of all possible Baronesses.

—It is clear, said he, that things cannot be otherwise than they are, for since everything is made to serve an end, everything necessarily serves the best end. Observe: noses were made to support spectacles, hence we have spectacles. Legs, as anyone can plainly see, were made to be breeched, and so we have breeches. Stones were made to be shaped and to build castles with; thus My Lord has a fine castle, for the greatest Baron in the province should have the finest house; and since pigs were made to be eaten, we eat pork all year round.[6] Consequently, those who say everything is well are uttering mere stupidities; they should say everything is for the best.

Candide listened attentively and believed implicitly; for he found Miss Cunégonde exceedingly pretty, though he never had the courage to tell her so. He decided that after the happiness of being born Baron of Thunder-Ten-Tronckh, the second order of happiness was to be Miss Cunégonde; the third was seeing her every day, and the fourth was listening to Master Pangloss, the greatest philosopher in the province and consequently in the entire world.

One day, while Cunégonde was walking near the castle in the little woods that they called a park, she saw Dr. Pangloss in the underbrush; he was giving a lesson in experimental physics to her mother's maid, a very attractive and obedient brunette. As Miss Cunégonde had a natural bent for the sci-

---

3. Genealogical divisions of one's family-tree. Seventy-one of them is a grotesque number to have, representing something over 2,000 years of uninterrupted nobility.   4. Cunégonde gets her odd name from Kunigunda (wife to Emperor Henry II) who walked barefoot and blindfolded on red-hot irons to prove her chastity; Pangloss gets his name from Greek words meaning all-tongue.   5. The "looney" buried in this burlesque word corresponds to a buried *nigaud*—"booby" in the French. Christian Wolff, disciple of Leibniz, invented and popularized the word "cosmology." The catch phrases in the following sentence, echoed by popularizers of Leibniz, make reference to the determinism of his system, its linking of cause with effect, and its optimism.   6. The argument from design supposes that everything in this world exists for a specific reason; Voltaire objects not to the argument as a whole, but to the abuse of it.

ences, she watched breathlessly the repeated experiments which were going on; she saw clearly the doctor's sufficient reason, observed both cause and effect, and returned to the house in a distracted and pensive frame of mind, yearning for knowledge and dreaming that she might be the sufficient reason of young Candide—who might also be hers.

As she was returning to the castle, she met Candide, and blushed; Candide blushed too. She greeted him in a faltering tone of voice; and Candide talked to her without knowing what he was saying. Next day, as everyone was rising from the dinner table, Cunégonde and Candide found themselves behind a screen; Cunégonde dropped her handkerchief, Candide picked it up; she held his hand quite innocently, he kissed her hand quite innocently with remarkable vivacity and emotion; their lips met, their eyes lit up, their knees trembled, their hands wandered. The Baron of Thunder-Ten-Tronckh passed by the screen and, taking note of this cause and this effect, drove Candide out of the castle by kicking him vigorously on the backside. Cunégonde fainted; as soon as she recovered, the Baroness slapped her face; and everything was confusion in the most beautiful and agreeable of all possible castles.

CHAPTER 2

What Happened to Candide Among the Bulgars[7]

Candide, ejected from the earthly paradise, wandered for a long time without knowing where he was going, weeping, raising his eyes to heaven, and gazing back frequently on the most beautiful of castles which contained the most beautiful of Baron's daughters. He slept without eating, in a furrow of a plowed field, while the snow drifted over him; next morning, numb with cold, he dragged himself into the neighboring village, which was called Waldberghoff-trarbk-dikdorff; he was penniless, famished, and exhausted. At the door of a tavern he paused forlornly. Two men dressed in blue[8] took note of him:

—Look, chum, said one of them, there's a likely young fellow of just about the right size.

They approached Candide and invited him very politely to dine with them.

—Gentlemen, Candide replied with charming modesty, I'm honored by your invitation, but I really don't have enough money to pay my share.

—My dear sir, said one of the blues, people of your appearance and your merit don't have to pay; aren't you five feet five inches tall?

—Yes, gentlemen, that is indeed my stature, said he, making a bow.

—Then, sir, you must be seated at once; not only will we pay your bill this time, we will never allow a man like you to be short of money; for men were made only to render one another mutual aid.

—You are quite right, said Candide; it is just as Dr. Pangloss always told me, and I see clearly that everything is for the best.

They beg him to accept a couple of crowns, he takes them, and offers an I.O.U.; they won't hear of it, and all sit down at table together.

7. Voltaire chose this name to represent the Prussian troops of Frederick the Great because he wanted to make an insinuation of pederasty against both the soldiers and their master. Cf. French *bougre*, English "bugger." 8. The recruiting officers of Frederick the Great, much feared in 18th-century Europe, wore blue uniforms. Frederick had a passion for sorting out his soldiers by size; several of his regiments would accept only six-footers.

—Don't you love dearly . . . ?

—I do indeed, says he, I dearly love Miss Cunégonde.

—No, no, says one of the gentlemen, we are asking if you don't love dearly the King of the Bulgars.

—Not in the least, says he, I never laid eyes on him.

—What's that you say? He's the most charming of kings, and we must drink his health.

—Oh, gladly, gentlemen; and he drinks.

—That will do, they tell him; you are now the bulwark, the support, the defender, the hero of the Bulgars; your fortune is made and your future assured.

Promptly they slip irons on his legs and lead him to the regiment. There they cause him to right face, left face, present arms, order arms, aim, fire, doubletime, and they give him thirty strokes of the rod. Next day he does the drill a little less awkwardly and gets only twenty strokes; the third day, they give him only ten, and he is regarded by his comrades as a prodigy.

Candide, quite thunderstruck, did not yet understand very clearly how he was a hero. One fine spring morning he took it into his head to go for a walk, stepping straight out as if it were a privilege of the human race, as of animals in general, to use his legs as he chose.[9] He had scarcely covered two leagues when four other heroes, each six feet tall, overtook him, bound him, and threw him into a dungeon. At the court-martial they asked which he preferred, to be flogged thirty-six times by the entire regiment or to receive summarily a dozen bullets in the brain. In vain did he argue that the human will is free and insist that he preferred neither alternative; he had to choose; by virtue of the divine gift called "liberty" he decided to run the gauntlet thirty-six times, and actually endured two floggings. The regiment was composed of two thousand men. That made four thousand strokes, which laid open every muscle and nerve from his nape to his butt. As they were preparing for the third beating, Candide, who could endure no more, begged as a special favor that they would have the goodness to smash his head. His plea was granted; they bandaged his eyes and made him kneel down. The King of the Bulgars, passing by at this moment, was told of the culprit's crime; and as this king had a rare genius, he understood, from everything they told him of Candide, that this was a young metaphysician, extremely ignorant of the ways of the world, so he granted his royal pardon, with a generosity which will be praised in every newspaper in every age. A worthy surgeon cured Candide in three weeks with the ointments described by Dioscorides.[1] He already had a bit of skin back and was able to walk when the King of the Bulgars went to war with the King of the Abares.[2]

---

9. This episode was suggested by the experience of a Frenchman named Courtilz, who had deserted from the Prussian army and been bastinadoed for it. Voltaire intervened with Frederick to gain his release. But it also reflects the story that Wolff, Leibniz's disciple, got into trouble with Frederick's father when someone reported that his doctrine denying free will had encouraged several soldiers to desert. "The argument of the grenadier," who was said to have pleaded preestablished harmony to justify his desertion, so infuriated the king that he had Wolff expelled from the country.   1. Dioscorides' treatise on *materia medica*, dating from the 1st century C.E., was not the most up to date.   2. A tribe of semicivilized Scythians, who might be supposed at war with the Bulgars; allegorically, the Abares are the French, who opposed the Prussians in the Seven Years' War (1756–63). According to the title page of 1761, "Doctor Ralph," the dummy author of *Candide*, himself perished at the battle of Minden (Westphalia) in 1759.

CHAPTER 3

How Candide Escaped from the Bulgars, and What Became of Him

Nothing could have been so fine, so brisk, so brilliant, so well-drilled as the two armies. The trumpets, the fifes, the oboes, the drums, and the cannon produced such a harmony as was never heard in hell. First the cannons battered down about six thousand men on each side; then volleys of musket fire removed from the best of worlds about nine or ten thousand rascals who were cluttering up its surface. The bayonet was a sufficient reason for the demise of several thousand others. Total casualties might well amount to thirty thousand men or so. Candide, who was trembling like a philosopher, hid himself as best he could while this heroic butchery was going on.

Finally, while the two kings in their respective camps celebrated the victory by having *Te Deums* sung, Candide undertook to do his reasoning of cause and effect somewhere else. Passing by mounds of the dead and dying, he came to a nearby village which had been burnt to the ground. It was an Abare village, which the Bulgars had burned, in strict accordance with the laws of war. Here old men, stunned from beatings, watched the last agonies of their butchered wives, who still clutched their infants to their bleeding breasts; there, disemboweled girls, who had first satisfied the natural needs of various heroes, breathed their last; others, half-scorched in the flames, begged for their death stroke. Scattered brains and severed limbs littered the ground.

Candide fled as fast as he could to another village; this one belonged to the Bulgars, and the heroes of the Abare cause had given it the same treatment. Climbing over ruins and stumbling over corpses, Candide finally made his way out of the war area, carrying a little food in his knapsack and never ceasing to dream of Miss Cunégonde. His supplies gave out when he reached Holland; but having heard that everyone in that country was rich and a Christian, he felt confident of being treated as well as he had been in the castle of the Baron before he was kicked out for the love of Miss Cunégonde.

He asked alms of several grave personages, who all told him that if he continued to beg, he would be shut up in a house of correction and set to hard labor.

Finally he approached a man who had just been talking to a large crowd for an hour on end; the topic was charity. Looking doubtfully at him, the orator demanded:

—What are you doing here? Are you here to serve the good cause?

—There is no effect without a cause, said Candide modestly; all events are linked by the chain of necessity and arranged for the best. I had to be driven away from Miss Cunégonde, I had to run the gauntlet, I have to beg my bread until I can earn it; none of this could have happened otherwise.

—Look here, friend, said the orator, do you think the Pope is Antichrist?[3]

—I haven't considered the matter, said Candide; but whether he is or not, I'm in need of bread.

—You don't deserve any, said the other; away with you, you rascal, you rogue, never come near me as long as you live.

---

3. Voltaire is satirizing extreme Protestant sects that have sometimes seemed to make hatred of Rome the sum and substance of their creed.

Meanwhile, the orator's wife had put her head out of the window, and, seeing a man who was not sure the Pope was Antichrist, emptied over his head a pot full of———Scandalous! The excesses into which women are led by religious zeal!

A man who had never been baptized, a good Anabaptist[4] named Jacques, saw this cruel and heartless treatment being inflicted on one of his fellow creatures, a featherless biped possessing a soul;[5] he took Candide home with him, washed him off, gave him bread and beer, presented him with two florins, and even undertook to give him a job in his Persian-rug factory—for these items are widely manufactured in Holland. Candide, in an ecstasy of gratitude, cried out:

—Master Pangloss was right indeed when he told me everything is for the best in this world; for I am touched by your kindness far more than by the harshness of that black-coated gentleman and his wife.

Next day, while taking a stroll about town, he met a beggar who was covered with pustules, his eyes were sunken, the end of his nose rotted off, his mouth twisted, his teeth black, he had a croaking voice and a hacking cough, and spat a tooth every time he tried to speak.

CHAPTER 4

*How Candide Met His Old Philosophy Tutor, Doctor Pangloss,
and What Came of It*

Candide, more touched by compassion even than by horror, gave this ghastly beggar the two florins that he himself had received from his honest Anabaptist friend Jacques. The phantom stared at him, burst into tears, and fell on his neck. Candide drew back in terror.

—Alas, said one wretch to the other, don't you recognize your dear Pangloss any more?

—What are you saying? You, my dear master! you, in this horrible condition? What misfortune has befallen you? Why are you no longer in the most beautiful of castles? What has happened to Miss Cunégonde, that pearl among young ladies, that masterpiece of Nature?

—I am perishing, said Pangloss.

Candide promptly led him into the Anabaptist's stable, where he gave him a crust of bread, and when he had recovered:—Well, said he, Cunégonde?

—Dead, said the other.

Candide fainted. His friend brought him around with a bit of sour vinegar which happened to be in the stable. Candide opened his eyes.

—Cunégonde, dead! Ah, best of worlds, what's become of you now? But how did she die? It wasn't of grief at seeing me kicked out of her noble father's elegant castle?

—Not at all, said Pangloss; she was disemboweled by the Bulgar soldiers, after having been raped to the absolute limit of human endurance; they smashed the Baron's head when he tried to defend her, cut the Baroness to

---

4. Holland, as the home of religious liberty, had offered asylum to the Anabaptists, whose radical views on property and religious discipline had made them unpopular during the 16th century. Granted tolerance, they settled down into respectable burghers. Since this behavior confirmed some of Voltaire's major theses, he had a high opinion of contemporary Anabaptists.   5. Plato's famous minimal definition of man, which he corrected by the addition of a soul to distinguish man from a plucked chicken.

bits, and treated my poor pupil exactly like his sister. As for the castle, not one stone was left on another, not a shed, not a sheep, not a duck, not a tree; but we had the satisfaction of revenge, for the Abares did exactly the same thing to a nearby barony belonging to a Bulgar nobleman.

At this tale Candide fainted again; but having returned to his senses and said everything appropriate to the occasion, he asked about the cause and effect, the sufficient reason, which had reduced Pangloss to his present pitiful state.

—Alas, said he, it was love; love, the consolation of the human race, the preservative of the universe, the soul of all sensitive beings, love, gentle love.

—Unhappy man, said Candide, I too have had some experience of this love, the sovereign of hearts, the soul of our souls; and it never got me anything but a single kiss and twenty kicks in the rear. How could this lovely cause produce in you such a disgusting effect?

Pangloss replied as follows:—My dear Candide! you knew Paquette, that pretty maidservant to our august Baroness. In her arms I tasted the delights of paradise, which directly caused these torments of hell, from which I am now suffering. She was infected with the disease, and has perhaps died of it. Paquette received this present from an erudite Franciscan, who took the pains to trace it back to its source; for he had it from an elderly countess, who picked it up from a captain of cavalry, who acquired it from a marquise, who caught it from a page, who had received it from a Jesuit, who during his novitiate got it directly from one of the companions of Christopher Columbus. As for me, I shall not give it to anyone, for I am a dying man.

—Oh, Pangloss, cried Candide, that's a very strange genealogy. Isn't the devil at the root of the whole thing?

—Not at all, replied that great man; it's an indispensable part of the best of worlds, a necessary ingredient; if Columbus had not caught, on an American island, this sickness which attacks the source of generation and sometimes prevents generation entirely—which thus strikes at and defeats the greatest end of Nature herself—we should have neither chocolate nor cochineal. It must also be noted that until the present time this malady, like religious controversy, has been wholly confined to the continent of Europe. Turks, Indians, Persians, Chinese, Siamese, and Japanese know nothing of it as yet; but there is a sufficient reason for which they in turn will make its acquaintance in a couple of centuries. Meanwhile, it has made splendid progress among us, especially among those big armies of honest, well-trained mercenaries who decide the destinies of nations. You can be sure that when thirty thousand men fight a pitched battle against the same number of the enemy, there will be about twenty thousand with the pox on either side.

—Remarkable indeed, said Candide, but we must see about curing you.

—And how can I do that, said Pangloss, seeing I don't have a cent to my name? There's not a doctor in the whole world who will let your blood or give you an enema without demanding a fee. If you can't pay yourself, you must find someone to pay for you.

These last words decided Candide; he hastened to implore the help of his charitable Anabaptist, Jacques, and painted such a moving picture of his friend's wretched state that the good man did not hesitate to take in Pangloss and have him cured at his own expense. In the course of the cure, Pangloss lost only an eye and an ear. Since he wrote a fine hand and knew arithmetic, the Anabaptist made him his bookkeeper. At the end of two months, being obliged to go to Lisbon on business, he took his two philosophers on the boat with him. Pangloss still maintained that everything was for the best, but Jacques didn't agree with him.

—It must be, said he, that men have corrupted Nature, for they are not born wolves, yet that is what they become. God gave them neither twenty-four-pound cannon nor bayonets, yet they have manufactured both in order to destroy themselves. Bankruptcies have the same effect, and so does the justice which seizes the goods of bankrupts in order to prevent the creditors from getting them.[6]

—It was all indispensable, replied the one-eyed doctor, since private misfortunes make for public welfare, and therefore the more private misfortunes there are, the better everything is.

While he was reasoning, the air grew dark, the winds blew from all directions, and the vessel was attacked by a horrible tempest within sight of Lisbon harbor.

CHAPTER 5

Tempest, Shipwreck, Earthquake, and What Happened to Doctor Pangloss, Candide, and the Anabaptist, Jacques

Half of the passengers, weakened by the frightful anguish of seasickness and the distress of tossing about on stormy waters, were incapable of noticing their danger. The other half shrieked aloud and fell to their prayers, the sails were ripped to shreds, the masts snapped, the vessel opened at the seams. Everyone worked who could stir, nobody listened for orders or issued them. The Anabaptist was lending a hand in the after part of the ship when a frantic sailor struck him and knocked him to the deck; but just at that moment, the sailor lurched so violently that he fell head first over the side, where he hung, clutching a fragment of the broken mast. The good Jacques ran to his aid, and helped him to climb back on board, but in the process was himself thrown into the sea under the very eyes of the sailor, who allowed him to drown without even glancing at him. Candide rushed to the rail, and saw his benefactor rise for a moment to the surface, then sink forever. He wanted to dive to his rescue; but the philosopher Pangloss prevented him by proving that the bay of Lisbon had been formed expressly for this Anabaptist to drown in. While he was proving the point *a priori*, the vessel opened up and everyone perished except for Pangloss, Candide, and the brutal sailor who had caused the virtuous Anabaptist to drown; this rascal swam easily to shore, while Pangloss and Candide drifted there on a plank.

When they had recovered a bit of energy, they set out for Lisbon; they still had a little money with which they hoped to stave off hunger after escaping the storm.

Scarcely had they set foot in the town, still bewailing the loss of their benefactor, when they felt the earth quake underfoot; the sea was lashed to a froth, burst into the port, and smashed all the vessels lying at anchor there. Whirlwinds of fire and ash swirled through the streets and public squares;

---

6. Voltaire had suffered losses from various bankruptcy proceedings.

houses crumbled, roofs came crashing down on foundations, foundations split; thirty thousand inhabitants of every age and either sex were crushed in the ruins.[7] The sailor whistled through his teeth, and said with an oath:— There'll be something to pick up here.

—What can be the sufficient reason of this phenomenon? asked Pangloss.

—The Last Judgment is here, cried Candide.

But the sailor ran directly into the middle of the ruins, heedless of danger in his eagerness for gain; he found some money, laid violent hands on it, got drunk, and, having slept off his wine, bought the favors of the first street-walker he could find amid the ruins of smashed houses, amid corpses and suffering victims on every hand. Pangloss however tugged at his sleeve.

—My friend, said he, this is not good form at all; your behavior falls short of that required by the universal reason; it's untimely, to say the least.

—Bloody hell, said the other, I'm a sailor, born in Batavia; I've been four times to Japan and stamped four times on the crucifix;[8] get out of here with your universal reason.

Some falling stonework had struck Candide; he lay prostrate in the street, covered with rubble, and calling to Pangloss:—For pity's sake bring me a little wine and oil; I'm dying.

—This earthquake is nothing novel, Pangloss replied; the city of Lima, in South America, underwent much the same sort of tremor, last year; same causes, same effects; there is surely a vein of sulphur under the earth's surface reaching from Lima to Lisbon.

—Nothing is more probable, said Candide; but, for God's sake, a little oil and wine.

—What do you mean, probable? replied the philosopher; I regard the case as proved.

Candide fainted and Pangloss brought him some water from a nearby fountain.

Next day, as they wandered amid the ruins, they found a little food which restored some of their strength. Then they fell to work like the others, bringing relief to those of the inhabitants who had escaped death. Some of the citizens whom they rescued gave them a dinner as good as was possible under the circumstances; it is true that the meal was a melancholy one, and the guests watered their bread with tears; but Pangloss consoled them by proving that things could not possibly be otherwise.

—For, said he, all this is for the best, since if there is a volcano at Lisbon, it cannot be somewhere else, since it is unthinkable that things should not be where they are, since everything is well.

A little man in black, an officer of the Inquisition,[9] who was sitting beside him, politely took up the question, and said:—It would seem that the gentleman does not believe in original sin, since if everything is for the best, man has not fallen and is not liable to eternal punishment.

---

7. The great Lisbon earthquake and fire occurred on November 1, 1755; between thirty and forty thousand deaths resulted.   8. The Japanese, originally receptive to foreign visitors, grew fearful that priests and proselytizers were merely advance agents of empire and expelled both the Portuguese and Spanish early in the 17th century. Only the Dutch were allowed to retain a small foothold, under humiliating conditions, of which the notion of stamping on the crucifix is symbolic. It was never what Voltaire suggests here, an actual requirement for entering the country.   9. Specifically, a *familier* or *poursuivant,* an undercover agent with powers of arrest.

—I most humbly beg pardon of your excellency, Pangloss answered, even more politely, but the fall of man and the curse of original sin entered necessarily into the best of all possible worlds.

—Then you do not believe in free will? said the officer.

—Your excellency must excuse me, said Pangloss; free will agrees very well with absolute necessity, for it was necessary that we should be free, since a will which is determined . . .

Pangloss was in the middle of his sentence, when the officer nodded significantly to the attendant who was pouring him a glass of port, or Oporto, wine.

CHAPTER 6

How They Made a Fine Auto-da-Fé to Prevent Earthquakes, and How Candide Was Whipped

After the earthquake had wiped out three quarters of Lisbon, the learned men of the land could find no more effective way of averting total destruction than to give the people a fine auto-da-fé;[1] the University of Coimbra had established that the spectacle of several persons being roasted over a slow fire with full ceremonial rites is an infallible specific against earthquakes.

In consequence, the authorities had rounded up a Biscayan convicted of marrying a woman who had stood godmother to his child, and two Portuguese who while eating a chicken had set aside a bit of bacon used for seasoning.[2] After dinner, men came with ropes to tie up Doctor Pangloss and his disciple Candide, one for talking and the other for listening with an air of approval; both were taken separately to a set of remarkably cool apartments, where the glare of the sun is never bothersome; eight days later they were both dressed in *san-benitos* and crowned with paper mitres;[3] Candide's mitre and *san-benito* were decorated with inverted flames and with devils who had neither tails nor claws; but Pangloss's devils had both tails and claws, and his flames stood upright. Wearing these costumes, they marched in a procession, and listened to a very touching sermon, followed by a beautiful concert of plainsong. Candide was flogged in cadence to the music; the Biscayan and the two men who had avoided bacon were burned, and Pangloss was hanged, though hanging is not customary. On the same day there was another earthquake, causing frightful damage.[4]

Candide, stunned, stupefied, despairing, bleeding, trembling, said to himself:—If this is the best of all possible worlds, what are the others like? The flogging is not so bad, I was flogged by the Bulgars. But oh my dear Pangloss, greatest of philosophers, was it necessary for me to watch you being hanged, for no reason that I can see? Oh my dear Anabaptist, best of men, was it necessary that you should be drowned in the port? Oh Miss Cunégonde, pearl of young ladies, was it necessary that you should have your belly slit open?

---

1. Literally, "act of faith," a public ceremony of repentance and humiliation. Such an auto-da-fé was actually held in Lisbon, June 20, 1756.   2. The Biscayan's fault lay in marrying someone within the forbidden bounds of relationship, an act of spiritual incest. The men who declined pork or bacon were understood to be crypto-Jews.   3. The cone-shaped paper cap (intended to resemble a bishop's mitre) and flowing yellow cape were customary garb for those pleading before the Inquisition.   4. In fact, the second quake occurred December 21, 1755.

He was being led away, barely able to stand, lectured, lashed, absolved, and blessed, when an old woman approached and said,—My son, be of good cheer and follow me.

CHAPTER 7

*How an Old Woman Took Care of Candide,
and How He Regained What He Loved*

Candide was of very bad cheer, but he followed the old woman to a shanty; she gave him a jar of ointment to rub himself, left him food and drink; she showed him a tidy little bed; next to it was a suit of clothing.

—Eat, drink, sleep, she said; and may Our Lady of Atocha, Our Lord St. Anthony of Padua, and Our Lord St. James of Compostela watch over you. I will be back tomorrow.

Candide, still completely astonished by everything he had seen and suffered, and even more by the old woman's kindness, offered to kiss her hand.

—It's not *my* hand you should be kissing, said she. I'll be back tomorrow; rub yourself with the ointment, eat and sleep.

In spite of his many sufferings, Candide ate and slept. Next day the old woman returned bringing breakfast; she looked at his back and rubbed it herself with another ointment; she came back with lunch; and then she returned in the evening, bringing supper. Next day she repeated the same routine.

—Who are you? Candide asked continually. Who told you to be so kind to me? How can I ever repay you?

The good woman answered not a word; she returned in the evening, and without food.

—Come with me, says she, and don't speak a word.

Taking him by the hand, she walks out into the countryside with him for about a quarter of a mile; they reach an isolated house, quite surrounded by gardens and ditches. The old woman knocks at a little gate, it opens. She takes Candide up a secret stairway to a gilded room furnished with a fine brocaded sofa; there she leaves him, closes the door, disappears. Candide stood as if entranced; his life, which had seemed like a nightmare so far, was now starting to look like a delightful dream.

Soon the old woman returned; on her feeble shoulder leaned a trembling woman, of a splendid figure, glittering in diamonds, and veiled.

—Remove the veil, said the old woman to Candide.

The young man stepped timidly forward, and lifted the veil. What an event! What a surprise! Could it be Miss Cunégonde? Yes, it really was! She herself! His knees give way, speech fails him, he falls at her feet, Cunégonde collapses on the sofa. The old woman plies them with brandy, they return to their senses, they exchange words. At first they could utter only broken phrases, questions and answers at cross purposes, sighs, tears, exclamations. The old woman warned them not to make too much noise, and left them alone.

—Then it's really you, said Candide, you're alive, I've found you again in Portugal. Then you never were raped? You never had your belly ripped open, as the philosopher Pangloss assured me?

—Oh yes, said the lovely Cunégonde, but one doesn't always die of these two accidents.

—But your father and mother were murdered then?

—All too true, said Cunégonde, in tears.

—And your brother?

—Killed too.

—And why are you in Portugal? and how did you know I was here? and by what device did you have me brought to this house?

—I shall tell you everything, the lady replied; but first you must tell me what has happened to you since that first innocent kiss we exchanged and the kicking you got because of it.

Candide obeyed her with profound respect; and though he was overcome, though his voice was weak and hesitant, though he still had twinges of pain from his beating, he described as simply as possible everything that had happened to him since the time of their separation. Cunégonde lifted her eyes to heaven; she wept at the death of the good Anabaptist and at that of Pangloss; after which she told the following story to Candide, who listened to every word while he gazed on her with hungry eyes.

CHAPTER 8

Cunégonde's Story

—I was in my bed and fast asleep when heaven chose to send the Bulgars into our castle of Thunder-Ten-Tronckh. They butchered my father and brother, and hacked my mother to bits. An enormous Bulgar, six feet tall, seeing that I had swooned from horror at the scene, set about raping me; at that I recovered my senses, I screamed and scratched, bit and fought, I tried to tear the eyes out of that big Bulgar—not realizing that everything which had happened in my father's castle was a mere matter of routine. The brute then stabbed me with a knife on my left thigh, where I still bear the scar.

—What a pity! I should very much like to see it, said the simple Candide.

—You shall, said Cunégonde; but shall I go on?

—Please do, said Candide.

So she took up the thread of her tale:—A Bulgar captain appeared, he saw me covered with blood and the soldier too intent to get up. Shocked by the monster's failure to come to attention, the captain killed him on my body. He then had my wound dressed, and took me off to his quarters, as a prisoner of war. I laundered his few shirts and did his cooking; he found me attractive, I confess it, and I won't deny that he was a handsome fellow, with a smooth, white skin; apart from that, however, little wit, little philosophical training; it was evident that he had not been brought up by Doctor Pangloss. After three months, he had lost all his money and grown sick of me; so he sold me to a Jew named Don Issachar, who traded in Holland and Portugal, and who was mad after women. This Jew developed a mighty passion for my person, but he got nowhere with it; I held him off better than I had done with the Bulgar soldier; for though a person of honor may be raped once, her virtue is only strengthened by the experience. In order to keep me hidden, the Jew brought me to his country house, which you see here. Till then I had thought there was nothing on earth so beautiful as the castle of Thunder-Ten-Tronckh; I was now undeceived.

—One day the Grand Inquisitor took notice of me at mass; he ogled me a good deal, and made known that he must talk to me on a matter of secret business. I was taken to his palace; I told him of my rank; he pointed out that it was beneath my dignity to belong to an Israelite. A suggestion was then conveyed to Don Issachar that he should turn me over to My Lord the Inquisitor. Don Issachar, who is court banker and a man of standing, refused out of hand. The inquisitor threatened him with an auto-da-fé. Finally my Jew, fearing for his life, struck a bargain by which the house and I would belong to both of them as joint tenants; the Jew would get Mondays, Wednesdays, and the Sabbath, the inquisitor would get the other days of the week. That has been the arrangement for six months now. There have been quarrels; sometimes it has not been clear whether the night from Saturday to Sunday belonged to the old or the new dispensation. For my part, I have so far been able to hold both of them off; and that, I think, is why they are both still in love with me.

—Finally, in order to avert further divine punishment by earthquake, and to terrify Don Issachar, My Lord the Inquisitor chose to celebrate an auto-da-fé. He did me the honor of inviting me to attend. I had an excellent seat; the ladies were served with refreshments between the mass and the execution. To tell you the truth, I was horrified to see them burn alive those two Jews and that decent Biscayan who had married his child's godmother; but what was my surprise, my terror, my grief, when I saw, huddled in a *san-benito* and wearing a mitre, someone who looked like Pangloss! I rubbed my eyes, I watched his every move, I saw him hanged; and I fell back in a swoon. Scarcely had I come to my senses again, when I saw you stripped for the lash; that was the peak of my horror, consternation, grief, and despair. I may tell you, by the way, that your skin is even whiter and more delicate than that of my Bulgar captain. Seeing you, then, redoubled the torments which were already overwhelming me. I shrieked aloud, I wanted to call out, 'Let him go, you brutes!' but my voice died within me, and my cries would have been useless. When you had been thoroughly thrashed: 'How can it be,' I asked myself, 'that agreeable Candide and wise Pangloss have come to Lisbon, one to receive a hundred whiplashes, the other to be hanged by order of My Lord the Inquisitor, whose mistress I am? Pangloss must have deceived me cruelly when he told me that all is for the best in this world.'

—Frantic, exhausted, half out of my senses, and ready to die of weakness, I felt as if my mind were choked with the massacre of my father, my mother, my brother, with the arrogance of that ugly Bulgar soldier, with the knife slash he inflicted on me, my slavery, my cookery, my Bulgar captain, my nasty Don Issachar, my abominable inquisitor, with the hanging of Doctor Pangloss, with that great plainsong *miserere* which they sang while they flogged you—and above all, my mind was full of the kiss which I gave you behind the screen, on the day I saw you for the last time. I praised God, who had brought you back to me after so many trials. I asked my old woman to look out for you, and to bring you here as soon as she could. She did just as I asked; I have had the indescribable joy of seeing you again, hearing you and talking with you once more. But you must be frightfully hungry; I am, myself; let us begin with a dinner.

So then and there they sat down to table; and after dinner, they adjourned to that fine brocaded sofa, which has already been mentioned; and there they were when the eminent Don Issachar, one of the masters of the house, appeared. It was the day of the Sabbath; he was arriving to assert his rights and express his tender passion.

CHAPTER 9

What Happened to Cunégonde, Candide, the Grand Inquisitor, and a Jew

This Issachar was the most choleric Hebrew seen in Israel since the Babylonian captivity.

—What's this, says he, you bitch of a Christian, you're not satisfied with the Grand Inquisitor? Do I have to share you with this rascal, too?

So saying, he drew a long dagger, with which he always went armed, and, supposing his opponent defenceless, flung himself on Candide. But our good Westphalian had received from the old woman, along with his suit of clothes, a fine sword. Out it came, and though his manners were of the gentlest, in short order he laid the Israelite stiff and cold on the floor, at the feet of the lovely Cunégonde.

—Holy Virgin! she cried. What will become of me now? A man killed in my house! If the police find out, we're done for.

—If Pangloss had not been hanged, said Candide, he would give us good advice in this hour of need, for he was a great philosopher. Lacking him, let's ask the old woman.

She was a sensible body, and was just starting to give her opinion of the situation, when another little door opened. It was just one o'clock in the morning, Sunday morning. This day belonged to the inquisitor. In he came, and found the whipped Candide with a sword in his hand, a corpse at his feet, Cunégonde in terror, and an old woman giving them both good advice.

Here now is what passed through Candide's mind in this instant of time; this is how he reasoned:—If this holy man calls for help, he will certainly have me burned, and perhaps Cunégonde as well; he has already had me whipped without mercy; he is my rival; I have already killed once; why hesitate?

It was a quick, clear chain of reasoning; without giving the inquisitor time to recover from his surprise, he ran him through, and laid him beside the Jew.

—Here you've done it again, said Cunégonde; there's no hope for us now. We'll be excommunicated, our last hour has come. How is it that you, who were born so gentle, could kill in two minutes a Jew and a prelate?

—My dear girl, replied Candide, when a man is in love, jealous, and just whipped by the Inquisition, he is no longer himself.

The old woman now spoke up and said:—There are three Andalusian steeds in the stable, with their saddles and bridles; our brave Candide must get them ready: my lady has some gold coin and diamonds; let's take to horse at once, though I can only ride on one buttock; we will go to Cadiz. The weather is as fine as can be, and it is pleasant to travel in the cool of the evening.

Promptly, Candide saddled the three horses. Cunégonde, the old woman, and he covered thirty miles without a stop. While they were fleeing, the Holy Brotherhood[5] came to investigate the house; they buried the inquisitor in a fine church, and threw Issachar on the dunghill.

Candide, Cunégonde, and the old woman were already in the little town of Avacena, in the middle of the Sierra Morena; and there, as they sat in a country inn, they had this conversation.

---

5. A semireligious order with police powers, very active in 18th-century Spain.

CHAPTER 10

In Deep Distress, Candide, Cunégonde, and the Old Woman Reach Cadiz; They Put to Sea

—Who then could have robbed me of my gold and diamonds? said Cunégonde, in tears. How shall we live? what shall we do? where shall I find other inquisitors and Jews to give me some more?

—Ah, said the old woman, I strongly suspect that reverend Franciscan friar who shared the inn with us yesterday at Badajoz. God save me from judging him unfairly! But he came into our room twice, and he left long before us.

—Alas, said Candide, the good Pangloss often proved to me that the fruits of the earth are a common heritage of all, to which each man has equal right. On these principles, the Franciscan should at least have left us enough to finish our journey. You have nothing at all, my dear Cunégonde?

—Not a maravedi, said she.

—What to do? said Candide.

—We'll sell one of the horses, said the old woman; I'll ride on the croup behind my mistress, though only on one buttock, and so we will get to Cadiz.

There was in the same inn a Benedictine prior; he bought the horse cheap. Candide, Cunégonde, and the old woman passed through Lucena, Chillas, and Lebrixa, and finally reached Cadiz. There a fleet was being fitted out and an army assembled, to reason with the Jesuit fathers in Paraguay, who were accused of fomenting among their flock a revolt against the kings of Spain and Portugal near the town of St. Sacrement.[6] Candide, having served in the Bulgar army, performed the Bulgar manual of arms before the general of the little army with such grace, swiftness, dexterity, fire, and agility, that they gave him a company of infantry to command. So here he is, a captain; and off he sails with Miss Cunégonde, the old woman, two valets, and the two Andalusian steeds which had belonged to My Lord the Grand Inquisitor of Portugal.

Throughout the crossing, they spent a great deal of time reasoning about the philosophy of poor Pangloss.

—We are destined, in the end, for another universe, said Candide; no doubt that is the one where everything is well. For in this one, it must be admitted, there is some reason to grieve over our physical and moral state.

—I love you with all my heart, said Cunégonde; but my soul is still harrowed by thoughts of what I have seen and suffered.

—All will be well, replied Candide; the sea of this new world is already better than those of Europe, calmer and with steadier winds. Surely it is the New World which is the best of all possible worlds.

—God grant it, said Cunégonde; but I have been so horribly unhappy in the world so far, that my heart is almost dead to hope.

—You pity yourselves, the old woman told them; but you have had no such misfortunes as mine.

---

6. Actually, Colonia del Sacramento. Voltaire took great interest in the Jesuit role in Paraguay, which he has much oversimplified and largely misrepresented here in the interests of his satire. In 1750 they did, however, offer armed resistance to an agreement made between Spain and Portugal. They were subdued and expelled in 1769.

Cunégonde nearly broke out laughing; she found the old woman comic in pretending to be more unhappy than she.

—Ah, you poor old thing, said she, unless you've been raped by two Bulgars, been stabbed twice in the belly, seen two of your castles destroyed, witnessed the murder of two of your mothers and two of your fathers, and watched two of your lovers being whipped in an auto-da-fé, I do not see how you can have had it worse than me. Besides, I was born a baroness, with seventy-two quarterings, and I have worked in a scullery.

—My lady, replied the old woman, you do not know my birth and rank; and if I showed you my rear end, you would not talk as you do, you might even speak with less assurance.

These words inspired great curiosity in Candide and Cunégonde, which the old woman satisfied with this story.

CHAPTER 11

The Old Woman's Story

—My eyes were not always bloodshot and red-rimmed, my nose did not always touch my chin, and I was not born a servant. I am in fact the daughter of Pope Urban the Tenth and the Princess of Palestrina.[7] Till the age of fourteen, I lived in a palace so splendid that all the castles of all your German barons would not have served it as a stable; a single one of my dresses was worth more than all the assembled magnificence of Westphalia. I grew in beauty, in charm, in talent, surrounded by pleasures, dignities, and glowing visions of the future. Already I was inspiring the young men to love; my breast was formed—and what a breast! white, firm, with the shape of the Venus de Medici; and what eyes! what lashes, what black brows! What fire flashed from my glances and outshone the glitter of the stars, as the local poets used to tell me! The women who helped me dress and undress fell into ecstasies, whether they looked at me from in front or behind; and all the men wanted to be in their place.

—I was engaged to the ruling prince of Massa-Carrara; and what a prince he was! as handsome as I, softness and charm compounded, brilliantly witty, and madly in love with me. I loved him in return as one loves for the first time, with a devotion approaching idolatry. The wedding preparations had been made, with a splendor and magnificence never heard of before; nothing but celebrations, masks, and comic operas, uninterruptedly; and all Italy composed in my honor sonnets of which not one was even passable. I had almost attained the very peak of bliss, when an old marquise who had been the mistress of my prince invited him to her house for a cup of chocolate. He died in less than two hours, amid horrifying convulsions. But that was only a trifle. My mother, in complete despair (though less afflicted than I), wished to escape for a while the oppressive atmosphere of grief. She owned a handsome property near Gaeta.[8] We embarked on a papal galley gilded like the altar of St. Peter's in Rome. Suddenly a pirate ship from Salé swept down and boarded us. Our soldiers defended themselves as papal troops usually

---

7. Voltaire left behind a comment on this passage, a note first published in 1829: "Note the extreme discretion of the author; hitherto there has never been a pope named Urban X; he avoided attributing a bastard to a known pope. What circumspection! what an exquisite conscience!"   8. About halfway between Rome and Naples.

do; falling on their knees and throwing down their arms, they begged of the corsair absolution *in articulo mortis.*[9]

—They were promptly stripped as naked as monkeys, and so was my mother, and so were our maids of honor, and so was I too. It's a very remarkable thing, the energy these gentlemen put into stripping people. But what surprised me even more was that they stuck their fingers in a place where we women usually admit only a syringe. This ceremony seemed a bit odd to me, as foreign usages always do when one hasn't traveled. They only wanted to see if we didn't have some diamonds hidden there; and I soon learned that it's a custom of long standing among the genteel folk who swarm the seas. I learned that my lords the very religious knights of Malta never overlook this ceremony when they capture Turks, whether male or female; it's one of those international laws which have never been questioned.

—I won't try to explain how painful it is for a young princess to be carried off into slavery in Morocco with her mother. You can imagine everything we had to suffer on the pirate ship. My mother was still very beautiful; our maids of honor, our mere chambermaids, were more charming than anything one could find in all Africa. As for myself, I was ravishing, I was loveliness and grace supreme, and I was a virgin. I did not remain so for long; the flower which had been kept for the handsome prince of Massa-Carrara was plucked by the corsair captain; he was an abominable negro, who thought he was doing me a great favor. My Lady the Princess of Palestrina and I must have been strong indeed to bear what we did during our journey to Morocco. But on with my story; these are such common matters that they are not worth describing.

—Morocco was knee deep in blood when we arrived. Of the fifty sons of the emperor Muley-Ismael,[1] each had his faction, which produced in effect fifty civil wars, of blacks against blacks, of blacks against browns, halfbreeds against halfbreeds; throughout the length and breadth of the empire, nothing but one continual carnage.

—Scarcely had we stepped ashore, when some negroes of a faction hostile to my captor arrived to take charge of his plunder. After the diamonds and gold, we women were the most prized possessions. I was now witness of a struggle such as you never see in the temperate climate of Europe. Northern people don't have hot blood; they don't feel the absolute fury for women which is common in Africa. Europeans seem to have milk in their veins; it is vitriol or liquid fire which pulses through these people around Mount Atlas. The fight for possession of us raged with the fury of the lions, tigers, and poisonous vipers of that land. A Moor snatched my mother by the right arm, the first mate held her by the left; a Moorish soldier grabbed one leg, one of our pirates the other. In a moment's time almost all our girls were being dragged four different ways. My captain held me behind him while with his scimitar he killed everyone who braved his fury. At last I saw all our Italian women, including my mother, torn to pieces, cut to bits, murdered by the monsters who were fighting over them. My captive companions, their captors, soldiers, sailors, blacks, browns, whites, mulattoes, and at last my captain,

9. Literally, when at the point of death. Absolution from a corsair in the act of murdering one is of very dubious validity.   1. Having reigned for more than fifty years, a potent and ruthless sultan of Morocco, he died in 1727 and left his kingdom in much the condition described.

all were killed, and I remained half dead on a mountain of corpses. Similar scenes were occurring, as is well known, for more than three hundred leagues around, without anyone skimping on the five prayers a day decreed by Mohammed.

—With great pain, I untangled myself from this vast heap of bleeding bodies, and dragged myself under a great orange tree by a neighboring brook, where I collapsed, from terror, exhaustion, horror, despair, and hunger. Shortly, my weary mind surrendered to a sleep which was more of a swoon than a rest. I was in this state of weakness and languor, between life and death, when I felt myself touched by something which moved over my body. Opening my eyes, I saw a white man, rather attractive, who was groaning and saying under his breath: 'O che sciagura d'essere senza coglioni!'[2]

CHAPTER 12

The Old Woman's Story Continued

—Amazed and delighted to hear my native tongue, and no less surprised by what this man was saying, I told him that there were worse evils than those he was complaining of. In a few words, I described to him the horrors I had undergone, and then fainted again. He carried me to a nearby house, put me to bed, gave me something to eat, served me, flattered me, comforted me, told me he had never seen anyone so lovely, and added that he had never before regretted so much the loss of what nobody could give him back.

'I was born at Naples,' he told me, 'where they caponize two or three thousand children every year; some die of it, others acquire a voice more beautiful than any woman's, still others go on to become governors of kingdoms.[3] The operation was a great success with me, and I became court musician to the Princess of Palestrina . . .'

'Of my mother,' I exclaimed.

'Of your mother,' cried he, bursting into tears; 'then you must be the princess whom I raised till she was six, and who already gave promise of becoming as beautiful as you are now!'

'I am that very princess; my mother lies dead, not a hundred yards from here, buried under a pile of corpses.'

—I told him my adventures, he told me his: that he had been sent by a Christian power to the King of Morocco, to conclude a treaty granting him gunpowder, cannon, and ships with which to liquidate the traders of the other Christian powers.

'My mission is concluded,' said this honest eunuch; 'I shall take ship at Ceuta and bring you back to Italy. *Ma che sciagura d'essere senza coglioni!*'

—I thanked him with tears of gratitude, and instead of returning me to Italy, he took me to Algiers and sold me to the dey of that country. Hardly had the sale taken place, when that plague which has made the rounds of Africa, Asia, and Europe broke out in full fury at Algiers. You have seen earthquakes; but tell me, young lady, have you ever had the plague?

—Never, replied the baroness.

—If you had had it, said the old woman, you would agree that it is far worse than an earthquake. It is very frequent in Africa, and I had it. Imag-

---

2. "Oh what a misfortune to have no testicles!" **3.** The castrato Farinelli (1705–1782), originally a singer, came to exercise considerable political influence on the kings of Spain, Philip V and Ferdinand VI.

ine, if you will, the situation of a pope's daughter, fifteen years old, who in three months' time had experienced poverty, slavery, had been raped almost every day, had seen her mother quartered, had suffered from famine and war, and who now was dying of pestilence in Algiers. As a matter of fact, I did not die; but the eunuch and the dey and nearly the entire seraglio of Algiers perished.

—When the first horrors of this ghastly plague had passed, the slaves of the dey were sold. A merchant bought me and took me to Tunis; there he sold me to another merchant, who resold me at Tripoli; from Tripoli I was sold to Alexandria, from Alexandria resold to Smyrna, from Smyrna to Constantinople. I ended by belonging to an aga of janizaries, who was shortly ordered to defend Azov against the besieging Russians.[4]

—The aga, who was a gallant soldier, took his whole seraglio with him, and established us in a little fort amid the Maeotian marshes,[5] guarded by two black eunuchs and twenty soldiers. Our side killed a prodigious number of Russians, but they paid us back nicely. Azov was put to fire and sword without respect for age or sex; only our little fort continued to resist, and the enemy determined to starve us out. The twenty janizaries had sworn never to surrender. Reduced to the last extremities of hunger, they were forced to eat our two eunuchs, lest they violate their oaths. After several more days, they decided to eat the women too.

—We had an imam,[6] very pious and sympathetic, who delivered an excellent sermon, persuading them not to kill us altogether.

'Just cut off a single rumpsteak from each of these ladies,' he said, 'and you'll have a fine meal. Then if you should need another, you can come back in a few days and have as much again; heaven will bless your charitable action, and you will be saved.'

—His eloquence was splendid, and he persuaded them. We underwent this horrible operation. The imam treated us all with the ointment that they use on newly circumcised children. We were at the point of death.

—Scarcely had the janizaries finished the meal for which we furnished the materials, when the Russians appeared in flat-bottomed boats; not a janizary escaped. The Russians paid no attention to the state we were in; but there are French physicians everywhere, and one of them, who knew his trade, took care of us. He cured us, and I shall remember all my life that when my wounds were healed, he made me a proposition. For the rest, he counselled us simply to have patience, assuring us that the same thing had happened in several other sieges, and that it was according to the laws of war.

—As soon as my companions could walk, we were herded off to Moscow. In the division of booty, I fell to a boyar who made me work in his garden, and gave me twenty whiplashes a day; but when he was broken on the wheel after about two years, with thirty other boyars, over some little court intrigue,[7] I seized the occasion; I ran away; I crossed all Russia; I was for a long time a chambermaid in Riga, then at Rostock, Vismara, Leipzig, Cassel,

---

4. Azov, near the mouth of the Don, was besieged by the Russians under Peter the Great in 1695–96. *Janizaries:* an elite corps of the Ottoman armies. 5. The Roman name of the so-called Sea of Azov, a shallow, swampy lake near the town. 6. In effect, a chaplain. 7. Voltaire had in mind an ineffectual conspiracy against Peter the Great known as the "revolt of the streltsy" or musketeers, which took place in 1698. Though easily put down, it provoked from the emperor a massive and atrocious program of reprisals.

Utrecht, Leyden, The Hague, Rotterdam; I grew old in misery and shame, having only half a backside and remembering always that I was the daughter of a Pope; a hundred times I wanted to kill myself, but always I loved life more. This ridiculous weakness is perhaps one of our worst instincts; is anything more stupid than choosing to carry a burden that really one wants to cast on the ground? to hold existence in horror, and yet to cling to it? to fondle the serpent which devours us till it has eaten out our heart?

—In the countries through which I have been forced to wander, in the taverns where I have had to work, I have seen a vast number of people who hated their existence; but I never saw more than a dozen who deliberately put an end to their own misery: three negroes, four Englishmen, four Genevans, and a German professor named Robeck.[8] My last post was as servant to the Jew Don Issachar; he attached me to your service, my lovely one; and I attached myself to your destiny, till I have become more concerned with your fate than with my own. I would not even have mentioned my own misfortunes, if you had not irked me a bit, and if it weren't the custom, on shipboard, to pass the time with stories. In a word, my lady, I have had some experience of the world, I know it; why not try this diversion? Ask every passenger on this ship to tell you his story, and if you find a single one who has not often cursed the day of his birth, who has not often told himself that he is the most miserable of men, then you may throw me overboard head first.

CHAPTER 13

How Candide Was Forced to Leave the Lovely Cunégonde and the Old Woman

Having heard out the old woman's story, the lovely Cunégonde paid her the respects which were appropriate to a person of her rank and merit. She took up the wager as well, and got all the passengers, one after another, to tell her their adventures. She and Candide had to agree that the old woman had been right.

—It's certainly too bad, said Candide, that the wise Pangloss was hanged, contrary to the custom of autos-da-fé; he would have admirable things to say of the physical evil and moral evil which cover land and sea, and I might feel within me the impulse to dare to raise several polite objections.

As the passengers recited their stories, the boat made steady progress, and presently landed at Buenos Aires. Cunégonde, Captain Candide, and the old woman went to call on the governor, Don Fernando d'Ibaraa y Figueroa y Mascarenes y Lampourdos y Souza. This nobleman had the pride appropriate to a man with so many names. He addressed everyone with the most aristocratic disdain, pointing his nose so loftily, raising his voice so mercilessly, lording it so splendidly, and assuming so arrogant a pose, that everyone who met him wanted to kick him. He loved women to the point of fury; and Cunégonde seemed to him the most beautiful creature he had ever seen. The first thing he did was to ask directly if she were the captain's wife. His manner of asking this question disturbed Candide; he did not dare say she was his wife, because in fact she was not; he did not dare say she was his

---

8. Johann Robeck (1672–1739) published a treatise advocating suicide and showed his conviction by drowning himself at the age of sixty-seven.

sister, because she wasn't that either; and though this polite lie was once common enough among the ancients,[9] and sometimes serves moderns very well, he was too pure of heart to tell a lie.

—Miss Cunégonde, said he, is betrothed to me, and we humbly beg your excellency to perform the ceremony for us.

Don Fernando d'Ibaraa y Figueroa y Mascarenes y Lampourdos y Souza twirled his moustache, smiled sardonically, and ordered Captain Candide to go drill his company. Candide obeyed. Left alone with My Lady Cunégonde, the governor declared his passion, and protested that he would marry her tomorrow, in church or in any other manner, as it pleased her charming self. Cunégonde asked for a quarter-hour to collect herself, consult the old woman, and make up her mind.

The old woman said to Cunégonde:—My lady, you have seventy-two quarterings and not one penny; if you wish, you may be the wife of the greatest lord in South America, who has a really handsome moustache; are you going to insist on your absolute fidelity? You have already been raped by the Bulgars; a Jew and an inquisitor have enjoyed your favors; miseries entitle one to privileges. I assure you that in your position I would make no scruple of marrying My Lord the Governor, and making the fortune of Captain Candide.

While the old woman was talking with all the prudence of age and experience, there came into the harbor a small ship bearing an alcalde and some alguazils.[1] This is what had happened.

As the old woman had very shrewdly guessed, it was a long-sleeved Franciscan who stole Cunégonde's gold and jewels in the town of Badajoz, when she and Candide were in flight. The monk tried to sell some of the gems to a jeweler, who recognized them as belonging to the Grand Inquisitor. Before he was hanged, the Franciscan confessed that he had stolen them, indicating who his victims were and where they were going. The flight of Cunégonde and Candide was already known. They were traced to Cadiz, and a vessel was hastily dispatched in pursuit of them. This vessel was now in the port of Buenos Aires. The rumor spread that an alcalde was aboard, in pursuit of the murderers of My Lord the Grand Inquisitor. The shrewd old woman saw at once what was to be done.

—You cannot escape, she told Cunégonde, and you have nothing to fear. You are not the one who killed my lord, and, besides, the governor, who is in love with you, won't let you be mistreated. Sit tight.

And then she ran straight to Candide:—Get out of town, she said, or you'll be burned within the hour.

There was not a moment to lose; but how to leave Cunégonde, and where to go?

CHAPTER 14

How Candide and Cacambo Were Received by the Jesuits of Paraguay

Candide had brought from Cadiz a valet of the type one often finds in the provinces of Spain and in the colonies. He was one quarter Spanish, son of a halfbreed in the Tucuman;[2] he had been choirboy, sacristan, sailor, monk,

9. Voltaire has in mind Abraham's adventures with Sarah (Genesis 12) and Isaac's with Rebecca (Genesis 26).   1. Police officers.   2. A province of Argentina, to the northwest of Buenos Aires.

merchant, soldier, and lackey. His name was Cacambo, and he was very fond of his master because his master was a very good man. In hot haste he saddled the two Andalusian steeds.

—Hurry, master, do as the old woman says; let's get going and leave this town without a backward look.

Candide wept:—O my beloved Cunégonde! must I leave you now, just when the governor is about to marry us! Cunégonde, brought from so far, what will ever become of you?

—She'll become what she can, said Cacambo; women can always find something to do with themselves; God sees to it; let's get going.

—Where are you taking me? where are we going? what will we do without Cunégonde? said Candide.

—By Saint James of Compostela, said Cacambo, you were going to make war against the Jesuits, now we'll go make war for them. I know the roads pretty well, I'll bring you to their country, they will be delighted to have a captain who knows the Bulgar drill; you'll make a prodigious fortune. If you don't get your rights in one world, you will find them in another. And isn't it pleasant to see new things and do new things?

—Then you've already been in Paraguay? said Candide.

—Indeed I have, replied Cacambo; I was cook in the College of the Assumption, and I know the government of Los Padres[3] as I know the streets of Cadiz. It's an admirable thing, this government. The kingdom is more than three hundred leagues across; it is divided into thirty provinces. Los Padres own everything in it, and the people nothing; it's a masterpiece of reason and justice. I myself know nothing so wonderful as Los Padres, who in this hemisphere make war on the kings of Spain and Portugal, but in Europe hear their confessions; who kill Spaniards here, and in Madrid send them to heaven; that really tickles me; let's get moving, you're going to be the happiest of men. Won't Los Padres be delighted when they learn they have a captain who knows the Bulgar drill!

As soon as they reached the first barricade, Cacambo told the frontier guard that a captain wished to speak with My Lord the Commander. A Paraguayan officer ran to inform headquarters by laying the news at the feet of the commander. Candide and Cacambo were first disarmed and deprived of their Andalusian horses. They were then placed between two files of soldiers; the commander was at the end, his three-cornered hat on his head, his cassock drawn up, a sword at his side, and a pike in his hand. He nods, and twenty-four soldiers surround the newcomers. A sergeant then informs them that they must wait, that the commander cannot talk to them, since the reverend father provincial has forbidden all Spaniards from speaking, except in his presence, and from remaining more than three hours in the country.

—And where is the reverend father provincial? says Cacambo.

—He is reviewing his troops after having said mass, the sergeant replies, and you'll only be able to kiss his spurs in three hours.

—But, says Cacambo, my master the captain, who, like me, is dying from hunger, is not Spanish at all, he is German; can't we have some breakfast while waiting for his reverence?

---

3. The Jesuit fathers.

The sergeant promptly went off to report this speech to the commander.

—God be praised, said this worthy; since he is German, I can talk to him; bring him into my bower.

Candide was immediately led into a leafy nook surrounded by a handsome colonnade of green and gold marble and trellises amid which sported parrots, birds of paradise,[4] hummingbirds, guinea fowl, and all the rarest species of birds. An excellent breakfast was prepared in golden vessels; and while the Paraguayans ate corn out of wooden bowls in the open fields under the glare of the sun, the reverend father commander entered into his bower.

He was a very handsome young man, with an open face, rather blonde in coloring, with ruddy complexion, arched eyebrows, liquid eyes, pink ears, bright red lips, and an air of pride, but a pride somehow different from that of a Spaniard or a Jesuit. Their confiscated weapons were restored to Candide and Cacambo, as well as their Andalusian horses; Cacambo fed them oats alongside the bower, always keeping an eye on them for fear of an ambush.

First Candide kissed the hem of the commander's cassock, then they sat down at the table.

—So you are German? said the Jesuit, speaking in that language.

—Yes, your reverence, said Candide.

As they spoke these words, both men looked at one another with great surprise, and another emotion which they could not control.

—From what part of Germany do you come? said the Jesuit.

—From the nasty province of Westphalia, said Candide; I was born in the castle of Thunder-Ten-Tronckh.

—Merciful heavens! cries the commander. Is it possible?

—What a miracle! exclaims Candide.

—Can it be you? asks the commander.

—It's impossible, says Candide.

They both fall back in their chairs, they embrace, they shed streams of tears.

—What, can it be you, reverend father! you, the brother of the lovely Cunégonde! you, who were killed by the Bulgars! you, the son of My Lord the Baron! you, a Jesuit in Paraguay! It's a mad world, indeed it is. Oh, Pangloss! Pangloss! how happy you would be, if you hadn't been hanged.

The commander dismissed his negro slaves and the Paraguayans who served his drink in crystal goblets. He thanked God and Saint Ignatius a thousand times, he clasped Candide in his arms, their faces were bathed in tears.

—You would be even more astonished, even more delighted, even more beside yourself, said Candide, if I told you that My Lady Cunégonde, your sister, who you thought was disemboweled, is enjoying good health.

—Where?

---

4. In this passage and several later ones, Voltaire uses in conjunction two words, both of which mean hummingbird. The French system of classifying hummingbirds, based on the work of the celebrated Buffon, distinguishes *oiseaux-mouches* with straight bills from *colibris* with curved bills. This distinction is wholly fallacious. Hummingbirds have all manner of shaped bills, and the division of species must be made on other grounds entirely. At the expense of ornithological accuracy, I have therefore introduced birds of paradise to get the requisite sense of glitter and sheen.

—Not far from here, in the house of the governor of Buenos Aires; and to think that I came to make war on you!

Each word they spoke in this long conversation added another miracle. Their souls danced on their tongues, hung eagerly at their ears, glittered in their eyes. As they were Germans, they sat a long time at table, waiting for the reverend father provincial; and the commander spoke in these terms to his dear Candide.

CHAPTER 15

How Candide Killed the Brother of His Dear Cunégonde

—All my life long I shall remember the horrible day when I saw my father and mother murdered and my sister raped. When the Bulgars left, that adorable sister of mine was nowhere to be found; so they loaded a cart with my mother, my father, myself, two serving girls, and three little murdered boys, to carry us all off for burial in a Jesuit chapel some two leagues from our ancestral castle. A Jesuit sprinkled us with holy water; it was horribly salty, and a few drops got into my eyes; the father noticed that my lid made a little tremor; putting his hand on my heart, he felt it beat; I was rescued, and at the end of three weeks was as good as new. You know, my dear Candide, that I was a very pretty boy; I became even more so; the reverend father Croust,[5] superior of the abbey, conceived a most tender friendship for me; he accepted me as a novice, and shortly after, I was sent to Rome. The Father General had need of a resupply of young German Jesuits. The rulers of Paraguay accept as few Spanish Jesuits as they can; they prefer foreigners, whom they think they can control better. I was judged fit, by the Father General, to labor in this vineyard. So we set off, a Pole, a Tyrolean, and myself. Upon our arrival, I was honored with the posts of subdeacon and lieutenant; today I am a colonel and a priest. We are giving a vigorous reception to the King of Spain's men; I assure you they will be excommunicated as well as trounced on the battlefield. Providence has sent you to help us. But is it really true that my dear sister, Cunégonde, is in the neighborhood, with the governor of Buenos Aires?

Candide reassured him with a solemn oath that nothing could be more true. Their tears began to flow again.

The baron could not weary of embracing Candide; he called him his brother, his savior.

—Ah, my dear Candide, said he, maybe together we will be able to enter the town as conquerors, and be united with my sister Cunégonde.

—That is all I desire, said Candide; I was expecting to marry her, and I still hope to.

—You insolent dog, replied the baron, you would have the effrontery to marry my sister, who has seventy-two quarterings! It's a piece of presumption for you even to mention such a crazy project in my presence.

Candide, terrified by this speech, answered:—Most reverend father, all the quarterings in the world don't affect this case; I have rescued your sister out of the arms of a Jew and an inquisitor; she has many obligations to me, she wants to marry me. Master Pangloss always taught me that men are equal; and I shall certainly marry her.

5. A Jesuit rector at Colmar with whom Voltaire had quarreled in 1754.

—We'll see about that, you scoundrel, said the Jesuit baron of Thunder-Ten-Tronckh; and so saying, he gave him a blow across the face with the flat of his sword. Candide immediately drew his own sword and thrust it up to the hilt in the baron's belly; but as he drew it forth all dripping, he began to weep.

—Alas, dear God! said he, I have killed my old master, my friend, my brother-in-law; I am the best man in the world, and here are three men I've killed already, and two of the three were priests.

Cacambo, who was standing guard at the entry of the bower, came running.

—We can do nothing but sell our lives dearly, said his master; someone will certainly come; we must die fighting.

Cacambo, who had been in similar scrapes before, did not lose his head; he took the Jesuit's cassock, which the commander had been wearing, and put it on Candide; he stuck the dead man's square hat on Candide's head, and forced him onto horseback. Everything was done in the wink of an eye.

—Let's ride, master; everyone will take you for a Jesuit on his way to deliver orders; and we will have passed the frontier before anyone can come after us.

Even as he was pronouncing these words, he charged off, crying in Spanish:—Way, make way for the reverend father colonel!

CHAPTER 16

What Happened to the Two Travelers with Two Girls, Two Monkeys, and the Savages Named Biglugs

Candide and his valet were over the frontier before anyone in the camp knew of the death of the German Jesuit. Foresighted Cacambo had taken care to fill his satchel with bread, chocolate, ham, fruit, and several bottles of wine. They pushed their Andalusian horses forward into unknown country, where there were no roads. Finally a broad prairie divided by several streams opened before them. Our two travelers turned their horses loose to graze; Cacambo suggested that they eat too, and promptly set the example. But Candide said:—How can you expect me to eat ham when I have killed the son of My Lord the Baron, and am now condemned never to see the lovely Cunégonde for the rest of my life? Why should I drag out my miserable days, since I must exist far from her in the depths of despair and remorse? And what will the *Journal de Trévoux*[6] say of all this?

Though he talked this way, he did not neglect the food. Night fell. The two wanderers heard a few weak cries which seemed to be voiced by women. They could not tell whether the cries expressed grief or joy; but they leaped at once to their feet, with that uneasy suspicion which one always feels in an unknown country. The outcry arose from two girls, completely naked, who were running swiftly along the edge of the meadow, pursued by two monkeys who snapped at their buttocks. Candide was moved to pity; he had learned marksmanship with the Bulgars, and could have knocked a nut off a bush without touching the leaves. He raised his Spanish rifle, fired twice, and killed the two monkeys.

—God be praised, my dear Cacambo! I've saved these two poor creatures from great danger. Though I committed a sin in killing an inquisitor and a

---

6. A newspaper published by the Jesuit order, founded in 1701 and consistently hostile to Voltaire.

Jesuit, I've redeemed myself by saving the lives of two girls. Perhaps they are two ladies of rank, and this good deed may gain us special advantages in the country.

He had more to say, but his mouth shut suddenly when he saw the girls embracing the monkeys tenderly, weeping over their bodies, and filling the air with lamentations.

—I wasn't looking for quite so much generosity of spirit, said he to Cacambo; the latter replied:—You've really fixed things this time, master; you've killed the two lovers of these young ladies.

—Their lovers! Impossible! You must be joking, Cacambo; how can I believe you?

—My dear master, Cacambo replied, you're always astonished by everything. Why do you think it so strange that in some countries monkeys succeed in obtaining the good graces of women? They are one quarter human, just as I am one quarter Spanish.

—Alas, Candide replied, I do remember now hearing Master Pangloss say that such things used to happen, and that from these mixtures there arose pans, fauns, and satyrs, and that these creatures had appeared to various grand figures of antiquity; but I took all that for fables.

—You should be convinced now, said Cacambo; it's true, and you see how people make mistakes who haven't received a measure of education. But what I fear is that these girls may get us into real trouble.

These sensible reflections led Candide to leave the field and to hide in a wood. There he dined with Cacambo; and there both of them, having duly cursed the inquisitor of Portugal, the governor of Buenos Aires, and the baron, went to sleep on a bed of moss. When they woke up, they found themselves unable to move; the reason was that during the night the Biglugs,[7] natives of the country, to whom the girls had complained of them, had tied them down with cords of bark. They were surrounded by fifty naked Biglugs, armed with arrows, clubs, and stone axes. Some were boiling a caldron of water, others were preparing spits, and all cried out:—It's a Jesuit, a Jesuit! We'll be revenged and have a good meal; let's eat some Jesuit, eat some Jesuit!

—I told you, my dear master, said Cacambo sadly, I said those two girls would play us a dirty trick.

Candide, noting the caldron and spits, cried out:—We are surely going to be roasted or boiled. Ah, what would Master Pangloss say if he could see these men in a state of nature? All is for the best, I agree; but I must say it seems hard to have lost Miss Cunégonde and to be stuck on a spit by the Biglugs.

Cacambo did not lose his head.

—Don't give up hope, said he to the disconsolate Candide; I understand a little of the jargon these people speak, and I'm going to talk to them.

—Don't forget to remind them, said Candide, of the frightful inhumanity of eating their fellow men, and that Christian ethics forbid it.

—Gentlemen, said Cacambo, you have a mind to eat a Jesuit today? An excellent idea; nothing is more proper than to treat one's enemies so.

---

7. Voltaire's name is "Oreillons" from Spanish "Orejones," a name mentioned in Garcilaso de Vega's *Historia General del Perú* (1609), on which Voltaire drew for many of the details in his picture of South America.

Indeed, the law of nature teaches us to kill our neighbor, and that's how men behave the whole world over. Though we Europeans don't exercise our right to eat our neighbors, the reason is simply that we find it easy to get a good meal elsewhere; but you don't have our resources, and we certainly agree that it's better to eat your enemies than to let the crows and vultures have the fruit of your victory. But, gentlemen, you wouldn't want to eat your friends. You think you will be spitting a Jesuit, and it's your defender, the enemy of your enemies, whom you will be roasting. For my part, I was born in your country; the gentleman whom you see is my master, and far from being a Jesuit, he has just killed a Jesuit, the robe he is wearing was stripped from him; that's why you have taken a dislike to him. To prove that I am telling the truth, take his robe and bring it to the nearest frontier of the kingdom of Los Padres; find out for yourselves if my master didn't kill a Jesuit officer. It won't take long; if you find that I have lied, you can still eat us. But if I've told the truth, you know too well the principles of public justice, customs, and laws, not to spare our lives.

The Biglugs found this discourse perfectly reasonable; they appointed chiefs to go posthaste and find out the truth; the two messengers performed their task like men of sense, and quickly returned bringing good news. The Biglugs untied their two prisoners, treated them with great politeness, offered them girls, gave them refreshments, and led them back to the border of their state, crying joyously:—He isn't a Jesuit, he isn't a Jesuit!

Candide could not weary of exclaiming over his preservation.

—What a people! he said. What men! what customs! If I had not had the good luck to run a sword through the body of Miss Cunégonde's brother, I would have been eaten on the spot! But, after all, it seems that uncorrupted nature is good, since these folk, instead of eating me, showed me a thousand kindnesses as soon as they knew I was not a Jesuit.

CHAPTER 17

Arrival of Candide and His Servant at the Country of Eldorado,
and What They Saw There

When they were out of the land of the Biglugs, Cacambo said to Candide:—You see that this hemisphere is no better than the other; take my advice, and let's get back to Europe as soon as possible.

—How to get back, asked Candide, and where to go? If I go to my own land, the Bulgars and Abares are murdering everyone in sight; if I go to Portugal, they'll burn me alive; if we stay here, we risk being skewered any day. But how can I ever leave that part of the world where Miss Cunégonde lives?

—Let's go toward Cayenne, said Cacambo, we shall find some Frenchmen there, for they go all over the world; they can help us; perhaps God will take pity on us.

To get to Cayenne was not easy; they knew more or less which way to go, but mountains, rivers, cliffs, robbers, and savages obstructed the way everywhere. Their horses died of weariness; their food was eaten; they subsisted for one whole month on wild fruits, and at last they found themselves by a little river fringed with coconut trees, which gave them both life and hope.

Cacambo, who was as full of good advice as the old woman, said to Candide:—We can go no further, we've walked ourselves out; I see an abandoned canoe on the bank, let's fill it with coconuts, get into the boat, and float with the current; a river always leads to some inhabited spot or other. If we don't find anything pleasant, at least we may find something new.

—Let's go, said Candide, and let Providence be our guide.

They floated some leagues between banks sometimes flowery, sometimes sandy, now steep, now level. The river widened steadily; finally it disappeared into a chasm of frightful rocks that rose high into the heavens. The two travelers had the audacity to float with the current into this chasm. The river, narrowly confined, drove them onward with horrible speed and a fearful roar. After twenty-four hours, they saw daylight once more; but their canoe was smashed on the snags. They had to drag themselves from rock to rock for an entire league; at last they emerged to an immense horizon, ringed with remote mountains. The countryside was tended for pleasure as well as profit; everywhere the useful was joined to the agreeable. The roads were covered, or rather decorated, with elegantly shaped carriages made of a glittering material, carrying men and women of singular beauty, and drawn by great red sheep which were faster than the finest horses of Andalusia, Tetuan, and Mequinez.

—Here now, said Candide, is a country that's better than Westphalia.

Along with Cacambo, he climbed out of the river at the first village he could see. Some children of the town, dressed in rags of gold brocade, were playing quoits at the village gate; our two men from the other world paused to watch them; their quoits were rather large, yellow, red, and green, and they glittered with a singular luster. On a whim, the travelers picked up several; they were of gold, emeralds, and rubies, and the least of them would have been the greatest ornament of the Great Mogul's throne.

—Surely, said Cacambo, these quoit players are the children of the king of the country.

The village schoolmaster appeared at that moment, to call them back to school.

—And there, said Candide, is the tutor of the royal household.

The little rascals quickly gave up their game, leaving on the ground their quoits and playthings. Candide picked them up, ran to the schoolmaster, and presented them to him humbly, giving him to understand by sign language that their royal highnesses had forgotten their gold and jewels. With a smile, the schoolmaster tossed them to the ground, glanced quickly but with great surprise at Candide's face, and went his way.

The travelers did not fail to pick up the gold, rubies, and emeralds.

—Where in the world are we? cried Candide. The children of this land must be well trained, since they are taught contempt for gold and jewels.

Cacambo was as much surprised as Candide. At last they came to the finest house of the village; it was built like a European palace. A crowd of people surrounded the door, and even more were in the entry; delightful music was heard, and a delicious aroma of cooking filled the air. Cacambo went up to the door, listened, and reported that they were talking Peruvian; that was his native language, for every reader must know that Cacambo was born in Tucuman, in a village where they talk that language exclusively.

—I'll act as interpreter, he told Candide; it's an hotel, let's go in.

Promptly two boys and two girls of the staff, dressed in cloth of gold, and wearing ribbons in their hair, invited them to sit at the host's table. The meal consisted of four soups, each one garnished with a brace of parakeets, a boiled condor which weighed two hundred pounds, two roast monkeys of an excellent flavor, three hundred birds of paradise in one dish and six hundred hummingbirds in another, exquisite stews, delicious pastries, the whole thing served up in plates of what looked like rock crystal. The boys and girls of the staff poured them various beverages made from sugar cane.

The diners were for the most part merchants and travelers, all extremely polite, who questioned Cacambo with the most discreet circumspection, and answered his questions very directly.

When the meal was over, Cacambo as well as Candide supposed he could settle his bill handsomely by tossing onto the table two of those big pieces of gold which they had picked up; but the host and hostess burst out laughing, and for a long time nearly split their sides. Finally they subsided.

—Gentlemen, said the host, we see clearly that you're foreigners; we don't meet many of you here. Please excuse our laughing when you offered us in payment a couple of pebbles from the roadside. No doubt you don't have any of our local currency, but you don't need it to eat here. All the hotels established for the promotion of commerce are maintained by the state. You have had meager entertainment here, for we are only a poor town; but everywhere else you will be given the sort of welcome you deserve.

Cacambo translated for Candide all the host's explanations, and Candide listened to them with the same admiration and astonishment that his friend Cacambo showed in reporting them.

—What is this country, then, said they to one another, unknown to the rest of the world, and where nature itself is so different from our own? This probably is the country where everything is for the best; for it's absolutely necessary that such a country should exist somewhere. And whatever Master Pangloss said of the matter, I have often had occasion to notice that things went badly in Westphalia.

CHAPTER 18

What They Saw in the Land of Eldorado

Cacambo revealed his curiosity to the host, and the host told him:—I am an ignorant man and content to remain so; but we have here an old man, retired from the court, who is the most knowing person in the kingdom, and the most talkative.

Thereupon he brought Cacambo to the old man's house. Candide now played second fiddle, and acted as servant to his own valet. They entered an austere little house, for the door was merely of silver and the paneling of the rooms was only gold, though so tastefully wrought that the finest paneling would not surpass it. If the truth must be told, the lobby was only decorated with rubies and emeralds; but the patterns in which they were arranged atoned for the extreme simplicity.

The old man received the two strangers on a sofa stuffed with bird-of-paradise feathers, and offered them several drinks in diamond carafes; then he satisfied their curiosity in these terms.

—I am a hundred and seventy-two years old, and I heard from my late father, who was liveryman to the king, about the astonishing revolutions in Peru which he had seen. Our land here was formerly part of the kingdom of the Incas, who rashly left it in order to conquer another part of the world, and who were ultimately destroyed by the Spaniards. The wisest princes of their house were those who had never left their native valley; they decreed, with the consent of the nation, that henceforth no inhabitant of our little kingdom should ever leave it; and this rule is what has preserved our innocence and our happiness. The Spaniards heard vague rumors about this land, they called it El Dorado;[8] and an English knight named Raleigh even came somewhere close to it about a hundred years ago; but as we are surrounded by unscalable mountains and precipices, we have managed so far to remain hidden from the rapacity of the European nations, who have an inconceivable rage for the pebbles and mud of our land, and who, in order to get some, would butcher us all to the last man.

The conversation was a long one; it turned on the form of the government, the national customs, on women, public shows, the arts. At last Candide, whose taste always ran to metaphysics, told Cacambo to ask if the country had any religion.

The old man grew a bit red.

—How's that? he said. Can you have any doubt of it? Do you suppose we are altogether thankless scoundrels?

Cacambo asked meekly what was the religion of Eldorado. The old man flushed again.

—Can there be two religions? he asked. I suppose our religion is the same as everyone's, we worship God from morning to evening.

—Then you worship a single deity? said Cacambo, who acted throughout as interpreter of the questions of Candide.

—It's obvious, said the old man, that there aren't two or three or four of them. I must say the people of your world ask very remarkable questions.

Candide could not weary of putting questions to this good old man; he wanted to know how the people of Eldorado prayed to God.

—We don't pray to him at all, said the good and respectable sage; we have nothing to ask him for, since everything we need has already been granted; we thank God continually.

Candide was interested in seeing the priests; he had Cacambo ask where they were. The old gentleman smiled.

—My friends, said he, we are all priests; the king and all the heads of household sing formal psalms of thanksgiving every morning, and five or six thousand voices accompany them.

—What! you have no monks to teach, argue, govern, intrigue, and burn at the stake everyone who disagrees with them?

—We should have to be mad, said the old man; here we are all of the same mind, and we don't understand what you're up to with your monks.

Candide was overjoyed at all these speeches, and said to himself:—This is very different from Westphalia and the castle of My Lord the Baron; if our

---

8. The myth of this land of gold somewhere in Central or South America had been widespread since the 16th century. *The Discovery of Guiana*, published in 1595, described Sir Walter Ralegh's infatuation with the myth of Eldorado and served to spread the story still further.

friend Pangloss had seen Eldorado, he wouldn't have called the castle of Thunder-Ten-Tronckh the finest thing on earth; to know the world one must travel.

After this long conversation, the old gentleman ordered a carriage with six sheep made ready, and gave the two travelers twelve of his servants for their journey to the court.

—Excuse me, said he, if old age deprives me of the honor of accompanying you. The king will receive you after a style which will not altogether displease you, and you will doubtless make allowance for the customs of the country if there are any you do not like.

Candide and Cacambo climbed into the coach; the six sheep flew like the wind, and in less than four hours they reached the king's palace at the edge of the capital. The entryway was two hundred and twenty feet high and a hundred wide; it is impossible to describe all the materials of which it was made. But you can imagine how much finer it was than those pebbles and sand which we call gold and jewels.

Twenty beautiful girls of the guard detail welcomed Candide and Cacambo as they stepped from the carriage, took them to the baths, and dressed them in robes woven of hummingbird feathers; then the high officials of the crown, both male and female, led them to the royal chamber between two long lines, each of a thousand musicians, as is customary. As they approached the throne room, Cacambo asked an officer what was the proper method of greeting his majesty: if one fell to one's knees or on one's belly; if one put one's hands on one's head or on one's rear; if one licked up the dust of the earth—in a word, what was the proper form?[9]

—The ceremony, said the officer, is to embrace the king and kiss him on both cheeks.

Candide and Cacambo fell on the neck of his majesty, who received them with all the dignity imaginable, and asked them politely to dine.

In the interim, they were taken about to see the city, the public buildings rising to the clouds, the public markets and arcades, the fountains of pure water and of rose water, those of sugar cane liquors which flowed perpetually in the great plazas paved with a sort of stone which gave off odors of gillyflower and rose petals. Candide asked to see the supreme court and the hall of parliament; they told him there was no such thing, that lawsuits were unknown. He asked if there were prisons, and was told there were not. What surprised him more, and gave him most pleasure, was the palace of sciences, in which he saw a gallery two thousand paces long, entirely filled with mathematical and physical instruments.

Having passed the whole afternoon seeing only a thousandth part of the city, they returned to the king's palace. Candide sat down to dinner with his majesty, his own valet Cacambo, and several ladies. Never was better food served, and never did a host preside more jovially than his majesty. Cacambo explained the king's witty sayings to Candide, and even when translated they still seemed witty. Of all the things which astonished Candide, this was not, in his eyes, the least astonishing.

9. Candide's questions are probably derived from those of Gulliver on a similar occasion, in the third part of *Gulliver's Travels*.

They passed a month in this refuge. Candide never tired of saying to Cacambo:—It's true, my friend, I'll say it again, the castle where I was born does not compare with the land where we now are; but Miss Cunégonde is not here, and you doubtless have a mistress somewhere in Europe. If we stay here, we shall be just like everybody else, whereas if we go back to our own world, taking with us just a dozen sheep loaded with Eldorado pebbles, we shall be richer than all the kings put together, we shall have no more inquisitors to fear, and we shall easily be able to retake Miss Cunégonde.

This harangue pleased Cacambo; wandering is such pleasure, it gives a man such prestige at home to be able to talk of what he has seen abroad, that the two happy men resolved to be so no longer, but to take their leave of his majesty.

—You are making a foolish mistake, the king told them; I know very well that my kingdom is nothing much; but when you are pretty comfortable somewhere, you had better stay there. Of course I have no right to keep strangers against their will, that sort of tyranny is not in keeping with our laws or our customs; all men are free; depart when you will, but the way out is very difficult. You cannot possibly go up the river by which you miraculously came; it runs too swiftly through its underground caves. The mountains which surround my land are ten thousand feet high, and steep as walls; each one is more than ten leagues across; the only way down is over precipices. But since you really must go, I shall order my engineers to make a machine which can carry you conveniently. When we take you over the mountains, nobody will be able to go with you, for my subjects have sworn never to leave their refuge, and they are too sensible to break their vows. Other than that, ask of me what you please.

—We only request of your majesty, Cacambo said, a few sheep loaded with provisions, some pebbles, and some of the mud of your country.

The king laughed.

—I simply can't understand, said he, the passion you Europeans have for our yellow mud; but take all you want, and much good may it do you.

He promptly gave orders to his technicians to make a machine for lifting these two extraordinary men out of his kingdom. Three thousand good physicists worked at the problem; the machine was ready in two weeks' time, and cost no more than twenty million pounds sterling, in the money of the country. Cacambo and Candide were placed in the machine; there were two great sheep, saddled and bridled to serve them as steeds when they had cleared the mountains, twenty pack sheep with provisions, thirty which carried presents consisting of the rarities of the country, and fifty loaded with gold, jewels, and diamonds. The king bade tender farewell to the two vagabonds.

It made a fine spectacle, their departure, and the ingenious way in which they were hoisted with their sheep up to the top of the mountains. The technicians bade them good-bye after bringing them to safety, and Candide had now no other desire and no other object than to go and present his sheep to Miss Cunégonde.

—We have, said he, enough to pay off the governor of Buenos Aires—if, indeed, a price can be placed on Miss Cunégonde. Let us go to Cayenne, take ship there, and then see what kingdom we can find to buy up.

CHAPTER 19

What Happened to Them at Surinam, and How Candide
Got to Know Martin

The first day was pleasant enough for our travelers. They were encouraged by the idea of possessing more treasures than Asia, Europe, and Africa could bring together. Candide, in transports, carved the name of Cunégonde on the trees. On the second day two of their sheep bogged down in a swamp and were lost with their loads; two other sheep died of fatigue a few days later; seven or eight others starved to death in a desert; still others fell, a little after, from precipices. Finally, after a hundred days' march, they had only two sheep left. Candide told Cacambo:—My friend, you see how the riches of this world are fleeting; the only solid things are virtue and the joy of seeing Miss Cunégonde again.

—I agree, said Cacambo, but we still have two sheep, laden with more treasure than the king of Spain will ever have; and I see in the distance a town which I suspect is Surinam; it belongs to the Dutch. We are at the end of our trials and on the threshold of our happiness.

As they drew near the town, they discovered a negro stretched on the ground with only half his clothes left, that is, a pair of blue drawers; the poor fellow was also missing his left leg and his right hand.

—Good Lord, said Candide in Dutch, what are you doing in that horrible condition, my friend?

—I am waiting for my master, Mr. Vanderdendur,[1] the famous merchant, answered the negro.

—Is Mr. Vanderdendur, Candide asked, the man who treated you this way?

—Yes, sir, said the negro, that's how things are around here. Twice a year we get a pair of linen drawers to wear. If we catch a finger in the sugar mill where we work, they cut off our hand; if we try to run away, they cut off our leg: I have undergone both these experiences. This is the price of the sugar you eat in Europe. And yet, when my mother sold me for ten Patagonian crowns on the coast of Guinea, she said to me: 'My dear child, bless our witch doctors, reverence them always, they will make your life happy; you have the honor of being a slave to our white masters, and in this way you are making the fortune of your father and mother.' Alas! I don't know if I made their fortunes, but they certainly did not make mine. The dogs, monkeys, and parrots are a thousand times less unhappy than we are. The Dutch witch doctors who converted me tell me every Sunday that we are all sons of Adam, black and white alike. I am no genealogist; but if these preachers are right, we must all be remote cousins; and you must admit no one could treat his own flesh and blood in a more horrible fashion.

—Oh Pangloss! cried Candide, you had no notion of these abominations! I'm through, I must give up your optimism after all.

—What's optimism? said Cacambo.

—Alas, said Candide, it is a mania for saying things are well when one is in hell.

---

1. A name perhaps intended to suggest VanDuren, a Dutch bookseller with whom Voltaire had quarreled. In particular, the incident of gradually raising one's price recalls VanDuren, to whom Voltaire had successively offered 1,000, 1,500, 2,000, and 3,000 florins for the return of the manuscript of Frederick the Great's *Anti-Machiavel*.

And he shed bitter tears as he looked at this negro, and he was still weeping as he entered Surinam.

The first thing they asked was if there was not some vessel in port which could be sent to Buenos Aires. The man they asked was a Spanish merchant who undertook to make an honest bargain with them. They arranged to meet in a café; Candide and the faithful Cacambo, with their two sheep, went there to meet with him.

Candide, who always said exactly what was in his heart, told the Spaniard of his adventures, and confessed that he wanted to recapture Miss Cunégonde.

—I shall take good care *not* to send you to Buenos Aires, said the merchant; I should be hanged, and so would you. The lovely Cunégonde is his lordship's favorite mistress.

This was a thunderstroke for Candide; he wept for a long time; finally he drew Cacambo aside.

—Here, my friend, said he, is what you must do. Each one of us has in his pockets five or six millions' worth of diamonds; you are cleverer than I; go get Miss Cunégonde in Buenos Aires. If the governor makes a fuss, give him a million; if that doesn't convince him, give him two millions; you never killed an inquisitor, nobody will suspect you. I'll fit out another boat and go wait for you in Venice. That is a free country, where one need have no fear either of Bulgars or Abares or Jews or inquisitors.

Cacambo approved of this wise decision. He was in despair at leaving a good master who had become a bosom friend; but the pleasure of serving him overcame the grief of leaving him. They embraced, and shed a few tears; Candide urged him not to forget the good old woman. Cacambo departed that very same day; he was a very good fellow, that Cacambo.

Candide remained for some time in Surinam, waiting for another merchant to take him to Italy, along with the two sheep which were left him. He hired servants and bought everything necessary for the long voyage; finally Mr. Vanderdendur, master of a big ship, came calling.

—How much will you charge, Candide asked this man, to take me to Venice—myself, my servants, my luggage, and those two sheep over there?

The merchant set a price of ten thousand piastres; Candide did not blink an eye.

—Oh, ho, said the prudent Vanderdendur to himself, this stranger pays out ten thousand piastres at once, he must be pretty well fixed.

Then, returning a moment later, he made known that he could not set sail under twenty thousand.

—All right, you shall have them, said Candide.

—Whew, said the merchant softly to himself, this man gives twenty thousand piastres as easily as ten.

He came back again to say he could not go to Venice for less than thirty thousand piastres.

—All right, thirty then, said Candide.

—Ah ha, said the Dutch merchant, again speaking to himself; so thirty thousand piastres mean nothing to this man; no doubt the two sheep are loaded with immense treasures; let's say no more; we'll pick up the thirty thousand piastres first, and then we'll see.

Candide sold two little diamonds, the least of which was worth more than all the money demanded by the merchant. He paid him in advance. The two sheep were taken aboard. Candide followed in a little boat, to board the vessel at its anchorage. The merchant bides his time, sets sail, and makes his escape with a favoring wind. Candide, aghast and stupefied, soon loses him from view.

—Alas, he cries, now there is a trick worthy of the old world!

He returns to shore sunk in misery; for he had lost riches enough to make the fortunes of twenty monarchs.

Now he rushes to the house of the Dutch magistrate, and, being a bit disturbed, he knocks loudly at the door; goes in, tells the story of what happened, and shouts a bit louder than is customary. The judge begins by fining him ten thousand piastres for making such a racket; then he listens patiently to the story, promises to look into the matter as soon as the merchant comes back, and charges another ten thousand piastres as the costs of the hearing.

This legal proceeding completed the despair of Candide. In fact he had experienced miseries a thousand times more painful, but the coldness of the judge, and that of the merchant who had robbed him, roused his bile and plunged him into a black melancholy. The malice of men rose up before his spirit in all its ugliness, and his mind dwelt only on gloomy thoughts. Finally, when a French vessel was ready to leave for Bordeaux, since he had no more diamond-laden sheep to transport, he took a cabin at a fair price, and made it known in the town that he would pay passage and keep, plus two thousand piastres, to any honest man who wanted to make the journey with him, on condition that this man must be the most disgusted with his own condition and the most unhappy man in the province.

This drew such a crowd of applicants as a fleet could not have held. Candide wanted to choose among the leading candidates, so he picked out about twenty who seemed companionable enough, and of whom each pretended to be more miserable than all the others. He brought them together at his inn and gave them a dinner, on condition that each would swear to tell truthfully his entire history. He would select as his companion the most truly miserable and rightly discontented man, and among the others he would distribute various gifts.

The meeting lasted till four in the morning. Candide, as he listened to all the stories, remembered what the old woman had told him on the trip to Buenos Aires, and of the wager she had made, that there was nobody on the boat who had not undergone great misfortunes. At every story that was told him, he thought of Pangloss.

—That Pangloss, he said, would be hard put to prove his system. I wish he was here. Certainly if everything goes well, it is in Eldorado and not in the rest of the world.

At last he decided in favor of a poor scholar who had worked ten years for the booksellers of Amsterdam. He decided that there was no trade in the world with which one should be more disgusted.

This scholar, who was in fact a good man, had been robbed by his wife, beaten by his son, and deserted by his daughter, who had got herself abducted by a Portuguese. He had just been fired from the little job on

which he existed; and the preachers of Surinam were persecuting him
because they took him for a Socinian.[2] The others, it is true, were at least as
unhappy as he, but Candide hoped the scholar would prove more amusing
on the voyage. All his rivals declared that Candide was doing them a great
injustice, but he pacified them with a hundred piastres apiece.

CHAPTER 20

What Happened to Candide and Martin at Sea

The old scholar, whose name was Martin, now set sail with Candide for
Bordeaux. Both men had seen and suffered much; and even if the vessel had
been sailing from Surinam to Japan via the Cape of Good Hope, they would
have been able to keep themselves amused with instances of moral evil and
physical evil during the entire trip.

However, Candide had one great advantage over Martin, that he still
hoped to see Miss Cunégonde again, and Martin had nothing to hope for;
besides, he had gold and diamonds, and though he had lost a hundred big
red sheep loaded with the greatest treasures of the earth, though he had
always at his heart a memory of the Dutch merchant's villainy, yet, when he
thought of the wealth that remained in his hands, and when he talked of
Cunégonde, especially just after a good dinner, he still inclined to the system of Pangloss.

—But what about you, Monsieur Martin, he asked the scholar, what do
you think of all that? What is your idea of moral evil and physical evil?

—Sir, answered Martin, those priests accused me of being a Socinian, but
the truth is that I am a Manichee.[3]

—You're joking, said Candide; there aren't any more Manichees in the
world.

—There's me, said Martin; I don't know what to do about it, but I can't
think otherwise.

—You must be possessed of the devil, said Candide.

—He's mixed up with so many things of this world, said Martin, that he
may be in me as well as elsewhere; but I assure you, as I survey this globe, or
globule, I think that God has abandoned it to some evil spirit—all of it
except Eldorado. I have scarcely seen one town which did not wish to
destroy its neighboring town, no family which did not wish to exterminate
some other family. Everywhere the weak loathe the powerful, before whom
they cringe, and the powerful treat them like brute cattle, to be sold for their
meat and fleece. A million regimented assassins roam Europe from one end
to the other, plying the trades of murder and robbery in an organized way for
a living, because there is no more honest form of work for them; and in the
cities which seem to enjoy peace and where the arts are flourishing, men are
devoured by more envy, cares, and anxieties than a whole town experiences
when it's under siege. Private griefs are worse even than public trials. In a
word, I have seen so much and suffered so much, that I am a Manichee.

2. A follower of Faustus and Laelius Socinus, 16th-century Polish theologians, who proposed a form of
"rational" Christianity which exalted the rational conscience and minimized such mysteries as the trinity.
The Socinians, by a special irony, were vigorous optimists.   3. Mani, a Persian sage and philosopher of
the 3rd century c.e., taught (probably under the influence of traditions stemming from Zoroaster and the
worshipers of the sun god Mithra) that the earth is a field of dispute between two almost equal powers, one
of light and one of darkness, both of which must be propitiated.

—Still there is some good, said Candide.

—That may be, said Martin, but I don't know it.

In the middle of this discussion, the rumble of cannon was heard. From minute to minute the noise grew louder. Everyone reached for his spyglass. At a distance of some three miles they saw two vessels fighting; the wind brought both of them so close to the French vessel that they had a pleasantly comfortable seat to watch the fight. Presently one of the vessels caught the other with a broadside so low and so square as to send it to the bottom. Candide and Martin saw clearly a hundred men on the deck of the sinking ship; they all raised their hands to heaven, uttering fearful shrieks; and in a moment everything was swallowed up.

—Well, said Martin, that is how men treat one another.

—It is true, said Candide, there's something devilish in this business.

As they chatted, he noticed something of a striking red color floating near the sunken vessel. They sent out a boat to investigate; it was one of his sheep. Candide was more joyful to recover this one sheep than he had been afflicted to lose a hundred of them, all loaded with big Eldorado diamonds.

The French captain soon learned that the captain of the victorious vessel was Spanish and that of the sunken vessel was a Dutch pirate. It was the same man who had robbed Candide. The enormous riches which this rascal had stolen were sunk beside him in the sea, and nothing was saved but a single sheep.

—You see, said Candide to Martin, crime is punished sometimes; this scoundrel of a Dutch merchant has met the fate he deserved.

—Yes, said Martin; but did the passengers aboard his ship have to perish too? God punished the scoundrel, and the devil drowned the others.

Meanwhile the French and Spanish vessels continued on their journey, and Candide continued his talks with Martin. They disputed for fifteen days in a row, and at the end of that time were just as much in agreement as at the beginning. But at least they were talking, they exchanged their ideas, they consoled one another. Candide caressed his sheep.

—Since I have found you again, said he, I may well rediscover Miss Cunégonde.

CHAPTER 21

Candide and Martin Approach the Coast of France: They Reason Together

At last the coast of France came in view.

—Have you ever been in France, Monsieur Martin? asked Candide.

—Yes, said Martin, I have visited several provinces. There are some where half the inhabitants are crazy, others where they are too sly, still others where they are quite gentle and stupid, some where they venture on wit; in all of them the principal occupation is love-making, the second is slander, and the third stupid talk.

—But, Monsieur Martin, were you ever in Paris?

—Yes, I've been in Paris; it contains specimens of all these types; it is a chaos, a mob, in which everyone is seeking pleasure and where hardly anyone finds it, at least from what I have seen. I did not live there for long; as I arrived, I was robbed of everything I possessed by thieves at the fair of St. Germain; I myself was taken for a thief, and spent eight days in jail, after which I took a proofreader's job to earn enough money to return on foot to Holland. I knew the writing gang, the intriguing gang, the gang with fits and convulsions.[4] They say there are some very civilized people in that town; I'd like to think so.

—I myself have no desire to visit France, said Candide; you no doubt realize that when one has spent a month in Eldorado, there is nothing else on earth one wants to see, except Miss Cunégonde. I am going to wait for her at Venice; we will cross France simply to get to Italy; wouldn't you like to come with me?

—Gladly, said Martin; they say Venice is good only for the Venetian nobles, but that on the other hand they treat foreigners very well when they have plenty of money. I don't have any; you do, so I'll follow you anywhere.

—By the way, said Candide, do you believe the earth was originally all ocean, as they assure us in that big book belonging to the ship's captain?[5]

—I don't believe that stuff, said Martin, nor any of the dreams which people have been peddling for some time now.

—But why, then, was this world formed at all? asked Candide.

—To drive us mad, answered Martin.

—Aren't you astonished, Candide went on, at the love which those two girls showed for the monkeys in the land of the Biglugs that I told you about?

—Not at all, said Martin, I see nothing strange in these sentiments; I have seen so many extraordinary things that nothing seems extraordinary any more.

—Do you believe, asked Candide, that men have always massacred one another as they do today? That they have always been liars, traitors, ingrates, thieves, weaklings, sneaks, cowards, backbiters, gluttons, drunkards, misers, climbers, killers, calumniators, sensualists, fanatics, hypocrites, and fools?

—Do you believe, said Martin, that hawks have always eaten pigeons when they could get them?

—Of course, said Candide.

—Well, said Martin, if hawks have always had the same character, why do you suppose that men have changed?

—Oh, said Candide, there's a great deal of difference, because freedom of the will . . .

As they were disputing in this manner, they reached Bordeaux.

CHAPTER 22

What Happened in France to Candide and Martin

Candide paused in Bordeaux only long enough to sell a couple of Dorado pebbles and to fit himself out with a fine two-seater carriage, for he could no longer do without his philosopher Martin; only he was very unhappy to part with his sheep, which he left to the academy of science in Bordeaux. They proposed, as the theme of that year's prize contest, the discovery of why the wool of the sheep was red; and the prize was awarded to a northern scholar[6]

---

4. The Jansenists, a sect of strict Catholics, became notorious for spiritual ecstasies. Their public displays reached a height during the 1720s, and Voltaire described them in *Le Siècle de Louis XIV* (chap. 37), as well as in the article "Convulsions" in the *Philosophical Dictionary.* 5. The Bible: Genesis 1. 6. Maupertuis Le Lapon, philosopher and mathematician, whom Voltaire had accused of trying to adduce mathematical proofs of the existence of God.

who demonstrated by A plus B minus C divided by Z that the sheep ought to be red and die of sheep rot.

But all the travelers with whom Candide talked in the roadside inns told him:—We are going to Paris.

This general consensus finally inspired in him too a desire to see the capital; it was not much out of his road to Venice.

He entered through the Faubourg Saint-Marceau,[7] and thought he was in the meanest village of Westphalia.

Scarcely was Candide in his hotel, when he came down with a mild illness caused by exhaustion. As he was wearing an enormous diamond ring, and people had noticed among his luggage a tremendously heavy safe, he soon found at his bedside two doctors whom he had not called, several intimate friends who never left him alone, and two pious ladies who helped to warm his broth. Martin said:—I remember that I too was ill on my first trip to Paris; I was very poor; and as I had neither friends, pious ladies, nor doctors, I got well.

However, as a result of medicines and bleedings, Candide's illness became serious. A resident of the neighborhood came to ask him politely to fill out a ticket, to be delivered to the porter of the other world.[8] Candide wanted nothing to do with it. The pious ladies assured him it was a new fashion; Candide replied that he wasn't a man of fashion. Martin wanted to throw the resident out the window. The cleric swore that without the ticket they wouldn't bury Candide. Martin swore that he would bury the cleric if he continued to be a nuisance. The quarrel grew heated; Martin took him by the shoulders and threw him bodily out the door; all of which caused a great scandal, from which developed a legal case.

Candide got better; and during his convalescence he had very good company in to dine. They played cards for money; and Candide was quite surprised that none of the aces were ever dealt to him, and Martin was not surprised at all.

Among those who did the honors of the town for Candide there was a little abbé from Perigord, one of those busy fellows, always bright, always useful, assured, obsequious, and obliging, who waylay passing strangers, tell them the scandal of the town, and offer them pleasures at any price they want to pay. This fellow first took Candide and Martin to the theatre. A new tragedy was being played. Candide found himself seated next to a group of wits. That did not keep him from shedding a few tears in the course of some perfectly played scenes. One of the commentators beside him remarked during the intermission:—You are quite mistaken to weep, this actress is very bad indeed; the actor who plays with her is even worse; and the play is even worse than the actors in it. The author knows not a word of Arabic, though the action takes place in Arabia; and besides, he is a man who doesn't believe in innate ideas. Tomorrow I will show you twenty pamphlets written against him.

---

7. A district on the left bank, notably grubby in the 18th century. "As I entered [Paris] through the Faubourg Saint-Marceau, I saw nothing but dirty stinking little streets, ugly black houses, a general air of squalor and poverty, beggars, carters, menders of clothes, sellers of herb-drinks and old hats." Jean-Jacques Rousseau, *Confessions*, Book IV.   8. In the middle of the 18th century, it became customary to require persons who were grievously ill to sign *billets de confession*, without which they could not be given absolution, admitted to the last sacraments, or buried in consecrated ground.

—Tell me, sir, said Candide to the abbé, how many plays are there for performance in France?

—Five or six thousand, replied the other.

—That's a lot, said Candide; how many of them are any good?

—Fifteen or sixteen, was the answer.

—That's a lot, said Martin.

Candide was very pleased with an actress who took the part of Queen Elizabeth in a rather dull tragedy[9] that still gets played from time to time.

—I like this actress very much, he said to Martin, she bears a slight resemblance to Miss Cunégonde; I should like to meet her.

The abbé from Perigord offered to introduce him. Candide, raised in Germany, asked what was the protocol, how one behaved in France with queens of England.

—You must distinguish, said the abbé; in the provinces, you take them to an inn; at Paris they are respected while still attractive, and thrown on the dunghill when they are dead.[1]

—Queens on the dunghill! said Candide.

—Yes indeed, said Martin, the abbé is right; I was in Paris when Miss Monime herself[2] passed, as they say, from this life to the other; she was refused what these folk call 'the honors of burial,' that is, the right to rot with all the beggars of the district in a dirty cemetery; she was buried all alone by her troupe at the corner of the Rue de Bourgogne; this must have been very disagreeable to her, for she had a noble character.

—That was extremely rude, said Candide.

—What do you expect? said Martin; that is how these folk are. Imagine all the contradictions, all the incompatibilities you can, and you will see them in the government, the courts, the churches, and the plays of this crazy nation.

—Is it true that they are always laughing in Paris? asked Candide.

—Yes, said the abbé, but with a kind of rage too; when people complain of things, they do so amid explosions of laughter; they even laugh as they perform the most detestable actions.

—Who was that fat swine, said Candide, who spoke so nastily about the play over which I was weeping, and the actors who gave me so much pleasure?

—He is a living illness, answered the abbé, who makes a business of slandering all the plays and books; he hates the successful ones, as eunuchs hate successful lovers; he's one of those literary snakes who live on filth and venom; he's a folliculator . . .

—What's this word *folliculator*? asked Candide.

—It's a folio filler, said the abbé, a Fréron.[3]

It was after this fashion that Candide, Martin, and the abbé from Perigord chatted on the stairway as they watched the crowd leaving the theatre.

---

9. *Le Comte d'Essex* by Thomas Corneille.   1. Voltaire engaged in a long and vigorous campaign against the rule that actors and actresses could not be buried in consecrated ground. The superstition probably arose from a feeling that by assuming false identities they drained their own souls.   2. Adrienne Lecouvreur (1690–1730), so called because she made her debut as Monime in Racine's *Mithridate*. Voltaire had assisted at her secret midnight funeral and wrote an indignant poem about it.   3. A successful and popular journalist, who had attacked several of Voltaire's plays, including *Tancrède*.

—Although I'm in a great hurry to see Miss Cunégonde again, said Candide, I would very much like to dine with Miss Clairon,[4] for she seemed to me admirable.

The abbé was not the man to approach Miss Clairon, who saw only good company.

—She has an engagement tonight, he said; but I shall have the honor of introducing you to a lady of quality, and there you will get to know Paris as if you had lived here for years.

Candide, who was curious by nature, allowed himself to be brought to the lady's house, in the depths of the Faubourg St.-Honoré; they were playing faro;[5] twelve melancholy punters held in their hands a little sheaf of cards, blank summaries of their bad luck. Silence reigned supreme, the punters were pallid, the banker uneasy; and the lady of the house, seated beside the pitiless banker, watched with the eyes of a lynx for the various illegal redoublings and bets at long odds which the players tried to signal by folding the corners of their cards; she had them unfolded with a determination which was severe but polite, and concealed her anger lest she lose her customers. The lady caused herself to be known as the Marquise of Parolignac.[6] Her daughter, fifteen years old, sat among the punters and tipped off her mother with a wink to the sharp practices of these unhappy players when they tried to recoup their losses. The abbé from Perigord, Candide, and Martin came in; nobody arose or greeted them or looked at them; all were lost in the study of their cards.

—My Lady the Baroness of Thunder-Ten-Tronckh was more civil, thought Candide.

However, the abbé whispered in the ear of the marquise, who, half rising, honored Candide with a gracious smile and Martin with a truly noble nod; she gave a seat and dealt a hand of cards to Candide, who lost fifty thousand francs in two turns; after which they had a very merry supper. Everyone was amazed that Candide was not upset over his losses; the lackeys, talking together in their usual lackey language, said:—He must be some English milord.

The supper was like most Parisian suppers: first silence, then an indistinguishable rush of words; then jokes, mostly insipid, false news, bad logic, a little politics, a great deal of malice. They even talked of new books.

—Have you seen the new novel by Dr. Gauchat, the theologian?[7] asked the abbé from Perigord.

—Oh yes, answered one of the guests; but I couldn't finish it. We have a horde of impudent scribblers nowadays, but all of them put together don't match the impudence of this Gauchat, this doctor of theology. I have been so struck by the enormous number of detestable books which are swamping us that I have taken up punting at faro.

—And the *Collected Essays* of Archdeacon T———[8] asked the abbé, what do you think of them?

---

4. Actually Claire Leris (1723–1803). She had played the lead role in *Tancrède* and was for many years a leading figure on the Paris stage.   5. A game of cards, about which it is necessary to know only that a number of punters play against a banker or dealer. The pack is dealt out two cards at a time, and each player may bet on any card as much as he pleases. The sharp practices of the punters consist essentially of tricks for increasing their winnings without corresponding risks.   6. A *paroli* is an illegal redoubling of one's bet; her name therefore implies a title grounded in cardsharping.   7. He had written against Voltaire, and Voltaire suspected him (wrongly) of having written the novel *L'Oracle des nouveaux philosophes*.   8. His name was Trublet, and he had said, among other disagreeable things, that Voltaire's epic poem, the *Henriade*, made him yawn and that Voltaire's genius was "the perfection of mediocrity."

—Ah, said Madame de Parolignac, what a frightful bore he is! He takes such pains to tell you what everyone knows; he discourses so learnedly on matters which aren't worth a casual remark! He plunders, and not even wittily, the wit of other people! He spoils what he plunders, he's disgusting! But he'll never disgust me again; a couple of pages of the archdeacon have been enough for me.

There was at table a man of learning and taste, who supported the marquise on this point. They talked next of tragedies; the lady asked why there were tragedies which played well enough but which were wholly unreadable. The man of taste explained very clearly how a play could have a certain interest and yet little merit otherwise; he showed succinctly that it was not enough to conduct a couple of intrigues, such as one can find in any novel, and which never fail to excite the spectator's interest; but that one must be new without being grotesque, frequently touch the sublime but never depart from the natural; that one must know the human heart and give it words; that one must be a great poet without allowing any character in the play to sound like a poet; and that one must know the language perfectly, speak it purely, and maintain a continual harmony without ever sacrificing sense to mere sound.

—Whoever, he added, does not observe all these rules may write one or two tragedies which succeed in the theatre, but he will never be ranked among the good writers; there are very few good tragedies; some are idylls in well-written, well-rhymed dialogue, others are political arguments which put the audience to sleep, or revolting pomposities; still others are the fantasies of enthusiasts, barbarous in style, incoherent in logic, full of long speeches to the gods because the author does not know how to address men, full of false maxims and emphatic commonplaces.

Candide listened attentively to this speech and conceived a high opinion of the speaker; and as the marquise had placed him by her side, he turned to ask her who was this man who spoke so well.

—He is a scholar, said the lady, who never plays cards and whom the abbé sometimes brings to my house for supper; he knows all about tragedies and books, and has himself written a tragedy that was hissed from the stage and a book, the only copy of which ever seen outside his publisher's office was dedicated to me.

—What a great man, said Candide, he's Pangloss all over.

Then, turning to him, he said:—Sir, you doubtless think everything is for the best in the physical as well as the moral universe, and that nothing could be otherwise than as it is?

—Not at all, sir, replied the scholar, I believe nothing of the sort. I find that everything goes wrong in our world; that nobody knows his place in society or his duty, what he's doing or what he ought to be doing, and that outside of mealtimes, which are cheerful and congenial enough, all the rest of the day is spent in useless quarrels, as of Jansenists against Molinists,[9] parliament-men against churchmen, literary men against literary men, courtiers against courtiers, financiers against the plebs, wives against husbands, relatives against relatives—it's one unending warfare.

---

9. The Jansenists (from Corneille Jansen, 1585–1638) were a relatively strict party of religious reform; the Molinists (from Luis Molina) were the party of the Jesuits. Their central issue of controversy was the relative importance of divine grace and human will to the salvation of man.

Candide answered:—I have seen worse; but a wise man, who has since had the misfortune to be hanged, taught me that everything was marvelously well arranged. Troubles are just the shadows in a beautiful picture.

—Your hanged philosopher was joking, said Martin; the shadows are horrible ugly blots.

—It is human beings who make the blots, said Candide, and they can't do otherwise.

—Then it isn't their fault, said Martin.

Most of the faro players, who understood this sort of talk not at all, kept on drinking; Martin disputed with the scholar, and Candide told part of his story to the lady of the house.

After supper, the marquise brought Candide into her room and sat him down on a divan.

—Well, she said to him, are you still madly in love with Miss Cunégonde of Thunder-Ten-Tronckh?

—Yes, ma'am, replied Candide. The marquise turned upon him a tender smile.

—You answer like a young man of Westphalia, said she; a Frenchman would have told me: 'It is true that I have been in love with Miss Cunégonde; but since seeing you, madame, I fear that I love her no longer.'

—Alas, ma'am, said Candide, I will answer any way you want.

—Your passion for her, said the marquise, began when you picked up her handkerchief; I prefer that you should pick up my garter.

—Gladly, said Candide, and picked it up.

—But I also want you to put it back on, said the lady; and Candide put it on again.

—Look you now, said the lady, you are a foreigner; my Paris lovers I sometimes cause to languish for two weeks or so, but to you I surrender the very first night, because we must render the honors of the country to a young man from Westphalia.

The beauty, who had seen two enormous diamonds on the two hands of her young friend, praised them so sincerely that from the fingers of Candide they passed over to the fingers of the marquise.

As he returned home with his Perigord abbé, Candide felt some remorse at having been unfaithful to Miss Cunégonde; the abbé sympathized with his grief; he had only a small share in the fifty thousand francs which Candide lost at cards, and in the proceeds of the two diamonds which had been half-given, half-extorted. His scheme was to profit, as much as he could, from the advantage of knowing Candide. He spoke at length of Cunégonde, and Candide told him that he would beg forgiveness for his beloved for his infidelity when he met her at Venice.

The Perigordian overflowed with politeness and unction, taking a tender interest in everything Candide said, everything he did, and everything he wanted to do.

—Well, sir, said he, so you have an assignation at Venice?

—Yes indeed, sir, I do, said Candide; it is absolutely imperative that I go there to find Miss Cunégonde.

And then, carried away by the pleasure of talking about his love, he recounted, as he often did, a part of his adventures with that illustrious lady of Westphalia.

—I suppose, said the abbé, that Miss Cunégonde has a fine wit and writes charming letters.

—I never received a single letter from her, said Candide; for, as you can imagine, after being driven out of the castle for love of her, I couldn't write; shortly I learned that she was dead; then I rediscovered her; then I lost her again, and I have now sent, to a place more than twenty-five hundred leagues from here, a special agent whose return I am expecting.

The abbé listened carefully, and looked a bit dreamy. He soon took his leave of the two strangers, after embracing them tenderly. Next day Candide, when he woke up, received a letter, to the following effect:

—Dear sir, my very dear lover, I have been lying sick in this town for a week, I have just learned that you are here. I would fly to your arms if I could move. I heard that you had passed through Bordeaux; that was where I left the faithful Cacambo and the old woman, who are soon to follow me here. The governor of Buenos Aires took everything, but left me your heart. Come; your presence will either return me to life or cause me to die of joy.

This charming letter, coming so unexpectedly, filled Candide with inexpressible delight, while the illness of his dear Cunégonde covered him with grief. Torn between these two feelings, he took gold and diamonds, and had himself brought, with Martin, to the hotel where Miss Cunégonde was lodging. Trembling with emotion, he enters the room; his heart thumps, his voice breaks. He tries to open the curtains of the bed, he asks to have some lights.

—Absolutely forbidden, says the serving girl; light will be the death of her. And abruptly she pulls shut the curtain.

—My dear Cunégonde, says Candide in tears, how are you feeling? If you can't see me, won't you at least speak to me?

—She can't talk, says the servant.

But then she draws forth from the bed a plump hand, over which Candide weeps a long time, and which he fills with diamonds, meanwhile leaving a bag of gold on the chair.

Amid his transports, there arrives a bailiff followed by the abbé from Perigord and a strong-arm squad.

—These here are the suspicious foreigners? says the officer; and he has them seized and orders his bullies to drag them off to jail.

—They don't treat visitors like this in Eldorado, says Candide.

—I am more a Manichee than ever, says Martin.

—But, please sir, where are you taking us? says Candide.

—To the lowest hole in the dungeons, says the bailiff.

Martin, having regained his self-possession, decided that the lady who pretended to be Cunégonde was a cheat, the abbé from Perigord was another cheat who had imposed on Candide's innocence, and the bailiff still another cheat, of whom it would be easy to get rid.

Rather than submit to the forms of justice, Candide, enlightened by Martin's advice and eager for his own part to see the real Cunégonde again, offered the bailiff three little diamonds worth about three thousand pistoles apiece.

—Ah, my dear sir! cried the man with the ivory staff, even if you have committed every crime imaginable, you are the most honest man in the world. Three diamonds! each one worth three thousand pistoles! My dear sir! I would gladly die for you, rather than take you to jail. All foreigners get arrested here; but let me manage it; I have a brother at Dieppe in Normandy; I'll take you to him; and if you have a bit of a diamond to give him, he'll take care of you, just like me.

—And why do they arrest all foreigners? asked Candide.

The abbé from Perigord spoke up and said:—It's because a beggar from Atrebatum[1] listened to some stupidities; that made him commit a parricide, not like the one of May, 1610, but like the one of December, 1594, much on the order of several other crimes committed in other years and other months by other beggars who had listened to stupidities.

The bailiff then explained what it was all about.[2]

—Foh! what beasts! cried Candide. What! monstrous behavior of this sort from a people who sing and dance? As soon as I can, let me get out of this country, where the monkeys provoke the tigers. In my own country I've lived with bears; only in Eldorado are there proper men. In the name of God, sir bailiff, get me to Venice where I can wait for Miss Cunégonde.

—I can only get you to Lower Normandy, said the guardsman.

He had the irons removed at once, said there had been a mistake, dismissed his gang, and took Candide and Martin to Dieppe, where he left them with his brother. There was a little Dutch ship at anchor. The Norman, changed by three more diamonds into the most helpful of men, put Candide and his people aboard the vessel, which was bound for Portsmouth in England. It wasn't on the way to Venice, but Candide felt like a man just let out of hell; and he hoped to get back on the road to Venice at the first possible occasion.

CHAPTER 23

Candide and Martin Pass the Shores of England; What They See There

—Ah, Pangloss! Pangloss! Ah, Martin! Martin! Ah, my darling Cunégonde! What is this world of ours? sighed Candide on the Dutch vessel.

—Something crazy, something abominable, Martin replied.

—You have been in England; are people as crazy there as in France?

—It's a different sort of crazy, said Martin. You know that these two nations have been at war over a few acres of snow near Canada, and that they are spending on this fine struggle more than Canada itself is worth.[3] As for telling you if there are more people in one country or the other who need a strait jacket, that is a judgment too fine for my understanding; I know only that the people we are going to visit are eaten up with melancholy.

As they chatted thus, the vessel touched at Portsmouth. A multitude of people covered the shore, watching closely a rather bulky man who was kneeling, his eyes blindfolded, on the deck of a man-of-war. Four soldiers,

1. The Latin name for the district of Artois, from which came Robert-François Damiens, who tried to stab Louis XV in 1757. The assassination failed, like that of Châtel, who tried to kill Henri IV in 1594, but unlike that of Ravaillac, who succeeded in killing him in 1610.   2. The point, in fact, is not too clear since arresting foreigners is an indirect way at best to guard against homegrown fanatics, and the position of the abbé from Perigord in the whole transaction remains confused. Has he called in the officer just to get rid of Candide? If so, why is he sardonic about the very suspicions he is trying to foster? Candide's reaction is to the notion that Frenchmen should be capable of political assassination at all; it seems excessive.   3. The wars of the French and English over Canada dragged intermittently through the 18th century till the peace of Paris sealed England's conquest (1763). Voltaire thought the French should concentrate on developing Louisiana, where the Jesuit influence was less marked.

stationed directly in front of this man, fired three bullets apiece into his brain, as peaceably as you would want; and the whole assemblage went home, in great satisfaction.[4]

—What's all this about? asked Candide. What devil is everywhere at work?

He asked who was that big man who had just been killed with so much ceremony.

—It was an admiral, they told him.

—And why kill this admiral?

—The reason, they told him, is that he didn't kill enough people; he gave battle to a French admiral, and it was found that he didn't get close enough to him.

—But, said Candide, the French admiral was just as far from the English admiral as the English admiral was from the French admiral.

—That's perfectly true, came the answer; but in this country it is useful from time to time to kill one admiral in order to encourage the others.

Candide was so stunned and shocked at what he saw and heard, that he would not even set foot ashore; he arranged with the Dutch merchant (without even caring if he was robbed, as at Surinam) to be taken forthwith to Venice.

The merchant was ready in two days; they coasted along France, they passed within sight of Lisbon, and Candide quivered. They entered the straits, crossed the Mediterranean, and finally landed at Venice.

—God be praised, said Candide, embracing Martin; here I shall recover the lovely Cunégonde. I trust Cacambo as I would myself. All is well, all goes well, all goes as well as possible.

CHAPTER 24

About Paquette and Brother Giroflée

As soon as he was in Venice, he had a search made for Cacambo in all the inns, all the cafés, all the stews—and found no trace of him. Every day he sent to investigate the vessels and coastal traders; no news of Cacambo.

—How's this? said he to Martin. I have had time to go from Surinam to Bordeaux, from Bordeaux to Paris, from Paris to Dieppe, from Dieppe to Portsmouth, to skirt Portugal and Spain, cross the Mediterranean, and spend several months at Venice—and the lovely Cunégonde has not come yet! In her place, I have met only that impersonator and that abbé from Perigord. Cunégonde is dead, without a doubt; and nothing remains for me too but death. Oh, it would have been better to stay in the earthly paradise of Eldorado than to return to this accursed Europe. How right you are, my dear Martin; all is but illusion and disaster.

He fell into a black melancholy, and refused to attend the fashionable operas or take part in the other diversions of the carnival season; not a single lady tempted him in the slightest. Martin told him:—You're a real simpleton if you think a half-breed valet with five or six millions in his pockets will go to the end of the world to get your mistress and bring her to Venice

---

4. Candide has witnessed the execution of Admiral John Byng, defeated off Minorca by the French fleet under Galisonnière and executed by firing squad on March 14, 1757. Voltaire had intervened to avert the execution.

for you. If he finds her, he'll take her for himself; if he doesn't, he'll take another. I advise you to forget about your servant Cacambo and your mistress Cunégonde.

Martin was not very comforting. Candide's melancholy increased, and Martin never wearied of showing him that there is little virtue and little happiness on this earth, except perhaps in Eldorado, where nobody can go.

While they were discussing this important matter and still waiting for Cunégonde, Candide noticed in St. Mark's Square a young Theatine[5] monk who had given his arm to a girl. The Theatine seemed fresh, plump, and flourishing; his eyes were bright, his manner cocky, his glance brilliant, his step proud. The girl was very pretty, and singing aloud; she glanced lovingly at her Theatine, and from time to time pinched his plump cheeks.

—At least you must admit, said Candide to Martin, that these people are happy. Until now I have not found in the whole inhabited earth, except Eldorado, anything but miserable people. But this girl and this monk, I'd be willing to bet, are very happy creatures.

—I'll bet they aren't, said Martin.

—We have only to ask them to dinner, said Candide, and we'll find out if I'm wrong.

Promptly he approached them, made his compliments, and invited them to his inn for a meal of macaroni, Lombardy partridges, and caviar, washed down with wine from Montepulciano, Cyprus, and Samos, and some Lacrima Christi. The girl blushed but the Theatine accepted gladly, and the girl followed him, watching Candide with an expression of surprise and confusion, darkened by several tears. Scarcely had she entered the room when she said to Candide:—What, can it be that Master Candide no longer knows Paquette?

At these words Candide, who had not yet looked carefully at her because he was preoccupied with Cunégonde, said to her:—Ah, my poor child! so you are the one who put Doctor Pangloss in the fine fix where I last saw him.

—Alas, sir, I was the one, said Paquette; I see you know all about it. I heard of the horrible misfortunes which befell the whole household of My Lady the Baroness and the lovely Cunégonde. I swear to you that my own fate has been just as unhappy. I was perfectly innocent when you knew me. A Franciscan, who was my confessor, easily seduced me. The consequences were frightful; shortly after My Lord the Baron had driven you out with great kicks on the backside, I too was forced to leave the castle. If a famous doctor had not taken pity on me, I would have died. Out of gratitude, I became for some time the mistress of this doctor. His wife, who was jealous to the point of frenzy, beat me mercilessly every day; she was a gorgon. The doctor was the ugliest of men, and I the most miserable creature on earth, being continually beaten for a man I did not love. You will understand, sir, how dangerous it is for a nagging woman to be married to a doctor. This man, enraged by his wife's ways, one day gave her as a cold cure a medicine so potent that in two hours' time she died amid horrible convulsions. Her relatives brought suit against the bereaved husband; he fled the country, and I was put in prison. My innocence would never have saved me if I had not been rather pretty. The

---

5. A Catholic order founded in 1524 by Cardinal Cajetan and G. P. Caraffa, later Pope Paul IV.

judge set me free on condition that he should become the doctor's successor. I was shortly replaced in this post by another girl, dismissed without any payment, and obliged to continue this abominable trade which you men find so pleasant and which for us is nothing but a bottomless pit of misery. I went to ply the trade in Venice. Ah, my dear sir, if you could imagine what it is like to have to caress indiscriminately an old merchant, a lawyer, a monk, a gondolier, an abbé; to be subjected to every sort of insult and outrage; to be reduced, time and again, to borrowing a skirt in order to go have it lifted by some disgusting man; to be robbed by this fellow of what one has gained from that; to be shaken down by the police, and to have before one only the prospect of a hideous old age, a hospital, and a dunghill, you will conclude that I am one of the most miserable creatures in the world.

Thus Paquette poured forth her heart to the good Candide in a hotel room, while Martin sat listening nearby. At last he said to Candide:—You see, I've already won half my bet.

Brother Giroflée[6] had remained in the dining room, and was having a drink before dinner.

—But how's this? said Candide to Paquette. You looked so happy, so joyous, when I met you; you were singing, you caressed the Theatine with such a natural air of delight; you seemed to me just as happy as you now say you are miserable.

—Ah, sir, replied Paquette, that's another one of the miseries of this business; yesterday I was robbed and beaten by an officer, and today I have to seem in good humor in order to please a monk.

Candide wanted no more; he conceded that Martin was right. They sat down to table with Paquette and the Theatine; the meal was amusing enough, and when it was over, the company spoke out among themselves with some frankness.

—Father, said Candide to the monk, you seem to me a man whom all the world might envy; the flower of health glows in your cheek, your features radiate pleasure; you have a pretty girl for your diversion, and you seem very happy with your life as a Theatine.

—Upon my word, sir, said Brother Giroflée, I wish that all the Theatines were at the bottom of the sea. A hundred times I have been tempted to set fire to my convent, and go turn Turk. My parents forced me, when I was fifteen years old, to put on this detestable robe, so they could leave more money to a cursed older brother of mine, may God confound him! Jealousy, faction, and fury spring up, by natural law, within the walls of convents. It is true, I have preached a few bad sermons which earned me a little money, half of which the prior stole from me; the remainder serves to keep me in girls. But when I have to go back to the monastery at night, I'm ready to smash my head against the walls of my cell; and all my fellow monks are in the same fix.

Martin turned to Candide and said with his customary coolness:

—Well, haven't I won the whole bet?

Candide gave two thousand piastres to Paquette and a thousand to Brother Giroflée.

—I assure you, said he, that with that they will be happy.

6. His name means "carnation" and Paquette means "daisy."

—I don't believe so, said Martin; your piastres may make them even more unhappy than they were before.

—That may be, said Candide; but one thing comforts me, I note that people often turn up whom one never expected to see again; it may well be that, having rediscovered my red sheep and Paquette, I will also rediscover Cunégonde.

—I hope, said Martin, that she will some day make you happy; but I very much doubt it.

—You're a hard man, said Candide.

—I've lived, said Martin.

—But look at these gondoliers, said Candide; aren't they always singing?

—You don't see them at home, said Martin, with their wives and squalling children. The doge has his troubles, the gondoliers theirs. It's true that on the whole one is better off as a gondolier than as a doge; but the difference is so slight, I don't suppose it's worth the trouble of discussing.

—There's a lot of talk here, said Candide, of this Senator Pococurante,[7] who has a fine palace on the Brenta and is hospitable to foreigners. They say he is a man who has never known a moment's grief.

—I'd like to see such a rare specimen, said Martin.

Candide promptly sent to Lord Pococurante, asking permission to call on him tomorrow.

CHAPTER 25

Visit to Lord Pococurante, Venetian Nobleman

Candide and Martin took a gondola on the Brenta, and soon reached the palace of the noble Pococurante. The gardens were large and filled with beautiful marble statues; the palace was handsomely designed. The master of the house, sixty years old and very rich, received his two inquisitive visitors perfectly politely, but with very little warmth; Candide was disconcerted and Martin not at all displeased.

First two pretty and neatly dressed girls served chocolate, which they whipped to a froth. Candide could not forbear praising their beauty, their grace, their skill.

—They are pretty good creatures, said Pococurante; I sometimes have them into my bed, for I'm tired of the ladies of the town, with their stupid tricks, quarrels, jealousies, fits of ill humor and petty pride, and all the sonnets one has to make or order for them; but, after all, these two girls are starting to bore me too.

After lunch, Candide strolled through a long gallery, and was amazed at the beauty of the pictures. He asked who was the painter of the two finest.

—They are by Raphael, said the senator; I bought them for a lot of money, out of vanity, some years ago; people say they're the finest in Italy, but they don't please me at all; the colors have all turned brown, the figures aren't well modeled and don't stand out enough, the draperies bear no resemblance to real cloth. In a word, whatever people may say, I don't find in them a real imitation of nature. I like a picture only when I can see in it a touch of nature itself, and there are none of this sort. I have many paintings, but I no longer look at them.

---

7. His name means "small care."

As they waited for dinner, Pococurante ordered a concerto performed. Candide found the music delightful.

—That noise? said Pococurante. It may amuse you for half an hour, but if it goes on any longer, it tires everybody though no one dares to admit it. Music today is only the art of performing difficult pieces, and what is merely difficult cannot please for long. Perhaps I should prefer the opera, if they had not found ways to make it revolting and monstrous. Anyone who likes bad tragedies set to music is welcome to them; in these performances the scenes serve only to introduce, inappropriately, two or three ridiculous songs designed to show off the actress's sound box. Anyone who wants to, or who can, is welcome to swoon with pleasure at the sight of a castrate wriggling through the role of Caesar or Cato, and strutting awkwardly about the stage. For my part, I have long since given up these paltry trifles which are called the glory of modern Italy, and for which monarchs pay such ruinous prices.

Candide argued a bit, but timidly; Martin was entirely of a mind with the senator.

They sat down to dinner, and after an excellent meal adjourned to the library. Candide, seeing a copy of Homer in a splendid binding, complimented the noble lord on his good taste.

—That is an author, said he, who was the special delight of great Pangloss, the best philosopher in all Germany.

—He's no special delight of mine, said Pococurante coldly. I was once made to believe that I took pleasure in reading him; but that constant recital of fights which are all alike, those gods who are always interfering but never decisively, that Helen who is the cause of the war and then scarcely takes any part in the story, that Troy which is always under siege and never taken—all that bores me to tears. I have sometimes asked scholars if reading it bored them as much as it bores me; everyone who answered frankly told me the book dropped from his hands like lead, but that they had to have it in their libraries as a monument of antiquity, like those old rusty coins which can't be used in real trade.

Your Excellence doesn't hold the same opinion of Virgil? said Candide.

—I concede, said Pococurante, that the second, fourth, and sixth books of his *Aeneid* are fine; but as for his pious Aeneas, and strong Cloanthes, and faithful Achates, and little Ascanius, and that imbecile King Latinus, and middle-class Amata, and insipid Lavinia, I don't suppose there was ever anything so cold and unpleasant. I prefer Tasso and those sleepwalkers' stories of Ariosto.

—Dare I ask, sir, said Candide, if you don't get great enjoyment from reading Horace?

—There are some maxims there, said Pococurante, from which a man of the world can profit, and which, because they are formed into vigorous couplets, are more easily remembered; but I care very little for his trip to Brindisi, his description of a bad dinner, or his account of a quibblers' squabble between some fellow Pupilus, whose words he says *were full of pus,* and another whose words *were full of vinegar.*[8] I feel nothing but extreme disgust

---

8. *Satires* I.vii; Pococurante, with gentlemanly negligence, has corrupted Rupilius to Pupilus. Horace's poems against witches are *Epodes* V, VIII, XII; the one about striking the stars with his lofty forehead is *Odes* I.i.

at his verses against old women and witches; and I can't see what's so great in his telling his friend Maecenas that if he is raised by him to the ranks of lyric poets, he will strike the stars with his lofty forehead. Fools admire everything in a well-known author. I read only for my own pleasure; I like only what is in my style.

Candide, who had been trained never to judge for himself, was much astonished by what he heard; and Martin found Pococurante's way of thinking quite rational.

—Oh, here is a copy of Cicero, said Candide. Now this great man I suppose you're never tired of reading.

—I never read him at all, replied the Venetian. What do I care whether he pleaded for Rabirius or Cluentius? As a judge, I have my hands full of lawsuits. I might like his philosophical works better, but when I saw that he had doubts about everything, I concluded that I knew as much as he did, and that I needed no help to be ignorant.

—Ah, here are eighty volumes of collected papers from a scientific academy, cried Martin; maybe there is something good in them.

—There would be indeed, said Pococurante, if one of these silly authors had merely discovered a new way of making pins; but in all those volumes there is nothing but empty systems, not a single useful discovery.

—What a lot of stage plays I see over there, said Candide, some in Italian, some in Spanish and French.

—Yes, said the senator, three thousand of them, and not three dozen good ones. As for those collections of sermons, which all together are not worth a page of Seneca, and all these heavy volumes of theology, you may be sure I never open them, nor does anybody else.

Martin noticed some shelves full of English books.

—I suppose, said he, that a republican must delight in most of these books written in the land of liberty.

—Yes, replied Pococurante, it's a fine thing to write as you think; it is mankind's privilege. In all our Italy, people write only what they do not think; men who inhabit the land of the Caesars and Antonines dare not have an idea without the permission of a Dominican. I would rejoice in the freedom that breathes through English genius, if partisan passions did not corrupt all that is good in that precious freedom.

Candide, noting a Milton, asked if he did not consider this author a great man.

—Who? said Pococurante. That barbarian who made a long commentary on the first chapter of Genesis in ten books of crabbed verse?[9] That clumsy imitator of the Greeks, who disfigures creation itself, and while Moses represents the eternal being as creating the world with a word, has the messiah take a big compass out of a heavenly cupboard in order to design his work? You expect me to admire the man who spoiled Tasso's hell and devil? who disguises Lucifer now as a toad, now as a pigmy? who makes him rehash the same arguments a hundred times over? who makes him argue theology? and who, taking seriously Ariosto's comic story of the invention of firearms, has the devils shooting off cannon in heaven? Neither I nor anyone else in Italy

---

9. The first edition of *Paradise Lost* had ten books, which Milton later expanded to twelve.

has been able to enjoy these gloomy extravagances. The marriage of Sin and Death, and the monster that Sin gives birth to, will nauseate any man whose taste is at all refined; and his long description of a hospital is good only for a gravedigger. This obscure, extravagant, and disgusting poem was despised at its birth; I treat it today as it was treated in its own country by its contemporaries. Anyhow, I say what I think, and care very little whether other people agree with me.

Candide was a little cast down by this speech; he respected Homer, and had a little affection for Milton.

—Alas, he said under his breath to Martin, I'm afraid this man will have a supreme contempt for our German poets.

—No harm in that, said Martin.

—Oh what a superior man, said Candide, still speaking softly, what a great genius this Pococurante must be! Nothing can please him.

Having thus looked over all the books, they went down into the garden. Candide praised its many beauties.

—I know nothing in such bad taste, said the master of the house; we have nothing but trifles here; tomorrow I am going to have one set out on a nobler design.

When the two visitors had taken leave of his excellency:—Well now, said Candide to Martin, you must agree that this was the happiest of all men, for he is superior to everything he possesses.

—Don't you see, said Martin, that he is disgusted with everything he possesses? Plato said, a long time ago, that the best stomachs are not those which refuse all food.

—But, said Candide, isn't there pleasure in criticizing everything, in seeing faults where other people think they see beauties?

—That is to say, Martin replied, that there's pleasure in having no pleasure?

—Oh well, said Candide, then I am the only happy man . . . or will be, when I see Miss Cunégonde again.

—It's always a good thing to have hope, said Martin.

But the days and the weeks slipped past; Cacambo did not come back, and Candide was so buried in his grief, that he did not even notice that Paquette and Brother Giroflée had neglected to come and thank him.

CHAPTER 26

About a Supper that Candide and Martin Had with Six Strangers,
and Who They Were

One evening when Candide, accompanied by Martin, was about to sit down for dinner with the strangers staying in his hotel, a man with a soot-colored face came up behind him, took him by the arm, and said:—Be ready to leave with us, don't miss out.

He turned and saw Cacambo. Only the sight of Cunégonde could have astonished and pleased him more. He nearly went mad with joy. He embraced his dear friend.

—Cunégonde is here, no doubt? Where is she? Bring me to her, let me die of joy in her presence.

—Cunégonde is not here at all, said Cacambo, she is at Constantinople.

—Good Heavens, at Constantinople! but if she were in China, I must fly there, let's go.

—We will leave after supper, said Cacambo; I can tell you no more; I am a slave, my owner is looking for me, I must go wait on him at table; mum's the word; eat your supper and be prepared.

Candide, torn between joy and grief, delighted to have seen his faithful agent again, astonished to find him a slave, full of the idea of recovering his mistress, his heart in a turmoil, his mind in a whirl, sat down to eat with Martin, who was watching all these events coolly, and with six strangers who had come to pass the carnival season at Venice.

Cacambo, who was pouring wine for one of the strangers, leaned respectfully over his master at the end of the meal, and said to him:—Sire, Your Majesty may leave when he pleases, the vessel is ready.

Having said these words, he exited. The diners looked at one another in silent amazement, when another servant, approaching his master, said to him:—Sire, Your Majesty's litter is at Padua, and the bark awaits you.

The master nodded, and the servant vanished. All the diners looked at one another again, and the general amazement redoubled. A third servant, approaching a third stranger, said to him:—Sire, take my word for it, Your Majesty must stay here no longer; I shall get everything ready.

Then he too disappeared.

Candide and Martin had no doubt, now, that it was a carnival masquerade. A fourth servant spoke to a fourth master:—Your Majesty will leave when he pleases—and went out like the others. A fifth followed suit. But the sixth servant spoke differently to the sixth stranger, who sat next to Candide. He said:—My word, sire, they'll give no more credit to Your Majesty, nor to me either; we could very well spend the night in the lockup, you and I. I've got to look out for myself, so good-bye to you.

When all the servants had left, the six strangers, Candide, and Martin remained under a pall of silence. Finally Candide broke it.

—Gentlemen, said he, here's a funny kind of joke. Why are you all royalty? I assure you that Martin and I aren't.

Cacambo's master spoke up gravely then, and said in Italian:—This is no joke, my name is Achmet the Third.[1] I was grand sultan for several years; then, as I had dethroned my brother, my nephew dethroned me. My viziers had their throats cut; I was allowed to end my days in the old seraglio. My nephew, the Grand Sultan Mahmoud, sometimes lets me travel for my health; and I have come to spend the carnival season at Venice.

A young man who sat next to Achmet spoke after him, and said:—My name is Ivan; I was once emperor of all the Russias.[2] I was dethroned while still in my cradle; my father and mother were locked up, and I was raised in prison; I sometimes have permission to travel, though always under guard, and I have come to spend the carnival season at Venice.

The third said:—I am Charles Edward, king of England;[3] my father yielded me his rights to the kingdom, and I fought to uphold them; but they

---

1. Ottoman ruler (1673–1736); he was deposed in 1730. 2. Ivan VI reigned from his birth in 1740 until 1756, then was confined in the Schlusselberg, and executed in 1764. 3. This is the Young Pretender (1720–1788), known to his supporters as Bonnie Prince Charlie. The defeat so theatrically described took place at Culloden, April 16, 1746.

tore out the hearts of eight hundred of my partisans, and flung them in their faces. I have been in prison; now I am going to Rome, to visit the king, my father, dethroned like me and my grandfather; and I have come to pass the carnival season at Venice.

The fourth king then spoke up, and said:—I am a king of the Poles;[4] the luck of war has deprived me of my hereditary estates; my father suffered the same losses; I submit to Providence like Sultan Achmet, Emperor Ivan, and King Charles Edward, to whom I hope heaven grants long lives; and I have come to pass the carnival season at Venice.

The fifth said:—I too am a king of the Poles;[5] I lost my kingdom twice, but Providence gave me another state, in which I have been able to do more good than all the Sarmatian kings ever managed to do on the banks of the Vistula. I too have submitted to Providence, and I have come to pass the carnival season at Venice.

It remained for the sixth monarch to speak.

—Gentlemen, said he, I am no such great lord as you, but I have in fact been a king like any other. I am Theodore; I was elected king of Corsica.[6] People used to call me *Your Majesty,* and now they barely call me *Sir;* I used to coin currency, and now I don't have a cent; I used to have two secretaries of state, and now I scarcely have a valet; I have sat on a throne, and for a long time in London I was in jail, on the straw; and I may well be treated the same way here, though I have come, like your majesties, to pass the carnival season at Venice.

The five other kings listened to his story with noble compassion. Each one of them gave twenty sequins to King Theodore, so that he might buy a suit and some shirts; Candide gave him a diamond worth two thousand sequins.

—Who in the world, said the five kings, is this private citizen who is in a position to give a hundred times as much as any of us, and who actually gives it?[7]

Just as they were rising from dinner, there arrived at the same establishment four most serene highnesses, who had also lost their kingdoms through the luck of war, and who came to spend the rest of the carnival season at Venice. But Candide never bothered even to look at these newcomers because he was only concerned to go find his dear Cunégonde at Constantinople.

4. Augustus III (1696–1763), Elector of Saxony and King of Poland, dethroned by Frederick the Great in 1756.   5. Stanislas Leczinski (1677–1766), father-in-law of Louis XV, who abdicated the throne of Poland in 1736, was made Duke of Lorraine and in that capacity befriended Voltaire.   6. Theodore von Neuhof (1690–1756), an authentic Westphalian, an adventurer and a soldier of fortune, who in 1736 was (for about eight months) the elected king of Corsica. He spent time in an Amsterdam as well as a London debtor's prison.   7. A late correction of Voltaire's makes this passage read:

—Who is this man who is in a position to give a hundred times as much as any of us, and who actually gives it? Are you a king too, sir?
—No, gentlemen, and I have no desire to be.

But this reading, though Voltaire's on good authority, produces a conflict with Candide's previous remark:—Why are you all royalty? I assure you that Martin and I aren't.
Thus, it has seemed better for literary reasons to follow an earlier reading. Voltaire was very conscious of his situation as a man richer than many princes; in 1758 he had money on loan to no fewer than three highnesses, Charles Eugene, Duke of Wurtemburg; Charles Theodore, Elector Palatine; and the Duke of Saxe-Gotha.

CHAPTER 27

Candide's Trip to Constantinople

Faithful Cacambo had already arranged with the Turkish captain who was returning Sultan Achmet to Constantinople to make room for Candide and Martin on board. Both men boarded ship after prostrating themselves before his miserable highness. On the way, Candide said to Martin:—Six dethroned kings that we had dinner with! and yet among those six there was one on whom I had to bestow charity! Perhaps there are other princes even more unfortunate. I myself have only lost a hundred sheep, and now I am flying to the arms of Cunégonde. My dear Martin, once again Pangloss is proved right, all is for the best.

—I hope so, said Martin.

—But, said Candide, that was a most unlikely experience we had at Venice. Nobody ever saw, or heard tell of, six dethroned kings eating together at an inn.

—It is no more extraordinary, said Martin, than most of the things that have happened to us. Kings are frequently dethroned; and as for the honor we had from dining with them, that's a trifle which doesn't deserve our notice.[8]

Scarcely was Candide on board than he fell on the neck of his former servant, his friend Cacambo.

—Well! said he, what is Cunégonde doing? Is she still a marvel of beauty? Does she still love me? How is her health? No doubt you have bought her a palace at Constantinople.

—My dear master, answered Cacambo, Cunégonde is washing dishes on the shores of the Propontis, in the house of a prince who has very few dishes to wash; she is a slave in the house of a onetime king named Ragotski,[9] to whom the Great Turk allows three crowns a day in his exile; but, what is worse than all this, she has lost all her beauty and become horribly ugly.

—Ah, beautiful or ugly, said Candide, I am an honest man, and my duty is to love her forever. But how can she be reduced to this wretched state with the five or six millions that you had?

—All right, said Cacambo, didn't I have to give two millions to Señor don Fernando d'Ibaraa y Figueroa y Mascarenes y Lampourdos y Souza, governor of Buenos Aires, for his permission to carry off Miss Cunégonde? And didn't a pirate cleverly strip us of the rest? And didn't this pirate carry us off to Cape Matapan, to Melos, Nicaria, Samos, Petra, to the Dardanelles, Marmora, Scutari? Cunégonde and the old woman are working for the prince I told you about, and I am the slave of the dethroned sultan.

—What a lot of fearful calamities linked one to the other, said Candide. But after all, I still have a few diamonds, I shall easily deliver Cunégonde. What a pity that she's become so ugly!

Then, turning toward Martin, he asked:—Who in your opinion is more to be pitied, the Emperor Achmet, the Emperor Ivan, King Charles Edward, or myself?

---

8. Another late change adds the following question:—*What does it matter whom you dine with as long as you fare well at table?* I have omitted it, again on literary grounds.   9. Francis Leopold Rakoczy (1676–1735), who was briefly king of Transylvania in the early 18th century. After 1720 he was interned in Turkey.

—I have no idea, said Martin; I would have to enter your hearts in order to tell.

—Ah, said Candide, if Pangloss were here, he would know and he would tell us.

—I can't imagine, said Martin, what scales your Pangloss would use to weigh out the miseries of men and value their griefs. All I will venture is that the earth holds millions of men who deserve our pity a hundred times more than King Charles Edward, Emperor Ivan, or Sultan Achmet.

—You may well be right, said Candide.

In a few days they arrived at the Black Sea canal. Candide began by repurchasing Cacambo at an exorbitant price; then, without losing an instant, he flung himself and his companions into a galley to go search out Cunégonde on the shores of Propontis, however ugly she might be.

There were in the chain gang two convicts who bent clumsily to the oar, and on whose bare shoulders the Levantine[1] captain delivered from time to time a few lashes with a bullwhip. Candide naturally noticed them more than the other galley slaves, and out of pity came closer to them. Certain features of their disfigured faces seemed to him to bear a slight resemblance to Pangloss and to that wretched Jesuit, that baron, that brother of Miss Cunégonde. The notion stirred and saddened him. He looked at them more closely.

—To tell you the truth, he said to Cacambo, if I hadn't seen Master Pangloss hanged, and if I hadn't been so miserable as to murder the baron, I should think they were rowing in this very galley.

At the names of 'baron' and 'Pangloss' the two convicts gave a great cry, sat still on their bench, and dropped their oars. The Levantine captain came running, and the bullwhip lashes redoubled.

—Stop, stop, captain, cried Candide. I'll give you as much money as you want.

—What, can it be Candide? cried one of the convicts.

—What, can it be Candide? cried the other.

—Is this a dream? said Candide. Am I awake or asleep? Am I in this galley? Is that My Lord the Baron, whom I killed? Is that Master Pangloss, whom I saw hanged?

—It is indeed, they replied.

—What, is that the great philosopher? said Martin.

—Now, sir, Mr. Levantine Captain, said Candide, how much money do you want for the ransom of My Lord Thunder-Ten-Tronckh, one of the first barons of the empire, and Master Pangloss, the deepest metaphysician in all Germany?

—Dog of a Christian, replied the Levantine captain, since these two dogs of Christian convicts are barons and metaphysicians, which is no doubt a great honor in their country, you will give me fifty thousand sequins for them.

—You shall have them, sir, take me back to Constantinople and you shall be paid on the spot. Or no, take me to Miss Cunégonde.

The Levantine captain, at Candide's first word, had turned his bow toward the town, and he had them rowed there as swiftly as a bird cleaves the air.

---

1. From the eastern Mediterranean.

A hundred times Candide embraced the baron and Pangloss.

—And how does it happen I didn't kill you, my dear baron? and my dear Pangloss, how can you be alive after being hanged? and why are you both rowing in the galleys of Turkey?

—Is it really true that my dear sister is in this country? asked the baron.

—Yes, answered Cacambo.

—And do I really see again my dear Candide? cried Pangloss.

Candide introduced Martin and Cacambo. They all embraced; they all talked at once. The galley flew, already they were back in port. A Jew was called, and Candide sold him for fifty thousand sequins a diamond worth a hundred thousand, while he protested by Abraham that he could not possibly give more for it. Candide immediately ransomed the baron and Pangloss. The latter threw himself at the feet of his liberator, and bathed them with tears; the former thanked him with a nod, and promised to repay this bit of money at the first opportunity.

—But is it really possible that my sister is in Turkey? said he.

—Nothing is more possible, replied Cacambo, since she is a dishwasher in the house of a prince of Transylvania.

At once two more Jews were called; Candide sold some more diamonds; and they all departed in another galley to the rescue of Cunégonde.

CHAPTER 28

What Happened to Candide, Cunégonde, Pangloss, Martin, &c.

—Let me beg your pardon once more, said Candide to the baron, pardon me, reverend father, for having run you through the body with my sword.

—Don't mention it, replied the baron. I was a little too hasty myself, I confess it; but since you want to know the misfortune which brought me to the galleys, I'll tell you. After being cured of my wound by the brother who was apothecary to the college, I was attacked and abducted by a Spanish raiding party; they jailed me in Buenos Aires at the time when my sister had just left. I asked to be sent to Rome, to the father general. Instead, I was named to serve as almoner in Constantinople, under the French ambassador. I had not been a week on this job when I chanced one evening on a very handsome young ichoglan.[2] The evening was hot; the young man wanted to take a swim; I seized the occasion, and went with him. I did not know that it is a capital offense for a Christian to be found naked with a young Moslem. A cadi sentenced me to receive a hundred blows with a cane on the soles of my feet, and then to be sent to the galleys. I don't suppose there was ever such a horrible miscarriage of justice. But I would like to know why my sister is in the kitchen of a Transylvanian king exiled among Turks.

—But how about you, my dear Pangloss, said Candide; how is it possible that we have met again?

—It is true, said Pangloss, that you saw me hanged; in the normal course of things, I should have been burned, but you recall that a cloudburst occurred just as they were about to roast me. So much rain fell that they despaired of lighting the fire; thus I was hanged, for lack of anything better to do with me. A surgeon bought my body, carried me off to his house, and

2. A page to the sultan.

dissected me. First he made a cross-shaped incision in me, from the navel to the clavicle. No one could have been worse hanged than I was. In fact, the executioner of the high ceremonials of the Holy Inquisition, who was a sub-deacon, burned people marvelously well, but he was not in the way of hanging them. The rope was wet, and tightened badly; it caught on a knot; in short, I was still breathing. The cross-shaped incision made me scream so loudly that the surgeon fell over backwards; he thought he was dissecting the devil, fled in an agony of fear, and fell downstairs in his flight. His wife ran in, at the noise, from a nearby room; she found me stretched out on the table with my cross-shaped incision, was even more frightened than her husband, fled, and fell over him. When they had recovered a little, I heard her say to him: 'My dear, what were you thinking of, trying to dissect a heretic? Don't you know those people are always possessed of the devil? I'm going to get the priest and have him exorcised.' At these words, I shuddered, and collected my last remaining energies to cry: 'Have mercy on me!' At last the Portuguese barber[3] took courage; he sewed me up again; his wife even nursed me; in two weeks I was up and about. The barber found me a job and made me lackey to a Knight of Malta who was going to Venice; and when this master could no longer pay me, I took service under a Venetian merchant, whom I followed to Constantinople.

—One day it occurred to me to enter a mosque; no one was there but an old imam and a very attractive young worshipper who was saying her prayers. Her bosom was completely bare; and between her two breasts she had a lovely bouquet of tulips, roses, anemones, buttercups, hyacinths, and primroses. She dropped her bouquet, I picked it up, and returned it to her with the most respectful attentions. I was so long getting it back in place that the imam grew angry, and, seeing that I was a Christian, he called the guard. They took me before the cadi, who sentenced me to receive a hundred blows with a cane on the soles of my feet, and then to be sent to the galleys. I was chained to the same galley and precisely the same bench as My Lord the Baron. There were in this galley four young fellows from Marseilles, five Neapolitan priests, and two Corfu monks, who assured us that these things happen every day. My Lord the Baron asserted that he had suffered a greater injustice than I; I, on the other hand, proposed that it was much more permissible to replace a bouquet in a bosom than to be found naked with an ichoglan. We were arguing the point continually, and getting twenty lashes a day with the bullwhip, when the chain of events within this universe brought you to our galley, and you ransomed us.

—Well, my dear Pangloss, Candide said to him, now that you have been hanged, dissected, beaten to a pulp, and sentenced to the galleys, do you still think everything is for the best in this world?

—I am still of my first opinion, replied Pangloss; for after all I am a philosopher, and it would not be right for me to recant since Leibniz could not possibly be wrong, and besides pre-established harmony is the finest notion in the world, like the plenum and subtle matter.[4]

3. The two callings of barber and surgeon, since they both involved sharp instruments, were interchangeable in the early days of medicine.   4. Rigorous determinism requires that there be no empty spaces in the universe, so wherever it seems empty, one posits the existence of the "plenum." "Subtle matter" describes the soul, the mind, and all spiritual agencies—which can, therefore, be supposed subject to the influence and control of the great world machine, which is, of course, visibly material. Both are concepts needed to round out the system of optimistic determinism.

CHAPTER 29

How Candide Found Cunégonde and the Old Woman Again

While Candide, the baron, Pangloss, Martin, and Cacambo were telling one another their stories, while they were disputing over the contingent or non-contingent events of this universe, while they were arguing over effects and causes, over moral evil and physical evil, over liberty and necessity, and over the consolations available to one in a Turkish galley, they arrived at the shores of Propontis and the house of the prince of Transylvania. The first sight to meet their eyes was Cunégonde and the old woman, who were hanging out towels on lines to dry.

The baron paled at what he saw. The tender lover Candide, seeing his lovely Cunégonde with her skin weathered, her eyes bloodshot, her breasts fallen, her cheeks seamed, her arms red and scaly, recoiled three steps in horror, and then advanced only out of politeness. She embraced Candide and her brother; everyone embraced the old woman; Candide ransomed them both.

There was a little farm in the neighborhood; the old woman suggested that Candide occupy it until some better fate should befall the group. Cunégonde did not know she was ugly, no one had told her; she reminded Candide of his promises in so firm a tone that the good Candide did not dare to refuse her. So he went to tell the baron that he was going to marry his sister.

—Never will I endure, said the baron, such baseness on her part, such insolence on yours; this shame at least I will not put up with; why, my sister's children would not be able to enter the Chapters in Germany.[5] No, my sister will never marry anyone but a baron of the empire.

Cunégonde threw herself at his feet, and bathed them with her tears; he was inflexible.

—You absolute idiot, Candide told him, I rescued you from the galleys, I paid your ransom, I paid your sister's; she was washing dishes, she is ugly, I am good enough to make her my wife, and you still presume to oppose it! If I followed my impulses, I would kill you all over again.

—You may kill me again, said the baron, but you will not marry my sister while I am alive.

CHAPTER 30

Conclusion

At heart, Candide had no real wish to marry Cunégonde; but the baron's extreme impertinence decided him in favor of the marriage, and Cunégonde was so eager for it that he could not back out. He consulted Pangloss, Martin, and the faithful Cacambo. Pangloss drew up a fine treatise, in which he proved that the baron had no right over his sister and that she could, according to all the laws of the empire, marry Candide morganatically.[6] Martin said they should throw the baron into the sea. Cacambo thought they should send him back to the Levantine captain to finish his time in the galleys, and then send him to the father general in Rome by the first vessel. This seemed

---

5. Knightly assemblies.   6. A morganatic marriage confers no rights on the partner of lower rank or on the offspring.

the best idea; the old woman approved, and nothing was said to his sister; the plan was executed, at modest expense, and they had the double pleasure of snaring a Jesuit and punishing the pride of a German baron.

It is quite natural to suppose that after so many misfortunes, Candide, married to his mistress, and living with the philosopher Pangloss, the philosopher Martin, the prudent Cacambo, and the old woman—having, besides, brought back so many diamonds from the land of the ancient Incas—must have led the most agreeable life in the world. But he was so cheated by the Jews[7] that nothing was left but his little farm; his wife, growing every day more ugly, became sour-tempered and insupportable; the old woman was ailing and even more ill-humored than Cunégonde. Cacambo, who worked in the garden and went into Constantinople to sell vegetables, was worn out with toil, and cursed his fate. Pangloss was in despair at being unable to shine in some German university. As for Martin, he was firmly persuaded that things are just as bad wherever you are; he endured in patience. Candide, Martin, and Pangloss sometimes argued over metaphysics and morals. Before the windows of the farmhouse they often watched the passage of boats bearing effendis, pashas, and cadis into exile on Lemnos, Mytilene, and Erzeroum; they saw other cadis, other pashas, other effendis coming, to take the place of the exiles and to be exiled in their turn. They saw various heads, neatly impaled, to be set up at the Sublime Porte.[8] These sights gave fresh impetus to their discussions; and when they were not arguing, the boredom was so fierce that one day the old woman ventured to say:—I should like to know which is worse, being raped a hundred times by negro pirates, having a buttock cut off, running the gauntlet in the Bulgar army, being flogged and hanged in an auto-da-fé, being dissected and rowing in the galleys—experiencing, in a word, all the miseries through which we have passed—or else just sitting here and doing nothing?

—It's a hard question, said Candide.

These words gave rise to new reflections, and Martin in particular concluded that man was bound to live either in convulsions of misery or in the lethargy of boredom. Candide did not agree, but expressed no positive opinion. Pangloss asserted that he had always suffered horribly; but having once declared that everything was marvelously well, he continued to repeat the opinion and didn't believe a word of it.

One thing served to confirm Martin in his detestable opinions, to make Candide hesitate more than ever, and to embarrass Pangloss. It was the arrival one day at their farm of Paquette and Brother Giroflée, who were in the last stages of misery. They had quickly run through their three thousand piastres, had split up, made up, quarreled, been jailed, escaped, and finally Brother Giroflée had turned Turk. Paquette continued to ply her trade everywhere, and no longer made any money at it.

—I told you, said Martin to Candide, that your gifts would soon be squandered and would only render them more unhappy. You have spent millions of piastres, you and Cacambo, and you are no more happy than Brother Giroflée and Paquette.

---

7. Voltaire's anti-Semitism, derived from various unhappy experiences with Jewish financiers, is not the most attractive aspect of his personality.   8. The gate of the sultan's palace is often used by extension to describe his government as a whole. But it was in fact a real gate where the heads of traitors and public enemies were gruesomely exposed.

—Ah ha, said Pangloss to Paquette, so destiny has brought you back in our midst, my poor girl! Do you realize you cost me the end of my nose, one eye, and an ear? And look at you now! eh! what a world it is, after all!

This new adventure caused them to philosophize more than ever.

There was in the neighborhood a very famous dervish, who was said to be the best philosopher in Turkey; they went to ask his advice. Pangloss was spokesman, and he said:—Master, we have come to ask you to tell us why such a strange animal as man was created.

—What are you getting into? answered the dervish. Is it any of your business?

—But, reverend father, said Candide, there's a horrible lot of evil on the face of the earth.

—What does it matter, said the dervish, whether there's good or evil? When his highness sends a ship to Egypt, does he worry whether the mice on board are comfortable or not?

—What shall we do then? asked Pangloss.

—Hold your tongue, said the dervish.

—I had hoped, said Pangloss, to reason a while with you concerning effects and causes, the best of possible worlds, the origin of evil, the nature of the soul, and pre-established harmony.

At these words, the dervish slammed the door in their faces.

During this interview, word was spreading that at Constantinople they had just strangled two viziers of the divan,[9] as well as the mufti, and impaled several of their friends. This catastrophe made a great and general sensation for several hours. Pangloss, Candide, and Martin, as they returned to their little farm, passed a good old man who was enjoying the cool of the day at his doorstep under a grove of orange trees. Pangloss, who was as inquisitive as he was explanatory, asked the name of the mufti who had been strangled.

—I know nothing of it, said the good man, and I have never cared to know the name of a single mufti or vizier. I am completely ignorant of the episode you are discussing. I presume that in general those who meddle in public business sometimes perish miserably, and that they deserve their fate; but I never listen to the news from Constantinople; I am satisfied with sending the fruits of my garden to be sold there.

Having spoken these words, he asked the strangers into his house; his two daughters and two sons offered them various sherbets which they had made themselves, Turkish cream flavored with candied citron, orange, lemon, lime, pineapple, pistachio, and mocha coffee uncontaminated by the inferior coffee of Batavia and the East Indies. After which the two daughters of this good Moslem perfumed the beards of Candide, Pangloss, and Martin.

—You must possess, Candide said to the Turk, an enormous and splendid property?

I have only twenty acres, replied the Turk; I cultivate them with my children, and the work keeps us from three great evils, boredom, vice, and poverty.

Candide, as he walked back to his farm, meditated deeply over the words of the Turk. He said to Pangloss and Martin:—This good old man seems to

---

9. Intimate advisers of the sultan.

have found himself a fate preferable to that of the six kings with whom we had the honor of dining.

—Great place, said Pangloss, is very perilous in the judgment of all the philosophers; for, after all, Eglon, king of the Moabites, was murdered by Ehud; Absalom was hung up by the hair and pierced with three darts; King Nadab, son of Jeroboam, was killed by Baasha; King Elah by Zimri; Ahaziah by Jehu; Athaliah by Jehoiada; and Kings Jehoiakim, Jeconiah, and Zedekiah were enslaved. You know how death came to Croesus, Astyages, Darius, Dionysius of Syracuse, Pyrrhus, Perseus, Hannibal, Jugurtha, Ariovistus, Caesar, Pompey, Nero, Otho, Vitellius, Domitian, Richard II of England, Edward II, Henry VI, Richard III, Mary Stuart, Charles I, the three Henrys of France, and the Emperor Henry IV? You know . . .

—I know also, said Candide, that we must cultivate our garden.

—You are perfectly right, said Pangloss; for when man was put into the garden of Eden, he was put there *ut operaretur eum,* so that he should work it; this proves that man was not born to take his ease.

—Let's work without speculation, said Martin; it's the only way of rendering life bearable

The whole little group entered into this laudable scheme; each one began to exercise his talents. The little plot yielded fine crops. Cunégonde was, to tell the truth, remarkably ugly; but she became an excellent pastry cook. Paquette took up embroidery; the old woman did the laundry. Everyone, down even to Brother Giroflée, did something useful; he became a very adequate carpenter, and even an honest man; and Pangloss sometimes used to say to Candide:—All events are linked together in the best of possible worlds' for, after all, if you had not been driven from a fine castle by being kicked in the backside for love of Miss Cunégonde, if you hadn't been sent before the Inquisition, if you hadn't traveled across America on foot, if you hadn't given a good sword thrust to the baron, if you hadn't lost all your sheep from the good land of Eldorado, you wouldn't be sitting here eating candied citron and pistachios.

—That is very well put, said Candide, but we must cultivate our garden.

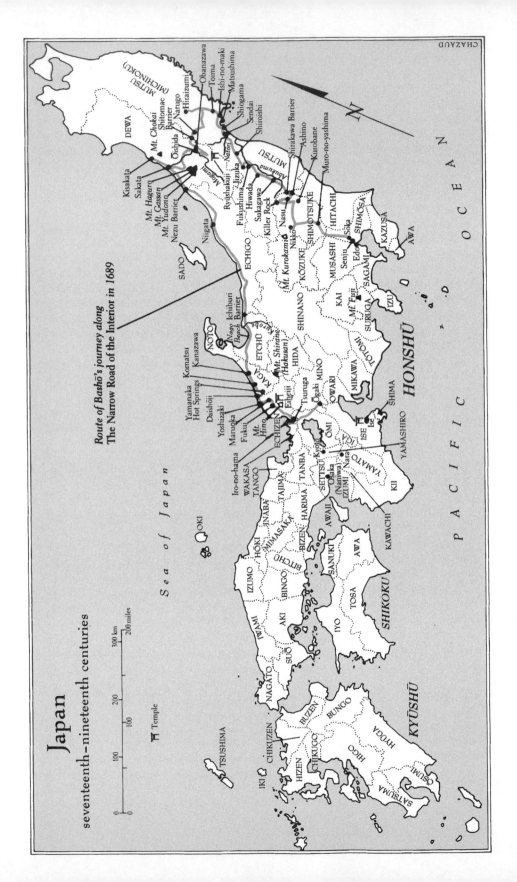

Japan
seventeenth–nineteenth centuries

Route of Bashō's journey along
The Narrow Road of the Interior in 1689

The Rise of Popular Arts
in Premodern Japan

In one of the grand ironies of history, Japan—a country whose prosperity now depends on intense cultivation of foreign markets—began its so-called early modern era as a world recluse. Its leaders chose to seal Japan from foreign influence, fearful that the toehold European traders and Christian missionaries had been gaining in Japan from the mid-sixteenth century through the early seventeenth would end up undermining their political control.

Since the late twelfth century, in the wake of the civil war chronicled in *The Tale of the Heike*, Japan had been governed by a series of military clans who held de facto power as peacekeepers and national administrators on behalf of the emperor, the formal if politically emasculated sovereign. In some periods the reigning military house succeeded as peacekeeper. In others, the country lapsed into disorder as rival clans jousted for supremacy. Gradually, the country splintered until chaos and bloodshed descended on Japan during 150 unruly years lasting from 1467 until the opening of the seventeenth century, when one clan, the Tokugawa, managed to dominate its rivals and thereby reunify the nation under strict but peaceful rule.

The Tokugawa shoguns quickly decided that the foreigners must go. They had seen the Portuguese missionaries play one feudal baron against another and, worse, claim to represent a higher authority to which the converted ranks must ultimately submit. In 1639, therefore, the government of Japan announced a policy of national seclusion. European traders and Christian missionaries were given a choice of expulsion or execution. The building of oceangoing vessels was prohibited, and any Japanese intrepid enough to venture abroad faced certain death if he got homesick. The country closed in on itself for two and a half centuries and, far from withering from a lack of outside stimulation, experienced one of its headiest periods of cultural ferment.

In sum, the shogunal authorities tried to stop time by freezing political, social, and economic conditions in a status quo that favored their predominance. For a remarkably long interval they did succeed in eradicating foreign influence. But they never succeeded in stopping time. When peace and stability returned to Japan, a new class quickly rose in economic and cultural significance. It was a bourgeois, mercantile class, and it came into being as the inevitable consequence of the new political administration. The shogun's vast bureaucracy was staffed by samurai retainers. With no more wars to fight, these former soldiers became bureaucrats, and with a government to run they clustered in the cities. Removed from the land and their previous military and agricultural pursuits, the urban samurai developed new needs, which were promptly met by enterprising merchants, artisans, and laborers whose numbers swelled in response to economic opportunity. City life and long-distance transport eventually made rice an unwieldy medium of exchange. Coin took its place in business transactions, and the growth of a money economy had a slow but irreversible effect on every aspect of Japanese life. Although the new commercial class was denied access to the political system, as the nation's bankers and suppliers it increasingly held the real power, which was financial.

These aggressive, upstart merchants were not hidebound by the traditions of another age, as could be said of both the samurai and their political predecessors, the sadly attenuated aristocrats, who barely kept the flame of classical Japanese convention from sputtering and dying out. Now and then the new merchant princes played dress-up with the trappings of high culture, but most of the time they were absorbed in a culture completely of their own making. As a reflection of their world, it was an urban culture. Woodblock prints, short stories, novels, poetry, and plays depicted city life—fast, varied, crowded, and competitive—where people lived by their wits and appreciated wit. Puns and parody took pride of place in the new popular literature, which itself became big business. Publishing proved yet another way of making money in this commercial age, so that for the first time books circulated in printed form rather than in manuscript. Literature came to the masses, or at least the urban masses.

To succeed, it had to meet their tastes. Like metropolitans the world over, Japanese townspeople of the seventeenth and eighteenth centuries moved to a faster beat. They were impatient, and it showed in their fiction. The stately pace of courtly prose yielded to narratives moving at a rapid clip, where action is compressed and any fine-grained analysis of character is likely to be jettisoned as a drag on the reader's fractured attention. The townspeople were also intensely rivalrous. By day they sweat to best the competition; by night they dressed to trump their neighbors in the social contest. Style was an essential component of success, and the new class demanded no less of its writers and artists, who were expected to capture the city scene with acuity and a sense of humor and to execute their work with verbal and visual panache.

Naturally, as tradesmen, the townspeople were nothing if not pragmatic, and naturally too their practical bent affected the literature they supported. The bourgeois audience had little use for tales of noble romance or martial prowess. The members of this new middle class demanded realism. What was real to them were other people like themselves, the gossip of their own tight world, the perils and the thrills of the marketplace, and the pleasures to be had from prosperity. For the first time, in other words, ordinary people became standard literary characters, and the material and sexual aspects of life were deemed worthy subjects of literature.

Inevitably, at times, there was a certain excess to this exuberant young culture, giddy and energized by the excitement of its own self-creation. It could be, for example, startlingly graphic: every artist of repute enjoyed a lucrative sideline producing erotic woodblock prints. It could also be vulgar, for the nouveaux riches of the merchant class were sometimes prone to a particularly mindless form of conspicuous consumption. A man dallies upstairs at a teahouse with his favorite courtesan. His friend sends over a giant dumpling, so enormous that it cannot be carried up the stairway. Instead of coming down to enjoy the dumpling, he hires six carpenters to widen the stairs. With events like this in the historical record, it is not surprising that caricature and lampoon compose the other side of popular "realism."

For the most part ignored by the samurai authorities and removed from foreign influence, the new urban culture developed organically. Actors, courtesans, adventurers, shopkeepers, rice brokers, moneylenders, fashion-plate wives, and precocious sons and daughters created their own cosmopolitan customs. Kabuki playwrights, haiku poets, woodblock artists, and best-selling novelists all captured in their own genres an intimate glimpse of kinetic bourgeois life—blunt, expansive, iconoclastic, irrepressibly playful. Few here ever heard of the Enlightenment or the scientific revolution. The walled garden of Japan in the seventeenth and eighteenth centuries bloomed nicely without the irrigation of European currents.

A note on the Japanese calendar and time-keeping practices will be helpful in reading the following selection. Until 1873, when Japan adopted the Gregorian calendar of the West, the official calendar was derived from China and was divided into twelve lunations (months) of twenty-nine or thirty days. The resulting lunar year was approximately eleven days shorter than the solar year, which required the insertion of a thirteenth intercalary month every third year or thereabout to align the calendrical year with the solar. In addition, by custom the Japanese year began slightly later than the Western, so that New Year's Day fell anywhere from January 15 to February 15. The beginning of the new year also marked an increase in one's age, in contrast to the Western practice of reckoning age by birthdays. A child born in the twelfth month, for instance, would turn two with the new year.

Years were numbered serially from the year when a reigning emperor ascended the throne. In the modern period (beginning in 1868) the reign of an emperor has one name for its duration. For example, the reign of Emperor Hirohito is called the Shōwa ("enlightened peace") era, which lasted from his ascension in 1926 until his death in 1989. In addition to following the Western practice of numbering years by the Gregorian calendar, the year 1930, say, is reckoned as Shōwa 5. In the premodern period, rather than having one name throughout, an emperor's reign was usually divided into various eras, each with its own name.

Both the months and the hours of the day were designated by the signs of the Chinese zodiac. The day was divided into twelve units, each equivalent to 120 minutes:

Hour	Modern Equivalent
1 Rat	11 P.M.–1 A.M.
2 Ox	1 A.M.–3 A.M.
3 Tiger	3 A.M.–5 A.M.
4 Rabbit	5 A.M.–7 A.M.
5 Dragon	7 A.M.–9 A.M.
6 Snake	9 A.M.–11 A.M.
7 Horse	11 A.M.–1 P.M.
8 Ram	1 P.M.–3 P.M.
9 Monkey	3 P.M.–5 P.M.
10 Rooster	5 P.M.–7 P.M.
11 Dog	7 P.M.–9 P.M.
12 Boar	9 P.M.–11 P.M.

PRONOUNCING GLOSSARY

The following list uses common English syllables to provide rough equivalents of selected words whose pronunciation may be unfamiliar to the general reader.

haiku: *hai-koo*

Heike: *hay-ke*

kabuki: *kah-boo-kee*

nō: *noh*

Tokugawa: *toh-koo-gah-wah*

Zeami: *ze-ah-mee*

TEXTS	CONTEXTS
	1600–1868 Edo period: Tokugawa family establishes dynasty of shoguns who rule from Edo (present-day Tokyo)
1609 Commercial publishing begins in Japan	
	1616–60 Imperial family commissions the Katsura Detached Palace (icon of modernism for twentieth-century architects)
	1620 The *Mayflower* carries Pilgrims to America
	ca. 1620–1716 Sōtatsu and Kōrin create masterpieces of Japanese screen painting
	1627 Korea becomes a tributary state of China
1639 Aesop's *Fables* translated into Japanese	**1639** Shogun proclaims policy of national isolation, expelling Portuguese and banning Christianity and foreign travel
1682 *The Life of a Sensuous Man* (Ihara Saikaku) launches comic realism and popular fiction	
1686 *The Barrelmaker Brimful of Love* published in Ihara Saikaku's collection *Five Women Who Loved Love*	
1690–94 *The Narrow Road of the Interior* (Matsuo Bashō), verse inset in a travel memoir written by the foremost haiku poet	
1721 *The Love Suicides at Amijima* (Chikamatsu Monzaemon), a masterpiece among tragedies of fatal love written for the puppet theater	
1745 Haiku poet Yosa Buson anticipates modern free verse with innovative poems in his *Elegy to Hokuju Rōsen*	

Boldface titles indicate works in the anthology.

TIME LINE

TEXTS	CONTEXTS
1748 *The Treasury of Loyal Retainers* (Takeda Izumo II), a popular play immortalizing the fealty of samurai who avenge their master's death	
1758–1801 Studies by Motoori Norinaga revive interest in *The Ten Thousand Leaves*, *The Tale of Genji*, and other Japanese classics	
	1760s Harunobu inaugurates heyday of color woodblock print
	1769–1800 James Watt's refinements of the steam engine fuel Industrial Revolution
1770–90 Center of literary activity shifts from Kyoto-Osaka area eastward to Edo (present-day Tokyo)	**1770–90** Glory days of Kabuki with actor Ichikawa Danjūrō V
ca. 1776 *Tales of Moonlight and Rain* (Ueda Akinari), a collection of supernatural stories, including *Bewitched*	**1776** American colonies adopt the Declaration of Independence
	1790 Utamaro's portraits of women add psychological depth to woodblock print tradition
	1810–80 Landscapes by Hokusai and Hiroshige take art of woodblock print to its zenith

MATSUO BASHŌ
1644–1694

Until the seventeenth century, Japanese literature was privileged property. Court aristocrats and provincial warlords (and the occasional member of the Buddhist clergy) had exclusive access to "books": a narrow supply of manuscript copies. Even when the first printed books began to appear at the beginning of the seventeenth century, they were still luxury items. Connoisseurs underwrote lavishly illustrated printings of the Japanese classics available in limited editions, usually of no more than one hundred copies and intended not for sale but for presentation. Like the manuscripts they replaced, the first printed books were an indulgence. But when printing and publishing became commercial endeavors around the second decade of the new century, books changed from being rare works of art, whose mysteries were known only to the chosen few, into tools and pastimes for the multitude.

The diffusion of literacy, and thus education, was both a cause and an effect of the diffusion of the printed word. Print not only provided new channels of communication, a new medium for artists, and new commercial opportunities, it created for the first time in Japan the conditions necessary for that peculiarly modern phenomenon, celebrity.

The haiku poet Matsuo Bashō was an odd candidate for the new renown. Born in 1644 as the second son of a low-ranking provincial samurai who cobbled a living by teaching calligraphy, he had little in his background or early years that augured celebrity. Adult life commenced in the most ordinary way, when Bashō entered the service of a cadet branch of the local ruling military house. But he became close to his employer, the young heir, who was a devotee of linked verse, and Bashō too developed a taste for the popular poetry. Together they studied with Kitamura Kigin, one of the leading poets of the day, and they shared the excitement of seeing their compositions—two by Bashō and one by his patron—published in a poetry anthology in 1664. The easygoing days of poetastering and unchallenging service must have been very pleasant for Bashō and must have seemed the shape his days would take for the rest of his life.

But everything changed suddenly with the premature death in 1666 of his master. Bashō lost not only a friend and poetry companion but the protector who would have guaranteed him security and advancement in the ranks of the samurai. In 1672 Bashō left for Edo (now Tokyo), the expanding military capital of the shogun's new government, where he decided to make his career as a professional poet. To do so he had to build a following. With some thirty of his verses now in anthologies and his first book recently published, the twenty-eight-year-old Bashō must have conjectured that he had a better chance of establishing himself in a new city, where the competition for income as a teacher and corrector of poetry (an expert paid to correct other people's poetry) would be less intense than in the old capital of Kyoto or the seasoned commercial town of Osaka. This departure for the east was in its own quiet way daring. By leaving his home district and the employ of the local clan, he was forfeiting his status as a samurai, a member (however lowly) of the elite ruling class. In relocating to the boomtown of Edo, with a population already over six hundred thousand and growing, Bashō was in fact courting fame.

It is not surprising that the first years in Edo were not easy. "Sometimes," he would later recall, "I grew weary of poetry and thought I would abandon it. Other times, I vowed to establish my name as the foremost poet. The two alternatives battled within, making me utterly restless." For a while, Bashō was forced to supplement his income with a post in the city's department of waterworks.

But ultimately he succeeded. Linked-verse anthologies sold well in the late seventeenth century, and Bashō's poems appeared in them with increasing frequency. Within eight years he had made a name for himself. He was asked to judge linked-verse competitions, and his published commentaries on these contests found a ready audience. Over time, he had gathered a stable of students large enough by 1680 for him to publish their best poems in an anthology. And Bashō's followers were so devoted that in the same year the more prosperous ones built a cottage for him in a quiet, still rural part of the city.

In front of this cottage, his students planted a banana tree. Its rare flowers were so small as to be unobtrusive, and the large, delicate leaves were easily torn when the wind blew in from the sea. The whole thing looked somehow lonesome. In a climate too cool for it to bear fruit, the tree was deprived of its purpose. Alone inside his hut, Bashō professed an affinity for his banana tree:

> Banana tree in autumn winds:
> a night passed hearing
> raindrops in a basin.

His persona was now complete: the lonely wayfarer who had traveled far from home, the man of simple tastes who had consecrated his life to poetry, the delicate sensibility as fragile as the leaves of a banana tree. It was only fitting that he took the word *banana*—Bashō—for his pen name.

One might well smile at Bashō's canniness. In the choice of his personal metaphor, he managed to join self-image and apparent, actual attributes with a public stance edited seamlessly into his literary product: like an actor so indistinguishable from his interchangeable roles that we think we know the "real" person. Bashō cast himself as a pilgrim, but the purpose of his frequent travels was a poetic devotion to nature—the beauty and truth it alone could reveal—not religious piety. Like a Zen monk, he shaved his head and donned the dark, drab garb of a cleric, setting off, as in *The Narrow Road of the Interior*, on paths by no means always certain, into wilderness not entirely safe. Whether home alone in his rustic cottage or enduring the ardors of the open road, Bashō sought an austere existence, as though he had taken a vow of poverty. *Economy* could have been his watchword.

In person and in art, he was the antithesis of Ihara Saikaku, that prosperous chronicler of rich, material life, and in fact Bashō appears to have disdained Saikaku's prolific literary output. To him, it was vulgar and excessive. (It is not surprising that Bashō-the-perfectionist's entire oeuvre, about 1,000 haiku, is an afternoon's work for Saikaku, whose most frenzied single sitting of solo linked-verse composition yielded 23,500 poems in twenty-four hours!) Perhaps Saikaku in turn disdained Bashō's fastidiousness, endlessly revising a mere seventeen syllables. In the world of poetry, however, the tortoise won the race. Bashō's lapidary style perfected a kind of epigram that indeed seems to capture the universe in a grain of sand. His sympathy with nature, and particularly with its frailest elements, which speak of the transience and vulnerability of living things, was permanently accepted as the essence of Japanese poetic feeling.

The haiku was the perfect form for Bashō's art: a flash of lyric verse as fleeting as the momentary impression it encapsulates—a scene from nature or a natural object that evokes a truth larger than itself—expressed in cryptic, unrhymed lines of five, seven, and five syllables:

> Upon a bare branch
> a crow has descended—
> autumn in evening.

It is a form of poetry that looks effortless. Anyone can string together seventeen syllables and make them sound ponderous or picturesque, which is probably why haiku have become so popular (though syntactic differences between Japanese and English can sometimes defeat translation attempts that hold to the exact syllable count). Only a true poet can work within the slender margins of this constricted form and create something beyond aphorism. It was Bashō's gift to fuse the transitory and the eternal, both the moment observed and its greater significance. The crow landing on the branch of a withered tree is the "now" of the poem; time's passing and loneliness are the universals.

Actually, haiku began as part of linked verse, and in this respect too its apparent simplicity is deceptive. In the composition of linked poetry, resulting normally in sequences of thirty-six or one hundred verses (although they could stretch into one thousand verses or more), several poets worked in tandem. They took turns composing alternating links, or verses, in three lines with syllable counts of five, seven, and five (identical in form to haiku) and in two lines with syllable counts of seven each. Eventually, anthologies of linked poetry began to appear, excerpting the opening verses from various sequences. Thus these short poems in three lines of seventeen syllables, originally intended as the base to which subsequent lines of verse would be added, came to stand on their own. Poets began to write haiku as self-contained lyrics. But however independent they became, for a long time haiku retained a vestigial sense that they were somehow part of a larger matrix, or ought to be. This is one reason that poems in *The Narrow Road of the Interior* are embedded in a travel narrative, the prose equivalent of a linked sequence. By subtly following some of the structural principles of linked verse, Bashō's narrative achieves a kind of covert unity. And by including an occasional poem by his traveling companion, Sora, it retains something of the feel of linked verse. Once again poets were collaborating.

The Narrow Road of the Interior was written, or begun, in 1689, when Bashō embarked on his most ambitious journey. It would cover fifteen hundred miles of hinterland and take Bashō and Sora to the far corners of northern Japan. Although he is first thought of as a haiku poet, many of Bashō's best poems originally appeared in the five travel memoirs that he wrote in the final decade of his life. *The Narrow Road* is the last of these travel diaries, the longest, and the most esteemed. It also represents the climax of a venerable tradition in Japan, where the travel diary as poetic memoir enjoyed a distinguished eight-hundred-year history.

This fact too is an indication that Bashō's poetry involves more than meets the eye. The journey depicted in *The Narrow Road* is another pilgrimage through nature, but it is also a very conscious emulation of the conventions of the past. "Bewitched by the god of restlessness" Bashō describes himself as the trip gets under way. "Seduced by the call of history" would be just as accurate. Bashō, or his literary persona, sets off as the hero on a quest. His goal is to seek inspiration from remote places made famous by literature and history. Reputation, celebrity, tradition intertwine.

In 1943, some 250 years later, a second diary was published. This was Sora's account of their trip together, and it came like a thunderclap. The man who represented himself as a frail pilgrim at the mercy of nature and fate, and who was later deified by the Shinto religion, is described by Sora as a much more practical and wily figure, who altered the facts of his trip, abridged, and deleted to maintain the ascetic tone appropriate for a poetic saint, a man who saw himself as the successor to all poet-travelers of the past and was not about to reveal that among the motives for his trip were cultivating patrons and recruiting new students.

But *The Narrow Road of the Interior* is a literary creation. Its spare, supple prose anchors wise poetic insights. Its haiku transcend entertainment. The material has been shaped only by taking great pains, and that is the nature of artistry.

PRONOUNCING GLOSSARY

The following list uses common English syllables to provide rough equivalents of selected words whose pronunciation may be unfamiliar to the general reader.

Atsumi: *ah-tsoo-mee*

Benkei: *ben-kay*

Butchō: *boot-choh*

Date: *dah-tay*

Echigo: *e-chee-goh*

Edo: *e-doh*

Fukuura: *foo-koo-oo-rah*

Genji: *gen-jee*

Genroku: *gen-roh-koo*

haikai: *hai-kai*

Heike: *hay-ke*

hototogisu: *hoh-toh-toh-gee-soo*

Ihara Saikaku: *ee-hah-rah sai-kah-koo*

Iizuka: *ee-ee-zoo-kah*

Ji: *jee*

Kanemori: *kah-ne-moh-ree*

Kawai: *kah-wai*

Kisakata: *kee-sah-kah-tah*

Kokinshū: *koh-keen-shoo*

konoshiro: *koh-noh-shee-roh*

koromogae: *koh-roh-moh-gah-e*

Kūkai: *koo-kai*

Kurokamiyama: *koo-roh-kah-mee-yah-mah*

Kyohaku: *kyoh-hah-koo*

Matsuo Bashō: *mah-tsoo-oh bah-shoh*

Minamidani: *mee-nah-mee-dah-nee*

Nikkō: *neek-koh*

Nōin: *noh-een*

Satō Shōji: *sah-toh shoh-jee*

Shinto: *sheen-toh*

Shiogoshi: *shee-oh-goh-shee*

Shirakawa: *shee-rah-kah-wah*

Sōgorō: *soh-goh-roh*

Tsuruga: *tsoo-roo-gah*

Yasuhira: *yah-soo-hee-rah*

Yoichi: *yoh-ee-chee*

Yudono: *yoo-doh-noh*

The Narrow Road of the Interior[1]

The sun and the moon are eternal voyagers; the years that come and go are travelers too. For those whose lives float away on boats, for those who greet old age with hands clasping the lead ropes of horses, travel is life, travel is home. And many are the men of old who have perished as they journeyed.

I myself fell prey to wanderlust some years ago, desiring nothing better than to be a vagrant cloud scudding before the wind. Only last autumn, after having drifted along the seashore for a time, had I swept away the old cobwebs from my dilapidated riverside hermitage. But the year ended before I knew it, and I found myself looking at hazy spring skies and thinking of crossing Shirakawa Barrier.[2] Bewitched by the god of restlessness, I lost my peace of mind; summoned by the spirits of the road, I felt unable to settle down to anything. By the time I had mended my torn trousers, put a new cord on my hat, and cauterized my legs with moxa,[3] I was thinking only of

---

1. Translated by Helen Craig McCullough and Steven D. Carter, with notes adapted from McCullough.
2. An old official checkpoint where travelers entered Mutsu Province.   3. A combustible substance used in traditional East Asian medicine. Moxa cones, made from pulverized plant leaves, were burned at specific therapeutic points on the skin, depending on the symptoms. The resulting heat was thought to adjust physical disorders by releasing energy obstructed at a crucial point and returning it to smooth circulation.

the moon at Matsushima. I turned over my dwelling to others, moved to a house belonging to Sanpū,[4] and affixed the initial page of a linked-verse sequence to one of the pillars at my cottage.

> Even my grass-thatched hut
> will have new occupants now:
> a display of dolls.[5]

It was the Twenty-seventh Day, almost the end of the Third Month. The wan morning moon retained little of its brilliance, but the silhouette of Mount Fuji was dimly visible in the first pale light of dawn. With a twinge of sadness, I wondered when I might see the flowering branches at Ueno and Yanaka again. My intimate friends, who had all assembled the night before, got on the boat to see me off.

We disembarked at Senju.[6] Transitory though I know this world to be, I shed tears when I came to the parting of the ways, overwhelmed by the prospect of the long journey ahead.

> Departing springtime:
> birds lament and fishes too
> have tears in their eyes.

With that as the initial entry in my journal, we started off, hard though it was to stride out in earnest. The others lined up part way along the road, apparently wanting to watch us out of sight.

That year was, I believe, the second of the Genroku[7] era [1689]. I had taken a sudden fancy to make the long pilgrimage on foot to Mutsu and Dewa[8]—to view places I had heard about but never seen, even at the cost of hardships severe enough to "whiten a man's hair under the skies of Wu."[9] The outlook was not reassuring, but I resolved to hope for the best and be content merely to return alive.

We barely managed to reach Sōka Post Station that night. My greatest trial was the pack I bore on my thin, bony shoulders. I had planned to set out with no baggage at all, but had ended by taking along a paper coat for cold nights, a cotton bath garment, rain gear, and ink and brushes, as well as certain farewell presents, impossible to discard, which simply had to be accepted as burdens on the way.

We went to pay our respects at Muro-no-yashima. Sora, my fellow pilgrim, said, "This shrine honors Ko-no-hana-sakuya-hime, the goddess worshipped at Mount Fuji. The name Muro-no-yashima is an allusion to the birth of Hohodemi-no-mikoto inside the sealed chamber the goddess entered and set ablaze in fulfillment of her vow. It is because of that same incident that poems about the shrine usually mention smoke. The passage in the shrine history telling of the prohibition against konoshiro fish[1] is also well known."

On the Thirtieth, we lodged at the foot of the Nikkō Mountains. "I am called Buddha Gozaemon," the master of the house informed us. "People

---

4. A disciple and patron. 5. It is the time of the Doll Festival, in the Third Month, when dolls representing the emperor, the empress, and their attendants are displayed in every household. 6. Near Edo (Tokyo). The path of Bashō's journey is traced on the map on p. 534. 7. The era name. For information on the Japanese calendar, see the period introduction (pp. 535–37). 8. Two northern provinces. 9. An allusion to a Chinese poem written by someone seeing off a monk on his travels: "Your hat will be heavy with the snows of Wu; / Your boots will be fragrant with the fallen blossoms of Chu." Snow on a traveler's hat was associated with hardships and with whitening hair. 1. Gizzard shad. It was taboo to eat the fish because, when broiled, it gave off a smell like flesh burning.

have given me that title because I make it a point to be honest in all my dealings. You may rest here tonight with your minds at ease."

"What kind of Buddha is it who has manifested himself in this impure world to help humble travelers like us—mendicant monks, as it were, on a pious pilgrimage?" I wondered. By paying close attention to his behavior, I satisfied myself that he was indeed a man of stubborn integrity, devoid of shrewdness and calculation. He was one of those, "firm, resolute, simple, and modest, who are near virtue,"[2] and I found his honorable, unassuming nature wholly admirable.

On the First of the Fourth Month, we went to worship at the shrine. In antiquity, the name of that holy mountain was written Nikōsan [Two-Storm Mountain], but the Great Teacher Kūkai changed it to Nikkō [Sunlight] when he founded the temple. It is almost as though the Great Teacher had been able to see 1,000 years into the future, for today the shrine's radiance extends throughout the realm, its beneficence overflows in the eight directions, and the four classes[3] of people dwell in security and peace. This is an awesome subject of which I shall write no more.

> Ah, awesome sight!
> on summer leaves and spring leaves,
> the radiance of the sun!

Kurokamiyama was veiled in haze, dotted with lingering patches of white snow. Sora composed this poem:

> Black hair shaved off,
> at Kurokamiyama[4]
> I change to new robes.

Sora is of the Kawai family; he was formerly called Sōgorō. He lived in a house adjoining mine, almost under the leaves of the banana plant, and used to help me with the chores of hauling wood and drawing water. Delighted by the thought of seeing Matsushima and Kisakata with me on this trip, and eager also to spare me some of the hardships of the road, he shaved his head at dawn on the day of our departure, put on a monk's black robe, and changed his name to Sōgo. That is why he composed the Kurokamiyama poem. The word koromogae ["I change to new robes"][5] was most effective.

There is a waterfall half a league or so up the mountain. The stream leaps with tremendous force over outthrust rocks at the top and descends 100 feet into a dark green pool strewn with 1,000 rocks. Visitors squeeze into the space between the rocks and the cascade to view it from the rear, which is why it is called Urami-no-take [Rearview Falls].

> In brief seclusion
> at a waterfall—the start
> of a summer retreat.

I knew someone at Kurobane in Nasu, so we decided to head straight across the plain from there. It began to rain as we walked along, taking our

2. From Confucius's *Analects*.   3. Samurai, farmer, artisan, and merchant. The shrine held the mausoleum of the founder of the Tokugawa shogunate.   4. Or Mount Kurokami, homonymous with "black hair."   5. The first day of the Fourth Month was the date for changing from winter to summer clothing.

bearings on a distant village, and the sun soon sank below the horizon. After borrowing accommodations for the night at a farmhouse, we started out across the plain again in the morning. A horse was grazing nearby. We appealed for help to a man who was cutting grass and found him by no means incapable of understanding other people's feelings, rustic though he was.

"What's the best thing to do, I wonder?" he said. "I can't leave my work. Still, inexperienced travelers are bound to get lost on this plain, what with all the trails branching off in every direction. Rather than see you go on alone, I'll let you take the horse. Send him back when he won't go any farther." With that, he lent us the animal.

Two small children came running behind the horse. One of them, a little girl, was called Kasane. Sora composed this poem:

> Kasane must be
> a name for a wild pink
> with double petals![6]

Before long, we arrived at a hamlet and turned the horse back with some money tied to the saddle.

We called on Jōbōji, the warden at Kurobane. Surprised and delighted to see us, he kept us in conversation day and night; and his younger brother, Tōsui, came morning and evening. We went with Tōsui to his own house and were also invited to the homes of various other relatives. So the time passed.

One day, we strolled into the outskirts of the town for a brief visit to the site of the old dog shoots, then pressed through the Nasu bamboo fields to Lady Tamamo's tumulus, and went on to pay our respects at Hachiman Shrine.[7] Someone told me that when Yoichi shot down the fan target, it was to this very shrine that he prayed, "and especially Shōhachiman, the tutelary deity of my province."[8] The thought of the divine response evoked deep emotion. We returned to Tōsui's house as darkness fell.

There was a mountain-cult temple, Kōmyōji, in the vicinity. We visited it by invitation and worshipped at the Ascetic's Hall.[9]

> Toward summer mountains
> we set off after prayers
> before the master's clogs.

The site of the Venerable Butchō's[1] hermitage was behind Unganji Temple in that province. Butchō once told me that he had used pine charcoal to inscribe a poem on a rock there:

> Ah, how I detest
> building any shelter at all,
> even a grass-thatched

---

6. This poem uses wordplay. The name *Kasane* can mean "double." The word for "wild pink" (a flower) can also mean "beloved child." 7. Dedicated to the god of war. According to legend, Lady Tamamo was a fox-woman with whom an emperor fell in love. After having been unmasked by a diviner, she fled to Nasu, where local warriors shot her down. Her vindictive spirit survived as Killer Rock, a large boulder that releases poisonous fumes, which Bashō will soon visit on his journey. "Dog shoots": for a brief time in the 13th century dog shooting had been a sport. 8. Refers to an episode in *The Tale of the Heike*. Yoichi is a minor samurai in the service of the Minamoto / Genji. An expert archer, he succeeds in shooting a fan suspended off the prow of an enemy ship, put there to taunt the Genji. 9. Dedicated to a miracle-working mountain ascetic of the 8th century, whose enshrined image is believed to have shown a holy man wearing high clogs (referred to in the following poem) and clothes made from leaves, holding a staff, and leaning against a rock. 1. A Zen master with whom Bashō had studied.

hovel less than five feet square!
Were it not for the rainstorms . . .

Staff in hand, I prepared to set out for the temple to see what was left of the hermitage. A number of people encouraged one another to accompany me, and I acquired a group of young companions who kept up a lively chatter along the way. We reached the lower limits of the temple grounds in no time. The mountains created an impression of great depth. The valley road stretched far into the distance, pines and cryptomerias rose in dark masses, the moss dripped with moisture, and there was a bite to the air, even though it was the Fourth Month. We viewed all of the Ten Sights[2] and entered the main gate by way of a bridge.

Eager to locate the hermitage, I scrambled up the hill behind the temple to a tiny thatched structure on a rock, a lean-to built against a cave. It was like seeing the holy Yuanmiao's Death Gate or the monk Fayun's[3] rock chamber. I left an impromptu verse on a pillar:

Even woodpeckers
seem to spare the hermitage
in the summer grove.

From Kurobane, I headed toward Killer Rock astride a horse lent us by the warden. When the groom asked if I would write a poem for him, I gave him this, surprised and impressed that he should exhibit such cultivated taste:

A cuckoo[4] song:
please make the horse angle off
across the field.

Killer Rock stands in the shadow of a mountain near a hot spring. It still emits poisonous vapors: dead bees, butterflies, and other insects lie in heaps near it, hiding the color of the sand.

The willow "where fresh spring water flowed"[5] survives on a ridge between two ricefields in Ashino Village. The district officer there, a man called Kohō, had often expressed a desire to show me the tree, and I had wondered each time about its exact location—but on this day I rested in its shade.

Ah, the willow tree:
a whole rice paddy planted
before I set out.

So the days of impatient travel had accumulated, until at last I had reached Shirakawa Barrier. It was there, for the first time, that I felt truly on the way. I could understand why Kanemori had been moved to say, "Would that there were a means somehow to send people word in the capital!"[6]

As one of the Three Barriers, Shirakawa has always attracted the notice of poets and other writers. An autumn wind seemed to sound in my ears, colored

2. Various rocks, peaks, buildings, etc., within the temple precincts. 3. A Chinese priest; he lived in a hut perched atop a high rock. Yuanmiao was a Chinese priest who confined himself for fifteen years to a cave he called Death's Gate. 4. In Japanese *hototogisu*; the name is an onomatopoeia derived from the bird's call: *ho-to-to*. Its song was deemed the quintessence of summer and is so beautiful that Bashō would like his horse to follow after it. 5. Refers to a verse by the famed poet-priest Saigyō (1118–1190): "On the wayside / where a clear spring flowed / in a willow's shade: / 'Just for a moment,' I thought, / but then I lingered there." Saigyō was an inveterate traveler and an important influence on Bashō. 6. Alludes to a poem by Kanemori (died 990): "Would there were means / To let them know, somehow, / the people of the capital: / 'Today I have crossed / Shirakawa Barrier.'"

leaves seemed to appear before my eyes—but even the leafy summer branches were delightful in their own way. Wild roses bloomed alongside the whiteness of the deutzia, making us feel as though we were crossing snow. I believe one of Kiyosuke's writings preserves a story about a man of the past who straightened his hat and adjusted his dress there.[7] Sora composed this poem:

> With deutzia[8] flowers
> we adorn our hats—formal garb
> for the barrier.

We passed beyond the barrier and crossed the Abukuma River. To the left, the peak of Aizu soared; to the right, the districts of Iwaki, Sōma, and Mihara lay extended; to the rear, mountains formed boundaries with Hitachi and Shimotsuke provinces. We passed Kagenuma Pond, but the sky happened to be overcast that day, so there were no reflections.[9]

At the post town of Sukagawa, we visited a man called Tōkyū, who persuaded us to stay four or five days. His first act was to inquire, "How did you feel when you crossed Shirakawa Barrier?"

"What with the fatigue of the long, hard trip, the distractions of the scenery, and the stress of so many nostalgic associations, I couldn't manage to think of a decent poem," I said. "Still, it seemed a pity to cross with nothing to show for it . . .":

> A start for connoisseurs
> of poetry—rice-planting song
> of Michinoku.

We added a second verse and then a third, and continued until we had completed three sequences.

Under a great chestnut tree in the corner of the town, there lived a hermit monk. It seemed to me that his cottage, with its aura of lonely tranquility, must resemble that other place deep in the mountains where someone had gathered horse chestnuts.[1] I set down a few words:

To form the character "chestnut," we write "tree of the west."[2] I have heard, I believe, that the bodhisattva Gyōgi perceived an affinity between this tree and the Western Paradise,[3] and that he used its wood for staffs and pillars throughout his life:

> Chestnut at the eaves—
> here are blossoms unremarked
> by ordinary folk.

Asakayama is just beyond Hiwada Post Station, about five leagues from Tōkyū's house. It is close to the road, and there are numerous marshes in

---

7. Fujiwara Kiyosuke (1104–1177) was a court noble and a poet-scholar. The man's actions show respect to Nōin (998–1050?), a monk and early poet-traveler who established Shirakawa Barrier as a place with poetic associations. In earlier times, travelers approaching checkpoints between provinces adjusted their clothes before crossing the barrier.   8. A shrub of the saxifrage family, an ornamental bush with white or pink flowers. It blooms in the Fourth Month.   9. The name of the pond is literally "Shadow Swamp"; with the sun obscured, it does not fulfill its reputation.   1. Refers to Saigyō and one of his poems: "In these remote hills, / I try to trap water / dripping onto the rocks; / I gather horse chestnuts / dropping to the ground." 2. The character for "chestnut" consists of the character for "tree" surmounted by an element resembling the character for "west." 3. One of the various "Buddha worlds" (Buddhist equivalents of Heaven); this one is located in the western sector of the universe and is presided over by Amida, the most popular Buddhist deity of the time. "Bodhisattva": a person who attains enlightenment but compassionately refrains from entering paradise to save others, a future Buddha. Gyōgi (668–749) was a Buddhist monk known for his asceticism and charisma.

the vicinity. It was almost the season for reaping *katsumi*.[4] We kept asking, "Which plant is the flowering *katsumi?*" But nobody knew. We wandered about, scrutinizing marshes, questioning people, and seeking "*katsumi, katsumi*" until the sun sank to the rim of the hills.

We turned off to the right at Nihonmatsu, took a brief look at Kurozuka Cave,[5] and stopped for the night at Fukushima.

On the following day, we went to Shinobu in search of the Fern-print Rock,[6] which proved to be half buried under the soil of a remote hamlet in the shadow of a mountain. Some village urchins came up and told us, "In the old days, the rock used to be on top of that mountain, but the farmers got upset because the people who passed would destroy the young grain so they could test it. They shoved it off into this valley; that's why it's lying upside down." A likely story, perhaps.

> Hands planting seedlings
> evoke Shinobu patterns
> of the distant past.

We crossed the river at Tsukinowa Ford and emerged at Senoue Post Station. Satō Shōji's[7] old home was about a league and a half away, near the mountains to the left. Told that we would find the site at Sabano in Iizuka Village, we went along, asking directions, until we came upon it at a place called Maruyama. That was where Shōji had had his house. I wept as someone explained that the front gate had been at the foot of the hill. Still standing at an old temple nearby were a number of stone monuments erected in memory of the family. It was especially moving to see the memorials to the two young wives.[8] "Women though they were, all the world knows of their bravery." The thought made me drench my sleeve. The Tablet of Tears[9] was not far to seek!

We entered the temple to ask for tea, and there we saw Yoshitsune's sword and Benkei's pannier,[1] preserved as treasures.

> Paper carp flying!
> Display pannier and sword, too,
> in the Fifth Month.

It was the First Day of the Fifth Month.

We lodged that night at Iizuka, taking advantage of the hot springs in the town to bathe before engaging a room. The hostelry turned out to be a wretched hovel, its straw mats spread over dirt floors. In the absence of a lamp, we prepared our beds and stretched out by the light from a fire-pit. Thunder rumbled during the night, and rain fell in torrents. What with the roof leaking right over my head and the fleas and mosquitoes biting, I got no sleep at all. To make matters worse, my old complaint[2] flared up, causing me such agony that I almost fainted.

---

4. Wild rice.   5. Rich in folklore. A witch was said to be interred beneath Kurozuka, a hillock whose name means "black mound," and the nearby rocky cave was thought a goblins' lair.   6. Said to have been used to imprint cloth with a moss-fern design, a specialty of the area.   7. A brave warrior and supporter of the Genji chieftain Yoshitsune (in *The Tale of the Heike*).   8. Of Satō Shōji's two sons, who died in battle. The young widows were said to have worn their husbands' suits of armor as a way of consoling their grieving mother-in-law, who still hoped to see her sons riding home victorious.   9. A memorial erected in China in honor of a virtuous official. All who saw it were said to weep.   1. A large basket. Yoshitsune is the great hero who leads his clan to victory in the war recounted in *The Tale of the Heike*. Benkei is his faithful lieutenant.   2. Bashō was troubled with stomachaches and hemorrhoids.

At long last, the short night ended and we set out again. Still feeling the effects of the night, I rode a rented horse to Kōri Post Station. It was unsettling to fall prey to an infirmity while so great a distance remained ahead. But I told myself that I had deliberately planned this long pilgrimage to remote areas, a decision that meant renouncing worldly concerns and facing the fact of life's uncertainty. If I were to die on the road—very well, that would be Heaven's decree. Such reflections helped to restore my spirits a bit, and it was with a jaunty step that I passed through the Great Gate into the Date[3] domain.

We entered Kasajima District by way of Abumizuri and Shiraishi Castle. I asked someone about the Fujiwara Middle Captain Sanekata's[4] grave and was told, "Those two villages far off to the right at the edge of the hills are Minowa and Kasajima. The Road Goddess's shrine and the 'memento miscanthus' are still there."[5] The road was in a dreadful state from the recent early-summer rains, and I was exhausted, so we contented ourselves with looking in that direction as we trudged on. Because the names Minowa and Kasajima suggested the rainy season,[6] I composed this verse.

> Where is Rain Hat Isle?
> Somewhere down the muddy roads
> of the Fifth Month!

We lodged at Iwanuma. It was exciting to see the Takekuma Pine. The trunk forks a bit above the ground, and one knows instantly that this is just how the old tree must have looked. My first thought was of Nōin. Did he compose the poem, "Not a trace this time of the pine" because a certain man, appointed long ago to serve as Governor of Mutsu, had felled the tree to get pilings for a bridge to span the Natori River? Someone told me that generations of people have been alternately cutting down the existing tree and planting a replacement. The present one is a magnificent specimen— quite capable, I should imagine, of living 1,000 years.

Kyohaku[7] had given me a poem as a farewell present:

> Late cherry blossoms:
> please show my friend the pine tree
> at Takekuma.

Thus:

> After three months:
> the twin-trunked pine awaited
> since the cherry trees bloomed.

We crossed the Natori River into Sendai on the day when people thatch their roofs with sweet-flag leaves.[8] We sought out a lodging and stayed four or five days.

---

3. A clan that included some of the richest and most powerful provincial barons. 4. Fujiwara Sanekata (died 998) was a court poet whose quarrel with a clansman led to his exile in the northern provinces. 5. Someone had planted a clump of miscanthus, a variety of ornamental grass, at Sanekata's grave in allusion to a memorial poem by Saigyō: "Only his name, / eternally withered, / has escaped decay: / we see, as a memento, / iscanthus on a dry plain." 6. *Mino* can mean "straw raincoat," and *kasa* can mean "rain hat." 7. A disciple. 8. On Boys' Day, a holiday on the fifth day of the Fifth Month, it was the custom for families with sons to fly carp streamers, a symbol of vigor and success. On the day before, irises ("sweet-flag"), because they were thought to ward off evil, were hung from the eaves. The holiday was also known as the Iris Festival.

I made the acquaintance of a local painter, Kaemon by name, who had been described to me as a man of cultivated taste. He told us he had devoted several years to locating famous old places that had become hard to identify, and took us to see some of them one day. The bush clover grew thick at Miyagino; I could imagine the sight in autumn. It was the season when the pieris[9] bloomed at Tamada, Yokono, and Tsutsuji-gaoka. We entered a pine grove where no sunlight penetrated—a place called Konoshita, according to Kaemon—and I thought it must have been the same kind of heavy moisture, dripping from those very trees long ago, that inspired the poem, "Suggest to your lord, attendants, that he wear his hat."[1] We paid our respects at the Yakushidō Hall and at Tenjin Shrine before the day ended.

Kaemon sent us off with a map on which he had drawn famous scenes of Shiogama and Matsushima. He also gave us two pairs of straw sandals, bound with dark blue cords, as a farewell present. The gifts showed him to be quite as cultivated as I had surmised.

> Let us bind sweet-flags
> to our feet, making of them
> cords for straw sandals.

Continuing on our way with the help of the map, we came to the *tofu* [ten-strand] sedge, growing at the base of the mountains where the "narrow road of the interior"[2] runs. I am told that the local people still make ten-strand mats every year for presentation to the provincial Governor.

We saw the Courtyard Monument Stone at Tagajō in Ichikawa Village. It was a little more than six feet tall and perhaps three feet wide. Some characters, faintly visible as depressions in the moss, listed distances to the provincial boundaries in the four directions. There was also an inscription: "This castle was erected in the first year of Jinki [724] by the Inspector-Garrison Commander ōno no Ason Azumabito. It was rebuilt in the sixth year of Tenpyō Hōji [762] by the Consultant-Garrison Commander Emi no Ason Asakari. First Day, Twelfth Month." That was in the reign of Emperor Shōmu.

Although we hear about many places celebrated in verse since antiquity, most of them have vanished with the passing of time. Mountains have crumbled, rivers have entered unaccustomed channels, roads have followed new routes, stones have been buried and hidden underground, aged trees have given way to saplings. But this monument was a genuine souvenir from 1,000 years ago, and to see it before my eyes was to feel that I could understand the sentiments of the old poets. "This is a traveler's reward," I thought. "This is the joy of having survived into old age." Moved to tears, I forgot the hardships of the road.

From there, we went to see Noda-no-tamagawa and Oki-no-ishi. A temple, Masshōzan, had been built at Sue-no-matsuyama, and there were graves everywhere among the pine trees, saddening reminders that such must be the end of all vows to "interchange wings and link branches."[3] The evening bell was tolling as we entered Shiogama.

---

9. Japanese andromeda (*Pieris japonica*), a broad-leafed evergreen with drooping clusters of white flowers. 1. A poem in the *Kokinshū*, the first of twenty-one imperially commissioned anthologies of classical Japanese poetry; it was completed around 905 and contains 1,111 poems. The poem referred to here is: "Suggest to your lord, / attendants, / that he wear his hat, / for beneath the trees of Miyagino / the dew comes down harder than the rain." 2. This road, the source of Bashō's title, extended from what is now northeastern Sendai to Tagajō City (see the map on p. 534). 3. An allusion to the pledge exchanged by the Chinese emperor and his beloved in the *Song of Everlasting Sorrow* by Po Chü-i: "In heaven, may we be birds with shared wings; / On earth, may we be trees with linked branches." The places mentioned here are in the vicinity of Sendai.

The perpetual overcast of the rainy season had lifted enough to reveal Magaki Island close at hand, faintly illuminated by the evening moon. A line of small fishing boats came rowing in. As I listened to the voices of the men dividing the catch, I felt that I understood the poet who sang, "There is deep pathos in a boat pulled by a rope," and my own emotion deepened.[4] That night, a blind singer recited a Michinoku ballad[5] to the accompaniment of his lute. He performed not far from where I was trying to sleep, and I found his loud, countrified falsetto rather noisy—a chanting style quite different from either *Heike* recitation or the *kōwaka-mai*[6] ballad drama. But then I realized how admirable it was that the fine old customs were still preserved in that distant land.

Early the next day, we visited Shiogama Shrine, which had been restored by the provincial Governor. Its pillars stood firm and majestic, its painted rafters sparkled, its stone steps rose in flight after flight, and its sacred red fences gleamed in the morning sunlight. With profound reverence, I reflected that it is the way of our land for the miraculous powers of the gods to manifest themselves even in such remote, out-of-the-way places as this.

In front of the sanctuary, there was a splendid old lantern with an inscription on its iron door: "Presented as an offering by Izumi no Saburō in the third year of Bunji [1187]." It was rare, indeed, to see before one's eyes an object that had remained unchanged for 500 years. Izumi no Saburō was a brave, honorable, loyal, and filial warrior. His fame endures even today; there is no one who does not admire him. How true it is that men must strive to walk in the Way and uphold the right! "Fame will follow of itself."

Noon was already approaching when we engaged a boat for the crossing to Matsushima, a distance of a little more than two leagues. We landed at Ojima Beach.

Trite though it may seem to say so, Matsushima is the most beautiful spot in Japan, by no means inferior to Dongting Lake or West Lake.[7] The sea enters from the southeast into a bay extending for three leagues, its waters as ample as the flow of the Zhejiang Bore.[8] There are more islands than anyone could count. The tall ones rear up as though straining toward the sky; the flat ones crawl on their bellies over the waves. Some seem made of two layers, others of three folds. To the left, they appear separate; to the right, linked. Here and there, one carries another on its back or cradles it in its arms, as though caring for a beloved child or grandchild. The pines are deep green in color, and their branches, twisted by the salt gales, have assumed natural shapes so dramatic that they seem the work of human hands. The tranquil charm of the scene suggests a beautiful woman who has just completed her toilette. Truly, Matsushima might have been made by Ōyamazumi[9] in the ancient age of the mighty gods! What painter can reproduce, what author can describe the wonder of the creator's divine handiwork?

---

4. Reference to a poem in the *Kokinshū:* "However it may be elsewhere / in Michinoku, / there is deep pathos / in a boat pulled by a rope / along Shiogama shore."   **5.** A local ballad. Bashō is now in the province of Michinoku.   **6.** Dramatic ballad-dances recounting military episodes from *The Tale of the Heike* (originally performed as an oral narrative) and other warrior stories. *Kōwaka-mai* were one of the precursors of *nō* plays.   **7.** Chinese sites (which Bashō had never seen) famed for their beauty.   **8.** In China.   **9.** A mountain god who was son of the gods who created the Japanese islands.

Ojima Island projects into the sea just offshore from the mainland. It is the site of the Venerable Ungo's[1] dwelling, and of the rock on which that holy man used to practice meditation. There also seemed to be a few recluses living among the pine trees. Upon seeing smoke rising from a fire of twigs and pine cones at one peaceful thatched hut, we could not help approaching the spot, even though we had no way of knowing what kind of man the occupant might be. Meanwhile, the moon began to shine on the water, transforming the scene from its daytime appearance.

We returned to the Matsushima shore to engage lodgings—a second-story room with a window on the sea. What marvelous exhilaration to spend the night so close to the winds and clouds! Sora recited this:

> Ah, Matsushima!
> Cuckoo, you ought to borrow
> the guise of the crane.[2]

I remained silent, trying without success to compose myself for sleep. At the time of my departure from the old hermitage, Sodō and Hara Anteki[3] had given me poems about Matsushima and Matsu-ga-urashima (the one in Chinese and the other in Japanese), and I got them out of my bag now to serve as companions for the evening. I also had some *hokku*, compositions by Sanpū and Jokushi.[4]

On the Eleventh, we visited Zuiganji.[5] Thirty-two generations ago, Makabe no Heishirō entered holy orders, went to China, and returned to found that temple. Later, through the virtuous influence of the Venerable Ungo, the seven old structures were transformed into a great religious center, a veritable earthly paradise, with dazzling golden walls and resplendent furnishings. I thought with respectful admiration of the holy Kenbutsu[6] and wondered where his place of worship might have been.

On the Twelfth, we left for Hiraizumi, choosing a little-frequented track used by hunters, grass-cutters, and woodchoppers, which was supposed to take us past the Aneha Pine and Odae Bridge. Blundering along, we lost our way and finally emerged at the port town of Ishino-maki. Kinkazan, the mountain of which the poet wrote, "Golden flowers have blossomed," was visible across the water.[7] Hundreds of coastal vessels rode together in the harbor, and smoke ascended everywhere from the cooking fires of houses jostling for space. Astonished to have stumbled on such a place, we looked for lodgings, but nobody seemed to have a room for rent, and we spent the night in a wretched shack.

The next morning, we set out again on an uncertain journey over strange roads, plodding along an interminable dike from which we could see Sode-

---

1. A monk who rebuilt a temple at Matsushima. He was the teacher of Butchō, Bashō's Zen master. 2. The gist of the poem is: "Your song is appealing, cuckoo, but the stately white crane is the bird we expect to see at Matsushima [Pine Isles]." Pines and cranes were a conventional pair, both symbols of longevity. Sora's poem alludes to an old poem of uncertain provenance and unstable wording, one version of which reads in part: "[When snow falls] does the plover borrow / The crane's [white] plumage?" 3. Two friends of Bashō, both amateur poets. Hara was also a physician. 4. Bashō's disciples. "*Hokku*": the first three lines of a linked-verse sequence, from which haiku evolved. 5. The temple restored by Ungo. 6. A monk who lived approximately six hundred years earlier and who confined himself to a small temple at Matsushima. 7. Refers to a poem in the *Man'yōshū* (The collection of ten thousand leaves), which was completed around 759 and is the earliest compilation of Japanese poetry, containing more than forty-five hundred poems. The poem referred to here was written when gold was discovered in the area: "For our sovereign's reign, / an auspicious augury: / among the mountains of Michinoku / in the east, / golden flowers have blossomed."

no-watari, Obuchi-no-maki, and Mano-no-kayahara[8] in the distance. We walked beside a long, dismal marsh to a place called Toima, where we stopped overnight, and finally arrived in Hiraizumi. I think the distance was something over twenty leagues.

The glory of three generations[9] was but a dozing dream. Paddies and wild fields have claimed the land where Hidehira's mansion stood, a league beyond the site of the great gate, and only Mount Kinkeizan looks as it did in the past. My first act was to ascend to Takadachi. From there, I could see both the mighty Kitakami River, which flows down from Nanbu, and the Koromo River, which skirts Izumi Castle and empties into the larger stream below Takadachi. Yasuhira's[1] castle, on the near side of Koromo Barrier, seems to have guarded the Nanbu entrance against barbarian encroachments. There at Takadachi, Yoshitsune shut himself up with a chosen band of loyal men—yet their heroic deeds lasted only a moment, and nothing remains but evanescent clumps of grass.

> The nation is destroyed; the mountains and rivers remain.
> Spring comes to the castle; the grasses are green.[2]

Sitting on my sedge hat with those lines running through my head, I wept for a long time.

> A dream of warriors,
> and after dreaming is done,
> the summer grasses.

> Ah, the white hair:
> vision of Kanefusa[3]
> in deutzia flowers.
>
> —Sora

The two halls of which we had heard so many impressive tales were open to visitors. The images of the three chieftains are preserved in the Sutra Hall, and in the Golden Hall there are the three coffins and the three sacred images.[4] In the past, the Golden Hall's seven precious substances were scattered and lost; gales ravaged the magnificent jewel-studded doors, and the golden pillars rotted in the frosts and snows. But just as it seemed that the whole building must collapse, leaving nothing but clumps of grass, new walls were put around it, and a roof was erected against the winds and rains. So it survives for a time, a memento of events that took place 1,000 years ago.

> Do the Fifth-Month rains
> stay away when they fall,
> sparing that Hall of Gold?

After journeying on with the Nanbu Road visible in the distance, we spent the night at Iwade-no-sato. From there, we passed Ogurazaki and Mizu-no-

8. All are located between Ishi-no-maki and Toima and had associations with earlier poetry.   9. That is, of the powerful Fujiwara family—Kiyohira, Motohira, and Hidehira—who created the so-called golden age of the north in the 12th century.   1. Son of Fujiwara Hidehira, whose fight with his brother destroyed the clan's prosperity in the region. After killing his brother, Yasuhira was in turn killed by the Minamoto / Genji chieftain Yoritomo.   2. A quote from the Chinese poet Tu Fu, lamenting the devastation caused by a rebellion in 755, from which the T'ang dynasty never fully recovered.   3. A loyal retainer of Yoshitsune.   4. Of Amida Buddha and his attendants Kannon and Seishi. The coffins contained the mummified remains of Hidehira, his father, and his grandfather.

ojima and arrived at Shitomae Barrier by way of Narugo Hot Springs, intending to cross into Dewa Province. The road was so little frequented by travelers that we excited the guards' suspicions, and we barely managed to get through the checkpoint. The sun had already begun to set as we toiled upward through the mountains, so we asked for shelter when we saw a border guard's house. Then the wind howled and the rain poured for three days, trapping us in those miserable hills.

> The fleas and the lice—
> and next to my pillow,
> a pissing horse.

The master of the house told us that our route into Dewa was an ill-marked trail through high mountains; we would be wise to engage a guide to help us with the crossing. I took his advice and hired a fine, stalwart young fellow, who strode ahead with a short, curved sword tucked into his belt and an oak staff in his hand. As we followed him, I felt an uncomfortable presentiment that this would be the day on which we would come face to face with danger at last. Just as our host had said, the mountains were high and thickly wooded, their silence unbroken even by the chirp of a bird. It was like traveling at night to walk in the dim light under the dense canopy. Feeling as though dust must be blowing down from the edge of the clouds,[5] we pushed through bamboo, forded streams, and stumbled over rocks, all the time in a cold sweat, until we finally emerged at Mogami-no-shō. Our guide took his leave in high spirits, after having informed us that the path we had followed was one on which unpleasant things were always happening, and that it had been a great stroke of luck to bring us through safely. Even though the danger was past, his words made my heart pound.

At Obanazawa, we called on Seifū, a man whose tastes were not vulgar despite his wealth. As a frequent visitor to the capital, he understood what it meant to be a traveler, and he kept us for several days, trying in many kind ways to make us forget the hardships of the long journey.

> I sit at ease,
> taking this coolness
> as my lodging place.

> Come on, show yourself!
> Under the silkworm nursery
> the croak of a toad.

> In my mind's eye,
> a brush for someone's brows:
> the safflower blossom.

> The silkworm nurses—
> figures reminiscent
> of a distant past.[6]
> —Sora

---

5. To emphasize the murkiness of the atmosphere, Bashō borrows from a poem in which Tu Fu compliments a princess by implying that she lives in the sky: "When I begin to ascend the breezy stone steps, / a dust storm blows down from the edge of the clouds."   6. The silkworm tenders (nurses) dress in an old style. Here, as Bashō does elsewhere, Sora expresses nostalgia for a way of life that had disappeared from the cities to the west.

In the Yamagata domain, there is a mountain temple called Ryū-shakuji, a serene, quiet seat of religion founded by the Great Teacher Jikaku.[7] Urged by others to see it, we retraced our steps some seven leagues from Obanazawa. We arrived before sundown, reserved accommodations in the pilgrims' hostel at the foot of the hill, and climbed to the halls above. The mountain consists of piles of massive rocks. Its pines and other evergreens bear the marks of many long years; its moss lies like velvet on the ancient rocks and soil. Not a sound emanated from the temple buildings at the summit, which all proved to be closed, but we skirted the cliffs and clambered over the rocks to view the halls. The quiet, lonely beauty of the environs purified the heart.

> Ah, tranquility!
> Penetrating the very rock,
> a cicada's voice.

At Ōishida, we awaited fair weather with a view to descending the Mogami River by boat. In that spot where the seeds of the old *haikai*[8] had fallen, some people still cherished the memory of the flowers. With hearts softened by poetry's civilizing touch, those onetime blowers of shrill reed flutes[9] had been groping for the correct way of practicing the art, so they told me, but had found it difficult to choose between the old styles and the new with no one to guide them. I felt myself under an obligation to leave them a sequence. Such was one result of this journey in pursuit of my art.

The Mogami River has its source deep in the northern mountains and its upper reaches in Yamagata. After presenting formidable hazards like Goten and Hayabusa,[1] it skirts Mount Itajiki on the north and finally empties into the sea at Sakata. Our boat descended amid luxuriant foliage, the mountains pressing overhead from the left and the right. It was probably similar craft,[2] loaded with sheaves, that the old song meant when it spoke of rice boats. Travelers can see the cascading waters of Shiraito Falls through gaps in the green leaves. The Sennindō Hall is there too, facing the bank.

The swollen waters made the journey hazardous:

> Bringing together
> the summer rains in swiftness:
> Mogami River!

On the Third of the Sixth Month, we climbed Mount Haguro. We called on Zushi Sakichi[3] and then were received by the Holy Teacher Egaku, the Abbot's deputy, who lodged us at the Minamidani Annex and treated us with great consideration.

On the Fourth, there was a *haikai* gathering at the Abbot's residence:

> Ah, what a delight!
> Cooled as by snow, the south wind
> at Minamidani.

---

7. Better known as Ennin (794–864), a famous priest who helped establish Buddhism in Japan. From the early 17th century until 1868, Japan was divided into domains, or fiefdoms, held directly by the shogun and his family or by the feudal barons who, to one degree or another, supported him. Yamagata was in the province of Dewa.   8. Nonstandard, or eccentric, linked verse. Masters from two older *haikai* schools had spent time in the area.   9. That is, untutored country people.   1. Two treacherous spots in the river, one with rocks and the other with swift currents.   2. Refers to a folk song whose chief interest lies in its puns on the word *rice*.   3. A dyer by trade and an amateur poet.

On the Fifth, we went to worship at Haguro Shrine. Nobody knows when the founder, the Great Teacher Nōjo, lived. The *Engi Canon*[4] mentions a shrine called "Satoyama in Dewa Province," which leads one to wonder if *sato* might be a copyist's error for *kuro*. Perhaps "Haguroyama" is a contraction of "Dewa no Kuroyama" [Kuroyama in Dewa Province]. I understand that the official gazetteer says Dewa acquired its name because the province used to present birds' feathers to the throne as tribute.[5]

Hagurosan, Gassan, and Yudono are known collectively as the Three Mountains. At Haguro, a subsidiary of Tōeizan Kan'eiji Temple in Edo, the moon of Tendai[6] enlightenment shines bright, and the lamp of the Law of perfect understanding and all-permeating vision burns high. The temple buildings stand roof to roof; the ascetics vie in the practice of rituals. We can but feel awe and trepidation before the miraculous powers of so holy a place, which may with justice be called a magnificent mountain, destined to flourish forever.

On the Eighth, we made the ascent of Gassan. Donning paper garlands, and with our heads wrapped in white turbans, we toiled upward for eight leagues, led by a porter guide through misty mountains with ice and snow underfoot. We could almost have believed ourselves to be entering the cloud barrier beyond which the sun and the moon traverse the heavens. The sun was setting and the moon had risen when we finally reached the summit, gasping for breath and numb with cold. We stretched out on beds of bamboo grass until dawn, and descended toward Yudono after the rising sun had dispersed the clouds.

Near a valley, we saw a swordsmith's cottage. The Dewa smiths, attracted by the miraculous waters, had purified themselves there before forging their famous blades, which they had identified by the carved signature, "Gassan."[7] I was reminded of the weapons tempered at Dragon Spring.[8] It also seemed to me that I could understand the dedication with which those men had striven to master their art, inspired by the ancient example of Gan Jiang and Moye.[9]

While seated on a rock for a brief rest, I noticed some half-opened buds on a cherry tree about three feet high. How admirable that those late blooms had remembered spring, despite the snowdrifts under which they had lain buried! They were like "plum blossoms in summer heat"[1] perfuming the air. The memory of Archbishop Gyōson's touching poem[2] added to the little tree's charm.

It is a rule among ascetics not to give outsiders details about Mount Yudono, so I shall lay aside my brush and write no more.

When we returned to our lodgings, Egaku asked us to inscribe poem cards with verses suggested by our pilgrimage to the Three Mountains:

---

4. An early collection of governmental regulations (compiled 905–927), designed to flesh out the broad administrative structure that was then being adapted from China.   5. The characters representing *sato* and *kuro* are similar in appearance, especially when written in cursive script. The *ha* of "Haguroyama" and the *wa* of "Dewa" can be written with the same phonetic symbol and were once the same sound. The connection between Dewa and birds' feathers is in the orthography: *wa* is written with the character for "feathers."   6. A Buddhist sect.   7. A famous swordsmith in the late 12th century.   8. In China; its waters were used for tempering sword blades.   9. Gan Jiang was a Chinese swordsmith. He and his wife, Moye, forged two famous swords.   1. A Zen metaphor for the rare and unusual and, by extension, for passing beyond this world to enlightenment.   2. A reference to a poem that Gyōson (1055–1135), an ascetic, composed when he discovered cherries blooming out of season: "Let us sympathize / with one another, / cherry tree on the mountain: / were it not for your blossoms, / I would have no friend at all."

Ah, what coolness!
Under a crescent moon,
Mount Haguro glimpsed.

Mountain of the Moon:
after how many cloud peaks
had formed and crumbled?

My sleeve was drenched
at Yudono, the mountain
of which none may speak.

Yudonoyama:
tears fall as I walk the path
where feet tread on coins.[3]

—Sora

After our departure from Haguro, we were invited to the warrior Nagayama Shigeyuki's home, where we composed a sequence. (Sakichi accompanied us that far.) Then we boarded a river boat and traveled downstream to Sakata Harbor. We stayed with a physician, En'an Fugyoku.

Evening cool!
A view from Mount Atsumi
to Fukuura.

Mogami River—
it has plunged the hot sun
into the sea.

I had already enjoyed innumerable splendid views of rivers and mountains, ocean and land; now I set my heart on seeing Kisakata. It was a journey of ten leagues northeast from Sakata, across mountains and along sandy beaches. A wind from the sea stirred the white sand early in the afternoon, and Mount Chōkai disappeared behind misting rain. "Groping in the dark," we found "the view in the rain exceptional too."[4] The surroundings promised to be beautiful once the skies had cleared. We crawled into a fisherman's thatched shanty to await the end of the rain.

The next day was fine, and we launched forth onto the bay in a boat as the bright morning sun rose. First of all, we went to Nōinjima to visit the spot where Saigyō had lived in seclusion for three years. Then we disembarked on the opposite shore and saw a memento of the poet, the old cherry tree that had suggested the verse, "rowing over flowers."[5] Near the water's edge, we noticed a tomb that was said to be the grave of Empress Jingu,[6] together

---

3. The coins have been strewn by pilgrims, but unlike the secular world, no one scrambles to pick them up. Sora sheds tears at this miraculous behavior, which he can only attribute to the power of the gods. **4.** Bashō compares Kisakata to the famous West Lake in China, of which Su Tongbo (1037–1101) wrote: "The sparkling, brimming waters are beautiful in sunshine." / The view when a misty rain veils the mountains is exceptional too." "'Groping in the dark,'": probably an allusion to a poem composed at the lake by a visiting Japanese monk, Sakugen (1501–1579): "The sun is setting beyond Yuhangmen; / All sights are indistinct, there is no view. / But I recall the poem, 'Exceptional in rain, beautiful in sunshine'; / Groping in the dark,: I feel West Lake's charm." **5.** From a poem attributed to Saigyō: "The cherry blossoms / at Kisakata / lie buried under waves: / seafolk in their fishing boat / go rowing over flowers." **6.** Legendary empress said to have ruled in the second half of the 4th century.

with a temple, Kanmanjuji. I had never heard that the Empress had gone to that place. I wonder how her grave happened to be there.

Seated in the temple's front apartment with the blinds raised, we commanded a panoramic view. To the south, Mount Chōkai propped up the sky, its image reflected in the bay; to the west, Muyamuya Barrier blocked the road; to the east, the Akita Road stretched far into the distance on an embankment; to the north, there loomed the majestic bulk of the sea, its waves entering the bay at a place called Shiogoshi.

The bay measures about a league in length and breadth. It resembles Matsushima in appearance but has a quality of its own: where Matsushima seems to smile, Kisakata droops in dejection. The lonely, melancholy scene suggests a troubled human spirit.

> Xi Shi's[7] drooping eyelids:
> mimosa in falling rain
> at Kisakata.

> At Shiogoshi
> crane legs drenched by high tide—
> and how cool the sea!

A festival:

> A shrine festival:
> what foods do worshippers eat
> at Kisakata?
>
> —Sora

> At fishers' houses,
> people lay down rain shutters,
> seeking evening cool.[8]
> —Teiji, a Mino merchant

Seeing an osprey nest on a rock:

> Might they have vowed,
> "Never shall waves cross here"[9]—
> those nesting ospreys?
>
> —Sora

After several days of reluctant farewells to friends in Sakata, we set out under the clouds of the Northern Land Road, quailing before the prospect of the long journey ahead. It was reported to be 130 leagues to the castle town of the Kaga domain. Once past Nezu Barrier, we made our way on foot through Echigo Province to Ichiburi Barrier in Etchū Province, a tiring journey of nine miserably hot, rainy days. I felt too ill to write anything.

---

7. A Chinese beauty of the 5th century B.C.E. Originally the consort of the king of Yue, she was later forced to wed his conqueror, the king of Wu. 8. That is, they remove the rain shutters from their houses and put them on the beach, where they sit, enjoying the evening cool. 9. This phrase constitutes a vow of eternal fidelity, derived from a poem in the *Kokinshū*: "Would I be the cast sort / To cast you aside / and turn to someone new? / Sooner would the waves traverse / Sue-no-matsu Mountain."

> In the Seventh Month,
> even the Sixth Day differs
> from ordinary nights.[1]

> Tumultuous seas:
> spanning the sky to Sado Isle,
> the Milky Way.

That night I drew up a pillow and lay down to sleep, exhausted after having traversed the most difficult stretches of road in all the north country—places with names like "Children Forget Parents," "Parents Forget Children," "Dogs Go Back," and "Horses Sent Back." The voices of young women drifted in from the adjoining room in front—two of them, it appeared, talking to an elderly man, whose voice was also audible. As I listened, I realized that they were prostitutes from Niigata in Echigo, bound on a pilgrimage to the Grand Shrines of Ise. The old man was to be sent home to Niigata in the morning, after having escorted them as far as this barrier, and they seemed to be writing letters and giving him inconsequential messages to take back. Adrift on "the shore where white breakers roll in," these "fishermen's daughters" had fallen low indeed, exchanging fleeting vows with every passerby.[2] How wretched the karma that had doomed them to such an existence! I fell asleep with their voices in my ears.

The next morning, the same two girls spoke to us as we were about to leave. "We're feeling terribly nervous and discouraged about going off on this hard trip over strange roads. Won't you let us join your party, even if we only stay close enough to catch a glimpse of you now and then? You wear the robes of mercy: please let us share the Buddha's compassion and form a bond with the Way," they said, weeping.

"I sympathize with you, but we'll be making frequent stops. Just follow others going to the same place; I'm sure the gods will see you there safely." We walked off without waiting for an answer, but it was some time before I could stop feeling sorry for them.

> Ladies of pleasure
> sleeping in the same hostel:
> bush clover and moon.[3]

I recited those lines to Sora, who wrote them down.

After crossing the "forty-eight channels" of the Kurobe River and innumerable other streams, we reached the coast at Nago. Even though the season was not spring, it seemed a shame to miss the wisteria at Tako in early autumn. We asked someone how to get there, but the answer frightened us off. "Tako is five leagues along the beach from here, in the hollow of those mountains. The only houses are a few ramshackle thatched huts belonging

---

1. Because people were preparing for the Tanabata Festival, which was held on the seventh day of the Seventh Month in honor of the stars Altair (the herd boy) and Vega (the weaver maiden). Legend held that the two lovers were separated by the Milky Way, except for this one night, when they would meet for their annual rendezvous.   2. Alludes to a classical poem: "I have no abode, / for I am but the daughter of a fisherman, / spending my life / on the shore / where white waves roll in." Prostitutes went out in small boats to greet incoming vessels.   3. In this much-discussed poem Bashō is probably not making an invidious comparison between the prostitutes (showy, ephemeral flowers) and himself (the pure remote moon) but simply using aspects of the scene at the inn to comment in amusement on a chance encounter between two very different types of people. It has often been suggested that he may have recorded the meeting at the barrier—or possibly invented it—as a means of including a reference to love, a standard topic in linked verse.

to fishermen; you probably wouldn't find anyone to put you up for the night."
Thus we went on into Kaga Province.

> Scent of ripening ears:[4]
> to the right as I push through,
> surf crashing onto rocks.

We arrived at Kanazawa on the Fifteenth of the Seventh Month, after
crossing Unohana Mountain and Kurikara Valley. There we met the merchant Kasho,[5] who had come up from Ōsaka, and joined him in his lodgings.
A certain Isshō had been living in Kanazawa—a man who had gradually come
to be known as a serious student of poetry, and who had gained a reputation
among the general public as well. I now learned that he had died last winter,
still in the prime of life. At the Buddhist service arranged by his older brother:

> Stir, burial mound!
> The voice I raise in lament
> is the autumn wind.

On being invited to a thatched cottage:

> The cool of autumn:
> let's each of us peel his own
> melons and eggplant.

Composed on the way:

> Despite the red blaze
> of the pitiless sun—
> an autumn breeze.

At Komatsu [Young Pines]:

> An appealing name:
> The wind in Young Pines ruffles
> bush clover and miscanthus.

At Komatsu we visited Tada Shrine, which numbers among its treasures a
helmet and a piece of brocade that once belonged to Sanemori.[6] We were
told that the helmet was a gift from Lord Yoshitomo in the old days when
Sanemori served the Genji—and indeed it was no ordinary warrior's head-
gear. From visor to earflaps, it was decorated with a gold-filled chrysanthe-
mum arabesque in the Chinese style, and the front was surmounted by a
dragon's head and a pair of horns. The shrine history tells in vivid language
of how Kiso no Yoshinaka[7] presented a petition there after Sanemori's death
in battle, and of how Higuchi no Jirō served as a messenger.

> A heartrending sound!
> Underneath the helmet,
> the cricket.

We could see Shirane's peaks behind us as we trudged toward Yamanaka
Hot Springs. The Kannon Hall[8] stood at the base of the mountains to the

---

4. That is, of the maturing rice crop.   5. Like others Bashō calls on during his journey, Kasho is an amateur poet.   6. Saitō Sanemori (1111–1183), a samurai in the service of the Minamoto/Genji who defects
to the Taira/Heike.   7. Leader of the northern Genji forces in the war against the Heike.   8. In honor
of Kannon, the bodhisattva of compassion and an attendant of the Buddha known as Amida.

left. Someone said the hall was founded by Retired Emperor Kazan, who enshrined an image of the bodhisattva there and named the spot Nata after completing a pious round of the Thirty-three Places. (The name Nata was explained to us as having been coined from Nachi and Tanigumi.[9]) It was a beautiful, impressive site, with many unusual rocks, rows of ancient pine trees, and a small thatched chapel, built on a rock against the cliff.

> Even whiter
> than the Ishiyama rocks—
> the wind of autumn.

We bathed in the hot springs, which were said to be second only to Ariake in efficacy.

> At Yamanaka,
> no need to pluck chrysanthemums:[1]
> the scent of the springs.

The master was a youth called Kumenosuke. His father, an amateur of *haikai*, had embarrassed Teishitsu[2] with his knowledge when the master visited Yamanaka from the capital as a young man. Teishitsu returned to the city, joined Teitoku's[3] school, and built up a reputation, but it is said that he never accepted money for reviewing the work of anyone from this village after he became famous. The story is an old one now.

Sora was suffering from a stomach complaint. Because he had relatives at Nagashima in Ise Province, he set off ahead of me. He wrote a poem as he was about to leave:

> Journeying onward:
> fall prostrate though I may—
> a bush-clover field!

The sorrow of the one who departed and the unhappiness of the one who remained resembled the feelings of a lapwing wandering lost in the clouds, separated from its friend.

> From this day forward,
> the legend will be erased:
> dewdrops on the hat.[4]

Still in Kaga, I lodged at Zenshōji, a temple outside the castle town of Daishōji. Sora had stayed there the night before and left this poem:

> All through the night,
> listening to the autumn wind—
> the mountain in back.

One night's separation is the same as 1,000 leagues. I too listened to the autumn wind as I lay in the guest dormitory. Toward dawn, I heard clear voices chanting a sutra, and then the sound of a gong beckoned me into the dining hall. I left the hall as quickly as possible, eager to reach Echizen

---

9. Two towns in different provinces; they were the beginning and ending points on an eleven-province tour of thirty-three places sacred to Kannon.   1. Flowers associated with longevity.   2. An adept of *haikai*.
3. Matsunaga Teitoku (1571–1653), one of the leading practitioners of linked verse.   4. A reference to a common practice when people traveled in pairs. They would write on their hats the phrase "Two persons following the same path."

Province that day, but a group of young monks pursued me to the foot of the stairs with paper and inkstone. Observing that some willow leaves had scattered in the courtyard, I stood there in my sandals and dashed off these lines:

> To sweep your courtyard
> of willow leaves, and then depart:
> that would be my wish!

At the Echizen border, I crossed Lake Yoshizaki by boat for a visit to the Shiogoshi pines.

> Inviting the gale
> to carry the waves ashore
> all through the night,
> they drip moonlight from their boughs—
> the pines of Shiogoshi!

> —Saigyō

In that single verse, the poet captures the essence of the scene at Shiozaki. For anyone to say more would be like "sprouting a useless digit."

In Maruoka, I called on the Tenryūji Abbot, an old friend.

A certain Hokushi from Kanazawa had planned to see me off a short distance, but had finally come all the way to Maruoka, reluctant to say goodbye. Always intent on conveying the effect of beautiful scenery in verse, he had produced some excellent poems from time to time. Now that we were parting, I composed this:

> Hard to say good-bye—
> to tear apart the old fan
> covered with scribbles.

I journeyed about a league and a half into the mountains to worship at Eiheiji, Dōen's[5] temple. I believe I have heard that Dōen had an admirable reason for avoiding the vicinity of the capital and founding his temple in those remote mountains.

After the evening meal, I set out for Fukui, three leagues away. It was a tedious, uncertain journey in the twilight.

A man named Tōsai had been living in Fukui as a recluse for a long time. He had come to Edo and visited me once—I was not sure just when, but certainly more than ten years earlier. I thought he must be very old and feeble by now, or perhaps even dead, but someone assured me that he was very much alive. Following my informant's directions into a quiet corner of the town, I came upon a poor cottage, its walls covered with moonflower and snake-gourd vines, and its door hidden by cockscomb and goosefoot.[6] That would be it, I thought. A woman of humble appearance emerged when I rapped on the gate.

"Where are you from, Reverend Sir? The master has gone to see someone in the neighborhood. Please look for him there if you have business with him." She was apparently the housewife.

---

5. Founder of one of the main sects of Zen Buddhism. 6. A plant with small greenish blossoms. "Cockscomb": a plant with fan-shaped clusters of red or yellow blossoms.

I hurried off to find Tōsai, feeling as though I had strayed into an old romance, and spent two nights at his house. Then I prepared to leave, hopeful of seeing the full moon at Tsuruga Harbor on the Fifteenth of the Eighth Month. Having volunteered to keep me company, Tōsai set out in high spirits as my guide, his skirts tucked jauntily into his sash.

The peaks of Shirane disappeared as Hina-ga-take came into view. We crossed Azamuzu Bridge, saw ears[7] on the reeds at Taema, journeyed beyond Uguisu Barrier and Yunoo Pass, heard the first wild geese of the season at Hiuchi Stronghold and Mount Kaeru, and took lodgings in Tsuruga at dusk on the Fourteenth. The sky was clear, the moon remarkably fine. When I asked if we might hope for the same weather on the following night, the landlord offered us wine, replying, "In the northern provinces, who knows whether the next night will be cloudy or fair?"

That night, I paid a visit to Kehi Shrine, the place where Emperor Chūai[8] is worshipped. An atmosphere of holiness pervaded the surroundings. Moonlight filtered in between the pine trees, and the white sand in front of the sanctuary glittered like frost. "Long ago, in pursuance of a great vow, the Second Pilgrim[9] himself cut grass and carried dirt and rock to fill a marsh that was a trial to worshippers going back and forth. The precedent is still observed; every new Pilgrim takes sand to the area in front of the shrine. The ceremony is called 'the Pilgrim's Carrying of the Sand,'" my landlord said.

> Shining on sand
> transported by pilgrims—
> pure light of the moon.

It rained on the Fifteenth, just as the landlord had warned it might.

> Night of the full moon:
> no predicting the weather
> in the northern lands.

The weather was fine on the Sixteenth, so we went in a boat to Irono-hama Beach to gather red shells. It was seven leagues by sea. A man named Ten'ya provided us with all kinds of refreshments—compartmented lunch boxes, wine flasks, and the like—and also ordered a number of servants to go along in the boat. A fair wind delivered us to our destination in no time. The beach was deserted except for a few fishermen's shacks and a forlorn Nichiren[1] temple. As we drank tea and warmed wine at the temple, I struggled to control feelings evoked by the loneliness of the evening.

> Ah, what loneliness!
> More desolate than Suma,[2]
> this beach in autumn.

> Between wave and wave:
> mixed with small shells, the remains
> of bush-clover bloom.

---

7. The spikes on a plant that contain the seeds.   8. According to tradition, the fourteenth emperor, married to Empress Jingū.   9. Taa Shōnin (1237–1319). "Pilgrim" was a title given to the patriarch of the Ji sect of Buddhism.   1. Buddhist monk (1222–1282) and founder of a sect that bore his name.
2. A coastal town made famous as the hero's place of exile in *The Tale of Genji*.

I persuaded Tōsai to write a description of the day's outing to be left at the temple.

Rōχu came to meet me at Tsuruga and accompanied me to Mino Province. Thus I arrived at Ōaki, my journey eased by a horse. Sora came from Ise, Etsujin galloped in on horseback, and we all gathered at Jokō's house. Zensenji, Keikō, Keikō's sons, and other close friends called day and night, rejoicing and pampering me as though I had returned from the dead.

Despite my travel fatigue, I set out again by boat on the Sixth of the Ninth Month to witness the relocation of the Ise sanctuaries.[3]

> Off to Futami,
> loath to part as clam from shell
> in waning autumn.

---

3. The two sanctuaries at the Grand Shrines of Ise, dedicated to the ancestral gods of the imperial family, are rebuilt every twenty years as a kind of repurification.

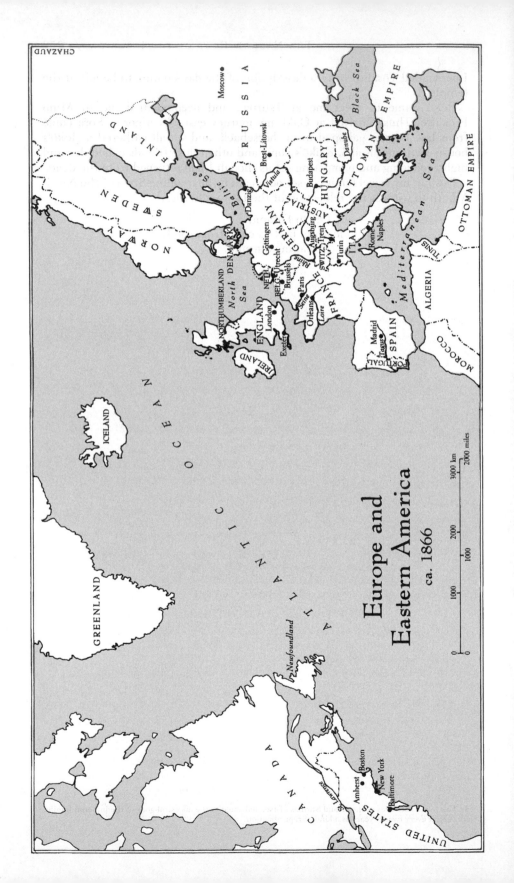

Europe and
Eastern America

ca. 1866

The Nineteenth Century:
Romanticism

"Bliss was it in that dawn to be alive, / But to be young was very heaven." William Wordsworth alludes here to his experience, at the age of seventeen, of the French Revolution. The possibility of referring to a national cataclysm in such terms suggests the remarkable shift in sensibility, in dominant assumptions, and in intellectual preoccupations that occurred late in the eighteenth century. We call the evidence of that shift "Romanticism"—a designation so grandly inclusive as to defy definition. If our terms for the late seventeenth and early eighteenth centuries ("Enlightenment," "Age of Reason") emphasize one aspect of the prevailing intellectual culture to the exclusion of others equally important, the label *Romanticism* refers to so many cultural manifestations that one can hardly pin it down. In general, it implies new emphases on imagination, on feeling, and on the value of the primitive and untrammeled, especially a narrowing of outlook from the universal to the particular, from humankind or "man" to nation or ethnic group, and from the stability of community to the "fulfillment" of the individual. Such shifts have important political and philosophical as well as literary implications.

In the writings of individuals, one finds lines of continuity between the late and early parts of the eighteenth century; but when it comes to generalizations, all the important truths appear to have reversed themselves. In the middle of the century, reason was the guide to certainty; at the century's end, *feeling* tested authenticity. Earlier, tradition still anchored experience; now, the ideal of joyous liberation implied rejection of traditional authority. Wisdom had long associated itself with maturity, even with old age; by the 1790s, William Blake hinted at the child's superior insight, and Wordsworth openly claimed for the infant holy wisdom inevitably lost in the process of aging. Johnson had valued experience as a vital path to knowledge; at the beginning of the nineteenth century, innocence—in its nature evanescent—provided a more generally treasured resource.

Cause and effect, in such massive shifts of perspective, can never be ascertained. The French Revolution derived from new ideas about the sacredness of the individual; it also helped generate such ideas. Without trying to distinguish causes from effects—indeed, with a strong suspicion that the period's striking phenomena constitute simultaneous causes and effects—one can specify a number of ways that the world appeared to change, as the eighteenth century approached the nineteenth, as well as ways that these changes both solidified themselves and evoked challenges later in the nineteenth century.

NEW AND OLD

The embattled farmers of Concord, Massachusetts, fired the shot heard round the world in 1775; fourteen years later, the Bastille fell. Both the American and the French revolutions developed out of strong convictions about the innate rights of individual human beings—in other words, Protestantism in political form. Those who developed revolutionary theory glimpsed new human possibility. The hope of salvation lay in overturning established institutions. The theory of revolution implied radical assault on virtually all social institutions. Fundamental hierarchies of government, notions of sovereignty and of aristocracy, inherited systems of distinction—all fell. Old conventions, once emblems of social and literary stability, now exemplified the dead hand of the past. Only a few years before, the old, the inherited, and the traditional had embodied truth, its power attested by its survival. But the revolutionaries felt themselves to be originators; the newness of what they proposed gave it the almost religious authority suggested by Wordsworth's allusions to "bliss" and "heaven."

The blessed state evoked by the new political thinkers embodied a sense of infinite possibility. Evidence of this fact abounds: in revolutionary sermons preached from pulpits even in England; in writings by such flamboyant defenders of human rights as Thomas Paine; even in the development of a political theory about women's social position. Mary Wollstonecraft was not the first to note the oppression of women; a century before her, Mary Astell had suggested the need for broader female education, and outcries on the subject emerged sporadically even earlier in the seventeenth century. But Wollstonecraft's *Vindication of the Rights of Woman* (1792) offered the first detailed argument to hold that the ideal of fulfilled human possibility for men and women demanded political acknowledgment of women's equality.

The very existence of such a work (which achieved a second edition in the year it was first published) testifies to the atmosphere of political expectancy in which men and women could rethink "self-evident" principles. Replacing the ideal of hierarchy, for example, was the revolutionary notion of human brotherhood. Liberty, equality, and fraternity, the French proclaimed; the new American nation celebrated essentially the same ideals. In practice, though, *fraternity* turned out to involve specifically the citizens of France or of the new United States. The emphasis on individual uniqueness extended itself to national uniqueness. In America particularly, ideas of national character and of national destiny developed almost talismanic force. Although peace generally prevailed among nations in the early nineteenth century, the developing distinctions dividing one country imaginatively from another foretold future danger.

New ideas with massive practical consequences included more than the political. In 1776, Adam Smith published *The Wealth of Nations,* a theory of laissez-faire economics presaging the enormous importance of money in subsequent history. Matters of exchange and acquisition, Smith argued, could be left to regulate themselves—a doctrine behind which still lurked unobtrusively the confidence, expressed in market terms, that Alexander Pope had expressed in religious ones: "All Chance, Direction, which thou canst not see, / All Discord, Harmony, not understood." As manufacturing and trade increased in vitality, however, their importance as financial resources in fact heightened discord through growing nationalism. Early in the century, at the end of *Windsor Forest* (1713), Pope had recognized in Britain's trade a form of power. A century later, the acceleration of this power would have astonished Pope. No longer did agriculture provide England's central economic resource. New forms of manufacture provided new substance for trade, generated new fortunes, produced a new social class—a "middle class" with the influence of wealth and without the inherited system of responsibilities, restrictions, and decorums that had helped control aristocratic possessors of wealth in preceding generations. Aristocrats had used their money, on the whole, to enlarge and beautify their estates. The newly monied developed original ideas about what money might do. Reinvested, it could support innovation in manufacture and trade. It could educate the children of the uneducated; it could buy them (as it had been doing for a century) husbands and wives from the aristocracy; it could help obviate ancient class distinctions. England's increasing economic ascendancy in the nineteenth century derived not only from new money but from the development of men willing and able to employ money ingeniously as power.

The expanded possibilities of manufacture testified to practical applications of scientific research, another area of activity in which the new overwhelmingly replaced the old. In England and America especially, inventions multiplied: the steam engine, the spinning jenny, the cotton gin. Increasingly often, and in increasing numbers, men and women left their native rural environments to congregate in cities, where opportunities for relatively unskilled workers abounded—and where more and more people lived in congestion, poverty, and misery.

More vividly, perhaps, than ever before, the world was changing—becoming, in fact, the world we ourselves assume, in which *mankind* as an ideal wanes, nations define themselves in psychic and military opposition to one another, money constitutes immediate power, and science serves manufacture and, hence, commerce. From the beginning of these crucial changes, certain thinkers and writers realized the destructive possibilities inherent in every form of "progress." Blake, for example, glimpsed London's economic brutality and human wastefulness; his "revolutionary" impulses expressed themselves partly in resistance to the consequences of the new. That is to say, the new gave way to the newer, as it had not previously done on such a scale.

INDIVIDUALISM

Immanuel Kant (1724–1804), a German philosopher whose work influenced virtually all philosophers after him, questioned the power of reason to provide the most significant forms of knowledge—knowledge of the ultimately real. Feeling, on the other hand, might offer a guide. The individual will must engage itself in ethical struggle to locate and experience the good. Such followers of Kant as Johann Fichte (1762–1814) more clearly suggested an identification between will and what we call ego. The idea of the self took on ever greater importance, for philosophers and poets, for political thinkers, autobiographers, and novelists.

To locate authority in the self rather than in society implies yet another radical break with the assumptions of the previous period. The idea of the self's importance is so familiar to us that it may be difficult to imagine the startling implications of the new focus. "I know my own heart, and understand my fellow man," Jean-Jacques Rousseau writes, at the beginning of his *Confessions*. "I am made unlike anyone I have ever met; I will even venture to say that I am like no one in the whole world." Samuel Johnson would have felt certain that a man who could write such words must be mad, like the astronomer in *Rasselas* who believes himself able to control the weather. Yet faith in the absolute uniqueness of every consciousness became increasingly prevalent. Rousseau's significance for his period derives partly from the fact that his stress on the feelings of his heart and on his own specialness aroused recognition in his audience. No longer did the universality of human nature supply comfort to individuals; now they might seek reassurance instead in their uniqueness.

Not only could individuals now see themselves as unique, but they could also understand themselves as *good*. In its earlier forms, Christianity had emphasized the fallen nature of the human soul. Every self, according to this view, contains the potential for violence and destructiveness. One must rely on God's grace for salvation, which cannot depend on human worth. At the secular level, human beings need institutions to provide the controls that save us from anarchy—from the evil latent in ourselves. Rousseau and his successors articulated the opposite position, stressing the essential goodness of human nature and the corresponding danger of institutional restraint. Repressiveness now became the fearful enemy, uniformity the menace. We may recognize the fear of external control today in the slogans of those celebrating the importance of "individual rights," and we still hear the older faith in institutions in the proponents of "law and order."

The new emphasis on the individual opened new possibilities for writers of poetry and prose alike. Even the grotesque and deviant became interesting. Victor Hugo could explore the psychology of Satan, for example: the angel cast out of heaven and falling through the abyss, undergoing a process of increasing horror, enduring the going out of light, but remaining defiant throughout his long ordeal. Unlike John Milton, who directed attention to cosmic drama on a large scale, Hugo concentrated his focus to create an impression of poignance as well as nightmare. In Russia, Alexander Pushkin investigated the psychology (as well as the social arrangements) of a group of people concerned only with money, generating a very different sense of horror.

As these instances suggest, stress on the individual implied revaluation of inner as opposed to outer experience. Previously, life in the public arena had been assumed to test human capacities and to provide meaningful forms of experience. After Rousseau, however, psychic experience could provide the proper measure of an individual's emotional capacity. To place value *there* opened the possibility of taking women as seriously as men, children as seriously as adults, "savages" as seriously as civilized beings. Indeed, women, children, and "primitive" peoples were often thought to exceed cultivated adult males in their capacity both to feel and to express their feelings spontaneously—although the social subordination of such groups continued unchanged.

Even before Rousseau, the novel of sensibility in England and on the Continent revealed interest in highly developed emotional responsiveness. Johann Wolfgang von Goethe's *The Sorrows of Young Werther* (1774) made its author famous and inspired a cult of introverted, melancholy young people. In England, Henry Mackenzie's *The Man of Feeling* (1771) associated intense emotion with benevolent action. By the latter part of the century, the Gothic novel had become an important form—a novelistic mode, often practiced by women, that typically placed a young woman at the center of the action. The heroines of such novels confront a kind of experience (usually involving at least apparent supernatural elements) for which their social training, that important resource of earlier heroines, provides no help; instead, quick intuitions and subtle feelings ensure their triumph over apparently insurmountable obstacles with no loss of feminine delicacy.

Given the view of feeling's centrality, which replaced the earlier stress on passion's fruitful tension with reason, a broader spectrum of feeling drew literary attention. From its beginnings the novel had tended to emphasize (usually in decorous terms) love between the sexes. Now romantic love became a central subject of poetry and drama as well. More surprising kinds of emotion also attracted notice. William Blake imagined a chimney sweep's emotional relation to the idea of heaven; Samuel Taylor Coleridge and Percy Bysshe Shelley made poetry of dejection; Alfred, Lord Tennyson, at the midpoint of the nineteenth century, wove his anxieties about the revelations of recent scientific inquiry into the texture of an elegiac poem. Rosalía de Castro wrote of the death of her child; Giacomo Leopardi could produce a lyric called "To Himself," exploring his personal relation to large ideas; Friedrich Hölderlin, in Germany, like Wordsworth and Coleridge in Engand, used the making of poetry as a subject for thought and feeling alike. As these examples indicate, painful as well as pleasurable emotion interested readers and writers. The poet, Wordsworth said, is a man speaking to men; poetry originates in recollected emotion and recapitulates lost feeling. Lyric, not epic, typifies poetry for Wordsworth, who understands his genre as a form of emotional communication.

Wordsworth's definition ignores the fact that women, too (including his own sister, Dorothy), write poetry. Emily Brontë, Christina Rossetti, Rosalía de Castro, Anna Petrovna Bunina, Emily Dickinson—such women writing in different countries evoked intense passion in verse. In the Romantic novel also, women excelled in the rendering of powerful feeling. The Brontë sisters, like George Eliot after them in England and the equally passionate George Sand in France, wrote under male pseudonyms but established distinctively female visions of the struggle not only for love but also for freedom and power within a context of social restriction. Mary Shelley (daughter of Mary Wollstonecraft and wife of the poet Shelley) in her eloquent fable of creativity, *Frankenstein* (1818), epitomizes the peculiar intensity of much women's writing in this period.

As the nineteenth century wore on, hope for a new earthly Eden faded. The flourishing of commerce and the innovations of science had negative as well as positive consequences. As the novels of Charles Dickens and William Thackeray insist, the new middle class frequently became the repository of moral mediocrity. The autocracy of money had effects more brutal than those of inherited privilege. Science, once the emblem of progress, began to generate theological confusion. Charles Darwin's *On the Origin of Species* (1859) stated clearly humanity's mean rather than transcendent origins: animal and plant species had evolved over the millennia, adapting themselves to their environment through the process of natural selection. Fossils found in rocks provided supporting evidence for this theory—an assertion troubling to many Christians because it contradicted the biblical account of creation. Eight years after Darwin's revolutionary work, Karl Marx published *Das Kapital*, with its dialectical theory of history and its vision of capitalism's eventual decay and of the working class's inevitable triumph. In the United States, civil war raged from 1861 to 1865, its central issue states' rights, a topic that, of course, involved the morality of slavery—that by-product of agricultural capitalism. Neither the making of money nor the effort to fathom natural law seemed merely reassuring.

In the face of history's threats—the menace of Marx's prophecy and of Darwin's biology, the chaos of civil war—to insist on the importance of private experience offered tentative security, a standing place, a temporary source of authority. The voices of blacks and, in increasing numbers, of women could now be heard: placing high value on the personal implied respecting all persons. The American Civil War made African Americans for the first time truly visible to the society that both included and denied them. Slave narratives—sometimes wholly or partly fictional, sometimes entirely authentic renditions of often horrifying experience—provided useful propaganda for the abolitionist cause, the ideology opposed to the institution of slavery. They also opened a new emotional universe. In their typical emphasis, for instance, on the salvationary force of reading and writing (officially forbidden to most slaves), these narratives illuminated a new area of the taken-for-granted, thus extending the enterprise of Romantic poetry.

The capacity for revelatory illumination belonged, according to the dominant nineteenth-century view, to imagination, a mysterious and virtually sacred power of individual consciousness. When Johnson, in *Rasselas*, suggested that the predominance of imagination over reason is insane, he intended, to put it crudely, an antithesis of true and false since imagination, the faculty of generating images, has no necessary anchor in the communal, historical experience that tests truth. For Wordsworth and Coleridge and those who came after them, imagination is a visionary and unifying force (a new incarnation of the seventeenth century's inner light or candle of the Lord) through which the gifted person discovers and communicates new truth. As Coleridge wrote,

> from the soul itself must issue forth
> A light, a glory, a fair luminous cloud
> Enveloping the Earth.

Imagination derives from the soul, that aspect of our being that links the human with the eternal. Through it, men and women can transcend earthly limitations, can express high aspiration, can escape—and help one another escape—the dreariness of mortality without necessarily admitting to a life beyond the present one.

A result of the high value attached to creative imagination was a new concern with originality. The notion of "the genius," the man or woman so gifted as to operate by principles unknown to ordinary mortals, developed only in the late eighteenth century. Previously, a person *had* genius rather than *was a* genius: the term designated a particular tendency or gift (a genius for cooking, say) rather than a human being with vast creative power. Now the genius was revered for his or her extraordinary difference from others, idealized as a being set apart; and the literary or artistic products of genius, it could be assumed, would correspondingly differ from everything previously produced. Yet the writers of this movement also recorded their anxiety about the claim of specialness implicit in the idea of genius. Goethe's *Faust*, a rewriting of an old legend, emphasizes the danger inherent in the desire to do what no one has ever done, to be what no one has ever been.

Despite all reservations, though, newness now became as never before a measure of value. The language, the themes, the forms of the preceding century would no longer suffice. In the early eighteenth century, literary figures wishing to congratulate themselves and their contemporaries would compare their artistic situation to that of Rome under the benevolent patronage of Augustus Caesar. A hundred years later, the note of self-congratulation would express itself in the claim of an unprecedented situation or unprecedented kinds of accomplishment. John Keats, in a letter, characterized Wordsworth as representing "the egotistical sublime." Such sublimity—authority and grandeur emanating from a unique self still in touch with something beyond itself—was the nineteenth century's special achievement.

NATURE

Nature and nature's laws, the rationally ordered universe, provided the foundation for much early eighteenth-century thought. In the nineteenth century, nature's importance possibly increased, but *nature* now meant something new. The physical reality of the natural world, in its varied abundance, became a matter of absorbing interest for poets and novelists. Nature provided an alternative to the human, a possibility for imaginative as well as literal escape. Its imagery—flowers, clouds, ocean—became the common poetic stock. Workers still hastened from the country to the city because the city housed possibilities of wealth; yet educated men and women increasingly declared their nostalgia for rural or sylvan landscapes embodying peace and beauty.

Nature, in the nineteenth-century mind, however, did not consist only in physical details. It also implied a totality, an enveloping whole greater than the sum of its parts, a vast unifying spirit. Wordsworth evokes

> a sense sublime
> Of something far more deeply interfused,
> Whose dwelling is the light of setting suns,
> And the round ocean and the living air,
> And the blue sky, and in the mind of man:
> A motion and a spirit, that impels
> All thinking things, all objects of all thought,
> And rolls through all things.

The unifying whole, as Wordsworth's language suggests, depends less on rational system than on emotional association. Human beings link themselves to the infinite by what Wordsworth elsewhere terms "wise passiveness," the capacity to submit to feeling and be led by it to transcendence. Natural detail, too, acquires value by evoking and symbolizing emotion. Nature belongs to the realm of the nonrational, the superrational. It can be linked to a sense of misery and pain, or it can evoke possibilities of utter joy and transcendence.

The idea of the natural can also imply the uncivilized or precivilized. Philosophers have differed dramatically in their hypotheses about what humankind was like in its "natural" state. Thomas Hobbes, in the seventeenth century, argued that the natural human condition was one of conflict. Society developed to curb the violent impulses that human beings would manifest without its restraint. The prevailing nineteenth-century view, on the other hand, made civilization the agent of corruption. Rousseau expounded the crippling effect of institutions. The child raised with the greatest possible freedom, he maintained, would develop in more admirable ways than one subjected to system. By the second half of the eighteenth century, a French novelist could contrast the decadent life of Europe unfavorably with existence on an unspoiled island (Jacques-Henri Bernardin de Saint-Pierre, *Paul and Virginia,* 1788); Thomas Chatterton, before committing suicide in 1770 at the age of eighteen, wrote poems rich in nostalgia for a more primitive stage of social development that he tried to pass off as medieval works; the forged Ossian poems (1760–63) of James Macpherson, purportedly ancient texts, attracted a large and enthusiastic audience. New interest manifested itself in ballads, poetic survivals of the primitive; Romantic poets imitated the form. The interest in a simpler past, a simpler life, continued throughout the nineteenth century.

The revolutionary fervor of the late eighteenth century had generated a vision of infinite human possibility, political and personal. The escapist implications of the increasing emphasis on nature, the primitive, the uncomplicated past suggest, however, a sense of alienation. "Society" would not help the individual work out his or her salvation; on the contrary, it embodied forces opposed to individual development. Indeed, the word *society* had come to embody the impulses that desecrated nature and oppressed the poor in the interests of industry and "progress." Melancholy marked the Romantic hero and tinged nineteenth-century poetry and fiction. The satiric spirit—that spirit of social reform—was suspended. Hope lay in the individual's separation from, not participation in, society. In the woods and mountains, one might feel free.

The Waste Land (1922), T. S. Eliot's twentieth-century epic, contains the line "In the mountains, there you feel free," a line given complex ironic overtones by its context. It reminds us how ideas that came into currency in the late eighteenth and early nineteenth centuries powerfully survive into our own time. The world of the Romantic period specifically prefigures our own, despite all the differences dividing the two cultures. We have developed more fully important Romantic tendencies: stress on the sacredness of the individual, suspicion of social institutions, belief in expressed feeling as the sign of authenticity, nostalgia for simpler ways of being, faith in genius, valuing of originality and imagination, an ambivalent relation to science. Although the authors represented in this section employ vocabularies and use references partly strange to us, they speak directly to the preoccupations of our time. By attending closely to their works, we may learn more about ourselves: not only in the common humanity that we share with all our predecessors but in our special historical situation as both direct heirs of nineteenth-century assumptions and rebels against them.

ROMANTICISM

TEXTS	CONTEXTS
1773 Thomas Hutchinson, Address to the Massachusetts Assembly	
1781–88 Jean-Jacques Rousseau, **Confessions**	1781 Immanuel Kant, *Critique of Pure Reason*
	1787 Wolfgang Amadeus Mozart's *Don Giovanni* is first performed
	1789 The National Assembly in France issues its charter, Declaration of the Rights of Man
1791 Germaine de Staël, *The Superiority of Moderation over Extremism*	
1792 Thomas Paine, Address to the People of France • Jean-Paul Marat, Address to the Convention on the Crimes of King Louis XVI	
1794 William Blake, **Songs of Innocence and of Experience**	
1798 William Wordsworth and Samuel Taylor Coleridge, **Lyrical Ballads** • Dorothy Wordsworth begins her journals	
1800 Novalis, *Hymns to the Night*	
	1801 United Kingdom of Great Britain (England and Scotland) and Ireland established
1802 Coleridge, "Dejection: An Ode"	1803 President Thomas Jefferson purchases French "Louisiana"
	1804 Napoleon has himself crowned emperor of France
1805 Mercy Otis Warren, *History of the Rise, Progress, and Termination of the American Revolution*	
1806 First published lyrics by Anna Petrovna Bunina	
1808 Johann Wolfgang von Goethe, **Faust, Part I** (*Part II,* 1832)	
1812–70 Charles Dickens, English novelist	
1812–18 George Gordon, Lord Byron, "Childe Harold's Pilgrimage"	1815 Battle of Waterloo, ending Napoleon's career
1816 Coleridge, "Kubla Khan" • John Keats, **"On First Looking into Chapman's Homer"**	

Boldface titles indicate works in the anthology.

ROMANTICISM

TEXTS	CONTEXTS
1818 Germaine de Staël, *Considerations on the Principal Events of the French Revolution*	
1818–20 Lyrics by Percy Bysshe Shelley and John Keats	
1820 Alphonse de Lamartine, *Poetic Meditations,* his first collection of poems	
1824 Giacomo Leopardi, **Canzoni**, his first collection of poems	
1826 Friedrich Hölderlin, *Gedichte*	
1827 Heinrich Heine, **Book of Songs**	
1828 Victor Hugo, **Odes and Ballads**	
	1831 First preparation of chloroform inaugurates a new medical era
1834 Alexander Sergeyevich Pushkin, **The Queen of Spades**	
1837 Mikhail Yuryevitch Lermontov, *The Poet's Death*	**1837** Victoria crowned queen of the United Kingdom • Electric telegraph patented
1840 Percy Bysshe Shelley, "A Defense of Poetry"; published posthumously	
1842 Alfred, Lord Tennyson, *Ulysses*	
1842–55 Robert Browning writes poems, including "Childe Roland to the Dark Tower Came"	
1845 Frederick Douglass, *Narrative of the Life of Frederick Douglass, an American Slave*	
1847 Charlotte Brontë, *Jane Eyre* • Emily Brontë, *Wuthering Heights*	
	1848 Karl Marx and Friedrich Engels, *Communist Manifesto* • Revolutions in France, Italy, Austria, Prague • Gold discovered in California
1850 Alfred, Lord Tennyson, "In Memoriam A. H. H."	
	1854 Electric lightbulb invented
1855 Walt Whitman, "Song of Myself" • Gérard de Nerval, *Aurélia*	
	1859 Charles Darwin's *On the Origin of Species,* presenting his theory of evolution
1860 Gustavo Adolfo Bécquer, *Rimas*	**1861** Serfs emancipated in Russia • Beginning of American Civil War

TEXTS	CONTEXTS
	1863 Emancipation Proclamation frees slaves in the Confederate States of America
	1864 Louis Pasteur, who formulated the germ theory of infection, invents pasteurization
	1865 American Civil War ends • President Abraham Lincoln assassinated • Thirteenth Amendment emancipates all slaves in the United States
	1867 Karl Marx, *Das Kapital*
	1874 First Impressionist exhibition, Paris
	1876 Alexander Graham Bell invents the telephone
1884 Rosalía de Castro, *Beside the River Sar*	
1890 Emily Dickinson, **Poems**, published posthumously	
1891 Herman Melville leaves manuscript of *Billy Budd, Sailor* at his death; not published until 1924	
	1895 X-rays discovered by Bavarian physicist Wilhelm Röntgen

JEAN-JACQUES ROUSSEAU
1712–1778

It would be difficult to overstate the historical importance of Jean-Jacques Rousseau's *Confessions* (composed between 1765 and 1770, published 1781–88), which inaugurated a new form of autobiography and suggested new ways of thinking about the self and its relation to others. Even for today's readers, the book's sheer audacity compels attention, demanding that we rethink easy assumptions about important and trivial, right and wrong.

The facts of Rousseau's life are unclear partly because the *Confessions,* despite its claim of absolute truthfulness, sometimes appears more concerned to create a self-justifying story than to confine itself strictly to reality. The son of a Geneva watchmaker, Rousseau left home in his teens and lived for some time with Françoise-Louise de Warens, his protector and eventually his mistress, the "mamma" of the *Confessions.* He worked at many occupations, from secretary to government official (under the king of Sardinia). In Paris, where he settled in 1745, he lived with Thérèse le Vasseur; he claims she bore him five children, all consigned to an orphanage, but the claim has never been substantiated (or, for that matter, disproved). At various times, his controversial writing forced Rousseau to leave France, usually for Switzerland; in 1766, he went to England as the guest of the philosopher David Hume. He was allowed to return to Paris in 1770 only on condition that he write nothing against the government or the church.

Rousseau's social ideas, elaborated in his didactic novels *Julie: or, The New Eloise* (1761) and *Émile* (1762) as well as in his autobiographical writings and political treatises (for example, *The Social Contract,* 1762), stirred much contemporary discussion. He believed in the destructiveness of institutions, the gradual corruption of humankind throughout history, and the importance of nature and of feeling in individual development and, consequently, in society. As he writes in *Émile,* "I hate books; they only teach us to talk about things we know nothing about." He proposes to teach children by immersing them first in the natural, then in the human world, preventing the corruption of their bodies and their feelings. For a time, he was a music teacher, and he published several works on music, including a dictionary, and composed a comic opera called *The Village Soothsayer* (1752).

The *Confessions* presents its subject as a person who always strives to express natural impulses and is recurrently frustrated by society's demands and assumptions. The central figure described here resembles Candide in his naïveté and good feeling. Experience chastens him less than it does Candide, however, although he reports many psychic hard knocks. For Voltaire's didactic purposes, his character's experience was more important than his personality; for Rousseau, his own nature is much more significant than anything that happens to him. His account of that nature becomes ever more complicated as the *Confessions* continues and the writer concerns himself increasingly with the problem of his relation to society at large. His sense of alienation alternates with wistful longing for inclusion as he delineates the dilemmas of the extraordinary individual in a world full of people primarily concerned with accumulating wealth and power.

To read even a few pages of the work reveals how completely Rousseau exemplifies several of his period's dominant values. He describes himself as a being of powerful passions but confused ideas, he makes feeling the guide of conduct, he glorifies imagination and romantic love, he believes the common people morally superior to the upper classes. The emphasis on imagination and passion for him seems not a matter of ideology but of experience: life presents itself to him in this way. The fact emphasizes the degree to which the movement we call Romanticism involved genuine revision. Everything looked different in the late eighteenth century, demanding that categories change from those previously accepted without question. The new way of looking at the world that characterizes the Romantic movement, inasmuch as it implies valuing the inner life of emotion and fancy for its own sake (not for the sake of any insight it might provide), always includes the danger of narcissism, a concentration on the self that shuts out awareness of the reality and integrity of others. Rousseau, in the *Confessions,* vividly expresses the narcissistic side of Romanticism.

Implicit in Rousseau's ways of understanding himself and his life are new moral assumptions as well. Honesty of a particular kind becomes the highest value; however disreputable his behavior, Rousseau can feel comfortable about it because he reports it accurately. To take the self this seriously as subject—not in relation to a progress of education or of salvation, but, merely in its moment-to-moment being—implies belief in self-knowledge (knowledge of feeling, thought, action) as a high moral achievement. This is not the slowly achieved, arduous discipline recommended by Socrates but a more indulgent form of self-contemplation. To connect it, as Rousseau does, with morality conveys the view that self-absorption without self-judgment provides valuable and sufficient insight.

In his presentation of self, Rousseau contrasts vividly with his great predecessor, Montaigne. Rousseau insists on his uniqueness: "I am made unlike any one I have ever met; I will even venture to say that I am like no one in the whole world." He presents himself for the reader's contemplation as a remarkable phenomenon. Montaigne, on the other hand, reminds us constantly of what author and reader (and humankind in general) have in common. "Not only does the wind of accidents stir me according to its blowing, but I am also stirred and troubled by the instability of my attitude; and he who examines himself closely will seldom find himself twice in the same state." The movement within the sentence from *I* to the universalizing *he* characterizes a more outward-looking mode.

It must be said, however, that the intensity of Rousseau's self-concentration makes his subject compelling for others as well. However distasteful one might find his obsessive focus, it is difficult to stop reading. The writer hints—makes us believe—that he will reveal all the secrets about himself; and learning such secrets, despite Rousseau's insistence on his own uniqueness, tells us of human weakness, inconsistency, power, scope—tells us, therefore, something about ourselves. Moreover, the writer's self-absorption causes him to examine minute shades of thought and feeling, thus depicting a personality of great subtlety and complexity. Rousseau is unafraid of exposing contradictions in his attitudes, unafraid of revealing sexual peculiarities, unafraid of acknowledging odd relationships. He makes vivid, in almost novelistic fashion, the intricacies of motivation and purpose.

The novel, already flourishing during the eighteenth century, would turn in the nineteenth century toward the psychological analysis of large groups of characters. Rousseau, making himself a "character," exemplifies a narrator's way of bringing personality to life as he not only examines himself but sketches the others who impinge upon him, often with flashes of brilliant selectivity. His art of detail and introspection provided a model for autobiographers and novelists alike.

PRONOUNCING GLOSSARY

The following list uses common English syllables and stress accents to provide rough equivalents of selected words whose pronunciation may be unfamiliar to the general reader.

de Vulson: *deu vyewl-sohnh'*

de Warens: *deu vah-rahnh'*

Lausanne: *loh-zahn'*

Montaigne: *mohn-ten'*

Nyon: *nee-yohnh'*

Jean-Jacques Rousseau: *zhahnh-zhahk roo-soh*

St. Marceau: *sanh mahr-soh'*　　　　Vaud: *voh*

Saône: *sohn*　　　　　　　　　　　Vévay: *vay-vay'*

Turin: *tyew-ranh'*

Confessions[1]

From Part I

FROM BOOK I

[*The Years 1712–1723*]

I have resolved on an enterprise which has no precedent, and which, once complete, will have no imitator. My purpose is to display to my kind a portrait in every way true to nature, and the man I shall portray will be myself.

Simply myself. I know my own heart and understand my fellow man. But I am made unlike any one I have ever met; I will even venture to say that I am like no one in the whole world. I may be no better, but at least I am different. Whether Nature did well or ill in breaking the mold in which she formed me, is a question which can only be resolved after the reading of my book.

Let the last trump sound when it will, I shall come forward with this work in my hand, to present myself before my Sovereign Judge, and proclaim aloud: "Here is what I have done, and if by chance I have used some immaterial embellishment it has been only to fill a void due to a defect of memory. I may have taken for fact what was no more than probability, but I have never put down as true what I knew to be false. I have displayed myself as I was, as vile and despicable when my behavior was such, as good, generous, and noble when I was so. I have bared my secret soul as Thou thyself hast seen it, Eternal Being! So let the numberless legion of my fellow men gather round me, and hear my confessions. Let them groan at my depravities, and blush for my misdeeds. But let each one of them reveal his heart at the foot of Thy throne with equal sincerity, and may any man who dares, say 'I was a better man than he.'"

* * *

I felt before I thought: which is the common lot of man, though more pronounced in my case than in another's. I know nothing of myself till I was five or six. I do not know how I learnt to read. I only remember my first books and their effect upon me; it is from my earliest reading that I date the unbroken consciousness of my own existence. My mother had possessed some novels, and my father and I began to read them after our supper. At first it was only to give me some practice in reading. But soon my interest in this entertaining literature became so strong that we read by

1. Translated by J. M. Cohen.

turns continuously, and spent whole nights so engaged. For we could never leave off till the end of the book. Sometimes my father would say with shame as we heard the morning larks: "Come, let us go to bed. I am more of a child than you are."

In a short time I acquired by this dangerous method, not only an extreme facility in reading and expressing myself, but a singular insight for my age into the passions. I had no idea of the facts, but I was already familiar with every feeling. I had grasped nothing; I had sensed everything. These confused emotions which I experienced one after another, did not warp my reasoning powers in any way, for as yet I had none. But they shaped them after a special pattern, giving me the strangest and most romantic notions about human life, which neither experience nor reflection has ever succeeded in curing me of.

*　*　*

I had one brother seven years older than myself, who was learning my father's trade. The extraordinary affection lavished upon me led to his being somewhat neglected, which I consider very wrong. Moreover his education had suffered by this neglect, and he was acquiring low habits even before he arrived at an age at which he could in fact indulge them. He was apprenticed to another master, with whom he took the same liberties as he had taken at home. I hardly ever saw him. Indeed, I can hardly say that I ever knew him, but I did not cease to love him dearly, and he loved me as well as a scoundrel can love. I remember once when my father was correcting him severely and angrily, throwing myself impetuously between them, and clasping my arms tightly around him. Thus I covered him with my body, and received the blows intended for him. So obstinately did I maintain my hold that, either as a result of my tearful cries or so as not to hurt me more than him, my father let him off his punishment. In the end my brother became so bad that he ran away and completely disappeared. We heard some time later that he was in Germany. But he did not write at all, and we had no more news of him after that. So it was that I became an only son.

But if that poor lad's upbringing was neglected, it was a different matter with his brother. No royal child could be more scrupulously cared for than I was in my early years. I was idolized by everyone around me and, what is rarer, always treated as a beloved son, never as a spoiled child. Never once, until I left my father's house, was I allowed to run out alone into the road with the other children. They never had to repress or to indulge in me any of those wayward humors that are usually attributed to Nature, but which are all the product of education alone. I had the faults of my years. I was a chatterer, I was greedy, and sometimes I lied. I would have stolen fruit or sweets or any kind of eatable; but I never took delight in being naughty or destructive, or in accusing other people or torturing poor animals. However, I do remember once having made water in one of our neighbor's cooking-pots while she was at church; her name was Mme Clot. I will even admit that the thought of it still makes me laugh, because Mme Clot, although a good woman on the whole, was the grumpiest old body I have ever met. And that is a brief and truthful account of all my childish misdeeds.

How could I have turned out wicked when I had nothing but examples of kindliness before my eyes, none but the best people in the world around me? My father, my aunt, my nurse, our friends and relations and everyone near me, may not have done my every bidding, but they did love me, and I loved them in return. My desires were so rarely excited and so rarely thwarted, that it never came into my head to have any. I could swear indeed that until I was put under a master I did not so much as know what it was to want my own way. When I was not reading or writing with my father, or going out for walks with my nurse, I spent all my time with my aunt, watching her embroider, hearing her sing, always sitting or standing beside her; and I was happy. Her cheerfulness and kindness and her pleasant face have left such an impression upon me that I can still remember her manner, her attitude and the way she looked. I recall too her affectionate little remarks, and I could still describe her clothes and her headdress, not forgetting the two curls of black hair she combed over her temples in the fashion of the day.

I am quite sure that it is to her I owe my taste, or rather my passion, for music, though it did not develop in me till long afterwards. She knew an enormous number of songs and tunes which she sang in a thin voice, that was very sweet. Such was the serenity of this excellent woman that it kept melancholy and sadness away, not only from her but from anyone who came near her; and such delight did I take in her singing that not only have many of her songs remained in my memory, but even now that I have lost her, others which I had completely forgotten since my childhood come back to me as I grow older, with a charm that I cannot express. It may seem incredible but, old dotard that I am, eaten up with cares and infirmities, I still find myself weeping like a child as I hum her little airs in my broken, tremulous voice.

* * *

The simplicity of this rural existence brought me one invaluable benefit; it opened my heart to friendship. Up to that time I had known nothing but lofty and theoretical emotions. Living peacefully side by side with my cousin Bernard gave me a bond of affection with him, and in a very short time I felt a greater attachment for him than I had ever felt for my brother, an attachment that has never disappeared. He was a tall, lank, sickly boy, as mild in spirit as he was weak in body, and he never abused his favored position in the house as my guardian's son. We shared the same studies, the same amusements, and the same tastes; we were on our own and of the same age, and each of us needed a companion; to be separated would have broken our hearts. Seldom though we had the opportunity of proving our attachment to one another, it was extremely strong. For not only could we not have lived one moment apart, but we never imagined that we could ever be parted. Being both of a nature easily swayed by affection, and tractable so long as there was no attempt at constraint, we were always in agreement on all subjects, and if the favor of our guardians gave him some advantage when they were present, the ascendancy was mine when we were alone—which redressed the balance. At our lessons I prompted him if he broke down; and when I had written my exercise I helped him with his. In our sports too I was the more active, and always took the lead. In fact our two natures agreed so well, and our friendship was so mutual and wholehearted that for five complete years, both at Bossey and at Geneva, we were almost inseparable. We

often fought, I confess, but no one ever had to part us. Not one of our quarrels lasted more than a quarter of an hour, and not once did either of us
complain of the other. It may be said that these observations are puerile, but
the relationship they describe is perhaps a unique one in all the history of
childhood.

The manner of my life at Bossey suited me so well that if only it had lasted
longer it could not have failed to fix my character forever. It was founded on
the affectionate, tender, and peaceable emotions. There was never, I believe,
a creature of our kind with less vanity than I. By sudden transports I
achieved moments of bliss, but immediately afterwards I relapsed into languor. My strongest desire was to be loved by everyone who came near me. I
was gentle, so was my cousin, and so were our guardians. For a whole two
years I was neither the witness nor the victim of any violence. Everything
served to strengthen the natural disposition of my heart. Nothing seemed to
me so delightful as to see everyone pleased with me and with everything. I
shall always remember repeating my catechism in my church, where nothing upset me more than the grieved and anxious look on Mlle Lambercier's
face when I hesitated. This made me unhappier than did my shame at faltering in public, though that too distressed me exceedingly. For although I
was not very susceptible to praise, I was always extremely sensitive to disgrace. But I may say now that the expectation of a scolding from Mlle Lambercier alarmed me less than the fear of annoying her.

Neither she nor her brother was lacking in severity when necessary. But as
their severity was almost always just and never excessive, I took it to heart
and never resented it. I was more upset at displeasing them, however, than
at being punished; and a word of rebuke was more painful to me than a
blow. It embarrasses me to be more explicit, but it is necessary nevertheless.
How differently people would treat children if only they saw the eventual
results of the indiscriminate, and often culpable, methods of punishment
they employ! The magnitude of the lesson to be derived from so common
and unfortunate a case as my own has resolved me to write it down.

Since Mlle Lambercier treated us with a mother's love, she had also a
mother's authority, which she exercised sometimes by inflicting on us such
childish chastisements as we had earned. For a long while she confined herself to threats, and the threat of a punishment entirely unknown to me
frightened me sufficiently. But when in the end I was beaten I found the
experience less dreadful in fact than in anticipation; and the very strange
thing was that this punishment increased my affection for the inflicter. It
required all the strength of my devotion and all my natural gentleness to
prevent my deliberately earning another beating; I had discovered in the
shame and pain of the punishment an admixture of sensuality which had
left me rather eager than otherwise for a repetition by the same hand. No
doubt, there being some degree of precocious sexuality in all this, the same
punishment at the hands of her brother would not have seemed pleasant at
all. But he was of too kindly a disposition to be likely to take over this duty;
and so, if I refrained from earning a fresh punishment, it was only out of
fear of annoying Mlle Lambercier; so much am I swayed by kindness, even
by kindness that is based on sensuality, that it has always prevailed with me
over sensuality itself.

The next occasion, which I postponed, although not through fear, occurred through no fault of mine—that is to say I did not act deliberately. But I may say that I took advantage of it with an easy conscience. This second occasion, however, was also the last. For Mlle Lambercier had no doubt detected signs that this punishment was not having the desired effect. She announced, therefore, that she would abandon it, since she found it too exhausting. Hitherto we had always slept in her room, and sometimes, in winter, in her bed. Two days afterwards we were made to sleep in another room, and henceforward I had the honor, willingly though I would have dispensed with it, of being treated as a big boy.

Who could have supposed that this childish punishment, received at the age of eight at the hands of a woman of thirty, would determine my tastes and desires, my passions, my very self for the rest of my life, and that in a sense diametrically opposed to the one in which they should normally have developed. At the moment when my senses were aroused my desires took a false turn and, confining themselves to this early experience, never set about seeking a different one. With sensuality burning in my blood almost from my birth, I kept myself pure and unsullied up to an age when even the coldest and most backward natures have developed. Tormented for a long while by I knew not what, I feasted feverish eyes on lovely women, recalling them ceaselessly to my imagination, but only to make use of them in my own fashion as so many Mlle Lamberciers.

My morals might well have been impaired by these strange tastes, which persisted with a depraved and insane intensity. But in fact they kept me pure even after the age of puberty. If ever education was chaste and decent, mine was. My three aunts were not only women of remarkable virtue, but examples of a modesty that has long since disappeared from womankind. My father was a pleasure lover, but a gallant of the old school, and never made a remark in the hearing of those women he loved most that would have brought a blush to a virgin's cheek; and never was the respect due to children more scrupulously observed than in my family and in my case. I did not find the slightest difference in this respect at M. Lambercier's; a very good servant maid was dismissed for a dubious word pronounced in our hearing. Not only had I not till adolescence any clear ideas concerning sexual intercourse, but my muddled thoughts on the subject always assumed odious and disgusting shapes. I had a horror of prostitutes which has never left me, and I could not look on a debauchee without contempt and even fear. Such had been my horror of immorality, even since the day when, on my way to Petit Saconex along the sunken road, I saw the holes in the earth on either side where I was told such people performed their fornications. When I thought of this I was always reminded of the coupling of dogs, and my stomach turned over at the very thought.

These adolescent prejudices would themselves have been sufficient to retard the first explosions of an inflammable temperament. But they were reinforced, as I have said, by the effect upon me of the promptings of sensuality. Imagining no pleasures other than those I had known, I could not, for all the restless tinglings in my veins, direct my desires towards any other form of gratification. Always I stopped short of imagining those satisfactions which I had been taught to loathe, and which, little though I suspected it, were in fact not so far divorced from those I envisaged. In my crazy fantasies, my wild fits of eroticism, and in the strange behavior which they sometimes drove me to, I always invoked, imaginatively, the aid of the opposite sex, without so much as dreaming that a woman could serve any other purpose than the one I lusted for.

Not only, therefore, did I, though ardent, lascivious, and precocious by nature, pass the age of puberty without desiring or knowing any other sensual pleasures than those which Mlle Lambercier had, in all innocence, acquainted me with; but when finally, in the course of years, I became a man I was preserved by that very perversity which might have been my undoing. My old childish tastes did not vanish, but became so intimately associated with those of maturity that I could never, when sensually aroused, keep the two apart. This peculiarity, together with my natural timidity, has always made me very backward with women, since I have never had the courage to be frank or the power to get what I wanted, it being impossible for the kind of pleasure I desired—to which the other kind is no more than a consummation—to be taken by him who wants it, or to be guessed at by the woman who could grant it. So I have spent my days in silent longing in the presence of those I most loved. I never dared to reveal my strange taste, but at least I got some pleasure from situations which pandered to the thought of it. To fall on my knees before a masterful mistress, to obey her commands, to have to beg for her forgiveness, have been to me the most delicate of pleasures; and the more my vivid imagination heated my blood the more like a spellbound lover I looked. As can be imagined, this way of making love does not lead to rapid progress, and is not very dangerous to the virtue of the desired object. Consequently I have possessed few women, but I have not failed to get a great deal of satisfaction in my own way, that is to say imaginatively. So it is that my sensibility, combined with my timidity and my romantic nature, have preserved the purity of my feelings and my morals, by the aid of those same tastes which might, with a little more boldness, have plunged me into the most brutal sensuality.

Now I have made the first and most painful step in the dark and miry maze of my confessions. It is the ridiculous and the shameful, not one's criminal actions, that it is hardest to confess. But henceforth I am certain of myself; after what I have just had the courage to say, nothing else will defeat me. How much it has cost me to make such revelations can be judged when I say that though sometimes laboring under passions that have robbed me of sight, of hearing, and of my senses, though sometimes trembling convulsively in my whole body in the presence of the woman I loved, I have never, during the whole course of my life, been able to force myself, even in moments of extreme intimacy, to confess my peculiarities and implore her to grant the one favor which was lacking. That confession I was only able to make once, when I was a child to a child of my own age, and then it was she who made the first overtures.

When I trace my nature back in this way to its earliest manifestations, I find features which may appear incompatible, but which have nevertheless combined to form a strong, simple, and uniform whole. I find other features, however, which, though similar in appearance, have formed by a concatenation of circumstances combinations so different that one could never suppose them to be in any way related to one another. Who would imagine, for instance, that I owe one of the most vigorous elements in my character to the same origins as the weakness and sensuality that flows in my veins?

Before we leave the subject I have been dwelling on, I will show it under a very different light.

One day I was learning my lessons alone in the room next to the kitchen, where the servant had left Mlle Lambercier's combs to dry on the stove top. Now when she came to take them off, she discovered that the teeth of one were broken off, all down one side. Who was to be blamed for this? I was the only person who had been in the room; but I said I had not touched it. M. and Mlle Lambercier jointly lectured, pressed, and threatened me; but I stubbornly maintained my denial. Appearances were too strong for me, however, and all my protests were overruled, although this was the first time that I had been convicted of a downright lie. They took the matter seriously, as it deserved. The mischief, the untruth, and my persistent denials, all seemed to deserve a punishment; but this time it was not Mlle Lambercier who inflicted it. They wrote to my Uncle Bernard, and he came. My cousin was accused of another crime no less grave; we were awarded the same chastisement, which was a severe one. If they had intended to allay my depraved tastes for ever by using the evil as its own remedy, they could not have gone about it in a better way. For a long time my desires left me in peace.

They were unable to force from me the confession they required. Though the punishment was several times repeated and I was reduced to the most deplorable condition, I remained inflexible. I would have died rather than give in, and I was resolved to. So force had to yield before the diabolical obstinacy of a child. For that is what they called my persistence. But finally I emerged from that cruel ordeal shattered but triumphant.

It is now nearly fifty years since this occurrence, and I have no fear of a fresh punishment for the offense. But I declare before Heaven that I was not guilty. I had not broken, nor so much as touched, the comb. I had not gone near the stove, nor so much as thought of doing so. But do not ask me how the mischief occurred. I have no idea, and I cannot understand it. But I do most positively know that I was innocent.

Imagine a person timid and docile in ordinary life, but proud, fiery, and inflexible when roused, a child who has always been controlled by the voice of reason, always treated with kindness, fairness, and indulgence, a creature without a thought of injustice, now for the first time suffering a most grave one at the hands of the people he loves best and mostly deeply respects. Imagine the revolution in his ideas, the violent change of his feelings, the confusion in his heart and brain, in his small intellectual and moral being! I say, imagine all this if you can. For myself I do not feel capable of unraveling the strands, or even remotely following all that happened at that time within me.

I had not yet sufficient reasoning power to realize the extent to which appearances were against me, to put myself in my elders' position. I clung to my own, and all I felt was the cruelty of an appalling punishment for a crime I had not committed. The physical pain was bad enough, but I hardly noticed it; what I felt was indignation, rage, and despair. My cousin was in a more or less similar case; he had been punished for what had only been a mistake but was taken for a premeditated crime, and he, following my example, got into a rage, and so to speak, worked himself up to the same pitch as myself. Lying together in the same bed, we embraced wildly, almost stifling one another; and when our young hearts were somewhat assuaged and we could give voice to our anger, we sat up and shouted a hundred times in unison at the tops of our voices: "Carnifex! carnifex! carnifex!"[2]

I feel my pulse beat faster once more as I write. I shall always remember that time if I live to be a thousand. That first meeting with violence and injustice has remained so deeply engraved on my heart that any thought which recalls it summons back this first emotion. The feeling was only a personal one in its origins, but it has since assumed such a consistency and has become so divorced from personal interests that my blood boils at the sight or the tale of any injustice, whoever may be the sufferer and wherever it may have taken place, in just the same way as if I were myself its victim. When I read of the cruelties of a fierce tyrant, of the subtle machinations of a rascally priest, I would gladly go and stab the wretch myself, even if it were to cost me my life a hundred times over. I have often run till I dropped, flinging stones at some cock or cow or dog, or any animal that I saw tormenting another because it felt itself the stronger. This is perhaps an innate characteristic in me. Indeed I think it is. But the memory of the first injustice I suffered was so painful, so persistent, and so intricately bound up with it that, however strong my initial bent in that direction, this youthful experience must certainly have powerfully reinforced it.

There ended the serenity of my childish life. From that moment I never again enjoyed pure happiness, and even today I am conscious that memory of childhood's delights stops short at that point. We stayed some months longer at Bossey. We lived as we are told the first man lived in the earthly paradise, but we no longer enjoyed it; in appearance our situation was unchanged, but in reality it was an entirely different kind of existence. No longer were we young people bound by ties of respect, intimacy, and confidence to our guardians; we no longer looked on them as gods who read our hearts; we were less ashamed of wrongdoing, and more afraid of being caught; we began to be secretive, to rebel, and to lie. All the vices of our years began to corrupt our innocence and to give an ugly turn to our amusements. Even the country no longer had for us those sweet and simple charms that touch the heart; it seemed to our eyes depressing and empty, as if it had been covered by a veil that cloaked its beauties. We gave up tending our little gardens, our herbs and flowers. We no longer went out to scratch the surface of the ground and shout with delight at finding one of the seeds we had sown beginning to sprout. We grew to dislike that life; and they grew to dislike us. So my uncle took us away, and we left M. and Mme Lambercier, with few regrets on either side, each party having grown weary of the other.

* * *

FROM BOOK II

[The Years 1728–1731]

Before I go further I must present my reader with an apology, or rather a justification, for the petty details I have just been entering into, and for those I shall enter into later, none of which may appear interesting in his eyes. Since I have undertaken to reveal myself absolutely to the public, nothing

2. Torturer! torturer! torturer! (Latin).

about me must remain hidden or obscure. I must remain incessantly beneath his gaze, so that he may follow me in all the extravagances of my heart and into every least corner of my life. Indeed, he must never lose sight of me for a single instant, for if he finds the slightest gap in my story, the smallest hiatus, he may wonder what I was doing at that moment and accuse me of refusing to tell the whole truth. I am laying myself sufficiently open to human malice by telling my story, without rendering myself more vulnerable by any silence.

* * *

Mine was no true childhood; I always felt and thought like a man. Only as I grew up did I become my true age, which I had not been at my birth. You may laugh at my modestly setting myself up as a prodigy. Very well, but when you have had your laugh, find a child who is attracted by novels at six, who is interested and moved by them to the point of weeping hot tears. Then I shall admit to being absurdly vain, and agree that I am wrong.

So, when I said that one should not talk to children about religion if one hopes that one day they will have some, and that they are incapable of knowing God, even in our imperfect way, I was basing my conviction on my observations, but not on my own experience. For I knew that my experience did not apply to others. Find me a Jean-Jacques Rousseau of six, talk to him of God at seven, and I promise you that you will be taking no risks.[3]

* * *

But, alas, I have not said all that I have to say about my time at Mme de Vercellis's. For though my condition was apparently unchanged I did not leave her house as I had entered it. I took away with me lasting memories of a crime and the unbearable weight of a remorse which, even after forty years, still burdens my conscience. In fact the bitter memory of it, far from fading, grows more painful with the years. Who would suppose that a child's wickedness could have such cruel results? It is for these only too probable consequences that I can find no consolation. I may have ruined a nice, honest, and decent girl, who was certainly worth a great deal more than I, and doomed her to disgrace and misery.

It is almost inevitable that the breaking up of an establishment should cause some confusion in the house, and that various things should be mislaid. But so honest were the servants and so vigilant were M. and Mme Lorenzi that nothing was found missing when the inventory was taken. Only Mlle Pontal lost a little pink and silver ribbon, which was quite old. Plenty of better things were within my reach, but this ribbon alone tempted me. I stole it, and as I hardly troubled to conceal it it was soon found. They inquired how I had got hold of it. I grew confused, stammered, and finally said with a blush that it was Marion who had given it to me. Marion was a young girl from the Maurienne whom Mme de Vercellis had taken as her cook when she had ceased to give dinners and had discharged her chef, since she had more need of good soup than of fine stews. Marion was not only pretty. She had that fresh complexion that one never finds except in the

3. That is, of turning the child into an atheist or agnostic because, if possessed of such exceptional gifts as Rousseau, he will not be susceptible. At this point in the narrative, Rousseau reports his own conversion to Catholicism and tells of his experience in Turin, where he eventually took service as a valet with Mme. de Vercellis.

mountains, and such a sweet and modest air that one had only to see her to love her. What is more she was a good girl, sensible and absolutely trustworthy. They were extremely surprised when I mentioned her name. But they had no less confidence in me than in her, and decided that it was important to find which of us was a thief. She was sent for, to face a considerable number of people, including the Comte de la Roque himself. When she came she was shown the ribbon. I boldly accused her. She was confused, did not utter a word, and threw me a glance that would have disarmed the devil, but my cruel heart resisted. In the end she firmly denied the theft. But she did not get indignant. She merely turned to me, and begged me to remember myself and not disgrace an innocent girl who had never done me any harm. But, with infernal impudence, I repeated my accusation, and declared to her face that she had given me the ribbon. The poor girl started to cry, but all she said to me was, "Oh, Rousseau, I thought you were a good fellow. You make me very sad, but I should not like to be in your place." That is all. She continued to defend herself with equal firmness and sincerity, but never allowed herself any reproaches against me. This moderation, contrasted with my decided tone, prejudiced her case. It did not seem natural to suppose such diabolical audacity on one side and such angelic sweetness on the other. They seemed unable to come to a definite decision, but they were prepossessed in my favor. In the confusion of the moment they had not time to get to the bottom of the business; and the Comte de la Roque, in dismissing us both, contented himself with saying that the guilty one's conscience would amply avenge the innocent. His prediction was not wide of the mark. Not a day passes on which it is not fulfilled.

I do not know what happened to the victim of my calumny, but she cannot possibly have found it easy to get a good situation after that. The imputation against her honor was cruel in every respect. The theft was only a trifle, but after all, it was a theft and, what is worse, had been committed in order to lead a boy astray. Theft, lying, and obstinacy—what hope was there for a girl in whom so many vices were combined? I do not even consider misery and friendlessness the worst dangers to which she was exposed. Who can tell to what extremes the depressed feeling of injured innocence might have carried her at her age? And if my remorse at having perhaps made her unhappy is unbearable, what can be said of my grief at perhaps having made her worse than myself?

This cruel memory troubles me at times and so disturbs me that in my sleepless hours I see this poor girl coming to reproach me for my crime, as if I had committed it only yesterday. So long as I have lived in peace it has tortured me less, but in the midst of a stormy life it deprives me of that sweet consolation which the innocent feel under persecution. It brings home to me indeed what I think I have written in one of my books, that remorse sleeps while fate is kind but grows sharp in adversity. Nevertheless I have never been able to bring myself to relieve my heart by revealing this in private to a friend. Not with the most intimate friend, not even with Mme de Warens,[4] has this been possible. The most that I could do was to confess

---

4. Françoise-Louise de Warens, whom Rousseau also refers to as "mamma." Rousseau had originally been sent to her home at Annecy, a town in southeastern France, so that she, herself a recent convert to Catholicism, could help him toward his own conversion. The two became devoted to one another.

that I had a terrible deed on my conscience, but I have never said in what it consisted. The burden, therefore, has rested till this day on my conscience without any relief; and I can affirm that the desire to some extent to rid myself of it has greatly contributed to my resolution of writing these *Confessions*.

I have been absolutely frank in the account I have just given, and no one will accuse me, I am certain, of palliating the heinousness of my offense. But I should not fulfill the aim of this book if I did not at the same time reveal my inner feelings and hesitated to put up such excuses for myself as I honestly could. Never was deliberate wickedness further from my intention than at that cruel moment. When I accused that poor girl, it is strange but true that my friendship for her was the cause. She was present in my thoughts, and I threw the blame on the first person who occurred to me. I accused her of having done what I intended to do myself. I said that she had given the ribbon to me because I meant to give it to her. When afterwards I saw her in the flesh my heart was torn. But the presence of all those people prevailed over my repentance. I was not much afraid of punishment, I was only afraid of disgrace. But that I feared more than death, more than crime, more than anything in the world. I should have rejoiced if the earth had swallowed me up and stifled me in the abyss. But my invincible sense of shame prevailed over everything. It was my shame that made me impudent, and the more wickedly I behaved the bolder my fear of confession made me. I saw nothing but the horror of being found out, of being publicly proclaimed, to my face, as a thief, a liar, and a slanderer. Utter confusion robbed me of all other feeling. If I had been allowed time to come to my senses, I should most certainly have admitted everything. If M. de la Roque had taken me aside and said: "Do not ruin that poor girl. If you are guilty tell me so," I should immediately have thrown myself at his feet, I am perfectly sure. But all they did was to frighten me, when what I needed was encouragement. My age also should be taken into account. I was scarcely more than a child. Indeed I still was one. In youth real crimes are even more reprehensible than in riper years; but what is no more than weakness is much less blameworthy, and really my crime amounted to no more than weakness. So the memory tortures me less on account of the crime itself than because of its possible evil consequences. But I have derived some benefit from the terrible impression left with me by the sole offense I have committed. For it has secured me for the rest of my life against any act that might prove criminal in its results. I think also that my loathing of untruth derives to a large extent from my having told that one wicked lie. If this is a crime that can be expiated, as I venture to believe, it must have been atoned for by all the misfortunes that have crowded the end of my life, by forty years of honest and upright behavior under difficult circumstances. Poor Marion finds so many avengers in this world that, however great my offense against her may have been, I have little fear of carrying the sin on my conscience at death. That is all I have to say on the subject. May I never have to speak of it again.

* * *

[*The Years 1731–1732*]

So there I was, settled at last in her[5] house. This, however, was still not the moment from which I date the happy period of my life, but it served to pave the way for it. Although the emotional sensibility that gives rise to real joy is a work of Nature, and perhaps innate in our constitutions, it stands in need of situations in which it can develop. Lacking the right circumstances, a man born with acute sensibility would feel nothing, and would die without ever having known his true nature. I had been more or less in that condition till then, and should have been so always perhaps had I never met Mme de Warens, or even, having known her, if I had not lived close to her for long enough to contract the sweet habit of affection with which she inspired me. I will venture to say that anyone who feels no more than love misses the sweetest thing in life. For I know another feeling, less impetuous perhaps but a thousand times more delightful, which is sometimes joined with love and sometimes separate from it. This feeling is something other than friendship, something less temperate and more tender. I do not think that it can be felt for anyone of the same sex. I have known friendship, at least, if ever a man has, and I have never had this feeling for any of my friends. This statement is obscure, but it will become clear in the sequel. Feelings can only be described in terms of their effects.

Mme de Warens lived in an old house, large enough to contain a fine spare room which she used as a drawing room, and it was here that I was put. It gave on to the passage * * * in which our first interview took place, and from it, on the far side of the stream and the gardens, one could see the country. This view was not a matter of indifference to the room's young occupant. Now, for the first time since Bossey, I had green fields outside my windows. Always shut in by walls, I had had nothing on which to gaze but the roofs of houses and the gray of the streets. I was truly sensitive, therefore, to the charm and novelty of my new situation, which greatly increased my susceptibility to tender feelings. I thought of this charming landscape as an additional gift from my dear patroness, who seemed to have placed it there deliberately for me. There I took my place peacefully beside her, and saw her everywhere among the flowers and the greenery. Her charms and the charms of spring became one in my eyes. My heart, constricted till then, felt more free before this open prospect, and among the orchards my sighs found easier vent.

* * *

She ran her household in exactly the way I should have chosen myself, and naturally I was only too pleased to take advantage of it. What somewhat displeased me, however, was having to spend a long time over meals. At the first smell of the soup and of the other dishes she almost fell into a faint. Indeed she could hardly bear these smells at all, and took some time to recover from her nausea. But little by little she felt better. Then she began to talk, but ate nothing. It would be half an hour before she would take her first mouthful. I could have eaten my dinner three times over in this time. My meal was fin-

---

5. He has returned to Mme. de Warens.

ished long before she had started hers. So I began again, to keep her company, and ate enough for two, without feeling any the worse for it.

In a word, I gave myself up to the sweet sense of well-being I felt in her company, a state of mind which was undisturbed by any concern as to the means of preserving it. Not being as yet in her close confidence, I supposed that the present state of affairs was likely always to continue. I found the same comforts again in her house in later days. But, knowing the true situation better, and seeing that she was anticipating her revenue,[6] I was not able to enjoy them so calmly. Looking ahead always ruins my enjoyment. It is never any good foreseeing the future. I have never known how to avoid it.

From the first day the sweetest intimacy was established between us, and it continued to prevail during the rest of her life. "Little one" was my name, hers was "Mamma," and we always remained "Little one" and "Mamma," even when the passage of the years had almost effaced the difference between our ages. The two names, I find, admirably express the tone of our behavior, the simplicity of our habits and, what is more, the relation between our hearts. To me she was the most tender of mothers, who never thought of her own pleasure but always of my good. And if there was a sensual side of my attachment to her, that did not alter its character, but only made it more enchanting. I was intoxicated with delight at having a young and pretty mamma whom I loved to caress. I use *caress* in the strict sense of the word, for she never thought of grudging me kisses or the tender caresses of a mother, and it never entered my thoughts to abuse them. It will be objected that we had in the end a relationship of a different character. I agree. But wait, I cannot tell everything at the same time.

The sudden moment of our first meeting was the only truly passionate one she ever made me feel. But that moment was the product of surprise. My glances never went wandering indiscreetly beneath her kerchief, though an ill-concealed plumpness in that region might well have attracted them. I felt neither emotions nor desires in her presence; my state was one of blissful calm, in which I enjoyed I knew not what. I could have spent my life like that and eternity as well, without a moment's boredom. She is the only person with whom I never suffered from that inability to find words that makes the maintenance of conversation such a penance to me. Our time together was spent less in conversation than in one interminable gossip, which required an interruption to bring it to an end. I needed no compulsion to talk; it almost needed compulsion to silence me. As she often thought over her plans, she often fell into reveries. I let her dream on. I gazed on her in silence and was the happiest of men. I had another singular habit. I never claimed the favor of being alone with her, but I ceaselessly sought opportunities for private interviews, which I enjoyed with a passion that turned to fury whenever troublesome visitors came to disturb us. As soon as anyone arrived—whether man or woman, it did not matter which—I went out grumbling, for I could never bear to remain with a third party. Then I would stay in her antechamber, counting the minutes and continually cursing her eternal visitors, quite unable to conceive how they could have so much to say since I had so much more.

---

6. Spending her money before she had it—that is, living on credit.

I only felt the full strength of my attachment to her when she was out of my sight. When I could see her I was merely happy. But my disquiet when she was away became almost painful. My inability to live without her caused me outbreaks of tenderness which often concluded with tears. I shall always remember how, on a Saint's day, while she was at vespers, I went for a walk outside the town, with my heart full of the thought of her and with a burning desire to spend my days beside her. I had sense enough to see that for the present this was impossible, that a happiness so deeply enjoyed must needs be short. This gave my thoughts a sad tinge, but not a gloomy one. For it was tempered by a flattering hope. The sound of the bells, which has always singularly moved me, the song of the birds, the beauty of the day, the calm of the countryside, the scattered country dwellings, one of which I fancifully pictured as our common home—all these produced so vivid an impression upon me, raised in me so tender, sad, and touching a mood, that I saw myself ecstatically transported into that happy time and place in which my heart would possess everything it could desire and in which I should enjoy it all with indescribable rapture, yet without so much as a thought of sensual pleasure. I do not remember ever having leapt into the future with greater force and illusion than I did then. And what has struck me most about my memory of this dream, now that it has been realized, is that eventually I found things exactly as I imagined them. If ever a waking man's dream seemed like a prophetic vision, that reverie of mine did. I was only deceived in my dream's seeming duration. For in it days and years and a whole life passed in changeless tranquillity, whilst in reality the whole experience was only a momentary one. Alas, my most lasting happiness was in a dream. Its fruition was almost immediately succeeded by my awakening.

I should never finish were I to describe in detail all the follies which the memory of my dear Mamma caused me to commit when I was out of her sight. How often have I kissed my bed because she had slept in it; my curtains, all the furniture of my room, since they belonged to her and her fair hand had touched them; even the floor on to which I threw myself, calling to mind how she had walked there! Sometimes even in her presence I fell into extravagances that seemed as if they could only have been inspired by the most violent love. One day at table, just as she had put some food into her mouth, I cried out that I had seen a hair in it. She spat the morsel back on her plate, whereupon I seized it greedily and swallowed it. In a word, there was but one difference between myself and the most passionate of lovers. But that difference was an essential one, and sufficient to render my whole condition inexplicable in the light of reason.

* * *

In me are united two almost irreconcilable characteristics, though in what way I cannot imagine. I have a passionate temperament, and lively and headstrong emotions. Yet my thoughts arise slowly and confusedly, and are never ready till too late. It is as if my heart and my brain did not belong to the same person. Feelings come quicker than lightning and fill my soul, but they bring me no illumination; they burn me and dazzle me. I feel everything and I see nothing; I am excited but stupid; if I want to think I must be cool. The astonishing thing is, though, that I have considerable tact, some understanding, and a certain skill with people so long as they will wait for me. I can make excellent replies impromptu, if I have a moment to think, but on the spur of the moment I can never say or do anything right. I could conduct a most delightful conversation by post, as they say the Spaniards play chess. When I read the story of that Duke of Savoy who turned round on his homeward journey to cry, "Mind out, my fine Paris merchant!" I recognize myself.

But I do not suffer from this combination of quick emotion and slow thoughts only in company. I know it too when I am alone and when I am working. Ideas take shape in my head with the most incredible difficulty. They go round in dull circles and ferment, agitating me and overheating me till my heart palpitates. During this stir of emotion I can see nothing clearly, and cannot write a word; I have to wait. Insensibly all this tumult grows quiet, the chaos subsides, and everything falls into place, but slowly, and after long and confused perturbations. Have you ever been to the opera in Italy? During changes of scenery wild and prolonged disorder reigns in their great theaters. The furniture is higgledy-piggledy; on all sides things are being shifted and everything seems upside down; it is as if they were bent on universal destruction; but little by little everything falls into place, nothing is missing, and, to one's surprise, all the long tumult is succeeded by a delightful spectacle. That is almost exactly the process that takes place in my brain when I want to write. If I had known in the past how to wait and then put down in all their beauty the scenes that painted themselves in my imagination, few authors would have surpassed me.

This is the explanation of the extreme difficulty I have in writing. My blotted, scratched, confused, illegible manuscripts attest to the pain they have cost me. There is not one that I have not had to rewrite four or five times before sending it to the printer. I have never been able to do anything with my pen in my hand, and my desk and paper before me; it is on my walks, among the rocks and trees, it is at night in my bed when I lie awake, that I compose in my head; and you can imagine how slowly, for I am completely without verbal memory and have never been able to memorize half a dozen verses in my life. Some of my paragraphs I have shaped and reshaped mentally for five or six nights before they were fit to be put down on paper. It is for that reason that I am more successful in works that demand labor than in things which need a light touch. I have never caught the knack of letter writing, for instance; it is a real torture to me. I never write a letter on the most trivial subject that does not cost me hours of weariness. For if I try to put down immediately what comes to me, I do not know how to begin or end; my letter is a long, muddled rigmarole, and scarcely understandable when it is read.

But not only do I find ideas difficult to express, I find them equally difficult to take in. I have studied men, and I think I am a fairly good observer. But all the same I do not know how to see what is before my eyes; I can only see clearly in retrospect, it is only in my memories that my mind can work. I have neither feeling nor understanding for anything that is said or done or that happens before my eyes. All that strikes me is the external manifestation. But afterwards it all comes back to me, I remember the place and the time, the tone of voice and look, the gesture and situation; nothing escapes me. Then from what a man has done or said I can read his thoughts, and I am rarely mistaken.

Seeing that I am so little master of myself when I am alone, imagine what

I am like in conversation, when in order to speak to the point one must think promptly of a dozen things at a time. The mere thought of all the conventions, of which I am sure to forget at least one, is enough to frighten me. I cannot understand how a man can have the confidence to speak in company. For not a word should be uttered without taking everyone present into account, without knowing their characters and their histories, in order to be certain of not offending anyone. In that respect men who live in society are at a great advantage. Knowing better what not to say, they are more certain of what they say. But even then they often make blunders. Consider then the predicament of a man who has come in out of the blue: it is almost impossible for him to talk for a moment without blundering.

In private conversation there is another difficulty, which I consider worse, the necessity of always talking. You have to reply each time you are spoken to, and if the conversation fails, to set it going again. This unbearable constraint would be enough in itself to disgust me with society. I can think of no greater torture than to be obliged to talk continually and without a moment for reflection. I do not know whether this is just an aspect of my mortal aversion to any sort of compulsion, but I have only to be absolutely required to speak and I infallibly say something stupid. But what is even more fatal is that, instead of keeping quiet when I have nothing to say, it is at just those times that I have a furious desire to chatter. In my anxiety to fulfill my obligations as quickly as possible I hastily gabble a few ill-considered words, and am only too glad if they mean nothing at all. So anxious am I to conquer or hide my ineptitude that I rarely fail to make it apparent. Among countless examples which I could cite I will relate one, which does not belong to my youth but to a time when I had lived for some while in society. By then I should have acquired a social manner and ease if that had been possible. One evening I was with two fine ladies and one gentleman whom I can name; it was the Duke de Gontaut. There was no one else in the room, and I compelled myself to contribute a few words—goodness knows what—to a four-cornered conversation, in which the other three had certainly no need of my help. The mistress of the house sent for a laudanum draft which she took twice a day for her digestion. The other lady, seeing her make a wry face, asked with a laugh, "Is that from Doctor Tronchin's prescription?" "I don't think so," answered the first lady in the same light tone. "That's about as good as she deserves," put in the gallant Rousseau in his witty way. Everyone was speechless; there was not a word, there was not a smile, and the next moment the conversation took another turn. Addressed to anyone else this blunder might have been only silly, but said to a lady too charming not to have some stories attached to her name, a lady whom I had certainly no wish to offend, it was dreadful; and I think the two witnesses of my discomfiture had all they could do not to burst out laughing. That is the kind of witticism I produce when I feel I must speak, but have nothing to say. It will be a long time before I forget that occasion. For not only is it very vivid in itself, but it had consequences that remain in my head to remind me of it only too often.

I think that I have sufficiently explained why, though I am not a fool, I am very often taken for one, even by people in a good position to judge.

*   *   *

FROM BOOK IV

[*The Year 1732*]

It is a very strange thing that my imagination never works more delightfully than when my situation is the reverse of delightful, and that, on the other hand, it is never less cheerful than when all is cheerful around me. My poor head can never submit itself to facts. It cannot beautify; it must create. It can depict real objects only more or less as they are, reserving its embellishments for the things of the imagination. If I want to describe the spring it must be in winter; if I want to describe a fine landscape I must be within doors; and as I have said a hundred times, if ever I were confined in the Bastille, there I would draw the picture of liberty. On leaving Lyons I could see none but agreeable prospects; I was as cheerful—and I had cause to be—as I had been the reverse when I set out from Paris. During this journey, however, I enjoyed none of those delicious daydreams that had accompanied me on my last trip. My heart was light, and that was all. I felt some emotion as I drew nearer to my excellent friend whom I was now to see again. I enjoyed some foretaste of the pleasure of living in her company, but I was not beside myself. I had always expected this; it was as if nothing new had happened. I felt a little anxious about my future employment, as if that had been a matter for much anxiety. My thoughts were calm and peaceful; they were not heavenly or ecstatic. Objects caught my eye. I observed the different landscapes I passed through. I noticed the trees, the houses, and the streams. I deliberated at crossroads. I was afraid of getting lost, but did not lose myself even once. In a word, I was no longer in the clouds. Sometimes I was where I was, sometimes already at my destination, but never did I soar off into the distance.

In telling the story of my travels, as in traveling itself, I never know how to stop.

* * *

These long details of my early youth may well seem extremely childish, and I am sorry for it. Although in certain respects I have been a man since birth, I was for a long time, and still am, a child in many others. I never promised to present the public with a great personage. I promised to depict myself as I am; and to know me in my latter years it is necessary to have known me well in my youth. As objects generally make less impression on me than does the memory of them, and as all my ideas take pictorial form, the first features to engrave themselves on my mind have remained there, and such as have subsequently imprinted themselves have combined with these rather than obliterated them. There is a certain sequence of impressions and ideas which modify those that follow them, and it is necessary to know the original set before passing any judgments. I endeavor in all cases to explain the prime causes, in order to convey the interrelation of results. I should like in some way to make my soul transparent to the reader's eye, and for that purpose I am trying to present it from all points of view, to show it in all lights, and to contrive that none of its movements shall escape his notice, so that he may judge for himself of the principle which has produced them.

If I made myself responsible for the result and said to him, "Such is my character," he might suppose, if not that I am deceiving him, at least that I am deceiving myself. But by relating to him in simple detail all that has happened to me, all that I have done, all that I have felt, I cannot lead him into error, unless willfully; and even if I wish to, I shall not easily succeed by this method. His task is to assemble these elements and to assess the being who is made up of them. The summing up must be his, and if he comes to wrong conclusions, the fault will be of his own making. But, with this in view, it is not enough for my story to be truthful, it must be detailed as well. It is not for me to judge of the relative importance of events; I must relate them all, and leave the selection to him. That is the task to which I have devoted myself up to this point with all my courage, and I shall not relax in the sequel. But memories of middle age are always less sharp than those of early youth. So I have begun by making the best possible use of the former. If the latter come back to me in the same strength, impatient readers will perhaps be bored, but I shall not be displeased with my labors. I have only one thing to fear in this enterprise; not that I may say too much or tell untruths, but that I may not tell everything and may conceal the truth.

* * *

FROM BOOK V

[The Years 1732–1738]

At Chambéry I often saw a Jacobin[7] who was professor of physics, a good-natured friar whose name I have forgotten, who frequently made small experiments that greatly amused me. Following his example, and with the assistance of Ozanam's *Mathematical Recreations*, I tried to make some sympathetic ink;[8] to which purpose I more than half-filled a bottle with quicklime, sulphide of arsenic, and water, and corked it tightly. Almost instantaneously the effervescence began most violently. I ran to the bottle to uncork it, but I was not in time; it burst in my face like a bomb. I swallowed so much of the sulphide and lime that it almost killed me. I was blinded for six weeks, and in that way I learnt not to meddle in experimental physics without knowing the rudiments of that science.

This accident came at an awkward moment, since for some time my health had been sensibly deteriorating. I do not know how it was, but, though of a sound constitution and indulging in no sort of excesses, I was visibly on the decline. I am pretty well built, my chest is broad and my lungs have room enough to expand. Nevertheless I was short of breath, felt constricted across the chest, gasped involuntarily, had palpitations and spat blood. On top of all this came a lingering fever which I have never entirely thrown off. How can a man fall into such a state in the flower of his youth, without any internal injury and having done nothing to destroy his health?

The sword wears out its sheath, as is sometimes said. That is my story. My passions have made me live, and my passions have killed me. What passions, it may be asked. Trifles, the most childish things in the world. Yet they

---

7. A member of a political group originally moderate, but becoming increasingly radical. Chambéry, in eastern France, is the town where Mme. de Warens was now living.   8. Ink that produces writing that remains invisible until a reagent is applied.

affected me as much as if the possession of Helen,[9] or of the throne of the Universe, had been at stake. In the first place, women. When I possessed one my senses were quiet, but my heart never. At the height of my pleasure the need for love devoured me. I had a tender mother, a dear friend; but I needed a mistress. In my imagination I put one in Mamma's place, endowing her with a thousand shapes in order to deceive myself. If I had thought I was holding Mamma in my arms when I embraced her, my embraces would have been just as tender, but all my desires would have died. I should have sobbed with affection but I should have had no physical pleasure. Physical pleasure! Is it the lot of man to enjoy it? Ah, if ever in all my life I had once tasted the delights of love to the full, I do not think that my frail existence could have endured them; I should have died on the spot.

So I was burning with love for no object, and it is perhaps love of this sort that is the most exhausting. I was restless, worried by the bad state of my poor Mamma's affairs and by her reckless conduct, which could not fail to bring on her ruin within a short time. My cruel imagination, which always outleaps my misfortunes, repeatedly showed me the approaching tragedy in all its hideous extent and with all its consequences. I already saw myself forcibly separated by poverty from one to whom I had consecrated my life, and without whom I could not enjoy it. That is why my soul was always disturbed. I was devoured alternately by desires and by fears.

* * *

FROM BOOK VI

[The Year 1738]

Here begins the short period of my life's happiness; here I come to those peaceful but transient moments that have given me the right to say I have lived. Precious and ever-regretted moments, begin to run your charming course again for me! Flow one after another through my memory, more slowly, if you can, than you did in your fugitive reality! What shall I do to prolong this touching and simple tale, as I should like to; endlessly to repeat the same words, and no more to weary my readers by their repetition than I wearied myself by beginning them for ever afresh? Indeed if it all consisted of facts, deeds, and words, I could describe it and in a sense convey its meaning. But how can I tell what was neither said, nor done, nor even thought, but only relished and felt, when I cannot adduce any other cause for my happiness but just this feeling? I rose with the sun, and I was happy; I went for walks, and I was happy; I saw Mamma, and I was happy; I left her, and I was happy; I strolled through the woods and over the hills, I wandered in the valleys, I read, I lazed, I worked in the garden, I picked the fruit, I helped in the household, and happiness followed me everywhere; it lay in no definable object, it was entirely within me; it would not leave me for a single moment.

Nothing that happened to me during that delightful time, nothing that I did, said, or thought all the while it lasted, has slipped from my memory. The period preceding it and following it recur to me at intervals; I recall them irregularly and confusedly; but I recall that time in its entirety, as if it existed

9. Helen of Troy, a woman of legendary beauty about whom the Trojan War was fought.

still. My imagination, which in my youth always looked forward but now looks back, compensates me with these sweet memories for the hope I have lost for ever. I no longer see anything in the future to attract me; only a return into the past can please me, and these vivid and precise returns into the period of which I am speaking often give me moments of happiness in spite of my misfortunes.[1]

I will present a single example of these memories, which will give some idea of their strength and precision. The first day we went out to sleep at Les Charmettes Mamma was in a sedan chair, and I followed on foot. The road climbed; she was rather heavy and, being afraid of overtiring her porters, she insisted on getting out at about halfway and completing the journey on foot. As she walked she saw something blue in the hedge, and said to me: "Look! There are some periwinkle still in flower." I had never seen a periwinkle, I did not stoop to examine it, and I am too shortsighted to distinguish plants on the ground without doing so. I merely gave it a passing glance, and nearly thirty years elapsed before I saw any periwinkle again, or at least before I noticed any. In 1764, when I was at Cressier with my friend M. du Peyrou, we were climbing a hill, on the top of which he has built a pretty little look out which he rightly calls Belle Vue. I was then beginning to botanize a little and, as I climbed and looked among the bushes, I gave a shout of joy: "Look, there are some periwinkle!," as in fact they were. Du Peyrou noticed my delight, but he did not know its cause; he will learn it, I hope, when one day he reads this. The reader can judge by the effect on me of something so small, the degree to which I have been moved by everything which relates to that stage in my life.

* * *

I should like to know whether such childish notions pass through other men's hearts as sometimes pass through mine. In the midst of my studies and of a life as innocent as any man could lead, I was still frequently disturbed by the fear of Hell, no matter what anyone might say. "In what state am I?" I asked myself. "If I were to die at this moment, should I be damned?" According to my Jansenists[2] the matter was past all doubt; but according to my conscience it seemed quite otherwise. Being always fearful, and now a prey to this cruel uncertainty, I resorted to the most ludicrous expedients to overcome it. I should not hesitate, in fact, to have a man shut up in a madhouse if I saw him acting as I did. One day, when brooding on this melancholy subject, I began throwing stones at the tree trunks, and this with my usual skill, which meant that I hardly hit one. While engaged in this noble exercise, it occurred to me to draw a sort of omen from it, to allay my anxiety. "I am going to throw this stone," I said to myself, "at the tree facing me. If I hit it, it is a sign that I am saved; if I miss it I am damned." As I said this I threw my stone with a trembling hand and a terrible throbbing of the heart, but so accurately that it hit the tree full in the middle; which really was not very difficult, since I had taken care to choose a very large tree very near to me. Since then I have never again doubted my salvation. But as I recall this incident I do not know whether I ought to laugh or weep. You great men, who are most certainly

---

1. Rousseau considered himself persecuted for his writing and his beliefs.   2. Proponents of Jansenism, a doctrine of moral determinism considered heretical by the Catholic Church.

laughing, are welcome to congratulate yourselves. But do not insult my misery, for I feel it most deeply, I assure you.

These troubles and alarms, however, though perhaps an inevitable part of the religious life, were not a permanent state. In general I was calm enough, and the effect on my mind of the prospect of early death was not so much one of sadness as of peaceful languor, which even had its charms. I have recently discovered amongst some old papers a kind of exhortation that I made for myself, congratulating myself upon dying at an age when a man has enough courage in his heart to envisage death, and without having suffered any great physical or mental ills in the course of my life. How right I was! I was frightened by the presentiment of living on only to suffer. It was as if I foresaw the fate that awaited me in my old age. I have never been so near to wisdom as during those happy days. Since I had no great remorse for the past, and was free of all care for the future, the dominant feeling in my heart was a constant enjoyment of the present. Religious people ordinarily possess a limited but very keen sensuality which makes them savor to the full such innocent pleasures as they are allowed. The worldly call this a crime, I do not know why; or rather I know very well. It is because they envy them the enjoyment of simple pleasures for which they have themselves lost the taste. I had that taste, and it delighted me to satisfy it with an easy conscience. My heart, which was still fresh, gave itself to everything with the joy of a child, or rather, if I may say so, with the rapture of an angel; for these quiet pleasures are in very truth as serene as the joys of Paradise. Picnic dinners at Montagnole, suppers in the arbor, the fruit picking, the grape harvest, the evenings stripping the hemp with our servants; all these were for us so many festivals, in which Mamma took as much pleasure as I. Our more solitary walks had a still greater charm, for the heart had then more freedom for its outpourings. One in particular forms a landmark in my memory. It is one which we took on a Saint Louis' day, which was Mamma's name day. We set out alone together in the early morning, after a mass that had been read by a visiting Carmelite at daybreak in a chapel belonging to the house. I had suggested walking along the opposite slope of the valley, where we had not yet been. We had sent our provisions on ahead, for the expedition was to take all day. Mamma, although somewhat round and fat, was not a bad walker, and we went from hill to hill and from wood to wood, sometimes in the sun and sometimes in the shade, resting from time to time and forgetting our cares for hours on end, talking of ourselves, of our relationship, and of the sweetness of our lot, and offering up prayers for its continuance, which were not granted. Everything seemed to conspire to add to the day's happiness. It had rained a short while before. There was no dust, and the streams were full. A little fresh wind shook the leaves. The air was clear and the horizon free from clouds. Serenity prevailed in the heavens, as it prevailed in our hearts. We took our dinner in a peasant's hut, sharing it with his family, who gave us their heartfelt blessings. These poor Savoyards are such good creatures! After dinner we went into the shade of some large trees where Mamma amused herself by botanizing amongst the undergrowth while I gathered dry twigs to boil our coffee. Then she took flowers from the bunch I had gathered for her on the way, and showed me a thousand curious details about their formation. This pleased me greatly and should have given me a taste for botany but the moment had not arrived. I was preoccupied with too many other studies. An idea struck me which diverted my mind from flowers and plants. The state of mind I was in, everything that we had said and done that day, all the objects which had caught my attention, combined to call to my mind the waking dream I had had at Annecy seven or eight years before, which I have already described in its place. The similarities were so striking that as I thought of it I was moved to tears. In an access of emotion I embraced my dear friend. "Mamma, Mamma," I cried passionately. "This day has long been promised to me, I can imagine nothing more beautiful. Thanks to you, my happiness is at its height. May it not decline hereafter! May it last as long as I continue to desire it, and it will only end with my life."

* * *

JOHANN WOLFGANG VON GOETHE
1749–1832

Recasting the ancient legend of Faust, Johann Wolfgang von Goethe created a powerful symbol of the Romantic imagination in all its aspiration and anxiety. Faust himself, central character of the epic drama, emerges as a Romantic hero, ever testing the limits of possibility. Yet to achieve his ends he must make a contract with the Devil—as if to say that giving full scope to imagination necessarily partakes of sin.

Goethe's *Faust* (Part I, 1808; Part II, 1832) constituted the crowning masterpiece of a life rich in achievement. Goethe exemplifies the nineteenth-century meaning of *genius*. Accomplished as poet, dramatist, novelist, and autobiographer, he also practiced law, served as a diplomat, and pursued scientific research. He had a happy childhood in Frankfurt, after which he studied law at Leipzig and then at Strasbourg, where in 1770–71 he met Johann Gottfried von Herder, a leader of a new literary movement called Sturm und Drang (Storm and Stress). Participants in this movement emphasized the importance of revolt against established standards; they interested Goethe in such newly discovered forms as the folk song and in the literary vitality of Shakespeare, as opposed to more formally constricted writers.

During the brief period when he practiced law, after an unhappy love affair, Goethe wrote *The Sorrows of Young Werther* (1774), a novel of immense influence in establishing the image of the introspective, self-pitying, melancholy Romantic hero. In 1775 he accepted an invitation to the court of Charles Augustus, Duke of Saxe-Weimar. He remained in Weimar for the rest of his life, for ten years serving the duke as chief minister. A trip to Italy from 1786 to 1788 aroused his interest in classic sources. He wrote dramas based on classic texts, most notably *Iphigenia in Tauris* (1787); novels (for example, *Elective Affinities*, 1809) that pointed the way to the psychological novel; lyric poetry; and an important autobiography, *Poetry and Truth* (1811–33). He also did significant work in botany and physiology. Increasingly famous, he became in his own lifetime a legendary figure; all Europe flocked to Weimar to visit him.

The legend of Dr. Faustus (the real Johannes Faustus, a scholar, lived from 1480 to 1540), in most versions a seeker after forbidden knowledge, had attracted other writers before Goethe. The most important previous literary embodiment of the tale was Christopher Marlowe's *Doctor Faustus* (ca. 1588), a drama ending in its protagonist's damnation as a result of his search for illegitimate power through learning. Goethe's Faust meets no such fate. Pursuing not knowledge but experience, he embodies the ideal of limitless aspiration in all its glamour and danger. His contract with Mephistopheles provides that he will die at the moment he declares himself satisfied, content to rest in the present; he stakes his life and his salvation on his capacity ever to yearn for something beyond.

In Part I of Goethe's play, the protagonist's vision of the impossible locates itself specifically in the figure of Margarete (or its diminutive, *Gretchen*), the simple, innocent girl whom he possesses physically but with whom he can never attain total union. In a speech epitomizing Romantic attitudes toward nature and toward emotion (especially the emotion of romantic love), Faust responds to his beloved's question about whether he believes in God:

> The sky it arches overhead,
> The earth lies firm beneath our feet,
> And the friendly shining stars, don't they
> Mount aloft eternally?
> Don't my eyes, seeking your eyes, meet?
> And all that there is, doesn't it press
> Close on your mind and heart,
> In eternal secrecy working,
> Visibly, invisibly about you?
> Fill heart with it to overflowing
> In an ecstasy of blissful feeling,
> Which then call what you would:
> Happiness! Heart! Love! Call it God!—
> Don't ask me his name, how should I know?
> Feeling is all,
> Names sound and smoke,
> Obscuring heaven's glow.

The idea of happiness here identifies an unnameable feeling derived from experience of nature and of romantic love, possibly identical with God, but valued partly for its very vagueness.

Modern readers may feel that Faust bullies Margarete, allowing her no reality except as instrument for his desires. In a poignant moment early in the play, interrupting Faust's rhapsody about her "meekness" and "lowliness," Margarete says, "You'll think of me for a moment or two." Faust seems incapable of any such awareness, too busy inventing his loved one to see her as she is. He dramatically represents the "egotistical sublime," with a kind of imaginative grandeur inseparable from his utter absorption in the wonder of his own being, his own experience.

Yet the action of Part I turns on Faust's development of just that consciousness of another's reality that seemed impossible for him, and Margarete is the agent of his development. In the great final scene—Margarete in prison, intermittently mad, condemned to death for murdering her illegitimate child by Faust—the woman again appeals to the man to think about her, to *know* her: "Have you any idea who you're letting go free?" Her anguish, his responsibility for it, force themselves on Faust. He wishes he had never been born: his lust for experience has resulted in this terrible culpability, this agonizing loss. At the final moment of separation, with Margaret's spiritual redemption proclaimed from above, Faust implicitly acknowledges the full reality of the woman he has lost and thus, even though he departs with Mephistopheles, distinguishes himself from his satanic mentor. Mephistopheles in his nature cannot grasp a reality utterly apart from his own; he can recognize only what belongs to him. Faust, at least fleetingly, realizes the otherness of the woman and the value of what he has lost.

Mephistopheles, at the outset witty and powerful in his own imagination, gradually reveals his limitations. In the "Prologue in Heaven," the Devil seems energetic, perceptive, enterprising, fearless: as the Lord says, a "railer," apparently more "trying" than malign. His bargain with the Lord turns on his belief in the essentially "beastly" nature of humankind: he emphasizes the human misuse of reason. Although the scene is modeled on the interchange between God and Satan in the Book of Job, it differs significantly in that the Lord gives an explicit reason for allowing the Tempter to function. "As long as man strives, he is bound to err," He says, but He adds that Mephistopheles's value is in prodding humanity into action. The introductory scene thus suggests that Mephistopheles will function as an agent of salvation rather than damnation. The Devil's subsequent exchanges with Faust, in Mephistopheles's mind predicated on his own superior knowledge and comprehension, gradually make one realize that the man in significant respects knows more than does the Devil. Mephistopheles, for example, can understand Faust's desire for Margarete only in sexual terms. His witty cynicism seems more and more inadequate to the actual situation. By the end of Part I, Faust's suffering has enlarged him; but from the beginning, his capacity for sympathy marks his potential superiority to the Devil.

The "Walpurgis Night" section, with the "Walpurgis Night's Dream," marks a stage in Faust's education and an extreme moment in the play's dramatic structure. Goethe here allows himself to indulge in unrestrained fantasy—grotesque, obscene, comic, with an explosion of satiric energy in the dream. The shifting tone and reference of these passages embody ways in which the diabolic might be thought to operate in human terms. While Margarete suffers the consequences of her sin, Faust experiences the ambiguous freedom of the imagination, always at the edge of horror.

The pattern of Faust's moral development in Part I prepares the reader for a non-tragic denouement to the drama as a whole. In Part II, which he worked on for some thirty years, completing it only the year before his death, Goethe moves from the individual to the social. Faust marries Helen of Troy, who gives birth to Euphorion, symbol of new humanity. He turns soldier to save a kingdom; he reclaims land from the sea; finally, he rests contented in a vision of happy community generated by the industry of humankind. Mephistopheles thinks this his moment of victory: now Faust has declared himself satisfied. But since his satisfaction depends still on aspiration, on a dream of the future, the angels rescue him at last and take him to heaven.

One cannot read *Faust* with twenty-first-century expectations of what a play should be like. This is above all *poetic* drama, to be read with pleasure in the richness of its language, the fertility and daring of its imagination. Although its cast of characters natural and supernatural and its sequence of supernaturally generated events are far from "realistic," it addresses problems still very much with us. How can individual ambition and desire be reconciled with responsibility to others? Does a powerful imagination—an artist's, say, or a scientist's—justify its possessor in ignoring social obligations? Goethe investigates such perplexing issues in symbolic terms, drawing his readers into personal involvement by playing on their emotions even as he questions the proper functions and limitations of commitment to desire—that form of emotional energy that leads to the greatest human achievements but involves the constant danger of debilitating narcissism.

PRONOUNCING GLOSSARY

The following list uses common English syllables and stress accents to provide rough equivalents of selected words whose pronunciation may be unfamiliar to the general reader.

Altmayer: *ahlt'-maier*

Auerbach: *aw'-er-bahk*

Elend: *ay'-lend*

encheirisis naturae: *en-kai-ray'-sis nahtu'-rai*

Euphorion: *oy-foh'-ree-on*

Faust: *fowst*

Goethe: *gur'te*

Leipzig: *laip'-zig*

Proktophantasmist: *prohk-toh-fan-tas'-mist*

Schierke: *sheer'ke*

Sturm und Drang: *shturm unt drahng*

Te Deum: *tay day'-um*

Wagner: *vahg'-ner*

Walpurgis: *vahl-poor'-gis*

Werther: *vayr'-ter*

Zenien: *tsay'-nee-en*

Faust[1]

Prologue in Heaven[2]

THE LORD. THE HEAVENLY HOST. *Then* MEPHISTOPHELES.[3] *The three* ARCHANGELS *advance to front.*

RAPHAEL   The sun sounds out his ancient measure
  In contest with each brother sphere,
  Marching around and around, with steps of thunder,
  His appointed circuit, year after year.
  To see him lends us angels strength,   5
  But what he *is*, oh who can say?
  The inconceivably great works are great
  As on the first creating day.
GABRIEL   And swift, past all conception swift,
  The jeweled globe spins on its axletree,   10
  Celestial brightness alternating
  With shuddering night's obscurity.
  Against earth's deep-based precipices
  The broad-running ocean tides are hurled,
  And rock and sea together hurtle   15
  With the eternally turning world.
MICHAEL   And hurricanes, contending, roar
  From sea to land, from land to sea,
  Linking in tremendous circuit
  A chain of blazing energy.   20
  The lightning bolt makes ready for
  The thunderclap a ruinous way—

---

1. Translated by Martin Greenberg.   2. The scene is patterned on Job 1.6–12 and 2.1–6.   3. The origin of the name remains debatable. It may come from Hebrew, Persian, or Greek, with such meanings as "destroyer-liar," "no friend of Faust," and "no friend of light."

Yet Lord, your servants reverence
The stiller motions of your day.

ALL THREE   From seeing this we draw our strength,   25
But what You *are*, oh who can say?
And all your great works are as great
As on the first creating day.

MEPHISTOPHELES   Lord, since you've stopped by here again,
liking to know
How all of us are doing, for which we're grateful,   30
And since you've never made me feel *de trop*,
Well, here I am too with your other people.
Excuse, I hope, my lack of eloquence,
Though this whole host, I'm sure, will think I'm stupid;
Coming from me, high-sounding sentiments   35
Would only make you laugh—that is, provided
Laughing was a thing Your Worship still did.
About suns and worlds I don't know beans, I only see
How mortals find their lives pure misery.
Earth's little god's shaped out of the same old clay,   40
He's the same queer fish he was on the first day.
He'd be much better off, in my opinion, without
The bit of heavenly light you dealt him out.
He calls it Reason and the use he puts it to?
To act more beastly than beasts ever do.   45
To me he seems, if you'll pardon my saying so,
Like a long-legged grasshopper all of whose leaping
Only lands him back in the grass again chirping
The tune he's always chirped. And if only he'd
Stay put in the grass! But no! It's an absolute need   50
With him to creep and crawl and strain and sweat
And stick his nose in every pile of dirt.

THE LORD   Is that all you have got to say to me?
Is that all you can do, accuse eternally?
Is nothing ever right for you down there, sir?   55

MEPHISTOPHELES   No, nothing, Lord—all's just as bad as ever.
I really pity humanity's myriad miseries,
I swear I hate tormenting the poor ninnies.

THE LORD   Do you know Faust?

MEPHISTOPHELES   The Doctor?[4]

THE LORD   My good servant!

MEPHISTOPHELES   You[5] don't say! Well, he serves you in a funny way,   60
Finds meat and drink, the fool, in nothing earthly,
Drives madly on, there's in him such a torment,
He himself is half aware he's crazy;
From Heaven he must have the brightest stars,
From earth the most ecstatic raptures,   65
And all that's near at hand or far and wide
Leaves your good servant quite unsatisfied.

---

4. Of philosophy.   5. In the German text, Mephistopheles shifts from *du* to *ihr*, indicating his lack of respect for God.

THE LORD   If today his service shows confused, disordered,
    With my help he'll see his way clearly forward.
    When the sapling greens, the gardener can feel certain   70
    Flower and fruit will follow in due season.
MEPHISTOPHELES   Would you care to bet on that? You'll lose, I tell you,
    If you'll just give me leave to lead the fellow
    Gently down my broad, my primrose path.
THE LORD   As long as Faustus walks the earth   75
    I shan't, I promise, interfere.
    Still as man strives, still he must err.
MEPHISTOPHELES   Well thanks, Lord, for it's not the dead and gone
    I like dealing with. By far what I prefer
    Are round and rosy cheeks. When corpses come   80
    A-knocking, sorry, Master's left the house;
    My way of working's the cat's way with a mouse.
THE LORD   So it's agreed, you have my full consent.
    Divert the soul of Faust from its true source
    And if you're able, lead him along, Hell bent   85
    With you, upon the downward course—
    Then blush for shame when you find you must admit:
    Stumbling along as he must, through darkness and confusion,
    A good man still knows which road is the right one.
MEPHISTOPHELES   Of course, of course! Yet I'll seduce him from it   90
    Soon enough. I'm not afraid I'll lose my bet.
    And after I have won it,
    You won't, I trust, begrudge me
    My whoops of triumph, shouts of victory.
    Dust he'll eat   95
    And find that he enjoys it, exactly like
    That old aunt of mine, the famous snake.
THE LORD   There too feel free, you have carte blanche.
    I've never hated your likes much;
    I find, of all the spirits of denial,   100
    You jeerers not my hardest trial.
    Man's very quick to slacken in his effort,
    What he likes best is Sunday peace and quiet;
    So I'm glad to give him a devil—for his own good,
    To prod and poke and incite him as a devil should.   105
    [To the ANGELS] But you who are God's true and faithful children—
    Delight in the world's wealth of living beauty!
    May that which moves the great work of creation,
    That makes all things to grow, evolve eternally,
    Bound you about with smiling love, fraternally,   110
    And the fitfulness, the flux of all appearance—
    By enduring thoughts give enduring forms to its transience.
        [The Heavens close, the ARCHANGELS withdraw.]
MEPHISTOPHELES   I like to see the Old Man now and then,
    And take good care I don't fall out with him.
    How very decent of a Lord Celestial
    To talk man to man with the Devil of all people.   115

Part I

NIGHT

In a narrow, high-vaulted Gothic room, FAUST, *seated restlessly in an armchair at his desk.*

FAUST   I've studied, alas, philosophy,
   Law and medicine, recto and verso,
   And how I regret it, theology also,
   Oh God, how hard I've slaved away,
   With what result? Poor foolish old man,   120
   I'm no whit wiser than when I began!
   I've got a Master of Arts degree,
   On top of that a Ph.D.,
   For ten long years, around and about,
   Upstairs, downstairs, in and out,   125
   I've led my students by the nose
   To what conclusion?—that nobody knows,
   Or ever can know, the tiniest crumb!
   Which is why I feel completely undone.
     Of course I'm cleverer than these stuffed shirts,   130
   These Doctors, Masters, Clerics, Priests,
   I'm not bothered by a doubt or a scruple,
   I'm not afraid of Hell or the Devil—
   But the consequence is, my mirth's all gone;
   No longer can I fool myself   135
   I'm able to teach anyone
   How to be better, love true worth;
   I've got no money or property,
   Worldly honors or celebrity;
   A dog wouldn't put up with this life!   140
   Which is why I've turned to magic,
   Seeking to know, by ways occult,
   From ghostly mouths, many a secret;
   So I no longer need to sweat
   Painfully explaining what   145
   I don't know anything about;
   So I may penetrate the power
   That holds the universe together,
   Its founts of energy, living seeds,
   And deal no more in words, words, words.   150

   O full moon, melancholy-bright,
   Friend I've watched for, many a night,
   Till your quiet-shining circle
   Appeared above my high-piled table,
   If only you might never again   155
   Look below down on my pain,
   If only I might stray at will

In your mild light, high on the hill,
Haunt with spirits upland hollows,
Fade with you in dim-lit meadows,   160
And soul no longer gasping in
The stink of learning's midnight oil,
Bathe in your dews till well again!

Oh misery! Oh am I still
Stuck here in this dismal prison?   165
A musty goddamned hole in the wall
Where even the golden light of heaven
Can only weakly make its way through
The painted panes of the gothic window;
Where all about me shelves of books   170
Rise up to the vault in stacks,
Books gray with dust, worm-eaten, rotten,
With soot-stained paper for a curtain;
Where instruments, retorts and glasses
Are crammed in everywhere a space is;   175
And stuck in somehow with these things
My family's ancient furnishings
Make complete the sad confusion—
Call this a world, this world you live in?

Can you still wonder why your heart   180
Should clench in your breast so anxiously?
Why your every impulse is stopped short
By an inexplicable misery?
Instead of Nature's flourishing garden
God created and man to dwell there,   185
Rubbish, dirt are everywhere
Your gaze turns, old bones, a skeleton.

Off, off, to the open countryside!
And this mysterious book, inscribed
By Nostradamus'[6] own hand—   190
What better help to master the secrets
Of how the stars turn in their orbits,
From Nature learn to understand
The spirits' power to speak to spirits;
Sitting here and racking your brains   195
To puzzle out the sacred signs—
What a sterile, futile business!
Spirits, I feel your presence around me:
Announce yourselves if you hear me!
    [*He opens the book and his eye encounters the sign of the Macrocosm.[7]*]

---

6. The Latin name of the French astrologer and physician Michel de Notredame (1503–1566). His collection of rhymed prophecies, *The Centuries*, appeared in 1555.   7. The great world (literal trans.); the universe as a whole. It represents the ordered, harmonious universe in its totality.

The pure bliss flooding all my senses   200
Seeing this! Through every nerve and vein
I feel youth's fiery, fresh spirit race again.
Was it a god marked out these signs
By which my agitated bosom's stilled,
By which my bleak heart's filled with joy,   205
By whose mysterious agency
The powers of Nature all around me stand revealed?
Am *I* a god? All's bright as day!
By these pure tracings I can see,
At my soul's feet, great Nature unconcealed.   210
And the sage's words—I understand them, finally:
"The spirit world is not barred shut,
It's your closed mind, your dead heart!
Stand up unappalled, my scholar,
And bathe your breast in the rose of Aurora!"   215
          [*He contemplates the sign.*]
How all is woven one, uniting,
Each in the other living, working!
How Heavenly Powers rise, descend,
Passing gold vessels from hand to hand!
On wings that scatter sweet-smelling blessings,   220
Everywhere they post in earth
And make a universal harmony sound forth!
Oh, what a sight! But a sight, and no more!
How, infinite Nature, lay hold of you, where?
Where find your all-life-giving fountains?—breasts that sustain   225
The earth and the heavens, which my shrunken breast
Yearns for with a feverish thirst—
You flow, overflow, must I keep on thirsting in vain?
          [*Morosely, he turns the pages of the book and comes on the sign of the
          Spirit of Earth.*[8]]
What a different effect this sign has on me!
Spirit of Earth, how nearer you are to me!   230
Already fresh lifeblood pours through every vein,
Already I'm aglow as if with new wine—
Now I have the courage to dare
To venture out into the world and bear
The ill and well of life, to battle   235
Storms, when the ship splits, not to tremble.

The air grows dark overhead—
The moon's put out her light,
The oil lamp looks like dying.
Vapors rise, red flashes dart   240
Around my head—fright,

---

8. This figure seems to be a symbol for the energy of terrestrial nature—neither good nor bad, merely powerful.

Shuddering down from the vault,
Seizes me by the throat!
Spirit I have invoked, hovering near:
Reveal yourself! 245
Ha! How my heart beats! All of my being's
Fumbling and groping amid never felt feelings!
Spirit, I feel I am yours, body and breath!
Appear! Oh, you must! Though it costs me my life!
> [*He seizes the book and pronounces the* SPIRIT's *mystic spell. A red flame flashes, in the midst of which the* SPIRIT *appears.*]

SPIRIT   Who's calling? 250
FAUST [*Averting his face.*]   Overpowering! Dreadful!
SPIRIT   Potently you've drawn me here,
A parched mouth sucking at my sphere.
And now—?
FAUST   Oh, you're unbearable!
SPIRIT   You're breathless from your implorations 255
To see my face, to hear me speak,
I've yielded to your supplications
And here I am.—Well, in a funk
I find the superman! I come at your bidding
And you're struck dumb! Is this the mind 260
That builds a whole interior world, doting
On its own creation, puffed to find
Itself quite on a par, the equal,
Of us spirits? Wherever is that Faust
Who urged himself just now with all 265
His strength on me, made such a fuss?
You're Faust? The one who at my breath's
Least touch, shudders to his depths,
A worm that wriggles off scared, a mouse!
FAUST   *I* shrink back from you, an airy flame? 270
I'm him, yes Faust, your equal, the same.
SPIRIT   I surge up and down
In the tides of being,
Drive forward and back
In the shocks of men's striving! 275
I am birth and the grave,
An eternal ocean,
A web changing momently,
A life burning fervently.
Thus seated at time's whirring loom 280
I weave the Godhead's living gown.
FAUST   We're equals, I know! I feel so close to you, near,
You busy spirit ranging everywhere!
SPIRIT   You equal the spirit you think I am,
Not me! [*Vanishes.*] 285
FAUST [*Deflated.*]   Not you?
Then who?
Me, made in God's own image,

Not even equal to you?
    [*A knocking.*]
Death! My famulus[9]—I know that knock.   290
Finis my supremest moment—worse luck!
That visions richer than I could have guessed
Should be scattered by a shuffling Dryasdust!
    [WAGNER *in dressing gown and nightcap, carrying a lamp.* FAUST *turns around impatiently.*]

WAGNER   Excuse me, sir, but wasn't that
Your voice I heard declaiming? A Greek tragedy,   295
I'm sure. Well, that's an art that comes in handy
Nowadays. I'd love to master it.
People say, how often I have heard it,
Actors could really give lessons to the clergy.

FAUST   Yes, so parsons can make a stage out of the pulpit—   300
Something I've seen done in more than one case.

WAGNER   Oh dear, to be so cooped up in one's study all day,
Seeing the world only now and then, on holiday,
Seeing people from far off, as if through a spyglass—
How can you persuade and direct them that way?   305

FAUST   You can't—unless you speak with feeling's own
True voice, unless your words are from
The soul and by their spontaneous power,
Seize with delight the soul of your hearer.
But no! Stick in your seats, you scholars!   310
Paste bits and pieces together, cook up
A beggar's stew from others' leftovers,
Over a flame you've sweated to coax up
From your own little heap of smoldering ashes,
Filling with wonder all the jackasses,   315
If that's the kind of stuff your taste favors—
But you'll never get heart to cleave to heart
Unless your words spring from the heart.

WAGNER   Still and all, a good delivery is what
Makes the orator. I'm far behind in that art.   320

FAUST   Advance yourself in an honest way!
Don't play the fool in cap and bells!
Good sense, good understanding, they
Are art enough, speak for themselves.
When you have something serious to say   325
What need is there for hunting up
Fancy words, high-sounding phrases?
Your brilliant speeches, polished up
With bits and pieces collected out
Of a miscellany of commonplaces   330
From all the languages spoken by all the races,
Are about as bracing as the foggy autumnal breeze
Swaying the last leaves on the trees.

---

9. Assistant to a medieval scholar.

WAGNER   Dear God, but art is long
   And our life—lots shorter.   335
   Often in the middle of my labor
   My confidence and courage falter.
   How hard it is to master all the stuff
   For dealing with each and every source,
   And before you've traveled half the course,   340
   Poor devil, you have gone and left this life.
FAUST   Parchment, tell me—that's the sacred fount
   You drink out of, to slake your eternal thirst?
   The only true refreshment that exists
   You get from where? Yourself—where all things start.   345
WAGNER   But sir, it's such a pleasure, isn't it,
   To enter into another age's spirit,
   To see what the sages before us thought
   And measure how far since then we've got.
FAUST   As far as to the stars, no doubt!   350
   Your history, why, it's a joke;
   Bygone times are a seven-sealed book.[1]
   What you call an age's spirit
   Is nothing more than your own spirit
   With the age reflected as you see it.   355
   And it's pathetic, what's to be seen in your mirror!
   One look and off I head for the exit:
   A trash can, strewn attic, junk-filled cellar,
   At best a blood-and-thunder thriller
   Improved with the most high-minded sentiments   360
   Exactly suited for mouthing by marionettes.
WAGNER   But this great world, the human mind and heart,
   They are things everyone wants to know about.
FAUST   Yes, know as the world, knows knowing!
   Who wants to know the real truth, tell me?   365
   Those few who had true understanding,
   Who failed to stand guard, most unwisely,
   Over their tongues, speaking their minds and hearts
   For the mob to hear—you know what's been their fate:
   They were crucified, burnt, torn to bits.   370
   But we must break off, friend, it's getting late.
WAGNER   I love such serious conversation, I do!
   I'd stay up all night gladly talking to you.
   But, sir, it's Easter Sunday in the morning
   And perhaps I may ask you a question or two then, if you're willing?   375
   I've studied hard, with unrelaxing zeal,
   I know a lot, but I want, sir, to know all. [*Exit.*]
FAUST [*Alone.*]   How such fellows keep their hopes up is a wonder!
   Their attention forever occupied with trivialities,
   Digging greedily in the ground for treasure,   380
   And when they've turned a worm up—what ecstacies!

---

1. Revelation 5.1.

That banal, commonplace human accents
Should fill air just now filled with spirits' voices!
Still, this one time you've earned my thanks,
Oh sorriest, oh shallowest of wretches!   385
You snatched me from the grip of a dejection
So profound I was nearly driven off
My head. So gigantic was the apparition
It made me feel no bigger than a dwarf—

Me, the image of God, absolutely sure in the belief   390
Soon, soon I'd behold the eternal mirror of truth
Whose near presence I felt; already basking in
Heaven's clear ether, mortal clothing stripped off;
Me, higher placed than the angels, presuming wildly
My strength was already streaming freely,   395
Creative as the gods, through Nature's live body—
Well, it had to be paid for: one word
Thundered out and I am knocked flat, all self-conceit curbed.
No, I can't claim we are equals, presumptuously!
Though I was strong enough to draw you down to me,   400
Holding on to you was another matter entirely.
In that exalted-humbling moment of pure delight
I felt myself at once both small and great.
And then you thrust me remorselessly back
Into uncertainty, which is all of humanity's fate.   405
Who'll tell me what to do? What not to do?
Still seek out the spirits to learn what they know?
Oh what we do, as much as what's done to us,
Hinders and frustrates our entire life's progress.

The noblest thoughts our minds are able to entertain   410
Are undermined by a corrupting grossness;
When we gain a bit of the good of the world as our prize,
Then the better's dismissed as delusion and lies;
Those radiant sentiments, once our breath of life,
Weaken and fade in the madding crowd's strife.   415
There was that hope and brave imagination
Boldly reached as far as to infinity,
But now misfortune piling on misfortune,
A little, confined space will satisfy.
It's then, heart-deep, Care builds her nest,   420
Dithering nervously, killing joy, ruining rest,
Masking herself as this, as that concern
For house and home, for wife and children,
Fearing fire and flood, daggers and poison;
You shrink back in terror from imagined blows   425
And cry over losing what you never in fact lose.

Oh no, I'm no god, only too well do I know it!
A worm's what I am, wriggling through the dirt

And finding his nourishment in it,
Whom the passerby treads underfoot.   430

These high walls, every shelf crammed, every niche,
Dust is what shrinks them to a stifling cell,
This moth-eaten world with its oddments and trash,
It's the reason I feel shut up in jail.
And here I'll discover what it is that I lack?   435
Devour thousands of books so as to learn, shall I,
Mankind has always been stretched on the rack,
With now and then somebody, somewhere, who's been happy?
You, empty skull there, smirking so, I know why—
What does it tell me if not that your brain,   440
Whirling like mine, sought the bright sun of truth,
Only to wander, night-bewildered, in vain.
And all that apparatus, you mock me, you laugh
With your every wheel, cylinder, cog and ratchet;
I stood at the door, sure you provided the key,   445
Yet for all the bit's cunning design you couldn't unlatch it.
Great Nature, so mysterious even in broad day,
Still hides her face, do what you may;
All those screws and levers can't make her reveal
The mystery hidden behind her veil.   450
You, ancient stuff I've left lying about,
You're here, and why?—my father[2] found you useful.
And you, old scrolls, have gathered soot
For as long as the lamp's smoked on this table.
Much better to have squandered the little I got   455
Than find myself sweating under the lot.
It's from our fathers, what we inherit,
To possess it really we have to earn it.
What's never used is a dead weight,
What's useful is what you spontaneously create.   460

But why do I find I must stare in that corner,
Is that bottle a magnet enchanting my sight?
Why is everything all at once brighter, clearer,
Like woods when the moon's up and floods them with light?

Vial, I salute you, exeptional, rare thing,   465
And reverently bring you down from the shelf,
Honoring in you man's craft and cunning;
Quintessence of easeful sleeping potions,
Pure distillation of subtle poisons,
Do your master the kindness that lies in your power!   470
One look at you and my agony lessens,
One touch and my feverish straining grows calmer

---

2. Later we find that Faust's father was a doctor of medicine.

And my tight-stretched spirit bit by bit slackens.
The spirit's flood tide runs more and more out,
My way is clear, into death's immense sea;   475
The bright waters glitter before my feet,
A new day is dawning, new shores calling to me.

A fiery chariot, bird-winged, swoops down on me,
I am ready to follow new paths and higher,
Aloft into new spheres of purest activity.   480
An existence so exalted, so godlike a rapture,
Does the worm of a minute ago deserve it?
No matter. Never falter! Turn your back bravely
On the sunlight, sweet sunlight, of our earth forever!
Tear wide open those dark gates boldly   485
Which the whole world skulks past with averted heads!
The time has come to disprove by deeds,
Because the gods are great, man's a derision,
To cringe back no more from that black pit
Whose unspeakable tortures are your own invention,   490
To struggle toward that narrow gate
Around which Hell fires flame in eternal eruption,
To do it calmly, without regret,
Even at the risk of utter extinction.
And now let me take this long forgotten   495
Crystal wine cup down out of its chest.
You used to shine bright at the family feast,
Making the solemn guests' faces lighten
When you went round with each lively toast.
The figures artfully cut in the crystal,   500
Which it was the duty of all at the table,
In turn, to make up rhymes about,
Then drain the cup at a single draught—
How they recall the nights of my youth!
But now there's no passing you on to my neighbor,   505
Or thinking up rhymes to parade my quick wit;[3]
Here is a juice that is quick too—to intoxicate,
A brownish liquid, see, filling the beaker,
Chosen by me, by me mixed together,
My last drink! Which now I lift up in festal greeting   510
To the bright new day I can see dawning!
        [*He raises the cup to his lips. Bells peal, a choir bursts into song.*]
CHORUS OF ANGELS
        Christ is arisen!
        Joy to poor mortals
        By their own baleful,
        Inherited, subtle   515
        Failings imprisoned.

---

3. Faust here alludes to the drinking of toasts. The maker of a toast often produced impromptu rhymes.

FAUST   What deep-sounding burden, what tremelo strain
    Arrest the glass before I can drink?
    Does that solemn ringing already proclaim
    The glorious advent of Holy Week?   520
    Already, choirs, are you intoning
    What angels' lips sang once, a comforting chant,
    Above the sepulcher's darkness sounding,
    Certain assurance of a new covenant?

CHORUS OF WOMEN
      With balm and with spices   525
      We anointed the man,
      We, his true, faithful ones,
      Laid him out in the tomb;
      In linen we wound him
      And bound up his hair—   530
      Oh, what do we find now?
      Christ is not here.

CHORUS OF ANGELS
      Christ is arisen!
      Blest is the man of love,
      He who in triumph passed   535
      The hard, the bitter test,
      Bringing salvation.

FAUST   But why do you seek me out in the dust,
    You music of Heaven, mild and magnificent?
    Ring out where men and women are simple,   540
    I hear your message but lack all belief in it,
    And where belief's lacking, no miracle's possible.
    The spheres whence those glad tidings come
    Are not for me to try and enter—
    Yet all's familiar from when I was young   545
    And back to life I feel myself sent for.
    Years ago the Heavenly Love
    Flew down to me in the Sabbath hush
    And caught me in His strong embrace;
    Oh, with what meaning the deep bells sounded,   550
    Praying to Jesus, oh what bliss!
    A yearning so sweet it was not to be fathomed
    Drove me out to the woods and the fields.
    Inside my soul a new world opened
    And my cheeks were streaming with scalding tears.   555
    Your song gave the signal for the games we rejoiced in
    When the springtime arrived with its gay festival,
    Innocent childhood's remembered feelings
    Hold me back from the last step of all.
    O sound away, sound away, sweet songs of Heaven,   560
    Tears fill my eyes, the earth claims me again!

CHORUS OF DISCIPLES
      He but now buried

Already's ascended,
Who while he dwelt below
Lived most sublimely,   565
Then rose up in glory
So he might share in
The bliss of creation.
But here on earth
We huddle afflicted—   570
He has left us, his children,
To wish for him, wait.
Master, we pity your bitter fate!

CHORUS OF ANGELS
Christ is arisen
From the womb of decay,   575
Strike off your fetters
And shout for joy!
Praise him by sweetest charity,
Loving-kindness, fraternity,
Relieving the least of all,   580
Preaching him east and west to all,
Promising Heaven's bliss to all.
You have the Master near,
You have him here, right here!

OUTSIDE THE CITY GATE

All sorts of people out walking.

SOME APPRENTICES   Where are you fellows off to?   585
OTHERS   To the hunters' lodge—over that way.
FIRST BUNCH   Well, we're on our way to the old mill.
ONE APPRENTICE   The river inn—that's what I say.
SECOND APPRENTICE   But the walk there's not pleasant, I feel.
SECOND BUNCH   And what about you?   590
THIRD APPRENTICE   I'll stick with the rest of us here.
FOURTH APPRENTICE   Let's go up to the village. There, I can promise
    you
   The best-looking girls, the best-tasting beer,
   And some very good roughhousing too.
FIFTH APPRENTICE   My, but aren't you greedy!
   A third bloody nose—don't you care?   595
   I'll never go there, it's too scary.
SERVANT GIRL   No, no, I'm turning back, now let me be.
ANOTHER   We're sure to find him at those poplar trees.
FIRST GIRL   Is that supposed to make me jump for joy?
   It's you he wants to walk with, wants to please,   600
   And you're the one he'll dance with. Fine
   For you. But what's it to me, your good time?
THE OTHER   He's not alone, I know, today. He said

He'd bring his friend—you know, that curlyhead.

A STUDENT   Those fast-stepping girls there, look at the heft of them!   605
   Into action, old fellow, we're taking out after them.
   Beer with body, tobacco with a good sharp taste
   And red-cheeked housemaids in their Sunday best
   Are just the things to make your Hermann happiest.

A BURGHER'S DAUGHTER   Oh look over there, such fine-looking boys!   610
   Really, I think they are so outrageous,
   They have their pick of the nicest girls,
   Instead they run after overweight wenches.

SECOND STUDENT [*To the first*]   Hold up, go slow! I see two more,
   And the pair of them dressed so pretty, so proper.   615
   But I know that one! She lives next door,
   And she, I can tell you, I think I could go for.
   They loiter along, eyes lowered decorously,
   But after saying no twice, they'll jump at our company.

FIRST STUDENT   No, no—all that bowing and scraping, it makes me feel ill
     at ease,   620
   If we don't get a move on we'll lose our two birds in the bushes!
   The work-reddened hand that swings the broom Saturdays
   On Sundays knows how to give the softest caresses.

A BURGHER   No, you can have him, our new Mayor,
   Since he took office he's been a dictator,   625
   All he's done is make the town poorer,
   Every day I get madder and madder,
   When he says a thing's so, not a peep, not a murmur,
   Dare we express—and the taxes climb higher.

A BEGGAR [*Singing.*]
     Good sirs and all you lovely ladies,   630
     Healthy in body and handsome in dress,
     Turn, oh turn your eyes on me, please,
     And pity the beggarman's distress!
     Must I grind the organ fruitlessly,
     Only the charitable know true joy.   635
     This day when all the world make merry,
     Oh make it for me a harvest day.

ANOTHER BURGHER   On a Sunday or holiday nothing in all my experience
   Beats talking about war and rumors of war,
   When leagues away, in Turkey, for instance,   640
   Armies are wading knee deep in gore.
   You stand at the window, take long pulls at your schooner,
   And watch the gaily colored boats glide past,
   And then at sunset go home in the best of humor
   And praise God for the peace by which we're blest.   645

THIRD BURGHER   Yes, neighbor, yes, exactly my opinion.
   Let them go and beat each other's brains in,
   Let them turn the whole world upside down,
   As long as things are just as always here at home.

OLD CRONE [*To the* BURGHERS' DAUGHTERS.]   Well, aren't we the smart ones!
     And so pretty and young!   650

I'd like to see the man who could resist you.
But not so proud, my dears! And never fear—I'm mum.
Oh, I know how to get what you want for you.

BURGHER'S DAUGHTER   Agatha, come, we've got to leave!
I'm afraid of being seen with that witchwoman.   655
Oh dear, and only last St. Andrew's Eve[4]
She showed me in a glass my very own one.

HER FRIEND   And mine she showed me in a crystal sphere
Looking a soldier, with swaggering friends around him,
And though I watch out everywhere,   660
I have no luck, I never seem to find him.

SOLDIERS
    Castles have ramparts,
    Great walls and towers,
    Girls turn their noses up
    At soldier-boy lovers—   665
    We'll make both ours!
    Boldly adventure
    And rake in the pay!

    Hear the shrill bugle
    Summon to battle,   670
    Forward to rapture
    Or forward to ruin!
    Oh what a struggle!
    Our life—oh how stirring!
    Haughty girls, high-walled castles,   675
    We'll make them surrender!
    Boldly adventure
    And rake in the pay!
    —And after, the soldiers
    Go marching away.   680
      [FAUST *and* WAGNER]

FAUST   The streams put off their icy mantle
Under the springtime's kindly smile;
Hope's green banner flies in the valley;
White-bearded winter, old and frail,
Retreats back up into the mountains,   685
And still retreating, down he sends
Feeble volleys of sleet showers,
Whitening in patches the green plains.
But the sun can bear with white no longer,
When life stirs, shaping all anew,   690
He wants a scene that has some color,
And since there's nowhere yet one flower,
Holiday crowds have got to do.

---

4. November 29, the traditional time for young girls to consult fortune-tellers about their future lovers or husbands.

Now face about, and looking down
From the hilltop back to town,   695
See the brightly colored crowd
Pouring like a spring flood
Through the gaping, gloomy arch
To bask in the sun all love so much.
They celebrate the Savior's Rising,   700
For they themselves are risen:
From airless rooms in huddled houses,
From drudgery at counters and benches,
From under cumbrous roofs and gables,
From crowded, suffocating alleys,   705
From the mouldering dimness of the churches,
All are brought forth into brightness.
And look there, how the eager crowd
Scatters through the fields and gardens.
How over the river's length and breadth   710
Skiffs and sculls are busily darting,
And that last boat, packed near to sinking,
Already's pulled a good ways off.
Even from distant mountain slopes
Bright colored clothes wink back at us.   715
Now I can hear it, the village commotion,
Out here, you can tell, is the people's true heaven,
Young and old crying exultingly:
Here I am human, here I can be free.

WAGNER To go for a walk with you, dear Doctor,   720
Is a treat for my mind as well as honoring me;
But by myself I'd never come near here,
For I can't abide the least vulgarity.
The fiddling, the shrieking, the clashing bowls
For me are all an unbearable uproar,   725
All scream and shout like possessed souls
And call it music, call it pleasure.

PEASANTS [Singing and dancing under the linden tree.]
The shepherd dressed up in his best,
Pantaloons and flowered vest,
    Oh my, how brave and handsome!   730
Within the broad-leaved linden's shade
Madly spun both man and maid,
        Hooray, hooray,
        Hurrah, hurrah, hooray!
The fiddle bow flew, and then some.   735
He flung himself into their midst
And seized a young thing round the waist,
    While saying, "Care to dance, ma'am?"
The snippy miss she tossed her head,
"You boorish shepherd boy!" she said,   740
    Hooray, hooray,
    Hurrah, hurrah, hooray!
"Observe, do, some decorum!"

But round the circle swiftly wheeled,
To right and left the dancers whirled,   745
   Till all the breath flew from them.
They got so red, they got so warm,
They rested, panting, arm in arm,
     Hooray, hooray,
      Hurrah, hurrah, hooray!   750
And breast to breast—a twosome.

"I'll thank you not to make so free!
We girls know well how men betray,
   What snakes lurk in your bosom!"
But still he wheedled her away—   755
Far off they heard the fiddles play,
     Hooray, hooray,
      Hurrah, hurrah, hooray!
   The shouting, uproar, bedlam.

OLD PEASANT   Professor, it's so good of you   760
  To join us common folk today,
Though such a wise and learned man,
Not to scorn our holiday.
So please accept our best cup, sir,
Brimful with the freshest beer;   765
We hope that it will quench your thirst,
But more than that, we pray and hope
Your sum of days may be increased
By as many drops as fill the cup!
FAUST   Friends, thanks for this refreshment, I   770
  In turn wish you all health and joy.
     [*The people make a circle around him.*]
OLD PEASANT   Indeed it's only right that you
  Should be with us this happy day,
Who when our times were bitter, proved
Himself our friend in every way.   775
Many a one stands in his boots here
Whom your good father, the last minute,
Snatched from the hot grip of the fever,
That time he quelled the epidemic.[5]
And you yourself, a youngster then,   780
Never shrank back; every house
The pest went in, you did too.
Out they carried many a corpse,
But never yours. Much you went through;
Us you saved, and God saved you.   785
ALL   Health to our tried and trusty friend,
  And may he help us yet again.

5. Pestilence or plague.

FAUST Bow down to him who dwells above,
    Whose love shows us how we should love.
       [He continues on with WAGNER.]

WAGNER   The gratification you must get from all of this,   790
    From knowing the reverence these people hold you in!
    The man whose gifts can gain him such advantages,
    Oh, he's a lucky one in my opinion.
    Who is it, each one asks as he runs to see,
    Fathers point you out to their boys,   795
    The fiddle stops, the dancers pause,
    And as you pass between the rows
    Of people, caps fly in the air, why,
    Next you know they'll all be on their knees
    As if the Host itself[6] were passing by.   800
FAUST   A few steps more to that rock where we'll rest
    A bit, shall we, from our walk. How often
    I would sit alone here thinking, thinking,
    And torture myself with praying hard and fasting.
    So much hope I had then, such great trust—   805
    I'd wring my hands, I'd weep, fall on my knees,
    Believing in this way the Lord being forced
    To look below, would cry halt to the disease.
    But now these people's generous praises are
    A mockery to me. If only you could peer   810
    Into my heart, you'd realize
    How little worthy father and son were really.
      My father was an upright man, a lonely,
    Brooding soul who searched great Nature's processes
    With a head crammed full of the most bizarre hypotheses.   815
    Shutting himself with fellow masters up in
    The vaulted confines of their vaporous Black Kitchen,
    He mixed together opposites according
    To innumerable recipes. A bold Red Lion,
    Handsome suitor he, took for wedding   820
    Partner a pure White Lily, the two uniting
    In a tepid bath; then being tested by fire,
    The pair precipitately fled
    From one bridal chamber to another,
    Till there appeared within the glass   825
    The young Queen, dazzlingly dressed
    In every color of the spectrum:
    The Sovereign Remedy—a futile nostrum.
    The patients died; none stopped to inquire
    How many there were who'd got better.[7]   830
      So with our infernal electuary
    We killed our way across the country.

---

6. The Eucharist, the consecrated bread and wine of the Sacrament.   7. This confusing sequence
evokes a kind of medicine closely allied to magic and inappropriate for the ill seeking help.

I poisoned, myself, by prescription, thousands,
They sickened and faded; yet I must live to see
On every side the murderers' fame emblazoned.   835
WAGNER   But why be so distressed, there is no reason.
If an honest man with conscientious devotion
Practises the arts his forebears practised,
It's understandable, it's what's to be expected.
A youth who is respectful of his father   840
Listens and soaks up all he has to teach;
If the grown man's able to lengthen science's reach,
His son in turn can reach goals even farther.
FAUST   Oh, he's a happy man who hopes
To keep from drowning in these seas of error!   845
What we know least about, we need the most,
And what we do know, is no use whatever.
      But we mustn't poison with our gloomy thoughts
The sweetness of the present hour!
Look how the sunset's level rays   850
Gild those cottages in their green bower,
The day fades quietly, the sun departs,
Hurrying off to kindle new life elsewhere—
If only I had wings to bear me up
Into the air and follow after!   855
Then I would see the whole world at my feet.
Quietly shining in the eternal sunset,
The peaks ablaze, the valleys gone to sleep,
And every silver stream a golden current.
The savage mountain with its plunging cliffs   860
Should never balk my godlike soaring,
And there's the ocean, see, already swelling
Before my wondering gaze, with its sun-warmed gulfs.
But finally the bright god looks like sinking,
Whereupon a renewed urgency   865
Drives me on to drink his eternal light,
The day always before, behind the night,
The heavens overhead, below the heaving sea . . .

      A lovely dream!—and meanwhile it grows dark.
Oh dear, oh dear, that our frames should lack   870
Wings with which to match the spirit's soaring.
Still our nature's such that all of us
Know feelings that strive upwards, always straining,
When high above, lost in the azure emptiness,
The skylark pours out his shrill rhapsody,   875
When over fir-clad mountain peaks
The eagle on his broad wings gyres silently,
And passing over prairies, over lakes,
The homeward-bound crane labors steadily.
WAGNER   Well, I've had more than one odd moment, I have,   880

But I have never felt those impulses you have.
Soon enough you get your fill of woods and things,
I don't really envy birds their wings.
How different are the pleasures of the intellect,
Sustaining one from page to page, from book to book,   885
And warming winter nights with dear employment
And with the consciousness your life's so lucky.
And goodness, when you spread out an old parchment,
Heaven's fetched straight down into your study.

FAUST   You know the one great driving force,   890
May you never know the other!
Two souls live in me, alas,
Forever warring with each other.
One, amorous of the world, with all its might
Grapples it close, greedy of all its pleasures;   895
The other fights to rise out of the dirt,
Up, up into the heaven of our great forebears.

You beings of the air, if such exist,
Holding sway between the skies and earth,
Come down to me out of the golden mist   900
And translate me to a new, a vivid life!
Oh, if I only had a magic mantle
To bear me off to unknown lands,
I'd never trade it for the costliest gowns,
Or for a cloak however rich and royal.   905

WAGNER   Never call them down, the dreadful swarm
That swoops and hovers through the atmosphere,
Bringing mankind every kind of harm
From every corner of the terrestrial sphere.
From the North they bare their razor teeth   910
And prick you with their arrow-pointed tongues,
From the East, sighing with parched breath,
They eat away your dessicated lungs;
And when from Southern wastes they gust and sough,
Fire on fire on your sunk head heaping,   915
From the West they send for your relief
Cooling winds—then drown fields just prepared for reaping.
Their ears are cocked, on trickery intent,
Seem dutiful while scheming to defeat us,
Their pretense is that they are heaven-sent   920
And lisp like angels even as they cheat us.
  However, come, let's go, the world's turned gray
And chilly, evening mists are rising!
At nightfall it's indoors you want to be.
But why should you stand still, astonished, staring?   925
What can you see in the dusk to find upsetting?

FAUST   Don't you see that black dog in the stubble,
Coursing back and forth?

WAGNER   I do. I noticed him.
  A while back. What about him?
FAUST   Look again.
  What kind of creature is it?   930
WAGNER   Kind? A poodle—
  Worried where his master is, and always
  Sniffing about to find his scent.
FAUST   Look, he's
  Circling around us, coming nearer and nearer.
  Unless I'm much mistaken, a wake of fire
  Is streaming after him.   935
WAGNER   I see nothing
  But a black-haired poodle. Your eyes are playing
  Tricks on you, perhaps.
FAUST   I think I see
  Him winding a magic snare, quietly,
  Around our feet, a noose which he'll pull tight
  In the future, when the time is right.   940
WAGNER   He's circling us because he's timid and uncertain;
  He's missed his master, come on men unknown to him.
FAUST   The circle's getting tighter, he's much closer!
WAGNER   You see!—a dog, it's no ghost, sir.
  He growls suspiciously, he hesitates,   945
  He wags his tail, lies down and waits.
  Never fear, it's all just dog behavior.
FAUST   Come here, doggie, here, to us!
WAGNER   A silly poodle, a poor creature,
  When you stop, he stops too at once,   950
  Speak to him, he'll leap and bark,
  Throw something and he'll fetch it back,
  Go after your stick right into the river.
FAUST   I guess you're right, it's just what he's been taught;
  I see no sign of anything occult.   955
WAGNER   A dog so good, so well-behaved by nature—
  Why, even a philosopher would like him.
  Some students trained him, found him an apt scholar—
  Sir, he deserves you should adopt him.
        [*They enter at the City Gate.*]

FAUST'S STUDY [I]

FAUST [*Entering with the poodle.*]
  Behind me lie the fields and meadows   960
  Shrouded in the lowering dark,
  In dread of what waits in the shadows
  Our better soul now starts awake.
  Our worser one, unruly, reckless,
  Quietens and starts to nod;   965
  In me the love of my own fellows

Begins to stir, and the love of God.

Poodle, stop! How you race round! A dozen
Dogs you seem. Why all that sniffing at the door?
Here's my best cushion, it's yours to doze on,   970
Behind the stove, there on the floor.
Just now when we came down the hillside
We found you a charming, playful beast.
I'm glad to welcome you in here, provide
Your keep—as long as you're a silent guest.   975

When once again the lamp light brightens
With its soft glow your narrow cell,
Oh then it lightens in your bosom,
And deeper in your heart as well.
Again you hear the voice of reason,   980
And hope revives, it breathes afresh,
You long to drink the living waters,
Mount upwards to our being's source.

You're growling, poodle! Animal squealings
Hardly suit the exalted feelings   985
Filling my soul to overflowing.
We're used to people ridiculing
What they hardly understand,
Grumbling at the good and beautiful—
It makes them so uncomfortable!   990
Do dogs now emulate mankind?
    Yet even with the best of will
I feel my new contentment fail.
Why must the waters cease so soon
And leave us thirsting once again?   995
Oh, this has happened much too often!
But there's an answer to it all:
I mean the supernatural,
I mean our hope of revelation,
Which nowhere shines so radiant   1000
As here in the New Testament.
I'll look right now at the original[8]
And see if it is possible
For me to make a true translation
Into my beloved German.   1005
    [*He opens the volume and begins.*]
"In the beginning was the Word"[9]—so goes
The text. And right off I am given pause!
A little help, please, someone, I'm unable
To see the *word* as first, most fundamental.
If I am filled with the true spirit   1010

8. That is, the Greek.   9. John 1.1.

I'll find a better way to say it.
So: "In the beginning *mind* was"—right?
Give plenty of thought to what you write,
Lest your pen prove too impetuous:
Is it mind that makes and moves the universe?   1015
Shouldn't it be: "In the beginning
Power was, before it nothing"?
Yet even as I write this down on paper
Something tells me don't stop there, go further.
The Spirit's prompt in aid; now, now, indeed   1020
I know for sure: "In the beginning was the *deed*!"

If this cell's one that we'll be sharing,
Poodle, stop that barking, yelping!
You're giving me a splitting headache,
I can't put up with such a roommate.   1025
I'm sorry to say that one of us
Has got to quit the premises.
It goes against the grain with me
To renege on hospitality,
But there's the door, dog, leave, goodbye.   1030

But what the devil's happening?
What I see's beyond belief!
Is it real, that monstrous thing?
My poodle's swelled up bigger than life!
Now he's heaving up his bulk—   1035
That's no dog, that great hulk!
What a dreadful spook I've brought
Into my house without a thought.
He looks, with his fierce eyes and jaws,
Just like a hippopotamus—   1040
But I have got you in my power!
With a demi-imp of Hell, as you are,
Solomon's Key[1] is what is called for.

SPIRITS [*Outside the door.*]
     Someone is locked in there!
     No one's allowed in there!   1045
     Like a fox hunters snared,
     Old Scratch, he shivers, scared.
     Be careful, watch out!
     Hover this way, now that,
     About and again about,   1050
     You'll soon find he's got out.
     If you can help him,
     Don't let him sit there,
     All of us owe him
     For many a favor.   1055

---

1. The *Clavicula Salomonis*, a standard work used by magicians for conjuring. In many medieval legends, Solomon was noted as a great magician.

FAUST   Against such a creature, my first defense:
  The Spell of the Four Elements.

> Salamander glow hot,
> Undine, undulate,
> Sylph, melt away quick,   1060
> Kobold,[2] off to work.

Ignorance
Of the elements,
Their powers and properties,
Denies you all mastery   1065
Over the demonry.

> Vanish in flames,
> Salamander!
> Undine, make babbling streams
> All flow together!   1070

> Glitter meteor-beauteous,
> Aërial Sylph!
> Give household help to us,
> Incubus! Incubus!
> Come out, come out, enough's enough.   1075

None of the four
Is in the cur.
Calmly he lies there, grinning at me,
My spells glance off him harmlessly.
   Now hear me conjure   1080
With something stronger.

> Are you, grim fellow,
> Escaped here from Hell below?
> Then look at this symbol
> Before which the legions   1085
> Of devils and demons
> Fearfully bow.

How his hair bristles, how he swells up now!

> Creature cast into darkness,
> Can you make out its meaning?   1090
> The never-begotten One.
> Wholly ineffable One,
> Cruelly pierced in the side One,
> Whose blood in the heavens
> Is everywhere streaming?   1095

2. A spirit of the earth. "Salamander": spirit of fire. "Undine": spirit of water. "Sylph": spirit of air.

Behind the stove, captive, the miscreant
Puffs himself up big as an elephant,
Filling the whole chamber
Disappearing into vapor.
—Now don't you try going through the ceiling!   1100
Down at my feet, do your master's bidding!
You see, my threats are scarcely idle—
With fire I'll rout you out, yes I will!
Wait if you wish,
For my triune[3] light's hot flash,   1105
Wait till you force me
To employ my most potent sorcery.

> [*The smoke clears, and* MEPHISTOPHELES, *dressed as an itinerant student, emerges from behind the stove.*]

MEPHISTO   Why all the racket? What's your wish, sir?
FAUST   So it's you who was the poodle!
   I have to laugh—a wandering scholar!   1110
MEPHISTO   My greetings to you, learned doctor,
   You really had me sweating hard there.
FAUST   And what's your name?
MEPHISTO   Your question's trivial
   From one who finds words superficial,
   Who strives to pass beyond mere seeming   1115
   And penetrate the heart of being.[4]
FAUST   With gentry like yourself, it's common
   To find the name declares what you are
   Very plainly. I'll just mention
   Lord of the Flies,[5] Destroyer, Liar.   1120
   So say who are you, if you would.
MEPHISTO   A humble part of that great power
   Which always means evil, always does good.
FAUST   Those ridding words mean what, I'd like to know.
MEPHISTO   I am the spirit that says no,   1125
   No always! And how right I am! For surely
   It's only fitting everything that comes to be
   Should cease to be. And so they do.
   Still better yet that nothing ever was. Hence sin,
   Destruction, ruin—all you call evil, in sum—   1130
   For me's the element that I swim in.
FAUST   A part, you say? You look like the whole works to me.
MEPHISTO   I say what's so, it isn't modesty—
   Man in his world of self's a fool,
   He likes to think he's all in all.   1135
   I'm part of the part which was all at first,
   A part of the dark from which light burst forth,
   Arrogant light which now usurps the air

---

3. Perhaps the Trinity or a triangle with divergent rays.   4. Mephistopheles refers to Faust's substitution of *Act* for *Word* in the passage from John (see line 1005).   5. An almost literal translation of the name of the Philistine deity Beelzebub.

And seeks to thrust Night from her ancient chair,
To no avail. Since light is one with all   1140
Things bodily, making them beautiful,
Streams from them, from them is reflected,
Since light by matter's manifested—
When by degrees all matter's burnt up and no more,
Why, then light shall not matter any more.   1145
FAUST   Oh, now I understand your office:
   Since you can't wreck Creation wholesale,
   You're going at it bit by bit, retail.
MEPHISTO   And making little headway, I confess.
   The opposite of nothing-at-all,   1150
   The *something*, this great shambling world,
   In spite of how I exert myself against it,
   Phlegmatically endures my every onset
   By earthquake, fire, tidal wave and storm:
   Next day the land and sea again are calm.   1155
   And all that *stuff*, those animal and human species—
   I can hardly make a dent in them.
   The numbers I've already buried, armies!
   Yet fresh troops keep on marching up again.
   That's how it is, it's enough to drive you crazy!   1160
   From air, from water, from the earth
   Seeds innumerable sprout forth
   In dry and wet and cold and warm!
   If I hadn't kept back fire for myself,
   What the devil could I call my own?   1165
FAUST   So against the good, the never-resting,
   All-powerful creative force
   In impotent spite you raise your fist and
   Try to arrest life's onward course?
   Look around for work that's more rewarding,   1170
   You singular son of old Chaos!
MEPHISTO   Well, it's a subject for discussion—
   At our next meeting. Now I wish
   To go. That is, with your permission.
FAUST   But why should *you* ask *me* for leave?   1175
   We've struck up an acquaintance, we two,
   Drop in on me whenever you please.
   There's the door and there's the window,
   And ever reliable, there's the chimney.
MEPHISTO   Well . . . you see . . . an obstacle   1180
   Keeps me from dropping *out*—so sorry!
   That witch's foot chalked on your doorsill.
FAUST   The pentagram's[6] the difficulty?
   But if it's that that has you stopped,
   How did you ever manage an entry?   1185
   And how should a devil like you get trapped?

---

6. A magic five-pointed star designed to keep away evil spirits.

MEPHISTO   Well, look close and you'll see that
   A corner's open: the outward pointing
   Angle's lines don't quite meet.
FAUST   What a stroke of luck! I'm thinking   1190
   Now you are my prisoner.
   Pure chance has put you in my power!
MEPHISTO   The poodle dashed right in, saw nothing;
   But now the case is the reverse:
   The Devil can't get out of the house!   1195
FAUST   There's the window, why don't you use it?
MEPHISTO   It's an iron law we devils can't flout,
   The way we come in, we've got to go out,
   We're free as to entrée, but not as to exit.
FAUST   So even in Hell there's law and order!   1200
   I'm glad, for then a man might sign
   A contract with you gentlemen.
MEPHISTO   Whatever we promise, you get, full measure,
   There's no cutting corners, no skulduggery—
   But it's not a thing to be done in a hurry;   1205
   Let's save the subject for our next get-together.
   And as for now, I beg you earnestly,
   Release me from the spell that binds me!
FAUST   Why rush off, stay a while, do.
   I'd love to hear some more from you.   1210
MEPHISTO   Let me go now. I swear I'll come back,
   Then you can ask me whatever you like.
FAUST   Don't blame me because you're caught;
   You trapped yourself, it's your own fault.
   Who's nabbed the Devil must keep a tight grip,   1215
   You don't grab him again once he gives you the slip.
MEPHISTO   Oh, all right! To please you I
   Will stay and keep you company;
   Provided with my arts you let me
   Entertain you in my own way.   1220
FAUST   Delighted, go ahead. But please
   Make sure those arts of yours amuse!
MEPHISTO   You'll find, my friend, your senses, in one hour,
   More teased and roused than all the long dull year.
   The songs the fluttering spirits murmur in your ear,   1225
   The visions they unfold of sweet desire,
   Oh they are more than just tricks meant to fool.
   By Arabian scents you'll be delighted,
   Your palate tickled, never sated,
   The ravishing sensations you will feel!   1230
   No preparation's needed, none.
   Here we are. Let the show begin!
SPIRITS   Open, you gloomy
     Vaulted ceiling above him,
     Let the blue ether   1235
     Look benignly in on him,

And dark cloudbanks scatter
So that all is fair for him!
Starlets are glittering,
Milder suns glowing,   1240
Angelic troops shining
In celestial beauty
Hover past smiling,
Swaying and stooping.
Ardent desire   1245
Follows them yearning;
And their robes streaming ribbons
Veil the fields, veil the meadows,
Veil the arbors where lovers
In pensive surrender   1250
Give themselves to each other
For ever and ever.
Arbor on arbor!
Vines clambering and twining!
Their heavy clusters,   1255
Poured into presses,
Pour out purple wines
Which descend in dark streams
Over beds of bright stones
Down the vineyards' steep slopes   1260
To broaden to lakes
At the foot of green hills.
Birds blissfully drink there,
With beating wings sunwards soar,
Soar towards the golden isles   1265
Shimmering hazily
On the horizon;
Where we hear voices
Chorusing jubilantly,
Where we see dancers   1270
Whirling exuberantly
Over the meadows,
Here, there and everywhere.
Some climb the heights,
Some swim in the lakes,   1275
Others float in the air—
Joying in life, all,
Beneath the paradisal
Stars glowing with love
Afar in the distance.   1280
MEPHISTO   Asleep! Oh bravely done, my airy younglings!
How duly to his slumbers you have sung him!
I am in your debt for this performance.
—As for you, sir, you were never born
To keep the Prince of Darkness down!   1285
Weave a net of sweet dreams all about him,

Drown him in a deep sea of delusion.
But to break the spell that holds me here,
A rat's tooth is what I require.
No need for conjuring long-windedly—   1290
Listen! I hear a rat rustling already.

The lord of flies and rats and mice,
Of frogs and bedbugs, worms and lice,
Commands you forth from your dark hole
To gnaw, beast, for me that doorsill   1295
Whereon I dab this drop of oil!
—And there you are! Begin, begin!
The corner that is pointing in,
That's the one that shuts me in;
One last crunch to clear my way: 1300
Now Faustus, till we meet next—dream away!
FAUST [*Awakening*.]   Deceived again, am I, by tricks,
Those vanished spirits just a hoax,
A dream the Devil, nothing more,
The dog I took home just a cur?   1305

FAUST'S STUDY [II]

FAUST, MEPHISTOPHELES.

FAUST   A knock, was that? Come in! Who is it this time?
MEPHISTO   Me.
FAUST   Come in!
MEPHISTO   You have to say it still a third time.
FAUST   All right, all right—come in!
MEPHISTO   Good, very good!
We two will get along, I see, just as we should.
I've come here dressed up as a grandee.[7] Why?   1310
To help you drive your blues away!
In a scarlet suit, all over gold braid,
Across my shoulders a stiff silk cape,
A gay cock's feather in my cap,
At my side a gallant's long blade—   1315
And bringing you advice that's short and sweet:
Put fine clothes on like me, cut loose a bit,
Be free and easy, man, throw off your yoke
And find out what real life is like.
FAUST   In any clothes, I'd feel the misery   1320
Of this cramped, suffocating life on earth.
I'm too old to live for amusement only,
Too young to live without desire or wish.
The world—what has it got to say to me?

---

7. In the popular plays based on the Faust legend, the Devil often appeared as a monk when the play catered to a Protestant audience and as a noble squire when the audience was mainly Catholic.

Renounce all that you long for, all—renounce!   1325
That's the everlasting song-and-dance
You are greeted by on every side,
The croak you hear year in, year out;
You can't have what you want, you can't!
I awake each morning, how? Horrified,   1330
On the verge of tears, to confront a day
Which at its close will not have satisfied
One smallest wish of mine, not one. Why,
Even the hope of a bit of pleasure, some pleasantness,
Withers in the atmosphere of mean-spirited fault-finding;   1335
My nature's active inventiveness
Is thwarted daily by endless interfering.
And when the night draws on and all is hushed,
I go to bed not soothed at last but apprehensively,
Well knowing what awaits me is not rest,   1340
But wild and whirling dreams that terrify me.
The god who thrones inside my bosom,
Able to shake me to the depths, so powerfully,
The lord and master of all my energies,
Is impotent to effect a single thing outside me;   1345
And so I find existence burdensome, wretched,
Death eagerly desired, my life hated.
MEPHISTO Yet the welcome men give death is never wholehearted.
FAUST Happy the man, even as he conquers gloriously,
Upon whose brow death sets the blood-stained laurel!   1350
Happy the man, after dancing the night through furiously,
Whom it finds out in the white arms of a girl!
If only, overwhelmed by the Spirit's power,
In raptures, I had died right then and there!
MEPHISTO And yet that very night, I seem to remember,   1355
A fellow didn't down a drink he'd prepared.
FAUST Spying around, I see, is what you like to do.
MEPHISTO I don't know everything, but I know a thing or two.
FAUST If a sweet, familiar strain of music,
When I was staggering, steadied me,   1360
Beguiled what's left of childhood feeling
With echoes of a happier day—
Well, never again! I pronounce a curse on
All tales that snare and cheat the soul,
All false and flattering persuasion   1365
That ties it to this *corpus vile*.
First I curse man's mind, for thinking
Much too well of itself; I curse
The show of things, so dazzling, glittering,
That assails us through our every sense;   1370
Our dreams of fame, of our name's enduring,
Oh what a sham, I curse them too;
I curse as hollow all our having,
Curse wife and child, peasant and plow;

I curse Mammon[8] when he incites us   1375
With dreams of treasure to reckless deeds,
Or plumps the cushions for our pleasure
As we lie lazily at ease;
Curse comfort sucked out of the grape,
Curse love on its pinnacle of bliss,   1380
Curse faith, so false, curse all vain hope,
And patience most of all I curse!

SPIRIT CHORUS [*Invisible.*]
          Oh, what a pity,
          Now you've destroyed it!
          The world once so lovely,   1385
          How you have wrecked it!
          Down it goes, smashed
          By a demigod's fist!
          Out of existence
          We sweep its poor remnants,   1390
          Sorrowing over
          Beauty now lost forever.
          —Then build again, better,
          Potent son of the earth,
          Build a new world, a fairer,   1395
          Inside your own self,
          Within your own heart!
          With a mind clear and strong,
          On your lips a new song,
          Come, make a fresh start!   1400

MEPHISTO   Do you hear them, my angels,
    My dear little wise ones,
    Sagely advising you
    To do things, be cheerful?
    Their wish is to draw you   1405
    Out of the shell you're shut up in,
    Out of your torpid stagnation
    Into the wide world before you.

    Stop making love to your misery,
    It gnaws away at you like a vulture;   1410
    Even in the meanest company
    You'd feel yourself a man like any other.
    Not that I'm advising you
    To mingle with the hoi poloi;
    Among demons I am not a V.I.P.,   1415
    But still, if you'll throw in with me,
    I'll walk beside you life's long route,
    Your good companion. If I suit,
    I'm ready to serve you hand and foot.

---

8. The Aramaic word for "riches," used in the New Testament of the Bible. Medieval writers interpreted the word as a proper noun, the name of the Devil, as representing greed.

FAUST   And in return what must I do?   1420
MEPHISTO   There's plenty of time for that, forget it.
FAUST   No, no, the Devil must have his due,
  He doesn't do things for the hell of it,
  Just to see another fellow through.
  So let's hear the terms, what the fine print is;   1425
  Having you for a servant's a tricky business.
MEPHISTO   I promise I will serve your wishes—here,
  A slave who'll do your bidding faithfully;
  But if we meet each other—there,
  Why, you must do the same for me.   1430
FAUST   That "there" of yours—it doesn't scare me off;
  If you pull this world down about my ears,
  Let the other one come on, who cares?
  My joys are part and parcel of this earth,
  It's under this sun that I suffer,   1435
  And once it's goodbye and I've left them
  Then let whatever happens happen,
  And that is that. About the hereafter
  We have had enough palaver,
  More than I want to hear, by far: 1440
  If still we love and hate each other,
  If some stand high and some stand lower,
  Et cetera, et cetera.
MEPHISTO   In that case an agreement's easy.
  Come, dare it! Come, your signature!   1445
  Oh, how my tricks will tickle your fancy!
  I'll show you things no man has seen before.
FAUST   You poor devil, really, what have you got to offer?
  The mind of man in its sublime endeavor,
  Tell me, have you ever understood it?   1450
  Oh yes indeed, you've bread, and when I eat it
  I'm hungry still; you've yellow gold, like yellow sand
  It runs away fast through the hand;
  Games of chance no man can win at ever;
  Girls who wind me in their arms, their lover,   1455
  While eyeing up a fresh one over my shoulder;
  There's fame, last failing of a noble nature;
  It shoots across the sky a second, then it's over—
  Oh yes, do show me fruit that rots as you try
  To pick it, trees whose leaves bud daily, daily die!   1460
MEPHISTO   Marvels like that? For a devil, not so daunting.
  I'm good for whatever you have in mind.
  —But friend, the day comes when you find
  A share of your own in life's good things,
  And peace and quiet, are what you're wanting.   1465
FAUST   If ever you see me loll at ease,
  Then it's all yours, you can have it, my life!
  If ever you fool me with flatteries
  Into feeling satisfied with myself,
  Or tempt me with visions of luxuries,   1470

That day's the last my voice on earth is heard,
I'll bet you!
MEPHISTO   Done! A bet!
FAUST   A bet—agreed!
  If ever I plead with the passing moment,
  "Linger awhile, you are so fair!"
  Then shut me up in close confinement,   1475
  I'll gladly breathe the air no more!
  Then let the death bell toll my finis,
  Then you are free of all your service,
  The clock may stop, hands break, fall off,
  And time for me be over with.   1480
MEPHISTO   Think twice. Forgetting's not a thing we do.
FAUST   Of course, quite right—a bet's a bet.
  This isn't anything I'm rushing into.
  But if I stagnate, fall into a rut,
  I'm a slave, it doesn't matter who to,   1485
  To this one, that one, or to you.
MEPHISTO   My service starts now—no procrastinating!—
  At the dinner tonight for the just-made Ph.D.s.
  But there's one thing: you know, for emergencies,
  I'd like to have our arrangement down in writing.   1490
FAUST   In black and white you want it! Oh, what pedantry!
  You've never learnt a *man's* word's your best guarantee?
  It's not enough for you that I'm committed
  By what I promise till the end of days?
  —Yet the world's a flood sweeps all along before it,   1495
  And why should I feel my word must hold always?
  A strange idea, but that's the way we are,
  And who would want it otherwise?
  That man's blessed who keeps his conscience clear,
  He'll regret no sacrifice.   1500
  But parchment signed and stamped and sealed,
  Is a bogey all recoil from, scared.
  The pen does in the living word,
  Only sealing wax and vellum count, honor must yield.
  Base spirit, say what you require!   1505
  Brass or marble, parchment or paper?
  Shall I write with quill, with stylus, chisel,
  I leave it up to you, you devil!
MEPHISTO   Why get so hot, make extravagant speeches?
  Ranting away does no good.   1510
  A scrap of paper takes care of the business.
  And sign it with a drop of blood.
FAUST   Oh, all right. If that's what makes you happy,
  I'll go along with the useless comedy.
MEPHISTO   Blood's a very special ink, you know.   1515
FAUST   Are you afraid that I won't keep our bargain?
  Till doomsday I will strive, I'll never slacken!
  So I've promised, that's what I will do.

I had ideas too big for me,
Your level's mine, that's all I'm good for.   1520
The Spirit laughed derisively,
Nature won't allow me near her.
With thinking, speculating, I'm through,
Learning and knowledge have sickened me.
—Then let's unloose our passions, dive into   1525
The depths of sensuality!
Bring on your miracles, each one,
Worked by inscrutable sorcery!
We'll plunge into time's racing current,
The vortex of activity,   1530
Where pleasure and distress,
Setbacks and success,
May come as they come, by turn-about, however;
To be always up and doing is man's nature.
MEPHISTO Try this, sample that, you're free, man, we impose no   1535
    limitations,
Whatever you like, snatch it up on the run,
And may they agree with you, all your pleasant diversions!
Only don't be bashful, wade right in.
FAUST I told you, I'm not out to enjoy myself, have fun,
I want frenzied excitements, gratifications that are painful,   1540
Love and hatred violently mixed,
Anguish that enlivens, inspiriting trouble.
Cured of my thirst to know at last,
I'll never again shun anything distressful;
From now on my wish is to undergo   1545
All that men everywhere undergo, their whole portion,
Make mine their heights and depths, their weal and woe,
Everything human embrace in my single person,
And so enlarge my soul to encompass all humanity,
And shipwreck with them when all shipwreck finally.   1550
MEPHISTO Believe me, I have chewed away in vain
At that tough meat, mankind, since long ago,
From birth to death's by far too short a time
For any man to digest such a lump of sourdough!
Only a God can take in all of them,   1555
The whole lot. For He dwells in eternal light,
While we poor devils are stuck down below
In darkness and gloom, lacking even candlelight,
And all *you* qualify for is, half day, half night.
FAUST Nevertheless I will!   1560
MEPHISTO   Bravely proclaimed!
Still, there's one thing worries me.
The time allotted you is very short,
But art has always been around and shall be,
So listen, hear what is my thought:
Hire a poet, learn by his instruction.   1565
Let the good gentleman rove through

All the realm of imagination,
And every noble attribute and virtue
He discovers, heap on you, his inspired creation:
    The lion's fierceness,   1570
    Mild hart's swiftness,
    Italian fieriness,
    Northern steadiness.
Let your poet solve that old conundrum,
How to be generous and also cunning;   1575
How, driven by youthful impulsiveness, unrestrained,
To fall in love as beforehand planned.
Such a creature—my, I'd love to know him!—
I'd call him Mr. Microcosm.
FAUST   What am I, then, if it can never be: 1580
The realization of all human possibility,
That crown my soul so avidly reaches for?
MEPHISTO   In the end you are—just what you are.
Wear wigs high-piled with curls, oh thousands,
Stick your legs in yard-high hessians,   1585
You're still you, the one you always were.
FAUST   I feel it now, how pointless my long grind
To make mine all the treasures of man's mind;
When I sit back and interrogate my soul,
No new powers answer to my call;   1590
I'm not a hair's breadth more in height,
A step nearer to the infinite.
MEPHISTO   Your understanding, my dear Faust,
Is commonplace, I must say vulgar,
We've got to understand things better   1595
Or lose our seat at life's rich feast.
Hell, man, you have hands and feet,
A headpiece and a pair of balls;
And pleasures freshly savored, don't
You have them too? They're no less yours.   1600
If I can keep six spanking stallions,
That horsepower's mine, my property,
My coach bowls on, ain't I the fellow,
Two dozen legs I've got for me!
    Sir, come on, quit all that thinking,   1605
Into the world, the pair of us!
The man who lives in his head only's
Like a donkey in the rough
Led round and round by the bad fairies,
While green grass grows a stone's throw off.   1610
FAUST   And how do we begin?
MEPHISTO   By clearing out—just leaving.
A torture chamber, that's what this place is!
You call it living, to be boring
Yourself and your young men to death?
Leave that to Dr. Bacon Fat next door!   1615

Why toil and moil at threshing heaps of straw?
Anyhow, the deepest knowledge you possess
You daren't let on to before your class.
—Oh now I hear one in the passageway!
FAUST   I can't see him—tell him to go away.   1620
MEPHISTO   The poor boy's been so patient, don't be cross;
We mustn't let him leave here *désolé*.
Let's have your cap and gown, Herr Doctor.
Won't I look the fine professor!
        [*Changes clothes.*]
Count on me to know just what to say!   1625
Fifteen minutes's all I need for it—
Meanwhile get ready for our little junket!

                                                                [*Exit* FAUST.]

MEPHISTO [*Wearing* FAUST's *gown.*]   Despise learning, heap
        contempt on reason,
The human race's best possession,
Only let the lying spirit draw you   1630
Over into mumbo-jumbo,
Make-believe and pure illusion—
And then you're mine for sure, I have you,
No matter what we just agreed to.
Fate's given him a spirit knows no measure,   1635
On and on it strives relentlessly,
It soars away disdaining every pleasure,
Yet I will lead him deep into debauchery
Where all proves shallow, meaningless,
Till he is limed and thrashes wildly, stuck;   1640
Before his greedy insatiableness
I'll dangle food and drink; he'll shriek
In vain for relief from his torturing dryness!
And even if he weren't the Devil's already,
He'd still be sure to perish miserably.   1645
        [*Enter a* STUDENT.]
STUDENT   Allow me, sir, but I am a beginner
And come in quest of an adviser,
One whom all the people here
Greatly esteem, indeed revere.
MEPHISTO   I thank you for your courtesy.   1650
But I'm a man, as you can see,
Like any other. Perhaps you should look further.
STUDENT   It's you, sir, you, I want for adviser!
I came here full of youthful zeal,
Eager to learn everything worthwhile.   1655
Mother cried to see me go;
I've got an allowance, not much, but it'll do.
MEPHISTO   You've come to the right place, my son.
STUDENT   But I'm ready to turn right around and run!
It seems so sad inside these walls,   1660
My heart misgives me; I find all's

Confined, shut in; there's nothing green,
Not even a single tree to be seen.
I can't, on the beach in the lecture hall,
Hear or see or think at all!   1665
MEPHISTO   It's a matter of getting used to things first.
At infant starts out fighting the breast,
But soon it's feeding lustily.
Just so your appetite will sharpen day by day
The more you nurse at Wisdom's bosom.   1670
STUDENT   I'll cling tight to her bosom, happily,
But where do I find her, by what way?
MEPHISTO   First of all, then—have you chosen
A faculty?
STUDENT   Well, you see,
I'd like to be a learned man.   1675
The earth below, the heavens on high—
All those things I long to understand,
All the sciences; all nature.
MEPHISTO   You've got the right idea; however,
It demands close application.   1680
STUDENT   Oh never fear, I'm in this heart and soul;
But still, a fellow gets so dull
Without time off for recreation,
In the long and lovely days of summer.
MEPHISTO   Time slips away so fast you need to use it   1685
Rationally, and not abuse it.
And for that reason I advise you:
The Principles of Logic *primo*!
We will drill your mind by rote,
Strap it in the Spanish boot   1690
So it never shall forget
The road that's been marked out for it
And stray about incautiously,
A will-o'-the-wisp, this way, that way.
Day after day you'll be taught   1695
All you once did just like that,
Like eating and drinking, thoughtlessly,
Now needs a methodology—
Order and system: *A, B, C!*
Our thinking instrument behaves   1700
Like a loom: every thread
At a step on the treadle's set in motion,
Back and forth the shuttle's sped,
The strands flow too fast for the eye,
A blow of the batten and there's cloth, woven!   1705
Now enter your philosopher, he
Proves all is just as it should be:
A being thus and *B* also,
Then *C* and *D* inevitably follow;
And if there were no *A* and *B*,   1710

There'd never be a C and D.
They're struck all of a heap, his admiring hearers,
But still, it doesn't make them weavers.
How do you study something living?
Drive out the spirit, deny it being, 1715
So there're just parts with which to deal,
Gone is what binds it all, the soul.
With lifeless pieces as the only things real,
The wonder's where's the life of the whole—
Encheiresis naturae,[9] the chemists then call it, 1720
Make fools of themselves and never know it.

STUDENT   I have trouble following what you say.

MEPHISTO   You'll get the hang of it by and by,
When you learn to distinguish and classify.

STUDENT   How stupid all this makes me feel; 1725
It spins around in my head like a wheel.

MEPHISTO   Next metaphysics—a vital part
Of scholarship, its very heart.
Exert your faculties to venture
Beyond the boundaries of our nature, 1730
Gain intelligence the brain
Has difficulty taking in,
And whether it goes in or not,
There's always a big word for it.
Be very sure, your first semester, 1735
To do things right, attend each lecture.
Five of them you'll have daily;
Be in your seat when the bell peals shrilly.
Come to class with your homework done,
The sections memorized, each one, 1740
So you are sure there's no mistake
And no word's said not in the book.
Still, all you hear set down in your notes
As if it came from the Holy Ghost.

STUDENT   No need to say that to me twice, 1745
I realize notes help a lot;
What you've got down in black and white
Goes home with you to a safe place.

MEPHISTO   But your faculty—you've still not told me!

STUDENT   Well, I think the law wouldn't suit me. 1750

MEPHISTO   I can't blame you for disliking it,
Jurisprudence's in a dreadful state,
Laws are like a disease we inherit,
Passed down through generations, spread about
From people to people, region to region; 1755
What once made sense in time becomes nonsensical,
What first was beneficial's lost all reason.
O grandsons coming after, how I wince for you all!

9. The natural process by which substances are united into a living organism—a name for an action no
one understands.

As for the rights we have from Nature as her heir—
Never a word about *them* will you hear! 1760
STUDENT   I hate the stuff now more than ever!
How lucky I am to have you for adviser.
Perhaps I'll take theology.
MEPHISTO   I shouldn't want to lead you astray,
But it's a science, if you'll allow me to say it, 1765
Where it's easy to lose your way.
There's so much poison hidden in it,
It's very nearly impossible
To tell what's toxic from what's medicinal.
Here again it's safer to choose 1770
One single master and echo his words dutifully—
As a general rule, put your trust in *words,*
They'll guide you safely past doubt and dubiety
Into the Temple of Absolute Certainty.
STUDENT   But shouldn't words convey ideas, a meaning? 1775
MEPHISTO   Of course they should! But why overdo it?
It's exactly when ideas are lacking
Words come in so handy as a substitute.
With words we argue pro and con,
With words invent a whole system. 1780
Believe in words! Have faith in them!
No jot or tittle shall pass from them.
STUDENT   Sorry to keep you; I've another query,
My last one and then I'll go.
Medicine, sir—what might you care to tell me 1785
About that study I should know?
Three years, my God, why, they're just minutes
For a field so vast—oh, it defeats me.
One or two professional shrewd hints
Could help one along wonderfully. 1790
MEPHISTO [*Aside*]   Enough of all this academic chatter.
Back again to deviltry!
[*Aloud*] Medicine's an easy art to master.
You study, study, man in himself and man abroad,
Only at last to see what happens happens at the pleasure 1795
Of the Lord.
Plough your way through all the sciences you please,
Each learns only what he can;
But the man who understands his opportunities,
Him I call a man. 1800
You seem a pretty strapping fellow,
Not one to hang back bashfully;
If you don't doubt yourself, I know
Nobody else will doubt you, nobody.
Above all learn your way with women; 1805
With their eternal sighs and groans,
Their never-ending aches and pains,
There's one way only, one, to treat them,

And if your manners are half decent,
You'll have them all just where you want them.   1810
With an M.D. you enjoy great credit,
Your art, they're sure, beats others' arts;
The doctor, when he pays a visit,
For greeting reaches for those parts
It takes a layman years to get at;   1815
You feel her pulse with extra emphasis,
And your arm slipping, with sly, burning glances,
Around her slender waist,
See if it's because she's so tight-laced.
STUDENT   Oh, that's much better—practical, down to earth!   1820
MEPHISTO   All theory, my dear boy, is gray,
And green the golden tree of life.
STUDENT   I swear it seems a dream to me!
Would you permit me, sir, to impose on
Your generous kindness another day   1825
And drink still more draughts of your wisdom?
MEPHISTO   I'm glad to help you in any way.
STUDENT   I mustn't leave without presenting
You my album. Do write something
In it for me, would you?
MEPHISTO   Happily.   1830
    [Writes and hands back the album.]
STUDENT [Reading.]   Eritis sicut Deus, scientes bonum et malum.[1]
    [Closes the book reverently and exits.]
MEPHISTO   Faithfully follow that good old verse,
That favorite line of my aunt's, the snake,
And for all your precious godlikeness,
You'll end up how? A nervous wreck.   1835
    [Enter FAUST.]
FAUST   And now where to?
MEPHISTO   Wherever you like.
First we'll mix with little people, then with great.
The pleasure and the profit you will get
From our course—and never pay tuition for it!
FAUST   But me and my long beard—we're hardly suited   1840
For the fast life. I feel myself defeated
Even before we start. I've never been
A fellow to fit in. Among other men
I feel so small, so mortified—I freeze.
Oh, in the world I'm always ill at ease!   1845
MEPHISTO   My friend, that's all soon changed, it doesn't matter;
With confidence comes savoir-vivre.
FAUST   But how do we get out of here?
Where are your horses, groom and carriage?
MEPHISTO   By air's how we make our departure,   1850

1. A slight alteration of the serpent's words to Eve in Genesis: "Ye shall be as God, knowing good and evil" (Latin).

On my cloak—you'll enjoy the voyage.
But take care, on so bold a venture,
You're sparing in the matter of luggage.
I'll heat some gas, that way we'll lift
Quickly off the face of earth;   1855
If we're light enough we'll rise right up—
I offer my congratulations, sir, on your new life!

AUERBACH'S CELLAR IN LEIPZIG

Drinkers carousing.

FROSCH   Faces glum and glasses empty?
I don't call this much of a party.
You fellows seem wet straw tonight,   1860
Who always used to blaze so bright.
BRANDER   It's your fault—he just sits there, hardly speaks!
Where's the horseplay, where the dirty jokes?
FROSCH [*Emptying a glass of wine on his head.*]
There! Both at once!
BRANDER   O horse and swine!
FROSCH   You asked for it, so don't complain.   1865
SIEBEL   Out in the street if you want to punch noses!
—Now take a deep breath and roar out a chorus
In praise of the grape and the jolly god Bacchus.
Come, all together with a rollicking round-o!
ALTMAYER   Stop, stop, man, I'm wounded, someone fetch me some   1870
cotton,
The terrible fellow has burst me an eardrum!
SIEBEL   Hear the sound rumble above in the vault?
That tells you you're hearing the true bass note.
FROSCH   That's right! Out the door, whoever don't like it!
With a do-re-mi,   1875
ALTMAYER   And a la-ti-do,
FROSCH   We will have us a concert!
[*Sings.*]
Our dear Holy Roman Empire,
How does the damn thing hold together?
BRANDER   Oh, but that's dreadful, and dreadfully sung,   1880
A dreary, disgusting *political* song!
Thank the Lord when you wake each morning
You're not the one must keep the Empire going.
It's a blessing I'm grateful for
To be neither Kaiser nor Chancellor.   1885
But we, too, need a chief for our group,
So let's elect ourselves a pope.
To all of us here I'm sure it's well known
What a man must do to sit on that throne.
FROSCH [*Singing.*]
Nightingale, fly away, o'er lawn, o'er bower,   1890
Tell her I love her ten thousand times over.

SIEBEL   Enough of that love stuff, it turns my stomach.
FROSCH   Ten thousand times, though it drives you frantic!
    [*Sings.*]
      Unbar the door, the night is dark!
      Unbar the door, my love, awake!   1895
      Bar up the door now it's daybreak.
SIEBEL   Go on, then, boast about her charms, her favor,
  But I will have the latest laugh of all.
  She played me false—just wait, she'll play you falser.
  A horned imp's what I wish her, straight from Hell,   1900
  To dawdle with her in the dust of crossroads;
  And may an old goat stinking from the Brocken
  Bleat "Goodnight, dearie," to her, galloping homewards.
  A fellow made of honest flesh and blood
  For a slut like that is much too good.   1905
  What love note would I send that scarecrow?—
  A beribboned rock through her kitchen window.
BRANDER   [*Banging on the table.*]
  Good fellows, your attention! None here will deny
  I know what should be done and shouldn't at all.
  Now we have lovers in our company   1910
  Whom we must treat in manner suitable
  To their condition, our jollity,
  With a song just lately written. So mind the air
  And come in on the chorus loud and clear!
    [*He sings.*]
      A rat lived downstairs in the cellar,   1915
      Dined every day on cheese and butter,
      His paunch grew round as any burgher's,
      As round as Dr. Martin Luther's.[2]
      The cook put poison down for it,
      Oh, how it groaned, the pangs it felt,   1920
        As if by Cupid smitten.
CHORUS   [*Loud and clear.*]
      As if by Cupid smitten!
BRANDER
      It rushed upstairs, it raced outdoors
      And drank from every gutter,
      It gnawed the woodwork, scratched the floors,   1925
      Its fever burned still hotter,
      In agony it hopped and leaped,
      Oh, piteously the creature squeaked,
        As if by Cupid smitten.
CHORUS
      As if by Cupid smitten!   1930
BRANDER
      Its torment drove it, in broad day,
      Out into the kitchen;

---

2. Martin Luther (1483–1546), German leader of the Protestant Reformation, hence an object of distaste for Catholics.

Collapsing on the hearth, it lay
Panting hard and twitching.
But that cruel Borgia smiled with pleasure,   1935
That's it, that's that beast's final seizure.
    As if by Cupid smitten.

CHORUS
    As if by Cupid smitten!
SIEBEL   You find it funny, you coarse louts,
  Oh, quite a stunt, so very cunning,   1940
  To put down poison for poor rats!
BRANDER   You like rats, do you, find them charming?
ALTMAYER   O big of gut and bald of pate!
  Losing out's subdued the oaf;
  What he sees in the bloated rat   1945
  'S the spitting image of himself.
     [FAUST *and* MEPHISTOPHELES *enter.*]
MEPHISTO   What your case calls for, Doctor, first,
  Is some diverting company,
  To teach you life affords some gaiety.
  For these men every night's a feast   1950
  And every day a holiday;
  With little wit but lots of zest
  All spin inside their little orbit
  Like young cats chasing their own tails.
  As long as the landlord grants them credit   1955
  And they are spared a splitting headache,
  They find life good, unburdened by travails.
BRANDER   They're travelers is what your Brander says,
  You can tell it by their foreign ways,
  They've not been here, I'll bet, an hour.   1960
FROSCH   Right, right! My Leipzig's an attraction, how I love her,
  A little Paris spreading light and culture!
SIEBEL   Who might they be? What's your guess?
FROSCH   Leave it to me. I'll fill their glass,
  Gently extract, as you do a baby's tooth,   1965
  All there is to know about them, the whole truth.
  I'd say we're dealing with nobility,
  They look so proud, so dissatisfied, to me.
BRANDER   They're pitchmen at the Fair, is what I think.
ALTMAYER   Maybe so.   1970
FROSCH   Now watch me go to work.
MEPHISTO [*To* FAUST.]
  These dolts can't ever recognize Old Nick
  Even when he's got them by the neck.
FAUST   Gentlemen, good day.
SIEBEL   Thank you, the same.
    [*Aside, obliquely studying* MEPHISTOPHELES.]
  What the hell, the fellow limps, he's lame![3]

3. By tradition, the Devil had a cloven foot, split like a sheep's hoof.

MEPHISTO   We'd like to join you, sirs, if you'll allow it.   1975
   Our landlord's wine looks so-so, I am thinking,
   So the company shall make up for it.
ALTMAYER   Particular, you are, about your drinking.
FROSCH   Fresh from Dogpatch, right? From supper
   On cabbage soup with Goodman Clodhopper?   1980
MEPHISTO   We couldn't stop on this trip, more's the pity!
   But last time he went on so tenderly
   About his Leipzig kith and kin,
   And sent his very best to you, each one.

                          [*Bowing to* FROSCH.]

ALTMAYER [*Aside to* FROSCH.]
   Score one for him. He's got some wit.   1985
SIEBEL   A sly one, he is.
FROSCH   Wait, I'll fix him yet!
MEPHISTO   Unless I err, weren't we just now hearing
   Some well-schooled voices joined in choral singing?
   Voices, I am sure, must resonate
   Inside this vault to very fine effect.   1990
FROSCH   You know music professionally, I think.
MEPHISTO   Oh no—the spirit's eager, but the voice is weak.
ALTMAYER   Give us a song!
MEPHISTO   Whatever you'd like to hear.
SIEBEL   The latest, nothing we've heard before.
MEPHISTO   Easily done. We've just come back from Spain,   1995
   Land where the air breathes song, the rivers run wine.
     [*Sings.*]
     Once upon a time a King
       Had a flea, a big one—
FROSCH   Did you hear that? A flea, goddamn!
   I'm all for fleas, myself, I am.   2000
MEPHISTO [*Sings.*]
     Once upon a time a King
       Had a flea, a big one,
     Doted fondly on the thing
       With fatherly affection.
     Calling his tailor in, he said,   2005
       Fetch needles, thread and scissors,
     Measure the Baron up for shirts,
       Measure him, too, for trousers.
BRANDER   And make it perfectly clear to the tailor
   He must measure exactly, sew perfect stitches,   2010
   If he's fond of his head, not the least little error,
   Not a wrinkle, you hear, not one, in those breeches!
MEPHISTO
     Glowing satins, gleaming silks
       Now were the flea's attire,
     Upon his chest red ribbons crossed   2015
       And a great star shone like fire,
     In sign of his exalted post

As the King's First Minister.
His sisters, cousins, uncles, aunts
    Enjoyed great influence too—   2020
The bitter torments that that Court's
    Nobility went through!
And the Queen as well, and her lady's maid,
    Though bitten till delirious,
Forbore to squash the fleas, afraid   2025
    To incur the royal animus.
But we free souls, we squash all fleas
    The instant they light on us!

CHORUS [*Loud and clear.*]
    But we free souls, we squash all fleas
      The instant they light on us!   2030

FROSCH   Bravo, bravo! That was fine!
SIEBEL   May every flea's fate be the same!
BRANDER   Between finger and nail, then crack! and they're done for.
ALTMAYER   Long live freedom, long live wine!
MEPHISTO   I'd gladly drink a glass in freedom's honor,   2035
  If only your wine was a little better.[4]
SIEBEL   Again! You try, sir, our good humor!
MEPHISTO   I'm sure our landlord wouldn't take it kindly,
  For otherwise I'd treat this company
  To wine that's wine—straight out of our own cellar.   2040
SIEBEL   Go on, go on, let the landlord be my worry.
FROSCH   You're princes, you are, if you're able
  To put good wine upon the table;
  But a drop or two, well, that's no trial at all,
  To judge right what I need's a real mouthful.   2045
ALTMAYER [*In an undertone.*]   They're from the Rhineland, I would swear.
MEPHISTO   Let's have an auger, please.
BRANDER   What for?
  Don't tell me you've barrels piled outside the door!
ALTMAYER   There's a basket of tools—look, over there.
MEPHISTO [*Picking out an auger, to* FROSCH.]
  Now gentlemen—name what you'll have, please?   2050
FROSCH   What do you mean? We have a choice?
MEPHISTO   Whatever you wish, I'll produce.
ALTMAYER [*To* FROSCH.]   Licking his lips already, he is!
FROSCH   Fine, fine! For me—a Rhine wine any day,
  The best stuff's from the Fatherland, I say.   2055
MEPHISTO [*Boring a hole in the table edge at* FROSCH's *place.*]
  Some wax to stop the holes with, quick!
ALTMAYER   Hell, it's just a sideshow trick.
MEPHISTO [*To* BRANDER.]
  And you?
BRANDER   The best champagne you have, friend, please,
  With lots of sparkle, lots of fizz.

---

4. That is, not cursed.

[MEPHISTOPHELES *goes round the table boring holes at all the places,*
which one of the drinkers stops with bungs made of wax.]

You can't always avoid what's foreign;   2060
About pleasure I'm nonpartisan.
A man who's a true German can't stand Frenchmen,
But he can stand their wine, oh how he can!
SIEBEL [*As* MEPHISTOPHELES *reaches his place.*]
I confess your dry wines don't
Please my palate, I'll take sweet.   2065
MEPHISTO   Tokay⁵ for you! Coming up shortly!
ALTMAYER   No, gentlemen! Look at me honestly,
The whole thing's meant to make fools of us.
MEPHISTO   Come on, my friend, I'm not so obtuse!
Trying something like that on you would be risky.   2070
So what's your pleasure, I'm waiting—speak!
ALTMAYER   Whatever you like, just don't take all week.
MEPHISTO [*All the holes are now bored and stopped; gesturing grotesquely*]
Grapes grow on the vine,
Horns on the head of the goat,
O vinestock of hard wood,   2075
O juice of the tender grape!
And a wooden table shall,
When summoned, yield wine as well!
O depths of Nature, mysterious, secret,
Here is a miracle—if you believe it!   2080
Now pull the plugs, all, drink and be merry!
ALL [*Drawing the bungs and the wine each drinker asked for gushing into*
his glass.]
Sweet fountain, flowing for us only!
MEPHISTO   But take good care you don't spill any.
[*They drink glass after glass.*]
ALL [*Singing.*]
How lovely everything is, I'm dreaming!
Like cannibals having a feast,   2085
Like pigs in a pen full of slops!
MEPHISTO   They feel so free, what a time they're having!
FAUST   I'd like to go now—nincompoops!
MEPHISTO   Before we do, you must admire
Their swinishness in its full splendor.   2090
SIEBEL [*Spilling wine on the floor, where it bursts into flame.*]
All Hell's afire, I burn, I burn!
MEPHISTO [*Conjuring the flame.*]
Peace, my own element, down, down!
[*To the drinkers.*]
Only a pinch, for the present, of the purgatorial fire.

---

5. A sweet Hungarian wine.

SIEBEL   What's going on here? For this you'll pay dear!
   You don't seem to know the kind of men you have here.   2095
FROSCH   Once is enough for that kind of business!
ALTMAYER   Throw him out on his ear, but quietly, no fuss!
SIEBEL   You've got your nerve, trying out
   Stuff like that—damned hocus-pocus!
MEPHISTO   Quiet, you tub of guts!   2100
SIEBEL   Bean pole, you!
   Now he insults us. I know what to do.
BRANDER   A taste of our fists is what: one-two, one-two.
ALTMAYER [*Drawing a bung and flames shooting out at him.*]
   I'm on fire, I'm on fire!
SIEBEL   It's witchcraft, no mistaking!
   Stick him, the rogue, he's free for the taking!
      [*They draw their knives and fall on* MEPHISTOPHELES.]
MEPHISTO [*Gesturing solemnly.*]
   False words, false shapes   2105
   Addle wits, muddle senses!
   Let here and otherwheres
   Change their places!
      [*All stand astonished and gape at each other.*]
ALTMAYER   Where am I? What a lovely country!
FROSCH   Such vineyards! Do my eyes deceive me?   2110
SIEBEL   And grapes you only need to reach for!
BRANDER   Just look inside this green arbor!
   What vines, what grapes! Cluster on cluster!
      [*He seizes* SIEBEL *by the nose. The others do the same to each other
      and raise their knives.*]
MEPHISTO   Unspell, illusion, eyes and ears!
   —Take note the Devil's a jester, my dears!   2115
      [*He vanishes with* FAUST; *the drinkers recoil from each other.*]
SIEBEL   What's happened?
ALTMAYER   What?
FROSCH   Was that your nose?
BRANDER [*To* SIEBEL.]   And I'm still holding on to yours!
ALTMAYER   The shock I felt—in every limb!
   Get me a chair, I'm caving in.
FROSCH   But what the devil was it, tell me.   2120
SIEBEL   If I ever catch that scoundrel,
   He won't go home alive, believe me!
ALTMAYER   I saw him, horsed upon a barrel,
   Vault straight out through the cellar door—
   My feet feel leaden, so unnatural.   2125
      [*Turning toward the table.*]
   Well—maybe some wine's still trickling here.
SIEBEL   Lies, all, lies! Oh how they duped us.
FROSCH   I was drinking wine, I'd swear.
BRANDER   And all those grapes—I know what a grape is!
ALTMAYER   Now try and tell me, you know-it-alls,   2130
   There's no such thing as miracles!

WITCH'S KITCHEN

A low hearth, and on the fire a large cauldron. In the steam rising up from it, various figures can be glimpsed. A SHE-APE *is seated by the cauldron, skimming it to keep it from boiling over. The* MALE *with their young crouches close by, warming himself. Hanging on the walls and from the ceiling are all sorts of strange objects, the household gear of a witch.*

FAUST, MEPHISTOPHELES.

FAUST Why, it's revolting, all this crazy witchery!
  Are you telling me I'll learn to be a new man
  Stumbling around in this lunatic confusion?
  Is an ancient hag the doctor who will cure me?   2135
  And that stuff that beast's stirring, that's the remedy
  To cancel thirty years, unbow my back?
  If you can do no better, the outlook's black
  For me, the hopes I nursed are dead already.
  Hasn't man's venturesome mind, instructed by Nature,   2140
  Discovered some sort of potent elixer?
MEPHISTO Now you're speaking sensibly!
  There *is* a natural way to recover your youth;
  But that's another business entirely
  And not your sort of thing, is my belief.   2145
FAUST No, no, come on, I want to hear it.
MEPHISTO All right. It's simple: you don't need to worry
  About money, doctors, necromancy.
  Go out into the fields right now, this minute,
  Start digging and hoeing with never a stop or a respite.   2150
  Confine yourself and your thoughts to the narrowest sphere,
  Eat nothing but the plainest kind of fare,
  Live with the cattle as cattle, don't think it too low
  To spread your own dung on the fields that you plow.
  So there you have it, the sane way, the healthy,   2155
  To keep yourself young till the age of eighty!
FAUST Yes, not my sort of thing, I'm afraid,
  Humbling myself to work with a spade;
  So straitened a life would never suit me.
MEPHISTO So it's back to the witch, my friend, are we?   2160
FAUST That horrible hag—no one else will do?
  Why can't *you* concoct the brew?
MEPHISTO A nice thing that, to waste the time of the Devil
  When his every moment is claimed by the business of evil!
  Please understand. Not only skill and science   2165
  Are called for here, but also patience:
  A mind must keep at it for years, very quietly,
  Only time can supply the mixture its potency.
  Such a deal of stuff goes into the process,
  All very strange, all so secret.   2170
  The Devil, it's true, taught her how to do it,
  But it's no business of his to brew it.

[*Seeing the* APES.]
See here, those creatures, aren't they pretty!
That one's the housemaid, that one's the flunkey.
    [*To the* APES.]
Madam is not at home, it seems?   2175
APES   Flew straight up the chimney
    To dine out with friends.
MEPHISTO   And her feasting, how long does it usually take her?
APES   As long as we warm our paws by the fire.
MEPHISTO [*To* FAUST.]   What do you think of this elegant troupe?   2180
FAUST   Nauseating—make me want to throw up.
MEPHISTO   Well, just this sort of causerie
    Is what I find most pleases me.
        [*To the* APES.]
    Tell me, you ugly things, oh do,
    What's that you're stirring there, that brew?   2185
APES   Beggars' soup, it's thin stuff, goes down easy.
MEPHISTO   Your public's assured—they like what's wishy-washy.
HE-APE [*Sidling up to* MEPHISTOPHELES *fawningly.*]
        Oh let the dice roll,
        I need money, and quick,
        Let me win, make me rich,   2190
        I'm so down on my luck.
        With a purse full of thaler,
        An ape passes for clever.
MEPHISTO   How very happy that monkey would be
    If he could buy chances in the lottery.   2195
        [*Meanwhile the young* APES *have been rolling around a big ball to
        which they now give a push forward.*]
HE-APE   The world, sirs, behold it!
        The up side goes down,
        The down side goes up,
        And there's never a respite.
        Touch it, it'll ring,   2200
        It's like glass, fractures easily.
        When all's said and done,
        A hollow, void thing.
        Here it shines brightly,
        And brighter here—tinsel!   2205
        —Oops, ain't I nimble!
        But you, son, take care
        And keep a safe distance,
        Or surely you'll die.
        The thing's made of clay,   2210
        A knock, and it's fragments.
MEPHISTO   What is that sieve for?
HE-APE [*Taking it down.*]
        If you came here to thieve,
        It would be my informer.

[*He scampers across to the* SHE-APE *and has her look through it.*]

Look through the sieve!   2215
Now say, do you know him?
Or you don't dare name him?

MEPHISTO [*Approaching the fire.*]   And this pot over here?

APES

Oh, you're a blockhead, sir—
Don't know what a pot's for!
Nor a kettle neither.   2220

MEPHISTO   What a rude creature!

HE-APE

Here, take this duster,
Sit down in the armchair.

[*Presses* MEPHISTOPHELES *down in the chair.*]

FAUST [*Who meanwhile has been standing in front of a mirror, going
forward to peer into it from close up and then stepping back.*]

What do I see? What a marvellous vision
Shows itself in this magic glass!   2225
Love, lend me your wings, your swiftest, to pass
Through the air to he heaven she must dwell in!
Oh dear, unless I stay fixed to this spot,
If I dare to move nearer even a bit,
Mist blurs the vision and obscures her quite.   2230
Woman unrivaled, beauty absolute!
Can such things be, a creature so lovely?
The body so indolently stretched out there
Surely epitomizes all that is heavenly.
Can such a marvel inhabit down here?   2235

MEPHISTO   Of course when a god's sweated six whole days,
And himself cries bravo in his works praise,
You can be certain the results are first class;
Look all you want now in the glass,
But I can find you just such a prize,   2240
And lucky the man, his bliss is assured,
Who can bring home such a beauty to his bed and board.

[FAUST *continues to stare into the mirror, while* MEPHISTOPHELES, *leaning back comfortably in the armchair and toying with the feather duster,
talks on.*]

Here I sit like a king on a throne,
Scepter in hand, all I'm lacking's my crown.

APES [*Who have been performing all sorts of queer, involved movements,
with loud cries bring* MEPHISTOPHELES *a crown.*]

Here, your majesty,   2245
If you would,
Glue up the crown
With sweat and blood!

[*Their clumsy handling of the crown causes it to break in two, and
they cavort around with the pieces.*]

Oh, oh, now it's broken!

We look and we listen,   2250
We chatter, scream curses,
And make up our verses—

FAUST [*Still gazing raptly into the mirror.*]
Good God, how my mind reels, it's going to snap!

MEPHISTO [*Nodding toward the* APES.]
My own head's starting to spin like a top.

APES
And if by some fluke   2255
The words happen to suit
Then the rhyme makes a thought!

FAUST [*As above.*]   I feel like my insides are on fire!
Let's go, we've got to get out of here.

MEPHISTO [*Keeping his seat.*]   They tell the truth, these poets do,   2260
You've got to give the creatures their due.

[*The cauldron, neglected by the* SHE-APE, *starts to boil over, causing a
great tongue of flame to shoot up in the chimney.* THE WITCH *comes in
riding down the flame, shrieking hideously.*]

THE WITCH   It hurts, it hurts!
Monkeys, apes, incompetent brutes!
Forgetting the pot and singeing your mistress—
The servants I have! Utterly useless!   2265

[*Catching sight of* FAUST *and* MEPHISTOPHELES.]
What's this? What's this?
Who are you? Explain!
What's your business?
Got in by chicane!
Hellfires parch and make   2270
Your bones crack and break!

[*She plunges the spoon into the cauldron and scatters fire over* FAUST,
MEPHISTOPHELES *and the* APES. *The apes whine.*]

MEPHISTOPHELES [*Turning the duster upside down and hitting out violently
among the glasses and jars with the butt end.*]
In pieces, in pieces,
Soup spilt, smashed the dishes!
It's all in fun, really—
Beating time, you old carcass,   2275
To your melody.

[THE WITCH *starts back in rage and fear.*]
Can't recognize me, rattlebones, old donkey you?
Can't recognize your lord and master?
Why I don't chop up you and your monkey crew
Into the littlest bits and pieces is a wonder!   2280
No respect at all for my red doublet?
And my cock's feather means nothing to you, beldam?
Is my face masked, or can you plainly see it?
Must I tell *you* of all people who I am?

THE WITCH   Oh sir, forgive my discourteous salute!   2285
But I look in vain for your cloven foot,
And your two ravens, where are they?

MEPHISTO   All right, this time you're let off—I remember,
   It's been so long since we've seen each other.
   Also, the world's grown so cultured today,   2290
   Even the Devil's been swept up in it;
   The northern bogey has made his departure,
   No horns now, no tail, to make people shiver;
   And as for my hoof, though I can't do without it,
   Socially it would raise too many eyebrows,   2295
   So like a lot of other young fellows,
   I've padded my calves to try and conceal it.
THE WITCH [*Dancing with glee.*]
   I'm out of my mind with delight, I swear!
   My lord Satan's dropped out of the air.
MEPHISTO   Woman, that name—I forbid you to use it.   2300
THE WITCH   Why not? Whyever now refuse it?
MEPHISTO   Since God knows when, it belongs to mythology,
   But that's hardly improved the morals of humanity.
   The Evil One's no more, evil ones more than ever.
   Address me as Baron, that will do,   2305
   A gentleman of rank like any other.
   And if you doubt my blood is blue,
   See, here's my house's arms, the noblest ever!
     [*He makes an indecent gesture.*]
THE WITCH [*Laughing excessively.*]
   Ha, ha! It's you, I see now, it's clear—
   The same old rascal you always were!   2310
MEPHISTO [*To* FAUST.]   Observe, friend, my diplomacy
   And learn the art of witch-mastery.
THE WITCH   Gentlemen, now what's your pleasure?
MEPHISTO   A generous glass of your famous liquor.
   But please, let it be from your oldest supply;   2315
   It doubles in strength as the years multiply.
THE WITCH   At once! Here I've got, as it happens, a bottle
   From which I myself every now and then tipple,
   And what is more, it's lost all its stink.
   I'll gladly pour you out a cup.   2320
     [*Under her breath.*]
   But if the fellow's unprepared, the drink
   Might kill him, you know, before an hour's up.
MEPHISTO   I know the man well, he'll thrive up on it.
   I wish him the best your kitchen affords.
   Now draw your circle, say the words,   2325
   And pour him out a brimming goblet.
     [*Making bizarre gestures,* THE WITCH *draws a circle and sets down an
     assortment of strange objects inside it. All the glasses start to ring and the
     pots to resound, providing a kind of musical accompaniment. Last of all,
     she brings out a great tome and stands the* APES *in the circle to serve as a
     lectern and to hold up the torches. Then she signals* FAUST *to approach.*]
FAUST [*To* MEPHISTOPHELES.]
   What's to be hoped from this, would you tell me?

That junk of hers, and her waving her arms crazily,
All the crude deceptions that she's practicing—
I know them too well, I find them disgusting.   2330
MEPHISTO   Nonsense, friend, it's not all that serious;
Really, you're being much too difficult.
Of course she employs hocus-pocus, she's a sorceress—
How else can her mixture produce a result?
   [*He presses* FAUST *inside the circle.*]
THE WITCH [*Declaiming from the book, with great emphasis.*]
   Listen and learn!   2335
   From one make ten,
   And let two go,
   And add three in,
   And you are rich.
   Now cancel four!   2340
   From five and six,
   So says the witch,
   Make seven and eight—
   Thus all's complete.
   And nine is one,   2345
   And ten is none,
   And that's the witch's one-times-one.
FAUST   I think the old woman's throwing a fit.
MEPHISTO   We're nowhere near the end of it.
   I know the book, it's all like that.   2350
   The time I've wasted over it!
   For a thoroughgoing paradox is what
   Bemuses fools and wise men equally.
   The trick's old as the hills yet it's still going strong:
   With Three-in-One and One-in-Three[6]   2355
   Lies are sown broadcast, truth may go hang.
   Who questions professors about the claptrap they teach—
   Who wants to debate and dispute with a fool?
   People dutifully think, hearing floods of fine speech,
   It can't be such big words mean nothing at all.   2360
THE WITCH [*Continuing.*]
   The power of science
   From the whole world kept hidden!
   Who don't have a thought,
   To them it is given
   Unbidden, unsought   2365
   It's theirs without sweat.
FAUST   Did you hear that, my God, what nonsense,
   It's giving me a headache, phew!
   It makes me think I'm listening to
   A hundred thousand fools in chorus.   2370
MEPHISTO   Enough, enough, O excellent Sibyl!
   Bring on the potion, fill the stoup,

---

6. The Christian doctrine of the Trinity.

Your drink won't give my friend here trouble,
He's earned his Ph.D. in many a bout.
> [THE WITCH *very ceremoniously pours the potion into a bowl; when*
> FAUST *raises it to his lips, a low flame plays over it.*]

Drink, now drink, no need to diddle,   2375
It'll put you into a fine glow.
When you've got a sidekick in the Devil,
Why should some fire frighten you so?
> [THE WITCH *breaks the circle and* FAUST *steps out.*]

Now let's be off, you mustn't dally.
THE WITCH   I hope that little nip, sir, hits the spot!   2380
MEPHISTO [*To* THE WITCH.]   Madam, thanks. If I can help *you* out,
Don't fail, upon Walpurgis Night,[7] to ask me.
THE WITCH [*To* FAUST.]   Here is a song, sir, carol it now and then,
You'll find it assists the medicine.
MEPHISTO   Come away quick! You must do as I say.   2385
To soak up the potion body and soul,
A man's got to sweat a bucketful.
And after, I'll teach you the gentleman's way
Of wasting your time expensively.
Soon yours the delight outdclights all things—   2390
Boy Cupid astir in you, stretching his wings.
FAUST   One more look in the mirror, let me—
That woman was inexpressibly lovely!
MEPHISTO   No, no, soon enough, before you, vis-à-vis,
Yours the fairest of fair women, I guarantee.   2395
[*Aside.*] With that stuff in him, old Jack will
Soon see a Helen in every Jill.

A STREET

FAUST. MARGARETE *passing by.*

FAUST   Pretty lady, here's my arm,
Would you allow me to see you home?
MARGARETE   I'm neither pretty nor a lady,   2400
And I can find my way unaided.
> [*She escapes his arm and passes by.*]

FAUST   By God, what a lovely girl,
I've never seen her like, a pearl!
A good girl, too, and quick-witted,
Her behavior modest and yet spirited,   2405
Those glowing cheeks, lips red as roses,
Will haunt me till my life closes!
The way she looked down shamefastly
Touched my heart, everlastingly;
And bringing me up short, quite speechless—   2410
Oh that was charming, that was priceless!

---

7. May Day Eve (April 30), when witches arc supposed to assemble on the Brocken, the highest peak in the Harz Mountains, which are in central Germany.

[*Enter* MEPHISTOPHELES.]

FAUST   Get me that girl, do you hear, you must!

MEPHISTO   What girl?

FAUST   The one who just went past.

MEPHISTO   Oh, her. She's just been to confession

To be absolved of all her sins.   2415

I sidled near the box to listen:

She could have spared herself her pains,

She is the soul of innocence

And has no reason, none at all,

To visit the confessional.   2420

Her kind is too much for me.

FAUST   She's over fourteen, isn't she?

MEPHISTO   Well, listen to him, the lady-killer,[8]

Eager to pluck every flower he sees,

Who's quite convinced that every favor   2425

Is his to have, hand it over, please.

But it doesn't go so easy always.

FAUST   Dear Doctor of What's Right and Proper,

Spare me your lectures, I can do without.

Let me tell you it straight out: 2430

If I don't hold that darling creature

Tight in my arms this very night,

We're through, we two, come twelve midnight.

MEPHISTO   Impossible! That's out of the question!

I must have two weeks at least   2435

To spy out a propitious occasion.

FAUST   With several hours or so, at the most,

I could seduce her handily—

Don't need the Devil to pimp for me.

MEPHISTO   You're talking like a Frenchman now.   2440

Calm down, there's no cause for vexation.

You'll find that instant gratification

Disappoints; if you allow

For compliments and billets doux,

Whisperings and rendezvous,   2445

The pleasure's felt so much more keenly.

Italian novels teach you exactly.

FAUST   I've no use for your slow-paced courting;

My appetite needs no whetting.

MEPHISTO   Please, I'm being serious.   2450

With such a pretty little miss

You mustn't be impetuous

And assault the fortress frontally.

What's called for here is strategy.

FAUST   Something of hers, do you hear, I require!   2455

Come, show me the way to the room she sleeps in,

Get me a scarf, a glove, a ribbon,

---

8. The German reads *Hans Liederlich,* meaning a profligate because *liederlich* means "careless" or "dissolute."

A garter with which to feed my desire!

MEPHISTO   To prove to you my earnest intention
  By every means to further your passion,   2460
  Not losing a minute, without delay
  I'll take you to her room today.

FAUST   I'll see her, yes? And have her?

MEPHISTO   No!
  She'll be at a neighbor's—you *must* go slow!
  Meanwhile alone there, in her room,   2465
  You'll breathe in her surrounding's perfume
  And dream of the delights to come.

FAUST   Can we start now?

MEPHISTO   Too soon! Be patient!

FAUST   Then find me a pretty thing for a present.

                                              [*Exit.*]

MEPHISTO   Presents already? The man's proving a lover!   2470
  Now for his gift. I know there's treasure
  Buried in many an out-of-the-way corner.
  Off I go to reconnoiter!

EVENING

A small room, very neat and clean.

MARGARETE [*As she braids her hair and puts it up.*]
  Who was he, I wonder, that gentleman,
  Who spoke to me this afternoon?   2475
  I wish I knew. He seemed very nice.
  I'm sure he's noble, from some great house;
  His look and manner told you that plainly,
  Who else would possess such effrontery?

                                            [*Exit.*]

    [MEPHISTOPHELES, *FAUST.*]

MEPHISTO   Come in now, in!—but take care, softly.   2480

FAUST [*After a silent interval.*]   Leave, please leave, I'd like
    to be alone.

MEPHISTO [*Sniffing around.*]   Not every girl keeps things so clean.

                                            [*Exit.*]

FAUST   Welcome, evening's twilight gloom,
  Stealing through this holy room.
  Possess my heart, O love's sweet anguish,   2485
  That lives in hope, in hope must languish.
  Stillness reigns here, breathing quietly
  Peace, good order and contentment—
  What riches in this poverty,
  What bliss there is in this confinement!   2490
      [*He flings himself into a leather armchair by the bed.*]
  Receive me as in generations past
  You received the happy and distressed,
  How often, I know, children crowded around

This chair where their grandsire sat enthroned.
Perhaps my darling too, a round-cheeked child,   2495
Grateful for her Christmas present, kissed
Reverentially his shrunken hand.
I feel, dear girl, where you are all is comfort,
Where you are order, goodness all abound;
Maternally instructed by your spirit,   2500
Daily you spread the clean cloth on the table,
Sprinkle the sand on the floor so very neatly—⁹
O lovely hand! Celestial!
That's made of this place something heavenly.
And here—!   2505
            [*He lifts a bed curtain.*]
                    I tremble, frightened, with delight!
Here I could linger hour after hour.
Here the dear creature, gently dreaming, slept,
Her angel substance slowly shaped by Nature.
Here warm life in her tender bosom swelled,
Here by a pure and holy weaving   2510
Of the strands, there was revealed
The celestial being.

But me? What is it brought me here?
See how shaken I am, how nervous!
What do I want? Why is my heart so anxious?   2515
Poor Faust, I hardly know you any more.

Has this room put a spell on me?
I came here burning up with lust,
And melt with love now, helplessly.
Are we blown about by every gust?   2520

And if she came in now, this minute,
How I would pay dear, I would, for it.
The big talker, Herr Professor,
Would dwindle to nothing, grovel before her.
MEPHISTO [*Entering.*]   Hurry! I saw her, she's coming up.   2525
FAUST   Hurry indeed, I'll never come here again!
MEPHISTO   Here's a jewel box I snatched up
    When I—but who cares how or when.
    Put it in the closet there,
    She'll jump for joy when she comes on it.   2530
    It's got a number of choice things in it,
    Meant for another—but I declare,
    Girls are girls, they're all the same,
    The only thing that matters is the game.
FAUST   Should I, I wonder?   2535
MEPHISTO   *Should* you, you say!

---

9. Floors were sprinkled with sand after cleaning.

Do you mean to keep it for yourself?
If what you're after's treasure, pelf,
Then I have wasted my whole day,
Been put to a lot of needless bother.
I hope you aren't some awful miser—   2540
After all my head-scratching, scheming, labor!
        [*He puts the box in the closet and shuts it.*]
Come on, let's go!
Our aim? Your darling's favor,
So you may do with her as you'd like to do.
And you do what?—only gape,   2545
As if going into your lecture hall,
There before you in human shape
Stood physics and metaphysics, old and stale.
                                                  [*Exit.*]

MARGARETE [*With a lamp.*]   How close, oppressive it's in here.
        [*She opens the window.*]
And yet outside it isn't warm.   2550
I feel, I don't know why, so queer—
I wish Mother would come home.
I shivering so in every limb.
What a foolish, frightened girl I am!
        [*She sings as she undresses.*]
        There was a king in Thule,[1]   2555
        No truer man drank up,
        To whom his mistress, dying,
        Gave a golden cup.

        Nothing he held dearer,
        And at the clamorous fête   2560
        Each time he raised the beaker
        All saw his eyes were wet.

        And when death knocked, he tallied
        His towns and treasure up,
        Yielded his heirs all gladly,   2565
        All except the cup.

        In the great hall of his fathers,
        In the castle by the sea,
        He and his knights sat down to
        Their last revelry.   2570

        Up stood the old carouser,
        A last time knew wine's warmth,
        Then pitched his beloved beaker
        Down into the gulf.

1. The fabled *ultima Thule* of Latin literature—those distant lands just beyond the reach of every explorer.
Goethe wrote the ballad in 1774; it was published in 1782 and set to music by several composers.

He saw it fall and founder,   2575
Beneath the waves it sank,
His eyes grew dim and never
Another drop he drank
    [*She opens the closet to put her clothes away and sees the jewel box.*]
How did this pretty box get here?
I locked the closet, I'm quite sure.   2580
Whatever's in the box? Maybe
Mother took it in pledge today.
And there's the little key on a ribbon.
I think I'd like to open it.
—Look at all this, God in Heaven!   2585
I've never seen the like of it!
Jewels! And *such* jewels, that a fine lady
Might wear on a great holiday.
How would the necklace look on me?
Who is it owns these wonderful things?   2590
    [*She puts the jewelry on and stands in front of the mirror.*]
I wish they were mine, these lovely earrings!
When you put them on, you're changed completely.
What good's your pretty face, your youth?
Fine to have but little worth.
Men praise you, do it half in pity,   2595
The thing on their mind is money, money.
Gold is their god, all,
Oh us poor people!

OUT WALKING

FAUST *strolling up and down, thinking. To him* MEPHISTOPHELES.

MEPHISTO   By true love cruelly scorned! By Hellfire fierce and fiery!
   If only I could think of worse to swear by!   2600
FAUST   What's eating you, now what's the trouble?
   Such a face I've not seen till today.
MEPHISTO   The Devil take me, that's what I would say,
   If it didn't so happen I'm the Devil.
FAUST   Are you in your right mind—behaving   2605
   Like a madman, wildly raving?
MEPHISTO   The jewels I got for Gretchen,[2] just imagine—
   Every piece a damned priest's stolen!
   The minute her mother saw them, she
   Began to tremble fearfully.   2610
   The woman has a nose! It's stuck
   Forever in her prayerbook;
   She knows right off, by the smell alone,
   If something's sacred or profane;
   One whiff of the jewelry was enough   2615
   To tell her something's wrong with the stuff.

---

2. Diminutive of the German *Margarete*. She is given this name through much of the play.

My child—she cried—and listen well to me,
All property obtained unlawfully
Does body and soul a mortal injury.
These jewels we'll consecrate to the Blessed Virgin,   2620
And for reward have showers of manna from Heaven.
Our little Margaret pouted, loath—
Why look a gift horse[3] in the mouth?
And surely the one to whom they owe it
Wasn't wicked for practising charity on the quiet.   2625
Her mother sent for the priest, and he,
When he saw how the land lay,
Was mightily pleased. You've done, he said,
Just as you should, mother and maid;
Who overcometh, is repaid.   2630
The Church's stomach's very capacious,
Gobbles up whole realms, anything precious,
Nor once suffers qualms, not even belches.
The Church alone, dear sister, God has named
Receiver of goods unlawfully obtained.   2635
FAUST   That's the way the whole world over,
From a king to a Jew, so all do, ever.
MEPHISTO   So then he pockets brooches, chains and rings
As if they were quite ordinary things,
And gives the women as much of a thank-you   2640
As a body gets for a mouldy potato,
In Heaven, he says, you'll be compensated—
And makes off leaving them feeling elevated.
FAUST   And Gretchen?
MEPHISTO   Sits there restlessly,
Her mind confused, her will uncertain,   2645
Thinks about jewels night and day,
Even more about her unknown patron.
FAUST   I can't bear that she should suffer.
Find her new ones immediately!
Poor stuff, those others, anyway.   2650
MEPHISTO   Oh yes indeed! With a snap of the fingers!
FAUST   Do what I say, march, man—how he lingers!
Insinuate yourself with her neighbor!
Damn it, devil, you move so sluggishly!
Fetch Gretchen new and better jewelry!   2655
MEPHISTO   Yes, yes, just as you wish, Your Majesty.

                                                [*Exit* FAUST.]
A lovesick fool! To amuse his girl he'd blow up
Sun, moon, stars, the whole damn shop.

THE NEIGHBOR'S HOUSE

MARTHE [*Alone.*]   May God forgive that man of mine,
He's done me wrong—disappeared   2660

---

3. Like the wooden horse in which Greek soldiers entered Troy to capture it; an emblem of treachery.

Into the night without a word
And left me here to sleep alone.
I never gave him cause for grief
But loved him as a faithful wife.
　　　[*She weeps.*]
Suppose he's dead—oh I feel hopeless!　　　　　　　　　　2665
If only I had an official notice.
　　　[*Enter* MARGARETE.]
MARGARETE　Frau Marthe!
MARTHE　　　　　　　　Gretel, what's wrong, tell me!
MARGARETE　I feel so weak I'm near collapse!
　Just now I found another box
　Inside my closet. Ebony,　　　　　　　　　　　　　　　2670
　And such things in it, much more splendid
　Than the first ones, I'm dumbfounded!
MARTHE　Never a word to your mother about it,
　Or the priest will have all the next minute.
MARGARETE　Just look at this, and this, and this here!　　　2675
MARTHE [*Decking her out in the jewels.*]
　Oh, what a lucky girl you are!
MARGARETE　But I mustn't be seen in the streets with such jewelry,
　And never in church. Oh, it's too cruel!
MARTHE　Come over to me whenever you're able,
　Here you can wear them without any worry,　　　　　　　2680
　March back and forth in front of the mirror—
　Won't we enjoy ourselves together!
　And when it's a holiday, some such occasion,
　You can start wearing them, with discretion.
　First a necklace, then a pearl earring,　　　　　　　　　2685
　Your mother'll never notice a thing.
　And if she does we'll think of something.
MARGARETE　Who put the jewelry in my closet?
　There's something that's not right about it.
　　　[*A knock.*]
　Dear God above, can that be Mother?　　　　　　　　　　2690
MARTHE [*Peeping through the curtain*]
　Please come in!—No, it's a stranger.
　　　[*Enter* MEPHISTOPHELES.]
MEPHISTO　With your permission, my good women!
　I beg you to excuse the intrusion.
　　　[*Steps back deferentially from* MARGARETE.]
　I'm looking for Frau Marthe Schwerdtlein.
MARTHE　I'm her. And what have you to say, sir?　　　　　2695
MEPHISTO [*Under his breath to her.*]
　Now I know who you are, that's enough.
　You have a lady under your roof,
　I'll go away and come back later.
MARTHE [*Aloud.*]　Goodness, child, you won't believe me,
　What the gentleman thinks is, you're a lady!　　　　　　2700
MARGARETE　A poor girl's what I am, no more.

The gentleman's kind—I thank you, sir.
These jewels don't belong to me.
MEPHISTO   Ah, it's not just the jewelry,
 It's the Fräulein herself, so clear-eyed, serene.   2705
 —So delighted I'm allowed to remain.
MARTHE   Why are you here, if you'll pardon the question?
MEPHISTO   I wish my news were pleasanter.
 Don't blame me, the messenger:
 Your husband's dead. He sent his affection.   2710
MARTHE   The good man's dead, gone, departed?
 Then I'll die too. Oh, I'm broken-hearted!
MARGARETE   Marthe dear, it's too violent, your sorrow!
MEPHISTO   Hear the sad story I've come to tell you.
MARGARETE   As long as I live I'll never love, no,   2715
 It would kill me with grief to lose my man so.
MEPHISTO   Joy's latter end is sorrow—and sorrow's joy.
MARTHE   Tell me how the dear man died.
MEPHISTO   He's buried in Padua, beside
 The blessed saint, sweet Anthony,   2720
 In hallowed ground where he can lie
 In rest eternal, quietly.
MARTHE   And nothing else, sir, that is all?
MEPHISTO   A last request. He enjoins you solemnly:
 Let three hundred masses be sung for his soul!   2725
 As for anything else, my pocket's empty.
MARTHE   What! No gold coin, jewel, souvenir,
 Such as every journeyman keeps in his wallet,
 And would sooner go hungry and beg than sell it?
MEPHISTO   Nothing, I'm sorry to say, Madam dear.   2730
 However—he never squandered his money,
 And he sincerely regretted his sins,
 Regretted even more he was so unlucky.
MARGARETE   Why must so many be so unhappy!
 I'll pray for him often, say requiems.   2735
MEPHISTO   What a lovable creature, there's none dearer!
 What you should have now, right away,
 Is a good husband. It's true what I say.
MARGARETE   Oh no, it's not time yet, that must come later.
MEPHISTO   If not now a husband, meanwhile a lover.   2740
 What blessing from Heaven, which one of life's charms
 Rivals holding a dear thing like you in one's arms.
MARGARETE   With us people here it isn't the custom.
MEPHISTO   Custom or not, it's what's done and by more than some.
MARTHE   Go on with your story, sir, go on!   2745
MEPHISTO   He lay on a bed of half-rotten straw,
 Better at least than a dunghill; and there
 He died as a Christian, knowing well
 Much remained outstanding on his bill.
 "Oh how," he cried, "I hate myself!   2750
 To abandon my trade, desert my wife!

It kills me even to think of it.
If only she would forgive and forget!"
MARTHE [*Weeping.*]   I did, long ago! He's forgiven, dear man.
MEPHISTO   "But she's more to blame, God knows, than I am."   2755
MARTHE   Liar! How shameless! At death's very door!
MEPHISTO   His mind wandered as the end drew near,
   If I'm anything of a connoisseur here.
   "No pleasure," he said, "no good times, nor anything nice;
   First getting children, then getting them fed,   2760
   By fed meaning lots more things than bread.
   With never a moment for having my bite in peace."
MARTHE   How could he forget my love and loyalty,
   My hard work day and night, the drudgery!
MEPHISTO   He didn't forget, he remembered all tenderly.   2765
   "When we set sail from Malta's port," he said,
   "For wife and children fervently I prayed.
   And Heaven, hearing, smiled down kindly,
   For we captured a Turkish vessel, stuffed
   With the Sultan's treasure. How we rejoiced!   2770
   Our courage being recompensed,
   I left the ship with a fatter purse
   Than ever I'd owned before in my life."
MARTHE   Treasure! Do you think he buried it?
MEPHISTO   Who knows what's become of it?   2775
   In Naples, where he wandered about,
   A pretty miss with a kind heart
   Showed the stranger such good will
   Till the day he died he felt it still.
MARTHE   The villain! Robbing his children, his wife!   2780
   And for all his misery, dire need,
   He would never give up his scandalous life.
MEPHISTO   Well, he's been paid, the man is dead.
   If I were in your shoes, my dear,
   I'd mourn him decently a year   2785
   And meanwhile keep an eye out for another.
MARTHE   Dear God, I'm sure it won't be easy
   To find, on this earth, his successor;
   So full of jokes he was, so jolly!
   But he was restless, always straying,   2790
   Loved foreign women, foreign wine,
   And how he loved, drat him, dice-playing!
MEPHISTO   Oh well, I'm sure things worked out fine
   If he was equally forgiving.
   With such an arrangement, why, I swear   2795
   I'd marry you myself, my dear!
MARTHE   Oh sir, you would? You're joking, I'm sure!
MEPHISTO [*Aside.*]   Time to leave! This one's an ogress,
   She'd sue the Devil for breach of promise!
        [*To* GRETCHEN.]
   And what's your love life like, my charmer?   2800

MARGARETE   What do you mean?

MEPHISTO [*Aside.*]   Oh you good girl,
  All innocence! [*Aloud.*] And now farewell.

MARGARETE   Farewell.

MARTHE   Quick, one last matter,
  If you would. I want to know
  If I might have some proof to show   2805
  How and when my husband died
  And where the poor man now is laid?
  I like to have things right and proper,
  With a notice published in the paper.

MEPHISTO   Madam, yes. To attest the truth,   2810
  Two witnesses must swear an oath.
  I know someone, a good man; we
  Will go before the notary.
  I'll introduce you to him.

MARTHE   Do.

MEPHISTO   And she'll be here, your young friend, too?—   2815
  A very fine fellow who's been all over,
  So polite to ladies, so urbane his behavior.

MARGARETE   I'd blush for shame before the gentleman.

MEPHISTO   No, not before a king or any man!

MARTHE   We'll wait for you tonight, the two of us,   2820
  Inside my garden, just behind the house.

A STREET

FAUST, MEPHISTOPHELES

FAUST   Well? What's doing? When am I going to have her?

MEPHISTO   Bravo, bravo, I can see you're all on fire!
  Very shortly Gretchen will be all yours.
  This evening you will meet her at her neighbor's.   2825
  Oh, that's a woman made to order
  To play the bawd, our Mistress Marthe.

FAUST   Good work.

MEPHISTO   There's something we must do for her, however.

FAUST   One good turn deserves another.

MEPHISTO   All it is is swear an oath   2830
  Her husband's buried in the earth,
  Interred in consecrated ground at Padua.

FAUST   So that means we must make a trip there—very clever!

MEPHISTO   *Sancta simplicitas!*[4] Whoever said that?
  Just swear an oath; that's all there's to it.   2835

FAUST   If that's your scheme, keep it, I'm through.

MEPHISTO   The saintly fellow! Just like you!
  Declaring falsely—Heaven forbid!—
  Is something Faustus never did.
  Haven't you pontificated   2840

4. Holy simplicity (Latin).

About God and the world, undisconcerted,
About man, man's mind and heart and being,
As bold as brass, without blushing?
Look at it closely and what's the truth?
You know as much about those things   2845
As you know about Herr Schwerdtlein's death.
FAUST   You always were a sophist and a liar.
MEPHISTO   Indeed, indeed. If we look ahead a little further,
To tomorrow, what do we see?
You swearing, oh so honorably,   2850
Your soul is Gretchen's—cajoling and deceiving her.
FAUST   My soul, and all my heart as well.
MEPHISTO   Oh wonderful!
You'll swear undying faith and love eternal,
Go on about desire unique and irresistible,
About longing, boundless, infinite: 2855
That, too, with all your heart—I'll bet!
FAUST   With all my heart! And now enough.
What I feel, an emotion of such depth,
Such turbulence—when I try to find
A name for it and nothing comes to mind,   2860
And cast about, search heaven and earth
For words to express its transcendent worth,
And call the fire in which I burn
Eternal, yes, eternal, never dying,
Do you really mean to tell me   2865
That's just devil's doing, deception, lying?
MEPHISTO   Say what you please, I'm right.
FAUST   One word more, one only,
And then I'll save my breath. A man who is unyielding,
Sure, absolutely, he's right, and has a tongue in his mouth—
Is right. So come, I'm sick of arguing.   2870
You're right, and the reason's simple enough:
I must do what I must, can't help myself.

A GARDEN

MARGARETE *with* FAUST, *her arm linked with his;* MARTHE *with* MEPHISTOPHELES.
The two couples stroll up and down.

MARGARETE   You are too kind, sir, I am sure it's meant
To spare a simple girl embarrassment.
A traveler finds whatever amusement he can,   2875
You've been all over, you're a gentleman—
How can anything I say
Interest you in any way?
FAUST   To me one word of yours, one look,
'S worth more than all the wisdom in the great world's book.   2880
    [*He kisses her hand.*]
MARGARETE   No, no, sir, please, you mustn't! How could you kiss
A hand so ugly—red and coarse?

You can't imagine all the work I have to do;
My mother must have things just so.
     [They walk on.]

MARTHE   And you, sir, I believe, you constantly travel?   2885
MEPHISTO   Business, business! It is so demanding!
    Leaving a place you like can be so painful,
    But there's no help for it, you have to keep on going.
MARTHE   How fine, how free, when you're young and full of ginger,
    To travel the world, see all that's doing.   2890
    But soon enough worse times arrive and worser;
    Where's the one can find it to his liking
    To crawl to his grave a lonely bachelor.
MEPHISTO   When I look at what's ahead, I tremble.
MARTHE   Then, sir, bethink yourself while you're still able.   2895
      [They walk on.]
MARGARETE   Yes, out of sight is out of mind.
    It's second nature with you, gallantry;
    But you have heaps and heaps of friends
    Cleverer by far, oh much, than me.
FAUST   Dear girl, believe me, what's called cleverness   2900
    Is mostly shallowness and vanity.
MARGARETE   What do you mean?
FAUST   God, isn't it a pity
    That unspoiled innocence and simpleness
    Should never know itself and its own worth,
    That meekness, lowliness, those highest gifts   2905
    Kindly Nature endows us with—
MARGARETE   You'll think of me for a moment or two,
    I'll have hours enough to think of you.
FAUST   You're alone a good deal, are you?
MARGARETE   Our family's very small, it's true,   2910
    But still it has to be looked to.
    We have no maid, I sweep the floors, I cook and knit
    And sew, do all the errands, morning and night;
    Mother's very careful about money,
    All's accounted for to the last penny.   2915
    Not that she really needs to pinch and save;
    We could afford much more than others have.
    My father left us a good bit,
    With a small dwelling added to it,
    And a garden just outside the city.   2920
    But lately I've lived quietly.
    My brother is a soldier. My little sister died.
    The trouble that she cost me, the poor child!
    But I loved her very much, I'd gladly do
    It all again.   2925
FAUST   An angel, if at all like you.
MARGARETE   All the care of her was mine,
    And she was very fond of her sister.
    My father died before she was born,

And Mother, well, we nearly lost her;
It took so long, oh many months, till she got better. 2930
It was out of the question she should nurse
The poor little crying thing herself,
So I nursed her, on milk and water.
I felt she was my own daughter.
In my arms, upon my lap, 2935
She smiled and kicked, grew round and plump.

FAUST   The happiness it must have given you!

MARGARETE   But it was hard on me so often, too.
Her crib stood at my bedside, near my head,
A slightest movement, cradle's creak, 2940
And instantly I was awake;
I'd give her a bottle, or take her into my bed;
If still she fretted, up I'd raise,
Walk up and down with her, swaying and crooning,
And be at the washtub early the next morning; 2945
To market after that, and getting the hearth to blaze,
And so it went, day after day, always.
Home's not always cheerful, be it said;
But still—how good your supper, good your bed.
[They walk on.]

MARTHE   It's very hard on us poor women; 2950
You bachelors don't listen, you're so stubborn!

MEPHISTO   What's needed are more charmers like yourself
To bring us bachelors down from off the shelf.

MARTHE   There's never, sir, been anyone? Confess!
You've never lost your heart to one of us? 2955

MEPHISTO   How does the proverb go? A loving wife,
And one's own hearthside, are more worth
Than all the gold that's hidden in the earth.

MARTHE   I mean, you've had no wish, yourself?

MEPHISTO   Oh, everywhere I've been received politely. 2960

MARTHE   No, what I mean is, hasn't there been somebody
Who ever made your heart beat? Seriously?

MEPHISTO   It's never a joking matter with women, believe me.

MARTHE   Oh, you don't understand!

MEPHISTO   So sorry! Still,
I can see that you are—amiable. 2965
[They walk on.]

FAUST   You recognized me, angel, instantly
When I came through the gate into the garden?

MARGARETE   I dropped my eyes. Didn't you see?

FAUST   And you'll forgive the liberty, you'll pardon
My swaggering up in that insulting fashion 2970
When you came out of the church door?

MARGARETE   I was bewildered. Never before
Had I been spoken to in that way.
I'm a good girl. Who would dare
To say a bad thing, ever, about me? 2975

Did he, I wondered, see a suggestion
Of something flaunting in my look?
There's a creature, he seemed to think,
With whom a man might strike a bargain
On the spot. But I'll confess,   2980
Something there was, I don't know what,
Spoke in your favor, here in my breast.
And oh how vexed I felt with myself
To find I wasn't vexed with you in the least.

FAUST   Dear girl!   2985

MARGARETE   Just wait.
        [*Picking a daisy and plucking the petals one by one.*]

FAUST   What is it for, a bouquet?

MARGARETE   Only a little game of ours.

FAUST   A game, is it?

MARGARETE   Never mind. I'm afraid you'll laugh at me.
        [*Murmuring to herself as she plucks the petals.*]

FAUST   What are you saying?

MARGARETE [*Under her breath.*]
                            Loves me—loves me not—

FAUST   Oh, what a creature, heavenly!

MARGARETE [*Continuing.*]   He loves me—not—he loves me—not—   2990
        [*Plucking the last petal and crying out delightedly.*]
He loves me.

FAUST   Dearest, yes! Yes, let the flower be
The oracle by which the truth is said.
He loves you! Do you understand?
He loves you! Let me take your hand.
        [*He takes her hands in his.*]

MARGARETE   I'm afraid!   2995

FAUST   No, no, never! Read the look
On my face, feel my hands gripping yours—
They tell you what's impossible
Ever to put in words:
Utter surrender, and such rapture   3000
As must never end, must last forever!
Yes, forever. An end—it would betoken
Utter despair, a heart forever broken!
No—no end! No end!
        [MARGARETE *squeezes his hands, frees herself and runs away. He doesn't*
        move for a moment, thinking, then follows her.]

MARTHE   It's getting dark.   3005

MEPHISTO   That's right. We have to go.

MARTHE   Please forgive me if I don't invite
You in. But ours is such a nasty-minded street,
You'd think people had no more to do
Than watch their neighbors' every coming and going.
The gossip that goes on here, about nothing!   3010
But where are they, our little couple?

MEPHISTO   Flew.

Up that path like butterflies.
MARTHE   He seems to like her.
MEPHISTO   And she him. Which is the way the world wags ever.

A SUMMERHOUSE

GRETCHEN *runs in and hides behind the door, putting her fingertips to her lips and peeping through a crack.*

MARGARETE   Here he comes!
FAUST   You're teasing me, are you?
I've got you now. [*Kisses her.*]   3015
MARGARETE [*Holding him around and returning the kiss.*]
                              I love you, yes, I do!
     [MEPHISTOPHELES *knocks.*]
FAUST [*Stamping his foot.*]
Who's there?
MEPHISTO   A friend.
FAUST   A fiend!
MEPHISTO   We must be on our way.
MARTHE [*Coming up.*]   Yes, sir, it's late.
FAUST   I'd like to walk you home.
MARGARETE   My mother, I'm afraid. . . . Goodbye!
FAUST   So we must say
Goodbye? Goodbye!
MARGARETE   I hope I'll see you soon.
                              [*Exit* FAUST *and* MEPHISTOPHELES.]
Good God, the thoughts that fill the head   3020
Of such a man, oh it's astounding!
I stand there dumbly, my face red,
And stammer yes to everything.
I don't understand. What in the world
Does he see in me, an ignorant child?   3025

A CAVERN IN THE FOREST

FAUST [*Alone.*]   Sublime Spirit, all that I asked for, all,
You gave me. Not for nothing was it,
The face you showed me, all ablaze with fire.
You gave me glorious Nature for my kingdom,
With the power to feel, to delight in her—nor as   3030
A spectator only, coolly admiring her wonders,
But letting me see deep into her bosom
As a man sees deep into a dear friend's heart.
Before me you make pass all living things,
From high to low, and teach me how to know   3035
My brother creatures in the silent woods, the streams, the air.
And when the shrieking storm winds make the forest
Groan, toppling the giant fir whose fall
Bears nearby branches down with it and crushes
Neighboring trees so that the hill returns   3040
A hollow thunder—oh, then you lead me to

The shelter of this cave, lay bare my being to myself,
And all the mysteries hidden in my depths
Unfold themselves and open to the day.
And when I see the moon ascend the sky,   3045
Shedding a pure, assuaging light, out
Of the walls of rock, the dripping bushes, drift
Silvery figures from the ancient world
And temper meditation's austere joy.

That nothing perfect's ever ours, oh but   3050
I know it now. Together with the rapture
That I owe you, by which I am exalted
Nearer and still nearer to the gods, you gave me
A familiar, a creature whom already I
Can't do without, though he's a cold   3055
And shameless devil who drags me down
In my own eyes and with a whispered word
Makes all you granted me to be as nothing.
The longing that I feel for that enchanting
Image of a woman, he busily blows up   3060
Into a leaping flame. And so desire
Whips me, stumbling on, to seize enjoyment,
And once enjoyed, I languish for desire.
       [*Enter* MEPHISTOPHELES.]
MEPHISTO   Aren't you fed up with it by now,
This mooning about? How can it still   3065
Amuse you? You do it for a while,
All right; but enough's enough, on to the new!
FAUST   Why, when I'm feeling a bit better,
Do you badger me with your insidious chatter?
MEPHISTO   All right, all right, a little breather, have it.   3070
But don't speak so, as if you really mean it—
I wouldn't shed tears, losing a companion
Who is so mad, so rude, so sullen.
I have my hands full every minute—
Impossible to tell what pleases you or doesn't.   3075
FAUST   Why, that's just perfect, isn't it?
He bores me stiff and wants praise for it.
MEPHISTO   You poor earthly creature, would
You ever have managed at all without me?
Whom do you have to thank for being cured   3080
Of your mad ideas, your feverish frenzy?
If not for me you would have disappeared
From off the face of earth already.
What kind of life do you call it, dully fretting
Owl-like in caves, or toad-like feeding   3085
On oozing moss and dripping stone?
That's a way to spend your time? Go on!
You're still living in your head—I have to say so;
Only the old Dr. Faust would carry on so.

FAUST   Try to understand: my life's renewed   3090
   When I wander, musing, in wild Nature.
   But even if you could, I know you would
   Begrudge me, Devil that you are, my rapture.
MEPHISTO   For sure, your rapture, spiritual, sublime!
   Sprawled on a mountain at night in the damp dewfall   3095
   And blissfully clasping heaven and earth to your bosom,
   A god no less, so great you've grown, so swollen,
   Penetrating the core of earth
   By sheer force of intuition,
   Feeling the six creation days unfold inside yourself,   3100
   In your pride of strength delighting in—what, I can't imagine,
   On the point of amorously over flowing the universe,
   The earthly creature transcended and forgotten—
   And how will it end, all your exalted insight?
       [*Making a gesture.*]
   I forbid myself to say, it's not polite.   3105
FAUST   For shame!
MEPHISTO   So that's not to your taste at all, sir?
   You're right, "shame"'s right, the moral comment called for.
   Never a word, when chaste ears are about,
   Of what chaste hearts can't do without
   I mean, feel free to fool yourself   3110
   As and when it pleases you.
   Yet you can't keep on doing as you do,
   You look a wreck again already;
   And if you do keep on, the time's not far
   When you'll go mad with horror, fear.   3115
   Enough, I say! Your sweetheart sits down there
   And all's a dismal prison for her.
   You haunt her mind continually,
   She's mad about you, oh completely.
   At first your passion, like a freshet,   3120
   Swollen with melted snow, overthrowing
   All barriers, engulfed a soul unknowing;
   But now the flood's thinned to a streamlet.
   Instead of playing monarch of the wood,
   My opinion is the Herr Professor   3125
   Should make the silly little creature
   Some return, in gratitude.
   For her the hours creep along,
   She stands at the window, watching the clouds
   Pass slowly over the old town walls,   3130
   "Lend me, sweet bird, your wings," is the song
   She sings all day and half the night.
   Sometimes she's cheerful, mostly she's downhearted,
   Sometimes she cries as if brokenhearted,
   Then she's calm again and seems all right,   3135
   And heart-sick always.
FAUST   Serpent! Snake!

MEPHISTO [*Aside.*] I'll have you yet!
FAUST   Get away from me, you fiend!
  Don't mention her, so beautiful, to me!   3140
  Don't make my half-crazed senses crave again
  The sweetness of that lovely body!
MEPHISTO   Then what? She thinks you've taken flight,
  And I must say, the girl's half right.
FAUST   However far I wander, I am near her,   3145
  I can't forget her for a minute.
  I even envy the Lord's body
  Her pressing her lips in church to it.[5]
MEPHISTO I understand. I've often envied *you*
  Her pair of does that feed among the lilies.[6]   3150
FAUST Pimp, you! I won't hear your blasphemies!
MEPHISTO   Fine! Insult me! And I laugh at you.
  The God that made you girls and boys
  Himself was first to recognize,
  And practice, what's the noblest calling,   3155
  The furnishing of opportunities.
  Away! A crying shame this, never linger!
  You act as if hard fate were dragging
  You to death, not to your true love's chamber.
FAUST   Heaven's out-heavened when she holds me tight,   3160
  I'm warmed to life upon her bosom—
  But it doesn't matter, still I feel her plight.
  A fugitive is what I am, a beast
  That's houseless, restless, purposeless,
  A furious, impatient cataract   3165
  That plunges down from rock to rock toward the abyss.
  And there she was, half grown up into womanhood,
  In her quiet cottage on the Alpine meadow,
  Her life the same unchanging quietude
  Within a little world where fell no shadow.   3170
  And I, abhorred by God,
  Was not content to batter
  Rocks to bits, I had
  To undermine her peace and overwhelm her!
  This sacrifice you claimed, Hell, as your due!   3175
  Help me, Devil, please, to shorten
  The anxious time I must go through!
  Let happen quick what has to happen!
  Let her fate fall on me, too, crushingly,
  And both together perish, her and me!   3180
MEPHISTO   All worked up again, all in a sweat!
  On your way, you fool, and comfort her.
  When blockheads think there's no way out,
  They give up instantly, they're done for.

---

5. When the bread of Communion miraculously turns to the body of Christ.   6. Compare Song of
Solomon 4.5: "Thy two breasts are like two young roes that are twins, which feed among the lilies."

Long live the man who keeps on undeterred!   3185
I'd rate your progress as a devil pretty fair;
But tell me, what is there that's more absurd
Than a moping devil, mewling in despair?

GRETCHEN'S ROOM

GRETCHEN [*Alone at her spinning wheel.*]
    My heart is sore,
    My peace is gone,   3190
    Gone, gone forever
    And evermore.

    Him gone, all's grief,
    All's death, the grave;
    The whole world   3195
    Gone sour, spoiled.

    My poor poor head,
    I tremble, nervous,
    I think I'm mad,
    My mind's a chaos.   3200

    My heart is sore,
    My peace is gone,
    Gone, gone forever
    And evermore.

    I peer out the window,   3205
    Walk out the door,
    It's him, only him,
    I look for.

    His bold brave walk,
    His princely person,   3210
    His laughing look,
    His eyes' persuasion,

    And his speech's grace—
    Magicalness!
    His hand's caress   3215
    And oh, his kiss!

    My heart is sore,
    My peace is gone,
    Gone, gone forever
    And evermore.   3220

    With blood and flesh
    I strain toward him,
    My only wish,
    To have and hold him,

And kiss and kiss him,   3225
Never ceasing,
Though I die in
His arms kissing.

MARTHE'S GARDEN

MARGARETE, FAUST

MARGARETE   Heinrich,[7] the truth—I have to insist!
FAUST   As far as I'm able.   3230
MARGARETE   Well, tell me, you must,
About your religion—how do you feel?
You're such a good man, kind and intelligent,
But I suspect you are indifferent.
FAUST   Enough of that, my child. You know quite well
I cherish you so very dearly,   3235
For those I love I'd give my life up gladly,
And I never interfere with people's faith.
MARGARETE   That isn't right, you've got to have belief!
FAUST   You do?
MARGARETE   I know you think I am a dunce!
You don't respect the sacraments.   3240
FAUST   I do respect them.
MARGARETE   Not enough to go to mass.
And tell me when you last went to confess?
Do you believe in God?
FAUST   Who, my dear,
Can say, I believe in God?
Ask any priest, philosopher,   3245
And what you get by way of answer
Sounds like a joke, pure mockery.
MARGARETE   So you don't believe in him?
FAUST   Don't misunderstand me, sweet.
Who is there dares to give him a name   3250
And affirm,
"I believe"? Who, feeling doubt,
Ventures to say right out,
"I don't believe"?
The All-embracing,   3255
All-sustaining
Sustains and embraces
You, me, himself.
The sky it arches overhead,
The earth lies firm beneath our feet,   3260
And the friendly shining stars, don't they
Mount aloft eternally?
Don't my eyes, seeking your eyes, meet?
And all that there is, doesn't it press

---

7. That is, Faust. In the legend, Faust's name was generally Johann (John). Goethe changed it to Heinrich (Henry).

Close on your mind and heart, 3265
In eternal secrecy working,
Visibly, invisibly about you?
Fill heart with it to overflowing
In an ecstasy of blissful feeling,
Which then call what you would: 3270
Happiness! Heart! Love! Call it God!—
Don't ask me his name, how should I know?
Feeling is all,
Names sound and smoke,
Obscuring heaven's glow. 3275

MARGARETE   I guess what you say is all right,
   The priest speaks so, or pretty near,
   Except his language isn't yours, not quite.

FAUST   I speak as all speak here below,
   All souls beneath the sun of heaven, 3280
   They use the language that they know,
   And I use mine. Are all mistaken?

MARGARETE   It sounds fine the way you put it,
   But something's wrong, there's still a question;
   The truth is, you are not a Christian. 3285

FAUST   Now darling!

MARGARETE   It is so upsetting, I can't bear it,
   To see the company you keep.

FAUST   Company?

MARGARETE   That man you always have with you,
   I loathe him, oh how much I do; 3290
   In all my life I can't remember
   Anything that's made me shiver
   More than his face has, so horrid, hateful!

FAUST   Silly thing, don't be so fearful.

MARGARETE   His presence puts my blood into a turmoil. 3295
   I like people, most of them indeed;
   But even as I long for you,
   I think of him with secret dread—
   And he's a scoundrel, he is too!
   If I'm unjust, forgive me, Lord. 3300

FAUST   It takes all kinds to make a world.

MARGARETE   I wouldn't want to have his kind around me!
   His lips curl so sarcastically,
   Half angrily,
   When he pokes his head inside the door; 3305
   You can see there's nothing he cares for;
   It's written on his face as plain as day
   He loves no one, we're all his enemy.
   I'm so happy with your arms around me,
   I'm yours, and feel so warm, so free, so easy, 3310
   But when he's here it knots up so inside me.

FAUST   You angel, you, atremble with foreboding!

MARGARETE   What I feel's so strong, so overwhelming,
  That let him join us anywhere
  And right away I almost fear   3315
  I don't love you anymore.
  And when he's near, my lips refuse to pray,
  Which causes me such agony.
  Don't you feel the same way too?
FAUST   It's just that you dislike him so.   3320
MARGARETE   I must go now.
FAUST   Shall we never
  Pass a quiet time alone together,
  Bosom pressed to bosom, two souls one?
MARGARETE   Oh, if I only slept alone!
  I'd draw the bolt for you tonight, yes, gladly;   3325
  But my mother sleeps so lightly,
  And if we were surprised by her
  I know I'd die right then and there.
FAUST   Angel, there's no need to worry.
  Here's a vial—three drops only   3330
  In her cup will subdue nature
  And lull her into pleasant slumber.
MARGARETE   What is there that I'd say no to
  When you ask?
  It won't harm her, though,   3335
  There is no risk?
FAUST   If there was anything to fear,
  Would I suggest you give it her?
MARGARETE   Let me only look at you
  And I don't know, I have to do   3340
  Your least wish.
  I have gone so far already,
  How much farther's left for me to go?

                                                                   [Exit.]
    [Enter MEPHISTOPHELES.]
MEPHISTO   The girl's a goose! I hope she's gone.
FAUST   Spying around, are you, again?   3345
MEPHISTO   I heard it all, yes, every bit of it,
  How she put the Doctor through his catechism,
  From which he'll have, I trust, much benefit.
  Does a fellow stick to the old, the true religion?—
  That's what all the girls are keen to know.   3350
  If he minds there, they think, then he'll mind us too.
FAUST   Monster, lacking the least comprehension
  How such a soul, so loving, pure,
  Whose faith is all in all to her,
  The sole means to obtain salvation,   3355
  Should be tormented by the fear
  The one she loves is damned forever!
MEPHISTO   You transcendental, hot and sensual Romeo,

See how a little skirt's got you in tow.

FAUST　You misbegotten thing of filth and fire!　　　　　　　　3360

MEPHISTO　And she's an expert, too, in physiognomy.
　When I come in, she feels—what, she's not sure;
　This face I wear hides a dark mystery;
　I am genius of some kind, a bad one,
　About that she is absolutely certain,　　　　　　　　　　3365
　Even the Devil, very possibly.
　Now about tonight—?

FAUST　　　　　　　　　　What's that to you?

MEPHISTO　I get my fun out of it too.

AT THE WELL

GRETCHEN *and* LIESCHEN *carrying pitchers.*

LIESCHEN　You've heard about that Barbara, have you?

GRETCHEN　No, not a word. I hardly see a soul.　　　　　　3370

LIESCHEN　Sybil told me; yes, the whole thing's true.
　She's gone and done it now, the little fool.
　You see what comes of being so stuck up!

GRETCHEN　What comes?

LIESCHEN　　　　　　　　Oh, it smells bad, I tell you, phew!—
　When she eats now, she's feeding two.　　　　　　　　　3375

GRETCHEN　Oh dear!

LIESCHEN　　　　　　　Serves her right, if you ask me.
　How she kept after him, without a letup
　Gadding about, the pair, and gallivanting
　Off to the village for the music, dancing,
　She had to be first always, everywhere,　　　　　　　　3380
　While he with wine and sweet cakes courted her.
　She thought her beauty echoed famously,
　Accepted his gifts shamelessly.
　They kissed and fondled by the hour,
　Till it was goodbye to her little flower.　　　　　　　　3385

GRETCHEN　The poor thing!

LIESCHEN　　　　　　　　　Poor thing, you say!
　While we two sat home spinning the whole day
　And our mothers wouldn't let us out at night,
　That one was outside, hugging her sweetheart
　On a bench, or up a dark alley,　　　　　　　　　　　3390
　And never found an hour passed too slowly.
　Well, now she's got to pay for it—
　Shiver in church, in her sinner's shirt.

GRETCHEN　He'll marry her, oh I feel certain.

LIESCHEN　Not him, he's too smart, is that one.　　　　　　　3395
　Elsewhere he'll find girls just as cordial.
　In fact he's gone.

GRETCHEN　　　　　　But that's not right, it's shameful!

LIESCHEN　And if he does, she'll rue the day,

The boys will snatch her bridal wreath away
And we'll throw dirty straw down in her doorway.[8]   3400
                                                          [*Exit.*]

GRETCHEN [*Turning to go home.*]
   How full of blame I used to be, how scornful
   Of any girl who got herself in trouble!
   I couldn't find words enough to express
   My disgust for others' sinfulness.
   Black as all their misdeeds seemed to be,   3405
   I blackened them still more, so cruelly,
   And still they weren't black enough for me.
   I blessed myself, was smug and proud
   To think I was so very good,
   And who's the sinner now? Me, me, oh God!   3410
   Yet everything that brought me to it,
   God, was so good, oh, was so sweet!

THE CITY WALL

*In a niche in the wall, an image of the Mater Dolorosa[9] at the foot of the cross,
with pots of flowers before it.*

GRETCHEN [*Putting fresh flowers in the pots.*]
   Incline, o
   Thou sorrow-rich Lady,
   Thy countenance kindly on me!   3415

   With the sword in your heart,
   Your torment, your hurt,
   To your dying son upwards you gaze.

   Up to the Father
   Your sighs race each other,   3420
   For his ordeal, your ordeal pleading.

   Who's there knows
   How it gnaws
   Deep inside me, the pain?
   The heart-anguish I suffer,   3425
   Fright, tremblings, desire?
   You only know, you alone!

   I go no matter where,
   The pain goes with me there,
   Aching, aching, aching!   3430
   No sooner I'm alone
   I moan, I moan, I moan—
   Mary, my heart is breaking!

---

8. In Germany, this treatment was reserved for young women who had sexual relations before marriage.
9. Sorrowful mother (Latin; literal trans.); that is, the Virgin Mary.

From the box outside my window,
Dropping tears like dew,   3435
Leaning into the dawning,
I picked these flowers for you.

Into my room early
The bright sun put his head,
Found me bolt upright sitting   3440
Miserably on my bed.

Help! Save me from shame and death!
Incline, o
Thou sorrow-rich Lady,
Thy countenance kindly on me!   3445

NIGHT

The street outside GRETCHEN's *door.*

VALENTINE [*A soldier,* GRETCHEN's *brother.*]
    Whenever at a bout the boys
    Would fill the tavern with the noise
    Of their loud bragging, swearing Mattie,
    Handsome Kate or blushing Mary
    The finest girl in all the country,   3450
    Confirming what they said by drinking
    Many a bumper, I'd say nothing,
    My elbows on the table propped
    Till all their boasting at last stopped;
    And then I'd stroke my beard and smiling,   3455
    Say there was no point to quarreling
    About taste; but tell me where
    There was one who could compare,
    A virgin who could hold a candle
    To my beloved sister, Gretel?   3460
    Clink, clank, you heard the tankards rattle
    All around and voices shout
    He's right, he is, she gets our vote,
    Among all her sex she has no equal!
    Which stopped those others cold. But now!—   3465
    I could tear my hair out, all,
    Run right up the side of the wall!
    All the drunks are free to crow
    Over me, to needle, sneer,
    And I'm condemned to sitting there   3470
    Like a man with debts unpaid
    Who sweats in fear what might be said.
    I itch to smash them all, those beggars,
    But still that wouldn't make them liars.

    Who's sneaking up here? Who is that?   3475
    There's two! And one I bet's that rat.

When I lay my hands on him
He won't be going home again!
[FAUST, MEPHISTOPHELES.]

FAUST How through the window of the vestry, look,
The flickering altar lamp that's always lit,   3480
Upward throws its light, while dim and weak,
By darkness choked, a gleam dies at our feet.
Just so all's night and gloom within my soul.

MEPHISTO And me, I'm itching like a tomcat on his prowls,
That slinks past fire escapes, hugs building walls.   3485
An honest devil I am, after all;
It's nothing serious, the little thievery
I have in mind, the little lechery—
It merely shows Walpurgis Night's already
Spooking up and down inside me.   3490
Still another night of waiting, then
The glorious season's here again
When a fellow finds out waking beats
Sleeping life away between the sheets.

FAUST That flickering light I see, is that   3495
Buried treasure rising, what?

MEPHISTO Very soon you'll have the pleasure
Of lifting out a pot of treasure.
The other day I stole a look—
Such lovely coins, oh you're in luck!   3500

FAUST No necklace, bracelet, some such thing
My darling can put on, a ring?

MEPHISTO I think I glimpsed a string of pearls—
Just the thing to please the girls.

FAUST Good, good. It makes me feel unhappy   3505
When I turn up with my hands empty.

MEPHISTO Why should you mind it if you can
Enjoy a drink on the house now and then?
Look up, how the heavens sparkle, starfull,
Time for a song, a cunning one, artful: 3510
I'll sing her a ballad that's moral, proper,
So as to delude the baggage the better.
[Sings to the guitar.]
    What business have you there,[1]
    Before your darling's door,
    O Katherine, my dear,   3515
        In dawning's chill?
    You pretty child, beware,
    The maid that enters there,
    Out she shall come ne'er
        A maiden still.   3520

    Girls, listen, trust no one,
    Or when all's said and done,

---

1. Lines 3515–30 are adapted by Goethe from Shakespeare's *Hamlet* 4.5.

> You'll find you are *un*done
>> And smart for it.
> Of your good selves take care,   3525
> Yield nothing though he swear,
> Until your finger wear
>> A ring on it.

VALENTINE [*Advancing.*]
> What's going on here with that braying?
> Abominable ratcatcher!   3530
> The devil take that thing you're playing,
> And then take you, foul serenader!

MEPHISTO   Smashed my guitar! Now it's no good at all.

VALENTINE   What I'll smash next is your thick skull.

MEPHISTO [*To* FAUST.]   Hold your ground, Professor! At the ready!   3535
> Stick close to me, I'll show you how.
> Out with your pigsticker now!
> You do the thrusting, I will parry.

VALENTINE   Parry that!

MEPHISTO   Why not?

VALENTINE   And this one too!

MEPHISTO   So delighted, I am, to oblige you.   3540

VALENTINE   It's the Devil I think I'm fighting!
> What's this? My hand is feeling feeble.

MEPHISTO [*To* FAUST.]   Stick him!

VALENTINE [*Falling.*]   Oh!

MEPHISTO   See how the lout's turned civil.
> What's called for now is legwork. Off and running!
> In no time they will raise a hue and cry.   3545
> I can manage sheriffs without trouble,
> But not the High Judiciary.

                                                        [*Exeunt.*]

MARTHE [*Leaning out of the window.*]
> Neighbors, help!

GRETCHEN [*Leaning out of her window.*]
>> A light, a light!

MARTHE   They curse and brawl, they scream and fight.

CROWD   Here's one on the ground. He's dead.   3550

MARTHE [*Coming out.*]   Where are the murderers? All fled?

GRETCHEN [*Coming out.*]
> Who's lying here?

CROWD   Your mother's son.

GRETCHEN   My God, the misery! On and on!

VALENTINE   I'm dying! Well, it's soon said, that,
> And sooner done. You women, don't   3555
> Stand there blubbering away.
> Come here, I've something I must say.
>> [*All gather around him.*]
> Gretchen, look here, you're young yet,
> A green girl, not so smart about

Managing her business.   3560
We know it, don't we, you and me,
You're a whore on the q.t.—
Go public, don't be shy, miss.
GRETCHEN   My brother! God! What wretchedness!
VALENTINE   You can leave God out of this.   3565
What's done can't ever be undone.
And as things went, so they'll go on.
You let in one at the back door,
Soon there'll be others, more and more—
A whole dozen, hot for pleasure,   3570
And then the whole town for good measure.

Shame is born in hugger-mugger,
The lying-in veiled in black night,
And she is swaddled up so tight
In hopes the ugly thing will smother.   3575
But as she thrives, grows bigger, bolder,
The hussy's eager to step out,
Though she has grown no prettier.
The more she's hateful to the sight,
The more the creature seeks the light.   3580

I look ahead and I see what?
The honest people of this place
Standing back from you, you slut,
As from a plague-infected corpse.
When they look you in the face   3585
You'll cringe with shame, pierced to the heart.
In church they'll drive you from the altar,
No wearing gold chains any more,
No putting on a fine lace collar
For skipping round on the dance floor.   3590
You'll hide in dark and dirty corners
With limping cripples, lousy beggars.
God may pardon you at last,
But here on earth you stand accurst!
MARTHE   Look up to God and ask his mercy!   3595
Don't add to all your other sins
Sacrilege and blasphemy.
VALENTINE   If I could only lay my hands
On your scrawny, dried-up body,
Vile panderer, repulsive bawd,   3600
Then I might hope to find forgiveness
Ten times over from the Lord!
GRETCHEN   My brother! Oh, what hellish anguish!
VALENTINE   Stop your bawling, all your to-do.
When you said goodbye to honor,   3605
That is what gave me the worst blow.

And now I go down in the earth,
Passing through the sleep of death
To God—who in his life was a brave soldier.

[*Dies.*]

THE CATHEDRAL

Requiem mass, organ music, singing. GRETCHEN *among a crowd of worshippers.*
Behind her an EVIL SPIRIT.

EVIL SPIRIT   Oh, it was different,   3610
   Wasn't it, Gretchen,
   When you then, an innocent,
   Used to come here
   To the altar and kneeling,
   Prattle out prayers   3615
   From the worn little prayer book,
   Half childish playing,
   Half God adoring,
   Gretchen!
   In your heart's hidden   3620
   What horrid sin?

   Do you pray for the soul of your mother,
   Who by your contriving slept on,
   On into unending pain?
   That blood on your doorstep, whose is it?   3625
   And under your heart, that faint stirring,
   A quickening in you, what is it?—
   Affrighting both you and itself
   With its foreboding presence.
GRETCHEN   Misery! Misery!   3630
   To be rid of these thoughts
   That go round and around in me,
   Accusing, accusing!
CHOIR   *Dies irae, dies illa*
   Solvet saeclum in favilla.[2]   3635
     [*Organ music.*]
EVIL SPIRIT   The wrath of God grips you!
   The trumpet is sounding,
   The sepulchers quaking,
   And your heart,
   From its ashen peace waking,   3640
   Trembles upwards in flames
   Of burning qualms!
GRETCHEN   To be out of here, gone!
   I feel as if drowning
   In the organ's sound,   3645

---

2. Day of wrath, that day that dissolves the world into ashes (Latin). The choir sings a famous mid-13th-century hymn by Thomas Celano (ca. 1200–ca. 1255).

Dissolving into nothing
In the singing's profound.
CHOIR   *Judex ergo cum sedebit,*
        Quidquid latet apparebit,
        Nil inultum remanebit.[3]   3650
GRETCHEN   I feel so oppressed here!
    The pillars imprison me!
    The vaulting presses
    Down on me! Air!
EVIL SPIRIT   Hide yourself, try! Sin and shame   3655
    Never stay hidden.
    Air! Light!
    Poor thing that you are!
CHOIR   *Quid sum miser tunc dicturus?*
        Quem patronum rogaturus,   3660
        Cum vix justus sit securus?[4]
EVIL SPIRIT   The blessed avert
    Their faces from you.
    Pure souls snatch back
    Hands once offered you.   3665
    Poor thing!
CHOIR   *Quid sum miser tunc dicturus?*
GRETCHEN   Neighbor, your smelling salts!
        [*She swoons.*]

WALPURGIS NIGHT

The Harz Mountains, near Schierke and Elend. FAUST, MEPHISTOPHELES.

MEPHISTO   What you would like now is a broomstick, right?
    Myself, give me a tough old billy goat.   3670
    We've got a ways to go, still, on this route.
FAUST   While legs hold up and breath comes freely,
    This knotty blackthorn's all I want.
    Hastening our journey, what's the point?
    To loiter through each winding valley,   3675
    Then clamber up this rocky slope
    Down which that stream there tumbles ceaselessly—
    That's what gives the pleasure to our tramp.
    The spring has laid her finger on the birch,
    Even the fir tree feels her touch,   3680
    Then mustn't our limbs feel new energy?
MEPHISTO   Must they? I don't feel that way, not me.
    My season's strictly wintertime,
    I'd much prefer we went through ice and snow.
    The waning moon, making its tardy climb   3685
    Up the sky, gives off a reddish glow

---

3. When the judge shall be seated, what is hidden shall appear, nothing shall remain unavenged (Latin).
4. What shall I say in my wretchedness? To whom shall I appeal when scarcely the righteous man is safe (Latin).

So sad and dim, at every step you run
Into a tree or stumble on a stone.
You won't mind me, will you, begging help
Of some quick-flitting will-o'-the-wisp?[5]   3690
I see one yonder, shining merrily.
—Hello there, friend, we'd like your company!
Why blaze away so uselessly, for nothing?
Do us a favor, light up this path we're climbing.

WILL-O'-THE-WISP   I hope the deep respect I hold you in, sir,   3695
    Will keep in check my all-too-skittish temper;
    The way we go is zigzag, that's our nature.

MEPHISTO   Trying to ape mankind, poor silly flame.
    Now listen to me: fly straight, in the Devil's name,
    Or I will blow your feeble flickering out!   3700

WILL-O'-THE-WISP   Yes, yes, you give the orders here, all right;
    I'll do what you require, eagerly.
    But don't forget, the mountain on this night
    Is mad with magic, witchcraft, sorcery,
    And if Jack-o'-Lantern is your guide,   3705
    Don't expect more than he can provide.

FAUST, MEPHISTOPHELES, WILL-O'-THE-WISP [*Singing in turn*]
    We have entered, as it seems,
    Realm of magic, realm of dreams.
    Lead us well and win the honor
    His to have, bright-shining creature,   3710
    By whose flicker we may hasten
    Forward through this wide, waste region!

    See the trees, one then another,
    Spinning past us fast and faster,
    And the cliffs impending over,   3715
    And the jutting crags, like noses
    Winds blow through with snoring noises!

    Over stones and through the heather
    Rills and runnels downwards hasten.
    Is that water splashing, listen,   3720
    Is it singing, that soft murmur,
    Is it love's sweet voice, lamenting
    For the days when all was heaven?
    How our hearts hoped, loving, yearning!
    And like a tale, an old, familiar,   3725
    Echo once more tells it over.

    Whoo-oo! owl's hoot's heard nearer,
    Cry of cuckoo and of plover—
    Still not nested, still awake?
    Are those lizards in the brake?   3730
    Straggle-legged, big of belly!
    And roots, winding every which way

---

5. *Ignis fatuus,* a wavering light formed by marsh gas. In German folklore, it was thought to lead travelers to their destruction.

In the rock and sand, send far out
Shoots to snare and make us cry out;
Tree warts, swollen, gross excrescents,   3735
Send their tentacles like serpents
Out to catch us. And mice scamper
In great packs of every color
Through the moss and through the heather.
And the glowworms swarm around us   3740
In dense clouds and only lead us
Hither, thither, to confuse us.

Tell me, are we standing still, or
Still advancing, climbing higher?
Everything spins round us wildly,   3745
Rocks and trees grin at us madly,
And the will-o'-the-wisps swell bigger
In their size and in their number.

MEPHISTO   Seize hold of my coattails, quick,
We're coming to a middling peak   3750
Where you'll marvel at the sight
Of Mammon's mountain, burning bright.[6]

FAUST   How strange that light is, there, far down,
Dim and reddish, like the dawn.
Its faint luminescence reaches   3755
Deep into the yawning gorges.
Mist rises here and streams away there,
Penetrated by pale fire.
Now the fire curls and winds in
A gold thread, now like a fountain   3760
Overflows, and spreading out
In branching veins, pours through the valley,
Or squeezed into a narrow gully,
Collects into a pool of light.
Sparks fly about as if a hand   3765
Were scattering golden grains of sand.
And look there, how from base to top
The whole cliffside is lit up.

MEPHISTO   At holiday time Lord Mammon stages
Quite a show, don't you agree?   3770
Oh, you're a lucky man to see this.
And here the guests come—not so quietly!

FAUST   What a gale of wind is blowing,
Buffeting my back and shoulders!

MEPHISTO   Clutch with your fingers that outcropping   3775
Or you'll fall to your death among the boulders.
The mist is making it darker than ever.
Hear how the trees are pitching and tossing!
Frightened, the owls fly up in a flutter.
The evergreen palace's pillars are creaking   3780

---

6. Mammon is imagined as leading a group of fallen angels in digging out gold and gems from the ground of hell, presumably for Satan's palace, as described in Milton's *Paradise Lost* 1.678 ff.

And cracking, boughs snapping and breaking,
As down the trunks thunder
With a shriek of roots tearing,
Piling up on each other
In a fearful disorder!   3785
And through the wreckage-strewn ravines
The hurtling storm blast howls and keens.
And hear those voices in the air,
Some faroff and others near?
That's the witches' wizard singing,   3790
Along the mountain shrilly ringing.

CHORUS OF WITCHES
            The witches ride up to the Brocken,
            Stubble's yellow, new grain green.
            The great host meets upon the peak and
            There Urian[7] mounts his throne.   3795
            So over stock and stone go stumping,
            Witches farting, billy goats stinking!

VOICE   Here comes Mother Baubo[8] now,
    Riding on an old brood sow.

CHORUS
            Honor to whom honor is due!   3800
            Old Baubo to the head of the queue!
            A fat pig and a fat frau on her,
            And all the witches following after!

VOICE   How did you come?
VOICE   Ilsenstein way.
    I peeked in an owl's nest, passing by,   3805
    Oh how it stared!
VOICE   Oh go to hell, all!
    Why such a rush, such a mad scramble?
VOICE   Too fast, too fast, my bottom's skinned sore!
    Oh my wounds! Look here and here!

CHORUS OF WITCHES
            Broad the way and long the road,   3810
            What a bumbling, stumbling crowd!
            Broomstraw scratches, pitchfork pokes,
            Mother's ripped and baby chokes.

HALF-CHORUS OF WARLOCKS
            We crawl like snails lugging their whorled shell,
            The women have got a good mile's lead.   3815
            When where you're going's to the Devil,
            It's woman knows how to get up speed.

OTHER HALF-CHORUS
            A mile or so, why should we care?
            Women may get the start of us,
            But for all of their forehandedness,   3820
            One jump carries a man right there.

7. A name for the devil.   8. In Greek mythology, the nurse of Demeter, noted for her obscenity and
bestiality.

VOICE [*Above.*]   Come along with us, you down at the lake.
VOICE [*From below.*]   Is there anything better we would like?
  We scrub ourselves clean as a whistle,
  But it's no use, still we're infertile.   3825
BOTH CHORUSES
     The wind is still, the stars are fled,
     The moon's relieved to hide her head.
     With a rush and a roar a magic chorus
     Scatters sparks by the thousands around us.
VOICE [*From below.*]   Wait, please wait, only a minute!   3830
VOICE [*Above.*]   From that crevice a voice, did y' hear it?
VOICE [*From below.*]   Take me along, don't forget me!
  For three hundred years I've tried to climb
  Up to the summit—all in vain.
  I long for creatures who are like me.   3835
BOTH CHORUSES
     Straddle a broomstick, a pitchfork's fine too,
     Get up on a goat, a plain stick will do.
     Who can't make it up today
     Forever is done for, and so bye-bye.
HALF-WITCH [*From below.*]   I trot breathlessly, and yet   3840
  How far ahead the rest have got.
  No peace at all at home, and here
  It's no better. Dear, oh dear!
CHORUS OF WITCHES
     The unction gives us hags a lift,
     A bit of rag will do for a sail,   3845
     Any tub's a fine sky boat—
     Don't fly now and you never will.
BOTH CHORUSES
     And when we've gained the very top,
     Light down, swooping, to a stop.
     We'll darken the heath entirely   3850
     With all our swarming witchery.
     [*They alight.*]
MEPHISTO   What a crowding and shoving, rushing and clattering,
  Hissing and shrieking, pushing and chattering,
  Burning and sparking, stinking and kicking!
  We're among witches, no mistaking!   3855
  Stick close to me or we'll lose each other.
  But where are you?
FAUST   Here, over here!
MEPHISTO   Already swept away so far!
  I must show this mob who's master.
  Out of the way of Voland the Devil,   3860
  Out of the way, you charming rabble!
  Doctor, hang on, we'll make a quick dash
  And get ourselves out of this terrible crush—
  Even for me it's too much to endure.
  Yonder's a light has a strange lure,   3865

Those bushes, I don't know why, attract me,
Quick now, dive in that shrubbery!
FAUST   Spirit of Contradiction! However,
Lead the way!—He's clever, my devil:
Walpurgis Night up the Brocken we scramble   3870
So as to do what? Hide ourselves in a corner!
MEPHISTO   Just look at that fire there, shining brightly,
Clubmen are meeting, how nice all looks, sprightly.
When the company's few, the feeling's jollier.
FAUST   But I would feel much happier   3875
To be on the summit. I can make out
A red glow and black smoke swirling,
Satanwards a great crowd's toiling,
And there, I don't have any doubt,
Many a riddle's at last resolved.   3880
MEPHISTO   And many another riddle revealed.
Let the great world rush on crazily,
We'll pass the time here cozily;
And doing what has been for a long time the thing done,
Inside that great world make us a little one.   3885
Look there, young witches, all stark naked,
And old ones wisely petticoated.
Don't sulk, be nice, if only to please me;
Much fun at small cost, really it's easy.
I hear music, a damned racket!   3890
You must learn not to mind it.
No backing out now, in with me!
You'll meet a distinguished company
And again be much obliged to me.
—Now what do you think of this place, my friend?   3895
Our eyes can hardly see to its end.
A hundred fires, in a row burning,
People around them dancing, carousing,
Talking and making love—oh, what a show!
Where's anything better, I'd like to know.   3900
FAUST   And when we enter into the revel,
What part will you play, magician or devil?
MEPHISTO   I travel incognito normally,
But when it comes to celebrations
A man must show his decorations.   3905
The Garter's never been awarded me,[9]
But in these parts the split hoof's much respected.
That snail there, do you see it, creeping forwards,
Its face pushing this way, that way, toward us?
Already I've been smelt out, I'm detected.   3910
Even if deception was my aim,
Here there's no denying who I am.

9. That is, he has no decoration of nobility, such as the Order of the Garter.

Come on, we'll go along from fire to fire,
Me the introducer, you the suitor.
     [*Addressing several figures huddled around a fading fire.*]
Old sirs, you keep apart, you're hardly merry,   3915
You'd please me better if you joined the party.
You ought to be carousing with the youngsters,
At home we're all alone enough, we oldsters.
GENERAL   Put no trust in nations, for the people,
In spite of all you've done, are never grateful.   3920
It's with them always as it is with women,
The young come first, and we—ignored, forgotten.
MINISTER OF STATE   The world has got completely off the track.
Oh, they were men, the older generation!
When we held every high position,   3925
That was the golden age, and no mistake.
PARVENU   We were no simpletons ourselves, we weren't,
And often did the things we shouldn't.
But everything's turned topsy-turvy, now
That we are foursquare with the status quo.   3930
AUTHOR   Who wants, today, to read a book
With a modicum of sense or wit?
And as for our younger folk,
I've never seen such rude conceit.
MEPHISTO [*Suddenly transformed into an old man.*]
For Judgment Day all now are ripe and ready   3935
Since I shan't ever again climb Brocken's top;
And considering, too, my wine of life is running cloudy,
The world also is coming to a stop.
JUNK-DEALER WITCH   Good sirs, don't pass me unawares,
Don't miss this opportunity!   3940
Look here, will you, at my wares,
What richness, what variety!
Yet there is not a single item
Hasn't served to claim a victim,
Nowhere on earth will you find such a stall!   3945
No dagger here but it has drunk hot blood,
No cup but from it deadly poison's flowed
To waste a body once robust and hale,
No gem but has seduced a loving girl,
No sword but has betrayed an ally or a friend,   3950
Or struck an adversary from behind.
MEPHISTO   Auntie, think about the times you live in—
What's past is done! Done and gone!
The new, the latest, that's what you should deal in;
The nouveau only, turns us on.   3955
FAUST   Am I me, I wonder, I'm so giddy.
This is a fair to beat all fairs, believe me!
MEPHISTO   The scrambling mob climbs upwards, jostling rushed,
You think you're pushing and you're being pushed.
FAUST   Who's that there?   3960

MEPHISTO   Take a good look.
   Lilith.[1]
FAUST   Lilith? Who is that?
MEPHISTO   Adam's wife, his first. Beware of her.
   Her beauty's one boast is her dangerous hair.
   When Lilith winds it tight around young men
   She doesn't soon let go of them again.   3965
FAUST   Look, one old witch, one young one, there they sit—
   They've waltzed around a lot already, I will bet!
MEPHISTO   Tonight's no night for resting. But for fun,
   Let's join the dance, a new one's just begun.
FAUST [Dancing with the YOUNG WITCH.]
   A lovely dream I dreamt one day: 3970
   I saw a green-leaved apple tree,
   Two apples swayed upon a stem,
   So tempting! I climbed up for them.
THE PRETTY WITCH   Ever since the days of Eden
   Apples have been man's desire.   3975
   How overjoyed I am to think, sir,
   Apples grow, too, in my garden.
MEPHISTO [Dancing with the OLD WITCH.]
   A naughty dream I one day:
   I saw a tree split up the middle—
   A huge cleft, phenomenal!   3980
   And yet it pleased me every way.
THE OLD WITCH   Welcome, welcome, to you, sire,
   Cloven-footed cavalier!
   Stand to with a proper stopper,
   Unless you fear to come a cropper.   3985
PROCTOPHANTASMIST[2] Accursed tribe, so bold, presumptuous!
   Hasn't it been proven past disputing
   Spirits all are footless, they lack standing?
   And here you're footing like the rest of us!
THE PRETTY WITCH [Dancing.]
   What's he doing here, at our party?   3990
FAUST [Dancing.]
   Him? You find him everywhere, that killjoy;
   We others dance, he does the criticizing.
   Every step one takes requires analyzing;
   Until it's jawed about, it hasn't yet occurred.
   He can't stand how we go forward undeterred;   3995
   If you keep going around in the same old circle,
   As he plods year in, year out on his treadmill,

1. According to rabbinical legend, Adam's first wife; the *female* mentioned in Genesis 1.27: "So God created man in his own image, in the image of God created he him; male and female created he them." After Eve was created, Lilith became a ghost who seduced men and inflicted evil on children.   2. A German coinage meaning "one who exorcises evil spirits by sitting in a pond and applying leeches to his behind" (see lines 4014–17). The figure caricatures Friedrich Nicolai (1733–1811), who opposed modern movements in German thought and literature and had parodied Goethe's *The Sorrows of Young Werther* (1774).

You might be favored with his good opinion,
  Provided you most humbly beg it of him.
PROCTOPHANTASMIST   Still here, are you? It's an outrage!   4000
  Vanish, ours is the Enlightened Age—
  You devils, no respect for rule and regulation.
  We've grown so wise, yet ghosts still walk in Tegel.[3]
  How long I've toiled to banish superstition,
  Yet it lives on. The whole thing is a scandal!   4005
THE PRETTY WITCH   Stop, stop, how boring, all your gabble!
PROCTOPHANTASMIST   I tell you to your face you ghostly freaks,
  I'll not endure this tyranny of spooks—
  My spirit finds you spirits much too spiritual!
      [*They go on dancing.*]
  I see I'm getting nowhere with these devils,   4010
  Still, it will add a chapter to my travels,
  And I hope, before my sands of life run out,
  To put foul fiends and poets all to rout.
MEPHISTO   He'll go and plump himself down in a puddle—
  It solaces him for all his ghostly trouble—   4015
  And purge away his spirit and these other spirits
  By having leeches feed on where the M'sieur sits.[4]
      [*To* FAUST, *who has broken off dancing and withdrawn.*]
  What's this? You've left your partner in the lurch
  As she was sweetly singing, pretty witch.
FAUST   Ugh! From her mouth a red mouse sprung   4020
  In the middle of her song.
MEPHISTO   Is that anything to fuss about?
  And anyway it wasn't gray, was it?
  To take on so, to me, seems simply rudeness
  When you are sporting with your Phyllis.   4025
FAUST   And then I saw—
MEPHISTO   Saw what?
FAUST   Look there, Mephisto,
  At that lovely child, so pale, so wistful,
  Standing by herself. How painfully
  She makes her way along, how lifelessly,
  As if her feet were chained. To me,   4030
  I must confess, it looks like Gretchen.
MEPHISTO   Let it be!
  It's bad, that thing, a lifeless shape, a wraith
  No man ever wants to meet up with.
  Your blood freezes under her dead stare,
  Almost turned to stone, you are.   4035
  Medusa,[5] did you ever hear of her?
FAUST   Yes, yes, those are a corpse's eyes
  No loving hand was by to close.

---

3. A town near Berlin where ghosts had been reported.   4. Nicolai claimed that he had been bothered by
ghosts but had repelled them by applying leeches to his rump.   5. The Gorgon with hair of serpents
whose glance turned people to stone.

That's Gretchen's breast, which she so often
Gave to me to rest my head on,   4040
That shape her dear, her lovely body
She gave to me to enjoy freely.

MEPHISTO It's all magic, hocus-pocus, idiot!
Her power is, each thinks she is his sweetheart.

FAUST What rapture! And what suffering!   4045
I stand here spellbound by her look.
How strange, that bit of scarlet string
That ornaments her lovely neck,
No thicker than a knife blade's back.

MEPHISTO Right you are. I see it, too.   4050
She's also perfectly able to
Tuck her head beneath her arm
And stroll about. Perseus—remember him?—
He was the one who hacked it off.
—Man, I'd think you'd have enough of   4055
The mad ideas your head is stuffed with!
Come, we'll climb this little hill where
All's as lively as inside the Prater.[6]
And unless somebody has bewitched me,
The thing I see there is a theater.   4060
What's happening?

SERVIBILIS   A play, a new one, starting shortly,
Last of seven. With us here it's customary
To offer a full repertory.
The playwright's a rank amateur,
Amateurs, too, the whole company.   4065
Well, I must hurry off now, please excuse me,
I need to raise the curtain—amateurishly!

MEPHISTO How right it is that I should find you here, sirs;
The Blocksberg's just the place for amateurs.

WALPURGIS NIGHT'S DREAM;
OR
OBERON AND TITANIA'S GOLDEN WEDDING

INTERMEZZO[7]

STAGE MANAGER [To crew.] Today we'll put by paint and canvas,   4070
Mieding's[8] brave sons, all.
Nature paints the scene for us:
Gray steep and mist-filled vale.

HERALD For the wedding to be golden,
Years must pass, full fifty;   4075
But if the quarrel is made up, then
It is golden truly.

---

6. A famous park in Vienna.   7. Brief interlude. Oberon and Titania are king and queen of the fairies.
8. Johann Martin Mieding (died 1782), a master carpenter and scene builder in the Weimar theater.

OBERON   Spirits hovering all around,
       Appear, dear imps, to me here!
       King and Queen are once more bound   4080
       Lovingly together.
PUCK[9] Here's Puck, my lord, who spins and whirls
       And cuts a merry caper,
       A hundred follow at his heels,
       Skipping to the measure.   4085
ARIEL[1] Ariel strikes up his song,
       The notes as pure as silver;
       Philistines all around him throng,
       But those, too, with true culture.
OBERON   Wives and husbands, learn from us   4090
       How two hearts unite:
       To find connubial happiness,
       Only separate.
TITANIA   If Master sulks and Mistress pouts,
       Here's the remedy: 4095
       Send her on a trip down south,
       Send him the other way.
FULL ORCHESTRA [*Fortissimo.*]   Buzzing fly and humming gnat
       And all their consanguinity,
       Frog's hoarse croak, cicada's chirp   4100
       Compose our symphony.
SOLO   Here I come, the bagpipes, who's
       Only a soap bubble.
       Hear me through my stumpy nose
       Go tootle-doodle-doodle.   4105
A BUDDING IMAGINATION   A spider's foot, a green toad's gut,
       Two winglets—though a travesty
       Devoid of life and nature, yet
       It does as nonsense poetry.
A YOUNG COUPLE   Short steps, smart leaps, all done neatly   4110
       On the scented lawn—
       I grant you foot it very featly,
       Yet we remain un-airborne.
AN INQUIRING TRAVELER   Can it be a fairground fraud,
       The shape at which I'm looking?
       Oberon the handsome god   4115
       Still alive and kicking?
A PIOUS BELIEVER   I don't see claws, nor any tail,
       And yet it's indisputable;
       Like Greece's gods, his dishabille   4120
       Shows he's a pagan devil.
AN ARTIST OF THE NORTH   Here everything I undertake
       Is weak, is thin, is sketchy;
       But I'm preparing soon to make
       My Italian journey.   4125

---

9. A mischievous spirit.   1. A helpful sprite.

A STICKLER FOR DECORUM   I'm here, and most unhappily,
  Where all's impure, improper;
  Among this riotous witchery
  There's only two wear powder.
A YOUNG WITCH   Powder, like a petticoat,   4130
  Is right for wives with gray hair;
  But I'll sit naked on my goat,
  Show off my strapping figure.
A MATRON   We are too well bred by far
  To bandy words about: 4135
  But may you, young thing that you are,
  Drop dead, and soon, cheap tart.
THE CONDUCTOR   Don't crowd so round the naked charmer,
  On with the concerto!
  Frog and blowfly, gnat, cicada—   4140
  Mind you keep the tempo.
A WEATHERCOCK [*Pointing one way.*]
  No better company than maids
  Like these, kind and complaisant,
  And bachelors to match, old boys
  Agog all, all impatient!   4145
WEATHERCOCK [*Pointing the other way.*]
  And if the earth don't open up
  And swallow this lewd rabble,
  Off I'll race at a great clip,
  Myself go to the Devil.
SATIRICAL EPIGRAMS [XENIEN[2]]   We are gadflies, plant our sting 4150
  In hides highborn and bourgeois,
  By so doing honoring
  Great Satan, our dear dada.
HENNINGS[3] Look there at the pack of them,
  Like schoolboys jeering meanly.   4155
  Next, I'm sure, they all will claim
  It's all in fun, friends, really.
MUSAGET[4] ["LEADER OF THE MUSES"]
  If I joined these witches here,
  I'm sure I'd not repine;
  I know I'd find it easier   4160
  To lead them than the Nine.
[A JOURNAL] FORMERLY [ENTITLED] "THE SPIRIT OF THE AGE"[5]
  What counts is knowing the right people,
  With me, sir, you'll go places;
  The Blocksberg's got a place for all,
  Like Germany's Parnassus.[6]   4165
THE INQUIRING TRAVELER   Who's that fellow who's so stiff

2. Literally, polemical verses written by Goethe and Friedrich von Schiller (1759–1805). The characters here are versions of Goethe himself.   3. August Adolf von Hennings (1746–1826), publisher of a journal called *Genius of the Age* that had attacked Schiller.   4. The title of a collection of Hennings's poetry. 5. That is, former "Genius of the Age"; probably alludes to the journal's change of title in 1800 to *Genius of the Nineteenth Century*.   6. A mountain sacred to Apollo and the Muses; hence, figuratively, the locale of poetic excellence.

And marches so majestical?
He sniffs away for all he's worth
"Pursuing things Jesuitical."

A CRANE   An earnest fisherman I am   4170
In clear and muddy waters,
And thus it is a pious man
'S seen hobnobbing with devils.

A CHILD OF THIS WORLD   All occasions serve the godly
In their work. Atop   4175
The Blocksberg, even there, they
Set up religious shop.

A DANCER   What's that drumming, a new bunch
Of musicians coming?
No, no, they're bitterns in the marsh   4180
In *unisono* booming.

THE DANCING MASTER   How cautiously each lifts a foot,
All the hard steps ducking,
The crippled hop, they jump the stout,
Heedless how they're looking.   4185

THE FIDDLER   This riffraff's so hate-filled, each lusts
To slit the other's throat;
Orpheus with his lute tamed beasts.[7]
These march to the bagpipes' note.

A DOGMATIST   You can't rattle me by all,   4190
Your questionings and quibbles;
The Devil is perfectly evil, hence real—
For perfection entails existence: so devils.

AN IDEALIST   The mind's creative faculty
This time has gone too far.   4195
If everything I see is me,
I'm crazy, that's for sure.

A REALIST   It's pandemonium, it's mad,
Oh, I feel so cast down;
This is the first time I have stood   4200
On such shaky ground.

A SUPERNATURALIST   The presence of these devils here
For me's reassuring evidence;
From the demonical I infer
The angelical's existence.   4205

A SKEPTIC   They see a flickering light and gloat,
There's treasure there, oh surely;
Devil's a word that pairs with doubt,
This is a place that suits me.

CONDUCTOR   Buzzing fly and humming gnat—   4210
What damned amateurs!
Frog's hoarse croak, cicada's chirp—
They call themselves performers!

THE SMART ONES   Sans all souci[8] we are, shift

7. In Greek mythology, Orpheus's music was said to have the power to quiet wild animals.   8. Without
any care or unhappiness (French).

About with lightning speed; 4215
When walking on the feet is out,
We walk upon the head.
THE NOT-SO-SMART ONES   At court we sat down to free dinners,
And now, dear God, there's naught!
We've worn out our dancing slippers 4220
And limp along barefoot.
WILL-O'-THE-WISPS   We're from the bottom lands, the swamps,
Such is our lowly origin;
But now we sparkle as gallants
And dance in the cotillion. 4225
A SHOOTING STAR   I shot across the sky's expanse,
A meteor, blazing bright.
Now fallen, I sprawl in the grass—
Who'll help me to my feet?
THE BRUISERS   Look out, look out, we're coming through, 4230
Trampling your lawn.
We're spirits too, but spirits who
Have lots of beef and brawn.
PUCK   Don't tramp like that, so heavily,
Like young elephants. 4235
Let robust Puck's own stamp today
Be the heaviest.
ARIEL   If you have wings, gift from kind Nature,
Or gift you owe the spirit,
As I fly, fly close after, 4240
Up to the rose hill's summit.
ORCHESTRA [*Pianissimo.*]
The shrouding mists and thick-massed clouds
Lighten in the dawn,
The breeze stirs leaves, wind rattles reeds,
And all is scattered, gone. 4245

AN OVERCAST DAY. A FIELD

FAUST *and* MEPHISTOPHELES.

FAUST   In misery! In despair! Stumbling about pitifully over the
earth for so long, and now a prisoner! A condemned criminal, shut
up in a dungeon and suffering horrible torments, the poor unfortunate child! It's come to this, to this! And not a word about it
breathed to me, you treacherous, odious spirit! Stand there rolling 4250
your Devil's eyes around in rage, oh do! Brazen it out with your
intolerable presence! A prisoner! In misery, irremediable misery!
Delivered up to evil spirits and the stony-hearted justice of
mankind! And meanwhile you distract me with your insipid enter-
tainments, keep her situation, more desperate every day, from me, 4255
and leave her to perish helplessly!
MEPHISTO   She's not the first.

FAUST   You dog, you monster! Change him, O you infinite Spirit,
change the worm back into a dog, give it back the shape it wore
those evenings when it liked to trot ahead of me and roll under the   4260
feet of some innocent wayfarer, tripping him up and leaping on
him as he fell. Give it back its favorite shape so it can crawl on its
belly in the sand before me, and I can kick it as it deserves, the
abomination!—Not the first!—Such misery, such misery! It's
inconceivable, humanly inconceivable, that more than one crea-   4265
ture should ever have plumbed such depths of misery, that the first
who did, writhing in her last agony under the eyes of the Eternal
Forgiveness, shouldn't have expiated the guilt of all the others who
came after! I am cut to the quick, pierced to the marrow, by the
suffering of this one being—you grin indifferently at the fate of   4270
thousands!

MEPHISTO   So once again we're at our wits' end, are we—reached
the point where you fellows start feeling your brain is about to
explode? Why did you ever throw in with us if you can't see the
thing through? You'd like to fly, but don't like heights. Did we force   4275
ourselves on you or you on us?

FAUST   Don't snarl at me that way with those wolfish fangs of yours,
it sickens me!—Great and glorious Spirit, Spirit who vouchsafed
to appear to me, who knows me in my heart and soul, why did you
fasten me to this scoundrel who diets on destruction, delights to   4280
hurt?

MEPHISTO   Finished yet?

FAUST   Save her or you'll pay for it! With a curse on you, the dread-
fulest there is, for thousands of years to come!

MEPHISTO   I'm powerless to strike off the Great Avenger's chains or
draw his bolts.—Save her indeed!—Who's the one who ruined her,   4285
I would like to know—you or me?

[FAUST looks around wildly.]

Looking for a thunderbolt, are you? A good thing you wretched mortals weren't given them. That's the tyrant's way of getting out of
difficulties—strike down any innocent person who makes an
objection, gets in his way.   4290

FAUST   Take me to where she is, you hear? She's got to be set free.

MEPHISTO   In spite of the risk you would run? There's blood guilt on
the town because of what you did. Where murder was, there the
avenging spirits hover, waiting for the murderer to return.

FAUST   That from you, that too? Death and destruction, a world's   4295
worth, on your head, you monster! Take me there, I say, and set her
free!

MEPHISTO   All right, all right, I'll carry you there. But hear what I
can do—do you think all the powers of heaven and earth are mine?
I'll muddle the turnkey's senses, then you seize his keys and lead   4300
her out. Only a human hand can do it. I'll keep watch. The spirit
horses are ready. Off I'll carry both of you. That's what I can do.

FAUST   Very well. Let's go!

NIGHT. OPEN COUNTRY

FAUST *and* MEPHISTOPHELES *going by on black horses at a furious gallop.*

FAUST   What's going on there, at the ravenstone?
MEPHISTO   Cooking up, getting up, something, who cares?   4305
FAUST   Now here, now there, hovering bowing, genuflecting.
MEPHISTO   A pack of witches.
FAUST   Hands strewing, consecrating.
MEPHISTO   Keep going, keep going!

A PRISON

FAUST [*With a bunch of keys and carrying a lamp, at a narrow iron door.*]
   I shudder as I haven't for so long—   4310
   It overcomes me, all of mankind's misery!
   She's shut up inside these dank walls, poor thing,
   And all her crime was love, the brave, the illusory.
   You're hanging back from going in!
   You're afraid of meeting her eyes again!   4315
   In, in, your hesitation's her death, hurry!
      [*He puts the key in the lock.*]
SINGING [*From within*]
         My mother, the whore,
         She's the one slew me!
         My father, the knave,
         He's the one ate me!   4320
         My sister, wee thing,
         Heaped up my bones
         Underneath stones.
         Then I became a pretty woodbird—
         Fly away, fly away!   4325
FAUST [*Unlocking the door*] She doesn't dream her lover's listening.
   Hears her chains rattle, the straw rustling.
      [*He enters.*]
MARGARETE [*Cowering on her paillasse*]
   They're coming, they're coming! How bitter, death, bitter!
FAUST [*Whispering*] Hush, dear girl, hush! You'll soon be free.
MARGARETE [*Groveling before him*]
   If your heart's human, think how I suffer.   4330
FAUST   You'll wake the guards. Speak quietly.
      [*Taking hold of the chains to unlock them.*]
MARGARETE   [*On her knees.*] Headsman, so early, it isn't right.
   Have mercy on me! Too soon, too soon!
   You come for me in the dead of night—
   Isn't it time enough at dawn?   4335
      [*Stands up.*]
   I'm still so young, too young surely—
   Still I must die.
   How pretty I was, that's what undid me.
   He held me so close, now he's far away,
   My wreath pulled apart, the flowers scattered.   4340

Don't grip me so hard, please, won't you spare me?
What did I ever do to you?
Don't let me beg in vain for mercy.
I never before laid eyes on you.

FAUST   It's unendurable, her misery,   4345

MARGARETE   What can I do, I'm in your power.
Only let me nurse my baby first,
All night long I hugged the dear creature;
How mean they were, snatched it from my breast,
And now they say I murdered it.   4350
And I'll never be happy, no, never again.
They sing songs about me in the street;
It's wicked of them.
There's an old fairy tale ends that way—
What has it got to do with me?   4355

FAUST [*Falling at her feet.*]   It's me here who loves you, me, at your feet,
To rescue you from this miserable fate.

MARGARETE [*Kneeling beside him.*]
We'll kneel down, that's right, and pray to the saints.
Look, under those steps,
Below the doorsill,   4360
All Hell's a-boil!
The Evil One
In his horrible rage
Makes such a noise.

FAUST [*Crying out.*]   Gretchen! Gretchen!   4365

MARGARETE [*Listening.*]   That was my darling's own dear voice!
      [*She jumps up, the chains fall away.*]
I heard him call. Where can he be?
No one may stop me now, I'm free!
Into his arms I'll run so fast,
Lie on his breast at last, at last.   4370
Gretchen, he called, from there on the sill.
Through all the howlings and gnashings of Hell,
Through the furious, devilish sneering and scorn,
I heard a dear voice, its sound so well known.

FAUST   It's me!   4375

MARGARETE   It's you! Oh, say it again.
      [*Catching hold of him.*]
It's him! Where is the torture now, it's him!
Where's my fear of the prison, the chains they put on me,
It's you, it's you, you've come here to save me!
I'm saved!
—I see it before me, so very clear,   4380
The street I saw you the first time on,
I see Marthe and me where we waited for you
In the sunlit garden.

FAUST [*Pulling her toward the door.*]
Come along, come!

MARGARETE   Don't go, stay here!

I love it so being wherever you are.   4385
    [*Caressing him.*]
FAUST   Hurry!
   If you don't hurry,
   The price we will pay!
MARGARETE   What? Don't know how to kiss anymore?
   Parted from me a short time only   4390
   And quite forgotten what lips are for?
   Why am I frightened with your arms around me?
   Time was, at a word or a look from you,
   Straight to heaven I was transported
   And you kissed me as if you'd devour me.   4395
   Kiss me, kiss me!
   Or I'll kiss you!
       [*She embraces him.*]
   What cold lips you have,
   You don't speak, look dumbly.
   What's become of your love?   4400
   Who took it from me?
       [*She turns away from him.*]
FAUST   Come, follow me! Darling, be brave!
   Oh, the kisses I'll give you, my love—
   Only come now, we'll slip through that door.
MARGARETE [*Turning back to him.*]
   Is it really you? Can I be sure?   4405
FAUST   Yes, it's me—you must come!
MARGARETE   You strike off my chains,
   Take me into your arms.
   How is it you don't shrink away from me?
   Have you any idea who you're letting go free?
FAUST   Hurry, hurry! The night's almost over.   4410
MARGARETE   I murdered my mother,
   Drowned my infant,
   Weren't both of us given it, you too its parent,
   Given you, too? It's you, I can hardly believe it.
   Give me your hand. No, I haven't dreamt it.   4415
   Your dear hand!—But your hand is wet!
   Wipe it off, there's blood on it!
   My God, my God, what did you do?
   Put away your sword,
   I beg you to!   4420
FAUST   What's past is done, forget it all.
   You're killing me.
MARGARETE   No, live on still.
   I'll tell you how the graves should be;
   Tomorrow you must see to it.   4425
   Give my mother the best spot,
   My brother put alongside her,
   Me, put me some distance off,
   Yet not too far,

And at my right breast put my baby. 4430
Nobody else shall lie beside me.
When I used to press up close to you,
How sweet it was, pure happiness,
But now I can't, it's over, all such bliss—
I feel it as an effort I must make, 4435
That I must force myself on you,
And you, I feel, resist me, push me back.
And yet it's you, with your good, kind look.

FAUST   If it's me, then come, we mustn't stay.

MARGARETE   Out there? 4440

FAUST   Out there, away!

MARGARETE   If the grave's out there, death waiting for me,
Come, yes, come! The two of us together!
But only to the last place, there, no other.
—You're going now?
I'd go too if I could, Heinrich, believe me! 4445

FAUST   You can! All you need is the will. Come on!
The way is clear.

MARGARETE   No, I mayn't, for me all hope is gone.
It's useless, flight. They'd keep, I'm sure,
A sharp watch out. I'd find it dreadful 4450
To have to beg my bread of people,
Beg with a bad conscience, too;
Dreadful to have to wander about
Where all is strange and new,
Only to end up getting caught. 4455

FAUST   But I'll stick to you!

MARGARETE   Quick, be quick!
Save your child, run!
Keep to the path
That goes up by the brook, 4460
Over the bridge,
Into the wood,
Left where the plank is,
There, in the pool—
Reach down and catch it! 4465
It wants to come up,
It's struggling still!
Save it, save it!

FAUST   Get hold of yourself!
One step and you're free, dear girl! 4470

MARGARETE   If only we were well past the hill!
On the rock over there Mother's sitting—
I'm shaking with fear, I'm cold, feel a chill.
She sits on the rock, her head heavy, nodding,
Doesn't look, doesn't wave, can't hold it up straight, 4475
Her sleep was so long she will never wake.
She slept so we might have our pleasure—
The happy hours we passed together!

FAUST   If all my persuading is no use,
   I'll have to carry you off by force.   4480
MARGARETE   Let go, let go, how dare you compel me!
   You're gripping me so brutally!
   I always did what you wanted, once.
FAUST   Soon day will be breaking! Darling, darling!
MARGARETE   Day? Yes, day, my last one, dawning,   4485
   My wedding day it should have been.
   Not a word to a soul, you've already been with your Gretchen.
   My poor wreath!
   Well, everything's finished, it's done.
   We'll see one another again,   4490
   But not to go dancing.
   The crowd's collecting, silent, numb,
   The square and the streets lack enough room.
   There goes the bell, now the staff shatters,
   They seize hold of me, fasten the fetters   4495
   And drag me bound to the block.
   How it twitches, the skin on each neck,
   As the axe-blade's about to strike mine.
   Dumb lies the world as the grave.
FAUST   I wish I had never been born!   4500
MEPHISTOPHELES [*Appearing outside*]
   Unless you come you are lost, now come on!
   Shilly-shallying, debating, jabbering!
   My horses are trembling.
   A minute or two and it's day.
MARGARETE   Who's that rising up out of the ground?   4505
   It's him, him, oh drive him away!
   It's holy here, what does he want?
   Me, he wants me!
FAUST   Live, I say!—live!
MARGARETE   It's the judgment of God! I submit!
MEPHISTO   Die both of you, I have to leave.   4510
MARGARETE   In your hands, our Father! Oh, save me!
   You angelical hosts, stand about me,
   Draw up in your ranks to protect me!
   I'm afraid of you, Heinrich, afraid!
MEPHISTO   She's condemned!   4515
VOICE [*From above.*]
                          She is saved!
MEPHISTO [*To* FAUST, *peremptorily.*]
   Now come on, I tell you, with me!
     [*He disappears with* FAUST.]
VOICE   [*From within, dying away.*]
   Heinrich! Heinrich!

WILLIAM BLAKE
1757–1827

Few works so ostentatiously "simple" as William Blake's *Songs of Innocence and of Experience* (1794) can ever have aroused such critical perplexity. Employing uncomplicated vocabulary and, often, variants of traditional ballad structure; describing the experience usually of naive subjects; supplying no obvious intellectual substance, these short lyrics have long fascinated and baffled their readers.

With no formal education, Blake, son of a London hosier, was at the age of fourteen apprenticed to the engraver James Basire. He developed both as painter and as engraver, partly influenced by the painter Henry Fuseli and the sculptor John Flaxman, both his friends, but remaining always highly individual in style and technique. An acknowledged mystic, he saw visions from the age of four: trees filled with angels, God looking at him through the window. His highly personal view of a world penetrated by the divine helped form both his visual and his verbal art. In 1800, Blake moved from London to Felpham, where the poet William Hayley was his patron. He returned to London in 1803 and remained there for the rest of his life, married but childless, engaged in writing, printing, and engraving.

Blake felt a close relation between the visual and the verbal; he illustrated the works of many poets, notably Milton and Dante. His first book, *Poetical Sketches* (1783), was conventionally published, but he produced all of his subsequent books himself, combining pictorial engravings with lettering, striking off only a few copies of each work by hand. Gradually, in increasingly long poems, he developed an elaborate private mythology, with important figures appearing in one work after another. His major mythic poems include *The Marriage of Heaven and Hell* (1793), *America* (1793), *The Book of Los* (1795), *Milton* (1804), *Jerusalem* (1804), and *The Four Zoas* (which he never completed).

As his short poem "Mock On, Mock On, Voltaire, Rousseau" testifies, Blake was bitterly opposed to what he thought the destructive and repressive rationalism of the eighteenth century. Voltaire and Rousseau might have been surprised to find themselves thus associated; they belong together, in Blake's view, because both implicitly oppose not only orthodox Christianity but the more private variety of revealed religion so vital to Blake himself. Although, like his contemporaries, Blake idealizes imagination and emotion and believes in the sacredness of the individual, he entirely avoids the "egotistical sublime," neither speaking directly of himself in his poetry, as Wordsworth did, nor, like Goethe, creating self-absorbed characters. In his short lyrics he adopts many different voices; the difficulties of interpretation stem partly from this fact. He insistently deals with metaphysical questions about our place in the universe and with social questions about the nature of human responsibility.

In *Songs of Innocence,* the speaker is often a child: asking questions of a lamb, meditating on his own blackness, describing the experience of a chimney sweep. Ostensibly these children in their innocence feel no anger or bitterness at the realities of the world in which they find themselves. The "little black boy" ensures himself a future when the "little English boy" will resemble him and love him; the child addressing the lamb evokes a realm of pure delight; the chimney sweep comforts himself with conventional morality and with a companion's dream. When an adult observer watches children, as in "Holy Thursday," he, too, sees a benign arrangement in which children are "flowers of London town," supervised by "agèd men, wise guardians of the poor." In the "Introduction" to the volume, the adult speaker receives empowering advice from a child, who instructs him to write. Everything is for the best in this best of all possible worlds.

But not quite. Disturbing undertones reverberate through even the most "innocent" of these songs. Innocence is, after all, by definition a state automatically lost through experience and impossible to regain. If the children evoked by the text still possess their innocence, the adult reader does not. "The Little Black Boy" suggests the kind of ambiguity evoked by the conjunction between innocent speaker and experienced reader. The poem opens with a situation that the speaker does not entirely understand but one likely to be painfully familiar to the reader. "White as an angel is the English child: / But I am black as if bereaved of light": the child's similes indicate how completely he has incorporated the value judgments of his society, in which white suggests everything good and black means deficiency and deprivation. In this context, the mother's teaching, a comforting myth, becomes comprehensible as a way of dealing with her child's bewilderment and anxiety about his difference. At the end of the poem, the boy extends his mother's story into a prophetic vision in which black means protective power ("I'll shade him from the heat till he can bear / To lean in joy upon our father's knee"), and difference disappears into likeness, hostility into love. The vision evokes an ideal situation located in an imagined afterlife; it has only an antithetical connection to present actuality. Its emphatic divergence from real social conditions creates the subterranean disturbance characteristic of Blake's lyrics, the disturbance that calls attention to the serious social criticism implicit even in lyrics that may appear sweet to the point of blandness.

For all Blake's dislike of the earlier eighteenth century, he shares with his forebears one important assumption: his poetry, too, instructs as well as pleases. The innocent chimney sweep evokes parental death and betrayal, horrifying working conditions (soot and nakedness, darkness and shaved heads), and compensatory dreams. He never complains, but when he ends with the tag "So if all do their duty, they need not fear harm," it generates moral shock. The discrepancy between the child's purity and his brutal exploitation indicts the society that allows such things. Innocence may be its own protection, these poems suggest, but that fact does not obviate social guilt.

If the *Songs of Innocence*, for all their atmosphere of brightness, cheer, and peace, convey outrage at the ways that social institutions harm those whom they should protect, the *Songs of Experience* more directly evoke a world worn, constricted, and burdened with misery created by human beings. Now a new version of "The Chimney Sweeper" openly states what the earlier poem suggested:

> "And because I am happy, & dance & sing,
> They think they have done me no injury,
> And are gone to praise God & his Priest & King,
> Who make up a heaven of our misery."

The child understands the protective self-blinding of adults.

"London," in its sixteen lines, sums up many of the collection's implications. Like most of the *Songs of Experience*, "London" presents an adult speaker, a wanderer through the city, who finds wherever he goes, in every face, "Marks of weakness, marks of woe." The city is the repository of suffering: men and infants and chimney sweepers cry; soldiers sigh; harlots curse. All are victims of corrupt institutions: blackening church, bloody palace. Marriage and death interpenetrate; the curses of illness and corruption pass through the generations. The speaker reports only what he sees and hears, without commentary. He evokes a society in dreadful decay, and he conveys his despairing rage at a situation he cannot remedy.

Blake's lyrics, in their mixture of the visionary and the observational, strike notes far different from those of satire. Like the visionary observations of Swift and Voltaire, though, they insist on the connection between literature and life. Literature has transformative capacity, but it works with the raw material of actual experience. And its visions have the power to insist on the necessity of change.

SONGS OF INNOCENCE AND OF EXPERIENCE

SHEWING THE TWO CONTRARY STATES OF THE HUMAN SOUL

From *Songs of Innocence*[1]

Introduction

Piping down the valleys wild
Piping songs of pleasant glee
On a cloud I saw a child,
And he laughing said to me,

"Pipe a song about a Lamb";   5
So I piped with merry chear;
"Piper pipe that song again"—
So I piped, he wept to hear.

"Drop thy pipe thy happy pipe
Sing thy songs of happy chear";   10
So I sung the same again
While he wept with joy to hear.

"Piper sit thee down and write
In a book that all may read"—
So he vanished from my sight.   15
And I plucked a hollow reed,

And I made a rural pen,
And I stained the water clear,
And I wrote my happy songs
Every child may joy to hear.   20

The Lamb

Little Lamb, who made thee?
 Dost thou know who made thee?
Gave thee life & bid thee feed,
By the stream & o'er the mead;
Gave thee clothing of delight,   5
Softest clothing wooly bright;
Gave thee such a tender voice,
Making all the vales rejoice!

---

1. The text for all of Blake's works is edited by David V. Erdman and Harold Bloom. *Songs of Innocence* (1789) was later combined with *Songs of Experience* (1794), and the poems were etched and accompanied by Blake's illustrations, the process accomplished by copper engravings stamped on paper, then colored by hand.

Little Lamb who made thee?
Dost thou know who made thee? 10

Little Lamb I'll tell thee,
Little Lamb I'll tell thee!
He is callèd by thy name,
For he calls himself a Lamb:
He is meek & he is mild, 15
He became a little child:
I a child & thou a lamb,
We are callèd by his name.[1]
Little Lamb God bless thee.
Little Lamb God bless thee. 20

The Little Black Boy

My mother bore me in the southern wild,
And I am black, but O! my soul is white;
White as an angel is the English child:
But I am black as if bereaved of light.

My mother taught me underneath a tree, 5
And sitting down before the heat of day,
She took me on her lap and kissèd me,
And pointing to the east, began to say:

"Look on the rising sun: there God does live,
And gives his light, and gives his heat away; 10
And flowers and trees and beasts and men receive
Comfort in morning, joy in the noon day.

"And we are put on earth a little space,
That we may learn to bear the beams of love,
And these black bodies and this sun-burnt face 15
Is but a cloud, and like a shady grove.

"For when our souls have learned the heat to bear,
The cloud will vanish; we shall hear his voice,
Saying: 'Come out from the grove, my love & care,
And round my golden tent like lambs rejoice.'" 20

Thus did my mother say, and kissèd me;
And thus I say to little English boy:
When I from black and he from white cloud free,
And round the tent of God like lambs we joy,

I'll shade him from the heat till he can bear 25
To lean in joy upon our father's knee;

1. Christians use the name of Christ to designate themselves.

And then I'll stand and stroke his silver hair,
And be like him, and he will then love me.

Holy Thursday[1]

'Twas on a Holy Thursday, their innocent faces clean,
The children walking two & two, in red & blue & green,[2]
Grey headed beadles[3] walked before with wands as white as snow,
Till into the high dome of Paul's they like Thames' waters flow.

O what a multitude they seemed, these flowers of London town!   5
Seated in companies they sit with radiance all their own.
The hum of multitudes was there, but multitudes of lambs,
Thousands of little boys & girls raising their innocent hands.

Now like a mighty wind they raise to heaven the voice of song,
Or like harmonious thunderings the seats of heaven among.   10
Beneath them sit the agèd men, wise guardians[4] of the poor;
Then cherish pity, lest you drive an angel from your door.[5]

The Chimney Sweeper

When my mother died I was very young,
And my father sold me[1] while yet my tongue
Could scarcely cry "'weep![2] "weep! "weep! "weep!"
So your chimneys I sweep & in soot I sleep.

There's little Tom Dacre, who cried when his head   5
That curled like a lamb's back, was shaved, so I said,
"Hush, Tom! never mind it, for when your head's bare,
You know that the soot cannot spoil your white hair."

And so he was quiet, & that very night,
As Tom was a-sleeping he had such a sight!   10
That thousands of sweepers, Dick, Joe, Ned, & Jack,
Were all of them locked up in coffins of black;

And by came an Angel who had a bright key,
And he opened the coffins & set them all free;
Then down a green plain, leaping, laughing they run,   15
And wash in a river and shine in the Sun;

1. Ascension Day, forty days after Easter, when children from charity schools were marched to St. Paul's
Cathedral.   2. Each school had its own distinctive uniform.   3. Ushers and minor functionaries, whose
job was to maintain order.   4. The governors of the charity schools.   5. See Hebrews 13.2: "Be not forgetful to entertain strangers: for thereby some have entertained angels unawares."   1. It was common
practice in Blake's day for fathers to sell, or indenture, their children to become chimney sweeps. The average age at which such children began working was six or seven; they were generally employed for seven
years, until they were too big to ascend the chimneys.   2. The child's lisping effort to say "sweep," as he
walks the streets looking for work.

Then naked[3] & white, all their bags left behind,
They rise upon clouds, and sport in the wind.
And the Angel told Tom, if he'd be a good boy,
He'd have God for his father & never want joy.   20

And so Tom awoke; and we rose in the dark
And got with our bags & our brushes to work.
Tho' the morning was cold, Tom was happy & warm;
So if all do their duty, they need not fear harm.

From *Songs of Experience*

Introduction

Hear the voice of the Bard!
Who Present, Past, & Future sees;
Whose ears have heard
The Holy Word
That walked among the ancient trees;[1]   5

Calling the lapsèd Soul
And weeping in the evening dew;[2]
That might control
The starry pole,
And fallen, fallen light renew!   10

"O Earth, O Earth, return!
Arise from out the dewy grass;
Night is worn,
And the morn
Rises from the slumberous mass.   15

"Turn away no more;
Why wilt thou turn away?
The starry floor
The watery shore
Is given thee till the break of day."   20

Earth's Answer

Earth raised up her head,
From the darkness dread & drear.

---

3. They climbed up the chimneys naked.   1. Genesis 3.8: "And [Adam and Eve] heard the voice of the
Lord God walking in the garden in the cool of the day."   2. Blake's ambiguous use of pronouns makes for
interpretative difficulties. It would seem that "The Holy Word" (Jehovah, a name for God in the Old Testament) calls *the* "lapsèd Soul," and weeps—not the Bard.

Her light fled:
Stony dread!
And her locks covered with grey despair.   5

"Prisoned on watery shore
Starry Jealousy does keep my den,
Cold and hoar
Weeping o'er
I hear the Father[1] of the ancient men.   10

"Selfish father of men,
Cruel, jealous, selfish fear!
Can delight
Chained in night
The virgins of youth and morning bear?   15

"Does spring hide its joy
When buds and blossoms grow?
Does the sower
Sow by night,
Or the plowman in darkness plow?   20

"Break this heavy chain
That does freeze my bones around;
Selfish! vain!
Eternal bane!
That free Love with bondage bound."   25

The Tyger

Tyger! Tyger! burning bright
In the forests of the night,
What immortal hand or eye
Could frame thy fearful symmetry?

In what distant deeps or skies   5
Burnt the fire of thine eyes?
On what wings dare he aspire?
What the hand dare seize the fire?

And what shoulder, & what art,
Could twist the sinews of thy heart?   10
And when thy heart began to beat,
What dread hand? & what dread feet?

---

1. In Blake's later prophetic works, one of the four Zoas, representing the four chief faculties of humankind, is Urizen. In general, he stands for the orthodox conception of the divine creator, sometimes Jehovah in the Old Testament, often the God conceived by Newton and Locke—in all instances a tyrant associated with excessive rationalism and sexual repression, and the opponent of the imagination and creativity. This may be "the Holy Word" in line 4 of "Introduction" (p. 712).

What the hammer? what the chain?
In what furnace was thy brain?
What the anvil? what dread grasp   15
Dare its deadly terrors clasp?

When the stars threw down their spears,
And watered heaven with their tears,
Did he smile his work to see?
Did he who made the Lamb make thee?   20

Tyger! Tyger! burning bright
In the forests of the night,
What immortal hand or eye
Dare frame thy fearful symmetry?

The Sick Rose

O Rose, thou art sick.
The invisible worm
That flies in the night
In the howling storm

Has found out thy bed   5
Of crimson joy,
And his dark secret love
Does thy life destroy.

London

I wander thro' each chartered[1] street,
Near where the chartered Thames does flow,
And mark in every face I meet
Marks of weakness, marks of woe.

In every cry of every Man,   5
In every Infant's cry of fear,
In every voice, in every ban,
The mind-forged manacles I hear:

How the Chimney-sweeper's cry
Every blackening Church appalls;[2]   10
And the hapless Soldier's sigh
Runs in blood down Palace walls.

1. Hired (literally). Blake implies that the streets and the river are controlled by commercial interests.
2. Makes white (literally), punning also on *appall* (to dismay) and *pall* (the cloth covering a corpse or bier).

But most thro' midnight streets I hear
How the youthful Harlot's curse
Blasts the new-born Infant's tear,[3]   15
And blights with plagues the Marriage hearse.

The Chimney Sweeper

A little black thing among the snow
Crying "'weep, 'weep," in notes of woe!
"Where are thy father & mother? say?"
"They are both gone up to the church to pray.

"Because I was happy upon the heath,   5
And smiled among the winter's snow;
They clothèd me in the clothes of death,
And taught me to sing the notes of woe.

"And because I am happy, & dance & sing,
They think they have done me no injury,   10
And are gone to praise God & his Priest & King,
Who make up a heaven of our misery."

Mock On, Mock On, Voltaire, Rousseau

Mock on, Mock on, Voltaire, Rousseau;
Mock on, Mock on, 'tis all in vain.
You throw the sand against the wind,
And the wind blows it back again.

And every sand becomes a Gem   5
Reflected in the beams divine;
Blown back, they blind the mocking Eye,
But still in Israel's paths they shine.

The Atoms of Democritus[1]
And Newton's Particles of light[2]   10
Are sands upon the Red sea shore,
Where Israel's tents do shine so bright.

---

3. The harlot infects the parents with venereal disease, and thus the infant is inflicted with neonatal blindness.   1. Greek philosopher (460?–362? B.C.E.), who advanced a theory that all things are merely patterns of atoms.   2. Sir Isaac Newton's (1642–1727) corpuscular theory of light. For Blake, both Newton and Democritus were condemned as materialists.

And Did Those Feet

And did those feet[1] in ancient time
Walk upon England's mountains green?
And was the holy Lamb of God
On England's pleasant pastures seen?

And did the Countenance Divine   5
Shine forth upon our clouded hills?
And was Jerusalem builded here,
Among those dark Satanic Mills?[2]

Bring me my Bow of burning gold:
Bring me my Arrows of desire: 10
Bring me my Spear: O clouds unfold!
Bring me my Chariot of fire!

I will not cease from Mental Fight,
Nor shall my Sword sleep in my hand,
Till we have built Jerusalem   15
In England's green & pleasant Land.

---

1. A reference to an ancient legend that Jesus came to England with Joseph of Arimathea.   2. Possibly industrial England, but *mills* also meant for Blake 18th-century arid, mechanistic philosophy.

FRIEDRICH HÖLDERLIN
1770–1843

Important partly for his capacity to combine classical and Romantic sensibility, the German poet Friedrich Hölderlin (*freed'-rick hul'der-lin*) wrote his considerable body of lyric verse early in his life, before becoming incurably schizophrenic at the age of thirty-six. He had prepared himself for the ministry but decided that he was unsuited for such a vocation and found work—not very successfully—as a tutor. In his lyrics, which have become celebrated since the twentieth century, he records and evokes intensities of personal feeling, with particular emphasis, as the selections printed here reveal, on what it means for human beings to live in time.

The Half of Life[1]

With yellow pears the country,
Brimming with wild roses,
Hangs into the lake,
You gracious swans,
And drunk with kisses   5

---

1. Translated by Christopher Middleton, who successfully evokes Hölderlin's range of tones and meters.

Your heads you dip
Into the holy lucid water.

Where, ah where shall I find,
When winter comes, the flowers,
And where the sunshine   10
And shadows of the earth?
Walls stand
Speechless and cold, in the wind
The weathervanes clatter.

Hyperion's[1] Song of Fate

You walk up there in the light
  On floors like velvet, blissful spirits.
    Shining winds divine
    Touch you lightly
      As a harper touches holy   5
      Strings with her fingers.

Fateless as babes asleep
  They breathe, the celestials.
    Chastely kept
    In a simple bud,   10
    For them the spirit
      Flowers eternal,
      And in bliss their eyes
      Gaze in eternal
      Calm clarity.   15

But to us it is given
  To find no resting place,
  We faint, we fall,
  Suffering, human,
  Blindly from one   20
  To the next moment
    Like water flung
    From rock to rock down
    Long years into uncertainty.

Brevity

Why make it so short? Have you lost your old liking
For song? Why, in days of hope, when young,
  You sang and sang,
  There scarce was an end of it.

1. In Greek mythology, a Titan, father of Aurora, goddess of dawn.

My song is short as my luck was. Who'd go 5
   Gaily swimming at sundown? It's gone, earth's cold,
      And the annoying nightbird
         Flits, close, blocking your vision.

To the Fates

Grant me a single summer, you lords of all,
   A single autumn, for the fullgrown song,
      So that, with such sweet playing sated,
         Then my heart may die more willing.

The soul, in life robbed of its godly right, 5
   Rests not, even in Orcus[1] down below;
      Yet should I once achieve my heart's
         First holy concern, the poem,

Welcome then, O stillness of the shadow world!
   Even if down I go without my 10
      Music, I shall be satisfied; once
         Like gods I shall have lived, more I need not.

1. Hades.

WILLIAM WORDSWORTH
1770–1850

William Wordsworth both proclaimed and embodied the *newness* of the Romantic movement. In his preface to the second edition of *Lyrical Ballads* (1800), a collection of poems by him and his friend Samuel Taylor Coleridge, he announced the advent of a poetic revolution. Like other revolutionaries, Wordsworth and Coleridge created their identities by rebelling against and parodying their predecessors. Now no longer would poets write in "dead" forms; now they had discovered a "new" direction, "new" subject matter; now poetry could at last serve as an important form of human communication. Reading Wordsworth's poems with the excitement of that revolution long past, we can still feel the power of his desire to communicate. The human heart is his subject; he writes, in particular, of growth and of memory and of the perplexities inherent in the human condition.

    Born at Cockermouth, Cumberland, to the family of an attorney, Wordsworth attended St. John's College, Cambridge, from 1787 to 1791. The next year, early in the French Revolution, he spent in France, where he met Annette Vallon and had a daughter by her. In 1795, Wordsworth met Coleridge; two years later, Wordsworth and his sister, Dorothy, moved to Alfoxden, near Coleridge's home in Nether Stowey, in Somerset. There the two men conceived the idea of collaboration; in 1798, the first edition of their *Lyrical Ballads* appeared, anonymously. The next year,

Wordsworth and his sister settled in the Lake District of northwest England. In 1802, the poet married Mary Hutchinson, with whom he had five children. He received the sinecure of stamp distributor in 1813 and in 1843 succeeded Robert Southey as England's poet laureate, having long since abandoned the political radicalism of his youth.

Wordsworth wrote little prose, except for the famous preface of 1800 and another preface in 1815; his accomplishment was almost entirely poetic. His early work employed conventional eighteenth-century techniques, but *Lyrical Ballads* marked a new direction: an effort to employ simple language and to reveal the high significance of simple themes, the transcendent importance of the everyday. Between 1798 and 1805 he composed his nineteenth-century version of an epic, *The Prelude*, an account of the development of a poet's mind—his own. His subsequent work included odes, sonnets, and many poems written to mark specific occasions.

It would be difficult to overestimate the extent of Wordsworth's historical and poetic importance. In *The Prelude*, not published until 1850, he not only made powerful poetry out of his own experience but also specified a way of valuing experience:

> There are in our existence spots of time,
> That with distinct pre-eminence retain
> A renovating virtue, whence, depressed
> By false opinion and contentious thought,
> Or aught of heavier or more deadly weight,
> In trivial occupations, and the round
> Of ordinary intercourse, our minds
> Are nourished and invisibly repaired;
> A virtue, by which pleasure is enhanced,
> That penetrates, enables us to mount
> When high, more high, and lifts us up when fallen.

To take seriously the moment, this passage suggests, enables us to resist the dulling force of everyday life ("trivial occupations") and provides the means of personal salvation.

Wordsworth often uses religious language (a religious reference is hinted in the idea of being lifted up when fallen) to insist on the importance of his doctrine. He inaugurated an attempt—lasting far into the century—to establish and sustain a secular religion to substitute for Christian faith. The attempt was, even for Wordsworth, only intermittently successful. *The Prelude* records experiences of persuasive visionary intensity, as when the poet speaks of seeing a shepherd in the distance:

> Or him have I descried in distant sky,
> A solitary object and sublime,
> Above all height! like an aerial cross
> Stationed alone upon a spiry rock
> Of the Chartreuse, for worship.

But such "spots of time" exist in isolation; it is difficult to maintain a saving faith on their basis.

The two long poems printed here treat the problem of discovering and sustaining faith. "Lines Composed a Few Miles above Tintern Abbey," first published in *Lyrical Ballads,* and "Ode on Intimations of Immortality," published in 1807 but written between 1802 and 1806, share a preoccupation with loss and with the saving power of memory. Both speak of personal experience, although the ode, a more formal poem, also generalizes to a hypothetical "we." Both insist that nature—the external world experienced through the senses and the containing pattern assumed beyond that world—offers the possibility of wisdom to combat the pain inherent in human growth.

But it would be a mistake to assume that these works exist to promulgate a doctrine of natural salvation, although some readers have considered the poems' "pantheism" (the belief that God pervades every part of His created universe) their most important aspect. Both poems evoke an intellectual and emotional process, not a conclusion; they sketch dramas of human development.

In "Tintern Abbey," the speaker conveys his relief at returning to a sylvan scene that has been important to him in memory. His recollections of this natural beauty, he says, have helped sustain him in the confusion and weariness of city life; he thinks that they may also have encouraged him toward goodness and serenity. But this second suggestion, that memories of nature have a moral effect, is only hypothetical, qualified in the text by such words and phrases as "I trust" and "perhaps." Indeed, the poem's next section opens with explicit statement that this may "Be but a vain belief." True or false, though, the belief comforts the speaker, who then recalls his more direct relation with nature in the past, when "The sounding cataract / Haunted me like a passion." He hopes, but cannot be sure, that his present awareness of "The still, sad music of humanity" and of the great "presence" that infuses nature compensates for what he has sacrificed in losing the immediacy of youthful experience.

The last section of "Tintern Abbey" emphasizes still more that the speaker is struggling with depression over his sense of loss; he observes that the presence of his "dearest Friend," his sister, would protect his "genial spirits" from decay even without his faith in what he has learned. That sister now becomes the focus for his thoughts about nature; he imagines her growth similar to his own, but perfected, and her power of memory as able to contain not only the beauties of the landscape but his presence as part of that landscape. The poem thus resolves itself with emphasis on a human relationship, between the man and his sister, as well as on the importance of nature. Its emotional power derives partly from its evocation of the *need* to believe in nature as a form of salvation and of the process of development through which that need manifests itself.

At about the same time that he wrote the "Ode on Intimations of Immortality," Wordsworth composed his sonnet "The World Is Too Much with Us":

> . . . we lay waste our powers
> Little we see in Nature that is ours;
> . . . we are out of tune.

Despite the rhapsodic tone that dominates the ode, it, too, reveals itself as a hard-won act of faith, an effort to combat the view of the present world conveyed in the sonnet.

The ode opens with insistence on loss: "The things which I have seen I now can see no more." The speaker feels grief; he tries to deny it because it seems at odds with the harmony and joy of the natural world. Yet the effort fails: even natural beauty speaks to him of what he no longer possesses. Stanzas V through VIII emphasize the association of infancy with natural communion and the inevitable deprivation attending growth. In stanza IX, the speaker attempts to value what still remains to him: it's all he has; he's grateful for it. In the concluding stanzas, however, he arrives at a new revelation: now nature acquires value not as a form of unmixed ecstasy, but in connection with the experience of human suffering:

> Though nothing can bring back the hour
> Of splendour in the grass, of glory in the flower;
> We will grieve not, rather find
> Strength in what remains behind; . . .
> In the soothing thoughts that spring
> Out of human suffering . . .

It is "the human heart by which we live" that finally enables the poet to experience the wonder of a flower, now become the source of "Thoughts that do often lie too deep for tears."

The view that the processes of maturing involve giving up a kind of wisdom accessible only to children belongs particularly to the Romantic period, but most people at least occasionally feel that in growing up they have left behind something they would rather keep. Wordsworth's poetic expression of the effort to come to terms with such feelings may remind his readers of barely noticed aspects of their own experience.

PRONOUNCING GLOSSARY

The following list uses common English syllables and stress accents to provide rough equivalents of selected words whose pronunciation may be unfamiliar to the general reader.

Proteus: *proh'-tee-us*   Triton: *try'-tun*

Lines Composed a Few Miles above Tintern Abbey

On Revisiting the Banks of the Wye During a Tour, July 13, 1798

Five years have past; five summers, with the length
Of five long winters! and again I hear
These waters, rolling from their mountain-springs
With a soft inland murmur.—Once again
Do I behold these steep and lofty cliffs,   5
That on a wild secluded scene impress
Thoughts of more deep seclusion; and connect
The landscape with the quiet of the sky.
The day is come when I again repose
Here, under this dark sycamore, and view   10
These plots of cottage-ground, these orchard-tufts,
Which at this season, with their unripe fruits,
Are clad in one green hue, and lose themselves
'Mid groves and copses. Once again I see
These hedge-rows, hardly hedge-rows, little lines   15
Of sportive wood run wild: these pastoral farms,
Green to the very door; and wreaths of smoke
Sent up, in silence, from among the trees!
With some uncertain notice, as might seem
Of vagrant dwellers in the houseless woods,   20
Or of some Hermit's cave, where by his fire
The Hermit sits alone.

              These beauteous forms,
Through a long absence, have not been to me
As is a landscape to a blind man's eye:
But oft, in lonely rooms, and 'mid the din   25
Of towns and cities, I have owed to them,
In hours of weariness, sensations sweet,
Felt in the blood, and felt along the heart;
And passing even into my purer mind,
With tranquil restoration:—feelings too   30

Of unremembered pleasure: such, perhaps,
As have no slight or trivial influence
On that best portion of a good man's life,
His little, nameless, unremembered, acts
Of kindness and of love. Nor less, I trust,   35
To them I may have owed another gift,
Of aspect more sublime; that blessèd mood,
In which the burthen of the mystery,
In which the heavy and the weary weight
Of all this unintelligible world,   40
Is lightened:—that serene and blessèd mood,
In which the affections gently lead us on,—
Until, the breath of this corporeal frame
And even the motion of our human blood
Almost suspended, we are laid asleep   45
In body, and become a living soul:
While with an eye made quiet by the power
Of harmony, and the deep power of joy,
We see into the life of things.

                                            If this
Be but a vain belief, yet, oh! how oft—   50
In darkness and amid the many shapes
Of joyless daylight; when the fretful stir
Unprofitable, and the fever of the world,
Have hung upon the beatings of my heart—
How oft, in spirit, have I turned to thee,   55
O sylvan Wye! thou wanderer thro' the woods,
How often has my spirit turned to thee!

    And now, with gleams of half-extinguished thought,
With many recognitions dim and faint,
And somewhat of a sad perplexity,   60
The picture of the mind revives again:
While here I stand, not only with the sense
Of present pleasure, but with pleasing thoughts
That in this moment there is life and food
For future years. And so I dare to hope,   65
Though changed, no doubt, from what I was when first
I came among these hills; when like a roe
I bounded o'er the mountains, by the sides
Of the deep rivers, and the lonely streams,
Wherever nature led: more like a man   70
Flying from something that he dreads, than one
Who sought the thing he loved. For nature then
(The coarser pleasures of my boyish days,
And their glad animal movements all gone by)
To me was all in all.—I cannot paint   75
What then I was. The sounding cataract
Haunted me like a passion: the tall rock,
The mountain, and the deep and gloomy wood,
Their colours and their forms, were then to me

An appetite; a feeling and a love,   80
That had no need of a remoter charm,
By thought supplied, nor any interest
Unborrowed from the eye.—That time is past,
And all its aching joys are now no more,
And all its dizzy raptures. Not for this   85
Faint I, nor mourn nor murmur; other gifts
Have followed; for such loss, I would believe,
Abundant recompense. For I have learned
To look on nature, not as in the hour
Of thoughtless youth; but hearing oftentimes   90
The still, sad music of humanity,
Nor harsh nor grating, though of ample power
To chasten and subdue. And I have felt
A presence that disturbs me with the joy
Of elevated thoughts; a sense sublime   95
Of something far more deeply interfused,
Whose dwelling is the light of setting suns,
And the round ocean and the living air,
And the blue sky, and in the mind of man:
A motion and a spirit, that impels   100
All thinking things, all objects of all thought,
And rolls through all things. Therefore am I still
A lover of the meadows and the woods,
And mountains; and of all that we behold
From this green earth; of all the mighty world   105
Of eye, and ear,—both what they half create,
And what perceive; well pleased to recognise
In nature and the language of the sense,
The anchor of my purest thoughts, the nurse,
The guide, the guardian of my heart, and soul   110
Of all my moral being.

          Nor perchance,
If I were not thus taught, should I the more
Suffer my genial[1] spirits to decay:
For thou art with me here upon the banks
Of this fair river; thou my dearest Friend,   115
My dear, dear Friend; and in thy voice I catch
The language of my former heart, and read
My former pleasures in the shooting lights
Of thy wild eyes. Oh! yet a little while
May I behold in thee what I was once,   120
My dear, dear Sister! and this prayer I make,
Knowing that Nature never did betray
The heart that loved her; 'tis her privilege,
Through all the years of this our life, to lead
From joy to joy: for she can so inform   125
The mind that is within us, so impress
With quietness and beauty, and so feed

---

1. Generative, creative.

With lofty thoughts, that neither evil tongues,
Rash judgments, nor the sneers of selfish men,
Nor greetings where no kindness is, nor all 130
The dreary intercourse of daily life,
Shall e'er prevail against us, or disturb
Our cheerful faith, that all which we behold
Is full of blessings. Therefore let the moon
Shine on thee in thy solitary walk; 135
And let the misty mountain-winds be free
To blow against thee: and, in after years,
When these wild ecstasies shall be matured
Into a sober pleasure; when thy mind
Shall be a mansion for all lovely forms, 140
Thy memory be as a dwelling-place
For all sweet sounds and harmonies; oh! then,
If solitude, or fear, or pain, or grief
Should be thy portion, with what healing thoughts
Of tender joy wilt thou remember me, 145
And these my exhortations! Nor, perchance—
If I should be where I no more can hear
Thy voice, nor catch from thy wild eyes these gleams
Of past existence—wilt thou then forget
That on the banks of this delightful stream 150
We stood together; and that I, so long
A worshipper of Nature, hither came
Unwearied in that service; rather say
With warmer love—oh! with far deeper zeal
Of holier love. Nor wilt thou then forget 155
That after many wanderings, many years
Of absence, these steep woods and lofty cliffs,
And this green pastoral landscape, were to me
More dear, both for themselves and for thy sake!

Ode on Intimations of Immortality

From Recollections of Early Childhood

> The Child is father of the Man;
> And I could wish my days to be
> Bound each to each by natural piety.

I

There was a time when meadow, grove, and stream,
The earth, and every common sight,
   To me did seem
  Apparelled in celestial light,
The glory and the freshness of a dream. 5
It is not now as it hath been of yore;—
   Turn wheresoe'er I may,

By night or day,
The things which I have seen I now can see no more.

II

The Rainbow comes and goes,   10
And lovely is the Rose;
The Moon doth with delight
Look round her when the heavens are bare,
    Waters on a starry night
    Are beautiful and fair;   15
The sunshine is a glorious birth;
But yet I know, where'er I go,
That there hath past away a glory from the earth.

III

Now, while the birds thus sing a joyous song,
    And while the young lambs bound   20
      As to the tabor's sound,
To me alone there came a thought of grief:
A timely utterance gave that thought relief,
    And I again am strong:
The cataracts blow their trumpets from the steep;   25
No more shall grief of mine the season wrong;
I hear the Echoes through the mountains throng,
The Winds come to me from the fields of sleep,
    And all the earth is gay;
      Land and sea   30
Give themselves up to jollity,
    And with the heart of May
Doth every Beast keep holiday;—
    Thou Child of Joy,
Shout round me, let me hear thy shouts, thou happy   35
  Shepherd-boy!

IV

Ye blessèd Creatures, I have heard the call
    Ye to each other make; I see
The heavens laugh with you in your jubilee;
    My heart is at your festival,   40
      My head hath its coronal,
The fulness of your bliss, I feel—I feel it all.
    Oh evil day! if I were sullen
    While Earth herself is adorning,
      This sweet May-morning,   45
    And the Children are culling
      On every side,
    In a thousand valleys far and wide,
    Fresh flowers; while the sun shines warm,
And the Babe leaps up on his Mother's arm:—   50
    I hear, I hear, with joy I hear!

—But there's a Tree, of many, one,
A single Field which I have looked upon,
Both of them speak of something that is gone:
  The Pansy at my feet   55
  Doth the same tale repeat:
Whither is fled the visionary gleam?
Where is it now, the glory and the dream?

        V

Our birth is but a sleep and a forgetting:
The Soul that rises with us, our life's Star,   60
  Hath had elsewhere its setting,
   And cometh from afar:
   Not in entire forgetfulness,
   And not in utter nakedness,
But trailing clouds of glory do we come   65
  From God, who is our home:
Heaven lies about us in our infancy!
Shades of the prison-house begin to close
  Upon the growing Boy,
But He beholds the light, and whence it flows,   70
  He sees it in his joy;
The Youth, who daily farther from the east
  Must travel, still is Nature's Priest,
  And by the vision splendid
  Is on his way attended;   75
At length the Man perceives it die away,
And fade into the light of common day.

        VI

Earth fills her lap with pleasures of her own;
Yearnings she hath in her own natural kind,
And, even with something of a Mother's mind,   80
  And no unworthy aim,
  The homely Nurse doth all she can
To make her Foster-child, her Inmate, Man,
  Forget the glories he hath known,
And that imperial palace whence he came.   85

        VII

Behold the Child among his new-born blisses,
A six years' Darling of a pigmy size!
See, where 'mid work of his own hand he lies,
Fretted by sallies of his mother's kisses,
With light upon him from his father's eyes!   90
See, at his feet, some little plan or chart,
Some fragment from his dream of human life,
Shaped by himself with newly-learnèd art;
  A wedding or a festival,
  A mourning or a funeral;   95

And this hath now his heart,
And unto this he frames his song:
Then will he fit his tongue
To dialogues of business, love, or strife;
But it will not be long   100
Ere this be thrown aside,
And with new joy and pride
The little Actor cons another part;
Filling from time to time his "humorous stage"
With all the Persons, down to palsied Age,   105
That Life brings with her in her equipage;
As if his whole vocation
Were endless imitation.

VIII

Thou, whose exterior semblance doth belie
Thy Soul's immensity;   110
Thou best Philosopher, who yet dost keep
Thy heritage, thou Eye among the blind,
That, deaf and silent, read'st the eternal deep,
Haunted for ever by the eternal mind,—
Mighty Prophet! Seer blest!   115
On whom those truths do rest,
Which we are toiling all our lives to find,
In darkness lost, the darkness of the grave;
Thou, over whom thy Immortality
Broods like the Day, a Master o'er a Slave,   120
A Presence which is not to be put by;
[To whom the grave
Is but a lonely bed without the sense or sight
Of day or the warm light,
A place of thought where we in waiting lie;]¹   125
Thou little Child, yet glorious in the might
Of heaven-born freedom on thy being's height,
Why with such earnest pains dost thou provoke
The years to bring the inevitable yoke,
Thus blindly with thy blessedness at strife?   130
Full soon thy Soul shall have her earthly freight,
And custom lie upon thee with a weight,
Heavy as frost, and deep almost as life!

IX

O joy! that in our embers
Is something that doth live,   135
That nature yet remembers
What was so fugitive!
The thought of our past years in me doth breed

---

1. The lines within brackets were included in the *Ode* in the 1807 and 1815 editions of Wordsworth's poems but were omitted in the 1820 and subsequent editions, as a result of Coleridge's severe censure of them.

Perpetual benediction: not indeed
For that which is most worthy to be blest;   140
Delight and liberty, the simple creed
Of Childhood, whether busy or at rest,
With new-fledged hope still fluttering in his breast—
    Not for these I raise
      The song of thanks and praise;   145
   But for those obstinate questionings
   Of sense and outward things,
   Fallings from us, vanishings;
   Blank misgivings of a Creature
Moving about in worlds not realized,   150
High instincts before which our mortal Nature
Did tremble like a guilty Thing surprised:
    But for those first affections,
    Those shadowy recollections,
     Which, be they what they may,   155
Are yet the fountain-light of all our day,
Are yet a master-light of all our seeing;
  Uphold us, cherish, and have power to make
Our noisy years seem moments in the being
Of the eternal Silence: truths that wake,   160
    To perish never;
Which neither listlessness, nor mad endeavour,
    Nor Man nor Boy,
Nor all that is at enmity with joy,
Can utterly abolish or destroy!   165
  Hence in a season of calm weather
    Though inland far we be,
Our Souls have sight of that immortal sea
    Which brought us hither,
    Can in a moment travel thither,   170
And see the Children sport upon the shore,
And hear the mighty waters rolling evermore.

X

Then sing, ye Birds, sing, sing a joyous song!
    And let the young Lambs bound
    As to the tabor's sound!   175
We in thought will join your throng,
    Ye that pipe and ye that play,
    Ye that through your hearts to-day
    Feel the gladness of the May!
What though the radiance which was once so bright   180
Be now for ever taken from my sight,
  Though nothing can bring back the hour
Of splendour in the grass, of glory in the flower;
    We will grieve not, rather find
    Strength in what remains behind;   185
    In the primal sympathy
    Which having been must ever be;

In the soothing thoughts that spring
Out of human suffering;
In the faith that looks through death, 190
In years that bring the philosophic mind.

XI

And O, ye Fountains, Meadows, Hills, and Groves,
Forebode not any severing of our loves!
Yet in my heart of hearts I feel your might;
I only have relinquished one delight 195
To live beneath your more habitual sway.
I love the Brooks which down their channels fret,
Even more than when I tripped lightly as they;
The innocent brightness of a new-born Day
Is lovely yet; 200
The Clouds that gather round the setting sun
Do take a sober colouring from an eye
That hath kept watch o'er man's mortality;
Another race hath been, and other palms are won.
Thanks to the human heart by which we live, 205
Thanks to its tenderness, its joys, and fears,
To me the meanest flower that blows can give
Thoughts that do often lie too deep for tears.

Composed upon Westminster Bridge, September 3, 1802

Earth has not anything to show more fair:
Dull would he be of soul who could pass by
A sight so touching in its majesty;
This City now doth, like a garment, wear
The beauty of the morning; silent, bare, 5
Ships, towers, domes, theatres, and temples lie
Open unto the fields, and to the sky;
All bright and glittering in the smokeless air.
Never did sun more beautifully steep
In his first splendour, valley, rock, or hill; 10
Ne'er saw I, never felt, a calm so deep!
The river glideth at his own sweet will:
Dear God! the very houses seem asleep;
And all that mighty heart is lying still!

The World Is Too Much with Us

The world is too much with us; late and soon,
Getting and spending, we lay waste our powers:
Little we see in Nature that is ours;

We have given our hearts away, a sordid boon![1]
This Sea that bares her bosom to the moon,   5
The winds that will be howling at all hours,
And are up-gathered now like sleeping flowers;
For this, for everything, we are out of tune;
It moves us not.—Great God! I'd rather be
A Pagan suckled in a creed outworn;   10
So might I, standing on this pleasant lea,
Have glimpses that would make me less forlorn;
Have sight of Proteus[2] rising from the sea;
Or hear old Triton[3] blow his wreathèd horn.

1. Gift. "Sordid": refers to the act of giving the heart away.   2. An old man of the sea who, in the *Odyssey*, could assume a variety of shapes.   3. A sea deity, usually represented as blowing on a conch shell.

JOHN KEATS
1795–1821

A poet "half in love with easeful Death," to quote a line from his "Ode to a Nightingale," John Keats expressed with compelling intensity the Romantic longing for the unattainable, a concept that he defined in ways very different from Goethe's. In a series of brilliant lyrics, he explored subtle links between the passion for absolute beauty, which provides an imagined alternative to the everyday world's sordidness and disappointment, and the desire to melt into extinction, another form of that alternative.

At the age of sixteen, Keats was apprenticed to a druggist and surgeon; in 1816, he was licensed as an apothecary—but almost immediately abandoned medicine for poetry. Son of a hostler (a groom for horses) at a London inn, he had earlier attended school at Enfield, where he manifested an interest in literature encouraged by his friend Charles Cowden Clarke, the headmaster's son. Through political radical, poet, and critic Leigh Hunt, whose literary circle he joined in 1816, Keats came to know Percy Bysshe Shelley, William Hazlitt, and Charles Lamb, important members of the Romantic movement. He had a brief love affair with Fanny Brawne, to whom he became engaged in 1819; the next year he went to Italy, seeking a cure for his tuberculosis, only to die in Rome.

Although his first book, *Poems* (1817), met with some critical success, the long mythological poem *Endymion*, which he published a year later, became an object of attack by conservative literary reviews (*Blackwood's* and the *Quarterly*). Shelley, in his elegy for Keats (*Adonais*, 1821), encouraged the myth that the harsh reviews caused the poet's death. In fact, Keats lived long enough to publish his most important volume—written scarcely five years after he first tried his hand at poetry—*Lamia, Isabella, The Eve of St. Agnes, and Other Poems* (1820), which won critical applause and contained most of the poems for which he is remembered today.

Some of Keats's greatest works return to a form popular in the eighteenth century: the ode addressed to an abstraction (for example, melancholy) or another nonhuman object (for example, a nightingale or an urn). Although the basic literary device seems highly artificial, Keats uses it powerfully to express his characteristic sense of beauty so intensely experienced that it almost corresponds to pain.

My heart aches, and a drowsy numbness pains
  My sense, as though of hemlock I had drunk . . .
'Tis not through envy of thy happy lot,
  But being too happy in thy happiness. . . .

"Ode on Melancholy," in its sharp contrast to Coleridge's and Shelley's poems on dejection as well as to seventeenth- and eighteenth-century evocations of melancholy, illustrates particularly well Keats's special exemplification of the Romantic sensibility. In the first stanza, the speaker explicitly rejects traditional accompaniments of melancholy—yew, the death's-head moth, the owl—because such associations suggest a kind of passivity or inertia that might "drown the wakeful anguish of the soul," interfering with the immediate and intense experience of melancholy that he actively seeks. Instead, he advocates trying to live as completely as possible in the immediacy of emotion. Melancholy, he continues, dwells with beauty and joy and pleasure, all in their nature evanescent. To fully feel the wonder of beauty or happiness implies awareness that it will soon vanish. Only those capable of active participation in their own positive emotions can hope to know melancholy; paradoxically, the result of energetic commitment to the life of feeling is the utter submission to melancholy's power: one can hope to "be among her cloudy trophies hung."

Prose summary of such an argument risks sounding ridiculous or incomprehensible, for Keats's emotional logic inheres in the imagery and the music of his poems, which exert their own compelling force. Without any previous belief in the desirability of melancholy as an emotion, the reader, absorbed into a rich sequence of images, feels swept into an experience comparable to that which the poem endorses. The ode generates its own sense of beauty and of melancholy, and of the close relation between the two. Its brilliantly evocative specificity of physical reference always suggests more than is directly said, more than paraphrase can encompass:

Aye, in the very temple of Delight
  Veiled Melancholy has her sovereign shrine,
    Though seen of none save him whose strenuous tongue
Can burst Joy's grape against his palate fine . . .

Everyone can recall the sensuous pleasure of a grape releasing its juice into the mouth, but it would be difficult to elucidate the full implications of the "strenuous tongue" or of "Joy's grape." Keat's great poetic gift manifests itself most unmistakably in his extraordinary power of suggestion—not only in the odes, but in the ballad imitation "La Belle Dame sans Merci," with its haunting, half-told story, and in the understated sonnets, asserting the speaker's feeling but always hinting more emotion than they directly affirm.

PRONOUNCING GLOSSARY

The following list uses common English syllables and stress accents to provide rough equivalents of selected words whose pronunciation may be unfamiliar to the general reader.

Arcady: *ahr'-kah-dee*

Darien: *day'-ree-en*

Hippocrene: *hip'-oh-kreen*

La Belle Dame sans Merci: *lah bel
  dahm sahnh mayr-see'*

Lethe: *lee'-thee*

Proserpine: *pro'-ser-pain*

Provençal: *proh-vahn-sahl'*

Tempe: *tem'-pee*

On First Looking into Chapman's Homer[1]

Much have I traveled in the realms of gold,
  And many goodly states and kingdoms seen;
  Round many western islands have I been
Which bards in fealty to Apollo[2] hold.
Oft of one wide expanse had I been told   5
  That deep-browed Homer ruled as his demesne;[3]
  Yet did I never breathe its pure serene
Till I heard Chapman speak out loud and bold:
Then felt I like some watcher of the skies
  When a new planet swims into his ken;   10
Or like stout Cortez[4] when with eagle eyes
  He stared at the Pacific—and all his men
Looked at each other with a wild surmise—
  Silent, upon a peak in Darien.

Bright Star

Bright star, would I were steadfast as thou art—
  Not in lone splendor hung aloft the night,
And watching, with eternal lids apart,
  Like nature's patient, sleepless Eremite,[1]
The moving waters at their priestlike task   5
  Of pure ablution round earth's human shores,
Or gazing on the new soft fallen mask
  Of snow upon the mountains and the moors—
No—yet still steadfast, still unchangeable,
  Pillowed upon my fair love's ripening breast,   10
To feel forever its soft fall and swell,
  Awake forever in a sweet unrest,
Still, still to hear her tender-taken breath,
And so live ever—or else swoon to death.

La Belle Dame sans Merci[1]

I

O what can ail thee, knight at arms,
  Alone and palely loitering?
The sedge has withered from the lake
  And no birds sing!

---

1. Keats's friend and former teacher Charles Cowden Clarke had introduced Keats to George Chapman's (1559?–1634) translations of the *Iliad* (1611) and the *Odyssey* (1616) the night before this poem was written.   **2.** The Greek god of poetic inspiration.   **3.** Realm, kingdom.   **4.** In fact, Vasco Núñez de Balboa (ca. 1475–1519), Spanish conquistador, not Hernando Cortés (1485–1547), another Spaniard, was the European explorer who first saw the Pacific from Darién, Panama.   **1.** Hermit.   **1.** The beautiful lady without pity (French); from a medieval poem by Alain Chartier.

II

O what can ail thee, knight at arms,   5
    So haggard, and so woebegone?
The squirrel's granary is full
    And the harvest's done.

III

I see a lily on thy brow
    With anguish moist and fever dew,   10
And on thy cheeks a fading rose
    Fast withereth too.

IV

I met a lady in the meads,[2]
    Full beautiful, a faery's child,
Her hair was long, her foot was light   15
    And her eyes were wild.

V

I made a garland for her head,
    And bracelets too, and fragrant zone;[3]
She looked at me as she did love
    And made sweet moan.   20

VI

I set her on my pacing steed
    And nothing else saw all day long,
For sidelong would she bend and sing
    A faery's song.

VII

She found me roots of relish sweet,   25
    And honey wild, and manna[4] dew,
And sure in language strange she said
    "I love thee true."

VIII

She took me to her elfin grot[5]
    And there she wept and sighed full sore,[6]   30
And there I shut her wild wild eyes
    With kisses four.

IX

And there she lullèd me asleep,
    And there I dreamed, ah woe betide!

2. Meadows. Here the knight answers the question asked in lines 5–6.   3. Girdle.   4. The supernatural substance with which God fed the children of Israel in the wilderness (Exodus 16 and Joshua 5.12). 5. Cavern.   6. With great grief.

The latest[7] dream I ever dreamt   35
   On the cold hill's side.

X

I saw pale kings, and princes too,
   Pale warriors, death-pale were they all;
They cried, "La belle dame sans merci
   Thee hath in thrall!"[8]   40

XI

I saw their starved lips in the gloam[9]
   With horrid warning gapèd wide,
And I awoke, and found me here
   On the cold hill's side.

XII

And this is why I sojourn here,   45
   Alone and palely loitering;
Though the sedge withered from the lake
   And no birds sing.

Ode on a Grecian Urn

I

Thou still unravished bride of quietness,
   Thou foster-child of silence and slow time,
Sylvan historian, who canst thus express
   A flowery tale more sweetly than our rhyme:
What leaf-fringed legend haunts about thy shape   5
   Of deities or mortals, or of both,
      In Tempe or the dales of Arcady?[1]
   What men or gods are these? What maidens loth?
What mad pursuit? What struggle to escape?
      What pipes and timbrels? What wild ecstasy?   10

II

Heard melodies are sweet, but those unheard
   Are sweeter; therefore, ye soft pipes, play on;
Not to the sensual ear, but, more endeared,
   Pipe to the spirit ditties of no tone:
Fair youth, beneath the trees, thou canst not leave   15
   Thy song, nor ever can those trees be bare;
      Bold lover, never, never canst thou kiss,

---

7. Last.   8. Bondage.   9. Twilight.   1. A mountainous region in the Peloponnese, traditionally regarded as the place of ideal rustic, bucolic contentment. Tempe is a valley in Thessaly between Mount Olympus and Mount Ossa.

Though winning near the goal—yet, do not grieve;
 She cannot fade, though thou hast not thy bliss,
For ever wilt thou love, and she be fair!   20

III

Ah, happy, happy boughs! that cannot shed
 Your leaves, nor ever bid the Spring adieu;
And, happy melodist, unwearièd,
 For ever piping songs for ever new;
More happy love! more happy, happy love!   25
 For ever warm and still to be enjoyed,
  For ever panting, and for ever young;
All breathing human passion far above,
 That leaves a heart high-sorrowful and cloyed,
  A burning forehead, and a parching tongue. 30

IV

Who are these coming to the sacrifice?
 To what green altar, O mysterious priest,
Lead'st thou that heifer lowing at the skies,
 And all her silken flanks with garlands drest?
What little town by river or sea shore,   35
 Or mountain-built with peaceful citadel,
  Is emptied of this folk, this pious morn?
And, little town, thy streets for evermore
Will silent be; and not a soul to tell
 Why thou art desolate, can e'er return.   40

V

O Attic shape! Fair attitude! with brede[2]
 Of marble men and maidens overwrought,
With forest branches and the trodden weed;
 Thou, silent form, dost tease us out of thought
As doth eternity: Cold Pastoral!   45
 When old age shall this generation waste,
  Thou shalt remain, in midst of other woe
Than ours, a friend to man, to whom thou say'st,
 "Beauty is truth, truth beauty,"—that is all
  Ye know on earth, and all ye need to know. 50

Ode to a Nightingale

I

My heart aches, and a drowsy numbness pains
 My sense, as though of hemlock I had drunk,

---

2. Pattern. "Attic": classical (literally, Athenian).

Or emptied some dull opiate to the drains
  One minute past, and Lethe-wards[1] had sunk:
'Tis not through envy of thy happy lot,   5
  But being too happy in thy happiness,
      That thou, light-winged Dryad[2] of the trees,
        In some melodious plot
  Of beechen green, and shadows numberless,
    Singest of summer in full-throated ease.   10

II

O for a draught of vintage! that hath been
  Cooled a long age in the deep-delvèd earth,
Tasting of Flora[3] and the country green,
  Dance, and Provençal[4] song, and sunburnt mirth!
O for a beaker full of the warm South!   15
  Full of the true, the blushful Hippocrene,[5]
      With beaded bubbles winking at the brim,
        And purple-stainèd mouth;
That I might drink, and leave the world unseen,
  And with thee fade away into the forest dim: 20

III

Fade far away, dissolve, and quite forget
  What thou among the leaves hast never known,
The weariness, the fever, and the fret
  Here, where men sit and hear each other groan;
Where palsy shakes a few, sad, last gray hairs,   25
    Where youth grows pale, and spectre-thin, and dies;
      Where but to think is to be full of sorrow
        And leaden-eyed despairs;
Where beauty cannot keep her lustrous eyes,
  Or new love pine at them beyond tomorrow.   30

IV

Away! away! for I will fly to thee,
  Not charioted by Bacchus and his pards,[6]
But on the viewless wings of Poesy,
  Though the dull brain perplexes and retards:
Already with thee! tender is the night,   35
    And haply[7] the Queen-Moon is on her throne,
      Clustered around by all her starry Fays;[8]
        But here there is no light,
Save what from heaven is with the breezes blown
  Through verdurous glooms and winding mossy ways.   40

1. That is, toward Lethe, the river of forgetfulness in Greek mythology.   2. Wood nymph.   3. The goddess of flowers and spring; here, flowers.   4. From Provence, the district in France associated with the troubadours.   5. The fountain on Mount Helicon, in Greece, sacred to the muse of poetry. 6. Leopards. Bacchus (Dionysus) was traditionally supposed to be accompanied by leopards, lions, goats, and so on.   7. Perhaps.   8. Fairies.

V

I cannot see what flowers are at my feet,
  Nor what soft incense hangs upon the boughs,
But, in embalmèd darkness, guess each sweet
  Wherewith the seasonable month endows
The grass, the thicket, and the fruit-tree wild;   45
    White hawthorn, and the pastoral eglantine;
      Fast-fading violets covered up in leaves;
        And mid-May's eldest child,
The coming musk-rose, full of dewy wine,
  The murmurous haunt of flies on summer eves.   50

VI

Darkling[9] I listen; and for many a time
  I have been half in love with easeful Death,
Called him soft names in many a musèd rhyme,
    To take into the air my quiet breath;
Now more than ever seems it rich to die,   55
  To cease upon the midnight with no pain,
    While thou art pouring forth thy soul abroad
      In such an ecstasy!
Still wouldst thou sing, and I have ears in vain—
  To thy high requiem become a sod.[1]   60

VII

Thou wast not born for death, immortal Bird!
  No hungry generations tread thee down;
The voice I hear this passing night was heard
  In ancient days by emperor and clown:
Perhaps the self-same song that found a path   65
  Through the sad heart of Ruth, when, sick for home,
    She stood in tears amid the alien corn;[2]
      The same that ofttimes hath
Charmed magic casements, opening on the foam
  Of perilous seas, in faery lands forlorn.   70

VIII

Forlorn! the very word is like a bell
  To toll me back from thee to my sole self!
Adieu! the fancy cannot cheat so well
  As she is famed to do, deceiving elf.
Adieu! adieu! thy plaintive anthem fades   75
  Past the near meadows, over the still stream,
    Up the hill-side; and now 'tis buried deep
      In the next valley-glades:
Was it a vision, or a waking dream?
  Fled is that music:—do I wake or sleep?   80

---

9. In the dark.   1. That is, like dirt, unable to hear.   2. See the book of Ruth. After her Ephrathite husband died, she returned to his native land with her mother-in-law.

Ode on Melancholy

I

No, no, go not to Lethe,[1] neither twist
  Wolfsbane, tight-rooted, for its poisonous wine;
Nor suffer thy pale forehead to be kissed
  By nightshade, ruby grape of Proserpine;[2]
Make not your rosary of yew-berries,[3]   5
  Nor let the beetle, nor the death-moth[4] be
    Your mournful Psyche,[5] nor the downy owl
A partner in your sorrow's mysteries;
  For shade to shade will come too drowsily,
    And drown the wakeful anguish of the soul.   10

II

But when the melancholy fit shall fall
  Sudden from heaven like a weeping cloud,
That fosters the droop-headed flowers all,
  And hides the green hill in an April shroud;
Then glut thy sorrow on a morning rose,   15
  Or on the rainbow of the salt sand-wave,
    Or on the wealth of globèd peonies;
Or if thy mistress some rich anger shows,
  Imprison her soft hand, and let her rave,
    And feed deep, deep upon her peerless eyes.   20

III

She[6] dwells with Beauty—Beauty that must die;
  And Joy, whose hand is ever at his lips
Bidding adieu; and aching Pleasure nigh,
  Turning to Poison while the bee-mouth sips:
Aye, in the very temple of Delight   25
  Veiled Melancholy has her sovereign shrine,
    Though seen of none save him whose strenuous tongue
  Can burst Joy's grape against his palate fine;
His soul shall taste the sadness of her might,
  And be among her cloudy trophies hung.[7]   30

To Autumn

I

Season of mists and mellow fruitfulness,
  Close bosom-friend of the maturing sun;
Conspiring with him how to load and bless

---

1. The river of forgetfulness in Hades.   2. Wife of Pluto, queen of the underworld.   3. Wolfsbane, nightshade, and yew berries are all poisonous.   4. The death's-head moth has markings that resemble a skull. The scarab beetle, depicted in Egyptian tombs, was an emblem of death.   5. The soul, portrayed by the Greeks as a butterfly.   6. Melancholy.   7. The Greeks placed war trophies in their temples to commemorate victories.

With fruit the vines that round the thatch-eaves run;
  To bend with apples the mossed cottage-trees,   5
    And fill all fruit with ripeness to the core;
      To swell the gourd, and plump the hazel shells
With a sweet kernel; to set budding more,
    And still more, later flowers for the bees,
    Until they think warm days will never cease,   10
      For Summer has o'er-brimmed their clammy cells.

II

Who hath not seen thee oft amid thy store?
  Sometimes whoever seeks abroad may find
Thee sitting careless on a granary floor,
    Thy hair soft-lifted by the winnowing wind;   15
Or on a half-reaped furrow sound asleep,
  Drowsed with the fume of poppies, while thy hook
    Spares the next swath and all its twinèd flowers:
And sometimes like a gleaner thou dost keep
  Steady thy laden head across a brook;   20
  Or by a cyder-press, with patient look,
    Thou watchest the last oozings hours by hours.

III

Where are the songs of Spring? Ay, where are they?
  Think not of them, thou hast thy music too,—
While barrèd clouds bloom the soft-dying day,   25
  And touch the stubble-plains with rosy hue;
Then in a wailful choir the small gnats mourn
  Among the river sallows,[1] borne aloft
    Or sinking as the light wind lives or dies;
And full-grown lambs loud bleat from hilly bourn;   30
  Hedge-crickets sing; and now with treble soft
  The red-breast whistles from a garden-croft;
    And gathering swallows twitter in the skies.

1. Willows.

HEINRICH HEINE
1797–1856

Born in Germany of Jewish parents, Heinrich Heine is most famous as a lyric poet, although he also composed drama, narrative poetry, political commentary, and literary criticism. As "The Silesian Weavers" suggests, he had strong revolutionary sympathies, which drew him to Paris in 1831. There he died, after a prolonged illness.

Simple diction and frequent reliance on the metrical patterns of traditional ballads characterize many of Heine's lyrics, which have frequently been set to music. Naive though the lyrics often seem, they have dark undertones. When Heine openly confronts political actualities, one ground for his despair becomes apparent: he sees German society as divided between the uncaring and tyrannical rich and the profoundly oppressed poor, and he finds the structure of social inequity intolerable.

PRONOUNCING GLOSSARY

The following list uses common English syllables and stress accents to provide rough equivalents of selected words whose pronunciation may be unfamiliar to the general reader.

Heinrich Heine: *hain'-rik hai'-ne*   Silesian: *sai-lee'-zhahn*

[A pine is standing lonely][1]

A pine is standing lonely
In the North on a bare plateau.
He sleeps; a bright white blanket
Enshrouds him in ice and snow.

He's dreaming of a palm tree   5
Far away in the Eastern land
Lonely and silently mourning
On a sunburnt rocky strand.

[A young man loves a maiden]

A young man loves a maiden
Who chooses another instead;
This other loves still another
And these two haply wed.

The maiden out of anger   5
Marries, with no regard,
The first good man she runs into—
The young lad takes it hard.

It is so old a story,
Yet somehow always new;   10
And he that has just lived it,
It breaks his heart in two.

[Ah, death is like the long cool night]

Ah, death is like the long cool night,
And life is like the sultry day.

---

1. All selections translated by Hal Draper.

Dusk falls now; I grow sleepy;
The day makes me tired of light.

Over my bed there's a tree that gleams—   5
   Young nightingales are singing there,
     Of love, love only, singing—
I hear it even in dreams.

The Silesian Weavers[1]

In somber eyes no tears of grieving;
Grinding their teeth, they sit at their weaving;
"O Germany, at your shroud we sit,
We're weaving a threefold curse in it—
   We're weaving, we're weaving!   5

"A curse on the god we prayed to, kneeling
With cold in our bones, with hunger reeling;
We waited and hoped, in vain persevered,
He scorned us and duped us, mocked and jeered—
   We're weaving, we're weaving!   10

"A curse on the king[2] of the rich man's nation
Who hardens his heart at our supplication,
Who wrings the last penny out of our hides
And lets us be shot like dogs besides—
   We're weaving, we're weaving!   15

"A curse on this false fatherland, teeming
With nothing but shame and dirty scheming,
Where every flower is crushed in a day,
Where worms are regaled on rot and decay—
   We're weaving, we're weaving!   20

"The shuttle flies, the loom creaks loud,
Night and day we weave your shroud—
Old Germany, at your shroud we sit,
We're weaving a threefold curse in it,
   We're weaving, we're weaving!"   25

---

1. Silesia was a province of the kingdom of Prussia in northeast Germany. This poem was occasioned by violent uprisings of weavers protesting intolerable working conditions during June 1844.   2. Friedrich Wilhelm IV (1795–1861). Heine's poem is prophetic: in 1848 the king, though not deposed, was forced by revolution to grant a constitution to Prussia.

GIACOMO LEOPARDI
1798–1837

The product of a rigid upbringing by aristocratic parents, the Italian Giacomo Leopardi (*jah'-koh-moh lay-oh-pahr'-dee*) grew to adulthood plagued by many ailments, a hunchback close to blindness. But his intellectual powers were highly developed, and he soon attained a fine reputation as scholar, poet, and translator. His poetry characteristically expresses a poignant sensitivity to the beauty and promise of every-day life, as well as despair at its inevitable destruction with the passage of time. Only the poetic imagination, which allows Leopardi to grasp and transcend his own mortality, offers an escape: "And sweet to me the foundering in this sea [of eternity]," he writes in "The Infinite."

The Infinite[1]

This lonely hill has always been so dear
To me, and dear the hedge which hides away
The reaches of the sky. But sitting here
And wondering, I fashion in my mind
The endless spaces far beyond, the more   5
Than human silences, and deepest peace;
So that the heart is on the edge of fear.
And when I hear the wind come blowing through
The trees, I pit its voice against that boundless
Silence and summon up eternity,   10
And the dead seasons, and the present one,
Alive with all its sound. And thus it is
In this immensity my thought is drowned:
And sweet to me the foundering in this sea.

To Himself

Now you may rest forever,
My tired heart. The last illusion is dead
That I believed eternal. Dead. I can
So clearly see—not only hope is gone
But the desire to be deceived as well.   5
Rest, rest forever.
You have beaten long enough. Nothing is worth
Your smallest motion, nor the earth your sighs.
This life is bitterness
And vacuum, nothing else. The world is mud.   10
From now on calm yourself.
Despair for the last time. The only gift
Fate gave our kind was death. Henceforth, heap scorn

---

1. All selections translated by Ottavio M. Casale, who skillfully conveys the rhythms of Leopardi's free verse.

Upon yourself, Nature, the ugly force
That, hidden, orders universal ruin,   15
And the boundless emptiness of everything.

To Sylvia

   Sylvia. Do you remember still
The moments of your mortal lifetime here,
When such a loveliness
Shone in the elusive laughter of your eyes,
And you, contemplative and gay, climbed toward   5
The summit of your youth?

   The tranquil chambers held,
The paths re-echoed, your perpetual song,
When at your woman's tasks
You sat, content to concentrate upon   10
The future beckoning within your mind.
It was the fragrant May,
And thus you passed your time.

   I often used to leave
The dear, belabored pages which consumed   15
So much of me and of my youth, and from
Ancestral balconies
Would lean to hear the music of your voice,
Your fingers humming through
The intricacies of the weaving work.   20
And I would gaze upon
The blue surrounding sky,
The paths and gardens golden in the sun,
And there the far-off sea, and here the mountain.
No human tongue can tell   25
What I felt then within my brimming heart.

   What tendernesses then,
What hopes, what hearts were ours, O Sylvia mine!
How large a thing seemed life, and destiny!
When I recall those bright anticipations,   30
Bitterness invades,
And I turn once again to mourn my lot.
O Nature, Nature, why
Do you not keep the promises you gave?
Why trick the children so?   35

   Before the winter struck the summer grass,
You died, my gentle girl,
Besieged by hidden illness and possessed.
You never saw the flowering of your years.
Your heart was never melted by the praise   40

Of your dark hair, your shy,
Enamoured eyes. Nor did you with your friends
Conspire on holidays to talk of love.
    The expectation failed
As soon for me, and fate denied my youth.   45
Ah how gone by, gone by,
You dear companion of my dawning time,
The hope that I lament!
Is this the world we knew? And these the joys
The love, the labors, happenings we shared?   50
And this the destiny
Of human beings? My poor one, when
The truth rose up, you fell,
And from afar you pointed me the way
To coldest death and the stark sepulchre.   55

The Village Saturday

    The sun is falling as the peasant girl
Returns from the open fields,
Bearing a swathe of grass and in her hand
Her customary bunch of violets
And roses which will grace   5
Her hair and breast the coming holiday.
And, spinning, the old woman sits upon
The steps among her neighbors,
Their faces turned against the dying light;
And she tells tales of her green days, when she   10
Adorned her body for the holidays
And, slenderly robust,
Would dance the night away
Among the companions of her lovely prime.
The very air seems now to deepen, the sky   15
Turns darker blue. Down from the hills and roofs
Returning shadows fall
At the whitening of the moon.

    Now bells declare the time
Is near, the festive day,   20
The hour of heart's renewal.
The shouting lads invade
The village square in troops,
Leaping now here, now there,
Making such happy chatter.   25
Meanwhile the whistling laborer comes back
To take his meager meal
And ruminate about his day of rest.

    And then, when every other lamp is out
And other sounds are stilled—   30

Listen—a pounding hammer and a saw:
It is the carpenter,
Awake and hurrying by lanternlight
Inside his shuttered shop
To end his task before the morning breaks.   35

Of all the seven days this is the one
Most cherished, full of joy and expectation.
The passing hours will bring tomorrow soon,
And tedium and sadness,
When each shall turn inside   40
His mind to his habitual travail.

O playful little boy,
Your flowering time is like a day of grace,
So brightly blue,
Anticipating the great feast of life.   45
My child, enjoy the season.
I will not tell you more; but if the day
Seems slow in coming, do not grieve too much.

ALEXANDER SERGEYEVICH PUSHKIN
1799–1837

In his best-known story, "The Queen of Spades," Alexander Pushkin combines familiar elements of Romantic fiction—the penniless young woman; the ambitious, passionate young man; the decayed beauty; the ghost—in a tale with intense ironic
overtones, a tale later a favorite of the great Russian novelist Fyodor Dostoevsky.
Pushkin's own life story sounds like a Romantic novel. Born into an aristocratic Russian family, neglected by his parents, he early began an extensive amatory and poetic
career, publishing his first poem at the age of fifteen and becoming notorious about
the same time for his many erotic involvements. At eighteen he graduated from a distinguished boarding school and accepted appointment in the Foreign Service; six
years later, the various instances of his defiance of authority resulted in expulsion
from the service and confinement, under police surveillance, on a paternal estate.
After the death of Czar Alexander I and the abortive military uprising that followed
(one involving several of Pushkin's friends, five of whom were subsequently hanged),
Pushkin—by then a well-known poet—was befriended (1826) by the new czar,
Nicholas. He moved back to Moscow, then to Petersburg, leading a moneyed and relatively carefree life. In 1831, however, he married a nineteen-year-old woman, whose
apparently flirtatious behavior embittered his subsequent life. He died after a duel
with his wife's putative lover.

Producing short lyrics, narrative poems, a great novel in verse (*Eugene Onegin*), lyrical drama (notably *Boris Gudonov*), versified folktales, and prose fiction, Pushkin
established himself as one of Russia's greatest writers. His interest in his nation's past,
his tendency to challenge authority, his fascination with the character and situation of
strong individuals—such obsessive concerns link his work with that of his Romantic
contemporaries elsewhere in Europe. Goethe, Byron, and early nineteenth-century

French novelists had a marked influence on him. He retained also, however, the kind of clarity, discipline, and ironic distance more often associated with the literature of the preceding century.

The treatment of love and sexuality in "The Queen of Spades" exemplifies the complexity of Pushkin's approach. First of all we hear the story of the "Muscovite Venus," the beautiful young gambler who pays her debts by learning the secret of three infallible cards. Then we encounter a young woman suffering in her dependent position and longing for a "deliverer." Hermann, the immediate object of Lisaveta's dreams, has his own sexual fantasies: himself a young man, he imagines becoming the lover of the eighty-seven-year-old countess. At this point, if not before, the reader begins to realize that something's wrong here: this is not the kind of romantic tale we're used to. Describing Hermann's first glimpse of Lisaveta, Pushkin writes, "Hermann saw a small, fresh face and a pair of dark eyes. That moment decided his fate." A Romantic cliché—except that the young man sees Lisaveta not as an object of devotion but as a means to an end. He sends her a love letter, copied word for word from a German novel. His rapidly developing passion focuses on financial, not erotic, gain.

Lisaveta's character is more ambiguous. The narrator invokes sympathy for her plight: she is at the mercy of a tyrannical employer who makes endless irrational demands and who never pays her. Her situation prohibits her from enjoying the kinds of amorous gratification other young women can expect. We can understand, therefore, why her dreams should concentrate specifically on a deliverer. Like Hermann, although far less unscrupulous, she may indulge in intrigues as a means to an end— in her case, not money but liberty.

"The Queen of Spades" contains no completely attractive characters. If Lisaveta's victimization arouses compassion, her lack of moral force or determination may also provoke irritation. Hermann's will to succeed, on the other hand, makes him a potential hero; but his obsession with money and his mean-spirited expediency alienate most readers. The countess, old and approaching death, uses the power of her money and rank with utter disregard for the needs or feelings of others. Even such a minor figure as the countess's grandson, Tomsky, playing with Lisaveta's feelings, going through his ritualized flirtation with Princess Polina, seems thoroughly contaminated by the values of the world he inhabits.

Indeed, those values provide the central subject of this tale. Pushkin employs conventions of the kind of ghost story common in folktales to convey serious criticism of a social structure corrupted by universal concentration on money. Gambling provides not only the chief male activity but also the central metaphor of the story. Everyone is out for what he or she can get. The countess, whose days at the card table are past, uses her money to buy subservience; Lisaveta is willing to risk her reputation, maybe even her chastity, for the possibility of escaping servitude; Hermann frightens someone to death in an effort to make his fortune; Tomsky plays elaborate social games of advance and retreat, trying to get his princess. The queen of spades is a conventional symbol of death; the kind of death most important in Pushkin's story is not literal— not the countess's demise—but figurative: it is the spiritual death suffered by the other characters, over whose world the countess/queen of spades metaphorically presides.

The Conclusion of "The Queen of Spades," a deadpan summary of the characters' future careers, epitomizes the story's central concerns. Hermann's madness dramatizes the financial obsession he has displayed from the beginning; Lisaveta's marriage, to an anonymous "very agreeable young man" with a good position "somewhere," emphasizes the degree to which she has always wished for marriage as rescue, not as attachment to a particular beloved other. In her married state, Lisaveta, ironically, "is bringing up a poor relative," recapitulating the structure of exploitation from which she herself suffered. Tomsky, relatively unimportant to the plot line, supplies the subject for the story's concluding sentence: his promotion and his "good" marriage remind us that everyone in the society here described seeks personal advantage at all costs. Hermann has simply paid the cost in the most dramatic way.

PRONOUNCING GLOSSARY

The following list uses common English syllables and stress accents to provide rough equivalents of selected words whose pronunciation may be unfamiliar to the general reader.

Chekalinsky: *che-kah-leen'-skee*

Eletskaya: *ye-lyet'-skah-yuh*

Fedotovna: *fye-daw'-tuv-nuh*

Ilyitch: *il-yeech'*

Lisaveta Ivanovna: *lyee-zah-vye'-tuh ee-vah'-nuv-nuh*

Richelieu: *ree'-she-lyeuh*

St-Germain: *sanh-zher-manh'*

The Queen of Spades[1]

CHAPTER ONE

And on rainy days
They gathered
Often;
Their stakes—God help them!—
Wavered from fifty
To a hundred,
And they won
And marked up their winnings
With chalk.
Thus on rainy days
Were they
Busy.[2]

There was a card party one day in the rooms of Narumov, an officer of the Horse Guards. The long winter evening slipped by unnoticed; it was five o'clock in the morning before the assembly sat down to supper. Those who had won ate with a big appetite; the others sat distractedly before their empty plates. But champagne was brought in, the conversation became more lively, and everyone took a part in it.

"And how did you get on, Surin?" asked the host.

"As usual, I lost. I must confess, I have no luck: I never vary my stake, never get heated, never lose my head, and yet I always lose!"

"And weren't you tempted even once to back[3] on a series? Your strength of mind astonishes me."

"What about Hermann then?" said one of the guests, pointing at the young Engineer.[4] "He's never held a card in his hand, never doubled a single stake in his life, and yet he sits up until five in the morning watching us play."

"The game fascinates me," said Hermann, "but I am not in the position to sacrifice the essentials of life in the hope of acquiring the luxuries."

---

1. Translated by Gillon R. Aitken.   2. Like most of the chapter epigraphs, this was presumably written by Pushkin himself.   3. Bet.   4. A member of the Corps of Engineers, concerned with fortifications.

"Hermann's a German: he's cautious—that's all," Tomsky observed. "But if there's one person I can't understand, it's my grandmother, the Countess Anna Fedotovna."

"How? Why?" the guests inquired noisily.

"I cannot understand why it is," Tomsky continued, "that my grandmother never gambles."

"But what's so astonishing about an old lady of eighty not gambling?" asked Narumov.

"Then you don't know . . . ?"

"No, indeed; I know nothing."

"Oh well, listen then:

"You must know that about sixty years ago my grandmother went to Paris, where she made something of a hit. People used to chase after her to catch a glimpse of *la Vénus moscovite;* Richelieu[5] paid court to her, and my grandmother vouches that he almost shot himself on account of her cruelty. At that time ladies used to play faro.[6] On one occasion at the Court, my grandmother lost a very great deal of money on credit to the Duke of Orleans. Returning home, she removed the patches[7] from her face, took off her hooped petticoat, announced her loss to my grandfather and ordered him to pay back the money. My late grandfather, as far as I can remember, was a sort of lackey to my grandmother. He feared her like fire; on hearing of such a disgraceful loss, however, he completely lost his temper; he produced his accounts, showed her that she had spent half a million francs in six months, pointed out that neither their Moscow nor their Saratov estates were in Paris, and refused point-blank to pay the debt. My grandmother gave him a box on the ear and went off to sleep on her own as an indication of her displeasure. In the hope that this domestic infliction would have had some effect on him, she sent for her husband the next day; she found him unshakeable. For the first time in her life she approached him with argument and explanation, thinking that she could bring him to reason by pointing out that there are debts and debts, that there is a big difference between a Prince and a coach-maker. But my grandfather remained adamant, and flatly refused to discuss the subject any further. My grandmother did not know what to do. A little while before, she had become acquainted with a very remarkable man. You have heard of Count St-Germain,[8] about whom so many marvellous stories are related. You know that he held himself out to be the Wandering Jew, and the inventor of the elixir of life, the philosopher's stone and so forth. Some ridiculed him as a charlatan and in his memoirs Casanova declares that he was a spy. However, St-Germain, in spite of the mystery which surrounded him, was a person of venerable appearance and much in demand in society. My grandmother remains quite infatuated with him and becomes quite angry if anyone speaks of him with disrespect. My grandmother knew that he had large sums of money at his disposal. She decided to have recourse to him, and wrote asking him to visit her without

5. Louis-François-Armand de Vignerod du Plessis, duc de Richelieu (1696–1788), French aristocrat renowned throughout the 18th century for both his military and his sexual exploits. "*La vénus moscovite*": the Venus of Moscow (French). Venus was the Roman goddess of love. 6. A card game much used for gambling. 7. That is, beauty patches, artificial "beauty marks" made of black silk or court plaster and worn on the face or neck. 8. A celebrated adventurer (ca. 1710–1784?) who frequented the French, German, and Russian courts.

delay. The eccentric old man at once called on her and found her in a state of terrible grief. She depicted her husband's barbarity in the blackest light, and ended by saying that she pinned all her hopes on his friendship and kindness.

"St-Germain reflected. 'I could let you have this sum,' he said, 'but I know that you would not be at peace while in my debt, and I have no wish to bring fresh troubles upon your head. There is another solution—you can win back the money.'"

"'But, my dear Count,' my grandmother replied, 'I tell you—we have no money at all.'

"'In this case money is not essential,' St-Germain replied. 'Be good enough to hear me out.'

"And at this point he revealed to her the secret for which any one of us here would give a very great deal . . ."

The young gamblers listened with still greater attention. Tomsky lit his pipe, drew on it and continued:

"That same evening my grandmother went to Versailles, *au jeu de la Reine*.[9] The Duke of Orleans kept the bank. Inventing some small tale, my grandmother lightly excused herself for not having brought her debt, and began to play against him. She chose three cards and played them one after the other: all three won and my grandmother recouped herself completely."

"Pure luck!" said one of the guests.

"A fairy-tale," observed Hermann.

"Perhaps the cards were marked!" said a third.

"I don't think so," Tomsky replied gravely.

"What!" cried Narumov. "You have a grandmother who can guess three cards in succession, and you haven't yet contrived to learn her secret."

"No, not much hope of that!" replied Tomsky. "She had four sons, including my father; all four were desperate gamblers, and yet she did not reveal her secret to a single one of them, although it would have been a good thing if she had told them—told me, even. But this is what I heard from my uncle, Count Ivan Ilyitch, and he gave me his word for its truth. The late Chaplitsky—the same who died a pauper after squandering millions—in his youth once lost nearly 300,000 roubles—to Zoritch, if I remember rightly. He was in despair. My grandmother, who was most strict in her attitude towards the extravagances of young men, for some reason took pity on Chaplitsky. She told him the three cards on condition that he played them in order; and at the same time she exacted his solemn promise that he would never play again as long as he lived. Chaplitsky appeared before his victor; they sat down to play. On the first card Chaplitsky staked 50,000 roubles and won straight off; he doubled his stake, redoubled—and won back more than he had lost . . .

"But it's time to go to bed; it's already a quarter to six."

Indeed, the day was already beginning to break. The young men drained their glasses and dispersed.

9. To the queen's game (French).

CHAPTER TWO

—Il paraît que monsieur est décidément pour les suivantes.
—Que voulez-vous, madame? Elles sont plus fraîches.[1]

FASHIONABLE CONVERSATION

The old Countess ***[2] was seated before the looking-glass in her dressing-room. Three lady's maids stood by her. One held a jar of rouge, another a box of hairpins, and the third a tall bonnet with flame-coloured ribbons. The Countess no longer had the slightest pretensions to beauty, which had long since faded from her face, but she still preserved all the habits of her youth, paid strict regard to the fashions of the 'seventies, and devoted to her dress the same time and attention as she had done sixty years before. At an embroidery frame by the window sat a young lady, her ward.

"Good morning, *grand'maman!*" said a young officer as he entered the room. "*Bonjour, mademoiselle Lise. Grand'maman,*[3] I have a request to make of you."

"What is it, Paul?"

"I want you to let me introduce one of my friends to you, and to allow me to bring him to the ball on Friday."

"Bring him straight to the ball and introduce him to me there. Were you at ***'s yesterday?"

"Of course. It was very merry; we danced until five in the morning. How charming Yeletskaya was!"

"But, my dear, what's charming about her? Isn't she like her grandmother, the Princess Darya Petrovna . . . ? By the way, I dare say she's grown very old now, the Princess Darya Petrovna?"

"What do you mean, 'grown old'?" asked Tomsky thoughtlessly. "She's been dead for seven years."

The young lady raised her head and made a sign to the young man. He remembered then that the death of any of her contemporaries was kept secret from the old Countess, and he bit his lip. But the Countess heard the news, previously unknown to her, with the greatest indifference.

"Dead!" she said. "And I didn't know it. We were maids of honour together, and when we were presented, the Empress . . ."

And for the hundredth time the Countess related the anecdote to her grandson.

"Come, Paul," she said when she had finished her story, "help me to stand up. Lisanka, where's my snuff-box?"

And with her three maids the Countess went behind a screen to complete her dress. Tomsky was left alone with the young lady.

"Whom do you wish to introduce?" Lisaveta Ivanovna asked softly.

"Narumov. Do you know him?"

"No. Is he a soldier or a civilian?"

"A soldier."

"An Engineer?"

"No, he's in the Cavalry. What made you think he was an Engineer?"

---

1. "It appears that the gentleman is decidedly in favor of servant girls." "What would you have me do, Madam? They are fresher [than upper-class women]" (French).   2. Asterisks in this selection are the author's and are intended to suggest that the proper name of an actual person has been omitted.   3. Russian aristocrats often spoke French. Lisaveta is here called by the French name Lise, and Pavel, Paul.

The young lady smiled but made no reply.

"Paul!" cried the Countess from behind the screen. "Bring along a new novel with you some time, will you, only please not one of those modern ones."

"What do you mean, *grand'maman*?"

"I mean not the sort of novel in which the hero strangles either of his parents or in which someone is drowned.[4] I have a great horror of drowned people."

"Such novels don't exist nowadays. Wouldn't you like a Russian one?"

"Are there such things? Send me one, my dear, please send me one."

"Will you excuse me now, *grand'maman*, I'm in a hurry. Good-bye, Lisaveta Ivanovna. What made you think that Narumov was in the Engineers?"

And Tomsky left the dressing-room.

Lisaveta Ivanovna was left on her own. She put aside her work and began to look out of the window. Presently a young officer appeared from behind the corner house on the other side of the street. A flush spread over her cheeks. She took up her work again and lowered her head over the frame. At this moment, the Countess returned, fully dressed.

"Order the carriage, Lisanka," she said, "and we'll go for a drive."

Lisanka got up from behind her frame and began to put her work away.

"What's the matter with you, my child? Are you deaf?" shouted the Countess. "Order the carriage this minute."

"I'll do so at once," the young lady replied softly and hastened into the ante-room.

A servant entered the room and handed the Countess some books from the Prince Pavel Alexandrovitch.

"Good, thank him," said the Countess. "Lisanka, Lisanka, where are you running to?"

"To get dressed."

"Plenty of time for that, my dear. Sit down. Open the first volume and read to me."

The young lady took up the book and read a few lines.

"Louder!" said the Countess. "What's the matter with you, my child? Have you lost your voice, or what . . . ? Wait . . . move that footstool up to me . . . nearer . . . that's right!"

Lisaveta Ivanovna read a further two pages. The Countess yawned.

"Put the book down," she said. "What rubbish! Have it returned to Prince Pavel with my thanks . . . But where is the carriage?"

"The carriage is ready," said Lisaveta Ivanovna, looking out into the street.

"Then why aren't you dressed?" asked the Countess. "I'm always having to wait for you—it's intolerable, my dear!"

Lisa ran up to her room. Not two minutes elapsed before the Countess began to ring with all her might. The three lady's maids came running in through one door and the valet through another.

"Why don't you come when you're called?" the Countess asked them. "Tell Lisaveta Ivanovna that I'm waiting for her."

---

4. Novels of the sort the countess does not wish to read were typical of the then current decadent movement in French literature.

Lisaveta Ivanovna entered the room wearing her hat and cloak.

"At last, my child!" said the Countess. "But what clothes you're wearing . . . ! Whom are you hoping to catch? What's the weather like? It seems windy."

"There's not a breath of wind, your Ladyship," replied the valet.

"You never know what you're talking about! Open that small window. There, as I thought: windy and bitterly cold. Unharness the horses. Lisaveta, we're not going out—there was no need to dress up like that."

"And this is my life," thought Lisaveta Ivanovna.

And indeed Lisaveta Ivanovna was a most unfortunate creature. As Dante says: "You shall learn the salt taste of another's bread, and the hard path up and down his stairs";[5] and who better to know the bitterness of dependence than the poor ward of a well-born old lady? The Countess *** was far from being wicked, but she had the capriciousness of a woman who has been spoiled by the world, and the miserliness and cold-hearted egotism of all old people who have done with loving and whose thoughts lie with the past. She took part in all the vanities of the *haut-monde*;[6] she dragged herself to balls, where she sat in a corner, rouged and dressed in old-fashioned style, like some misshapen but essential ornament of the ball-room. On arrival, the guests would approach her with low bows, as if in accordance with an established rite, but after that, they would pay no further attention to her. She received the whole town at her house, and although no longer able to recognise the faces of her guests, she observed the strictest etiquette. Her numerous servants, grown fat and grey in her hall and servants' room, did exactly as they pleased, vying with one another in stealing from the dying old lady. Lisaveta Ivanovna was the household martyr. She poured out the tea, and was reprimanded for putting in too much sugar; she read novels aloud, and was held guilty of all the faults of the authors; she accompanied the Countess on her walks, and was made responsible for the state of the weather and the pavement. There was a salary attached to her position, but it was never paid. Meanwhile, it was demanded of her to be dressed like everybody else—that is, like the very few who could afford to dress well. In society she played the most pitiable role. Everybody knew her, but nobody took any notice of her; at balls she danced only when there was a partner short, and ladies only took her arm when they needed to go to the dressing-room to make some adjustment to their dress. She was proud and felt her position keenly, and looked around her in impatient expectation of a deliverer; but the young men, calculating in their flightiness, did not honour her with their attention, despite the fact that Lisaveta Ivanovna was a hundred times prettier than the cold, arrogant but more eligible young ladies on whom they danced attendance. Many a time did she creep softly away from the bright but wearisome drawing-room to go and cry in her own poor room, where stood a papered screen, a chest of drawers, a small looking-glass and a painted bedstead, and where a tallow candle burned dimly in its copper candlestick.

One day—two days after the evening described at the beginning of this story, and about a week previous to the events just recorded—Lisaveta Ivanovna was sitting at her embroidery frame by the window when, happening to glance out into the street, she saw a young Engineer, standing motion-

5. *Paradiso* 17.59.   6. High society (French).

less with his eyes fixed upon her window. She lowered her head and continued with her work; five minutes later she looked out again—the young officer was still standing in the same place. Not being in the habit of flirting with passing officers, she ceased to look out of the window, and sewed for about two hours without raising her head. Dinner was announced. She got up and began to put away her frame, and, glancing casually out into the street, she again saw the officer. She was considerably puzzled by this. After dinner, she approached the window with a feeling of some disquiet, but the officer was no longer outside, and she thought no more of him.

Two days later, while preparing to enter the carriage with the Countess, she saw him again. He was standing just by the front door, his face concealed by a beaver collar; his dark eyes shone from beneath his cap. Without knowing why, Lisaveta Ivanovna felt afraid, and an unaccountable trembling came over her as she sat down in the carriage.

On her return home, she hastened to the window—the officer was standing in the same place as before, his eyes fixed upon her. She drew back, tormented by curiosity and agitated by a feeling that was quite new to her.

Since then, not a day had passed without the young man appearing at the customary hour beneath the windows of their house. A sort of mute acquaintance grew up between them. At work in her seat, she used to feel him approaching, and would raise her head to look at him—for longer and longer each day. The young man seemed to be grateful to her for this: she saw, with the sharp eye of youth, how a sudden flush would spread across his pale cheeks on each occasion that their glances met. After a week she smiled at him . . .

When Tomsky asked leave of the Countess to introduce one of his friends to her; the poor girl's heart beat fast. But on learning that Narumov was in the Horse Guards, and not in the Engineers, she was sorry that, by an indiscreet question, she had betrayed her secret to the light-hearted Tomsky.

Hermann was the son of a Russianised German, from whom he had inherited a small amount of money. Being firmly convinced of the necessity of ensuring his independence, Hermann did not draw on the income that this yielded, but lived on his pay, forbidding himself the slightest extravagance. Moreover, he was secretive and ambitious, and his companions rarely had occasion to laugh at his excessive thrift. He had strong passions and a fiery imagination, but his tenacity of spirit saved him from the usual errors of youth. Thus, for example, although at heart a gambler, he never took a card in his hand, for he reckoned that his position did not allow him (as he put it) "to sacrifice the essentials of life in the hope of acquiring the luxuries"—and, meanwhile, he would sit up at the card table for whole nights at a time, and follow the different turns of the game with feverish anxiety.

The story of the three cards had made a strong impression on his imagination, and he could think of nothing else all night.

"What if the old Countess should reveal her secret to me?" he thought the following evening as he wandered through the streets of Petersburg. "What if she should tell me the names of those three winning cards? Why not try my luck . . . ? Become introduced to her, try to win her favour, perhaps become her lover . . . ? But all that demands time, and she's eighty-seven; she might die in a week, in two days . . . ! And the story itself . . . ? Can one really believe it . . . ? No! Economy, moderation and industry: these are my three winning cards, these will treble my capital, increase it sevenfold, and earn for me ease and independence!"

Reasoning thus, he found himself in one of the principal streets of Petersburg, before a house of old-fashioned architecture. The street was crowded with vehicles; one after another, carriages rolled up to the lighted entrance. From them there emerged, now the shapely little foot of some beautiful young woman, now a rattling jack-boot, now the striped stocking and elegant shoe of a diplomat. Furs and capes flitted past the majestic hall-porter. Hermann stopped.

"Whose house is this?" he asked the watchman at the corner.

"The Countess ***'s," the watchman replied.

Hermann started. His imagination was again fired by the amazing story of the three cards. He began to walk around near the house, thinking of its owner and her mysterious faculty. It was late when he returned to his humble rooms. For a long time he could not sleep, and when at last he did drop off, cards, a green table,[7] heaps of banknotes and piles of golden coins appeared to him in his dreams. He played one card after the other, doubled his stake decisively, won unceasingly, and raked in the golden coins and stuffed his pockets with the banknotes. Waking up late, he sighed at the loss of his imaginary fortune, again went out to wander about the town and again found himself outside the house of the Countess ***. Some unknown power seemed to have attracted him to it. He stopped and began to look at the windows. At one he saw a head with long black hair, probably bent down over a book or a piece of work. The head was raised. Hermann saw a small, fresh face and a pair of dark eyes. That moment decided his fate.

CHAPTER THREE

*Vous m'écrivez, mon ange, des lettres de
quatre pages plus vite que je ne puis
les lire.*[8]

CORRESPONDENCE

Scarcely had Lisaveta Ivanovna taken off her hat and cloak when the Countess sent for her and again ordered her to have the horses harnessed. They went out to take their seats in the carriage. At the same moment as the old lady was being helped through the carriage doors by two footmen, Lisaveta Ivanovna saw her Engineer standing close by the wheel. He seized her hand and, before she could recover from her fright the young man had disappeared—leaving a letter in her hand. She hid it in her glove and throughout the whole of the drive neither heard nor saw a thing. As was her custom when riding in her carriage, the Countess kept up a ceaseless flow of questions: "Who was it who met us just now? What's this bridge called? What's written on that signboard?" This time Lisaveta Ivanovna's answers were so vague and inappropriate that the Countess became angry.

"What's the matter with you, my child? Are you in a trance or something? Don't you hear me or understand what I'm saying? Heaven be thanked that I'm still sane enough to speak clearly."

---

7. Tables on which gambling took place were typically covered with green baize.   8. My angel, you write me four-page-long letters faster than I can read them (French).

Lisaveta Ivanovna did not listen to her. On returning home, she ran up to her room and drew the letter from her glove; it was unsealed. Lisaveta Ivanovna read it through. The letter contained a confession of love; it was tender, respectful and taken word for word from a German novel. But Lisaveta Ivanovna had no knowledge of German and was most pleased by it.

Nevertheless, the letter made her feel extremely uneasy. For the first time in her life she was entering into a secret and confidential relationship with a young man. His audacity shocked her. She reproached herself for her imprudent behaviour, and did not know what to do. Should she stop sitting at the window and by a show of indifference cool off the young man's desire for further acquaintance? Should she send the letter back to him? Or answer it with cold-hearted finality? There was nobody to whom she could turn for advice: she had no friend or preceptress. Lisaveta Ivanovna resolved to answer the letter.

She sat down at her small writing-table, took a pen and some paper, and lost herself in thought. Several times she began her letter—and then tore it up: her manner of expression seemed to her to be either too condescending or too heartless. At last she succeeded in writing a few lines that satisfied her:

> "I am sure that your intentions are honourable, and that you did not wish to offend me by your rash behaviour, but our acquaintance must not begin in this way. I return your letter to you and hope that in the future I shall have no cause to complain of undeserved disrespect."

The next day, as soon as she saw Hermann approach, Lisaveta Ivanovna rose from behind her frame, went into the ante-room, opened a small window, and threw her letter into the street, trusting to the agility of the young officer to pick it up. Hermann ran forward, took hold of the letter and went into a confectioner's shop. Breaking the seal of the envelope, he found his own letter and Lisaveta Ivanovna's answer. It was as he had expected, and he returned home, deeply preoccupied with his intrigue.

Three days afterwards, a bright-eyed young girl brought Lisaveta Ivanovna a letter from a milliner's shop. Lisaveta Ivanovna opened it uneasily, envisaging a demand for money, but she suddenly recognised Hermann's handwriting.

"You have made a mistake, my dear," she said: "this letter is not for me."

"Oh, but it is!" the girl answered cheekily and without concealing a sly smile. "Read it."

Lisaveta Ivanovna ran her eyes over the note. Hermann demanded a meeting.

"It cannot be," said Lisaveta Ivanovna, frightened at the haste of his demand and the way in which it was made: "this is certainly not for me."

And she tore the letter up into tiny pieces.

"If the letter wasn't for you, why did you tear it up?" asked the girl. "I would have returned it to the person who sent it."

"Please, my dear," Lisaveta Ivanovna said, flushing at the remark, "don't bring me any more letters in the future. And tell the person who sent you that he should be ashamed of . . ."

But Hermann was not put off. By some means or other, he sent a letter to Lisaveta Ivanovna every day. The letters were no longer translated from the German. They were inspired by passion and written in a language, true to Hermann's character, which expressed his obsessive desires and the disorder of an unfettered imagination. Lisaveta Ivanovna no longer thought of returning them to him: she revelled in them, began to answer them, and with each day, her replies became longer and more tender. Finally, she threw out of the window the following letter:

"This evening there is a ball at the *** Embassy. The Countess will be there. We will stay until about two o'clock. Here is your chance to see me alone. As soon as the Countess has left the house, the servants will probably go to their quarters—with the exception of the hall-porter, who normally goes out to his closet anyway. Come at half-past eleven. Walk straight upstairs. If you meet anybody in the ante-room, ask whether the Countess is at home. You will be told 'No'—and there will be nothing you can do but go away. But it is unlikely that you will meet anybody. The lady's maids sit by themselves, all in the one room. On leaving the hall, turn to the left and walk straight on until you come to the Countess' bedroom. In the bedroom, behind a screen, you will see two small doors: the one on the right leads into the study, which the Countess never goes into; the one on the left leads into a corridor and thence to a narrow winding staircase: this staircase leads to my bedroom."

Hermann quivered like a tiger as he awaited the appointed hour. He was already outside the Countess' house at ten o'clock. The weather was terrible; the wind howled, and a wet snow fell in large flakes upon the deserted streets, where the lamps shone dimly. Occasionally a passing cab-driver leaned forward over his scrawny nag, on the look-out for a late passenger. Feeling neither wind nor snow, Hermann waited, dressed only in his frock-coat. At last the Countess' carriage was brought round. Hermann saw two footmen carry out in their arms the bent old lady, wrapped in a sable fur, and immediately following her, the figure of Lisaveta Ivanovna, clad in a light cloak and with her head adorned with fresh flowers. The doors were slammed and the carriage rolled heavily away along the soft snow. The hall-porter closed the front door. The windows became dark. Hermann began to walk about near the deserted house. He went up to a lamp and looked at his watch; it was twenty minutes past eleven. He remained beneath the lamp, his eyes fixed upon the hands of his watch, waiting for the remaining minutes to pass. At exactly half-past eleven, Hermann ascended the steps of the Countess' house and reached the brightly-lit porch. The hall-porter was not there. Hermann ran up the stairs, opened the door into the ante-room and saw a servant asleep by the lamp in a soiled antique armchair. With a light, firm tread Hermann stepped past him. The drawing-room and reception-room were in darkness, but the lamp in the ante-room sent through a feeble light. Hermann passed through into the bedroom. Before an icon-case, filled with old-fashioned images,[9] glowed a gold sanctuary lamp. Faded brocade armchairs and dull gilt divans with soft cushions were ranged in sad symmetry around the room, the walls of which were hung with Chinese silk. Two portraits, painted in Paris by Madame Lebrun,[1] hung on one of the walls. One of these featured a plump, red-faced man of about forty, in a light-green uniform and with a star pinned to his breast; the other—a beautiful young woman with an aquiline nose and powdered hair, brushed back at the tem-

9. That is, religious images.   1. Marie-Louise-Élisabeth Vigée-Lebrun (1755–1842), French portrait painter, particularly of the aristocracy and royalty.

ples and adorned with a rose. In the corners of the room stood porcelain shepherdesses, table clocks from the workshop of the celebrated Leroy, little boxes, roulettes, fans and the various lady's playthings which had been popular at the end of the last century, when the Montgolfiers' balloon and Mesmer's magnetism[2] were invented. Hermann went behind the screen, where stood a small iron bedstead; on the right was the door leading to the study; on the left the one which led to the corridor. Hermann opened the latter, and saw the narrow, winding staircase which led to the poor ward's room . . . But he turned back and stepped into the dark study.

The time passed slowly. Everything was quiet. The clock in the drawing-room struck twelve; one by one the clocks in all the other rooms sounded the same hour, and then all was quiet again. Hermann stood leaning against the cold stove. He was calm; his heart beat evenly, like that of a man who has decided upon some dangerous but necessary action. One o'clock sounded; two o'clock; he heard the distant rattle of the carriage. He was seized by an involuntary agitation. The carriage drew near and stopped. He heard the sound of the carriage-steps being let down. The house suddenly came alive. Servants ran here and there, voices echoed through the house and the rooms were lit. Three old maidservants hastened into the bedroom, followed by the Countess, who, tired to death, lowered herself into a Voltairean armchair.[3] Hermann peeped through a crack. Lisaveta Ivanovna went past him. Hermann heard her hurried steps as she went up the narrow staircase. In his heart there echoed something like the voice of conscience, but it grew silent, and his heart once more turned to stone.

The Countess began to undress before the looking-glass. Her rose-bedecked cap was unfastened; her powdered wig was removed from her grey, closely-cropped hair. Pins fell in showers around her. Her yellow dress, embroidered with silver, fell at her swollen feet. Hermann witnessed all the loathsome mysteries of her toilet. At last the Countess stood in her dressing-gown and night-cap; in this attire, more suitable to her age, she seemed less hideous and revolting.

Like most old people, the Countess suffered from insomnia. Having undressed, she sat down in the Voltairean armchair by the window and dismissed her maidservants. The candles were carried out; once again the room was lit by a single sanctuary lamp. Looking quite yellow, the Countess rocked from side to side in her chair, her flabby lips moving. Her dim eyes reflected a total absence of thought; looking at her, one would have thought that the awful old woman's rocking came not of her own volition, but by the action of some hidden galvanism.

Suddenly, an indescribable change came over her death-like face. Her lips ceased to move, her eyes came to life: before the Countess stood an unknown man.

"Don't be alarmed, for God's sake, don't be alarmed," he said in a clear, low voice. "I have no intention of harming you; I have come to beseech a favour of you."

2. Franz Anton Mesmer (1734–1815) argued that a person can transmit personal force to others in the form of "animal magnetism." Julien Leroy (1686–1759), famous French clockmaker. "Roulettes": little balls; or possibly portable devices for playing the gambling game of roulette. Joseph-Michel (1740–1810) and Jacques-Étienne (1745–1799) Montgolfier, French brothers, helped develop the hot-air balloon and conducted the first untethered flights. 3. A large armchair with a high back.

The old woman looked at him in silence, as if she had not heard him. Hermann imagined that she was deaf, and bending right down over her ear, he repeated what he had said. The old woman kept silent as before.

"You can ensure the happiness of my life," Hermann continued, "and it will cost you nothing: I know that you can guess three cards in succession . . ."

Hermann stopped. The Countess appeared to understand what was demanded of her; she seemed to be seeking words for her reply.

"It was a joke," she said at last. "I swear to you, it was a joke."

"There's no joking about it," Hermann retorted angrily. "Remember Chaplitsky whom you helped to win."

The Countess was visibly disconcerted, and her features expressed strong emotion; but she quickly resumed her former impassivity.

"Can you name these three winning cards?" Hermann continued.

The Countess was silent. Hermann went on:

"For whom do you keep your secret? For your grandsons? They are rich and they can do without it; they don't know the value of money. Your three cards will not help a spendthrift. He who cannot keep his paternal inheritance will die in want, even if he has the devil at his side. I am not a spendthrift; I know the value of money. Your three cards will not be lost on me. Come . . . !"

He stopped and awaited her answer with trepidation. The Countess was silent. Hermann fell upon his knees.

"If your heart has ever known the feeling of love," he said, "if you remember its ecstasies, if you ever smiled at the wailing of your new-born son, if ever any human feeling has run through your breast, I entreat you by the feelings of a wife, a lover, a mother, by everything that is sacred in life, not to deny my request! Reveal your secret to me! What is it to you . . . ? Perhaps it is bound up with some dreadful sin, with the loss of eternal bliss, with some contract made with the devil . . . Consider: you are old; you have not long to live—I am prepared to take your sins on my own soul. Only reveal to me your secret. Realise that the happiness of a man is in your hands, that not only I, but my children, my grandchildren, my great-grandchildren will bless your memory and will revere it as something sacred . . ."

The old woman answered not a word.

Hermann stood up.

"You old witch!" he said, clenching his teeth. "I'll force you to answer . . ."

With these words he drew a pistol from his pocket. At the sight of the pistol, the Countess, for the second time, exhibited signs of strong emotion. She shook her head and, raising her hand as though to shield herself from the shot, she rolled over on her back and remained motionless.

"Stop this childish behaviour now," Hermann said, taking her hand. "I ask you for the last time: will you name your three cards or won't you?"

The Countess made no reply. Hermann saw that she was dead.

CHAPTER FOUR

*7 Mai 18**

Homme sans moeurs et sans religion![4]

CORRESPONDENCE

Still in her ball dress, Lisaveta Ivanovna sat in her room, lost in thought. On her arrival home, she had quickly dismissed the sleepy maid who had reluctantly offered her services, had said that she would undress herself, and with a tremulous heart had gone up to her room, expecting to find Hermann there and yet hoping not to find him. Her first glance assured her of his absence and she thanked her fate for the obstacle that had prevented their meeting. She sat down, without undressing, and began to recall all the circumstances which had lured her so far in so short a time. It was not three weeks since she had first seen the young man from the window—and yet she was already in correspondence with him, and already he had managed to persuade her to grant him a nocturnal meeting! She knew his name only because some of his letters had been signed; she had never spoken to him, nor heard his voice, nor heard anything about him . . . until that very evening. Strange thing! That very evening, Tomsky, vexed with the Princess Polina *** for not flirting with him as she usually did, had wished to revenge himself by a show of indifference: he had therefore summoned Lisaveta Ivanovna and together they had danced an endless mazurka. All the time they were dancing, he had teased her about her partiality to officers of the Engineers, had assured her that he knew far more than she would have supposed possible, and indeed, some of his jests were so successfully aimed that on several occasions Lisaveta Ivanovna had thought that her secret was known to him.

"From whom have you discovered all this?" she asked, laughing.

"From a friend of a person you know well," Tomsky answered. "From a most remarkable man!"

"Who is this remarkable man?"

"He is called Hermann."

Lisaveta made no reply, but her hands and feet turned quite numb.

"This Hermann," Tomsky continued, "is a truly romantic figure: he has the profile of a Napoleon, and the soul of a Mephistopheles. I should think he has at least three crimes on his conscience . . . How pale you have turned . . . !"

"I have a headache . . . What did this Hermann—or whatever his name is—tell you?"

"Hermann is most displeased with his friend: he says that he would act quite differently in his place. I even think that Hermann himself has designs on you; at any rate he listens to the exclamations of his enamoured friend with anything but indifference."

"But where has he seen me?"

"At church, perhaps; on a walk—God only knows! Perhaps in your room, whilst you were asleep: he's quite capable of it . . ."

Three ladies approaching him with the question: *"Oublie ou regret?"*[5]

---

4. A man without morals and without religion! (French).   5. The ladies cut in, offering the man a choice: *oublie* ("forgetting") or *regret*. He does not know which lady is which. He chooses correctly the one with whom he wants to dance.

interrupted the conversation which had become so agonisingly interesting to Lisaveta Ivanovna.

The lady chosen by Tomsky was the Princess Polina *** herself. She succeeded in clearing up the misunderstanding between them during the many turns and movements of the dance, after which he conducted her to her chair. Tomsky returned to his own place. He no longer had any thoughts for Hermann or Lisaveta Ivanovna, who desperately wanted to renew her interrupted conversation; but the mazurka came to an end and shortly afterwards the old Countess left.

Tomsky's words were nothing but ball-room chatter, but they made a deep impression upon the mind of the young dreamer. The portrait, sketched by Tomsky, resembled the image she herself had formed of Hermann, and thanks to the latest romantic novels, Hermann's quite commonplace face took on attributes that both frightened and captivated her imagination. Now she sat, her uncovered arms crossed, her head, still adorned with flowers, bent over her bare shoulders . . . Suddenly the door opened, and Hermann entered. She shuddered.

"Where have you been?" she asked in a frightened whisper.

"In the old Countess' bedroom," Hermann answered. "I have just left it. The Countess is dead."

"Good God! What are you saying?"

"And it seems," Hermann continued, "that I am the cause of her death."

Lisaveta Ivanovna looked at him, and the words of Tomsky echoed in her mind: "He has at least three crimes on his conscience!" Hermann sat down beside her on the window sill and told her everything.

Lisaveta Ivanovna listened to him with horror. So those passionate letters, those ardent demands, the whole impertinent and obstinate pursuit—all that was not love! Money—that was what his soul craved! It was not she who could satisfy his desire and make him happy! The poor ward had been nothing but the unknowing assistant of a brigand, of the murderer of her aged benefactress! She wept bitterly, in an agony of belated repentance. Hermann looked at her in silence. His heart was also tormented; but neither the tears of the poor girl nor the astounding charm of her grief disturbed his hardened soul. He felt no remorse at the thought of the dead old lady. He felt dismay for only one thing: the irretrievable loss of the secret upon which he had relied for enrichment.

"You are a monster!" Lisaveta Ivanovna said at last.

"I did not wish for her death," Hermann answered. "My pistol wasn't loaded."

They were silent.

The day began to break. Lisaveta Ivanovna extinguished the flickering candle. A pale light lit up her room. She wiped her tear-stained eyes and raised them to Hermann. He sat by the window, his arms folded and with a grim frown on his face. In this position, he bore an astonishing resemblance to a portrait of Napoleon. Even Lisaveta Ivanovna was struck by the likeness.

"How am I going to get you out of the house?" Lisaveta Ivanovna said at last. "I had thought of leading you down the secret staircase, but that would mean going past the Countess' bedroom, and I am afraid."

"Tell me how to find this secret staircase. I'll go on my own."

Lisaveta Ivanovna stood up, took a key from her chest of drawers, handed it to Hermann and gave him detailed instructions. Hermann pressed her cold, unresponsive hand, kissed her bowed head and left.

He descended the winding staircase and once more entered the Countess' bedroom. The dead old lady sat as if turned to stone; her face expressed a deep calm. Hermann stopped in front of her and gazed at her for a long time, as if wishing to assure himself of the dreadful truth. Finally, he went into the study, felt for the door behind the silk wall hangings and, agitated by strange feelings, began to descend the dark staircase.

"Along this very staircase," he thought, "perhaps at this same hour sixty years ago, in an embroidered coat, his hair dressed à l'oiseau royal,[6] his three-cornered hat pressed to his heart, there may have crept into this very bedroom a young and happy man now long since turned to dust in his grave—and to-day the aged heart of his mistress ceased to beat."

At the bottom of the staircase Hermann found a door, which he opened with the key Lisaveta Ivanovna had given to him, and he found himself in a corridor which led to the street.

CHAPTER FIVE

That evening there appeared before me
the figure of the late Baroness von V**.
She was all in white and she said to me:
"How are you, Mr. Councillor!"
SWEDENBORG[7]

Three days after the fateful night, at nine o'clock in the morning, Hermann set out for the *** monastery, where a funeral service for the dead Countess was going to be held. Although unrepentant, he could not altogether silence the voice of conscience, which kept repeating: "You are the murderer of the old woman!" Having little true religious belief, he was extremely superstitious. He believed that the dead Countess could exercise a harmful influence on his life and he had therefore resolved to be present at her funeral, in order to ask for forgiveness.

The church was full. Hermann could scarcely make his way through the crowd of people. The coffin stood on a rich catafalque beneath a velvet canopy. Within it lay the dead woman, her arms folded upon her chest, dressed in a white satin robe and with a lace cap on her head. Around her stood the members of her household: servants in black coats, with armorial ribbons upon their shoulders and candles in their hands; the relatives—children, grandchildren, great-grandchildren—in deep mourning. Nobody cried; tears would have been une affectation. The Countess was so old that her death could have surprised nobody, and her relatives had long considered her as having outlived herself. A young bishop pronounced the funeral sermon. In simple, moving words, he described the peaceful end of the righteous woman, who for many years had been in quiet and touching preparation for a Christian end. "The angel of death found her," the speaker said, "waiting for the midnight bridegroom, vigilant in godly meditation." The service was completed with sad decorum. The relatives were the first to take

---

6. In the style of the royal bird (French, literal trans.); an antiquated and elaborate hairstyle.
7. Emanuel Swedenborg (1688–1772), Swedish theologian, believed that he had several experiences of divine revelation, some involving appearances to him of the dead.

leave of the body. Then the numerous guests went up to pay final homage to her who had so long participated in their frivolous amusements. They were followed by all the members of the Countess' household, the last of whom was an old housekeeper of the same age as the Countess. She was supported by two young girls who led her up to the coffin. She had not the strength to bow down to the ground—and merely shed a few tears as she kissed the cold hand of her mistress. After her, Hermann decided to approach the coffin. He knelt down and for several minutes lay on the cold floor, which was strewn with fir branches. At last he stood up, as pale as the dead woman herself, ascended the steps of the catafalque and bent his head over the body of the Countess . . . At that very moment, it seemed to him that the dead woman gave him a mocking glance, and winked at him. Hermann, hurriedly stepping back, missed his footing and crashed on to his back against the ground. He was helped to his feet. Simultaneously, Lisaveta Ivanovna was carried out in a faint to the porch of the church. These events disturbed the solemnity of the gloomy ceremony for a few moments. A subdued murmur arose among the congregation, and a tall, thin chamberlain, a near relative of the dead woman, whispered in the ear of an Englishman standing by him that the young officer was the Countess' illegitimate son, to which the Englishman replied coldly: "Oh?"

For the whole of that day Hermann was exceedingly troubled. He went to a secluded inn for dinner and, contrary to his usual custom and in the hope of silencing his inward agitation, he drank heavily. But the wine fired his imagination still more. Returning home, he threw himself on to his bed without undressing and fell into a heavy sleep.

It was already night when he awoke: the moon lit up his room. He glanced at his watch; it was a quarter to three. He found he could not go back to sleep; he sat on his bed and thought about the funeral of the old Countess.

Just then, someone in the street glanced in at his window and immediately went away. Hermann paid no heed to the incident. A minute or so later, he heard the door into the front room being opened. Hermann imagined that it was his orderly, drunk as usual, returning from some nocturnal outing. But he heard unfamiliar footsteps and the soft shuffling of slippers. The door opened: a woman in a white dress entered. Hermann mistook her for his old wet-nurse and wondered what could have brought her out at this time of the night. But the woman in white glided across the room and suddenly appeared before him—and Hermann recognised the Countess!

"I have come to you against my will," she said in a firm voice, "but I have been ordered to fulfill your request. Three, seven, ace, played in that order, will win for you, but only on condition that you play not more than one card in twenty-four hours, and that you never play again for the rest of your life. I'll forgive you my death if you marry my ward, Lisaveta Ivanovna . . ."

With these words, she turned round quietly, walked towards the door and disappeared, her slippers shuffling. Herman heard the door in the hall bang, and again saw somebody look in at him through the window.

For a long time Hermann could not collect his senses. He went into the next room. His orderly was lying asleep on the floor. Hermann could scarcely awaken him. As usual, the orderly was drunk, and it was impossible to get any sense out of him. The door into the hall was locked. Hermann returned to his room, lit a candle, and recorded the details of his vision.

CHAPTER SIX

—Attendez![8]
—How dare you say to me: "Attendez!"?
—Your Excellency, I said: "Attendez, sir!"

Two fixed ideas can no more exist in one mind than, in the physical sense, two bodies can occupy one and the same place. "Three, seven, ace" soon eclipsed from Hermann's mind the form of the dead old lady. "Three, seven, ace" never left his thoughts, were constantly on his lips. At the sight of a young girl, he would say: "How shapely she is! Just like the three of hearts." When asked the time, he would reply: "About seven." Every potbellied man he saw reminded him of an ace. "Three, seven, ace," assuming all possible shapes, persecuted him in his sleep: the three bloomed before him in the shape of some luxuriant flower, the seven took on the appearance of a Gothic gateway, the ace—of an enormous spider. To the exclusion of all others, one thought alone occupied his mind—making use of the secret which had cost him so much. He began to think of retirement and of travel. He wanted to try his luck in the public gaming-houses of Paris. Chance spared him the trouble.

There was in Moscow a society of rich gamblers, presided over by the celebrated Chekalinsky, a man whose whole life had been spent at the card-table, and who had amassed millions long ago, accepting his winnings in the form of promissory notes and paying his losses with ready money. His long experience had earned him the confidence of his companions, and his open house, his famous cook and his friendliness and gaiety had won him great public respect. He arrived in Petersburg. The younger generation flocked to his house, forgetting balls for cards, and preferring the enticements of faro to the fascinations of courtship. Narumov took Hermann to meet him.

They passed through a succession of magnificent rooms, full of polite and attentive waiters. Several generals and privy councillors were playing whist; young men, sprawled out on brocade divans, were eating ices and smoking their pipes. In the drawing-room, seated at the head of a long table, around which were crowded about twenty players, the host kept bank. He was a most respectable-looking man of about sixty; his head was covered with silvery grey hair, and his full, fresh face expressed good nature; his eyes, enlivened by a perpetual smile, shone brightly. Narumov introduced Hermann to him. Chekalinsky shook his hand warmly, requested him not to stand on ceremony and went on dealing.

The game lasted a long time. More than thirty cards lay on the table. Chekalinsky paused after each round, in order to give the players time to arrange their cards, and wrote down their losses. He listened politely to their demands, and more politely still allowed them to retract any stake accidentally left on the table. At last the game finished. Chekalinsky shuffled the cards and prepared to deal again.

"Allow me to place a stake," Hermann said, stretching out his hand from behind a fat gentleman who was punting[9] there.

Chekalinsky smiled and nodded silently, as a sign of his consent. Narumov laughingly congratulated Hermann on forswearing a longstanding principle and wished him a lucky beginning.

---

8. Wait! (French). Attendants at the gaming table called "Attendez" to indicate the end of the period to place bets.   9. Betting against the dealer.

"I've staked," Hermann said, as he chalked up the amount, which was very considerable, on the back of his card.

"How much is it?" asked the banker, screwing up his eyes. "Forgive me, but I can't make it out."

"47,000 roubles," Hermann replied.

At these words every head in the room turned, and all eyes were fixed on Hermann.

"He's gone out of his mind!" Narumov thought.

"Allow me to observe to you," Chekalinsky said with his invariable smile, "that your stake is extremely high: nobody here has ever put more than 275 roubles on any single card."

"What of it?" retorted Hermann. "Do you take me or not?"

Chekalinsky, bowing, humbly accepted the stake.

"However, I would like to say," he said, "that, being judged worthy of the confidence of my friends, I can only bank against ready money. For my own part, of course, I am sure that your word is enough, but for the sake of the order of the game and of the accounts, I must ask you to place your money on the card."

Hermann drew a banknote from his pocket and handed it to Chekalinsky who, giving it a cursory glance, put it on Hermann's card.

He began to deal. On the right a nine turned up, on the left a three.[1]

"The three wins," said Hermann, showing his card.

A murmur arose among the players. Chekalinsky frowned, but instantly the smile returned to his face.

"Do you wish to take the money now?" he asked Hermann.

"If you would be so kind."

Chekalinsky drew a number of banknotes from his pocket and settled up immediately. Hermann took up his money and left the table. Narumov was too astounded even to think. Hermann drank a glass of lemonade and went home.

The next evening he again appeared at Chekalinsky's. The host was dealing. Hermann walked up to the table; the players already there immediately gave way to him. Chekalinsky bowed graciously.

Hermann waited for the next deal, took a card and placed on it his 47,000 roubles together with the winnings of the previous evening.

Chekalinsky began to deal. A knave turned up on the right, a seven on the left.

Hermann showed his seven.

There was a general cry of surprise, and Chekalinsky was clearly disconcerted. He counted out 94,000 roubles and handed them to Hermann, who pocketed them coolly and immediately withdrew.

The following evening Hermann again appeared at the table. Everyone was expecting him. The generals and privy councillors abandoned their whist in order to watch such unusual play. The young officers jumped up from their divans; all the waiters gathered in the drawing-room. Hermann was surrounded by a crowd of people. The other players held back their cards, impatient to see how Hermann would get on. Hermann stood at the

---

1. Bets in faro are made on the positions of cards. A player selects a card and places it facedown in front of him or her; if the card turns up on the dealer's left, the player wins; if on the right, the dealer wins.

table and prepared to play alone against the pale but still smiling Chekalinsky. Each unsealed a pack of cards. Chekalinsky shuffled. Hermann drew and placed his card, covering it with a heap of banknotes. It was like a duel. A deep silence reigned all around.

His hands shaking, Chekalinsky began to deal. On the right lay a queen, on the left an ace.

"The ace wins," said Hermann and showed his card.

"Your queen has lost," Chekalinsky said kindly.

Hermann started: indeed, instead of an ace, before him lay the queen of spades. He could not believe his eyes, could not understand how he could have slipped up.

At that moment it seemed to him that the queen of spades winked at him and smiled. He was struck by an unusual likeness . . .

"The old woman!" he shouted in terror.

Chekalinsky gathered up his winnings. Hermann stood motionless. When he left the table, people began to converse noisily.

"Famously punted!" the players said.

Chekalinsky shuffled the cards afresh; play went on as usual.

CONCLUSION

Hermann went mad. He is now installed in Room 17 at the Obukhov Hospital, he answers no questions, but merely mutters with unusual rapidity: "Three, seven, ace! Three, seven, queen!"

Lisaveta Ivanovna married a very agreeable young man, the son of the old Countess's former steward and with a good position in the Service somewhere. Lisaveta Ivanovna is bringing up a poor relative.

Tomsky has been promoted to the rank of Captain and is going to be married to Princess Polina.

VICTOR HUGO
1802–1885

Celebrated as poet, dramatist, and novelist, Victor Hugo (pronounced *vik-tor' ew-goh'*) was a towering figure in his generation of French literary figures. He wrote in virtually every available genre and explored an enormous range of subjects and feelings, helping throughout to articulate the principles of Romanticism. His various political allegiances determined some of his actions: for twenty years he exiled himself to the island of Guernsey (a possession of the British Crown), believing his life in danger after President Louis-Napoléon seized power. Always, though, he devoted himself to writing. *Et nox facta est*, printed here, is the first section of the epic *The End of Satan* and depicts the fallen angel's defiant plunge from heaven. Hugo's portrait of Satan demonstrates both psychological acuity and powerful identification with the figure of a rebel. The poem makes one feel both the terror and the ugliness of Satan's nay-saying and the splendor of his refusal.

Et nox facta est[1]

I

He[2] had been falling in the abyss some four thousand years.

Never had he yet managed to grasp a peak,
Nor lift even once his towering forehead.
He sank deeper in the dark and the mist, aghast,
Alone, and behind him, in the eternal nights,   5
His wing feathers fell more slowly still.
He fell dumbfounded, grim, and silent,
Sad, his mouth open and his feet towards the heavens,
The horror of the chasm imprinted on his livid face.
He cried: "Death!" his fists stretched out in the empty dark.   10
Later this word was man and was named Cain.[3]

He was falling. A rock struck his hand quite suddenly;
He held on to it, as a dead man holds on to his tomb,
And stopped. Someone, from on high, cried out to him: "Fall!
The suns will go out around you, accursed!"   15
And the voice was lost in the immensity of horror.
And pale, he looked toward the eternal dawn.
The suns were far off, but shone still.
Satan raised his head and spoke, his arms in the air:
"You lie!" This word was later the soul of Judas.[4]   20

Like the gods of bronze erect upon their pilasters,
He waited a thousand years, eyes fixed upon the stars.
The suns were far off, but were still shining.
The thunder then rumbled in the skies unhearing, cold.
Satan laughed, and spat towards the thunder.   25
Filled by the visionary shadow, the immensity
Shivered. This spitting out was later Barabbas.[5]

A passing breath made him fall lower still.

II

The fall of the damned one began once again.—Terrible,
Somber, and pierced with holes luminous as a sieve,   30
The sky full of suns withdrew, brightness
Trembled, and in the night the great fallen one,
Naked, sinister, and pulled by the weight of his crime,
Fell, and his head wedging the abyss apart.
Lower! Lower, and still lower! Everything presently   35

1. Translated by Mary Ann Caws, who has evoked the dignity and the intensity of Hugo's verse. Written as part of *The End of Satan*, an epic poem never completed. The Latin title (And there was night) contrasts with the biblical "And there was light" (Genesis 1.3).   2. Satan, formerly the rebellious archangel Lucifer, thrown out of heaven by God (Revelation 12.7–9 and Isaiah 14.12).   3. The first murderer, son of Adam and brother of Abel, the victim (Genesis 4.1–15).   4. Judas Iscariot, the apostle who betrayed Jesus (Matthew 26.47–50, 27.3–5).   5. The condemned criminal who was freed instead of Jesus (Mark 15.6–15).

Fled from him; no obstacle to seize in passing,
No mountain, no crumbling rock, no stone,
Nothing, shadow! and from fright he closed his eyes.

And when they opened, three suns only
Shone, and shadow had eaten away the firmament.   40
All the other suns had perished.

III

A rock
Emerged from blackest mist like some arm approaching.
He grasped it, and his feet touched summits.

Then the dreadful being called Never
Dreamed. His forehead sank between his guilty hands.   45
The three suns, far off, like three great eyes,
Watched him, and he watched them not.
Space resembled our earthly plains,
At evening, when the horizon sinking, retreating,
Blackens under the white eyes of the ghostly twilight.   50
Long rays entwined the feet of the great exile.
Behind him his shadow filled the infinite.
The peaks of chaos mingled in themselves.
In an instant he felt some horrendous growth of wings;
He felt himself become a monster, and that the angel in him   55
Was dying, and the rebel then knew regret.
He felt his shoulder, so bright before,
Quiver in the hideous cold of membraned wing,
And folding his arms with his head lifted high,
This bandit, as if grown greater through affront,   60
Alone in these depths that only ruin inhabits,
Looked steadily at the shadow's cave.
The noiseless darkness grew in the nothingness.
Obscure opacity closed off the gaping sky;
And making beyond the last promontory   65
A triple crack in the black pane,
The three suns mingled their three lights.
You would have thought them three wheels of a chariot of fire,
Broken after some battle in the high firmament.
Like prows, the mountains from the mist emerged.   70
"So," cried Satan, "so be it! still I can see!
He shall have the blue sky, the black sky is mine.
Does he think I will come weeping to his door?
I hate him. Three suns suffice. What do I care?
I hate the day, the blueness, fragrance and the light."   75

Suddenly he shivered; there remained only one.

IV

The abyss was fading. Nothing kept its shape.
Darkness seemed to swell its giant wave.

Something nameless and submerged, something
That is no longer, takes its leave, falls silent;   80
And no one could have said, in this deep horror,
If this frightful remnant of a mystery or a world,
Like the vague mist where the dream takes flight,
Was called shipwreck or was called night;
And the archangel felt himself become a phantom.   85
He shouted: "Hell!" This word later made Sodom.[6]

And the voice repeated slowly on his forehead:
"Accursed! all about you the stars will go dark."

And already the sun was only a star.

                            V

And all disappeared slowly under a veil.   90
Then the archangel quaked; Satan learned to shiver.
Toward the star trembling livid on the horizon
He hurled himself, leaping from peak to peak.
Then, although with horror at the wings of a beast,
Although it was the clothing of emprisonment,   95
Like a bird going from bush to bush,
Horrendous he took his flight from mount to mount,
And this convict began running in his cell.
He ran, he flew, he shouted: "Star of gold! Brother![7]
Wait for me! I'm running! Don't go out yet!   100
Don't leave me alone!"

                    Thus the monster
Crossed the first lakes of the dead immensity,
Former chaos, emptied and already stagnant,
And into the lugubrious depths he plunged.

Now the star was only a spark.   105

He went down further in universal shadow,
Sank further, cast himself wallowing in the night,
Climbed the filthy mountains, their damp gleaming front,
Whose base is unsteady in the cesspool deeps,
And trembling stared before him.

                            The spark   110
Was only a red dot in the depth of the dark abyss.

                            VI

As between two battlements the archer leans
On the wall, when twilight has reached his keep,
Wild he leaned from the mountain top,

---

6. Biblical city, with Gomorrah a symbol of corruption and decadence. Both were destroyed by God (Genesis 18.20–19.28).   7. Lucifer means "Light Bearer."

And upon the star, hoping to arouse its flame,   115
He started to blow as upon some ember.
And anguish caused his fierce nostrils to swell.
The breath rushing from his chest
Is now upon earth and called hurricane.

With his breath a great noise stirred the shadow, an ocean   120
No being dwells in and no fires illumine.
The mountains found nearby took their flight,
The monstrous chaos full of fright arose
And began to shriek: Jehovah Jehovah!
The infinite opened, rent apart like a cloth,   125
But nothing moved in the lugubrious star;
And the damned one, crying: "Don't go out yet! I'll go on!
I'll get there!" resumed again his desperate flight.
And the glaciers mingled with the nights resembling them
Turned on their backs like frightened beasts,   130
And the black tornadoes and the hideous chasms
Bent in terror, while above them,
Flying toward the star like some arrow to the goal,
There passed, wild and haggard, this terrible supplicant.

And ever since it has seen this frightening flight,   135
This bitter abyss, aghast like a fleeing man
Retains forever the horror and the craze,
So monstrous was it to see, in the shadow immense,
Opening his atrocious wing far from the heavens,
This bat flying from his eternal prison!   140

VII

He flew for ten thousand years.

For ten thousand years,
Stretching forth his livid neck and his frenzied hands,
He flew without finding a peak on which to rest.
The star seemed sometimes to fade and to go out,   145
And the horror of the tomb caused the angel to shiver;
Then a pale brightness, vague, strange, uncertain,
Reappeared: and in joy, he cried: "Onward!"
Around him hovered the north wind birds.
He was flying. The infinite never ceases to start again.   150
His flight circled immense in that sea.
The night watched his horrible talons fleeing.
As a cloud feels its whirlwinds fall,
He felt his strength crumble in the chasm.
The winter murmured: tremble! and the shadow said: suffer!   155

Finally he perceived a black peak far off
Which a fearsome reflection in the shadow inflamed.
Satan, like a swimmer in his effort supreme,
Stretched out his wing, with claws and bald, and specter-pale,

Panting, broken, tired, and smoking with sweat,   160
He sank down on the edge of the abrupt descent.[8]

VIII

There was the sun dying in the abyss.
The star, in the deepest fog had no air to revive it,
Grew cold, dim, and was slowly destroyed.
Its sinister round was seen in the night;   165
And in this somber silence its fiery ulcers were seen
Subsiding under a leprosy of dark.
Coal of a world put out! torch blown out by God!
Its crevices still showed a trace of fire,
As if the soul could be seen through holes in the skull.   170
At the center there quivered and flickered a flame
Now and then licking the outermost edge,
And from each crater flashes came
Shivering like flaming swords,
And fading noiselessly as dreams.   175
The star was almost black. The archangel was tired
Beyond voice or breath, a pity to see.
And the star in death throes under his savage glance,
Was dying, doing battle. With its somber apertures
Into the cold darkness it spewed now and again   180
Burning streams, crimson lumps, and smoking hills,
Rocks foaming with initial brightness:
As if this giant of life and light
Engulfed by the mist where all is fading,
Had refused to die without insulting the night   185
And spitting its lava in the shadow's face.
About it time and space and number,
Form, and noise expired, making
The forbidding and black oneness of void.
Then the specter Nothing[9] raised its head from the abyss.   190

Suddenly, from the heart of the star, a jet of sulphur
Sharp, clamorous like one dying in delirium,
Burst sudden, shining, splendid with surprise,
And lighting from far a thousand deathly forms,
Massive, pierced to the shadow's depths   195
The monstrous porches of endless deep.
Night and immensity formed
Their angels. Satan, wild and out of breath,
His vision dazzled and full of this flashing,
Beat with his wing, opened his hands and then shivered   200
And cried: "Despair! see it growing pale!"

The archangel understood, as does the mast in its sinking,
That he was the drowned man of the shadows' flood;
He furled once more his wing with its granite nails,
And wrung his hands. And the star went out.   205

8. Literally, escarpment, the steep wall before a fortification or cliff.   9. Satan.

IX

Now, near the skies, at chasm's edge where nothing changes,
One feather escaped from the archangel's wing
Remained and quivered, pure and white.
The angel on whose forehead the dazzling dawn is born
Saw and grasped it, observing the sublime sky: 210
"Lord, must it too fall into the abyss?"
God turned about, absorbed in being and in Life,
And said "Do not discard what has not fallen."[1]

* * *

Black caves of the past, porches of time passed
With no date and no radiance, somber, unmeasured,   215
Cycles previous to man, chaos, heavens,
World terrible and rich in prodigious beings,
Oh fearful fog where the preadamites
Appeared, standing in limitless shadow.
Who could fathom you, oh chasms, oh unknown times.   220
The thinker barefoot like the poor,
Through respect for the One unseen, the sage,
Digs in the depths of origin and age,
Fathoms and seeks beyond the colossi,[2] further
Than the facts witnessed by the present sky,   225
Reaches with pale visage suspected things,
And finds, lifting the darkness of years
And the layers of days, worlds, voids,
Gigantic centuries dead beneath giants of centuries.
And thus the wise man dreams in the deep of the night   230
His face illumined by glints of the abyss.

1. In the second part of *The End of Satan—Satan's Feather*—the feather is brought to life by a divine glance and becomes the female spirit Liberty. She wins God's permission to plunge into hell in an attempt to redeem her father (part 3), and in part 4 the repentant archangel is released and re-created as Lucifer. 2. Giants of preadamic time.

WALT WHITMAN
1819–1892

As insistently as Rousseau, but with a far richer sense of the nature and the importance of his social context, Walt Whitman in his poetry makes himself the center of the universe. He brings to his emphatic self-presentation a detailed, partly ironic, partly celebratory sense of what it means to be an American; his poetry suggests something of what life in the United States must have felt like in the middle of the nineteenth century.

Born on New York's Long Island, Whitman in his childhood moved with his family to Brooklyn. He was christened Walter, but shortened his first name to distinguish himself from his father. As a young man, he worked as schoolteacher, builder, bookstore owner, journalist, and poet, before moving to Washington, D.C., to work as a government clerk. There he also served as a volunteer nurse, helping to care for the Civil War wounded. In 1873 he settled in Camden, New Jersey, where he remained for the rest of his life.

Whitman began writing in his youth, producing a good deal of bad poetry and a novel, a fictionalized temperance tract. He first published *Leaves of Grass* in 1855, after having become an admirer of Emerson and a Jeffersonian Democrat; he continued enlarging and revising the book for the rest of his life. In 1865, he published *Drum Taps,* poems derived from his Civil War experiences; in 1871, *Democratic Vistas,* a collection of political and philosophical essays.

Whitman's shifting diction—familiar, even slangy, to formal and rhetorical—makes possible a large range of tones in *Song of Myself.* In a single section (21), for example, these two sequences occur in close conjunction:

> I chant the chant of dilation or pride,
> We have had ducking and deprecating about enough,
> I show that size is only development.
>
> Smile O voluptuous cool-breathed earth!
> Earth of the slumbering and liquid trees!
> Earth of departed sunset—earth of the mountains misty-topt!
> Earth of the vitreous pour of the full moon just tinged with blue!

The first three-line passage, after its formal opening, falls into a pattern like that of colloquial speech. "About enough" belongs to an informal vocabulary; the final line, turning on the word *only,* makes the kind of joke one might make in conversation. ("Size doesn't matter, really, it only comes from growing.") The speaker's claim that he does not endorse conventional judgments, by which bigger is better, and his slightly mocking tone declare his independence and his willingness not to take himself with undue seriousness. Only a few lines later, when he turns to the "voluptuous cool-breathed earth," he sounds like a different person, entirely serious, almost grandiose, about his personal perceptions. Now his rhapsodic tone unites him with the Romantic poets, although his vocabulary still insists on his individuality. The conjunction of "voluptuous" with "cool-breathed," the use of "vitreous" (glasslike) to modify "pour" used as a noun, the idea of "liquid trees": such choices demand the reader's close attention to figure out exactly what the poem is saying, and they emphasize a fresh way of seeing, a precise attention to the look of things. But they also sound like poetry, in a sense familiar to readers of earlier nineteenth-century works—unlike the lines quoted just before, which resemble colloquial prose.

The range of tones used in the given example helps communicate an important theme of Whitman's poem: the tension and exchange between desire for individuality and for community. *Song of Myself* alternates between assertions of specialness and of identification with others.

> I am of old and young, of the foolish as much as the wise,. . . .
> One of the Nation of many nations, the smallest the same and the largest the same,
> A Southerner soon as a Northerner, a planter nonchalant and hospitable down by
>   the Oconee I live, . . .
> At home on Kanadian snow-shoes or up in the bush, or with fishermen off New-
>   foundland,
> At home in the fleet of ice-boats, sailing with the rest and tacking.

Declaring his union not, like Wordsworth, with the natural universe, but with the society of his compatriots, Whitman identifies himself with the enormous variety he perceives and celebrates in his country. But his poem opens "I celebrate myself, and sing myself, / And what I assume you shall assume," insisting on his uniqueness and dominance. Toward the end, these two lines occur: "I too am not a bit tamed, I too am untranslatable, / I sound my barbaric yawp over the roofs of the world." One hears the note of defiant specialness, another characteristic aspect of *Song of Myself*. The poem's power derives partly from its capacity to embody both feelings, the feeling of uniqueness and the sense of shared humanity, feelings that most people experience, sometimes in confusing conjunction. Like his Romantic predecessors, Whitman values emotion, every kind of emotion, for its own sake. He suggests the irrelevance of the notion of contradiction to any understanding of inner life. In the realm of emotion, everything coexists. *Song of Myself* attempts to include all of it.

The poetic daring of *Song of Myself* expresses itself not only in choice of subject matter but in poetic technique. Whitman's lines are unrhymed and avoid the blank verse that had been the norm, instead establishing a new sort of rhythm—one that proved of crucial importance to twentieth-century American poets, who adapted it to their own purposes. Not metrical in any familiar sense, the verse establishes its own hypnotic rhythms, evoking an individual speaking voice, an individual idiom. It even risks the prosaic in its insistence that poetry implies, above all, personal perception and personal voice: "everything" can be included in technique as well as in material.

"Out of the Cradle Endlessly Rocking," another of Whitman's best-known pre–Civil War poems, develops a child's imaginative relation with nature in a way that Wordsworth might have approved. A man hears a birdsong that evokes for him a past experience—just as, at the beginning of *Remembrance of Things Past,* Proust's narrator finds his childhood returning to his memory at the taste of a madeleine. Reduced to tears by the song and the memory, the speaker, "chanter of pains and joys, uniter of here and hereafter," records and explores his youthful revelation of lyric power, achieved by identification with the bird mourning the loss of its mate.

> Now in a moment I know what I am for, I awake,
> And already a thousand singers, a thousand songs, clearer, louder and more
>   sorrowful than yours,
> A thousand warbling echoes have started to life within me, never to die.

The poem concludes with the adult speaker meditating on the nature of his creative force in terms recalling Keats's in "Ode to a Nightingale." Whitman, too, muses about the attraction of death, feels the demonic and the beautiful united in the song that inspires him. His own songs merge in his imagination with the "strong and delicious word" spoken by the sea, another aspect of nature and one traditionally associated with death (as well as with birth). In poetry marked, like *Song of Myself,* by his powerfully individual rhythm and meter, Whitman reminds us once more of a great Romantic theme: the mystery of creativity.

From Song of Myself[1]

1

I celebrate myself, and sing myself,
And what I assume you shall assume,
For every atom belonging to me as good belongs to you.

---

1. First published in 1855. This text is from the 1891–92 edition of *Leaves of Grass,* the so-called Deathbed Edition.

I loafe and invite my soul,
I lean and loafe at my ease observing a spear of summer grass.   5

My tongue, every atom of my blood, formed from this soil, this air,
Born here of parents born here from parents the same, and their parents
     the same,
I, now thirty-seven years old in perfect health begin,
Hoping to cease not till death.

Creeds and schools in abeyance,   10
Retiring back a while sufficed at what they are, but never forgotten,
I harbor for good or bad, I permit to speak at every hazard,
Nature without check with original energy.

                              *   *   *

                              4

Trippers and askers surround me,
People I meet, the effect upon me of my early life or the ward and city I
     live in, or the nation,
The latest dates, discoveries, inventions, societies, authors old and new,
My dinner, dress, associates, looks, compliments, dues,
The real or fancied indifference of some man or woman I love,   5
The sickness of one of my folks or of myself, or ill-doing or loss or lack
     of money, or depressions or exaltations,
Battles, the horrors of fratricidal war, the fever of doubtful news, the
     fitful events;
These come to me days and nights and go from me again,
But they are not the Me myself.

Apart from the pulling and hauling stands what I am,   10
Stands amused, complacent, compassionating, idle, unitary,
Looks down, is erect, or bends an arm on an impalpable certain rest,
Looking with side-curved head curious what will come next,
Both in and out of the game and watching and wondering at it.

Backward I see in my own days where I sweated through fog with
     linguists and contenders,   15
I have no mockings or arguments, I witness and wait.

                              *   *   *

                              7

Has any one supposed it lucky to be born?
I hasten to inform him or her it is just as lucky to die, and I know it.

I pass death with the dying and birth with the new-washed babe, and am
     not contained between my hat and boots,
And peruse manifold objects, no two alike and every one good,
The earth good and the stars good, and their adjuncts all good.   5

I am not an earth nor an adjunct of an earth,
I am the mate and companion of people, all just as immortal and
    fathomless as myself,
(They do not know how immortal, but I know.)

Every kind for itself and its own, for me mine male and female,
For me those that have been boys and that love women,   10
For me the man that is proud and feels how it stings to be slighted,
For me the sweet-heart and the old maid, for me mothers and the mothers
    of mothers,
For me lips that have smiled, eyes that have shed tears,
For me children and the begetters of children.

Undrape! you are not guilty to me, nor stale nor discarded,   15
I see through the broadcloth and gingham whether or no,
And am around, tenacious, acquisitive, tireless, and cannot be shaken
    away.

* * *

16

I am of old and young, of the foolish as much as the wise,
Regardless of others, ever regardful of others,
Maternal as well as paternal, a child as well as a man,
Stuffed with the stuff that is coarse and stuffed with the stuff that is fine,
One of the Nation of many nations, the smallest the same and the
    largest the same,   5
A Southerner soon as a Northerner, a planter nonchalant and hospitable
    down by the Oconee[2] I live,
A Yankee bound my own was ready for trade, my joints the limberest
    joints on earth and the sternest joints on earth,
A Kentuckian walking the vale of the Elkhorn in my deer-skin leggings,
    a Louisianian or Georgian,
A boatman over lakes or bays or along coasts, a Hoosier, Badger,
    Buckeye;
At home on Kanadian snow-shoes or up in the bush, or with fishermen
    off Newfoundland,   10
At home in the fleet of ice-boats, sailing with the rest and tacking,
At home on the hills of Vermont or in the woods of Maine, or the Texan
    ranch,
Comrade of Californians, comrade of free North-Westerners, (loving their
    big proportions,)
Comrade of raftsmen and coalmen, comrade of all who shake hands and
    welcome to drink and meat,
A learner with the simplest, a teacher of the thoughtfullest,   15
A novice beginning yet experient of myriads of seasons,
Of every hue and caste am I, of every rank and religion,
A farmer, mechanic, artist, gentleman, sailor, quaker,
Prisoner, fancy-man, rowdy, lawyer, physician, priest.

---

2. River in Georgia.

I resist any thing better than my own diversity,   20
Breathe the air but leave plenty after me,
And am not stuck up, and am in my place.

(The moth and the fish-eggs are in their place,
The bright suns I see and the dark suns I cannot see are in their place,
The palpable is in its place and the impalpable is in its place.)   25

* * *

21

I am the poet of the Body and I am the poet of the Soul,
The pleasures of heaven are with me and the pains of hell are with me,
The first I graft and increase upon myself, the latter I translate into a new
    tongue.

I am the poet of the woman the same as the man,
And I say it is as great to be a woman as to be a man,   5
And I say there is nothing greater than the mother of men.

I chant the chant of dilation or pride,
We have had ducking and deprecating about enough,
I show that size is only development.

Have you outstript the rest? are you the President?   10
It is a trifle, they will more than arrive there every one, and still pass on.

I am he that walks with the tender and growing night,
I call to the earth and sea half-held by the night.

Press close bare-bosomed night—press close magnetic nourishing night!
Night of south winds—night of the large few stars!   15
Still nodding night—mad naked summer night.

Smile O voluptuous cool-breathed earth!
Earth of the slumbering and liquid trees!
Earth of departed sunset—earth of the mountains misty-topt!
Earth of the vitreous pour of the full moon just tinged with blue!   20
Earth of shine and dark mottling the tide of the river!
Earth of the limpid gray of clouds brighter and clearer for my sake!
Far-swooping elbowed earth—rich apple-blossomed earth!
Smile, for your lover comes.

Prodigal, you have given me love—therefore I to you give love!   25
O unspeakable passionate love.

* * *

24

Walt Whitman, a kosmos, of Manhattan the son,
Turbulent, fleshy, sensual, eating, drinking and breeding,

No sentimentalist, no stander above men and women or apart from them,
No more modest than immodest.

Unscrew the locks from the doors!   5
Unscrew the doors themselves from their jambs!

Whoever degrades another degrades me,
And whatever is done or said returns at last to me.

Through me the afflatus surging and surging, through me the current and
    index.

I speak the pass-word primeval, I give the sign of democracy,   10
By God! I will accept nothing which all cannot have their counterpart of
    on the same terms.

✻ ✻ ✻

32

I think I could turn and live with animals, they are so placid and self-
    contained,
I stand and look at them long and long.

They do not sweat and whine about their condition,
They do not lie awake in the dark and weep for their sins,
They do not make me sick discussing their duty to God,   5
Not one is dissatisfied, not one is demented with the mania of owning
    things,
Not one kneels to another, nor to his kind that lived thousands of years
    ago,
Not one is respectable or unhappy over the whole earth.

So they show their relations to me and I accept them,
They bring me tokens of myself, they evince them plainly in their
    possession.   10
I wonder where they get those tokens,
Did I pass that way huge times ago and negligently drop them?

Myself moving forward then and now and forever,
Gathering and showing more always and with velocity,
Infinite and omnigenous,[3] and the like of these among them,   15
Not too exclusive toward the reachers of my remembrancers,
Picking out here one that I love, and now go with him on brotherly terms.

A gigantic beauty of a stallion, fresh and responsive to my caresses,
Head high in the forehead, wide between the ears,
Limbs glossy and supple, tail dusting the ground,   20
Eyes full of sparkling wickedness, ears finely cut, flexibly moving.

---

3. Belonging to all races.

His nostrils dilate as my heels embrace him,
His well-built limbs tremble with pleasure as we race around and return.

I but use you a minute, then I resign you, stallion,
Why do I need your paces when I myself out-gallop them?   25
Even as I stand or sit passing faster than you.

*   *   *

46

I know I have the best of time and space, and was never measured and
    never will be measured.

I tramp a perpetual journey, (come listen all!)
My signs are a rain-proof coat, good shoes, and a staff cut from the
    woods,
No friend of mine takes his ease in my chair,
I have no chair, no church, no philosophy,   5
I lead no man to a dinner-table, library, exchange,
But each man and each woman of you I lead upon a knoll,
My left hand hooking you round the waist,
My right hand pointing to landscapes of continents and the public road.
Not I, not any one else can travel that road for you,   10
You must travel it for yourself.

It is not far, it is within reach,
Perhaps you have been on it since you were born and did not know,
Perhaps it is everywhere on water and on land.

Shoulder your duds dear son, and I will mine, and let us hasten forth,   15
Wonderful cities and free nations we shall fetch as we go.

*   *   *

51

The past and present wilt—I have filled them, emptied them,
And proceed to fill my next fold of the future.

Listener up there! what have you to confide to me?
Look in my face while I snuff the sidle of evening,[4]
(Talk honestly, no one else hears you, and I stay only a minute longer.)   5

Do I contradict myself?
Very well then I contradict myself,
(I am large, I contain multitudes.)

I concentrate toward them that are nigh, I wait on the door-slab.

---

4. That is, smell the fragrance of the slowly descending evening.

Who has done his day's work? who will soonest be through with his
    supper? 10
Who wishes to walk with me?

Will you speak before I am gone? will you prove already too late?

52

The spotted hawk swoops by and accuses me, he complains of my gab and
    my loitering.

I too am not a bit tamed, I too am untranslatable,
I sound my barbaric yawp over the roofs of the world.

The last scud of day holds back for me,
It flings my likeness after the rest and true as any on the shadowed wilds, 5
It coaxes me to the vapor and the dusk.

I depart as air, I shake my white locks at the runaway sun,
I effuse my flesh in eddies, and drift it in lacy jags.

I bequeath myself to the dirt to grow from the grass I love,
If you want me again look for me under your boot-soles. 10

You will hardly know who I am or what I mean,
But I shall be good health to you nevertheless,
And filter and fibre your blood.

Failing to fetch me at first keep encouraged,
Missing me one place search another, 15
I stop somewhere waiting for you.

Out of the Cradle Endlessly Rocking

Out of the cradle endlessly rocking,
Out of the mocking-bird's throat, the musical shuttle,
Out of the Ninth-month[1] midnight,
Over the sterile sands and the fields beyond, where the child leaving his
    bed wandered alone, bareheaded, barefoot,
Down from the showered halo, 5
Up from the mystic play of shadows twining and twisting as if they were
    alive,
Out from the patches of briers and blackberries,
From the memories of the bird that chanted to me,
From your memories sad brother, from the fitful risings and fallings I
    heard,
From under that yellow half-moon late-risen and swollen as if with
    tears, 10

---

1. September, in Quaker usage.

From those beginning notes of yearning and love there in the mist,
From the thousand responses of my heart never to cease,
From the myriad thence-aroused words,
From the word stronger and more delicious than any,
From such as now they start the scene revisiting,   15
As a flock, twittering, rising, or overhead passing,
Borne hither, ere all eludes me, hurriedly,
A man, yet by these tears a little boy again,
Throwing myself on the sand, confronting the waves,
I, chanter of pains and joys, uniter of here and hereafter,   20
Taking all hints to use them, but swiftly leaping beyond them,
A reminiscence sing.

Once Paumanok,[2]
When the lilac-scent was in the air and Fifth-month[3] grass was growing,
Up this seashore in some briers,   25
Two feathered guests from Alabama, two together,
And their nest, and four light-green eggs spotted with brown,
And every day the he-bird to and fro near at hand,
And every day the she-bird crouched on her nest, silent, with bright eyes,
And every day I, a curious boy, never too close, never disturbing them,   30
Cautiously peering, absorbing, translating.

Shine! shine! shine!
Pour down your warmth, great sun!
While we bask, we two together.

Two together!   35
Winds blow south, or winds blow north,
Day come white, or night come black,

Home, or rivers and mountains from home,
Singing all time, minding no time,
While we two keep together.   40

Till of a sudden,
Maybe killed, unknown to her mate,
One forenoon the she-bird crouched not on the nest,
Nor returned that afternoon, nor the next,
Nor ever appeared again.   45

And thenceforward all summer in the sound of the sea,
And at night under the full of the moon in calmer weather,
Over the hoarse surging of the sea,
Or flitting from brier to brier by day,
I saw, I heard at intervals the remaining one, the he-bird,   50
The solitary guest from Alabama.

Blow! blow! blow!
Blow up sea-winds along Paumanok's shore;
I wait and I wait till you blow my mate to me.

---

2. Pronounced *paw-mah'-nok*. The Native American name for Long Island, where Whitman grew up.
3. May.

Yes, when the stars glistened,   55
All night long on the prong of a moss-scalloped stake,
Down almost amid the slapping waves,
Sat the lone singer wonderful causing tears.

He called on his mate,
He poured forth the meanings which I of all men know.   60

Yes my brother I know,
The rest might not, but I have treasured every note,
For more than once dimly down to the beach gliding,
Silent, avoiding the moonbeams, blending myself with the shadows,
Recalling now the obscure shapes, the echoes, the sounds and sights
    after their sorts,   65
The white arms out in the breakers tirelessly tossing,
I, with bare feet, a child, the wind wafting my hair,
Listened long and long.

Listened to keep, to sing, now translating the notes,
Following you my brother.   70

Soothe! soothe! soothe!
Close on its wave soothes the wave behind,
And again another behind embracing and lapping, every one close,
But my love soothes not me, not me.

Low hangs the moon, it rose late,   75
It is lagging—O I think it is heavy with love, with love.

O madly the sea pushes upon the land,
With love, with love.

O night! do I not see my love fluttering out among the breakers?
What is that little black thing I see there in the white?   80
Loud! loud! loud!
Loud I call to you, my love!
High and clear I shoot my voice over the waves,
Surely you must know who is here, is here,
You must know who I am, my love.   85

Low-hanging moon!
What is that dusky spot in your brown yellow?
O it is the shape, the shape of my mate!
O moon do not keep her from me any longer.

Land! land! O land!   90
Whichever way I turn, O I think you could give me my mate back again if
*   you only would,*
For I am almost sure I see her dimly whichever way I look.

O rising stars!
Perhaps the one I want so much will rise, will rise with some of you.

O throat! O trembling throat!   95
Sound clearer through the atmosphere!
Pierce the woods, the earth,
Somewhere listening to catch you must be the one I want.

Shake out carols!
Solitary here, the night's carols!   100
Carols of lonesome love! death's carols!
Carols under that lagging, yellow, waning moon!
O under that moon where she droops almost down into the sea!
O reckless despairing carols.

But soft! sink low!   105
Soft! let me just murmur,
And do you wait a moment you husky-noised sea,
For somewhere I believe I heard my mate responding to me,
So faint, I must be still, be still to listen,
But not altogether still, for then she might not come immediately to me.   110

Hither my love!
Here I am! here!
With this just-sustained note I announce myself to you,
This gentle call is for you my love, for you.

Do not be decoyed elsewhere,   115
That is the whistle of the wind, it is not my voice,
That is the fluttering, the fluttering of the spray,
Those are the shadows of leaves.

O darkness! O in vain!
O I am very sick and sorrowful.   120

O brown halo in the sky near the moon, drooping upon the sea!
O troubled reflection in the sea!
O throat! O throbbing heart!
And I singing uselessly, uselessly all the night.

O past! O happy life! O songs of joy!   125
In the air, in the woods, over fields,
Loved! loved! loved! loved! loved!
But my mate no more, no more with me!
We two together no more.

The aria sinking,   130
All else continuing, the stars shining,
The winds blowing, the notes of the bird continuous echoing,
With angry moans the fierce old mother incessantly moaning,
On the sands of Paumanok's shore gray and rustling,
The yellow half-moon enlarged, sagging down, drooping, the face of
        the sea almost touching,   135
The boy ecstatic, with his bare feet the waves, with his hair the
        atmosphere dallying,

The love in the heart long pent, now loose, now at last tumultuously
    bursting,
The aria's meaning, the ears, the soul, swiftly depositing,
The strange tears down the cheeks coursing,
The colloquy there, the trio, each uttering,   140
The undertone, the savage old mother incessantly crying,
To the boy's soul's questions sullenly timing, some drowned secret hissing,
To the outsetting bard.

Demon or bird! (said the boy's soul,)
Is it indeed toward your mate you sing? or is it really to me?   145
For I, that was a child, my tongue's use sleeping, now I have heard you,
Now in a moment I know what I am for, I awake,
And already a thousand singers, a thousand songs, clearer, louder and more
    sorrowful than yours,
A thousand warbling echoes have started to life within me, never to die.

O you singer solitary, singing by yourself, projecting me,   150
O solitary me listening, never more shall I cease perpetuating you,
Never more shall I escape, never more the reverberations,
Never more the cries of unsatisfied love be absent from me,
Never again leave me to be the peaceful child I was before what there in
    the night,
By the sea under the yellow and sagging moon,   155
The messenger there aroused, the fire, the sweet hell within,
The unknown want, the destiny of me.

O give me the clue! (it lurks in the night here somewhere,)
O if I am to have so much, let me have more!

A word then, (for I will conquer it,)   160
The word final, superior to all,
Subtle, sent up—what is it?—I listen;
Are you whispering it, and have been all the time, you sea-waves?
Is that it from your liquid rims and wet sands?
Whereto answering, the sea,   165
Delaying not, hurrying not,
Whispered me through the night, and very plainly before daybreak,
Lisped to me the low and delicious word death,
And again death, death, death, death,
Hissing melodious, neither like the bird nor like my aroused child's
    heart,   170
But edging near as privately for me rustling at my feet,
Creeping thence steadily up to my ears and laving me softly all over.
Death, death, death, death, death.

Which I do not forget,
But fuse the song of my dusky demon and brother,   175
That he sang to me in the moonlight on Paumanok's gray beach,
With the thousand responsive songs at random,
My own songs awaked from that hour,
And with them the key, the word up from the waves,

The word of the sweetest song and all songs,   180
That strong and delicious word which, creeping to my feet,
(Or like some old crone rocking the cradle, swathed in sweet garments,
    bending aside,)
The sea whispered me.

EMILY DICKINSON
1830–1886

Emily Dickinson forces her readers to acknowledge the startling aspects of ordinary life. "Ordinary life" includes the mysterious actuality of death, but it also includes birds and woods and oceans, arguments between people, the weight of depression. In small facts and large, Dickinson perceives enormous meaning.

The poet's life, like her verse, was somewhat mysterious. Born to a prosperous and prominent Amherst, Massachusetts, family (her father, a lawyer, was also treasurer of Amherst College), Dickinson attended Amherst Academy and later, for a year, the Mount Holyoke Female Seminary. Thereafter, however, she remained almost entirely in her father's house, leading the life of a recluse. She had close family attachments and a few close friendships, pursued mainly through correspondence. The most important of these relationships, from a literary point of view, was with the Boston writer and critic Thomas Wentworth Higginson, who eventually published her poems. She had begun writing verse in the late 1850s; in 1862, after seeing an essay of Higginson's in the *Atlantic Monthly,* Dickinson wrote him to ask his opinion of her poems, about three hundred of them in existence by this time. The correspondence thus begun continued to the end of Dickinson's life; Higginson also visited her in Amherst.

At Dickinson's death, 1,775 poems survived; only seven had been published, anonymously. With the help of another friend, Mabel Todd Loomis, Higginson selected poems for a volume, published in 1890, which proved extremely popular. Further selections continued to appear, but not until 1955 did Dickinson's entire body of work reach print.

By 1843, the English poet Elizabeth Barrett Browning had written in verse an exhortation to social reform ("The Cry of the Children"); in 1857, she published a long poem, *Aurora Leigh,* commenting on the oppressed situation of women. Christina Rossetti, born the same year as Dickinson and like her unmarried, in poems like "Goblin Market" (1862) found indirect ways to meditate on female predicaments. Dickinson, on the other hand, seems only peripherally aware of social facts. She alludes to church services, locomotives, female costume; very occasionally (for example, in "My Life had stood—a Loaded Gun—") she refers to the way a woman's life is defined in relation to a man's. More centrally, she finds brilliant and provocative formulations of the emotional import of universal phenomena. We may feel already that death amounts to an incomprehensible and indigestible fact, but we are unlikely to have imagined conversations within a tomb or a personified version of death as carriage driver. By using such images, Dickinson disarmingly suggests a kind of playful innocence. Only gradually does one realize that the naive, childlike perception, devoid of obviously ominous suggestion, conceals a complex, disturbing sense of human self-deception and reluctance to face the truth of experience.

Truth is an important word in Dickinson's poetry. "Tell all the Truth but tell it slant," she advises, pointing out that "The Truth must dazzle gradually / Or every man be blind—." She tells of a man who preaches about "'Truth' until it proclaimed him a Liar—": truth remains an absolute, both challenging and judging us all. In one of her most haunting poems, she claims the identity of Beauty and Truth (an identity tellingly asserted earlier in Keats's "Ode on a Grecian Urn") through the fiction of two dead people discussing their profound commitments:

> I died for Beauty—but was scarce
> Adjusted in the Tomb
> When One who died for Truth, was lain
> In an adjoining Room—

Her neighbor asks her why she "failed"; when she explains, he says that beauty and truth "are One":

> And so, as Kinsmen, met a Night—
> We talked between the Rooms—
> Until the Moss had reached our lips—
> And covered up—our names—

Until the last two lines, about the moss, the poem appears to evoke a rather cozy vision of death: neighbors amiably conversing from one room to another, as though at a slumber party ("met a Night"), two "Kinsmen" dedicated to noble abstractions and comforted by the companionship of their dedication. Only the word *failed* (meaning "died") disturbs the comfortable atmosphere, by suggesting a view of death as defeat.

The Keats poem that ends by asserting the identity of truth and beauty implies the permanence of both, as embodied in the work of art, the Grecian urn that stimulates the poet's reflections. Dickinson's poem concludes with troubling suggestions of impermanence. Talk of beauty and truth may reassure the talkers, but death necessarily implies forgetfulness: the dead forget and are forgotten, their very identities ("names") lost, their capacity for communication eliminated. Death *is* defeat; the high Romanticism of Keats's ode, on which this poem implicitly comments, blurs that fact. Despite Dickinson's fanciful images and allegories, her poems insist on their own kind of uncompromising realism. They speak of the universal human effort to imagine experience in reassuring terms, but they do not suggest that reality offers much in the way of reassurance: only brief experiences of natural beauty; and even those challenge human constructions. "I started Early—Took my dog—" a poem about visiting the sea begins; but it ends with the sea encountering "the Solid Town— / No One He seemed to know—" and withdrawing.

Dickinson's eccentric punctuation, with dashes as the chief mark of emphasis and interruption, emphasizes the movements of consciousness in her lyrics. In their early publication, the poems were typically given conventional punctuation; only in 1955 did the body of work appear as Dickinson wrote it. The highly personal mode of punctuation emphasizes the fact that this verse contains also a personal and demanding vision.

216

> Safe in their Alabaster Chambers—
> Untouched by Morning
> And untouched by Noon—
> Sleep the meek members of the Resurrection—
> Rafter of satin,
> And Roof of stone.   5

Light laughs the breeze
In her Castle above them—
Babbles the Bee in a stolid Ear,
Pipe the Sweet Birds in ignorant cadence—   10
Ah, what sagacity perished here!

258

There's a certain Slant of light,
Winter Afternoons—
That oppresses, like the Heft
Of Cathedral Tunes—

Heavenly Hurt, it gives us—   5
We can find no scar,
But internal difference,
Where the Meanings, are—

None may teach it—Any—
'Tis the Seal Despair—   10
An imperial affliction
Sent us of the Air—

When it comes, the Landscape listens—
Shadows—hold their breath—
When it goes, 'tis like the Distance   15
On the look of Death—

303

The Soul selects her own Society—
Then—shuts the Door—
To her divine Majority—
Present no more—

Unmoved—she notes the Chariots—pausing   5
At her low Gate—
Unmoved—an Emperor be kneeling
Upon her Mat—

I've known her—from an ample nation—
Choose One—   10
Then—close the Valves of her attention—
Like Stone—

328

A Bird came down the Walk—
He did not know I saw—
He bit an Angleworm in halves
And ate the fellow, raw,

And then he drank a Dew   5
From a convenient Grass—
And then hopped sidewise to the Wall
To let a Beetle pass—

He glanced with rapid eyes
That hurried all around—   10
They looked like frightened Beads, I thought—
He stirred his Velvet Head

Like one in danger, Cautious,
I offered him a Crumb
And he unrolled his feathers   15
And rowed him softer home—

Than Oars divide the Ocean,
Too silver for a seam—
Or Butterflies, off Banks of Noon
Leap, plashless as they swim.   20

341

After great pain, a formal feeling comes—
The Nerves sit ceremonious, like Tombs—
The stiff Heart questions was it He, that bore,
And Yesterday, or Centuries before?

The Feet, mechanical, go round—   5
Of Ground, or Air, or Ought[1]—
A Wooden way
Regardless grown,
A Quartz contentment, like a stone—

This is the Hour of Lead—
Remembered, if outlived,   10
As Freezing persons, recollect the Snow—
First—Chill—then Stupor—then the letting go—

1. Zero.

435

Much Madness is divinest Sense—
To a discerning Eye—
Much Sense—the starkest Madness—
'Tis the Majority

In this, as All, prevail—   5
Assent—and you are sane—
Demur—you're straightway dangerous—
And handled with a Chain—

449

I died for Beauty—but was scarce
Adjusted in the Tomb
When One who died for Truth, was lain
In an adjoining Room—

He questioned softly "Why I failed"?   5
"For Beauty", I replied—
"And I—for Truth—Themself are One—
We Brethren, are", He said—

And so, as Kinsmen, met a Night—
We talked between the Rooms—   10
Until the Moss had reached our lips—
And covered up—our names—

465

I heard a Fly buzz—when I died—
The Stillness in the Room
Was like the Stillness in the Air—
Between the Heaves of Storm—

The Eyes around—had wrung them dry—   5
And Breaths were gathering firm
For that last Onset—when the King
Be witnessed—in the Room—

I willed my Keepsakes—Signed away
What portion of me be   10
Assignable—and then it was
There interposed a Fly—

With Blue—uncertain stumbling Buzz—
Between the light—and me—
And then the Windows failed—and then   15
I could not see to see—

519

'Twas warm—at first—like Us—
Until there crept upon
A Chill—like frost upon a Glass—
Till all the scene—be gone.

The Forehead copied Stone—   5
The Fingers grew too cold
To ache—and like a Skater's Brook—
The busy eyes—congealed—

It straightened—that was all—
It crowded Cold to Cold   10
It multiplied indifference—
As[1] Pride were all it could—

And even when with Cords—
'Twas lowered, like a Weight—
It made no Signal, nor demurred,   15
But dropped like Adamant.

585

I like to see it lap the Miles—
And lick the Valleys up—
And stop to feed itself at Tanks—
And then—prodigious step

Around a Pile of Mountains—   5
And supercilious peer
In Shanties—by the sides of Roads—
And then a Quarry pare

To fit its Ribs
And crawl between   10
Complaining all the while
In horrid—hooting stanza—
Then chase itself down Hill—

And neigh like Boanerges[1]—
Then—punctual as a Star
Stop—docile and omnipotent   15
At its own stable door—

---

1. As if.   1. "Sons of thunder," name given by Jesus to the brothers and disciples James and John, presumably because they were thunderous preachers.

632

The Brain—is wider than the Sky—
For—put them side by side—
The one the other will contain
With ease—and You—beside—

The Brain is deeper than the sea—   5
For—hold them—Blue to Blue—
The one the other will absorb—
As Sponges—Buckets—do—

The Brain is just the weight of God—
For—Heft them—Pound for Pound—   10
And they will differ—if they do—
As Syllable from Sound—

657

I dwell in Possibility—
A fairer House than Prose—
More numerous of Windows—
Superior—for Doors—

Of Chambers as the Cedars—   5
Impregnable of Eye—
And for an Everlasting Roof
The Gambrels[1] of the Sky—

Of Visitors—the fairest—
For Occupation—This—   10
The spreading wide my narrow Hands
To gather Paradise—

712

Because I could not stop for Death—
He kindly stopped for me—
The Carriage held but just Ourselves—
And Immortality.

We slowly drove—He knew no haste   5
And I had put away
My labor and my leisure too,
For His Civility—

---

1. Slopes, as in the large, arched roofs often seen on barns.

We passed the School, where Children strove
At Recess—in the Ring—
We passed the Fields of Gazing Grain—
We passed the Setting Sun—

Or rather—He passed Us—
The Dews drew quivering and chill—
For only Gossamer, my Gown—
My Tippet—only Tulle[1]—

We paused before a House that seemed
A Swelling of the Ground—
The Roof was scarcely visible—
The Cornice—in the Ground—

Since then—'tis Centuries—and yet
Feels shorter than the Day
I first surmised the Horses' Heads
Were toward Eternity—

754

My Life had stood—a Loaded Gun—
In Corners—till a Day
The Owner passed—identified—
And carried Me away—

And now We roam in Sovereign Woods—
And now We hunt the Doe—
And every time I speak for Him—
The Mountains straight reply—

And do I smile, such cordial light
Upon the Valley glow—
It is as a Vesuvian face[1]
Had let its pleasure through—

And when at Night—Our good Day done—
I guard My Master's Head—
'Tis better than the Eider-Duck's
Deep Pillow—to have shared—

To foe of His—I'm deadly foe—
None stir the second time—
On whom I lay a Yellow Eye—
Or an emphatic Thumb—

10

15

20

5

10

15

20

---

1. Fine, silken netting. "Tippet": a scarf.   1. A face glowing with light like that from an erupting volcano.

Though I than He—may longer live
He longer must—than I—
For I have but the power to kill,
Without—the power to die—

1084

At Half past Three, a single Bird
Unto a silent Sky
Propounded but a single term
Of cautious melody.

At Half past Four, Experiment   5
Had subjugated test
And lo, Her silver Principle
Supplanted all the rest.

At Half past Seven, Element
Nor Implement, be seen—   10
And Place was where the Presence was
Circumference between.

1129

Tell all the Truth but tell it slant—
Success in Circuit lies
Too bright for our infirm Delight
The Truth's superb surprise

As Lightning to the Children eased   5
With explanation kind
The Truth must dazzle gradually
Or every man be blind—

1207

He preached upon "Breadth" till it argued him narrow—
The Broad are too broad to define
And of "Truth" until it proclaimed him a Liar—
The Truth never flaunted a Sign—

Simplicity fled from his counterfeit presence   5
As Gold the Pyrites[1] would shun—
What confusion would cover the innocent Jesus
To meet so enabled[2] a Man!

1. Iron bisulfide, sometimes called fool's gold.   2. Competent.

1564

Pass to thy Rendezvous of Light,
Pangless except for us—
Who slowly ford the Mystery
Which thou hast leaped across!

1593

There came a Wind like a Bugle—
It quivered through the Grass
And a Green Chill upon the Heat
So ominous did pass
We barred the Windows and the Doors   5
As from an Emerald Ghost—
The Doom's electric Moccasin[1]
That very instant passed—
On a strange Mob of panting Trees
And Fences fled away   10
And Rivers where the Houses ran
Those looked that lived—that Day—
The Bell within the steeple wild
The flying tidings told—
How much can come   15
And much can go,
And yet abide the World!

---

1. That is, water moccasin, a poisonous snake.

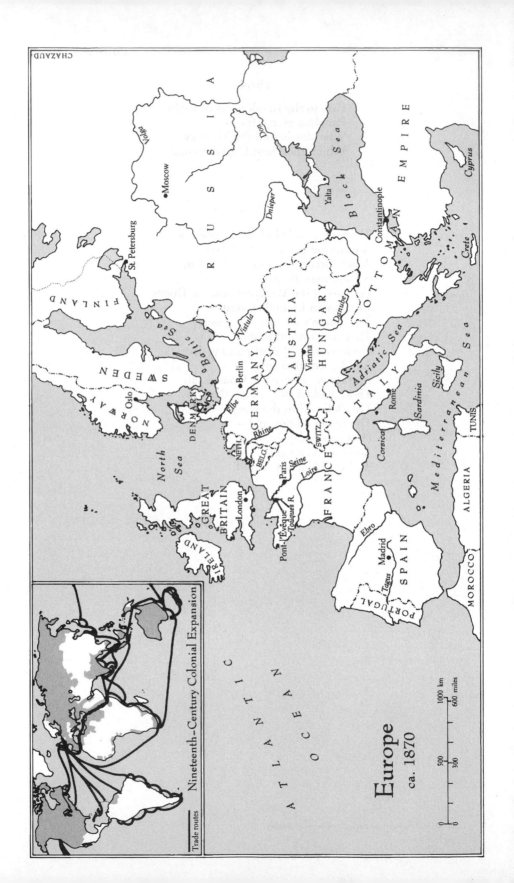

Europe
ca. 1870

Nineteenth-Century Colonial Expansion

Trade routes

CHAZAUD

The Nineteenth Century: Realism and Symbolism

The nineteenth century saw enormous changes in the history of Western civilization. The upheavals following the French Revolution broke up the old order of Europe. The Holy Roman empire and the Papal States were dissolved. Nationalism, nourished by the political and social aspirations of the middle classes, grew by leaps and bounds. Colonial empires were created and vast sections of the globe opened up forcibly to Western trade. "Liberty" became the dominant political slogan of the century, although the various calls for liberty focused on Western society and not on the colonies. In different countries and in different decades, *liberty* meant different things: here liberation from the rule of the foreigner, there the emancipation of the serf; here the removal of economic restrictions on trade and manufacturing, there the introduction of a constitution, free speech, parliamentary institutions, and agitation for the rights of women. Almost everywhere in Europe, the middle classes established their effective rule, though revolutions in 1830 and 1848 were crushed across Europe and monarchs remained in more or less nominal power. Two large European countries, Germany and Italy, achieved their centuries-old dream of political unification. The predominance of France, still marked at the beginning of the century, was broken, and England—or, rather, Great Britain—ruled the seas throughout the century. The smaller European nations, especially in the Balkans, began to emancipate themselves from foreign rule.

These major political changes were caused by—and, in their turn, caused—great social and economic changes. The Industrial Revolution, which had begun in England in the eighteenth century, spread throughout the Continent and transformed living conditions radically. The enormous increase in the speed and availability of transportation due to the development of railroads and steamships as well as the rapid urbanization following the establishment of industries changed the pattern of human life in most countries and caused, within a century, an unprecedented increase in population (as much as threefold in most of Europe), which was also fostered by advances in medicine and hygiene. The development of transportation and communication systems brought the world closer and prepared the way for global economic and political systems. The existence of widespread wealth and prosperity is undeniable, although it coexisted with wretched living conditions and other hardships for the early factory workers, many of them women. As the social and political power of the aristocracy declined, the barriers between the social classes also diminished. Middle-class values dominated, and the industrial laborer began to be felt as a political force.

These social and economic changes were closely bound up with shifts in prevailing outlooks and philosophies. Technological innovation is impossible without scientific discoveries. The scientific viewpoint, hitherto dominant only in a comparatively limited area, spread widely and permeated almost all fields of human thought and endeavor. It raised enormous hopes for the future betterment of humankind, especially when Charles Darwin's evolutionary theories fortified the earlier, vaguer faith in unlimited progress. "Liberty," "science," "progress," and "evolution" are the concepts that define the mental atmosphere of the nineteenth century in Europe.

But tendencies hostile to these were by no means absent. Feudal or Catholic conservatism succeeded, especially in Austria-Hungary, Russia, and much of southern Europe, in preserving old regimes, and the philosophies of a conservative and religious society were reformulated in modern terms. At the same time in England, the very assumptions of the new industrial middle-class society were powerfully attacked by writers such as Carlyle and Ruskin, who recommended a return to medieval forms of social cooperation and handicraft. The industrial civilization of the nineteenth century was also opposed by the fierce individualism of many artists and thinkers who were unhappy in the ugly, commercial, and "Philistine" society of the age. The writings of Friedrich Nietzsche, toward the end of the century, and the whole movement of art for art's sake, which asserted the independence of the artist from society, are the most obvious symptoms of this revolt. The free-enterprise system and the liberalism of the ruling middle classes also clashed early with the rising proletariat; diverse forms of socialism developed, preaching a new collectivism that stressed equality. Socialism could have Christian or romantic motivations, or it could become "scientific" and revolutionary, as Karl Marx's brand of socialism (a certain stage of which he called "communism") claimed to be.

While up through the eighteenth century religion was, at least in name, a major force in European civilization, in the nineteenth century there was a marked decrease in its influence on both intellectual leaders and ordinary people. Local, intense revivals of religious consciousness, such as the Oxford movement in England, did occur, and the traditional religious institutions were preserved everywhere; but the impact of science on religion was such that many tenets of the old faiths crumbled or were severely weakened. The discoveries of astronomy, geology, evolutionary biology, and archaeology as well as biblical criticism forced, almost everywhere, a restatement of the old creeds. Religion, especially in Protestant countries, was frequently confined to an inner feeling of religiosity or to a system of morality that preserved the ancient Christian virtues. In Germany during the early nineteenth century, Hegel and his predecessors and followers tried to interpret the world in spiritual terms, outside the bounds of traditional religion. There were many attempts even late in the century to restate this view, but the methods and discoveries of science seemed to invalidate it, and various formulas that took science as their base in building new lay religions of hope in humanity gained popularity. French positivism, English utilitarianism, the evolutionism of Herbert Spencer are some of the best-known examples. Meanwhile, for the first time in history—at least in Europe—profoundly pessimistic and atheistic philosophies arose, of which Arthur Schopenhauer's was the most subtle, while extreme materialism was the most widespread. Thus the whole gamut of views of the universe was represented during the century in new and impressive formulations.

The visual arts did not show a similar vitality. For a long time in most countries, painting and architecture floundered in a sterile eclecticism—in a bewildering variety of historical masquerades in which the neo-Gothic style was replaced by the neo-Renaissance and that by the neo-Baroque and other decorative revivals of past forms. Only in France did painting (with the Impressionists) find a new style that was genuinely original. In music, the highly Romantic art of Richard Wagner attracted the most attention. Wagner's concept of the *Gesamtkunstwerk* (*ge-zamt-koonst'-vehrk*)— the "total work," combining music, drama, poetry, and spectacle—influenced Symbolist writers and encouraged the tendency to break down distinctions between genres. Otherwise, the individual national schools either continued in their tradition, like Italian opera (Verdi), or founded an idiom of their own, often based on a revival of folklore, as in Russia (Tchaikovsky), Poland (Chopin), Bohemia (Dvořák), and Norway (Grieg).

But literature was the most representative and most widely influential art of nineteenth-century Europe. It found new forms and methods, and expressed the social and intellectual situation of the time most fully and memorably. It was this literature, moreover, that served as a model for many non-Western writers seeking to modernize their own literary traditions on the basis of European masterworks. Nowadays, many writers are unwilling to emulate foreign models and seek instead to rediscover an earlier, precolonial tradition. The literature of nineteenth-century Europe continues nonetheless to be read and admired in its own right.

REALISM

After the great wave of Romanticism had spent its force in the fourth decade of the nineteenth century, European literature moved in the direction of what is usually called *realism*. Realism was not a coherent general movement that established itself unchallenged for a long period of time, as classicism had done during the eighteenth century. Exceptions and reservations there were, and debates over the best way of reproducing reality. But still, in retrospect, the nineteenth century appears as the period of the great realistic writers: Gustave Flaubert in France, Fyodor Dostoevsky and Leo Tolstoy in Russia, Charles Dickens in England, Henry James in America, Henrik Ibsen in Norway.

What is meant by *realism*? The term, in literary use (there is a much older philosophical use), apparently dates back to the Germans at the turn of the nineteenth century—to Friedrich Schiller and August and Friedrich Schlegel. It cropped up in France as early as 1826 but became a commonly accepted literary and artistic slogan only in the 1850s. When an academically minded jury rejected Gustave Courbet's painting *The Artist's Studio* for Paris's Exposition Universelle of 1855, the artist exhibited a collection of his paintings separately as "realist" art and wrote a preface to the exhibit catalog that became an unofficial manifesto for realist art. In the following year, a review called *Réalisme* began publication, and in 1857 a novelist and critic, Champfleury (the pseudonym of Jules-François-Félix Husson), published a volume of critical articles with the title *Le Réalisme*. Since then, the word has been bandied about, discussed, analyzed, and abused, as all slogans are. It is frequently confused with *naturalism*, an ancient philosophical term for materialism, epicureanism, or any secularism. As a specifically literary term, *naturalism* crystallized only in France, where it meant simply the study of nature, and the analogy between the writer and the naturalist was ready at hand. Émile Zola, in an essay called "The Experimental Novel," derived a method of naturalist writing from Dr. Claude Bernard's principles of experimental medicine and claimed that his early novel *Thérèse Raquin* (1866), was "an analytical labor on two living bodies like that of a surgeon on corpses."

The program of the groups of writers and critics who used these terms can be easily summarized. Realists like Flaubert and Guy de Maupassant wanted a truthful representation of reality—that is, the reality of contemporary life and manners. They thought of their method as inductive, observational, and, hence, "objective." The personality of the author was to be suppressed or was at least to recede into the background because reality was to be seen "as it is." The naturalistic program, as formulated by Zola, was substantially the same, except that Zola put greater stress on the analogies to science, considering the procedure of the novelist as identical with that of the experimenting scientist. He also more definitely and exclusively embraced the philosophy of scientific materialism, with its deterministic implications and its stress on heredity and environment, while the older realists were not always as clear in drawing the philosophical consequences.

These French theories were anticipated, paralleled, or imitated all over the world of Western literature. In Germany, the movement called Young Germany, with which Heinrich Heine was associated, had propounded a substantially anti-Romantic realistic program as early as the 1830s, but versions of the French theories definitely triumphed there only in the 1880s. In Russia, as early as the 1840s, the most prominent critic of the time, Vissarion Belinsky, praised the early Gogol as a "poet of reality" and later supported the "natural" school of Russian fiction, which described contemporary Russia with fidelity. In Italy, Giovanni Verga and Luigi Capuana founded an analogous movement called *verismo*. The English-speaking countries were the last to adopt the critical programs and slogans of the Continent: George Moore and George Gissing brought the French theories to England in the late 1880s, and in the United States William Dean Howells began his campaign for realism in 1886, when he became editor of *Harper's Magazine*. Realistic and naturalistic theories of literature have since been widely accepted, either as the basis of writing or as a standard against which later generations rebel. The officially promoted doctrine of Soviet Russia was called "socialist realism," a combination of factual observation and implied socialist message; the realistic novel in the United States is usually considered naturalistic and judged by the standards of nature and truth. Yet twentieth-century novelists in Europe and America also pushed realism to an extreme in the "literature of fact," in documentary novels, and in narratives that foreground a series of undifferentiated "objective" perceptions.

The slogans "realism" and "naturalism" were thus new to the nineteenth century and served as effective formulas directed against the Romantic creed. Truth, contemporaneity, and objectivity were the obvious counterparts of Romantic imagination, of Romantic historicism and its glorification of the past, and of Romantic subjectivity, the exaltation of the ego and the individual. But, of course, the emphasis on truth and objectivity was not really new: these qualities had been demanded by many older, classical theories of imitation, and in the eighteenth century there were great writers such as Denis Diderot who wanted a literal "imitation of life" even on the stage.

The practice of realism, it could be argued, is very old indeed. There are realistic scenes in the *Iliad* and *Odyssey*, and there is plenty of realism in ancient comedy and satire, in medieval stories (*fabliaux*) like some of Chaucer's and Boccaccio's, in many Elizabethan plays, in the Spanish rogue novels, in the English eighteenth-century novel beginning with Daniel Defoe, and so on almost ad infinitum. But while it would be easy to find in early literature anticipations of almost every element of modern realism, still the systematic description of contemporary society, with a serious purpose, often even with a tragic tone, and with sympathy for heroes drawn from the middle and lower classes, was a real innovation of the nineteenth century.

It is usually rash to explain a literary movement in social and political terms. But the new realistic art surely had something to do with the triumph of the middle classes in France after the July Revolution in 1830 and in England after the passage of the Reform Bill in 1832, and with the increasing influence of the middle classes in almost every country. Russia is an exception since no large middle class could develop there during the nineteenth century. An absolute feudal régime continued in power, and the special character of most of Russian literature must be the result of this distinction. But even in Russia, there emerged an "intelligentsia" (the term comes from Russia) that was open to Western ideas and was highly critical of the czarist regime and its official ideology.

Although much nineteenth-century literature reflects the triumph of the middle classes, it would be wrong to think of the great realistic writers as spokespeople or mouthpieces of the middle-class society they described. Honoré de Balzac was politically a Catholic monarchist who applauded the Bourbon restoration after the fall of Napoleon, but he had an extraordinary imaginative insight into the processes leading to the victory of the middle classes. Both Flaubert and Maupassant despised the middle-class society of the Third Empire with an intense hatred and the pride of a self-conscious artist. Dickens became increasingly critical of the middle classes and the assumptions of industrial civilization. Dostoevsky, even though he took part in a conspiracy against the Russian government early in his life and spent ten years in exile in Siberia, became the propounder of an extremely conservative nationalistic and religious creed that was definitely directed against the revolutionary forces in Russia. Tolstoy, himself a count and a landowner, was violent in his criticism of the czarist regime, especially later in his life, but he cannot be described as friendly to the middle classes, to the aims of the democratic movements in Western Europe, or to the science of the time. Ibsen's political attitude was that of a proud individualist who condemns the "compact majority" and its tyranny. Possibly all art is critical of its society. But in the nineteenth century, this criticism became much more explicit, as social and political issues became much more urgent or, at least, were regarded as more urgent by those writing about or within them. To a far greater degree than in earlier centuries, writers felt their isolation from society, viewed the structure and problems of the prevailing order as debatable and reformable, and, in spite of all demands for objectivity, became in many cases social propagandists and reformers in their own right.

The program of realism, while defensible enough as a reaction against Romanticism, raises many critical questions. What is meant by *truth of representation?* Photographic copying? This seems the implication of many famous pronouncements: "A novel is a mirror walking along the road," said Stendhal (the pseudonym of Marie-Henri Beyle) as early as 1830. But such statements can hardly be taken literally. All art must select and represent; it cannot be, and has never been, a simple transcript of reality. What such analogies are intended to convey is rather a claim for an all-inclusiveness of subject matter, a protest against the exclusion of themes that before were considered low, sordid, or trivial (like the puddles on the road along which the mirror walks). Anton Chekhov formulated this protest with the usual parallel between the scientist and the writer: "To a chemist nothing on earth is unclean. A writer must be as objective as a chemist; he must abandon the subjective line: he must know that dung heaps play a very respectable part in a landscape, and that evil passions are as inherent in life as good ones." Thus the truth of realistic art includes the sordid, the low, the disgusting, and the evil; and the implication is that the subject is treated objectively, without interference and falsification by the artist's personality and his own desires.

But in practice, while realistic art succeeded in expanding the themes of art, it could not fulfill the demand for total objectivity. Works of art are written by human beings and inevitably express their personalities and their points of view. As Joseph Conrad admitted, "Even the most artful of writers will give himself (and his morality) away in about every third sentence." Objectivity, in the sense that Zola had in mind when he proposed a scientific method in the writing of novels and conceived of the novelist as a sociologist collecting human documents, is impossible in practice. Surely Maupassant was right when he said that it "would be impossible to describe everything, for you would need at least a book a day to list the multitude of trivial incidents that fill our existence," and concluded that the writer must select and organize details to give the *impression* of truth. The demand for objectivity can be understood only as a demand for a specific method of narration in which the author does not interfere explicitly, in his or her own name, and as a rejection of personal themes of introspection and reverie.

The realistic program, while it made innumerable new subjects available to art, also implied a narrowing of its themes and methods to exclude anything that did not seem a direct representation of reality. Romantic art could, without offending its readers, use coincidences, improbabilities, and even impossibilities that were not, theoretically at least, tolerated in realistic art. Realism professes to present us with a slice of life, but one should recognize that both realism and naturalism are artistic methods and conventions like any other mode of writing. The complete representation of reality in literature is unachievable and not merely because it would take too long: like all art, literature is a *making*, a creating of a world of symbols that differs radically from the world that we call reality. The value of realism lies in its negation of the conventions of Romanticism, its expansion of the themes of art, and its new demonstration (never forgotten by artists) that literature has to deal also with its time and society and has, at its best, an insight into reality (not only social reality) that is not necessarily identical with that of science. Many of the great writers make us realize the world of their time, evoke an imaginative picture of it that seems truer and will last longer than that of historians and sociologists. But this achievement is due to their imagination and to their art or craft, two requisites that realistic theory tended to forget or minimize. One could assert, in short, that all the great realists were simply artists who created worlds of imagination and knew (at least instinctively) that in art one can say something about reality only through language.

SYMBOLISM

Where prose fiction and drama faced outward, aiming to mirror the real world, Symbolist poetry turned its attention to the mirror itself: to the *words* that reflect reality. Symbolist poets found their own way to address the same questions of truth and reality that preoccupied the novelists, and they embarked on an exploration of language that would influence all forms of twentieth-century literature. Preserving the Romantic notion of the poet as seer or visionary but experimenting with language to communicate that vision, they played with multiple and shifting perspectives in a manner that heralded not only modern free verse, prose poems, and spatial poetry, but also the innovative language of novelists such as James Joyce, William Faulkner, Alain Robbe-Grillet, and Marguerite Duras.

The evolution was gradual until the middle of the century. In England, the Pre-Raphaelite movement upheld a Romantic, escapist, and antirealist program. In France, a large and diverse group of Parnassians retained Romantic themes while focusing on a precise and delicate use of detail. The most important writer at mid-century is Charles Baudelaire (1821–1867), whose poetry and writings on art deeply influenced the course of European poetry. Baudelaire's major collection of poems, *The Flowers of Evil*, was published in 1857, the same year that Flaubert was brought to trial for *Madame Bovary*. Inspiring a poetic movement that would later be called Symbolism, Baudelaire remains today the French poet most widely read outside France. Oddly enough, the great poets who are usually called Symbolist (Baudelaire, Stéphane Mallarmé, Paul Verlaine, Arthur Rimbaud) are more accurately "pre-Symbolist" since they were writing well before the official Symbolist movement and the Symbolist Manifesto of 1886. Yet there are elements in common, and the precursors of Symbolism are often discussed in the same breath as their descendants.

Symbolist poetry generally tries to organize patterns of association and allusion to evoke another set of meanings hidden behind appearances. A "symbol" here is not a linear substitution (of the type $A=B$ or *a rose=love*) but is more likely to be an image or group of images created to suggest, as a *whole*, another dimension, a plane of reality, that cannot be expressed in more direct, rational terms. In Baudelaire's poem "Correspondences," for example, the five senses fuse to evoke a primitive level of being, a preconscious world where colors have taste, sights have physical texture, sounds have odors, and so on. (This fusion is called *synesthesia*.) Baudelaire's poetry may lead to abstract or visionary conclusions, but it is firmly based in images as realistic as a rotting carcass ("A Carcass"), logs falling on the pavement ("Song of Autumn I"), and a mangy cat trying to find a comfortable spot in rainy weather ("Spleen LXXVIII"). The imagined scene is not an escape from natural reality as much as a transformation of it, the creation of a new world reassembled in the mind from pieces of the old.

After Symbolic allusion, the second great theme of Symbolist poetry is language—as a means of communication and as the necessary, but flawed, tool of poetic creation. Like Flaubert seeking *le mot juste* ("the exact word"), Symbolist poets are haunted by the difficulty of writing: Baudelaire described his exhausted brain as a graveyard; Mallarmé felt paralyzed by "the empty paper whose whiteness defends it." The difficulty for the Symbolists is that their ideal poetic language must be distilled out of ordinary language through a totally controlled arrangement of all possible levels of form. Sound patterns, image clusters, and intertwined systems of logical and psychological associations act to create a complex architecture of inner reference. It is the relationship of words that counts, not just their dictionary definitions; the artist is, in a sense, a technician. The extraordinary self-consciousness of the Symbolist poet soon became an accepted element of the poem itself. Some poems focused on difficulties of communication (a characteristic Romantic theme); others, like Baudelaire's "Windows," asserted the joy of using language to imagine other existences and to gain, in return, a better sense of their own reality. The Symbolists' acute awareness of the possibilities and limitations of language influenced both philosophers of language and literary theorists in the twentieth century.

Symbolist writers frequently compared their poetry to music, whose characteristics they tried to reproduce. Both poetry and music were felt to be pure arts in which line and harmony (including calculated dissonance) meant more than separate notes or the definitions of individual words. They saw analogies, too, between their art and painting, where distinctive new methods of depicting reality were being developed. Symbolist poetry and Impressionist art both represented moves away from the conventional realistic representation of reality; and in the poetic as in the art world, they both outraged the average citizen by their apparent betrayal of common sense.

PRONOUNCING GLOSSARY

The following list uses common English syllables and stress accents to provide rough equivalents of selected words whose pronunciation may be unfamiliar to the general reader.

Balzac: *bahl-zahk'*

Baudelaire: *boh-d'lair'*

Champfleury: *shom-fler-ee'*

Chekhov: *cheh'-hoff*

Corbière: *cohr-bee-ehr'*

Courbet: *coor-bay'*

Dostoevsky: *dos-toy-eff'-skee*

fabliaux: *fah-blee-oh'*

Flaubert: *floh-bair'*

Mallarmé: *mahl-ahr-may'*

Moréas: *moh-ray-ahs'*

Proust: *Proost*

réalisme: *ray-al-eezm'*

Rilke: *ril'-kuh*

Rimbaud: *ram-boh'*

Schlegel: *shlay'-gel*

Stendhal: *ston-dahl'*

verismo: *vehr-eez'-moh*

Verlaine: *vehr-len'*

Wagner: *vahg'-ner*

Zola: *zoh-lah'*

REALISM AND SYMBOLISM

TEXTS	CONTEXTS
1835 Thomas Babington Macaulay, [Minute on Indian Education, February 2, 1835]	
1842 Nikolai Gogol, *Dead Souls* and *The Overcoat*	
1848 Karl Marx and Friedrich Engels, "Manifesto of the Communist Party"	
1856 Gustave Flaubert, *Madame Bovary*	
1857 Charles Baudelaire, **The Flowers of Evil**	
1859 Charles Darwin, *The Origin of Species*	
1860 Giuseppe Garibaldi, "Memorandum" to the heads of Europe	**1861** Serfs emancipated in Russia
	1861–65 Civil War in the United States
1864 Fyodor Dostoyevsky, **Notes from Underground**	
1866 Fyodor Dostoyevsky, *Crime and Punishment* • Émile Zola's essay "The Experimental Novel" argues for a "naturalist" style analogous to methods in experimental science	
1867 Karl Marx, *Capital*	
1869 Leo Tolstoy, *War and Peace*	**1869** Suez Canal completed
1870 Ernest Renan's *Life of Jesus* offers a historical approach to the New Testament	
1871 George Eliot (Mary Ann Evans), *Middlemarch* • Charles Darwin, *The Descent of Man*	
1874 Paul Verlaine, *Songs without Words*	**1874** Claude Monet's painting *Impression: Rising Sun* launches Impressionism as a style
1876 Stéphane Mallarmé, *The Afternoon of a Faun*	**1876** Invention of the telephone
1882 Friedrich Nietzsche, *The Gay Science* (1882–87)	
1883 Giovanni Verga, *Freedom*	**1884–85** Berlin Conference agrees on procedures for European acquisition of African territory; by 1914, all Africa, except Ethiopia and Liberia, succumbs to European rule

Boldface titles indicate works in the anthology.

REALISM AND SYMBOLISM

TEXTS	CONTEXTS
1886 Arthur Rimbaud, ***Illuminations*** • Leo Tolstoy, ***The Death of Ivan Ilyich*** • Friedrich Nietzsche's *Beyond Good and Evil* proclaims a "life force," a "will to power," and a "superman" who embodies these qualities	
	1887 Eiffel Tower built for the 1889 Paris World's Fair • Gottlieb Daimler's internal combustion engine for the automobile
1889 Guy de Maupassant, *Hautot and His Son*	
1890 Henrik Ibsen, ***Hedda Gabler*** • *Poems* of Emily Dickinson (1830–86) published posthumously • Chief Machemba of the Yao refuses to accept colonial rule in his "Letter to Major von Wissmann"	
1893 Émile Zola completes a twenty-volume series of naturalist novels begun in 1871, *Les Rougon-Macquart*	
	1894 X-rays discovered
	1894–1906 In the Dreyfus Affair, anti-Semitic sentiment polarizes France
1897 Mona Caird, "The Emancipation of the Family" • Mary Kingsley, *Travels in West Africa*	
1898 Émile Zola's "Letter to Félix Faure" denounces governmental corruption in the Dreyfus Case	**1898** Radium discovered by Marie and Pierre Curie • Spanish-American War breaks out
1899 Anton Chekhov, "The Lady with the Dog" • Cecil Rhodes, "Speech at Drill Hall, Cape Town, South Africa," articulates the imperialist view of African colonialism • Olive Schreiner, *An English–South African's View of the Situation*	
1899–1900 Sol T. Plaatje, *Mafeking Diary*, describes the Boer siege of Mafeking from a black perspective	
1904 Anton Chekhov's ***The Cherry Orchard*** performed	

GUSTAVE FLAUBERT
1821–1880

Gustave Flaubert is rightly considered the exemplary realist novelist. He displays the objectivity, the detachment from his characters demanded by the theory, and is a great virtuoso of the art of composition and of style while giving a clear picture of the society of his time. It is likewise a picture in which we can see much of ourselves.

Flaubert was born in Rouen, Normandy, on December 12, 1821, to the chief surgeon of the Hôtel Dieu. He was extremely precocious; by the age of sixteen he was writing stories in the Romantic taste, which were published only after his death. In 1840 he went to Paris to study law (he had received his baccalaureate from the local *lycée*), but he failed in his examinations and in 1843 suffered a sudden nervous breakdown that kept him at home. In 1846 he moved to Croisset, just outside of Rouen on the Seine, where he made his home for the rest of his life, devoting himself to writing. The same year, in Paris, Flaubert met Louise Colet, a minor poet and lady about town, who became his mistress. In 1849–51 he visited the Levant, traveling extensively in Greece, Syria, and Egypt. After his return he settled down to the writing of *Madame Bovary*, which took him five full years and which was a great popular success. The remainder of his life was uneventful. He made occasional trips to Paris, and one trip, in 1860, to Tunisia to see the ruins of Carthage in preparation for the writing of his novel *Salammbô*. Three more novels followed: *The Sentimental Education* (1869), *The Temptation of St. Anthony* (1874), and the unfinished *Bouvard and Pecuchet* (1881), as well as *Three Tales* (1877), consisting of "A Simple Heart," "The Legend of St. Julian the Hospitaler," and "Herodias." Flaubert died at Croisset on May 8, 1880.

Flaubert's novel *Madame Bovary* (1856) is deservedly considered the showpiece of French realism. It would be impossible to find a novel, certainly before Flaubert, in which humble persons in a humble setting (the story concerns the adulteries and final suicide of the wife of a simple country doctor) are treated with such seriousness, restraint, verisimilitude, and imaginative clarity. There is nothing of Balzac's lurid melodrama, high-pitched tone, and passionate eloquence in Flaubert's masterpiece. At first sight, *Madame Bovary* is the prosaic description of a prosaic life, set in its daily surroundings, the French province of Normandy about the middle of the nineteenth century. Everything is told soberly, objectively. The author hides his feelings completely behind his personages. All the light falls on Emma Bovary, as we follow the story of her romantic dreams, disillusionment, despair. Every scene is superbly realized, with an extraordinary accuracy of observation, and details, which at times are based on scientific information. The topography of the two villages, the interior of the houses, great scenes—such as those of the ball, the cattle show, the operation of clubfoot, the opera in Rouen, the arsenic poisoning—imprint themselves vividly on our memory. Early readers were puzzled by Flaubert's attitude toward Emma Bovary, so accustomed were they to the usual commentary of an author, approving or condemning every action of his characters. But today, when we know the early unpublished writings of Flaubert and his revealing correspondence, there cannot be any doubt about the tone of the book. Behind all the detachment there is a victory of art over temperament, a self-imposed discipline and restraint. It is, in part, the result of a theory of the objectivity, the complete impersonality of art. According to this view, the artist has to disappear behind his or her creation as God does behind His. Future ages should hardly believe that the artist lived.

If we listen more carefully, however, we become aware of the author's savage satiric attitude toward the romantic illusions of poor Emma, his hatred for the complacent freethinking apothecary Homais, his contempt for the stupid husband and the callous, weak lovers. The pity of it all comes through only because the author lets the facts speak for themselves.

The story of the composition of *Madame Bovary,* which we know from Flaubert's letters, is one of self-inflicted martyrdom, of an artist perversely clinging to an uncongenial and even repulsive subject because he believes that the subject itself is of no importance and that the artist should, by his art, purge himself of personal indulgences and preferences. It is also the story of a struggle for style, for the "right word" (*mot juste*), for which Flaubert worked with the suppressed fury of a galley slave.

"A Simple Heart," a late story published in the collection *Three Tales,* is clearly related to *Madame Bovary.* It has the same setting of the Norman countryside, the same houses and farms, some of the same kind of people. And it has the same theme of disillusionment. Félicité is anticipated in *Madame Bovary* by the figure of Catherine Leroux, who at the great agricultural show receives a silver medal, worth twenty-five francs, for fifty-four years of service at one farm. The little old woman, with the "monastic rigidity" of her face, the dumbness and calm of her animal look, has to be almost pushed by the audience to receive her prize. When she walks away with the medal, she is heard muttering, "I'll give it to our *curé* up home, to say some masses for me."

"A Simple Heart," like *Madame Bovary,* treats the life of a humble person with complete objectivity, with vivid concrete imagination, clear in every detail. We see and smell the interiors of the houses and farms and can visualize the scenes of almost Dutch simplicity. But the story is also connected with the two other stories in the collection, "The Legend of St. Julian the Hospitaler" and "Hérodias." Like these it is a saint's legend: like a saint, Félicité undergoes a Calvary of suffering—the betrayal of her lover, the death of the little girl Virginie, the loss of her nephew, the loss of the parrot. Like a saint, too, she meets savage beasts (a bull in the fields), is lashed by a whip on the road, tends the running ulcer of a dying old man, and finally sees a beatific vision, during the Corpus Christi procession, in which the Holy Ghost and the parrot fuse into one.

But one would miss the implications of Flaubert's sophisticated art if one thought of the story merely as a realistic picture of a servant girl's plight or even as a traditional saint's legend in modern times. It is no doubt a combination of these two apparently very different types: we can see a social purpose in the picture of the poor oppressed woman, her devotion to a selfish mistress, her frustration, resignation, and final dying happiness; and we can sense the author's restraint as a device of simplicity to make the tone of the tale approach that of a legend. But such a reading would not capture all the undertones of Flaubert's style. There are disturbing elements in the story, which show that a simple interpretation is insufficient. We have glimpses, for instance, of Flaubert's predilection for the exotic and strange, for the deliberately decorative mosaic: the exotic pictures that constitute "the whole of [Félicité's] literary education," the curious color combinations of the scene at Virginie's deathbed (the spots of red of the candles, the white mist, the yellow face, the blue lips), and the gorgeous Corpus Christi wayside altar—all these clash with the otherwise sober and gray tone of the narrative. More disturbing, there is an undertone of satire and contemptuous mockery of this humble world. In a letter to a correspondent (Madame Roger de Genettes; June 19, 1876) Flaubert denied that "there is anything ironical as you suppose," and went on to declare that "on the contrary, it is very serious and very sad. I want to excite pity, I want to make sensitive souls weep, as I am one of them myself." But surely this professed intention is hard to reconcile with the passages about the parrot, who is shown as grotesque and absurd, an icon of the Holy Ghost (traditionally represented as a dove) but also a moth-eaten relic with a broken wing and stuffing protruding from its stomach.

There is "something of the parrot" in the church window's image of the Holy Ghost, a likeness that is confirmed by the highly colored religious print that gives the dove purple wings and an emerald body. Some readers would find not only satire but blasphemy in the description of Félicité swerving toward the parrot from time to time as she says her prayers or glimpsing, on her deathbed, "an opening in the heavens, and a gigantic parrot hovering above her head." Yet there is also imaginative power in this grotesque deathbed vision. The parrot is not absurd in itself but only when seen from an external perspective that measures spiritual insight by traditional religious iconography. Viewed from a different angle, this subversive distortion is part of a creative process by which Félicité re-creates the world around her in the image of her own intense feelings. She enters passionately into the priest's stories of sacred history, trying to understand the various images of divinity in terms of her own experience. After learning that God is "not merely a bird, but a flame as well, and a breath of other times," she interprets these images through her own narration: "It may be His light, she thought, which flits at night about the edge of the marshes, His breathing which drives on the clouds, His voice which gives harmony to the bells." Flaubert insists on Félicité's capacity for reimagining the world: she *becomes* Virginie during the latter's first communion, and she expects to see Victor's house on the map, "so stunted was her mind!" A logic of personal need governs her imaginings; by linking the religious print to the parrot, Félicité both "consecrates" her beloved Loulou and makes the Holy Ghost "more vivid to her eye and more intelligible." Seeking intelligibility (to *know* God, in the tradition of the mystics), she decides that the bird who expresses God's meaning must be one who can speak: therefore, a parrot. If the gigantic parrot of the conclusion seems to mock traditional religious imagery, which it clearly does, it also presides over a world of will and imagination that Félicité—a secular saint—has made her own.

PRONOUNCING GLOSSARY

The following list uses common English syllables and stress accents to provide rough equivalents of selected words whose pronunciation may be unfamiliar to the general reader.

Aubain: *oh-banh'*

Félicité: *fay-lee-see-tay'*

Flaubert: *floh-bair'*

Pont l'Evêque: *pohnh lay-veck'*

Virginie: *veer-zheen-ee'*

A Simple Heart[1]

I

Madame Aubain's servant Félicité was the envy of the ladies of Pont-l'Évêque[2] for half a century.

She received a hundred francs a year. For that she was cook and general servant, and did the sewing, washing, and ironing; she could bridle a horse, fatten poultry, and churn butter—and she remained faithful to her mistress, unamiable as the latter was.

Mme. Aubain had married a gay bachelor without money who died at the beginning of 1809, leaving her with two small children and a quantity of

---

1. Translated by Arthur MacDowall.　　2. A village in Normandy on the Toucques River, twenty-five miles from Caen.

debts. She then sold all her property except the farms of Toucques and Geffosses, which brought in five thousand francs a year at most, and left her
house in Saint-Melaine for a less expensive one that had belonged to her
family and was situated behind the market.

This house had a slate roof and stood between an alley and a lane that
went down to the river. There was an unevenness in the levels of the rooms
which made you stumble. A narrow hall divided the kitchen from the "parlour" where Mme. Aubain spent her day, sitting in a wicker easy chair by the
window. Against the panels, which were painted white, was a row of eight
mahogany chairs. On an old piano under the barometer a heap of wooden
and cardboard boxes rose like a pyramid. A stuffed armchair stood on either
side of the Louis-Quinze chimney-piece, which was in yellow marble with a
clock in the middle of it modelled like a temple of Vesta.[3] The whole room
was a little musty, as the floor was lower than the garden.

The first floor began with "Madame's" room: very large, with a pale-
flowered wall-paper and a portrait of "Monsieur" as a dandy of the period. It
led to a smaller room, where there were two children's cots without mattresses. Next came the drawing-room, which was always shut up and full of
furniture covered with sheets. Then there was a corridor leading to a study.
The shelves of a large bookcase were respectably lined with books and
papers, and its three wings surrounded a broad writing-table in darkwood.
The two panels at the end of the room were covered with pen-drawings,
water-colour landscapes, and engravings by Audran,[4] all relics of better days
and vanished splendour. Félicité's room on the top floor got its light from a
dormer-window, which looked over the meadows.

She rose at daybreak to be in time for Mass, and worked till evening without stopping. Then, when dinner was over, the plates and dishes in order,
and the door shut fast, she thrust the log under the ashes and went to sleep
in front of the hearth with her rosary in her hand. Félicité was the stub-
bornest of all bargainers; and as for cleanness, the polish on her saucepans
was the despair of other servants. Thrifty in all things, she ate slowly, gathering off the table in her fingers the crumbs of her loaf—a twelve-pound
loaf expressly baked for her, which lasted for three weeks.

At all times of year she wore a print handkerchief fastened with a pin
behind, a bonnet that covered her hair, grey stockings, a red skirt, and a
bibbed apron—such as hospital nurses wear—over her jacket.

Her face was thin and her voice sharp. At twenty-five she looked like forty.
From fifty onwards she seemed of no particular age; and with her silence,
straight figure, and precise movements she was like a woman made of wood,
and going by clockwork.

II

She had had her love-story like another.

Her father, a mason, had been killed by falling off some scaffolding. Then
her mother died, her sisters scattered, and a farmer took her in and

---

3. Temple of the Roman goddess of the hearth; it was round and enclosed by columns.   4. Gérard
Audran (1640–1703) made engravings of many paintings by Poussin, Mignard, and others.

employed her, while she was still quite little, to herd the cows at pasture. She shivered in rags and would lie flat on the ground to drink water from the ponds; she was beaten for nothing, and finally turned out for the theft of thirty sous which she did not steal. She went to another farm, where she became dairy-maid; and as she was liked by her employers her companions were jealous of her.

One evening in August (she was then eighteen) they took her to the assembly at Colleville. She was dazed and stupefied in an instant by the noise of the fiddlers, the lights in the trees, the gay medley of dresses, the lace, the gold crosses, and the throng of people jigging all together. While she kept shyly apart a young man with a well-to-do air, who was leaning on the shaft of a cart and smoking his pipe, came up to ask her to dance. He treated her to cider, coffee, and cake, and bought her a silk handkerchief; and then, imagining she had guessed his meaning, offered to see her home. At the edge of a field of oats he pushed her roughly down. She was frightened and began to cry out; and he went off.

One evening later she was on the Beaumont road. A big haywagon was moving slowly along; she wanted to get in front of it, and as she brushed past the wheels she recognized Theodore. He greeted her quite calmly, saying she must excuse it all because it was "the fault of the drink." She could not think of any answer and wanted to run away.

He began at once to talk about the harvest and the worthies of the commune, for his father had left Colleville for the farm at Les Écots, so that now he and she were neighbours. "Ah!" she said. He added that they thought of settling him in life. Well, he was in no hurry; he was waiting for a wife to his fancy. She dropped her head; and then he asked her if she thought of marrying. She answered with a smile that it was mean to make fun of her.

"But I am not, I swear!"—and he passed his left hand round her waist. She walked in the support of his embrace; their steps grew slower. The wind was soft, the stars glittered, the huge wagon-load of hay swayed in front of them, and dust rose from the dragging steps of the four horses. Then, without a word of command, they turned to the right. He clasped her once more in his arms, and she disappeared into the shadow.

The week after Theodore secured some assignations with her.

They met at the end of farmyards, behind a wall, or under a solitary tree. She was not innocent as young ladies are—she had learned knowledge from the animals—but her reason and the instinct of her honour would not let her fall. Her resistance exasperated Theodore's passion; so much so that to satisfy it—or perhaps quite artlessly—he made her an offer of marriage. She was in doubt whether to trust him, but he swore great oaths of fidelity.

Soon he confessed to something troublesome; the year before his parents had bought him a substitute for the army, but any day he might be taken again, and the idea of serving was a terror to him. Félicité took this cowardice of his as a sign of affection, and it redoubled hers. She stole away at night to see him, and when she reached their meeting-place Theodore racked her with his anxieties and urgings.

At last he declared that he would go himself to the prefecture for information, and would tell her the result on the following Sunday, between eleven and midnight.

When the moment came she sped towards her lover. Instead of him she found one of his friends.

He told her that she would not see Theodore any more. To ensure himself against conscription he had married an old woman, Madame Lehoussais, of Toucques, who was very rich.

There was an uncontrollable burst of grief. She threw herself on the ground, screamed, called to the God of mercy, and moaned by herself in the fields till daylight came. Then she came back to the farm and announced that she was going to leave; and at the end of the month she received her wages, tied all her small belongings with a handkerchief, and went to Pont-l'Évêque.

In front of the inn there she made inquiries of a woman in a widow's cap, who, as it happened, was just looking for a cook. The girl did not know much, but her willingness seemed so great and her demands so small that Mme. Aubain ended by saying:

"Very well, then, I will take you."

A quarter of an hour afterwards Félicité was installed in her house.

She lived there at first in a tremble, as it were, at "the style of the house" and the memory of "Monsieur" floating over it all. Paul and Virginie, the first aged seven and the other hardly four, seemed to her beings of a precious substance; she carried them on her back like a horse; it was a sorrow to her that Mme. Aubain would not let her kiss them every minute. And yet she was happy there. Her grief had melted in the pleasantness of things all round.

Every Thursday regular visitors came in for a game of boston, and Félicité got the cards and foot-warmers ready beforehand. They arrived punctually at eight and left before the stroke of eleven.

On Monday mornings the dealer who lodged in the covered passage spread out all his old iron on the ground. Then a hum of voices began to fill the town, mingled with the neighing of horses, bleating of lambs, grunting of pigs, and the sharp rattle of carts along the street. About noon, when the market was at its height, you might see a tall, hook-nosed old countryman with his cap pushed back making his appearance at the door. It was Robelin, the farmer of Geffosses. A little later came Liébard, the farmer from Toucques—short, red, and corpulent—in a grey jacket and gaiters shod with spurs.

Both had poultry or cheese to offer their landlord. Félicité was invariably a match for their cunning, and they went away filled with respect for her.

At vague intervals Mme. Aubain had a visit from the Marquis de Gremanville, one of her uncles, who had ruined himself by debauchery and now lived at Falaise on his last remaining morsel of land. He invariably came at the luncheon hour, with a dreadful poodle whose paws left all the furniture in a mess. In spite of efforts to show his breeding, which he carried to the point of raising his hat every time he mentioned "my late father," habit was too strong for him; he poured himself out glass after glass and fired off improper remarks. Félicité edged him politely out of the house—"You have had enough, Monsieur de Gremanville! Another time!"—and she shut the door on him.

She opened it with pleasure to M. Bourais, who had been a lawyer. His baldness, his white stock, frilled shirt, and roomy brown coat, his way of rounding the arm as he took snuff—his whole person, in fact, created that disturbance of mind which overtakes us at the sight of extraordinary men.

As he looked after the property of "Madame" he remained shut up with her for hours in "Monsieur's" study, though all the time he was afraid of compromising himself. He respected the magistracy immensely, and had some pretensions to Latin.

To combine instruction and amusement he gave the children a geography book made up of a series of prints. They represented scenes in different parts of the world: cannibals with feathers on their heads, a monkey carrying off a young lady, Bedouins in the desert, the harpooning of a whale, and so on. Paul explained these engravings to Félicité; and that, in fact, was the whole of her literary education. The children's education was undertaken by Guyot, a poor creature employed at the town hall, who was famous for his beautiful hand and sharpened his penknife on his boots.

When the weather was bright the household set off early for a day at Geffosses Farm.

Its courtyard is on a slope, with the farmhouse in the middle, and the sea looks like a grey streak in the distance.

Félicité brought slices of cold meat out of her basket, and they breakfasted in a room adjoining the dairy. It was the only surviving fragment of a country house which was now no more. The wallpaper hung in tatters, and quivered in the draughts. Mme. Aubain sat with bowed head, overcome by her memories; the children became afraid to speak. "Why don't you play, then?" she would say, and off they went.

Paul climbed into the barn, caught birds, played at ducks and drakes over the pond, or hammered with his stick on the big casks which boomed like drums. Virginie fed the rabbits or dashed off to pick cornflowers, her quick legs showing their embroidered little drawers.

One autumn evening they went home by the fields. The moon was in its first quarter, lighting part of the sky; and mist floated like a scarf over the windings of the Toucques. Cattle, lying out in the middle of the grass, looked quietly at the four people as they passed. In the third meadow some of them got up and made a half-circle in front of the walkers. "There's nothing to be afraid of," said Félicité, as she stroked the nearest on the back with a kind of crooning song; he wheeled round and the others did the same. But when they crossed the next pasture there was a formidable bellow. It was a bull, hidden by the mist. Mme. Aubain was about to run. "No! no! don't go so fast!" They mended their pace, however, and heard a loud breathing behind them which came nearer. His hoofs thudded on the meadow grass like hammers; why, he was galloping now! Félicité turned round, and tore up clods of earth with both hands and threw them in his eyes. He lowered his muzzle, waved his horns, and quivered with fury, bellowing terribly. Mme. Aubain, now at the end of the pasture with her two little ones, was looking wildly for a place to get over the high bank. Félicité was retreating, still with her face to the bull, keeping up a shower of clods which blinded him, and crying all the time, "Be quick! be quick!"

Mme. Aubain went down into the ditch, pushed Virginie first and then Paul, fell several times as she tried to climb the bank, and managed it at last by dint of courage.

The bull had driven Félicité to bay against a rail-fence; his slaver was streaming into her face; another second, and he would have gored her. She had just time to slip between two of the rails, and the big animal stopped short in amazement.

This adventure was talked of at Pont-l'Évêque for many a year. Félicité did not pride herself on it in the least, not having the barest suspicion that she had done anything heroic.

Virginie was the sole object of her thoughts, for the child developed a nervous complaint as a result of her fright, and M. Poupart, the doctor, advised sea-bathing at Trouville.[5] It was not a frequented place then. Mme. Aubain collected information, consulted Bourais, and made preparations as though for a long journey.

Her luggage started a day in advance, in Liébard's cart. The next day he brought round two horses, one of which had a lady's saddle with a velvet back to it, while a cloak was rolled up to make a kind of seat on the crupper of the other. Mme. Aubain rode on that, behind the farmer. Félicité took charge of Virginie, and Paul mounted M. Lechaptois' donkey, lent on condition that great care was taken of it.

The road was so bad that its five miles took two hours. The horses sank in the mud up to their pasterns, and their haunches jerked abruptly in the effort to get out; or else they stumbled in the ruts, and at other moments had to jump. In some places Liébard's mare came suddenly to a halt. He waited patiently until she went on again, talking about the people who had properties along the road, and adding moral reflections to their history. So it was that as they were in the middle of Toucques, and passed under some windows bowered with nasturtiums, he shrugged his shoulders and said: "There's a Mme. Lehoussais lives there; instead of taking a young man she . . ." Félicité did not hear the rest; the horses were trotting and the donkey galloping. They all turned down a bypath; a gate swung open and two boys appeared; and the party dismounted in front of a manure-heap at the very threshold of the farmhouse door.

When Mme. Liébard saw her mistress she gave lavish signs of joy. She served her a luncheon with a sirloin of beef, tripe, black-pudding, a fricasse of chicken, sparkling cider, a fruit tart, and brandied plums; seasoning it all with compliments to Madame, who seemed in better health; Mademoiselle, who was "splendid" now; and Monsieur Paul, who had "filled out" wonderfully. Nor did she forget their deceased grandparents, whom the Liébards had known, as they had been in the service of the family for several generations. The farm, like them, had the stamp of antiquity. The beams on the ceiling were worm-eaten, the walls blackened with smoke, and the windowpanes grey with dust. There was an oak dresser laden with every sort of useful article—jugs, plates, pewter bowls, wolf-traps, and sheep-shears; and a huge syringe made the children laugh. There was not a tree in the three courtyards without mushrooms growing at the bottom of it or a tuft of mistletoe on its boughs. Several of them had been thrown down by the wind. They had taken root again at the middle; and all were bending under their wealth of apples. The thatched roofs, like brown velvet and of varying thickness, withstood the heaviest squalls. The cart-shed, however, was falling into ruin. Mme. Aubain said she would see about it, and ordered the animals to be saddled again.

5. A town on the English Channel, now a popular resort, some five miles from Pont-l'Évêque.

It was another half-hour before they reached Trouville. The little caravan dismounted to pass Écores—it was an overhanging cliff with boats below it—and three minutes later they were at the end of the quay and entered the courtyard of the Golden Lamb, kept by good Mme. David.

From the first days of their stay Virginie began to feel less weak, thanks to the change of air and the effect of the sea-baths. These, for want of a bathing-dress, she took in her chemise; and her nurse dressed her afterwards in a coastguard's cabin which was used by the bathers.

In the afternoons they took the donkey and went off beyond the Black Rocks, in the direction of Hennequeville. The path climbed at first through ground with dells in it like the green sward of a park, and then reached a plateau where grass fields and arable lay side by side. Hollies rose stiffly out of the briary tangle at the edge of the road; and here and there a great withered tree made zigzags in the blue air with its branches.

They nearly always rested in a meadow, with Deauville on their left, Havre on their right, and the open sea in front. It glittered in the sunshine, smooth as a mirror and so quiet that its murmur was scarcely to be heard; sparrows chirped in hiding and the immense sky arched over it all. Mme. Aubain sat doing her needlework; Virginie plaited rushes by her side; Félicité pulled up lavender, and Paul was bored and anxious to start home.

Other days they crossed the Toucques in a boat and looked for shells. When the tide went out sea-urchins, starfish, and jelly-fish were left exposed; and the children ran in pursuit of the foam-flakes which scudded in the wind. The sleepy waves broke on the sand and unrolled all along the beach; it stretched away out of sight, bounded on the land-side by the dunes which parted it from the Marsh, a wide meadow shaped like an arena. As they came home that way, Trouville, on the hill-slope in the background, grew bigger at every step, and its miscellaneous throng of houses seemed to break into a gay disorder.

On days when it was too hot they did not leave their room. From the dazzling brilliance outside light fell in streaks between the laths of the blinds. There were no sounds in the village; and on the pavement below not a soul. This silence round them deepened the quietness of things. In the distance, where men were caulking, there was a tap of hammers as they plugged the hulls, and a sluggish breeze wafted up the smell of tar.

The chief amusement was the return of the fishing-boats. They began to tack as soon as they had passed the buoys. The sails came down on two of the three masts; and they drew on with the foresail swelling like a balloon, gliding through the splash of the waves, and when they had reached the middle of the harbour suddenly dropped anchor. Then the boats drew up against the quay. The sailors threw quivering fish over the side; a row of carts was waiting, and women in cotton bonnets darted out to take the baskets and give their men a kiss.

One of them came up to Félicité one day, and she entered the lodgings a little later in a state of delight. She had found a sister again—and then Nastasie Barette, "wife of Leroux," appeared, holding an infant at her breast and another child with her right hand, while on her left was a little cabin boy with his hands on his hips and a cap over his ear.

After a quarter of an hour Mme. Aubain sent them off; but they were always to be found hanging about the kitchen, or encountered in the course of a walk. The husband never appeared.

Félicité was seized with affection for them. She bought them a blanket, some shirts, and a stove; it was clear that they were making a good thing out of her. Mme. Aubain was annoyed by this weakness of hers, and she did not like the liberties taken by the nephew, who said "thee" and "thou"[6] to Paul. So as Virginie was coughing and the fine weather gone, she returned to Pont-l'Évêque.

There M. Bourais enlightened her on the choice of a boys' school. The one at Caen was reputed to be the best, and Paul was sent to it. He said his good-byes bravely, content enough at going to live in a house where he would have companions.

Mme. Aubain resigned herself to her son's absence as a thing that had to be. Virginie thought about it less and less. Félicité missed the noise he made. But she found an occupation to distract her; from Christmas onward she took the little girl to catechism every day.

III

After making a genuflexion at the door she walked up between the double rows of chairs under the lofty nave, opened Mme. Aubain's pew, sat down, and began to look about her. The choir stalls were filled with the boys on the right and the girls on the left, and the curé stood by the lectern. On a painted window in the apse the Holy Ghost looked down upon the Virgin. Another window showed her on her knees before the child Jesus, and a group carved in wood behind the altar-shrine represented St. Michael over-throwing the dragon.

The priest began with a sketch of sacred history. The Garden, the Flood, the Tower of Babel, cities in flames, dying nations, and overturned idols passed like a dream before her eyes; and the dizzying vision left her with reverence for the Most High and fear of his wrath. Then she wept at the story of the Passion. Why had they crucified Him, when He loved the children, fed the multitudes, healed the blind, and had willed, in His meekness, to be born among the poor, on the dung-heap of a stable? The sowings, harvests, wine-presses, all the familiar things that the Gospel speaks of, were a part of her life. They had been made holy by God's passing; and she loved the lambs more tenderly for her love of the Lamb, and the doves because of the Holy Ghost.

She found it hard to imagine Him in person, for He was not merely a bird, but a flame as well, and a breath at other times. It may be His light, she thought, which flits at night about the edge of the marshes, His breathing which drives on the clouds, His voice which gives harmony to the bells; and she would sit rapt in adoration, enjoying the cool walls and the quiet of the church.

Of doctrines she understood nothing—did not even try to understand. The curé discoursed, the children repeated their lesson, and finally she went to sleep, waking up with a start when their wooden shoes clattered on the flagstones as they went away.

It was thus that Félicité, whose religious education had been neglected in her youth, learned the catechism by dint of hearing it; and from that time

---

6. That is, used the familiar *tu* and *toi* rather than the more respectful *vous*.

she copied all Virginie's observances, fasting as she did and confessing with her. On Corpus Christi Day[7] they made a festal altar together.

The first communion loomed distractingly ahead. She fussed over the shoes, the rosary, the book and gloves; and how she trembled as she helped Virginie's mother to dress her!

All through the mass she was racked with anxiety. She could not see one side of the choir because of M. Bourais but straight in front of her was the flock of maidens, with white crowns above their hanging veils, making the impression of a field of snow; and she knew her dear child at a distance by her dainty neck and thoughtful air. The bell tinkled. The heads bowed, and there was silence. As the organ pealed, singers and congregation took up the "Agnus Dei";[8] then the procession of the boys began, and after them the girls rose. Step by step, with their hands joined in prayer, they went towards the lighted altar, knelt on the first step, received the sacrament in turn, and came back in the same order to their places. When Virginie's turn came Félicité leaned forward to see her; and with the imaginativeness of deep and tender feeling it seemed to her that she actually was the child; Virginie's face became hers, she was dressed in her clothes, it was her heart beating in her breast. As the moment came to open her mouth she closed her eyes and nearly fainted.

She appeared early in the sacristy next morning for Monsieur the curé to give her the communion. She took it with devotion, but it did not give her the same exquisite delight.

Mme. Aubain wanted to make her daughter into an accomplished person; and as Guyot could not teach her music or English she decided to place her in the Ursuline Convent at Honfleur[9] as a boarder. The child made no objection. Félicité sighed and thought that Madame lacked feeling. Then she reflected that her mistress might be right; matters of this kind were beyond her.

So one day an old spring-van drew up at the door, and out of it stepped a nun to fetch the young lady. Félicité hoisted the luggage on to the top, admonished the driver, and put six pots of preserves, a dozen pears, and a bunch of violets under the seat.

At the last moment Virginie broke into a fit of sobbing; she threw her arms round her mother, who kissed her on the forehead, saying over and over "Come be brave! be brave!" The step was raised, and the carriage drove off.

Then Mme. Aubain's strength gave way; and in the evening all her friends—the Lormeau family, Mme. Lechaptois, the Rochefeuille ladies, M. de Houppeville, and Bourais—came in to console her.

To be without her daughter was very painful for her at first. But she heard from Virginie three times a week, wrote to her on the other days, walked in the garden, and so filled up the empty hours.

From sheer habit Félicité went into Virginie's room in the mornings and gazed at the walls. It was boredom to her not to have to comb the child's hair now, lace up her boots, tuck her into bed—and not to see her charming face perpetually and hold her hand when they went out together. In this idle con-

7. Feast day commemorating the founding of the Sacrament of the Eucharist (Corpus Christi is Latin for body of Christ). 8. "Lamb of God" (Latin)—that is, Jesus; a part of the Roman Catholic Mass. 9. At the mouth of the Seine River, twelve miles from Pont-l'Évêque.

dition she tried making lace. But her fingers were too heavy and broke the threads; she could not attend to anything, she had lost her sleep, and was, in her own words, "destroyed."

To "divert herself" she asked leave to have visits from her nephew Victor.

He arrived on Sundays after mass, rosy-cheeked, bare-chested, with the scent of the country he had walked through still about him. She laid her table promptly and they had lunch, sitting opposite each other. She ate as little as possible herself to save expense, but stuffed him with food so generous that at last he went to sleep. At the first stroke of vespers she woke him up, brushed his trousers, fastened his tie, and went to church, leaning on his arm with maternal pride.

Victor was always instructed by his parents to get something out of her— a packet of moist sugar, it might be, a cake of soap, spirits, or even money at times. He brought his things for her to mend and she took over the task, only too glad to have a reason for making him come back.

In August his father took him off on a coasting voyage. It was holiday time, and she was consoled by the arrival of the children. Paul, however, was getting selfish, and Virginie was too old to be called "thou" any longer; this put a constraint and barrier between them.

Victor went to Morlaix, Dunkirk, and Brighton[1] in succession and made Félicité a present on his return from each voyage. It was a box made of shells the first time, a coffee cup the next, and on the third occasion a large gingerbread man. Victor was growing handsome. He was well made, had a hint of a moustache, good honest eyes, and a small leather hat pushed backwards like a pilot's. He entertained her by telling stories embroidered with nautical terms.

On a Monday, July 14, 1819 (she never forgot the date), he told her that he had signed on for the big voyage and next night but one he would take the Honfleur boat and join his schooner, which was to weigh anchor from Havre before long. Perhaps he would be gone two years.

The prospect of this long absence threw Félicité into deep distress; one more good-bye she must have, and on the Wednesday evening, when Madame's dinner was finished, she put on her clogs and made short work of the twelve miles between Pont-l'Évêque and Honfleur.

When she arrived in front of the Calvary she took the turn to the right instead of the left, got lost in the timber-yards, and retraced her steps; some people to whom she spoke advised her to be quick. She went all round the harbour basin, full of ships, and knocked against hawsers; then the ground fell away, lights flashed across each other, and she thought her wits had left her, for she saw horses up in the sky.

Others were neighing by the quay-side, frightened at the sea. They were lifted by a tackle and deposited in a boat, where passengers jostled each other among cider casks, cheese baskets, and sacks of grain; fowls could be heard clucking, the captain swore; and a cabin-boy stood leaning over the bows, indifferent to it all. Félicité, who had not recognized him, called "Victor!" and he raised his head; all at once, as she was darting forwards, the gangway was drawn back.

1. In England, across the channel. Morlaix and Dunkirk are in Brittany and Flanders, respectively.

The Honfleur packet, women singing as they hauled it, passed out of harbour. Its framework creaked and the heavy waves whipped its bows. The canvas had swung round, no one could be seen on board now; and on the moon-silvered sea the boat made a black speck which paled gradually, dipped, and vanished.

As Félicité passed by the Calvary she had a wish to commend to God what she cherished most, and she stood there praying a long time with her face bathed in tears and her eyes towards the clouds. The town was asleep, coastguards were walking to and fro; and water poured without cessation through the holes in the sluice, with the noise of a torrent. The clocks struck two.

The convent parlour would not be open before day. If Félicité were late Madame would most certainly be annoyed; and in spite of her desire to kiss the other child she turned home. The maids at the inn were waking up as she came in to Pont-l'Évêque.

So the poor slip of a boy was going to toss for months and months at sea! She had not been frightened by his previous voyages. From England or Brittany you came back safe enough; but America, the colonies, the islands—these were lost in a dim region at the other end of the world.

Félicité's thoughts from that moment ran entirely on her nephew. On sunny days she was harassed by the idea of thirst; when there was a storm she was afraid of the lightning on his account. As she listened to the wind growling in the chimney or carrying off the slates she pictured him lashed by that same tempest, at the top of a shattered mast, with his body thrown backwards under a sheet of foam; or else (with a reminiscence of the illustrated geography) he was being eaten by savages, captured in a wood by monkeys, or dying on a desert shore. And never did she mention her anxieties.

Mme. Aubain had anxieties of her own, about her daughter. The good sisters found her an affectionate but delicate child. The slightest emotion unnerved her. She had to give up the piano.

Her mother stipulated for regular letters from the convent. She lost patience one morning when the postman did not come, and walked to and fro in the parlour from her armchair to the window. It was really amazing; not a word for four days!

To console Mme. Aubain by her own example Félicité remarked:

"As for me, Madame, it's six months since I heard . . ."

"From whom, pray?"

"Why . . . from my nephew," the servant answered gently.

"Oh! your nephew!" And Mme. Aubain resumed her walk with a shrug of the shoulders, as much as to say: "I was not thinking of him! And what is more, it's absurd! A scamp of a cabin-boy—what does he matter? . . . whereas my daughter . . . why, just think!"

Félicité, though she had been brought up on harshness, felt indignant with Madame—and then forgot. It seemed the simplest thing in the world to her to lose one's head over the little girl. For her the two children were equally important; a bond in her heart made them one, and their destinies must be the same.

She heard from the chemist that Victor's ship had arrived at Havana. He had read this piece of news in a gazette.

Cigars—they made her imagine Havana as a place where no one does anything but smoke, and there was Victor moving among the negroes in a cloud of tobacco. Could you, she wondered, "in case you needed," return by land? What was the distance from Pont-l'Évêque? She questioned M. Bourais to find out.

He reached for his atlas and began explaining the longitudes; Félicité's consternation provoked a fine pedantic smile. Finally, he marked with his pencil a black, imperceptible point in the indentations of an oval spot, and said as he did so, "Here it is." She bent over the map; the maze of coloured lines wearied her eyes without conveying anything; and on an invitation from Bourais to tell him her difficulty she begged him to show her the house where Victor was living. Bourais threw up his arms, sneezed, and laughed immensely: a simplicity like hers was a positive joy. And Félicité did not understand the reason; how could she when she expected, bvery likely to see the actual image of her nephew—so stunted was her mind!

A fortnight afterwards Liébard came into the kitchen at market-time as usual and handed her a letter from her brother-in-law. As neither of them could read she took it to her mistress.

Mme. Aubain, who was counting the stitches in her knitting, put the work down by her side, broke the seal of the letter, started, and said in a low voice, with a look of meaning:

"It is bad news . . . that they have to tell you. Your nephew . . ."

He was dead. The letter said no more.

Félicité fell on to a chair, leaning her head against the wainscot; and she closed her eyelids, which suddenly flushed pink. Then with bent forehead, hands hanging, and fixed eyes, she said at intervals:

"Poor little lad! poor little lad!"

Liébard watched her and heaved sighs. Mme. Aubain trembled a little.

She suggested that Félicité should go to see her sister at Trouville. Félicité answered by a gesture that she had no need.

There was a silence. The worthy Liébard thought it was time for them to withdraw.

Then Félicité said:

"They don't care, not they!"

Her head dropped again; and she took up mechanically, from time to time, the long needles on her work-table.

Women passed in the yard with a barrow of dripping linen.

As she saw them through the window-panes, she remembered her washing; she had put it to soak the day before, to-day she must wring it out; and she left the room.

Her plank and tub were at the edge of the Toucques. She threw a pile of linen on the bank, rolled up her sleeves, and taking her wooden beater dealt lusty blows whose sound carried to the neighbouring gardens. The meadows were empty, the river stirred in the wind; and down below long grasses wavered, like the hair of corpses floating in the water. She kept her grief down and was very brave until the evening; but once in her room she surrendered to it utterly, lying stretched on the mattress with her face in the pillow and her hands clenched against her temples.

Much later she heard, from the captain himself, the circumstances of Victor's end. They had bled him too much at the hospital for yellow fever. Four doctors held him at once. He had died instantly, and the chief had said:

"Bah! there goes another!"

His parents had always been brutal to him. She preferred not to see them again; and they made no advances, either because they forgot her or from the callousness of the wretchedly poor.

Virginie began to grow weaker.

Tightness in her chest, coughing, continual fever, and veinings on her cheek-bones betrayed some deep-seated complaint. M. Poupart had advised a stay in Provence.[2] Mme. Aubain determined on it, would have brought her daughter home at once but for the climate of Pont-l'Évêque.

She made an arrangement with a job-master, and he drove her to the convent every Tuesday. There is a terrace in the garden, with a view over the Seine. Virginie took walks there over the fallen vine-leaves, on her mother's arm. A shaft of sunlight through the clouds made her blink sometimes, as she gazed at the sails in the distance and the whole horizon from the castle of Tancarville to the lighthouses at Havre. Afterwards they rested in the arbour. Her mother had secured a little cask of excellent Malaga;[3] and Virginie, laughing at the idea of getting tipsy, drank a thimble-full of it, no more.

Her strength came back visibly. The autumn glided gently away. Félicité reassured Mme. Aubain. But one evening, when she had been out on a commission in the neighbourhood, she found M. Poupart's gig at the door. He was in the hall, and Mme. Aubain was tying her bonnet.

"Give me my foot-warmer, purse, gloves. Quicker, come!"

Virginie had inflammation of the lungs; perhaps it was hopeless.

"Not yet!" said the doctor, and they both got into the carriage under whirling flakes of snow. Night was coming on and it was very cold.

Félicité rushed into the church to light a taper. Then she ran after the gig, came up with it in an hour, and jumped lightly in behind. As she hung on by the fringes a thought came into her mind: "The courtyard has not been shut up; supposing burglars got in!" And she jumped down.

At dawn next day she presented herself at the doctor's. He had come in and started for the country again. Then she waited in the inn, thinking that a letter would come by some hand or other. Finally, when it was twilight, she took the Lisieux coach.

The convent was at the end of a steep lane. When she was about half-way up it she heard strange sounds—a death-bell tolling. "It is for someone else," thought Félicité, and she pulled the knocker violently.

After some minutes there was a sound of trailing slippers, the door opened ajar, and a nun appeared.

The good sister, with an air of compunction, said that "she had just passed away." On the instant the bell of St. Leonard's tolled twice as fast.

Félicité went up to the second floor.

From the doorway she saw Virginie stretched on her back, with her hands joined, her mouth open, and head thrown back under a black crucifix that leaned towards her, between curtains that hung stiffly, less pale than was her face. Mme. Aubain, at the foot of the bed which she clasped with her arms, was choking with sobs of agony. The mother superior stood on the right. Three candlesticks on the chest of drawers made spots of red, and the

2. In southern France. 3. A sweet wine.

mist came whitely through the windows. Nuns came and took Mme. Aubain away.

For two nights Félicité never left the dead child. She repeated the same prayers, sprinkled holy water over the sheets, came and sat down again, and watched her. At the end of the first vigil she noticed that the face had grown yellow, the lips turned blue, the nose was sharper, and the eyes sunk in. She kissed them several times, and would not have been immensely surprised if Virginie had opened them again; to minds like hers the supernatural is quite simple. She made the girl's toilette, wrapped her in her shroud, lifted her down into her bier, put a garland on her head, and spread out her hair. It was fair, and extraordinarily long for her age. Félicité cut off a big lock and slipped half of it into her bosom, determined that she should never part with it.

The body was brought back to Pont-l'Évêque, as Mme. Aubain intended; she followed the hearse in a closed carriage.

It took another three-quarters of an hour after the mass to reach the cemetery. Paul walked in front, sobbing. M. Bourais was behind, and then came the chief residents, the women shrouded in black mantles, and Félicité. She thought of her nephew; and because she had not been able to pay these honours to him her grief was doubled, as though the one were being buried with the other.

Mme. Aubain's despair was boundless. It was against God that she first rebelled, thinking it unjust of Him to have taken her daughter from her—she had never done evil and her conscience was so clear! Ah, no!—she ought to have taken Virginie off to the south. Other doctors would have saved her. She accused herself now, wanted to join her child, and broke into cries of distress in the middle of her dreams. One dream haunted her above all. Her husband, dressed as a sailor, was returning from a long voyage, and shedding tears he told her that he had been ordered to take Virginie away. Then they consulted how to hide her somewhere.

She came in once from the garden quite upset. A moment ago—and she pointed out the place—the father and daughter had appeared to her, standing side by side, and they did nothing, but they looked at her.

For several months after this she stayed inertly in her room. Félicité lectured her gently; she must live for her son's sake, and for the other, in remembrance of "her."

"Her?" answered Mme. Aubain, as though she were just waking up. "Ah, yes! . . . yes! . . . You do not forget her!" This was an allusion to the cemetery, where she was strictly forbidden to go.

Félicité went there every day.

Precisely at four she skirted the houses, climbed the hill, opened the gate, and came to Virginie's grave. It was a little column of pink marble with a stone underneath and a garden plot enclosed by chains. The beds were hidden under a coverlet of flowers. She watered their leaves, freshened the gravel, and knelt down to break up the earth better. When Mme. Aubain was able to come there she felt a relief and a sort of consolation.

Then years slipped away, one like another, and their only episodes were the great festivals as they recurred—Easter, the Assumption, All Saints' Day. Household occurrences marked dates that were referred to afterwards. In 1825, for instance, two glaziers white-washed the hall; in 1827 a piece of the roof fell into the courtyard and nearly killed a man. In the summer of

1828 it was Madame's turn to offer the consecrated bread; Bourais, about this time, mysteriously absented himself; and one by one the old acquaintances passed away: Guyot, Liébard, Mme. Lechaptois, Robelin, and Uncle Gremanville, who had been paralysed for a long time.

One night the driver of the mail-coach announced the Revolution of July[4] in Pont-l'Évêque. A new sub-prefect was appointed a few days later—Baron de Larsonnière, who had been consul in America, and brought with him, besides his wife, a sister-in-law and three young ladies, already growing up. They were to be seen about on their lawn, in loose blouses, and they had a negro and a parrot. They paid a call on Mme. Aubain which she did not fail to return. The moment they were seen in the distance Félicité ran to let her mistress know. But only one thing could really move her feelings—the letters from her son.

He was swallowed up in a tavern life and could follow no career. She paid his debts, he made new ones; and the sighs that Mme. Aubain uttered as she sat knitting by the window reached Félicité at her spinning-wheel in the kitchen.

They took walks together along the espaliered wall, always talking of Virginie and wondering if such and such a thing would have pleased her and what, on some occasion, she would have been likely to say.

All her small belongings filled a cupboard in the two-bedded room. Mme. Aubain inspected them as seldom as she could. One summer day she made up her mind to it—and some moths flew out of the wardrobe.

Virginie's dresses were in a row underneath a shelf, on which there were three dolls, some hoops, a set of toy pots and pans, and the basin that she used. They took out her petticoats as well, and the stockings and handkerchiefs, and laid them out on the two beds before folding them up again. The sunshine lit up these poor things, bringing out their stains and the creases made by the body's movements. The air was warm and blue, a blackbird warbled, life seemed bathed in a deep sweetness. They found a little plush hat with thick, chestnut-coloured pile; but it was eaten all over by moth. Félicité begged it for her own. Their eyes met fixedly and filled with tears; at last the mistress opened her arms, the servant threw herself into them, and they embraced each other, satisfying their grief in a kiss that made them equal.

It was the first time in their lives, Mme. Aubain's nature not being expansive. Félicité was as grateful as though she had received a favour; and cherished her mistress from that moment with the devotion of an animal and a religious worship.

The kindness of her heart unfolded.

When she heard the drums of a marching regiment in the street she posted herself at the door with a pitcher of cider and asked the soldiers to drink. She nursed cholera patients and protected the Polish refugees;[5] one of these even declared that he wished to marry her. They quarrelled, however; for when she came back from the Angelus one morning she found that he had got into her kitchen and made himself a vinegar salad which he was quietly eating.

After the Poles came father Colmiche, an old man who was supposed to have committed atrocities in '93.[6] He lived by the side of the river in the

---

4. In 1830 the Bourbons were driven out, and Louis-Philippe became king of France. **5.** After the Polish uprising against Russia in 1831 was suppressed, many Poles came to France. **6.** In 1793 the Reign of Terror during the French Revolution began.

ruins of a pigsty. The little boys watched him through the cracks in the wall, and threw pebbles at him which fell on the pallet where he lay constantly shaken by a catarrh; his hair was very long, his eyes inflamed, and there was a tumour on his arm bigger than his head. She got him some linen and tried to clean up his miserable hole; her dream was to establish him in the bake-house without letting him annoy Madame. When the tumour burst she dressed it every day; sometimes she brought him cake, and would put him in the sunshine on a truss of straw. The poor old man, slobbering and trembling, thanked her in his worn-out voice, was terrified that he might lose her, and stretched out his hands when he saw her go away. He died; and she had a mass said for the repose of his soul.

That very day a great happiness befell her; just at dinner-time appeared Mme. de Larsonnière's negro, carrying the parrot in its cage, with perch, chain, and padlock. A note from the baroness informed Mme. Aubain that her husband had been raised to a prefecture and they were starting that evening; she begged her to accept the bird as a memento and mark of her regard.

For a long time he had absorbed Félicité's imagination, because he came from America; and that name reminded her of Victor, so much so that she made inquiries of the negro. She had once gone so far as to say "How Madame would enjoy having him!"

The negro repeated the remark to his mistress; and as she could not take the bird away with her she chose this way of getting rid of him.

IV

His name was Loulou. His body was green and the tips of his wings rose-pink; his forehead was blue and his throat golden.

But he had the tiresome habits of biting his perch, tearing out his feathers, sprinkling his dirt about, and spattering the water of his tub. He annoyed Mme. Aubain, and she gave him to Félicité for good.

She endeavoured to train him; soon he could repeat "Nice boy! Your servant, sir! Good morning, Marie!" He was placed by the side of the door, and astonished several people by not answering to the name Jacquot, for all parrots are called Jacquot. People compared him to a turkey and a log of wood, and stabbed Félicité to the heart each time. Strange obstinacy on Loulou's part!—directly you looked at him he refused to speak.

None the less he was eager for society; for on Sundays, while the Rochefeuille ladies, M. de Houppeville, and new familiars—Onfroy the apothecary, Monsieur Varin, and Captain Mathieu—were playing their game of cards, he beat the windows with his wings and threw himself about so frantically that they could not hear each other speak.

Bourais' face, undoubtedly, struck him as extremely droll. Directly he saw it he began to laugh—and laugh with all his might. His peals rang through the courtyard and were repeated by the echo; the neighbours came to their windows and laughed too; while M. Bourais, gliding along under the wall to escape the parrot's eye, and hiding his profile with his hat, got to the river and then entered by the garden gate. There was a lack of tenderness in the looks which he darted at the bird.

Loulou had been slapped by the butcher-boy for making so free as to plunge his head into his basket; and since then he was always trying to nip him through his shirt. Fabu threatened to wring his neck, although he was not cruel, for all his tattooed arms and large whiskers. Far from it; he really rather liked the parrot, and in a jovial humour even wanted to teach him to swear. Félicité, who was alarmed by such proceedings, put the bird in the kitchen. His little chain was taken off and he roamed about the house.

His way of going downstairs was to lean on each step with the curve of his beak, raise the right foot, and then the left; and Félicité was afraid that these gymnastics brought on fits of giddiness. He fell ill and could not talk or eat any longer. There was a growth under his tongue, such as fowls have sometimes. She cured him by tearing the pellicle off with her finger-nails. Mr. Paul was thoughtless enough one day to blow some cigar smoke into his nostrils, and another time when Mme. Lormcau was teasing him with the end of her umbrella he snapped at the ferrule. Finally he got lost.

Félicité had put him on the grass to refresh him, and gone away for a minute, and when she came back—no sign of the parrot! She began by looking for him in the shrubs, by the waterside, and over the roofs, without listening to her mistress's cries of "Take care, do! You are out of your wits!" Then she investigated all the gardens in Pont-l'Évêque, and stopped the passers-by. "You don't ever happen to have seen my parrot, by any chance, do you?" And she gave a description of the parrot to those who did not know him. Suddenly, behind the mills at the foot of the hill she thought she could make out something green that fluttered. But on the top of the hill there was nothing. A hawker assured her that he had come across the parrot just before, at Saint-Melaine, in Mère Simon's shop. She rushed there; they had no idea of what she meant. At last she came home exhausted, with her slippers in shreds and despair in her soul; and as she was sitting in the middle of the garden-seat at Madame's side, telling the whole story of her efforts, a light weight dropped on to her shoulder—it was Loulou! What on earth had he been doing? Taking a walk in the neighbourhood, perhaps!

She had some trouble in recovering from this, or rather never did recover. As the result of a chill she had an attack of quinsy, and soon afterwards an earache. Three years later she was deaf; and she spoke very loud, even in church. Though Félicité's sins might have been published in every corner of the diocese without dishonour to her or scandal to anybody, his Reverence the priest thought it right now to hear her confession in the sacristy only.

Imaginary noises in the head completed her upset. Her mistress often said to her, "Heavens! how stupid you are!" "Yes, Madame," she replied, and looked about for something.

Her little circle of ideas grew still narrower; the peal of churchbells and the lowing of cattle ceased to exist for her. All living beings moved as silently as ghosts. One sound only reached her ears now—the parrot's voice.

Loulou, as though to amuse her, reproduced the click-clack of the turnspit, the shrill call of a man selling fish, and the noise of the saw in the joiner's house opposite; when the bell rang he imitated Mme. Aubain's "Félicité! the door! the door!"

They carried on conversations, he endlessly reciting the three phrases in his repertory, to which she replied with words that were just as disconnected but uttered what was in her heart. Loulou was almost a son and a lover to her in her isolated state. He climbed up her fingers, nibbled at her lips, and clung to her kerchief; and when she bent her forehead and shook her head gently to and fro, as nurses do, the great wings of her bonnet and the bird's wings quivered together.

When the clouds massed and the thunder rumbled Loulou broke into cries, perhaps remembering the downpours in his native forests. The streaming rain made him absolutely mad; he fluttered wildly about, dashed up to the ceiling, upset everything, and went out through the window to dabble in the garden; but he was back quickly to perch on one of the fire-dogs and hopped about to dry himself, exhibiting his tail and his beak in turn.

One morning in the terrible winter of 1837 she had put him in front of the fireplace because of the cold. She found him dead, in the middle of his cage: head downwards, with his claws in the wires. He had died from congestion, no doubt. But Félicité thought he had been poisoned with parsley, and though there was no proof of any kind her suspicions inclined to Fabu.

She wept so piteously that her mistress said to her, "Well, then, have him stuffed!"

She asked advice from the chemist, who had always been kind to the parrot. He wrote to Havre, and a person called Fellacher undertook the business. But as parcels sometimes got lost in the coach she decided to take the parrot as far as Honfleur herself.

Along the sides of the road were leafless apple-trees, one after the other. Ice covered the ditches. Dogs barked about the farms; and Félicité, with her hands under her cloak, her little black sabots and her basket, walked briskly in the middle of the road.

She crossed the forest, passed High Oak, and reached St. Gatien.

A cloud of dust rose behind her, and in it a mail-coach, carried away by the steep hill, rushed down at full gallop like a hurricane. Seeing this woman who would not get out of the way, the driver stood up in front and the postilion shouted too. He could not hold in his four horses, which increased their pace, and the two leaders were grazing her when he threw them to one side with a jerk of the reins. But he was wild with rage, and lifting his arm as he passed at full speed, gave her such a lash from waist to neck with his big whip that she fell on her back.

Her first act, when she recovered consciousness, was to open her basket. Loulou was happily none the worse. She felt a burn in her right cheek, and when she put her hands against it they were red; the blood was flowing.

She sat down on a heap of stones and bound up her face with her handkerchief. Then she ate a crust of bread which she had put in the basket as a precaution, and found a consolation for her wound in gazing at the bird.

When she reached the crest of Ecquemauville she saw the Honfleur lights sparkling in the night sky like a company of stars; beyond, the sea stretched dimly. Then a faintness overtook her and she stopped; her wretched childhood, the disillusion of her first love, her nephew's going away, and Virginie's death all came back to her at once like the waves of an oncoming tide, rose to her throat, and choked her.

Afterwards, at the boat, she made a point of speaking to the captain, begging him to take care of the parcel, though she did not tell him what was in it.

Fellacher kept the parrot a long time. He was always promising it for the following week. After six months he announced that a packing-case had started, and then nothing more was heard of it. It really seemed as though Loulou was never coming back. "Ah, they have stolen him!" she thought.

He arrived at last, and looked superb. There he was, erect upon a branch which screwed into a mahogany socket, with a foot in the air and his head on one side, biting a nut which the bird-stuffer—with a taste for impressiveness-had gilded.

Félicité shut him up in her room. It was a place to which few people were admitted, and held so many religious objects and miscellaneous things that it looked like a chapel and bazaar in one.

A big cupboard impeded you as you opened the door. Opposite the window commanding the garden a little round one looked into the court; there was a table by the folding-bed with a water-jug, two combs, and a cube of blue soap in a chipped plate. On the walls hung rosaries, medals, several benign Virgins, and a holy water vessel made out of cocoa-nut; on the chest of drawers, which was covered with a cloth like an altar, was the shell box that Victor had given her, and after that a watering-can, a toy-balloon, exercise-books, the illustrated geography, and a pair of young lady's boots; and, fastened by its ribbons to the nail of the looking-glass, hung the little plush hat! Félicité carried observances of this kind so far as to keep one of Monsieur's frock-coats. All the old rubbish which Mme. Aubain did not want any longer she laid hands on for her room. That was why there were artificial flowers along the edge of the chest of drawers and a portrait of the Comte d'Artois[7] in the little window recess.

With the aid of a bracket Loulou was established over the chimney, which jutted into the room. Every morning when she woke up she saw him there in the dawning light, and recalled old days and the smallest details of insignificant acts in a deep quietness which knew no pain.

Holding, as she did, no communication with anyone, Félicité lived as insensibly as if she were walking in her sleep. The Corpus Christi processions roused her to life again. Then she went round begging mats and candlesticks from the neighbours to decorate the altar they put up in the street.

In church she was always gazing at the Holy Ghost in the window, and observed that there was something of the parrot in him. The likeness was still clearer, she thought, on a crude colour-print representing the baptism of Our Lord. With his purple wings and emerald body he was the very image of Loulou.

She bought him, and hung him up instead of the Comte d'Artois, so that she could see them both together in one glance. They were linked in her thoughts; and the parrot was consecrated by his association with the Holy Ghost, which became more vivid to her eye and more intelligible. The Father could not have chosen to express Himself through a dove, for such creatures cannot speak; it must have been one of Loulou's ancestors, surely. And though Félicité looked at the picture while she said her prayers she swerved a little from time to time towards the parrot.

---

7. Title of Charles X, the last of the Bourbons, the youngest brother of Louis XVI and Louis XVIII. He was king between 1824 and 1830 and died in exile in 1836.

She wanted to join the Ladies of the Virgin, but Mme. Aubain dissuaded her.

And then a great event loomed up before them—Paul's marriage.

He had been a solicitor's clerk to begin with, and then tried business, the Customs, the Inland Revenue, and made efforts, even, to get into the Rivers and Forests. By an inspiration from heaven he had suddenly, at thirty-six, discovered his real line—the Registrar's Office. And there he showed such marked capacity that an inspector had offered him his daughter's hand and promised him his influence.

So Paul, grown serious, brought the lady to see his mother.

She sniffed at the ways of Pont-l'évêque, gave herself great airs, and wounded Félicité's feelings. Mme. Aubain was relieved at her departure.

The week after came news of M. Bourais' death in an inn in Lower Brittany. The rumour of suicide was confirmed, and doubts arose as to his honesty. Mme. Aubain studied his accounts, and soon found out the whole tale of his misdoings—embezzled arrears, secret sales of wood, forged receipts, etc. Besides that he had an illegitimate child, and "relations with a person at Dozulé."

These shameful facts distressed her greatly. In March 1853 she was seized with a pain in the chest; her tongue seemed to be covered with film, and leeches did not ease the difficult breathing. On the ninth evening of her illness she died, just at seventy-two.

She passed as being younger, owing to the bands of brown hair which framed her pale, pock-marked face. There were few friends to regret her, for she had a stiffness of manner which kept people at a distance.

But Félicité mourned for her as one seldom mourns for a master. It upset her ideas and seemed contrary to the order of things, impossible and monstrous, that Madame should die before her.

Ten days afterwards, which was the time it took to hurry there from Besançon,[8] the heirs arrived. The daughter-in-law ransacked the drawers, chose some furniture, and sold the rest; and then they went back to their registering.

Madame's armchair, her small round table, her foot-warmer, and the eight chairs were gone! Yellow patches in the middle of the panels showed where the engravings had hung. They had carried off the two little beds and the mattresses, and all Virginie's belongings had disappeared from the cupboard. Félicité went from floor to floor dazed with sorrow.

The next day there was a notice on the door, and the apothecary shouted in her ear that the house was for sale.

She tottered, and was obliged to sit down. What distressed her most of all was to give up her room, so suitable as it was for poor Loulou. She enveloped him with a look of anguish when she was imploring the Holy Ghost, and formed the idolatrous habit of kneeling in front of the parrot to say her prayers. Sometimes the sun shone in at the attic window and caught his glass eye, and a great luminous ray shot out of it and put her in an ecstasy.

She had a pension of three hundred and eighty francs a year which her mistress had left her. The garden gave her a supply of vegetables. As for

8. In eastern France, near the Swiss border.

clothes, she had enough to last her to the end of her days, and she economized in candles by going to bed at dusk.

She hardly ever went out, as she did not like passing the dealer's shop, where some of the old furniture was exposed for sale. Since her fit of giddiness she dragged one leg; and as her strength was failing Mère Simon, whose grocery business had collapsed, came every morning to split the wood and pump water for her.

Her eyes grew feeble. The shutters ceased to be thrown open. Years and years passed, and the house was neither let nor sold.

Félicité never asked for repairs because she was afraid of being sent away. The boards on the roof rotted; her bolster was wet for a whole winter. After Easter she spat blood.

Then Mère Simon called in a doctor. Félicité wanted to know what was the matter with her. But she was too deaf to hear, and the only word which reached her was "pneumonia." It was a word she knew, and she answered softly "Ah! like Madame," thinking it natural that she should follow her mistress.

The time for the festal shrines was coming near. The first one was always at the bottom of the hill, the second in front of the post-office, and the third towards the middle of the street. There was some rivalry in the matter of this one, and the women of the parish ended by choosing Mme. Aubain's courtyard.

The hard breathing and fever increased. Félicité was vexed at doing nothing for the altar. If only she could at least have put something there! Then she thought of the parrot. The neighbours objected that it would not be decent. But the priest gave her permission, which so intensely delighted her that she begged him to accept Loulou, her sole possession, when she died.

From Tuesday to Saturday, the eve of the festival, she coughed more often. By the evening her face had shrivelled, her lips stuck to her gums, and she had vomitings; and at twilight next morning, feeling herself very low, she sent for a priest.

Three kindly women were round her during the extreme unction. Then she announced that she must speak to Fabu. He arrived in his Sunday clothes, by no means at his ease in the funereal atmosphere.

"Forgive me," she said, with an effort to stretch out her arm; "I thought it was you who had killed him."

What did she mean by such stories? She suspected him of murder—a man like him! He waxed indignant, and was on the point of making a row. "There," said the women, "she is no longer in her senses, you can see it well enough!"

Félicité spoke to shadows of her own from time to time. The women went away, and Mère Simon had breakfast. A little later she took Loulou and brought him close to Félicité with the words:

"Come, now, say good-bye to him!"

Loulou was not a corpse, but the worms devoured him; one of his wings was broken, and the tow was coming out of his stomach. But she was blind now; she kissed him on the forehead and kept him close against her cheek. Mère Simon took him back from her to put him on the altar.

V

Summer scents came up from the meadows; flies buzzed; the sun made the river glitter and heated the slates. Mère Simon came back into the room and fell softly asleep.

She woke at the noise of bells; the people were coming out from vespers. Félicité's delirium subsided. She thought of the procession and saw it as if she had been there.

All the school children, the church-singers, and the firemen walked on the pavement, while in the middle of the road the verger armed with his halle-bard and the beadle with a large cross advanced in front. Then came the schoolmaster, with an eye on the boys, and the sister, anxious about her lit-tle girls; three of the daintiest, with angelic curls, scattered rose-petals in the air; the deacon controlled the band with outstretched arms; and two censer-bearers turned back at every step towards the Holy Sacrament, which was borne by Monsieur the curé, wearing his beautiful chasuble, under a canopy of dark-red velvet held by four churchwardens. A crowd of people pressed behind, between the white cloths covering the house walls, and they reached the bottom of the hill.

A cold sweat moistened Félicité's temples. Mère Simon sponged her with a piece of linen, saying to herself that one day she would have to go that way.

The hum of the crowd increased, was very loud for an instant and then went further away.

A fusillade shook the window-panes. It was the postilions saluting the monstrance. Félicité rolled her eyes and said as audibly as she could: "Does he look well?" The parrot was weighing on her mind.

Her agony began. A death-rattle that grew more and more convulsed made her sides heave. Bubbles of froth came at the corners of her mouth and her whole body trembled.

Soon the booming of the ophicleides,[9] the high voices of the children, and the deep voices of the men were distinguishable. At intervals all was silent, and the tread of feet, deadened by the flowers they walked on, sounded like a flock pattering on grass.

The clergy appeared in the courtyard. Mère Simon clambered on to a chair to reach the attic window, and so looked down straight upon the shrine. Green garlands hung over the altar, which was decked with a flounce of English lace. In the middle was a small frame with relics in it; there were two orange-trees at the corners, and all along stood silver candlesticks and china vases, with sun-flowers, lilies, peonies, foxgloves, and tufts of hortensia. This heap of blazing colour slanted from the level of the altar to the carpet which went on over the pavement; and some rare objects caught the eye. There was a silver-gilt sugar-basin with a crown of violets; pendants of Alençon stone glittered on the moss, and two Chinese screens displayed their landscapes. Loulou was hidden under roses, and showed nothing but his blue forehead, like a plaque of lapis lazuli.

The churchwardens, singers, and children took their places round the three sides of the court. The priest went slowly up the steps, and placed his great, radiant golden sun[1] upon the lace. Everyone knelt down. There was a

9. An old large brass-wind instrument now replaced by the tuba.   1. The monstrance containing the consecrated Host.

deep silence; and the censers glided to and fro on the full swing of their chains.

An azure vapour rose up into Félicité's room. Her nostrils met it; she inhaled it sensuously, mystically; and then closed her eyes. Her lips smiled. The beats of her heart lessened one by one, vaguer each time and softer, as a fountain sinks, an echo disappears; and when she sighed her last breath she thought she saw an opening in the heavens, and a gigantic parrot hovering above her head.

FYODOR DOSTOEVSKY
1821–1881

Fyodor Dostoevsky has been a central figure in the formation of the modern sensibility. His works are fundamental to the Western tradition of the novel and a strong influence on modern literature in China and Japan. Dostoevsky formulated in fictional terms, in dramatic and even sensational scenes, some of the central predicaments of our time: the choices between God and atheism, good and evil, freedom and tyranny; the recognition of the limits and even of the fall of humanity against the belief in progress, revolution, and utopia. Most important, he captured unforgettably the enormous contradictions of which our common human nature is capable and by which it is torn.

Fyodor Mikhailovich Dostoevsky was born in Moscow on October 30, 1821. His father was a staff doctor at the Hospital for the Poor. Later he acquired an estate and serfs. In 1839 he was killed by one of his peasants in a quarrel. Dostoevsky was sent to the Military Engineering Academy in St. Petersburg, from which he graduated in 1843. He became a civil servant, a draftsman in the St. Petersburg Engineering Corps, but resigned soon because he feared that he would be transferred to the provinces when his writing was discovered. His first novel, *Poor People* (1846), proved a great success with the critics; his second, *The Double* (1846), which followed immediately, was a failure.

Subsequently, Dostoevsky became involved in the Petrashevsky circle, a secret society of antigovernment and socialist tendencies. He was arrested on April 23, 1849, and condemned to be shot. On December 22 he was led to public execution, but he was reprieved at the last moment and sent to penal servitude in Siberia (near Omsk), where he worked for four years in a stockade, wearing fetters, completely cut off from communications with Russia. On his release in February 1854, he was assigned as a common soldier to Semipalatinsk, a small town near the Mongolian frontier. There he received several promotions (eventually becoming an ensign); his rank of nobility, forfeited by his sentence, was restored; and he married the widow of a customs official. In July 1859, Dostoevsky was permitted to return to Russia, and finally, in December 1859, to St. Petersburg—after ten years of his life had been spent in Siberia.

In the last year of his exile, Dostoevsky had resumed writing, and in 1861, shortly after his return, he founded a review, *Time (Vremya)*. This was suppressed in 1863, though Dostoevsky had changed his political opinions and was now strongly nationalistic and conservative in outlook. He made his first trip to France and England in 1862, and traveled in Europe again in 1863 and 1865, to follow a young woman friend, Apollinaria Suslova, and to indulge in gambling. After his wife's death in 1864, and another unsuccessful journalistic venture, *The Epoch* (*Epokha*, 1864–65), Dostoevsky was for a time almost crushed by gambling debts, emotional entanglements, and frequent epileptic seizures. He barely managed to return from Germany in 1865. In the winter of 1866 he wrote *Crime and Punishment* and, before he had finished it, dictated a shorter novel, *The Gambler*, to meet a deadline. He married his secretary, Anna Grigoryevna Snitkina, early in 1867 and left Russia with her to avoid his creditors. For years they wandered over Germany, Italy, and Switzerland, frequently in abject poverty. Their first child died. In 1871, when the initial chapters of *The Possessed* proved a popular success, Dostoevsky returned to St. Petersburg. He became the editor of a weekly, *The Citizen* (*Grazhdanin*), for a short time and then published a periodical written by himself, *The Diary of a Writer* (1876–81), which won great acclaim. His last novel, *The Brothers Karamazov* (1880), was an immense success, and honors and some prosperity came to him at last. At a Pushkin anniversary celebrated in Moscow in 1880 he gave the main speech. But soon after his return to St. Petersburg he died, on January 28, 1881, not yet sixty years old.

Dostoevsky, like every great writer, can be approached in different ways and read on different levels. We can try to understand him as a religious philosopher, a political commentator, a psychologist, and a novelist, and if we know much about his fascinating and varied life, we might also interpret his works as biographical.

The biographical interpretation is the one that has been pushed furthest. The lurid crimes of Dostoevsky's characters (such as the rape of a young girl) have been ascribed to him, and all his novels have been studied as if they constituted a great personal confession. Dostoevsky certainly did draw from his experiences in his books, as every writer does: he several times described the feelings of a man facing a firing squad as he himself faced it on December 22, 1849, only to be reprieved at the last moment. His writings also reflect his years in Siberia: four years working in a loghouse, in chains, as he describes it in an oddly impersonal book, *Memoirs from the House of the Dead* (1862), and six more years as a common soldier on the borders of Mongolia, in a small, remote provincial town. Similarly, he used the experience of his disease (epilepsy), ascribing great spiritual significance to the ecstatic rapture preceding the actual seizure. He assigned his disease to both his most angelic "good" man, the "Idiot," Prince Myshkin, and his most diabolical, inhuman figure, the cold-blooded unsexed murderer of the old Karamazov, the flunky Smerdyakov. Dostoevsky also used something of his experiences in Germany, where in the 1860s he succumbed to a passion for gambling, which he overcame only much later, during his second marriage. The short novel *The Gambler* (1866) gives an especially vivid account of this life and its moods.

There are other autobiographical elements in Dostoevsky's works, but it seems a gross misunderstanding of his methods and the procedures of art in general to conclude from his writings (as Thomas Mann has done) that he was a "saint and criminal" in one. Dostoevsky, after all, was an extremely hard worker who wrote and rewrote some twenty volumes. He was a novelist who employed the methods of the French sensational novel; he was constantly on the lookout for the most striking occurrences—the most shocking crimes and the most horrible disasters and scandals—because only in such fictional situations could he exalt his characters to their highest pitch, bringing out the clash of ideas and temperaments, revealing the deepest layers of their souls. But these fictions cannot be taken as literal transcriptions of reality and actual experience.

Whole books have been written to explain Dostoevsky's religious philosophy and conception of human nature. The Russian philosopher Berdyayev concludes his excellent study by saying, "So great is the value of Dostoevsky that to have produced him is by itself sufficient justification for the existence of the Russian people in the world." But there is no need for such extravagance. Dostoevsky's philosophy of religion is rather a personal version of extreme mystical Christianity, and assumes flesh and blood only in the context of the novels. Reduced to the bare bones of abstract propositions, it amounts to saying that humanity is fallen but is free to choose between evil and Christ. And choosing Christ means taking on oneself the burden of humanity in love and pity, since "everybody is guilty for all and before all." Hence in Dostoevsky there is tremendous stress on personal freedom of choice, and his affirmation of the worth of every individual is combined, paradoxically, with an equal insistence on the substantial identity of all human beings, their equality before God, the bond of love that unites them.

Dostoevsky also develops a philosophy of history, with practical political implications, based on this point of view. According to him, the West is in complete decay; only Russia has preserved Christianity in its original form. The West is either Catholic (and Catholicism is condemned by Dostoevsky as an attempt to force salvation by magic and authority) or bourgeois, and hence materialistic and fallen away from Christ, or socialist, and socialism is to Dostoevsky identical with atheism, as it dreams of a utopia in which human beings would not be free to choose even at the expense of suffering. Dostoevsky—who himself had belonged to a revolutionary group and come into contact with Russian revolutionaries abroad—had an extraordinary insight into the mentality of the Russian underground. In *The Possessed* (1871–72) he gives a lurid satiric picture of these would-be saviors of Russia and humankind. But while he was afraid of the revolution, Dostoevsky himself hoped and prophesied that Russia would save Europe from the dangers of communism, as Russia alone was the uncorrupted Christian land. Put in terms of political propositions (as Dostoevsky himself preaches them in his journal, *The Diary of a Writer*, 1876–81), what he propounds is a conservative Russian nationalism with messianic hopes for Russian Christianity.

When translated into abstractions, Dostoevsky's psychology is as unimpressive as his political theory. It is merely a derivative of theories propounded by German writers about the unconscious, the role of dreams, the ambivalence of human feelings. What makes it electric in the novels is his ability to dramatize it in scenes of sudden revelation, in characters who in today's terminology would be called split personalities, in people twisted by isolation, lust, humiliation, and resentment. The dreams of Raskolnikov may be interpreted according to Freudian psychology, but to the reader without any knowledge of science they are comprehensible in their place in the novel and function as warnings and anticipations.

Dostoevsky was first of all an artist—a novelist who succeeded in using his ideas (many old and venerable, many new and fantastic) and psychological insights for the writing of stories of absorbing interest. As an artist, Dostoevsky treated the novel like a drama, constructing it in large, vivid scenes that end with a scandal or a crime or some act of violence, filling it with unforgettable "stagelike" figures torn by great passions and swayed by great ideas. Then he set this world in an environment of St. Petersburg slums or of towns, monasteries, and country houses, all so vividly realized that we forget how the setting, the figures, and the ideas blend together into one cosmos of the imagination only remotely and obliquely related to any reality of nineteenth-century Russia. We take part in a great drama of pride and humility, good and evil, in a huge allegory of humanity's search for God and itself. We understand and share in this world because it is not merely Russia in the nineteenth century, where people could hardly have talked and behaved as Dostoevsky's people do, but a myth of humanity, universalized as all art is.

Notes from Underground (1864) precedes the four great novels: *Crime and Punishment* (1866), *The Idiot* (1868), *The Possessed*, and *The Brothers Karamazov* (1880). The *Notes* can be viewed as a prologue, an important introduction to the cycle of the four great novels, an anticipation of the mature Dostoevsky's method and thought. Though it cannot compare in dramatic power and scope with these, the story has its own peculiar and original artistry. It is made up of two parts, at first glance seemingly independent: the monologue of the Underground man and the confession that he makes about himself, called "Apropos of Wet Snow." The monologue, though it includes no action, is dramatic—a long address to an imaginary hostile reader, whom the Underground man ridicules, defies, jeers at, but also flatters. The confession is an autobiographical reminiscence of the Underground man. It describes events that occurred long before the delivery of the monologue, but it functions as a confirmation in concrete terms of the self-portrait drawn in the monologue and as an explanation of the isolation of the hero.

The narrative of the confession is a comic variation on the old theme of the rescue of a fallen woman from vice, a seesaw series of humiliations permitting Dostoevsky to display all the cruelty of his probing psychology. The hero, out of spite and craving for human company, forces himself into the company of former schoolfellows and is shamefully humiliated by them. He reasserts his ego (as he cannot revenge himself on them) in the company of a humble prostitute by impressing her with florid and moving speeches, which he knows to be insincere, about her horrible future. Ironically, he converts her, but when she comes to him and surprises him in a degrading scene with his servant, he humiliates her again. When, even then, she understands and forgives and thus shows her moral superiority, he crowns his spite by deliberately misunderstanding her and forcing money on her. She is the moral victor and the Underground man returns to his hideout to jeer at humanity. It is hard not to feel that we are shown a tortured and twisted soul almost too despicable to elicit our compassion.

Still it would be a complete misunderstanding of Dostoevsky's story to take the philosophy expounded jeeringly in the long monologue of the first part merely as the irrational railings of a sick personality. The Underground man, though abject and spiteful, represents not only a specific Russian type of the time—the intellectual divorced from the soil and his nation—but also modern humanity, even Everyman, and strangely enough, even the author, who through the mouth of this despicable character, as through a mask, expresses his boldest and most intimate convictions. In spite of all the exaggerated pathos, wild paradox, and jeering irony used by the speaker, his self-criticism and his criticism of society and history must be taken seriously and interpreted patiently if we are to extract the meaning accepted by Dostoevsky.

The Underground man is also the hyperconscious man who examines himself as if in a mirror, and sees himself with pitiless candor. His very self-consciousness cripples his will and poisons his feelings. He cannot escape from his ego; he knows that he has acted badly toward the woman but at the same time he cannot help acting as he does. He knows that he is alone, that there is no bridge from him to humanity, that the world is hostile to him, and that he is humiliated by everyone he meets. But though he resents the humiliation, he cannot help courting it, provoking it, and even enjoying it in his perverse manner. He understands (and knows from his own experience) that something within us all enjoys evil and destruction.

His self-criticism widens, then, into a criticism of the assumptions of modern civilization, of nineteenth-century optimism about human nature and progress, of utilitarianism, and of all kinds of utopias. It is possible to identify specific allusions to a contemporary novel by a radical socialist and revolutionary, Chernyshevsky, titled *What Shall We Do?* (1863), but we do not need to know the exact target of Dostoevsky's satire to recognize what he attacks: the view that human nature is good, that we generally seek our enlightened self-interest, that science propounds immutable truths, and that a paradise on earth will be just around the corner once society is reformed along scientific lines. In a series of vivid symbols these assumptions are represented, parodied, exposed. Science says that "twice two makes four" but the Underground man laughs that "twice two makes five is sometimes a very charming thing too." Science means to him (and to Dostoevsky) the victory of the doctrine of fatality, of iron necessity, of determinism, and thus finally of death. Humanity would become an "organ stop," a "piano key," if deterministic science were valid.

Equally disastrous are the implications of the social philosophy of liberalism and of socialism (which Dostoevsky considers its necessary consequence). In this view, we need only follow our enlightened self-interest, need only be rational, and we will become noble and good and the earth will be a place of prosperity and peace. But the Underground man knows that this conception of human nature is entirely false. What if humankind does not follow, and never will follow, its own enlightened self-interest, is consciously and purposely irrational, even bloodthirsty and evil? History seems to the Underground man to speak a clear language: "civilization has made mankind if not more bloodthirsty, at least more vilely, more loathsomely blood-thirsty." Humanity wills the irrational and evil because it does not want to become an organ stop, a piano key, because it wants to be left with the freedom to choose between good and evil. This freedom of choice, even at the expense of chaos and destruction, is what makes us human.

Actually, we love something other than our own well-being and happiness, love even suffering and pain, because we are human and not animals inhabiting some great organized rational "ant heap." The ant heap, the hen house, the block of tenements, and finally the Crystal Palace (then the newest wonder of architecture, a great hall of iron and glass erected for the Universal Exhibition in London) are the images used by the Underground man to represent his hated utopia. The heroine of *What Shall We Do?* had dreamed of a building, made of cast iron and glass and placed in the middle of a beautiful garden where there would be eternal spring and summer, eternal joy. Dostoevsky had recognized there the utopian dream of Charles Fourier, the French socialist whom he had admired in his youth and whose ideals he had come to hate with a fierce revulsion. But we must realize that the Underground man, and Dostoevsky, despise this "ant heap," this perfectly organized society of automatons, in the name of something higher, in the name of freedom. Dostoevsky does not believe that humanity can achieve freedom and happiness at the same time; happiness can be bought only at the expense of freedom, and all utopian schemes seem to him devices to lure us into the yoke of slavery. This freedom is, of course, not political freedom but freedom of choice, indeterminism, even caprice and willfulness, in the paradoxical formulation of the Underground man.

There are hints at a positive solution only in the one chapter (Part I, chapter X) that was mutilated by the censor. A letter by Dostoevsky to his brother about the "swine of a censor who let through the passages where I jeered at everything and blasphemed ostensibly" refers to the fact that he "suppressed everything where I drew the conclusion that faith in Christ is needed." In Part I, chapter XI, of the present text (and Dostoevsky never restored the suppressed passages) the Underground man says merely, "I am lying because I know myself that it is not underground that is better, but something different, quite different, for which I am thirsting, but which I cannot find!" This "something . . . quite different" all the other writings of Dostoevsky show to be the voluntary following of the Christian savior even at the expense of suffering and pain.

In a paradoxical form, through the mouth of one of his vilest characters, Dostoevsky reveals in the story his view of humanity and history—of the evil in human nature and of the blood and tragedy in history—and his criticism of the optimistic, utilitarian, utopian, progressive view of humanity that was spreading to Russia from the West during the nineteenth century and that found its most devoted adherents in the Russian revolutionaries. Preoccupied with criticism, Dostoevsky does not here suggest any positive remedy. But if we understand the *Notes* we can understand how Raskolnikov, the murderer out of intellect in *Crime and Punishment,* can find salvation at last, and how Dmitri, the guilty-guiltless parricide of *The Brothers Karamazov,* can sing his hymn to joy in the Siberian mines. We can even understand the legend of the Grand Inquisitor told by Ivan Karamazov, in which we meet the same criticism of a utopia (this time that of Catholicism) and the same exaltation of human freedom even at the price of suffering.

PRONOUNCING GLOSSARY

The following list uses common English syllables and stress accents to provide rough equivalents of selected words whose pronunciation may be unfamiliar to the general reader.

Anton Antonych: *ahn-tawn' ahn-taw'-nich*

Apollon: *ah-pah-lawn'*

Ferfichkin: *fehr-feech'-keen*

Fyodor Dostoevsky: *fyo'dor dos-toy-eff'-skee*

Karamazov: *kuh-rah-mah'-zuf*

Kolya: *kawl'-yuh*

Podkharzhevsky: *put-khar-zhef'-skee*

Simonov: *see-muh-nuf*

Trudolyubov: *troo-dah-lyoo'-buf*

Zverkov: *zvyehr-kof'*

From Notes from Underground[1]

I

Underground[2]

I

I am a sick man. . . . [3] I am a spiteful man. I am a most unpleasant man. I think my liver is diseased. Then again, I don't know a thing about my illness; I'm not even sure what hurts. I'm not being treated and never have been, though I respect both medicine and doctors. Besides, I'm extremely superstitious—well at least enough to respect medicine. (I'm sufficiently educated not to be superstitious; but I am, anyway.) No, gentlemen, it's out of spite that I don't wish to be treated. Now then, that's something you probably won't understand. Well, I do. Of course, I won't really be able to explain to you precisely who will be hurt by my spite in this case; I know perfectly well that I can't possibly "get even" with doctors by refusing their treatment; I know better than anyone that all this is going to hurt me alone, and no one else. Even so, if I refuse to be treated, it's out of spite. My liver hurts? Good, let it hurt even more!

I've been living this way for some time—about twenty years. I'm forty now. I used to be in the civil service. But no more. I was a nasty official. I was rude and took pleasure in it. After all, since I didn't accept bribes, at least I had to reward myself in some way. (That's a poor joke, but I won't cross it out. I wrote it thinking that it would be very witty; but now, having realized

1. Translated by Michael Katz.   2. Both the author of these notes and the *Notes* themselves are fictitious, of course. Nevertheless, people like the author of these notes not only may, but actually must exist in our society, considering the general circumstances under which our society was formed. I wanted to bring before the public with more prominence than usual one of the characters of the recent past. He's a representative of the current generation. In the excerpt entitled "Underground" this person introduces himself and his views, and, as it were, wants to explain the reasons why he appeared and why he had to appear in our midst. The following excerpt ["Apropos of Wet Snow"] contains the actual "notes" of this person about several events in his life [Author's note].   3. The ellipses are the author's and do not indicate omissions from this text.

that I merely wanted to show off disgracefully, I'll make a point of not cross-ing it out!) When petitioners used to approach my desk for information, I'd gnash my teeth and feel unending pleasure if I succeeded in causing some-one distress. I almost always succeeded. For the most part they were all timid people: naturally, since they were petitioners. But among the dandies there was a certain officer whom I particularly couldn't bear. He simply refused to be humble, and he clanged his saber in a loathsome manner. I waged war with him over that saber for about a year and a half. At last I pre-vailed. He stopped clanging. All this, however, happened a long time ago, during my youth. But do you know, gentlemen, what the main component of my spite really was? Why, the whole point, the most disgusting thing, was the fact that I was shamefully aware at every moment, even at the moment of my greatest bitterness, that not only was I not a spiteful man, I was not even an embittered one, and that I was merely scaring sparrows to no effect and consoling myself by doing so. I was foaming at the mouth—but just bring me some trinket to play with, just serve me a nice cup of tea with sugar, and I'd probably have calmed down. My heart might even have been touched, although I'd probably have gnashed my teeth out of shame and then suffered from insomnia for several months afterward. That's just my usual way.

I was lying about myself just now when I said that I was a nasty official. I lied out of spite. I was merely having some fun at the expense of both the petitioners and that officer, but I could never really become spiteful. At all times I was aware of a great many elements in me that were just the opposite of that. I felt how they swarmed inside me, these contradictory elements. I knew that they had been swarming inside me my whole life and were beg-ging to be let out; but I wouldn't let them out, I wouldn't, I deliberately wouldn't let them out. They tormented me to the point of shame; they drove me to convulsions and—and finally I got fed up with them, oh how fed up! Perhaps it seems to you, gentlemen, that I'm repenting about something, that I'm asking your forgiveness for something? I'm sure that's how it seems to you. . . . But really, I can assure you, I don't care if that's how it seems. . . .

Not only couldn't I become spiteful, I couldn't become anything at all: nei-ther spiteful nor good, neither a scoundrel nor an honest man, neither a hero nor an insect. Now I live out my days in my corner, taunting myself with the spiteful and entirely useless consolation that an intelligent man cannot seriously become anything and that only a fool can become some-thing. Yes, sir, an intelligent man in the nineteenth century must be, is morally obliged to be, principally a characterless creature; a man possessing character, a man of action, is fundamentally a limited creature. That's my conviction at the age of forty. I'm forty now; and, after all, forty is an entire lifetime; why it's extreme old age. It's rude to live past forty, it's indecent, immoral! Who lives more than forty years? Answer sincerely, honestly. I'll tell you who: only fools and rascals. I'll tell those old men that right to their faces, all those venerable old men, all those silver-haired and sweet-smelling old men! I'll say it to the whole world right to its face! I have a right to say it because I myself will live to sixty! I'll make it to seventy! Even to eighty! . . . Wait! Let me catch my breath. . . .

You probably think, gentlemen, that I want to amuse you. You're wrong about that, too. I'm not at all the cheerful fellow I seem to be, or that I may seem to be; however, if you're irritated by all this talk (and I can already sense that you are irritated), and if you decide to ask me just who I really am, then I'll tell you: I'm a collegiate assessor. I worked in order to have something to eat (but only for that reason); and last year, when a distant relative of mine left me six thousand rubles in his will, I retired immediately and settled down in this corner. I used to live in this corner before, but now I've settled down in it. My room is nasty, squalid, on the outskirts of town. My servant is an old peasant woman, spiteful out of stupidity; besides, she has a foul smell. I'm told that the Petersburg climate is becoming bad for my health, and that it's very expensive to live in Petersburg with my meager resources. I know all that; I know it better than all those wise and experienced advisers and admonishers. But I shall remain in Petersburg; I shall not leave Petersburg! I shall not leave here because . . . Oh, what difference does it really make whether I leave Petersburg or not?

Now, then, what can a decent man talk about with the greatest pleasure? Answer: about himself.

Well, then, I too will talk about myself.

II

Now I would like to tell you, gentlemen, whether or not you want to hear it, why it is that I couldn't even become an insect. I'll tell you solemnly that I wished to become an insect many times. But not even that wish was granted. I swear to you, gentlemen, that being overly conscious is a disease, a genuine, full-fledged disease. Ordinary human consciousness would be more than sufficient for everyday human needs—that is, even half or a quarter of the amount of consciousness that's available to a cultured man in our unfortunate nineteenth century, especially to one who has the particular misfortune of living in St. Petersburg, the most abstract and premeditated city in the whole world.[4] (Cities can be either premeditated or unpremeditated.) It would have been entirely sufficient, for example, to have the consciousness with which all so-called spontaneous people and men of action are endowed. I'll bet that you think I'm writing all this to show off, to make fun of these men of action, that I'm clanging my saber just like that officer did to show off in bad taste. But, gentlemen, who could possibly be proud of his illnesses and want to show them off?

But what am I saying? Everyone does that; people do take pride in their illnesses, and I, perhaps, more than anyone else. Let's not argue; my objection is absurd. Nevertheless, I remain firmly convinced that not only is being overly conscious a disease, but so is being conscious at all. I insist on it. But let's leave that alone for a moment. Tell me this: why was it, as if on purpose, at the very moment, indeed, at the precise moment that I was most capable of becoming conscious of the subtleties of everything that

---

4. Petersburg was conceived as an imposing city; plans called for regular streets, broad avenues, and spacious squares.

was "beautiful and sublime,"[5] as we used to say at one time, that I didn't become conscious, and instead did such unseemly things, things that . . . well, in short, probably everyone does, but it seemed as if they occurred to me deliberately at the precise moment when I was most conscious that they shouldn't be done at all? The more conscious I was of what was good, of everything "beautiful and sublime," the more deeply I sank into the morass and the more capable I was of becoming entirely bogged down in it. But the main thing is that all this didn't seem to be occurring accidentally; rather, it was as if it all had to be so. It was as if this were my most normal condition, not an illness or an affliction at all, so that finally I even lost the desire to struggle against it. It ended when I almost came to believe (perhaps I really did believe) that this might really have been my normal condition. But at first, in the beginning, what agonies I suffered during that struggle! I didn't believe that others were experiencing the same thing; therefore, I kept it a secret about myself all my life. I was ashamed (perhaps I still am even now); I reached the point where I felt some secret, abnormal, despicable little pleasure in returning home to my little corner on some disgusting Petersburg night, acutely aware that once again I'd committed some revolting act that day, that what had been done could not be undone, and I used to gnaw and gnaw at myself inwardly, secretly, nagging away, consuming myself until finally the bitterness turned into some kind of shameful, accursed sweetness and at last into genuine, earnest pleasure! Yes, into pleasure, real pleasure! I absolutely mean that. . . . That's why I first began to speak out, because I want to know for certain whether other people share this same pleasure. Let me explain: the pleasure resulted precisely from the overly acute consciousness of one's own humiliation; from the feeling that one had reached the limit; that it was disgusting, but couldn't be otherwise; you had no other choice—you could never become a different person; and that even if there were still time and faith enough for you to change into something else, most likely you wouldn't even want to change, and if you did, you wouldn't have done anything, perhaps because there really was nothing for you to change into. But the main thing and the final point is that all of this was taking place according to normal and fundamental laws of overly acute consciousness and of the inertia which results directly from these laws; consequently, not only couldn't one change, one simply couldn't do anything at all. Hence it follows, for example, as a result of this overly acute consciousness, that one is absolutely right in being a scoundrel, as if this were some consolation to the scoundrel. But enough of this. . . . Oh, my, I've gone on rather a long time, but have I really explained anything? How can I explain this pleasure? But I will explain it! I shall see it through to the end! That's why I've taken up my pen. . . .

For example, I'm terribly proud. I'm as mistrustful and as sensitive as a hunchback or a dwarf; but, in truth, I've experienced some moments when, if someone had slapped my face, I might even have been grateful for it. I'm being serious. I probably would have been able to derive a peculiar sort of pleasure from it—the pleasure of despair, naturally, but the most intense

5. This phrase originated in Edmund Burke's (1729–1797) *Philosophical Inquiry into the Origin of Our Ideas of the Sublime and Beautiful* (1756) and was repeated in Immanuel Kant's (1724–1804) *Observations on the Feeling of the Beautiful and the Sublime* (1756). It became a cliché in the writings of Russian critics during the 1830s.

pleasures occur in despair, especially when you're very acutely aware of the hopelessness of your own predicament. As for a slap in the face—why, here the consciousness of being beaten to a pulp would overwhelm you. The main thing is, no matter how I try, it still turns out that I'm always the first to be blamed for everything and, what's even worse, I'm always the innocent victim, so to speak, according to the laws of nature. Therefore, in the first place, I'm guilty inasmuch as I'm smarter than everyone around me. (I've always considered myself smarter than everyone around me, and sometimes, believe me, I've been ashamed of it. At the least, all my life I've looked away and never could look people straight in the eye.) Finally, I'm to blame because even if there were any magnanimity in me, it would only have caused more suffering as a result of my being aware of its utter uselessness. After all, I probably wouldn't have been able to make use of that magnanimity: neither to forgive, as the offender, perhaps, had slapped me in accordance with the laws of nature, and there's no way to forgive the laws of nature; nor to forget, because even if there were any laws of nature, it's offensive nonetheless. Finally, even if I wanted to be entirely unmagnanimous, and had wanted to take revenge on the offender, I couldn't be revenged on anyone for anything because, most likely, I would never have decided to do anything, even if I could have. Why not? I'd like to say a few words about that separately.

Summary   In chapters III and IV, the Underground Man discusses the difficulty, for an overly conscious person, of having simple feelings (such as the desire for pure vengeance); he describes his vain search for a "primary cause" on which to base any action or belief, his refusal to be governed by "the laws of nature, the conclusions of natural science and mathematics," and his insistence on self–assertion and individual will despite logic and "natural law."

VII

But these are all golden dreams. Oh, tell me who was first to announce, first to proclaim that man does nasty things simply because he doesn't know his own true interest; and that if he were to be enlightened, if his eyes were to be opened to his true, normal interests, he would stop doing nasty things at once and would immediately become good and noble, because, being so enlightened and understanding his real advantage, he would realize that his own advantage really did lie in the good; and that it's well known that there's not a single man capable of acting knowingly against his own interest; consequently, he would, so to speak, begin to do good out of necessity. Oh, the child! Oh, the pure, innocent babe! Well, in the first place, when was it during all these millennia, that man has ever acted only in his own self interest? What does one do with the millions of facts bearing witness to the one fact that people knowingly, that is, possessing full knowledge of their own true interests, have relegated them to the background and have rushed down a different path, that of risk and chance, compelled by no one and nothing, but merely as if they didn't want to follow the beaten track, and so they stubbornly, willfully forged another way, a difficult and absurd one, searching for it almost in the darkness? Why, then, this means that stubbornness and willfulness were really more pleasing to them than any kind of advantage. . . . Advantage! What is advantage? Will you take it upon yourself to define with absolute precision what constitutes man's advantage? And what if it turns out that man's advantage sometimes not only may, but even must in certain circumstances, consist precisely in his desiring something harmful to himself instead of something advantageous? And if this is so, if this can ever occur, then the whole theory falls to pieces. What do you think, can such a thing happen? You're laughing; laugh, gentlemen, but answer me: have man's advantages ever been calculated with absolute certainty? Aren't there some which don't fit, can't be made to fit into any classification? Why, as far as I know, you gentlemen have derived your list of human advantages from averages of statistical data and from scientific-economic formulas. But your advantages are prosperity, wealth, freedom, peace, and so on and so forth; so that a man who, for example, expressly and knowingly acts in opposition to this whole list, would be, in you opinion, and in mine, too, of course, either an obscurantist or a complete madman, wouldn't he? But now here's what's astonishing: why is it that when all these statisticians, sages, and lovers of humanity enumerate man's advantages, they invariably leave one out? They don't even take it into consideration in the form in which it should be considered, although the entire calculation depends upon it. There would be no great harm in considering it, this advantage, and adding it to the list. But the whole point is that this particular advantage doesn't fit into any classification and can't be found on any list. I have a friend, for instance. . . . But gentlemen! Why, he's your friend, too! In fact, he's everyone's friend! When he's preparing to do something, this gentleman straight away explains to you eloquently and clearly just how he must act according to the laws of nature and truth. And that's not all: with excitement and passion he'll tell you all about genuine, normal human interests; with scorn he'll reproach the shortsighted fools who understand neither their own advantage nor the real meaning of virtue; and then—exactly a quarter of an hour later, without any sudden outside cause, but precisely because of something internal that's stronger than all his interests—he does a complete about-face; that is, he does something which clearly contradicts what he's been saying: it goes against the laws of reason and his own advantage, in a word, against everything. . . . I warn you that my friend is a collective personage; therefore it's rather difficult to blame only him. That's just it, gentlemen; in fact, isn't there something dearer to every man than his own best advantage, or (so as not to violate the rules of logic) isn't there one more advantageous advantage (exactly the one omitted, the one we mentioned before), which is more important and more advantageous than all others and, on behalf of which, a man will, if necessary, go against all laws, that is, against reason, honor, peace, and prosperity—in a word, against all those splendid and useful things, merely in order to attain this fundamental, most advantageous advantage which is dearer to him than everything else?

"Well, it's advantage all the same," you say, interrupting me. Be so kind as to allow me to explain further; besides, the point is not my pun, but the fact that this advantage is remarkable precisely because it destroys all our classifications and constantly demolishes all systems devised by lovers of humanity for the happiness of mankind. In a word, it interferes with everything. But, before I name this advantage, I want to compromise myself personally; therefore I boldly declare that all these splendid systems, all these theories to explain to mankind its real, normal interests so that, by necessarily striving to achieve them, it would immediately become good and noble—are, for the time being, in my opinion, nothing more than logical exercises! Yes, sir, logical exercises! Why, even to maintain a theory of mankind's regeneration through a system of its own advantages, why, in my opinion, that's almost the same as . . . well, claiming, for instance, following Buckle,[6] that man has become kinder as a result of civilization; consequently, he's becoming less bloodthirsty and less inclined to war. Why, logically it all even seems to follow. But man is so partial to systems and abstract conclusions that he's ready to distort the truth intentionally, ready to deny everything that he himself has ever seen and heard, merely in order to justify his own logic. That's why I take this example, because it's such a glaring one. Just look around: rivers of blood are being spilt, and in the most cheerful way, as if it were champagne. Take this entire nineteenth century of ours during which even Buckle lived. Take Napoleon—both the great and the present one.[7] Take North America— that eternal union.[8] Take, finally, that ridiculous Schleswig-Holstein[9]. . . . What is it that civilization makes kinder in us? Civilization merely promotes a wider variety of sensations in man and . . . absolutely nothing else. And through the development of this variety man may even reach the point where he takes pleasure in spilling blood. Why, that's even happened to him already. Haven't you noticed that the most refined blood-shedders are almost always the most civilized gentlemen to whom all these Attila the Huns and Stenka Razins[1] are scarcely fit to hold a candle; and if they're not as conspicuous as Attila and Stenka Razin, it's precisely because they're too common and have become too familiar to us. At least if man hasn't become more bloodthirsty as a result of civilization, surely he's become bloodthirsty in a nastier, more repulsive way than before. Previously man saw justice in bloodshed and exterminated whomever he wished with a clear conscience; whereas now, though we consider bloodshed to be abominable, we nevertheless engage in this abomination even more than before. Which is worse? Decide for yourselves. They say that Cleopatra (forgive an example from Roman history) loved to stick gold pins into the breasts of her slave girls and take pleasure in their screams and writhing. You'll say that this took place, relatively speaking, in barbaric times; that these are barbaric times too, because (also comparatively speaking), gold pins are used even now; that even now, although man has learned on occasion to see more clearly than in barbaric times, *he's still far from having learned* how to act in accordance with the dictates of reason and science. Nevertheless, you're still absolutely convinced that he will learn how to do so, as soon as he gets rid of some bad, old habits and as soon as common sense and science have completely re-educated human nature and have turned it in the proper direction. You're convinced that then man will voluntarily stop committing blunders, and that he will, so to speak, never willingly set his own will in opposition to his own normal interests. More than that: then, you say, science itself will teach man (though, in my opinion, that's already a luxury) that in fact he possesses nei-

6. In his *History of Civilization in England* (1857–61), Henry Thomas Buckle (1821–1862) argued that the development of civilization necessarily leads to the cessation of war. Russia had recently been involved in fierce fighting in the Crimea (1853–56).   7. The French emperors Napoleon I (1769–1821) and his nephew Napoleon III (1808–1873), both of whom engaged in numerous wars, though on vastly different scales.   8. The United States was in the middle of its Civil War (1861–65).   9. The German duchies of Schleswig and Holstein, held by Denmark since 1773, were reunited with Prussia after a brief war in 1864.   1. Cossack leader (died 1671) who organized a peasant rebellion in Russia. Attila (406?–453 C.E.), king of the Huns, who conducted devastating wars against the Roman emperors.

ther a will nor any whim of his own, that he never did, and that he himself is nothing more than a kind of piano key or an organ stop;[2] that, moreover, there still exist laws of nature, so that everything he's done has been not in accordance with his own desire, but in and of itself, according to the laws of nature. Consequently, we need only discover these laws of nature, and man will no longer have to answer for his own actions and will find it extremely easy to live. All human actions, it goes without saying, will then be tabulated according to these laws, mathematically, like tables of logarithms up to 108,000, and will be entered on a schedule; or even better, certain edifying works will be published, like our contemporary encyclopedic dictionaries, in which everything will be accurately calculated and specified so that there'll be no more actions or adventures left on earth.

At that time, it's still you speaking, new economic relations will be established, all ready-made, also calculated with mathematical precision, so that all possible questions will disappear in a single instant, simply because all possible answers will have been provided. Then the crystal palace[3] will be built. And then . . . Well, in a word, those will be our halcyon days. Of course, there's no way to guarantee (now this is me talking) that it won't be, for instance, terribly boring then (because there won't be anything left to do, once everything has been calculated according to tables); on the other hand, everything will be extremely rational. Of course, what don't people think up out of boredom! Why, even gold pins get stuck into other people out of boredom, but that wouldn't matter. What's really bad (this is me talking again) is that for all I know, people might even be grateful for those gold pins. For man is stupid, phenomenally stupid. That is, although he's not really stupid at all, he's really so ungrateful that it's hard to find another being quite like him. Why, I, for example, wouldn't be surprised in the least, if, suddenly, for no reason at all, in the midst of this future, universal rationalism, some gentleman with an offensive, rather, a retrograde and derisive expression on his face were to stand up, put his hands on his hips, and declare to us all: "How about it, gentlemen, what if we knock over all this rationalism with one swift kick for the sole purpose of sending all these logarithms to hell, so that once again we can live according to our own stupid will!" But that wouldn't matter either; what's so annoying is that he would undoubtedly find some followers; such is the way man is made. And all because of the most foolish reason, which, it seems, is hardly worth mentioning: namely, that man, always and everywhere, whoever he is, has preferred to act as he wished, and not at all as reason and advantage have dictated; one might even desire something opposed to one's own advantage, and sometimes (this is now my idea) one *positively must do so*. One's very own free, unfettered desire, one's own whim, no matter how wild, one's own fantasy, even though sometimes roused to the point of madness—all this constitutes precisely that previously omitted, most advantageous advantage which isn't included under any classification and because of which all systems and theories are constantly smashed to smithereens. Where did these sages ever get the idea that man

---

2. A reference to the last discourse of the French philosopher Denis Diderot (1713–1784) in the *Conversation of D'Alembert and Diderot* (1769).   3. An allusion to the crystal palace described in Vera Pavlovna's fourth dream in Chernyshevsky's *What Is to Be Done?* as well as to the actual building designed by Sir Joseph Paxton, erected for the Great Exhibition in London in 1851 and at that time admired as the newest wonder of architecture; Dostoevsky described it in *Winter Notes on Summer Impressions* (1863).

needs any normal, virtuous desire? How did they ever imagine that man needs any kind of rational, advantageous desire? Man needs only one thing—his own *independent* desire, whatever that independence might cost and wherever it might lead. And as far as desire goes, the devil only knows. . . .

<h2 style="text-align:center">VIII</h2>

"Ha, ha, ha! But in reality even this desire, if I may say so, doesn't exist!" you interrupt me with a laugh. "Why science has already managed to dissect man so now we know that desire and so-called free choice are nothing more than . . ."

"Wait, gentlemen, I myself wanted to begin like that. I must confess that even I got frightened. I was just about to declare that the devil only knows what desire depends on and perhaps we should be grateful for that, but then I remembered about science and I . . . stopped short. But now you've gone and brought it up. Well, after all, what if someday they really do discover the formula for all our desires and whims, that is, the thing that governs them, precise laws that produce them, how exactly they're applied, where they lead in each and every case, and so on and so forth, that is, the genuine mathematical formula—why, then all at once man might stop desiring, yes, indeed, he probably would. Who would want to desire according to some table? And that's not all: he would immediately be transformed from a person into an organ stop or something of that sort; because what is man without desire, without will, and without wishes if not a stop in an organ pipe? What do you think? Let's consider the probabilities—can this really happen or not?"

"Hmmm . . . ," you decide, "our desires are mistaken for the most part because of an erroneous view of our own advantage. Consequently, we sometimes desire pure rubbish because, in our own stupidity, we consider it the easiest way to achieve some previously assumed advantage. Well, and when all this has been analyzed, calculated on paper (that's entirely possible, since it's repugnant and senseless to assume in advance that man will never come to understand the laws of nature) then, of course, all so-called desires will no longer exist. For if someday desires are completely reconciled with reason, we'll follow reason instead of desire simply because it would be impossible, for example, while retaining one's reason, to *desire* rubbish, and thus knowingly oppose one's reason, and desire something harmful to oneself. . . . And, since all desires and reasons can really be tabulated, since someday the laws of our so-called free choice are sure to be discovered, then, all joking aside, it may be possible to establish something like a table, so that we could actually desire according to it. If, for example, someday they calculate and demonstrate to me that I made a rude gesture because I couldn't possibly refrain from it, that I had to make precisely that gesture, well, in that case, what sort of *free choice* would there be, especially if I'm a learned man and have completed a course of study somewhere? Why, then I'd be able to calculate in advance my entire life for the next thirty years; in a word, if such a table were to be drawn up, there'd be nothing left for us to do; we'd simply have to accept it. In general, we should be repeating endlessly to ourselves that at such a time and in such circumstances nature certainly won't ask our opinion; that we must accept it as is, and not as we fantasize it, and that if we really aspire to prepare a table, a schedule, and, well . . . well, even a laboratory test tube, there's nothing to be done—one must even accept the test tube! If not, it'll be accepted even without you. . . .

"Yes, but that's just where I hit a snag! Gentlemen, you'll excuse me for all this philosophizing; it's a result of my forty years in the underground! Allow me to fantasize. Don't you see: reason is a fine thing, gentlemen, there's no doubt about it, but it's only reason, and it satisfies only man's rational faculty, whereas desire is a manifestation of all life, that is, of all human life, which includes both reason, as well as all of life's itches and scratches. And although in this manifestation life often turns out to be fairly worthless, it's life all the same, and not merely the extraction of square roots. Why, take me, for instance; I quite naturally want to live in order to satisfy all my faculties of life, not merely my rational faculty, that is, some one-twentieth of all my faculties. What does reason know? Reason knows only what it's managed to learn. (Some things it may never learn; while this offers no comfort, why not admit it openly?) But human nature acts as a whole, with all that it contains, consciously and unconsciously; and although it may tell lies, it's still alive. I suspect, gentlemen, that you're looking at me with compassion; you repeat that an enlightened and cultured man, in a word, man as he will be in the future, cannot knowingly desire something disadvantageous to himself, and that this is pure mathematics. I agree with you: it really is mathematics. But I repeat for the one-hundredth time, there is one case, only one, when a man may intentionally, consciously desire even something harmful to himself, something stupid, even very stupid, namely: in order *to have the right* to desire something even very stupid and not be bound by an obligation to desire only what's smart. After all, this very stupid thing, one's own whim, gentlemen, may in fact be the most advantageous thing on earth for people like me, especially in certain cases. In particular, it may be more advantageous than any other advantage, even in a case where it causes obvious harm and contradicts the most sensible conclusions of reason about advantage—because in any case it preserves for us what's most important and precious, that is, our personality and our individuality. There are some people who maintain that in fact this is more precious to man than anything else; of course, desire can, if it so chooses, coincide with reason, especially if it doesn't abuse this option, and chooses to coincide in moderation; this is useful and sometimes even commendable. But very often, even most of the time, desire absolutely and stubbornly disagrees with reason and . . . and . . . and, do you know, sometimes this is also useful and even very commendable? Let's assume, gentlemen, that man isn't stupid. (And really, this can't possibly be said about him at all, if only because if he's stupid, then who on earth is smart?) But even if he's not stupid, he is, nevertheless, monstrously ungrateful. Phenomenally ungrateful. I even believe that the best definition of man is this: a creature who walks on two legs and is ungrateful. But that's still not all; that's still not his main defect. His main defect is his perpetual misbehavior, perpetual from the time of the Great Flood to the Schleswig-Holstein period of human destiny. Misbehavior, and consequently, imprudence; for it's long been known that imprudence results from nothing else but misbehavior. Just cast a glance at the history of mankind; well, what do you see? Is it majestic? Well, perhaps it's majestic; why, the

Colossus of Rhodes,[4] for example—that alone is worth something! Not without reason did Mr Anaevsky[5] report that some people consider it to be the product of human hands, while others maintain that it was created by nature itself. Is it colorful? Well, perhaps it's also colorful; just consider the dress uniforms, both military and civilian, of all nations at all times—why, that alone is worth something, and if you include everyday uniforms, it'll make your eyes bulge; not one historian will be able to sort it all out. Is it monotonous? Well, perhaps it's monotonous, too: men fight and fight; now they're fighting; they fought first and they fought last—you'll agree that it's really much too monotonous. In short, anything can be said about world history, anything that might occur to the most disordered imagination. There's only one thing that can't possibly be said about it—that it's rational. You'll choke on the word. Yet here's just the sort of thing you'll encounter all the time: why, in life you're constantly running up against people who are so well-behaved and so rational, such wise men and lovers of humanity who set themselves the lifelong goal of behaving as morally and rationally as possible, so to speak, to be a beacon for their nearest and dearest, simply in order to prove that it's really possible to live one's life in a moral and rational way. And so what? It's a well-known fact that many of these lovers of humanity, sooner or later, by the end of their lives, have betrayed themselves: they've pulled off some caper, sometimes even quite an indecent one. Now I ask you: what can one expect from man as a creature endowed with such strange qualities? Why, shower him with all sorts of earthly blessings, submerge him in happiness over his head so that only little bubbles appear on the surface of this happiness, as if on water, give him such economic prosperity that he'll have absolutely nothing left to do except sleep, eat gingerbread, and worry about the continuation of world history—even then, out of pure ingratitude, sheer perversity, he'll commit some repulsive act. He'll even risk losing his gingerbread, and will intentionally desire the most wicked rubbish, the most uneconomical absurdity, simply in order to inject his own pernicious fantastic element into all this positive rationality. He wants to hold onto those most fantastic dreams, his own indecent stupidity solely for the purpose of assuring himself (as if it were necessary) that men are still men and not piano keys, and that even if the laws of nature play upon them with their own hands, they're still threatened by being overplayed until they won't possibly desire anything more than a schedule. But that's not all: even if man really turned out to be a piano key, even if this could be demonstrated to him by natural science and pure mathematics, even then he still won't become reasonable; he'll intentionally do something to the contrary, simply out of ingratitude, merely to have his own way. If he lacks the means, he'll cause destruction and chaos, he'll devise all kinds of suffering and have his own way! He'll leash a curse upon the world; and, since man alone can do so (it's his privilege and the thing that most distinguishes him from other animals), perhaps only through this curse will he achieve his goal, that is, become really convinced that he's a man and not a piano key! If you say that one can also calculate all this according to a table,

4. A large bronze statue of the sun god, Helios, built between 292 and 280 b.c.e. in the harbor of Rhodes (an island in the Aegean Sea) and considered one of the Seven Wonders of the Ancient World.   5. A. E. Anaevsky was a critic whose articles were frequently ridiculed in literary polemics of the period.

this chaos and darkness, these curses, so that the mere possibility of calculating it all in advance would stop everything and that reason alone would
prevail—in that case man would go insane deliberately in order not to have
reason, but to have his own way! I believe this, I vouch for it, because, after
all, the whole of man's work seems to consist only in proving to himself constantly that he's a man and not an organ stop! Even if he has to lose his own
skin, he'll prove it; even if he has to become a troglodyte, he'll prove it. And
after that, how can one not sin, how can one not praise the fact that all this
hasn't yet come to pass and that desire still depends on the devil knows
what . . . ?"

You'll shout at me (if you still choose to favor me with your shouts) that no
one's really depriving me of my will; that they're merely attempting to
arrange things so that my will, by its own free choice, will coincide with my
normal interests, with the laws of nature, and with arithmetic.

"But gentlemen, what sort of free choice will there be when it comes down
to tables and arithmetic, when all that's left is two times two makes four?
Two times two makes four even without my will. Is that what you call free
choice?"

IX

Gentlemen, I'm joking of course, and I myself know that it's not a very
good joke; but, after all, you can't take everything as a joke. Perhaps I'm
gnashing my teeth while I joke. I'm tormented by questions, gentlemen;
answer them for me. Now, for example, you want to cure man of his old
habits and improve his will according to the demands of science and common sense. But how do you know not only whether it's possible, but even if
it's *necessary* to remake him in this way? Why do you conclude that human
desire *must* undoubtedly be improved? In short, how do you know that such
improvement will really be to man's advantage? And, to be perfectly frank,
why are you so *absolutely* convinced that not to oppose man's real, normal
advantage guaranteed by the conclusions of reason and arithmetic is really
always to man's advantage and constitutes a law for all humanity? After all,
this is still only an assumption of yours. Let's suppose that it's a law of logic,
but perhaps not a law of humanity. Perhaps, gentlemen, you're wondering if
I'm insane? Allow me to explain. I agree that man is primarily a creative animal, destined to strive consciously toward a goal and to engage in the art of
engineering, that, is, externally and incessantly building new roads for himself *wherever they lead*. But sometimes he may want to swerve aside precisely
because he's *compelled* to build these roads, and perhaps also because, no
matter how stupid the spontaneous man of action may generally be, nevertheless it sometimes occurs to him that the road, as it turns out, almost
always leads *somewhere or other*, and that the main thing isn't so much
where it goes, but the fact that it does, and that the well-behaved child, dis-
regarding the art of engineering, shouldn't yield to pernicious idleness
which, as is well known, constitutes the mother of all vices. Man loves to
create and build roads; that's indisputable. But why is he also so passionately fond of destruction and chaos? Now, then, tell me. But I myself want
to say a few words about this separately. Perhaps the reason that he's so fond
of destruction and chaos (after all, it's indisputable that he sometimes really

loves it, and that's a fact) is that he himself has an instinctive fear of achieving his goal and completing the project under construction? How do you know if perhaps he loves his building only from afar, but not from close up; perhaps he only likes building it, but not living in it, leaving it afterward *aux animaux domestiques*,[6] such as ants or sheep, or so on and so forth. Now ants have altogether different tastes. They have one astonishing structure of a similar type, forever indestructible—the anthill.

The worthy ants began with the anthill, and most likely, they will end with the anthill, which does great credit to their perseverance and steadfastness. But man is a frivolous and unseemly creature and perhaps, like a chess player, he loves only the process of achieving his goal, and not the goal itself. And, who knows (one can't vouch for it), perhaps the only goal on earth toward which mankind is striving consists merely in this incessant process of achieving or to put it another way, in life itself, and not particularly in the goal which, of course, must always be none other than two times two makes four, that is, a formula; after all, two times two makes four is no longer life, gentlemen, but the beginning of death. At least man has always been somewhat afraid of this two times two makes four, and I'm afraid of it now, too. Let's suppose that the only thing man does is search for this two times two makes four; he sails across oceans, sacrifices his own life in the quest; but to seek it out and find it—really and truly, he's very frightened. After all, he feels that as soon as he finds it, there'll be nothing left to search for. Workers, after finishing work, at least receive their wages, go off to a tavern, and then wind up at a police station—now that's a full week's occupation. But where will man go? At any rate a certain awkwardness can be observed each time he approaches the achievement of similar goals. He loves the process, but he's not so fond of the achievement, and that, of course is terribly amusing. In short, man is made in a comical way; obviously there's some sort of catch in all this. But two times two makes four is an insufferable thing, nevertheless. Two times two makes four—why, in my opinion, it's mere insolence. Two times two makes four stands there brazenly with its hands on its hips, blocking your path and spitting at you. I agree that two times two makes four is a splendid thing; but if we're going to lavish praise, then two times two makes five is sometimes also a very charming little thing.

And why are you so firmly, so triumphantly convinced that only the normal and positive—in short, only well-being is advantageous to man? Doesn't reason ever make mistakes about advantage? After all, perhaps man likes something other than well-being? Perhaps he loves suffering just as much? Perhaps suffering is just as advantageous to him as well-being? Man sometimes loves suffering terribly, to the point of passion, and that's a fact. There's no reason to study world history on this point; if indeed you're a man and have lived at all, just ask yourself. As far as my own personal opinion is concerned, to love only well-being is somehow even indecent. Whether good or bad, it's sometimes also very pleasant to demolish something. After all, I'm not standing up for suffering here, nor for well-being, either. I'm standing up for . . . my own whim and for its being guaranteed

6. To domestic animals (French).

to me whenever necessary. For instance, suffering is not permitted in vaudevilles,[7] that I know. It's also inconceivable in the crystal palace; suffering is doubt and negation. What sort of crystal palace would it be if any doubt were allowed? Yet, I'm convinced that man will never renounce real suffering, that is, destruction and chaos. After all, suffering is the sole cause of consciousness. Although I stated earlier that in my opinion consciousness is man's greatest misfortune, still I know that man loves it and would not exchange it for any other sort of satisfaction. Consciousness, for example, is infinitely higher than two times two. Of course, after two times two, there's nothing left, not merely nothing to do, but nothing to learn. Then the only thing possible will be to plug up your five senses and plunge into contemplation. Well, even if you reach the same result with consciousness, that is, having nothing left to do, at least you'll be able to flog yourself from time to time, and that will liven things up a bit. Although it may be reactionary, it's still better than nothing.

X[8]

You believe in the crystal palace, eternally indestructible, that is, one at which you can never stick out your tongue furtively nor make a rude gesture, even with your fist hidden away. Well, perhaps I'm so afraid of this building precisely because it's made of crystal and it's eternally indestructible, and because it won't be possible to stick one's tongue out even furtively.

Don't you see: if it were a chicken coop instead of a palace, and if it should rain, then perhaps I could crawl into it so as not to get drenched; but I would still not mistake a chicken coop for a palace out of gratitude, just because it sheltered me from the rain. You're laughing, you're even saying that in this case there's no difference between a chicken coop and a mansion. Yes, I reply, if the only reason for living is to keep from getting drenched.

But what if I've taken it into my head that this is not the only reason for living, and, that if one is to live at all, one might as well live in a mansion? Such is my wish, my desire. You'll expunge it from me only when you've changed my desires. Well, then, change them, tempt me with something else, give me some other ideal. In the meantime, I still won't mistake a chicken coop for a palace. But let's say that the crystal palace is a hoax, that according to the laws of nature it shouldn't exist, and that I've invented it only out of my own stupidity, as a result of certain antiquated, irrational habits of my generation. But what do I care if it doesn't exist? What difference does it make if it exists only in my own desires, or, to be more precise, if it exists as long as my desires exist? Perhaps you're laughing again? Laugh, if you wish; I'll resist all your laughter and I still won't say I'm satiated if I'm really hungry; I know all the same that I won't accept a compromise, an infinitely recurring zero, just because it exists according to the laws of nature and it *really* does exist. I won't accept as the crown of my desires a large building with tenements for poor tenants to be rented for a thousand years and, just in case, with the name of the dentist Wagenheim on the sign. Destroy my desires, eradicate

---

7. A dramatic genre, popular on the Russian stage, consisting of scenes from contemporary life acted with a satirical twist, often in racy dialogue.   8. This chapter was badly mutilated by the censor, as Dostoevsky makes clear in the letter to his brother Mikhail, dated March 26, 1864 (see the headnote).

my ideals, show me something better and I'll follow you. You may say, perhaps, that it's not worth getting involved; but, in that case, I'll say the same thing in reply. We're having a serious discussion; if you don't grant me your attention, I won't grovel for it. I still have my underground.

And, as long as I'm still alive and feel desire—may my arm wither away before it contributes even one little brick to that building! Never mind that I myself have just rejected the crystal palace for the sole reason that it won't be possible to tease it by sticking out one's tongue at it. I didn't say that because I'm so fond of sticking out my tongue. Perhaps the only reason I got angry is that among all your buildings there's still not a single one where you don't feel compelled to stick out your tongue. On the contrary, I'd let my tongue be cut off out of sheer gratitude, if only things could be so arranged that I'd no longer want to stick it out. What do I care if things can't be so arranged and if I must settle for some tenements? Why was I made with such desires? Can it be that I was made this way only in order to reach the conclusion that my entire way of being is merely a fraud? Can this be the whole purpose? I don't believe it.

By the way, do you know what? I'm convinced that we underground men should be kept in check. Although capable of sitting around quietly in the underground for some forty years, once he emerges into the light of day and bursts into speech, he talks on and on and on. . . .

XI

The final result, gentlemen, is that it's better to do nothing! Conscious inertia is better! And so, long live the underground! Even though I said that I envy the normal man to the point of exasperation, I still wouldn't want to be him under the circumstances in which I see him (although I still won't keep from envying him. No, no, in any case the underground is more advantageous!) At least there one can . . . Hey, but I'm lying once again! I'm lying because I know myself as surely as two times two, that it isn't really the underground that's better, but something different, altogether different, something that I long for, but I'll never be able to find! To hell with the underground! Why, here's what would be better: if I myself were to believe even a fraction of everything I've written. I swear to you, gentlemen, that I don't believe one word, not one little word of all that I've scribbled. That is, I do believe it, perhaps, but at the very same time, I don't know why, I feel and suspect that I'm lying like a trooper.

"Then why did you write all this?" you ask me.

"What if I'd shut you up in the underground for forty years with nothing to do and then came back forty years later to see what had become of you? Can a man really be left alone for forty years with nothing to do?"

"Isn't it disgraceful, isn't it humiliating!" you might say, shaking your head in contempt. "You long for life, but you try to solve life's problems by means of a logical tangle. How importunate, how insolent your outbursts, and how frightened you are at the same time! You talk rubbish, but you're constantly afraid of them and make apologies. You maintain that you fear nothing, but at the same time you try to ingratiate yourself with us. You assure us that you're gnashing your teeth, yet at the same time you try to be witty and amuse us. You know that your witticisms are not very clever, but apparently you're pleased by their literary merit. Perhaps you really have suffered, but you don't even respect your own suffering. There's some truth in you, too, but no chastity; out of the pettiest vanity you bring your truth out into the open, into the marketplace, and you shame it. . . . You really want to say something, but you conceal your final word out of fear because you lack the resolve to utter it; you have only cowardly impudence. You boast about your consciousness, but you merely vacillate, because even though your mind is working, your heart has been blackened by depravity, and without a pure heart, there can be no full, genuine consciousness. And how importunate you are; how you force yourself upon others; you behave in such an affected manner. Lies, lies, lies!"

Of course, it was I who just invented all these words for you. That, too, comes from the underground. For forty years in a row I've been listening to all your words through a crack. I've invented them myself, since that's all that's occurred to me. It's no wonder that I've learned it all by heart and that it's taken on such a literary form. . . .

But can you really be so gullible as to imagine that I'll print all this and give it to you to read? And here's another problem I have: why do I keep calling you "gentlemen"? Why do I address you as if you really were my readers? Confessions such as the one I plan to set forth here aren't published and given to other people to read. Anyway, I don't possess sufficient fortitude, nor do I consider it necessary to do so. But don't you see, a certain notion has come into my mind, and I wish to realize it at any cost. Here's the point.

Every man has within his own reminiscences certain things he doesn't reveal to anyone, except, perhaps, to his friends. There are also some that he won't reveal even to his friends, only to himself perhaps, and even then, in secret. Finally, there are some which a man is afraid to reveal even to himself; every decent man has accumulated a fair number of such things. In fact, it can even be said that the more decent the man, the more of these things he's accumulated. Anyway, only recently I myself decided to recall some of my earlier adventures; up to now I've always avoided them, even with a certain anxiety. But having decided not only to recall them, but even to write them down, now is when I wish to try an experiment: is it possible to be absolutely honest even with one's own self and not to fear the whole truth? Incidentally, I'll mention that Heine maintains that faithful autobiographies are almost impossible, and that a man is sure to lie about himself.[9] In Heine's opinion, Rousseau, for example, undoubtedly told untruths about himself in his confession and even lied intentionally, out of vanity. I'm convinced that Heine is correct; I understand perfectly well that sometimes it's possible out of vanity alone to impute all sorts of crimes to oneself, and I can even understand what sort of vanity that might be. But Heine was making judgments about a person who confessed to the public. I, however, am writing for myself alone and declare once and for all that if I write as if I were addressing readers, that's only for show, because it's easier for me to write that way. It's a form, simply a form; I shall never have any readers. I've already stated that. . . . I don't want to be restricted in any way by editing my notes. I won't attempt to introduce any order or system. I'll write down whatever comes to mind.

9. A reference to the work *On Germany* (1853–54) by the German poet Heinrich Heine (1797–1856), in which on the very first page Heine speaks of Rousseau as lying and inventing disgraceful incidents about himself for his *Confessions*.

Well, now, for example, someone might seize upon my words and ask me, if you really aren't counting on any readers, why do you make such compacts with yourself, and on paper no less; that is, if you're not going to introduce any order or system, if you're going to write down whatever comes to mind, etc., etc.? Why do you go on explaining? Why do you keep apologizing?

"Well, imagine that," I reply.

This, by the way, contains an entire psychology. Perhaps it's just that I'm a coward. Or perhaps it's that I imagine an audience before me on purpose, so that I behave more decently when I'm writing things down. There may be a thousand reasons.

But here's something else: why is it that I want to write? If it's not for the public, then why can't I simply recall it all in my own mind and not commit it to paper?

Quite so; but somehow it appears more dignified on paper. There's something more impressive about it; I'll be a better judge of myself; the style will be improved. Besides, perhaps I'll actually experience some relief from the process of writing it all down. Today, for example, I'm particularly oppressed by one very old memory from my distant past. It came to me vividly several days ago and since then it's stayed with me, like an annoying musical motif that doesn't want to leave you alone. And yet you must get rid of it. I have hundreds of such memories; but at times a single one emerges from those hundreds and oppresses me. For some reason I believe that if I write it down I can get rid of it. Why not try?

Lastly, I'm bored, and I never do anything. Writing things down actually seems like work. They say that work makes a man become good and honest. Well, at least there's a chance.

It's snowing today, an almost wet, yellow, dull snow. It was snowing yesterday too, a few days ago as well. I think it was apropos of the wet snow that I recalled this episode and now it doesn't want to leave me alone. And so, let it be a tale apropos of wet snow.

II

Apropos of Wet Snow

> When from the darkness of delusion
> I saved your fallen soul
> With ardent words of conviction,
> And, full of profound torment,
> Wringing your hands, you cursed
> The vice that had ensnared you;
> When, punishing by recollection
> Your forgetful conscience,
> You told me the tale
> Of all that had happened before,
> And, suddenly, covering your face,
> Full of shame and horror,
> You tearfully resolved,
> Indignant, shaken . . .
> Etc., etc., etc.
> From the poetry of N. A. Nekrasov[1]

1. Nikolay A. Nekrasov (1821–1878) was a famous Russian poet and editor of radical sympathies. The poem quoted dates from 1845, and is without title. It ends with the lines, "And enter my house bold and free / To become its full mistress!"

I

At that time I was only twenty-four years old. Even then my life was gloomy, disordered, and solitary to the point of savagery. I didn't associate with anyone; I even avoided talking, and I retreated further and further into my corner. At work in the office I even tried not to look at anyone; I was aware not only that my colleagues considered me eccentric, but that they always seemed to regard me with a kind of loathing. Sometimes I wondered why it was that no one else thinks that others regard him with loathing. One of our office-workers had a repulsive pock-marked face which even appeared somewhat villainous. It seemed to me that with such a disreputable face I'd never have dared look at anyone. Another man had a uniform so worn that there was a foul smell emanating from him. Yet, neither of these two gentlemen was embarrassed—neither because of his clothes, nor his face, nor in any moral way. Neither one imagined that other people regarded him with loathing; and if either had so imagined, it wouldn't have mattered at all, as long as their supervisor chose not to view him that way. It's perfectly clear to me now, because of my unlimited vanity and the great demands I accordingly made on myself, that I frequently regarded myself with a furious dissatisfaction verging on loathing; as a result, I intentionally ascribed my own view to everyone else. For example, I despised my own face; I considered it hideous, and I even suspected that there was something repulsive in its expression. Therefore, every time I arrived at work, I took pains to behave as independently as possible, so that I couldn't be suspected of any malice, and I tried to assume as noble an expression as possible. "It may not be a handsome face," I thought, "but let it be noble, expressive, and above all, extremely *intelligent*." But I was agonizingly certain that my face couldn't possibly express all these virtues. Worst of all, I considered it positively stupid. I'd have been reconciled if it had looked intelligent. In fact, I'd even have agreed to have it appear repulsive, on the condition that at the same time people would find my face terribly intelligent.

Of course, I hated all my fellow office-workers from the first to the last and despised every one of them; yet, at the same time it was as if I were afraid of them. Sometimes it happened that I would even regard them as superior to me. At this time these changes would suddenly occur: first I would despise them, then I would regard them as superior to me. A cultured and decent man cannot be vain without making unlimited demands on himself and without hating himself, at times to the point of contempt. But, whether hating them or regarding them as superior, I almost always lowered my eyes when meeting anyone. I even conducted experiments: could I endure someone's gaze? I'd always be the first to lower my eyes. This infuriated me to the point of madness. I slavishly worshipped the conventional in everything external. I embraced the common practice and feared any eccentricity with all my soul. But how could I sustain it? I was morbidly refined, as befits any cultured man of our time. All others resembled one another as sheep in a flock. Perhaps I was the only one in the whole office who constantly thought of himself as a coward and a slave; and I thought so precisely because I was so cultured. But not only did I think so, it actually was so: I was a coward and a slave. I say this without any embarrassment. Every decent man of our time is and must be a coward and a slave. This is his normal condition. I'm deeply convinced of it. This is how he's made and what he's meant to be. And not only at the present time, as the result of some accidental circumstance, but in general at all times, a decent man must be a coward and a slave. This is a law of nature for all decent men on earth. If one of them should happen to be brave about something or other, we shouldn't be comforted or distracted: he'll still lose his nerve about something else. That's the single and eternal way out. Only asses and their mongrels are brave, and even then, only until they come up against a wall. It's not worthwhile paying them any attention because they really don't mean anything at all.

There was one more circumstance tormenting me at that time: no one was like me, and I wasn't like anyone else. "I'm alone," I mused, "and they are *everyone*"; and I sank deep into thought.

From all this it's clear that I was still just a boy.

The exact opposite would also occur. Sometimes I would find it repulsive to go to the office: it reached the point where I would often return home from work ill. Then suddenly, for no good reason at all, a flash of skepticism and indifference would set in (everything came to me in flashes); I would laugh at my own intolerance and fastidiousness, and reproach myself for my *romanticism*. Sometimes I didn't even want to talk to anyone; at other times it reached a point where I not only started talking, but I even thought about striking up a friendship with others. All my fastidiousness would suddenly disappear for no good reason at all. Who knows? Perhaps I never really had any, and it was all affected, borrowed from books. I still haven't answered this question, even up to now. And once I really did become friends with others; I began to visit their houses, play préférance,[2] drink vodka, talk about promotions. . . . But allow me to digress.

We Russians, generally speaking, have never had any of those stupid, transcendent German romantics, or even worse, French romantics, on whom nothing produces any effect whatever: the earth might tremble beneath them, all of France might perish on the barricades, but they remain the same, not even changing for decency's sake; they go on singing their transcendent songs, so to speak, to their dying day, because they're such fools. We here on Russian soil have no fools. It's a well-know fact; that's precisely what distinguishes us from foreigners. Consequently, transcendent natures cannot be found among us in their pure form. That's the result of our "positive" publicists and critics of that period, who hunted for the Kostanzhonglo and the Uncle Pyotr Ivanoviches,[3] foolishly mistaking them for our ideal and slandering our own romantics, considering them to be the same kind of transcendents as one finds in Germany or France. On the contrary, the characteristics of our romantics are absolutely and directly opposed to the transcendent Europeans; not one of those European standards can apply here. (Allow me to use the word "romantic"—it's an old-fashioned little word, well-respected and deserving, familiar to

---

2. A card game for three players.   3. A character in Ivan Goncharov's novel *A Common Story* (1847); a high bureaucrat, a factory owner who teaches lessons of sobriety and good sense to the romantic hero, Alexander Aduyev. Konstanzhonglo is the ideal efficient landowner in the second part of Nikolai Gogol's novel *Dead Souls* (1852).

everyone.) The characteristics of our romantics are to understand everything, *to see everything, often to see it much more clearly than our most positive minds*; not to be reconciled with anyone or anything, but, at the same time, not to balk at anything; to circumvent everything, to yield on every point, to treat everyone diplomatically; never to lose sight of some useful, practical goal (an apartment at government expense, a nice pension, a decoration)—to keep an eye on that goal through all his excesses and his volumes of lyrical verse, and, at the same time, to preserve intact the "beautiful and sublime" to the end of their lives; and, incidentally, to preserve themselves as well, wrapped up in cotton like precious jewelry, if only, for example, for the sake of that same "beautiful and sublime." Our romantic has a very broad nature and is the biggest rogue of all, I can assure you of that . . . even by my own experience. Of course, all this is true if the romantic is smart. But what am I saying? A romantic is always smart; I merely wanted to observe that although we've had some romantic fools, they really don't count at all, simply because while still in their prime they would degenerate completely into Germans, and, in order to preserve their precious jewels more comfortably, they'd settle over there, either in Weimar or in the Black Forest. For instance, I genuinely despised my official position and refrained from throwing it over merely out of necessity, because I myself sat there working and received good money for doing it. And, as a result, please note, I still refrained from throwing it over. Our romantic would sooner lose his mind (which, by the way, very rarely occurs) than give it up, if he didn't have another job in mind; nor is he ever kicked out, unless he's hauled off to the insane asylum as the "King of Spain,"[4] and only if he's gone completely mad. Then again, it's really only the weaklings and towheads who go mad in our country. An enormous number of romantics later rise to significant rank. What extraordinary versatility! And what a capacity for the most contradictory sensations! I used to be consoled by these thoughts back then, and still am even nowadays. That's why there are so many "broad natures" among us, people who never lose their ideals, no matter how low they fall; even though they never lift a finger for the sake of their ideals, even though they're outrageous villains and thieves, nevertheless they respect their original ideals to the point of tears and are extremely honest men at heart. Yes, only among us Russians can the most outrageous scoundrel be absolutely, even sublimely honest at heart, while at the same time never ceasing to be a scoundrel. I repeat, nearly always do our romantics turn out to be very efficient rascals (I use the word "rascal" affectionately); they suddenly manifest such a sense of reality and positive knowledge that their astonished superiors and the general public can only click their tongues at them in amazement.

Their versatility is really astounding; God only knows what it will turn into, how it will develop under subsequent conditions, and what it holds for us in the future. The material is not all that bad! I'm not saying this out of some ridiculous patriotism or jingoism. However, I'm sure that once again

4. An allusion to the hero of Gogol's short story "Diary of a Madman" (1835). Poprishchin, a low-ranking civil servant, sees his aspirations crushed by the enormous bureaucracy. He ends by going insane and imagining himself to be king of Spain.

you think I'm joking. But who knows? Perhaps it's quite the contrary, that is, you're convinced that this is what I really think. In any case, gentlemen, I'll consider that both of these opinions constitute an honor and a particular pleasure. And do forgive me for this digression.

Naturally, I didn't sustain any friendships with my colleagues, and soon I severed all relations after quarreling with them; and, because of my youthful inexperience at the same time, I even stopped greeting them, as if I'd cut them off entirely. That, however, happened to me only once. On the whole, I was always alone.

At home I spent most of my time reading. I tried to stifle all that was constantly seething within me with external sensations. And of all external sensations available, only reading was possible for me. Of course, reading helped a great deal—it agitated, delighted, and tormented me. But at times it was terribly boring. I still longed to be active; and suddenly I sank into dark, subterranean, loathsome depravity—more precisely, petty vice. My nasty little passions were sharp and painful as a result of my constant, morbid irritability. I experienced hysterical fits accompanied by tears and convulsions. Besides reading, I had nowhere else to go—that is, there was nothing to respect in my surroundings, nothing to attract me. In addition, I was overwhelmed by depression; I possessed a hysterical craving for contradictions and contrasts; and, as a result, I plunged into depravity. I haven't said all this to justify myself. . . . But, no, I'm lying. I did want to justify myself. It's for myself, gentlemen, that I include this little observation. I don't want to lie. I've given my word.

I indulged in depravity all alone, at night, furtively, timidly, sordidly, with a feeling of shame that never left me even in my most loathsome moments and drove me at such times to the point of profanity. Even then I was carrying around the underground in my soul. I was terribly afraid of being seen, met, recognized. I visited all sorts of dismal places.

Once, passing by some wretched little tavern late at night, I saw through a lighted window some gentlemen fighting with billiard cues; one of them was thrown out the window. At some other time I would have been disgusted; but just then I was overcome by such a mood that I envied the gentleman who'd been tossed out; I envied him so much that I even walked into the tavern and entered the billiard room. "Perhaps," I thought, "I'll get into a fight, and they'll throw me out the window, too."

I wasn't drunk, but what could I do—after all, depression can drive a man to this kind of hysteria. But nothing came of it. It turned out that I was incapable of being tossed out the window; I left without getting into a fight.

As soon as I set foot inside, some officer put me in my place.

I was standing next to the billiard table inadvertently blocking his way as he wanted to get by; he took hold of me by the shoulders and without a word of warning or explanation, moved me from where I was standing to another place, and he went past as if he hadn't even noticed me. I could have forgiven even a beating, but I could never forgive his moving me out of the way and entirely failing to notice me.

The devil knows what I would have given for a genuine, ordinary quarrel, a decent one, a more *literary* one, so to speak. But I'd been treated as if I were a fly. The officer was about six feet tall, while I'm small and scrawny.

The quarrel, however, was in my hands; all I had to do was protest, and of course they would've thrown me out the window. But I reconsidered and preferred . . . to withdraw resentfully.

I left the tavern confused and upset and went straight home; the next night I continued my petty vice more timidly, more furtively, more gloomily than before, as if I had tears in my eyes—but I continued nonetheless. Don't conclude, however, that I retreated from that officer as a result of any cowardice; I've never been a coward at heart, although I've constantly acted like one in deed, but—wait before you laugh—I can explain this. I can explain anything, you may rest assured.

Oh, if only this officer had been the kind who'd have agreed to fight a duel! But no, he was precisely one of those types (alas, long gone) who preferred to act with their billiard cues or, like Gogol's Lieutenant Pirogov,[5] by appealing to the authorities. They didn't fight duels; in any case, they'd have considered fighting a duel with someone like me, a lowly civilian, to be indecent. In general, they considered duels to be somehow inconceivable, freethinking, French, while they themselves, especially if they happened to be six feet tall, offended other people rather frequently.

In this case I retreated not out of any cowardice, but because of my unlimited vanity. I wasn't afraid of his height, nor did I think I'd receive a painful beating and get thrown out the window. In fact, I'd have had sufficient physical courage; it was moral fortitude I lacked. I was afraid that everyone present—from the insolent billiard marker to the foul-smelling, pimply little clerks with greasy collars who used to hang about—wouldn't understand and would laugh when I started to protest and speak to them in literary Russian. Because, to this very day, it's still impossible for us to speak about a point of honor, that is, not about honor itself, but a point of honor (*point d'honneur*), except in literary language. One can't even refer to a "point of honor" in everyday language. I was fully convinced (a sense of reality, in spite of all my romanticism!) that they would all simply split their sides laughing, and that the officer, instead of giving me a simple beating, that is, an inoffensive one, would certainly apply his knee to my back and drive me around the billiard table; only then perhaps would he have the mercy to throw me out the window. Naturally, this wretched story of mine couldn't possibly end with this alone. Afterward I used to meet this officer frequently on the street and I observed him very carefully. I don't know whether he ever recognized me. Probably not; I reached that conclusion from various observations. As for me, I stared at him with malice and hatred, and continued to do so for several years! My malice increased and became stronger over time. At first I began to make discreet inquiries about him. This was difficult for me to do, since I had so few acquaintances. But once, as I was following him at a distance as though tied to him, someone called to him on the street: that's how I learned his name. Another time I followed him back to his own apartment and for a ten-kopeck piece learned from the doorman where and how he lived, on

5. One of two main characters in Gogol's short story "Nevsky Prospect" (1835). A shallow and self-satisfied officer, he mistakes the wife of a German artisan for a woman of easy virtue and receives a sound thrashing. He decides to lodge an official complaint, but after consuming a cream-filled pastry, thinks better of it.

what floor, with whom, etc.—in a word, all that could be learned from a doorman. One morning, although I never engaged in literary activities, it suddenly occurred to me to draft a description of this officer as a kind of exposé, a caricature, in the form of a tale. I wrote it with great pleasure. I exposed him; I even slandered him. At first I altered his name only slightly, so that it could be easily recognized; but then, upon careful reflection, I changed it. Then I sent the tale off to *Notes of the Fatherland*.[6] But such exposés were no longer in fashion, and they didn't publish my tale. I was very annoyed by that. At times I simply choked on my spite. Finally, I resolved to challenge my opponent to a duel. I composed a beautiful, charming letter to him, imploring him to apologize to me; in case he refused, I hinted rather strongly at a duel. The letter was composed in such a way that if that officer had possessed even the smallest understanding of the "beautiful and sublime," he would have come running, thrown his arms around me, and offered his friendship. That would have been splendid! We would have led such a wonderful life! Such a life! He would have shielded me with his rank; I would have ennobled him with my culture, and, well, with my ideas. Who knows what might have come of it! Imagine it, two years had already passed since he'd insulted me; my challenge was the most ridiculous anachronism, in spite of all the cleverness of my letter in explaining and disguising that fact. But, thank God (to this day I thank the Almighty with tears in my eyes), I didn't send that letter. A shiver runs up and down my spine when I think what might have happened if I had. Then suddenly . . . suddenly, I got my revenge in the simplest manner, a stroke of genius! A brilliant idea suddenly occurred to me. Sometimes on holidays I used to stroll along Nevsky Prospect at about four o'clock in the afternoon, usually on the sunny side. That is, I didn't really stroll; rather, I experienced innumerable torments, humiliations, and bilious attacks. But that's undoubtedly just what I needed. I darted in and out like a fish among the strollers, constantly stepping aside before generals, cavalry officers, hussars, and young ladies. At those moments I used to experience painful spasms in my heart and a burning sensation in my back merely at the thought of my dismal apparel as well as the wretchedness and vulgarity of my darting little figure. This was sheer torture, uninterrupted and unbearable humiliation at the thought, which soon became an incessant and immediate sensation, that I was a fly in the eyes of society, a disgusting, obscene fly—smarter than the rest, more cultured, even nobler—all that goes without saying, but a fly, nonetheless, who incessantly steps aside, insulted and injured by everyone. For what reason did I inflict this torment on myself? Why did I stroll along Nevsky Prospect? I don't know. But something simply *drew* me there at every opportunity.

Then I began to experience surges of that pleasure about which I've already spoken in the first chapter. After the incident with the officer I was drawn there even more strongly; I used to encounter him along Nevsky most often, and it was there that I could admire him. He would also go there, mostly on holidays. He, too, would give way before generals and individuals of superior rank; he, too, would spin like a top among them. But he would

6. A radical literary and political journal published in Petersburg from 1839 to 1867.

simply trample people like me, or even those slightly superior; he would walk directly toward them, as if there were empty space ahead of him; and under no circumstance would he ever step aside. I revelled in my malice as I observed him, and . . . bitterly stepped aside before him every time. I was tortured by the fact that even on the street I found it impossible to stand on an equal footing with him. "Why is it you're always first to step aside?" I badgered myself in insane hysteria, at times waking up at three in the morning. "Why always you and not he? After all, there's no law about it; it isn't written down anywhere. Let it be equal, as it usually is when people of breeding meet: he steps aside halfway and you halfway, and you pass by showing each other mutual respect." But that was never the case, and I continued to step aside, while he didn't even notice that I was yielding to him. Then a most astounding idea suddenly dawned on me. "What if," I thought, "what if I were to meet him and . . . not step aside? Deliberately not step aside, even if it meant bumping into him: how would that be?" This bold idea gradually took such a hold that it afforded me no peace. I dreamt about it incessantly, horribly, and even went to Nevsky more frequently so that I could imagine more clearly how I would do it. I was in ecstasy. The scheme was becoming more and more possible and even probable to me. "Of course, I wouldn't really collide with him," I thought, already feeling more generous toward him in my joy, "but I simply won't turn aside. I'll bump into him, not very painfully, but just so, shoulder to shoulder, as much as decency allows. I'll bump into him the same amount as he bumps into me." At last I made up my mind completely. But the preparations took a very long time. First, in order to look as presentable as possible during the execution of my scheme, I had to worry about my clothes. "In any case, what if, for example, it should occasion a public scandal? (And the public there was *superflu*:[7] a countess, Princess D., and the entire literary world.) It was essential to be well-dressed; that inspires respect and in a certain sense will place us immediately on an equal footing in the eyes of high society." With that goal in mind I requested my salary in advance, and I purchased a pair of black gloves and a decent hat at Churkin's store. Black gloves seemed to me more dignified, more *bon ton*[8] than the lemon-colored ones I'd considered at first. "That would be too glaring, as if the person wanted to be noticed"; so I didn't buy the lemon-colored ones. I'd already procured a fine shirt with white bone cufflinks; but my overcoat constituted a major obstacle. In and of itself it was not too bad at all; it kept me warm; but it was quilted and had a raccoon collar, the epitome of bad taste. At all costs I had to replace the collar with a beaver one, just like on an officer's coat. For this purpose I began to frequent the Shopping Arcade; and, after several attempts, I turned up some cheap German beaver. Although these German beavers wear out very quickly and soon begin to look shabby, at first, when they're brand new, they look very fine indeed; after all, I only needed it for a single occasion. I asked the price: it was still expensive. After considerable reflection I resolved to sell my raccoon collar. I decided to request a loan for the remaining amount—a rather significant sum for me—from Anton Antonych Setochkin, my office chief, a modest man, but a serious and solid one, who never lent money to anyone, but to whom, upon entering the civil service, I'd once been specially recom-

7. Excessively refined (French).   8. In good taste (French).

mended by an important person who'd secured the position for me. I suffered terribly. It seemed monstrous and shameful to ask Anton Antonych for money. I didn't sleep for two or three nights in a row; in general I wasn't getting much sleep those days, and I always had a fever. I would have either a vague sinking feeling in my heart, or else my heart would suddenly begin to thump, thump, thump! . . . At first Anton Antonych was surprised, then he frowned, thought it over, and finally gave me the loan, after securing from me a note authorizing him to deduct the sum from my salary two weeks later. In this way everything was finally ready; the splendid beaver reigned in place of the mangy raccoon, and I gradually began to get down to business. It was impossible to set about it all at once, in a foolhardy way; one had to proceed in this matter very carefully, step by step. But I confess that after many attempts I was ready to despair: we didn't bump into each other, no matter what! No matter how I prepared, no matter how determined I was— it seems that we're just about to bump, when I look up—and once again I've stepped aside while he's gone by without even noticing me. I even used to pray as I approached him that God would grant me determination. One time I'd fully resolved to do it, but the result was that I merely stumbled and fell at his feet because, at the very last moment, only a few inches away from him, I lost my nerve. He stepped over me very calmly, and I bounced to one side like a rubber ball. That night I lay ill with a fever once again and was delirious. Then, everything suddenly ended in the best possible way. The night before I decided once and for all not to go through with my pernicious scheme and to give it all up without success; with that in mind I went to Nevsky Prospect for one last time simply in order to see how I'd abandon the whole thing. Suddenly, three paces away from my enemy, I made up my mind unexpectedly; I closed my eyes and—we bumped into each other forcefully, shoulder to shoulder! I didn't yield an inch and walked by him on a completely equal footing! He didn't even turn around to look at me and pretended that he hadn't even noticed; but he was merely pretending, I'm convinced of that. To this very day I'm convinced of that! Naturally, I got the worst of it; he was stronger, but that wasn't the point. The point was that I'd achieved my goal, I'd maintained my dignity, I hadn't yielded one step, and I'd publicly placed myself on an equal social footing with him. I returned home feeling completely avenged for everything. I was ecstatic. I rejoiced and sang Italian arias. Of course, I won't describe what happened to me three days later; if you've read the first part entitled "Underground," you can guess for yourself. The officer was later transferred somewhere else; I haven't seen him for some fourteen years. I wonder what he's doing nowadays, that dear friend of mine! Whom is he trampling underfoot?

Summary   In chapter II, the Underground Man examines his daydreams of being rich, famous, a hero and saint; he describes his everyday life and goes to visit his former schoolmate Simonov.

III

I found two more of my former schoolmates there with him. Apparently they were discussing some important matter. None of them paid any attention to me when I entered, which was strange since I hadn't seen them for several years. Evidently they considered me some sort of ordinary house fly. They hadn't even treated me like that when we were in school together, although they'd all hated me. Of course, I understood that they must despise me now for my failure in the service and for the fact that I'd sunk so low, was badly dressed, and so on, which, in their eyes, constituted proof of my ineptitude and insignificance. But I still hadn't expected such a degree of contempt. Simonov was even surprised by my visits. All this disconcerted me; I sat down in some distress and began to listen to what they were saying.

The discussion was serious, even heated, and concerned a farewell dinner which these gentlemen wanted to organize jointly as early as the following day for their friend Zverkov, an army officer who was heading for a distant province. Monsieur Zverkov had also been my schoolmate all along. I'd begun to hate him especially in the upper grades. In the lower grades he was merely an attractive, lively lad whom everyone liked. However, I'd hated him in the lower grades, too, precisely because he was such an attractive, lively lad. He was perpetually a poor student and had gotten worse as time went on; he managed to graduate, however, because he had influential connections. During his last year at school he'd come into an inheritance of some two hundred serfs, and, since almost all the rest of us were poor, he'd even begun to brag. He was an extremely uncouth fellow, but a nice lad nonetheless, even when he was bragging. In spite of our superficial, fantastic, and high-flown notions of honor and pride, all of us, except for a very few, would fawn upon Zverkov, the more so the more he bragged. They didn't fawn for any advantage; they fawned simply because he was a man endowed by nature with gifts. Moreover, we'd somehow come to regard Zverkov as a cunning fellow and an expert on good manners. This latter point particularly infuriated me. I hated the shrill, self-confident tone of his voice, his adoration for his own witticisms, which were terribly stupid in spite of his bold tongue; I hated his handsome, stupid face (for which, however, I'd gladly have exchanged my own intelligent one), and the impudent bearing typical of officers during the 1840s. I hated the way he talked about his future successes with women. (He'd decided not to get involved with them yet, since he still hadn't received his officer's epaulettes; he awaited those epaulettes impatiently.) And he talked about all the duels he'd have to fight. I remember how once, although I was usually very taciturn, I suddenly clashed with Zverkov when, during our free time, he was discussing future exploits with his friends; getting a bit carried away with the game like a little puppy playing in the sun, he suddenly declared that not a single girl in his village would escape his attention—that it was his *droit de seigneur*,[9] and that if the peasants even dared protest, he'd have them all flogged, those bearded rascals; and he'd double their quit-rent.[1] Our louts applauded, but I attacked him—not out of any pity for the poor girls or their fathers, but simply because

---

9. Lord's privilege (French); the feudal lord's right to spend the first night with the bride of a newly married serf.   1. The annual sum paid in cash or produce by serfs to landowners for the right to farm their land in feudal Russia, as opposed to the *corvée*, a certain amount of labor owed.

everyone else was applauding such a little insect. I got the better of him that time, but Zverkov, although stupid, was also cheerful and impudent. Therefore he laughed it off to such an extent that, in fact, I really didn't get the better of him. The laugh remained on his side. Later he got the better of me several times, but without malice, just so, in jest, in passing, in fun. I was filled with spite and hatred, but I didn't respond. After graduation he took a few steps toward me; I didn't object strongly because I found it flattering; but soon we came to a natural parting of the ways. Afterward I heard about his barrack-room successes as a lieutenant and about his *binges*. Then there were other rumors—about his *successes* in the service. He no longer bowed to me on the street; I suspected that he was afraid to compromise himself by acknowledging such an insignificant person as myself. I also saw him in the theater once, in the third tier, already sporting an officer's gold braids. He was fawning and grovelling before the daughters of some aged general. In those three years he'd let himself go, although he was still as handsome and agile as before; he sagged somehow and had begun to put on weight; it was clear that by the age of thirty he'd be totally flabby. So it was for this Zverkov, who was finally ready to depart, that our schoolmates were organizing a farewell dinner. They'd kept up during these three years, although I'm sure that inwardly they didn't consider themselves on an equal footing with him.

One of Simonov's two guests was Ferfichkin, a Russified German, a short man with a face like a monkey, a fool who made fun of everybody, my bitterest enemy from the lower grades—a despicable, impudent show-off who affected the most ticklish sense of ambition, although, of course, he was a coward at heart. He was one of Zverkov's admirers and played up to him for his own reasons, frequently borrowing money from him. Simonov's other guest, Trudolyubov, was insignificant, a military man, tall, with a cold demeanor, rather honest, who worshipped success of any kind and was capable of talking only about promotions. He was a distant relative of Zverkov's, and that, silly to say, lent him some importance among us. He'd always regarded me as a nonentity; he treated me not altogether politely, but tolerably.

"Well, if each of us contributes seven rubles," said Trudolyubov, "with three of us that makes twenty-one altogether—we can have a good dinner. Of course, Zverkov won't have to pay."

"Naturally," Simonov agreed, "since we're inviting him."

"Do you really think," Ferfichkin broke in arrogantly and excitedly, just like an insolent lackey bragging about his master-the-general's medals, "do you really think Zverkov will let us pay for everything? He'll accept out of decency, but then he'll order *half a dozen bottles* on his own."

"What will the four of us do with half a dozen bottles?" asked Trudolyubov, only taking note of the number.

"So then, three of us plus Zverkov makes four, twenty-one rubles, in the Hôtel de Paris, tomorrow at five o'clock," concluded Simonov definitively, since he'd been chosen to make the arrangements.

"Why only twenty-one?" I asked in trepidation, even, apparently, somewhat offended. "If you count me in, you'll have twenty-eight rubles instead of twenty-one."

It seemed to me that to include myself so suddenly and unexpectedly would appear as quite a splendid gesture and that they'd all be smitten at once and regard me with respect.

"Do you really want to come, too?" Simonov inquired with displeasure, managing somehow to avoid looking at me. He knew me inside out.

It was infuriating that he knew me inside out.

"And why not? After all, I was his schoolmate, too, and I must admit that I even feel a bit offended that you've left me out," I continued, just about to boil over again.

"And how were we supposed to find you?" Ferfichkin interjected rudely.

"You never got along very well with Zverkov," added Trudolyubov frowning. But I'd already latched on and wouldn't let go.

"I think no one has a right to judge that," I objected in a trembling voice, as if God knows what had happened. "Perhaps that's precisely why I want to take part now, since we didn't get along so well before."

"Well, who can figure you out . . . such lofty sentiments . . . ," Trudolyubov said with an ironic smile.

"We'll put your name down," Simonov decided, turning to me. "Tomorrow at five o'clock at the Hôtel de Paris. Don't make any mistakes."

"What about the money?" Ferfichkin started to say in an undertone to Simonov while nodding at me, but he broke off because Simonov looked embarrassed.

"That'll do," Trudolyubov said getting up. "If he really wants to come so much, let him."

"But this is our own circle of friends," Ferfichkin grumbled, also picking up his hat. "It's not an official gathering. Perhaps we really don't want you at all. . . ."

They left. Ferfichkin didn't even say goodbye to me as he went out; Trudolyubov barely nodded without looking at me. Simonov, with whom I was left alone, was irritated and perplexed, and he regarded me in a strange way. He neither sat down nor invited me to.

"Hmmm . . . yes . . . , so, tomorrow. Will you contribute your share of the money now? I'm asking just to know for sure," he muttered in embarrassment.

I flared up; but in doing so, I remembered that I'd owed Simonov fifteen rubles for a very long time, which debt, moreover, I'd forgotten, but had also never repaid.

"You must agree, Simonov, that I couldn't have known when I came here . . . oh, what a nuisance, but I've forgotten. . . ."

He broke off and began to pace around the room in even greater irritation. As he paced, he began to walk on his heels and stomp more loudly.

"I'm not detaining you, am I?" I asked after a few moments of silence.

"Oh, no!" he replied with a start. "That is, in fact, yes. You see, I still have to stop by at . . . It's not very far from here . . . ," he added in an apologetic way with some embarrassment.

"Oh, good heavens! Why didn't you say so?" I exclaimed, seizing my cap; moreover I did so with a surprisingly familiar air, coming from God knows where.

"But it's really not far . . . only a few steps away . . . ," Simonov repeated, accompanying me into the hallway with a bustling air which didn't suit him well at all. "So, then, tomorrow at five o'clock sharp!" he shouted to me on the stairs. He was very pleased that I was leaving. However, I was furious.

"What possessed me, what on earth possessed me to interfere?" I gnashed my teeth as I walked along the street. "And for such a scoundrel, a pig like

Zverkov! Naturally, I shouldn't go. Of course, to hell with them. Am I bound to go, or what? Tomorrow I'll inform Simonov by post. . . ."

But the real reason I was so furious was that I was sure I'd go. I'd go on purpose. The more tactless, the more indecent it was for me to go, the more certain I'd be to do it.

There was even a definite impediment to my going: I didn't have any money. All I had was nine rubles. But of those, I had to hand over seven the next day to my servant Apollon for his monthly wages; he lived in and received seven rubles for his meals.

Considering Apollon's character it was impossible not to pay him. But more about that rascal, that plague of mine, later.

In any case, I knew that I wouldn't pay him his wages and that I'd definitely go.

That night I had the most hideous dreams. No wonder: all evening I was burdened with recollections of my years of penal servitude at school and I couldn't get rid of them. I'd been sent off to that school by distant relatives on whom I was dependent and about whom I've heard nothing since. They dispatched me, a lonely boy, crushed by their reproaches, already introspective, taciturn, and regarding everything around him savagely. My schoolmates received me with spiteful and pitiless jibes because I wasn't like any of them. But I couldn't tolerate their jibes; I couldn't possibly get along with them as easily as they got along with each other. I hated them all at once and took refuge from everyone in fearful, wounded and excessive pride. Their crudeness irritated me. Cynically they mocked my face and my awkward build; yet, what stupid faces they all had! Facial expressions at our school somehow degenerated and became particularly stupid. Many attractive lads had come to us, but in a few years they too were repulsive to look at. When I was only sixteen I wondered about them gloomily; even then I was astounded by the pettiness of their thoughts and the stupidity of their studies, games and conversations. They failed to understand essential things and took no interest in important, weighty subjects, so that I couldn't help considering them beneath me. It wasn't my wounded vanity that drove me to it; and, for God's sake, don't repeat any of those nauseating and hackneyed clichés, such as, "I was merely a dreamer, whereas they already understood life." They didn't understand a thing, not one thing about life, and I swear, that's what annoyed me most about them. On the contrary, they accepted the most obvious, glaring reality in a fantastically stupid way, and even then they'd begun to worship nothing but success. Everything that was just, but oppressed and humiliated, they ridiculed hard-heartedly and shamelessly. They mistook rank for intelligence; at the age of sixteen they were already talking about occupying comfortable little niches. Of course, much of this was due to their stupidity and the poor examples that had constantly surrounded them in their childhood and youth. They were monstrously depraved. Naturally, even this was more superficial, more affected cynicism; of course, their youth and a certain freshness shone through their depravity; but even this freshness was unattractive and manifested itself in a kind of rakishness. I hated them terribly, although, perhaps, I was even worse than they were. They returned the feeling and didn't conceal their loathing for me. But I no longer wanted their affection; on the contrary, I constantly longed for their humiliation. In order to avoid their jibes, I began to study as hard as I could on purpose and made my way to the top of the class. That impressed them. In addition, they all began to realize that I'd read certain books which they could never read and that I understood certain things (not included in our special course) about which they'd never even heard. They regarded this with savagery and sarcasm, but they submitted morally, all the more since even the teachers paid me some attention on this account. Their jibes ceased, but their hostility remained, and relations between us became cold and strained. In the end I myself couldn't stand it: as the years went by, my need for people, for friends, increased. I made several attempts to get closer to some of them; but these attempts always turned out to be unnatural and ended of their own accord. Once I even had a friend of sorts. But I was already a despot at heart; I wanted to exercise unlimited power over his soul; I wanted to instill in him contempt for his surroundings; and I demanded from him a disdainful and definitive break with those surroundings. I frightened him with my passionate friendship, and I reduced him to tears and convulsions. He was a naive and giving soul, but as soon as he'd surrendered himself to me totally, I began to despise him and reject him immediately—as if I only needed to achieve a victory over him, merely to subjugate him. But I was unable to conquer them all; my one friend was not at all like them, but rather a rare exception. The first thing I did upon leaving school was abandon the special job in the civil service for which I'd been trained, in order to sever all ties, break with my past, cover it over with dust. . . . The devil only knows why, after all that, I'd dragged myself over to see this Simonov! . . .

Early the next morning I roused myself from bed, jumped up in anxiety, just as if everything was about to start happening all at once. But I believed that some radical change in my life was imminent and was sure to occur that very day. Perhaps because I wasn't used to it, but all my life, at any external event, albeit a trivial one, it always seemed that some sort of radical change would occur. I went off to work as usual, but returned home two hours earlier in order to prepare. The most important thing, I thought, was not to arrive there first, or else they'd all think I was too eager. But there were thousands of most important things, and they all reduced me to the point of impotence. I polished my boots once again with my own hands. Apollon wouldn't polish them twice in one day for anything in the world; he considered it indecent. So I polished them myself, after stealing the brushes from the hallway so that he wouldn't notice and then despise me for it afterward. Next I carefully examined my clothes and found that everything was old, shabby, and worn out. I'd become too slovenly. My uniform was in better shape, but I couldn't go to dinner in a uniform. Worst of all, there was an enormous yellow stain on the knee of my trousers. I had an inkling that the spot alone would rob me of nine-tenths of my dignity. I also knew that it was unseemly for me to think that. "But this isn't the time for thinking. Reality is now looming," I thought, and my heart sank. I also knew perfectly well at that time, that I was monstrously exaggerating all these facts. But what could be done? I was no longer able to control myself, and was shaking with fever. In despair I imagined how haughtily and coldly that "scoundrel" Zverkov would greet me; with what dull and totally relentless contempt that dullard Trudolyubov would regard me; how nastily and impudently that insect Ferfichkin would giggle at me in order to win Zverkov's approval; how well Simonov would understand all this and how he'd despise me for my wretched vanity and cowardice; and worst of all, how petty all this would be, not *literary*, but commonplace. Of course, it would have been better not to go at all. But that was no longer possible; once I began to feel drawn to something, I plunged right in, head first. I'd have reproached myself for the rest of my life: "So, you retreated, you retreated before reality, you retreated!" On the contrary, I desperately wanted to prove to all this "rabble" that I really wasn't the coward I imagined myself to be. But that's not all: in the strongest paroxysm of cowardly fever I dreamt of gaining the upper hand, of conquering them, of carrying them away, compelling them to love me—if only "for the nobility of my thought and my indisputable wit." They would abandon Zverkov; he'd sit by in silence and embarassment, and I'd crush him. Afterward, perhaps, I'd be reconciled with Zverkov and drink to our *friendship*, but what was most spiteful and insulting for me was that I knew even then, I knew completely and for sure, that I didn't need any of this at all; that in fact I really didn't want to crush them, conquer them, or attract them, and that if I could have ever achieved all that, I'd be the first to say that it wasn't worth a damn. Oh, how I prayed to God that this day would pass quickly! With inexpressible anxiety I approached the window, opened the transom,[2] and peered out into the murky mist of the thickly falling wet snow. . . .

At last my worthless old wall clock sputtered out five o'clock. I grabbed my hat, and, trying not to look at Apollon—who'd been waiting since early morning to receive his wages, but didn't want to be the first one to mention it out of pride—I slipped out the door past him and intentionally hired a smart cab with my last half-ruble in order to arrive at the Hôtel de Paris in style.

Summary   In chapters IV and V, the Underground Man quarrels with the others at Zverkov's farewell party; intoxicated, he insults Zverkov and challenges Ferfichkin to a duel. The others leave for a brothel; he borrows money to go there too but arrives late. A young girl is brought to him.

VI

Somewhere behind a partition a clock was wheezing as if under some strong pressure, as though someone were strangling it. After this unnaturally prolonged wheezing there followed a thin, nasty, somehow unexpectedly hurried chime, as if someone had suddenly leapt forward. It struck two. I recovered, although I really hadn't been asleep, only lying there half-conscious.

It was almost totally dark in the narrow, cramped, low-ceilinged room, which was crammed with an enormous wardrobe and cluttered with cartons, rags, and all sorts of old clothes. The candle burning on the table at one end of the room flickered faintly from time to time, and almost went out completely. In a few moments total darkness would set in.

It didn't take long for me to come to my senses; all at once, without any effort, everything returned to me, as though it had been lying in ambush ready to pounce on me again. Even in my unconscious state some point had

---

2. A small hinged pane in the window of a Russian house, used for ventilation especially during the winter when the main part of the window is sealed.

constantly remained in my memory, never to be forgotten, around which my sleepy visions had gloomily revolved. But it was a strange thing: everything that had happened to me that day now seemed, upon awakening, to have occurred in the distant past, as if I'd long since left it all behind.

My mind was in a daze. It was as though something were hanging over me, provoking, agitating, and disturbing me. Misery and bile were welling inside me, seeking an outlet. Suddenly I noticed beside me two wide-open eyes, examining me curiously and persistently. The gaze was coldly detached, sullen, as if belonging to a total stranger. I found it oppressive.

A dismal thought was conceived in my brain and spread throughout my whole body like a nasty sensation, such as one feels upon entering a damp, mouldy underground cellar. It was somehow unnatural that only now these two eyes had decided to examine me. I also recalled that during the course of the last two hours I hadn't said one word to this creature, and that I had considered it quite unnecessary; that had even given me pleasure for some reason. Now I'd suddenly realized starkly how absurd, how revolting as a spider, was the idea of debauchery, which, without love, crudely and shamelessly begins precisely at the point where genuine love is consummated. We looked at each other in this way for some time, but she didn't lower her gaze before mine, nor did she alter her stare, so that finally, for some reason, I felt very uneasy.

"What's your name?" I asked abruptly, to put an end to it quickly.

"Liza," she replied, almost in a whisper, but somehow in a very unfriendly way; and she turned her eyes away.

I remained silent.

"The weather today . . . snow . . . foul!" I observed, almost to myself, drearily placing one arm behind my head and staring at the ceiling.

She didn't answer. The whole thing was obscene.

"Are you from around here?" I asked her a moment later, almost angrily, turning my head slightly toward her.

"No."

"Where are you from?"

"Riga," she answered unwillingly.

"German?"

"No, Russian."

"Have you been here long?"

"Where?"

"In this house."

"Two weeks." She spoke more and more curtly. The candle had gone out completely; I could no longer see her face.

"Are your mother and father still living?"

"Yes . . . no . . . they are."

"Where are they?"

"There . . . in Riga."

"Who are they?"

"Just . . ."

"Just what? What do they do?"

"Tradespeople."

"Have you always lived with them?"

"Yes."

"How old are you?"

"Twenty."

"Why did you leave them?"

"Just because . . ."

That "just because" meant: leave me alone, it makes me sick. We fell silent.

Only God knows why, but I didn't leave. I too started to feel sick and more depressed. Images of the previous day began to come to mind all on their own, without my willing it, in a disordered way. I suddenly recalled a scene that I'd witnessed on the street that morning as I was anxiously hurrying to work. "Today some people were carrying a coffin and nearly dropped it," I suddenly said aloud, having no desire whatever to begin a conversation, but just so, almost accidentally.

"A coffin?"

"Yes, in the Haymarket; they were carrying it up from an underground cellar."

"From a cellar?"

"Not a cellar, but from a basement . . . well, you know . . . from downstairs . . . from a house of ill repute . . . There was such filth all around. . . . Eggshells, garbage . . . it smelled foul . . . it was disgusting."

Silence.

"A nasty day to be buried!" I began again to break the silence.

"Why nasty?"

"Snow, slush . . ." (I yawned.)

"It doesn't matter," she said suddenly after a brief silence.

"No, it's foul. . . ." (I yawned again.) "The grave diggers must have been cursing because they were getting wet out there in the snow. And there must have been water in the grave."

"Why water in the grave?" she asked with some curiosity, but she spoke even more rudely and curtly than before. Something suddenly began to goad me on.

"Naturally, water on the bottom, six inches or so. You can't ever dig a dry grave at Volkovo cemetery."

"Why not?"

"What do you mean, why not? The place is waterlogged. It's all swamp. So they bury them right in the water. I've seen it myself . . . many times. . . ."

(I'd never seen it, and I'd never been to Volkovo cemetery, but I'd heard about it from other people.)

"Doesn't it matter to you if you die?"

"Why should I die?" she replied, as though defending herself.

"Well, someday you'll die; you'll die just like that woman did this morning. She was a . . . she was also a young girl . . . she died of consumption."

"The wench should have died in the hospital. . . ." (She knows all about it, I thought, and she even said "wench" instead of "girl.")

"She owed money to her madam," I retorted, more and more goaded on by the argument. "She worked right up to the end, even though she had consumption. The cabbies standing around were chatting with the soldiers, telling them all about it. Her former acquaintances, most likely. They were all laughing. They were planning to drink to her memory at the tavern." (I invented a great deal of this.)

Silence, deep silence. She didn't even stir.

"Do you think it would be better to die in a hospital?"

"Isn't it just the same? . . . Besides, why should I die?" she added irritably.

"If not now, then later?"

"Well, then later . . ."

"That's what you think! Now you're young and pretty and fresh—that's your value. But after a year of this life, you won't be like that any more; you'll fade."

"In a year?"

"In any case, after a year your price will be lower," I continued, gloating. "You'll move out of here into a worse place, into some other house. And a year later, into a third, each worse and worse, and seven years from now you'll end up in a cellar on the Haymarket. Even that won't be so bad. The real trouble will come when you get some disease, let's say a weakness in the chest . . . or you catch cold or something. In this kind of life it's no laughing matter to get sick. It takes hold of you and may never let go. And so, you die."

"Well, then, I'll die," she answered now quite angrily and stirred quickly.

"That'll be a pity."

"For what?"

"A pity to lose a life."

Silence.

"Did you have a sweetheart? Huh?"

"What's it to you?"

"Oh, I'm not interrogating you. What do I care? Why are you angry? Of course, you may have had your own troubles. What's it to me? Just the same, I'm sorry."

"For whom?"

"I'm sorry for you."

"No need . . . ," she whispered barely audibly and stirred once again.

That provoked me at once. What! I was being so gentle with her, while she . . .

"Well, and what do you think? Are you on the right path then?"

"I don't think anything."

"That's just the trouble—you don't think. Wake up, while there's still time. And there is time. You're still young and pretty; you could fall in love, get married, be happy.[3] . . ."

"Not all married women are happy," she snapped in her former, rude manner.

"Not all, of course, but it's still better than this. A lot better. You can even live without happiness as long as there's love. Even in sorrow life can be good; it's good to be alive, no matter how you live. But what's there besides . . . stench? Phew!"

I turned away in disgust; I was no longer coldly philosophizing. I began to feel what I was saying and grew excited. I'd been longing to expound these cherished *little ideas* that I'd been nurturing in my corner. Something had suddenly caught fire in me, some kind of goal had "manifested itself" before me.

---

3. A popular theme treated by Gogol, Chernyshevsky, and Nekrasov, among others. Typically, an innocent and idealistic young man attempts to rehabilitate a prostitute or "fallen woman."

"Pay no attention to the fact that I'm here. I'm no model for you. I may be even worse than you are. Moreover, I was drunk when I came here." I hastened nonetheless to justify myself. "Besides, a man is no example to a woman. It's a different thing altogether; even though I degrade and defile myself, I'm still no one's slave; if I want to leave, I just get up and go. I shake it all off and I'm a different man. But you must realize right from the start that you're a slave. Yes, a slave! You give away everything, all your freedom. Later, if you want to break this chain, you won't be able to; it'll bind you ever more tightly. That's the kind of evil chain it is. I know. I won't say anything else; you might not even understand me. But tell me this, aren't you already in debt to your madam? There, you see!" I added, even though she hadn't answered, but had merely remained silent; but she was listening with all her might. "There's your chain! You'll never buy yourself out. That's the way it's done. It's just like selling your soul to the devil. . . .

"And besides . . . I may be just as unfortunate, how do you know, and I may be wallowing in mud on purpose, also out of misery. After all, people drink out of misery. Well, I came here out of misery. Now, tell me, what's so good about this place? Here you and I were . . . intimate . . . just a little while ago, and all that time we didn't say one word to each other; afterward you began to examine me like a wild creature, and I did the same. Is that the way people love? Is that how one person is supposed to encounter another? It's a disgrace, that's what it is!"

"Yes!" she agreed with me sharply and hastily. The haste of her answer surprised even me. It meant that perhaps the very same idea was flitting through her head while she'd been examining me earlier. It meant that she too was capable of some thought. . . . "Devil take it; this is odd, this *kinship*," I thought, almost rubbing my hands together. "Surely I can handle such a young soul."

It was the sport that attracted me most of all.

She turned her face closer to mine, and in the darkness it seemed that she propped her head up on her arm. Perhaps she was examining me. I felt sorry that I couldn't see her eyes. I heard her breathing deeply.

"Why did you come here?" I began with some authority.

"Just so . . ."

"But think how nice it would be living in your father's house! There you'd be warm and free; you'd have a nest of your own."

"And what if it's worse than that?"

"I must establish the right tone," flashed through my mind. "I won't get far with sentimentality."

However, that merely flashed through my mind. I swear that she really did interest me. Besides, I was somewhat exhausted and provoked. After all, artifice goes along so easily with feeling.

"Who can say?" I hastened to reply. "All sorts of things can happen. Why, I was sure that someone had wronged you and was more to blame than you are. After all, I know nothing of your life story, but a girl like you doesn't wind up in this sort of place on her own accord. . . ."

"What kind of a girl am I?" she whispered hardly audibly; but I heard it.

"What the hell! Now I'm flattering her. That's disgusting! But, perhaps it's a good thing. . . ." She remained silent.

"You see, Liza, I'll tell you about myself. If I'd had a family when I was growing up, I wouldn't be the person I am now. I think about this often. After all, no matter how bad it is in your own family—it's still your own father and mother, and not enemies or strangers. Even if they show you their love only once a year, you still know that you're at home. I grew up without a family; that must be why I turned out the way I did—so unfeeling."

I waited again.

"She might not understand," I thought. "Besides, it's absurd—all this moralizing."

"If I were a father and had a daughter, I think that I'd have loved her more than my sons, really," I began indirectly, talking about something else in order to distract her. I confess that I was blushing.

"Why's that?"

Ah, so she's listening!

"Just because. I don't know why, Liza. You see, I knew a father who was a stern, strict man, but he would kneel before his daughter and kiss her hands and feet; he couldn't get enough of her, really. She'd go dancing at a party, and he'd stand in one spot for five hours, never taking his eyes off her. He was crazy about her; I can understand that. At night she'd be tired and fall asleep, but he'd wake up, go in to kiss her, and make the sign of the cross over her while she slept. He used to wear a dirty old jacket and was stingy with everyone else, but would spend his last kopeck on her, buying her expensive presents; it afforded him great joy if she liked his presents. A father always loves his daughters more than their mother does. Some girls have a very nice time living at home. I think that I wouldn't even have let my daughter get married."

"Why not?" she asked with a barely perceptible smile.

"I'd be jealous, so help me God. Why, how could she kiss someone else? How could she love a stranger more than her own father? It's even painful to think about it. Of course, it's all nonsense; naturally, everyone finally comes to his senses. But I think that before I'd let her marry, I'd have tortured myself with worry. I'd have found fault with all her suitors. Nevertheless, I'd have ended up by allowing her to marry whomever she loved. After all, the one she loves always seems the worst of all to the father. That's how it is. That causes a lot of trouble in many families."

"Some are glad to sell their daughters, rather than let them marry honorably," she said suddenly.

Aha, so that's it!

"That happens, Liza, in those wretched families where there's neither God nor love," I retorted heatedly. "And where there's no love, there's also no good sense. There are such families, it's true, but I'm not talking about them. Obviously, from the way you talk, you didn't see much kindness in your own family. You must be very unfortunate. Hmm . . . But all this results primarily from poverty."

"And is it any better among the gentry? Honest folk live decently even in poverty."

"Hmmm . . . Yes. Perhaps. There's something else, Liza. Man only likes to count his troubles; he doesn't calculate his happiness. If he figured as he should, he'd see that everyone gets his share. So, let's say that all goes well in a particular family; it enjoys God's blessing, the husband turns out to be a good man, he loves you, cherishes you, and never leaves you. Life is good in that family. Sometimes, even though there's a measure of sorrow, life's still good. Where isn't there sorrow? If you choose to get married, *you'll find out for yourself*. Consider even the first years of a marriage to the one you love: what happiness, what pure bliss there can be sometimes! Almost without exception. At first even quarrels with your husband turn out well. For some women, the more they love their husbands, the more they pick fights with them. It's true; I once knew a woman like that. 'That's how it is,' she'd say. 'I love you very much and I'm tormenting you out of love, so that you'll feel it.' Did you know that one can torment a person intentionally out of love? It's mostly women who do that. Then she thinks to herself, 'I'll love him so much afterward, I'll be so affectionate, it's no sin to torment him a little now.' At home everyone would rejoice over you, and it would be so pleasant, cheerful, serene, and honorable. . . . Some other women are very jealous. If her husband goes away, I knew one like that, she can't stand it; she jumps up at night and goes off on the sly to see. Is he there? Is he in that house? Is he with that one? Now that's bad. Even she herself knows that it's bad; her heart sinks and she suffers because she really loves him. It's all out of love. And how nice it is to make up after a quarrel, to admit one's guilt or forgive him! How nice it is for both of them, how good they both feel at once, just as if they'd met again, married again, and begun their love all over again. No one, no one at all has to know what goes on between a husband and wife, if they love each other. However their quarrel ends, they should never call in either one of their mothers to act as judge or to hear complaints about the other one. They must act as their own judges. Love is God's mystery and should be hidden from other people's eyes, no matter what happens. This makes it holier, much better. They respect each other more, and a great deal is based on this respect. And, if there's been love, if they got married out of love, why should love disappear? Can't it be sustained? It rarely happens that it can't be sustained. If the husband turns out to be a kind and honest man, how can the love disappear? The first phase of married love will pass, that's true, but it's followed by an even better kind of love. Souls are joined together and all their concerns are managed in common; there'll be no secrets from one another. When children arrive, each and every stage, even a very difficult one, will seem happy, as long as there's both love and courage. Even work is cheerful; even when you deny yourself bread for your children's sake, you're still happy. After all, they'll love you for it afterward; you're really saving for your own future. Your children will grow up, and you'll feel that you're a model for them, a support. Even after you die, they'll carry your thoughts and feelings all during their life. They'll take on your image and likeness, since they received it from you. Consequently, it's a great obligation. How can a mother and father keep from growing closer? They say it's difficult to raise children. Who says that? It's heavenly joy! Do you love little children, Liza? I love them dearly. You know—a rosy little boy, suckling at your breast; what husband's heart could turn against his wife seeing her sitting there holding his child? The chubby, rosy little baby sprawls and snuggles; his little hands and feet are plump; his little nails are clean and tiny, so tiny it's even funny to see them; his little eyes look as if he already understood everything. As he suckles, he tugs at your breast playfully with his little hand. When the father approaches, the child lets go of the breast, bends way back, looks at his father, and laughs—as if God only knows how funny it is—and then takes to suckling again. Afterward, when he starts cutting teeth, he'll sometimes bite his mother's breast; looking at her sideways his little eyes seem to say, 'See, I bit you!' Isn't this pure bliss— the three of them, husband, wife, and child, all together? You can forgive a great deal for such moments. No, Liza, I think you must first learn how to live by yourself, and only afterward blame others."

"It's by means of images," I thought to myself, "just such images that I can get to you," although I was speaking with considerable feeling, I swear it; and all at once I blushed. "And what if she suddenly bursts out laughing— where will I hide then?" That thought drove me into a rage. By the end of my speech I'd really become excited, and now my pride was suffering somehow. The silence lasted for a while. I even considered shaking her.

"Somehow you . . ." she began suddenly and then stopped.

But I understood everything already: something was trembling in her voice now, not shrill, rude or unyielding as before, but something soft and timid, so timid that I suddenly was rather ashamed to watch her and felt guilty.

"What?" I asked with tender curiosity.

"Well, you . . ."

"What?"

"You somehow . . . it sounds just like a book," she said, and once again something which was noticeably sarcastic was suddenly heard in her voice.

Her remark wounded me dreadfully. That's not what I'd expected.

Yet, I didn't understand that she was intentionally disguising her feelings with sarcasm; that was usually the last resort of people who are timid and chaste of heart, whose souls have been coarsely and impudently invaded; and who, until the last moment, refuse to yield out of pride and are afraid to express their own feelings to you. I should've guessed it from the timidity with which on several occasions she tried to be sarcastic, until she finally managed to express it. But I hadn't guessed, and a malicious impulse took hold of me.

"Just you wait," I thought.

VII

"That's enough, Liza. What do books have to do with it, when this disgusts me as an outsider? And not only as an outsider. All this has awakened in my heart . . . Can it be, can it really be that you don't find it repulsive here? No, clearly habit means a great deal. The devil only knows what habit can do to a person. But do you seriously think that you'll never grow old, that you'll always be pretty, and that they'll keep you on here forever and ever? I'm not even talking about the filth. . . . Besides, I want to say this about your present life: even though you're still young, good-looking, nice, with soul and feelings, do you know, that when I came to a little while ago, I was immediately disgusted to be here with you! Why, a man has to be drunk to wind up here. But if you were in a different place, living as nice people do, I might not only chase after you, I might actually fall in love with you. I'd rejoice at a look from you, let alone a word; I'd wait for you at the gate and kneel down before you; I'd think of you as my betrothed and even consider that an honor. I wouldn't dare have any impure thoughts about you. But here, I know that I need only whistle, and you, whether you want to or not, will come to me, and that I don't have to do your bidding, whereas you have to do mine. The lowliest peasant may hire himself out as a laborer, but he doesn't make a complete slave of himself; he knows that it's only for a limited term. But what's your term? Just think about it. What are you giving up here? What are you enslaving? Why, you're enslaving your soul, something you don't really own, together with your body! You're giving away your love to be defiled by any drunkard! Love! After all, that's all there is! It's a precious jewel, a maiden's treasure, that's what it is! Why, to earn that love a man might be ready to offer up his own soul, to face death. But what's your love worth now? You've been bought, all of you; and why should anyone strive for your love, when you offer everything even without it? Why, there's no greater insult for a girl, don't you understand? Now, I've heard that they console you foolish girls, they allow you to see your own lovers here. But that's merely child's play, deception, making fun of you, while you believe it. And do you really think he loves you, that lover of yours? I don't believe it. How can he, if he knows that you can be called away from him at any moment? He'd have to be depraved after all that. Does he possess even one drop of respect for you? What do you have in common with him? He's laughing at you and stealing from you at the same time—so much for his love. It's not too bad, as long as he doesn't beat you. But perhaps he does. Go on, ask him, if you have such a lover, whether he'll ever marry you. Why, he'll burst out laughing right in your face, if he doesn't spit at you or smack you. He himself may be worth no more than a few lousy kopecks. And for what, do you think, did you ruin your whole life here? For the coffee they give you to drink, or for the plentiful supply of food? Why do you think they feed you so well? Another girl, an honest one, would choke on every bite, because she'd know why she was being fed so well. You're in debt here, you'll be in debt, and will remain so until the end, until such time comes as the customers begin to spurn you. And that time will come very soon; don't count on your youth. Why, here youth flies by like a stagecoach. They'll kick you out. And they'll not merely kick you out, but for a long time before that they'll pester you, reproach you, and abuse you—as if you hadn't ruined your health for the madam, hadn't given up your youth and your soul for her in vain, but rather, as if you'd ruined her, ravaged her, and robbed her. And don't expect any support. Your friends will also attack you to curry her favor, because they're all in bondage here and have long since lost both conscience and pity. They've become despicable, and there's nothing on earth more despicable, more repulsive, or more insulting than their abuse. You'll lose everything here, everything, without exception—your health, youth, beauty, and hope— and at the age of twenty-two you'll look as if you were thirty-five, and even that won't be too awful if you're not ill. Thank God for that. Why, you probably think that you're not even working, that it's all play! But there's no harder work or more onerous task than this one in the whole world and there never has been. I'd think that one's heart alone would be worn out by crying. Yet you dare not utter one word, not one syllable; when they drive you out, you leave as if you were the guilty one. You'll move to another place, then to a third, then somewhere else, and finally you'll wind up in the Haymarket. And there they'll start beating you for no good reason at all; it's a local custom; the clients there don't know how to be nice without beating you. You don't think it's so disgusting there? Maybe you should go and have a look sometime, and see it with your own eyes. Once, at New Year's, I saw a woman in a doorway. Her own kind had pushed her outside as a joke, to freeze her for a little while because she was wailing too much; they shut the door behind her. At nine o'clock in the morning she was already dead drunk, dishevelled, half-naked, and all beaten up. Her face was powdered, but her eyes were bruised; blood was streaming from her nose and mouth; a certain cabby had just fixed her up. She was sitting on a stone step, holding a piece of salted fish in her hand; she was howling, wailing something about her 'fate,' and slapping the fish against the stone step. Cabbies and drunken soldiers had gathered around the steps and were taunting her. Don't you think you'll wind up the same way? I wouldn't want to believe it myself, but how do you know, perhaps eight or ten years ago this same girl, the one with the salted fish, arrived here from somewhere or other, all fresh like a little cherub, innocent, and pure; she knew no evil and blushed at every word. Perhaps she was just like you—proud, easily offended, unlike all the rest; she looked like a queen and knew that total happiness awaited the man who would love her and whom she would also love. Do you see how it all ended? What if at the very moment she was slapping the fish against that filthy step, dead drunk and dishevelled, what if, even at that very moment she'd recalled her earlier, chaste years in her father's house when she was still going to school, and when her neighbor's son used to wait for her along the path and assure her that he'd love her all his life and devote himself entirely to her, and when they vowed to love one another forever and get married as soon as they grew up! No, Liza, you'd be lucky, very lucky, if you died quickly from consumption somewhere in a corner, in a cellar, like that other girl. In a hospital, you say? All right—they'll take you off, but what if the madam still requires your services? Consumption is quite a disease—it's not like dying from a fever. A person continues to hope right up until the last minute and declares that he's in good health. He consoles himself. Now that's useful for your madam. Don't worry, that's the way it is. You've sold your soul; besides, you owe her money—that means you don't dare say a thing. And while you're dying, they'll all abandon you, turn away from you—because there's nothing left to get from you. They'll even reproach you for taking up space for no good reason and for taking so long to die. You won't even be able to ask for something to drink, without their hurling abuse at you: 'When will you croak, you old bitch? You keep on moaning and don't let us get any sleep—and you drive our customers away.' That's for sure; I've overheard such words myself. And as you're breathing your last, they'll shove you into the filthiest corner of the cellar—into darkness and dampness; lying there alone, what will you think about then? After you die, some stranger will lay you out hurriedly, grumbling all the while, impatiently—no one will bless you, no one will sigh over you; they'll merely want to get rid of you as quickly as possible. They'll buy you a wooden trough and carry you out as they did that poor woman I saw today; then they'll go off to a tavern and drink to your memory. There'll be slush, filth, and wet snow in your grave—why bother for the likes of you? 'Let her down, Vanyukha; after all, it's her fate to go down with her legs up, that's the sort of girl she was. Pull up on that rope, you rascal!' 'It's okay like that.' 'How's it okay? See, it's lying on its side. Was she a human being or not? Oh, never mind, cover it up.' They won't want to spend much time arguing over you. They'll cover your coffin quickly with wet, blue clay and then go off to the tavern. . . . That'll be the end of your memory on earth; for other women, children will visit their graves, fathers, husbands— but for you—no tears, no sighs; no remembrances. No one, absolutely no one in the whole world, will ever come to visit you; your name will disappear from the face of the earth, just as if you'd never been born and had never existed. Mud and filth, no matter how you pound on the lid of your coffin at night when other corpses arise: 'Let me out, kind people, let me live on earth for a little while! I lived, but I didn't really see life; my life went down the drain; they drank it away in a tavern at the Haymarket; let me out, kind people, let me live in the world once again!'"

I was so carried away by my own pathos that I began to feel a lump forming in my throat, and . . . I suddenly stopped, rose up in fright, and, leaning over apprehensively, I began to listen carefully as my own heart pounded. There was cause for dismay.

For a while I felt that I'd turned her soul inside out and had broken her heart; the more I became convinced of this, the more I strived to reach my goal as quickly and forcefully as possible. It was the sport, the sport that attracted me; but it wasn't only the sport. . . .

I knew that I was speaking clumsily, artificially, even bookishly; in short, I didn't know how to speak except "like a book." But that didn't bother me, for I knew, I had a premonition, that I would be understood and that this bookishness itself might even help things along. But now, having achieved this effect, I suddenly lost all my nerve. No, never, never before had I witnessed such despair! She was lying there, her face pressed deep into a pillow she was clutching with her hands. Her heart was bursting. Her young body was shuddering as if she were having convulsions. Suppressed sobs shook her breast, tore her apart, and suddenly burst forth in cries and moans. Then she pressed her face even deeper into the pillow: she didn't want anyone, not one living soul, to hear her anguish and her tears. She bit the pillow; she bit her hand until it bled (I noticed that afterward); or else, thrusting her fingers into her dishevelled hair, she became rigid with the strain, holding her breath and clenching her teeth. I was about to say something, to ask her to calm down; but I felt that I didn't dare. Suddenly, all in a kind of chill, almost in a panic, I groped hurriedly to get out of there as quickly as possible. It was dark: no matter how I tried, I couldn't end it quickly. Suddenly I felt a box of matches and a candlestick with a whole unused candle. As soon as the room was lit up, Liza started suddenly, sat up, and looked at me almost senselessly, with a distorted face and a half-crazy smile. I sat down next to her and took her hands; she came to and threw herself at me, wanting to embrace me, yet not daring to. Then she quietly lowered her head before me.

"Liza, my friend, I shouldn't have . . . you must forgive me," I began, but she squeezed my hands so tightly in her fingers that I realized I was saying the wrong thing and stopped.

"Here's my address, Liza. Come to see me."

"I will," she whispered resolutely, still not lifting her head.

"I'm going now, good-bye . . . until we meet again."

I stood up; she did, too, and suddenly blushed all over, shuddered, seized a shawl lying on a chair, threw it over her shoulders, and wrapped herself up to her chin. After doing this, she smiled again somewhat painfully, blushed, and looked at me strangely. I felt awful. I hastened to leave, to get away.

"Wait," she said suddenly as we were standing in the hallway near the door, and she stopped me by putting her hand on my overcoat. She quickly put the candle down and ran off; obviously she'd remembered something or wanted to show me something. As she left she was blushing all over, her eyes were gleaming, and a smile had appeared on her lips—what on earth did it all mean? I waited against my own will; she returned a moment later with a glance that seemed to beg forgiveness for something. All in all it was no longer the same face or the same glance as before—sullen, distrustful, obstinate. Now her glance was imploring, soft, and, at the same time, trusting, affectionate, and timid. That's how children look at people whom they love very much, or when they're asking for something. Her eyes were light hazel, lovely, full of life, as capable of expressing love as brooding hatred.

Without any explanation, as if I were some kind of higher being who was supposed to know everything, she held a piece of paper out toward me. At that moment her whole face was shining with a most naive, almost childlike triumph. I unfolded the paper. It was a letter to her from some medical student containing a high-flown, flowery, but very respectful declaration of love. I don't remember the exact words now, but I can well recall the genuine emotion that can't be feigned shining through that high style. When I'd finished reading the letter, I met her ardent, curious, and childishly impatient gaze. She'd fixed her eyes on my face and was waiting eagerly to see what I'd say. In a few words, hurriedly, but with some joy and pride, she explained that she'd once been at a dance somewhere, in a private house, at the home of some "very, very good people, *family people*, where they *knew nothing*, nothing at all," because she'd arrived at this place only recently and was just . . . well, she hadn't quite decided whether she'd stay here and she'd certainly leave as soon as she'd paid off her debt. . . . Well, and this student was there; he danced with her all evening and talked to her. It turned out he was from Riga; he'd known her as a child, they'd played together, but that had been a long time ago; he was acquainted with her parents—but he knew nothing, absolutely nothing *about this place* and he didn't even suspect it! And so, the very next day, after the dance, (only some three days ago), he'd sent her this letter through the friend with whom she'd gone to the party . . . and . . . well, that's the whole story."

She lowered her sparkling eyes somewhat bashfully after she finished speaking.

The poor little thing, she'd saved this student's letter as a treasure and had run to fetch this one treasure of hers, not wanting me to leave without knowing that she too was the object of sincere, honest love, and that someone exists who had spoken to her respectfully. Probably that letter was fated to lie in her box without results. But that didn't matter; I'm sure that she'll guard it as a treasure her whole life, as her pride and vindication; and now, at a moment like this, she remembered it and brought it out to exult naively before me, to raise herself in my eyes, so that I could see it for myself and could also think well of her. I didn't say a thing; I shook her hand and left. I really wanted to get away. . . . I walked all the way home in spite of the fact that wet snow was still falling in large flakes. I was exhausted, oppressed, and perplexed. But the truth was already glimmering behind that perplexity. The ugly truth!

Summary   In chapter VIII, the Underground Man, back at home, worries that Liza will visit him and see his poverty; alternately humiliated and enraged, he quarrels with his valet, Apollon. Liza arrives.

IX

And enter my house bold and free,
To become its full mistress!
From the same poem.[4]

I stood before her, crushed, humiliated, abominably ashamed; I think I was smiling as I tried with all my might to wrap myself up in my tattered, quilted dressing gown—exactly as I'd imagined this scene the other day during a fit of depression. Apollon, after standing over us for a few minutes, left, but that didn't make things any easier for me. Worst of all was that she suddenly became embarrassed too, more than I'd ever expected. At the sight of me, of course.

"Sit down," I said mechanically and moved a chair up to the table for her, while I sat on the sofa. She immediately and obediently sat down, staring at me wide-eyed, and, obviously, expecting something from me at once. This naive expectation infuriated me, but I restrained myself.

She should have tried not to notice anything, as if everything were just as it should be, but she . . . And I vaguely felt that she'd have to pay dearly *for everything*.

"You've found me in an awkward situation, Liza," I began, stammering and realizing that this was precisely the wrong way to begin.

"No, no, don't imagine anything!" I cried, seeing that she'd suddenly blushed. "I'm not ashamed of my poverty. . . . On the contrary, I regard it with pride. I'm poor, but noble. . . . One can be poor and noble," I muttered. "But . . . would you like some tea?"

"No . . . ," she started to say.

"Wait!"

I jumped up and ran to Apollon. I had to get away somehow.

"Apollon," I whispered in feverish haste, tossing down the seven rubles which had been in my fist the whole time, "here are your wages. There, you see, I've given them to you. But now you must rescue me: bring us some tea and a dozen rusks from the tavern at once. If you don't go, you'll make me a very miserable man. You have no idea who this woman is. . . . This means— everything! You may think she's . . . But you've no idea at all who this woman really is!"

Apollon, who'd already sat down to work and had put his glasses on again, at first glanced sideways in silence at the money without abandoning his needle; then, paying no attention to me and making no reply, he continued to fuss with the needle he was still trying to thread. I waited there for about three minutes standing before him with my arms folded *à la Napoleon*.[5] My temples were soaked in sweat. I was pale, I felt that myself. But, thank God,

4. See n. 1, p. 849.   5. In the style of Napoleon.

he must have taken pity just looking at me. After finishing with the thread, he stood up slowly from his place, slowly pushed back his chair, slowly took off his glasses, slowly counted the money and finally, after inquiring over his shoulder whether he should get a whole pot, slowly walked out of the room. As I was returning to Liza, it occurred to me: shouldn't I run away just as I was, in my shabby dressing gown, no matter where, and let come what may.

I sat down again. She looked at me uneasily. We sat in silence for several minutes.

"I'll kill him." I shouted suddenly, striking the table so hard with my fist that ink splashed out of the inkwell.

"Oh, what are you saying?" she exclaimed, startled.

"I'll kill him, I'll kill him!" I shrieked, striking the table in an absolute frenzy, but understanding full well at the same time how stupid it was to be in such a frenzy.

"You don't understand, Liza, what this executioner is doing to me. He's my executioner. . . . He's just gone out for some rusks; he . . ."

And suddenly I burst into tears. It was a nervous attack. I felt so ashamed amidst my sobs, but I couldn't help it. She got frightened.

"What's the matter? What's wrong with you?" she cried, fussing around me.

"Water, give me some water, over there!" I muttered in a faint voice, realizing full well, however, that I could've done both without the water and without the faint voice. But I was *putting on an act*, as it's called, in order to maintain decorum, although my nervous attack was genuine.

She gave me some water while looking at me like a lost soul. At that very moment Apollon brought in the tea. It suddenly seemed that this ordinary and prosaic tea was horribly inappropriate and trivial after everything that had happened, and I blushed. Liza stared at Apollon with considerable alarm. He left without looking at us.

"Liza, do you despise me?" I asked, looking her straight in the eye, trembling with impatience to find out what she thought.

She was embarrassed and didn't know what to say.

"Have some tea," I said angrily. I was angry at myself, but she was the one who'd have to pay, naturally. A terrible anger against her suddenly welled up in my heart; I think I could've killed her. To take revenge I swore inwardly not to say one more word to her during the rest of her visit. "She's the cause of it all," I thought.

Our silence continued for about five minutes. The tea stood on the table; we didn't touch it. It reached the point of my not wanting to drink on purpose, to make it even more difficult for her; it would be awkward for her to begin alone. Several times she glanced at me in sad perplexity. I stubbornly remained silent. I was the main sufferer, of course, because I was fully aware of the despicable meanness of my own spiteful stupidity; yet, at the same time, I couldn't restrain myself.

"I want to . . . get away from . . . that place . . . once and for all," she began just to break the silence somehow; but, poor girl, that was just the thing she shouldn't have said at that moment, stupid enough as it was to such a person as me, stupid as I was. My own heart even ached with pity for her tactlessness and unnecessary straightforwardness. But something hideous immediately suppressed all my pity; it provoked me even further. Let the whole world go to hell. Another five minutes passed.

"Have I disturbed you?" she began timidly, barely audibly, and started to get up.

But as soon as I saw this first glimpse of injured dignity, I began to shake with rage and immediately exploded.

"Why did you come here? Tell me why, please," I began, gasping and neglecting the logical order of my words. I wanted to say it all at once, without pausing for breath; I didn't even worry about how to begin.

"Why did you come here? Answer me! Answer!" I cried, hardly aware of what I was saying. "I'll tell you, my dear woman, why you came here. You came here because I spoke some *words of pity* to you that time. Now you've softened, and want to hear more 'words of pity.' Well, you should know that I was laughing at you then. And I'm laughing at you now. Why are you trembling? Yes, I was laughing at you! I'd been insulted, just prior to that, at dinner, by those men who arrived just before me that evening. I came intending to thrash one of them, the officer; but I didn't succeed; I couldn't find him; I had to avenge my insult on someone, to get my own back; you turned up and I took my anger out at you, and I laughed at you. I'd been humiliated, and I wanted to humiliate someone else; I'd been treated like a rag, and I wanted to exert some power. . . . That's what it was; you thought that I'd come there on purpose to save you, right? Is that what you thought? Is that it?"

I knew that she might get confused and might not grasp all the details, but I also knew that she'd understand the essence of it very well. That's just what happened. She turned white as a sheet; she wanted to say something. Her lips were painfully twisted, but she collapsed onto a chair just as if she'd been struck down with an ax. Subsequently she listened to me with her mouth gaping, her eyes wide open, shaking with awful fear. It was the cynicism, the cynicism of my words that crushed her. . . .

"To save you!" I continued, jumping up from my chair and rushing up and down the room in front of her, "to save you from what? Why, I may be even worse than you are. When I recited that sermon to you, why didn't you throw it back in my face? You should have said to me, 'Why did you come here? To preach morality or what?' Power, it was the power I needed then, I craved the sport, I wanted to reduce you to tears, humiliation, hysteria— that's what I needed then! But I couldn't have endured it myself, because I'm such a wretch. I got scared. The devil only knows why I foolishly gave you my address. Afterward, even before I got home, I cursed you like nothing on earth on account of that address. I hated you already because I'd lied to you then, because it was all playing with words, dreaming in my own mind. But, do you know what I really want now? For you to get lost, that's what! I need some peace. Why, I'd sell the whole world for a kopeck if people would only stop bothering me. Should the world go to hell, or should I go without my tea? I say, let the world go to hell as long as I can always have my tea. Did you know that or not? And I know perfectly well that I'm a scoundrel, a bastard, an egotist, and a sluggard. I've been shaking from fear for the last three days wondering whether you'd ever come. Do you know what disturbed me most of all these last three days? The fact that I'd appeared to you then as such a hero, and that now you'd suddenly see me in this torn dressing gown, dilapidated and revolting. I said before that I wasn't ashamed of my poverty; well, you should know that I am ashamed, I'm ashamed of it more than anything, more afraid of it than anything, more than if I were a thief, because I'm so vain; it's as if the skin's been stripped away from my body so that even wafts of air cause pain. By now surely even you've guessed that I'll never forgive you for having come upon me in this dressing gown as I was attacking Apollon like a vicious dog. Your saviour, your former hero, behaving like a mangy, shaggy mongrel, attacking his own lackey, while that lackey stood there laughing at me! Nor will I ever forgive you for those tears which, like an embarrassed old woman, I couldn't hold back before you. And I'll never forgive *you* for all that I'm confessing now. Yes—you, you alone must pay for everything because you turned up like this, because I'm a scoundrel, because I'm the nastiest, most ridiculous, pettiest, stupidest, most envious worm of all those living on earth who're no better than me in any way, but who, the devil knows why, never get embarrassed, while all my life I have to endure insults from every louse—that's my fate. What do I care that you don't understand any of this? What do I care, what do I care about you and whether or not you perish there? Why, don't you realize how much I'll hate you now after having said all this with your being here listening to me? After all, a man can only talk like this once in his whole life, and then only in hysteria! . . . What more do you want? Why, after all this, are you still hanging around here tormenting me? Why don't you leave?"

But at this point a very strange thing suddenly occurred.

I'd become so accustomed to inventing and imagining everything according to books, and picturing everything on earth to myself just as I'd conceived of it in my dreams, that at first I couldn't even comprehend the meaning of this strange occurrence. But here's what happened: Liza, insulted and crushed by me, understood much more than I'd imagined. She understood out of all this what a woman always understands first of all, if she sincerely loves—namely, that I myself was unhappy.

The frightened and insulted expression on her face was replaced at first by grieved amazement. When I began to call myself a scoundrel and a bastard, and my tears had begun to flow (I'd pronounced this whole tirade in tears), her whole face was convulsed by a spasm. She wanted to get up and stop me; when I'd finished, she paid no attention to my shouting, "Why are you here? Why don't you leave?" She only noticed that it must have been very painful for me to utter all this. Besides, she was so defenseless, the poor girl. She considered herself immeasurably beneath me. How could she get angry or take offense? Suddenly she jumped up from the chair with a kind of uncontrollable impulse, and yearning toward me, but being too timid and not daring to stir from her place, she extended her arms in my direction. . . . At this moment my heart leapt inside me, too. Then suddenly she threw herself at me, put her arms around my neck, and burst into tears. I, too, couldn't restrain myself and sobbed as I'd never done before.

"They won't let me . . . I can't be . . . good!"[6] I barely managed to say; then I went over to the sofa, fell upon it face down, and sobbed in genuine hysterics for a quarter of an hour. She knelt down, embraced me, and remained motionless in that position.

---

6. This epithet *dobryi* ("good") must be read in combination with that in the second sentence of the work, where the hero describes himself as *zloi*—not only "spiteful" but also "evil."

But the trouble was that my hysterics had to end sometime. And so (after all, I'm writing the whole loathsome truth), lying there on the sofa and pressing my face firmly into that nasty leather cushion of mine, I began to sense gradually, distantly, involuntarily, but irresistibly, that it would be awkward for me to raise my head and look Liza straight in the eye. What was I ashamed of? I don't know, but I was ashamed. It also occurred to my overwrought brain that now our roles were completely reversed; now she was the heroine, and I was the same sort of humiliated and oppressed creature she'd been in front of me that evening—only four days ago. . . . And all this came to me during those few minutes as I lay face down on the sofa!

My God! Was it possible that I envied her?

I don't know; to this very day I still can't decide. But then, of course, I was even less able to understand it. After all, I couldn't live without exercising power and tyrannizing over another person. . . . But . . . but, then, you really can't explain a thing by reason; consequently, it's useless to try.

However, I regained control of myself and raised my head; I had to sooner or later. . . . And so, I'm convinced to this day that it was precisely because I felt too ashamed to look at her, that another feeling was suddenly kindled and burst into flame in my heart—the feeling of domination and possession. My eyes gleamed with passion; I pressed her hands tightly. How I hated her and felt drawn to her simultaneously! One feeling intensified the other. It was almost like revenge! . . . At first there was a look of something resembling bewilderment, or even fear, on her face, but only for a brief moment. She embraced me warmly and rapturously.

X

A quarter of an hour later I was rushing back and forth across the room in furious impatience, constantly approaching the screen to peer at Liza through the crack. She was sitting on the floor, her head leaning against the bed, and she must have been crying. But she didn't leave, and that's what irritated me. By this time she knew absolutely everything. I'd insulted her once and for all, but . . . there's nothing more to be said. She guessed that my outburst of passion was merely revenge, a new humiliation for her, and that to my former, almost aimless, hatred there was added now a *personal, envious* hatred of her. . . . However, I don't think that she understood all this explicitly; on the other hand, she fully understood that I was a despicable man, and, most important, that I was incapable of loving her.

I know that I'll be told this is incredible—that it's impossible to be as spiteful and stupid as I am; you may even add that it was impossible not to return, or at least to appreciate, this love. But why is this so incredible? In the first place, I could no longer love because, I repeat, for me love meant tyrannizing and demonstrating my moral superiority. All my life I could never even conceive of any other kind of love, and I've now reached the point that I sometimes think that love consists precisely in a voluntary gift by the beloved person of the right to tyrannize over him. Even in my underground dreams I couldn't conceive of love in any way other than a struggle. It always began with hatred and ended with moral subjugation; afterward, I could never imagine what to do with the subjugated object. And what's so incredible about that, since I'd previously managed to corrupt myself morally; I'd already become unaccustomed to "real life," and only a short while ago had taken it into my head to reproach her and shame her for having come to hear "words of pity" from me. But I never could've guessed that she'd come not to hear words of pity at all, but to love me, because it's in that kind of love that a woman finds her resurrection, all her salvation from whatever kind of ruin, and her rebirth, as it can't appear in any other form. However, I didn't hate her so much as I rushed around the room and peered through the crack behind the screen. I merely found it unbearably painful that she was still there. I wanted her to disappear. I longed for "peace and quiet"; I wanted to remain alone in my underground. "Real life" oppressed me—so unfamiliar was it—that I even found it hard to breathe.

But several minutes passed, and she still didn't stir, as if she were oblivious. I was shameless enough to tap gently on the screen to remind her. . . . She started suddenly, jumped up, and hurried to find her shawl, hat, and coat, as if she wanted to escape from me. . . . Two minutes later she slowly emerged from behind the screen and looked at me sadly. I smiled spitefully; it was forced, however, for *appearance's sake only*; and I turned away from her look.

"Good-bye," she said, going toward the door.

Suddenly I ran up to her, grabbed her hand, opened it, put something in . . . and closed it again. Then I turned away at once and bolted to the other corner, so that at least I wouldn't be able to see. . . .

I was just about to lie—to write that I'd done all this accidentally, without knowing what I was doing, in complete confusion, out of foolishness. But I don't want to lie; therefore I'll say straight out, that I opened her hand and placed something in it . . . out of spite. It occurred to me to do this while I was rushing back and forth across the room and she was sitting there behind the screen. But here's what I can say for sure: although I did this cruel thing deliberately, it was not from my heart, but from my stupid head. This cruelty of mine was so artificial, cerebral, intentionally invented, *bookish*, that I couldn't stand it myself even for one minute—at first I bolted to the corner so as not to see, and then, out of shame and in despair, I rushed out after Liza. I opened the door into the hallway and listened. "Liza! Liza!" I called down the stairs, but timidly, in a soft voice.

There was no answer; I thought I could hear her footsteps at the bottom of the stairs.

"Liza!" I cried more loudly.

No answer. But at that moment I heard down below the sound of the tight outer glass door opening heavily with a creak and then closing again tightly. The sound rose up the stairs.

She'd gone. I returned to my room deep in thought. I felt horribly oppressed.

I stood by the table near the chair where she'd been sitting and stared senselessly into space. A minute or so passed, then I suddenly started: right before me on the chair I saw . . . in a word, I saw the crumpled blue five-ruble note, the very one I'd thrust into her hand a few moments before. It was the same one; it couldn't be any other; I had none other in my apartment. So she'd managed to toss it down on the table when I'd bolted to the other corner.

So what? I might have expected her to do that. Might have expected it?

No. I was such an egotist, in fact, I so lacked respect for other people, that I couldn't even conceive that she'd ever do that. I couldn't stand it. A moment later, like a madman, I hurried to get dressed. I threw on whatever I happened to find, and rushed headlong after her. She couldn't have gone more than two hundred paces when I ran out on the street.

It was quiet; it was snowing heavily, and the snow was falling almost perpendicularly, blanketing the sidewalk and the deserted street. There were no passers-by; no sound could be heard. The street lights were flickering dismally and vainly. I ran about two hundred paces to the crossroads and stopped.

"Where did she go? And why am I running after her? Why? To fall down before her, sob with remorse, kiss her feet, and beg her forgiveness! That's just what I wanted. My heart was being torn apart; never, never will I recall that moment with indifference. But—why?" I wondered. "Won't I grow to hate her, perhaps as soon as tomorrow, precisely because I'm kissing her feet today? Will I ever be able to make her happy? Haven't I found out once again today, for the hundredth time, what I'm really worth? Won't I torment her?"

I stood in the snow, peering into the murky mist, and thought about all this.

"And wouldn't it be better, wouldn't it," I fantasized once I was home again, stifling the stabbing pain in my heart with such fantasies, "wouldn't it be better if she were to carry away the insult with her forever? Such an insult—after all, is purification; it's the most caustic and painful form of consciousness. Tomorrow I would have defiled her soul and wearied her heart. But now that insult will never die within her; no matter how abominable the filth that awaits her, that insult will elevate and purify her . . . by hatred . . . hmm . . . perhaps by forgiveness as well. But will that make it any easier for her?"

And now, in fact, I'll pose an idle question of my own. Which is better: cheap happiness or sublime suffering? Well, come on, which is better?

These were my thoughts as I sat home that evening, barely alive with the anguish in my soul. I'd never before endured so much suffering and remorse; but could there exist even the slightest doubt that when I went rushing out of my apartment, I'd turn back again after going only halfway? I never met Liza afterward, and I never heard anything more about her. I'll also add that for a long time I remained satisfied with my theory about the use of insults and hatred, in spite of the fact that I myself almost fell ill from anguish at the time.

Even now, after so many years, all this comes back to me as *very unpleasant*. A great deal that comes back to me now is very unpleasant, but . . . perhaps I should end these *Notes* here? I think that I made a mistake in beginning to write them. At least, I was ashamed all the time I was writing this *tale*; consequently, it's not really literature, but corrective punishment. After all, to tell you long stories about how, for example, I ruined my life through moral decay in my corner, by the lack of appropriate surroundings, by isolation from any living beings, and by futile malice in the underground— so help me God, that's not very interesting. A novel needs a hero, whereas here all the traits of an anti-hero have been assembled *deliberately*; but the most important thing is that all this produces an extremely unpleasant impression because we've all become estranged from life, we're all cripples, every one of us, more or less. We've become so estranged that at times we feel some kind of revulsion for genuine "real life," and therefore we can't bear to be reminded of it. Why, we've reached a point where we almost regard "real life" as hard work, as a job, and we've all agreed in private that it's really better in books. And why do we sometimes fuss, indulge in whims, and make demands? We don't know ourselves. It'd be even worse if all our whimsical desires were fulfilled. Go on, try it. Give us, for example, a little more independence; untie the hands of any one of us, broaden our sphere of activity, relax the controls, and . . . I can assure you, we'll immediately ask to have the controls reinstated. I know that you may get angry at me for saying this, you may shout and stamp your feet: "Speak for yourself," you'll say, "and for your own miseries in the underground, but don't you dare say '*all of us.*'" If you'll allow me, gentlemen; after all, I'm not trying to justify myself by saying *all of us*. What concerns me in particular, is that in my life I've only taken to an extreme that which you haven't even dared to take halfway; what's more, you've mistaken your cowardice for good sense; and, in so deceiving yourself, you've consoled yourself. So, in fact, I may even be "more alive" than you are. Just take a closer look! Why, we don't even know where this "real life" lives nowadays, what it really is, and what it's called. Leave us alone without books and we'll get confused and lose our way at once—we won't know what to join, what to hold on to, what to love or what to hate, what to respect or what to despise. We're even oppressed by being men—men with real bodies and blood of *our very own*. We're ashamed of it; we consider it a disgrace and we strive to become some kind of impossible "general-human-beings." We're stillborn; for some time now we haven't been conceived by living fathers; we like it more and more. We're developing a taste for it. Soon we'll conceive of a way to be born from ideas. But enough; I don't want to write any more "from Underground. . . ."

However, the "notes" of this paradoxalist don't end here. He couldn't resist and kept on writing. But it also seems to us that we might as well stop here.

CHARLES BAUDELAIRE
1821–1867

Few writers have had such impact on succeeding generations as Charles Baudelaire, called both the "first modern poet" and the "father of modern criticism." Nor is his reputation confined to the West, for Baudelaire is the most widely read French poet around the globe. Yet for a long time Baudelaire's literary image was dominated by his reputation as a scandalous writer whose blatant eroticism and open fascination with evil outraged all right-thinking people. Both he and Flaubert were brought to trial in 1857 for "offenses against public and religious morals"—Flaubert for *Madame Bovary* and Baudelaire for his just-published book of poetry *Les Fleurs de Mal* (The flowers of evil). Some of this reputation is justified; the poet did intend to shock, and he displayed in painfully vivid scenes his own spiritual and sensual torment. Haunted by a religiously framed vision of human nature as fallen and corrupt, he lucidly analyzed his own weaknesses as well as the hypocrisy and sins he found in society. Lust, hatred, laziness, a disabling self-awareness that ironized all emotions, a horror of death and decay, and finally an apathy that swallowed up all other vices— all contrasted bitterly with the poet's dreams of a lost Eden, an ideal harmony of being. Perfection existed only in the distance: in scenes of erotic love, faraway voyages, or artistic beauty created often out of ugliness and crude reality. Baudelaire's ability to present realistic detail inside larger symbolic horizons, his constant use of imagery and suggestion, his consummate craftsmanship and the intense musicality of his verse made him a precursor of Symbolism and, in the words of T. S. Eliot, "the greatest exemplar in *modern* poetry in any language."

Baudelaire was born in Paris on April 9, 1821. His father died when he was six, and his widowed mother married Captain (later General) Jacques Aupick a year later. In 1832 the family moved to Lyons, and young Charles was placed in boarding school; in 1836, Aupick and his family were reassigned to Paris. Throughout his life Baudelaire remained greatly attached to his mother and detested his disciplinarian stepfather. He was a rebellious and difficult youth whose unconventional behavior and extravagant lifestyle continued to worry his family, especially after he turned twenty-one and received his father's inheritance. In 1844, they obtained a court order to supervise his finances, and from then on the poet subsisted on allowances paid by a notary.

In contrast to the Romantics with their love of nature and pastoral scenes, Baudelaire was a city poet fascinated by the variety and excitement of modern urban life. Living in Paris, he collaborated with other writers, published poems, translations, and criticism in different journals, and in 1842 began a lifelong liaison with Jeanne Duval, the "black Venus" of many poems. When he read Edgar Allan Poe for the first time, he was struck by the similarity of their ideas: by Poe's dedication to beauty, his fascination with bizarre images and death, and above all by his emphasis on craftsmanship and perfectly controlled art. Baudelaire's translations of Poe, collected in five volumes published from 1856 to 1865, were immensely popular and introduced the American writer to a broad European audience.

Public scandal greeted the appearance in 1857 of Baudelaire's major work, *The Flowers of Evil*. French authorities, already annoyed at Flaubert's acquittal, seized the book immediately. Less than two months later, the poet and his publisher were condemned to pay a fine and to delete six poems. A second edition with more poems appeared in 1861, and new lyrics were added to later printings. By now the poet was also well known as a critic. He championed the modern art of his time, interpreting and upholding the spirit of modernity in the art criticism of his 1845, 1846, and 1859 *Salons*, in remarkable studies of the painters Eugène Delacroix and Constantin Guys, and in a spirited defense of the German composer Richard Wagner. Baudelaire started publishing prose poetry at the beginning of the 1860s, experimenting with a form that was almost unknown in France and in which he hoped to achieve "the miracle of a poetic prose, musical without rhythm or rhyme, able . . . to adapt itself to the soul's lyric movements, to the undulations of reverie, to the sudden starts of consciousness." A slim book of twenty prose poems appeared in 1862; the complete *Prose Poems* (also called *Paris Spleen*) would contain fifty poems in all. Baudelaire's health was precarious during these years. In 1862, he had what was apparently a minor stroke, which he called a "warning" and described with characteristically vivid imagery: "I felt pass over me a draft of wind from imbecility's wing." Four years later, in Belgium, he was stricken with aphasia and hemiplegia; unable to speak, he was brought back to Paris where he died on August 31, 1867.

His audience was never far from Baudelaire's mind. He wished to shock, to startle, to make the reader rethink cherished ideas and values. In the prefatory poem to *The Flowers of Evil*, "To the Reader," Baudelaire ends a catalogue of human vices by insisting that both he and the reader are caught in a common guilt: "You—hypocrite

Reader—my double—my brother!" The poet's insistent theme of *ennui* (pathological boredom or apathy) occurs here at the beginning of the book: it is the melancholy inertia that keeps human beings from acting either for good or for evil, placing them outside the realm of choice much as Dante relegated to Limbo those who were unwilling to take a moral stand. (In Catholic theology, such spiritual inertia is termed *acedia*.) This *spleen*, as it is also called (from the part of the body governing a splenetic or bilious humor), appears throughout *The Flowers of Evil* as an insidious, debilitating force. In "To the Reader" Baudelaire argues that the Devil's most terrifying weapon against humankind is not the litany of sins so colorfully described, but rather his ability to diminish the possibility of action: to evaporate—like a chemist in a laboratory—the precious metal of human will.

Baudelaire alternates between acid melancholy and glimpses of happiness. One of his rare contented and even tender poems is the lyrical "Invitation to the Voyage," a lover's invitation to an exotic land of peace, beauty, and sensuous harmony. The voyage is imaginary, of course, implying two forms of escape from reality: an escape out of real time into a primeval accord of the senses, and an escape into another artistic vision—the glowing interiors painted by such Dutch masters as Jan Vermeer. A similar but more cynical voyage of escape occurs in "Her Hair." Here the poet, abandoning himself to passion, buries his face in the dark tide of his mistress's hair as if to submerge himself in the dark ocean of dream. This escape is available only on a temporary basis, however; the woman remains his "oasis" only so long as he adorns her hair with jewels. In both these poems, and in Baudelaire's poetry in general, we must admit that women do not exist as separate personalities but rather as foils for poetic inspiration: conventional images of beauty, coldness, vision, or vice given one or another form. Similarly, the woman in "A Carcass" exists only as an appropriate listener in a poem that mocks Petrarchan ideals of feminine beauty. Nor are men better treated; they appear not as individuals but generically, in groups, or they are addressed as brothers (or doubles) of the poet himself. Baudelaire's poetry is governed by a strong subjective impulse, no matter how much he reaches into the world for the raw material of his complex imaginative universe.

Baudelaire was convinced that "every good poet has always been a realist," and he himself was a master of realistic details used for effects that go beyond conventional or photographic realism. The rhythmic thump of firewood being delivered is repeated throughout "Song of Autumn I," where it coordinates ascending images of death. Maggots swarm over a dead body in "A Carcass," and yet there is a strange beauty in this evocation of a buzzing, vibrating new life superimposed on the now-blurred outlines of a decaying animal carcass. The poem's ostensible theme is familiar—*carpe diem*, "seize the day" or "think of the future and love me now," since only a poet can preserve beauty—but one has only to compare Yeats's poem, "When You Are Old" to recognize the harshness of this address to the beloved. The mixture of tones is more subtle in the *Spleen* poems, celebrated for their evocation of gray misery. Here Baudelaire inserts mundane items like mangy cats, decks of cards, old-fashioned clothes, uncorked perfume bottles, and noisy rainspouts. Such down-to-earth details give substance to concurrent mythical or allegorical scenes. A chill revelation of mortality emerges from the sequence of thoroughly practical references to water in "Spleen LXXVIII," beginning with the rain and fog in the city and including a cat twisting and turning uncomfortably on clammy tiles, the whine of a rainspout, the wheeze of wet wood and a damp clock pendulum, and finally a deck of cards left by an old woman who died of dropsy. If the sequence is interesting as a tour de force of linked images, it also serves cumulatively to evoke an atmosphere of lethargy and decay climaxing in a tiny, altogether unrealistic final scene in which two face cards talk sinisterly of their past loves.

Similar themes are to be found in the prose poems published as *Little Poems in Prose* or *Paris Spleen* and generally seen as the first important example of the prose poem although Baudelaire did not actually originate the genre. He was keenly aware, however, of the need for poetic prose to also find its own way to be musical "without rhyme." Stanzas become paragraphs; rhythm is created through variations in sentence length, syntax, and sound patterns, and also through the juxtaposition of scenes and tones. Rhythm is undeniably present, however changed: it is audible, for example, in the contrasting dialogue leading up to the soul's explosion at the end of "Anywhere out of the World."

Baudelaire is a complex and ironic poet, an inheritor of that Romantic irony that wishes to embrace all the opposites of human existence: good and evil, love and hate, self and other, dream and reality. His is a universe of relationships, of echoes and correspondences. His best-known poem, in fact, is the sonnet "Correspondences." This poem describes a vision of the mystic unity of all nature, which is demonstrated by the reciprocity of our five senses (*synesthesia*). Nature, says the poet, is a system of perpetual analogies in which one thing always corresponds to another—physical objects to each other (colonnades in a temple, for example, to trees in the forest), spiritual reality to physical reality, and the five senses (taste, smell, touch, sight, and hearing) among themselves—to produce such combinations as "bitter green," a "soft look," or "a harsh sound." Human beings are not usually aware of the "universal analogy"—the forest of the first stanza watches us without our knowing it—but it is the role of the poet to act as seer and guide, urging us toward a state of awareness where both mind and senses fuse in another dimension. "Correspondences" is no vaguely intuitive poem, however. Even though it describes a state of ecstatic awareness, it works through the stages of a logical argument. The thesis is set out in the first stanza, explained in the second, and illustrated with cumulative examples in the third and fourth. Baudelaire's yearning for mystic harmony does not make him neglect either a base in reality or a rigorous application of intellect. His fusion of idealist vision, realistic detail, and artistic discipline made him the most influential poet of the nineteenth century, and the first poet of the modern age.

The selections printed here, from a range of Baudelaire's most influential lyric and prose poems, are translated by different modern poets. While remaining faithful to the original text, each translation necessarily stresses different aspects (for example, images, meter and rhyme, word order, tone, a particular set of associations when more than one is possible) to create a genuine English poem. The footnotes occasionally point out elements that are especially significant in the French text.

PRONOUNCING GLOSSARY

The following list uses common English syllables and stress accents to provide rough equivalents of selected words whose pronunciation may be unfamiliar to the general reader.

Baudelaire: *boh-d'lair'*   Pylades: *pill'-ah-deez*

ennui: *on-wee'*

THE FLOWERS OF EVIL

To the Reader[1]

Infatuation, sadism, lust avarice
possess our souls and drain the body's force;
we spoonfeed our adorable remorse,
like whores or beggars nourishing their lice.

Our sins are mulish, our confessions lies;   5
we play to the grandstand with our promises,
we pray for tears to wash our filthiness,
importantly pissing hogwash through our styes.

The devil, watching by our sickbeds, hissed
old smut and folk-songs to our soul, until   10
the soft and precious metal of our will
boiled off in vapor for this scientist.

Each day his flattery[2] makes us eat a toad,
and each step forward is a step to hell,
unmoved, though previous corpses and their smell   15
asphyxiate our progress on this road.

Like the poor lush who cannot satisfy,
we try to force our sex with counterfeits,
die drooling on the deliquescent tits,
mouthing the rotten orange we suck dry.   20

Gangs of demons are boozing in our brain—
ranked, swarming, like a million warrior-ants,[3]
they drown and choke the cistern of our wants;
each time we breathe, we tear our lungs with pain.

If poison, arson, sex, narcotics, knives   25
have not yet ruined us and stitched their quick,
loud patterns on the canvas of our lives,
it is because our souls are still too sick.[4]

Among the vermin, jackals, panthers, lice,
gorillas and tarantulas that suck   30
and snatch and scratch and defecate and fuck
in the disorderly circus of our vice,

there's one more ugly and abortive birth.
It makes no gestures, never beats its breast,
yet it would murder for a moment's rest,[5]   35
and willingly annihilate the earth.

---

1. Translated by Robert Lowell. The translation pays primary attention to the insistent rhythm of the original poetic language and keeps the *abba* rhyme scheme.   2. The Devil is literally described as a puppet master controlling our strings.   3. Literally, intestinal worms.   4. Literally, not bold enough.
5. Literally, swallow the world in a yawn.

It's BOREDOM. Tears have glued its eyes together.
You know it well, my Reader. This obscene
beast chain-smokes yawning for the guillotine—
you— hypocrite Reader—my double—my brother!   40

Correspondences[1]

Nature is a temple whose living colonnades
Breathe forth a mystic speech in fitful sighs;
Man wanders among symbols in those glades
Where all things watch him with familiar eyes.

Like dwindling echoes gathered far away   5
Into a deep and thronging unison
Huge as the night or as the light of day,
All scents and sounds and colors meet as one.

Perfumes there are as sweet as the oboe's sound,
Green as the prairies, fresh as a child's caress,[2]   10
—And there are others, rich, corrupt, profound[3]

And of an infinite pervasiveness,
Like myrrh, or musk, or amber,[4] that excite
The ecstasies of sense, the soul's delight.

Correspondances

La Nature est un temple où de vivants piliers
Laissent parfois sortir de confuses paroles;
L'homme y passe à travers des forêts de symboles
Qui l'observent avec des regards familiers.

Comme de longs échos qui de loin se confondent   5
Dans une ténébreuse et profonde unité,
Vaste comme la nuit et comme la clarté,
Les parfums, les couleurs et les sons se répondent.

Il est des parfums frais comme des chairs d'enfants,
Doux comme les hautbois, verts comme les prairies,   10
—Et d'autres, corrompus, riches et triomphants,

Ayant l'expansion des choses infinies,
Comme l'ambre, le musc, le benjoin et l'encens,
Qui chantent les transports de l'esprit et des sens.

1. Translated by Richard Wilbur. The translation keeps the intricate melody of the sonnet's original rhyme
scheme.   2. Literally, flesh.   3. Literally, triumphant.   4. Or ambergris, a substance secreted by
whales. Ambergris and musk (a secretion of the male musk deer) are used in making perfume.

Her Hair[1]

O fleece, that down the neck waves to the nape!
O curls! O perfume nonchalant and rare!
O ecstacy! To fill this alcove[2] shape
With memories that in these tresses sleep,
I would shake them like pennons in the air!   5

Languorous Asia, burning Africa,
And a far world, defunct almost, absent,
Within your aromatic forest stay!
As other souls on music drift away,
Mine, o my love! still floats upon your scent.   10

I shall go there where, full of sap, both tree
And man swoon in the heat of southern climes;
Strong tresses, be the swell that carries me!
I dream upon your sea of ebony
Of dazzling sails, of oarsmen, masts and flames: 15

A sun-drenched and reverberating port,
Where I imbibe color and sound and scent;
Where vessels, gliding through the gold and moire,
Open their vast arms as they leave the shore
To clasp the pure and shimmering firmament.   20

I'll plunge my head, enamored of its pleasure,
In this black ocean where the other hides;
My subtle spirit then will know a measure
Of fertile idleness and fragrant leisure,
Lulled by the infinite rhythm of its tides!   25

Pavilion, of blue-shadowed tresses spun,
You give me back the azure from afar;
And where the twisted locks are fringed with down
Lurk mingled odors I grow drunk upon
Of oil of coconut, of musk and tar.   30

A long time! always! my hand in your hair
Will sow the stars of sapphire, pearl, ruby,
That you be never deaf to my desire,
My oasis and gourd whence I aspire
To drink deep of the wine of memory![3]   35

---

1. Translated by Doreen Bell. The translation emulates the French original's challenging *abaab* rhyme pattern. 2. Bedroom. 3. The last two lines are a question: "Are you not . . . ?"

A Carcass[1]

Remember, my love, the item you saw
    That beautiful morning in June:
By a bend in the path a carcass reclined
    On a bed sown with pebbles and stones;

Her legs were spread out like a lecherous whore,   5
    Sweating out poisonous fumes,
Who opened in slick invitational style
    Her stinking and festering womb.

The sun on this rottenness focused its rays
    To cook the cadaver till done,   10
And render to Nature a hundredfold gift
    Of all she'd united in one.

And the sky cast an eye on this marvelous meat
    As over the flowers in bloom.
The stench was so wretched that there on the grass   15
    You nearly collapsed in a swoon.

The flies buzzed and droned on these bowels of filth
    Where an army of maggots arose,
Which flowed like a liquid and thickening stream
    On the animate rags of her clothes.[2]   20

And it rose and it fell, and pulsed like a wave,
    Rushing and bubbling with health.
One could say that this carcass, blown with vague breath,
    Lived in increasing itself.

And this whole teeming world made a musical sound   25
    Like babbling brooks and the breeze,
Or the grain that a man with a winnowing-fan
    Turns with a rhythmical ease.

The shapes wore away as if only a dream
    Like a sketch that is left on the page   30
Which the artist forgot and can only complete
    On the canvas, with memory's aid.

From back in the rocks, a pitiful bitch
    Eyed us with angry distaste,
Awaiting the moment to snatch from the bones   35
    The morsel she'd dropped in her haste.

---

1. Translated by James McGowan with special attention to imagery. The alternation of long and short lines in English emulates the French meter's rhythmic swing between twelve-syllable and eight-syllable lines in an *abab* rhyme scheme.   **2.** By extension. The torn flesh is described as "living rags."

—And you, in your turn, will be rotten as this:
   Horrible, filthy, undone,
Oh sun of my nature and star of my eyes,
   My passion, my angel[3] in one!   40

Yes, such will you be, oh regent of grace,
   After the rites have been read,
Under the weeds, under blossoming grass
   As you molder with bones of the dead.

Ah then, oh my beauty, explain to the worms   45
   Who cherish your body so fine,
That I am the keeper for corpses of love
   Of the form, and the essence divine![4]

Invitation to the Voyage[1]

My child, my sister, dream
   How sweet all things would seem
Were we in that kind land to live together,
   And there love slow and long,
   There love and die among   5
Those scenes that image you, that sumptuous weather.
   Drowned suns that glimmer there
   Through cloud-disheveled air
Move me with such a mystery as appears
   Within those other skies   10
   Of your treacherous eyes
When I behold them shining through their tears.

There, there is nothing else but grace and measure,
Richness, quietness, and pleasure.

   Furniture that wears   15
   The lustre of the years
Softly would glow within our glowing chamber,
   Flowers of rarest bloom
   Proffering their perfume
Mixed with the vague fragrances of amber;   20
   Gold ceilings would there be,
   Mirrors deep as the sea,
The walls all in an Eastern splendor hung—
   Nothing but should address

3. Series of conventional Petrarchan images that idealize the beloved.   4. "Any form created by man is immortal. For form is independent of matter . . ." from Baudelaire's journal *My Heart Laid Bare* LXXX. 1. Translated by Richard Wilbur. The translation maintains both the rhyme scheme and the rocking motion of the original meter, which follows an unusual pattern of two five-syllable lines followed by one seven-syllable line, and a seven-syllable couplet as refrain.

The soul's loneliness,   25
Speaking her sweet and secret native tongue.

There, there is nothing else but grace and measure,
Richness, quietness, and pleasure.

    See, sheltered from the swells
    There in the still canals   30
Those drowsy ships that dream of sailing forth;
    It is to satisfy
    Your least desire, they ply
Hither through all the waters of the earth.
    The sun at close of day   35
    Clothes the fields of hay,
Then the canals, at last the town entire
    In hyacinth and gold:
    Slowly the land is rolled
Sleepward under a sea of gentle fire.   40

There, there is nothing else but grace and measure,
Richness, quietness, and pleasure.

Song of Autumn I[1]

Soon we shall plunge into the chilly fogs;
Farewell, swift light! our summers are too short!
I hear already the mournful fall of logs
Re-echoing from the pavement of the court.

All of winter will gather in my soul: 5
Hate, anger, horror, chills, the hard forced work;
And, like the sun in his hell by the north pole,
My heart will be only a red and frozen block.

I shudder, hearing every log that falls;
No scaffold could be built with hollower sounds.   10
My spirit is like a tower whose crumbling walls
The tireless battering-ram brings to the ground.

It seems to me, lulled by monotonous shocks,
As if they were hastily nailing a coffin today.
For whom?—Yesterday was summer. Now autumn knocks.   15
That mysterious sound is like someone's going away.

---

1. Translated by C. F. MacIntyre to follow the original rhyme pattern.

Spleen LXXVIII[1]

Old Pluvius,[2] month of rains, in peevish mood
Pours from his urn chill winter's sodden gloom
On corpses fading in the near graveyard,
On foggy suburbs pours life's tedium.

My cat seeks out a litter on the stones,   5
Her mangy body turning without rest.
An ancient poet's soul in monotones
Whines in the rain-spouts like a chilblained ghost.

A great bell mourns, a wet log wrapped in smoke
Sings in falsetto to the wheezing clock,   10
While from a rankly perfumed deck of cards
(A dropsical old crone's fatal bequest)
The Queen of Spades, the dapper Jack of Hearts
Speak darkly of dead loves, how they were lost.

Spleen LXXIX[1]

I have more memories than if I had lived a thousand years.

Even a bureau crammed with souvenirs,
Old bills, love letters, photographs, receipts,
Court depositions, locks of hair in plaits,
Hides fewer secrets than my brain could yield.   5
It's like a tomb, a corpse-filled Potter's Field,[2]
A pyramid where the dead lie down by scores.
I am a graveyard that the moon abhors:
Like guilty qualms, the worms burrow and nest
Thickly in bodies that I loved the best.   10
I'm a stale boudoir where old-fashioned clothes
Lie scattered among wilted fern and rose,
Where only the Boucher girls[3] in pale pastels
Can breathe the uncorked scents and faded smells.

Nothing can equal those days for endlessness   15
When in the winter's blizzardy caress
Indifference expanding to Ennui[4]
Takes on the feel of Immortality.
O living matter, henceforth you're no more
Than a cold stone encompassed by vague fear   20

1. Translated by Kenneth O. Hanson, with emphasis on the imagery. The French original uses identical *abab* rhymes in the two quatrains and shifts to *ccd, eed* in the tercets.   2. Pluvius is literally "the rainy time" (Latin), a period extending from January 20 to February 18 as the fifth month of the French Revolutionary calendar.   1. Translated by Anthony Hecht. The translation follows the original rhymed couplets except for one technical impossibility: Baudelaire's repetition (in a poem about monotony) of an identical rhyme for eight lines (lines 11–18, the sound of long *a*).   2. A general term describing the common cemetery for those buried at public expense.   3. François Boucher (1703–1770), court painter for Louis XV of France, drew many pictures of young women clothed and nude.   4. Melancholy, paralyzing boredom.

And by the desert, and the mist and sun;
An ancient Sphinx ignored by everyone,
Left off the map, whose bitter irony
Is to sing as the sun sets in that dry sea.[5]

PARIS SPLEEN[1]

Anywhere out of the World[2]

Life is a hospital where every patient is obsessed by the desire of changing beds. One would like to suffer opposite the stove, another is sure he would get well beside the window.

It always seems to me that I should be happy anywhere but where I am, and this question of moving is one that I am eternally discussing with my soul.

"Tell me, my soul, poor chilly soul, how would you like to live in Lisbon? It must be warm there, and you would be as blissful as a lizard in the sun. It is a city by the sea; they say that it is built of marble, and that its inhabitants have such a horror of the vegetable kingdom that they tear up all the trees. You see it is a country after my own heart; a country entirely made of mineral and light, and with liquid to reflect them."

My soul does not reply.

"Since you are so fond of being motionless and watching the pageantry of movement, would you like to live in the beatific land of Holland? Perhaps you could enjoy yourself in that country which you have so long admired in paintings on museum walls. What do you say to Rotterdam,[3] you who love forests of masts, and ships that are moored on the doorsteps of houses?"

My soul remains silent.

"Perhaps you would like Batavia[4] better? There, moreover, we should find the wit of Europe wedded to the beauty of the tropics."

Not a word. Can my soul be dead?

"Have you sunk into so deep a stupor that you are happy only in your unhappiness? If that is the case, let us fly to countries that are the counterfeits of Death. I know just the place for us, poor soul. We will pack up our trunks for Torneo.[5] We will go still farther, to the farthest end of the Baltic Sea; still farther from life if possible; we will settle at the Pole. There the sun only obliquely grazes the earth, and the slow alternations of daylight and night abolish variety and increase that other half of nothingness, monotony. There we can take deep baths of darkness, while sometimes for our entertainment, the Aurora Borealis will shoot up its rose-red sheafs like the reflections of the fireworks of hell!"

At last my soul explodes! "Anywhere! Just so it is out of the world!"

5. Baudelaire combines two references to ancient Egypt, the sphinx and the legendary statue of Memnon at Thebes, which was supposed to sing at sunset.   **1.** Translated by Louis Varèse.   **2.** The title (given in English by Baudelaire) is based on a line from Thomas Hood's poem "Bridge of Sighs": "Anywhere, anywhere—out of the world." Baudelaire probably found the reference in Poe's "Poetic Principle." **3.** Large Dutch seaport.   **4.** Former name of Djakarta, capital of the Dutch East Indies and now the capital city of Indonesia.   **5.** A city in Finland.

LEO TOLSTOY
1828–1910

Count Leo Tolstoy excited the interest of Europe mainly as a public figure: a count owning large estates who decided to give up his wealth and live like a simple Russian peasant—to dress in a blouse, to eat peasant food, and even to plow the fields and make shoes with his own hands. By the time of his death he had become the leader of a religious cult, the propounder of a new religion. It was, in substance, a highly simplified primitive Christianity that he reduced to a few moral commands (such as, "Do not resist evil") and from which he drew, with radical consistency, a complete condemnation of modern civilization: the state, courts and law, war, patriotism, marriage, modern art and literature, science and medicine. In debating this Christian anarchism people have tended to forget that Tolstoy established his command of the public ear as a novelist, or they have exaggerated the contrast between the early worldly novelist and the later prophet who repudiated all his early, great novelistic work: *War and Peace*, the enormous epic of the 1812 invasion of Russia, and *Anna Karenina*, the story of an adulterous love, superbly realized in accurately imagined detail.

Tolstoy was born at Yásnaya Polyána, his mother's estate near Tula (about 130 miles south of Moscow), on August 28, 1828. His father was a retired lieutenant colonel; one of his ancestors, the first count, had served Peter the Great as an ambassador. His mother's father was a Russian general-in-chief. Tolstoy lost both parents early in his life and was brought up by aunts. He went to the University of Kazan between 1844 and 1847, drifted along aimlessly for a few years more, and in 1851 became a cadet in the Caucasus. As an artillery officer he saw action in the wars with the mountain tribes and again, in 1854–55, during the Crimean War against the French and English. Tolstoy had written fictional reminiscences of his childhood while he was in the Caucasus, and during the Crimean War he wrote war stories, which established his literary reputation. For some years he lived on his estate, where he founded and himself taught an extremely "progressive" school for peasant children. He made two trips to western Europe, in 1857 and in 1860–61. In 1862 he married the daughter of a physician, Sonya Bers, with whom he had thirteen children.

In the first years of his married life, between 1863 and 1869, he wrote his enormous novel *War and Peace*. The book made him famous in Russia but was not translated into English until long afterward. Superficially, *War and Peace* is an historical novel about the Napoleonic invasion of Russia in 1812, a huge swarming epic of a nation's resistance to the foreigner. Tolstoy himself interprets history in general as a struggle of anonymous collective forces that are moved by unknown irrational impulses, waves of communal feeling. Heroes, great men and women, are actually not heroes but merely insignificant puppets; the best general is the one who does nothing to prevent the unknown course of Providence. But *War and Peace* is not only an impressive and vivid panorama of historical events but also the profound story— centered in two main characters, Pierre Bezukhov and Prince Andrey Bolkonsky—of a search for meaning in life. Andrey finds meaning in love and forgiveness of his enemies. Pierre, at the end of a long groping struggle, an education by suffering, finds it in an acceptance of ordinary existence, its duties and pleasures, the family, the continuity of the race.

Tolstoy's next long novel, *Anna Karenina* (1875–77), resumes this second thread of *War and Peace*. It is a novel of contemporary manners, a narrative of adultery and suicide. But this vivid story, told with incomparable concrete imagination, is counterpointed and framed by a second story, that of Levin, another seeker after the meaning of life, a figure who represents the author as Pierre did in the earlier book; the work ends with a promise of salvation, with the ideal of a life in which we should "remember God." Thus *Anna Karenina* also anticipates the approaching crisis in Tolstoy's life. When it came, with the sudden revulsion he describes in *A Confession* (1879), he condemned his earlier books and spent the next years in writing pamphlets and tracts expounding his religion.

Only slowly did Tolstoy return to the writing of fiction, now regarded entirely as a means of presenting his creed. The earlier novels seemed to him unclear in their message, overdetailed in their method. Hence Tolstoy tried to simplify his art; he wrote plays with a thesis, stories that are like fables or parables, and one long, rather inferior novel, *The Resurrection* (1899), his most savage satire on Russian and modern institutions.

In 1901 Tolstoy was excommunicated. A disagreement with his wife about the nature of the good life and about financial matters sharpened into a conflict over his last will, which finally led to a complete break: he left home in the company of a doctor friend. He caught cold on the train journey south and died in the house of the stationmaster of Astápovo, on November 20, 1910.

If we look back on Tolstoy's work as a whole, we must recognize its continuity. From the very beginning he was a Rousseauist. As early as 1851, when he was in the Caucasus, his diary announced his intention of founding a new, simplified religion. Even as a young man on his estate he had lived quite simply, like a peasant, except for occasional sprees and debauches. He had been horrified by war from the very beginning, though he admired the heroism of the individual soldier and had remnants of patriotic feeling. All his books concern the same theme, the good life, and they all say that the good life lies outside civilization, near the soil, in simplicity and humility, in love of one's neighbor. Power, the lust for power, luxury, are always evil.

Tolstoy's roots as a novelist are part of another, older realistic tradition. He read and knew the English writers of the eighteenth century—and also William Makepeace Thackeray and Anthony Trollope—though he did not care for the recent French writers (he was strong in his disapproval of Gustave Flaubert) except for Guy de Maupassant, who struck him as truthful and useful in his struggle against hypocrisy. Tolstoy's long novels are loosely plotted, though they have large overall designs. They work by little scenes vividly visualized, by an accumulation of exact detail. Each character is drawn by means of repeated emphasis on certain physical traits, like Pierre's shortsightedness and his hairy, clumsy hands, or Princess Marya's luminous eyes, the red patches on her face, and her shuffling gait. This concretely realized surface, however, everywhere recedes into depths: to the depiction of disease, delirium, and death and to glimpses into eternity. In *War and Peace* the blue sky is the recurrent symbol for the metaphysical spirit within us. Tolstoy is so robust, has his feet so firmly on the ground, presents what he sees with such clarity and objectivity, that one can be easily deluded into considering his dominating quality to be physical, sensual, antithetical to Dostoevsky's spirituality. The contrasts between the two greatest Russian novelists are indeed obvious. While Tolstoy's method can be called epic, Dostoevsky's is dramatic; while Tolstoy's view of humanity is Rousseauistic, Dostoevsky stresses the Fall; while Tolstoy rejects history and status, Dostoevsky appeals to the past and desires a hierarchical society, and so on. But these profound differences should not obscure one basic similarity: the deep spirituality of both writers, their rejection of the basic materialism and the conception of truth propounded by modern science and theorists of realism.

"The Death of Iván Ilyich" (1886) belongs to the period after Tolstoy's religious conversion when he slowly returned to fiction writing. It represents a happy medium between his early and late manner. Its story and moral are simple and obvious, as always with Tolstoy (in contrast to Dostoevsky). And it expresses what almost all of his works are intended to convey—that humanity is leading the wrong kind of life, that we should return to essentials, to "nature." In "The Death of Iván Ilyich" Tolstoy combines a savage satire on the futility and hypocrisy of conventional life with a powerful symbolic presentation of isolation in the struggle with death and of hope for a final resurrection. Iván Ilyich is a Russian judge, an official, but he is also the average man of the prosperous middle classes of his time and ours, and he is also Everyman confronted with disease and dying and death. He is an ordinary person, neither virtuous nor particularly vicious, a "go-getter" in his profession, a "family man," as marriages go, who has children but has drifted apart from his wife. Through his disease, which comes about by a trivial accident in the trivial business of fixing a curtain, Iván Ilyich is slowly awakened to self-consciousness and a realization of the falsity of his life and ambitions. The isolation that disease imposes on him, the wall of hypocrisy erected around him by his family and his doctors, his suffering and pain, drive him slowly to the recognition of *It*: to a knowledge, not merely theoretical but proved on his pulses, of his own mortality. At first he would like simply to return to his former pleasant and normal life—even in the last days of his illness, knowing he must die, he screams in his agony, "I won't!"—but at the end, struggling in the black sack into which he is being pushed, he sees the light at the bottom. "'Death is finished,' he said to himself. 'It is no more!'"

The people around him are egotists and hypocrites: his wife, who can remember only how she suffered during his agony; his daughter, who thinks only of the delay in her marriage; his colleagues, who speculate only about the room his death will make for promotions in the court; the doctors, who think only of the name of the disease and not of the patient; all except his shy and frightened son, Vásya, and the servant Gerásim. Because he is young, near to "nature," and free from hypocrisy, Gerásim is able to make his master more comfortable, and even to mention death, while all the others conceal the truth from him. The doctors, especially, are shown as mere specialists, inhuman and selfish. The first doctor is like a judge—like Iván himself when he sat in court—summing up and cutting off further questions of the patient. The satire at points appears ineffectively harsh in its violence, but it will not seem exceptional to those who know the older Tolstoy's general attitude toward courts, medicine, marriage, and even modern literature. The cult of art is jeered at, in small touches, only incidentally; it belongs, according to Tolstoy, to the falsities of modern civilization, alongside marriage (which merely hides bestial sensuality), and science (which merely hides rapacity and ignorance).

The story is deliberately deprived of any element of suspense, not only by the announcement contained in the title but by the technique of the cutback. We first hear of Iván Ilyich's death and see the reaction of the widow and friends, and only then listen to the story of his life. The detail, as always in Tolstoy, is superbly concrete and realistic: he does not shy away from the smell of disease, the physical necessity of using a chamber pot, or the sound of screaming. He can employ the creaking of a hassock as a recurrent motif to point out the comedy of hypocrisy played by the widow and her visitor. He can seriously and tragically use the humble image of a black sack or the illusion of the movement of a train.

But all this naturalistic detail serves the one purpose of making us come to realize, as Iván Ilyich realizes, that not only is Caius mortal but you and I also, and that the life of "civilized" people is a great lie simply because it disguises and ignores its dark background, the metaphysical abyss, the reality of Death. While the presentation of "The Death of Iván Ilyich" approaches, at moments, the tone of a legend or fable ("Iván Ilyich's life had been most simple and most ordinary and therefore most terrible"), Tolstoy in this story manages to stay within the concrete situation of his society and to combine the aesthetic method of realism with the universalizing power of symbolic art.

PRONOUNCING GLOSSARY

The following list uses common English syllables and stress accents to provide rough equivalents of selected words whose pronunciation may be unfamiliar to the general reader.

Fëdor Petróvich: *fyaw'-dur pe-traw'-veech*

Fëdor Vasílievich: *fyaw'-dur vah-seel'-ye-veech*

Gerásim: *gye-rah'-syeem*

Golovín: *guh-lah-veen'*

Iván Ilyich: *ee-vahn' il-yeech'*

Ivánovich: *ee-vah'-nuh-veech*

Karenina: *kah-re'-nyee-nuh*

The Death of Iván Ilyich[1]

I

During an interval in the Melvínski trial in the large building of the Law Courts the members and public prosecutor met in Iván Egórovich Shébek's private room, where the conversation turned on the celebrated Krasóvski case. Fëdor Vasílievich warmly maintained that it was not subject to their jurisdiction, Iván Egórovich maintained the contrary, while Peter Ivánovich, not having entered into the discussion at the start, took no part in it but looked through the *Gazette* which had just been handed in.

"Gentlemen," he said, "Iván Ilyich has died!"

"You don't say!"

"Here read it yourself," replied Peter Ivánovich, handing Fëdor Vasílievich the paper still damp from the press. Surrounded by a black border were the words: "Praskóvya Fëdorovna Goloviná, with profound sorrow, informs relatives and friends of the demise of her beloved husband Iván Ilyich Golovín, Member of the Court of Justice, which occurred on February the 4th of this year 1882. The funeral will take place on Friday at one o'clock in the afternoon."

Iván Ilyich had been a colleague of the gentlemen present and was liked by them all. He had been ill for some weeks with an illness said to be incurable. His post had been kept open for him, but there had been conjectures that in case of his death Alexéev might receive his appointment, and that either Vínnikov or Shtábel would succeed Alexéev. So on receiving the news of Iván Ilyich's death the first thought of each of the gentlemen in that private room was of the changes and promotions it might occasion among themselves or their acquaintances.

"I shall be sure to get Shtábel's place or Vínnikov's," thought Fëdor Vasílievich. "I was promised that long ago, and the promotion means an extra eight hundred rubles a year for me besides the allowance."

"Now I must apply for my brother-in-law's transfer from Kalúga," thought Peter Ivánovich. "My wife will be very glad, and then she won't be able to say that I never do anything for her relations."

---

1. Translated by Louise Maude and Aylmer Maude.

"I thought he would never leave his bed again," said Peter Ivánovich aloud. "It's very sad."

"But what really was the matter with him?"

"The doctors couldn't say—at least they could, but each of them said something different. When last I saw him I thought he was getting better."

"And I haven't been to see him since the holidays. I always meant to go."

"Had he any property?"

"I think his wife had a little—but something quite trifling."

"We shall have to go to see her, but they live so terribly far away."

"Far away from you, you mean. Everything's far away from your place."

"You see, he never can forgive my living on the other side of the river," said Peter Ivánovich, smiling at Shébek. Then, still talking of the distances between different parts of the city, they returned to the Court.

Besides considerations as to the possible transfers and promotions likely to result from Iván Ilyich's death, the mere fact of the death of a near acquaintance aroused, as usual, in all who heard of it the complacent feeling that, "it is he who is dead and not I."

Each one thought or felt, "Well, he's dead but I'm alive!" But the more intimate of Iván Ilyich's acquaintances, his so-called friends, could not help thinking also that they would now have to fulfil the very tiresome demands of propriety by attending the funeral service and paying a visit of condolence to the widow.

Fëdor Vasílievich and Peter Ivánovich had been his nearest acquaintances. Peter Ivánovich had studied law with Iván Ilyich and had considered himself to be under obligations to him.

Having told his wife at dinner-time of Iván Ilyich's death, and of his conjecture that it might be possible to get her brother transferred to their circuit, Peter Ivánovich sacrificed his usual nap, put on his evening clothes, and drove to Iván Ilyich's house.

At the entrance stood a carriage and two cabs. Leaning against the wall in the hall downstairs near the cloak-stand was a coffin-lid covered with cloth of gold, ornamented with gold cord and tassels, that had been polished up with metal powder. Two ladies in black were taking off their fur cloaks. Peter Ivánovich recognized one of them as Iván Ilyich's sister, but the other was a stranger to him. His colleague Schwartz was just coming downstairs, but on seeing Peter Ivánovich enter he stopped and winked at him, as if to say: "Iván Ilyich has made a mess of things—not like you and me."

Schwartz's face with his Piccadilly whiskers, and his slim figure in evening dress, had as usual an air of elegant solemnity which contrasted with the playfulness of his character and had a special piquancy here, or so it seemed to Peter Ivánovich.

Peter Ivánovich allowed the ladies to precede him and slowly followed them upstairs. Schwartz did not come down but remained where he was, and Peter Ivánovich understood that he wanted to arrange where they should play bridge that evening. The ladies went upstairs to the widow's room, and Schwartz with seriously compressed lips but a playful look in his eyes, indicated by a twist of his eyebrows the room to the right where the body lay.

Peter Ivánovich, like everyone else on such occasions, entered feeling uncertain what he would have to do. All he knew was that at such times it is always safe to cross oneself. But he was not quite sure whether one should make obeisances while doing so. He therefore adopted a middle course. On entering the room he began crossing himself and made a slight movement resembling a bow. At the same time, as far as the motion of his head and arm allowed, he surveyed the room. Two young men—apparently nephews, one of whom was a high-school pupil—were leaving the room, crossing themselves as they did so. An old woman was standing motionless, and a lady with strangely arched eyebrows was saying something to her in a whisper. A vigorous, resolute Church Reader, in a frock-coat, was reading something in a loud voice with an expression that precluded any contradiction. The butler's assistant, Gerásim, stepping lightly in front of Peter Ivánovich, was strewing something on the floor. Noticing this, Peter Ivánovich was immediately aware of a faint odour of a decomposing body.

The last time he had called on Iván Ilyich, Peter Ivánovich had seen Gerásim in the study. Iván Ilyich had been particularly fond of him and he was performing the duty of a sick nurse.

Peter Ivánovich continued to make the sign of the cross slightly inclining his head in an intermediate direction between the coffin, the Reader, and the icons on the table in a corner of the room. Afterwards, when it seemed to him that this movement of his arm in crossing himself had gone on too long, he stopped and began to look at the corpse.

The dead man lay, as dead men always lie, in a specially heavy way, his rigid limbs sunk in the soft cushions of the coffin, with the head forever bowed on the pillow. His yellow waxen brow with bald patches over his sunken temples was thrust up in the way peculiar to the dead, the protruding nose seeming to press on the upper lip. He was much changed and had grown even thinner since Peter Ivánovich had last seen him, but, as is always the case with the dead, his face was handsomer and above all more dignified than when he was alive. The expression on the face said that what was necessary had been accomplished, and accomplished rightly. Besides this there was in that expression a reproach and a warning to the living. This warning seemed to Peter Ivánovich out of place, or at least not applicable to him. He felt a certain discomfort and so he hurriedly crossed himself once more and turned and went out of the door—too hurriedly and too regardless of propriety, as he himself was aware.

Schwartz was waiting for him in the adjoining room with legs spread wide apart and both hands toying with his top-hat behind his back. The mere sight of that playful, well-groomed, and elegant figure refreshed Peter Ivánovich. He felt that Schwartz was above all these happenings and could not surrender to any depressing influences. His very look said that this incident of a church service for Iván Ilyich could not be a sufficient reason for infringing the order of the session—in other words, that it would certainly not prevent his unwrapping a new pack of cards and shuffling them that evening while a footman placed four fresh candles on the table: in fact, that there was no reason for supposing that this incident would hinder their spending the evening agreeably. Indeed he said this in a whisper as Peter Ivánovich passed him, proposing that they should meet for a game at Fëdor Vasílievich's. But apparently Peter Ivánovich was not destined to play bridge that evening. Praskóvya Fëdorovna (a short, fat woman who despite all efforts to the contrary had continued to broaden steadily from her shoulders downwards and who had the same extraordinary arched eyebrows as the lady who had been standing by the coffin), dressed all in black, her head covered with lace, came out of her own room with some other ladies, conducted them to the room where the dead body lay, and said: "The service will begin immediately. Please go in."

Schwartz, making an indefinite bow, stood still, evidently neither accepting nor declining this invitation. Praskóvya Fëdorovna recognizing Peter Ivánovich, sighed, went close up to him, took his hand, and said: "I know you were a true friend to Iván Ilyich . . ." and looked at him awaiting some suitable response. And Peter Ivánovich knew that, just as it had been the right thing to cross himself in that room, so what he had to do here was to press her hand, sigh, and say, "Believe me . . ." So he did all this and as he did it felt that the desired result had been achieved: that both he and she were touched.

"Come with me. I want to speak to you before it begins," said the widow. "Give me your arm."

Peter Ivánovich gave her his arm and they went to the inner rooms, passing Schwartz who winked at Peter Ivánovich compassionately.

"That does for our bridge! Don't object if we find another player. Perhaps you can cut in when you do escape," said his playful look.

Peter Ivánovich sighed still more deeply and despondently, and Praskóvya Fëdorovna pressed his arm gratefully. When they reached the drawing-room, upholstered in pink cretonne and lighted by a dim lamp, they sat down at the table—she on a sofa and Peter Ivánovich on a low hassock, the springs of which yielded spasmodically under his weight. Praskóvya Fëdorovna had been on the point of warning him to take another seat, but felt that such a warning was out of keeping with her present condition and so changed her mind. As he sat down on the hassock Peter Ivánovich recalled how Iván Ilyich had arranged this room and had consulted him regarding this pink cretonne with green leaves. The whole room was full of furniture and knick-knacks, and on her way to the sofa the lace of the widow's black shawl caught on the carved edge of the table. Peter Ivánovich rose to detach it, and the springs of the hassock, relieved of his weight, rose also and gave him a push. The widow began detaching her shawl herself, and Peter Ivánovich again sat down, suppressing the rebellious springs of the hassock under him. But the widow had not quite freed herself and Peter Ivánovich got up again, and again the hassock rebelled and even creaked. When this was all over she took out a clean cambric handkerchief and began to weep. The episode with the shawl and the struggle with the hassock had cooled Peter Ivánovich's emotions and he sat there with a sullen look on his face. This awkward situation was interrupted by Sokolóv, Iván Ilyich's butler, who came to report that the plot in the cemetery that Praskóvya Fëdorovna had chosen would cost two hundred rubles. She stopped weeping and, looking at Peter Ivánovich with the air of a victim, remarked in French that it was very hard for her. Peter Ivánovich made a silent gesture signifying his full conviction that it must indeed be so.

"Please smoke," she said in a magnanimous yet crushed voice, and turned to discuss with Sokolóv the price of the plot for the grave.

Peter Ivánovich while lighting his cigarette heard her inquiring very circumstantially into the prices of different plots in the cemetery and finally decide which she would take. When that was done she gave instructions about engaging the choir. Sokolóv then left the room.

"I look after everything myself," she told Peter Ivánovich, shifting the albums that lay on the table; and noticing that the table was endangered by his cigarette-ash, she immediately passed him an ashtray, saying as she did so: "I consider it an affectation to say that my grief prevents my attending to practical affairs. On the contrary, if anything can—I won't say console me, but—distract me, it is seeing to everything concerning him." She again took out her handkerchief as if preparing to cry, but suddenly, as if mastering her feeling, she shook herself and began to speak calmly. "But there is something I want to talk to you about."

Peter Ivánovich bowed, keeping control of the springs of the hassock, which immediately began quivering under him.

"He suffered terribly the last few days."

"Did he?" said Peter Ivánovich.

"Oh, terribly! He screamed unceasingly, not for minutes but for hours. For the last three days he screamed incessantly. It was unendurable. I cannot understand how I bore it; you could hear him three rooms off. Oh, what I have suffered!"

"Is it possible that he was conscious all that time?" asked Peter Ivánovich.

"Yes," she whispered. "To the last moment. He took leave of us a quarter of an hour before he died, and asked us to take Vásya away."

The thought of the sufferings of this man he had known so intimately, first as a merry little boy, then as a school-mate, and later as a grown-up colleague, suddenly struck Peter Ivánovich with horror, despite an unpleasant consciousness of his own and this woman's dissimulation. He again saw that brow, and that nose pressing down on the lip, and felt afraid for himself.

"Three days of frightful suffering and then death! Why, that might suddenly, at any time, happen to me," he thought, and for a moment felt terrified. But—he did not himself know how—the customary reflection at once occurred to him that this had happened to Iván Ilyich and not to him, and that it should not and could not happen to him, and that to think that it could would be yielding to depression which he ought not to do, as Schwartz's expression plainly showed. After which reflection Peter Ivánovich felt reassured, and began to ask with interest about the details of Iván Ilyich's death, as though death was an accident natural to Iván Ilyich but certainly not to himself.

After many details of the really dreadful physical sufferings Iván Ilyich had endured (which details he learnt only from the effect those sufferings had produced on Praskóvya Fëdorovna's nerves) the widow apparently found it necessary to get to business.

"Oh, Peter Ivánovich, how hard it is! How terribly, terribly hard!" and she again began to weep.

Peter Ivánovich sighed and waited for her to finish blowing her nose. When she had done so he said, "Believe me . . ." and she again began talking and brought out what was evidently her chief concern with him—namely, to question him as to how she could obtain a grant of money from the government on the occasion of her husband's death. She made it appear that she was asking Peter Ivánovich's advice about her pension, but he soon saw that she already knew about that to the minutest detail, more even than he did

himself. She knew how much could be got out of the government in consequence of her husband's death, but wanted to find out whether she could
possibly extract something more. Peter Ivánovich tried to think of some
means of doing so, but after reflecting for a while and, out of propriety, condemning the government for its niggardliness, he said he thought that nothing more could be got. Then she sighed and evidently began to devise means
of getting rid of her visitor. Noticing this, he put out his cigarette, rose,
pressed her hand, and went out into the anteroom.

In the dining-room where the clock stood that Iván Ilyich had liked so
much and had bought at an antique shop, Peter Ivánovich met a priest and a
few acquaintances who had come to attend the service, and he recognized
Iván Ilyich's daughter, a handsome young woman. She was in black and her
slim figure appeared slimmer than ever. She had a gloomy, determined,
almost angry expression, and bowed to Peter Ivánovich as though he were in
some way to blame. Behind her, with the same offended look, stood a
wealthy young man, an examining magistrate, whom Peter Ivánovich also
knew and who was her fiancé, as he had heard. He bowed mournfully to
them and was about to pass into the death-chamber, when from under the
stairs appeared the figure of Iván Ilyich's schoolboy son, who was extremely
like this father. He seemed a little Iván Ilyich, such as Peter Ivánovich
remembered when they studied law together. His tear-stained eyes had in
them the look that is seen in the eyes of boys of thirteen or fourteen who are
not pure-minded.

When he saw Peter Ivánovich he scowled morosely and shamefacedly.
Peter Ivánovich nodded to him and entered the death-chamber. The service
began: candles, groans, incense, tears, and sobs. Peter Ivánovich stood looking gloomily down at his feet. He did not look once at the dead man, did not
yield to any depressing influence, and was one of the first to leave the room.
There was no one in the anteroom, but Gerásim darted out of the dead
man's room, rummaged with his strong hands among the fur coats to find
Peter Ivánovich's and helped him on with it.

"Well, friend Gerásim," said Peter Ivánovich, so as to say something. "It's
a sad affair, isn't it?"

"It's God's will. We shall all come to it some day," said Gerásim, displaying
his teeth—the even, white teeth of a healthy peasant—and, like a man in
the thick of urgent work, he briskly opened the front door, called the coachman, helped Peter Ivánovich into the sledge, and sprang back to the porch
as if in readiness for what he had to do next.

Peter Ivánovich found the fresh air particularly pleasant after the smell of
incense, the dead body, and carbolic acid.

"Where to, sir?" asked the coachman.

"It's not too late even now. . . . I'll call round on Fëdor Vasílievich."

He accordingly drove there and found them just finishing the first rubber,
so that it was quite convenient for him to cut in.

II

Iván Ilyich's life had been most simple and most ordinary and therefore
most terrible.

He had been a member of the Court of Justice, and died at the age of forty-five. His father had been an official who after serving in various ministries and departments in Petersburg had made the sort of career which brings men to positions from which by reason of their long service they cannot be dismissed, though they are obviously unfit to hold any responsible position, and for whom therefore posts are specially created, which though fictitious, carry salaries of from six to ten thousand rubles that are not fictitious, and in receipt of which they live on to a great age.

Such was the Privy Councillor and superfluous member of various superfluous institutions, Ilya Efímovich Golovín.

He had three sons, of whom Iván Ilyich was the second. The eldest son was following in his father's footsteps only in another department, and was already approaching that stage in the service at which a similar sinecure would be reached. The third son was a failure. He had ruined his prospects in a number of positions and was now serving in the railway department. His father and brothers, and still more their wives, not merely disliked meeting him, but avoided remembering his existence unless compelled to do so. His sister had married Baron Greff, a Petersburg official of her father's type. Iván Ilyich was *le phénix de la famille*[2] as people said. He was neither as cold and formal as his elder brother nor as wild as the younger, but was a happy mean between them—an intelligent, polished, lively and agreeable man. He had studied with his younger brother at the School of Law, but the latter had failed to complete the course and was expelled when he was in the fifth class. Iván Ilyich finished the course well. Even when he was at the School of Law he was just what he remained for the rest of his life: a capable, cheerful, good-natured, and sociable man, though strict in the fulfilment of what he considered to be his duty: and he considered his duty to be what was so considered by those in authority. Neither as a boy nor as a man was he a toady, but from early youth was by nature attracted to people of high station as a fly is drawn to the light, assimilating their ways and views of life and establishing friendly relations with them. All the enthusiasms of childhood and youth passed without leaving much trace on him; he succumbed to sensuality, to vanity, and latterly among the highest classes to liberalism, but always within limits which his instinct unfailingly indicated to him as correct.

At school he had done things which had formerly seemed to him very horrid and made him feel disgusted with himself when he did them; but when later on he saw that such actions were done by people of good position and that they did not regard them as wrong, he was able not exactly to regard them as right, but to forget about them entirely or not be at all troubled at remembering them.

Having graduated from the School of Law and qualified for the tenth rank of the civil service, and having received money from his father for his equipment, Iván Ilyich ordered himself clothes at Scharmer's, the fashionable tailor, hung a medallion inscribed *respice finem*[3] on his watchchain, took leave of his professor and the prince who was patron of the school, had a farewell dinner with his comrades at Donon's first-class restaurant, and with his new and fashionable portmanteau, linen, clothes,

2. The phoenix of the family (French). The word *phoenix* is used here to mean "rare bird," "prodigy."
3. Regard the end (a Latin motto).

shaving and other toilet appliances, and a travelling rug, all purchased at the best shops, he set off for one of the provinces where, through his father's influence, he had been attached to the governor as an official for special service.

In the province Iván Ilyich soon arranged as easy and agreeable a position for himself as he had at the School of Law. He performed his official tasks, made his career, and at the same time amused himself pleasantly and decorously. Occasionally he paid official visits to country districts, where he behaved with dignity both to his superiors and inferiors, and performed the duties entrusted to him, which related chiefly to the sectarians,[4] with an exactness and incorruptible honesty of which he could not but feel proud.

In official matters, despite his youth and taste for frivolous gaiety, he was exceedingly reserved, punctilious, and even severe; but in society he was often amusing and witty, and always good-natured, correct in his manner, and *bon enfant*, as the governor and his wife—with whom he was like one of the family—used to say of him.

In the province he had an affair with a lady who made advances to the elegant young lawyer, and there was also a milliner; and there were carousals with aides-de-camp who visited the district, and after-supper visits to a certain outlying street of doubtful reputation; and there was too some obsequiousness to his chief and even to his chief's wife, but all this was done with such a tone of good breeding that no hard names could be applied to it. It all came under the heading of the French saying: *"Il faut que jeunesse se passe."*[5] It was all done with clean hands, in clean linen, with French phrases, and above all among people of the best society and consequently with the approval of people of rank.

So Iván Ilyich served for five years and then came a change in his official life. The new and reformed judicial institutions were introduced, and new men were needed. Iván Ilyich became such a new man. He was offered the post of Examining Magistrate, and he accepted it though the post was in another province and obliged him to give up the connexions he had formed and to make new ones. His friends met to give him a send-off; they had a group-photograph taken and presented him with a silver cigarette-case, and he set off to his new post.

As examining magistrate Iván Ilyich was just as *comme il faut* and decorous a man, inspiring general respect and capable of separating his official duties from his private life, as he had been when acting as an official on special service. His duties now as examining magistrate were far more interesting and attractive than before. In his former position it had been pleasant to wear an undress uniform made by Scharmer, and to pass through the crowd of petitioners and officials who were timorously awaiting an audience with the governor, and who envied him as with free and easy gait he went straight into his chief's private room to have a cup of tea and a cigarette with him. But not many people had then been directly dependent on him—only police officials and the sectarians when he went on special missions—and he liked to treat them politely, almost as comrades, as if he were letting them feel

4. The Old Believers, a large group of Russians (about twenty-five million in 1900), members of a sect that originated in a break with the Orthodox Church in the 17th century; they were subject to many legal restrictions. 5. Youth must have its fling [translator's note].

that he who had the power to crush them was treating them in this simple, friendly way. There were then but few such people. But now, as an examining magistrate, Iván Ilyich felt that everyone without exception, even the most important and self-satisfied, was in his power, and that he need only write a few words on a sheet of paper with a certain heading, and this or that important, self-satisfied person would be brought before him in the role of an accused person or a witness, and if he did not choose to allow him to sit down, would have to stand before him and answer his questions. Iván Ilyich never abused his power; he tried on the contrary to soften its expression, but the consciousness of it and of the possibility of softening its effect, supplied the chief interest and attraction of his office. In his work itself, especially in his examinations, he very soon acquired a method of eliminating all considerations irrelevant to the legal aspect of the case, and reducing even the most complicated case to a form in which it would be presented on paper only in its externals, completely excluding his personal opinion of the matter, while above all observing every prescribed formality. The work was new and Iván Ilyich was one of the first men to apply the new Code of 1864.[6]

On taking up the post of examining magistrate in a new town, he made new acquaintances and connexions, placed himself on a new footing, and assumed a somewhat different tone. He took up an attitude of rather dignified aloofness towards the provincial authorities, but picked out the best circle of legal gentlemen and wealthy gentry living in the town and assumed a tone of slight dissatisfaction with the government, of moderate liberalism, and of enlightened citizenship. At the same time, without at all altering the elegance of his toilet, he ceased shaving his chin and allowed his beard to grow as it pleased.

Iván Ilyich settled down very pleasantly in this new town. The society there, which inclined towards opposition to the governor, was friendly, his salary was larger, and he began to play *vint* [a form of bridge], which he found added not a little to the pleasure of life, for he had a capacity for cards, played good-humouredly, and calculated rapidly and astutely, so that he usually won.

After living there for two years he met his future wife, Praskóvya Fëdorovna Míkhel, who was the most attractive, clever, and brilliant girl of the set in which he moved, and among other amusements and relaxations from his labours as examining magistrate, Iván Ilyich established light and playful relations with her.

While he had been an official on special service he had been accustomed to dance, but now as an examining magistrate it was exceptional for him to do so. If he danced now, he did it as if to show that though he served under the reformed order of things, and had reached the fifth official rank, yet when it came to dancing he could do it better than most people. So at the end of an evening he sometimes danced with Praskóvya Fëdorovna, and it was chiefly during these dances that he captivated her. She fell in love with him. Iván Ilyich had at first no definite intention of marrying, but when the girl fell in love with him he said to himself: "Really, why shouldn't I marry?"

---

6. The emancipation of the serfs in 1861 was followed by a thorough all-round reform of judicial proceedings [translator's note].

Praskóvya Fëdorovna came of a good family, was not bad looking, and had some little property. Iván Ilyich might have aspired to a more brilliant match, but even this was good. He had his salary, and she, he hoped, would have an equal income. She was well connected, and was a sweet, pretty, and thoroughly correct young woman. To say that Iván Ilyich married because he fell in love with Praskóvya Fëdorovna and found that she sympathized with his views of life would be as incorrect as to say that he married because his social circle approved of the match. He was swayed by both these considerations: the marriage gave him personal satisfaction, and at the same time it was considered the right thing by the most highly placed of his associates.

So Iván Ilyich got married.

The preparations for marriage and the beginning of married life, with its conjugal caresses, the new furniture, new crockery, and new linen, were very pleasant until his wife became pregnant—so that Iván Ilyich had begun to think that marriage would not impair the easy, agreeable, gay, and always decorous character of his life, approved of by society and regarded by himself as natural, but would even improve it. But from the first months of his wife's pregnancy, something new, unpleasant, depressing, and unseemly, and from which there was no way of escape, unexpectedly showed itself.

His wife, without any reason—*de gaieté de coeur*[7] as Iván Ilyich expressed it to himself—began to disturb the pleasure and propriety of their life. She began to be jealous without any cause, expected him to devote his whole attention to her, found fault with everything, and made coarse and ill-mannered scenes.

At first Iván Ilyich hoped to escape from the unpleasantness of this state of affairs by the same easy and decorous relation to life that had served him heretofore: he tried to ignore his wife's disagreeable moods, continued to live in his usual easy and pleasant way, invited friends to his house for a game of cards, and also tried going out to his club or spending his evenings with friends. But one day his wife began upbraiding him so vigorously, using such coarse words, and continued to abuse him every time he did not fulfil her demands, so resolutely and with such evident determination not to give way till he submitted—that is, till he stayed at home and was bored just as she was—that he became alarmed. He now realized that matrimony—at any rate with Praskóvya Fëdorovna—was not always conducive to the pleasures and amenities of life, but on the contrary often infringed both comfort and propriety, and that he must therefore entrench himself against such infringement. And Iván Ilyich began to seek for means of doing so. His official duties were the one thing that imposed upon Praskóvya Fëdorovna, and by means of his official work and the duties attached to it he began struggling with his wife to secure his own independence.

With the birth of their child, the attempts to feed it and the various failures in doing so, and with the real and imaginary illnesses of mother and child, in which Iván Ilyich's sympathy was demanded but about which he understood nothing, the need of securing for himself an existence outside his family life became still more imperative.

---

7. From sheer animal spirits (French).

As his wife grew more irritable and exacting and Iván Ilyich transferred the centre of gravity of his life more and more to his official work, so did he grow to like his work better and became more ambitious than before.

Very soon, within a year of his wedding, Iván Ilyich had realized that marriage, though it may add some comforts to life, is in fact a very intricate and difficult affair towards which in order to perform one's duty, that is, to lead a decorous life approved of by society, one must adopt a definite attitude just as towards one's official duties.

And Iván Ilyich evolved such an attitude towards married life. He only required of it those conveniences—dinner at home, housewife, and bed—which it could give him, and above all that propriety of external forms required by public opinion. For the rest he looked for light-hearted pleasure and propriety, and was very thankful when he found them, but if he met with antagonism and querulousness he at once retired into his separate fenced-off world of official duties, where he found satisfaction.

Iván Ilyich was esteemed a good official, and after three years was made Assistant Public Prosecutor. His new duties, their importance, the possibility of indicting and imprisoning anyone he chose, the publicity his speeches received, and the success he had in all these things, made his work still more attractive.

More children came. His wife became more and more querulous and ill-tempered, but the attitude Iván Ilyich had adopted towards his home life rendered him almost impervious to her grumbling.

After seven years' service in that town he was transferred to another province as Public Prosecutor. They moved, but were short of money and his wife did not like the place they moved to. Though the salary was higher the cost of living was greater, besides which two of their children died and family life became still more unpleasant for him.

Praskóvya Fëdorovna blamed her husband for every inconvenience they encountered in their new home. Most of the conversations between husband and wife, especially as to the children's education, led to topics which recalled former disputes, and those disputes were apt to flare up again at any moment. There remained only those rare periods of amorousness which still came to them at times but did not last long. These were islets at which they anchored for a while and then again set out upon that ocean of veiled hostility which showed itself in their aloofness from one another. This aloofness might have grieved Iván Ilyich had he considered that it ought not to exist, but he now regarded the position as normal, and even made it the goal at which he aimed in family life. His aim was to free himself more and more from those unpleasantnesses and to give them a semblance of harmlessness and propriety. He attained this by spending less and less time with his family, and when obliged to be at home he tried to safeguard his position by the presence of outsiders. The chief thing however was that he had his official duties. The whole interest of his life now centered in the official world and that interest absorbed him. The consciousness of his power, being able to ruin anybody he wished to ruin, the importance, even the external dignity of his entry into court, or meetings with his subordinates, his success with superiors and inferiors, and above all his masterly handling of cases, of which he was conscious—all this gave him pleasure and filled his life, together with chats with his colleagues, dinners, and bridge. So that on the

whole Iván Ilyich's life continued to flow as he considered it should do—
pleasantly and properly.

So things continued for another seven years. His eldest daughter was
already sixteen, another child had died, and only one son was left, a schoolboy and a subject of dissensions. Iván Ilyich wanted to put him in the School
of Law, but to spite him Praskóvya Fëdorovna entered him at the High
School. The daughter had been educated at home and had turned out well:
the boy did not learn badly either.

III

So Iván Ilyich lived for seventeen years after his marriage. He was already
a Public Prosecutor of long standing, and had declined several proposed
transfers while awaiting a more desirable post, when an unanticipated and
unpleasant occurrence quite upset the peaceful course of his life. He was
expecting to be offered the post of presiding judge in a University town, but
Hoppe somehow came to the front and obtained the appointment instead.
Iván Ilyich became irritable, reproached Hoppe, and quarrelled both with
him and with his immediate superiors—who became colder to him and again
passed him over when other appointments were made.

This was in 1880, the hardest year of Iván Ilyich's life. It was then that it
became evident on the one hand that his salary was insufficient for them to
live on, and on the other that he had been forgotten, and not only this, but
that what was for him the greatest and most cruel injustice appeared to others a quite ordinary occurrence. Even his father did not consider it his duty
to help him. Iván Ilyich felt himself abandoned by everyone, and that they
regarded his position with a salary of 3,500 rubles as quite normal and even
fortunate. He alone knew that with the consciousness of the injustices done
him, with his wife's incessant nagging, and with the debts he had contracted
by living beyond his means his position was far from normal.

In order to save money that summer he obtained leave of absence and
went with his wife to live in the country at her brother's place.

In the country, without his work, he experienced *ennui* for the first time in
his life, and not only *ennui* but intolerable depression, and he decided that
it was impossible to go on living like that, and that it was necessary to take
energetic measures.

Having passed a sleepless night pacing up and down the veranda, he
decided to go to Petersburg and bestir himself, in order to punish those who
had failed to appreciate him and to get transferred to another ministry.

Next day, despite many protests from his wife and her brother, he started
for Petersburg with the sole object of obtaining a post with a salary of five
thousand rubles a year. He was no longer bent on any particular department,
or tendency, or kind of activity. All he now wanted was an appointment to
another post with a salary of five thousand rubles, either in the administration, in the banks, with the railways, in one of the Empress Marya's Institutions,[8] or even in the customs—but it had to carry with it a salary of five
thousand rubles and be in a ministry other than that in which they had
failed to appreciate him.

8. Reference to the charitable organization founded by the Empress Márya, wife of Paul I, late in the 18th
century.

And this quest of Iván Ilyich's was crowned with remarkable and unexpected success. At Kursk an acquaintance of his, F.I. Ilyín, got into the first-class carriage, sat down beside Iván Ilyich, and told him of a telegram just received by the governor of Kursk announcing that a change was about to take place in the ministry: Peter Ivánovich was to be superseded by Iván Semënovich.

The proposed change, apart from its significance for Russia, had a special significance for Iván Ilyich, because by bringing forward a new man, Peter Petróvich, and consequently his friend Zachár Ivánovich, it was highly favourable for Iván Ilyich, since Zachár Ivánovich was a friend and colleague of his.

In Moscow his news was confirmed, and on reaching Petersburg Iván Ilyich found Zachár Ivánovich and received a definite promise of an appointment in his former department of Justice.

A week later he telegraphed to his wife: "Zachár in Miller's place. I shall receive appointment on presentation of report."

Thanks to this change of personnel, Iván Ilyich had unexpectedly obtained an appointment in his former ministry which placed him two stages above his former colleagues besides giving him five thousand rubles salary and three thousand five hundred rubles for expenses connected with his removal. All his ill humour towards his former enemies and the whole department vanished, and Iván Ilyich was completely happy.

He returned to the country more cheerful and contented than he had been for a long time. Praskóvya Fëdorovna also cheered up and a truce was arranged between them. Iván Ilyich told of how he had been fêted by everybody in Petersburg, how all those who had been his enemies were put to shame and now fawned on him, how envious they were of his appointment, and how much everybody in Petersburg had liked him.

Praskóvya Fëdorovna listened to all this and appeared to believe it. She did not contradict anything, but only made plans for their life in the town to which they were going. Iván Ilyich saw with delight that these plans were his plans, that he and his wife agreed, and that, after a stumble, his life was regaining its due and natural character of pleasant lightheartedness and decorum.

Iván Ilyich had come back for a short time only, for he had to take up his new duties on the 10th of September. Moreover, he needed time to settle into the new place, to move all his belongings from the province, and to buy and order many additional things: in a word, to make such arrangements as he had resolved on, which were almost exactly what Praskóvya Fëdorovna too had decided on.

Now that everything had happened so fortunately, and that he and his wife were at one in their aims and moreover saw so little of one another they got on together better than they had done since the first years of marriage. Iván Ilyich had thought of taking his family away with him at once, but the insistence of his wife's brother and her sister-in-law, who had suddenly become particularly amiable and friendly to him and his family, induced him to depart alone.

So he departed, and the cheerful state of mind induced by his success and by the harmony between his wife and himself, the one intensifying the other, did not leave him. He found a delightful house, just the thing both he and his wife had dreamt of. Spacious, lofty reception rooms in the old style, a convenient and dignified study, rooms for his wife and daughter, a study for his son—it might have been specially built for them. Iván Ilyich himself superintended the arrangements, chose the wallpapers, supplemented the furniture (preferably with antiques which he considered particularly *comme il faut*), and supervised the upholstering. Everything progressed and progressed and approached the ideal he had set himself: even when things were only half completed they exceeded his expectations. He saw what a refined and elegant character, free from vulgarity, it would all have when it was ready. On falling asleep he pictured to himself how the reception-room would look. Looking at the yet unfinished drawing-room he could see the fireplace, the screen, the what-not, the little chairs dotted here and there, the dishes and plates on the walls, and the bronzes, as they would be when everything was in place. He was pleased by the thought of how his wife and daughter, who shared his taste in this matter, would be impressed by it. They were certainly not expecting as much. He had been particularly successful in finding, and buying cheaply, antiques which gave a particularly aristocratic character to the whole place. But in his letters he intentionally understated everything in order to be able to surprise them. All this so absorbed him that his new duties—though he liked his official work—interested him less than he had expected. Sometimes he even had moments of absentmindedness during the Court Sessions, and would consider whether he should have straight or curved cornices for his curtains. He was so interested in it all that he often did things himself, rearranging the furniture, or rehanging the curtains. Once when mounting a step-ladder to show the upholsterer, who did not understand, how he wanted the hangings draped, he made a false step and slipped, but being a strong and agile man he clung on and only knocked his side against the knob of the window frame. The bruised place was painful but the pain soon passed, and he felt particularly bright and well just then. He wrote: "I feel fifteen years younger." He thought he would have everything ready by September, but it dragged on till mid-October. But the result was charming not only in his eyes but to everyone who saw it.

In reality it was just what is usually seen in the houses of people of moderate means who want to appear rich, and therefore succeed only in resembling others like themselves: there were damasks, dark wood, plants, rugs, and dull and polished bronzes—all the things people of a certain class have in order to resemble other people of that class. His house was so like the others that it would never have been noticed, but to him it all seemed to be quite exceptional. He was very happy when he met his family at the station and brought them to the newly furnished house all lit up, where a footman in a white tie opened the door into the hall decorated with plants, and when they went on into the drawing room and the study uttering exclamations of delight. He conducted them everywhere, drank in their praises eagerly, and beamed with pleasure. At tea that evening, when Praskóvya Fëdorovna among other things asked him about his fall, he laughed, and showed them how he had gone flying and had frightened the upholsterer.

"It's a good thing I'm a bit of an athlete. Another man might have been killed, but I merely knocked myself, just here; it hurts when it's touched, but it's passing off already—it's only a bruise."

So they began living in their new home—in which, as always happens, when they got thoroughly settled in they found they were just one room short—and with the increased income, which as always was just a little (some five hundred rubles) too little, but it was all very nice.

Things went particularly well at first, before everything was finally arranged and while something had still to be done: this thing bought, that thing ordered, another thing moved, and something else adjusted. Though there were some disputes between husband and wife, they were both so well satisfied and had so much to do that it all passed off without any serious quarrels. When nothing was left to arrange it became rather dull and something seemed to be lacking, but they were then making acquaintances, forming habits, and life was growing fuller.

Iván Ilyich spent his mornings at the law court and came home to dinner, and at first he was generally in a good humour, though he occasionally became irritable just on account of his house. (Every spot on the tablecloth or the upholstery, and every broken window-blind string, irritated him. He had devoted so much trouble to arranging it all that every disturbance of it distressed him.) But on the whole his life ran its course as he believed life should do: easily, pleasantly, and decorously.

He got up at nine, drank his coffee, read the paper, and then put on his undress uniform and went to the law courts. There the harness in which he worked had already been stretched to fit him and he donned it without a hitch: petitioners, inquiries at the chancery, the chancery itself, and the sittings public and administrative. In all this the thing was to exclude everything fresh and vital, which always disturbs the regular course of official business, and to admit only official relations with people, and then only on official grounds. A man would come, for instance, wanting some information. Iván Ilyich, as one in whose sphere the matter did not lie, would have nothing to do with him: but if the man had some business with him in his official capacity, something that could be expressed on officially stamped paper, he would do everything, positively everything he could within the limits of such relations, and in doing so would maintain the semblance of friendly human relations, that is, would observe the courtesies of life. As soon as the official relations ended, so did everything else. Iván Ilyich possessed this capacity to separate his real life from the official side of affairs and not mix the two, in the highest degree, and by long practice and natural aptitude had brought it to such a pitch that sometimes, in the manner of a virtuoso, he would even allow himself to let the human and official relations mingle. He let himself do this just because he felt that he could at any time he chose resume the strictly official attitude again and drop the human relation. And he did it all easily, pleasantly, correctly, and even artistically. In the intervals between the sessions he smoked, drank tea, chatted a little about politics, a little about general topics, a little about cards, but most of all about official appointments. Tired, but with the feelings of a virtuoso—one of the first violins who has played his part in an orchestra with precision—he would return home to find that his wife and daughter had been out paying calls, or had a visitor, and that his son had been to school, had done his homework with his tutor, and was duly learning what is taught at High Schools. Everything was as it should be. After dinner, if they had no visitors, Iván Ilyich sometimes read a book that was being much discussed at the time, and in the evening settled down to work, that is, read official papers, compared the depositions of witnesses, and noted paragraphs of the Code applying to them. This was neither dull nor amusing. It was dull when he might have been playing bridge, but if no bridge was available it was at any rate better than doing nothing or sitting with his wife. Iván Ilyich's chief pleasure was giving little dinners to which he invited men and women of good social position, and just as his drawing-room resembled all other drawing-rooms so did his enjoyable little parties resemble all other such parties.

Once they even gave a dance. Iván Ilyich enjoyed it and everything went off well, except that it led to a violent quarrel with his wife about the cakes and sweets. Praskóvya Fëdorovna had made her own plans, but Iván Ilyich insisted on getting everything from an expensive confectioner and ordered too many cakes, and the quarrel occurred because some of those cakes were left over and the confectioner's bill came to forty-five rubles. It was a great and disagreeable quarrel. Praskóvya Fëdorovna called him "a fool and an imbecile," and he clutched at his head and made angry allusions to divorce.

But the dance itself had been enjoyable. The best people were there, and Iván Ilyich had danced with Princess Trúfonova, a sister of the distinguished founder of the Society "Bear my Burden."

The pleasures connected with his work were pleasures of ambition; his social pleasures were those of vanity; but Iván Ilyich's greatest pleasure was playing bridge. He acknowledged that whatever disagreeable incident happened in his life, the pleasure that beamed like a ray of light above everything else was to sit down to bridge with good players, not noisy partners, and of course to four-handed bridge (with five players it was annoying to have to stand out, though one pretended not to mind), to play a clever and serious game (when the cards allowed it) and then to have supper and drink a glass of wine. After a game of bridge, especially if he had won a little (to win a large sum was unpleasant), Iván Ilyich went to bed in specially good humour.

So they lived. They formed a circle of acquaintances among the best people and were visited by people of importance and by young folk. In their views as to their acquaintances, husband, wife, and daughter were entirely agreed, and tacitly and unanimously kept at arm's length and shook off the various shabby friends and relations who, with much show of affection, gushed into the drawing-room with its Japanese plates on the walls. Soon these shabby friends ceased to obtrude themselves and only the best people remained in the Golovíns' set.

Young men made up to Lisa, and Petríshchev, an examining magistrate and Dmítri Ivánovich Petríschchev's son and sole heir, began to be so attentive to her that Iván Ilyich had already spoken to Praskóvya Fëdorovna about it, and considered whether they should not arrange a party for them, or get up some private theatricals.

So they lived, and all went well, without change, and life flowed pleasantly.

IV

They were all in good health. It could not be called ill health if Iván Ilyich sometimes said that he had a queer taste in his mouth and felt some discomfort in his left side.

But this discomfort increased and, though not exactly painful, grew into a sense of pressure in his side accompanied by ill humour. And his irritability became worse and worse and began to mar the agreeable, easy, and correct life that had established itself in the Golovín family. Quarrels between husband and wife became more and more frequent, and soon the ease and amenity disappeared and even the decorum was barely maintained. Scenes again became frequent, and very few of those islets remained on which husband and wife could meet without an explosion. Praskóvya Fëdorovna now had good reason to say that her husband's temper was trying. With characteristic exaggeration she said he had always had a dreadful temper, and that it had needed all her good nature to put up with it for twenty years. It was true that now the quarrels were started by him. His bursts of temper always came just before dinner, often just as he began to eat his soup. Sometimes he noticed that a plate or dish was chipped, or the food was not right, or his son put his elbow on the table, or his daughter's hair was not done as he liked it, and for all this he blamed Praskóvya Fëdorovna. At first she retorted and said disagreeable things to him, but once or twice he fell into such a rage at the beginning of dinner that she realized it was due to some physical derangement brought on by taking food, and so she restrained herself and did not answer, but only hurried to get the dinner over. She regarded this self-restraint as highly praiseworthy. Having come to the conclusion that her husband had a dreadful temper and made her life miserable, she began to feel sorry for herself, and the more she pitied herself the more she hated her husband. She began to wish he would die; yet she did not want him to die because then his salary would cease. And this irritated her against him still more. She considered herself dreadfully unhappy just because not even his death could save her, and though she concealed her exasperation, that hidden exasperation of hers increased his irritation also.

After one scene in which Iván Ilyich had been particularly unfair and after which he had said in explanation that he certainly was irritable but that it was due to his not being well, she said that if he was ill it should be attended to, and insisted on his going to see a celebrated doctor.

He went. Everything took place as he had expected and as it always does. There was the usual waiting and the important air assumed by the doctor, with which he was so familiar (resembling that which he himself assumed in court), and the sounding and listening, and the questions which called for answers that were foregone conclusions and were evidently unnecessary, and the look of importance which implied that "if only you put yourself in our hands we will arrange everything—we know indubitably how it has to be done, always in the same way for everybody alike." It was all just as it was in the law courts. The doctor put on just the same air towards him as he himself put on towards an accused person.

The doctor said that so-and-so indicated that there was so-and-so inside the patient, but if the investigation of so-and-so did not confirm this, then he must assume that and that. If he assumed that and that, then . . . and so on. To Iván Ilyich only one question was important: was his case serious or not? But the doctor ignored that inappropriate question. From his point of view it was not the one under consideration, the real question was to decide between a floating kidney, chronic catarrh, or appendicitis. It was not a question of Iván Ilyich's life or death, but one between a floating kidney and appendicitis. And that question the doctor solved brilliantly, as it seemed to Iván Ilyich, in favour of the appendix, with the reservation that should an examination of the urine give fresh indications the matter would be reconsidered. All this was just what Iván Ilyich had himself brilliantly accomplished a thousand times in dealing with men on trial. The doctor summed up just as brilliantly, looking over his spectacles triumphantly and even gaily at the accused. From the doctor's summing up Iván Ilyich concluded that things were bad, but that for the doctor, and perhaps for everybody else, it was a matter of indifference, though for him it was bad. And this conclusion struck him painfully, arousing in him a great feeling of pity for himself and of bitterness towards the doctor's indifference to a matter of such importance.

He said nothing of this, but rose, placed the doctor's fee on the table, and remarked with a sigh: "We sick people probably often put inappropriate questions. But tell me, in general, is this complaint dangerous or not? . . ."

The doctor looked at him sternly over his spectacles with one eye, as if to say: "Prisoner, if you will not keep to the questions put to you, I shall be obliged to have you removed from the court."

"I have already told you what I consider necessary and proper. The analysis may show something more." And the doctor bowed.

Iván Ilyich went out slowly, seated himself disconsolately in his sledge, and drove home. All the way home he was going over what the doctor had said, trying to translate those complicated, obscure, scientific phrases into plain language and find in them an answer to the question: "Is my condition bad? Is it very bad? Or is there as yet nothing much wrong?" And it seemed to him that the meaning of what the doctor had said was it was very bad. Everything in the streets seemed depressing. The cabmen, the houses, the passers-by, and the shops, were dismal. His ache, this dull gnawing ache that never ceased for a moment, seemed to have acquired a new and more serious significance from the doctor's dubious remarks. Iván Ilyich now watched it with a new and oppressive feeling.

He reached home and began to tell his wife about it. She listened, but in the middle of his account his daughter came in with her hat on, ready to go out with her mother. She sat down reluctantly to listen to this tedious story, but could not stand it long, and her mother too did not hear him to the end.

"Well, I am very glad," she said. "Mind now to take your medicine regularly. Give me the prescription and I'll send Gerásim to the chemist's." And she went to get ready to go out.

While she was in the room Iván Ilyich had hardly taken time to breathe, but he sighed deeply when she left it.

"Well," he thought, "perhaps it isn't so bad after all."

He began taking his medicine and following the doctor's directions, which had been altered after the examination of the urine. But then it happened that there was a contradiction between the indications drawn from the examination of the urine and the symptoms that showed themselves. It turned out that what was happening differed from what the doctor had told him, and that he had either forgotten, or blundered, or hidden something from him. He could not, however, be blamed for that, and Iván Ilyich still obeyed his orders implicitly and at first derived some comfort from doing so.

From the time of his visit to the doctor, Iván Ilyich's chief occupation was the exact fulfilment of the doctor's instructions regarding hygiene and the taking of medicine, and the observation of his pain and his excretions. His chief interests came to be people's ailments and people's health. When sickness, deaths, or recoveries were mentioned in his presence, especially when the illness resembled his own, he listened with agitation which he tried to hide, asked questions, and applied what he heard to his own case.

The pain did not grow less, but Iván Ilyich made efforts to force himself to think that he was better. And he could do this so long as nothing agitated him. But as soon as he had any unpleasantness with his wife, any lack of success in his official work, or held bad cards at bridge, he was at once acutely sensible of his disease. He had formerly borne such mischances, hoping soon to adjust what was wrong, to master it and attain success, or make a grand slam. But now every mischance upset him and plunged him into despair. He would say to himself. "There now, just as I was beginning to get better and the medicine had begun to take effect, comes this accursed misfortune, or unpleasantness . . ." And he was furious with the mishap, or with the people who were causing the unpleasantness and killing him, for he felt that this fury was killing him but could not restrain it. One would have thought that it should have been clear to him that this exasperation with circumstances and people aggravated his illness, and that he ought therefore to ignore unpleasant occurrences. But he drew the very opposite conclusion: he said that he needed peace, and he watched for everything that might disturb it and became irritable at the slightest infringement of it. His condition was rendered worse by the fact that he read medical books and consulted doctors. The progress of his disease was so gradual that he could deceive himself when comparing one day with another—the difference was so slight. But when he consulted the doctors it seemed to him that he was getting worse, and even very rapidly. Yet despite this he was continually consulting them.

That month he went to see another celebrity, who told him almost the same as the first had done but put his questions rather differently, and the interview with this celebrity only increased Iván Ilyich's doubts and fears. A friend of a friend of his, a very good doctor, diagnosed his illness again quite differently from the others, and though he predicted recovery, his questions and suppositions bewildered Iván Ilyich still more and increased his doubts. A homeopathist diagnosed the disease in yet another way, and prescribed medicine which Iván Ilyich took secretly for a week. But after a week, not feeling any improvement and having lost confidence both in the former doctor's treatment and in this one's, he became still more despondent. One day a lady acquaintance mentioned a cure effected by a wonder-working icon. Iván Ilyich caught himself listening attentively and beginning to believe that it had occurred. This incident alarmed him. "Has my mind really weakened to such an extent?" he asked himself. "Nonsense! It's all rubbish. I mustn't give way to nervous fears but having chosen a doctor must keep strictly to his treatment. That is what I will do. Now it's all settled. I won't think about it, but will follow the treatment seriously till summer, and then we shall see. From now there must be no more of this wavering!" This was easy to say but impossible to carry out. The pain in his side oppressed him and seemed to grow worse and more incessant, while the taste in his mouth grew stranger and stranger. It seemed to him that his breath had a disgusting smell, and he was conscious of a loss of appetite and strength. There was no deceiving himself: something terrible, new, and more important than anything before in his life, was taking place within him of which he alone was aware. Those about him did not understand or would not understand it, but thought everything in the world was going on as usual. That tormented Iván Ilyich more than anything. He saw that his household, especially his wife and daughter who were in a perfect whirl of visiting, did not understand anything of it and were annoyed that he was so depressed and so exacting, as if he were to blame for it. Though they tried to disguise it he saw that he was an obstacle in their path, and that his wife had adopted a definite line in regard to his illness and kept to it regardless of anything he said or did. Her attitude was this: "You know," she would say to her friends, "Iván Ilyich can't do as other people do, and keep to the treatment prescribed for him. One day he'll take his drops and keep strictly to his diet and go to bed in good time, but the next day unless I watch him he'll suddenly forget his medicine, eat sturgeon—which is forbidden—and sit up playing cards till one o'clock in the morning."

"Oh, come, when was that?" Iván Ilyich would ask in vexation. "Only once at Peter Ivánovich's."

"And yesterday with Shébek."

"Well, even if I hadn't stayed up, this pain would have kept me awake."

"Be that as it may you'll never get well like that, but will always make us wretched."

Praskóvya Fédorovna's attitude to Iván Ilyich's illness, as she expressed it both to others and to him, was that it was his own fault and was another of the annoyances he caused her. Iván Ilyich felt that this opinion escaped her involuntarily—but that did not make it easier for him.

At the law courts too, Iván Ilyich noticed, or thought he noticed, a strange attitude towards himself. It sometimes seemed to him that people were watching him inquisitively as a man whose place might soon be vacant. Then again, his friends would suddenly begin to chaff him in a friendly way about his low spirits, as if the awful, horrible, and unheard-of thing that was going on within him, incessantly gnawing at him and irresistibly drawing him away, was a very agreeable subject for jests. Schwartz in particular irritated him by his jocularity, vivacity, and *savoir-faire*, which reminded him of what he himself had been ten years ago.

Friends came to make up a set and they sat down to cards. They dealt, bending the new cards to soften them, and he sorted the diamonds in his hand and found he had seven. His partner said "No trumps" and supported him with two diamonds. What more could be wished for? It ought to be jolly and lively. They would make a grand slam. But suddenly Iván Ilyich was conscious of that gnawing pain, that taste in his mouth, and it seemed ridiculous that in such circumstances he should be pleased to make a grand slam.

He looked at his partner Mikháil Mikháylovich, who rapped the table with his strong hand and instead of snatching up the tricks pushed the cards courteously and indulgently towards Iván Ilyich that he might have the pleasure of gathering them up without the trouble of stretching out his hand for them. "Does he think I am too weak to stretch out my arm?" thought Iván Ilyich, and forgetting what he was doing he over-trumped his partner, missing the grand slam by three tricks. And what was most awful of all was that he saw how upset Mikháil Mikháylovich was about it but did not himself care. And it was dreadful to realize why he did not care.

They all saw that he was suffering, and said: "We can stop if you are tired. Take a rest." Lie down? No, he was not at all tired, and he finished the rubber. All were gloomy and silent. Iván Ilyich felt that he had diffused this gloom over them and could not dispel it. They had supper and went away, and Iván Ilyich was left alone with the consciousness that his life was poisoned and was poisoning the lives of others, and that this poison did not weaken but penetrated more and more deeply into his whole being.

With this consciousness, and with physical pain besides the terror, he must go to bed, often to lie awake the greater part of the night. Next morning he had to get up again, dress, go to the law courts, speak, and write; or if he did not go out, spend at home those twenty-four hours a day each of which was a torture. And he had to live thus all alone on the brink of an abyss, with no one who understood or pitied him.

V

So one month passed and then another. Just before the New Year his brother-in-law came to town and stayed at their house. Iván Ilyich was at the law courts and Praskóvya Fëdorovna had gone shopping. When Iván Ilyich came home and entered his study he found his brother-in-law there—a healthy, florid man—unpacking his portmanteau himself. He raised his head on hearing Iván Ilyich's footsteps and looked up at him for a moment without a word. That stare told Iván everything. His brother-in-law opened his mouth to utter an exclamation of surprise but checked himself, and that action confirmed it all.

"I have changed, eh?"

"Yes, there is a change."

And after that, try as he would to get his brother-in-law to return to the subject of his looks, the latter would say nothing about it. Praskóvya Fëdorovna came home and her brother went out to her. Iván Ilyich locked the door and began to examine himself in the glass, first full face, then in profile. He took up a portrait of himself taken with his wife, and compared it with what he saw in the glass. The change in him was immense. Then he bared his arms to the elbow, looked at them, drew the sleeves down again, sat down on an ottoman, and grew blacker than night.

"No, no, this won't do!" he said to himself, and jumped up, went to the table, took up some law papers and began to read them, but could not continue. He unlocked the door and went into the reception-room. The door leading to the drawing-room was shut. He approached it on tiptoe and listened.

"No, you are exaggerating!" Praskóvya Fëdorovna was saying.

"Exaggerating! Don't you see it? Why, he's a dead man! Look at his eyes—there's no light in them. But what is it that is wrong with him?"

"No one knows. Nikoláevich [that was another doctor] said something, but I don't know what. And Leshchetítsky [this was the celebrated specialist] said quite the contrary . . ."

Iván Ilyich walked away, went to his own room, lay down and began musing: "The kidney, a floating kidney." He recalled all the doctors had told him of how it detached itself and swayed about. And by an effort of imagination he tried to catch that kidney and arrest it and support it. So little was needed for this, it seemed to him. "No, I'll go to see Peter Ivánovich again." [That was the friend whose friend was a doctor.] He rang, ordered the carriage, and got ready to go.

"Where are you going, *Jean?*" asked his wife, with a specially sad and exceptionally kind look.

This exceptionally kind look irritated him. He looked morosely at her.

"I must go to see Peter Ivánovich."

He went to see Peter Ivánovich, and together they went to see his friend, the doctor. He was in, and Iván Ilyich had a long talk with him.

Reviewing the anatomical and physiological details of what in the doctor's opinion was going on inside him, he understood it all.

There was something, a small thing, in the vermiform appendix. It might all come right. Only stimulate the energy of one organ and check the activity of another, then absorption would take place and everything would come right. He got home rather late for dinner, ate his dinner, and conversed cheerfully, but could not for a long time bring himself to go back to work in his room. At last, however, he went to his study and did what was necessary, but the consciousness that he had put something aside—an important, intimate matter which he would revert to when his work was done—never left him. When he had finished his work he remembered that this intimate matter was the thought of his vermiform appendix. But he did not give himself up to it, and went to the drawing-room for tea. There were callers there, including the examining magistrate who was a desirable match for his daughter, and they were conversing, playing the piano, and singing. Iván Ilyich, as Praskóvya Fëdorovna remarked, spent that evening more cheerfully than usual, but he never for a moment forgot that he had postponed the important matter of the appendix. At eleven o'clock he said good-night and went to his bedroom. Since his illness he had slept alone in a small room next to his study. He undressed and took up a novel by Zola,[9] but instead of reading it he fell into thought, and in his imagination that desired improvement in the verm[iform appendix occurred. There was the absorption and evacuation and the reestablishment of normal activity. "Yes, that's it!" he said to himself. "One need only assist nature, that's all." He remembered his medicine, rose, took it, and lay down on his back watching for the beneficent action of the medicine and for it to lessen the pain. "I need only take it regularly and avoid all injurious influences. I am already feeling better, much better." He began touching his side: it was not painful to the touch. "There, I really don't feel it. It's much better already." He put out the light and turned on his side. . . . "The appendix is getting better, absorption is occurring." Suddenly he felt the old, familiar, dull, gnawing pain, stubborn and serious. There was the same familiar loathsome taste in his mouth. His heart sank and he felt dazed. "My God! My God!" he muttered. "Again, again! And it will never cease." And suddenly the matter presented itself in a quite different aspect. "Vermiform appendix! Kidney!" he said to himself. "It's not a question of appendix or kidney, but of life and . . . death. Yes, life

---

9. Émile Zola (1840—1902), French novelist, author of the *Rougon-Macquart* novels (*Nana, Germinal,* and so on). Tolstoy condemned Zola for his naturalistic theories and considered his novels crude and gross.

was there and now it is going, going and I cannot stop it. Yes. Why deceive myself? Isn't it obvious to everyone but me that I'm dying, and that it's only a question of weeks, days . . . it may happen this moment. There was light and now there is darkness. I was here and now I'm going there! Where?" A chill came over him, his breathing ceased, and he felt only the throbbing of his heart.

"When I am not, what will there be? There will be nothing. Then where shall I be when I am no more? Can this be dying? No, I don't want to!" He jumped up and tried to light the candle, felt for it with trembling hands, dropped candle and candlestick on the floor, and fell back on his pillow.

"What's the use? It makes no difference," he said to himself, staring with wide-open eyes into the darkness. "Death. Yes, death. And none of them know or wish to know it, and they have no pity for me. Now they are playing." (He heard through the door the distant sound of a song and its accompaniment.) "It's all the same to them, but they will die too! Fools! I first, and they later, but it will be the same for them. And now they are merry . . . the beasts!"

Anger choked him and he was agonizingly, unbearably miserable. "It is impossible that all men have been doomed to suffer this awful horror!" He raised himself.

"Something must be wrong. I must calm myself—must think it all over from the beginning." And he again began thinking. "Yes, the beginning of my illness: I knocked my side, but I was still quite well that day and the next. It hurt a little, then rather more. I saw the doctors, then followed despondency and anguish, more doctors, and I drew nearer to the abyss. My strength grew less and I kept coming nearer and nearer, and now I have wasted away and there is no light in my eyes. I think of the appendix—but this is death! I think of mending the appendix, and all the while here is death! Can it really be death!" Again terror seized him and he gasped for breath. He leant down and began feeling for the matches, pressing with his elbow on the stand beside the bed. It was in his way and hurt him, he grew furious with it, pressed on it still harder, and upset it. Breathless and in despair he fell on his back, expecting death to come immediately.

Meanwhile the visitors were leaving. Praskóvya Fëdorovna was seeing them off. She heard something fall and came in.

"What has happened?"

"Nothing. I knocked it over accidentally."

She went out and returned with a candle. He lay there panting heavily, like a man who has run a thousand yards, and stared upwards at her with a fixed look.

"What is it, *Jean?*"

"No . . . o . . . thing. I upset it." ("Why speak of it? She won't understand," he thought.)

And in truth she did not understand. She picked up the stand, lit his candle, and hurried away to see another visitor off. When she came back he still lay on his back, looking upwards.

"What is it? Do you feel worse?"

"Yes."

She shook her head and sat down.

"Do you know, *Jean,* I think we must ask Leshchetítsky to come and see you here."

This meant calling in the famous specialist, regardless of expense. He smiled malignantly and said "No." She remained a little longer and then went up to him and kissed his forehead.

While she was kissing him he hated her from the bottom of his soul and with difficulty refrained from pushing her away.

"Good-night. Please God you'll sleep."

"Yes."

VI

Iván Ilyich saw that he was dying, and he was in continual despair.

In the depth of his heart he knew he was dying, but not only was he not accustomed to the thought, he simply did not and could not grasp it.

The syllogism he had learned from Kiesewetter's *Logic:*[1] "Caius is a man, men are mortal, therefore Caius is mortal," had always seemed to him correct as applied to Caius, but certainly not as applied to himself. That Caius—man in the abstract—was mortal, was perfectly correct, but he was not Caius, not an abstract man, but a creature quite, quite separate from all others. He had been little Ványa, with a mamma and a papa, with Mítya and Volódya, with the toys, a coachman and a nurse, afterwards with Kátenka and with all the joys, griefs, and delights of childhood, boyhood, and youth. What did Caius know of the smell of that striped leather ball Ványa had been so fond of? Had Caius kissed his mother's hand like that, and did the silk of her dress rustle so for Caius? Had he rioted like that at school when the pastry was bad? Had Caius been in love like that? Could Caius preside at a session as he did? "Caius really was mortal, and it was right for him to die; but for me, little Ványa, Iván Ilyich, with all my thoughts and emotions, it's altogether a different matter. It cannot be that I ought to die. That would be too terrible."

Such was his feeling.

"If I had to die like Caius I should have known it was so. An inner voice would have told me so, but there was nothing of the sort in me and I and all my friends felt that our case was quite different from that of Caius. And now here it is!" he said to himself. "It can't be. It's impossible! But here it is. How is this? How is one to understand it?"

He could not understand it, and tried to drive this false, incorrect, morbid thought away and to replace it by other proper and healthy thoughts. But that thought, and not the thought only but the reality itself, seemed to come and confront him.

And to replace that thought he called up a succession of others, hoping to find in them some support. He tried to get back into the former current of thoughts that had once screened the thought of death from him. But strange to say, all that had formerly shut off, hidden, and destroyed, his consciousness of death, no longer had that effect. Iván Ilyich now spent most of his time in attempting to re-establish that old current. He would say to himself: "I will take up my duties again—after all I used to live by them." And banishing all doubts he would go to the law courts, enter into conversation with his colleagues, and sit carelessly as was his wont, scanning the crowd with a

---

1. Karl Kiesewetter (1766—1819) was a German popularizer of Kant's philosophy. His *Outline of Logic According to Kantian Principles* (1796) was widely used in Russian adaptations as a schoolbook.

thoughtful look and leaning both his emaciated arms on the arms of his oak chair; bending over as usual to a colleague and drawing his papers nearer he would interchange whispers with him, and then suddenly raising his eyes and sitting erect would pronounce certain words and open the proceedings. But suddenly in the midst of those proceedings the pain in his side, regardless of the stage the proceedings had reached, would begin its own gnawing work. Iván Ilyich would turn his attention to it and try to drive the thought of it away, but without success. *It* would come and stand before him and look at him, and he would be petrified and the light would die out of his eyes, and he would again begin asking himself whether *It* alone was true. And his colleagues and subordinates would see with surprise and distress that he, the brilliant and subtle judge, was becoming confused and making mistakes. He would shake himself, try to pull himself together, manage somehow to bring the sitting to a close, and return home with the sorrowful consciousness that his judicial labours could not as formerly hide from him what he wanted them to hide, and could not deliver him from *It*. And what was worst of all was that *It* drew his attention to itself not in order to make him take some action but only that he should look at *It*, look it straight in the face: look at it without doing anything, suffer inexpressibly.

And to save himself from this condition Iván Ilyich looked for consolations—new screens—and new screens were found and for a while seemed to save him, but then they immediately fell to pieces or rather became transparent, as *It* penetrated them and nothing could veil *It*.

In these latter days he would go into the drawing-room he had arranged—that drawing-room where he had fallen and for the sake of which (how bitterly ridiculous it seemed) he had sacrificed his life—for he knew that his illness originated with that knock. He would enter and see that something had scratched the polished table. He would look for the cause of this and find that it was the bronze ornamentation of an album, that had got bent. He would take up the expensive album which he had lovingly arranged, and feel vexed with his daughter and her friends for their untidiness—for the album was torn here and there and some of the photographs turned upside down. He would put it carefully in order and bend the ornamentation back into position. Then it would occur to him to place all those things in another corner of the room, near the plants. He would call the footman, but his daughter or wife would contradict him, and he would dispute and grow angry. But that was all right, for then he did not think about *It*. *It* was invisible.

But then, when he was moving something himself, his wife would say: "Let the servants do it. You will hurt yourself again." And suddenly *It* would flash through the screen and he would see it. It was just a flash, and he hoped it would disappear, but he would involuntarily pay attention to his side. "It sits there as before, gnawing just the same!" And he could no longer forget *It*, but could distinctly see it looking at him from behind the flowers. "What is it all for?"

"It really is so! I lost my life over that curtain as I might have done when storming a fort. Is that possible? How terrible and how stupid. It can't be true! It can't, but it is."

He would go to his study, lie down, and again be alone with *It* face to face with *It*. And nothing could be done with *It* except to look at it and shudder.

VII

How it happened it is impossible to say because it came about step by step, unnoticed, but in the third month of Iván Ilyich's illness, his wife, his daughter, his son, his acquaintances, the doctors, the servants, and above all he himself, were aware that the whole interest he had for other people was whether he would soon vacate his place, and at last release the living from the discomfort caused by his presence and be himself released from his sufferings.

He slept less and less. He was given opium and hypodermic injections of morphine, but this did not relieve him. The dull depression he experienced in a somnolent condition at first gave him a little relief, but only as something new; afterwards it became as distressing as the pain itself or even more so.

Special foods were prepared for him by the doctors' orders, but all those foods became increasingly distasteful and disgusting to him.

For his excretions also special arrangements had to be made, and this was a torment to him every time—a torment from the uncleanliness, the unseemliness, and the smell, and from knowing that another person had to take part in it.

But just through this most unpleasant matter, Iván Ilyich obtained comfort. Gerásim, the butler's young assistant, always came in to carry the things out. Gerásim was a clean, fresh peasant lad, grown stout on town food and always cheerful and bright. At first the sight of him, in his clean Russian peasant costume, engaged on that disgusting task embarrassed Iván Ilyich.

Once when he got up from the commode too weak to draw up his trousers, he dropped into a soft armchair and looked with horror at his bare, enfeebled thighs with the muscles so sharply marked on them.

Gerásim with a firm light tread, his heavy boots emitting a pleasant smell of tar and fresh winter air, came in wearing a clean Hessian apron, the sleeves of his print shirt tucked up over his strong bare young arms; and refraining from looking at his sick master out of consideration for his feelings, and restraining the joy of life that beamed from his face, he went up to the commode.

"Gerásim!" said Iván Ilyich in a weak voice.

Gerásim started, evidently afraid he might have committed some blunder, and with a rapid movement turned his fresh, kind, simple young face which just showed the first downy sign of a beard.

"Yes, sir?"

"That must be very unpleasant for you. You must forgive me. I am helpless."

"Oh, why, sir," and Gerásim's eyes beamed and he showed his glistening white teeth, "what's a little trouble? It's a case of illness with you, sir."

And his deft strong hands did their accustomed task, and he went out of the room stepping lightly. Five minutes later he as lightly returned.

Iván Ilyich was still sitting in the same position in the armchair.

"Gerásim," he said when the latter had replaced the freshly-washed utensil. "Please come here and help me." Gerásim went up to him. "Lift me up. It is hard for me to get up, and I have sent Dmítri away."

Gerásim went up to him, grasped his master with his strong arms deftly but gently, in the same way that he stepped—lifted him, supported him with one hand, and with the other drew up his trousers and would have set him down again, but Iván Ilyich asked to be led to the sofa. Gerásim, without an effort and without apparent pressure, led him, almost lifting him, to the sofa and placed him on it.

"Thank you. How easily and well you do it all!"

Gerásim smiled again and turned to leave the room. But Iván Ilyich felt his presence such a comfort that he did not want to let him go.

"One thing more, please move up that chair. No, the other one—under my feet. It is easier for me when my feet are raised."

Gerásim brought the chair, set it down gently in place, and raised Iván Ilyich's legs on to it. It seemed to Iván Ilyich that he felt better while Gerásim was holding up his legs.

"It's better when my legs are higher," he said. "Place that cushion under them."

Gerásim did so. He again lifted the legs and placed them, and again Iván Ilyich felt better while Gerásim held his legs. When he set them down Iván Ilyich fancied he felt worse.

"Gerásim," he said. "Are you busy now?"

"Not at all, sir," said Gerásim, who had learnt from the townsfolk how to speak to gentlefolk.

"What have you still to do?"

"What have I to do? I've done everything except chopping the logs for to-morrow."

"Then hold my legs up a bit higher, can you?"

"Of course I can. Why not?" And Gerásim raised his master's legs higher and Iván Ilyich thought that in that position he did not feel any pain at all.

"And how about the logs?"

"Don't trouble about that, sir. There's plenty of time."

Iván Ilyich told Gerásim to sit down and hold his legs, and began to talk to him. And strange to say it seemed to him that he felt better while Gerásim held his legs up.

After that Iván Ilyich would sometimes call Gerásim and get him to hold his legs on his shoulders, and he liked talking to him. Gerásim did it all easily, willingly, simply, and with a good nature that touched Iván Ilyich. Health, strength, and vitality in other people were offensive to him, but Gerásim's strength and vitality did not mortify but soothed him.

What tormented Iván Ilyich most was the deception, the lie, which for some reason they all accepted, that he was not dying but was simply ill, and that he only need keep quiet and undergo a treatment and then something very good would result. He however knew that do what they would nothing would come of it, only still more agonizing suffering and death. This deception tortured him—their not wishing to admit what they all knew and what he knew, but wanting to lie to him concerning his terrible condition, and wishing and forcing him to participate in that lie. Those lies—lies enacted over him on the eve of his death and destined to degrade this awful, solemn act to the level of their visitings, their curtains, their sturgeon for dinner—were a terrible agony for Iván Ilyich. And strangely enough, many times when they were going through their antics over him he had been within a hairbreadth of calling out to them: "Stop lying! You know and I know that I am dying. Then at least stop lying about it!" But he had never had the spirit to do it. The awful, terrible act of his dying was, he could see, reduced by those about him to the level of a casual, unpleasant, and almost indecorous incident (as if someone entered a drawing-room diffusing an unpleasant odour) and this was done by that very decorum which he had served all his life long. He saw that no one felt for him, because no one even wished to grasp his position. Only Gerásim recognized and pitied him. And so Iván Ilyich felt at ease only with him. He felt comforted when Gerásim supported his legs (sometimes all night long) and refused to go to bed, saying: "Don't you worry, Iván Ilyich. I'll get sleep enough later on," or when he suddenly became familiar and exclaimed: "If you weren't sick it would be another matter, but as it is, why should I grudge a little trouble?" Gerásim alone did not lie; everything showed that he alone understood the facts of the case and did not consider it necessary to disguise them, but simply felt sorry for his emaciated and enfeebled master. Once when Iván Ilyich was sending him away he even said straight out: "We shall all of us die, so why should I grudge a little trouble?"—expressing the fact that he did not think his work burdensome, because he was doing it for a dying man and hoped someone would do the same for him when his time came.

Apart from this lying, or because of it, what most tormented Iván Ilyich was that no one pitied him as he wished to be pitied. At certain moments after prolonged suffering he wished most of all (though he would have been ashamed to confess it) for someone to pity him as a sick child is pitied. He longed to be petted and comforted. He knew he was an important functionary, that he had a beard turning grey, and that therefore what he longed for was impossible, but still he longed for it. And in Gerásim's attitude towards him there was something akin to what he wished for, and so that attitude comforted him. Iván Ilyich wanted to weep, wanted to be petted and cried over, and then his colleague Shébek would come, and instead of weeping and being petted, Iván Ilyich would assume a serious, severe, and profound air, and by force of habit would express his opinion on a decision of the Court of Appeal and would stubbornly insist on that view. This falsity around him and within him did more than anything else to poison his last days.

VIII

It was morning. He knew it was morning because Gerásim had gone, and Peter the footman had come and put out the candles, drawn back one of the curtains, and begun quietly to tidy up. Whether it was morning or evening, Friday or Sunday, made no difference, it was all just the same: the gnawing, unmitigated, agonizing pain, never ceasing for an instant, the consciousness of life inexorably waning but not yet extinguished, the approach of that ever dreaded and hateful Death which was the only reality, and always the same falsity. What were days, weeks, hours, in such a case?

"Will you have some tea, sir?"

"He wants things to be regular, and wishes the gentlefolk to drink tea in the morning," thought Iván Ilyich, and only said "No."

"Wouldn't you like to move onto the sofa, sir?"

"He wants to tidy up the room, and I'm in the way. I am uncleanliness and disorder," he thought, and said only:

"No, leave me alone."

The man went on bustling about. Iván Ilyich stretched out his hand. Peter came up, ready to help.

"What is it, sir?"

"My watch."

Peter took the watch which was close at hand and gave it to his master.

"Half-past eight. Are they up?"

"No sir, except Vladímir Ivánich" (the son) "who has gone to school. Praskóvya Fëdorovna ordered me to wake her if you asked for her. Shall I do so?"

"No, there's no need to." "Perhaps I'd better have some tea," he thought, and added aloud: "Yes, bring me some tea."

Peter went to the door, but Iván Ilyich dreaded being left alone. "How can I keep him here? Oh yes, my medicine." "Peter, give me my medicine." "Why not? Perhaps it may still do me some good." He took a spoonful and swallowed it. "No, it won't help. It's all tomfoolery, all deception," he decided as soon as he became aware of the familiar, sickly, hopeless taste. "No, I can't believe in it any longer. But the pain, why this pain? If it would only cease just for a moment!" And he moaned. Peter turned towards him. "It's all right. Go and fetch me some tea."

Peter went out. Left alone Iván Ilyich groaned not so much with pain, terrible though that was, as from mental anguish. Always and forever the same, always these endless days and nights. If only it would come quicker! If only *what* would come quicker? Death, darkness? . . . No, no! Anything rather than death!

When Peter returned with the tea on a tray, Iván Ilyich stared at him for a time in perplexity, not realizing who and what he was. Peter was disconcerted by that look and his embarrassment brought Iván Ilyich to himself.

"Oh, tea! All right, put it down. Only help me to wash and put on a clean shirt."

And Iván Ilyich began to wash. With pauses for rest, he washed his hands and then his face, cleaned his teeth, brushed his hair, and looked in the glass. He was terrified by what he saw, especially by the limp way in which his hair clung to his pallid forehead.

While his shirt was being changed he knew that he would be still more frightened at the sight of his body, so he avoided looking at it. Finally he was ready. He drew on a dressing-gown, wrapped himself in a plaid, and sat down in the armchair to take his tea. For a moment he felt refreshed, but as soon as he began to drink the tea he was again aware of the same taste, and the pain also returned. He finished it with an effort, and then lay down stretching out his legs, and dismissed Peter.

Always the same. Now a spark of hope flashes up, then a sea of despair rages, and always pain; always pain, always despair, and always the same. When alone he had a dreadful and distressing desire to call someone, but he knew beforehand that with others present it would be still worse. "Another dose of morphine—to lose consciousness. I will tell him, the doctor, that he must think of something else. It's impossible, impossible, to go on like this."

An hour and another pass like that. But now there is a ring at the door bell. Perhaps it's the doctor? It is. He comes in fresh, hearty, plump, and cheerful, with that look on his face that seems to say: "There now, you're in a panic about something, but we'll arrange it all for you directly!" The doctor knows this expression is out of place here, but he has put it on once for all and can't take it off—like a man who has put on a frock-coat in the morning to pay a round of calls.

The doctor rubs his hands vigorously and reassuringly.

"Brr! How cold it is! There's such a sharp frost; just let me warm myself!" he says, as if it were only a matter of waiting till he was warm, and then he would put everything right.

"Well now, how are you?"

Iván Ilyich feels that the doctor would like to say: "Well, how are our affairs?" but that even he feels that this would not do, and says instead: "What sort of a night have you had?"

Iván Ilyich looks at him as much as to say: "Are you really never ashamed of lying?" But the doctor does not wish to understand this question, and Iván Ilyich says: "Just as terrible as ever. The pain never leaves me and never subsides. If only something . . ."

"Yes, you sick people are always like that. . . . There, now I think I'm warm enough. Even Praskóvya Fëdorovna, who is so particular, could find no fault with my temperature. Well, now I can say good-morning," and the doctor presses his patient's hand.

Then, dropping his former playfulness, he begins with a most serious face to examine the patient, feeling his pulse and taking his temperature, and then begins the sounding and auscultation.

Iván Ilyich knows quite well and definitely that all this is nonsense and pure deception, but when the doctor, getting down on his knee, leans over him, putting his ear first higher then lower, and performs various gymnastic movements over him with a significant expression on his face, Iván Ilyich submits to it all as he used to submit to the speeches of the lawyers, though he knew very well that they were all lying and why they were lying.

The doctor, kneeling on the sofa, is still sounding him when Praskóvya Fëdorovna's silk dress rustles at the door and she is heard scolding Peter for not having let her know of the doctor's arrival.

She comes in, kisses her husband, and at once proceeds to prove that she has been up a long time already, and only owing to a misunderstanding failed to be there when the doctor arrived.

Iván Ilyich looks at her, scans her all over, sets against her the whiteness and plumpness and cleanness of her hands and neck, the gloss of her hair, and the sparkle of her vivacious eyes. He hates her with his whole soul. And the thrill of hatred he feels for her makes him suffer from her touch.

Her attitude towards him and his disease is still the same. Just as the doctor had adopted a certain relation to his patient which he could not abandon, so had she formed one towards him—that he was not doing something he ought to do and was himself to blame, and that she reproached him lovingly for this—and she could not now change that attitude.

"You see he doesn't listen to me and doesn't take his medicine at the proper time. And above all he lies in a position that is no doubt bad for him—with his legs up."

She described how he made Gerásim hold his legs up.

The doctor smiled with a contemptuous affability that said: "What's to be done? These sick people do have foolish fancies of that kind, but we must forgive them."

When the examination was over the doctor looked at his watch, and then Praskóvya Fëdorovna announced to Iván Ilyich that it was of course as he pleased, but she had sent to-day for a celebrated specialist who would examine him and have a consultation with Michael Danílovich (their regular doctor).

"Please don't raise any objections. I am doing this for my own sake," she said ironically, letting it be felt that she was doing it all for his sake and only said this to leave him no right to refuse. He remained silent, knitting his brows. He felt that he was so surrounded and involved in a mesh of falsity that it was hard to unravel anything.

Everything she did for him was entirely for her own sake, and she told him she was doing for herself what she actually was doing for herself, as if that was so incredible that he must understand the opposite.

At half-past eleven the celebrated specialist arrived. Again the sounding began and the significant conversations in his presence and in other rooms, about the kidneys and the appendix, and the questions and answers, with such an air of importance that again, instead of the real question of life and death which now alone confronted him, the question arose of the kidney and the appendix which were not behaving as they ought to and would now be attacked by Michael Danílovich and the specialist and forced to amend their ways.

The celebrated specialist took leave of him with a serious though not hopeless look, and in reply to the timid question in Iván Ilyich, with eyes glistening with fear and hope, put to him as to whether there was a chance of recovery, said that he could not vouch for it but there was a possibility. The look of hope with which Iván Ilyich watched the doctor out was so pathetic that Praskóvya Fëdorovna, seeing it, even wept as she left the room to hand the doctor his fee.

The gleam of hope kindled by the doctor's encouragement did not last long. The same room, the same pictures, curtains, wallpaper, medicine bottles, were all there, and the same aching suffering body, and Iván Ilyich began to moan. They gave him a subcutaneous injection and he sank into oblivion.

It was twilight when he came to. They brought him his dinner and he swallowed some beef tea with difficulty, and then everything was the same again and night was coming on.

After dinner, at seven o'clock, Praskóvya Fëdorovna came into the room in evening dress, her full bosom pushed up by her corset, and with traces of powder on her face. She had reminded him in the morning that they were going to the theatre. Sarah Bernhardt[2] was visiting the town and they had a box, which he had insisted on their taking. Now he had forgotten about it and her toilet offended him, but he concealed his vexation when he remembered that he had himself insisted on their securing a box and going because it would be an instructive and aesthetic pleasure for the children.

2. Stage name of Rosine Bernard (1844–1923), famed for romantic and tragic roles.

Praskóvya Fëdorovna came in, self-satisfied but yet with a rather guilty air. She sat down and asked how he was, but, as he saw, only for the sake of asking and not in order to learn about it, knowing that there was nothing to learn—and then went on to what she really wanted to say: that she would not on any account have gone but that the box had been taken and Helen and their daughter were going, as well as Petríshchev (the examining magistrate, their daughter's fiancé) and that it was out of the question to let them go alone; but that she would have much preferred to sit with him for a while; and he must be sure to follow the doctor's orders while she was away.

"Oh, and Fëdor Petróvich" (the fiancé) "would like to come in. May he? And Lisa?"

"All right."

Their daughter came in in full evening dress, her fresh young flesh exposed (making a show of that very flesh which in his own case caused so much suffering), strong, healthy, evidently in love, and impatient with illness, suffering, and death, because they interfered with her happiness.

Fëdor Petróvich came in too, in evening dress, his hair curled à la Capoul, a tight stiff collar round his long sinewy neck, an enormous white shirt-front and narrow black trousers tightly stretched over his strong thighs. He had one white glove tightly drawn on, and was holding his opera hat in his hand.

Following him the schoolboy crept in unnoticed, in a new uniform, poor little fellow, and wearing gloves. Terribly dark shadows showed under his eyes, the meaning of which Iván Ilyich knew well.

His son had always seemed pathetic to him, and now it was dreadful to see the boy's frightened look of pity. It seemed to Iván Ilyich that Vásya was the only one besides Gerásim who understood and pitied him.

They all sat down and again asked how he was. A silence followed. Lisa asked her mother about the opera-glasses, and there was an altercation between mother and daughter as to who had taken them and where they had been put. This occasioned some unpleasantness.

Fëdor Petróvich inquired of Iván Ilyich whether he had ever seen Sarah Bernhardt. Iván Ilyich did not at first catch the question, but then replied: "No, have you seen her before?"

"Yes, in *Adrienne Lecouvreur*."[3]

Praskóvya Fëdorovna mentioned some rôles in which Sarah Bernhardt was particularly good. Her daughter disagreed. Conversation sprang up as to the elegance and realism of her acting—the sort of conversation that is always repeated and is always the same.

In the midst of the conversation Fëdor Petróvich glanced at Iván Ilyich and became silent. The others also looked at him and grew silent. Iván Ilyich was staring with glittering eyes straight before him, evidently indignant with them. This had to be rectified, but it was impossible to do so. The silence had to be broken, but for a time no one dared to break it and they all became afraid that the conventional deception would suddenly become obvious and the truth become plain to all. Lisa was the first to pluck up

---

3. A play (1849) by the French dramatist Eugène Scribe (1791–1861), in which the heroine was a famous actress of the 18th century. Tolstoy considered Scribe, who wrote over four hundred plays, a shoddy, commercial playwright.

courage and break that silence, but by trying to hide what everybody was feeling, she betrayed it.

"Well, if we are going it's time to start," she said, looking at her watch, a present from her father, and with a faint and significant smile at Fëdor Petróvich relating to something known only to them. She got up with a rustle of her dress.

They all rose, said good-night, and went away.

When they had gone it seemed to Iván Ilyich that he felt better; the falsity had gone with them. But the pain remained—that same pain and that same fear that made everything monotonously alike, nothing harder and nothing easier. Everything was worse.

Again minute followed minute and hour followed hour. Everything remained the same and there was no cessation. And the inevitable end of it all became more and more terrible.

"Yes, send Gerásim here," he replied to a question Peter asked.

IX

His wife returned late at night. She came in on tiptoe, but he heard her, opened his eyes, and made haste to close them again. She wished to send Gerásim away and to sit with him herself, but he opened his eyes and said: "No, go away."

"Are you in great pain?"

"Always the same."

"Take some opium."

He agreed and took some. She went away.

Till about three in the morning he was in a state of stupefied misery. It seemed to him that he and his pain were being thrust into a narrow, deep black sack, but though they were pushed further and further in they could not be pushed to the bottom. And this, terrible enough in itself, was accompanied by suffering. He was frightened yet wanted to fall through the sack, he struggled but yet co-operated. And suddenly he broke through, fell, and regained consciousness. Gerásim was sitting at the foot of the bed dozing quietly and patiently, while he himself lay with his emaciated stockinged legs resting on Gerásim's shoulders; the same shaded candle was there and the same unceasing pain.

"Go away, Gerásim," he whispered.

"It's all right, sir. I'll stay a while."

"No. Go away."

He removed his legs from Gerásim's shoulders, turned sideways onto his arm, and felt sorry for himself. He only waited till Gerásim had gone into the next room and then restrained himself no longer but wept like a child. He wept on account of his helplessness, his terrible loneliness, the cruelty of man, the cruelty of God, and the absence of God.

"Why hast Thou done all this? Why hast Thou brought me here? Why, dost Thou torment me so terribly?"

He did not expect an answer and yet wept because there was no answer and could be none. The pain again grew more acute, but he did not stir and did not call. He said to himself: "Go on! Strike me! But what is it for? What have I done to Thee? What is it for?"

Then he grew quiet and not only ceased weeping but even held his breath and became all attention. It was as though he were listening not to an audible voice but to a voice of his soul, to the current of thoughts arising within him.

"What is it you want?" was the first clear conception capable of expression in words, that he heard.

"What do you want? What do you want?" he repeated to himself.

"What do I want? To live and not to suffer," he answered.

And again he listened with such concentrated attention that even his pain did not distract him.

"To live? How?" asked his inner voice.

"Why, to live as I used to—well and pleasantly."

"As you lived before, well and pleasantly?" the voice repeated.

And in imagination he began to recall the moments of his pleasant life. But strange to say none of those best moments of his pleasant life now seemed at all what they had then seemed—none of them except the first recollections of childhood. There, in childhood, there had been something really pleasant with which it would be possible to live if it could return. But the child who had experienced that happiness existed no longer, it was like a reminiscence of somebody else.

As soon as the period began which had produced the present Iván Ilyich, all that had then seemed joys now melted before his sight and turned into something trivial and often nasty.

And the further he departed from childhood and the nearer he came to the present the more worthless and doubtful were the joys. This began with the School of Law. A little that was really good was still found there—there was light-heartedness, friendship, and hope. But in the upper classes there had already been fewer of such good moments. Then during the first years of his official career, when he was in the service of the Governor, some pleasant moments again occurred: they were the memories of love for a woman. Then all became confused and there was still less of what was good; later on again there was still less that was good, and the further he went the less there was. His marriage, a mere accident, then the disenchantment that followed it, his wife's bad breath and the sensuality and hypocrisy: then that deadly official life and those preoccupations about money, a year of it, and two, and ten, and twenty, and always the same thing. And the longer it lasted the more deadly it became. "It is as if I had been going downhill while I imagined I was going up. And that is really what it was. I was going up in public opinion, but to the same extent life was ebbing away from me. And now it is all done and there is only death."

"Then what does it mean? Why? It can't be that life is so senseless and horrible. But if it really has been so horrible and senseless, why must I die and die in agony? There is something wrong!"

"Maybe I did not live as I ought to have done," it suddenly occurred to him. "But how could that be, when I did everything properly?" he replied, and immediately dismissed from his mind this, the sole solution of all the riddles of life and death, as something quite impossible.

"Then what do you want now? To live? Live how? Live as you lived in the law courts when the usher proclaimed 'The judge is coming!' The judge is coming, the judge!" he repeated to himself. "Here he is, the judge. But I am not guilty!" he exclaimed angrily. "What is it for?" And he ceased crying, but turning his face to the wall continued to ponder on the same question: Why, and for what purpose, is there all this horror? But however much he pondered he found no answer. And whenever the thought occurred to him, as it often did, that it all resulted from his not having lived as he ought to have done, he at once recalled the correctness of his whole life, and dismissed so strange an idea.

X

Another fortnight passed. Iván Ilyich now no longer left his sofa. He would not lie in bed but lay on the sofa, facing the wall nearly all the time. He suffered ever the same unceasing agonies and in his loneliness pondered always on the same insoluble question: "What is this? Can it be that it is Death?" And the inner voice answered: "Yes, it is Death."

"Why these sufferings?" And the voice answered, "For no reason—they just are so." Beyond and besides this there was nothing.

From the very beginning of his illness, ever since he had first been to see the doctor, Iván Ilyich's life had been divided between two contrary and alternating moods: now it was despair and the expectation of this uncomprehended and terrible death, and now hope and an intently interested observation of the functioning of his organs. Now before his eyes there was only a kidney or an intestine that temporarily evaded its duty, and now only that incomprehensible and dreadful death from which it was impossible to escape.

These two states of mind had alternated from the very beginning of his illness, but the further it progressed the more doubtful and fantastic became the conception of the kidney, and the more real the sense of impending death.

He had but to call to mind what he had been three months before and what he was now, to call to mind with what regularity he had been going downhill, for every possibility of hope to be shattered.

Latterly during that loneliness in which he found himself as he lay facing the back of the sofa, a loneliness in the midst of a populous town and surrounded by numerous acquaintances and relations but that yet could not have been more complete anywhere—either at the bottom of the sea or under the earth—during that terrible loneliness Iván Ilyich had lived only in memories of the past. Pictures of his past rose before him one after another. They always began with what was nearest in time and then went back to what was most remote—to his childhood—and rested there. If he thought of the stewed prunes that had been offered him that day, his mind went back to the raw shrivelled French plums of his childhood, their peculiar flavour and the flow of saliva when he sucked their stones, and along with the memory of that taste came a whole series of memories of those days: his nurse, his brother, and their toys. "No, I mustn't think of that. . . . It is too painful," Iván Ilyich said to himself, and brought himself back to the present—to the button on the back of the sofa and the creases in its morocco. "Morocco is expensive, but it does not wear well: there had been a quarrel about it. It was a different kind of quarrel and a different kind of morocco that time when we tore father's portfolio and were punished, and mamma brought us some tarts. . . ." And again his thoughts dwelt on his childhood, and again it was painful and he tried to banish them and fix his mind on something else.

Then again together with that chain of memories another series passed through his mind—of how his illness had progressed and grown worse. There also the further back he looked the more life there had been. There had been more of what was good in life and more of life itself. The two merged together. "Just as the pain went on getting worse and worse, so my life grew worse and worse," he thought. "There is one bright spot there at the back, at the beginning of life, and afterwards all becomes blacker and blacker and proceeds more and more rapidly—in inverse ratio to the square of the distance from death," thought Iván Ilyich. And the example of a stone falling downwards with increasing velocity entered his mind. Life, a series of increasing sufferings, flies further and further towards its end—the most terrible suffering. "I am flying. . . ." He shuddered, shifted himself, and tried to resist, but was already aware that resistance was impossible, and again with eyes weary of gazing but unable to cease seeing what was before them, he stared at the back of the sofa and waited—awaiting that dreadful fall and shock and destruction.

"Resistance is impossible!" he said to himself. "If I could only understand what it is all for! But that too is impossible. An explanation would be possible if it could be said that I have not lived as I ought to. But it is impossible to say that," and he remembered all the legality, correctitude, and propriety of his life. "That at any rate can certainly not be admitted," he thought, and his lips smiled ironically as if someone could see that smile and be taken in by it. "There is no explanation! Agony, death. . . . What for?"

XI

Another two weeks went by in this way and during that fortnight an event occurred that Iván Ilyich and his wife had desired. Petríshchev formally proposed. It happened in the evening. The next day Praskóvya Fëdorovna came into her husband's room considering how best to inform him of it, but that very night there had been a fresh change for the worse in his condition. She found him still lying on the sofa but in a different position. He lay on his back, groaning and staring fixedly straight in front of him.

She began to remind him of his medicines, but he turned his eyes towards her with such a look that she did not finish what she was saying; so great an animosity, to her in particular, did that look express.

"For Christ's sake let me die in peace!" he said.

She would have gone away, but just then their daughter came in and went up to say good morning. He looked at her as he had done at his wife, and in reply to her inquiry about his health said dryly that he would soon free them all of himself. They were both silent and after sitting with him for a while went away.

"Is it our fault?" Lisa said to her mother. "It's as if we were to blame! I am sorry for papa, but why should we be tortured?"

The doctor came at his usual time. Iván Ilyich answered "Yes" and "No," never taking his angry eyes from him, and at last said: "You know you can do nothing for me, so leave me alone."

"We can ease your sufferings."

"You can't even do that. Let me be."

The doctor went into the drawing-room and told Praskóvya Fëdorovna that the case was very serious and that the only resource left was opium to allay her husband's sufferings, which must be terrible.

It was true, as the doctor said, that Iván Ilyich's physical sufferings were terrible, but worse than the physical sufferings were his mental sufferings which were his chief torture.

His mental sufferings were due to the fact that that night, as he looked at Gerásim's sleepy, good-natured face with its prominent cheek-bones, the question suddenly occurred to him: "What if my whole life has really been wrong?"

It occurred to him that what had appeared perfectly impossible before, namely that he had not spent his life as he should have done, might after all be true. It occurred to him that his scarcely perceptible attempts to struggle against what was considered good by the most highly placed people, those scarcely noticeable impulses which he had immediately suppressed, might have been the real thing, and all the rest false. And his professional duties and the whole arrangement of his life and of his family, and all his social and official interests, might all have been false. He tried to defend all those things to himself and suddenly felt the weakness of what he was defending. There was nothing to defend.

"But if that is so," he said to himself, "and I am leaving this life with the consciousness that I have lost all that was given me and it is impossible to rectify it—what then?"

He lay on his back and began to pass his life in review in quite a new way. In the morning when he saw first his footman, then his wife, then his daughter, and then the doctor, their every word and movement confirmed to him the awful truth that had been revealed to him during the night. In them he saw himself—all that for which he had lived—and saw clearly that it was not real at all, but a terrible and huge deception which had hidden both life and death. This consciousness intensified his physical suffering tenfold. He groaned and tossed about, and pulled at his clothing which choked and stifled him. And he hated them on that account.

He was given a large dose of opium and became unconscious, but at noon his sufferings began again. He drove everybody away and tossed from side to side.

His wife came to him and said:

"*Jean,* my dear, do this for me. It can't do any harm and often helps. Healthy people often do it."

He opened his eyes wide.

"What? Take communion? Why? It's unnecessary! However . . ."

She began to cry.

"Yes, do, my dear. I'll send for our priest. He is such a nice man."

"All right. Very well," he muttered.

When the priest came and heard his confession, Iván Ilyich was softened and seemed to feel a relief from his doubts and consequently from his sufferings, and for a moment there came a ray of hope. He again began to think of the vermiform appendix and the possibility of correcting it. He received the sacrament with tears in his eyes.

When they laid him down again afterwards he felt a moment's ease, and the hope that he might live awoke in him again. He began to think of the operation that had been suggested to him. "To live! I want to live!" he said to himself.

His wife came in to congratulate him after his communion, and when uttering the usual conventional words she added:

"You feel better, don't you?"

Without looking at her he said "Yes."

Her dress, her figure, the expression of her face, the tone of her voice, all revealed the same thing. "This is wrong, it is not as it should be. All you have lived for and still live for is falsehood and deception, hiding life and death from you." And as soon as he admitted that thought, his hatred and his agonizing physical suffering again sprang up, and with that suffering a consciousness of the unavoidable, approaching end. And to this was added a new sensation of grinding shooting pain and a feeling of suffocation.

The expression of his face when he uttered that "yes" was dreadful. Having uttered it, he looked her straight in the eyes, turned on his face with a rapidity extraordinary in his weak state and shouted:

"Go away! Go away and leave me alone!"

XII

From that moment the screaming began that continued for three days, and was so terrible that one could not hear it through two closed doors without horror. At the moment he answered his wife he realized that he was lost, that there was no return, that the end had come, the very end, and his doubts were still unsolved and remained doubts.

"Oh! Oh! Oh!" he cried in various intonations. He had begun by screaming "I won't!" and continued screaming on the letter "o."

For three whole days, during which time did not exist for him, he struggled in that black sack into which he was being thrust by an invisible, resistless force. He struggled as a man condemned to death struggles in the hands of the executioner, knowing that he cannot save himself. And every moment he felt that despite all his efforts he was drawing nearer and nearer to what terrified him. He felt that his agony was due to his being thrust into that black hole and still more to his not being able to get right into it. He was hindered from getting into it by his conviction that his life had been a good one. That very justification of his life held him fast and prevented his moving forward, and it caused him most torment of all.

Suddenly some force struck him in the chest and side, making it still harder to breathe, and he fell through the hole and there at the bottom was a light. What had happened to him was like the sensation one sometimes experiences in a railway carriage when one thinks one is going backwards while one is really going forwards and suddenly becomes aware of the real direction.

"Yes, it was all not the right thing," he said to himself, "but that's no matter. It can be done. But what *is* the right thing?" he asked himself, and suddenly grew quiet.

This occurred at the end of the third day, two hours before his death. Just then his schoolboy son had crept softly in and gone up to the bedside. The dying man was still screaming desperately and waving his arms. His hand fell on the boy's head, and the boy caught it, pressed it to his lips, and began to cry.

At that very moment Iván Ilyich fell through and caught sight of the light, and it was revealed to him that though his life had not been what it should have been, this could still be rectified. He asked himself, "What *is* the right thing?" and grew still, listening. Then he felt that someone was kissing his hand. He opened his eyes, looked at his son, and felt sorry for him. His wife came up to him and he glanced at her. She was gazing at him open-mouthed, with undried tears on her nose and cheek and a despairing look on her face. He felt sorry for her too.

"Yes, I am making them wretched," he thought. "They are sorry, but it will be better for them when I die." He wished to say this but had not the strength to utter it. "Besides, why speak? I must act," he thought. With a look at his wife he indicated his son and said: "Take him away . . . sorry for him . . . sorry for you too. . . ." He tried to add, "forgive me," but said "forgo" and waved his hand, knowing that He whose understanding mattered would understand.

And suddenly it grew clear to him that what had been oppressing him and would not leave him was all dropping away at once from two sides, from ten sides, and from all sides. He was sorry for them, he must act so as not to hurt them: release them and free himself from these sufferings. "How good and how simple!" he thought. "And the pain?" he asked himself. "What has become of it? Where are you, pain?"

He turned his attention to it.

"Yes, here it is. Well, what of it? Let the pain be."

"And death . . . where is it?"

He sought his former accustomed fear of death and did not find it. "Where is it? What death?" There was no fear because there was no death.

In place of death there was light.

"So that's what it is!" he suddenly exclaimed aloud. "What joy!"

To him all this happened in a single instant, and the meaning of that instant did not change. For those present his agony continued for another two hours. Something rattled in his throat, his emaciated body twitched, then the gasping and rattle became less and less frequent.

"It is finished!" said someone near him.

He heard these words and repeated them in his soul.

"Death is finished," he said to himself. "It is no more!"

He drew in a breath, stopped in the midst of a sigh, stretched out, and died.

HENRIK IBSEN

1828–1906

Henrik Ibsen was the foremost playwright of his time—treating social themes and ideas and often satirizing the nineteenth-century bourgeoisie—and not only in Norway, his native land. His plays may be viewed historically as the culmination of the bourgeois drama that has flourished fitfully, in France and Germany particularly, since the eighteenth century, when Diderot advocated and wrote plays about the middle classes and their "conditions" and problems. But they may also be seen as the beginning of realistic prose plays about modern life, from George Bernard Shaw and John Galsworthy to a wide range of soap operas on radio and TV. Even in China, Ibsen's drama of domestic and political crisis was immensely popular and influenced a generation of modern playwrights.

Ibsen was born at Skien, in Norway, on March 20, 1828. His family had sunk into poverty and at one point was forced to sell their possessions to pay off creditors. In 1844, at the age of sixteen, he was sent to Grimstad, another small coastal town, as an apothecary's apprentice. There he lived in almost complete isolation and cut himself off from his family, except for his sister Hedvig. In 1850 he managed to get to Oslo (then Christiania) and to enroll at the university. But he never passed his examinations and in the following year left for Bergen, where he had acquired the position of playwright and assistant stage manager at the newly founded Norwegian Theater. Ibsen supplied the small theater with several historical and romantic plays. In 1857 he was appointed artistic director at the Mollergate Theater in Christiania, and a year later he married Susannah Thoresen. Love's Comedy, his first major play, caused a scandal when it was published in a journal in 1862. Ibsen was roundly denounced in the press for the play's apparent attack on the institution of marriage, and the Christiana theater refused to stage it. His depression at the attacks on his play increased when Norway refused to support Denmark in its war with Prussia and Austria over Schleswig-Holstein. Ibsen was at that time deeply affected by Scandinavianism, the movement for solidarity of the northern nations, and he was ready to leave Norway when he received a government grant in 1863 to study European art. He settled in Rome with his family and lived for the following twenty-seven years in Rome, Dresden, Munich, and various smaller summer resorts, during which time he wrote all of his later plays.

After a long period of incubation and experimentation with romantic and historical themes, Ibsen wrote a series of "problem" plays, beginning with The Pillars of Society (1877), which in their time created a furor by their fearless criticism of the nineteenth-century social scene: the subjection of women, hypocrisy, hereditary disease, seamy politics, and corrupt journalism. He wrote these plays using realistic modes of presentation: ordinary colloquial speech, a simple setting in a drawing room or study, a natural way of introducing or dismissing characters. Ibsen had learned from the "well-made" Parisian play (typified by those of Eugène Scribe) how to confine his action to one climactic situation and how gradually to uncover the past by retrogressive exposition. But he went far beyond Scribe in technical skill and intellectual honesty.

The success of Ibsen's problem plays was international. But we must not forget that he was a Norwegian, the first writer of his small nation (its population at that time was less than 2 million) to win a reputation outside of Norway. Ibsen more than anyone else widened the scope of world literature beyond the confines of the "great" modern nations, which had entered its community roughly in this order: Italy, Spain, France, England, Germany, Russia. Since the time of Ibsen, other small nations have begun to play their part in the concert of world literature. Paradoxically, however, Ibsen rejected his own land. He had dreamed of becoming a great national poet. Instead, the plays he wrote during his voluntary exile depicted Norwegian society as consisting largely of a stuffy, provincial middle class, redeemed by a few upright, even fiery, individuals of initiative and courage. Only in 1891, when he was sixty-three, did Ibsen return to Christiania for good. He was then famous and widely honored, but lived a very retired life. In 1900 he suffered a stroke that made him a complete invalid for the last years of his life. He died on May 23, 1906.

Ibsen could hardly have survived his time if he had been merely a painter of society, a dialectician of social issues, and a magnificent technician of the theater. True, many of his discussions are now dated. We smile at some of what happens in A Doll's House (1879) and Ghosts (1881). His realistic stagecraft is familiar to modern audi-

The definitive meeting between alien cultures, an event unmatched in world history, took place the morning of November 8, 1519, as the conquistador Hernán Cortés with his band of four hundred soldiers entered the Aztec capital of Tenochtitlán. Surrounded by the dazzling architecture of a city larger than Rome, the newly arrived Spaniards compared the scene before them to the fantasies of which they had read in chivalric romances. To the Aztecs, the newcomers were none other than spirits stepped out of the pages of the Quetzalcoatl cycle, a body of narrative chronicling the deeds of a hero god who had fled eastward in disgrace but had vowed return. Upon their meeting, Montezuma, the Aztec emperor, was said to have greeted Cortés with the title exclamation "O Our Lord!" (i.e., Quetzalcoatl).

The events that led to the fall of Tenochtitlán in 1521 were painstakingly re-created in Spanish chronicles, in Cortes's own letters, and in the native-language Florentine Codex. A generation later, Aztec singers were still lamenting the conquest, yet they hopefully compared it with the struggle their ancestors had endured two hundred years earlier at the time of Tenochtitlán's founding. Through the power of music the heroic forebears were brought back to life, at least in song, re-creating "that time of our utmost eagerness"—as phrased in one of the song texts in the sixteenth-century codex Cantares Mexicanos.

Shown here on a page from another of the sixteenth-century codices—the Codex Mendoza—are the heroes who had founded Tenochtitlán in the 1300s, including the principal chief Tenoch (or Tenuch) at center left, seated on the special mat of authority and with a speech glyph issuing from his mouth, indicating that he is the "speaker," or ruler. In the center is the famous eagle alighting on the prickly-pear cactus, a symbol of both Tenochtitlán and, prophetically, the modern Mexican state.

From 1421 to 1911—during most of the Ming dynasty and all of the Qing dynasty—the Forbidden City in Beijing was the imperial seat of power in China. Although it has been refurbished over the centuries, its overall look and layout (based on ancient Chinese diagrams of the universe) have remained remarkably consistent. Spread over an area of more than two million square feet and surrounded by a ten-foot wall that in turn is encircled by a moat, the city contains many buildings and courtyards that served as the settings for various ceremonial and administrative functions. Shown above is the Hall of Supreme Harmony, which was the site of most official celebrations, including the enthronement of new emperors.

Emperor Qianlong's reign—from 1736 to 1799—was the longest in Chinese history, and marked a concerted return to Confucian ideals after a period (during the last phase of the Ming dynasty) of heightened individualism. Attempting to consolidate Chinese cultural history around a definable canon, Qianlong ordered the assemblage of a massive anthology of China's most famous literary and historical works. This collection, called the Four Treasuries, offered 3,450 works copied in their entirety and accompanied by learned commentaries. Completed ten years after Qianlong's decree, the Four Treasuries ultimately filled 36,000 manuscript volumes. Although clearly a monumental achievement, the assemblage of the Four Treasuries also amounted to a cultural purge. Scholars searched private libraries throughout the empire, confiscated and destroyed works deemed harmful or critical of the ruling Manchus, and severely punished those who owned such books.

The portrait above of Qianlong and his empress (a detail of a larger work that also features the portraits of the emperor's eleven consorts) was painted by a westerner—the Italian Jesuit Giuseppe Castiglione—in commemoration of Qianlong's inauguration. Castiglione merged Western visual ideas with traditional Chinese watercolor techniques to render this sensitive likeness of the new emperor (which no doubt helped him occupy a favored position in Qianlong's court). The Jesuits had had a presence in China at least from the late Ming dynasty.

The greatest scientific work of the era we familiarly call "the Enlightenment," and one of the greatest such works in all of human history, is Sir Isaac Newton's *Philosophiae Naturalis Principia Mathematica* (*Mathematical Principles of Natural Philosophy*, 1687), in which he outlined the principles of universal gravitation. By the time Newton published the *Principia*, he had also essentially invented integral and (simultaneously with Wilhelm Leibniz) differential calculus and had made several significant discoveries in optics. (His study of optics led him to propose and construct the world's first reflecting telescope, pictured to the right next to the *Principia* manuscript.) Although many others contributed to the feeling during the seventeenth century that the universe was rational and comprehensible, Newton did more than anyone to provide concrete justification for that view.

Accompanying Europe's intellectual optimism during the Enlightenment was a continued recognition of the contingencies of the human condition. Perhaps no European capital was more aware of
these contingencies than London during the 1660s. After having suffered through a severe outbreak
of plague during the spring and summer of 1665—an outbreak that killed nearly 15 percent of the
city's population—London suffered a devastating fire during early September of 1666, re-created in
this seventeenth-century woodcut. Nearly three-quarters of the city's buildings were destroyed by
the fire, including over twelve thousand houses. Although only six people were reported to have
died in the fire, thousands were left without homes, belongings, or livelihoods.

Throughout the Edo period in Japan, an emerging merchant class became the primary consumer—and thus, the primary patron—of literary and visual arts. In the visual arts, the *ukiyo-e* style of painting, marked by its subject matter of theater, dance, and erotic intrigue, was extremely popular among the middle classes, especially since individual works were available in multiple prints.

The image above is by Utamaro, an artist working in the late eighteenth century who was celebrated for the psychological depth that he added to the formulaic *ukiyo-e* style. The scene pictured is from an immensely popular play of the period—*Kanadehon Chushingura*—which was inspired by an actual revenge killing that had occurred in 1703 in Ako province.

When this portrait was painted in 1787, Johann Wolfgang von Goethe had already published the immensely popular and influential novel *The Sorrows of Young Werther*, the work that almost single-handedly established the image of the introspective, self-pitying, melancholy Romantic hero. His masterpiece, *Faust*, published twenty-one years after this portrait, secured Goethe's reputation as an authentic Romantic genius and made him a legendary figure in his own lifetime.

This picture, *Goethe in the Campagna* (the countryside around Rome, shown here with artfully scattered classical ruins), was painted in 1786 by the German classical painter Johann Tischbein during the writer's two-year tour of Italy. Its carefully posed and idealized portrait of the handsome writer meditating in the midst of nature and the ruins of classical antiquity can be seen as the eighteenth-century equivalent of modern celebrity posters, and gives a hint of the international adulation that Goethe would enjoy as a quintessential genius during the latter half of his life.

"Bliss was it in that dawn to be alive," wrote William Wordsworth about his feelings witnessing the events of the French Revolution. His enthusiasm for the political transformation of France from an absolute monarchy to a representative republic was shared by many artists and intellectuals of the late eighteenth century, including Jacques Louis David, a French painter whose images of the Revolution and its aftermath are the most famous visual chronicles of its ideals and tragedies.

The image above, a drawing made by David in preparation for a massive painting that he never managed to complete, celebrates a moment of great courage and idealism at the beginning of the Revolution: the Tennis Court Oath of June 1789. Deputies of the Third Estate (commoners, as distinct from the nobles and the clergy), outraged at being locked out of the meeting hall where they were scheduled to discuss reforms, adjourned to a nearby indoor tennis court. Here, the revolutionaries vowed to remain united as the "National Assembly," until they produced a new constitution for France based on ideals that would soon afterward be made explicit in the Declaration of the Rights of Man: "liberty, property, security, and resistance to oppression."

After the great wave of the international Romantic movement had spent its force in the fourth decade of the nineteenth century, and as photography set a new standard for capturing reality visually, many artists and writers in Europe moved in a direction that we now call *realism*. The realists wanted a truthful representation of contemporary life and manners, and saw their method as inductive, observational, and hence "objective." The realist program in literature and in art aimed at providing a "slice of life," a glimpse into everyday existence that might well include the sordid, the banal, the ugly, and the evil. Artists and writers found interest in the lives of the middle and lower classes, both of which had previously been neglected.

In the visual arts, Honoré Daumier stands a quintessential realist, offering by turns sympathetic views of the lives of those on the bottom rungs of society, as in *Third Class Carriage* (ca. 1860), above, and satirical jabs at the puffery of the privileged, as in his famous illustrations of lawyers, judges, and other members of the professional classes.

Impressionism emerged in opposition to the prevailing official styles of realism, which claimed to represent objective reality, and of romanticism, which favored the depiction of human emotions. French artists like Claude Monet and Pierre-August Renoir turned to explorations of light and color and new techniques of painting. Bright colors and combinations of colors, and the manipulation of light and shadow, suggested that reality was not permanent or monolithic but fluid, existing in the viewer's eye and seized moment by moment.

Monet began painting the cathedral at Rouen during a visit in February 1892. Fascinated by the changing appearance of the stone at different times of day, he became obsessed with capturing these moments and created and reworked a series of thirty linked canvases over the next two and a half years. "Everything changes, even stone," he wrote. Monet painted the cathedral in different weather and from morning to night, recording what he called its "enveloppe" of air, light, and color. We see here the west façade first as a "harmony of blue and gold" in the full noon sun and then in gray weather. As with many Impressionist paintings, the images are best viewed at a distance, so that the thick brush strokes and juxtaposition of myriad colors blend into a single harmonious vision.

[1]

"Post-Impressionist" is the name given to a series of late-nineteenth-century European artists who rejected both Impressionist ideals and traditional Academic realism. Developing a range of personal styles, these artists abandoned Impressionist sensitivity and delicate shades to work with vibrant colors, bold, defining lines, and a direct presentation of the subject. Echoing Romantic and Symbolist practice, they evoked moods and emotions and suggested larger hidden meanings, many of which implied a critique of modern industrial society.

Dreams of exotic escape to a freer, more primitive existence appear in both these pictures, by Paul Gauguin and Henri Rousseau. Gauguin fled Paris for tropical islands, painting idealized scenes of a purer "primitive" life, as in *Tahitian Women/On the Beach* (1891) [1]; Rousseau, whose "naïve" or "primitive" style masks great technical mastery, never left France and painted his fantastic landscapes, such as *The Dream* (1910) [2], on the basis of books and the Paris Zoo.

[2]

[1]

Radical questions of perspective began to dominate Western art at the beginning of the twentieth century. Despite recent stylistic innovations, the Renaissance concept of a unified spatial perspective—an anchor point around which the work of art could be organized in depth—remained unchanged. Pablo Picasso's *Les Demoiselles d'Avignon* (1907) [1], often called the "first painting of the twentieth century," fractures this organizational model, breaking up images (and human figures) into a complex arrangement of planes and geometric shapes. On one level, the painting represents five prostitutes in a Barcelona brothel; its distorted images also include echoes of Cézanne's *Bathers*, of early Iberian sculpture, and—in the two figures on the right—of African masks.

[2]

The Belgian surrealist René Magritte plays with perspective in an entirely different manner. In *La Trahison des images* (1929) [2], also called *Ceci n'est pas une pipe* (this is not a pipe), the artist moves humorously back and forth between language and art, neither of which completely captures reality. The painting depicts a pipe as if in a class illustration—yet the sign says it is *not* a pipe, and of course it is not a *real* pipe; yet it *is* a pipe . . .

[1]

Post-Impressionism took many forms, one of which explored the expression of human emotions and developed into an international movement called Expressionism. Although German Expressionism is best known, Expressionist principles and techniques were employed in many countries and in diverse media. In art, literature, dance, music, and theater, conventional representations of reality were distorted to provide deeper insights into human emotions and thought processes. Often these insights were tragic, showing ordinary people under great stress and at moments of spiritual crisis. The Norwegian painter and graphic artist Edvard Munch, a strong influence on the formation of German Expressionism, produced violent images that gave terrifying expression to his own anxieties and fears. An exhibit of his woodcuts closed in Berlin in 1892 because it frightened the viewers. Munch was working from what he heard as "the scream of nature," a scream that echoes in the bold, black lines of *The Scream* (1896) [1]. Its timeless, free-floating anguish has become an icon of solitary psychic torment. In contrast, the etching *Woman with Dead Child* [2], by the German printmaker and sculptor Käthe Kollwitz, depicts two interrelated figures and thus focuses its monumental grief on a particular event. Each scene emblematizes a dimension of human suffering.

[2]

[1]

In the first quarter of the twentieth century, Latin American artists and writers began to question the supremacy of European cultural tradition and to look for a new, appropriately Latin American identity that recognized the role of indigenous culture. Diego Rivera, who had studied Modernist techniques in France and Spain, returned home when he was asked to use his art to help define

[2]

Mexican national identity after the Revolution of 1910. Public murals were considered the most effective form of proletarian art, and Rivera embarked on a career that would bring him world-wide renown as a muralist, painting not only modern subjects but also—to inspire citizens with pride in their cultural roots—scenes that recalled earlier eras of Mexican history. *The Totonac Civilization* (1942) [1] is part of a series depicting pre-Hispanic civilization, and shows the gaily dressed inhabitants of a prosperous city with a large pyramidal temple and buildings as far as the eye can see. Frida Kahlo's imagery is more personal, but she reveals a similar dedication to *Mexicanidad* and includes emblems from folk art and Aztec culture in many of her paintings. The monkey in *Self-Portrait with Monkey* (1940) [2] is often taken to be an allusion to the Aztec belief in animals as alter egos.

[1]

Traditional Chinese painting underwent a change in the twentieth century that corresponded to political developments in China. As part of the national drive to modernize society (and modernization meant learning the Western model), art instruction included courses in the principles and techniques of Western art. It is not surprising that a blend of traditions occurred. The anonymous *Industrialization along the Yang-Tse-Kiang River* [1] introduces factories and smokestacks and tall buildings into an otherwise traditional landscape, transforming its natural setting with an overlay of the industrial development that meant economic and social progress. Socialist realist style, approved by the Communist governments of the Soviet Union and China, held that artists and writers should subordinate their identity to the group, and give an optimistic and even utopian picture of blissful life in the well-organized socialist society. *Fish Pond of the Commune* [2], an energetic and light-hearted picture of unbelievable success at fishing when the group gets to work, is an attractive example of propaganda art "painted by peasants from Houhsien" after 1958, the year of the Great Leap Forward, announced by Chairman Mao Zedong.

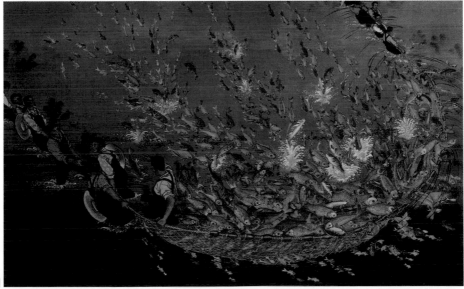

[2]

The African masks that were part of indigenous society—used in rituals, dance, and ceremonies—were welcomed by European modernists both as exotic images of non-Western culture and as models of sculptural form whose balanced planes had much in common with contemporary Cubist tendencies. This mask [1] comes from the Adouma people of Gabon in southwest Africa. The figure in *Ibaye* [2] by Cuban artist Wilfredo Lam, by contrast, sets out as a conscious blend of two traditions. Lam left his native Cuba in 1923 to study painting under Salvador Dalí and later moved to Paris, where he became friends with both Pablo Picasso and the Surrealist writer André Breton. The influences of Picasso's imagery and Surrealism persist throughout Lam's work, fused with a new preoccupation. Fleeing war-torn Europe in 1941, the painter returned to Cuba, where he became interested in Afro-Cuban society and religion, and undertook to express its spirit in his art.

[1]

[2]

ences because it has become part of our dramatic tradition. But Ibsen stays with us because he has more to offer—because he was an artist who managed to create, at his best, works of poetry that, under their mask of sardonic humor, express his dream of humanity reborn by intelligence and self-sacrifice.

Hedda Gabler (1890) surprised and puzzled the large audience all over Europe that Ibsen had won in the 1880s. The play shows nothing of Ibsen's reforming zeal: no general theme emerges that could be used in spreading progressive ideas such as the emancipation of women dramatized in *A Doll's House* (1879), nor is the play an example of Ibsen's peculiar technique of retrospective revelation exhibited in *Rosmersholm* (1886). At first glance it seems mainly a study of a complex, exceptional, and even unique woman. Henry James, reviewing the first English performance, saw it as the picture of "a state of nerves as well as of soul, a state of temper, of health, of chagrin, of despair." Undoubtedly, Hedda is the central figure of the play, but she is no conventional heroine. She behaves atrociously to everyone with whom she comes in contact, and her moral sense is thoroughly defective: she is perverse, egotistical, sadistic, callous, even evil and demonic, truly a *femme fatale*. Still, this impression, while not mistaken, ignores another side of her personality and her situation. The play is, after all, a tragedy (though there are comic touches), and we are to feel pity and terror. Hedda is not simply evil and perverse. Born, she feels, for a greater destiny and imbued with romantic visions of genius that include making one's own life a work of art, she cannot accept the practical compromises and mediocre aspirations with which she is surrounded. We must imagine her as distinguished, well bred, proud, beautiful, and even grand in her defiance of her surroundings and in the final gesture of her suicide. Not for nothing have great actresses excelled in this role. We must pity her as a tortured, tormented creature caught in a web of circumstance, as a victim, in spite of her desperate struggles to dominate and control the fate of those around her.

We are carefully prepared to understand her heritage. She is General Gabler's daughter. Ibsen tells us himself (in a letter to Count Moritz Prozor, dated December 4, 1890) that "I intended to indicate thereby that as a personality she is to be regarded rather as her father's daughter than as her husband's wife." She has inherited an aristocratic view of life. Her father's portrait hangs in her apartment. His pistols tell of the code of honor and the ready escape they offer in a self-inflicted death. Hedda lives in Ibsen's Norway, a stuffy, provincial, middle-class society, and is acutely, even morbidly, afraid of scandal. She has, to her own regret, rejected the advances of Eilert, theatrically threatening him with her father's pistol. She envies Thea for the boldness with which she deserted her husband to follow Eilert. She admires Eilert for his escapades, which she romanticizes with the recurrent metaphor of his returning with "vine leaves in his hair." But she cannot break out of the narrow confines of her society. She is not an emancipated woman.

When she is almost thirty, in reduced circumstances, she accepts a suitable husband, George Tesman. The marriage of convenience turns out to be a ghastly error for which she cannot forgive herself: Tesman is an amiable bore absorbed in his research into the "Domestic Craftsmanship Practices of Medieval Brabant." His expectations of a professorship in his hometown turn out to be uncertain. He has gone into debt, even to his guileless old aunt, in renting an expensive house, and, supreme humiliation for her, Hedda is pregnant by him. The dream of luxury, of becoming a hostess, of keeping Thoroughbred horses, is shattered the very first day after their return from the prolonged honeymoon, which for Tesman was also a trip to rummage around in archives. Hedda is deeply stirred by the return of Eilert, her first suitor. She seems vaguely to think of a new relationship, at least, by spoiling his friendship with Thea. She plays with the attentions of Judge Brack. But everything quickly comes to naught: she is trapped in her marriage, unable and unwilling to become unfaithful to her husband; she is deeply disappointed by Eilert's ugly death, saying, "Oh absurdity—! It hangs like a curse over everything I so much as touch." She fears the scandal that will follow when her role in Eilert's suicide is discovered and she is called before the police; she can avoid it only by coming under the power of Judge Brack, who is prepared to blackmail her with his knowledge of the circumstances. Her plot to destroy Thea and Eilert's brainchild is frustrated by Thea's having preserved notes and drafts, which Thea eagerly uses to start to reconstruct with the help of Tesman. Still, while Hedda is in a terrible impasse, her suicide remains a shock, an abrupt, even absurd deed, eliciting the final line from the commonsensical Judge Brack: "But God have mercy—People just don't act that way!" But we must assume that Hedda had pondered suicide long before: the pistol she gave to Eilert implies an unspoken suicide pact. He bungled it; she does it the right way, dying in beauty, shot in the temple and not in the abdomen.

The play is not, however, simply a character study, though Hedda is an extraordinarily complex, contradictory, subtle woman whose portrait, at least on the stage, could not be easily paralleled before Ibsen. It is also an extremely effective, swiftly moving play of action, deftly plotted in its clashes and climaxes. At the end of Act One Hedda seems to have won. The Tesmans, husband and aunt, are put in their place. Thea is lured into making confidences. The scene in Act Two in which Hedda appeals to Eilert's pride in his independence and induces him to join in Judge Brack's party is a superb display of Hedda's power and skill. Act Two ends with Eilert going off and the two women left alone in their tense though suppressed antagonism. Act III ends with Hedda alone, burning the precious manuscript about the "cultural forces which will shape the future and . . . the future course of civilization," an obvious contrast to Tesman's research into an irrelevant past. (Ibsen himself always believed in progress, in a utopia he called "the Third Empire.")

The action is compressed into about thirty-six hours and located in a house where only the moving of furniture (the piano into the back room) or the change of light or costumes indicates the passing of time. Tesman is something of a fool. He is totally unaware of Hedda's inner turmoil, he obtusely misunderstands allusions to her pregnancy, he comically encourages the advances of Judge Brack, he complacently settles down to the task of assembling the fragments of Eilert's manuscript, recognizing that "finding the order in other people's papers—that's precisely what I'm meant for." Though he seems amiably domestic in his love for his aunts, proud of having won Hedda, ambitious to provide an elegant home for her, his behavior is by no means above reproach. He envies and fears Eilert, gloats over his bad reputation, surreptitiously brings home the lost manuscript, conceals its recovery from Thea; when Hedda tells of its being burned, he is at first shocked, reacting comically with the legal phrase about "criminal appropriation of lost property," but is then easily persuaded to accept it when Hedda tells him that she did it for his sake and is completely won over when she reveals her pregnancy. After Eilert's death he feels, however, some guilt and tries to make up by helping in the reconstruction of the manuscript, now that his rival no longer threatens his career. Tesman is given strong speech mannerisms: the frequent use of "what?"—which Hedda, commenting at the end on the progress of the work on the manuscript, imitates sarcastically—and the use of "Just think." His last inappropriate words, "Shot herself! Shot herself in the temple! Just think!" lend a grotesque touch to the tragic end. Aunt Juliane belongs with him: she is a fussy, kindly person, proud of her nephew, awed by his new wife, eager to help with the expected baby, but also easily consoled after the death of her sister: "Oh, there's always some poor invalid or other who needs care and attention."

The other pair, Eilert Løvborg and Thea Elvsted, are sharply contrasted. Thea had the courage to leave her husband; she is devoted to Eilert and seems to have cured him of his addiction to drink but fears that he cannot resist a new temptation. Eilert tells Hedda unkindly that Thea is "stupid," and there is some truth to that, inasmuch as she is so easily taken in by Hedda. Her quick settling down to work on the manuscript after Eilert's death suggests some obtuseness, though we must, presumably, excuse it as a theatrical foreshortening.

Judge Brack is a "man of the world," a sensualist who hardly conceals his desire to make Hedda his mistress, by blackmail if necessary, and is dismayed when she escapes his clutches: in his facile philosophy, "one can usually learn to live with the inevitable."

Eilert, we must assume, is some kind of genius. His book, we have to take on trust, is an important work. We are told that he had squandered an inheritance, had engaged in orgies, and had regaled Hedda with tales of his exploits before she chased him with her pistol. When he comes back to town, ostensibly reformed, dressed conventionally, he immediately starts courting Hedda again. Stung by her contempt for his abstinence, he rushes off to Brack's party, which degenerates into a disgraceful brawl in a brothel. His relapse and the loss of the manuscript destroy his self-esteem and hope for any future. He accepts Hedda's pistol but dies an ignominious, ugly death. We see Eilert mainly reflected in Hedda's imagination as a figure of pagan freedom who, she thinks, has done something noble, beautiful, and courageous in "to break away from the banquet of life—so soon." She dies in beauty as she wanted Eilert to die.

This aesthetic suicide must seem to us a supremely futile gesture of revolt. Ibsen always admired the great rebels, the fighters for freedom, but *Hedda Gabler* will appear almost a parodic version of his persistent theme: the individual against society, defying it and escaping it in death.

PRONOUNCING GLOSSARY

The following list uses common English syllables and stress accents to provide rough equivalents of selected words whose pronunciation may be unfamiliar to the general reader.

Berta: *behr'-tuh*
Eilert Løvborg: *ai'-lert leuhv'-borg*
fjord: *fyoord*

Rosmersholm: *ross'-merss-holm*
Thea Elvsted: *tay'-ah aelf'-sted*

Hedda Gabler[1]

CHARACTERS

GEORGE TESMAN, *reseach fellow in*
   cultural history
HEDDA TESMAN, *his wife*
MISS JULIANE TESMAN, *his aunt*

MRS. ELEVSTED
JUDGE BRACK
EILERT LØVBORG
BERTA, *the maid to the Tesmans*

The action takes place in the fashionable west side of Christiania, Norway's capital.

---

1. Translated by Rick Davis and Brian Johnston.

Act I

A large, pleasantly and tastefully furnished drawing room, decorated in somber tones. In the rear wall is a wide doorway with the curtains pulled back. This doorway leads into a smaller room decorated in the same style. In the right wall of the drawing room is a folding door leading into the hall. In the opposite wall, a glass door, also with its curtains pulled back. Outside, through the windows, part of a covered veranda can be seen, along with trees in their autumn colors. In the foreground, an oval table surrounded by chairs. Downstage, near the right wall, is a broad, dark porcelain stove, a high-backed armchair, a footstool with cushions and two stools. Up in the right-hand corner, a corner-sofa and a small round table. Downstage, on the left side, a little distance from the wall, a sofa. Beyond the glass door, a piano. On both sides of the upstage doorway stand shelves displaying terra cotta and majolica objects. By the back wall of the inner room, a sofa, a table and a couple of chairs can be seen. Above the sofa hangs the portrait of a handsome elderly man in a general's uniform. Above the table, a hanging lamp with an opalescent glass shade. There are many flowers arranged in vases and glasses all around the drawing room. More flowers lie on the tables. The floors of both rooms are covered with thick rugs.

Morning light. The sun shines in through the glass door.

[MISS JULIE TESMAN, *with hat and parasol, comes in from the hall, followed by* BERTA, *who carries a bouquet wrapped in paper.* MISS TESMAN *is a kindly, seemingly good-natured lady of about sixty-five, neatly but simply dressed in a grey visiting outfit.* BERTA *is a housemaid, getting on in years, with a homely and somewhat rustic appearance.*]

MISS TESMAN [*Stops just inside the doorway, listens, and speaks softly.*] Well—I believe they're just now getting up!

BERTA [*Also softly.*] That's what I said, Miss. Just think—the steamer got in so late last night, and then—Lord, the young mistress wanted so much unpacked before she could settle down.

MISS TESMAN Well, well. Let them have a good night's sleep at least. But— they'll have some fresh morning air when they come down. [*She crosses to the glass door and throws it wide open.*]

BERTA [*By the table, perplexed, holding the bouquet.*] Hmm. Bless me if I can find a spot for these. I think I'd better put them down here, Miss. [*Puts the bouquet down on the front of the piano.*]

MISS TESMAN So, Berta dear, now you have a new mistress. As God's my witness, giving you up was a heavy blow.

BERTA And me, Miss—what can I say? I've been in yours and Miss Rina's service for so many blessed years—

MISS TESMAN We must bear it patiently, Berta. Truly, there's no other way. You know George has to have you in the house with him—he simply has to. You've looked after him since he was a little boy.

BERTA Yes, but Miss—I keep worrying about her, lying there at home—so completely helpless, poor thing. And that new girl! She'll never learn how to take care of sick people.

MISS TESMAN Oh, I'll teach her how soon enough. And I'll be doing most of the work myself, you know. Don't you worry about my sister, Berta dear.

BERTA   Yes, but there's something else, Miss. I'm so afraid I won't satisfy the new mistress—

MISS TESMAN   Ffft—Good Lord—there might be a thing or two at first—

BERTA   Because she's so particular about things—

MISS TESMAN   Well, what do you expect? General Gabler's daughter—the way she lived in the general's day! Do you remember how she would go out riding with her father? In that long black outfit, with the feather in her hat?

BERTA   Oh, yes—I remember that all right. But I never thought she'd make a match with our Mr. Tesman.

MISS TESMAN   Neither did I. But—while I'm thinking about it, don't call George "Mister Tesman" any more. Now it's "Doctor Tesman."

BERTA   Yes—that's what the young mistress said as soon as they came in last night. So it's true?

MISS TESMAN   Yes, it's really true. Think of it, Berta—they've made him a doctor. While he was away, you understand. I didn't know a thing about it, until he told me himself, down at the pier.

BERTA   Well, he's so smart he could be anything he wanted to be. But I never thought he'd take up curing people too!

MISS TESMAN   No, no, no. He's not that kind of doctor. [Nods significantly.] As far as that goes, you might have to start calling him something even grander soon.

BERTA   Oh no! What could that be?

MISS TESMAN   [Smiling.]   Hmm—wouldn't you like to know? [Emotionally.] Oh, dear God . . . if our sainted Joseph could look up from his grave and see what's become of his little boy. [She looks around.] But, Berta—what's this now? Why have you taken all the slipcovers off the furniture?

BERTA   The mistress told me to. She said she can't stand covers on chairs.

MISS TESMAN   But are they going to use this for their everyday living room?

BERTA   Yes, they will. At least she will. He—the doctor—he didn't say anything.

[GEORGE TESMAN enters, humming, from the right of the inner room, carrying an open, empty suitcase. He is a youthful-looking man of thirty-three, of medium height, with an open, round, and cheerful face, blond hair and beard. He wears glasses and is dressed in comfortable, somewhat disheveled clothes.]

MISS TESMAN   Good morning, good morning, George!

TESMAN   Aunt Julie! Dear Aunt Julie! [Goes over and shakes her hand.] All the way here—so early in the day! Hm!

MISS TESMAN   Yes, you know me—I just had to peek in on you a little.

TESMAN   And after a short night's sleep at that!

MISS TESMAN   Oh, that's nothing at all to me.

TESMAN   So—you got home all right from the pier, hm?

MISS TESMAN   Yes, as it turned out, thanks be to God. The Judge was kind enough to see me right to the door.

TESMAN   We felt so bad that we couldn't take you in the carriage—but you saw how many trunks and boxes Hedda had to bring.

MISS TESMAN   Yes, it was amazing.

BERTA [*To* TESMAN.]   Perhaps I should go in and ask the mistress if there's anything I can help her with.

TESMAN   No, thank you, Berta. You don't have to do that. If she needs you, she'll ring—that's what she said.

BERTA [*Going out to right.*]   Very well.

TESMAN   Ah—but—Berta—take this suitcase with you.

BERTA [*Takes the case.*]   I'll put it in the attic.

TESMAN   Just imagine, Auntie. I'd stuffed that whole suitcase with notes—just notes! The things I managed to collect in those archives—really incredible! Ancient, remarkable things that no one had any inkling of.

MISS TESMAN   Ah yes—you certainly haven't wasted any time on your honeymoon.

TESMAN   Yes—I can really say that's true. But, Auntie, take off your hat—Here, let's see. Let me undo that ribbon, hm?

MISS TESMAN [*While he does so.*]   Ah, dear God—this is just what it was like when you were home with us.

TESMAN [*Examining the hat as he holds it.*]   My, my—isn't this a fine, elegant hat you've got for yourself.

MISS TESMAN   I bought it for Hedda's sake.

TESMAN   For Hedda's—hm?

MISS TESMAN   Yes, so Hedda won't feel ashamed of me if we go out for a walk together.

TESMAN [*Patting her cheek.*]   You think of everything, Auntie Julie, don't you? [*Putting her hat on a chair by the table.*] And now—let's just settle down here on the sofa until Hedda comes. [*They sit. She puts her parasol down near the sofa.*]

MISS TESMAN [*Takes both his hands and gazes at him.*]   What a blessing to have you here, bright as day, right before my eyes again, George. Sainted Joseph's own boy!

TESMAN   For me too. To see you again, Aunt Julie—who've been both father and mother to me.

MISS TESMAN   Yes, I know you'll always have a soft spot for your old aunts.

TESMAN   But no improvement at all with Rina, hm?

MISS TESMAN   Oh dear no—and none to be expected poor thing. She lies there just as she has all these years. But I pray that Our Lord lets me keep her just a little longer. Otherwise I don't know what I'd do with my life, George. Especially now, you know—when I don't have you to take care of any more.

TESMAN [*Patting her on the back.*]   There. There. There.

MISS TESMAN   Oh—just to think that you've become a married man, George. And that you're the one who carried off Hedda Gabler! Beautiful Hedda Gabler. Imagine—with all her suitors.

TESMAN [*Hums a little and smiles complacently.*]   Yes, I believe I have quite a few friends in town who envy me, hm?

MISS TESMAN   And then—you got to take such a long honeymoon—more than five—almost six months . . .

TESMAN   Yes, but it was also part of my research, you know. All those archives I had to wade through—and all the books I had to read!

MISS TESMAN   I suppose you're right. [*Confidentially and more quietly.*] But listen, George—isn't there something—something extra you want to tell me?

TESMAN   About the trip?

MISS TESMAN   Yes.

TESMAN   No—I can't think of anything I didn't mention in my letters. I was given my doctorate—but I told you that yesterday.

MISS TESMAN   So you did. But I mean—whether you might have any—any kind of—prospects—?

TESMAN   Prospects?

MISS TESMAN   Good Lord, George—I'm your old aunt.

TESMAN   Well of course I have prospects.

MISS TESMAN   Aha!

TESMAN   I have excellent prospects of becoming a professor one of these days. But Aunt Julie dear, you already know that.

MISS TESMAN   [*With a little laugh.*]   You're right, I do. [*Changing the subject.*] But about your trip. It must have cost a lot.

TESMAN   Well, thank God, that huge fellowship paid for a good part of it.

MISS TESMAN   But how did you make it last for the both of you?

TESMAN   That's the tricky part, isn't it?

MISS TESMAN   And on top of that, when you're travelling with a lady! That's always going to cost you more, or so I've heard.

TESMAN   You're right—it was a bit more costly. But Hedda just had to have that trip, Auntie. She really had to. There was no choice.

MISS TESMAN   Well, I suppose not. These days a honeymoon trip is essential, it seems. But now tell me—have you had a good look around the house?

TESMAN   Absolutely! I've been up since dawn.

MISS TESMAN   And what do you think about all of it?

TESMAN   It's splendid! Only I can't think of what we'll do with those two empty rooms between the back parlor and Hedda's bedroom.

MISS TESMAN   [*Lightly laughing.*]   My dear George—when the time comes, you'll think of what to do with them.

TESMAN   Oh, of course—as I add to my library, hm?

MISS TESMAN   That's right, my boy—of course I was thinking about your library.

TESMAN   Most of all I'm just so happy for Hedda. Before we got engaged she'd always say how she couldn't imagine living anywhere but here—in Prime Minister Falk's house.

MISS TESMAN   Yes—imagine. And then it came up for sale just after you left for your trip.

TESMAN   Aunt Julie, we really had luck on our side, hm?

MISS TESMAN   But the expense, George. This will all be costly for you.

TESMAN [*Looks at her disconcertedly.*]   Yes. It might be. It might be, Auntie.

MISS TESMAN   Ah, God only knows.

TESMAN   How much, do you think? Approximately. Hm?

MISS TESMAN   I can't possibly tell before all the bills are in.

TESMAN   Luckily Judge Brack lined up favorable terms for me—he wrote as much to Hedda.

MISS TESMAN   That's right—don't you ever worry about that, my boy. All this furniture, and the carpets? I put up the security for it.

TESMAN   Security? You? Dear Auntie Julie, what kind of security could you give?

MISS TESMAN   I took out a mortgage on our annuity.

TESMAN   What? On your—and Aunt Rina's annuity!

MISS TESMAN   I couldn't think of any other way.

TESMAN [*Standing in front of her.*]   Have you gone completely out of your mind, Auntie? That annuity is all you and Aunt Rina have to live on.

MISS TESMAN   Now, now, take it easy. It's just a formality, you understand. Judge Brack said so. He was good enough to arrange it all for me. Just a formality, he said.

TESMAN   That could very well be, but all the same . . .

MISS TESMAN   You'll be earning your own living now, after all. And, good Lord, so what if we do have to open the purse a little, spend a little bit at first? That would only make us happy.

TESMAN   Auntie . . . you never get tired of sacrificing yourself for me.

MISS TESMAN [*Rises and lays her hands on his shoulders.*]   What joy do I have in the world, my dearest boy, other than smoothing out the path for you? You, without a father or mother to take care of you . . . but we've reached our destination, my dear. Maybe things looked black from time to time. But, praise God, George, you've come out on top!

TESMAN   Yes, it's really amazing how everything has gone according to plan.

MISS TESMAN   And those who were against you—those who would have blocked your way—they're at the bottom of the pit. They've fallen, George. And the most dangerous one, he fell the farthest. Now he just lies there where he fell, the poor sinner.

TESMAN   Have you heard anything about Eilert—since I went away, I mean?

MISS TESMAN   Nothing, except they say he published a new book.

TESMAN   What? Eilert Løvborg? Just recently, hm?

MISS TESMAN   That's what they say. God only knows how there could be anything to it. But when *your* book comes out—now that will be something else again, won't it, George? What's it going to be about?

TESMAN   It will deal with the Domestic Craftsmanship Practices of Medieval Brabant.[2]

MISS TESMAN   Just think—you can write about that kind of thing too.

TESMAN   However, it might be quite a while before that book is ready. I've got all these incredible collections that have to be put in order first.

MISS TESMAN   Ordering and collecting—you're certainly good at that. You're not the son of sainted Joseph for nothing.

TESMAN   And I'm so eager to get going. Especially now that I've got my own snug house and home to work in.

MISS TESMAN   And most of all, now that you've got her—your heart's desire, dear, dear George!

2. In the Middle Ages, Brabant was a duchy located in parts of what are now Belgium and the Netherlands.

TESMAN [*Embracing her.*] Yes, Auntie Julie! Hedda . . . that's the most beautiful thing of all! [*Looking toward the doorway.*] I think that's her, hm?

> [HEDDA *comes in from the left side of the inner room. She is a lady of twenty-nine. Her face and figure are aristocratic and elegant. Her complexion is pale. Her eyes are steel-grey, cold and clear. Her hair is an attractive medium brown but not particularly full. She is wearing a tasteful, somewhat loose-fitting morning gown.*]

MISS TESMAN [*Going to meet* HEDDA.] Good morning, Hedda, my dear. Good morning.

HEDDA [*Extending her hand.*] Good morning, Miss Tesman, my dear. You're here so early. How nice of you.

MISS TESMAN [*Looking somewhat embarrassed.*] Well now, how did the young mistress sleep in her new home?

HEDDA Fine thanks. Well enough.

TESMAN [*Laughing.*] Well enough! That's a good one, Hedda. You were sleeping like a log when I got up.

HEDDA Yes, lucky for me. But of course you have to get used to anything new, Miss Tesman. A little at a time. [*Looks toward the window.*] Uch! Look at that. The maid opened the door. I'm drowning in all this sunlight.

MISS TESMAN [*Going to the door.*] Well then, let's close it.

HEDDA No, no, don't do that. Tesman my dear, just close the curtains. That gives a gentler light.

TESMAN [*By the door.*] All right, all right. Now then, Hedda. You've got both fresh air and sunlight.

HEDDA Yes, fresh air. That's what I need with all these flowers all over the place. But Miss Tesman, won't you sit down?

MISS TESMAN No, but thank you. Now that I know everything's all right here, I've got to see about getting home again. Home to that poor dear who's lying there in pain.

TESMAN Be sure to give her my respects, won't you? And tell her I'll stop by and look in on her later today.

MISS TESMAN Yes, yes I'll certainly do that. But would you believe it, George? [*She rustles around in the pocket of her skirt.*] I almost forgot. Here, I brought something for you.

TESMAN And what might that be, Auntie, hm?

MISS TESMAN [*Brings out a flat package wrapped in newspaper and hands it to him.*] Here you are, my dear boy.

TESMAN [*Opening it.*] Oh my Lord. You kept them for me, Aunt Julie. Hedda, isn't this touching, hm?

HEDDA Well, what is it?

TESMAN My old house slippers. My slippers.

HEDDA Oh yes, I remember how often you talked about them on our trip.

TESMAN Yes, well, I really missed them. [*Goes over to her.*] Now you can see them for yourself, Hedda.

HEDDA [*Moves over to the stove.*] Oh, no thanks, I don't really care to.

TESMAN [*Following after her.*] Just think, Aunt Rina lying there embroidering for me, sick as she was. Oh, you couldn't possibly believe how many memories are tangled up in these slippers.

HEDDA [*By the table.*] Not for me.

MISS TESMAN Hedda's quite right about that, George.

TESMAN Yes, but now that she's in the family I thought—

HEDDA That maid won't last, Tesman.

MISS TESMAN Berta—?

TESMAN What makes you say that, hm?

HEDDA [*Pointing.*] Look, she's left her old hat lying there on that chair.

TESMAN [*Terrified, dropping the slippers on the floor.*] Hedda—!

HEDDA What if someone came in and saw that.

TESMAN But Hedda—that's Aunt Julie's hat.

HEDDA Really?

MISS TESMAN [*Taking the hat.*] Yes, it really is. And for that matter it's not so old either, my dear little Hedda.

HEDDA Oh, I really didn't get a good look at it, Miss Tesman.

MISS TESMAN [*Tying the hat on her head.*] Actually I've never worn it before today—and the good Lord knows that's true.

TESMAN And an elegant hat it is too. Really magnificent.

MISS TESMAN [*She looks around.*] Oh that's as may be, George. My parasol? Ah, here it is. [*She takes it.*] That's mine too. [*She mutters.*] Not Berta's.

TESMAN A new hat and a new parasol. Just think, Hedda.

HEDDA Very charming, very attractive.

TESMAN That's true, hm? But Auntie, take a good look at Hedda before you go. Look at how charming and attractive she is.

MISS TESMAN Oh my dear, that's nothing new. Hedda's been lovely all her life. [*She nods and goes across to the right.*]

TESMAN [*Following her.*] Yes, but have you noticed how she's blossomed, how well she's filled out on our trip?

HEDDA Oh, leave it alone!

MISS TESMAN [*Stops and turns.*] Filled out?

TESMAN Yes, Aunt Julie. You can't see it so well right now in that gown— but I, who have a little better opportunity to—

HEDDA [*By the glass door impatiently.*] Oh you don't have the opportunity for anything.

TESMAN It was that mountain air down in the Tyrol.

HEDDA [*Curtly interrupting.*] I'm the same as when I left.

TESMAN You keep saying that. But it's true, isn't it Auntie?

MISS TESMAN [*Folding her hands and gazing at* HEDDA.] Lovely . . . lovely . . . lovely. That's Hedda. [*She goes over to her and with both her hands takes her head, bends it down, kisses her hair.*] God bless and keep Hedda Tesman for George's sake.

HEDDA [*Gently freeing herself.*] Ah—! Let me out!

MISS TESMAN [*With quiet emotion.*] I'll come look in on you two every single day.

TESMAN Yes, Auntie, do that, won't you, hm?

MISS TESMAN Good-bye, good-bye.

> [*She goes out through the hall door.* TESMAN *follows her out. The door remains half open.* TESMAN *is heard repeating his greetings to Aunt Rina and his thanks for the slippers. While this is happening,* HEDDA *walks around the room raising her arms and clenching her fists as if in a rage. Then she draws the curtains back from the door, stands there and looks out. After a short time,* TESMAN *comes in and closes the door behind him.*]

TESMAN [*Picking up the slippers from the floor.*]   What are you looking at, Hedda?

HEDDA [*Calm and controlled again.*]   Just the leaves. So yellow and so withered.

TESMAN [*Wrapping up the slippers and placing them on the table.*]   Yes, well—we're into September now.

HEDDA [*Once more uneasy.*]   Yes—It's already—already September.

TESMAN   Didn't you think Aunt Julie was acting strange just now, almost formal? What do you suppose got into her?

HEDDA   I really don't know her. Isn't that the way she usually is?

TESMAN   No, not like today.

HEDDA [*Leaving the glass door.*]   Do you think she was upset by the hat business?

TESMAN   Not really. Maybe a little, for just a moment—

HEDDA   But where did she get her manners, flinging her hat around any way she likes here in the drawing room. People just don't act that way.

TESMAN   Well, I'm sure she won't do it again.

HEDDA   Anyway, I'll smooth everything over with her soon enough.

TESMAN   Yes, Hedda, if you would do that.

HEDDA   When you visit them later today, invite her here for the evening.

TESMAN   Yes, that's just what I'll do. And there's one more thing you can do that would really make her happy.

HEDDA   Well?

TESMAN   If you just bring yourself to call her Aunt Julie, for my sake, Hedda, hm?

HEDDA   Tesman, for God's sake, don't ask me to do that. I've told you that before. I'll try to call her Aunt once in a while and that's enough.

TESMAN   Oh well, I just thought that now that you're part of the family . . .

HEDDA   Hmm. I don't know—[*She crosses upstage to the doorway.*]

TESMAN [*After a pause.*]   Is something the matter, Hedda?

HEDDA   I was just looking at my old piano. It really doesn't go with these other things.

TESMAN   As soon as my salary starts coming in, we'll see about trading it in for a new one.

HEDDA   Oh, no, don't trade it in. I could never let it go. We'll leave it in the back room instead. And then we'll get a new one to put in here. I mean, as soon as we get the chance.

TESMAN [*A little dejectedly.*]   Yes, I suppose we could do that.

HEDDA [*Taking the bouquet from the piano.*]   These flowers weren't here when we got in last night.

TESMAN   I suppose Aunt Julie brought them.

HEDDA [*Looks into the bouquet.*]   Here's a card. [*Takes it out and reads.*]   "Will call again later today." Guess who it's from.

TESMAN   Who is it, hm?

HEDDA   It says Mrs. Elvsted.

TESMAN   Really. Mrs. Elvsted. She used to be Miss Rysing.

HEDDA   Yes, that's the one. She had all that irritating hair she'd always be fussing with. An old flame of yours, I've heard.

TESMAN [*Laughs.*]   Oh, not for long and before I knew you, Hedda. And she's here in town. How about that.

HEDDA   Strange that she should come visiting us. I hardly know her except from school.

TESMAN   Yes, and of course I haven't seen her since—well God knows how long. How could she stand it holed up out there so far from everything, hm?

HEDDA [*Reflects a moment and then suddenly speaks.*]   Just a minute, Tesman. Doesn't he live out that way, Eilert Løvborg, I mean?

TESMAN   Yes, right up in that area.

[BERTA *comes in from the hallway.*]

BERTA   Ma'am, she's back again. The lady who came by with the flowers an hour ago. [*Pointing.*] Those you've got in your hand, Ma'am.

HEDDA   Is she then? Please ask her to come in.

[BERTA *opens the door for* MRS. ELVSTED *and then leaves.* MRS. ELVSTED *is slender with soft, pretty features. Her eyes are light blue, large, round and slightly protruding. Her expression is one of alarm and question. Her hair is remarkably light, almost a white gold and exceptionally rich and full. She is a couple of years younger than Hedda. Her costume is a dark visiting dress, tasteful but not of the latest fashion.*]

HEDDA [*Goes to meet her in a friendly manner.*]   Hello my dear Mrs. Elvsted. So delightful to see you again.

MRS. ELVSTED [*Nervous, trying to control herself.*]   Yes, it's been so long since we've seen each other.

TESMAN [*Shakes her hand.*]   And we could say the same, hm?

HEDDA   Thank you for the lovely flowers.

MRS. ELVSTED   I would have come yesterday right away but I heard you were on a trip—

TESMAN   So you've just come into town, hm?

MRS. ELVSTED   Yesterday around noon. I was absolutely desperate when I heard you weren't home.

HEDDA   Desperate, why?

TESMAN   My dear Miss Rysing—I mean Mrs. Elvsted.

HEDDA   There isn't some sort of trouble—?

MRS. ELVSTED   Yes there is—and I don't know another living soul to turn to here in town.

HEDDA [*Sets the flowers down on the table.*]   All right then, let's sit down here on the sofa.

MRS. ELVSTED   Oh no, I'm too upset to sit down.

HEDDA   No you're not. Come over here. [*She draws* MRS. ELVSTED *to the sofa and sits beside her.*]

TESMAN   Well, and now Mrs.—

HEDDA   Did something happen up at your place?

MRS. ELVSTED   Yes—That's it—well, not exactly—Oh, I don't want you to misunderstand me—

HEDDA   Well then the best thing is just to tell it straight out, Mrs. Elvsted—why?

TESMAN   That's why you came here, hm?

MRS. ELVSTED   Yes, of course. So I'd better tell you, if you don't already know, that Eilert Løvborg is in town.

HEDDA   Løvborg?

TESMAN   Eilert Løvborg's back again? Just think, Hedda.

HEDDA   Good Lord, Tesman, I can hear.

MRS. ELVSTED   He's been back now for about a week. The whole week alone here where he can fall in with all kinds of bad company. This town's a dangerous place for him.

HEDDA   But my dear Mrs. Elvsted, how does this involve you?

MRS. ELVSTED   [*With a scared expression, speaking quickly.*]   He was the children's tutor.

HEDDA   Your children?

MRS. ELVSTED   My husband's. I don't have any.

HEDDA   The stepchildren then?

MRS. ELVSTED   Yes.

TESMAN   [*Somewhat awkwardly.*]   But was he sufficiently—I don't know how to say this—sufficiently regular in his habits to be trusted with that kind of job, hm?

MRS. ELVSTED   For the past two years no one could say anything against him.

TESMAN   Really, nothing. Just think, Hedda.

HEDDA   I hear.

MRS. ELVSTED   Nothing at all I assure you. Not in any way. But even so, now that I know he's here in the city alone and with money in his pocket I'm deathly afraid for him.

TESMAN   But why isn't he up there with you and your husband, hm?

MRS. ELVSTED   When the book came out he was too excited to stay up there with us.

TESMAN   Yes, that's right. Aunt Julie said he'd come out with a new book.

MRS. ELVSTED   Yes, a major new book on the progress of civilization—in its entirely I mean. That was two weeks ago. And it's been selling wonderfully. Everyone's reading it. It's created a huge sensation—why?

TESMAN   All that really? Must be something he had lying around from his better days.

MRS. ELVSTED   From before, you mean?

TESMAN   Yes.

MRS. ELVSTED   No, he wrote the whole thing while he was up there living with us. Just in the last year.

TESMAN   That's wonderful to hear, Hedda. Just think!

MRS. ELVSTED   Yes, if only it continues.

HEDDA   Have you met him here in town?

MRS. ELVSTED   No, not yet. I had a terrible time hunting down his address but this morning I finally found it.

HEDDA   [*Looks searchingly.*]   I can't help thinking this is a little odd on your husband's part.

MRS. ELVSTED   [*Starts nervously.*] My husband—What?

HEDDA   That he'd send you to town on this errand. That he didn't come himself to look for his friend.

MRS. ELVSTED   Oh no, no, no. My husband doesn't have time for that. And anyway I had to do some shopping too.

HEDDA   [*Smiling slightly.*]   Oh well, that's different then.

MRS. ELVSTED   [*Gets up quickly, ill at ease.*]   And now I beg you, Mr. Tesman, please be kind to Eilert Løvborg if he comes here—and I'm sure he will. You were such good friends in the old days. You have interests in common. The same area of research, as far as I can tell.

TESMAN   Yes, that used to be the case anyway.

MRS. ELVSTED   Yes, that's why I'm asking you—from the bottom of my heart to be sure to—that you'll—that you'll keep a watchful eye on him. Oh, Mr. Tesman, will you do that—will you promise me that?

TESMAN   Yes, with all my heart, Mrs. Rysing.

HEDDA   Elvsted.

TESMAN   I'll do anything in my power for Eilert. You can be sure of it.

MRS. ELVSTED   Oh, that is so kind of you. [*She presses his hands.*] Many, many thanks. [*Frightened.*] Because my husband thinks so highly of him.

HEDDA [*Rising.*]   You should write to him, Tesman. He might not come to you on his own.

TESMAN   Yes, that's the way to do it, Hedda, hm?

HEDDA   And the sooner the better. Right now, I think.

MRS. ELVSTED [*Beseechingly.*]   Yes, if you only could.

TESMAN   I'll write to him this moment. Do you have his address, Mrs. Elvsted?

MRS. ELVSTED   Yes. [*She takes a small slip of paper from her pocket and hands it to him.*] Here it is.

TESMAN   Good, good. I'll go write him—[*Looks around just a minute.*]— Where are my slippers? Ah, here they are. [*Takes the packet and is about to leave.*]

HEDDA   Make sure your note is very friendly—nice and long too.

TESMAN   Yes, you can count on me.

MRS. ELVSTED   But please don't say a word about my asking you to do it.

TESMAN   Oh, that goes without saying.

[TESMAN *leaves to the right through the rear room.*]

HEDDA [*Goes over to* MRS. ELVSTED, *smiles and speaks softly.*]   There, now we've killed two birds with one stone.

MRS. ELVSTED   What do you mean?

HEDDA   Didn't you see that I wanted him out of the way?

MRS. ELVSTED   Yes, to write the letter—

HEDDA   So I could talk to you alone.

MRS. ELVSTED [*Confused.*]   About this thing?

HEDDA   Yes, exactly, about this thing.

MRS. ELVSTED [*Apprehensively.*]   But there's nothing more to it, Mrs. Tesman, really there isn't.

HEDDA   Ah, but there is indeed. There's a great deal more. I can see that much. Come here, let's sit down together. Have a real heart-to-heart talk. [*She forces* MRS. ELVSTED *into the armchair by the stove and sits down herself on one of the small stools.*]

MRS. ELVSTED [*Nervously looking at her watch.*]   Mrs. Tesman, I was just thinking of leaving.

HEDDA   Now you can't be in such a hurry, can you? Talk to me a little bit about how things are at home.

MRS. ELVSTED   Oh, that's the last thing I want to talk about.

HEDDA   But to me? Good Lord, we went to the same school.

MRS. ELVSTED   Yes, but you were one class ahead of me. Oh, I was so afraid of you then.

HEDDA   Afraid of me?

MRS. ELVSTED Horribly afraid. Whenever we'd meet on the stairs you always used to pull my hair.

HEDDA No, did I do that?

MRS. ELVSTED Yes, you did—and once you said you'd burn it off.

HEDDA Oh, just silly talk, you know.

MRS. ELVSTED Yes, but I was so stupid in those days and anyway since then we've gotten to be so distant from each other. Our circles have just been totally different.

HEDDA Well let's see if we can get closer again. Listen now, I know we were good friends in school. We used to call each other by our first names.

MRS. ELVSTED No, no, I think you're mistaken.

HEDDA I certainly am not. I remember it perfectly and so we have to be perfectly open with each other just like in the old days. [*Moves the stool closer.*] There now. [*Kisses her cheek.*] Now you must call me Hedda.

MRS. ELVSTED [*Pressing and patting her hands.*] Oh, you're being so friendly to me. I'm just not used to that.

HEDDA There, there, there. I'll stop being so formal with you and I'll call you my dear Thora.

MRS. ELVSTED My name is Thea.

HEDDA That's right, of course, I meant Thea. [*Looks at her compassionately.*] So you're not used to friendship, Thea, in your own home?

MRS. ELVSTED If I only had a home, but I don't. I've never had one.

HEDDA [*Glances at her.*] I suspected it might be something like that.

MRS. ELVSTED [*Staring helplessly before her.*] Yes, yes, yes.

HEDDA I can't exactly remember now, but didn't you go up to Sheriff Elvsted's as a housekeeper?

MRS. ELVSTED Actually I was supposed to be a governess but his wife—at that time—she was an invalid, mostly bedridden, so I had to take care of the house too.

HEDDA So in the end you became mistress of your own house.

MRS. ELVSTED [*Heavily.*] Yes, that's what I became.

HEDDA Let me see. How long has that been?

MRS. ELVSTED Since I was married?

HEDDA Yes.

MRS. ELVSTED Five years now.

HEDDA That's right, it must be about that.

MRS. ELVSTED Oh these five years—! Or the last two or three anyway—! Ah, Mrs. Tesman, if you could just imagine.

HEDDA [*Slaps her lightly on the hand.*] Mrs. Tesman; really, Thea.

MRS. ELVSTED No, no, of course, I'll try to remember. Anyway, Hedda, if you could only imagine.

HEDDA [*Casually.*] It seems to me that Eilert, Løvborg's been living up there for about three years, hasn't he?

MRS. ELVSTED [*Looks uncertainly at her.*] Eilert Løvborg? Yes, that's about right.

HEDDA Did you know him from before—from here in town?

MRS. ELVSTED Hardly at all. I mean his name of course.

HEDDA But up there he'd come to visit you at the house?

MRS. ELVSTED Yes, every day. He'd read to the children. I couldn't manage everything myself, you see.

HEDDA   No, of course not. And what about your husband? His work must take him out of the house quite a bit.

MRS. ELVSTED   Yes, as you might imagine. He's the sheriff so he has to go traveling around the whole district.

HEDDA [*Leaning against the arm of the chair.*]   Thea, my poor sweet Thea— You've got to tell me everything just the way it is.

MRS. ELVSTED   All right, but you've got to ask the questions.

HEDDA   So, Thea, what's your husband really like? I mean, you know, to be with? Is he good to you?

MRS. ELVSTED [*Evasively.*]   He thinks he does everything for the best.

HEDDA   I just think he's a little too old for you. He's twenty years older, isn't he?

MRS. ELVSTED [*Irritatedly.*]   There's that too. There's a lot of things. I just can't stand being with him. We don't have a single thought in common, not a single thing in the world, he and I.

HEDDA   But doesn't he care for you at all in his own way?

MRS. ELVSTED   I can't tell what he feels. I think I'm just useful to him, and it doesn't cost very much to keep me. I'm very inexpensive.

HEDDA   That's a mistake.

MRS. ELVSTED [*Shaking her head.*]   Can't be any other way, not with him. He only cares about himself and maybe about the children a little.

HEDDA   And also for Eilert Løvborg, Thea.

MRS. ELVSTED [*Stares at her.*]   For Eilert Løvborg? Why do you think that?

HEDDA   Well, my dear, he sent you all the way into town to look for him. [*Smiling almost imperceptibly.*] And besides, you said so yourself, to Tesman.

MRS. ELVSTED [*With a nervous shudder.*]   Oh yes, I suppose I did. No, I'd better just tell you the whole thing. It's bound to come to light sooner or later anyway.

HEDDA   But my dear Thea.

MRS. ELVSTED   All right, short and sweet. My husband doesn't know that I'm gone.

HEDDA   What, your husband doesn't know?

MRS. ELVSTED   Of course not. Anyway he's not at home. He was out traveling. I just couldn't stand it any longer, Hedda, it was impossible. I would have been so completely alone up there.

HEDDA   Well, then what?

MRS. ELVSTED   Then I packed some of my things, just the necessities, all in secret, and I left the house.

HEDDA   Just like that?

MRS. ELVSTED   Yes, and I took the train to town.

HEDDA   Oh, my good, dear Thea. You dared to do that!

MRS. ELVSTED [*Gets up and walks across the floor.*]   Well, what else could I do?

HEDDA   What do you think your husband will say when you go home again?

MRS. ELVSTED [*By the table looking at her.*]   Up there to him?

HEDDA   Of course, of course.

MRS. ELVSTED   I'm never going back up there.

HEDDA [*Gets up and goes closer to her.*]   So you've really done it? You've really run away from everything?

MRS. ELVSTED   Yes, I couldn't think of anything else to do.

HEDDA   But you did it—so openly.

MRS. ELVSTED   Oh, you can't keep something like that a secret anyway.

HEDDA   Well, what do you think people will say about you, Thea?

MRS. ELVSTED   They'll say whatever they want, God knows. [*She sits tired and depressed on the sofa.*] But I only did what I had to do.

HEDDA [*After a brief pause.*]   So what will you do with yourself now?

MRS. ELVSTED   I don't know yet. All I know is that I've got to live here where Eilert Løvborg lives if I'm going to live at all.

HEDDA [*Moves a chair closer from the table, sits beside her and strokes her hands.*]   Thea, my dear, how did it come about, this—bond between you and Eilert Løvborg?

MRS. ELVSTED   Oh, it just happened, little by little. I started to have a kind of power over him.

HEDDA   Really?

MRS. ELVSTED   He gave up his old ways—and not because I begged him to. I never dared do that. But he started to notice that those kinds of things upset me, so he gave them up.

HEDDA [*Concealing an involuntary, derisive smile.*]   So you rehabilitated him, as they say. You, little Thea.

MRS. ELVSTED   That's what he said, anyway. And for his part he's made a real human being out of me. Taught me to think, to understand all sorts of things.

HEDDA   So he read to you too, did he?

MRS. ELVSTED   No, not exactly, but he talked to me. Talked without stopping about all sorts of great things. And then there was that wonderful time when I shared in his work, when I helped him.

HEDDA   You got to do that?

MRS. ELVSTED   Yes. Whenever he wrote anything, we had to agree on it first.

HEDDA   Like two good comrades.

MRS. ELVSTED [*Eagerly.*]   Yes, comrades. Imagine, Hedda, that's what he called it too. I should feel so happy, but I can't yet because I don't know how long it will last.

HEDDA   Are you that unsure of him?

MRS. ELVSTED [*Dejectedly.*]   There's the shadow of a woman between Eilert Løvborg and me.

HEDDA [*Stares intently at her.*]   Who could that be?

MRS. ELVSTED   I don't know. Someone from his past. Someone he's never really been able to forget.

HEDDA   What has he told you about all this?

MRS. ELVSTED   He's only talked about it once and very vaguely.

HEDDA   Yes, what did he say?

MRS. ELVSTED   He said that when they broke up she was going to shoot him with a pistol.

HEDDA [*Calm and controlled.*]   That's nonsense, people just don't act that way here.

MRS. ELVSTED   No they don't—so I think it's got to be that red-haired singer that he once—

HEDDA   Yes, that could well be.

MRS. ELVSTED   Because I remember they used to say about her that she went around with loaded pistols.

HEDDA   Well, then it's her, of course.

MRS. ELVSTED [*Wringing her hands.*]   Yes, but Hedda, just think, I hear this singer is in town again. Oh, I'm so afraid.

HEDDA [*Glancing toward the back room.*]   Shh, here comes Tesman. [*She gets up and whispers.*] Now, Thea, all of this is strictly between you and me.

MRS. ELVSTED [*Jumping up.*]   Oh yes, yes, for God's sake!

[GEORGE TESMAN, *a letter in his hand, comes in from the right side of the inner room.*]

TESMAN   There now, the epistle is prepared.

HEDDA   Well done—but Mrs. Elvsted's got to leave now, I think. Just a minute, I'll follow you as far as the garden gate.

TESMAN   Hedda dear, do you think Berta could see to this?

HEDDA [*Takes the letter.*]   I'll instruct her.

[BERTA *comes in from the hall.*]

BERTA   Judge Brack is here. Says he'd like to pay his respects.

HEDDA   Yes, ask the Judge to be so good as to come in, and then—listen here now—Put this letter in the mailbox.

BERTA [*Takes the letter.*]   Yes, ma'am.

[*She opens the door for* JUDGE BRACK *and then goes out.* JUDGE BRACK *is forty-five years old, short, well built and moves easily. He has a round face and an aristocratic profile. His short hair is still almost black. His eyes are lively and ironic. He has thick eyebrows and a thick moustache, trimmed square at the ends. He is wearing outdoor clothing, elegant, but a little too young in style. He has a monocle in one eye. Now and then he lets it drop.*]

BRACK [*Bows with his hat in his hand.*]   Does one dare to call so early?

HEDDA   One does dare.

TESMAN [*Shakes his hand.*]   You're welcome any time. Judge Brack, Mrs. Rysing. [HEDDA *sighs.*]

BRACK [*Bows.*]   Aha, delighted.

HEDDA [*Looks at him laughing.*]   Nice to see you by daylight for a change, Judge.

BRACK   Do I look different?

HEDDA   Yes, younger,

BRACK   You're too kind.

TESMAN   Well, how about Hedda, hm? Doesn't she look fine? Hasn't she filled out?

HEDDA   Stop it now. You should be thanking Judge Brack for all of his hard work—

BRACK   Nonsense. It was my pleasure.

HEDDA   There's a loyal soul. But here's my friend burning to get away. Excuse me, Judge, I'll be right back.

[*Mutual good-byes.* MRS. ELVSTED *and* HEDDA *leave by the hall door.*]

BRACK   Well, now, your wife's satisfied, more or less?

TESMAN   Oh yes, we can't thank you enough. I gather there might be a little more rearrangement here and there and one or two things still missing. A couple of small things yet to be procured.

BRACK   Is that so?

TESMAN   But nothing for you to worry about. Hedda said that she'd look for everything herself. Let's sit down.

BRACK   Thanks. Just for a minute. [*Sits by the table.*] Now, my dear Tesman, there's something we need to talk about.

TESMAN   Oh yes, ah, I understand. [*Sits down.*] Time for a new topic. Time for the serious part of the celebration, hm?

BRACK   Oh, I wouldn't worry too much about the finances just yet— although I must tell you that it would have been better if we'd managed things a little more frugally.

TESMAN   But there was no way to do that. You know Hedda, Judge, you know her well. I couldn't possibly ask her to live in a middle-class house.

BRACK   No, that's precisely the problem.

TESMAN   And luckily it can't be too long before I get my appointment.[3]

BRACK   Well, you know, these things often drag on and on.

TESMAN   Have you heard anything further, hm?

BRACK   Nothing certain. [*Changing the subject.*] But there is one thing. I've got a piece of news for you.

TESMAN   Well?

BRACK   Your old friend Eilert Løvborg's back in town.

TESMAN   I already know.

BRACK   Oh, how did you find out?

TESMAN   She told me, that lady who just left with Hedda.

BRACK   Oh, I see. I didn't quite get her name.

TESMAN   Mrs. Elvsted.

BRACK   Ah yes, the sheriff's wife. Yes, he's been staying up there with them.

TESMAN   And I'm so glad to hear that he's become a responsible person again.

BRACK   Yes, one is given to understand that.

TESMAN   And he's come out with a new book, hm?

BRACK   He has indeed.

TESMAN   And it's caused quite a sensation.

BRACK   It's caused an extraordinary sensation.

TESMAN   Just think, isn't that wonderful to hear. With all his remarkable talents, I was absolutely certain he was down for good.

BRACK   That was certainly the general opinion.

TESMAN   But I can't imagine what he'll do with himself now. What will he live on, hm?

[*During these last words,* HEDDA *has entered from the hallway.*]

HEDDA [*To* BRACK, *laughing a little scornfully.*]   Tesman is constantly going around worrying about what to live on.

TESMAN   My Lord, we're talking about Eilert Løvborg, dear.

HEDDA [*Looking quickly at him.*]   Oh yes? [*Sits down in the armchair by the stove and asks casually.*] What's the matter with him?

TESMAN   Well, he must have spent his inheritance along time ago, and he can't really write a new book every year, hm? So I was just asking what was going to become of him.

BRACK   Perhaps I can enlighten you on that score.

TESMAN   Oh?

BRACK   You might remember that he has some relatives with more than a little influence.

---

3. Tesman expects to be appointed to a professorship. These positions were much less numerous and more socially prominent than their contemporary American counterparts.

TESMAN   Unfortunately they've pretty much washed their hands of him.

BRACK   In the old days they thought of him as the family's great shining hope.

TESMAN   Yes, in the old days, possibly, but he took care of that himself.

HEDDA   Who knows? [*Smiles slightly.*] Up at the Elvsteds' he's been the target of a reclamation project.

BRACK   And there's this new book.

TESMAN   Well, God willing, they'll help him out some way or another. I've just written to him, Hedda, asking him to come over this evening.

BRACK   But my dear Tesman, you're coming to my stag party[4] this evening. You promised me on the pier last night.

HEDDA   Had you forgotten, Tesman?

TESMAN   Yes, to be perfectly honest, I had.

BRACK   For that matter, you can be sure he won't come.

TESMAN   Why do you say that, hm?

BRACK [*Somewhat hesitantly getting up and leaning his hands on the back of his chair.*]   My dear Tesman, you too, Mrs. Tesman, in good conscience I can't let you go on living in ignorance of something like this.

TESMAN   Something about Eilert, hm?

BRACK   About both of you.

TESMAN   My dear Judge, tell me what it is.

BRACK   You ought to prepare yourself for the fact that your appointment might not come through as quickly as you expect.

TESMAN [*Jumps up in alarm.*]   Has something held it up?

BRACK   The appointment might just possibly be subject to a competition.

TESMAN   A competition! Just think of that, Hedda!

HEDDA [*Leans further back in her chair.*]   Ah yes—yes.

TESMAN   But who on earth would it—surely not with—?

BRACK   Yes, precisely, with Eilert Løvborg.

TESMAN [*Clasping his hands together.*]   No, no, this is absolutely unthinkable, absolutely unthinkable, hm?

BRACK   Hmm—well, we might just have to learn to get used to it.

TESMAN   No, but Judge Brack, that would be incredibly inconsiderate. [*Waving his arms.*]   Because—well—just look, I'm a married man. We went and got married on this very prospect, Hedda and I. Went and got ourselves heavily into debt. Borrowed money from Aunt Julie too. I mean, good Lord, I was as much as promised the position, hm?

BRACK   Now, now, you'll almost certainly get it but first there'll have to be a contest.

HEDDA [*Motionless in the armchair.*]   Just think, Tesman, it will be a sort of match.

TESMAN   But Hedda, my dear, how can you be so calm about this?

HEDDA   Oh I'm not, not at all. I can't wait for the final score.

BRACK   In any case, Mrs. Tesman, it's a good thing that you know how matters stand. I mean, before you embark on any more of these little purchases I hear you're threatening to make.

HEDDA   What's that got to do with this?

---

4. A party for men only, whether single or married.

BRACK   Well, well, that's another matter. Good-bye. [*To* TESMAN.]   I'll come by for you when I take my afternoon walk.

TESMAN   Oh yes, yes, forgive me—I don't know if I'm coming or going.

HEDDA [*Reclining, stretching out her hand.*]   Good-bye, Judge, and do come again.

BRACK   Many thanks. Good-bye, good-bye.

TESMAN [*Following him to the door.*]   Good-bye, Judge. You'll have to excuse me.

[JUDGE BRACK *goes out through the hallway door.*]

TESMAN [*Pacing about the floor.*]   We should never let ourselves get lost in a wonderland, Hedda, hm?

HEDDA [*Looking at him and smiling.*]   Do you do that?

TESMAN   Yes, well, it can't be denied. It was like living in wonderland to go and get married and set up housekeeping on nothing more than prospects.

HEDDA   You may be right about that.

TESMAN   Well, at least we have our home, Hedda, our wonderful home. The home both of us dreamt about, that both of us craved, I could almost say, hm?

HEDDA [*Rises slowly and wearily.*]   The agreement was that we would live in society, that we would entertain.

TESMAN   Yes, good Lord, I was so looking forward to that. Just think, to see you as a hostess in our own circle. Hm. Well, well, well, for the time being at least we'll just have to make do with each other, Hedda. We'll have Aunt Julie here now and then. Oh you, you should have such a completely different—

HEDDA   To begin with, I suppose I can't have the liveried footmen.[5]

TESMAN   Ah no, unfortunately not. No footmen. We can't even think about that right now.

HEDDA   And the horse!

TESMAN [*Horrified.*]   The horse.

HEDDA   I suppose I mustn't think about that any more.

TESMAN   No, God help us, you can see that for yourself.

HEDDA [*Walking across the floor.*]   Well, at least I've got one thing to amuse myself with.

TESMAN [*Beaming with pleasure.*]   Ah, thank God for that, and what is that, Hedda?

HEDDA [*In the center doorway looking at him with veiled scorn.*]   My pistols, George.

TESMAN [*Alarmed.*]   Pistols?

HEDDA [*With cold eyes.*]   General Gabler's pistols.

[*She goes through the inner room and out to the left.*]

TESMAN [*Running to the center doorway and shouting after her.*]   No, for the love of God, Hedda, dearest, don't touch those dangerous things. For my sake, Hedda, hm?

5. Uniformed servants.

Act II

The TESMANS' *rooms as in the first act except that the piano has been moved out and an elegant little writing table with a bookshelf has been put in its place. Next to the sofa a smaller table has been placed. Most of the bouquets have been removed.* MRS. ELVSTED's *bouquet stands on the larger table in the foreground. It is afternoon.*

[HEDDA, *dressed to receive visitors, is alone in the room. She stands by the open glass door loading a pistol. The matching pistol lies in an open pistol case on the writing table.*]

HEDDA [*Looking down into the garden and calling.*]   Hello again, Judge.

BRACK [*Is heard some distance below.*]   Likewise, Mrs. Tesman.

HEDDA [*Raises the pistol and aims.*]   Now, Judge Brack, I am going to shoot you.

BRACK [*Shouting from below.*]   No, no, no. Don't stand there aiming at me like that.

HEDDA   That's what you get for coming up the back way. [*She shoots.*]

BRACK   Are you out of your mind?

HEDDA   Oh, good Lord, did I hit you?

BRACK [*Still outside.*]   Stop this nonsense.

HEDDA   Then come on in, Judge.
[JUDGE BRACK, *dressed for a bachelor party, comes in through the glass doors. He carries a light overcoat over his arm.*]

BRACK   In the devil's name, are you still playing this game? What were you shooting at?

HEDDA   Oh, I just stand here and shoot at the sky.

BRACK [*Gently taking the pistol out of her hands.*]   With your permission, ma'am? [*Looks at it.*] Ah, this one. I know it well. [*Looks around.*] And where do we keep the case? I see, here it is. [*Puts the pistol inside and shuts the case.*] All right, we're through with these little games for today.

HEDDA   Then what in God's name am I to do with myself?

BRACK   No visitors?

HEDDA [*Closes the glass door.*]   Not a single one. Our circle is still in the country.

BRACK   Tesman's not home either, I suppose.

HEDDA [*At the writing table, locks the pistol case in the drawer.*]   No, as soon as he finished eating he was off to the aunts. He wasn't expecting you so early.

BRACK   Hmm, I never thought of that. Stupid of me.

HEDDA [*Turns her head, looks at him.*]   Why stupid?

BRACK   Then I would have come a little earlier.

HEDDA [*Going across the floor.*]   Then you wouldn't have found anyone here at all. I've been in my dressing room since lunch.

BRACK   Isn't there even one little crack in the door wide enough for a negotiation?

HEDDA   Now that's something you forgot to provide for.

BRACK   That was also stupid of me.

HEDDA   So we'll just have to flop down here and wait. Tesman won't be home any time soon.

BRACK   Well, well, Lord knows I can be patient.

[HEDDA *sits in the corner of the sofa.* BRACK *lays his overcoat over the back of the nearest chair and sits down, keeps his hat in his hand. Short silence. They look at each other.*]

HEDDA   So?

BRACK [*In the same tone.*]   So?

HEDDA   I asked first.

BRACK [*Leaning a little forward.*]   Yes, why don't we allow ourselves a cozy little chat, Mrs. Hedda.

HEDDA [*Leaning further back in the sofa.*]   Doesn't it feel like an eternity since we last talked together? A few words last night and this morning, but I don't count them.

BRACK   Like this, between ourselves, just the two of us?

HEDDA   Well, yes, more or less.

BRACK   I wished you were back home every single day.

HEDDA   The whole time I was wishing the same thing.

BRACK   You, really, Mrs. Hedda? Here I thought you were having a wonderful time on your trip.

HEDDA   Oh yes, you can just imagine.

BRACK   But that's what Tesman always wrote.

HEDDA   Yes, him! He thinks it's the greatest thing in the world to go scratching around in libraries. He loves sitting and copying out old parchments or whatever they are.

BRACK [*Somewhat maliciously.*]   Well, that's his calling in the world, at least in part.

HEDDA   Yes, so it is, and no doubt it's—but for me, oh dear Judge, I've been so desperately bored.

BRACK [*Sympathetically.*]   Do you really mean that? You're serious?

HEDDA   Yes, you can imagine it for yourself. Six whole months never meeting with a soul who knew the slightest thing about our circle. No one we could talk with about our kinds of things.

BRACK   Ah no, I'd agree with you there. That would be a loss.

HEDDA   Then what was most unbearable of all.

BRACK   Yes?

HEDDA   To be together forever and always—with one and the same person.

BRACK [*Nodding agreement.*]   Early and late, yes, night and day, every waking and sleeping hour.

HEDDA   That's it, forever and always.

BRACK   Yes, all right, but with our excellent Tesman I would have imagined that you might—

HEDDA   Tesman is—a specialist, dear Judge.

BRACK   Undeniably.

HEDDA   And specialists aren't so much fun to travel with. Not for the long run anyway.

BRACK   Not even the specialist that one loves?

HEDDA   Uch, don't use that syrupy word.

BRACK [*Startled.*]   Mrs. Hedda.

HEDDA [*Half laughing, half bitterly.*] Well, give it a try for yourself. Hearing about the history of civilization every hour of the day.

BRACK Forever and always.

HEDDA Yes, yes, yes. And then his particular interest, domestic crafts in the Middle Ages. Uch, the most revolting thing of all.

BRACK [*Looks at her curiously.*] But, tell me now, I don't quite understand how—hmmm.

HEDDA That we're together? George Tesman and I, you mean?

BRACK Well, yes. That's a good way of putting it.

HEDDA Good Lord, do you think it's so remarkable?

BRACK I think—yes and no, Mrs. Hedda.

HEDDA I'd danced myself out, dear Judge. My time was up. [*Shudders slightly.*] Uch, no, I'm not going to say that or even think it.

BRACK You certainly have no reason to think it.

HEDDA Ah, reasons—[*Looks watchfully at him.*] And George Tesman? Well, he'd certainly be called a most acceptable man in every way.

BRACK Acceptable and solid, God knows.

HEDDA And I can't find anything about him that's actually ridiculous, can you?

BRACK Ridiculous? No—I wouldn't quite say that.

HEDDA Hmm. Well, he's a very diligent archivist anyway. Some day he might do something interesting with all of it. Who knows.

BRACK [*Looking at her uncertainly.*] I thought you believed, like everyone else, that he'd turn out to be a great man.

HEDDA [*With a weary expression.*] Yes, I did. And then when he went around constantly begging with all his strength, begging for permission to let him take care of me, well, I didn't see why I shouldn't take him up on it.

BRACK Ah well, from that point of view . . .

HEDDA It was a great deal more than any of my other admirers were offering.

BRACK [*Laughing.*] Well, of course I can't answer for all the others, but as far as I'm concerned you know very well that I've always maintained a certain respect for the marriage bond, that is, in an abstract kind of way, Mrs. Hedda.

HEDDA [*Playfully.*] Oh, I never had any hopes for you.

BRACK All I ask is an intimate circle of good friends, friends I can be of service to in any way necessary. Places where I am allowed to come and go as a trusted friend.

HEDDA Of the man of the house, you mean.

BRACK [*Bowing.*] No, to be honest, of the lady. Of the man as well, you understand, because you know that kind of—how should I put this—that kind of triangular arrangement is really a magnificent convenience for everyone concerned.

HEDDA Yes, you can't imagine how many times I longed for a third person on that trip. Ach, huddled together alone in a railway compartment.

BRACK Fortunately, the wedding trip is over now.

HEDDA [*Shaking her head.*] Oh no, it's a very long trip. It's nowhere near over. I've only come to a little stopover on the line.

BRACK Then you should jump out, stretch your legs a little, Mrs. Hedda.

HEDDA I'd never jump out.

BRACK Really?

HEDDA No, because there's always someone at the stop who—

BRACK [*Laughing.*] Who's looking at your legs, you mean?

HEDDA Yes, exactly.

BRACK Yes, but for heaven's sake.

HEDDA [*With a disdainful gesture.*] I don't hold with that sort of thing. I'd rather remain sitting, just like I am now, a couple alone. On a train.

BRACK But what if a third man climbed into the compartment with the couple?

HEDDA Ah yes. Now that's quite different.

BRACK An understanding friend, a proven friend—

HEDDA Who can be entertaining on all kinds of topics—

BRACK And not a specialist in any way!

HEDDA [*With an audible sigh.*] Yes, that would be a relief.

BRACK [*Hears the front door open and glances toward it.*] The triangle is complete.

HEDDA [*Half audibly.*] And there goes the train.

> [GEORGE TESMAN *in a gray walking suit and with a soft felt hat comes in from the hallway. He is carrying a large stack of unbound books under his arm and in his pockets.*]

TESMAN [*Goes to the table by the corner, sofa.*] Phew—hot work lugging all these here. [*Puts the books down.*] Would you believe I'm actually sweating, Hedda? And you're already here, Judge, hm. Berta didn't mention anything about that.

BRACK [*Getting up.*] I came up through the garden.

HEDDA What are all those books you've got there?

TESMAN [*Stands leafing through them.*] All the new works by my fellow specialists. I've absolutely got to have them.

HEDDA By your fellow specialists.

BRACK Ah, the specialists, Mrs. Tesman. [BRACK *and* HEDDA *exchange a knowing smile.*]

HEDDA You need even more of these specialized works?

TESMAN Oh, yes, my dear Hedda, you can never have too many of these. You have to keep up with what's being written and published.

HEDDA Yes, you certainly must do that.

TESMAN [*Searches among the books.*] And look here, I've got Eilert Løvborg's new book too. (*Holds it out.*) Maybe you'd like to look at it, Hedda, hm?

HEDDA No thanks—or maybe later.

TESMAN I skimmed it a little on the way.

HEDDA And what's your opinion as a specialist?

TESMAN I think the argument's remarkably thorough. He never wrote like this before. [*Collects the books together*] Now I've got to get all these inside. Oh, it's going to be such fun to cut the pages.[6] Then I'll go and change. [*To* BRACK.] We don't have to leave right away, hm?

BRACK No, not at all. No hurry at all.

---

6. Books used to be sold with the pages folded but uncut; the owner had to cut the pages to read the book.

TESMAN   Good, I'll take my time then. [*Leaves with the books but stands in the doorway and turns.*] Oh, Hedda, by the way, Aunt Julie won't be coming over this evening.

HEDDA   Really? Because of that hat business?

TESMAN   Not at all. How could you think that of Aunt Julie? No, it's just that Aunt Rina is very ill.

HEDDA   She always is.

TESMAN   Yes, but today she's gotten quite a bit worse.

HEDDA   Well, then it's only right that the other one should stay at home with her. I'll just have to make the best of it.

TESMAN   My dear, you just can't believe how glad Aunt Julie was, in spite of everything, at how healthy and rounded out you looked after the trip.

HEDDA [*Half audibly getting up.*]   Oh, these eternal aunts.

TESMAN   Hm?

HEDDA [*Goes over to the glass door.*]   Nothing.

TESMAN   Oh, all right. [*He goes out through the rear room and to the right.*]

BRACK   What were you saying about a hat?

HEDDA   Oh, just a little run-in with Miss Tesman this morning. She'd put her hat down there on that chair [*Looks at him smiling.*] and I pretended I thought it was the maid's.

BRACK [*Shaking his head.*]   My dear Mrs. Hedda, how could you do such a thing to that harmless old lady.

HEDDA [*Nervously walking across the floor.*]   Oh, you know—these things just come over me like that and I can't resist them. [*Flings herself into the armchair by the stove.*] I can't explain it, even to myself.

BRACK [*Behind the armchair.*]   You're not really happy—that's the heart of it.

HEDDA [*Staring in front of her.*]   And why should I be happy? Maybe you can tell me.

BRACK   Yes. Among other things, be happy you've got the home that you've always longed for.

HEDDA [*Looks up at him and laughs.*]   You also believe that myth?

BRACK   There's nothing to it?

HEDDA   Yes, heavens, there's something to it.

BRACK   So?

HEDDA   And here's what it is. I used George Tesman to walk me home from parties last summer.

BRACK   Yes, regrettably I had to go another way.

HEDDA   Oh yes, you certainly were going a different way last summer.

BRACK [*Laughs.*]   Shame on you, Mrs. Hedda. So you and Tesman . . .

HEDDA   So we walked past here one evening and Tesman, the poor thing, was twisting and turning in his agony because he didn't have the slightest idea what to talk about and I felt sorry that such a learned man—

BRACK [*Smiling skeptically.*]   You did . . .

HEDDA   Yes, if you will, I did, and so just to help him out of his torment I said, without really thinking about it, that this was the house I would love to live in.

BRACK   That was all?

HEDDA   For that evening.

BRACK   But afterward?

HEDDA   Yes, dear Judge, my thoughtlessness has had its consequences.

BRACK   Unfortunately, our thoughtlessness often does, Mrs. Hedda.

HEDDA   Thanks, I'm sure. But it so happens that George Tesman and I found our common ground in this passion for Prime Minister Falk's villa. And after that it all followed. The engagement, the marriage, the honeymoon and everything else. Yes, yes, Judge, I almost said: you make your bed, you have to lie in it.

BRACK   That's priceless. Essentially what you're telling me is you didn't care about any of this here.

HEDDA   God knows I didn't.

BRACK   What about now, now that we've made it into a lovely home for you?

HEDDA   Ach, I feel an air of lavender and dried roses in every room—or maybe Aunt Julie brought that in with her.

BRACK [*Laughing.*]   No, I think that's probably a relic of the eminent prime minister's late wife.

HEDDA   Yes, that's it, there's something deathly about it. It reminds me of a corsage the day after the ball. [*Folds her hands at the back of her neck, leans back in her chair and gazes at him.*] Oh, my dear Judge, you can't imagine how I'm going to bore myself out here.

BRACK   What if life suddenly should offer you some purpose or other, something to live for? What about that, Mrs. Hedda?

HEDDA   A purpose? Something really tempting for me?

BRACK   Preferably something like that, of course.

HEDDA   God knows what sort of purpose that would be. I often wonder if— [*Breaks off.*] No, that wouldn't work out either.

BRACK   Who knows. Let me hear.

HEDDA   If I could get Tesman to go into politics, I mean.

BRACK [*Laughing.*]   Tesman? No, you have to see that politics, anything like that, is not for him. Not in his line at all.

HEDDA   No, I can see that. But what if I could get him to try just the same?

BRACK   Yes, but why should he do that if he's not up to it? Why would you want him to?

HEDDA   Because I'm bored, do you hear me? [*After a pause.*] So you don't think there's any way that Tesman could become a cabinet minister?

BRACK   Hmm, you see my dear Mrs. Hedda, that requires a certain amount of wealth in the first place.

HEDDA [*Rises impatiently.*]   Yes, that's it, this shabby little world I've ended up in. [*Crosses the floor.*] That's what makes life so contemptible, so completely ridiculous. That's just what it is.

BRACK   I think the problem's somewhere else.

HEDDA   Where's that?

BRACK   You've never had to live through anything that really shakes you up.

HEDDA   Anything serious, you mean.

BRACK   Yes, you could call it that. Perhaps now, though, it's on its way.

HEDDA [*Tosses her head.*]   You mean that competition for that stupid professorship? That's Tesman's business. I'm not going to waste a single thought on it.

BRACK   No, forget about that. But when you find yourself facing what one calls in elegant language a profound and solemn calling—[*Smiling.*] a new calling, my dear little Mrs. Hedda.

HEDDA [*Angry.*]   Quiet. You'll never see anything like that.

BRACK [*Gently.*]   We'll talk about it again in a year's time, at the very latest.

HEDDA [*Curtly.*]   I don't have any talent for that, Judge. I don't want anything to do with that kind of calling.

BRACK   Why shouldn't you, like most other women, have an innate talent for a vocation that—

HEDDA [*Over by the glass door.*]   Oh, please be quiet. I often think I only have one talent, one talent in the world.

BRACK [*Approaching.*]   And what is that may I ask?

HEDDA [*Standing, staring out.*]   Boring the life right out of me. Now you know. [*Turns, glances toward the inner room and laughs.*] Perfect timing; here comes the professor.

BRACK [*Warning softly.*]   Now, now, now, Mrs. Hedda.

[GEORGE TESMAN, *in evening dress, carrying his gloves and hat, comes in from the right of the rear room.*]

TESMAN   Hedda, no message from Eilert Løvborg?

HEDDA   No.

BRACK   Do you really think he'll come?

TESMAN   Yes, I'm almost certain he will. What you told us this morning was just idle gossip.

BRACK   Oh?

TESMAN   Yes, at least Aunt Julie said she couldn't possibly believe that he would stand in my way anymore. Just think.

BRACK   So, then everything's all right.

TESMAN [*Puts his hat with his gloves inside on a chair to the right.*]   Yes, but I'd like to wait for him as long as I can.

BRACK   We have plenty of time. No one's coming to my place until seven or even half past.

TESMAN   Meanwhile, we can keep Hedda company and see what happens, hm?

HEDDA [*Sets* BRACK's *overcoat and hat on the corner sofa.*]   At the very worst, Mr. Løvborg can stay here with me.

BRACK [*Offering to take his things.*]   At the worst, Mrs. Tesman, what do you mean?

HEDDA   If he won't go out with you and Tesman.

TESMAN [*Looking at her uncertainly.*]   But, Hedda dear, do you think that would be quite right, him staying here with you? Remember, Aunt Julie can't come.

HEDDA   No, but Mrs. Elvsted will be coming and the three of us can have a cup of tea together.

TESMAN   Yes, that's all right then.

BRACK [*Smiling.*]   And I might add, that would be the best plan for him.

HEDDA   Why so?

BRACK   Good Lord, Mrs. Tesman, you've had enough to say about my little bachelor parties in the past. Don't you agree they should be open only to men of the highest principle?

HEDDA   That's just what Mr. Løvborg is now, a reclaimed sinner.

[BERTA *comes in from the hall doorway.*]

BERTA   Madam, there's a gentleman who wishes to—

HEDDA   Yes, please, show him in.

TESMAN [*Softly.*]   It's got to be him. Just think.

> [EILERT LØVBORG *enters from the hallway. He is slim and lean, the same age as* TESMAN, *but he looks older and somewhat haggard. His hair and beard are dark brown. His face is longish, pale, with patches of red over the cheekbones. He is dressed in an elegant suit, black, quite new dark gloves and top hat. He stops just inside the doorway and bows hastily. He seems somewhat embarrassed.*]

TESMAN [*Goes to him and shakes his hands.*]   Oh my dear Eilert, we meet again at long last.

LØVBORG [*Speaks in a low voice.*]   Thanks for the letter, George. [*Approaches* HEDDA.] May I shake your hand also, Mrs. Tesman?

HEDDA [*Takes his hand.*]   Welcome, Mr. Løvborg. [*With a gesture.*] I don't know if you two gentlemen—

LØVBORG [*Bowing.*]   Judge Brack, I believe.

BRACK [*Similarly.*]   Indeed. It's been quite a few years—

TESMAN [*To* LØVBORG, *his hands on his shoulders.*]   And now Eilert, make yourself completely at home. Right, Hedda? I hear you're going to settle down here in town, hm?

LØVBORG   Yes, I will.

TESMAN   Well, that's only sensible. Listen, I got your new book. I haven't really had time to read it yet.

LØVBORG   You can save yourself the trouble.

TESMAN   What do you mean?

LØVBORG   There's not much to it.

TESMAN   How can you say that?

BRACK   But everyone's been praising it so highly.

LØVBORG   Exactly as I intended—so I wrote the sort of book that everyone can agree with.

BRACK   Very clever.

TESMAN   Yes, but my dear Eilert.

LØVBORG   Because I want to reestablish my position, begin again.

TESMAN [*A little downcast.*]   Yes, I suppose you'd want to, hm.

LØVBORG [*Smiling, putting down his hat and pulling a package wrapped in paper from his coat pocket.*]   But when this comes out, George Tesman— this is what you should read. It's the real thing. I've put my whole self into it.

TESMAN   Oh yes? What's it about?

LØVBORG   It's the sequel.

TESMAN   Sequel to what?

LØVBORG   To my book.

TESMAN   The new one?

LØVBORG   Of course.

TESMAN   But my dear Eilert, that one takes us right to the present day.

LØVBORG   So it does—and this one takes us into the future.

TESMAN   The future. Good Lord! We don't know anything about that.

LØVBORG   No, we don't—but there are still one or two things to say about it, just the same. [*Opens the packages.*]   Here, you'll see.

TESMAN   That's not your handwriting, is it?

LØVBORG   I dictated it. [*Turns the pages.*] It's written in two sections. The first is about the cultural forces which will shape the future, and this other section [*Turning the pages.*]   is about the future course of civilization.

TESMAN   Extraordinary. It would never occur to me to write about something like that.

HEDDA [*By the glass door, drumming on the pane.*]   Hmm, no, no.

LØVBORG [*Puts the papers back in the packet and sets it on the table.*]   I brought it along because I thought I might read some of it to you tonight.

TESMAN   Ah, that was very kind of you, Eilert, but this evening [*Looks at* BRACK.] I'm not sure it can be arranged—

LØVBORG   Some other time then, there's no hurry.

BRACK   I should tell you, Mr. Løvborg, we're having a little party at my place this evening, mostly for Tesman, you understand—

LØVBORG [*Looking for his hat.*]   Aha, well then I'll—

BRACK   No, listen, why don't you join us?

LØVBORG [*Briefly but firmly.*]   No, that I can't do, but many thanks just the same.

BRACK   Oh come now, you certainly can do that. We'll be a small, select circle and I guarantee we'll be "lively," as Mrs. Hed—Mrs. Tesman would say.

LØVBORG   No doubt, but even so—

BRACK   And then you could bring your manuscript along and read it to Tesman at my place. I've got plenty of rooms.

TESMAN   Think about that, Eilert. You could do that, hm?

HEDDA [*Intervening.*]   Now, my dear, Mr. Løvborg simply doesn't want to. I'm quite sure Mr. Løvborg would rather settle down here and have supper with me.

LØVBORG [*Staring at her.*]   With you, Mrs. Tesman?

HEDDA   And with Mrs. Elvsted.

LØVBORG   Ah—[*Casually.*] I saw her this morning very briefly.

HEDDA   Oh did you? Well, she's coming here; so you might almost say it's essential that you stay here, Mr. Løvborg. Otherwise she'll have no one to see her home.

LØVBORG   That's true. Yes, Mrs. Tesman, many thanks. I'll stay.

HEDDA   I'll go and have a word with the maid.
   [*She goes over to the hall door and rings.* BERTA *enters.* HEDDA *speaks quietly to her and points toward the rear room.* BERTA *nods and goes out again.*]

TESMAN [*At the same time to* LØVBORG.]   Listen, Eilert, your lecture—Is it about this new subject? About the future?

LØVBORG   Yes.

TESMAN   Because I heard down at the bookstore that you'd be giving a lecture series here this fall.

LØVBORG   I plan to. Please don't hold it against me.

TESMAN   No, God forbid, but—?

LØVBORG   I can easily see how this might make things awkward.

TESMAN [*Dejectedly.*]   Oh, for my part, I can't expect you to—

LØVBORG   But I'll wait until you get your appointment.

TESMAN   You will? Yes but—yes but—you won't be competing then?

LØVBORG   No. I only want to conquer you in the marketplace of ideas.

TESMAN   But, good Lord, Aunt Julie was right after all. Oh yes, yes, I was quite sure of it. Hedda, imagine, my dear—Eilert Løvborg won't stand in our way.

HEDDA [*Curtly.*]   Our way? Leave me out of it.

> [*She goes up toward the rear room where* BERTA *is placing a tray with decanters and glasses on the table.* HEDDA *nods approvingly, comes forward again.* BERTA *goes out.*]

TESMAN [*Meanwhile.*]   So, Judge Brack, what do you say about all this?

BRACK   Well now, I say that honor and victory, hmm—they have a powerful appeal—

TESMAN   Yes, yes, I suppose they do but all the same—

HEDDA [*Looking at* TESMAN *with a cold smile.*]   You look like you've been struck by lightning.

TESMAN   Yes, that's about it—or something like that, I think—

BRACK   That was quite a thunderstorm that passed over us, Mrs. Tesman.

HEDDA [*Pointing toward the rear room.*]   Won't you gentlemen go in there and have a glass of punch?

BRACK [*Looking at his watch.*]   For the road? Yes, not a bad idea.

TESMAN   Wonderful, Hedda, wonderful! And I'm in such a fantastic mood now.

HEDDA   You too, Mr. Løvborg, if you please.

LØVBORG [*Dismissively.*]   No, thank you, not for me.

BRACK   Good Lord, cold punch isn't exactly poison, you know.

LØVBORG   Maybe not for everybody.

HEDDA   Then I'll keep Mr. Løvborg company in the meantime.

TESMAN   Yes, yes, Hedda dear, you do that.

> [TESMAN *and* BRACK *go into the rear room, sit down and drink punch, smoking cigarettes and talking animatedly during the following.* EILERT LØVBORG *remains standing by the stove and* HEDDA *goes to the writing table.*]

HEDDA [*In a slightly raised voice.*]   Now, if you like, I'll show you some photographs. Tesman and I—we took a trip to the Tyrol on the way home.

> [*She comes over with an album and lays it on the table by the sofa, seating herself in the farthest corner.* EILERT LØVBORG *comes closer, stooping and looking at her. Then he takes a chair and sits on her left side with his back to the rear room.*]

HEDDA [*Opening the album.*]   Do you see these mountains, Mr. Løvborg? That's the Ortler group. Tesman's written a little caption. Here. "The Ortler group near Meran."[7]

LØVBORG [*Who has not taken his eyes off her from the beginning, says softly and slowly.*]   Hedda Gabler.

HEDDA [*Glances quickly at him.*]   Shh, now.

LØVBORG [*Repeating softly.*]   Hedda Gabler.

HEDDA [*Staring at the album.*]   Yes, so I was once, when we knew each other.

LØVBORG   And from now—for the rest of my life—do I have to teach myself never to say Hedda Gabler?

HEDDA [*Turning the pages.*]   Yes, you have to. And I think you'd better start practicing now. The sooner the better, I'd say.

---

7. That is, Merano, a city in the Austrian Tyrol, since 1918 in Italy. The scenic features mentioned here and later are tourist attractions. The Ortler group and the Dolomites are Alpine mountain ranges. The Ampezzo Valley lies beyond the Dolomites to the east. The Brenner Pass is a major route through the Alps to Austria.

LØVBORG [*In a resentful voice.*]   Hedda Gabler married—and then—with
George Tesman.

HEDDA   That's how it goes.

LØVBORG   Ah, Hedda, Hedda—how could you have thrown yourself away
like that?

HEDDA [*Looks sharply at him.*]   What? Now stop that.

LØVBORG   Stop what, what do you mean?

HEDDA   Calling me Hedda and—[8]

[TESMAN *comes in and goes toward the sofa.*]

HEDDA [*Hears him approaching and says casually.*]   And this one here, Mr.
Løvborg, this was taken from the Ampezzo Valley. Would you just look at
these mountain peaks. [*Looks warmly up at* TESMAN.] George, dear, what
were these extraordinary mountains called?

TESMAN   Let me see. Ah, yes, those are the Dolomites.

HEDDA   Of course. Those, Mr. Løvborg, are the Dolomites.

TESMAN   Hedda, dear, I just wanted to ask you if we should bring some
punch in here, for you at least.

HEDDA   Yes, thank you my dear. And a few pastries perhaps.

TESMAN   Any cigarettes?

HEDDA   No.

TESMAN   Good.

[*He goes into the rear room and off to the right.* BRACK *remains sitting,
from time to time keeping his eye on* HEDDA *and* LØVBORG.]

LØVBORG [*Quietly, as before.*]   Then answer me, Hedda—how could you go
and do such a thing?

HEDDA [*Apparently absorbed in the album.*]   If you keep talking to me that
way, I just won't speak to you.

LØVBORG   Not even when we're alone together?

HEDDA   No. You can think whatever you want but you can't talk about it.

LØVBORG   Ah, I see. It offends your love for George Tesman.

HEDDA [*Glances at him and smiles.*]   Love? Don't be absurd.

LØVBORG   Not love then either?

HEDDA   But even so—nothing unfaithful. I will not allow it.

LØVBORG   Answer me just one thing—

HEDDA   Shh.

[TESMAN, *with a tray, enters from the rear room.*]

TESMAN   Here we are, here come the treats. [*He places the tray on the
table.*]

HEDDA   Why are you serving us yourself?

TESMAN [*Filling the glasses.*]   I have such a good time waiting on you,
Hedda.

HEDDA   But now you've gone and poured two drinks and Mr. Løvborg definitely does not want—

TESMAN   No, but Mrs. Elvsted's coming soon.

HEDDA   Yes, that's right, Mrs. Elvsted.

TESMAN   Did you forget about her?

---

8. This line is interpolated in an attempt to suggest the difference between the informal *du* (three or thy)
and the formal *de* (you) in the Norwegian text. Løvborg has just addressed Hedda in the informal manner
and she is warning him not to [translators' note].

HEDDA   We were just sitting here so completely wrapped up in these. [*Shows him a picture.*] *Do you remember this little village?*

TESMAN   Yes, that's the one below the Brenner Pass. We spent the night there—

HEDDA   —and ran into all those lively summer visitors.

TESMAN   Ah yes, that was it. Imagine—if you could have been with us, Eilert, just think. [*He goes in again and sits with* BRACK.]

LØVBORG   Just answer me one thing—

HEDDA   Yes?

LØVBORG   In our relationship—wasn't there any love there either? No trace? Not a glimmer of love in any of it?

HEDDA   I wonder if there really was. For me it was like we were two good comrades, two really good, faithful friends. [*Smiling.*] I remember you were particularly frank and open.

LØVBORG   That's how you wanted it.

HEDDA   When I look back on it, there was something really beautiful—something fascinating, something brave about this secret comradeship, this secret intimacy that no living soul had any idea about.

LØVBORG   Yes, Hedda, that's true isn't it? That was it. When I'd come to your father's in the afternoon—and the General would sit in the window reading his newspaper with his back toward the room—

HEDDA   And us on the corner sofa.

LØVBORG   Always with the same illustrated magazine in front of us.

HEDDA   Instead of an album, yes.

LØVBORG   Yes, Hedda—and when I made all those confessions to you—telling you things about myself that no one else knew in those days. Sat there and told you how I'd lost whole days and nights in drunken frenzy, frenzy that would last for days on end. Ah, Hedda—what kind of power was in you that drew these confessions out of me?

HEDDA   You think it was a power in me?

LØVBORG   Yes. I can't account for it in any other way. And you'd ask me all those ambiguous leading questions—

HEDDA   Which you understood implicity—

LØVBORG   How did you sit there and question me so fearlessly?

HEDDA   Ambiguously?

LØVBORG   Yes, but fearlessly all the same. Questioning me about—About things like that.

HEDDA   And how could you answer them, Mr. Løvborg?

LØVBORG   Yes, yes. That's just what I don't understand anymore. But now tell me, Hedda, wasn't it love underneath it all? Wasn't that part of it? You wanted to purify me, to cleanse me—when I'd seek you out to make my confessions. Wasn't that it?

HEDDA   No, no, not exactly.

LØVBORG   Then what drove you?

HEDDA   Do you find it so hard to explain that a young girl—when it becomes possible—in secret—

LØVBORG   Yes?

HEDDA   That she wants a glimpse of a world that—

LØVBORG   That—

HEDDA   That is not permitted to her.

LØVBORG   So that was it.

HEDDA   That too, that too—I almost believe it.

LØVBORG   Comrades in a quest for life. So why couldn't it go on?

HEDDA   That was your own fault.

LØVBORG   You broke it off.

HEDDA   Yes, when it looked like reality threatened to spoil the situation. Shame on you, Eilert Løvborg, how could you do violence to your comrade in arms?

LØVBORG   [Clenching his hands together.]   Well, why didn't you do it for real? Why didn't you shoot me dead right then and there like you threatened to?

HEDDA   Oh, I'm much too afraid of scandal.

LØVBORG   Yes, Hedda, underneath it all, you're a coward.

HEDDA   A terrible coward. [Changes her tone.] Lucky for you. And now you've got plenty of consolation up there at the Elvsteds'.

LØVBORG   I know what Thea's confided to you.

HEDDA   And no doubt you've confided to her about us.

LØVBORG   Not one word. She's too stupid to understand things like this.

HEDDA   Stupid?

LØVBORG   In things like this she's stupid.

HEDDA   And I'm a coward. [Leans closer to him without looking him in the eyes and says softly.] Now I'll confide something to you.

LØVBORG   [In suspense.]   What?

HEDDA   My not daring to shoot you—

LØVBORG   Yes?!

HEDDA   —that wasn't my worst cowardice that evening.

LØVBORG   [Stares at her a moment, understands and whispers passionately.] Ah, Hedda Gabler, now I see the hidden reason why we're such comrades. This craving for life in you—

HEDDA   [Quietly, with a sharp glance at him.]   Watch out, don't believe anything of the sort.

        [It starts to get dark. The hall door is opened by BERTA.]

HEDDA   [Clapping the album shut and crying out with a smile.]   Ah, finally. Thea, darling, do come in.

        [MRS. ELVSTED enters from the hall. She is in evening dress. The door is closed after her.]

HEDDA   [On the sofa, stretching out her arms.]   Thea, my sweet, you can't imagine how I've been expecting you.

        [MRS. ELVSTED, in passing, exchanges a greeting with the gentlemen in the inner room, crosses to the table, shakes HEDDA's hand. EILERT LØVBORG has risen. He and MRS. ELVSTED greet each other with a single nod.]

MRS. ELVSTED   Perhaps I should go in and have a word with your husband.

HEDDA   Not at all. Let them sit there. They'll be on their way soon.

MRS. ELVSTED   They're leaving?

HEDDA   Yes, they're going out on a little binge.

MRS. ELVSTED   [Quickly to LØVBORG.]   You're not?

LØVBORG   No.

HEDDA   Mr. Løvborg . . . he'll stay here with us.

MRS. ELVSTED [*Takes a chair and sits down beside him.*] It's so nice to be here.

HEDDA No, you don't, little Thea, not there. Come right over here next to me. I want to be in the middle between you.

MRS. ELVSTED All right, whatever you like. [*She goes around the table and sits on the sofa to the right of* HEDDA. LØVBORG *takes his chair again.*]

LØVBORG [*After a brief pause, to* HEDDA.] Isn't she lovely to look at?

HEDDA [*Gently stroking her hair.*] Only to look at?

LØVBORG Yes. We're true comrades, the two of us. We trust each other completely and that's why we can sit here and talk so openly and boldly together.

HEDDA With no ambiguity, Mr. Løvborg.

LØVBORG Well—

MRS. ELVSTED [*Softly, clinging to* HEDDA.] Oh, Hedda, I'm so lucky. Just think, he says I've inspired him too.

HEDDA [*Regards her with a smile.*] No, dear, does he say that?

LØVBORG And she has the courage to take action, Mrs. Tesman.

MRS. ELVSTED Oh God, me, courage?

LØVBORG Tremendous courage when it comes to comradeship.

HEDDA Yes, courage—yes! That's the crucial thing.

LØVBORG Why is that, do you suppose?

HEDDA Because then—maybe—life has a chance to be lived. [*Suddenly changing her tone.*] But now, my dearest Thea. Why don't you treat yourself to a nice cold glass of punch?

MRS. ELVSTED No thank you, I never drink anything like that.

HEDDA Then for you, Mr. Løvborg.

LØVBORG No thank you, not for me either.

MRS. ELVSTED No, not for him either.

HEDDA [*Looking steadily at him.*] But if I insisted.

LØVBORG Doesn't matter.

HEDDA [*Laughing.*] Then I have absolutely no power over you? Ah, poor me.

LØVBORG Not in that area.

HEDDA But seriously now, I really think you should, for your own sake.

MRS. ELVSTED No, Hedda—

LØVBORG Why is that?

HEDDA Or to be more precise, for others' sakes.

LØVBORG Oh?

HEDDA Because otherwise people might get the idea that you don't, deep down inside, feel really bold, really sure of yourself.

LØVBORG Oh, from now on people can think whatever they like.

MRS. ELVSTED Yes, that's right, isn't it.

HEDDA I saw it so clearly with Judge Brack a few minutes ago.

LØVBORG What did you see?

HEDDA That condescending little smile when you didn't dare join them at the table.

LØVBORG Didn't dare? I'd just rather stay here and talk with you, of course.

MRS. ELVSTED That's only reasonable, Hedda.

HEDDA How was the Judge supposed to know that? I saw how he smiled and shot a glance at Tesman when you didn't dare join them in their silly little party.

LØVBORG   Didn't dare. You're saying I don't dare.

HEDDA   Oh, I'm not. But that's how Judge Brack sees it.

LØVBORG   Well let him.

HEDDA   So you won't join them?

LØVBORG   I'm staying here with you and Thea.

MRS. ELVSTED   Yes, Hedda, you can be sure he is.

HEDDA [*Smiling and nodding approvingly to* LØVBORG.]   What a strong foundation you've got. Principles to last a lifetime. That's what a man ought to have. [*Turns to* MRS. ELVSTED.] See now, wasn't that what I told you when you came here this morning in such a panic—

LØVBORG [*Startled.*]   Panic?

MRS. ELVSTED [*Terrified.*]   Hedda, Hedda, no.

HEDDA   Just see for yourself. No reason at all to come running here in mortal terror. [*Changing her tone.*] There, now all three of us can be quite jolly.

LØVBORG [*Shocked.*]   What does this mean, Mrs. Tesman?

MRS. ELVSTED   Oh God, oh God, Hedda. What are you doing? What are you saying?

HEDDA   Keep calm now. That disgusting Judge is sitting there watching you.

LØVBORG   In mortal terror on my account?

MRS. ELVSTED [*Quietly wailing.*]   Oh, Hedda—

LØVBORG [*Looks at her steadily for a moment; his face is drawn.*]   So that, then, was how my brave, bold comrade trusted me.

MRS. ELVSTED [*Pleading.*]   Oh, my dearest friend, listen to me—

LØVBORG [*Takes one of the glasses of punch, raises it and says in a low, hoarse voice.*]   Your health, Thea. [*Empties the glass, takes another.*]

MRS. ELVSTED [*Softly.*]   Oh Hedda, Hedda—how could you want this to happen?

HEDDA   Want it? I want this? Are you mad?

LØVBORG   And your health too, Mrs. Tesman. Thanks for the truth. Long may it live. [*He drinks and goes to refill the glass.*]

HEDDA [*Placing her hand on his arm.*]   That's enough for now. Remember, you're going to the party.

MRS. ELVSTED   No, no, no.

HEDDA   Shh. They're watching us.

LØVBORG [*Putting down the glass.*]   Thea, be honest with me now.

MRS. ELVSTED   Yes.

LØVBORG   Was your husband told that you came here to look for me?

MRS. ELVSTED [*Wringing her hands.*]   Oh, Hedda, listen to what he's asking me!

LØVBORG   Did he arrange for you to come to town to spy on me? Maybe he put you up to it himself. Aha, that's it. He needed me back in the office again. Or did he just miss me at the card table?

MRS. ELVSTED [*Softly moaning.*]   Oh, Løvborg, Løvborg—

LØVBORG [*Grabs a glass intending to fill it.*]   Skøal to the old Sheriff too.

HEDDA [*Preventing him.*]   No more now. Remember, you're going out to read to Tesman.

LØVBORG [*Calmly putting down his glass.*]   Thea, that was stupid of me. What I did just now. Taking it like that I mean. Don't be angry with me, my dear, dear comrade. You'll see. Both of you and everyone else will see that even though I once was fallen—now I've raised myself up again, with your help, Thea.

MRS. ELVSTED [*Radiant with joy.*]   Oh God be praised.

    [*Meanwhile* BRACK *has been looking at his watch. He and* TESMAN *get up and come into the drawing room.*]

BRACK [*Taking his hat and overcoat.*]   Well, Mrs. Tesman, our time is up.

HEDDA   Yes, it must be.

LØVBORG [*Rising.*]   Mine too.

MRS. ELVSTED [*Quietly pleading.*]   Løvborg, don't do it.

HEDDA [*Pinching her arm.*]   They can hear you.

MRS. ELVSTED [*Crying out faintly.*]   Ow.

LØVBORG [*To* BRACK.]   You were kind enough to ask me along.

BRACK   So you're coming after all.

LØVBORG   Yes, thanks.

BRACK   I'm delighted.

LØVBORG [*Putting the manuscript packet in his pocket and saying to* TESMAN.] I'd really like you to look at one or two things before I send it off.

TESMAN   Just think, that will be splendid. But, Hedda dear, how will you get Mrs. Elvsted home?

HEDDA   Oh, there's always a way out.

LØVBORG [*Looking at the ladies.*]   Mrs. Elvsted? Well, of course, I'll come back for her. [*Coming closer.*] Around ten o'clock, Mrs. Tesman, will that do?

HEDDA   Yes, that will be fine.

TESMAN   Well, everything's all right then; but don't expect me that early, Hedda.

HEDDA   No dear, you stay just as long—as long as you like.

MRS. ELVSTED [*With suppressed anxiety.*]   Mr. Løvborg—I'll stay here until you come.

LØVBORG [*His hat in his hand.*]   That's understood.

BRACK   All aboard then, the party train's pulling out. Gentlemen, I trust it will be a lively trip, as a certain lovely lady suggested.

HEDDA   Ah yes, if only that lovely lady could be there—invisible, of course.

BRACK   Why invisible?

HEDDA   To hear a little of your liveliness, Judge, uncensored.

BRACK [*Laughing.*]   Not recommended for the lovely lady.

TESMAN [*Also laughing.*]   You really are the limit, Hedda. Think of it.

BRACK   Well, well, my ladies. Good night. Good night.

LØVBORG [*Bowing as he leaves.*]   Until ten o'clock, then.

    [BRACK, LØVBORG *and* TESMAN *leave through the hall door. At the same time* BERTA *comes in from the rear room with a lighted lamp which she places on the drawing room table, going out the way she came in.*]

MRS. ELVSTED [*Has gotten up and wanders uneasily about the room.*]   Oh, Hedda, where is all this going?

HEDDA   Ten o'clock—then he'll appear. I see him before me with vine leaves in his hair,[9] burning bright and bold.

---

9. Like Bacchus, the Greek god of wine, and his followers.

MRS. ELVSTED   Yes, if only it could be like that.

HEDDA   And then you'll see—then he'll have power over himself again. Then he'll be a free man for the rest of his days.

MRS. ELVSTED   Oh God yes—if only he'd come back just the way you see him.

HEDDA   He'll come back just that way and no other. [*Gets up and comes closer.*] You can doubt him as much as you like. I believe in him. And so we'll see—

MRS. ELVSTED   There's something behind this, something else you're trying to do.

HEDDA   Yes, there is. Just once in my life I want to help shape someone's destiny.

MRS. ELVSTED   Don't you do that already?

HEDDA   I don't and I never have.

MRS. ELVSTED   Not even your husband?

HEDDA   Oh yes, that was a real bargain. Oh, if you could only understand how destitute I am while you get to be so rich. [*She passionately throws her arms around her.*] I think I'll burn your hair off after all.

MRS. ELVSTED   Let me go, let me go. I'm afraid of you.

BERTA [*In the doorway.*]   Tea is ready in the dining room, Madam.

HEDDA   Good. We're on our way.

MRS. ELVSTED   No, no, no! I'd rather go home alone! Right now!

HEDDA   Nonsense! First you're going to have some tea, you little bubble-head, and then—at ten o'clock—Eilert Løvborg—with vine leaves in his hair! [*She pulls* MRS. ELVSTED *toward the doorway almost by force.*]

Act III

The room at the TESMANS'. *The curtains are drawn across the center doorway and also across the glass door. The lamp covered with a shade burns low on the table. In the stove, with its door standing open, there has been a fire that is almost burned out.*

[MRS. ELVSTED, *wrapped in a large shawl and with her feet on a footstool, sits sunk back in an armchair.* HEDDA, *fully dressed, lies sleeping on the sofa with a rug over her.*]

MRS. ELVSTED [*After a pause suddenly straightens herself in the chair and listens intently. Then she sinks back wearily and moans softly.*]   Still not back . . . Oh God, oh God . . . Still not back.

    [BERTA *enters tiptoeing carefully through the hall doorway; she has a letter in her hand.*]

MRS. ELVSTED   Ah—did someone come?

BERTA   Yes, a girl came by just now with this letter.

MRS. ELVSTED [*Quickly stretching out her hand.*]   A letter? Let me have it.

BERTA   No ma'am, it's for the doctor.

MRS. ELVSTED   Oh.

BERTA   It was Miss Tesman's maid who brought it. I'll put it on the table here.

MRS. ELVSTED   Yes, do that.

BERTA [*Puts down the letter.*]   I'd better put out the lamp; it's starting to smoke.

MRS. ELVSTED   Yes, put it out. It'll be light soon anyway.

BERTA [*Putting out the light.*]   Oh, ma'am, it's already light.

MRS. ELVSTED   So, morning and still not back—!

BERTA   Oh, dear Lord—I knew all along it would go like this.

MRS. ELVSTED   You knew?

BERTA   Yes, when I saw a certain person was back in town. And then when he went off with them—oh we'd heard plenty about that gentleman.

MRS. ELVSTED   Don't speak so loud, you'll wake your mistress.

BERTA [*Looks over to the sofa and sighs.*]   No, dear Lord—let her sleep, poor thing. Shouldn't I build the stove up a little more?

MRS. ELVSTED   Not for me, thanks.

BERTA   Well, well then. [*She goes out quietly through the hall doorway.*]

HEDDA [*Awakened by the closing door, looks up.*]   What's that?

MRS. ELVSTED   Only the maid.

HEDDA [*Looking around.*]   In here—! Oh, now I remember.
       [*Straightens up, stretches sitting on the sofa and rubs her eyes.*]
   What time is it, Thea?

MRS. ELVSTED [*Looks at her watch.*]   It's after seven.

HEDDA   What time did Tesman get in?

MRS. ELVSTED   He hasn't.

HEDDA   Still?

MRS. ELVSTED [*Getting up.*]   No one's come back.

HEDDA   And we sat here waiting and watching until almost four.

MRS. ELVSTED [*Wringing her hands.*]   Waiting for him!

HEDDA [*Yawning and speaking with her hand over her mouth.*]   Oh yes—we could have saved ourselves the trouble.

MRS. ELVSTED   Did you finally manage to sleep?

HEDDA   Yes, I think I slept quite well. Did you?

MRS. ELVSTED   Not a wink. I couldn't, Hedda. It was just impossible for me.

HEDDA [*Gets up and goes over to her.*]   Now, now, now. There's nothing to worry about. I know perfectly well how it all turned out.

MRS. ELVSTED   Yes, what do you think? Can you tell me?

HEDDA   Well, of course they dragged it out dreadfully up at Judge Brack's.

MRS. ELVSTED   Oh God yes—that must be true. But all the same—

HEDDA   And then you see, Tesman didn't want to come home and create a fuss by ringing the bell in the middle of the night. [*Laughing.*] He probably didn't want to show himself either right after a wild party like that.

MRS. ELVSTED   For goodness sake—where would he have gone?

HEDDA   Well, naturally, he went over to his aunt's and laid himself down to sleep there. They still have his old room standing ready for him.

MRS. ELVSTED   No, he's not with them. A letter just came for him from Miss Tesman. It's over there.

HEDDA   Oh? [*Looks at the inscription.*] Yes, that's Aunt Julie's hand all right. So then, he's still over at Judge Brack's and Eilert Løvborg—he's sitting—reading aloud with vine leaves in his hair.

MRS. ELVSTED   Oh, Hedda, you don't even believe what you're saying.

HEDDA   You are such a little noodlehead, Thea.

MRS. ELVSTED   Yes, unfortunately I probably am.

HEDDA   And you look like you're dead on your feet.

MRS. ELVSTED   Yes, I am. Dead on my feet.

HEDDA   And so now you're going to do what I tell you. You'll go into my room and lie down on my bed.

MRS. ELVSTED   Oh no, no—I couldn't get to sleep anyway.

HEDDA   Yes, you certainly will.

MRS. ELVSTED   But your husband's bound to be home any time now and I've got to find out right away—

HEDDA   I'll tell you as soon as he comes.

MRS. ELVSTED   Promise me that, Hedda?

HEDDA   Yes, that you can count on. Now just go in and sleep for a while.

MRS. ELVSTED   Thanks. At least I'll give it a try. [*She goes in through the back room.*]

[HEDDA *goes over to the glass door and draws back the curtains. Full daylight floods the room. She then takes a small hand mirror from the writing table, looks in it and arranges her hair. Then she goes to the hall door and presses the bell. Soon after* BERTA *enters the doorway.*]

BERTA   Did Madam want something?

HEDDA   Yes, build up the stove a little bit. I'm freezing in here.

BERTA   Lord, in no time at all it'll be warm in here. [*She rakes the embers and puts a log inside. She stands and listens.*] There's the front doorbell, Madam.

HEDDA   So, go answer it. I'll take care of the stove myself.

BERTA   It'll be burning soon enough. [*She goes out through the hall door.*]

[HEDDA *kneels on the footstool and puts more logs into the stove. After a brief moment,* GEORGE TESMAN *comes in from the hall. He looks weary and rather serious. He creeps on tiptoes toward the doorway and is about to slip through the curtains.*]

HEDDA [*By the stove, without looking up.*]   Good morning.

TESMAN [*Turning around.*]   Hedda. [*Comes nearer.*] What in the world— Up so early, hm?

HEDDA   Yes, up quite early today.

TESMAN   And here I was so sure you'd still be in bed. Just think, Hedda.

HEDDA   Not so loud. Mrs. Elvsted's lying down in my room.

TESMAN   Has Mrs. Elvsted been here all night?

HEDDA   Yes. No one came to pick her up.

TESMAN   No, no, they couldn't have.

HEDDA [*Shuts the door of the stove and gets up.*]   So, did you have a jolly time at the Judge's?

TESMAN   Were you worried about me?

HEDDA   No, that would never occur to me. I asked if you had a good time.

TESMAN   Yes, I really did, for once, in a manner of speaking—Mostly in the beginning, I'd say. We'd arrived an hour early. How about that? And Brack had so much to get ready. But then Eilert read to me.

HEDDA [*Sits at the right of the table.*]   So, tell me.

TESMAN   Hedda, you can't imagine what this new work will be like. It's one of the most brilliant things ever written, no doubt about it. Think of that.

HEDDA   Yes, yes, but that's not what I'm interested in.

TESMAN   But I have to confess something, Hedda. After he read—
something horrible came over me.

HEDDA   Something horrible?

TESMAN   I sat there envying Eilert for being able to write like that. Think
of it, Hedda.

HEDDA   Yes, yes, I'm thinking.

TESMAN   And then, that whole time, knowing that he—even with all the
incredible powers at his command—is still beyond redemption.

HEDDA   You mean he's got more of life's courage in him than the others?

TESMAN   No, for heaven sakes—he just has no control over his pleasures.

HEDDA   And what happened then—at the end?

TESMAN   Well, Hedda, I guess you'd have to say it was a bacchanal.

HEDDA   Did he have vine leaves in his hair?

TESMAN   Vine leaves? No, I didn't see anything like that. But he did make
a long wild speech for the woman who had inspired him in his work. Yes—
that's how he put it.

HEDDA   Did he name her?

TESMAN   No, he didn't, but I can only guess that it must be Mrs. Elvsted.
Wouldn't you say?

HEDDA   Hmm—where did you leave him?

TESMAN   On the way back. Most of our group broke up at the same time
and Brack came along with us to get a little fresh air. And you see, we
agreed to follow Eilert home because—well—he was so far gone.

HEDDA   He must have been.

TESMAN   But here's the strangest part, Hedda! Or maybe I should say the
saddest. I'm almost ashamed for Eilert's sake—to tell you—

HEDDA   So?

TESMAN   There we were walking along, you see, and I happened to drop
back a bit, just for a couple of minutes, you understand.

HEDDA   Yes, yes, good Lord but—

TESMAN   And then when I was hurrying to catch up—can you guess what
I found in the gutter, hm?

HEDDA   How can I possibly guess?

TESMAN   Don't ever tell a soul, Hedda. Do you hear? Promise me that for
Eilert's sake. [*Pulls a package out of his coat pocket.*] Just think—this is
what I found.

HEDDA   That's the package he had with him here yesterday, isn't it?

TESMAN   That's it. His precious, irreplaceable manuscript—all of it. And he's
lost it—without even noticing it. Oh just think, Hedda—the pity of it—

HEDDA   Well, why didn't you give it back to him right away?

TESMAN   Oh, I didn't dare do that—The condition he was in—

HEDDA   You didn't tell any of the others that you found it either?

TESMAN   Absolutely not. I couldn't, you see, for Eilert's sake.

HEDDA   So nobody knows you have Eilert's manuscript? Nobody at all?

TESMAN   No. And they mustn't find out either.

HEDDA   What did you talk to him about later?

TESMAN   I didn't get a chance to talk to him any more. We got to the city
limits, and he and a couple of the others went a different direction. Just
think—

HEDDA   Aha, they must have followed him home then.

TESMAN   Yes, I suppose so. Brack also went his way.

HEDDA   And, in the meantime, what became of the bacchanal?

TESMAN   Well, I and some of the others followed one of the revelers up to his place and had morning coffee with him—or maybe we should call it morning-after coffee, hm? Now, I'll rest a bit—and as soon as I think Eilert has managed to sleep it off, poor man, then I've got to go over to him with this.

HEDDA [*Reaching out for the envelope.*]   No, don't give it back. Not yet, I mean. Let me read it first.

TESMAN   Oh no.

HEDDA   Oh, for God's sake.

TESMAN   I don't dare do that.

HEDDA   You don't dare?

TESMAN   No, you can imagine how completely desperate he'll be when he wakes up and realizes he can't find the manuscript. He's got no copy of it. He said so himself.

HEDDA [*Looks searchingly at him.*]   Couldn't it be written again?

TESMAN   No, I don't believe that could ever be done because the inspiration—you see—

HEDDA   Yes, yes—That's the thing, isn't it? [*Casually.*] But, oh yes—there's a letter here for you.

TESMAN   No, think of that.

HEDDA [*Hands it to him.*]   It came early this morning.

TESMAN   From Aunt Julie, Hedda. What can it be? [*Puts the manuscript on the other stool, opens the letter and jumps up.*] Oh Hedda—poor Aunt Rina's almost breathing her last.

HEDDA   It's only what's expected.

TESMAN   And if I want to see her one more time, I've got to hurry. I'll charge over there right away.

HEDDA [*Suppressing a smile.*]   You'll charge?

TESMAN   Oh, Hedda dearest—if you could just bring yourself to follow me. Just think.

HEDDA [*Rises and says wearily and dismissively.*]   No, no. Don't ask me to do anything like that. I won't look at sickness and death. Let me stay free from everything ugly.

TESMAN   Oh, good Lord, then—[*Darting around.*] My hat—? My overcoat—? Ah, in the hall—Oh, I hope I'm not too late, Hedda, hm?

HEDDA   Then charge right over—

[BERTA *appears in the hallway.*]

BERTA   Judge Brack is outside.

HEDDA   Ask him to come in.

TESMAN   At a time like this! No, I can't possibly deal with him now.

HEDDA   But I can. [*To* BERTA.] Ask the Judge in.

[BERTA *goes out.*]

HEDDA [*In a whisper.*]   The package, Tesman. [*She snatches it off the stool.*]

TESMAN   Yes, give it to me.

HEDDA   No, I'll hide it until you get back.

[*She goes over to the writing table and sticks the package in the bookcase.* TESMAN *stands flustered, and can't get his gloves on.* BRACK *enters through the hall doorway.*]

HEDDA [*Nodding to him.*]   Well, you're an early bird.

BRACK   Yes, wouldn't you say. [*To* TESMAN.] You're going out?

TESMAN   Yes, I've got to go over to my aunt's. Just think, the poor dear is dying.

BRACK   Good Lord, is she really? Then don't let me hold you up for even a moment, at a time like this—

TESMAN   Yes, I really must run—Good-bye. Good-bye. [*He hurries through the hall doorway.*]

HEDDA [*Approaches.*]   So, things were livelier than usual at your place last night, Judge.

BRACK   Oh yes, so much so that I haven't even been able to change clothes, Mrs. Hedda.

HEDDA   You too.

BRACK   As you see. But, what has Tesman been telling you about last night's adventures?

HEDDA   Oh, just some boring things. He went someplace to drink coffee.

BRACK   I've already looked into the coffee party. Eilert Løvborg wasn't part of that group, I presume.

HEDDA   No, they followed him home before that.

BRACK   Tesman too?

HEDDA   No, but a couple of others, he said.

BRACK [*Smiles.*]   George Tesman is a very naive soul, Mrs. Hedda.

HEDDA   God knows, he is. But is there something more behind this?

BRACK   I'd have to say so.

HEDDA   Well then, Judge, let's be seated. Then you can speak freely. [*She sits to the left side of the table,* BRACK *at the long side near her.*] Well, then—

BRACK   I had certain reasons for keeping track of my guests—or, more precisely, some of my guests' movements last night.

HEDDA   For example, Eilert Løvborg?

BRACK   Yes, indeed.

HEDDA   Now I'm hungry for more.

BRACK   Do you know where he and a couple of the others spent the rest of the night, Mrs. Hedda?

HEDDA   Why don't you tell me, if it can be told.

BRACK   Oh, it's certainly worth the telling. It appears that they found their way into a particularly animated soirée.[1]

HEDDA   A lively one?

BRACK   The liveliest.

HEDDA   Tell me more, Judge.

BRACK   Løvborg had received an invitation earlier—I knew all about that. But he declined because, as you know, he's made himself into a new man.

HEDDA   Up at the Elvsteds', yes. But he went just the same?

BRACK   Well, you see, Mrs. Hedda—unfortunately, the spirit really seized him at my place last evening.

HEDDA   Yes, I hear he was quite inspired.

---

1. Evening party (French).

BRACK Inspired to a rather powerful degree. And so, he started to reconsider, I assume, because we men, alas, are not always so true to our principles as we ought to be.

HEDDA Present company excepted, Judge Brack. So, Løvborg—?

BRACK Short and sweet—He ended up at the salon of a certain Miss Diana.

HEDDA Miss Diana?

BRACK Yes, it was Miss Diana's soirée for a select circle of ladies and their admirers.

HEDDA Is she a redhead?

BRACK Exactly.

HEDDA A sort of a—singer?

BRACK Oh, yes—She's also that. And a mighty huntress—of men, Mrs. Hedda. You must have heard of her. Eilert Løvborg was one of her most strenuous admirers—in his better days.

HEDDA And how did all this end?

BRACK Apparently less amicably than it began. Miss Diana, after giving him the warmest of welcomes, soon turned to assault and battery.

HEDDA Against Løvborg?

BRACK Oh, yes. He accused her, or one of her ladies, or robbing him. He insisted that his pocketbook was missing, along with some other things. In short, he seems to have created a dreadful spectacle.

HEDDA And what did that lead to?

BRACK A regular brawl between both the men and the women. Luckily the police finally got there.

HEDDA The police too?

BRACK Yes. It's going to be quite a costly little romp for Eilert Løvborg. What a madman.

HEDDA Well!

BRACK Apparently, he resisted arrest. It seems he struck one of the officers on the ear, and ripped his uniform to shreds, so he had to go to the police station.

HEDDA How do you know all this?

BRACK From the police themselves.

HEDDA [*Gazing before her.*] So, that's how it ended? He had no vine leaves in his hair.

BRACK Vine leaves, Mrs. Hedda?

HEDDA [*Changing her tone.*] Tell me now, Judge, why do you go around snooping and spying on Eilert Løvborg?

BRACK For starters, I'm not a completely disinterested party—especially if the hearing uncovers the fact that he came straight from my place.

HEDDA There's going to be a hearing?

BRACK You can count on it. Be that as it may, however—My real concern was my duty as a friend of the house to inform you and Tesman of Løvborg's nocturnal adventures.

HEDDA Why, Judge Brack?

BRACK Well, I have an active suspicion that he'll try to use you as a kind of screen.

HEDDA Oh! What makes you think that?

BRACK   Good God—we're not that blind, Mrs. Hedda. Wait and see. This Mrs. Elvsted—she won't be in such a hurry to leave town again.

HEDDA   If there's anything going on between those two, there's plenty of places they can meet.

BRACK   Not one single home. Every respectable house will be closed to Eilert Løvborg from now on.

HEDDA   And mine should be too—Is that what you're saying?

BRACK   Yes. I have to admit it would be more than painful for me if this man secured a foothold here. If this—utterly superfluous—and intrusive individual—were to force himself into—

HEDDA   Into the triangle?

BRACK   Precisely! It would leave me without a home.

HEDDA   [Looks smilingly at him.]   I see—The one cock of the walk—That's your goal.

BRACK   [Slowly nodding and dropping his voice.]   Yes, that's my goal. And it's a goal that I'll fight for—with every means at my disposal.

HEDDA   [Her smile fading.]   You're really a dangerous man, aren't you— when push comes to shove.

BRACK   You think so?

HEDDA   Yes, I'm starting to. And that's all right—just as long as you don't have any kind of hold on me.

BRACK   [Laughing ambiguously.]   Yes, Mrs. Hedda—you might be right about that. Of course, then, who knows whether I might not find some way or other—

HEDDA   Now listen, Judge Brack! That sounds like you're threatening me.

BRACK   [Gets up.] Oh, far from it. A triangle, you see—is best fortified by free defenders.

HEDDA   I think so too.

BRACK   Well, I've had my say so I should be getting back. Good-bye, Mrs. Hedda. [He goes toward the glass doors.]

HEDDA   Out through the garden?

BRACK   Yes, it's shorter for me.

HEDDA   And then, it's also the back way.

BRACK   That's true. I have nothing against back ways. Sometimes they can be very piquant.

HEDDA   When there's sharpshooting.

BRACK   [In the doorway, laughing at her.]   Oh, no—you never shoot your tame cocks.

HEDDA   [Also laughing.]   Oh, no, especially when there's only one—
[Laughing and nodding they take their farewells. He leaves. She closes the door after him. HEDDA stands for a while, serious, looking out. Then she goes and peers through the curtains in the back wall. She goes to the writing table, takes Løvborg's package from the bookcase, and is about to leaf through it. BERTA's voice, raised in indignation, is heard out in the hall. HEDDA turns and listens. She quickly locks the package in the drawer and sets the key on the writing table. EILERT LØVBORG, wearing his overcoat and carrying his hat, bursts through the hall doorway. He looks somewhat confused and excited.]

LØVBORG [*Turned toward the hallway.*] And I'm telling you, I've got to go in! And that's that! [*He closes the door, sees* HEDDA, *controls himself immediately, and bows.*]

HEDDA [*By the writing table.*] Well, Mr. Løvborg, it's pretty late to be calling for Thea.

LØVBORG Or a little early to be calling on you. I apologize.

HEDDA How do you know that she's still here?

LØVBORG I went to where she was staying. They told me she'd been out all night.

HEDDA [*Goes to the table.*] Did you notice anything special when they told you that?

LØVBORG [*Looks inquiringly at her.*] Notice anything?

HEDDA I mean—did they seem to have any thought on the subject—one way or the other?

LØVBORG [*Suddenly understanding.*] Oh, of course, it's true. I'm dragging her down with me. Still, I didn't notice anything. Tesman isn't up yet, I suppose?

HEDDA No, I don't think so.

LØVBORG When did he get home?

HEDDA Very late.

LØVBORG Did he tell you anything?

HEDDA Yes. I heard Judge Brack's was very lively.

LØVBORG Nothing else?

HEDDA No, I don't think so. I was terribly tired, though—
  [MRS. ELVSTED *comes in through the curtains at the back.*]

MRS. ELVSTED [*Runs toward him.*] Oh, Løvborg—at last!

LØVBORG Yes, at last, and too late.

MRS. ELVSTED [*Looking anxiously at him.*] What's too late?

LØVBORG Everything's too late. I'm finished.

MRS. ELVSTED Oh no, no—Don't say that!

LØVBORG You'll say it too, when you've heard—

MRS. ELVSTED I won't listen—

HEDDA Shall I leave you two alone?

LØVBORG No, stay—You too, I beg you.

MRS. ELVSTED But I won't listen to anything you tell me.

LØVBORG I don't want to talk about last night.

MRS. ELVSTED What is it, then?

LØVBORG We've got to go our separate ways.

MRS. ELVSTED Separate!

HEDDA [*Involuntarily.*] I knew it!

LØVBORG Because I have no more use for you, Thea.

MRS. ELVSTED You can stand there and say that! No more use for me! Can't I help you now, like I did before? Won't we go on working together?

LØVBORG I don't plan to work any more.

MRS. ELVSTED [*Desperately.*] Then what do I have to live for?

LØVBORG Just try to live your life as if you'd never known me.

MRS. ELVSTED I can't do that.

LØVBORG Try, Thea. Try, if you can. Go back home.

MRS. ELVSTED [*Defiantly.*] Where you are, that's where I want to be. I won't let myself be just driven off like this. I want to stay at your side—be with you when the book comes out.

HEDDA [*Half aloud, tensely.*] Ah, the book—Yes.

LØVBORG [*Looking at her.*] Mine and Thea's, because that's what it is.

MRS. ELVSTED Yes, that's what I feel it is. That's why I have a right to be with you when it comes out. I want to see you covered in honor and glory again, and the joy. I want to share that with you too.

LØVBORG Thea—our book's never coming out.

HEDDA Ah!

MRS. ELVSTED Never coming out?

LØVBORG It can't ever come out.

MRS. ELVSTED [*In anxious foreboding.*] Løvborg, what have you done with the manuscript?

HEDDA [*Looking intently at him.*] Yes, the manuscript—?

MRS. ELVSTED What have you—?

LØVBORG Oh, Thea, don't ask me that.

MRS. ELVSTED Yes, yes, I've got to know. I have the right to know.

LØVBORG The manuscript—all right then, the manuscript—I've ripped it up into a thousand pieces.

MRS. ELVSTED [*Screams.*] Oh no, no!

HEDDA [*Involuntarily.*] But that's just not—!

LØVBORG [*Looking at her.*] Not true, you think?

HEDDA [*Controls herself.*] All right then. Of course it is, if you say so. It sounds so ridiculous.

LØVBORG But it's true, just the same.

MRS. ELVSTED [*Wringing her hands.*] Oh God—oh God, Hedda. Torn his own work to pieces.

LØVBORG I've torn my own life to pieces. I might as well tear up my life's work too—

MRS. ELVSTED And you did that last night!

LØVBORG Yes. Do you hear me? A thousand pieces. Scattered them all over the fjord.[2] Way out where there's pure salt water. Let them drift in it. Drift with the current in the wind. Then, after a while, they'll sink. Deeper and deeper. Like me, Thea.

MRS. ELVSTED You know, Løvborg, all this with the book—? For the rest of my life, it will be just like you'd killed a little child.

LØVBORG You're right. Like murdering a child.

MRS. ELVSTED But then, how could you—! That child was partly mine, too.

HEDDA [*Almost inaudibly.*] Ah, the child—

MRS. ELVSTED [*Sighs heavily.*] So it's finished? All right, Hedda, now I'm going.

HEDDA You're not going back?

MRS. ELVSTED Oh, I don't know what I'm going to do. I can't see anything out in front of me. [*She goes out through the hall doorway.*]

HEDDA [*Standing a while, waiting.*] Don't you want to see her home, Mr. Løvborg?

2. Inlet of the sea (Norwegian).

LØVBORG   Through the streets? So that people can get a good look at us together?

HEDDA   I don't know what else happened to you last night but if it's so completely beyond redemption—

LØVBORG   It won't stop there. I know that much. And I can't bring myself to live that kind of life again either. Not again. Once I had the courage to live life to the fullest, to break every rule. But she's taken that out of me.

HEDDA [*Staring straight ahead.*]   That sweet little fool has gotten hold of a human destiny. [*Looks at him.*]   And you're so heartless to her.

LØVBORG   Don't call it heartless.

HEDDA   To go and destroy the thing that has filled her soul for this whole long, long time. You don't call that heartless?

LØVBORG   I can tell you the truth, Hedda.

HEDDA   The truth?

LØVBORG   First, promise me—Give me your word that Thea will never find out what I'm about to confide to you.

HEDDA   You have my word.

LØVBORG   Good. Then I'll tell you—What I stood here and described—It wasn't true.

HEDDA   About the manuscript?

LØVBORG   Yes. I haven't ripped it up. I didn't throw it in the fjord, either.

HEDDA   No, well—so—Where is it?

LØVBORG   I've destroyed it just the same. Utterly and completely, Hedda!

HEDDA   I don't understand any of this.

LØVBORG   Thea said that what I'd done seemed to her like murdering a child.

HEDDA   Yes, she did.

LØVBORG   But killing his child—that's not the worst thing a father can do to it.

HEDDA   Not the worst?

LØVBORG   No. And the worst—that is what I wanted to spare Thea from hearing.

HEDDA   And what is the worst?

LØVBORG   Imagine, Hedda, a man—in the very early hours of the morning—after a wild night of debauchery, came home to the mother of his child and said, "Listen—I've been here and there to this place and that place, and I had our child with me in this place and that place. And the child got away from me. Just got away. The devil knows whose hands it's fallen into, who's got a hold of it."

HEDDA   Well—when you get right down to it—it's only a book—

LØVBORG   All of Thea's soul was in that book.

HEDDA   Yes, I can see that.

LØVBORG   And so, you must also see that there's no future for her and me.

HEDDA   So, what will your road be now?

LØVBORG   None. Only to see to it that I put an end to it all. The sooner the better.

HEDDA [*Comes a step closer.*]   Eilert Løvborg—Listen to me now—Can you see to it that—that when you do it, you bathe it in beauty?

LØVBORG   In beauty? [*Smiles.*]   With vine leaves in my hair, as you used to imagine?

HEDDA Ah, no. No vine leaves—I don't believe in them any longer. But in beauty, yes! For once! Good-bye. You've got to go now. And don't come here any more.

LØVBORG Good-bye, Mrs. Tesman. And give my regards to George Tesman. [*He is about to leave.*]

HEDDA No, wait! Take a souvenir to remember me by.
[*She goes over to the writing table, opens the drawer and the pistol case. She returns to* LØVBORG *with one of the pistols.*]

LØVBORG [*Looks at her.*] That's the souvenir?

HEDDA [*Nodding slowly.*] Do you recognize it? It was aimed at you once.

LØVBORG You should have used it then.

HEDDA Here, you use it now.

LØVBORG [*Puts the pistol in his breast pocket.*] Thanks.

HEDDA In beauty, Eilert Løvborg. Promise me that.

LØVBORG Good-bye, Hedda Gabler. [*He goes out the hall doorway.*]
[HEDDA *listens a moment at the door. Afterward, she goes to the writing table and takes out the package with the manuscript, looks inside the wrapper, pulls some of the pages half out and looks at them. She then takes it all over to the armchair by the stove and sits down. She has the package in her lap. Soon after she opens the stove door and then opens the package.*]

HEDDA [*Throws one of the sheets into the fire and whispers to herself.*] Now, I'm burning your child, Thea—You with your curly hair. [*Throws a few more sheets into the fire.*] Your child and Eilert Løvborg's. [*Throws in the rest.*] Now I'm burning—burning the child.

Act IV

The same room at the TESMANS'. *It is evening. The drawing room is in darkness. The rear room is lit with a hanging lamp over the table. The curtains are drawn across the glass door.*

[HEDDA, *dressed in black, wanders up and down in the darkened room. Then she goes into the rear room, and over to the left side. Some chords are heard from the piano. Then she emerges again, and goes into the drawing room.* BERTA *comes in from the right of the rear room, with a lighted lamp, which she places on the table in front of the sofa, in the salon. Her eyes show signs of crying, and she has black ribbons on her cap. She goes quietly and carefully to the right.* HEDDA *goes over to the glass door, draws the curtains aside a little, and stares out into the darkness. Soon after,* MISS TESMAN *enters from the hallway dressed in black with a hat and a veil.* HEDDA *goes over to her and shakes her hand.*]

MISS TESMAN Yes, here I am, Hedda—in mourning black. My poor sister's struggle is over at last.

HEDDA As you can see, I've already heard. Tesman sent me a note.

MISS TESMAN Yes, he promised he would but I thought I should bring the news myself. This news of death into this house of life.

HEDDA That was very kind of you.

MISS TESMAN Ah, Rina shouldn't have left us right now. Hedda's house is no place for sorrow at a time like this.

HEDDA [*Changing the subject.*] She died peacefully, Miss Tesman?

MISS TESMAN Yes, so gently—Such a peaceful release. And she was happy beyond words that she got to see George once more and could say a proper good-bye to him. Is it possible he's not home yet?

HEDDA No. He wrote saying I shouldn't expect him too early. But, please sit down.

MISS TESMAN No, thank you, my dear—blessed Hedda. I'd like to, but I have so little time. She'll be dressed and arranged the best that I can. She'll look really splendid when she goes to her grave.

HEDDA Can I help you with anything?

MISS TESMAN Oh, don't even think about it. These kinds of things aren't for Hedda Tesman's hands or her thoughts either. Not at this time. No, no.

HEDDA Ah—thoughts—Now they're not so easy to master—

MISS TESMAN [*Continuing.*] Yes, dear God, that's how this world goes. Over at my house we'll be sewing a linen shroud for Aunt Rina, and here there will be sewing too, but of a whole different kind, praise God.

[GEORGE TESMAN *enters through a hall door.*]

HEDDA Well, it's good you're finally here.

TESMAN You here, Aunt Julie, with Hedda. Just think.

MISS TESMAN I was just about to go, my dear boy. Well. Did you manage to finish everything you promised to?

TESMAN No, I'm afraid I've forgotten half of it. I have to run over there tomorrow again. Today my brain is just so confused. I can't keep hold of two thoughts in a row.

MISS TESMAN George, my dear, you mustn't take it like that.

TESMAN Oh? How should I take it, do you think?

MISS TESMAN You must be joyful in your sorrow. You must be glad for what has happened, just as I am.

TESMAN Ah, yes. You're thinking of Aunt Rina.

HEDDA You'll be lonely now, Miss Tesman.

MISS TESMAN For the first few days, yes. But that won't last long, I hope. Our sainted Rina's little room won't stand empty. That much I know.

TESMAN Really? Who'll be moving in there, hm?

MISS TESMAN Oh, there's always some poor invalid or other who needs care and attention, unfortunately.

HEDDA You'd really take on a cross like that again?

MISS TESMAN Cross? God forgive you child. It's not a cross for me.

HEDDA But a complete stranger—

MISS TESMAN It's easy to make friends with sick people. And I so badly need someone to live for. Well, God be praised and thanked—there'll be a thing or two to keep an old aunt busy here in this house soon enough.

HEDDA Oh, please don't think about us.

TESMAN Yes. The three of us could be quite cozy here if only—

HEDDA If only—?

TESMAN [*Uneasily.*] Oh, it's nothing. Everything'll be fine. Let's hope, hm?

MISS TESMAN Well, well, you two have plenty to talk about, I'm sure. [*Smiling.*] And Hedda may have something to tell you, George. Now it's home to Rina. [*Turning in the doorway.*] Dear Lord, isn't it strange to think about. Now Rina's both with me and our sainted Joseph.

TESMAN Yes, just think, Aunt Julie, hm?

[MISS TESMAN *leaves through the hall door.*]

HEDDA [*Follows* TESMAN *with cold, searching eyes.*] I think all this has hit you harder than your aunt.

TESMAN Oh, it's not just this death. It's Eilert I'm worried about.

HEDDA [*Quickly.*] Any news?

TESMAN I wanted to run to him this afternoon and tell him that his manuscript was safe—in good hands.

HEDDA Oh? Did you find him?

TESMAN No, he wasn't home. But later I met Mrs. Elvsted, and she told me he'd been here early this morning.

HEDDA Yes, just after you left.

TESMAN And apparently he said that he'd ripped the manuscript up into a thousand pieces, hm?

HEDDA That's what he said.

TESMAN But, good God, he must have been absolutely crazy. So you didn't dare give it back to him, Hedda?

HEDDA No, he didn't get it back.

TESMAN But, you told him we had it?

HEDDA No. [*Quickly.*] Did you tell Mrs. Elvsted?

TESMAN No, I didn't want to. But you should have told him. What would happen if in his desperation he went and did something to himself? Let me have the manuscript, Hedda. I'll run it over to him right away. Where did you put it?

HEDDA [*Cold and impassively leaning on the armchair.*] I don't have it any more.

TESMAN Don't have it! What in the world do you mean?

HEDDA I burned it up—every page.

TESMAN [*Leaps up in terror.*] Burned? Burned? Eilert's manuscript!

HEDDA Don't shout like that. The maid will hear you.

TESMAN Burned! But good God—! No, no, no—That's absolutely impossible.

HEDDA Yes, but all the same it's true.

TESMAN Do you have any idea what you've done, Hedda? That's—that's criminal appropriation of lost property. Think about that. Yes, just ask Judge Brack, then you'll see.

HEDDA Then it's probably wise for you not to talk about it, isn't it? To the Judge or anyone else.

TESMAN How could you have gone and done something so appalling? What came over you? Answer me that, Hedda, hm?

HEDDA [*Suppressing an almost imperceptible smile.*] I did it for your sake, George.

TESMAN My sake?

HEDDA Remember you came home this morning and talked about how he had read to you?

TESMAN Yes, yes.

HEDDA You confessed that you envied him.

TESMAN Good God, I didn't mean it literally.

HEDDA   Nevertheless, I couldn't stand the idea that someone would overshadow you.

TESMAN [*Exclaiming between doubt and joy.*]   Hedda—Oh, is this true?— What you're saying?—Yes, but. Yes, but. I never noticed that you loved me this way before. Think of that!

HEDDA   Well, you need to know—that at a time like this—[*Violently breaking off.*] No, no—go and ask your Aunt Julie. She'll provide all the details.

TESMAN   Oh, I almost think I understand you, Hedda. [*Clasps his hands together.*] No, good God—Can it be, hm?

HEDDA   Don't shout like that. The maid can hear you.

TESMAN [*Laughing in extraordinary joy.*]   The maid! Oh, Hedda, you are priceless. The maid—why it's—why it's Berta. I'll go tell Berta myself.

HEDDA [*Clenching her hands as if frantic.*]   Oh, I'm dying—Dying of all this.

TESMAN   All what, Hedda, what?

HEDDA [*Coldly controlled again.*]   All this—absurdity—George.

TESMAN   Absurdity? I'm so incredibly happy. Even so, maybe I shouldn't say anything to Berta.

HEDDA   Oh yes, go ahead. Why not?

TESMAN   No, no. Not right now. But Aunt Julie, yes, absolutely. And then, you're calling me George. Just think. Oh, Aunt Julie will be so happy—so happy.

HEDDA   When she hears I've burned Eilert Løvborg's manuscript for your sake?

TESMAN   No, no, you're right. All this with the manuscript. No. Of course, nobody can find out about that. But, Hedda—you're burning for me— Aunt Julie really must share in that. But I wonder—all this—I wonder if it's typical with young wives, hm?

HEDDA   You'd better ask Aunt Julie about that too.

TESMAN   Oh yes, I certainly will when I get the chance. [*Looking uneasy and thoughtful again.*] No, but, oh no, the manuscript. Good Lord, it's awful to think about poor Eilert, just the same.

　　　　[MRS. ELVSTED, *dressed as for her first visit with hat and coat, enters through the hall door.*]

MRS. ELVSTED [*Greets them hurriedly and speaks in agitation.*]   Oh, Hedda, don't be offended that I've come back again.

HEDDA   What happened to you, Thea?

TESMAN   Something about Eilert Løvborg?

MRS. ELVSTED   Oh yes, I'm terrified that he's had an accident.

HEDDA [*Grips her arm.*]   Ah, do you think so?

TESMAN   Good Lord, where did you get that idea, Mrs. Elvsted?

MRS. ELVSTED   I heard them talking at the boarding house—just as I came in. There are the most incredible rumors about him going around town today.

TESMAN   Oh yes, imagine, I heard them too. And still I can swear he went straight home to sleep. Just think.

HEDDA   So—What were they saying at the boarding house?

MRS. ELVSTED   Oh, I couldn't get any details, either because they didn't know or—or they saw me and stopped talking. And I didn't dare ask.

TESMAN [*Uneasily pacing the floor.*]   Let's just hope—you misunderstood.

MRS. ELVSTED   No, I'm sure they were talking about him. Then I heard them say something about the hospital—

TESMAN   Hospital?

HEDDA   No—That's impossible.

MRS. ELVSTED   I'm deathly afraid for him, so I went up to his lodgings and asked about him there.

HEDDA   You dared to do that?

MRS. ELVSTED   What else should I have done? I couldn't stand the uncertainty any longer.

TESMAN   You didn't find him there either, hm?

MRS. ELVSTED   No. And the people there didn't know anything at all. They said he hadn't been home since yesterday afternoon.

TESMAN   Yesterday? How could they say that?

MRS. ELVSTED   It could only mean one thing—Something terrible's happened to him.

TESMAN   You know, Hedda—What if I were to go into town and ask around at different places—?

HEDDA   No! You stay out of this.

[JUDGE BRACK, *carrying his hat, enters through the hall door, which* BERTA *opens and closes after him. He looks serious and bows in silence.*]

TESMAN   Oh, here you are, Judge, hm?

BRACK   Yes, it was essential for me to see you this evening.

TESMAN   I see you got the message from Aunt Julie.

BRACK   Yes, that too.

TESMAN   Isn't it sad, hm?

BRACK   Well, my dear Tesman, that depends on how you look at it.

TESMAN   [*Looks at him uneasily.*]   Has anything else happened?

BRACK   Yes, it has.

HEDDA   [*Tensely.*]   Something sad, Judge Brack?

BRACK   Once again, it depends on how you look at it, Mrs. Tesman.

MRS. ELVSTED   [*In an uncontrollable outburst.*]   It's Eilert Løvborg.

BRACK   [*Looks briefly at her.*]   How did you guess, Mrs. Elvsted? Do you already know something—?

MRS. ELVSTED   [*Confused.*]   No, no, I don't know anything but—

TESMAN   Well, for God's sake, tell us what it is.

BRACK   [*Shrugging his shoulders.*]   Well then—I'm sorry to tell you—that Eilert Løvborg has been taken to the hospital. He is dying.

MRS. ELVSTED   [*Crying out.*]   Oh God, oh God.

TESMAN   Dying?

HEDDA   [*Involuntarily.*]   So quickly—?

MRS. ELVSTED   [*Wailing.*]   And we were quarrelling when we parted, Hedda.

HEDDA   [*Whispers.*]   Now, Thea—Thea.

MRS. ELVSTED   [*Not noticing her.*]   I'm going to him. I've got to see him alive.

BRACK   It would do you no good, Mrs. Elvsted. No visitors are allowed.

MRS. ELVSTED   At least tell me what happened. What—?

TESMAN   Yes, because he certainly wouldn't have tried to—hm?

HEDDA   Yes, I'm sure that's what he did.

TESMAN   Hedda. How can you—

BRACK   [*Who is watching her all the time.*]   Unfortunately, Mrs. Tesman, you've guessed right.

MRS. ELVSTED   Oh, how awful.

TESMAN   To himself, too. Think of it.

HEDDA   Shot himself!

BRACK   Right again, Mrs. Tesman.

MRS. ELVSTED [*Tries to compose herself*.]   When did this happen, Mr. Brack?

BRACK   Just this afternoon, between three and four.

TESMAN   Oh, my God—Where did he do it, hm?

BRACK [*Slightly uncertain*.]   Where? Oh, I suppose at his lodgings.

MRS. ELVSTED   No, that can't be. I was there between six and seven.

BRACK   Well then, some other place. I don't know precisely. All I know is that he was found—he'd shot himself—in the chest.

MRS. ELVSTED   Oh, how awful to think that he should die like that.

HEDDA [*To* BRACK.]   In the chest?

BRACK   Yes, like I said.

HEDDA   Not through the temple?

BRACK   The chest, Mrs. Tesman.

HEDDA   Well, well. The chest is also good.

BRACK   What was that, Mrs. Tesman?

HEDDA [*Evasively*.]   Oh, nothing—nothing.

TESMAN   And the wound is fatal, hm?

BRACK   The wound is absolutely fatal. In fact, it's probably already over.

MRS. ELVSTED   Yes, yes, I can feel it. It's over. It's all over. Oh, Hedda—!

TESMAN   Tell me, how did you find out about all this?

BRACK [*Curtly*.]   From a police officer. One I spoke with.

HEDDA [*Raising her voice*.]   Finally—an action.

TESMAN   God help us, Hedda, what are you saying?

HEDDA   I'm saying that here, in this—there is beauty.

BRACK   Uhm, Mrs. Tesman.

TESMAN   Beauty! No, don't even think it.

MRS. ELVSTED   Oh, Hedda. How can you talk about beauty?

HEDDA   Eilert Løvborg has come to terms with himself. He's had the courage to do what had to be done.

MRS. ELVSTED   No, don't ever believe it was anything like that. What he did, he did in a moment of madness.

TESMAN   It was desperation.

MRS. ELVSTED   Yes, madness. Just like when he tore his book in pieces.

BRACK [*Startled*.]   The book. You mean his manuscript? Did he tear it up?

MRS. ELVSTED   Yes, last night.

TESMAN [*Whispering softly*.]   Oh, Hedda, we'll never get out from under all this.

BRACK   Hmm, that's very odd.

TESMAN [*Pacing the floor*.]   To think that Eilert Løvborg should leave the world this way. And then not to leave behind the work that would have made his name immortal.

MRS. ELVSTED   Oh, what if it could be put together again.

TESMAN   Yes—just think—what if it could? I don't know what I wouldn't give—

MRS. ELVSTED   Maybe it can, Mr. Tesman.

TESMAN   What do you mean?

MRS. ELVSTED [*Searching in the pocket of her skirt.*] See this? I saved all the notes he dictated from.

HEDDA [*A step closer.*] Ah.

TESMAN You saved them, Mrs. Elvsted, hm?

MRS. ELVSTED Yes, they're all here. I brought them with me when I came to town, and here they've been. Tucked away in my pocket—

TESMAN Oh, let me see them.

MRS. ELVSTED [*Gives him a bundle of small papers.*] But they're all mixed up, completely out of order.

TESMAN Just think. What if we could sort them out. Perhaps if the two of us helped each other.

MRS. ELVSTED Oh yes. Let's at least give it a try—

TESMAN It will happen. It must happen. I'll give my whole life to this.

HEDDA You, George, your life?

TESMAN Yes, or, anyway, all the time I have. Every spare minute. My own research will just have to be put aside. Hedda—you understand, don't you, hm? I owe this to Eilert's memory.

HEDDA Maybe so.

TESMAN Now, my dear Mrs. Elvsted, let's pull ourselves together. God knows there's no point brooding about what's happened. We've got to try to find some peace of mind so that—

MRS. ELVSTED Yes, yes, Mr. Tesman. I'll do my best.

TESMAN Well. So, come along then. We've got to get started on these notes right away. Where should we sit? Here? No. In the back room. Excuse us, Judge. Come with me, Mrs. Elvsted.

MRS. ELVSTED Oh God—if only it can be done.

[TESMAN *and* MRS. ELVSTED *go into the rear room. She takes her hat and coat off. Both sit at the table under the hanging lamp and immerse themselves in eager examination of the papers. Hedda goes across to the stove and sits in the armchair. Soon after,* BRACK *goes over to her.*]

HEDDA [*Softly.*] Ah, Judge—This act of Eilert Løvborg's—there's a sense of liberation in it.

BRACK Liberation, Mrs. Hedda? Yes, I guess it's a liberation for him, all right.

HEDDA I mean, for me. It's a liberation for me to know that in this world an act of such courage, done in full, free will, is possible. Something bathed in a bright shaft of sudden beauty.

BRACK [*Smiles.*] Hmm—Dear Mrs. Hedda—

HEDDA Oh, I know what you're going to say, because you're a kind of specialist too, after all, just like—Ah well.

BRACK [*Looking steadily at her.*] Eilert Løvborg meant more to you than you might admit—even to yourself. Or am I wrong?

HEDDA I don't answer questions like that. All I know is that Eilert Løvborg had the courage to live life his own way, and now—his last great act—bathed in beauty. He—had the will to break away from the banquet of life—so soon.

BRACK It pains me, Mrs. Hedda—but I'm forced to shatter this pretty illusion of yours.

HEDDA Illusion?

BRACK Which would have been taken away from you soon enough.

HEDDA   And what's that?

BRACK   He didn't shoot himself—so freely.

HEDDA   Not freely?

BRACK   No. This whole Eilert Løvborg business didn't come off exactly the way I described it.

HEDDA [*In suspense.*]   Are you hiding something? What is it?

BRACK   I employed a few euphemisms for poor Mrs. Elvsted's sake.

HEDDA   Such as—?

BRACK   First, of course, he's already dead.

HEDDA   At the hospital?

BRACK   Yes. And without regaining consciousness.

HEDDA   What else?

BRACK   The incident took place somewhere other than his room.

HEDDA   That's insignificant.

BRACK   Not completely. I have to tell you—Eilert Løvborg was found shot in—Miss Diana's boudoir.

HEDDA [*About to jump up but sinks back again.*]   That's impossible, Judge. He can't have gone there again today.

BRACK   He was there this afternoon. He came to demand the return of something that he said they'd taken from him. He talked crazily about a lost child.

HEDDA   Ah, so that's why—

BRACK   I thought maybe he was referring to his manuscript but I hear he'd already destroyed that himself so I guess it was his pocketbook.

HEDDA   Possibly. So—that's where he was found.

BRACK   Right there, with a discharged pistol in his coat pocket, and a fatal bullet wound.

HEDDA   In the chest, yes?

BRACK   No—lower down.

HEDDA [*Looks up at him with an expression of revulsion.*]   That too! Oh absurdity—! It hangs like a curse over everything I so much as touch.

BRACK   There's still one more thing, Mrs. Hedda. Also in the ugly category.

HEDDA   And what is that?

BRACK   The pistol he had with him—

HEDDA [*Breathless.*]   Well, what about it?

BRACK   He must have stolen it.

HEDDA [*Jumping up.*]   Stolen? That's not true. He didn't.

BRACK   There's no other explanation possible. He must have stolen it—Shh.

[TESMAN *and* MRS. ELVSTED *have gotten up from the table in the rear room and come into the living room.*]

TESMAN [*With papers in both hands.*]   Hedda, my dear—I can hardly see anything in there under that lamp. Just think—

HEDDA   I'm thinking.

TESMAN   Do you think you might let us sit a while at your desk, hm?

HEDDA   Oh, gladly. [*Quickly.*]   No, wait. Let me just clean it up a bit first.

TESMAN   Oh, not necessary, Hedda. There's plenty of room.

HEDDA   No, no, I'll just straighten it up, I'm telling you. I'll just move these things here under the piano for a while.

[*She has pulled an object covered with sheet music out of the bookcase.*

She adds a few more sheets and carries the whole pile out to the left of the rear room. TESMAN *puts the papers on the desk and brings over the lamp from the corner table. He and* MRS. ELVSTED *sit and continue their work.*]

HEDDA   Well, Thea, my sweet. Are things moving along with the memorial?

MRS. ELVSTED [*Looks up at her dejectedly.*]   Oh, God—It's going to be so difficult to find the order in all of this.

TESMAN   But it must be done. There's simply no other choice. And finding the order in other people's papers—that's precisely what I'm meant for.

[HEDDA *goes over to the stove and sits on one of the stools.* BRACK *stands over her, leaning over the armchair.*]

HEDDA [*Whispers.*]   What were you saying about the pistol?

BRACK [*Softly.*]   That he must have stolen it.

HEDDA   Why stolen exactly?

BRACK   Because there shouldn't be any other way to explain it, Mrs. Hedda.

HEDDA   I see.

BRACK [*Looks briefly at her.*]   Eilert Løvborg was here this morning, am I correct?

HEDDA   Yes.

BRACK   Were you alone with him?

HEDDA   Yes, for a while.

BRACK   You didn't leave the room at all while he was here?

HEDDA   No.

BRACK   Think again. Weren't you out of the room, even for one moment?

HEDDA   Yes. Perhaps. Just for a moment—out in the hallway.

BRACK   And where was your pistol case at that time?

HEDDA   I put it under the—

BRACK   Well, Mrs. Hedda—

HEDDA   It was over there on the writing table.

BRACK   Have you looked since then to see if both pistols are there?

HEDDA   No.

BRACK   It's not necessary. I saw the pistol Løvborg had, and I recognized it immediately from yesterday, and from before as well.

HEDDA   Have you got it?

BRACK   No, the police have it.

HEDDA   What will the police do with that pistol?

BRACK   Try to track down its owner.

HEDDA   Do you think they can do that?

BRACK [*Bends over her and whispers.*]   No, Hedda Gabler, not as long as I keep quiet.

HEDDA [*Looking fearfully at him.*]   And what if you don't keep quiet—then what?

BRACK   Then the way out is to claim that the pistol was stolen.

HEDDA   I'd rather die.

BRACK [*Smiling.*]   People make those threats but they don't act on them.

HEDDA [*Without answering.*]   So—let's say the pistol is not stolen and the owner is found out? What happens then?

BRACK   Well, Hedda—then there'll be a scandal.

HEDDA   A scandal?

BRACK   Oh, yes, a scandal. Just what you're so desperately afraid of. You'd have to appear in court, naturally. You and Miss Diana. She'd have to detail how it all occurred. Whether it was an accident or a homicide. Was he trying to draw the pistol to threaten her? Is that when the gun went off? Did she snatch it out of his hands to shoot him, and then put the pistol back in his pocket? That would be thoroughly in character for her. She's a feisty little thing, that Miss Diana.

HEDDA   But all this ugliness has got nothing to do with me.

BRACK   No. But you would have to answer one question. Why did you give the pistol to Eilert Løvborg? And what conclusions would people draw from the fact that you gave it to him?

HEDDA [*Lowers her head.*]   That's true. I didn't think of that.

BRACK   Well. Fortunately you have nothing to worry about as long as I keep quiet.

HEDDA [*Looking up at him.*]   So I'm in your power now, Judge. You have a hold over me from now on.

BRACK [*Whispering more softly.*]   Dearest Hedda—Believe me—I won't abuse my position.

HEDDA   But in your power. Totally subject to your demands—And your will. Not free. Not free at all. [*She gets up silently.*] No, that's one thought I just can't stand. Never!

BRACK [*Looks mockingly at her.*]   One can usually learn to live with the inevitable.

HEDDA [*Returning his look.*]   Maybe so. [*She goes over to the writing table, suppressing an involuntary smile and imitating* TESMAN's *intonation.*] Well, George, this is going to work out, hm?

TESMAN   Oh, Lord knows, dear. Anyway, at this rate, it's going to be months of work.

HEDDA [*As before.*]   No, just think. [*Runs her fingers lightly through* MRS. ELVSTED's *hair.*] Doesn't it seem strange, Thea. Here you are, sitting together with Tesman—just like you used to sit with Eilert Løvborg.

MRS. ELVSTED   Oh, God, if only I could inspire your husband too.

HEDDA   Oh, that will come—in time.

TESMAN   Yes, you know what, Hedda—I really think I'm beginning to feel something like that. But why don't you go over and sit with Judge Brack some more.

HEDDA   Can't you two find any use for me here?

TESMAN   No, nothing in the world. [*Turning his head.*] From now on, my dear Judge, you'll have to be kind enough to keep Hedda company.

BRACK [*With a glance at* HEDDA.]   That will be an infinite pleasure for me.

HEDDA   Thanks, but I'm tired tonight. I'll go in there and lie down on the sofa for a while.

TESMAN   Yes, do that, Hedda, hm?

[HEDDA *goes into the rear room and draws the curtains after her. Short pause. Suddenly she is heard to play a wild dance melody on the piano.*]

MRS. ELVSTED [*Jumping up from her chair.*]   Oh—what's that?

TESMAN [*Running to the doorway.*]   Oh, Hedda, my dear—Don't play dance music tonight. Just think of poor Aunt Rina and of Eilert Løvborg too.

HEDDA [*Putting her head out from between the curtains.*]   And Aunt Julie and all the rest of them too. From now on I shall be quiet. [*She closes the curtains again.*]

TESMAN [*At the writing table.*]   This can't be making her very happy— Seeing us at this melancholy work. You know what, Mrs. Elvsted—You're going to move in with Aunt Julie. Then I can come over in the evening, and we can sit and work there, hm?

MRS. ELVSTED   Yes, maybe that would be the best—

HEDDA [*From the rear room.*]   I can hear you perfectly well, Tesman. So, how am I supposed to get through the evenings out here?

TESMAN [*Leafing through the papers.*]   Oh, I'm sure Judge Brack will be good enough to call on you.

BRACK [*In the armchair, shouts merrily.*]   I'd be delighted, Mrs. Tesman. Every evening. Oh, we're going to have some good times together, the two of us.

HEDDA [*Loudly and clearly.*]   Yes, that's what you're hoping for, isn't it, Judge? You, the one and only cock of the walk—

[*A shot is heard within.* TESMAN, MRS. ELVSTED *and* BRACK *all jump to their feet.*]

TESMAN   Oh, she's playing around with those pistols again.

[*He pulls the curtains aside and runs in.* MRS. ELVSTED *follows.* HEDDA *is stretched out lifeless on the sofa. Confusion and cries.* BERTA *comes running in from the right.*]

[Shrieking to BRACK.]   Shot herself! Shot herself in the temple! Just think!

BRACK [*Half prostrate in the armchair.*]   But God have mercy—People just don't act that way!

END OF PLAY

ARTHUR RIMBAUD
1854–1891

In a dazzlingly brief literary career, which he abandoned at the age of twenty, Arthur Rimbaud (*ram-boh'*) put his indelible stamp on the visionary and experimental aspects of modern poetry. Taking literally the ancient (and Romantic) notion of the poet as prophet, he determined to make himself a seer, or *voyant*, by whatever violent means were necessary. His writing reveals the mixture of idealism, hope, and faith in his own genius that led him to believe in the possibility of a self-produced apocalypse. It also recounts a futile search for love that permeates his poetic quest; a stormy relationship with the older poet Paul Verlaine; and finally, the bitterness and sense of defeat that drove him to abandon his former life and become a fortune hunter in Africa. Rimbaud was an especially strong model for the Surrealists and for others in twentieth-century literature who saw in him an example of complete dedication to a poetic ideal that surpassed mere written words: he exemplified a revolutionary reimagining of human experience that would open vistas, explode harmful patterns of thought, and thus bring about a better future. Despite—or perhaps because of—Rimbaud's admission of defeat, he became a mythic figure whose brilliant poems and prose were markers on the way of a career that, in the words of one admirer, passed like a lightning bolt through French literature.

Jean-Nicolas-Arthur Rimbaud was born on October 20, 1854, in Charleville, a town in northeastern France. Rimbaud's father abandoned the family when Arthur was seven, and his embittered mother raised her children in a repressive and disciplinarian atmosphere. In 1870, Rimbaud made the first of his flights from home and spent ten days in jail as a vagrant. Yet he proved to be an unusually gifted student and was encouraged in his literary tastes and endeavors by a sympathetic teacher who introduced him to current poetry. It was this teacher, Georges Izambard, to whom Rimbaud first wrote of his poetic ambitions and his desire to make himself a seer by the systematic "derangement of all the senses." In 1871, the poet Paul Verlaine (to whom Rimbaud had sent some of his work) invited Rimbaud to Paris. It was the beginning of a stormy two-year relationship in Paris, London, and Brussels that ended in 1873 when Verlaine shot Rimbaud through the wrist and was sentenced to two years' imprisonment. In that year, at the age of nineteen, Rimbaud decided to give up writing and seek his fortune in commerce. He found his way to many parts of Europe, to Cyprus, to Java, and to Aden, where he worked for an exporting firm, later moving to Harar in Abyssinia. As an independent trader he went on expeditions in Abyssinia and engaged in gun running; despite rumor, it does not appear that he trafficked in slaves. Falling ill with a cancerous tumor on one knee and unable to find adequate treatment, Rimbaud returned to France with a gangrenous leg in May 1891. His leg was amputated at a Marseille hospital, and he died six months later on November 10, 1891.

In a short and violent literary career—he wrote all his poetry between the ages of fifteen and twenty—Rimbaud combines an aggressive, cynical realism and attempts to transform both self and surroundings into a magically perfect whole. The visionary image sequences of his first major poem (a symbolic voyage titled "The Drunken Boat"), the agonized and mocking autobiographical prose of *A Season in Hell*, and finally the transfigured scenes from real life called *Illuminations* together represent stages in this endeavor to discover—or create—a state of natural innocence and harmony. For a while, Rimbaud believed that he could manipulate language to create the vision of an ideal world. "I have strung ropes from steeple to steeple; garlands from window to window; golden chains from star to star, and I dance."

"The Drunken Boat," written when the poet was still sixteen and had never seen the sea, uses the traditional literary theme of the voyage to express his rebellion against guides and restraints. Speaking as a boat let loose on the high seas, the narrator describes a gradually intensifying series of encounters with a total reality—at once beautiful and terrifying—that goes beyond his individual power to sustain. Yet the concluding section is not a resolution of the original need for flight: Rimbaud's boat cannot accept the world of proud commercial shipping or of prison ships, and dreams of the childhood world of a solitary paper boat set adrift in a small pool. The poem ends in a clearer restatement of its original alienation and in an attitude that many have interpreted as prefiguring Rimbaud's eventual departure from Europe and his rejection of poetry.

Rimbaud's attempt to become a *voyant*, to transform his everyday reality by means of the re-creating power of poetry, is both summarized and mocked in the bitter autobiographical prose poem *A Season in Hell*. In an atmosphere of perpetual crisis, alternating between agonized idealism and cynical disbelief, he reviews his quest for perfect truth and love and vividly describes his effort to reach the unknown by pure hallucination. "I saw very plainly a mosque in place of a factory, a school of drummers composed of angels . . . a drawing room at the bottom of the lake . . . I became a fabulous opera." At the end of *A Season in Hell* he tells us that he has rejected these earlier illusions and embraced earth and rugged reality. Yet he never wrote poetry to celebrate his newly rediscovered realism (and may well have completed the

Illuminations after that point), so that he remains best known for the passion and beauty of his apocalyptic vision.

The Illuminations offers a series of transformations that leave only traces of their varied points of departure: bridges in London, plowed fields, a park statue, dawn. They parade illusions and free association, and they cut short logical sequences to develop an almost musical organization of themes and images. Almost all are prose poems, intricately organized in complex rhythmic and visual patterns. Some echo autobiographical themes, but the scenes and allusions are transformed. "The Bridges" recalls the London where Rimbaud lived for a time, but it is an impressionistic memory that transforms the real scene. "Barbarian" may echo a previous sea voyage and drug use, but the poem transcends the question of any single source in reality. Set outside normal time and space, "Long after the days and the seasons, and the creatures and the countries," it enacts a withdrawal that moves gradually from echoes of the real world to an elemental core of tenderness and beauty, completely inside the world of imagination.

"Barbarian" is not, however, merely an impressionistic, unstructured collection of words. It is carefully organized according to an almost musical development of themes and pattern of oppositions: red and white (raw meat and arctic flowers, embers and frost, fire and diamonds, flames and drift ice), heat and cold, subterranean volcanoes and starry sky. On a more fundamental level, it is a world that swings between the real and the ideal, from echoes of a former reality to an ideal world where there are ultimately no complete images, only "forms, sweats, eyes" that will be part of a new creation heralded by a feminine voice reaching into the very heart of this fiery, icy vortex.

From Letter of the Seer [Letter to Paul Demeny][1]

Charleville
May 15, 1871

* * *

Here is some prose on the future of poetry:

All ancient poetry culminated in the poetry of the Greeks. Harmonious life. From Greece to the Romantic movement—the Middle Ages—there are writers and versifiers. From Ennius to Theroldus, from Theroldus to Casimir Delavigne, everything is rhymed prose, a game, the stupidity and glory of endless idiotic generations. Racine alone is pure, strong, and great. But had his rhymes been twisted, his hemistichs[2] messed up, the Divine Dumbhead would be as unknown today as the latest-come author of the *Origins*. . . . After Racine, the game gets moldy. It's been going on for two hundred years!

No joke, and no paradox. My reason inspires me with more certainty on the subject than a young radical has fits. Anyway, *newcomers* can swear at their ancestors; it's their house and they've got all the time in the world.

Romanticism has never been fairly judged. Who's to judge it? The Critics!!

---

1. Translated by Paul Schmidt. Rimbaud had met the young poet Paul Demeny through his teacher, Georges Izambard. In this letter, called the *Lettre du Voyant* (Letter of the seer), the sixteen-year-old poet alternates flippant remarks with a theory of the poet as impersonal visionary. Throughout, the word for *poet* is written without the customary accent, thus suggesting the ancient Greek word for "creator" or "maker."
2. Half a line of verse.

The Romantics? They illustrate perfectly the fact that the song is very rarely the work of the singer—that is, his thought, snug and understood.

For *I* is an *other*. If brass wakes as a bugle, it is not its fault at all. That is quite clear to me: I am a spectator at the flowering of my thought: I watch it, I listen to it: I draw a bow across a string: a symphony stirs in the depths, or surges onto the stage.

If those old idiots hadn't discovered only the false meaning of EGO, we wouldn't have to sweep away the millions of skeletons that have for ages and ages piled up the products of their one-eyed intelligence, and acclaimed themselves their authors!

In Greece, as I said, words and music gave a rhythm to Action. Afterward music and rhymes became toys, pastimes. Studying this past has a certain charm for the curious: some people delight in reworking these antiquities: that's their business. The universal intelligence has always cast off its ideas naturally; men would pick up some of these fruits of the mind: they were acted upon, they inspired books: and so it went; man didn't develop himself, not yet awake, or not yet aware of the great dream. Pen pushers, these writers: the author, the creator, the poet; that man has never existed!

The first task of the man who wants to be a poet is to study his own awareness of himself, in its entirety; he seeks out his soul, he inspects it, he tests it, he learns it. As soon as he knows it, he must cultivate it! That seems simple: every brain experiences a certain natural development; hundreds of *egoists* call themselves authors; there are many more who attribute their intellectual progress to themselves!—But the problem is to make the soul into a monster, like the comprachicos,[3] you know? Think of a man grafting warts onto his face and growing them there.

I say you have to be a visionary, make yourself a visionary.

A Poet makes himself a visionary through a long, boundless, and systematized *disorganization of all the senses*. All forms of love, of suffering, of madness; he searches himself, he exhausts within himself all poisons, and preserves their quintessences. Unspeakable torment, where he will need the greatest faith, a superhuman strength, where he becomes among all men the great invalid, the great criminal, the great accursed—and the Supreme Scientist! For he attains the *unknown!* Because he has cultivated his soul, already rich, more than anyone! He attains the unknown, and if, demented, he finally loses the understanding of his visions, he will at least have seen them! So what if he is destroyed in his ecstatic flight through things unheard of, unnameable: other horrible workers will come; they will begin at the horizons where the first one has fallen!

—Back in six minutes—

I interrupt my discourse with another psalm: be kind enough to lend a willing ear, and everybody will be delighted. Bow in hand, I begin:

MY LITTLE LOVELIES . . .

There. And please note that if I were not afraid of making you spend more than 60 centimes on postage due—poor starving me who hasn't had a single centime in the last seven months!—I would send you also my "Amant de Paris," one hundred hexameters, and my "Mort de Paris," two hundred hexameters!

---

3. Kidnappers who mutilated children to make money by exhibiting them as freaks; described in Victor Hugo's novel *The Man Who Laughs* (1869).

Here we go again:

The poet, therefore, is truly the thief of fire.[4]

He is responsible for humanity, for *animals* even; he will have to make sure his visions can be smelled, fondled, listened to; if what he brings back from *beyond* has form, he gives it form; if it has none, he gives it none. A language must be found; besides, all speech being idea, a time of universal language will come! Only an academic—deader than a fossil—could compile a dictionary, in no matter what language. Weaklings who begin to *think* about the first letter of the alphabet would quickly go mad!

This language will be of the soul, for the soul, and will include everything: perfumes, sounds, colors, thought grappling with thought. The poet would make precise the quantity of the unknown arising in his time in the universal soul: he would provide more than the formula of his thought, the record *of his path to Progress!* Enormity becoming norm, absorbed into everything, he would truly become a *multiplier of progress!*

That future will be materialistic, as you see. Always full of *Number* and *Harmony*, these poems will be made to last. Essentially, it will again be Greek Poetry,[5] in a way.

This eternal art will be functional, since poets are citizens. Poetry will no longer give rhythm to action; it *will be in advance.*

And there will be poets like this! When the eternal slavery of Women is destroyed, when she lives for herself and through herself, when man—up till now abominable—will have set her free, she will be a poet as well! Woman will discover the unknown! Will her world of ideas differ from ours? She will discover strange things, unfathomable, repulsive, delightful; we will accept and understand them.

While we wait, let us ask the *poet* for *something new*—ideas and forms.

The Drunken Boat[1]

As I descended black, impassive Rivers,
I sensed that haulers[2] were no longer guiding me:
Screaming Redskins took them for their targets,
Nailed nude to colored stakes: barbaric trees.

I was indifferent to all my crews;   5
I carried English cottons, Flemish wheat.
When the disturbing din of haulers ceased,
The Rivers let me ramble where I willed.

Through the furious ripping of the sea's mad tides,
Last winter, deafer than an infant's mind,   10
I ran! And drifting, green Peninsulas
Did not know roar more gleefully unkind.

---

4. In Greek myth, Prometheus stole fire from the gods to give to human beings, thus lifting them above the condition of animals.   **5.** Rimbaud has earlier praised ancient Greek poetry for the way it combined music and words, giving rhythm to action (probably an allusion to Homer).   **1.** Translated by Stephen Stepanchev.   **2.** The image is of a commercial barge being towed along a canal.

A tempest blessed my vigils on the sea.
Lighter than a cork I danced on the waves,
Those endless rollers, as they say, of graves:[3]   15
Ten nights beyond a lantern's[4] silly eye!

Sweeter than sourest apple-flesh to children,
Green water seeped into my pine-wood hull
And washed away blue wine[5] stains, vomitings,
Scattering rudder, anchor, man's lost rule.   20

And then I, trembling, plunged into the Poem
Of the Sea,[6] infused with stars, milk-white,
Devouring azure greens; where remnants, pale
And gnawed, of pensive corpses fell from light;

Where, staining suddenly the blueness, delirium.   25
The slow rhythms of the pulsing glow of day,
Stronger than alcohol and vaster than our lyres,
The bitter reds of love ferment the way!

I know skies splitting into light, whirled spouts
Of water, surfs, and currents: I know the night,   30
The dawn exalted like a flock of doves, pure wing,
And I have seen what men imagine they have seen.

I saw the low sun stained with mystic horrors,
Lighting long, curdled clouds of violet,
Like actors in a very ancient play,   35
Waves rolling distant thrills like lattice[7] light!

I dreamed of green night, stirred by dazzling snows,
Of kisses rising to the sea's eyes, slowly,
The sap-like coursing of surprising currents,
And singing phosphors,[8] flaring blue and gold!   40

I followed, for whole months, a surge like herds
Of insane cattle in assault on the reefs,
Unhopeful that three Marys,[9] come on luminous feet,
Could force a muzzle on the panting seas!

Yes, I struck incredible Floridas[1]   45
That mingled flowers and the eyes of panthers
In skins of men! And rainbows bridled green
Herds beneath the horizon of the seas.

---

3. Victor Hugo's *Oceano nox* (Night on the ocean; Latin) describes the sea as a graveyard in which sailors' corpses roll eternally.   4. Port beacon.   5. A cheap, ordinary, bitter wine.   6. A play on words. "Poem" suggests "creation" (Greek *poiein*, "making"); "Sea," the source or "mother" of life, sounds the same as "mother" in French (*mer / mère*).   7. Like the ripple of venetian blinds.   8. *Noctiluca*, tiny marine animals.   9. A legend that the three biblical Marys crossed the sea during a storm to land in Camargue, a region in southern France famous for its horses and bulls.   1. A name (plural) given to any exotic country.

I saw the ferment of enormous marshes, weirs
Where a whole Leviathan[2] lies rotting in the weeds!   50
Collapse of waters within calms at sea,
And distances in cataract toward chasms!

Glaciers, silver suns, pearl waves, and skies like coals,
Hideous wrecks at the bottom of brown gulfs
Where giant serpents eaten by red bugs   55
Drop from twisted trees and shed a black perfume!

I should have liked to show the young those dolphins
In blue waves, those golden fish, those fish that sing.
—Foam like flowers rocked my sleepy drifting,
And, now and then, fine winds supplied me wings.   60

When, feeling like a martyr, I tired of poles and zones,
The sea, whose sobbing made my tossing sweet,
Raised me its dark flowers, deep and yellow whirled,
And, like a woman, I fell on my knees . . . [3]

Peninsula, I tossed upon my shores   65
The quarrels and droppings of clamorous, blond-eyed birds.
I sailed until, across my rotting cords,
Drowned men, spinning backwards, fell asleep! . . .

Now I, a lost boat in the hair of coves,[4]
Hurled by tempest into a birdless air,   70
I, whose drunken carcass neither Monitors
Nor Hansa ships[5] would fish back for men's care;

Free, smoking, rigged with violet fogs,
I, who pierced the red sky like a wall
That carries exquisite mixtures for good poets,   75
Lichens of sun and azure mucus veils;

Who, spotted with electric crescents, ran
Like a mad plank, escorted by seashores,
When cudgel blows of hot Julys struck down
The sea-blue skies upon wild water spouts;   80

I, who trembled, feeling the moan at fifty leagues
Of rutting Behemoths[6] and thick Maelstroms, I,
Eternal weaver of blue immobilities,
I long for Europe with its ancient quays!

I saw sidereal archipelagoes! and isles   85
Whose delirious skies are open to the voyager:

---

2. Vast biblical sea monster (Job 41.1–10).   3. The poet's ellipses; nothing has been omitted.   4. Seaweed.   5. Vessels belonging to the German Hanseatic League of commercial maritime cities. "Monitors": armored coast-guard ships, after the iron-clad Union warship *Monitor* of the American Civil War.   6. Biblical animal resembling a hippopotamus (Job 40.15–24).

—Is it in depthless nights you sleep your exile,
A million golden birds, O future Vigor?—

But, truly, I have wept too much! The dawns disturb.
All moons are painful, and all suns break bitterly: 90
Love has swollen me with drunken torpors.
Oh, that my keel might break and spend me in the sea!

Of European waters I desire
Only the black, cold puddle in a scented twilight
Where a child of sorrows squats and sets the sails   95
Of a boat as frail as a butterfly in May.

I can no longer, bathed in languors, O waves,
Cross the wake of cotton-bearers on long trips,
Nor ramble in a pride of flags and flares,
Nor swim beneath the horrible eyes of prison ships.[7]   100

A Season in Hell[1]

Night of Hell

I have swallowed a first-rate draught of poison.—Thrice blessed be the counsel that came to me!—My entrails are on fire. The violence of the venom wrings my limbs, deforms me, fells me. I am dying of thirst, I am suffocating, I cannot cry out. This is hell, the everlasting punishment! Mark how the fire surges up again! I am burning properly. There you are, demon!

I had caught a glimpse of conversion to righteousness and happiness, salvation. May I describe the vision; the atmosphere of hell does not permit hymns! It consisted of millions of charming creatures, a sweet sacred concert, power and peace, noble ambitions, and goodness knows what else.

Noble ambitions![2]

And yet this is life!—What if damnation is eternal! A man who chooses to mutilate himself is rightly damned, isn't he? I believe that I am in hell, consequently I am there.[3] This is the effect of the catechism. I am the slave of my baptism.[4] Parents, you have caused my affliction and you have caused your own. Poor innocent!—Hell cannot assail pagans.—This is life, nevertheless! Later, the delights of damnation will be deeper. A crime, quickly, that I may sink to nothingness, in accordance with human law.

Be silent, do be silent! . . . There is shame, reproof, in this place: Satan who says that the fire is disgraceful, that my wrath is frightfully foolish.—Enough! . . . The errors that are whispered to me, enchantments, false per-

---

7. Portholes of ships tied at anchor and used as prisons.   1. Translated by Enid Rhodes Peschel. "Night of Hell" is the second section (after the Preface) of the autobiographical *A Season in Hell*. The first section, "Bad Blood," describes his solitary childhood and sense of being a member of an "inferior race." It also contrasts an authoritarian and hypocritical European society with African paganism, which is seen as a freer and more natural existence.   2. Mockery of his childhood idealism and attraction to traditional Catholicism.   3. A parody of French philosopher René Descartes's (1596–1650) phrase "I think, therefore I am," which had become a symbol of well-ordered thought.   4. Since baptism creates the possibility of both heaven and hell.

fumes, childish melodies.[5]—And to say that I possess truth, that I understand justice: I have a sound and steady judgment, I am prepared for perfection . . . Pride.—The skin of my head is drying up. Pity! Lord, I am terrified. I am thirsty, so thirsty! Ah! childhood, the grass, the rain, the lake upon the stones, *the moonlight when the bell tower was striking twelve*[6] . . . the devil is in the bell tower, at that hour. Mary! Blessed Virgin! . . . —The horror of my stupidity.

Over there, are they not honest-souls, who wish me well? . . . Come . . . I have a pillow over my mouth, they don't hear me, they are phantoms. Besides, no one ever thinks of others. Let no one approach. I reek of burning, that's certain.

The hallucinations are countless. It's exactly what I've always had: no more faith in history, neglect of principles. I shall be silent about this: poets and visionaries would be jealous. I am a thousand times the richest, let us be avaricious like the sea.

Now then! the clock of life has just stopped. I am no longer in the world.—Theology is serious, hell is certainly *below*—and heaven above.—Ecstasy, nightmare, sleep in a nest of flames.

What pranks during my vigilance in the country . . . Satan, Ferdinand,[7] races with the wild seeds . . . Jesus walks on the purplish briers, without bending them . . . Jesus used to walk on the troubled waters.[8] The lantern revealed him to us, a figure standing, pale and with brown tresses, beside a wave of emerald . . .

I am going to unveil all the mysteries: mysteries religious or natural, death, birth, futurity, antiquity, cosmogony, nothingness, I am a master of phantasmagories.

Listen! . . .

I have all the talents!—There is nobody here and there is somebody: I would not wish to scatter my treasure.—Do you wish for Negro chants, dances of houris?[9] Do you wish me to vanish, to dive in search of the *ring?*[1] Do you? I shall produce gold, cures.

Rely, then, upon me: faith comforts, guides, heals. All of you, come,—even the little children,[2]—that I may console you, that one may pour out his heart for you,—the marvelous heart!—Poor men, laborers! I do not ask for prayers; with your confidence alone, I shall be happy.

—And let's think of me. This makes me miss the world very little. I have the good fortune not to suffer any longer. My life was nothing but sweet follies, regrettably.

Bah! let's make all the grimaces imaginable.

Decidedly, we are out of the world. No more sound. My sense of touch has disappeared. Ah! my castle, my Saxony,[3] my forest of willows. The evenings, the mornings, the nights, the days . . . Am I weary!

I ought to have my hell for wrath, my hell for pride,—and the hell of the caress; a concert of hells.

---

5. The poetic visions and harmonies that Rimbaud explored with Paul Verlaine.   6. A collection of romanticized childhood memories.   7. Peasant name for the devil.   8. Jesus' disciples saw him walking on the sea at night (John 6.16–21).   9. Beautiful virgins in the Koranic paradise.   1. At the end of Wagner's opera *Götterdämmerung*, Hagen plunges into the river Rhine to recapture the golden ring of world power.   2. Parody of Jesus' words "Suffer little children, and forbid them not, to come unto me" (Matthew 19.14).   3. Germanic duchy, part of Rimbaud's visionary memories.

I am dying of weariness. This is the tomb, I am going to the worms, horror of horrors! Satan, jester, you wish to undo me, with your spells. I protest. I protest! one jab of the pitchfork, one lick of fire.

Ah! to rise again to life! To cast eyes upon our deformities. And that poison, that kiss a thousand times accursed! My weakness, the cruelty of the world! Dear God, your mercy, hide me, I regard myself too poorly!—I am hidden and I am not.

It is the fire that rises again with the soul condemned to it.

THE ILLUMINATIONS[1]

The Bridges[2]

Crystalline gray skies. A strange pattern of bridges, these straight, those arched, others descending obliquely at angles to the first, and these configurations repeating themselves in the other illuminated circuits of the canal,[3] but all so long and light that the shores, laden with domes, sink and diminish. Some of these bridges are still encumbered with hovels.[4] Others support masts, signals, frail parapets. Minor chords interweave, and flow smoothly; ropes rise from the steep banks. One detects a red jacket, perhaps other costumes and musical instruments. Are these popular tunes, fragments of manorial concerts, remnants of public anthems? The water is gray and blue, ample as an arm of the sea.

A white ray, falling from the summit of the sky, reduces to nothingness this theatrical performance.

Barbarian

Long after the days and the seasons, and the creatures and the countries,
The banner of bleeding meat[1] on the silk of the seas and of the arctic flowers; (they do not exist.)
Delivered from the old fanfares of heroism—that still attack our heart and our head—far from the former assassins.
—Oh! the banner of bleeding meat on the silk of the seas and of the arctic flowers; (they do not exist.)
Delights!
Blazing coals, raining in squalls of hoarfrost—Delights!—fires in the rain of the wind of diamonds, rain hurled down by the earthly heart eternally carbonized for us—O world!—

---

1. Translated by Enid Rhodes Peschel. 2. An impressionistic memory of London. 3. The river Thames as it winds through the city. 4. Houses were once built on London Bridge. 1. Perhaps a description of the Danish flag (a white cross on a red field), which Rimbaud would have seen on a visit to Iceland, then a Danish possession.

(Far from the old retreats and the old flames, that are known, that are felt,)

Blazing coals and froths. Music, veering of whirlpools and collisions of drift ice with the stars.

O Delights, oh world, oh music! And there, the forms, the sweats, the heads of hair and the eyes, floating. And the white tears, boiling—oh delights!—and the feminine voice borne down to the bottom of the volcanoes and the arctic grottoes.

The banner . . .

ANTON CHEKHOV
1860–1904

In plays and stories Anton Chekhov depicts Russia around the turn of the twentieth century with great pity, gentleness, and kindness of heart. More important, with a deep humanity that has outlasted all the problems of his time, he dramatizes universal and almost timeless feelings rather than ideas that date and pass. He differs sharply from the two giants of Russian literature, Dostoevsky and Tolstoy. For one thing, his work is of smaller scope. With the exception of an immature, forgotten novel and a travel book, he wrote only short stories and plays. He belongs, furthermore, to a very different moral and spiritual atmosphere. Chekhov had studied medicine and practiced it for a time. He shared the scientific outlook of his age and had too skeptical a mind to believe in Christianity or in any metaphysical system. He confessed that an intelligent believer was a puzzle to him. His attitude toward his materials and characters is detached, "objective," and his letters to friends insist that a good writer must present both physical details and a character's state of mind without overt interpretation or judgment. He is thus much more in the stream of Western realism than either Tolstoy or Dostoevsky, and the delicate, precise realism of his short stories has served as a model for later writers in Europe, China, and the United States. But extended reading of Chekhov does convey an impression of his view of life. There is implied in his stories a philosophy of kindness and humanity, a love of beauty, a sense of the unexplainable mystery of life, a sense, especially, of the individual's utter loneliness in this universe and among other people. Chekhov's pessimism has nothing of the defiance of the universe or the horror at it which we meet in other writers with similar attitudes; it is somehow merely sad, often pathetic, and yet also comforting and comfortable.

The Russia depicted in Chekhov's stories and plays is of a later period than that presented by Tolstoy and Dostoevsky. It seems to be nearing its end; there is a sense of decadence and frustration which heralds the approach of catastrophe. The aristocracy still keeps up a beautiful front but is losing its fight without much resistance, resignedly. Officialdom is stupid and venal. The church is backward and narrowminded. The intelligentsia are hopelessly ineffectual, futile, lost in the provinces or absorbed in their egos. The peasants live subject to the lowest degradations of poverty and drink, apparently rather aggravated than improved since the muchheralded emancipation of the serfs in 1861. There seems no hope for society except in a gradual spread of enlightenment, good sense, and hygiene, for Chekhov is skeptical of the revolution and revolutionaries as well as of Tolstoy's followers.

Anton Pavlovich Chekhov was born on January 17, 1860, at Taganrog, a small town on the Sea of Azov. His father was a grocer and haberdasher; his grandfather, a serf who had bought his freedom. Chekhov's father went bankrupt in 1876, and the family moved to Moscow, leaving Anton to finish school in his home town. After his graduation in 1879, he followed his family to Moscow, where he studied medicine. To earn additional money for his family and himself, he started to write humorous sketches and stories for magazines. In 1884 he became a doctor and published his first collection of stories, *Tales of Melpomene*. In the same year he had his first hemorrhage. All the rest of his life he struggled against tuberculosis. His first play, *Ivanov*, was performed in 1887. Three years later, he undertook an arduous journey through Siberia to the island of Sakhalin (north of Japan) and back by boat through the Suez Canal. He saw there the Russian penal settlements and wrote a moving account of his trip in *Sakhalin Island* (1892). In 1898 his play *The Sea Gull* was a great success at the Moscow Art Theater. The next year he moved to Yalta, in the Crimea, and in 1901 married the actress Olga Knipper. He died on July 2, 1904, at Badenweiler in the Black Forest.

The plays of Chekhov seem to go furthest in the direction of naturalism, the depiction of a "slice of life," on stage. Compared with Ibsen's plays they seem plotless; they could be described as a succession of little scenes, composed like a mosaic or like the dots or strokes in an Impressionist painting. The characters rarely engage in the usual dialogue; they speak often in little soliloquies, hardly justified by the situation; and they often do not listen to the words of their ostensible partners. They seem alone even in a crowd. Human communication seems difficult and even impossible. There is no clear message, no zeal for social reform; life seems to flow quietly, even sluggishly, until interrupted by some desperate outbreak or even a pistol shot.

Chekhov's last play, *The Cherry Orchard* (composed in 1903, first performed at the Moscow Art Theater on January 17, 1904), differs, however, from this pattern in several respects. It has a strongly articulated central theme—the loss of the orchard—and it has a composition that roughly follows the traditional scheme of a well-made play. Arrival and departure from the very same room, the nursery, frame the two other acts: the outdoor idyll of Act II and the dance in Act III. Act III is the turning point of the action: Lopahin appears and announces, somewhat shamefacedly, that he has bought the estate. The orchard was lost from the very beginning—there is no real struggle to prevent its sale—but still the news of Lopahin's purchase is a surprise as he had no intention of buying it but did so only when during the auction sale a rival seemed to have a chance of acquiring it. A leading action runs its course, and many—one may even argue too many—subplots crisscross each other: the shy and awkward love affair of the student Trofimov and the daughter Anya; the love triangle among the three dependents, Yepihodov (the unlucky clerk), Dunyasha (the chambermaid), and Yasha (the conceited and insolent footman). Varya, the practical stepdaughter, has her troubles with Lopahin, and Simeonov-Pishchik is beset by the same financial problems as the owners of the orchard and is rescued by the discovery of some white clay on his estate. The German governess Charlotta drifts around alluding to her obscure origins and past. There are undeveloped references to events preceding the action on stage—the lover in Paris, the drowned boy Grisha—but there is no revelation of the past as in Ibsen, no mystery, no intrigue.

While the events on the stage follow each other naturally, though hardly always in a logical, causal order, a symbolic device is used conspicuously: in Act II after a pause, "suddenly a distant sound is heard, coming from the sky as it were, the sound of a snapping string, mournfully dying away." It occurs again at the very end of the play followed by "the strokes of the ax against a tree far away in the orchard." An attempt is made to explain this sound at its first occurrence as a bucket's fall in a faraway pit or as the cries of a heron or an owl, but the effect is weird and even super-natural; it establishes an ominous mood. Even the orchard carries more than its obvi-ous meaning: it is white, drowned in blossoms when the party arrives in the spring; it is bare and desolate in the autumn when the axes are heard cutting it down. "The old bark on the trees gleams faintly, and the cherry trees seem to be dreaming of things that happened a hundred, two hundred years ago and to be tormented by painful visions," declaims Trofimov, defining his feeling for the orchard as a symbol of repres-sion and serfdom. For Lubov Ranevskaya it is an image of her lost innocence and of the happier past, while Lopahin sees it only as an investment. It seems to draw together the meaning of the play.

But what is this meaning? Can we even decide whether it is a tragedy or a comedy? It has been commonly seen as the tragedy of the downfall of the Russian aristocracy (or more correctly, the landed gentry) victimized by the newly rich, upstart peasantry. One could see the play as depicting the defeat of a group of feckless people at the hand of a ruthless "developer" who destroys nature and natural beauty for profit. Or one can see it as prophesying, through the mouth of the student Trofimov, the approaching end of feudal Russia and the coming happier future. Soviet interpreta-tions and performances lean that way.

Surely none of these interpretations can withstand inspection in the light of the actual play. They all run counter to Chekhov's professed intentions. He called the play a comedy. In a letter of September 15, 1903, he declared expressly that the play "has not turned out as drama but as comedy, in places even a farce" and a few days later (September 21, 1903) he wrote that "the whole play is gay and frivolous." Chekhov did not like the staging of the play at the Moscow Art Theater and com-plained of its tearful tone and its slow pace. He objected that "they obstinately call my play a drama in playbill and newspaper advertisements" while he had called it a comedy (April 10, 1904).

No doubt, there are many comical and even farcical characters and scenes in the play. Charlotta with her nut-eating dog, her card tricks, her ventriloquism, her disap-pearing acts, is a clownish figure. Gayev, the landowner, though "suave and elegant," is a boor, obsessed by his passion for billiards, constantly popping candy into his mouth, telling the waiters in a restaurant about the "decadents" in Paris. Yepihodov, the clerk, carries a revolver and, threatening suicide, asks foolishly whether you have read Buckle (the English historian) and complains of his ill-luck: a spider on his chest, a cockroach in his drink. Simeonov-Pishchik empties a whole bottle of pills, eats half a bucket of pickles, quotes Nietzsche supposedly recommending the forging of banknotes, and, fat as he is, puffs and prances at the dance ordering the "cavaliers à genoux." Even the serious characters are put into ludicrous predicaments: Trofimov falls down the stairs; Lopahin, coming to announce the purchase of the estate, is almost hit with a stick by Varya (and was hit in the original version). Lopahin, teas-ing his intended Varya, "moos like a cow." The ball, the hunting for the galoshes, and the champagne drinking by Yasha in the last act have all a touch of absurdity. The grand speeches, Gayev's addresses to the bookcase and to nature or Trofimov's about "mankind going forward" and "All Russia is our orchard," are undercut by the con-trast between words and character: Gayev is callous and shallow; the "perpetual stu-dent," Trofimov never did a stitch of work. He is properly ridiculed and insulted by Lubov for his scant beard and his silly professions of being "above love." One can sympathize with Chekhov's irritation at the pervading gloom imposed by the Moscow production.

Still, we cannot, in spite of the author, completely dismiss the genuine pathos of the central situation and of the central figure, Lubov Ranevskaya. Whatever one may say about her recklessness in financial matters and her guilt in relation to her lover in France, we must feel her deep attachment to the house and the orchard, to the past and her lost innocence, clearly and unhumorously expressed in the first act on her arrival, again and again at the impending sale of the estate, and finally at the parting from her house: "Oh, my orchard—my dear, sweet, beautiful orchard! . . . My life, my youth, my happiness—Good-bye!" That Gayev, before the final parting, seems to have overcome the sense of loss and even looks forward to his job in the bank and that Lubov acknowledges that her "nerves are better" and that "she sleeps well" testifies to the indestructible spirit of brother and sister, but cannot minimize the sense of loss, the pathos of parting, the nostalgia for happier times. Nor is the conception of Lopahin simple. Chekhov emphasized, in a letter to Konstantin Stanislavsky, who was to play the part, that "Lopahin is a decent person in the full sense of the word, and his bearing must be that of a completely dignified and intelligent man." He is not, he says, a profiteering peasant (*kulachok,* October 30, 1903). He admires Lubov and thinks of her with gratitude. He senses the beauty of the poppies in his fields. Even the scene of the abortive encounter with Varya at the end has its quiet pathos in spite of all its awkwardness and the comic touches such as the reference to the broken thermometer. Firs, the eighty-seven-year-old valet, may be grotesque in his deafness and his nostalgia for the good old days of serfdom, but the very last scene when we see him abandoned in the locked-up house surely ends the play on a note of desolation and even despair.

Chekhov, we must conclude, achieved a highly original and even paradoxical blend of comedy and tragedy, or rather of farce and pathos. The play presents a social picture firmly set in a specific historical time—the dissolution of the landed gentry, the rise of the peasant, the encroachment of the city—but it does not propound an obvious social thesis. Chekhov, in his tolerance and tenderness, in his distrust of ideologies and heroics, extends his sympathy to all his characters (with the exception of the crudely ambitious valet Yasha). The glow of his humanity, untrammeled by time and place, keeps *The Cherry Orchard* alive in quite different social and political conditions, as it has the universalizing power of great art.

PRONOUNCING GLOSSARY

The following list uses common English syllables and stress accents to provide rough equivalents of selected words whose pronunciation may be unfamiliar to the general reader.

Anton Chekhov: *ahn-tawn' che'-khuf*

Charlotta Ivanovna: *shar-law'-tuh ee-vah'-nuv-nuh*

Firs: *feers*

Leonid Andreyevich Gayev: *lay-ah-neet' ahn-dray'-uh-veech gah'-yef*

Lubov Andreyevna Ranevskaya: *lyu-bawf' ahn-dray'-uv-nuh rah-nyef'-skah-yuh*

Pyotr Sergeyevich Trofimov: *pyaw'-tr sehr-gay'-eh-veech trah-fee'-muf*

Semyon Yepihodov: *seem-yawn' ye-pee-khaw'-duf*

Simeonov-Pishchik: *see-may-awn'-uf peesh'-cheek*

Yermolay Alexeyevich Lopahin: *yehr-mah-lai' ah-lex-ay'-eh-veech lah-pah'-kheen*

The Cherry Orchard[1]

CHARACTERS

LUBOV ANDREYEVNA RANEVSKAYA, *a landowner*

ANYA, *her seventeen-year-old daughter*

VARYA, *her adopted daughter, twenty-four years old*

LEONID ANDREYEVICH GAYEV, *Mme. Ranevskaya's brother*

YERMOLAY ALEXEYEVICH LOPAHIN, *a merchant*

PYOTR SERGEYEVICH TROFIMOV, *a student*

SIMEONOV-PISHCHIK, *a landowner*

CHARLOTTA IVANOVNA, *a governess*

SEMYON YEPIHODOV, *a clerk*

DUNYASHA, *a maid*

FIRS, *a manservant, aged eighty-seven*

YASHA, *a young valet*

A TRAMP

STATIONMASTER

POST OFFICE CLERK

GUESTS

SERVANTS

The action takes place on MME. RANEVSKAYA'S *estate.*

Act I

A room that is still called the nursery. One of the doors leads into ANYA'S *room. Dawn, the sun will soon rise. It is May, the cherry trees are in blossom, but it is cold in the orchard; there is a morning frost. The windows are shut. Enter* DUN-YASHA *with a candle, and* LOPAHIN *with a book in his hand.*

LOPAHIN   The train is in, thank God. What time is it?

DUNYASHA   Nearly two. [*Puts out the candle.*]   It's light already.

LOPAHIN   How late is the train, anyway? Two hours at least. [*Yawns and stretches.*] I'm a fine one! What a fool I've made of myself! I came here on purpose to meet them at the station, and then I went and overslept. I fell asleep in my chair. How annoying! You might have waked me . . .

DUNYASHA   I thought you'd left. [*Listens.*] I think they're coming!

LOPAHIN [*Listens.*]   No, they've got to get the luggage, and one thing and another . . . [*Pause.*] Lubov Andreyevna spent five years abroad, I don't know what she's like now. . . . She's a fine person—lighthearted, simple. I remember when I was a boy of fifteen, my poor father—he had a shop here in the village then—punched me in the face with his fist and made my nose bleed. We'd come into the yard, I don't know what for, and he'd had a drop too much. Lubov Andreyevna, I remember her as if it were yesterday—she was still young and so slim—led me to the washbasin, in this very room . . . in the nursery. "Don't cry, little peasant," she said, "it'll heal in time for your wedding . . ." [*Pause.*] Little peasant . . . my father was a peasant, it's true, and here I am in a white waistcoat and yellow shoes. A pig in a pastry shop, you might say. It's true I'm rich. I've got a lot of money. . . . But when you look at it closely, I'm a peasant through

---

1. Translated by Avrahm Yarmolinsky.

and through. [*Pages the book.*] Here I've been reading this book and I didn't understand a word of it. . . . I was reading it and fell asleep . . . [*Pause.*]

DUNYASHA   And the dogs were awake all night, they feel that their masters are coming.

LOPAHIN   Dunyasha, why are you so—

DUNYASHA: My hands are trembling. I'm going to faint.

LOPAHIN   You're too soft, Dunyasha. You dress like a lady, and look at the way you do your hair. That's not right. One should remember one's place.
[*Enter* YEPIHODOV *with a bouquet; he wears a jacket and highly polished boots that squeak badly. He drops the bouquet as he comes in.*]

YEPIHODOV [*Picking up the bouquet.*]   Here, the gardener sent these, said you're to put them in the dining room. [*Hands the bouquet to* DUNYASHA.]

LOPAHIN   And bring me some kvass.[2]

DUNYASHA   Yes, sir. [*Exits.*]

YEPIHODOV   There's a frost this morning—three degrees below—and yet the cherries are all in blossom. I cannot approve of our climate. [*Sighs.*] I cannot. Our climate does not activate properly. And, Yermolay Alexeyevich, allow me to make a further remark. The other day I bought myself a pair of boots, and I make bold to assure you, they squeak so that it is really intolerable. What should I grease them with?

LOPAHIN   Oh, get out! I'm fed up with you.

YEPIHODOV   Every day I meet with misfortune. And I don't complain, I've got used to it, I even smile.
[DUNYASHA *enters, hands* LOPAHIN *the kvass.*]

YEPIHODOV   I am leaving. [*Stumbles against a chair, which falls over.*] There! [*Triumphantly, as it were.*] There again, you see what sort of circumstance, pardon the expression. . . . It is absolutely phenomenal! [*Exits.*]

DUNYASHA   You know, Yermolay Alexeyevich, I must tell you, Yepihodov has proposed to me.

LOPAHIN   Ah!

DUNYASHA   I simply don't know . . . he's a quiet man, but sometimes when he starts talking, you can't make out what he means. He speaks nicely— and it's touching—but you can't understand it. I sort of like him though, and he is crazy about me. He's an unlucky man . . . every day something happens to him. They tease him about it here . . . they call him, Two-and-Twenty Troubles.

LOPAHIN [*Listening.*]   There! I think they're coming.

DUNYASHA   They *are* coming! What's the matter with me? I feel cold all over.

LOPAHIN   They really are coming. Let's go and meet them. Will she recognize me? We haven't seen each other for five years.

DUNYASHA: [*In a flutter.*]   I'm going to faint this minute. . . . Oh, I'm going to faint!
[*Two carriages are heard driving up to the house.* LOPAHIN *and* DUNYASHA *go out quickly. The stage is left empty. There is a noise in the adjoining rooms.* FIRS, *who had driven to the station to meet* LUBOV

---

2. Russian beer, made from rye or barley.

ANDREYEVNA RANEVSKAYA, *crosses the stage hurriedly, leaning on a stick. He is wearing an old-fashioned livery and a tall hat. He mutters to himself indistinctly. The hubbub offstage increases. A* VOICE: "Come, let's go this way." *Enter* LUBOV ANDREYEVNA, ANYA, *and* CHARLOTTA IVANOVNA *with a pet dog on a leash, all in traveling dresses;* VARYA, *wearing a coat and kerchief;* GAYEV, SIMEONOV-PISHCHIK, LOPAHIN, DUNYASHA, *with a bag and an umbrella, servants with luggage. All walk across the room.*]

ANYA Let's go this way. Do you remember what room this is, Mamma?

MME. RANEVSKAYA [*Joyfully, through her tears.*] The nursery!

VARYA How cold it is! My hands are numb. [*To* MME. RANEVSKAYA] Your rooms are just the same as they were, Mamma, the white one and the violet.

MME. RANEVSKAYA The nursery! My darling, lovely room! I slept here when I was a child . . . [*Cries.*] And here I am, like a child again! [*Kisses her brother and* VARYA, *and then her brother again.*] Varya's just the same as ever, like a nun. And I recognized Dunyasha. [*Kisses* DUNYASHA.]

GAYEV The train was two hours late. What do you think of that? What a way to manage things!

CHARLOTTA [*To* PISHCHIK.] My dog eats nuts, too.

PISHCHIK [*In amazement.*] You don't say!

[*All go out, except* ANYA *and* DUNYASHA.]

DUNYASHA We've been waiting for you for hours. [*Takes* ANYA'*s hat and coat.*]

ANYA I didn't sleep on the train for four nights and now I'm frozen . . .

DUNYASHA It was Lent when you left; there was snow and frost, and now . . . My darling! [*Laughs and kisses her.*] I have been waiting for you, my sweet, my darling! But I must tell you something . . . I can't put it off another minute . . .

ANYA [*Listlessly.*] What now?

DUNYASHA The clerk, Yepihodov, proposed to me, just after Easter.

ANYA There you are, at it again . . . [*Straightening her hair.*] I've lost all my hairpins . . . [*She is staggering with exhaustion.*]

DUNYASHA Really, I don't know what to think. He loves me—he loves me so!

ANYA [*Looking toward the door of her room, tenderly.*] My own room, my windows, just as though I'd never been away. I'm home! Tomorrow morning I'll get up and run into the orchard. Oh, if I could only get some sleep. I didn't close my eyes during the whole journey—I was so anxious.

DUNYASHA Pyotr Sergeyevich came the day before yesterday.

ANYA [*Joyfully.*] Petya!

DUNYASHA He's asleep in the bathhouse. He has settled there. He said he was afraid of being in the way. [*Looks at her watch.*] I should wake him, but Miss Varya told me not to. "Don't you wake him," she said.

[*Enter* VARYA *with a bunch of keys at her belt.*]

VARYA Dunyasha, coffee, and be quick . . . Mamma's asking for coffee.

DUNYASHA In a minute. [*Exits.*]

VARYA Well, thank God, you've come. You're home again. [*Fondling* ANYA.] My darling is here again. My pretty one is back.

ANYA Oh, what I've been through!

VARYA I can imagine.

ANYA   When we left, it was Holy Week, it was cold then, and all the way
    Charlotta chattered and did her tricks. Why did you have to saddle me
    with Charlotta?

VARYA   You couldn't have travelled all alone, darling—at seventeen!

ANYA   We got to Paris, it was cold there, snowing. My French is dreadful.
    Mamma lived on the fifth floor; I went up there, and found all kinds of
    Frenchmen, ladies, an old priest with a book. The place was full of
    tobacco smoke, and so bleak. Suddenly I felt sorry for Mamma, so sorry,
    I took her head in my arms and hugged her and couldn't let go of her.
    Afterward Mamma kept fondling me and crying . . .

VARYA   [Through tears.]   Don't speak of it . . . don't.

ANYA   She had already sold her villa at Mentone, she had nothing left, noth-
    ing. I hadn't a kopeck left either, we had only just enough to get home.
    And Mamma wouldn't understand! When we had dinner at the stations,
    she always ordered the most expensive dishes, and tipped the waiters a
    whole ruble. Charlotta, too. And Yasha kept ordering, too—it was simply
    awful. You know Yasha's Mamma's footman now, we brought him here
    with us.

VARYA   Yes, I've seen the blackguard.

ANYA   Well, tell me—have you paid the interest?

VARYA   How could we?

ANYA   Good heavens, good heavens!

VARYA   In August the estate will be put up for sale.

ANYA   My God!

LOPAHIN   [Peeps in at the door and bleats.]   Meh-h-h. [Disappears.]

VARYA   [Through tears.]   What I couldn't do to him! [Shakes her fist threat-
    eningly.]

ANYA   [Embracing VARYA, gently.]   Varya, has he proposed to you? [VARYA
    shakes her head.] But he loves you. Why don't you come to an under-
    standing? What are you waiting for?

VARYA   Oh, I don't think anything will ever come of it. He's too busy, he has
    no time for me . . . pays no attention to me. I've washed my hands of
    him—I can't bear the sight of him. They all talk about our getting mar-
    ried, they all congratulate me—and all the time there's really nothing to
    it—it's all like a dream. [In another tone.] You have a new brooch—like a
    bee.

ANYA   [Sadly.] Mamma bought it. [She goes into her own room and speaks
    gaily like a child.] And you know, in Paris I went up in a balloon.

VARYA   My darling's home, my pretty one is back! [DUNYASHA returns with
    the coffeepot and prepares coffee. VARYA stands at the door of ANYA's room.]
    All day long, darling, as I go about the house, I keep dreaming. If only we
    could marry you off to a rich man, I should feel at ease. Then I would go
    into a convent, and afterward to Kiev, to Moscow . . . I would spend my
    life going from one holy place to another . . . I'd go on and on . . . What
    a blessing that would be!

ANYA   The birds are singing in the orchard. What time is it?

VARYA   It must be after two. Time you were asleep, darling. [Goes into ANYA's
    room.] What a blessing that would be!

    [YASHA enters with a plaid and a traveling bag, crosses the stage.]

YASHA   [Finically.] May I pass this way, please?

DUNYASHA   A person could hardly recognize you, Yasha. Your stay abroad has certainly done wonders for you.

YASHA   Hm-m . . . and who are you?

DUNYASHA   When you went away I was that high—[*Indicating with her hand.*] I'm Dunyasha—Fyodor Kozoyedev's daughter. Don't you remember?

YASHA   Hm! What a peach!

[*He looks round and embraces her. She cries out and drops a saucer. YASHA leaves quickly.*]

VARYA   [*In the doorway, in a tone of annoyance.*] What's going on here?

DUNYASHA   [*Through tears.*] I've broken a saucer.

VARYA   Well, that's good luck.

ANYA   [*Coming out of her room.*] We ought to warn Mamma that Petya's here.

VARYA   I left orders not to wake him.

ANYA   [*Musingly.*] Six years ago father died. A month later brother Grisha was drowned in the river. . . . Such a pretty little boy he was—only seven. It was more than Mamma could bear, so she went away, went away without looking back . . . [*Shudders.*] How well I understand her, if she only knew! [*Pause.*] And Petya Trofimov was Grisha's tutor, he may remind her of it all . . .

[*Enter FIRS, wearing a jacket and a white waistcoat. He goes up to the coffeepot.*]

FIRS   [*Anxiously.*] The mistress will have her coffee here. [*Puts on white gloves.*] Is the coffee ready? [*Sternly, to DUNYASHA.*] Here, you! And where's the cream?

DUNYASHA   Oh, my God! [*Exits quickly.*]

FIRS   [*Fussing over the coffeepot.*] Hah! the addlehead! [*Mutters to himself.*] Home from Paris. And the old master used to go to Paris too . . . by carriage. [*Laughs.*]

VARYA   What is it, Firs?

FIRS   What is your pleasure, Miss? [*Joyfully.*] My mistress has come home, and I've seen her at last! Now I can die. [*Weeps with joy.*]

[*Enters MME. RANEVSKAYA, GAYEV, and SIMEONOV-PISHCHIK: The latter is wearing a tight-waisted, pleated coat of fine cloth, and full trousers. GAYEV, as he comes in, goes through the motions of a billiard player with his arms and body.*]

MME. RANEVSKAYA   Let's see, how does it go? Yellow ball in the corner! Bank shot in the side pocket!

GAYEV   I'll tip it in the corner! There was a time, Sister, when you and I used to sleep in this very room and now I'm fifty-one, strange as it may seem.

LOPAHIN   Yes, time flies.

GAYEV   Who?

LOPAHIN   I say, time flies.

GAYEV   It smells of patchouli here.

ANYA   I'm going to bed. Good night, Mamma. [*Kisses her mother.*]

MME. RANEVSKAYA   My darling child! [*Kisses her hands.*] Are you happy to be home? I can't come to my senses.

ANYA   Good night, Uncle.

GAYEV   [*Kissing her face and hands.*] God bless you, how like your mother you are! [*To his sister.*] At her age, Luba, you were just like her.

[ANYA *shakes hands with* LOPAHIN *and* PISHCHIK, *then goes out, shutting the door behind her.*]

MME. RANEVSKAYA She's very tired.

PISHCHIK Well, it was a long journey.

VARYA [*To* LOPAHIN *and* PISHCHIK.] How about it, gentlemen? It's past two o'clock—isn't it time for you to go?

MME. RANEVSKAYA [*Laughs.*] You're just the same as ever, Varya. [*Draws her close and kisses her.*] I'll have my coffee and then we'll all go. [FIRS *puts a small cushion under her feet.*] Thank you, my dear. I've got used to coffee. I drink it day and night. Thanks, my dear old man. [*Kisses him.*]

VARYA I'd better see if all the luggage has been brought in. [*Exits.*]

MME. RANEVSKAYA Can it really be I sitting here? [*Laughs.*] I feel like dancing, waving my arms about. [*Covers her face with her hands.*] But maybe I am dreaming! God knows I love my country, I love it tenderly; I couldn't look out of the window in the train, I kept crying so. [*Through tears.*] But I must have my coffee. Thank you, Firs, thank you, dear old man. I'm so happy that you're still alive.

FIRS Day before yesterday.

GAYEV He's hard of hearing.

LOPAHIN I must go soon, I'm leaving for Kharkov about five o'clock. How annoying! I'd like to have a good look at you, talk to you. . . . You're just as splendid as ever.

PISHCHIK [*Breathing heavily.*] She's even better-looking. . . . Dressed in the latest Paris fashion . . . Perish my carriage and all its four wheels. . . .

LOPAHIN Your brother, Leonid Andreyevich, says I'm a vulgarian and an exploiter. But it's all the same to me—let him talk. I only want you to trust me as you used to. I want you to look at me with your touching, wonderful eyes, as you used to. Dear God! My father was a serf of your father's and grandfather's, but you, you yourself, did so much for me once . . . so much . . . that I've forgotten all about that; I love you as though you were my sister—even more.

MME. RANEVSKAYA I can't sit still, I simply can't. [*Jumps up and walks about in violent agitation.*] This joy is too much for me. . . . Laugh at me, I'm silly! My own darling bookcase! My darling table! [*Kisses it.*]

GAYEV While you were away, nurse died.

MME. RANEVSKAYA [*Sits down and takes her coffee.*] Yes, God rest her soul; they wrote me about it.

GAYEV And Anastasy is dead. Petrushka Kossoy has left me and has gone into town to work for the police inspector. [*Takes a box of sweets out of his pocket and begins to suck one.*]

PISHCHIK My daughter Dashenka sends her regards.

LOPAHIN I'd like to tell you something very pleasant—cheering. [*Glancing at his watch.*] I am leaving directly. There isn't much time to talk. But I will put it in a few words. As you know, your cherry orchard is to be sold to pay your debts. The sale is to be on the twenty-second of August; but don't you worry, my dear, you may sleep in peace; there is a way out. Here is my plan. Give me your attention! Your estate is only fifteen miles from the town; the railway runs close by it; and if the cherry orchard and the

land along the riverbank were cut up into lots and these leased for summer cottages, you would have an income of at least 25,000 rubles a year
out of it.

GAYEV   Excuse me. . . . What nonsense.

MME. RANEVSKAYA   I don't quite understand you, Yermolay Alexeyevich.

LOPAHIN   You will get an annual rent of at least ten rubles per acre, and if
you advertise at once, I'll give you any guarantee you like that you won't
have a square foot of ground left by autumn, all the lots will be snapped
up. In short, congratulations, you're saved. The location is splendid—by
that deep river. . . . Only, of course, the ground must be cleared . . . all
the old buildings, for instance, must be torn down, and this house, too,
which is useless, and, of course, the old cherry orchard must be cut
down.

MME. RANEVSKAYA   Cut down? My dear, forgive me, but you don't know
what you're talking about. If there's one thing that's interesting—
indeed, remarkable—in the whole province, it's precisely our cherry
orchard.

LOPAHIN   The only remarkable thing about this orchard is that it's a very
large one. There's a crop of cherries every other year, and you can't do
anything with them; no one buys them.

GAYEV   This orchard is even mentioned in the encyclopedia.

LOPAHIN   [Glancing at his watch.]   If we can't think of a way out, if we don't
come to a decision, on the twenty-second of August the cherry orchard
and the whole estate will be sold at auction. Make up your minds! There's
no other way out—I swear. None, none.

FIRS   In the old days, forty or fifty years ago, the cherries were dried,
soaked, pickled, and made into jam, and we used to—

GAYEV   Keep still, Firs.

FIRS   And the dried cherries would be shipped by the cartload. It meant a
lot of money! And in those days the dried cherries were soft and juicy,
sweet, fragrant. . . . They knew the way to do it, then.

MME. RANEVSKAYA   And why don't they do it that way now?

FIRS   They've forgotten. Nobody remembers it.

PISHCHIK   [To MME. RANEVSKAYA.]   What's doing in Paris? Eh? Did you eat
frogs there?

MME. RANEVSKAYA   I ate crocodiles.

PISHCHIK   Just imagine!

LOPAHIN   There used to be only landowners and peasants in the country,
but now these summer people have appeared on the scene. . . . All the
towns, even the small ones, are surrounded by these summer cottages;
and in another twenty years, no doubt, the summer population will have
grown enormously. Now the summer resident only drinks tea on his
porch, but maybe he'll take to working his acre, too, and then your cherry
orchard will be a rich, happy, luxuriant place.

GAYEV   [Indignantly.]   Poppycock!

[Enter VARYA and YASHA.]

VARYA   There are two telegrams for you, Mamma dear. [Picks a key from the
bunch at her belt and noisily opens an old-fashioned bookcase.] Here they
are.

MME. RANEVSKAYA They're from Paris. [*Tears them up without reading them.*] I'm through with Paris.

GAYEV Do you know, Luba, how old this bookcase is? Last week I pulled out the bottom drawer and there I found the date burnt in it. It was made exactly a hundred years ago. Think of that! We could celebrate its centenary. True, it's an inanimate object, but nevertheless, a bookcase . . .

PISHCHIK [*Amazed.*] A hundred years! Just imagine!

GAYEV Yes. [*Tapping it.*] That's something. . . . Dear, honored bookcase, hail to you who for more than a century have served the glorious ideals of goodness and justice! Your silent summons to fruitful toil has never weakened in all those hundred years [*through tears*], sustaining, through successive generations of our family, courage and faith in a better future, and fostering in us ideals of goodness and social consciousness. . . . [*Pauses.*]

LOPAHIN Yes . . .

MME. RANEVSKAYA You haven't changed a bit, Leonid.

GAYEV [*Somewhat embarrassed.*] I'll play it off the red in the corner! Tip it in the side pocket!

LOPAHIN [*Looking at his watch.*] Well, it's time for me to go . . .

YASHA [*Handing pillbox to* MME. RANEVSKAYA.] Perhaps you'll take your pills now.

PISHCHIK One shouldn't take medicines, dearest lady, they do neither harm nor good. . . . Give them here, my valued friend. [*Takes the pillbox, pours the pills into his palm, blows on them, puts them in his mouth, and washes them down with some kvass.*] There!

MME. RANEVSKAYA [*Frightened.*] You must be mad!

PISHCHIK I've taken all the pills.

LOPAHIN What a glutton!
[*All laugh.*]

FIRS The gentleman visited us in Easter week, ate half a bucket of pickles, he did . . . [*Mumbles.*]

MME. RANEVSKAYA What's he saying?

VARYA He's been mumbling like that for the last three years—we're used to it.

YASHA His declining years!
[CHARLOTTA IVANOVNA, *very thin, tightly laced, dressed in white, a lorgnette at her waist, crosses the stage.*]

LOPAHIN Forgive me, Charlotta Ivanovna, I've not had time to greet you. [*Tries to kiss her hand.*]

CHARLOTTA [*Pulling away her hand.*] If I let you kiss my hand, you'll be wanting to kiss my elbow next, and then my shoulder.

LOPAHIN I've no luck today. [*All laugh.*] Charlotta Ivanovna, show us a trick.

MME. RANEVSKAYA Yes, Charlotta, do a trick for us.

CHARLOTTA I don't see the need. I want to sleep. [*Exits.*]

LOPAHIN In three weeks we'll meet again. [*Kisses* MME. RANEVSKAYA'S *hand.*] Good-bye till then. Time's up. [*To* GAYEV.] Bye-bye. [*Kisses* PISHCHIK.] Bye-bye. [*Shakes hands with* VARYA, *then with* FIRS *and* YASHA.] I hate to leave. [*To* MME. RANEVSKAYA.] If you make up your mind about the cottages, let me know; I'll get you a loan of 50,000 rubles.[3] Think it over seriously.

VARYA [*Crossly.*]   Will you never go!

LOPAHIN   I'm going, I'm going. [*Exits.*]

GAYEV   The vulgarian. But, excuse me . . . Varya's going to marry him, he's Varya's fiancé.

VARYA   You talk too much, Uncle.

MME. RANEVSKAYA   Well, Varya, it would make me happy. He's a good man.

PISHCHIK   Yes, one must admit, he's a most estimable man. And my Dashenka . . . she too says that . . . she says . . . lots of things. [*Snores; but wakes up at once.*] All the same, my valued friend, could you oblige me . . . with a loan of 240 rubles? I must pay the interest on the mortgage tomorrow.

VARYA [*Alarmed.*]   We can't, we can't!

MME. RANEVSKAYA   I really haven't any money.

PISHCHIK   It'll turn up. [*Laughs.*] I never lose hope, I thought everything was lost, that I was done for, when lo and behold, the railway ran through my land . . . and I was paid for it. . . . And something else will turn up again, if not today, then tomorrow . . . Dashenka will win two hundred thousand . . . she's got a lottery ticket.

MME. RANEVSKAYA   I've had my coffee, now let's go to bed.

FIRS [*Brushes off* GAYEV; *admonishingly.*]   You've got the wrong trousers on again. What am I to do with you?

VARYA [*Softly.*]   Anya's asleep. [*Gently opens the window.*] The sun's up now, it's not a bit cold. Look, Mamma dear, what wonderful trees. And heavens, what air! The starlings are singing!

GAYEV [*Opens the other window.*]   The orchard is all white. You've not forgotten it? Luba? That's the long alley that runs straight, straight as an arrow; how it shines on moonlight nights, do you remember? You've not forgotten?

MME. RANEVSKAYA [*Looking out of the window into the orchard.*]   Oh, my childhood, my innocent childhood. I used to sleep in this nursery—I used to look out into the orchard, happiness waked with me every morning, the orchard was just the same then . . . nothing has changed. [*Laughs with joy.*] All, all white! Oh, my orchard! After the dark, rainy autumn and the cold winter, you are young again, and full of happiness, the heavenly angels have not left you. . . . If I could free my chest and my shoulders from this rock that weighs on me, if I could only forget the past!

GAYEV   Yes, and the orchard will be sold to pay our debts, strange as it may seem.

MME. RANEVSKAYA   Look! There is our poor mother walking in the orchard . . . all in white . . . [*Laughs with joy.*] It is she!

GAYEV   Where?

VARYA   What are you saying, Mamma dear!

MME. RANEVSKAYA   There's no one there, I just imagined it. To the right, where the path turns toward the arbor, there's a little white tree, leaning over, that looks like a woman . . .

---

3. The basic unit of currency. One ruble is equal to one hundred kopecks.

[TROFIMOV *enters, wearing a shabby student's uniform and specta-cles.*]

MME. RANEVSKAYA   What an amazing orchard! White masses of blossom, the blue sky . . .

TROFIMOV   Lubov Andreyevna! [*She looks round at him.*]   I just want to pay my respects to you, then I'll leave at once. [*Kisses her hand ardently.*] I was told to wait until morning, but I hadn't the patience . . .

[MME. RANEVSKAYA   *looks at him, perplexed.*]

VARYA [*Through tears.*]   This is Petya Trofimov.

TROFIMOV   Petya Trofimov, formerly your Grisha's tutor. . . . Can I have changed so much?

[MME. RANEVSKAYA *embraces him and weeps quietly.*]

GAYEV [*Embarrassed.*]   Don't, don't, Luba.

VARYA [*Crying.*]   I told you, Petya, to wait until tomorrow.

MME. RANEVSKAYA   My Grisha . . . my little boy . . . Grisha . . . my son.

VARYA   What can one do, Mamma dear, it's God's will.

TROFIMOV [*Softly, through tears.*]   There . . . there.

MME. RANEVSKAYA [*Weeping quietly.*]   My little boy was lost . . . drowned. Why? Why, my friend? [*More quietly.*]   Anya's asleep in there, and here I am talking so loudly . . . making all this noise . . . But tell me, Petya, why do you look so badly? Why have you aged so?

TROFIMOV   A mangy master, a peasant woman in the train called me.

MME. RANEVSKAYA   You were just a boy then, a dear little student, and now your hair's thin—and you're wearing glasses! Is it possible you're still a student? [*Goes toward the door.*]

TROFIMOV   I suppose I'm a perpetual student.

MME. RANEVSKAYA [*Kisses her brother, then* VARYA.]   Now, go to bed. . . . You have aged, too, Leonid.

PISHCHIK [*Follows her.*]   So now we turn in. Oh, my gout! I'm staying the night here . . . Lubov Andreyevna, my angel, tomorrow morning . . . I do need 240 rubles.

GAYEV   He keeps at it.

PISHCHIK   I'll pay it back, dear . . . it's a trifling sum.

MME. RANEVSKAYA   All right, Leonid will give it to you. Give it to him, Leonid.

GAYEV   Me give it to him! That's a good one!

MME. RANEVSKAYA   It can't be helped. Give it to him! He needs it. He'll pay it back.

[MME. RANEVSKAYA, TROFIMOV, PISHCHIK, *and* FIRS *go out;* GAYEV, VARYA, *and* YASHA *remain.*]

GAYEV   Sister hasn't got out of the habit of throwing money around. [*To* YASHA.] Go away, my good fellow, you smell of the barnyard.

YASHA [*With a grin.*]   And you, Leonid Andreyevich, are just the same as ever.

GAYEV   Who? [*To* VARYA.]   What did he say?

VARYA [*To* YASHA.]   Your mother's come from the village; she's been sitting in the servants' room since yesterday, waiting to see you.

YASHA   Botheration!

VARYA   You should be ashamed of yourself!

YASHA   She's all I needed! She could have come tomorrow. [*Exits.*]

VARYA   Mamma is just the same as ever; she hasn't changed a bit. If she had her own way, she'd keep nothing for herself.

GAYEV   Yes . . . [*Pauses.*]   If a great many remedies are offered for some disease, it means it is incurable; I keep thinking and racking my brains; I have many remedies, ever so many, and that really means none. It would be fine if we came in for a legacy; it would be fine if we married off our Anya to a very rich man; or we might go to Yaroslavl and try our luck with our aunt, the Countess. She's very rich, you know . . .

VARYA [*Weeping.*]   If only God would help us!

GAYEV   Stop bawling. Aunt's very rich, but she doesn't like us. In the first place, Sister married a lawyer who was no nobleman . . . [ANYA   *appears in the doorway.*] She married beneath her, and it can't be said that her behavior has been very exemplary. She's good, kind, sweet, and I love her, but no matter what extenuating circumstances you may adduce, there's no denying that she has no morals. You sense it in her least gesture.

VARYA [*In a whisper.*]   Anya's in the doorway.

GAYEV   Who? [*Pauses.*]   It's queer, something got into my right eye—my eyes are going back on me. . . . And on Thursday, when I was in the circuit court—

[*Enter* ANYA.]

VARYA   Why aren't you asleep, Anya?

ANYA   I can't get to sleep, I just can't.

GAYEV   My little pet! [*Kisses* ANYA's *face and hands.*]   My child! [*Weeps.*] You are not my niece, you're my angel! You're everything to me. Believe me, believe—

ANYA   I believe you, Uncle. Everyone loves you and respects you . . . but, Uncle dear, you must keep still. . . . You must. What were you saying just now about my mother? Your own sister? What made you say that?

GAYEV   Yes, yes . . . [*Covers his face with her hand.*]   Really, that was awful! Good God! Heaven help me! Just now I made a speech to the bookcase . . . so stupid! And only after I was through, I saw how stupid it was.

VARYA   It's true, Uncle dear, you ought to keep still. Just don't talk, that's all.

ANYA   If you could only keep still, it would make things easier for you, too.

GAYEV   I'll keep still. [*Kisses* ANYA's *and* VARYA's *hands.*]   I will. But now about business. On Thursday I was in court; well, there were a number of us there, and we began talking of one thing and another, and this and that, and do you know, I believe it will be possible to raise a loan on a promissory note to pay the interest at the bank.

VARYA   If only God would help us!

GAYEV   On Tuesday I'll go and see about it again. [*To* VARYA.]   Stop bawling. [*To* ANYA.] Your mamma will talk to lopahin, and he, of course, will not refuse her . . . and as soon as you're rested, you'll go to Yaroslavl to the Countess, your great-aunt. So we'll be working in three directions at once, and the thing is in the bag. We'll pay the interest—I'm sure of it. [*Puts a candy in his mouth.*] I swear on my honor, I swear by anything you like, the estate shan't be sold. [*Excitedly.*] I swear by my own happiness! Here's my hand on it, you can call me a swindler and a scoundrel if I let it come to an auction! I swear by my whole being.

ANYA [*Relieved and quite happy again.*]   How good you are, Uncle, and how clever! [*Embraces him.*] Now I'm at peace, quite at peace, I'm happy.

[*Enter* FIRS.]

firs [*Reproachfully*.]   Leonid Andreyevich, have you no fear of God? When are you going to bed?

gayev   Directly, directly. Go away, Firs, I'll . . . yes, I will undress myself. Now, children, 'nightie-'nightie. We'll consider details tomorrow, but now go to sleep. [*Kisses* anya *and* varya.] I am a man of the eighties; they have nothing good to say of that period nowadays. Nevertheless, in the course of my life, I have suffered not a little for my convictions. It's not for nothing that the peasant loves me; one should know the peasant; one should know from which—

anya   There you go again, Uncle.

varya   Uncle dear, be quiet.

firs [*Angrily*.]   Leonid Andreyevich!

gayev   I'm coming, I'm coming! Go to bed! Double bank shot in the side pocket! Here goes a clean shot . . .

[*Exits,* firs *hobbling after him.*]

anya   I am at peace now. I don't want to go to Yaroslavl—I don't like my great-aunt, but still, I am at peace, thanks to Uncle. [*Sits down.*]

varya   We must get some sleep. I'm going now. While you were away, something unpleasant happened. In the old servants' quarters, there are only the old people as you know; Yefim, Polya, Yevstigney, and Karp, too. They began letting all sorts of rascals in to spend the night. . . . I didn't say anything. Then I heard they'd been spreading a report that I gave them nothing but dried peas to eat—out of stinginess, you know . . . and it was all Yevstigney's doing. . . . All right, I thought, if that's how it is, I thought, just wait. I sent for Yevstigney . . . [*Yawns.*] He comes. . . . "How's this, Yevstigney?" I say, "You fool . . ." [*Looking at* anya.] Anichka! [*Pauses.*] She's asleep. [*Puts her arm around* anya.] Come to your little bed. . . . Come . . . [*Leads her.*] My darling has fallen asleep. . . . Come.

[*They go out. Far away beyond the orchard, a shepherd is piping.* trofimov *crosses the stage and, seeing* varya *and* anya, *stands still.*]

varya   Sh! She's asleep . . . asleep. . . . Come, darling.

anya [*Softly, half-asleep.*]   I'm so tired. Those bells . . . Uncle . . . dear. . . . Mamma and Uncle . . .

varya   Come, my precious, come along. [*They go into* anya*'s room.*]

trofimov [*With emotion.*]   My sunshine, my spring!

Act II

A meadow. An old, long-abandoned, lopsided little chapel; near it a well, large slabs, which had apparently once served as tombstones, and an old bench. In the background the road to the Gayev estate. To one side poplars loom darkly, where the cherry orchard begins. In the distance a row of telegraph poles, and far off, on the horizon, the faint outline of a large city which is seen only in fine, clear weather. The sun will soon be setting. charlotta, yasha, *and* dunyasha *are seated on the bench.* yepihodov *stands near and plays a guitar. All are pensive.* charlotta *wears an old peaked cap. She has taken a gun from her shoulder and is straightening the buckle on the strap.*

charlotta [*Musingly.*]   I haven't a real passport, I don't know how old I am, and I always feel that I am very young. When I was a little girl, my father and mother used to go from fair to fair and give performances, very good ones. And I used to do the *salto mortale*,[4] and all sorts of other tricks. And when papa and mamma died, a German lady adopted me and began to educate me. Very good. I grew up and became a governess. But where I come from and who am I, I don't know. . . . Who were my parents? Perhaps they weren't even married. . . . I don't know . . . [*Takes a cucumber out of her pocket and eats it.*] I don't know a thing. [*Pause.*] One wants so much to talk, and there isn't anyone to talk to. . . . I haven't anybody.

YEPIHODOV [*Plays the guitar and sings.*] "What care I for the jarring world? What's friend or foe to me? . . ." How agreeable it is to play the mandolin.

DUNYASHA That's a guitar, not a mandolin. [*Looks in a hand mirror and powders her face.*]

YEPIHODOV To a madman in love it's a mandolin. [*Sings.*] "Would that the heart were warmed by the fire of mutual love!"

[YASHA *joins in.*]

CHARLOTTA How abominably these people sing. Pfui! Like jackals!

DUNYASHA [*To* YASHA.] How wonderful it must be though to have stayed abroad!

YASHA Ah, yes, of course, I cannot but agree with you there. [*Yawns and lights a cigar.*]

YEPIHODOV Naturally. Abroad, everything has long since achieved full perfection.

YASHA That goes without saying.

YEPIHODOV I'm a cultivated man, I read all kinds of remarkable books. And yet I can never make out what direction I should take, what is it that I want, properly speaking. Should I live, or should I shoot myself, properly speaking? Nevertheless, I always carry a revolver about me. . . . Here it is . . . [*Shows revolver.*]

CHARLOTTA I've finished. I'm going. [*Puts the gun over her shoulder.*] You are a very clever man, Yepihodov, and a very terrible one; women must be crazy about you. Br-r-r! [*Starts to go.*] These clever men are all so stupid; there's no one for me to talk to . . . always alone, alone, I haven't a soul . . . and who I am, and why I am, nobody knows. [*Exits unhurriedly.*]

YEPIHODOV Properly speaking and letting other subjects alone, I must say regarding myself, among other things, that fate treats me mercilessly, like a storm treats a small boat. If I am mistaken, let us say, why then do I wake up this morning, and there on my chest is a spider of enormous dimensions . . . like this . . . [*Indicates with both hands.*] Again, I take up a pitcher of kvass to have a drink, and in it there is something unseemly to the highest degree, something like a cockroach. [*Pause.*] Have you read Buckle?[5] [*Pause.*] I wish to have a word with you, Avdotya Fyodorovna, if I may trouble you.

DUNYASHA Well, go ahead.

YEPIHODOV I wish to speak with you alone. [*Sighs.*]

---

4. Somersault (Italian).   5. Henry Thomas Buckle (1821–1862) wrote a *History of Civilization in England* (1857–61), which was considered daringly materialistic and freethinking.

DUNYASHA [*Embarrassed.*] Very well. Only first bring me my little cape. You'll find it near the wardrobe. It's rather damp here.

YEPIHODOV Certainly, ma'am; I will fetch it, ma'am. Now I know what to do with my revolver. [*Takes the guitar and goes off playing it.*]

YASHA Two-and-Twenty Troubles! An awful fool, between you and me. [*Yawns.*]

DUNYASHA I hope to God he doesn't shoot himself! [*Pause.*] I've become so nervous, I'm always fretting. I was still a little girl when I was taken into the big house, I am quite unused to the simple life now, and my hands are white, as white as a lady's. I've become so soft, so delicate, so refined, I'm afraid of everything. It's so terrifying; and if you deceive me, Yasha, I don't know what will happen to my nerves. [YASHA *kisses her.*]

YASHA You're a peach! Of course, a girl should never forget herself; and what I dislike more than anything is when a girl doesn't behave properly.

DUNYASHA I've fallen passionately in love with you; you're educated—you have something to say about everything. [*Pause.*]

YASHA [*Yawns.*] Yes, ma'am. Now the way I look at it, if a girl loves someone, it means she is immoral. [*Pause.*] It's agreeable smoking a cigar in the fresh air. [*Listens.*] Someone's coming this way. . . . It's our madam and the others. [DUNYASHA *embraces him impulsively.*] You go home, as though you'd been to the river to bathe; go to the little path, or else they'll run into you and suspect me of having arranged to meet you here. I can't stand that sort of thing.

DUNYASHA [*Coughing softly.*] Your cigar's made my head ache.

[*Exits.* YASHA *remains standing near the chapel. Enter* MME. RANEVSKAYA, GAYEV, *and* LOPAHIN.]

LOPAHIN You must make up your mind once and for all—there's no time to lose. It's quite a simple question, you know. Do you agree to lease your land for summer cottages or not? Answer in one word, yes or no; only one word!

MME. RANEVSKAYA Who's been smoking such abominable cigars here? [*Sits down.*]

GAYEV Now that the railway line is so near, it's made things very convenient. [*Sits down.*] Here we've been able to have lunch in town. Yellow ball in the side pocket! I feel like going into the house and playing just one game.

MME. RANEVSKAYA You can do that later.

LOPAHIN Only one word! [*Imploringly.*] Do give me an answer!

GAYEV [*Yawning.*] Who?

MME. RANEVSKAYA [*Looks into her purse.*] Yesterday I had a lot of money and now my purse is almost empty. My poor Varya tries to economize by feeding us just milk soup; in the kitchen the old people get nothing but dried peas to eat, while I squander money thoughtlessly. [*Drops the purse, scattering gold pieces.*] You see, there they go . . . [*Shows vexation.*]

YASHA Allow me—I'll pick them up. [*Picks up the money.*]

MME. RANEVSKAYA Be so kind. Yasha. And why did I go to lunch in town? That nasty restaurant, with its music and the tablecloth smelling of soap. . . . Why drink so much, Leonid? Why eat so much? Why talk so much? Today again you talked a lot, and all so inappropriately about the seventies, about the decadents.[6] And to whom? Talking to waiters about decadents!

LOPAHIN Yes.

GAYEV [*Waving his hand.*] I'm incorrigible; that's obvious. [*Irritably, to* YASHA.] Why do you keep dancing about in front of me?

YASHA [*Laughs.*] I can't hear your voice without laughing—

GAYEV Either he or I—

MME. RANEVSKAYA Go away, Yasha; run along.

YASHA [*Handing* MME. RANEVSKAYA *her purse.*] I'm going at once. [*Hardly able to suppress his laughter.*] This minute. [*Exits.*]

LOPAHIN That rich man, Deriganov, wants to buy your estate. They say he's coming to the auction himself.

MME. RANEVSKAYA Where did you hear that?

LOPAHIN That's what they are saying in town.

GAYEV Our aunt in Yaroslavl has promised to help, but when she will send the money, and how much, no one knows.

LOPAHIN How much will she send? A hundred thousand? Two hundred?

MME. RANEVSKAYA Oh, well, ten or fifteen thousand; and we'll have to be grateful for that.

LOPAHIN Forgive me, but such frivolous people as you are, so queer and unbusinesslike—I never met in my life. One tells you in plain language that your estate is up for sale, and you don't seem to take it in.

MME. RANEVSKAYA What are we to do? Tell us what to do.

LOPAHIN I do tell you, every day; every day I say the same thing! You must lease the cherry orchard and the land for summer cottages, you must do it and as soon as possible—right away. The auction is close at hand. Please understand! Once you've decided to have the cottages, you can raise as much money as you like, and you're saved.

MME. RANEVSKAYA Cottages—summer people—forgive me, but it's all so vulgar.

GAYEV I agree with you absolutely.

LOPAHIN I shall either burst into tears or scream or faint! I can't stand it! You've worn me out! [*To* GAYEV.] You're an old woman!

GAYEV Who?

LOPAHIN An old woman! [*Gets up to go.*]

MME. RANEVSKAYA [*Alarmed.*] No, don't go! Please stay, I beg you, my dear. Perhaps we shall think of something.

LOPAHIN What is there to think of?

MME. RANEVSKAYA Don't go, I beg you. With you here it's more cheerful anyway. [*Pause.*] I keep expecting something to happen, it's as though the house were going to crash about our ears.

GAYEV [*In deep thought.*] Bank shot in the corner. . . . Three cushions in the side pocket. . . .

MME. RANEVSKAYA We have been great sinners . . .

LOPAHIN What sins could you have committed?

GAYEV [*Putting a candy in his mouth.*] They say I've eaten up my fortune in candy! [*Laughs.*]

6. A group of French poets of the 1880s (Mallarmé is today the most famous) were labeled "decadents" by their enemies and sometimes adopted the name themselves, proud of their refinement and sensitivity.

MME. RANEVSKAYA Oh, my sins! I've squandered money away recklessly, like a lunatic, and I married a man who made nothing but debts. My husband drank himself to death on champagne, he was a terrific drinker. And then, to my sorrow, I fell in love with another man, and I lived with him. And just then—that was my first punishment—a blow on the head: my little boy was drowned here in the river. And I went abroad, went away forever . . . never to come back, never to see this river again . . . I closed my eyes and ran, out of my mind. . . . But he followed me, pitiless, brutal. I bought a villa near Mentone, because he fell ill there; and for three years, day and night, I knew no peace, no rest. The sick man wore me out, he sucked my soul dry. Then last year, when the villa was sold to pay my debts, I went to Paris, and there he robbed me, abandoned me, took up with another woman, I tried to poison myself—it was stupid, so shameful—and then suddenly I felt drawn back to Russia, back, to my own country, to my little girl. [*Wipes her tears away.*] Lord, Lord! Be merciful, forgive me my sins—don't punish me anymore! [*Takes a telegram out of her pocket.*] This came today from Paris—he begs me to forgive him, implores me to go back . . . [*Tears up the telegram.*] Do I hear music? [*Listens.*]

GAYEV That's our famous Jewish band, you remember? Four violins, a flute, and a double bass.

MME. RANEVSKAYA Does it still exist? We ought to send for them some evening and have a party.

LOPAHIN [*Listens.*] I don't hear anything. [*Hums softly.*] "The Germans for a fee will Frenchify a Russian."[7] [*Laughs.*] I saw a play at the theater yesterday—awfully funny.

MME. RANEVSKAYA There was probably nothing funny about it. You shouldn't go to see plays, you should look at yourselves more often. How drab your lives are—how full of unnecessary talk.

LOPAHIN That's true; come to think of it, we do live like fools. [*Pause.*] My pop was a peasant, an idiot; he understood nothing, never taught me anything, all he did was beat me when he was drunk, and always with a stick. Fundamentally, I'm just the same kind of blockhead and idiot. I was never taught anything—I have a terrible handwriting. I write so that I feel ashamed before people, like a pig.

MME. RANEVSKAYA You should get married, my friend.

LOPAHIN Yes . . . that's true.

MME. RANEVSKAYA To our Varya, she's a good girl.

LOPAHIN Yes.

MME. RANEVSKAYA She's a girl who comes of simple people, she works all day long; and above all, she loves you. Besides, you've liked her for a long time now.

LOPAHIN Well, I've nothing against it. She's a good girl. [*Pause.*]

GAYEV I've been offered a place in the bank—6,000 a year. Have you heard?

MME. RANEVSKAYA You're not up to it. Stay where you are.

[FIRS *enters, carrying an overcoat.*]

---

7. Satirical reference to Russian efforts, from the time of Peter the Great (1672–1725), to imitate western Europe and particularly Parisian culture.

FIRS [*To* GAYEV.] Please put this on, sir, it's damp.

GAYEV [*Putting it on.*] I'm fed up with you, brother.

FIRS Never mind. This morning you drove off without saying a word. [*Looks him over.*]

MME. RANEVSKAYA How you've aged, Firs.

FIRS I beg your pardon?

LOPAHIN The lady says you've aged.

FIRS I've lived a long time; they were arranging my wedding and your papa wasn't born yet. [*Laughs.*] When freedom came[8] I was already head footman. I wouldn't consent to be set free then; I stayed on with the master . . . [*Pause.*] I remember they were all very happy, but why they were happy, they didn't know themselves.

LOPAHIN It was fine in the old days! At least there was flogging!

FIRS [*Not hearing.*] Of course. The peasants kept to the masters, the masters kept to the peasants; but now they've all gone their own ways, and there's no making out anything.

GAYEV Be quiet, Firs. I must go to town tomorrow. They've promised to introduce me to a general who might let us have a loan.

LOPAHIN Nothing will come of that. You won't even be able to pay the interest, you can be certain of that.

MME. RANEVSKAYA He's raving, there isn't any general.

[*Enter* TROFIMOV, ANYA, *and* VARYA.]

GAYEV Here come our young people.

ANYA There's Mamma, on the bench.

MME. RANEVSKAYA [*Tenderly.*] Come here, come along, my darlings. [*Embraces* ANYA *and* VARYA.] If you only knew how I love you both! Sit beside me—there, like that. [*All sit down.*]

LOPAHIN Our perpetual student is always with the young ladies.

TROFIMOV That's not any of your business.

LOPAHIN He'll soon be fifty, and he's still a student!

TROFIMOV Stop your silly jokes.

LOPAHIN What are you so cross about, you queer bird?

TROFIMOV Oh, leave me alone.

LOPAHIN [*Laughs.*] Allow me to ask you, what do you think of me?

TROFIMOV What I think of you, Yermolay Alexeyevich, is this: you are a rich man who will soon be a millionaire. Well, just as a beast of prey, which devours everything that comes in its way, is necessary for the process of metabolism to go on, so you, too, are necessary. [*All laugh.*]

VARYA Better tell us something about the planets, Petya.

MME. RANEVSKAYA No, let's go on with yesterday's conversation.

TROFIMOV What was it about?

GAYEV About man's pride.

TROFIMOV Yesterday we talked a long time, but we came to no conclusion. There is something mystical about man's pride in your sense of the word. Perhaps you're right, from your own point of view. But if you reason simply, without going into subtleties, then what call is there for pride? Is there any sense in it, if man is so poor a thing physiologically, and if, in the great

---

8. Czar Alexander II (ruled 1855–81) emancipated the serfs in 1861.

majority of cases, he is coarse, stupid, profoundly unhappy? We should stop admiring ourselves. We should work, and that's all.

GAYEV You die, anyway.

TROFIMOV Who knows? And what does it mean—to die? Perhaps man has a hundred senses, and at his death only the five we know perish, while the other ninety-five remain alive.

MME. RANEVSKAYA How clever you are, Petya!

LOPAHIN [*Ironically.*] Awfully clever!

TROFIMOV Mankind goes forward, developing its powers. Everything that is now unattainable for it will one day come within man's reach and be clear to him; only we must work, helping with all our might those who seek the truth. Here among us in Russia only the very few work as yet. The great majority of the intelligentsia, as far as I can see, seek nothing, do nothing, are totally unfit for work of any kind. They call themselves the intelligentsia, yet they are uncivil to their servants, treat the peasants like animals, are poor students, never read anything serious, do absolutely nothing at all, only talk about science, and have little appreciation of the arts. They are all solemn, have grim faces, they all philosophize and talk of weighty matters. And meanwhile the vast majority of us, ninety-nine out of a hundred, live like savages. At the least provocation—a punch in the jaw, and curses. They eat disgustingly, sleep in filth and stuffiness, bedbugs everywhere, stench and damp and moral slovenliness. And obviously, the only purpose of all our fine talk is to hoodwink ourselves and others. Show me where the public nurseries are that we've heard so much about, and the libraries. We read about them in novels, but in reality they don't exist, there is nothing but dirt, vulgarity, and Asiatic backwardness. I don't like very solemn faces, I'm afraid of them, I'm afraid of serious conversations. We'd do better to keep quiet for a while.

LOPAHIN Do you know, I get up at five o'clock in the morning, and I work from morning till night; and I'm always handling money, my own and other people's, and I see what people around me are really like. You've only to start doing anything to see how few honest, decent people there are. Sometimes when I lie awake at night, I think: "Oh, Lord, thou hast given us immense forests, boundless fields, the widest horizons, and living in their midst, we ourselves ought really to be giants."

MME. RANEVSKAYA Now you want giants! They're only good in fairy tales; otherwise they're frightening.

[YEPIHODOV *crosses the stage at the rear, playing the guitar.*]

MME. RANEVSKAYA [*Pensively.*] There goes Yepihodov.

GAYEV Ladies and gentlemen, the sun has set.

TROFIMOV Yes.

GAYEV [*In a low voice, declaiming as it were.*] Oh, Nature, wondrous Nature, you shine with eternal radiance, beautiful and indifferent! You, whom we call our mother, unite within yourself life and death! You animate and destroy!

VARYA [*Pleadingly.*] Uncle dear!

ANYA Uncle, again!

TROFIMOV You'd better bank the yellow ball in the side pocket.

GAYEV I'm silent, I'm silent . . .

[*All sit plunged in thought. Stillness reigns. Only* FIRS*'s muttering is audible. Suddenly a distant sound is heard, coming from the sky as it were, the sound of a snapping string, mournfully dying away.*]

MME. RANEVSKAYA   What was that?

LOPAHIN   I don't know. Somewhere far away, in the pits, a bucket's broken loose; but somewhere very far away.

GAYEV   Or it might be some sort of bird, perhaps a heron.

TROFIMOV   Or an owl . . .

MME. RANEVSKAYA [*Shudders.*]   It's weird, somehow. [*Pause.*]

FIRS   Before the calamity the same thing happened—the owl screeched, and the samovar hummed all the time.

GAYEV   Before what calamity?

FIRS   Before the Freedom. [*Pause.*]

MME. RANEVSKAYA   Come, my friends, let's be going. It's getting dark. [*To* ANYA.] You have tears in your eyes. What is it, my little one? [*Embraces her.*]

ANYA   I don't know, Mamma; it's nothing.

TROFIMOV   Somebody's coming.

[A TRAMP *appears, wearing a shabby white cap and an overcoat. He is slightly drunk.*]

TRAMP   Allow me to inquire, will this short cut take me to the station?

GAYEV   It will. Just follow that road.

TRAMP   My heartfelt thanks. [*Coughing.*] The weather is glorious. [*Recites.*] "My brother, my suffering brother. . . . Go down to the Volga![9] Whose groans . . . ?" [*To* VARYA.] Mademoiselle, won't you spare 30 kopecks for a hungry Russian?

[VARYA, *frightened, cries out.*]

LOPAHIN [*Angrily.*]   Even panhandling has its proprieties.

MME. RANEVSKAYA [*Scared.*]   Here, take this. [*Fumbles in her purse.*] I haven't any silver . . . never mind, here's a gold piece.

TRAMP   My heartfelt thanks. [*Exits. Laughter.*]

VARYA [*Frightened.*]   I'm leaving. I'm leaving. . . . Oh, Mamma dearest, at home the servants have nothing to eat, and you gave him a gold piece!

MME. RANEVSKAYA   What are you going to do with me? I'm such a fool. When we get home, I'll give you everything I have. Yermolay Alexeyevich, you'll lend me some more . . .

LOPAHIN   Yes, ma'am.

MME. RANEVSKAYA   Come, ladies and gentlemen, it's time to be going. Oh! Varya, we've settled all about your marriage. Congratulations!

VARYA [*Through tears.*]   Really, Mamma, that's not a joking matter.

LOPAHIN   "Aurelia, get thee to a nunnery, go . . ."

GAYEV   And do you know, my hands are trembling: I haven't played billiards in a long time.

LOPAHIN   "Aurelia, nymph, in your orisons, remember me!"[1]

MME. RANEVSKAYA   Let's go, it's almost suppertime.

---

9. Lines from poems by Semyon Nadson (1826–1878) and Nikolay Nekrasov (1821–1878).   1. Lopahin makes comic use of Hamlet's meeting with Ophelia. (Here *Aurelia* conveys the Russian text's distortion of "Ophelia" as "Okhmelia.") Hamlet, seeing her approaching, says: "Nymph, in thy orisons / Be all my sins remembered" (III. 89–90), and later, suspecting her of spying for her father, sends her off with "Get thee to a nunnery" (III.121).

VARYA   He frightened me! My heart's pounding.

LOPAHIN   Let me remind you, ladies and gentlemen, on the twenty-second of August the cherry orchard will be up for sale. Think about that! Think!

[*All except* TROFIMOV *and* ANYA *go out.*]

ANYA [*Laughs.*]   I'm grateful to that tramp, he frightened Varya and so we're alone.

TROFIMOV   Varya's afraid we'll fall in love with each other all of a sudden. She hasn't left us alone for days. Her narrow mind can't grasp that we're above love. To avoid the petty and illusory, everything that prevents us from being free and happy—that is the goal and meaning of our life. Forward! Do not fall behind, friends!

ANYA [*Strikes her hands together.*]   How well you speak! [*Pause.*] It's wonderful here today.

TROFIMOV   Yes, the weather's glorious.

ANYA   What have you done to me, Petya? Why don't I love the cherry orchard as I used to? I loved it so tenderly. It seemed to me there was no spot on earth lovelier than our orchard.

TROFIMOV   All Russia is our orchard. Our land is vast and beautiful, there are many wonderful places in it. [*Pause.*] Think of it, Anya, your grandfather, your great-grandfather and all your ancestors were serf owners, owners of living souls, and aren't human beings looking at you from every tree in the orchard, from every leaf, from every trunk? Don't you hear voices? Oh, it's terrifying! Your orchard is a fearful place, and when you pass through it in the evening or at night, the old bark on the trees gleams faintly, and the cherry trees seem to be dreaming of things that happened a hundred, two hundred years ago and to be tormented by painful visions. What is there to say? We're at least two hundred years behind, we've really achieved nothing yet, we have no definite attitude to the past, we only philosophize, complain of the blues, or drink vodka. It's all so clear: in order to live in the present, we should first redeem our past, finish with it, and we can expiate it only by suffering, only by extraordinary, unceasing labor. Realize that, Anya.

ANYA   The house in which we live has long ceased to be our own, and I will leave it, I give you my word.

TROFIMOV   If you have the keys, fling them into the well and go away. Be free as the wind.

ANYA [*In ecstasy.*]   How well you put that!

TROFIMOV   Believe me, Anya, believe me! I'm not yet thirty, I'm young, I'm still a student—but I've already suffered so much. In winter I'm hungry, sick, harassed, poor as a beggar, and where hasn't Fate driven me? Where haven't I been? And yet always, every moment of the day and night, my soul is filled with inexplicable premonitions. . . . I have a premonition of happiness, Anya. . . . I see it already!

ANYA [*Pensively.*]   The moon is rising.

[YEPIHODOV *is heard playing the same mournful tune on the guitar. The moon rises. Somewhere near the poplars* VARYA *is looking for* ANYA *and calling,* "Anya, where are you?"]

TROFIMOV   Yes, the moon is rising. [*Pause.*] There it is, happiness, it's approaching, it's coming nearer and nearer, I can already hear its footsteps. And if we don't see it, if we don't know it, what does it matter? Others will!

VARYA'S VOICE   Anya! Where are you?

TROFIMOV   That Varya again! [*Angrily.*] It's revolting!

ANYA   Never mind, let's go down to the river. It's lovely there.

TROFIMOV   Come on. [*They go.*]

VARYA'S VOICE   Anya! Anya!

Act III

A drawing room separated by an arch from a ballroom. Evening. Chandelier burning. The Jewish band is heard playing in the anteroom. In the ballroom they are dancing the Grand Rond.[2] PISCHIK   *is heard calling, "Promenade à une paire!"*[3] PISHCHIK *and* CHARLOTTA, TROFIMOV *and* MME. RANEVSKAYA, ANYA *and the* POST OFFICE CLERK, VARYA *and the* STATIONMASTER, *and others enter the drawing room in couples.* DUNYASHA *is in the last couple.* VARYA *weeps quietly, wiping her tears as she dances. All parade through drawing room,* PISHCHIK *calling, "Grand rond, balancez!"*[4] *and "Les cavaliers à genoux et remerciez vos dames!"*[5] FIRS, *wearing a dress coat, brings in soda water on a tray.* PISHCHIK *and* TROFIMOV *enter the drawing room.*

PISHCHIK   I have high blood pressure; I've already had two strokes. Dancing's hard work for me; but as they say, "If you run with the pack, you can bark or not, but at least wag your tail." Still, I'm as strong as a horse. My late lamented father, who would have his joke, God rest his soul, used to say, talking about our origin, that the ancient line of the Simeonov-Pishchiks was descended from the very horse that Caligula had made a senator.[6] [*Sits down.*] But the trouble is, I have no money. A hungry dog believes in nothing but meat. [*Snores, and wakes up at once.*] It's the same with me—I can think of nothing but money.

TROFIMOV   You know, there *is* something equine about your figure.

PISHCHIK   Well, a horse is a fine animal—one can sell a horse.

   [*Sound of billiards being played in an adjoining room.* VARYA: *appears in the archway.*]

TROFIMOV [*Teasing her.*]   Madam Lopahina! Madam Lopahina!

VARYA [*Angrily.*]   Mangy master!

TROFIMOV   Yes, I am a mangy master and I'm proud of it.

VARYA [*Reflecting bitterly.*]   Here we've hired musicians, and what shall we pay them with? [*Exits.*]

TROFIMOV [*To* PISHCHIK.]   If the energy you have spent during your lifetime looking for money to pay interest had gone into something else, in the end you could have turned the world upside down.

PISHCHIK   Nietzsche,[7] the philosopher, the greatest, most famous of men,

2. A ring dance.   3. Promenade with your partner! (French).   4. Make a large circle, get set! (French).   5. Gentlemen, on your knees and thank your ladies! (French).   6. The mad emperor Caligula (12–41 C.E.) brought his favorite horse into the Roman senate to make it a senator.
7. Friedrich W. Nietzsche (1844–1900), German philosopher.

that colossal intellect, says in his works that it is permissible to forge banknotes.

TROFIMOV   Have you read Nietzsche?

PISHCHIK   Well . . . Dashenka told me. . . . And now I've got to the point where forging banknotes is the only way out for me. . . . The day after tomorrow I have to pay 310 rubles—I already have 130 . . . [*Feels in his pockets. In alarm.*] The money's gone! I've lost my money! [*Through tears.*] Where's my money? [*Joyfully.*] Here it is! Inside the lining . . . I'm all in a sweat . . .

> [*Enter* MME. RANEVSKAYA *and* CHARLOTTA.]

MME. RANEVSKAYA [*Hums the "Lezginka."*8]   Why isn't Leonid back yet? What is he doing in town? [*To* DUNYASHA.] Dunyasha, offer the musicians tea.

TROFIMOV   The auction hasn't taken place, most likely.

MME. RANEVSKAYA   It's the wrong time to have the band, and the wrong time to give a dance. Well, never mind. [*Sits down and hums softly.*]

CHARLOTTA. [*Hands* PISHCHIK *a pack of cards.*]   Here is a pack of cards. Think of any card you like.

PISHCHIK   I've thought of one.

CHARLOTTA   Shuffle the pack now. That's right. Give it here, my dear Mr. Pishchik. *Eins, zwei, drei!*9 Now look for it—it's in your side pocket.

PISHCHIK [*Taking the card out of his pocket.*]   The eight of spades! Perfectly right! Just imagine!

CHARLOTTA [*Holding the pack of cards in her hands. To* TROFIMOV.] Quickly, name the top card.

TROFIMOV   Well, let's see—the queen of spades.

CHARLOTTA   Right! [*To* PISHCHIK.]   Now name the top card.

PISHCHIK   The ace of hearts.

CHARLOTTA   Right! [*Claps her hands and the pack of cards disappears.*] Ah, what lovely weather it is today! [*A mysterious feminine* VOICE, *which seems to come from under the floor, answers her:* "Oh, yes, it's magnificent weather, madam."] You are my best ideal. [VOICE: "And I find you pleasing too, madam."]

STATIONMASTER [*Applauding.*]   The lady ventriloquist, bravo!

PISHCHIK [*Amazed.*]   Just imagine! Enchanting Charlotta Ivanovna, I'm simply in love with you.

CHARLOTTA   In love? [*Shrugs her shoulders.*]   Are you capable of love? *Guter Mensch, aber schlechter Musikant!*1

TROFIMOV [*Claps* PISHCHIK *on the shoulder.*]   You old horse, you!

CHARLOTTA   Attention please! One more trick! [*Takes a plaid*2 *from a chair.*] Here is a very good plaid; I want to sell it. [*Shaking it out.*] Does anyone want to buy it?

PISHCHIK [*In amazement.*]   Just imagine!

CHARLOTTA   *Eins, zwei, drei!* [*Raises the plaid quickly, behind it stands* ANYA.

---

8. The music that in the Caucasus mountains accompanies a courtship dance in which the man dances with abandon around the woman, who moves with grace and ease.   9. One, two, three (German).   1. "A good man, but a bad musician" (German), usually quoted in the plural: *"Gute Leute, schlechte Musikanten."* It comes from *Das Buch le Grand* (1826) by the German poet Heinrich Heine (1799–1856). Here it suggests that Pishchik may be a good man but a bad lover.   2. A small plaid blanket, or lap robe.

*She curtsies, runs to her mother, embraces her, and runs back into the ball-
room, amid general enthusiasm.*]

MME. RANEVSKAYA [*Applauds.*]   Bravo! Bravo!

CHARLOTTA   Now again! *Eins, zwei, drei!* [*Lifts the plaid; behind it stands*
VARYA, *bowing.*]

PISHCHIK [*In amazement.*]   Just imagine!

[CHARLOTTA *throws the plaid at* PISHCHIK, *curtsies, and runs into the
ballroom.*]

PISHCHIK [*Running after her.*]   The rascal! What a woman, what a woman!
[*Exits.*]

MME. RANEVSKAYA   And Leonid still isn't here. What is he doing in town so
long? I don't understand. It must be all over by now. Either the estate has
been sold, or the auction hasn't taken place. Why keep us in suspense so
long?

VARYA [*Trying to console her.*]   Uncle's bought it, I feel sure of that.

TROFIMOV [*Mockingly.*]   Oh, yes!

VARYA   Great-aunt sent him an authorization to buy it in her name, and to
transfer the debt. She's doing it for Anya's sake. And I'm sure that God
will help us, and Uncle will buy it.

MME. RANEVSKAYA   Great-aunt sent fifteen thousand to buy the estate in her
name, she doesn't trust us, but that's not even enough to pay the interest.
[*Covers her face with her hands.*] Today my fate will be decided, my fate—

TROFIMOV [*Teasing* VARYA.]   Madam Lopahina!

VARYA [*Angrily.*]   Perpetual student! Twice already you've been expelled
from the university.

MME. RANEVSKAYA   Why are you so cross, Varya? He's teasing you about
Lopahin. Well, what of it? If you want to marry Lopahin, go ahead. He's
a good man, and interesting; if you don't want to, don't. Nobody's compelling you, my pet!

VARYA   Frankly, Mamma dear, I take this thing seriously; he's a good man
and I like him.

MME. RANEVSKAYA: All right then, marry him. I don't know what you're
waiting for.

VARYA   But, Mamma, I can't propose to him myself. For the last two years,
everyone's been talking to me about him—talking. But he either keeps
silent, or else cracks jokes. I understand; he's growing rich, he's absorbed
in business—he has no time for me. If I had money, even a little, say, 100
rubles, I'd throw everything up and go far away—I'd go into a nunnery.

TROFIMOV   What a blessing . . .

VARYA   A student ought to be intelligent. [*Softly, with tears in her voice.*]
How homely you've grown, Petya! How old you look! [*To* MME.
RANEVSKAYA, *with dry eyes.*] But I can't live without work, Mamma dear; I
must keep busy every minute.

[*Enter* YASHA.]

YASHA [*Hardly restraining his laughter.*]   Yepihodov has broken a billiard
cue! [*Exits.*]

VARYA   Why is Yepihodov here? Who allowed him to play billiards? I don't
understand these people! [*Exits.*]

MME. RANEVSKAYA   Don't tease her, Petya. She's unhappy enough without
that.

TROFIMOV She bustles so—and meddles in other people's business. All summer long she's given Anya and me no peace. She's afraid of a love affair between us. What business is it of hers? Besides, I've given no grounds for it, and I'm far from such vulgarity. We are above love.

MME. RANEVSKAYA And I suppose I'm beneath love? [*Anxiously.*] What can be keeping Leonid? If I only knew whether the estate has been sold or not. Such a calamity seems so incredible to me that I don't know what to think—I feel lost. . . . I could scream. . . . I could do something stupid. . . . Save me, Petya, tell me something, talk to me!

TROFIMOV Whether the estate is sold today or not, isn't it all one? That's all done with long ago—there's no turning back, the path is overgrown. Calm yourself, my dear. You mustn't deceive yourself. For once in your life you must face the truth.

MME. RANEVSKAYA What truth? You can see the truth, you can tell it from falsehood, but I seem to have lost my eyesight, I see nothing. You settle every great problem so boldly, but tell me, my dear boy, isn't it because you're young, because you don't yet know what one of your problems means in terms of suffering? You look ahead fearlessly, but isn't it because you don't see and don't expect anything dreadful, because life is still hidden from your young eyes? You're bolder, more honest, more profound than we are, but think hard, show just a bit of magnanimity, spare me. After all, I was born here, my father and mother lived here, and my grandfather; I love this house. Without the cherry orchard, my life has no meaning for me, and if it really must be sold, then sell me with the orchard. [*Embraces* TROFIMOV, *kisses him on the forehead.*] My son was drowned here. [*Weeps.*] Pity me, you good, kind fellow!

TROFIMOV You know, I feel for you with all my heart.

MME. RANEVSKAYA But that should have been said differently, so differently! [*Takes out her handkerchief—a telegram falls on the floor.*] My heart is so heavy today—you can't imagine! The noise here upsets me—my inmost being trembles at every sound—I'm shaking all over. But I can't go into my own room; I'm afraid to be alone. Don't condemn me, Petya. . . . I love you as though you were one of us, I would gladly let you marry Anya—I swear I would—only, my dear boy, you must study—you must take your degree—you do nothing, you let yourself be tossed by Fate from place to place—it's so strange. It's true, isn't it? And you should do something about your beard, to make it grow somehow! [*Laughs.*] You're so funny!

TROFIMOV [*Picks up the telegram.*] I've no wish to be a dandy.

MME. RANEVSKAYA That's a telegram from Paris. I get one every day. One yesterday and one today. That savage is ill again—he's in trouble again. He begs forgiveness, implores me to go to him, and really I ought to go to Paris to be near him. Your face is stern, Petya; but what is there to do, my dear boy? What am I to do? He's ill, he's alone and unhappy, and who is to look after him, who is to keep him from doing the wrong thing, who is to give him his medicine on time? And why hide it or keep still about it—I love him! That's clear. I love him, love him! He's a millstone round my neck, he'll drag me to the bottom, but I love that stone, I can't live without it. [*Presses* TROFIMOV's *hand.*] Don't think badly of me, Petya, and don't say anything, don't say . . .

TROFIMOV [*Through tears.*] Forgive me my frankness in heaven's name; but, you know, he robbed you!

MME. RANEVSKAYA No, no, no, you mustn't say such things! [*Covers her ears.*]

TROFIMOV But he's a scoundrel! You're the only one who doesn't know it. He's a petty scoundrel—a nonentity!

MME. RANEVSKAYA [*Controlling her anger.*] You are twenty-six or twenty-seven years old, but you're still a schoolboy.

TROFIMOV That may be.

MME. RANEVSKAYA You should be a man at your age. You should understand people who love—and ought to be in love yourself. You ought to fall in love! [*Angrily.*] Yes, yes! And it's not purity in you, it's prudishness, you're simply a queer fish, a comical freak!

TROFIMOV [*Horrified.*] What is she saying?

MME. RANEVSKAYA "I am above love!" You're not above love, but simple, as our Firs says, you're an addlehead. At your age not to have a mistress!

TROFIMOV [*Horrified.*] This is frightful! What is she saying! [*Goes rapidly into the ballroom, clutching his head.*] It's frightful—I can't stand it, I won't stay! [*Exits, but returns at once.*] All is over between us! [*Exits into anteroom.*]

MME. RANEVSKAYA [*Shouts after him.*] Petya! Wait! You absurd fellow, I was joking. Petya!

[*Sound of somebody running quickly downstairs and suddenly falling down with a crash.* ANYA *and* VARYA *scream. Sound of laughter a moment later.*]

MME. RANEVSKAYA What's happened?

[ANYA *runs in.*]

ANYA [*Laughing.*] Petya's fallen downstairs! [*Runs out.*]

MME. RANEVSKAYA What a queer bird that Petya is!

[STATIONMASTER, *standing in the middle of the ballroom, recites Alexey Tolstoy's "Magdalene,"*[3] *to which all listen, but after a few lines, the sound of a waltz is heard from the anteroom and the reading breaks off. All dance.* TROFIMOV, ANYA, VARYA *and* MME. RANEVSKAYA *enter from the anteroom.*]

MME. RANEVSKAYA Petya, you pure soul, please forgive me. . . . Let's dance. [*Dances with* PETYA, ANYA *and* VARYA *dance.* FIRS *enters, puts his stick down by the side door.* YASHA *enters from the drawing room and watches the dancers.*]

YASHA Well, Grandfather?

FIRS I'm not feeling well. In the old days it was generals, barons, and admirals that were dancing at our balls, and now we have to send for the Post Office Clerk and the Stationmaster, and even they aren't too glad to come. I feel kind of shaky. The old master that's gone, their grandfather, dosed everyone with sealing wax, whatever ailed 'em. I've been taking sealing wax every day for twenty years or more. Perhaps that's what's kept me alive.

YASHA I'm fed up with you, Grandpop. [*Yawns.*] It's time you croaked.

FIRS Oh, you addlehead! [*Mumbles.*]

---

3. Called "The Sinning Woman" in Russian, it begins: "A bustling crowd with happy laughter, / with twanging lutes and clashing cymbals / with flowers and foliage all around / the colonnaded portico." Alexey Tolstoy (1817–1875), popular in his time as a dramatist and poet, was a distant relative of Leo Tolstoy.

[TROFIMOV *and* MME. RANEVSKAYA *dance from the ballroom into the drawing room.*]

MME. RANEVSKAYA   Merci. I'll sit down a while. [*Sits down.*] I'm tired.
  [*Enter* ANYA.]

ANYA [*Excitedly.*]   There was a man in the kitchen just now who said the cherry orchard was sold today.

MME. RANEVSKAYA   Sold to whom?

ANYA   He didn't say. He's gone. [*Dances off with* TROFIMOV.]

YASHA   It was some old man gabbing, a stranger.

FIRS   And Leonid Andreyevich isn't back yet, he hasn't come. And he's wearing his lightweight between-season overcoat; like enough, he'll catch cold. Ah, when they're young they're green.

MME. RANEVSKAYA   This is killing me. Go, Yasha, find out to whom it has been sold.

YASHA   But the old man left long ago. [*Laughs.*]

MME RANEVSKAYA   What are you laughing at? What are you pleased about?

YASHA   That Yepihodov is such a funny one. A funny fellow, Two-and-Twenty Troubles!

MME. RANEVSKAYA   Firs, if the estate is sold, where will you go?

FIRS   I'll go where you tell me.

MME. RANEVSKAYA   Why do you look like that? Are you ill? You ought to go to bed.

FIRS   Yes! [*With a snigger.*]   Me go to bed, and who's to hand things round? Who's to see to things? I'm the only one in the whole house.

YASHA [*To* MME. RANEVSKAYA.]   Lubov Andreyevna, allow me to ask a favor of you, be so kind! If you go back to Paris, take me with you, I beg you. It's positively impossible for me to stay here. [*Looking around; sotto voce.*] What's the use of talking? You see for yourself, it's an uncivilized country, the people have no morals, and then the boredom! The food in the kitchen's revolting, and besides there's this Firs wanders about mumbling all sorts of inappropriate words. Take me with you, be so kind!
  [*Enter* PISHCHIK.]

PISHCHIK   May I have the pleasure of a waltz with you, charming lady? [MME. RANEVSKAYA *accepts.*] All the same, enchanting lady, you must let me have 180 rubles. . . . You must let me have [*dancing*] just one hundred and eighty rubles. [*They pass into the ballroom.*]

YASHA [*Hums softly.*]   "Oh, wilt thou understand the tumult in my soul?"
  [*In the ballroom a figure in a gray top hat and checked trousers is jumping about and waving its arms; shouts:* "Bravo, Charlotta Ivanovna!"]

DUNYASHA [*Stopping to powder her face; to* FIRS.]   The young miss has ordered me to dance. There are so many gentlemen and not enough ladies. But dancing makes me dizzy, my heart begins to beat fast, Firs Nikolayevich. The Post Office Clerk said something to me just now that quite took my breath away.
  [*Music stops.*]

FIRS   What did he say?

DUNYASHA   "You're like a flower," he said.

YASHA [*Yawns.*]   What ignorance. [*Exits.*]

DUNYASHA   "Like a flower!" I'm such a delicate girl. I simply adore pretty speeches.

FIRS You'll come to a bad end.

[*Enter* YEPIHODOV.]

YEPIHODOV [*To* DUNYASHA.] You have no wish to see me, Avdotya Fyodorovna . . . as though I was some sort of insect. [*Sighs.*] Ah, life!

DUNYASHA What is it you want?

YEPIHODOV Indubitably you may be right. [*Sighs.*] But of course, if one looks at it from the point of view, if I may be allowed to say so, and apologizing for my frankness, you have completely reduced me to a state of mind. I know my fate. Every day some calamity befalls me, and I grew used to it long ago, so that I look upon my fate with a smile. You gave me your word, and though I—

DUNYASHA Let's talk about it later, please. But just now leave me alone, I am daydreaming. [*Plays with a fan.*]

YEPIHODOV A misfortune befalls me every day; and if I may be allowed to say so, I merely smile, I even laugh.

[*Enter* VARYA.]

VARYA [*To* YEPIHODOV.] Are you still here? What an impertinent fellow you are really! Run along, Dunyasha. [*To* YEPIHODOV.] Either you're playing billiards and breaking a cue, or you're wandering about the drawing room as though you were a guest.

YEPIHODOV You cannot, permit me to remark, penalize me.

VARYA I'm not penalizing you; I'm just telling you. You merely wander from place to place, and don't do your work. We keep you as a clerk, but heaven knows what for.

YEPIHODOV [*Offended.*] Whether I work or whether I walk, whether I eat or whether I play billiards, is a matter to be discussed only by persons of understanding and of mature years.

VARYA [*Enraged.*] You dare say that to me—you dare? You mean to say I've no understanding? Get out of here at once! This minute!

YEPIHODOV [*Scared.*] I beg you to express yourself delicately.

VARYA [*Beside herself.*] Clear out this minute! Out with you!

[YEPIHODOV *goes toward the door,* VARYA *following.*]

VARYA Two-and-Twenty Troubles! Get out—don't let me set eyes on you again!

[*Exit* YEPIHODOV. *His voice is heard behind the door: "I shall lodge a complaint against you!"*]

VARYA Oh, you're coming back? [*She seizes the stick left near door by* FIRS.] Well, come then . . . come . . . I'll show you. . . . Ah, you're coming? You're coming? . . . Come . . . [*Swings the stick just as* LOPAHIN *enters.*]

LOPAHIN Thank you kindly.

VARYA [*Angrily and mockingly.*] I'm sorry.

LOPAHIN It's nothing. Thank you kindly for your charming reception.

VARYA Don't mention it. [*Walks away, looks back and asks softly.*] I didn't hurt you, did I?

LOPAHIN Oh, no, not at all. I shall have a large bump, though.

[*Voices from the ballroom: "Lopahin is here! Lopahin!"* Enter PISHCHIK.]

PISHCHIK My eyes do see, my ears do hear! [*Kisses* LOPAHIN.] You smell of cognac, my dear friend. And we've been celebrating here, too.

[*Enter* MME. RANEVSKAYA.]

MME. RANEVSKAYA   Is that you, Yermolay Alexeyevich? What kept you so long? Where's Leonid?

LOPAHIN   Leonid Andreyevich arrived with me. He's coming.

MME. RANEVSKAYA   Well, what happened? Did the sale take place? Speak!

LOPAHIN [*Embarrassed, fearful of revealing his joy.*]   The sale was over at four o'clock. We missed the train—had to wait till half-past nine. [*Sighing heavily.*] Ugh. I'm a little dizzy.

> [*Enter* GAYEV: *In his right hand he holds parcels, with his left he is wiping away his tears.*]

MME. RANEVSKAYA   Well, Leonid? What news? [*Impatiently, through tears.*] Be quick, for God's sake!

GAYEV [*Not answering, simply waves his hand. Weeping, to* FIRS.]   Here, take these; anchovies, Kerch herrings . . . I haven't eaten all day. What I've been through! [*The click of billiard balls comes through the open door of the billiard room and* YASHA's *voice is heard:* "Seven and eighteen!" GAYEV's *expression changes, he no longer weeps.*] I'm terribly tired. Firs, help me change. [*Exits, followed by* FIRS.]

PISHCHIK   How about the sale? Tell us what happened.

MME. RANEVSKAYA   Is the cherry orchard sold?

LOPAHIN   Sold.

MME. RANEVSKAYA   Who bought it?

LOPAHIN   I bought it.

> [*Pause.* MME. RANEVSKAYA *is overcome. She would fall to the floor, were it not for the chair and table near which she stands.* VARYA *takes the keys from her belt, flings them on the floor in the middle of the drawing room and goes out.*]

LOPAHIN   I bought it. Wait a bit, ladies and gentlemen, please, my head is swimming, I can't talk. [*Laughs.*] We got to the auction and Deriganov was there already. Leonid Andreyevich had only 15,000 and straight off Deriganov bid 30,000 over and above the mortgage. I saw how the land lay, got into the fight, bid 40,000. He bid 45,000. I bid fifty-five. He kept adding five thousands, I ten. Well . . . it came to an end. I bid ninety above the mortgage and the estate was knocked down to me. Now the cherry orchard's mine! Mine! [*Laughs uproariously.*] Lord! God in Heaven! The cherry orchard's mine! Tell me that I'm drunk—out of my mind—that it's all a dream. [*Stamps his feet.*] Don't laugh at me! If my father and my grandfather could rise from their graves and see all that has happened—how their Yermolay, who used to be flogged, their half-literate Yermolay, who used to run about barefoot in winter, how that very Yermolay has bought the most magnificent estate in the world. I bought the estate where my father and grandfather were slaves, where they weren't even allowed to enter the kitchen. I am asleep—it's only a dream—I only imagine it. . . . It's the fruit of your imagination, wrapped in the darkness of the unknown! [*Picks up the keys, smiling genially.*] She threw down the keys, wants to show she's no longer mistress here. [*Jingles keys.*] Well, no matter. [*The band is warming up.*] Hey, musicians! Strike up! I want to hear you! Come, everybody, and see how Yermolay Lopahin will lay the ax to the cherry orchard and how the trees will fall to the ground. We will build summer cottages there, and our grandsons and great grandsons will see a new life here. Music! Strike up!

[*The band starts to play.* MME. RANEVSKAYA *has sunk into a chair and is weeping bitterly.*]

LOPAHIN [*Reproachfully.*] Why, why didn't you listen to me? My dear friend, my poor friend, you can't bring it back now. [*Tearfully.*] Oh, if only this were over quickly! Oh, if only our wretched, disordered life were changed!

PISHCHIK [*Takes him by the arm; sotto voce.*] She's crying. Let's go into the ballroom. Let her be alone. Come. [*Takes his arm and leads him into the ballroom.*]

LOPAHIN What's the matter? Musicians, play so I can hear you! Let me have things the way I want them. [*Ironically.*] Here comes the new master, the owner of the cherry orchard. [*Accidentally he trips over a little table, almost upsetting the candelabra.*] I can pay for everything. [*Exits with* PISHCHIK.]

[MME. RANEVSKAYA, *alone, sits huddled up, weeping bitterly. Music plays softly. Enter* ANYA *and* TROFIMOV *quickly.* ANYA *goes to her mother and falls on her knees before her.* TROFIMOV *stands in the doorway.*]

ANYA Mamma, Mamma, you're crying! Dear, kind, good Mamma, my precious, I love you, I bless you! The cherry orchard is sold, it's gone, that's true, quite true. But don't cry, Mamma, life is still before you, you still have your kind, pure heart. Let us go, let us go away from here, darling. We will plant a new orchard, even more luxuriant than this one. You will see it, you will understand, and like the sun at evening, joy—deep, tranquil joy—will sink into your soul, and you will smile, Mamma. Come, darling, let us go.

Act IV

Scene as in Act I. No window curtains or pictures, only a little furniture, piled up in a corner, as if for sale. A sense of emptiness. Near the outer door and at the back, suitcases, bundles, etc., are piled up. A door open on the left and the voices of VARYA *and* ANYA *are heard.* LOPAHIN *stands waiting.* YASHA *holds a tray with glasses full of champagne.* YEPIHODOV *in the anteroom is tying up a box. Behind the scene a hum of voices: peasants have come to say good-bye. Voice of* GAYEV: "Thanks, brothers, thank you."*

YASHA The country folk have come to say good-bye. In my opinion, Yermolay Alexeyevich, they are kindly souls, but there's nothing in their heads.

[*The hum dies away. Enter* MME. RANEVSKAYA *and* GAYEV: *She is not crying, but is pale, her face twitches and she cannot speak.*]

GAYEV You gave them your purse, Luba. That won't do! That won't do!

MME. RANEVSKAYA I couldn't help it! I couldn't! [*They go out.*]

LOPAHIN [*Calls after them.*] Please, I beg you, have a glass at parting. I didn't think of bringing any champagne from town and at the station I could find only one bottle. Please, won't you? [*Pause.*] What's the matter, ladies and gentlemen, don't you want any? [*Moves away from the door.*] If I'd known, I wouldn't have bought it. Well, then I won't drink any, either. [YASHA *carefully sets the tray down on a chair.*] At least you have a glass, Yasha.

YASHA Here's to the travelers! And good luck to those that stay! [*Drinks.*] This champagne isn't the real stuff, I can assure you.

LOPAHIN Eight rubles a bottle. [*Pause.*] It's devilishly cold here.

YASHA They didn't light the stoves today—it wasn't worth it, since we're leaving. [*Laughs.*]

LOPAHIN Why are you laughing?

YASHA It's just that I'm pleased.

LOPAHIN It's October, yet it's as still and sunny as though it were summer. Good weather for building. [*Looks at his watch, and speaks off.*] Bear in mind, ladies and gentlemen, the train goes in forty-seven minutes, so you ought to start for the station in twenty minutes. Better hurry up!

[*Enter* TROFIMOV, *wearing an overcoat.*]

TROFIMOV I think it's time to start. The carriages are at the door. The devil only knows what's become of my rubbers; they've disappeared. [*Calling off.*] Anya! My rubbers are gone. I can't find them.

LOPAHIN I've got to go to Kharkov. I'll take the same train you do. I'll spend the winter in Kharkov. I've been hanging round here with you, till I'm worn out with loafing. I can't live without work—I don't know what to do with my hands, they dangle as if they didn't belong to me.

TROFIMOV Well, we'll soon be gone, then you can go on with your useful labors again.

LOPAHIN Have a glass.

TROFIMOV No, I won't.

LOPAHIN So you're going to Moscow now?

TROFIMOV Yes, I'll see them into town, and tomorrow I'll go on to Moscow.

LOPAHIN Well, I'll wager the professors aren't giving any lectures, they're waiting for you to come.

TROFIMOV That's none of your business.

LOPAHIN: Just how many years have you been at the university?

TROFIMOV Can't you think of something new? Your joke's stale and flat. [*Looking for his rubbers.*] We'll probably never see each other again, so allow me to give you a piece of advice at parting: don't wave your hands about! Get out of the habit. And another thing: building bungalows, figuring that summer residents will eventually become small farmers, figuring like that is just another form of waving your hands about. . . . Never mind, I love you anyway; you have fine, delicate fingers, like an artist; you have a fine delicate soul.

LOPAHIN [*Embracing him.*] Good-bye, my dear fellow. Thank you for everything. Let me give you some money for the journey, if you need it.

TROFIMOV What for? I don't need it.

LOPAHIN But you haven't any.

TROFIMOV Yes, I have, thank you. I got some money for a translation—here it is in my pocket. [*Anxiously.*] But where are my rubbers?

VARYA [*From the next room.*] Here! Take the nasty things. [*Flings a pair of rubbers onto the stage.*]

TROFIMOV What are you so cross about, Varya? Hm . . . and these are not my rubbers.

LOPAHIN I sowed three thousand acres of poppies in the spring, and now I've made 40,000 on them, clear profit; and when my poppies were in bloom, what a picture it was! So, as I say, I made 40,000; and I am offering you a loan because I can afford it. Why turn up your nose at it? I am a peasant—I speak bluntly.

TROFIMOV Your father was a peasant, mine was a druggist—that proves absolutely nothing whatever. [LOPAHIN *takes out his wallet.*] Don't, put that away! If you were to offer me two hundred thousand, I wouldn't take it. I'm a free man. And everything that all of you, rich and poor alike, value so highly and hold so dear hasn't the slightest power over me. It's like so much fluff floating in the air. I can get on without you, I can pass you by, I'm strong and proud. Mankind is moving toward the highest truth, toward the highest happiness possible on earth, and I am in the front ranks.

LOPAHIN Will you get there?

TROFIMOV I will. [*Pause.*] I will get there, or I will show others the way to get there.

[*The sound of axes chopping down trees is heard in the distance.*]

LOPAHIN Well, good-bye, my dear fellow. It's time to leave. We turn up our noses at one another, but life goes on just the same. When I'm working hard, without resting, my mind is easier, and it seems to me that I, too, know why I exist. But how many people are there in Russia, brother, who exist nobody knows why? Well, it doesn't matter. That's not what makes the wheels go round. They say Leonid Andreyevich has taken a position in the bank, 6,000 rubles a year. Only, of course, he won't stick to it, he's too lazy. . . .

ANYA [*In the doorway.*] Mamma begs you not to start cutting down the cherry trees until she's gone.

TROFIMOV Really, you should have more tact! [*Exits.*]

LOPAHIN Right away—right away! Those men . . . [*Exits.*]

ANYA Has Firs been taken to the hospital?

YASHA I told them this morning. They must have taken him.

ANYA [*To* YEPIHODOV, *who crosses the room.*] Yepihodov, please find out if Firs has been taken to the hospital.

YASHA [*Offended.*] I told Yegor this morning. Why ask a dozen times?

YEPIHODOV The aged Firs, in my definitive opinion, is beyond mending. It's time he was gathered to his fathers. And I can only envy him. [*Puts a suitcase down on a hat box and crushes it.*] There now, of course, I knew it! [*Exits.*]

YASHA [*Mockingly.*] Two-and-Twenty Troubles!

VARYA [*Through the door.*] Has Firs been taken to the hospital?

ANYA Yes.

VARYA Then why wasn't the note for the doctor taken too?

ANYA Oh! Then someone must take it to him. [*Exits.*]

VARYA [*From adjoining room.*] Where's Yasha? Tell him his mother's come and wants to say good-bye.

YASHA [*Waves his hand.*] She tries my patience.

[DUNYASHA *has been occupied with the luggage. Seeing* YASHA *alone, she goes up to him.*]

DUNYASHA You might just give me one little look, Yasha. You're going away. . . . You're leaving me . . . [*Weeps and throws herself on his neck.*]

YASHA What's there to cry about? [*Drinks champagne.*] In six days I shall be in Paris again. Tomorrow we get into an express train and off we go, that's the last you'll see of us. . . . I can scarcely believe it. *Vive la France!*[4] It don't suit me here, I just can't live here. That's all there is to it. I'm fed up with the ignorance here, I've had enough of it. [*Drinks champagne.*] What's there to cry about? Behave yourself properly, and you'll have no cause to cry.

DUNYASHA [*Powders her face, looking in pocket mirror.*] Do send me a letter from Paris. You know I loved you, Yasha, how I loved you! I'm a delicate creature, Yasha.

YASHA Somebody's coming! [*Busies himself with the luggage; hums softly.*]
[*Enter* MME. RANEVSKAYA, GAYEV, ANYA, *and* CHARLOTTA.]

GAYEV We ought to be leaving. We haven't much time. [*Looks at* YASHA.] Who smells of herring?

MME. RANEVSKAYA In about ten minutes we should be getting into the carriages. [*Looks around the room.*] Good-bye, dear old home, good-bye, grandfather. Winter will pass, spring will come, you will no longer be here, they will have torn you down. How much these walls have seen! [*Kisses* ANYA *warmly.*] My treasure, how radiant you look! Your eyes are sparkling like diamonds. Are you glad? Very?

ANYA [*Gaily.*] Very glad. A new life is beginning, Mamma.

GAYEV: Well, really, everything is all right now. Before the cherry orchard was sold, we all fretted and suffered; but afterward, when the question was settled finally and irrevocably, we all calmed down, and even felt quite cheerful. I'm a bank employee now, a financier. The yellow ball in the side pocket! And anyhow, you are looking better, Luba, there's no doubt of that.

MME. RANEVSKAYA Yes, my nerves are better, that's true. [*She is handed her hat and coat.*] I sleep well. Carry out my things, Yasha. It's time. [*To* ANYA.] We shall soon see each other again, my little girl. I'm going to Paris, I'll live there on the money your great-aunt sent us to buy the estate with— long live Auntie! But that money won't last long.

ANYA You'll come back soon, soon, Mamma, won't you? Meanwhile I'll study. I'll pass my high school examination, and then I'll go to work and help you. We'll read all kinds of books together, Mamma, won't we? [*Kisses her mother's hands.*] We'll read in the autumn evenings, we'll read lots of books, and a new wonderful world will open up before us. [*Falls into a revery.*] Mamma, do come back.

MME. RANEVSKAYA I will come back, my precious.
[*Embraces her daughter. Enter* LOPAHIN *and* CHARLOTTA, *who is humming softly.*]

GAYEV Charlotta's happy: she's singing.

CHARLOTTA [*Picks up a bundle and holds it like a baby in swaddling clothes.*] Bye, baby, bye. [*A baby is heard crying:* "Wah! Wah!"] Hush, hush, my pet, my little one. ["Wah! Wah!"] I'm so sorry for you! [*Throws the bundle down.*] You will find me a position, won't you? I can't go on like this.

LOPAHIN We'll find one for you, Charlotta Ivanovna, don't worry.

GAYEV Everyone's leaving us. Varya's going away. We've suddenly become of no use.

---

4. Long live France! (French).

CHARLOTTA There's no place for me to live in town, I must go away. [*Hums.*]

[*Enter* PISHCHIK.]

LOPAHIN There's nature's masterpiece!

PISHCHIK [*Gasping.*] Oh . . . let me get my breath . . . I'm in agony. . . . Esteemed friends . . . Give me a drink of water. . . .

GAYEV Wants some money, I suppose. No, thank you . . . I'll keep out of harm's way. [*Exits.*]

PISHCHIK It's a long while since I've been to see you, most charming lady. [*To* LOPAHIN.] So you are here . . . glad to see you, you intellectual giant . . . There . . . [*Gives* LOPAHIN *money.*] Here's 400 rubles, and I still owe you 840.

LOPAHIN [*Shrugging his shoulders in bewilderment.*] I must be dreaming. . . . Where did you get it?

PISHCHIK Wait a minute . . . it's hot. . . . A most extraordinary event! Some Englishmen came to my place and found some sort of white clay on my land . . . [*To* MME. RANEVSKAYA.] And 400 for you . . . most lovely . . . most wonderful . . . [*Hands her the money.*] The rest later. [*Drinks water.*] A young man in the train was telling me just now that a great philosopher recommends jumping off roofs. "Jump!" says he; "that's the long and the short of it!" [*In amazement.*] Just imagine! Some more water!

LOPAHIN What Englishmen?

PISHCHIK I leased them the tract with the clay on it for twenty-four years. . . . And now, forgive me, I can't stay. . . . I must be dashing on. . . . I'm going over to Znoikov . . . to Kardamanov . . . I owe them all money . . . [*Drinks water.*] Good-bye, everybody . . . I'll look in on Thursday . . .

MME. RANEVSKAYA We're just moving into town; and tomorrow I go abroad.

PISHCHIK [*Upset.*] What? Why into town? That's why the furniture is like that . . . and the suitcases. . . . Well, never mind! [*Through tears.*] Never mind . . . men of colossal intellect, these Englishmen. . . . Never mind . . . Be happy. God will come to your help. . . . Never mind . . . everything in this world comes to an end. [*Kisses* MME. RANEVSKAYA's *hand.*] If the rumor reaches you that it's all up with me, remember this old . . . horse, and say: "Once there lived a certain . . . Simeonov-Pishchik . . . the kingdom of Heaven be his. . . ." Glorious weather! . . . Yes . . . [*Exits, in great confusion, but at once returns and says in the doorway.*] My daughter Dashenka sends her regards. [*Exits.*]

MME. RANEVSKAYA Now we can go. I leave with two cares weighing on me. The first is poor old Firs. [*Glancing at her watch.*] We still have about five minutes.

ANYA Mamma, Firs has already been taken to the hospital. Yasha sent him there this morning.

MME. RANEVSKAYA My other worry is Varya. She's used to getting up early and working; and now, with no work to do, she is like a fish out of water. She has grown thin and pale, and keeps crying, poor soul. [*Pause.*] You know this very well, Yermolay Alexeyevich; I dreamed of seeing her married to you, and it looked as though that's how it would be. [*Whispers to* ANYA, *who nods to* CHARLOTTA *and both go out.*] She loves you. You find her attractive. I don't know, I don't know why it is you seem to avoid each other; I can't understand it.

LOPAHIN   To tell you the truth, I don't understand it myself. It's all a puzzle. If there's still time, I'm ready now, at once. Let's settle it straight off, and have done with it! Without you, I feel I'll never be able to propose.

MME. RANEVSKAYA   That's splendid. After all, it will only take a minute. I'll call her at once. . . .

LOPAHIN   And luckily, here's champagne, too. [*Looks at the glasses.*] Empty! Somebody's drunk it all. [*Yasha coughs.*] That's what you might call guzzling . . .

MME. RANEVSKAYA [*Animatedly.*]   Excellent! We'll go and leave you alone. Yasha, *allez!*[5] I'll call her. [*At the door.*] Varya, leave everything and come here. Come! [*Exits with* YASHA.]

LOPAHIN [*Looking at his watch.*]   Yes . . . [*Pause behind the door, smothered laughter and whispering; at last, enter* VARYA.]

VARYA [*Looking over the luggage in leisurely fashion.*]   Strange, I can't find it . . .

LOPAHIN   What are you looking for?

VARYA   Packed it myself, and I don't remember . . . [*Pause.*]

LOPAHIN   Where are you going now, Varya?

VARYA   I? To the Ragulins'. I've arranged to take charge there—as housekeeper, if you like.

LOPAHIN   At Yashnevo? About fifty miles from here. [*Pause.*] Well, life in this house is ended!

VARYA [*Examining luggage.*]   Where is it? Perhaps I put it in the chest. Yes, life in this house is ended. . . . There will be no more of it.

LOPAHIN   And I'm just off to Kharkov—by this next train. I've a lot to do there. I'm leaving Yepihodov here . . . I've taken him on.

VARYA   Oh!

LOPAHIN   Last year at this time, it was snowing, if you remember, but now it's sunny and there's no wind. It's cold, though. . . . It must be three below.

VARYA   I didn't look. [*Pause.*] And besides, our thermometer's broken. [*Pause.* VOICE   *from the yard:* "Yermolay Alexeyevich!"]

LOPAHIN [*As if he had been waiting for the call.*]   This minute! [*Exits quickly.*]

[VARYA: *sits on the floor and sobs quietly, her head on a bundle of clothes. Enter* MME. RANEVSKAYA *cautiously.*]

MME. RANEVSKAYA   Well? [*Pause.*] We must be going.

VARYA [*Wiping her eyes.*]   Yes, it's time, Mamma dear. I'll be able to get to the Ragulins' today, if only we don't miss the train.

MME. RANEVSKAYA [*At the door.*]   Anya, put your things on.

[*Enter* ANYA, GAYEV, CHARLOTTA. GAYEV *wears a heavy overcoat with a hood. Enter servants and coachmen.* YEPIHODOV *bustles about the luggage.*]

MME. RANEVSKAYA   Now we can start on our journey.

ANYA [*Joyfully.*]   On our journey!

GAYEV   My friends, my dear, cherished friends, leaving this house forever, can I be silent? Can I, at leave-taking, refrain from giving utterance to those emotions that now fill my being?

5. Go on! (French).

ANYA [*Imploringly.*]   Uncle!

VARYA   Uncle, Uncle dear, don't.

GAYEV [*Forlornly.*]   I'll bank the yellow in the side pocket . . . I'll be silent . . .

>[*Enter* TROFIMOV, *then* LOPAHIN.]

TROFIMOV   Well, ladies and gentlemen, it's time to leave.

LOPAHIN   Yepihodov, my coat.

MME. RANEVSKAYA   I'll sit down just a minute. It seems as though I'd never before seen what the walls of this house were like, the ceilings, and now I look at them hungrily, with such tender affection.

GAYEV   I remember when I was six years old sitting on that window sill on Whitsunday,[6] watching my father going to church.

MME. RANEVSKAYA   Has everything been taken?

LOPAHIN   I think so. [*Putting on his overcoat.*] Yepihodov, see that everything's in order.

YEPIHODOV [*In a husky voice.*]   You needn't worry, Yermolay Alexeyevich.

LOPAHIN   What's the matter with your voice?

YEPIHODOV   I just had a drink of water. I must have swallowed something.

YASHA [*Contemptuously.*]   What ignorance!

MME. RANEVSKAYA   When we're gone, not a soul will be left here.

LOPAHIN   Until the spring.

>[VARYA *pulls an umbrella out of a bundle, as though about to hit someone with it.* LOPAHIN *pretends to be frightened.*]

VARYA   Come, come, I had no such idea!

TROFIMOV   Ladies and gentlemen, let's get into the carriages—it's time. The train will be in directly.

VARYA   Petya, there they are, your rubbers, by that trunk. [*Tearfully.*] And what dirty old things, they are!

TROFIMOV [*Puts on rubbers.*]   Let's go, ladies and gentlemen.

GAYEV [*Greatly upset, afraid of breaking down.*]   The train . . . the station. . . . Three cushions in the side pocket, I'll bank this one in the corner . . .

MME. RANEVSKAYA   Let's go.

LOPAHIN   Are we all here? No one in there? [*Locks the side door on the left.*] There are some things stored here, better lock up. Let us go!

ANYA   Good-bye, old house! Good-bye, old life!

TROFIMOV   Hail to you, new life!

>[*Exits with* ANYA: VARYA *looks round the room and goes out slowly.* YASHA *and* CHARLOTTA *with her dog go out.*]

LOPAHIN   And so, until the spring. Go along, friends . . . Bye-bye! [*Exits.*]

>[MME. RANEVSKAYA *and* GAYEV *remain alone. As though they had been waiting for this, they throw themselves on each other's necks, and break into subdued, restrained sobs, afraid of being overheard.*]

GAYEV [*In despair.*]   My sister! My sister!

MME. RANEVSKAYA   Oh, my orchard—my dear, sweet, beautiful orchard! My life, my youth, my happiness—good-bye! Good-bye!

>[*Voice of* ANYA, *gay and summoning:* "*Mamma!*" *Voice of* TROFIMOV, *gay and excited:* "*Halloo!*"]

---

6. Or Pentecost, a Christian festival occurring on the seventh Sunday after Easter.

MME. RANEVSKAYA   One last look at the walls, at the windows. . . . Our poor
mother loved to walk about this room . . .

GAYEV   My sister, my sister!

[*Voice of* ANYA: "Mamma!" *Voice of* TROFIMOV: "Halloo!"]

MME. RANEVSKAYA   We're coming.

> [*They go out. The stage is empty. The sound of doors being locked, of carriages driving away. Then silence. In the stillness is heard the muffled sound of the ax striking a tree, a mournful, lonely sound.*
>
> *Footsteps are heard.* FIRS *appears in the doorway on the right. He is dressed as usual in a jacket and white waistcoat and wears slippers. He is ill.*]

FIRS [*Goes to the door, tries the handle.*]   Locked! They've gone . . . [*Sits down on the sofa.*] They've forgotten me. . . . Never mind . . . I'll sit here a bit . . . I'll wager Leonid Andreyevich hasn't put his fur coat on, he's gone off in his light overcoat . . . [*Sighs anxiously.*] I didn't keep an eye on him. . . . Ah, when they're young, they're green . . . [*Mumbles something indistinguishable.*] Life has gone by as if I had never lived. [*Lies down.*] I'll lie down a while . . . There's no strength left in you, old fellow; nothing is left, nothing. Ah, you addlehead!

> [*Lies motionless. A distant sound is heard coming from the sky, as it were, the sound of a snapping string mournfully dying away. All is still again, and nothing is heard but the strokes of the ax against a tree far away in the orchard.*]

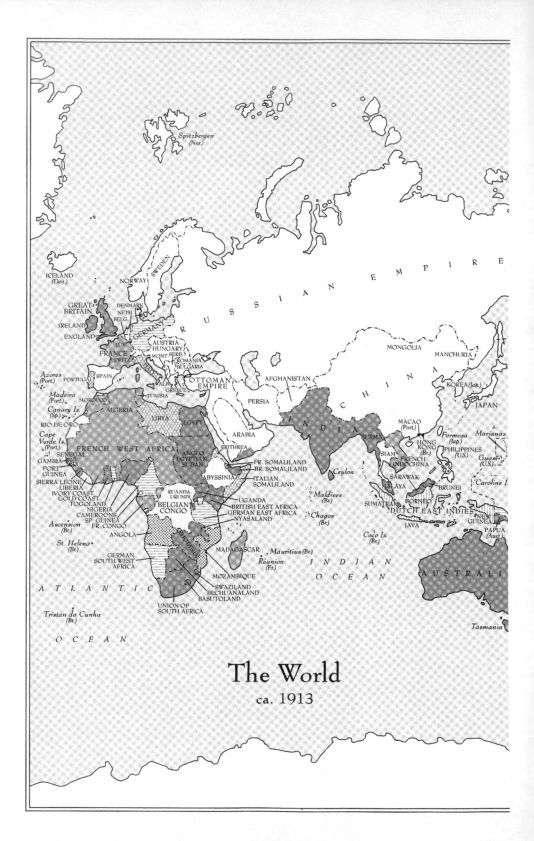

The World

ca. 1913

GREENLAND
(Den.)

ALASKA
(U.S.)

C A N A D A

A T L A N T I C

O C E A N

U N I T E D
S T A T E S

P A C I F I C

O C E A N

Bermuda
(Br.)

Bahamas (Br.)

HAITI
DOMINICAN REPUBLIC
Puerto Rico (U.S.)

Hawaiian Islands
(U.S.)

BR.
HONDURAS

CUBA

Guadeloupe (Fr.)
Martinique (Fr.)

JAMAICA

Grenada
(Br.)

Barbados (Br.)
Trinidad (Br.)

Marshall Is.

German
Pacific
Islands

GUATEMALA
EL SALVADOR
HONDURAS
NICARAGUA
COSTA RICA

VENEZUELA

PANAMA

BR. GUIANA
DUTCH GUIANA
FR. GUIANA

Bismarck
Archipelago

P A C I F I C

COLOMBIA

Solomon Is. (Br.)

Galapagos Is.

ECUADOR

New Hebrides
(Br. & Fr.)

Marquesas Is.

French Polynesia

B R A Z I L

PERU

New Caledonia
(Fr.)

Tahiti

BOLIVIA

O C E A N

NEW
ZEALAND

CHILE

ARGENTINA

PARAGUAY

URUGUAY

Colonial Empires

Falkland Is.
(Br.)

British

Dutch

French

Italian

German

Portuguese

Chazaud

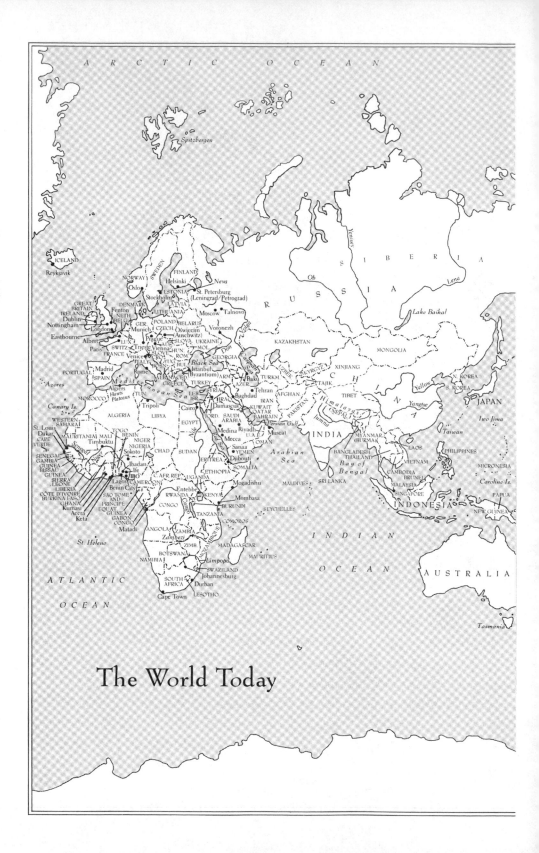

The World Today

The Twentieth Century

The twentieth century was not the first age to consider itself modern. Other periods have made a point of being consciously new: the Renaissance, with the dawn of secular humanism and "modern" artistic perspectives; the Enlightenment, with its "quarrel of the ancients and moderns"; or even the late fifth century B.C.E. in Athens, in the cultural battles celebrated by Aristophanes. The Victorians of the late nineteenth century believed that they ushered in a truly modern age, created by the achievements of science and the Industrial Revolution. Their faith in progress was echoed in art and literature that—although it often rejected industrial society—was intent on forcing open new horizons of thought. "One must be absolutely modern," proclaimed the poet Arthur Rimbaud.

There is, nonetheless, a particular stamp to the twentieth century's idea of modernity: it was not so much comparative as *interrogative*, and it inquired *how* we know *what* we know, rather than merely rejecting previous modes of thought (which it also did). Employing the tools of reason and scientific investigation, uncovering more and more complex structures of the natural universe, it also confronted the possibility that "knowledge" was not fixed or stable and that much of what we think we know reflects the questions we ask and the methods we use to obtain answers. Modernity in the twentieth century was not merely an opposition of old and new perspectives, but a philosophical interrogation of what it means to have a perspective at all. For writers and artists, this interrogation brought new insights as well as further questions about the means of expression available for representing them.

These insights did not remain static, nor did the literature related to them: the "modernism" that emerged as an innovative literary style early in the century evolved over many years before being absorbed into diverse approaches that emphasized cultural contexts rather than the implications of form. Its formal innovations were not lost, nor was their significance forgotten: they simply became part of the writer's trade. If the first half of the century became known as a period of modernist and then "high modernist" style, the second half extended the exploration of modernity into different fields with "postmodernist" thought that criticized the universalist assumptions of modernist thought or with "postcolonial" and related views that considered "postmodern" merely a label, an outgrowth of modernism, and turned to their own separately defined missions.

In science, philosophy, social theory, and the arts, the nineteenth century defined many of the issues that would become crucial in the twentieth. Unprecedented developments in science had encouraged people to believe that they would soon master all the secrets of the universe and revealed a faith in progress and rational solutions that had not been seen since the Enlightenment. The discovery of important underlying structures in chemistry (atomic theory, the periodic table of elements), physics (unified field theory), and astronomy seemed to make the universe more rational and, hence, predictable. Technological applications suggested that these discoveries would serve humanity, not master it: photography provided unique documentary records, for example, and locomotives and steamships exploited discoveries in thermodynamics to offer rapid transportation throughout the world. The history of living nature itself became an object of study when Charles Darwin (1809–1882) examined the evolution of species according to material evidence, without reference to divine laws or purpose, and proposed his enormously influential theories of natural selection and the mutability of species.

The appeal of large explanatory systems was seen in other fields as well, notably in the positivist philosophy of Auguste Comte (1798–1857) and in the economic and social theories of Karl Marx (1818–1883). Comte held that scientific method constituted a total worldview by which everything would ultimately be explained, including human society. He outlined a science of humanity that would analyze and define the laws governing human society (the beginning of sociology). Comte's positivism has come to stand for an excessive faith in the power of science and rational inquiry to discover unambiguous answers for all problems. Twentieth-century writers pointed out that positivism's belief in the scientific "rightness" of certain ideas made it blind to its own bias and created inflexible attitudes with damaging consequences in real life. Marx's "Manifesto of the Communist Party" (1848) and *Capital* (1867) proposed that the most basic material needs—food, shelter, and the social relationships enabling group survival—provided an economic foundation from which all other aspects of human culture were derived. His vision of modern workers as alienated cogs in the industrial economic machine, no longer owning their own labor, expressed for many the antihuman aspect of modern technological progress. Yet he also believed in the power of rational systems to find answers for social ills; he described the division of modern industrial society into the two competing forces of capital and labor (the proletariat), and proposed the theory of dialectical materialism to explain the processes of history.

One of the strongest opponents of positivism and its faith in rational solutions was the German philosopher Friedrich Nietzsche (1844–1900). Nietzsche focused on the individual, not society, and admired only the *Übermensch*, the superhuman being who refuses to be bound by the prevailing social paradigms of nationalism, Christianity, faith in science, loyalty to the state, or bourgeois civilized comfort. Nietzsche's insistence on the individual's complete freedom (and responsibility) in a world that lacks transcendental law ("God is dead") and his attack on the unimaginative mediocrity of mass society in the modern industrial world made him a powerful influence in the early years of the twentieth century.

The shape and intensity of this debate as well as its impact on the world at large were dictated for many years by a historical event that turned the generations of the early twentieth century against everything inherited from the recent past: the Great War, World War I (1914–18). Despite the confident rationalism of the political leaders of "Papa's Europe" (a term of resentment used by many to describe an authoritarian, patriarchal society that claimed to have all the answers), World War I had for the first time involved the whole continent of Europe and the United States in battle and was the first "total war" in which modern weapons spared no one, including civilians. Clearly, something was wrong. A generation of European and American youth was lost in the trenches, and many of the survivors resolved to reexamine the bases of certainty, the structures of knowledge, the systems of belief, and the repositories of authority in a society that had allowed such a war to occur. Their reaction would also be reflected in literature—not only in subject matter but, for many, in a new use of language, in new ways of representing our knowledge of the world, and, most especially, in new hesitations about subscribing to any single mode of understanding. They drew on areas beyond the intellect and interrogated the whole of human consciousness.

Various thinkers helped formulate alternatives to positivist rationalism. The French philosopher Henri Bergson (1859–1941) criticized scientific rationality as a mode of knowledge because human experience, he felt, could only be apprehended by consciousness. Instead of quantitative and logical inquiry, Bergson proposed intuiting the "immediate data of consciousness" as an alternate, nonscientific means of knowledge. Sigmund Freud (1856–1939), the founder of psychoanalysis, studied subconscious motives and instinctual drives to gain insights into human behavior. His essays and case studies argued that dreams and manias contain their own networks of meaning and that human beings cannot properly be understood without taking into consideration both the irrational and the rational levels of their existence. All are caught up, he suggested, in the process of mediating the same sexual drives and civilizational repressions that caused neurosis in his own patients. Freud focused attention on the way that everyday, "rational" behavior is shaped by unconscious impulses and hidden motivations, and on the way human beings actually create (and modify) their images of self through engaging in dialogue with others. His influence is so widespread that it is probably impossible for any post-Freud poet, novelist, or playwright—whether or not the author has ever read the psychoanalyst—to write without taking into consideration the psychological undercurrents of human behavior.

Positivism had assumed that language was an unambiguous tool for representing reality (a view parodied in "The sun is called a sun because it *looks* like a sun"). In contrast, the Swiss linguist Ferdinand de Saussure (1857–1913) and the Austrian philosopher Ludwig Wittgenstein (1889–1951) emphasized that language does not give us the "real thing" but a series of labels—"signifiers" pointing to a "signified." What works in conversation is not the thing itself but the way the label—the word used to describe it—provides a recognizable common ground for different speakers. In this perspective, both literature and linguistic systems are seen as *games*, combinations of pieces (words) and rules (grammar, syntax, and other conventions). Twentieth-century writers stressing the gamelike nature of language combine words and word fragments to exhibit the play of relationships, instead of struggling to find the "right word" dear to Gustave Flaubert.

Ever since Plato, philosophers have struggled systematically to understand the relationship between appearance and reality. Such issues were the central concern of the twentieth-century philosophy phenomenology (phenomena are literally "things as they appear") and its offshoot, existentialism. Both approaches investigated the role of perception in establishing our ideas of what is real. The phenomenology proposed by Edmund Husserl (1859–1938) described all consciousness as consciousness *of* something *by* someone and concluded that every object of study should be imagined in "brackets"—not as a thing in itself, but as implicated in a relationship between perceiver and perceived.

The ethical implications of this view were taken up by the philosophers Martin Heidegger (1889–1976) and Jean-Paul Sartre (1905–1980), who questioned the meaning of existence in a world without preexisting truths, values, or general laws. Heidegger's profoundly somber vision defined the "absurd" condition of human beings "thrown into the world" without any understanding of their fate. Sartre, more interested in social activism, derived from the same "absurd" freedom an ideal of human authenticity that consists in choosing our actions at each point and avoiding the bad faith of pretending that others are responsible for our choices. Albert Camus (1913–1960), writing at the same time as Sartre, offers in *The Guest* a good example of existentialism's emphasis on freedom, responsibility, and social "engagement."

Existentialism's popular appeal in the 1940s and 1950s was undoubtedly enhanced by the fact that it was a philosophic attempt to recover clear vision—and a basis for action—in a confused and meaningless world. The notion of philosophical absurdity corresponded to a very real confusion caused by the radical historical changes taking place in the first half of the century. By 1950, there had been two world wars, the second of which was truly global, and a sweeping realignment of geopolitical forces that saw the flourishing of Marxism and the establishment of major Communist states. Almost all the old monarchies had been overthrown, and colonial empires were being dismantled as the emerging nations of Africa and Asia struggled for independence and self-definition. The wielders of authority became the enormous buck-passing bureaucracies of the modern state, multinational corporations, international governmental organizations, and ethnic alliances. Transportation and telecommunications progressed to an extent envisaged only in earlier ages' science fiction and effectively shrank the global community. The rise of the modern industrial state set up new political, cultural, and economic tensions, the most important of which was a widening gulf between the West and "less developed" countries.

These changes in historical conditions had visible effects on literature and art. Cultural parochialism—the belief that there is only one correct view of the world (one's own)—was much harder to maintain when people traveled widely and experienced different ways of life. Racial and ethnic stereotypes were challenged, and traditional ideas of identity and social class were broken down. Romantic heroism and aristocratic rank seemed irrelevant to soldiers who died anonymously in the trenches of World War I, or to civilians killed at a distance by bombing raids, or to the millions of refugees and displaced persons created by wars and political persecution throughout the century. The conventional roles of the sexes came under examination. Women achieved civil rights that they had been denied for centuries: the right to vote (1920 in the United States), the right to have bank accounts and to own and control their own property, the right to be educated equally with men, and the right to enter professions not previously open to them. Technology became part of the modern literary consciousness, inspiring both enthusiasm and fear, and initiating all over again the question of human values in a society where so much could be done (and so many controlled) by the use of machines and mass media.

The literary and artistic movements of the twentieth century are part of this evolution; they were shaped by it and helped shape it for others. Many of these movements flourished in Europe or America and were exported to other parts of the globe, where they flourished or failed, according to their relevance for local conditions. Expressionism, Dadaism, Surrealism, and Futurism—each worth exploring—are all different ways of expressing the reality of the world.

Dada-Surrealism is the best-known and most influential twentieth-century movement, and the only one to have followers today. Dada began in Zürich, Switzerland, in 1916 as a movement of absolute revolt that set out to subvert authority and break all the rules (including those of art), hoping to liberate the creative imagination. Dada creations were attacks on the mind and emotions; both Dadaists and Surrealists emphasized a "revolution of the mind" that destabilized ordinary ways of looking at things. Freedom from conventional perspectives, they felt, was a first step in reforming society. Surrealists especially aimed to bring about a fuller awareness of human experience, including both conscious and unconscious states. In France, the *Surrealist Manifestoes* of 1924 and 1930 proclaimed that Surrealism was a means of expressing "the actual functioning of thought," "the total recuperation of our psychic force by a means that is nothing else than the dizzying descent into ourselves." The Surrealists experimented with various means to liberate the unconscious imagination and reach a sublime state they called "the marvelous": Dream writing, automatic writing (writing rapidly and continuously whatever comes to mind), riddle games, interruption and collage, and chiefly the creation of startling images opened the mind to new possibilities.

Known for its intensity, playfulness, and openness to change, Surrealism proved to be the most influential and enduring of these movements of revolt. By the end of the twentieth century, art and literature had absorbed the characteristic Surrealist themes of free play, antirationality, and the importance of the unconscious mind, and employed the preferred Surrealist techniques of collage, metamorphosis, and the blurring of dream and reality. In an ironic mark of success, commercial advertising also adopted Surrealist strategies, and the term *surrealist* became a convenient for unconventional or fantastic works whether or not they were connected to the movement.

Modernism is the usual term for a general change in attitudes and artistic strategy occurring at the beginning of the century, but there are many modernisms. Taken more narrowly, it refers to a group of Anglo-American writers (many associated with the Imagists of 1908–17) who favored clear, precise images and common speech and who thought of the work as an art object produced by consummate craft rather than as a statement of emotion. James Joyce, Ezra Pound, T. S. Eliot, William Faulkner, and Virginia Woolf are examples of Anglo-American modernism and of the larger modernism, too. In its broader sense, modernism reconstructed conventional images of the world and of human nature by changing the forms in which reality was usually represented. Modernist writers played with shifting and contradictory appearances to suggest the changing and uncertain nature of reality (Pirandello); they broke up the logically developing plot typical of the nineteenth-century novel and offered instead unexpected connections or sudden changes of perspective (Woolf, Faulkner); they used interior monologues and free association to express the rhythms of consciousness (Joyce). They drew attention to style instead of trying to make it transparent and made much greater use of image clusters, thematic associations, and musical patterning to supply the basic structures of both fiction and poetry. Modernists blended fantasy with reality while representing real historical or psychological dilemmas (Kafka) and explored age-old questions of human identity in terms of contemporary philosophy and psychology. These experiments with perspective and language, as disorienting as they often were, were still defined within the traditional concepts of individual psychological depth and the idea of the artwork as a coherent aesthetic whole. The combination of discontinuous, experimental style and a continuing belief in the wholeness of the human personality and of the artwork generally marks the early modernist tradition.

Modernism evolved after the mid-century, questioning—as "postmodernism"—some of its philosophical premises while continuing to explore the implications of language and linguistic form. Postmodernist writers viewed their recently canonized predecessors—Joyce, Proust, Eliot, Woolf, Mann, and Stevens, for example—as part of a conservative "high modernism" that championed formal innovation but preserved traditional roots in mainstream thought. In this view, the high-modernist quest for more profound insight and inclusive vision does not so much break with the past as it continues an idealist tradition reaching back to Homer and the Bible. In contrast, postmodernist writers created a network of allusions, interruptions, contradictions, and blurred reference as if to disorient a reader who seeks to reduce human events to one demonstrated meaning. Where high modernism wished to reveal a core of profound experience through innovative form, these rhetorical writers were suspicious of profundity: calling something "profound," after all, implies that it is especially true and valuable, and reflects the speaker's own value judgment. Modern authors who wished to avoid such judgments rejected images of depth and profundity, and limited themselves to inconclusive surface images. Readers will find that certain easily identified strategies are at work in much of this literature, strategies whose general aim is to avoid creating any fixed reference point or sense of completeness.

Without diminishing the description of social reality in earlier twentieth-century literature, one may say that Western literature in the latter half of the twentieth century gave unprecedented recognition to different ethnic, sexual, and cultural identities, both depicted as subject matter and embodied in narrative perspective. In many ways, the pluralism of literary styles and the willingness to blur the boundaries of previous generic and descriptive conventions corresponded to the diversity of a new geopolitical age as well as the increasing sophistication of scientific theory. Late-twentieth-century writers inhabited a world of shifting frontiers and massive waves of migration; of global markets and volatile economic conditions; of famines, continental epidemics, and terrorist attacks appearing in the daily news. The United Nations had 191 members, and about sixty-eight hundred languages were spoken around the globe: at the same time, English emerged as a medium of global communication. Postcolonial societies struggled with a mixed heritage of indigenous and colonial traditions, debating whether to reject (with difficulty) the colonizer's language and culture or to develop and control the rich hybridity of existing cultural consciousness. Cultural, racial, religious, and gender issues came to the forefront of political controversy, assuming different values in different parts of the world. Writers in the later twentieth century did not emulate the essentialism of earlier literature, therefore, but gave difference its due; instead of revealing the similarities among human beings, they were likely to represent a profusion of styles and perspectives that expressed the range and diversity of individual experience and contemporary cultural perspectives. Chinua Achebe has described this impulse to see life from different angles in terms of an old Igbo belief: "Wherever Something stands, Something Else will stand beside it. Nothing is absolute." Some—those as far apart as Alexander Solzhenitsyn and Chinua Achebe—chose to work in a more realistic vein; others, like Gabriel García Márquez, expanded into "magical realist" realms that blurred the frontiers between dreamlike visions and physical or political reality. Leslie Marmon Silko's *Yellow Woman* used its setting in the American Southwest as a point of departure for a (possibly) mystical meeting based on Laguna Indian legend. By the end of the century, contemporary writers continued to profit from modernist innovations in language and perspective at the same time that they found different ways to articulate the world of *their* experience. Modernism, as an exploration of literary and linguistic forms employed to express the twentieth century's ongoing interrogation of reality, continued to exert its influence throughout the century and to change the contexts of modern experience.

THE TWENTIETH CENTURY

TEXTS	CONTEXTS
1893 Rabindranath Tagore, "**Punishment**"	
1895 Higuchi Ichiyō, *Child's Play*	
ca. 1897–1902 Washington Matthews conducts studies of the Navajo "Night Chant"	1899–1902 Boer War in South Africa
	1900 Boxer uprisings in China protest European presence • Max Planck proposes quantum theory, the first step in the discovery of the atom
1902 Joseph Conrad, **Heart of Darkness**	
1903 Henry James, *The Ambassadors*	1903 Wright brothers invent the powered airplane
1905 Sigmund Freud, *Dora (Fragment of an Analysis of a Case of Hysteria)* • F. T. Marinetti, *Futurist Manifesto*	1905 Modern labor movement begins with foundation of International Workers of the World (IWW) • Partition of Bengal based on Hindu and Muslim populations
1907 August Strindberg, *The Ghost Sonata*	1907 Japanese immigration to the United States prohibited
1908 Gertrude Stein, *Three Lives*	
	1909 Commercial manufacture of plastic begins
	1910 China abolishes slavery • Mexican Revolution (1910–11) • NAACP founded in United States • Post-Impressionist Exhibition in London
	1911 Revolution establishes Chinese Republic after 267 years of Manchu rule
1912 Rabindranath Tagore, *Gitanjali*	1912–13 Balkan wars
1913 Marcel Proust, *Swann's Way,* first volume of *Remembrance of Things Past* (1913–27) • Thomas Mann, *Death in Venice* • D. H. Lawrence, *Sons and Lovers*	
	1914–18 World War I involves Europe, Turkey, and the United States

Boldface titles indicate works in the anthology.

THE TWENTIETH CENTURY

TEXTS	CONTEXTS
	1915 Albert Einstein formulates general theory of relativity • First transcontinental phone call, in America
1916 Franz Kafka, **The Metamorphosis** • James Joyce, A *Portrait of the Artist as a Young Man*	
1917 T. S. Eliot, **Prufrock and Other Observations**	1917 Russian Revolution overthrows Romanov Dynasty
1918 Lu Xun, **"Diary of a Madman,"** the first story in Chinese vernacular	1918 Women over thirty given vote in Great Britain
	1918–20 Global influenza epidemic kills millions
	1919 League of Nations formed (U.S. Senate rejects membership, 1920)
1920 Edith Wharton, *The Age of Innocence*	1920 Mahatma Gandhi leads India's struggle for independence from Britain
1921 Luigi Pirandello, **Six Characters in Search of an Author** •	1921–29 Harlem Renaissance, black literary and artistic movement
1921–24 Knud Rasmussen documents Inuit culture and collects Inuit songs during the Fifth Thule Expedition	
1922 T. S. Eliot, **The Waste Land** • Paris publication of James Joyce, *Ulysses* (imported copies burned in U.S. Post Office) • Rainer Maria Rilke, *Sonnets to Orpheus*	1922 Turkey becomes a republic • Irish Free State established • USSR formed • Discovery of Egyptian pharaoh Tutankhamen's tomb
1923 Rainer Maria Rilke, *Duino Elegies*	1923 Earthquakes destroy centers of Tokyo and Yokohama
1924 Thomas Mann, *The Magic Mountain* • André Breton, *First Surrealist Manifesto* • Premchand, *The Road to Salvation*	1924 Insecticides first used
1925 *Geriguigatugo* and other tales narrated by Úke Iwágu Úo published in Italian and Bororo	

Boldface titles indicate works in the anthology.

THE TWENTIETH CENTURY

TEXTS	CONTEXTS
1926 Franz Kafka, *The Castle*	
1927 Virginia Woolf, *To the Lighthouse*	
1928 William Butler Yeats, *The Tower*	1928 Sixty-five states sign Kellogg-Briand antiwar pact in Paris • First Five Year Plan in USSR • Penicillin discovered • First scheduled television broadcasts
1929 William Faulkner, *The Sound and the Fury*	1929 Stock market crash heralds beginning of world economic crisis; Great Depression lasts until 1937
1932 Zuni ritual poetry published by anthropologist Ruth L. Bunzel	
1933 Federico García Lorca, *Blood Wedding*	1933 Adolf Hitler given dictatorial powers in Germany • Nazis build first concentration camps
	1934 Stalin begins purges of Communist Party
1935–47 Kawabata Yasunari, *Snow Country*	
1936 Premchand, *The Cow* • Leo Frobenius, *History of African Civilizations*	
1937 Wallace Stevens, *The Man with the Blue Guitar*	
1939 Aimé Césaire, *Notebook of a Return to the Native Land*	1939 Germany invades Poland and all Europe is drawn into World War II
1940 Richard Wright, *Native Son*	
1941 Bertolt Brecht, *Mother Courage and Her Children*	1941 United States and Japan enter World War II
1942 Albert Camus, *The Stranger*	
1943 T. S. Eliot, *Four Quartets*	
1944 Jorge Luis Borges, **"The Garden of Forking Paths"** • Ralph Ellison, *King of the Bingo Game*	

THE TWENTIETH CENTURY

TEXTS	CONTEXTS
1945 Leopold Sedar Senghor, *Chants d'ombre*	1945 World War II ends with dropping of atomic bombs on Hiroshima and Nagasaki • United Nations, Arab League founded
	1946 Churchill's "Iron Curtain" speech marks beginning of Cold War • Pan-African Federation formed
1947 Birago Diop, *Tales of Amadou Koumba*	1947 Religious massacres accompany partition of India and Pakistan into independent states • Transistor invented
1948 Ezra Pound, *Pisan Cantos*	1948 Creation of Jewish state in Palestine
	1949 Communist People's Republic of China established • Apartheid instituted in South Africa
	1950–53 Korean War involves North and South Korea, the United Nations, and China
1952 Ralph *Ellison, Invisible Man*	1952 Revolution in Egypt, which becomes a republic in 1953 • First hydrogen bomb
	1953 Discovery of DNA structure launches modern genetic science
1954 Kojima Nobuo, *The American School*	
1955 Alain Robbe-Grillet, *The Voyeur*	
1956 Tanizaki Jun'ichiro, *The Key*	1956 First Congress of Black Writers meets in Paris
1956–57 Naguib Mahfouz, *The Cairo Trilogy*	
1957 Samuel Beckett, *Endgame* • Albert Camus, *Exile and the Kingdom*, which includes "The Guest"	
1958 Chinua Achebe, **Things Fall Apart**	1958 European Common Market established • Algerian War of Independence (1958–62)

Boldface titles indicate works in the anthology.

THE TWENTIETH CENTURY

TEXTS	CONTEXTS
1959 Tawfiq al-Hakim, *The Sultan's Dilemma*	
1960 Marguerite Duras, *Hiroshima mon amour* • Shōno Junzō, *Still Life*	1960–62 Independence for Belgian Congo, Uganda, Tanganyika, Nigeria
	1961 Soviet astronaut orbits earth
1962 Doris Lessing, *The Golden Notebook* • Alain Robbe-Grillet, *Snapshots,* which includes **"The Secret Room"**	1962–73 United States engaged in Vietnam War
1963 Anna Akhmatova, **Requiem** • Naguib Mahfouz, *God's World*, which includes **"Zaabalawi"**	
1965 Recorded performance by Andrew Peynetsa of "The Boy and the Deer"	
	1966 Mao Tse-tung's *Cultural Revolution* attacks Confucian tradition and intellectuals in China (1966–69) • First Dakar Arts Festival provides showcase for African culture
1967 Gabriel García Márquez, *One Hundred Years of Solitude*	
1968 Kamau Brathwaite, *Masks*	
	1969 American astronaut is first man on moon
1970 Derek Walcott, *Dream on Monkey Mountain* • A. B. Yehoshua, *Three Days and a Child* • Gabriel García Márquez, *Death Constant Beyond Love*	
1972 Ingeborg Bachmann, *Three Paths to the Lake*	
	1973 Arab oil producers cut off shipments to nations supporting Israel; ensuing energy crisis reshapes global economy

THE TWENTIETH CENTURY

TEXTS	CONTEXTS
1975 Wole Soyinka, *Death and the King's Horseman*	
1979 Mariama Bâ, So *Long a Letter*	
1980 Nadine Gordimer, A *Soldier's Embrace* • Mahasweta *Devi,* "**Breast-Giver**" • Anita Desai, *Clear Light of Day* • Lorna Goodison, *Tamarind Season*	**1980s** Widespread concern as damage to the environment is increasingly documented
1981 Leslie Marmon Silko, *Ceremony* and *Storyteller,* which includes "**Yellow Woman**"	
	1983–84 Famine in Ethiopia • Ethnic and religious riots throughout India
	1986 Nuclear disaster in Chernobyl spreads radiation contamination throughout Europe
	1987 Floods destroy homes of millions in Bangladesh • World stock market crash
1989 Murakami Haruki, *TV People*	**1989** Mikhail Gorbachev restructures the Soviet state • Chinese government shoots thousands of protesters gathered in Tiananmen Square • Berlin Wall demolished
	1990 East and West Germany united
	1991 United States and USSR agree to arms reduction • Economic chaos and nationalist unrest bring end of Soviet Union
	1994 Nelson Mandela becomes president of South Africa after first multiracial elections • Israel and PLO sign peace agreement establishing a Palestinian state

Boldface titles indicate works in the anthology.

JOSEPH CONRAD
1857–1924

Born in Russia to Polish parents, learning English at twenty-one, and then serving as a sailor for sixteen years, Joseph Conrad nonetheless became a prolific writer of English fiction and, in his best work, a master of evocative modernist prose. His ability to suggest the vibration, color, and form of distant places as well as the complexity of human responses to moments of moral crisis stamped works like *Heart of Darkness* and *Lord Jim,* and made them permanent points of reference. Conrad's own sense of separation and exile, his yearning for the kinship and solidarity of the larger humanity he describes in the Preface to *The Nigger of the "Narcissus,"* permeates these works along with the despairing vision of a universe in which even the most ardent idealist finds no ultimate meaning or moral value.

He was born Jozef Teodor Konrad Korzeniowski on December 3, 1857, the only child of Polish patriots who were involved in Polish resistance to Russian rule. (He changed his name to Conrad, more pronounceable in English, for the publication of his first novel in 1895.) When his father was condemned for conspiracy in 1862, the family went together into exile in northern Russia, where Conrad's mother died three years later from tuberculosis. Conrad's father, who was a poet and translator, supported the small family by translating Shakespeare and Victor Hugo, and Conrad himself read novels by William Makepeace Thackeray, Walter Scott, and Charles Dickens in Polish and French. When his father died a few years later, in 1869, the eleven-year-old orphan went to live with his maternal uncle, Tadeusz Bobrowski, who sent him to school in Cracow (Poland) and Switzerland. Bobrowski supported his orphaned nephew both financially and emotionally, and, when Conrad asked to fulfill a long-standing dream of going to sea, gave him an annual allowance and helped him find a berth in the merchant marine.

During the next few years, he worked on French ships, traveling to the West Indies and participating in various activities—some of which were probably illegal—that would play a role in future novels of the sea. He also lost money at the casino in Monte Carlo, may have had an unhappy romance, and attempted suicide. Signing on to a British ship in 1878 to avoid conscription by the French (he had just turned twenty-one), Conrad visited England for the first time, knowing only a few words of English. He served for sixteen years on British merchant ships, earning his Master's Certificate in 1886 (the same year that he became a British subject) and learning English fast and well. Trips to the Far East and India gave him material for future novels, among them *The Nigger of the "Narcissus"* (1897) and *Typhoon* (1903), and two early novels set in Malaya, *Almayer's Folly* (1895) and *An Outcast of the Islands* (1896). For a long time, on the basis of these first works, Conrad was viewed as an exotic storyteller and a novelist of the sea. He turned his back on the sea as a profession when he married in 1896 and, buoyed by the publication of his first novel, chose writing as his career.

Among the various voyages that furnished material for his fiction, one stands out as the most intense, emotional, and subsequently controversial of them all: the trip up the Congo River that he made in 1890, straight into the heart of King Leopold's privately owned Congo Free State. Like many nineteenth-century explorers, Conrad was fascinated by the mystery of this dark (because uncharted by Europeans) continent, and he persuaded a relative to find him a job as pilot on a Belgian merchant steamer. Circumstances from then on are much as described by Marlow in *Heart of Darkness* (1899). The steamer that Conrad was supposed to pilot had been damaged, and while waiting for a replacement he was shifted to another one to help out and to learn about the river. This second trip is the journey recounted in *Heart of Darkness:* the boat traveled upstream to collect a seriously ill trader, Georges Antoine Klein (who died on the return trip), and Conrad, after speaking with Klein and observing the inhuman conditions imposed by slave labor and the ruthless search for ivory, returned seriously ill and traumatized by his journey. The experience marked him both physically and mentally. After a few years, he began to write about it with a moral rage that emerged openly at first and subsequently in more complex, ironic form. "An Outpost of Progress." a harshly satirical story of two murderous incompetents in a jungle trading post, was published in 1897, and Conrad wrote *Heart of Darkness* two years later.

The "darkness" of the title is both a conventional metaphor for obscurity and evil, and a common cliché referring to Africa and the "unenlightened" state of its indigenous population. Leopold II of Belgium, who owned the trading company that effectively was the Congo Free State, gained a free hand in the area after calling an international conference in 1876 "to open to civilization the only part of our globe where Christianity has not penetrated and to pierce the darkness which envelops the entire population." Conrad plays on images of darkness and savagery throughout the novella and complicates any simple opposition by associating moral darkness, the evil that lurks in human beings and underlies their predatory idealism, with a white exterior, beginning with the town that is the headquarters of the Belgian firm and is described as a "whited sepulcher." It is not surprising, however, that Chinua Achebe should have criticized *Heart of Darkness* for its racist picture of Africans. Marlow's words and behavior—indeed, the selectivity of his narrative—are as distant and cruelly patronizing as those of any European colonialist. They constitute the background for the strange figure of Kurtz, the charismatic, once idealistic, and now totally corrupt trader whose report to the International Society for the Suppression of Savage Customs concludes seventeen pages of benevolent rhetoric with the scrawl "Exterminate all the brutes!" Marlow's strange bond with this soul gone mad stems initially from a desire to see a man described as a universal genius, an "emissary of pity, and science, and progress" and part of the "gang of virtue." It continues as a horrified fascination with someone who has explored moral extremes up to the end. Kurtz is, for Marlow, the "inconceivable mystery of a soul that knew no restraint," and his dying judgment—"The horror! The horror!"—encompasses a more than personal despair.

Heart of Darkness

1

The *Nellie,* a cruising yawl,[1] swung to her anchor without a flutter of the sails, and was at rest. The flood had made, the wind was nearly calm, and being bound down the river, the only thing for it was to come to and wait for the turn of the tide.

The sea-reach of the Thames stretched before us like the beginning of an interminable waterway. In the offing the sea and the sky were welded together without a joint, and in the luminous space the tanned sails of the barges drifting up with the tide seemed to stand still in red clusters of canvas sharply peaked, with gleams of varnished sprits. A haze rested on the low shores that ran out to sea in vanishing flatness. The air was dark above Gravesend,[2] and farther back still seemed condensed into a mournful gloom, brooding motionless over the biggest, and the greatest, town on earth.

---

1. A two-masted boat.   2. A port on the Thames River, the last major town in the estuary.

The Director of Companies was our captain and our host. We four affectionately watched his back as he stood in the bows looking to seaward. On the whole river there was nothing that looked half so nautical. He resembled a pilot, which to a seaman is trustworthiness personified. It was difficult to realise his work was not out there in the luminous estuary, but behind him, within the brooding gloom.

Between us there was, as I have already said somewhere, the bond of the sea. Besides holding our hearts together through long periods of separation, it had the effect of making us tolerant of each other's yarns—and even convictions. The Lawyer—the best of old fellows—had, because of his many years and many virtues, the only cushion on deck, and was lying on the only rug. The Accountant had brought out already a box of dominoes, and was toying architecturally with the bones. Marlow sat cross-legged right aft, leaning against the mizzenmast. He had sunken cheeks, a yellow complexion, a straight back, an ascetic aspect, and, with his arms dropped, the palms of hands outwards, resembled an idol. The Director, satisfied the anchor had good hold, made his way aft and sat down amongst us. We exchanged a few words lazily. Afterwards there was silence on board the yacht. For some reason or other we did not begin that game of dominoes. We felt meditative, and fit for nothing but placid staring. The day was ending in a serenity of still and exquisite brilliance. The water shone pacifically; the sky, without a speck, was a benign immensity of unstained light; the very mist on the Essex marshes was like a gauzy and radiant fabric, hung from the wooded rises inland, and draping the low shores in diaphanous folds. Only the gloom to the west, brooding over the upper reaches, became more sombre every minute, as if angered by the approach of the sun.

And at last, in its curved and imperceptible fall, the sun sank low, and from glowing white changed to a dull red without rays and without heat, as if about to go out suddenly, stricken to death by the touch of that gloom brooding over a crowd of men.

Forthwith a change came over the waters, and the serenity became less brilliant but more profound. The old river in its broad reach rested unruffled at the decline of day, after ages of good service done to the race that peopled its banks, spread out in the tranquil dignity of a waterway leading to the uttermost ends of the earth. We looked at the venerable stream not in the vivid flush of a short day that comes and departs for ever, but in the august light of abiding memories. And indeed nothing is easier for a man who has, as the phrase goes, "followed the sea" with reverence and affection, than to evoke the great spirit of the past upon the lower reaches of the Thames. The tidal current runs to and fro in its unceasing service, crowded with memories of men and ships it has borne to the rest of home or to the battles of the sea. It had known and served all the men of whom the nation is proud, from Sir Francis Drake to Sir John Franklin, knights all, titled and untitled—the great knights-errant of the sea. It had borne all the ships whose names are like jewels flashing in the night of time, from the *Golden Hind* returning with her round flanks full of treasure, to be visited by the Queen's Highness and thus pass out of the gigantic tale, to the *Erebus* and *Terror*,[3] bound on

3. The *Erebus* and the *Terror* were ships commanded by Arctic explorer Sir John Franklin (1786–1847) and lost in an attempt to find a passage from the Atlantic Ocean to the Pacific. "*Golden Hind*": the ship that Elizabethan explorer Sir Francis Drake (1540–1596) used to sail around the world.

other conquests—and that never returned. It had known the ships and the men. They had sailed from Deptford, from Greenwich, from Erith—the adventurers and the settlers; kings' ships and the ships of men on 'Change; captains, admirals, the dark "interlopers"[4] of the Eastern trade, and the commissioned "generals" of East India fleets. Hunters for gold or pursuers of fame, they all had gone out on that stream, bearing the sword, and often the torch, messengers of the might within the land, bearers of a spark from the sacred fire. What greatness had not floated on the ebb of that river into the mystery of an unknown earth! . . . The dreams of men, the seed of commonwealths, the germs of empires.

The sun set; the dusk fell on the stream, and lights began to appear along the shore. The Chapman lighthouse, a three-legged thing erect on a mud-flat, shone strongly. Lights of ships moved in the fairway—a great stir of lights going up and going down. And farther west on the upper reaches the place of the monstrous town was still marked ominously on the sky, a brooding gloom in sunshine, a lurid glare under the stars.

"And this also," said Marlow suddenly, "has been one of the dark places of the earth."

He was the only man of us who still "followed the sea." The worst that could be said of him was that he did not represent his class. He was a sea-man, but he was a wanderer too, while most seamen lead, if one may so express it, a sedentary life. Their minds are of the stay-at-home order, and their home is always with them—the ship; and so is their country—the sea. One ship is very much like another, and the sea is always the same. In the immutability of their surroundings the foreign shores, the foreign faces, the changing immensity of life, glide past, veiled not by a sense of mystery but by a slightly disdainful ignorance; for there is nothing mysterious to a sea-man unless it be the sea itself, which is the mistress of his existence and as inscrutable as Destiny. For the rest, after his hours of work, a casual stroll or a casual spree on shore suffices to unfold for him the secret of a whole con-tinent, and generally he finds the secret not worth knowing. The yarns of seamen have a direct simplicity, the whole meaning of which lies within the shell of a cracked nut. But Marlow was not typical (if his propensity to spin yarns be excepted), and to him the meaning of an episode was not inside like a kernel but outside, enveloping the tale which brought it out only as a glow brings out a haze, in the likeness of one of these misty halos that sometimes are made visible by the spectral illumination of moonshine.

His remark did not seem at all surprising. It was just like Marlow. It was accepted in silence. No one took the trouble to grunt even; and presently he said, very slow:

"I was thinking of very old times, when the Romans first came here, nine-teen hundred years ago—the other day. . . . Light came out of this river since—you say Knights? Yes; but it is like a running blaze on a plain, like a flash of lightning in the clouds. We live in the flicker—may it last as long as the old earth keeps rolling! But darkness was here yesterday. Imagine the feelings of a commander of a fine—what d'ye call 'em?—trireme[5] in the

---

4. Private ships intruding on the East India Company's monopoly of trade. Deptford, Greenwich, and Erith are ports on the Thames between London and Gravesend. "'Change": the stock exchange.   5. A Roman galley with three banks of oars.

Mediterranean, ordered suddenly to the north; run overland across the Gauls in a hurry; put in charge of one of these craft the legionaries—a wonderful lot of handy men they must have been too—used to build, apparently by the hundred, in a month or two, if we may believe what we read. Imagine him here—the very end of the world, a sea the colour of lead, a sky the colour of smoke, a kind of ship about as rigid as a concertina—and going up this river with stores, or orders, or what you like. Sandbanks, marshes, forests, savages—precious little to eat fit for a civilised man, nothing but Thames water to drink. No Falernian wine[6] here, no going ashore. Here and there a military camp lost in a wilderness, like a needle in a bundle of hay—cold, fog, tempests, disease, exile, and death—death skulking in the air, in the water, in the bush. They must have been dying like flies here. Oh yes—he did it. Did it very well, too, no doubt, and without thinking much about it either, except afterwards to brag of what he had gone through in his time, perhaps. They were men enough to face the darkness. And perhaps he was cheered by keeping his eye on a chance of promotion to the fleet at Ravenna[7] by and by, if he had good friends in Rome and survived the awful climate. Or think of a decent young citizen in a toga—perhaps too much dice, you know—coming out here in the train of some prefect, or tax-gatherer, or trader, even, to mend his fortunes. Land in a swamp, march through the woods, and in some inland post feel the savagery, the utter savagery, had closed round him—all that mysterious life of the wilderness that stirs in the forest, in the jungles, in the hearts of wild men. There's no initiation either into such mysteries. He has to live in the midst of the incomprehensible, which is also detestable. And it has a fascination, too, that goes to work upon him. The fascination of the abomination—you know. Imagine the growing regrets, the longing to escape, the powerless disgust, the surrender, the hate."

He paused.

"Mind," he began again, lifting one arm from the elbow, the palm of the hand outwards, so that, with his legs folded before him, he had the pose of a Buddha preaching in European clothes and without a lotus-flower—"Mind, none of us would feel exactly like this. What saves us is efficiency—the devotion to efficiency. But these chaps were not much account, really. They were no colonists; their administration was merely a squeeze, and nothing more, I suspect. They were conquerors, and for that you want only brute force—nothing to boast of, when you have it, since your strength is just an accident arising from the weakness of others. They grabbed what they could get for the sake of what was to be got. It was just robbery with violence, aggravated murder on a great scale, and men going at it blind—as is very proper for those who tackle a darkness. The conquest of the earth, which mostly means the taking it away from those who have a different complexion or slightly flatter noses than ourselves, is not a pretty thing when you look into it too much. What redeems it is the idea only. An idea at the back of it; not a sentimental pretence but an idea; and an unselfish belief in the idea—something you can set up, and bow down before, and offer a sacrifice to. . . ."

6. Wine from a famous wine-making district in southern Italy.   7. Once a major Roman port on the Adriatic Sea.

He broke off. Flames glided in the river, small green flames, red flames, white flames, pursuing, overtaking, joining, crossing each other—then separating slowly or hastily. The traffic of the great city went on in the deepening night upon the sleepless river. We looked on, waiting patiently—there was nothing else to do till the end of the flood; but it was only after a long silence, when he said, in a hesitating voice, "I suppose you fellows remember I did once turn fresh-water sailor for a bit," that we knew we were fated, before the ebb began to run, to hear about one of Marlow's inconclusive experiences.

"I don't want to bother you much with what happened to me personally," he began, showing in this remark the weakness of many tellers of tales who seem so often unaware of what their audience would best like to hear; "yet to understand the effect of it on me you ought to know how I got out there, what I saw, how I went up that river to the place where I first met the poor chap. It was the farthest point of navigation and the culminating point of my experience. It seemed somehow to throw a kind of light on everything about me—and into my thoughts. It was sombre enough too—and pitiful—not extraordinary in any way—not very clear either. No, not very clear. And yet it seemed to throw a kind of light.

"I had then, as you remember, just returned to London after a lot of Indian Ocean, Pacific, China Seas—a regular dose of the East—six years or so, and I was loafing about, hindering you fellows in your work and invading your homes, just as though I had got a heavenly mission to civilise you. It was very fine for a time, but after a bit I did get tired of resting. Then I began to look for a ship—I should think the hardest work on earth. But the ships wouldn't even look at me. And I got tired of that game too.

"Now when I was a little chap I had a passion for maps. I would look for hours at South America, or Africa, or Australia, and lose myself in all the glories of exploration. At that time there were many blank spaces on the earth, and when I saw one that looked particularly inviting on a map (but they all look that) I would put my finger on it and say, When I grow up I will go there. The North Pole was one of these places, I remember. Well, I haven't been there yet, and shall not try now. The glamour's off. Other places were scattered about the Equator, and in every sort of latitude all over the two hemispheres. I have been in some of them, and . . . well, we won't talk about that. But there was one yet—the biggest, the most blank, so to speak—that I had a hankering after.

"True, by this time it was not a blank space any more. It had got filled since my boyhood with rivers and lakes and names. It had ceased to be a blank space of delightful mystery—a white patch for a boy to dream gloriously over. It had become a place of darkness. But there was in it one river especially, a mighty big river, that you could see on the map, resembling an immense snake uncoiled, with its head in the sea, its body at rest curving afar over a vast country, and its tail lost in the depths of the land. And as I looked at the map of it in a shop-window, it fascinated me as a snake would a bird—a silly little bird. Then I remembered there was a big concern, a Company for trade on that river. Dash it all! I thought to myself, they can't trade without using some kind of craft on that lot of fresh water—steamboats! Why shouldn't I try to get charge of one? I went on along Fleet Street,[8] but could not shake off the idea. The snake had charmed me.

"You understand it was a Continental concern, that Trading Society;[9] but I have a lot of relations living on the Continent, because it's cheap and not so nasty as it looks, they say.

"I am sorry to own I began to worry them. This was already a fresh departure for me. I was not used to get things that way, you know. I always went my own road and on my own legs where I had a mind to go. I wouldn't have believed it of myself; but, then—you see—I felt somehow I must get there by hook or by crook. So I worried them. The men said, 'My dear fellow,' and did nothing. Then—would you believe it?—I tried the women. I, Charlie Marlow, set the women to work—to get a job. Heavens! Well, you see, the notion drove me. I had an aunt, a dear enthusiastic soul. She wrote: 'It will be delightful. I am ready to do anything, anything for you. It is a glorious idea. I know the wife of a very high personage in the Administration, and also a man who has lots of influence with,' etc. etc. She was determined to make no end of fuss to get me appointed skipper of a river steamboat, if such was my fancy.

"I got my appointment—of course; and I got it very quick. It appears the Company had received news that one of their captains had been killed in a scuffle with the natives. This was my chance, and it made me the more anxious to go. It was only months and months afterwards, when I made the attempt to recover what was left of the body, that I heard the original quarrel arose from a misunderstanding about some hens. Yes, two black hens. Fresleven—that was the fellow's name, a Dane—thought himself wronged somehow in the bargain, so he went ashore and started to hammer the chief of the village with a stick. Oh, it didn't surprise me in the least to hear this, and at the same time to be told that Fresleven was the gentlest, quietest creature that ever walked on two legs. No doubt he was; but he had been a couple of years already out there engaged in the noble cause, you know, and he probably felt the need at last of asserting his self-respect in some way. Therefore he whacked the old nigger mercilessly, while a big crowd of his people watched him, thunderstruck, till some man—I was told the chief's son—in desperation at hearing the old chap yell, made a tentative jab with a spear at the white man—and of course it went quite easy between the shoulder-blades. Then the whole population cleared into the forest, expecting all kinds of calamities to happen, while, on the other hand, the steamer Fresleven commanded left also in a bad panic, in charge of the engineer, I believe. Afterwards nobody seemed to trouble much about Fresleven's remains, till I got out and stepped into his shoes. I couldn't let it rest, though; but when an opportunity offered at last to meet my predecessor, the grass growing through his ribs was tall enough to hide his bones. They were all there. The supernatural being had not been touched after he fell. And the village was deserted, the huts gaped black, rotting, all askew within the fallen enclosures. A calamity had come to it, sure enough. The people had vanished. Mad terror had scattered them, men, women, and children,

8. A major street in central London, famous as a publishing headquarter.   9. The trading company—specifically, a Belgian company that operated ships on the Congo River in the protectorate of King Leopold II of Belgium.

through the bush, and they had never returned. What became of the hens I don't know either. I should think the cause of progress got them, anyhow. However, through this glorious affair I got my appointment, before I had fairly begun to hope for it.

"I flew around like mad to get ready, and before forty-eight hours I was crossing the Channel to show myself to my employers, and sign the contract. In a very few hours I arrived in a city that always makes me think of a whited sepulchre. Prejudice no doubt. I had no difficulty in finding the Company's offices. It was the biggest thing in the town, and everybody I met was full of it. They were going to run an oversea empire, and make no end of coin by trade.

"A narrow and deserted street in deep shadow, high houses, innumerable windows with venetian blinds, a dead silence, grass sprouting between the stones, imposing carriage archways right and left, immense double doors standing ponderously ajar. I slipped through one of these cracks, went up a swept and ungarnished staircase, as arid as a desert, and opened the first door I came to. Two women, one fat and the other slim, sat on straw-bottomed chairs, knitting black wool. The slim one got up and walked straight at me—still knitting with downcast eyes—and only just as I began to think of getting out of her way, as you would for a somnambulist, stood still, and looked up. Her dress was as plain as an umbrella-cover, and she turned round without a word and preceded me into a waiting-room. I gave my name, and looked about. Deal table in the middle, plain chairs all round the walls, on one end a large shining map, marked with all the colours of a rainbow. There was a vast amount of red—good to see at any time, because one knows that some real work is done in there, a deuce of a lot of blue, a little green, smears of orange, and, on the East Coast, a purple patch, to show where the jolly pioneers of progress drink the jolly lager-beer. However, I wasn't going into any of these. I was going into the yellow. Dead in the centre. And the river was there—fascinating—deadly—like a snake. Ough! A door opened, a white-haired secretarial head, but wearing a compassionate expression, appeared, and a skinny forefinger beckoned me into the sanctuary. Its light was dim, and a heavy writing desk squatted in the middle. From behind that structure came out an impression of pale plumpness in a frock-coat. The great man himself. He was five feet six, I should judge, and had his grip on the handle-end of ever so many millions. He shook hands, I fancy, murmured vaguely, was satisfied with my French. *Bon voyage.*

"In about forty-five seconds I found myself again in the waiting-room with the compassionate secretary, who, full of desolation and sympathy, made me sign some document. I believe I undertook amongst other things not to disclose any trade secrets. Well, I am not going to.

"I began to feel slightly uneasy. You know I am not used to such ceremonies, and there was something ominous in the atmosphere. It was just as though I had been let into some conspiracy—I don't know—something not quite right; and I was glad to get out. In the outer room the two women knitted black wool feverishly. People were arriving, and the younger one was walking back and forth introducing them. The old one sat on her chair. Her flat cloth slippers were propped up on a foot-warmer, and a cat reposed on her lap. She wore a starched white affair on her head, had a wart on one cheek, and silver-rimmed spectacles hung on the tip of her nose. She glanced at me above the glasses. The swift and indifferent placidity of that look troubled me. Two youths with foolish and cheery countenances were being piloted over, and she threw at them the same quick glance of unconcerned wisdom. She seemed to know all about them and about me too. An eerie feeling came over me. She seemed uncanny and fateful. Often far away there I thought of these two, guarding the door of Darkness, knitting black wool as for a warm pall, one introducing, introducing continuously to the unknown, the other scrutinising the cheery and foolish faces with unconcerned old eyes. *Ave!* Old knitter of black wool. *Morituri te salutant.*[1] Not many of those she looked at ever saw her again—not half, by a long way.

"There was yet a visit to the doctor. 'A simple formality,' assured me the secretary, with an air of taking an immense part in all my sorrows. Accordingly a young chap wearing his hat over the left eyebrow, some clerk I suppose—there must have been clerks in the business, though the house was as still as a house in a city of the dead—came from somewhere upstairs, and led me forth. He was shabby and careless, with ink-stains on the sleeves of his jacket, and his cravat was large and billowy, under a chin shaped like the toe of an old boot. It was a little too early for the doctor, so I proposed a drink, and thereupon he developed a vein of joviality. As we sat over our vermuths he glorified the Company's business, and by and by I expressed casually my surprise at him not going out there. He became very cool and collected all at once. 'I am not such a fool as I look, quoth Plato to his disciples,' he said sententiously, emptied his glass with great resolution, and we rose.

"The old doctor felt my pulse, evidently thinking of something else the while. 'Good, good for there,' he mumbled, and then with a certain eagerness asked me whether I would let him measure my head. Rather surprised, I said Yes, when he produced a thing like callipers and got the dimensions back and front and every way, taking notes carefully. He was an unshaven little man in a threadbare coat like a gaberdine, with his feet in slippers, and I thought him a harmless fool. 'I always ask leave, in the interests of science, to measure the crania of those going out there,' he said. 'And when they come back too?' I asked. 'Oh, I never see them,' he remarked; 'and, moreover, the changes take place inside, you know.' He smiled, as if at some quiet joke. 'So you are going out there. Famous. Interesting too.' He gave me a searching glance, and made another note. 'Ever any madness in your family?' he asked, in a matter-of-fact tone. I felt very annoyed. 'Is that question in the interests of science too?' 'It would be,' he said, without taking notice of my irritation, 'interesting for science to watch the mental changes of individuals, on the spot, but . . .' 'Are you an alienist?'[2] I interrupted. 'Every doctor should be—a little,' answered that original[3] imperturbably. 'I have a little theory which you Messieurs who go out there must help me to prove. This is my share in the advantages my country shall reap from the possession of such a magnificent dependency. The mere wealth I leave to others. Pardon my questions, but you are the first Englishman coming under my observation . . .' I hastened to assure him I was not in the least typical. 'If I were,' said I, 'I wouldn't be talking like this with you.' 'What you say is rather profound, and

---

1. "Those who are about to die salute you" (Latin): the greeting of gladiators to the Roman emperor before beginning combat in the arena.   2. An early term for a psychiatrist.   3. Unusual or eccentric person.

probably erroneous,' he said, with a laugh. 'Avoid irritation more than expo-
sure to the sun. Adieu. How do you English say, eh? Good-bye. Ah! Good-
bye. Adieu. In the tropics one must before everything keep calm.' . . . He
lifted a warning forefinger. . . . '*Du calme, du calme. Adieu.*'[4]

"One thing more remained to do—say good-bye to my excellent aunt. I
found her triumphant. I had a cup of tea—the last decent cup of tea for
many days—and in a room that most soothingly looked just as you would
expect a lady's drawing-room to look, we had a long quiet chat by the fire-
side. In the course of these confidences it became quite plain to me I had
been represented to the wife of the high dignitary, and goodness knows to
how many more people besides, as an exceptional and gifted creature—a
piece of good fortune for the Company—a man you don't get hold of every
day. Good heavens! and I was going to take charge of a two-penny-halfpenny
river-steamboat with a penny whistle attached! It appeared, however, I was
also one of the Workers, with a capital—you know. Something like an emissary of light, something like a lower sort of apostle. There had been a lot of
such rot let loose in print and talk just about that time, and the excellent
woman, living right in the rush of all that humbug, got carried off her feet.
She talked about 'weaning those ignorant millions from their horrid ways,'
till, upon my word, she made me quite uncomfortable. I ventured to hint
that the Company was run for profit.

" 'You forget, dear Charlie, that the labourer is worthy of his hire,' she said
brightly. It's queer how out of touch with truth women are. They live in a
world of their own, and there had never been anything like it, and never can
be. It is too beautiful altogether, and if they were to set it up it would go to
pieces before the first sunset. Some confounded fact we men have been living contentedly with ever since the day of creation would start up and knock
the whole thing over.

"After this I got embraced, told to wear flannel, be sure to write often, and
so on—and I left. In the street—I don't know why—a queer feeling came to
me that I was an impostor. Odd thing that I, who used to clear out for any
part of the world at twenty-four hours' notice, with less thought than most
men give to the crossing of a street, had a moment—I won't say of hesitation, but of startled pause, before this commonplace affair. The best way I
can explain it to you is by saying that, for a second or two, I felt as though,
instead of going to the centre of a continent, I were about to set off for the
centre of the earth.

"I left in a French steamer, and she called in every blamed port they have
out there, for, as far as I could see, the sole purpose of landing soldiers and
custom-house officers. I watched the coast. Watching a coast as it slips by
the ship is like thinking about an enigma. There it is before you—smiling,
frowning, inviting, grand, mean, insipid, or savage, and always mute with an
air of whispering, Come and find out. This one was almost featureless, as if
still in the making, with an aspect of monotonous grimness. The edge of a
colossal jungle, so dark green as to be almost black, fringed with white surf,
ran straight, like a ruled line, far, far away along a blue sea whose glitter was
blurred by a creeping mist. The sun was fierce, the land seemed to glisten
and drip with steam. Here and there greyish-whitish specks showed up clus-

4. "Be calm, be calm. Good-bye" (French).

tered inside the white surf, with a flag flying above them perhaps—settlements some centuries old, and still no bigger than pin-heads on the untouched expanse of their background. We pounded along, stopped, landed soldiers; went on, landed custom-house clerks to levy toll in what looked like a God-forsaken wilderness, with a tin shed and a flag-pole lost in it; landed more soldiers—to take care of the custom-house clerks presumably. Some, I heard, got drowned in the surf; but whether they did or not, nobody seemed particularly to care. They were just flung out there, and on we went. Every day the coast looked the same, as though we had not moved; but we passed various places—trading places—with names like Gran' Bassam, Little Popo; names that seemed to belong to some sordid farce acted in front of a sinister back-cloth. The idleness of a passenger, my isolation amongst all these men with whom I had no point of contact, the oily and languid sea, the uniform sombreness of the coast, seemed to keep me away from the truth of things, within the toil of a mournful and senseless delusion. The voice of the surf heard now and then was a positive pleasure, like the speech of a brother. It was something natural, that had its reason, that had a meaning. Now and then a boat from the shore gave one a momentary contact with reality. It was paddled by black fellows. You could see from afar the white of their eyeballs glistening. They shouted, sang; their bodies streamed with perspiration; they had faces like grotesque masks—these chaps; but they had bone, muscle, a wild vitality, an intense energy of movement, that was as natural and true as the surf along their coast. They wanted no excuse for being there. They were a great comfort to look at. For a time I would feel I belonged still to a world of straightforward facts; but the feeling would not last long. Something would turn up to scare it away. Once, I remember, we came upon a man-of-war anchored off the coast. There wasn't even a shed there, and she was shelling the bush. It appears the French had one of their wars going on thereabouts. Her ensign dropped limp like a rag; the muzzles of the long six-inch guns stuck out all over the low hull; the greasy, slimy swell swung her up lazily and let her down, swaying her thin masts. In the empty immensity of earth, sky, and water, there she was, incomprehensible, firing into a continent. Pop, would go one of the six-inch guns; a small flame would dart and vanish, a little white smoke would disappear, a tiny projectile would give a feeble screech—and nothing happened. Nothing could happen. There was a touch of insanity in the proceeding, a sense of lugubrious drollery in the sight; and it was not dissipated by somebody on board assuring me earnestly there was a camp of natives—he called them enemies!—hidden out of sight somewhere.

"We gave her her letters (I heard the men in that lonely ship were dying of fever at the rate of three a day) and went on. We called at some more places with farcical names, where the merry dance of death and trade goes on in a still and earthy atmosphere as of an overheated catacomb; all along the formless coast bordered by dangerous surf, as if Nature herself had tried to ward off intruders; in and out of rivers, streams of death in life, whose banks were rotting into mud, whose waters, thickened into slime, invaded the contorted mangroves, that seemed to writhe at us in the extremity of an impotent despair. Nowhere did we stop long enough to get a particularised impression, but the general sense of vague and oppressive wonder grew upon me. It was like a weary pilgrimage amongst hints for nightmares.

"It was upward of thirty days before I saw the mouth of the big river. We anchored off the seat of the government. But my work would not begin till some two hundred miles farther on. So as soon as I could I made a start for a place thirty miles higher up.

"I had my passage on a little sea-going steamer. Her captain was a Swede, and knowing me for a seaman, invited me on the bridge. He was a young man, lean, fair, and morose, with lanky hair and a shuffling gait. As we left the miserable little wharf, he tossed his head contemptuously at the shore. 'Been living there?' he asked. I said, 'Yes.' 'Fine lot these government chaps—are they not?' he went on, speaking English with great precision and considerable bitterness. 'It is funny what some people will do for a few francs a month. I wonder what becomes of that kind when it goes up country?' I said to him I expected to see that soon. 'So-o-o!' he exclaimed. He shuffled athwart, keeping one eye ahead vigilantly. 'Don't be too sure,' he continued. 'The other day I took up a man who hanged himself on the road. He was a Swede, too.' 'Hanged himself! Why, in God's name?' I cried. He kept on looking out watchfully. 'Who knows? The sun too much for him, or the country perhaps.'

"At last we opened a reach. A rocky cliff appeared, mounds of turned-up earth by the shore, houses on a hill, others with iron roofs, amongst a waste of excavations, or hanging to the declivity. A continuous noise of the rapids above hovered over this scene of inhabited devastation. A lot of people, mostly black and naked, moved about like ants. A jetty projected into the river. A blinding sunlight drowned all this at times in a sudden recrudescence of glare. 'There's your Company's station,' said the Swede, pointing to three wooden barrack-like structures on the rocky slope. 'I will send your things up. Four boxes did you say? So. Farewell.'

"I came upon a boiler wallowing in the grass, then found a path leading up the hill. It turned aside for the boulders, and also for an undersized railway truck lying there on its back with its wheels in the air. One was off. The thing looked as dead as the carcass of some animal. I came upon more pieces of decaying machinery, a stack of rusty nails. To the left a clump of trees made a shady spot, where dark things seemed to stir feebly. I blinked, the path was steep. A horn tooted to the right, and I saw the black people run. A heavy and dull detonation shook the ground, a puff of smoke came out of the cliff, and that was all. No change appeared on the face of the rock. They were building a railway. The cliff was not in the way or anything; but this objectless blasting was all the work going on.

"A slight clinking behind me made me turn my head. Six black men advanced in a file, toiling up the path. They walked erect and slow, balancing small baskets full of earth on their heads, and the clink kept time with their footsteps. Black rags were wound round their loins, and the short ends behind waggled to and fro like tails. I could see every rib, the joints of their limbs were like knots in a rope; each had an iron collar on his neck, and all were connected together with a chain whose bights swung between them, rhythmically clinking. Another report from the cliff made me think suddenly of that ship of war I had seen firing into a continent. It was the same kind of ominous voice; but these men could by no stretch of imagination be called enemies. They were called criminals, and the outraged law, like the bursting shells, had come to them, an insoluble mystery from the sea. All their meagre breasts panted together, the violently dilated nostrils quivered, the eyes stared stonily uphill. They passed me within six inches, without a glance, with that complete, deathlike indifference of unhappy savages. Behind this raw matter one of the reclaimed, the product of the new forces at work, strolled despondently, carrying a rifle by its middle. He had a uniform jacket with one button off, and seeing a white man on the path, hoisted his weapon to his shoulder with alacrity. This was simple prudence, white men being so much alike at a distance that he could not tell who I might be. He was speedily reassured, and with a large, white, rascally grin, and a glance at his charge, seemed to take me into partnership in his exalted trust. After all, I also was a part of the great cause of these high and just proceedings.

"Instead of going up, I turned and descended to the left. My idea was to let that chain-gang get out of sight before I climbed the hill. You know I am not particularly tender; I've had to strike and to fend off. I've had to resist and to attack sometimes—that's only one way of resisting—without counting the exact cost, according to the demands of such sort of life as I had blundered into. I've seen the devil of violence, and the devil of greed, and the devil of hot desire; but, by all the stars! these were strong, lusty, red-eyed devils, that swayed and drove men—men, I tell you. But as I stood on this hillside, I foresaw that in the blinding sunshine of that land I would become acquainted with a flabby, pretending, weak-eyed devil of a rapacious and pitiless folly. How insidious he could be, too, I was only to find out several months later and a thousand miles farther. For a moment I stood appalled, as though by a warning. Finally I descended the hill, obliquely, towards the trees I had seen.

"I avoided a vast artificial hole somebody had been digging on the slope, the purpose of which I found it impossible to divine. It wasn't a quarry or a sandpit, anyhow. It was just a hole. It might have been connected with the philanthropic desire of giving the criminals something to do. I don't know. Then I nearly fell into a very narrow ravine, almost no more than a scar in the hillside. I discovered that a lot of imported drainage-pipes for the settlement had been tumbled in there. There wasn't one that was not broken. It was a wanton smash-up. At last I got under the trees. My purpose was to stroll into the shade for a moment; but no sooner within than it seemed to me I had stepped into the gloomy circle of some Inferno. The rapids were near, and an uninterrupted, uniform, headlong, rushing noise filled the mournful stillness of the grove, where not a breath stirred, not a leaf moved, with a mysterious sound—as though the tearing pace of the launched earth had suddenly become audible.

"Black shapes crouched, lay, sat between the trees, leaning against the trunks, clinging to the earth, half coming out, half effaced within the dim light, in all the attitudes of pain, abandonment, and despair. Another mine[5] on the cliff went off, followed by a slight shudder of the soil under my feet. The work was going on. The work! And this was the place where some of the helpers had withdrawn to die.

"They were dying slowly—it was very clear. They were not enemies, they were not criminals, they were nothing earthly now—nothing but black shadows of disease and starvation, lying confusedly in the greenish gloom.

5. Explosive charge.

Brought from all the recesses of the coast in all the legality of time con-
tracts, lost in uncongenial surroundings, fed on unfamiliar food, they sickened, became inefficient, and were then allowed to crawl away and rest.
These moribund shapes were free as air—and nearly as thin. I began to distinguish the gleam of eyes under the trees. Then, glancing down, I saw a
face near my hand. The black bones reclined at full length with one shoulder
against the tree, and slowly the eyelids rose and the sunken eyes looked up
at me, enormous and vacant, a kind of blind, white flicker in the depths of
the orbs, which died out slowly. The man seemed young—almost a boy—but
you know with them it's hard to tell. I found nothing else to do but to offer
him one of my good Swede's ship's biscuits I had in my pocket. The fingers
closed slowly on it and held—there was no other movement and no other
glance. He had tied a bit of white worsted[6] round his neck—Why? Where
did he get it? Was it a badge—an ornament—a charm—a propitiatory act?
Was there any idea at all connected with it? It looked startling round his
black neck, this bit of white thread from beyond the seas.

"Near the same tree two more bundles of acute angles sat with their legs
drawn up. One, with his chin propped on his knees, stared at nothing, in an
intolerable and appalling manner: his brother phantom rested its forehead,
as if overcome with a great weariness; and all about others were scattered in
every pose of contorted collapse, as in some picture of a massacre or a pestilence. While I stood horror-struck, one of these creatures rose to his hands
and knees, and went off on all-fours towards the river to drink. He lapped
out of his hand, then sat up in the sunlight, crossing his shins in front of
him, and after a time let his woolly head fall on his breastbone.

"I didn't want any more loitering in the shade, and I made haste towards
the station. When near the buildings I met a white man, in such an unexpected elegance of get-up that in the first moment I took him for a sort of
vision. I saw a high starched collar, white cuffs, a light alpaca[7] jacket, snowy
trousers, a clear necktie, and varnished boots. No hat. Hair parted, brushed,
oiled, under a green-lined parasol held in a big white hand. He was amazing,
and had a penholder behind his ear.

"I shook hands with this miracle, and I learned he was the Company's
chief accountant, and that all the book-keeping was done at this station. He
had come out for a moment, he said, 'to get a breath of fresh air.' The expression sounded wonderfully odd, with its suggestion of sedentary desk-life. I
wouldn't have mentioned the fellow to you at all, only it was from his lips
that I first heard the name of the man who is so indissolubly connected with
the memories of that time. Moreover, I respected the fellow. Yes; I respected
his collars, his vast cuffs, his brushed hair. His appearance was certainly that
of a hairdresser's dummy; but in the great demoralisation of the land he kept
up his appearance. That's backbone. His starched collars and got-up shirt-
fronts were achievements of character. He had been out nearly three years;
and, later, I could not help asking him how he managed to sport such linen.
He had just the faintest blush, and said modestly, 'I've been teaching one of
the native women about the station. It was difficult. She had a distaste for
the work.' Thus this man had verily accomplished something. And he was
devoted to his books, which were in apple-pie order.

6. Wool fabric.   7. An expensive fine wool that comes from a South American animal of the same name.

"Everything else in the station was in a muddle,—heads, things, buildings. Strings of dusty niggers with splay feet arrived and departed; a stream of manufactured goods, rubbishy cottons, beads, and brass-wire sent into the depths of darkness, and in return came a precious trickle of ivory.

"I had to wait in the station for ten days—an eternity. I lived in a hut in the yard, but to be out of the chaos I would sometimes get into the accountant's office. It was built of horizontal planks, and so badly put together that, as he bent over his high desk, he was barred from neck to heels with narrow strips of sunlight. There was no need to open the big shutter to see. It was hot there too; big flies buzzed fiendishly, and did not sting, but stabbed. I sat generally on the floor, while, of faultless appearance (and even slightly scented), perching on a high stool, he wrote, he wrote. Sometimes he stood up for exercise. When a truckle-bed[8] with a sick man (some invalided agent from up country) was put in there, he exhibited a gentle annoyance. 'The groans of this sick person' he said, 'distract my attention. And without that it is extremely difficult to guard against clerical errors in this climate.'

"One day he remarked, without lifting his head, 'In the interior you will no doubt meet Mr Kurtz.' On my asking who Mr Kurtz was, he said he was a first-class agent; and seeing my disappointment at this information, he added slowly, laying down his pen, 'He is a very remarkable person.' Further questions elicited from him that Mr Kurtz was at present in charge of a trading-post, a very important one, in the true ivory-country, at 'the very bottom of there. Sends in as much ivory as all the others put together . . .' He began to write again. The sick man was too ill to groan. The flies buzzed in a great peace.

"Suddenly there was a growing murmur of voices and a great tramping of feet. A caravan had come in. A violent babble of uncouth sounds burst out on the other side of the planks. All the carriers were speaking together, and in the midst of the uproar the lamentable voice of the chief agent was heard 'giving it up' tearfully for the twentieth time that day. . . . He rose slowly. 'What a frightful row,' he said. He crossed the room gently to look at the sick man, and returning, said to me, 'He does not hear.' 'What! Dead?' I asked, startled. 'No, not yet,' he answered, with great composure. Then, alluding with a toss of the head to the tumult in the station-yard, 'When one has got to make correct entries, one comes to hate those savages—hate them to the death.' He remained thoughtful for a moment. 'When you see Mr Kurtz,' he went on, 'tell him from me that everything here'—he glanced at the desk—'is very satisfactory. I don't like to write to him—with those messengers of ours you never know who may get hold of your letter—at that Central Station.' He stared at me for a moment with his mild, bulging eyes. 'Oh, he will go far, very far,' he began again. 'He will be a somebody in the Administration before long. They, above—the Council in Europe, you know—mean him to be.'

"He turned to his work. The noise outside had ceased, and presently in going out I stopped at the door. In the steady buzz of flies the homeward-bound agent was lying flushed and insensible; the other, bent over his books, was making correct entries of perfectly correct transactions; and fifty feet below the doorstep I could see the still tree-tops of the grove of death.

8. That is, trundle bed, a low portable bed that is on castors and that may be slid under a higher bed when it is not being used.

"Next day I left that station at last, with a caravan of sixty men, for a two-hundred-mile tramp.

"No use telling you much about that. Paths, paths, everywhere; a stamped-in network of paths spreading over the empty land, through long grass, through burnt grass, through thickets, down and up chilly ravines, up and down stony hills ablaze with heat; and a solitude, a solitude, nobody, not a hut. The population had cleared out a long time ago. Well, if a lot of mysterious niggers armed with all kinds of fearful weapons suddenly took to travelling on the road between Deal and Gravesend, catching the yokels right and left to carry heavy loads for them, I fancy every farm and cottage thereabouts would get empty very soon. Only here the dwellings were gone too. Still, I passed through several abandoned villages. There's something pathetically childish in the ruins of grass walls. Day after day, with the stamp and shuffle of sixty pair of bare feet behind me, each pair under a 60-lb. load. Camp, cook, sleep, strike camp, march. Now and then a carrier dead in harness, at rest in the long grass near the path, with an empty water-gourd and his long staff lying by his side. A great silence around and above. Perhaps on some quiet night the tremor of far-off drums, sinking, swelling, a tremor vast, faint; a sound weird, appealing, suggestive, and wild—and perhaps with as profound a meaning as the sound of bells in a Christian country. Once a white man in an unbuttoned uniform, camping on the path with an armed escort of lank Zanzibaris,[9] very hospitable and festive—not to say drunk. Was looking after the upkeep of the road, he declared. Can't say I saw any road or any upkeep, unless the body of a middle-aged negro, with a bullet-hole in the forehead, upon which I absolutely stumbled three miles farther on, may be considered as a permanent improvement. I had a white companion too, not a bad chap, but rather too fleshy and with the exasperating habit of fainting on the hot hillsides, miles away from the least bit of shade and water. Annoying, you know, to hold your own coat like a parasol over a man's head while he is coming-to. I couldn't help asking him once what he meant by coming there at all. 'To make money, of course. What do you think?' he said scornfully. Then he got fever, and had to be carried in a hammock slung under a pole. As he weighed sixteen stone[1] I had no end of rows with the carriers. They jibbed, ran away, sneaked off with their loads in the night—quite a mutiny. So, one evening, I made a speech in English with gestures, not one of which was lost to the sixty pairs of eyes before me, and the next morning I started the hammock off in front all right. An hour afterwards I came upon the whole concern wrecked in a bush—man, hammock, groans, blankets, horrors. The heavy pole had skinned his poor nose. He was very anxious for me to kill somebody, but there wasn't the shadow of a carrier near. I remembered the old doctor—'It would be interesting for science to watch the mental changes of individuals, on the spot.' I felt I was becoming scientifically interesting. However, all that is to no purpose. On the fifteenth day I came in sight of the big river again, and hobbled into the Central Station. It was on a back water surrounded by scrub and forest, with a pretty border of smelly mud on one side, and on the three others enclosed by a crazy fence of rushes. A neglected gap was all the gate it had, and the

9. Mercenary soldiers from the island of Zanzibar off the east African coast.   1. That is, pounds (1 stone equals 14 pounds).

first glance at the place was enough to let you see the flabby devil was running that show. White men with long staves in their hands appeared languidly from amongst the buildings, strolling up to take a look at me, and then retired out of sight somewhere. One of them, a stout, excitable chap with black moustaches, informed me with great volubility and many digressions, as soon as I told him who I was, that my steamer was at the bottom of the river. I was thunderstruck. What, how, why? Oh, it was 'all right.' The 'manager himself' was there. All quite correct. 'Everybody had behaved splendidly! splendidly!'—'You must,' he said in agitation, 'go and see the general manager at once. He is waiting!'

"I did not see the real significance of that wreck at once. I fancy I see it now, but I am not sure—not at all. Certainly the affair was too stupid—when I think of it—to be altogether natural. Still . . . But at the moment it presented itself simply as a confounded nuisance. The steamer was sunk. They had started two days before in a sudden hurry up the river with the manager on board, in charge of some volunteer skipper, and before they had been out three hours they tore the bottom out of her on stones, and she sank near the south bank. I asked myself what I was to do there, now my boat was lost. As a matter of fact, I had plenty to do in fishing my command out of the river. I had to set about it the very next day. That, and the repairs when I brought the pieces to the station, took some months.

"My first interview with the manager was curious. He did not ask me to sit down after my twenty-mile walk that morning. He was commonplace in complexion, in feature, in manners, and in voice. He was of middle size and of ordinary build. His eyes, of the usual blue, were perhaps remarkably cold, and he certainly could make his glance fall on one as trenchant and heavy as an axe. But even at these times the rest of his person seemed to disclaim the intention. Otherwise there was only an indefinable, faint expression of his lips, something stealthy—a smile—not a smile—I remember it, but I can't explain. It was unconscious, this smile was, though just after he had said something it got intensified for an instant. It came at the end of his speeches like a seal applied on the words to make the meaning of the commonest phrase appear absolutely inscrutable. He was a common trader, from his youth up employed in these parts—nothing more. He was obeyed, yet he inspired neither love nor fear, nor even respect. He inspired uneasiness. That was it! Uneasiness. Not a definite mistrust—just uneasiness—nothing more. You have no idea how effective such a . . . a . . . faculty can be. He had no genius for organising, for initiative, or for order even. That was evident in such things as the deplorable state of the station. He had no learning, and no intelligence. His position had come to him—why? Perhaps because he was never ill . . . He had served three terms of three years out there . . . Because triumphant health in the general rout of constitutions is a kind of power in itself. When he went home on leave he rioted on a large scale—pompously. Jack ashore—with a difference—in externals only. This one could gather from his casual talk. He originated nothing, he could keep the routine going—that's all. But he was great. He was great by this little thing that it was impossible to tell what could control such a man. He never gave that secret away. Perhaps there was nothing within him. Such a suspicion made one pause—for out there there were no external checks. Once when various tropical diseases had laid low almost every 'agent' in the station, he was heard to say, 'Men who come out here should have no entrails.' He sealed the utterance with that smile of his, as though it had been a door opening into a darkness he had in his keeping. You fancied you had seen things—but the seal was on. When annoyed at meal-times by the constant quarrels of the white men about precedence, he ordered an immense round table to be made, for which a special house had to be built. This was the station's mess-room. Where he sat was the first place—the rest were nowhere. One felt this to be his unalterable conviction. He was neither civil nor uncivil. He was quiet. He allowed his 'boy'—an overfed young negro from the coast—to treat the white men, under his very eyes, with provoking insolence.

"He began to speak as soon as he saw me. I had been very long on the road. He could not wait. Had to start without me. The up-river stations had to be relieved. There had been so many delays already that he did not know who was dead and who was alive, and how they got on—and so on, and so on. He paid no attention to my explanations, and, playing with a stick of sealing-wax, repeated several times that the situation was 'very grave, very grave.' There were rumours that a very important station was in jeopardy, and its chief, Mr Kurtz, was ill. Hoped it was not true. Mr Kurtz was . . . I felt weary and irritable. Hang Kurtz, I thought. I interrupted him by saying I had heard of Mr Kurtz on the coast. 'Ah! So they talk of him down there,' he murmured to himself. Then he began again, assuring me Mr Kurtz was the best agent he had, an exceptional man, of the greatest importance to the Company; therefore I could understand his anxiety. He was, he said, 'very, very uneasy.' Certainly he fidgeted on his chair a good deal, exclaimed, 'Ah, Mr Kurtz!' broke the stick of sealing-wax and seemed dumbfounded by the accident. Next thing he wanted to know 'how long it would take to' . . . I interrupted him again. Being hungry, you know, and kept on my feet too, I was getting savage. 'How can I tell?' I said, 'I haven't even seen the wreck yet—some months, no doubt.' All this talk seemed to me so futile. 'Some months,' he said. 'Well, let us say three months before we can make a start. Yes. That ought to do the affair.' I flung out of his hut (he lived all alone in a clay hut with a sort of verandah) muttering to myself my opinion of him. He was a chattering idiot. Afterwards I took it back when it was borne in upon me startlingly with what extreme nicety he had estimated the time requisite for the 'affair.'

"I went to work the next day, turning, so to speak, my back on that station. In that way only it seemed to me I could keep my hold on the redeeming facts of life. Still, one must look about sometimes; and then I saw this station, these men strolling aimlessly about in the sunshine of the yard. I asked myself sometimes what it all meant. They wandered here and there with their absurd long staves in their hands, like a lot of faithless pilgrims bewitched inside a rotten fence. The word 'ivory' rang in the air, was whispered, was sighed. You would think they were praying to it. A taint of imbecile rapacity blew through it all, like a whiff from some corpse. By Jove! I've never seen anything so unreal in my life. And outside, the silent wilderness surrounding this cleared speck on the earth struck me as something great and invincible, like evil or truth, waiting patiently for the passing away of this fantastic invasion.

"Oh, these months! Well, never mind. Various things happened. One evening a grass shed full of calico, cotton prints, beads, and I don't know what else, burst into a blaze so suddenly that you would have thought the earth had opened to let an avenging fire consume all that trash. I was smoking my pipe quietly by my dismantled steamer, and saw them all cutting capers in the light, with their arms lifted high, when the stout man with moustaches came tearing down to the river, a tin pail in his hand, assured me that everybody was 'behaving splendidly, splendidly,' dipped about a quart of water and tore back again. I noticed there was a hole in the bottom of his pail.

"I strolled up. There was no hurry. You see the thing had gone off like a box of matches. It had been hopeless from the very first. The flame had leaped high, driven everybody back, lighted up everything—and collapsed. The shed was already a heap of embers glowing fiercely. A nigger was being beaten near by. They said he had caused the fire in some way; be that as it may, he was screeching most horribly. I saw him, later, for several days, sitting in a bit of shade looking very sick and trying to recover himself: afterwards he arose and went out—and the wilderness without a sound took him into its bosom again. As I approached the glow from the dark I found myself at the back of two men, talking. I heard the name of Kurtz pronounced, then the words, 'take advantage of this unfortunate accident.' One of the men was the manager. I wished him a good evening. 'Did you ever see anything like it—eh? it is incredible,' he said, and walked off. The other man remained. He was a first-class agent, young, gentlemanly, a bit reserved, with a forked little beard and a hooked nose. He was standoffish with the other agents, and they on their side said he was the manager's spy upon them. As to me, I had hardly ever spoken to him before. We got into talk, and by and by we strolled away from the hissing ruins. Then he asked me to his room, which was in the main building of the station. He struck a match, and I perceived that this young aristocrat had not only a silver-mounted dressing-case but also a whole candle all to himself. Just at that time the manager was the only man supposed to have any right to candles. Native mats covered the clay walls; a collection of spears, assegais,[2] shields, knives, was hung up in trophies. The business entrusted to this fellow was the making of bricks—so I had been informed; but there wasn't a fragment of a brick anywhere in the station, and he had been there more than a year—waiting. It seems he could not make bricks without something, I don't know what— straw maybe. Anyway, it could not be found there, and as it was not likely to be sent from Europe, it did not appear clear to me what he was waiting for. An act of special creation perhaps. However, they were all waiting—all the sixteen or twenty pilgrims of them—for something; and upon my word it did not seem an uncongenial occupation, from the way they took it, though the only thing that ever came to them was disease—as far as I could see. They beguiled the time by backbiting and intriguing against each other in a foolish kind of way. There was an air of plotting about that station, but nothing came of it, of course. It was as unreal as everything else—as the philanthropic pretence of the whole concern, as their talk, as their government, as their show of work. The only real feeling was a desire to get appointed to a trading-post where ivory was to be had, so that they could earn percentages. They intrigued and slandered and hated each other only on that account—but

---

2. Slender hardwood javelins used as weapons.

as to effectually lifting a little finger—oh no. By heavens! there is something after all in the world allowing one man to steal a horse while another must not look at a halter. Steal a horse straight out. Very well. He has done it. Perhaps he can ride. But there is a way of looking at a halter that would provoke the most charitable of saints into a kick.

"I had no idea why he wanted to be sociable, but as we chatted in there it suddenly occurred to me the fellow was trying to get at something—in fact, pumping me. He alluded constantly to Europe, to the people I was supposed to know there—putting leading questions as to my acquaintances in the sepulchral city, and so on. His little eyes glittered like mica[3] discs—with curiosity—though he tried to keep up a bit of superciliousness. At first I was astonished, but very soon I became awfully curious to see what he would find out from me. I couldn't possibly imagine what I had in me to make it worth his while. It was very pretty to see how he baffled himself, for in truth my body was full only of chills, and my head had nothing in it but that wretched steamboat business. It was evident he took me for a perfectly shameless prevaricator. At last he got angry, and, to conceal a movement of furious annoyance, he yawned. I rose. Then I noticed a small sketch in oils, on a panel, representing a woman, draped and blindfolded, carrying a lighted torch. The background was sombre—almost black. The movement of the woman was stately, and the effect of the torchlight on the face was sinister.

"It arrested me, and he stood by civilly, holding an empty half-pint champagne bottle (medical comforts) with the candle stuck in it. To my question he said Mr Kurtz had painted this—in this very station more than a year ago—while waiting for means to go to his trading-post. 'Tell me, pray,' said I, 'who is this Mr Kurtz?'

"'The chief of the Inner Station,' he answered in a short tone, looking away. 'Much obliged,' I said, laughing. 'And you are the brickmaker of the Central Station. Every one knows that.' He was silent for a while. 'He is a prodigy,' he said at last. 'He is an emissary of pity, and science, and progress, and devil knows what else. We want,' he began to declaim suddenly, 'for the guidance of the cause entrusted to us by Europe, so to speak, higher intelligence, wide sympathies, a singleness of purpose.' 'Who says that?' I asked. 'Lots of them,' he replied. 'Some even write that; and so *he* comes here, a special being, as you ought to know.' 'Why ought I to know?' I interrupted, really surprised. He paid no attention. 'Yes. To-day he is chief of the best station, next year he will be assistant-manager, two years more and . . . but I daresay you know what he will be in two years' time. You are of the new gang—the gang of virtue. The same people who sent him specially also recommended you. Oh, don't say no. I've my own eyes to trust.' Light dawned upon me. My dear aunt's influential acquaintances were producing an unexpected effect upon that young man. I nearly burst into a laugh. 'Do you read the Company's confidential correspondence?' I asked. He hadn't a word to say. It was great fun. 'When Mr Kurtz,' I continued severely, 'is General Manager, you won't have the opportunity.'

"He blew the candle out suddenly, and we went outside. The moon had risen. Black figures strolled about listlessly, pouring water on the glow,

3. A mineral silicate that separates into glittering layers.

whence proceeded a sound of hissing; steam ascended in the moonlight; the beaten nigger groaned somewhere. 'What a row the brute makes!' said the indefatigable man with the moustaches, appearing near us. 'Serve him right. Transgression—punishment—bang! Pitiless, pitiless. That's the only way. This will prevent all conflagrations for the future. I was just telling the manager . . .' He noticed my companion, and became crestfallen all at once. 'Not in bed yet,' he said, with a kind of servile heartiness; 'it's so natural. Ha! Danger—agitation.' He vanished. I went on to the river-side, and the other followed me. I heard a scathing murmur at my ear, 'Heap of muffs—go to.' The pilgrims could be seen in knots gesticulating, discussing. Several had still their staves in their hands. I verily believe they took these sticks to bed with them. Beyond the fence the forest stood up spectrally in the moonlight, and through the dim stir, through the faint sounds of that lamentable courtyard, the silence of the land went home to one's very heart—its mystery, its greatness, the amazing reality of its concealed life. The hurt nigger moaned feebly somewhere near by, and then fetched a deep sigh that made me mend my pace away from there. I felt a hand introducing itself under my arm. 'My dear sir,' said the fellow, 'I don't want to be misunderstood, and especially by you, who will see Mr Kurtz long before I can have that pleasure. I wouldn't like him to get a false idea of my disposition. . . .'

"I let him run on, this papier-mâché Mephistopheles, and it seemed to me that if I tried I could poke my forefinger through him, and would find nothing inside but a little loose dirt, maybe. He, don't you see, had been planning to be assistant-manager by and by under the present man, and I could see that the coming of that Kurtz had upset them both not a little. He talked precipitately, and I did not try to stop him. I had my shoulders against the wreck of my steamer, hauled up on the slope like a carcass of some big river animal. The smell of mud, of primeval mud, by Jove! was in my nostrils, the high stillness of primeval forest was before my eyes; there were shiny patches on the black creek. The moon had spread over everything a thin layer of silver—over the rank grass, over the mud, upon the wall of matted vegetation standing higher than the wall of a temple, over the great river I could see through a sombre gap glittering, glittering, as it flowed broadly by without a murmur. All this was great, expectant, mute, while the man jabbered about himself. I wondered whether the stillness on the face of the immensity looking at us two were meant as an appeal or as a menace. What were we who had strayed in here? Could we handle that dumb thing, or would it handle us? I felt how big, how confoundedly big, was that thing that couldn't talk and perhaps was deaf as well. What was in there? I could see a little ivory coming out from there, and I had heard Mr Kurtz was in there. I had heard enough about it too—God knows! Yet somehow it didn't bring any image with it—no more than if I had been told an angel or a fiend was in there. I believed it in the same way one of you might believe there are inhabitants in the planet Mars. I knew once a Scotch sailmaker who was certain, dead sure, there were people in Mars. If you asked him for some idea how they looked and behaved, he would get shy and mutter something about 'walking on all-fours.' If you as much as smiled, he would—though a man of sixty—offer to fight you. I would not have gone so far as to fight for Kurtz, but I went for him near enough to a lie. You know I hate, detest, and can't bear a lie, not because I am straighter than the rest of us, but simply because it appals me. There is a taint of death, a flavour of mortality in lies—which is exactly what I hate and detest in the world—what I want to forget. It makes me miserable and sick, like biting something rotten would do. Temperament, I suppose. Well, I went near enough to it by letting the young fool there believe anything he liked to imagine as to my influence in Europe. I became in an instant as much of a pretence as the rest of the bewitched pilgrims. This simply because I had a notion it somehow would be of help to that Kurtz whom at the time I did not see—you understand. He was just a word for me. I did not see the man in the name any more than you do. Do you see him? Do you see the story? Do you see anything? It seems to me I am trying to tell you a dream—making a vain attempt, because no relation of a dream can convey the dream-sensation, that commingling of absurdity, surprise, and bewilderment in a tremor of struggling revolt, that notion of being captured by the incredible which is of the very essence of dreams. . . ."

He was silent for a while.

". . . No, it is impossible; it is impossible to convey the life-sensation of any given epoch of one's existence—that which makes its truth, its meaning—its subtle and penetrating essence. It is impossible. We live, as we dream—alone. . . ."

He paused again as if reflecting, then added:

"Of course in this you fellows see more than I could then. You see me, whom you know. . . ."

It had become so pitch dark that we listeners could hardly see one another. For a long time already he, sitting apart, had been no more to us than a voice. There was not a word from anybody. The others might have been asleep, but I was awake. I listened, I listened on the watch for the sentence, for the word, that would give me the clue to the faint uneasiness inspired by this narrative that seemed to shape itself without human lips in the heavy night-air of the river.

". . . Yes—I let him run on," Marlow began again, "and think what he pleased about the powers that were behind me. I did! And there was nothing behind me! There was nothing but that wretched, old, mangled steamboat I was leaning against, while he talked fluently about 'the necessity for every man to get on.' 'And when one comes out here, you conceive, it is not to gaze at the moon.' Mr Kurtz was a 'universal genius,' but even a genius would find it easier to work with 'adequate tools—intelligent men.' He did not make bricks—why, there was a physical impossibility in the way—as I was well aware; and if he did secretarial work for the manager, it was because 'no sensible man rejects wantonly the confidence of his superiors.' Did I see it? I saw it. What more did I want? What I really wanted was rivets, by heaven! Rivets. To get on with the work—to stop the hole. Rivets I wanted. There were cases of them down at the coast—cases—piled up—burst—split! You kicked a loose rivet at every second step in that station yard on the hillside. Rivets had rolled into the grove of death. You could fill your pockets with rivets for the trouble of stooping down—and there wasn't one rivet to be found where it was wanted. We had plates that would do, but nothing to fasten them with. And every week the messenger, a lone negro, letter-bag on shoulder and staff in hand, left our station for the coast. And several times a week a coast caravan came in with trade goods—ghastly glazed calico that made you shudder only to look at it, glass beads value about a penny a quart, confounded spotted cotton handkerchiefs. And no rivets. Three carriers could have brought all that was wanted to set that steamboat afloat.

"He was becoming confidential now, but I fancy my unresponsive attitude must have exasperated him at last, for he judged it necessary to inform me he feared neither God nor devil, let alone any mere man. I said I could see that very well, but what I wanted was a certain quantity of rivets—and rivets were what really Mr Kurtz wanted, if he had only known it. Now letters went to the coast every week. . . . 'My dear sir,' he cried, 'I write from dictation.' I demanded rivets. There was a way—for an intelligent man. He changed his manner; became very cold, and suddenly began to talk about a hippopotamus; wondered whether sleeping on board the steamer (I stuck to my salvage night and day) I wasn't disturbed. There was an old hippo that had the bad habit of getting out on the bank and roaming at night over the station grounds. The pilgrims used to turn out in a body and empty every rifle they could lay hands on at him. Some even had sat up o' nights for him. All this energy was wasted, though. 'That animal has a charmed life,' he said; 'but you can say this only of brutes in this country. No man—you apprehend me?—no man here bears a charmed life.' He stood there for a moment in the moonlight with his delicate hooked nose set a little askew, and his mica eyes glittering without a wink, then, with a curt Good-night, he strode off. I could see he was disturbed and considerably puzzled, which made me feel more hopeful than I had been for days. It was a great comfort to turn from that chap to my influential friend, the battered, twisted, ruined, tinpot steamboat. I clambered on board. She rang under my feet like an empty Huntley & Palmer biscuit-tin kicked along a gutter; she was nothing so solid in make, and rather less pretty in shape, but I had expended enough hard work on her to make me love her. No influential friend would have served me better. She had given me a chance to come out a bit—to find out what I could do. No, I don't like work. I had rather laze about and think of all the fine things that can be done. I don't like work—no man does—but I like what is in the work—the chance to find yourself. Your own reality—for yourself, not for others—what no other man can ever know. They can only see the mere show, and never can tell what it really means.

"I was not surprised to see somebody sitting aft, on the deck, with his legs dangling over the mud. You see I rather chummed with the few mechanics there were in that station, whom the other pilgrims naturally despised—on account of their imperfect manners, I suppose. This was the foreman—a boiler-maker by trade—a good worker. He was a lank, bony, yellow-faced man, with big intense eyes. His aspect was worried, and his head was as bald as the palm of my hand; but his hair in falling seemed to have stuck to his chin, and had prospered in the new locality, for his beard hung down to his waist. He was a widower with six young children (he had left them in charge of a sister of his to come out there), and the passion of his life was pigeon-flying. He was an enthusiast and a connoisseur. He would rave about pigeons. After work hours he used sometimes to come over from his hut for a talk about his children and his pigeons; at work, when he had to crawl in the mud under the bottom of the steamboat, he would tie up that beard of his in a kind of white serviette[4] he brought for the purpose. It had loops to

4. Table napkin (French).

go over his ears. In the evening he could be seen squatted on the bank rinsing that wrapper in the creek with great care, then spreading it solemnly on a bush to dry.

"I slapped him on the back and shouted 'We shall have rivets!' He scrambled to his feet exclaiming 'No! Rivets!' as though he couldn't believe his ears. Then in a low voice, 'You . . . eh?' I don't know why we behaved like lunatics. I put my finger to the side of my nose and nodded mysteriously. 'Good for you!' he cried, snapped his fingers above his head, lifting one foot. I tried a jig. We capered on the iron deck. A frightful clatter came out of that hulk, and the virgin forest on the other bank of the creek sent it back in a thundering roll upon the sleeping station. It must have made some of the pilgrims sit up in their hovels. A dark figure obscured the lighted doorway of the manager's hut, vanished, then, a second or so after, the doorway itself vanished too. We stopped, and the silence driven away by the stamping of our feet flowed back again from the recesses of the land. The great wall of vegetation, an exuberant and entangled mass of trunks, branches, leaves, boughs, festoons, motionless in the moonlight, was like a rioting invasion of soundless life, a rolling wave of plants, piled up, crested, ready to topple over the creek, to sweep every little man of us out of his little existence. And it moved not. A deadened burst of mighty splashes and snorts reached us from afar, as though an ichthyosaurus[5] had been taking a bath of glitter in the great river. 'After all,' said the boiler-maker in a reasonable tone, 'why shouldn't we get the rivets?' Why not, indeed! I did not know of any reason why we shouldn't. 'They'll come in three weeks,' I said confidently.

"But they didn't. Instead of rivets there came an invasion, an infliction, a visitation. It came in sections during the next three weeks, each section headed by a donkey carrying a white man in new clothes and tan shoes, bowing from that elevation right and left to the impressed pilgrims. A quarrelsome band of footsore sulky niggers trod on the heels of the donkey; a lot of tents, camp-stools, tin boxes, white cases, brown bales would be shot down in the courtyard, and the air of mystery would deepen a little over the muddle of the station. Five such instalments came, with their absurd air of disorderly flight with the loot of innumerable outfit shops and provision stores, that, one would think, they were lugging, after a raid, into the wilderness for equitable division. It was an inextricable mess of things decent in themselves but that human folly made look like the spoils of thieving.

"This devoted band called itself the Eldorado[6] Exploring Expedition, and I believe they were sworn to secrecy. Their talk, however, was the talk of sordid buccaneers: it was reckless without hardihood, greedy without audacity, and cruel without courage; there was not an atom of foresight or of serious intention in the whole batch of them, and they did not seem aware these things are wanted for the work of the world. To tear treasure out of the bowels of the land was their desire, with no more moral purpose at the back of it than there is in burglars breaking into a safe. Who paid the expenses of the noble enterprise I don't know; but the uncle of our manager was leader of that lot.

---

5. An extinct prehistoric marine animal combining aspects of a crocodile and a fish.   6. *El Dorado* (literally, "the gilded one," Spanish), the land of gold sought by the Spanish conquistadors in South America.

"In exterior he resembled a butcher in a poor neighbourhood, and his eyes had a look of sleepy cunning. He carried his fat paunch with ostentation on his short legs, and during the time his gang infested the station spoke to no one but his nephew. You could see these two roaming about all day long with their heads close together in an everlasting confab.[7]

"I had given up worrying myself about the rivets. One's capacity for that kind of folly is more limited than you would suppose. I said Hang!—and let things slide. I had plenty of time for meditation, and now and then I would give some thought to Kurtz. I wasn't very interested in him. No. Still, I was curious to see whether this man, who had come out equipped with moral ideas of some sort, would climb to the top after all, and how he would set about his work when there."

2

"One evening as I was lying flat on the deck of my steamboat, I heard voices approaching—and there were the nephew and the uncle strolling along the bank. I laid my head on my arm again, and had nearly lost myself in a doze, when somebody said in my ear, as it were: 'I am as harmless as a little child, but I don't like to be dictated to. Am I the manager—or am I not? I was ordered to send him there. It's incredible.' . . . I became aware that the two were standing on the shore alongside the forepart of the steamboat, just below my head. I did not move; it did not occur to me to move: I was sleepy. 'It *is* unpleasant,' grunted the uncle. 'He has asked the Administration to be sent there,' said the other, 'with the idea of showing what he could do; and I was instructed accordingly. Look at the influence that man must have. Is it not frightful?' They both agreed it was frightful, then made several bizarre remarks: 'Make rain and fine weather—one man—the Council—by the nose'—bits of absurd sentences that got the better of my drowsiness, so that I had pretty near the whole of my wits about me when the uncle said, 'The climate may do away with this difficulty for you. Is he alone there?' 'Yes,' answered the manager; 'he sent his assistant down the river with a note to me in these terms: "Clear this poor devil out of the country, and don't bother sending more of that sort. I had rather be alone than have the kind of men you can dispose of with me." It was more than a year ago. Can you imagine such impudence?' 'Anything since then?' asked the other hoarsely. 'Ivory,' jerked the nephew; 'lots of it—prime sort—lots—most annoying, from him.' 'And with that?' questioned the heavy rumble. 'Invoice,' was the reply fired out, so to speak. Then silence. They had been talking about Kurtz.

"I was broad awake by this time, but, lying perfectly at ease, remained still, having no inducement to change my position. 'How did that ivory come all this way?' growled the elder man, who seemed very vexed. The other explained that it had come with a fleet of canoes in charge of an English half-caste clerk Kurtz had with him; that Kurtz had apparently intended to return himself, the station being by that time bare of goods and stores, but after coming three hundred miles, had suddenly decided to go back, which he started to do alone in a small dugout with four paddlers, leaving the half-caste to continue down the river with the ivory. The two fellows there

7. Conversation.

seemed astounded at anybody attempting such a thing. They were at a loss for an adequate motive. As for me, I seemed to see Kurtz for the first time. It was a distinct glimpse: the dugout, four paddling savages, and the lone white man turning his back suddenly on the headquarters, on relief, on thoughts of home—perhaps; setting his face towards the depths of the wilderness, towards his empty and desolate station. I did not know the motive. Perhaps he was just simply a fine fellow who stuck to his work for its own sake. His name, you understand, had not been pronounced once. He was 'that man.' The half-caste, who, as far as I could see, had conducted a difficult trip with great prudence and pluck, was invariably alluded to as 'that scoundrel.' The 'scoundrel' had reported that the 'man' had been very ill—had recovered imperfectly. . . . The two below me moved away then a few paces, and strolled back and forth at some little distance. I heard: 'Military post—doctor—two hundred miles—quite alone now—unavoidable delays—nine months—no news—strange rumours.' They approached again, just as the manager was saying, 'No one, as far as I know, unless a species of wandering trader—a pestilential fellow, snapping ivory from the natives.' Who was it they were talking about now? I gathered in snatches that this was some man supposed to be in Kurtz's district, and of whom the manager did not approve. 'We will not be free from unfair competition till one of these fellows is hanged for an example,' he said. 'Certainly,' grunted the other; 'get him hanged! Why not? Anything—anything can be done in this country. That's what I say; nobody here, you understand, *here*, can endanger your position. And why? You stand the climate—you outlast them all. The danger is in Europe; but there before I left I took care to—' They moved off and whispered, then their voices rose again. 'The extraordinary series of delays is not my fault. I did my possible.' The fat man sighed, 'Very sad.' 'And the pestiferous absurdity of his talk,' continued the other; 'he bothered me enough when he was here. "Each station should be like a beacon on the road towards better things, a centre for trade of course, but also for humanising, improving, instructing." Conceive you[8]—that ass! And he wants to be manager! No, it's—' Here he got choked by excessive indignation, and I lifted my head the least bit. I was surprised to see how near they were—right under me. I could have spat upon their hats. They were looking on the ground, absorbed in thought. The manager was switching his leg with a slender twig: his sagacious relative lifted his head. 'You have been well since you came out this time?' he asked. The other gave a start. 'Who? I? Oh! Like a charm—like a charm. But the rest—oh, my goodness! All sick. They die so quick, too, that I haven't the time to send them out of the country—it's incredible!' 'H'm. Just so,' grunted the uncle. 'Ah! my boy, trust to this—I say, trust to this.' I saw him extend his short flipper of an arm for a gesture that took in the forest, the creek, the mud, the river—seemed to beckon with a dishonouring flourish before the sunlit face of the land a treacherous appeal to the lurking death, to the hidden evil, to the profound darkness of its heart. It was so startling that I leaped to my feet and looked back at the edge of the forest, as though I had expected an answer of some sort to that black display

---

8. "Just imagine." This phrase—like "I did my possible" (I did the best I could), above, and others throughout the novel—is a literal translation of the French spoken by Belgian traders. Conrad reminds us of the setting: the Belgian Congo was an international scandal for its brutal treatment of Africans.

of confidence. You know the foolish notions that come to one sometimes. The high stillness confronted these two figures with its ominous patience, waiting for the passing away of a fantastic invasion.

"They swore aloud together—out of sheer fright, I believe—then, pretending not to know anything of my existence, turned back to the station. The sun was low; and leaning forward side by side, they seemed to be tugging painfully uphill their two ridiculous shadows of unequal length, that trailed behind them slowly over the tall grass without bending a single blade.

"In a few days the Eldorado Expedition went into the patient wilderness, that closed upon it as the sea closes over a diver. Long afterwards the news came that all the donkeys were dead. I know nothing as to the fate of the less valuable animals. They, no doubt, like the rest of us, found what they deserved. I did not inquire. I was then rather excited at the prospect of meeting Kurtz very soon. When I say very soon I mean it comparatively. It was just two months from the day we left the creek when we came to the bank below Kurtz's station.

"Going up that river was like travelling back to the earliest beginnings of the world, when vegetation rioted on the earth and the big trees were kings. An empty stream, a great silence, an impenetrable forest. The air was warm, thick, heavy, sluggish. There was no joy in the brilliance of sunshine. The long stretches of the waterway ran on, deserted, into the gloom of overshadowed distances. On silvery sandbanks hippos and alligators sunned themselves side by side. The broadening waters flowed through a mob of wooded islands; you lost your way on that river as you would in a desert, and butted all day long against shoals, trying to find the channel, till you thought yourself bewitched and cut off for ever from everything you had known once—somewhere—far away—in another existence perhaps. There were moments when one's past came back to one, as it will sometimes when you have not a moment to spare to yourself; but it came in the shape of an unrestful and noisy dream, remembered with wonder amongst the overwhelming realities of this strange world of plants, and water, and silence. And this stillness of life did not in the least resemble a peace. It was the stillness of an implacable force brooding over an inscrutable intention. It looked at you with a vengeful aspect. I got used to it afterwards; I did not see it any more; I had no time. I had to keep guessing at the channel; I had to discern, mostly by inspiration, the signs of hidden banks; I watched for sunken stones; I was learning to clap my teeth smartly before my heart flew out, when I shaved by a fluke some infernal sly old snag that would have ripped the life out of the tin-pot steamboat and drowned all the pilgrims; I had to keep a look-out for the signs of dead wood we could cut up in the night for next day's steaming. When you have to attend to things of that sort, to the mere incidents of the surface, the reality—the reality, I tell you—fades. The inner truth is hidden—luckily, luckily. But I felt it all the same; I felt often its mysterious stillness watching me at my monkey tricks, just as it watches you fellows performing on your respective tight-ropes for—what is it? half a crown a tumble—"

"Try to be civil, Marlow," growled a voice, and I knew there was at least one listener awake besides myself.

"I beg your pardon. I forgot the heartache which makes up the rest of the price. And indeed what does the price matter, if the trick be well done? You do your tricks very well. And I didn't do badly either, since I managed not to sink that steamboat on my first trip. It's a wonder to me yet. Imagine a blindfolded man set to drive a van over a bad road. I sweated and shivered over that business considerably, I can tell you. After all, for a seaman, to scrape the bottom of the thing that's supposed to float all the time under his care is the unpardonable sin. No one may know of it, but you never forget the thump—eh? A blow on the very heart. You remember it, you dream of it, you wake up at night and think of it—years after—and go hot and cold all over. I don't pretend to say that steamboat floated all the time. More than once she had to wade for a bit, with twenty cannibals splashing around and pushing. We had enlisted some of these chaps on the way for a crew. Fine fellows—cannibals—in their place. They were men one could work with, and I am grateful to them. And, after all, they did not eat each other before my face: they had brought along a provision of hippo-meat which went rotten, and made the mystery of the wilderness stink in my nostrils. Phoo! I can sniff it now. I had the manager on board and three or four pilgrims with their staves—all complete. Sometimes we came upon a station close by the bank, clinging to the skirts of the unknown, and the white men rushing out of a tumble-down hovel, with great gestures of joy and surprise and welcome, seemed very strange—had the appearance of being held there captive by a spell. The word 'ivory' would ring in the air for a while—and on we went again into the silence, along empty reaches, round the still bends, between the high walls of our winding way, reverberating in hollow claps the ponderous beat of the stern-wheel. Trees, trees, millions of trees, massive, immense, running up high; and at their foot, hugging the bank against the stream, crept the little begrimed steamboat, like a sluggish beetle crawling on the floor of a lofty portico. It made you feel very small, very lost, and yet it was not altogether depressing, that feeling. After all, if you were small, the grimy beetle crawled on—which was just what you wanted it to do. Where the pilgrims imagined it crawled to I don't know. To some place where they expected to get something, I bet! For me it crawled towards Kurtz—exclusively; but when the steam-pipes started leaking we crawled very slow. The reaches opened before us and closed behind, as if the forest had stepped leisurely across the water to bar the way for our return. We penetrated deeper and deeper into the heart of darkness. It was very quiet there. At night sometimes the roll of drums behind the curtain of trees would run up the river and remain sustained faintly, as if hovering in the air high over our heads, till the first break of day. Whether it meant war, peace, or prayer we could not tell. The dawns were heralded by the descent of a chill stillness; the woodcutters slept, their fires burned low; the snapping of a twig would make you start. We were wanderers on a prehistoric earth, on an earth that wore the aspect of an unknown planet. We could have fancied ourselves the first of men taking possession of an accursed inheritance, to be subdued at the cost of profound anguish and of excessive toil. But suddenly, as we struggled round a bend, there would be a glimpse of rush walls, of peaked grass-roofs, a burst of yells, a whirl of black limbs, a mass of hands clapping, of feet stamping, of bodies swaying, of eyes rolling, under the droop of heavy and motionless foliage. The steamer toiled along slowly on the edge of a black and incomprehensible frenzy. The prehistoric man was cursing us, praying to us, welcoming us—who could tell? We were cut off from the comprehension of our surroundings; we glided past like phantoms, wondering and secretly appalled, as sane men would be before an enthusiastic outbreak in a madhouse. We could not understand because we were too far and could not remember, because we were travelling in the night of first ages, of those ages that are gone, leaving hardly a sign—and no memories.

"The earth seemed unearthly. We are accustomed to look upon the shackled form of a conquered monster, but there—there you could look at a thing monstrous and free. It was unearthly, and the men were—No, they were not inhuman. Well, you know, that was the worst of it—this suspicion of their not being inhuman. It would come slowly to one. They howled and leaped, and spun, and made horrid faces; but what thrilled you was just the thought of their humanity—like yours—the thought of your remote kinship with this wild and passionate uproar. Ugly. Yes, it was ugly enough; but if you were man enough you would admit to yourself that there was in you just the faintest trace of a response to the terrible frankness of that noise, a dim suspicion of there being a meaning in it which you—you so remote from the night of first ages—could comprehend. And why not? The mind of man is capable of anything—because everything is in it, all the past as well as all the future. What was there after all? Joy, fear, sorrow, devotion, valour, rage—who can tell?—but truth—truth stripped of its cloak of time. Let the fool gape and shudder—the man knows, and can look on without a wink. But he must at least be as much of a man as these on the shore. He must meet that truth with his own true stuff—with his own inborn strength. Principles? Principles won't do. Acquisitions, clothes, pretty rags—rags that would fly off at the first good shake. No; you want a deliberate belief. An appeal to me in this fiendish row—is there? Very well; I hear; I admit, but I have a voice too, and for good or evil mine is the speech that cannot be silenced. Of course, a fool, what with sheer fright and fine sentiments, is always safe. Who's that grunting? You wonder I didn't go ashore for a howl and a dance? Well, no—I didn't. Fine sentiments, you say? Fine sentiments be hanged! I had no time. I had to mess about with white-lead and strips of woollen blanket helping to put bandages on those leaky steam-pipes—I tell you. I had to watch the steering, and circumvent those snags, and get the tin-pot along by hook or by crook. There was surface-truth enough in these things to save a wiser man. And between whiles I had to look after the savage who was fireman. He was an improved specimen; he could fire up a vertical boiler.[9] He was there below me, and, upon my word, to look at him was as edifying as seeing a dog in a parody of breeches and a feather hat, walking on his hind legs. A few months of training had done for that really fine chap. He squinted at the steam-gauge and at the water-gauge with an evident effort of intrepidity—and he had filed teeth too, the poor devil, and the wool of his pate shaved into queer patterns, and three ornamental scars on each of his cheeks. He ought to have been clapping his hands and stamping his feet on the bank, instead of which he was hard at work, a thrall to strange witchcraft, full of improving knowledge. He was useful because he had been instructed; and what he knew was this—that should the water in that transparent thing disappear, the evil spirit inside the boiler would get angry through the greatness of his thirst, and take a terrible vengeance. So

9. A simple and easily fired narrow boiler.

he sweated and fired up and watched the glass fearfully (with an impromptu charm, made of rags, tied to his arm, and a piece of polished bone, as big as a watch, stuck flatways through his lower lip), while the wooded banks slipped past us slowly, the short noise was left behind, the interminable miles of silence—and we crept on, towards Kurtz. But the snags were thick, the water was treacherous and shallow, the boiler seemed indeed to have a sulky devil in it, and thus neither that fireman nor I had any time to peer into our creepy thoughts.

"Some fifty miles below the Inner Station we came upon a hut of reeds, an inclined and melancholy pole, with the unrecognisable tatters of what had been a flag of some sort flying from it, and a neatly stacked wood-pile. This was unexpected. We came to the bank, and on the stack of firewood found a flat piece of board with some faded pencil-writing on it. When deciphered it said: 'Wood for you. Hurry up. Approach cautiously.' There was a signature, but it was illegible—not Kurtz—a much longer word. Hurry up. Where? Up the river? 'Approach cautiously.' We had not done so. But the warning could not have been meant for the place where it could be only found after approach. Something was wrong above. But what—and how much? That was the question. We commented adversely upon the imbecility of that tele-graphic style. The bush around said nothing, and would not let us look very far, either. A torn curtain of red twill hung in the doorway of the hut, and flapped sadly in our faces. The dwelling was dismantled; but we could see a white man had lived there not very long ago. There remained a rude table— a plank on two posts; a heap of rubbish reposed in a dark corner, and by the door I picked up a book. It had lost its covers, and the pages had been thumbed into a state of extremely dirty softness; but the back had been lov-ingly stitched afresh with white cotton thread, which looked clean yet. It was an extraordinary find. Its title was, *An Inquiry into some Points of Seaman-ship*, by a man Towser, Towson—some such name—Master in His Majesty's Navy. The matter looked dreary reading enough, with illustrative diagrams and repulsive tables of figures, and the copy was sixty years old. I handled this amazing antiquity with the greatest possible tenderness, lest it should dissolve in my hands. Within, Towson or Towser was inquiring earnestly into the breaking strain of ships' chains and tackle, and other such matters. Not a very enthralling book; but at the first glance you could see there a singleness of intention, an honest concern for the right way of going to work, which made these humble pages, thought out so many years ago, luminous with another than a professional light. The simple old sailor, with his talk of chains and purchases, made me forget the jungle and the pilgrims in a deli-cious sensation of having come upon something unmistakably real. Such a book being there was wonderful enough; but still more astounding were the notes pencilled in the margin, and plainly referring to the text. I couldn't believe my eyes! They were in cipher! Yes, it looked like cipher. Fancy a man lugging with him a book of that description into this nowhere and studying it—and making notes—in cipher at that! It was an extravagant mystery.

"I had been dimly aware for some time of a worrying noise, and when I lifted my eyes I saw the wood-pile was gone, and the manager, aided by all the pilgrims, was shouting at me from the river-side. I slipped the book into my pocket. I assure you to leave off reading was like tearing myself away from the shelter of an old and solid friendship.

"I started the lame engine ahead. 'It must be this miserable trader—this intruder,' exclaimed the manager, looking back malevolently at the place we had left. 'He must be English,' I said. 'It will not save him from getting into trouble if he is not careful,' muttered the manager darkly. I observed with assumed innocence that no man was safe from trouble in this world.

"The current was more rapid now, the steamer seemed at her last gasp, the stern-wheel flopped languidly, and I caught myself listening on tiptoe for the next beat of the float,[1] for in sober truth I expected the wretched thing to give up every moment. It was like watching the last flickers of a life. But still we crawled. Sometimes I would pick out a tree a little way ahead to measure our progress towards Kurtz by, but I lost it invariably before we got abreast. To keep the eyes so long on one thing was too much for human patience. The manager displayed a beautiful resignation. I fretted and fumed and took to arguing with myself whether or no I would talk openly with Kurtz; but before I could come to any conclusion it occurred to me that my speech or my silence, indeed any action of mine, would be a mere futility. What did it matter what any one knew or ignored? What did it matter who was manager? One gets sometimes such a flash of insight. The essentials of this affair lay deep under the surface, beyond my reach, and beyond my power of meddling.

"Towards the evening of the second day we judged ourselves about eight miles from Kurtz's station. I wanted to push on; but the manager looked grave, and told me the navigation up there was so dangerous that it would be advisable, the sun being very low already, to wait where we were till next morning. Moreover, he pointed out that if the warning to approach cautiously were to be followed, we must approach in daylight—not at dusk, or in the dark. This was sensible enough. Eight miles meant nearly three hours' steaming for us, and I could also see suspicious ripples at the upper end of the reach. Nevertheless, I was annoyed beyond expression at the delay, and most unreasonably too, since one night more could not matter much after so many months. As we had plenty of wood, and caution was the word, I brought up in the middle of the stream. The reach was narrow, straight, with high sides like a railway cutting. The dusk came gliding into it long before the sun had set. The current ran smooth and swift, but a dumb immobility sat on the banks. The living trees, lashed together by the creepers and every living bush of the undergrowth, might have been changed into stone, even to the slenderest twig, to the lightest leaf. It was not sleep—it seemed unnatural, like a state of trance. Not the faintest sound of any kind could be heard. You looked on amazed, and began to suspect yourself of being deaf—then the night came suddenly, and struck you blind as well. About three in the morning some large fish leaped, and the loud splash made me jump as though a gun had been fired. When the sun rose there was a white fog, very warm and clammy, and more blinding than the night. It did not shift or drive; it was just there, standing all round you like something solid. At eight or nine, perhaps, it lifted as a shutter lifts. We had a glimpse of the towering multitude of trees, of the immense matted jungle, with the blazing little ball of the sun hanging over it—all perfectly still—and then the white shutter came down again, smoothly, as if sliding in greased grooves. I ordered the

1. The sound of the paddle ("paddle float") as it hits the water.

chain, which we had begun to heave in, to be paid out again. Before it stopped running with a muffled rattle, a cry, a very loud cry, as of infinite desolation, soared slowly in the opaque air. It ceased. A complaining clamour, modulated in savage discords, filled our ears. The sheer unexpectedness of it made my hair stir under my cap. I don't know how it struck the others: to me it seemed as though the mist itself had screamed, so suddenly, and apparently from all sides at once, did this tumultuous and mournful uproar arise. It culminated in a hurried outbreak of almost intolerably excessive shrieking, which stopped short, leaving us stiffened in a variety of silly attitudes, and obstinately listening to the nearly as appalling and excessive silence. 'Good God! What is the meaning—?' stammered at my elbow one of the pilgrims—a little fat man, with sandy hair and red whiskers, who wore side-spring boots, and pink pyjamas tucked into his socks. Two others remained open-mouthed a whole minute, then dashed into the little cabin, to rush out incontinently and stand darting scared glances, with Winchesters[2] at 'ready' in their hands. What we could see was just the steamer we were on, her outlines blurred as though she had been on the point of dissolving, and a misty strip of water, perhaps two feet broad, around her—and that was all. The rest of the world was nowhere, as far as our eyes and ears were concerned. Just nowhere. Gone, disappeared; swept off without leaving a whisper or a shadow behind.

"I went forward, and ordered the chain to be hauled in short, so as to be ready to trip the anchor and move the steamboat at once if necessary. 'Will they attack?' whispered an awed voice. 'We will all be butchered in this fog,' murmured another. The faces twitched with the strain, the hands trembled slightly, the eyes forgot to wink. It was very curious to see the contrast of expressions of the white men and of the black fellows of our crew, who were as much strangers to that part of the river as we, though their homes were only eight hundred miles away. The whites, of course greatly discomposed, had besides a curious look of being painfully shocked by such an outrageous row. The others had an alert, naturally interested expression; but their faces were essentially quiet, even those of the one or two who grinned as they hauled at the chain. Several exchanged short, grunting phrases, which seemed to settle the matter to their satisfaction. Their headman, a young, broad-chested black, severely draped in dark-blue fringed cloths, with fierce nostrils and his hair all done up artfully in oily ringlets, stood near me. 'Aha!' I said, just for good fellowship's sake. 'Catch 'im,' he snapped, with a blood-shot widening of his eyes and a flash of sharp teeth—'catch 'im. Give 'im to us.' 'To you, eh?' I asked; 'what would you do with them?' 'Eat 'im!' he said curtly, and, leaning his elbow on the rail, looked out into the fog in a dignified and profoundly pensive attitude. I would no doubt have been properly horrified, had it not occurred to me that he and his chaps must be very hungry: that they must have been growing increasingly hungry for at least this month past. They had been engaged for six months (I don't think a single one of them had any clear idea of time, as we at the end of countless ages have. They still belonged to the beginnings of time—had no inherited experience to teach them, as it were), and of course, as long as there was a piece of paper written over in accordance with some farcical law or other made

---

2. Breech-loading rifles.

down the river, it didn't enter anybody's head to trouble how they would live. Certainly they had brought with them some rotten hippo-meat, which couldn't have lasted very long, anyway, even if the pilgrims hadn't, in the midst of a shocking hullabaloo, thrown a considerable quantity of it overboard. It looked like a high-handed proceeding; but it was really a case of legitimate self-defence. You can't breathe dead hippo waking, sleeping, and eating, and at the same time keep your precarious grip on existence. Besides that, they had given them every week three pieces of brass wire, each about nine inches long; and the theory was they were to buy their provisions with that currency in river-side villages. You can see how *that* worked. There were either no villages, or the people were hostile, or the director, who like the rest of us fed out of tins, with an occasional old he-goat thrown in, didn't want to stop the steamer for some more or less recondite reasons. So, unless they swallowed the wire itself, or made loops of it to snare the fishes with, I don't see what good their extravagant salary could be to them. I must say it was paid with a regularity worthy of a large and honourable trading company. For the rest, the only thing to eat—though it didn't look eatable in the least—I saw in their possession was a few lumps of some stuff like half-cooked dough, of a dirty lavender colour, they kept wrapped in leaves, and now and then swallowed a piece of, but so small that it seemed done more for the look of the thing than for any serious purpose of sustenance. Why in the name of all the gnawing devils of hunger they didn't go for us—they were thirty to five—and have a good tuck-in for once, amazes me now when I think of it. They were big powerful men, with not much capacity to weigh the consequences, with courage, with strength, even yet, though their skins were no longer glossy and their muscles no longer hard. And I saw that something restraining, one of those human secrets that baffle probability, had come into play there. I looked at them with a swift quickening of interest—not because it occurred to me I might be eaten by them before very long, though I own to you that just then I perceived—in a new light, as it were—how unwholesome the pilgrims looked, and I hoped, yes, I positively hoped, that my aspect was not so—what shall I say?—so—unappetising: a touch of fantastic vanity which fitted well with the dream-sensation that pervaded all my days at that time. Perhaps I had a little fever too. One can't live with one's finger everlastingly on one's pulse. I had often 'a little fever,' or a little touch of other things—the playful paw-strokes of the wilderness, the preliminary trifling before the more serious onslaught which came in due course. Yes; I looked at them as you would on any human being, with a curiosity of their impulses, motives, capacities, weaknesses, when brought to the test of an inexorable physical necessity. Restraint! What possible restraint? Was it superstition, disgust, patience, fear—or some kind of primitive honour? No fear can stand up to hunger, no patience can wear it out, disgust simply does not exist where hunger is; and as to superstition, beliefs, and what you may call principles, they are less than chaff in a breeze. Don't you know the devilry of lingering starvation, its exasperating torment, its black thoughts, its sombre and brooding ferocity? Well, I do. It takes a man all his inborn strength to fight hunger properly. It's really easier to face bereavement, dishonour, and the perdition of one's soul—than this kind of prolonged hunger. Sad, but true. And these chaps too had no earthly reason for any kind of scruple. Restraint! I would just as soon have expected restraint from a hyena prowling amongst the corpses of a battlefield. But there was the fact facing me—the fact dazzling, to be seen, like the foam on the depths of the sea, like a ripple on an unfathomable enigma, a mystery greater—when I thought of it—than the curious, inexplicable note of desperate grief in this savage clamour that had swept by us on the river-bank, behind the blind whiteness of the fog.

"Two pilgrims were quarrelling in hurried whispers as to which bank. 'Left.' 'No, no; how can you? Right, right, of course.' 'It is very serious,' said the manager's voice behind me; 'I would be desolated if anything should happen to Mr. Kurtz before we came up.' I looked at him, and had not the slightest doubt he was sincere. He was just the kind of man who would wish to preserve appearances. That was his restraint. But when he muttered something about going on at once, I did not even take the trouble to answer him. I knew, and he knew, that it was impossible. Were we to let go our hold of the bottom, we would be absolutely in the air—in space. We wouldn't be able to tell where we were going to—whether up or down stream, or across—till we fetched against one bank or the other—and then we wouldn't know at first which it was. Of course I made no move. I had no mind for a smash-up. You couldn't imagine a more deadly place for a shipwreck. Whether drowned at once or not, we were sure to perish speedily in one way or another. 'I authorise you to take all the risks,' he said, after a short silence. 'I refuse to take any,' I said shortly; which was just the answer he expected, though its tone might have surprised him. 'Well, I must defer to your judgment. You are captain,' he said, with marked civility. I turned my shoulder to him in sign of my appreciation, and looked into the fog. How long would it last? It was the most hopeless look-out. The approach to this Kurtz grubbing for ivory in the wretched bush was beset by as many dangers as though he had been an enchanted princess sleeping in a fabulous castle. 'Will they attack, do you think?' asked the manager, in a confidential tone.

"I did not think they would attack, for several obvious reasons. The thick fog was one. If they left the bank in their canoes they would get lost in it, as we would be if we attempted to move. Still, I had also judged the jungle of both banks quite impenetrable—and yet eyes were in it, eyes that had seen us. The river-side bushes were certainly very thick; but the undergrowth behind was evidently penetrable. However, during the short lift I had seen no canoes anywhere in the reach—certainly not abreast of the steamer. But what made the idea of attack inconceivable to me was the nature of the noise—of the cries we had heard. They had not the fierce character boding of immediate hostile intention. Unexpected, wild, and violent as they had been, they had given me an irresistible impression of sorrow. The glimpse of the steamboat had for some reason filled those savages with unrestrained grief. The danger, if any, I expounded, was from our proximity to a great human passion let loose. Even extreme grief may ultimately vent itself in violence—but more generally takes the form of apathy. . . .

"You should have seen the pilgrims stare! They had no heart to grin, or even to revile me; but I believe they thought me gone mad—with fright, maybe. I delivered a regular lecture. My dear boys, it was no good bothering. Keep a look-out? Well, you may guess I watched the fog for the signs of lifting as a cat watches a mouse; but for anything else our eyes were of no more use to us than if we had been buried miles deep in a heap of cotton-wool. It felt like it too—choking, warm, stifling. Besides, all I said, though it sounded extravagant, was absolutely true to fact. What we afterwards alluded to as an attack was really an attempt at repulse. The action was very far from being aggressive—it was not even defensive, in the usual sense: it was undertaken under the stress of desperation, and in its essence was purely protective.

"It developed itself, I should say, two hours after the fog lifted, and its commencement was at a spot, roughly speaking, about a mile and a half below Kurtz's station. We had just floundered and flopped round a bend, when I saw an islet, a mere grassy hummock of bright green, in the middle of the stream. It was the only thing of the kind; but as we opened the reach more, I perceived it was the head of a long sandbank, or rather of a chain of shallow patches stretching down the middle of the river. They were discoloured, just awash, and the whole lot was seen just under the water, exactly as a man's backbone is seen running down the middle of his back under the skin. Now, as far as I did see, I could go to the right or to the left of this. I didn't know either channel, of course. The banks looked pretty well alike, the depth appeared the same; but as I had been informed the station was on the west side, I naturally headed for the western passage.

"No sooner had we fairly entered it than I became aware it was much narrower than I had supposed. To the left of us there was the long uninterrupted shoal, and to the right a high steep bank heavily overgrown with bushes. Above the bush the trees stood in serried ranks. The twigs overhung the current thickly, and from distance to distance a large limb of some tree projected rigidly over the stream. It was then well on in the afternoon, the face of the forest was gloomy, and a broad strip of shadow had already fallen on the water. In this shadow we steamed up—very slowly, as you may imagine. I sheered her well inshore—the water being deepest near the bank, as the sounding-pole informed me.

"One of my hungry and forbearing friends was sounding in the bows just below me. This steamboat was exactly like a decked scow. On the deck there were two little teak-wood houses, with doors and windows. The boiler was in the fore-end, and the machinery right astern. Over the whole there was a light roof, supported on stanchions. The funnel projected through that roof, and in front of the funnel a small cabin built of light planks served for a pilot-house. It contained a couch, two camp-stools, a loaded Martini-Henry[3] leaning in one corner, a tiny table, and the steering-wheel. It had a wide door in front and a broad shutter at each side. All these were always thrown open, of course. I spent my days perched up there on the extreme fore-end of that roof, before the door. At night I slept, or tried to, on the couch. An athletic black belonging to some coast tribe, and educated by my poor predecessor, was the helmsman. He sported a pair of brass earrings, wore a blue cloth wrapper from the waist to the ankles, and thought all the world of himself. He was the most unstable kind of fool I had ever seen. He steered with no end of a swagger while you were by; but if he lost sight of you, he became instantly the prey of an abject funk, and would let that cripple of a steamboat get the upper hand of him in a minute.

3. A breech-loading rifle taking an especially powerful charge.

"I was looking down at the sounding-pole, and feeling much annoyed to see at each try a little more of it stick out of that river, when I saw my pole-man give up the business suddenly, and stretch himself flat on the deck, without even taking the trouble to haul his pole in. He kept hold on it though, and it trailed in the water. At the same time the fireman, whom I could also see below me, sat down abruptly before his furnace and ducked his head. I was amazed. Then I had to look at the river mighty quick, because there was a snag in the fairway. Sticks, little sticks, were flying about—thick; they were whizzing before my nose, dropping below me, striking behind me against my pilot-house. All this time the river, the shore, the woods, were very quiet—perfectly quiet. I could only hear the heavy splashing thump of the stern-wheel and the patter of these things. We cleared the snag clumsily. Arrows, by Jove! We were being shot at! I stepped in quickly to close the shutter on the land-side. That fool-helmsman, his hands on the spokes, was lifting his knees high, stamping his feet, champing his mouth, like a reined-in horse. Confound him! And we were staggering within ten feet of the bank. I had to lean right out to swing the heavy shutter, and I saw a face amongst the leaves on the level with my own, looking at me very fierce and steady; and then suddenly, as though a veil had been removed from my eyes, I made out, deep in the tangled gloom, naked breasts, arms, legs, glaring eyes—the bush was swarming with human limbs in movement, glistening, of bronze colour. The twigs shook, swayed, and rustled, the arrows flew out of them, and then the shutter came to. 'Steer her straight,' I said to the helmsman. He held his head rigid, face forward; but his eyes rolled, he kept on lifting and setting down his feet gently, his mouth foamed a little. 'Keep quiet!' I said in a fury. I might just as well have ordered a tree not to sway in the wind. I darted out. Below me there was a great scuffle of feet on the iron deck; confused exclamations; a voice screamed, 'Can you turn back?' I caught sight of a V-shaped ripple on the water ahead. What? Another snag! A fusillade burst out under my feet. The pilgrims had opened with their Winchesters, and were simply squirting lead into that bush. A deuce of a lot of smoke came up and drove slowly forward. I swore at it. Now I couldn't see the ripple or the snag either. I stood in the doorway, peering, and the arrows came in swarms. They might have been poisoned, but they looked as though they wouldn't kill a cat. The bush began to howl. Our wood-cutters raised a warlike whoop; the report of a rifle just at my back deafened me. I glanced over my shoulder, and the pilot-house was yet full of noise and smoke when I made a dash at the wheel. The fool-nigger had dropped everything, to throw the shutter open and let off that Martini-Henry. He stood before the wide opening, glaring, and I yelled at him to come back, while I straightened the sudden twist out of that steamboat. There was no room to turn even if I had wanted to, the snag was somewhere very near ahead in that confounded smoke, there was no time to lose, so I just crowded her into the bank—right into the bank, where I knew the water was deep.

"We tore slowly along the overhanging bushes in a whirl of broken twigs and flying leaves. The fusillade below stopped short, as I had foreseen it would when the squirts got empty. I threw my head back to a glinting whizz that traversed the pilot-house, in at one shutter-hole and out at the other. Looking past that mad helmsman, who was shaking the empty rifle and yelling at the shore, I saw vague forms of men running bent double, leaping, gliding, distinct, incomplete, evanescent. Something big appeared in the air before the shutter, the rifle went overboard, and the man stepped back swiftly, looked at me over his shoulder in an extraordinary, profound, familiar manner, and fell upon my feet. The side of his head hit the wheel twice, and the end of what appeared a long cane clattered round and knocked over a little camp-stool. It looked as though after wrenching that thing from somebody ashore he had lost his balance in the effort. The thin smoke had blown away, we were clear of the snag, and looking ahead I could see that in another hundred yards or so I would be free to sheer off, away from the bank; but my feet felt so very warm and wet that I had to look down. The man had rolled on his back and stared straight up at me; both his hands clutched that cane. It was the shaft of a spear that, either thrown or lunged through the opening, had caught him in the side just below the ribs; the blade had gone in out of sight, after making a frightful gash; my shoes were full; a pool of blood lay very still, gleaming dark-red under the wheel; his eyes shone with an amazing lustre. The fusillade burst out again. He looked at me anxiously, gripping the spear like something precious, with an air of being afraid I would try to take it away from him. I had to make an effort to free my eyes from his gaze and attend to the steering. With one hand I felt above my head for the line of the steam whistle, and jerked out screech after screech hurriedly. The tumult of angry and warlike yells was checked instantly, and then from the depths of the woods went out such a tremulous and prolonged wail of mournful fear and utter despair as may be imagined to follow the flight of the last hope from the earth. There was a great commotion in the bush; the shower of arrows stopped, a few dropping shots rang out sharply—then silence, in which the languid beat of the stern-wheel came plainly to my ears. I put the helm hard a-starboard at the moment when the pilgrim in pink pyjamas, very hot and agitated, appeared in the doorway. 'The manager sends me—' he began in an official tone, and stopped short. 'Good God!' he said, glaring at the wounded man.

"We two whites stood over him, and his lustrous and inquiring glance enveloped us both. I declare it looked as though he would presently put to us some question in an understandable language; but he died without uttering a sound, without moving a limb, without twitching a muscle. Only in the very last moment, as though in response to some sign we could not see, to some whisper we could not hear, he frowned heavily, and that frown gave to his black death-mask an inconceivably sombre, brooding, and menacing expression. The lustre of inquiring glance faded swiftly into vacant glassiness. 'Can you steer?' I asked the agent eagerly. He looked very dubious; but I made a grab at his arm, and he understood at once I meant him to steer whether or no. To tell you the truth, I was morbidly anxious to change my shoes and socks. 'He is dead,' murmured the fellow, immensely impressed. 'No doubt about it,' said I, tugging like mad at the shoe-laces. 'And by the way, I suppose Mr Kurtz is dead as well by this time.'

"For the moment that was the dominant thought. There was a sense of extreme disappointment, as though I had found out I had been striving after something altogether without a substance. I couldn't have been more disgusted if I had travelled all this way for the sole purpose of talking with Mr Kurtz. Talking with . . . I flung one shoe overboard, and became aware that that was exactly what I had been looking forward to—a talk with Kurtz.

I made the strange discovery that I had never imagined him as doing, you know, but as discoursing. I didn't say to myself, 'Now I will never see him,' or 'Now I will never shake him by the hand,' but, 'Now I will never hear him.' The man presented himself as a voice. Not of course that I did not connect him with some sort of action. Hadn't I been told in all the tones of jealousy and admiration that he had collected, bartered, swindled, or stolen more ivory than all the other agents together? That was not the point. The point was in his being a gifted creature, and that of all his gifts the one that stood out pre-eminently, that carried with it a sense of real presence, was his ability to talk, his words—the gift of expression, the bewildering, the illuminating, the most exalted and the most contemptible, the pulsating stream of light, or the deceitful flow from the heart of an impenetrable darkness.

"The other shoe went flying unto the devil-god of that river. I thought, By Jove! it's all over. We are too late; he has vanished—the gift has vanished, by means of some spear, arrow, or club. I will never hear that chap speak after all—and my sorrow had a startling extravagance of emotion, even such as I had noticed in the howling sorrow of these savages in the bush. I couldn't have felt more of lonely desolation somehow, had I been robbed of a belief or had missed my destiny in life. . . . Why do you sigh in this beastly way, somebody? Absurd? Well, absurd. Good Lord! mustn't a man ever—Here, give me some tobacco." . . .

There was a pause of profound stillness, then a match flared, and Marlow's lean face appeared, worn, hollow, with downward folds and dropped eyelids, with an aspect of concentrated attention; and as he took vigorous draws at his pipe, it seemed to retreat and advance out of the night in the regular flicker of the tiny flame. The match went out.

"Absurd!" he cried. "This is the worst of trying to tell . . . Here you all are, each moored with two good addresses, like a hulk with two anchors, a butcher round one corner, a policeman round another, excellent appetites, and temperature normal—you hear—normal from year's end to year's end. And you say, Absurd! Absurd be—exploded! Absurd! My dear boys, what can you expect from a man who out of sheer nervousness had just flung overboard a pair of new shoes? Now I think of it, it is amazing I did not shed tears. I am, upon the whole, proud of my fortitude. I was cut to the quick at the idea of having lost the inestimable privilege of listening to the gifted Kurtz. Of course I was wrong. The privilege was waiting for me. Oh yes, I heard more than enough. And I was right, too. A voice. He was very little more than a voice. And I heard—him—it—this voice—other voices—all of them were so little more than voices—and the memory of that time itself lingers around me, impalpable, like a dying vibration of one immense jabber, silly, atrocious, sordid, savage, or simply mean, without any kind of sense. Voices, voices—even the girl herself—now—"

He was silent for a long time.

"I laid the ghost of his gifts at last with a lie," he began suddenly. "Girl! What? Did I mention a girl? Oh, she is out of it—completely. They—the women I mean—are out of it—should be out of it. We must help them to stay in that beautiful world of their own, lest ours gets worse. Oh, she had to be out of it. You should have heard the disinterred body of Mr Kurtz saying, 'My Intended.' You would have perceived directly then how completely she was out of it. And the lofty frontal bone of Mr Kurtz! They say the hair goes on growing sometimes, but this—ah—specimen was impressively bald. The wilderness had patted him on the head, and, behold, it was like a ball—an ivory ball; it had caressed him, and—lo!—he had withered; it had taken him, loved him, embraced him, got into his veins, consumed his flesh, and sealed his soul to its own by the inconceivable ceremonies of some devilish initiation. He was its spoiled and pampered favourite. Ivory? I should think so. Heaps of it, stacks of it. The old mud shanty was bursting with it. You would think there was not a single tusk left either above or below the ground in the whole country. 'Mostly fossil,' the manager had remarked disparagingly. It was no more fossil than I am; but they call it fossil when it is dug up. It appears these niggers do bury the tusks sometimes—but evidently they couldn't bury this parcel deep enough to save the gifted Mr Kurtz from his fate. We filled the steamboat with it, and had to pile a lot on the deck. Thus he could see and enjoy as long as he could see, because the appreciation of this favour had remained with him to the last. You should have heard him say, 'My ivory.' Oh yes, I heard him. 'My Intended, my ivory, my station, my river, my—' everything belonged to him. It made me hold my breath in expectation of hearing the wilderness burst into a prodigious peal of laughter that would shake the fixed stars in their places. Everything belonged to him—but that was a trifle. The thing was to know what he belonged to, how many powers of darkness claimed him for their own. That was the reflection that made you creepy all over. It was impossible—it was not good for one either—trying to imagine. He had taken a high seat amongst the devils of the land—I mean literally. You can't understand. How could you?—with solid pavement under your feet, surrounded by kind neighbours ready to cheer you or to fall on you, stepping delicately between the butcher and the policeman, in the holy terror of scandal and gallows and lunatic asylums—how can you imagine what particular region of the first ages a man's untrammelled feet may take him into by the way of solitude—utter solitude without a policeman—by the way of silence—utter silence, where no warning voice of a kind neighbour can be heard whispering of public opinion? These little things make all the great difference. When they are gone you must fall back upon your own innate strength, upon your own capacity for faithfulness. Of course you may be too much of a fool to go wrong—too dull even to know you are being assaulted by the powers of darkness. I take it, no fool ever made a bargain for his soul with the devil: the fool is too much of a fool, or the devil too much of a devil—I don't know which. Or you may be such a thunderingly exalted creature as to be altogether deaf and blind to anything but heavenly sights and sounds. Then the earth for you is only a standing place—and whether to be like this is your loss or your gain I won't pretend to say. But most of us are neither one nor the other. The earth for us is a place to live in, where we must put up with sights, with sounds, with smells, too, by Jove!—breathe dead hippo, so to speak, and not be contaminated. And there, don't you see? your strength comes in, the faith in your ability for the digging of unostentatious holes to bury the stuff in—your power of devotion, not to yourself, but to an obscure, back-breaking business. And that's difficult enough. Mind, I am not trying to excuse or even explain—I am trying to account to myself for—for—Mr Kurtz—for the shade of Mr Kurtz. This initiated wraith from the back of Nowhere honoured me with its amazing confidence before it vanished altogether. This was because it could speak English to me. The original Kurtz had been educated partly in England, and—as he was good enough to say himself—his sympathies were in the right place. His mother was half-English, his father was half-French. All Europe contributed to the making of Kurtz; and by and by I learned that, most appropriately, the International Society for the Suppression of Savage Customs had entrusted him with the making of a report, for its future guidance. And he had written it too. I've seen it. I've read it. It was eloquent, vibrating with eloquence, but too high-strung, I think. Seventeen pages of close writing he had found time for! But this must have been before his—let us say—nerves went wrong, and caused him to preside at certain midnight dances ending with unspeakable rites, which—as far as I reluctantly gathered from what I heard at various times—were offered up to him—do you understand?—to Mr Kurtz himself. But it was a beautiful piece of writing. The opening paragraph, however, in the light of later information, strikes me now as ominous. He began with the argument that we whites, from the point of development we had arrived at, 'must necessarily appear to them [savages] in the nature of supernatural beings—we approach them with the might as of a deity,' and so on, and so on. 'By the simple exercise of our will we can exert a power for good practically unbounded,' etc. etc. From that point he soared and took me with him. The peroration was magnificent, though difficult to remember, you know. It gave me the notion of an exotic Immensity ruled by an august Benevolence. It made me tingle with enthusiasm. This was the unbounded power of eloquence—of words— of burning noble words. There were no practical hints to interrupt the magic current of phrases, unless a kind of note at the foot of the last page, scrawled evidently much later, in an unsteady hand, may be regarded as the exposition of a method. It was very simple, and at the end of that moving appeal to every altruistic sentiment it blazed at you, luminous and terrifying, like a flash of lightning in a serene sky: 'Exterminate all the brutes!' The curious part was that he had apparently forgotten all about that valuable postscriptum, because, later on, when he in a sense came to himself, he repeatedly entreated me to take good care of 'my pamphlet' (he called it), as it was sure to have in the future a good influence upon his career. I had full information about all these things, and, besides, as it turned out, I was to have the care of his memory. I've done enough for it to give me the indisputable right to lay it, if I choose, for an everlasting rest in the dust-bin of progress, amongst all the sweepings and, figuratively speaking, all the dead cats of civilisation. But then, you see, I can't choose. He won't be forgotten. Whatever he was, he was not common. He had the power to charm or frighten rudimentary souls into an aggravated witchdance in his honour; he could also fill the small souls of the pilgrims with bitter misgivings: he had one devoted friend at least, and he had conquered one soul in the world that was neither rudimentary nor tainted with self-seeking. No; I can't forget him, though I am not prepared to affirm the fellow was exactly worth the life we lost in getting to him. I missed my late helmsman awfully—I missed him even while his body was still lying in the pilot-house. Perhaps you will think it passing strange this regret for a savage who was no more account than a grain of sand in a black Sahara. Well, don't you see, he had done something, he had steered; for months I had him at my back—a help—an instrument. It was a kind of partnership. He steered for me—I had to look after him, I worried about his deficiencies, and thus a subtle bond had been created, of which I only became aware when it was suddenly broken. And the intimate profundity of that look he gave me when he received his hurt remains to this day in my memory—like a claim of distant kinship affirmed in a supreme moment.

"Poor fool! If he had only left that shutter alone. He had no restraint, no restraint—just like Kurtz—a tree swayed by the wind. As soon as I had put on a dry pair of slippers, I dragged him out, after first jerking the spear out of his side, which operation I confess I performed with my eyes shut tight. His heels leaped together over the little doorstep; his shoulders were pressed to my breast; I hugged him from behind desperately. Oh! he was heavy, heavy; heavier than any man on earth, I should imagine. Then without more ado I tipped him overboard. The current snatched him as though he had been a wisp of grass, and I saw the body roll over twice before I lost sight of it for ever. All the pilgrims and the manager were then congregated on the awning-deck about the pilot-house, chattering at each other like a flock of excited magpies, and there was a scandalised murmur at my heartless promptitude. What they wanted to keep that body hanging about for I can't guess. Embalm it, maybe. But I had also heard another, and a very ominous, murmur on the deck below. My friends the wood-cutters were likewise scandalised, and with a better show of reason—though I admit that the reason itself was quite inadmissible. Oh, quite! I had made up my mind that if my late helmsman was to be eaten, the fishes alone should have him. He had been a very second-rate helmsman while alive, but now he was dead he might have become a first-class temptation, and possibly cause some startling trouble. Besides, I was anxious to take the wheel, the man in pink pyjamas showing himself a hopeless duffer at the business.

"This I did directly the simple funeral was over. We were going half-speed, keeping right in the middle of the stream, and I listened to the talk about me. They had given up Kurtz, they had given up the station; Kurtz was dead, and the station had been burnt—and so on—and so on. The red-haired pilgrim was beside himself with the thought that at least this poor Kurtz had been properly revenged. 'Say! We must have made a glorious slaughter of them in the bush. Eh? What do you think? Say?' He positively danced, the bloodthirsty little gingery beggar.[4] And he had nearly fainted when he saw the wounded man! I could not help saying, 'You made a glorious lot of smoke, anyhow.' I had seen, from the way the tops of the bushes rustled and flew, that almost all the shots had gone too high. You can't hit anything unless you take aim and fire from the shoulder; but these chaps fired from the hip with their eyes shut. The retreat, I maintained—and I was right— was caused by the screeching of the steam-whistle. Upon this they forgot Kurtz, and began to howl at me with indignant protests.

"The manager stood by the wheel murmuring confidentially about the necessity of getting well away down the river before dark at all events, when I saw in the distance a clearing on the river-side and the outlines of some sort of building. 'What's this?' I asked. He clapped his hands in wonder. 'The station!' he cried. I edged in at once, still going half-speed.

4. Red-haired rascal (British).

"Through my glasses I saw the slope of a hill interspersed with rare trees and perfectly free from undergrowth. A long decaying building on the summit was half buried in the high grass; the large holes in the peaked roof gaped black from afar; the jungle and the woods made a background. There was no enclosure or fence of any kind; but there had been one apparently, for near the house half a dozen slim posts remained in a row, roughly trimmed, and with their upper ends ornamented with round carved balls. The rails, or whatever there had been between, had disappeared. Of course the forest surrounded all that. The river-bank was clear, and on the water side I saw a white man under a hat like a cart-wheel beckoning persistently with his whole arm. Examining the edge of the forest above and below, I was almost certain I could see movements—human forms gliding here and there. I steamed past prudently, then stopped the engines and let her drift down. The man on the shore began to shout, urging us to land. 'We have been attacked,' screamed the manager. 'I know—I know. It's all right,' yelled back the other, as cheerful as you please. 'Come along. It's all right. I am glad.'

"His aspect reminded me of something I had seen—something funny I had seen somewhere. As I manœuvred to get alongside, I was asking myself, 'What does this fellow look like?' Suddenly I got it. He looked like a harlequin.[5] His clothes had been made of some stuff that was brown holland[6] probably, but it was covered with patches all over, with bright patches, blue, red, and yellow—patches on the back, patches on the front, patches on elbows, on knees; coloured binding round his jacket, scarlet edging at the bottom of his trousers; and the sunshine made him look extremely gay and wonderfully neat withal, because you could see how beautifully all this patching had been done. A beardless, boyish face, very fair, no features to speak of, nose peeling, little blue eyes, smiles and frowns chasing each other over that open countenance like sunshine and shadow on a wind-swept plain. 'Look out, captain!' he cried; 'there's a snag lodged in here last night.' What! Another snag? I confess I swore shamefully. I had nearly holed my cripple, to finish off that charming trip. The harlequin on the bank turned his little pug nose up to me. 'You English?' he asked, all smiles. 'Are you?' I shouted from the wheel. The smiles vanished, and he shook his head as if sorry for my disappointment. Then he brightened up. 'Never mind!' he cried encouragingly. 'Are we in time?' I asked. 'He is up there,' he replied, with a toss of the head up the hill, and becoming gloomy all of a sudden. His face was like the autumn sky, overcast one moment and bright the next.

"When the manager, escorted by the pilgrims, all of them armed to the teeth, had gone to the house, this chap came on board. 'I say, I don't like this. These natives are in the bush,' I said. He assured me earnestly it was all right. 'They are simple people,' he added; 'well, I am glad you came. It took me all my time to keep them off.' 'But you said it was all right,' I cried. 'Oh, they meant no harm,' he said; and as I stared he corrected himself, 'Not exactly.' Then vivaciously, 'My faith, your pilot-house wants a clean up!' In the next breath he advised me to keep enough steam on the boiler to blow the whistle in case of any trouble. 'One good screech will do more for you than all your rifles. They are simple people,' he repeated. He rattled away at such a rate he quite overwhelmed me. He seemed to be trying to make up for lots of silence,

---

5. A traditional clown figure known by his multicolored costume.   6. Unbleached linen fabric.

and actually hinted, laughing, that such was the case. 'Don't you talk with Mr Kurtz?' I said. 'You don't talk with that man—you listen to him,' he exclaimed with severe exaltation. 'But now—' He waved his arm, and in the twinkling of an eye was in the uttermost depths of despondency. In a moment he came up again with a jump, possessed himself of both my hands, shook them continuously, while he gabbled: 'Brother sailor . . . honour . . . pleasure . . . delight . . . introduce myself . . . Russian . . . son of an arch-priest . . . Government of Tambov . . . What? Tobacco! English tobacco; the excellent English tobacco! Now, that's brotherly. Smoke? Where's a sailor that does not smoke?'

"The pipe soothed him, and gradually I made out he had run away from school, had gone to sea in a Russian ship; ran away again; served some time in English ships; was now reconciled with the arch-priest. He made a point of that. 'But when one is young one must see things, gather experience, ideas; enlarge the mind.' 'Here!' I interrupted. 'You can never tell! Here I met Mr Kurtz,' he said, youthfully solemn and reproachful. I held my tongue after that. It appears he had persuaded a Dutch trading-house on the coast to fit him out with stores and goods, and had started for the interior with a light heart, and no more idea of what would happen to him than a baby. He had been wandering about that river for nearly two years alone, cut off from everybody and everything. 'I am not so young as I look. I am twenty-five,' he said. 'At first old Van Shuyten would tell me to go to the devil,' he narrated with keen enjoyment; 'but I stuck to him, and talked and talked, till at last he got afraid I would talk the hind-leg off his favourite dog, so he gave me some cheap things and a few guns, and told me he hoped he would never see my face again. Good old Dutchman, Van Shuyten. I sent him one small lot of ivory a year ago, so that he can't call me a little thief when I get back. I hope he got it. And for the rest I don't care. I had some wood stacked for you. That was my old house. Did you see?'

"I gave him Towson's book. He made as though he would kiss me, but restrained himself. 'The only book I had left, and I thought I had lost it,' he said, looking at it ecstatically. 'So many accidents happen to a man going about alone, you know. Canoes get upset sometimes—and sometimes you've got to clear out so quick when the people get angry.' He thumbed the pages. 'You made notes in Russian?' I asked. He nodded. 'I thought they were written in cipher,' I said. He laughed, then became serious. 'I had lots of trouble to keep these people off,' he said. 'Did they want to kill you?' I asked. 'Oh no!' he cried, and checked himself. 'Why did they attack us?' I pursued. He hesitated, then said shamefacedly, 'They don't want him to go.' 'Don't they?' I said curiously. He nodded a nod full of mystery and wisdom. 'I tell you,' he cried, 'this man has enlarged my mind.' He opened his arms wide, staring at me with his little blue eyes that were perfectly round."

3

"I looked at him, lost in astonishment. There he was before me, in motley, as though he had absconded from a troupe of mimes, enthusiastic, fabulous. His very existence was improbable, inexplicable, and altogether bewildering. He was an insoluble problem. It was inconceivable how he had existed, how he had succeeded in getting so far, how he had managed to remain—why he did not instantly disappear. 'I went a little farther,' he said, 'then still a little farther—till I had gone so far that I don't know how I'll ever get back. Never mind. Plenty time. I can manage. You take Kurtz away quick—quick—I tell you.' The glamour of youth enveloped his particoloured rags, his destitution, his loneliness, the essential desolation of his futile wanderings. For months—for years—his life hadn't been worth a day's purchase; and there he was gallantly, thoughtlessly alive, to all appearance indestructible solely by the virtue of his few years and of his unreflecting audacity. I was seduced into something like admiration—like envy. Glamour urged him on, glamour kept him unscathed. He surely wanted nothing from the wilderness but space to breathe in and to push on through. His need was to exist, and to move onwards at the greatest possible risk, and with a maximum of privation. If the absolutely pure, uncalculating, unpractical spirit of adventure had ever ruled a human being, it ruled this be-patched youth. I almost envied him the possession of this modest and clear flame. It seemed to have consumed all thought of self so completely, that, even while he was talking to you, you forgot that it was he—the man before your eyes—who had gone through these things. I did not envy him his devotion to Kurtz, though. He had not meditated over it. It came to him, and he accepted it with a sort of eager fatalism. I must say that to me it appeared about the most dangerous thing in every way he had come upon so far.

"They had come together unavoidably, like two ships becalmed near each other, and lay rubbing sides at last. I suppose Kurtz wanted an audience, because on a certain occasion, when encamped in the forest, they had talked all night, or more probably Kurtz had talked. 'We talked of everything,' he said, quite transported at the recollection. 'I forgot there was such a thing as sleep. The night did not seem to last an hour. Everything! Everything! . . . Of love too.' 'Ah, he talked to you of love!' I said, much amused. 'It isn't what you think,' he cried, almost passionately. 'It was in general. He made me see things—things.'

"He threw his arms up. We were on deck at the time, and the head-man of my wood-cutters, lounging near by, turned upon him his heavy and glittering eyes. I looked around, and I don't know why, but I assure you that never, never before, did this land, this river, this jungle, the very arch of this blazing sky, appear to me so hopeless and so dark, so impenetrable to human thought, so pitiless to human weakness. 'And, ever since, you have been with him, of course?' I said.

"On the contrary. It appears their intercourse had been very much broken by various causes. He had, as he informed me proudly, managed to nurse Kurtz through two illnesses (he alluded to it as you would to some risky feat), but as a rule Kurtz wandered alone, far in the depths of the forest. 'Very often coming to this station, I had to wait days and days before he would turn up,' he said. 'Ah, it was worth waiting for!—sometimes.' 'What was he doing? exploring or what?' I asked. 'Oh yes, of course'; he had discovered lots of villages, a lake too—he did not know exactly in what direction; it was dangerous to inquire too much—but mostly his expeditions had been for ivory. 'But he had no goods to trade with by that time,' I objected. 'There's a good lot of cartridges left even yet,' he answered, looking away. 'To speak plainly, he raided the country,' I said. He nodded. 'Not alone, surely!' He muttered something about the villages round that lake. 'Kurtz got the tribe to follow him, did he?' I suggested. He fidgeted a little. 'They adored him,' he said. The tone of these words was so extraordinary that I looked at him searchingly. It was curious to see his mingled eagerness and reluctance to speak of Kurtz. The man filled his life, occupied his thoughts, swayed his emotions. 'What can you expect?' he burst out; 'he came to them with thunder and lightning, you know—and they had never seen anything like it—and very terrible. He could be very terrible. You can't judge Mr Kurtz as you would an ordinary man. No, no, no! Now—just to give you an idea—I don't mind telling you, he wanted to shoot me too one day—but I don't judge him.' 'Shoot you!' I cried. 'What for?' 'Well, I had a small lot of ivory the chief of that village near my house gave me. You see I used to shoot game for them. Well, he wanted it, and wouldn't hear reason. He declared he would shoot me unless I gave him the ivory and then cleared out of the country, because he could do so, and had a fancy for it, and there was nothing on earth to prevent him killing whom he jolly well pleased. And it was true too. I gave him the ivory. What did I care! But I didn't clear out. No, no. I couldn't leave him. I had to be careful, of course, till we got friendly again for a time. He had his second illness then. Afterwards I had to keep out of the way; but I didn't mind. He was living for the most part in those villages on the lake. When he came down to the river, sometimes he would take to me, and sometimes it was better for me to be careful. This man suffered too much. He hated all this, and somehow he couldn't get away. When I had a chance I begged him to try and leave while there was time; I offered to go back with him. And he would say yes, and then he would remain; go off on another ivory hunt; disappear for weeks; forget himself amongst these people— forget himself—you know.' 'Why! he's mad,' I said. He protested indignantly. Mr Kurtz couldn't be mad. If I had heard him talk, only two days ago, I wouldn't dare hint at such a thing. . . . I had taken up my binoculars while we talked, and was looking at the shore, sweeping the limit of the forest at each side and at the back of the house. The consciousness of there being people in that bush, so silent, so quiet—as silent and quiet as the ruined house on the hill—made me uneasy. There was no sign on the face of nature of this amazing tale that was not so much told as suggested to me in desolate exclamations, completed by shrugs, in interrupted phrases, in hints ending in deep sighs. The woods were unmoved, like a mask—heavy, like the closed door of a prison—they looked with their air of hidden knowledge, of patient expectation, of unapproachable silence. The Russian was explaining to me that it was only lately that Mr Kurtz had come down to the river, bringing along with him all the fighting men of that lake tribe. He had been absent for several months—getting himself adored, I suppose—and had come down unexpectedly, with the intention to all appearance of making a raid either across the river or down stream. Evidently the appetite for more ivory had got the better of the—what shall I say?—less material aspirations. However, he had got much worse suddenly. 'I heard he was lying helpless, and so I came up—took my chance,' said the Russian. 'Oh, he is bad, very bad.' I directed my glass to the house. There were no signs of life, but there was the ruined roof, the long mud wall peeping above the grass, with three little square window-holes, no two of the same size; all this brought within reach of my hand, as it were. And then I made a brusque movement, and one of the remaining posts of that vanished fence leaped up in the field of my glass.

You remember I told you I had been struck at the distance by certain attempts at ornamentation, rather remarkable in the ruinous aspect of the place. Now I had suddenly a nearer view, and its first result was to make me throw my head back as if before a blow. Then I went carefully from post to post with my glass, and I saw my mistake. These round knobs were not ornamental but symbolic; they were expressive and puzzling, striking and disturbing—food for thought and also for the vultures if there had been any looking down from the sky; but at all events for such ants as were industrious enough to ascend the pole. They would have been even more impressive, those heads on the stakes, if their faces had not been turned to the house. Only one, the first I had made out, was facing my way. I was not so shocked as you may think. The start back I had given was really nothing but a movement of surprise. I had expected to see a knob of wood there, you know. I returned deliberately to the first I had seen—and there it was, black, dried, sunken, with closed eyelids—a head that seemed to sleep at the top of that pole, and, with the shrunken dry lips showing a narrow white line of the teeth, was smiling too, smiling continuously at some endless and jocose dream of that eternal slumber.

"I am not disclosing any trade secrets. In fact the manager said afterwards that Mr Kurtz's methods had ruined the district. I have no opinion on that point, but I want you clearly to understand that there was nothing exactly profitable in these heads being there. They only show that Mr Kurtz lacked restraint in the gratification of his various lusts, that there was something wanting in him—some small matter which, when the pressing need arose, could not be found under his magnificent eloquence. Whether he knew of this deficiency himself I can't say. I think the knowledge came to him at last—only at the very last. But the wilderness had found him out early, and had taken on him a terrible vengeance for the fantastic invasion. I think it had whispered to him things about himself which he did not know, things of which he had no conception till he took counsel with this great solitude—and the whisper had proved irresistibly fascinating. It echoed loudly within him because he was hollow at the core. . . . I put down the glass, and the head that had appeared near enough to be spoken to seemed at once to have leaped away from me into inaccessible distance.

"The admirer of Mr Kurtz was a bit crestfallen. In a hurried, indistinct voice he began to assure me he had not dared to take these—say, symbols—down. He was not afraid of the natives; they would not stir till Mr Kurtz gave the word. His ascendancy was extraordinary. The camps of these people surrounded the place, and the chiefs came every day to see him. They would crawl . . . 'I don't want to know anything of the ceremonies used when approaching Mr Kurtz,' I shouted. Curious, this feeling that came over me that such details would be more intolerable than those heads drying on the stakes under Mr Kurtz's windows. After all, that was only a savage sight, while I seemed at one bound to have been transported into some lightless region of subtle horrors, where pure, uncomplicated savagery was a positive relief, being something that had a right to exist—obviously—in the sunshine. The young man looked at me with surprise. I suppose it did not occur to him that Mr Kurtz was no idol of mine. He forgot I hadn't heard any of these splendid monologues on, what was it? on love, justice, conduct of life—or what not. If it had come to crawling before Mr Kurtz, he crawled as much as the veriest savage of them all. I had no idea of the conditions, he said: these heads were the heads of rebels. I shocked him excessively by laughing. Rebels! What would be the next definition I was to hear? There had been enemies, criminals, workers—and these were rebels. Those rebellious heads looked very subdued to me on their sticks. 'You don't know how such a life tries a man like Kurtz,' cried Kurtz's last disciple. 'Well, and you?' I said. 'I! I! I am a simple man. I have no great thoughts. I want nothing from anybody. How can you compare me to . . . ?' His feelings were too much for speech, and suddenly he broke down. 'I don't understand,' he groaned. 'I've been doing my best to keep him alive, and that's enough. I had no hand in all this. I have no abilities. There hasn't been a drop of medicine or a mouthful of invalid food for months here. He was shamefully abandoned. A man like this, with such ideas. Shamefully! Shamefully! I—I—haven't slept for the last ten nights. . . .'

"His voice lost itself in the calm of the evening. The long shadows of the forest had slipped down hill while we talked, had gone far beyond the ruined hovel, beyond the symbolic row of stakes. All this was in the gloom, while we down there were yet in the sunshine, and the stretch of the river abreast of the clearing glittered in a still and dazzling splendour, with a murky and overshadowed bend above and below. Not a living soul was seen on the shore. The bushes did not rustle.

"Suddenly round the corner of the house a group of men appeared, as though they had come up from the ground. They waded waist-deep in the grass, in a compact body, bearing an improvised stretcher in their midst. Instantly, in the emptiness of the landscape, a cry arose whose shrillness pierced the still air like a sharp arrow flying straight to the very heart of the land; and, as if by enchantment, streams of human beings—of naked human beings—with spears in their hands, with bows, with shields, with wild glances and savage movements, were poured into the clearing by the dark-faced and pensive forest. The bushes shook, the grass swayed for a time, and then everything stood still in attentive immobility.

"'Now, if he does not say the right thing to them we are all done for,' said the Russian at my elbow. The knot of men with the stretcher had stopped too, half-way to the steamer, as if petrified. I saw the man on the stretcher sit up, lank and with an uplifted arm, above the shoulders of the bearers. 'Let us hope that the man who can talk so well of love in general will find some particular reason to spare us this time,' I said. I resented bitterly the absurd danger of our situation, as if to be at the mercy of that atrocious phantom had been a dishonouring necessity. I could not hear a sound, but through my glasses I saw the thin arm extended commandingly, the lower jaw moving, the eyes of that apparition shining darkly far in its bony head that nodded with grotesque jerks. Kurtz—Kurtz—that means 'short' in German—don't it? Well, the name was as true as everything else in his life— and death. He looked at least seven feet long. His covering had fallen off, and his body emerged from it pitiful and appalling as from a winding-sheet. I could see the cage of his ribs all astir, the bones of his arm waving. It was as though an animated image of death carved out of old ivory had been shaking its hand with menaces at a motionless crowd of men made of dark and glittering bronze. I saw him open his mouth wide—it gave him a weirdly voracious aspect, as though he had wanted to swallow all the air, all the earth, all the men before him. A deep voice reached me faintly. He must have been shouting. He fell back suddenly. The stretcher shook as the bearers staggered forward again, and almost at the same time I noticed that the crowd of savages was vanishing without any perceptible movement of retreat, as if the forest that had ejected these beings so suddenly had drawn them in again as the breath is drawn in a long aspiration.

"Some of the pilgrims behind the stretcher carried his arms—two shotguns, a heavy rifle, and a light revolver-carbine—the thunderbolts of that pitiful Jupiter. The manager bent over him murmuring as he walked beside his head. They laid him down in one of the little cabins—just a room for a bedplace and a camp-stool or two, you know. We had brought his belated correspondence, and a lot of torn envelopes and open letters littered his bed. His hand roamed feebly amongst these papers. I was struck by the fire of his eyes and the composed languor of his expression. It was not so much the exhaustion of disease. He did not seem in pain. This shadow looked satiated and calm, as though for the moment it had had its fill of all the emotions.

"He rustled one of the letters, and looking straight in my face said, 'I am glad.' Somebody had been writing to him about me. These special recommendations were turning up again. The volume of tone he emitted without effort, almost without the trouble of moving his lips, amazed me. A voice! a voice! It was grave, profound, vibrating, while the man did not seem capable of a whisper. However, he had enough strength in him—factitious no doubt—to very nearly make an end of us, as you shall hear directly.

"The manager appeared silently in the doorway; I stepped out at once and he drew the curtain after me. The Russian, eyed curiously by the pilgrims, was staring at the shore. I followed the direction of his glance.

"Dark human shapes could be made out in the distance, flitting indistinctly against the gloomy border of the forest, and near the river two bronze figures, leaning on tall spears, stood in the sunlight under fantastic headdresses of spotted skins, warlike and still in statuesque repose. And from right to left along the lighted shore moved a wild and gorgeous apparition of a woman.

"She walked with measured steps, draped in striped and fringed cloths, treading the earth proudly, with a slight jingle and flash of barbarous ornaments. She carried her head high; her hair was done in the shape of a helmet; she had brass leggings to the knee, brass wire gauntlets to the elbow, a crimson spot on her tawny cheek, innumerable necklaces of glass beads on her neck; bizarre things, charms, gifts of witch-men, that hung about her, glittered and trembled at every step. She must have had the value of several elephant tusks upon her. She was savage and superb, wild-eyed and magnificent; there was something ominous and stately in her deliberate progress. And in the hush that had fallen suddenly upon the whole sorrowful land, the immense wilderness, the colossal body of the fecund and mysterious life seemed to look at her, pensive, as though it had been looking at the image of its own tenebrous and passionate soul.

"She came abreast of the steamer, stood still, and faced us. Her long shadow fell to the water's edge. Her face had a tragic and fierce aspect of wild sorrow and of dumb pain mingled with the fear of some struggling, half-shaped resolve. She stood looking at us without a stir, and like the wilderness itself, with an air of brooding over an inscrutable purpose. A whole minute passed, and then she made a step forward. There was a low jingle, a glint of yellow metal, a sway of fringed draperies, and she stopped as if her heart had failed her. The young fellow by my side growled. The pilgrims murmured at my back. She looked at us all as if her life had depended upon the unswerving steadiness of her glance. Suddenly she opened her bared arms and threw them up rigid above her head, as though in an uncontrollable desire to touch the sky, and at the same time the swift shadows darted out on the earth, swept around on the river, gathering the steamer into a shadowy embrace. A formidable silence hung over the scene.

"She turned away slowly, walked on, following the bank, and passed into the bushes to the left. Once only her eyes gleamed back at us in the dusk of the thickets before she disappeared.

"'If she had offered to come aboard I really think I would have tried to shoot her,' said the man of patches nervously. 'I had been risking my life every day for the last fortnight to keep her out of the house. She got in one day and kicked up a row about those miserable rags I picked up in the storeroom to mend my clothes with. I wasn't decent. At least it must have been that, for she talked like a fury to Kurtz for an hour, pointing at me now and then. I don't understand the dialect of this tribe. Luckily for me, I fancy Kurtz felt too ill that day to care, or there would have been mischief. I don't understand. . . . No—it's too much for me. Ah, well, it's all over now.'

"At this moment I heard Kurtz's deep voice behind the curtain: 'Save me!—save the ivory, you mean. Don't tell me. Save *me*! Why, I've had to save you. You are interrupting my plans now. Sick! Sick! Not so sick as you would like to believe. Never mind. I'll carry my ideas out yet—I will return. I'll show you what can be done. You with your little peddling notions—you are interfering with me. I will return. I . . .'

"The manager came out. He did me the honour to take me under the arm and lead me aside. 'He is very low, very low,' he said. He considered it necessary to sigh, but neglected to be consistently sorrowful. 'We have done all we could for him—haven't we? But there is no disguising the fact, Mr Kurtz has done more harm than good to the Company. He did not see the time was not ripe for vigorous action. Cautiously, cautiously—that's my principle. We must be cautious yet. The district is closed to us for a time. Deplorable! Upon the whole, the trade will suffer. I don't deny there is a remarkable quantity of ivory—mostly fossil. We must save it, at all events—but look how precarious the position is—and why? Because the method is unsound.' 'Do you,' said I, looking at the shore, 'call it "unsound method"?' 'Without doubt,' he exclaimed hotly, 'Don't you?' . . . 'No method at all,' I murmured after a while. 'Exactly,' he exulted. 'I anticipated this. Shows a complete want of judgment. It is my duty to point it out in the proper quarter.' 'Oh,' said I, 'that fellow—what's his name?—the brickmaker, will make a readable report for you.' He appeared confounded for a moment. It seemed to me I had never breathed an atmosphere so vile, and I turned mentally to Kurtz for relief—positively for relief. 'Nevertheless, I think Mr Kurtz is a remarkable man,' I said with emphasis. He started, dropped on me a cold heavy glance, said very quietly, 'He *was*,' and turned his back on me. My hour of favour was over; I found myself lumped along with Kurtz as a partisan of methods for which the time was not ripe: I was unsound! Ah! but it was something to have at least a choice of nightmares.

"I had turned to the wilderness really, not to Mr Kurtz, who, I was ready to admit, was as good as buried. And for a moment it seemed to me as if I also were buried in a vast grave full of unspeakable secrets. I felt an intolerable weight oppressing my breast, the smell of the damp earth, the unseen presence of victorious corruption, the darkness of an impenetrable night. . . . The Russian tapped me on the shoulder. I heard him mumbling and stammering something about 'brother seaman—couldn't conceal—knowledge of matters that would affect Mr Kurtz's reputation.' I waited. For him evidently Mr Kurtz was not in his grave; I suspect that for him Mr Kurtz was one of the immortals. 'Well!' said I at last, 'speak out. As it happens, I am Mr Kurtz's friend—in a way.'

"He stated with a good deal of formality that had we not been 'of the same profession,' he would have kept the matter to himself without regard to consequences. He suspected 'there was an active ill-will towards him on the part of these white men that—' 'You are right,' I said, remembering a certain conversation I had overheard. 'The manager thinks you ought to be hanged.' He showed a concern at this intelligence which amused me at first. 'I had better get out of the way quietly,' he said earnestly. 'I can do no more for Kurtz now, and they would soon find some excuse. What's to stop them? There's a military post three hundred miles from here.' 'Well, upon my word,' said I, 'perhaps you had better go if you have any friends amongst the savages near by.' 'Plenty,' he said. 'They are simple people—and I want nothing, you know.' He stood biting his lip, then: 'I don't want any harm to happen to these whites here, but of course I was thinking of Mr Kurtz's reputation—but you are a brother seaman and—' 'All right,' said I, after a time. 'Mr Kurtz's reputation is safe with me.' I did not know how truly I spoke.

"He informed me, lowering his voice, that it was Kurtz who had ordered the attack to be made on the steamer. 'He hated sometimes the idea of being taken away—and then again . . . But I don't understand these matters. I am a simple man. He thought it would scare you away—that you would give it up, thinking him dead. I could not stop him. Oh, I had an awful time of it this last month.' 'Very well,' I said. 'He is all right now.' 'Ye-e-es,' he muttered, not very convinced apparently. 'Thanks,' said I; 'I shall keep my eyes open.' 'But quiet—eh?' he urged anxiously. 'It would be awful for his reputation if anybody here—' I promised a complete discretion with great gravity. 'I have a canoe and three black fellows waiting not very far. I am off. Could you give me a few Martini-Henry cartridges?' I could, and did, with proper secrecy. He helped himself, with a wink at me, to a handful of my tobacco. 'Between sailors—you know—good English tobacco.' At the door of the pilot-house he turned round—'I say, haven't you a pair of shoes you could spare?' He raised one leg. 'Look.' The soles were tied with knotted strings sandal-wise under his bare feet. I rooted out an old pair, at which he looked with admiration before tucking it under his left arm. One of his pockets (bright red) was bulging with cartridges, from the other (dark blue) peeped 'Towson's Inquiry,' etc. etc. He seemed to think himself excellently well equipped for a renewed encounter with the wilderness. 'Ah! I'll never, never meet such a man again. You ought to have heard him recite poetry—his own too it was, he told me. Poetry!' He rolled his eyes at the recollection of these delights. 'Oh, he enlarged my mind!' 'Good-bye,' said I. He shook hands and vanished in the night. Sometimes I ask myself whether I had ever really seen him—whether it was possible to meet such a phenomenon! . . .

"When I woke up shortly after midnight his warning came to my mind with its hint of danger that seemed, in the starred darkness, real enough to make me get up for the purpose of having a look round. On the hill a big fire burned, illuminating fitfully a crooked corner of the station-house. One of the agents with a picket of a few of our blacks, armed for the purpose, was keeping guard over the ivory; but deep within the forest, red gleams that wavered, that seemed to sink and rise from the ground amongst confused columnar shapes of intense blackness, showed the exact position of the camp where Mr Kurtz's adorers were keeping their uneasy vigil. The monotonous beating of a big drum filled the air with muffled shocks and a lingering vibration. A steady droning sound of many men chanting each to himself some weird incantation came out from the black, flat wall of the woods as the humming of bees comes out of a hive, and had a strange narcotic effect upon my half-awake senses. I believe I dozed off leaning over the rail, till an abrupt burst of yells, an overwhelming outbreak of a pent-up and mysterious frenzy, woke me up in a bewildered wonder. It was cut short all at once, and the low droning went on with an effect of audible and soothing silence. I glanced casually into the little cabin. A light was burning within, but Mr Kurtz was not there.

"I think I would have raised an outcry if I had believed my eyes. But I didn't believe them at first—the thing seemed so impossible. The fact is I was completely unnerved by a sheer blank fright, pure abstract terror, unconnected with any distinct shape of physical danger. What made this emotion so overpowering was—how shall I define it?—the moral shock I received, as if something altogether monstrous, intolerable to thought and odious to the soul, had been thrust upon me unexpectedly. This lasted of course the merest fraction of a second, and then the usual sense of commonplace, deadly danger, the possibility of a sudden onslaught and massacre, or something of the kind, which I saw impending, was positively welcome and composing. It pacified me, in fact, so much, that I did not raise an alarm.

"There was an agent buttoned up inside an ulster[7] and sleeping on a chair on deck within three feet of me. The yells had not awakened him; he snored very slightly; I left him to his slumbers and leaped ashore. I did not betray Mr Kurtz—it was ordered I should never betray him—it was written I should be loyal to the nightmare of my choice. I was anxious to deal with this shadow by myself alone—and to this day I don't know why I was so jealous of sharing with any one the peculiar blackness of that experience.

"As soon as I got on the bank I saw a trail—a broad trail through the grass. I remember the exultation with which I said to myself, 'He can't walk—he is crawling on all-fours—I've got him.' The grass was wet with dew. I strode rapidly with clenched fists. I fancy I had some vague notion of falling upon him and giving him a drubbing. I don't know. I had some imbecile thoughts. The knitting old woman with the cat obtruded herself upon my memory as a most improper person to be sitting at the other end of such an affair. I saw a row of pilgrims squirting lead in the air out of Winchesters held to the hip. I

---

7. A long, loose overcoat often with a belt.

thought I would never get back to the steamer, and imagined myself living alone and unarmed in the woods to an advanced age. Such silly things—you know. And I remember I confounded the beat of the drum with the beating of my heart, and was pleased at its calm regularity.

"I kept to the track though—then stopped to listen. The night was very clear; a dark blue space, sparkling with dew and starlight, in which black things stood very still. I thought I could see a kind of motion ahead of me. I was strangely cocksure of everything that night. I actually left the track and ran in a wide semicircle (I verily believe chuckling to myself) so as to get in front of that stir, of that motion I had seen—if indeed I had seen anything. I was circumventing Kurtz as though it had been a boyish game.

"I came upon him, and, if he had not heard me coming, I would have fallen over him too, but he got up in time. He rose, unsteady, long, pale, indistinct, like a vapour exhaled by the earth, and swayed slightly, misty and silent before me; while at my back the fires loomed between the trees, and the murmur of many voices issued from the forest. I had cut him off cleverly; but when actually confronting him I seemed to come to my senses, I saw the danger in its right proportion. It was by no means over yet. Suppose he began to shout? Though he could hardly stand, there was still plenty of vigour in his voice. 'Go away—hide yourself,' he said, in that profound tone. It was very awful. I glanced back. We were within thirty yards of the nearest fire. A black figure stood up, strode on long black legs, waving long black arms, across the glow. It had horns—antelope horns, I think—on its head. Some sorcerer, some witch-man no doubt: it looked fiend-like enough. 'Do you know what you are doing?' I whispered. 'Perfectly,' he answered, raising his voice for that single word: it sounded to me far off and yet loud, like a hail through a speaking-trumpet. If he makes a row we are lost, I thought to myself. This clearly was not a case for fisticuffs, even apart from the very natural aversion I had to beat that Shadow—this wandering and tormented thing. 'You will be lost,' I said—'utterly lost.' One gets sometimes such a flash of inspiration, you know. I did say the right thing, though indeed he could not have been more irretrievably lost than he was at this very moment, when the foundations of our intimacy were being laid—to endure—to endure—even to the end—even beyond.

"'I had immense plans,' he muttered irresolutely. 'Yes,' said I; 'but if you try to shout I'll smash your head with—' There was not a stick or a stone near. 'I will throttle you for good,' I corrected myself. 'I was on the threshold of great things,' he pleaded, in a voice of longing, with a wistfulness of tone that made my blood run cold. 'And now for this stupid scoundrel—' 'Your success in Europe is assured in any case,' I affirmed steadily. I did not want to have the throttling of him, you understand—and indeed it would have been very little use for any practical purpose. I tried to break the spell—the heavy, mute spell of the wilderness—that seemed to draw him to its pitiless breast by the awakening of forgotten and brutal instincts, by the memory of gratified and monstrous passions. This alone, I was convinced, had driven him out to the edge of the forest, to the bush, towards the gleam of fires, the throb of drums, the drone of weird incantations; this alone had beguiled his unlawful soul beyond the bounds of permitted aspirations. And, don't you see, the terror of the position was not in being knocked on the head—though I had a very lively sense of that danger too—but in this, that I had to deal with a being to whom I could not appeal in the name of anything high or low. I had, even like the niggers, to invoke him—himself—his own exalted and incredible degradation. There was nothing either above or below him, and I knew it. He had kicked himself loose of the earth. Confound the man! he had kicked the very earth to pieces. He was alone, and I before him did not know whether I stood on the ground or floated in the air. I've been telling you what we said—repeating the phrases we pronounced—but what's the good? They were common everyday words—the familiar, vague sounds exchanged on every waking day of life. But what of that? They had behind them, to my mind, the terrific suggestiveness of words heard in dreams, of phrases spoken in nightmares. Soul! If anybody had ever struggled with a soul, I am the man. And I wasn't arguing with a lunatic either. Believe me or not, his intelligence was perfectly clear—concentrated, it is true, upon himself with horrible intensity, yet clear; and therein was my only chance— barring, of course, the killing him there and then, which wasn't so good, on account of unavoidable noise. But his soul was mad. Being alone in the wilderness, it had looked within itself, and, by heavens! I tell you, it had gone mad. I had—for my sins, I suppose, to go through the ordeal of looking into it myself. No eloquence could have been so withering to one's belief in mankind as his final burst of sincerity. He struggled with himself too. I saw it—I heard it. I saw the inconceivable mystery of a soul that knew no restraint, no faith, and no fear, yet struggling blindly with itself. I kept my head pretty well; but when I had him at last stretched on the couch, I wiped my forehead, while my legs shook under me as though I had carried half a ton on my back down that hill. And yet I had only supported him, his bony arm clasped round my neck—and he was not much heavier than a child.

"When next day we left at noon, the crowd, of whose presence behind the curtain of trees I had been acutely conscious all the time, flowed out of the woods again, filled the clearing, covered the slope with a mass of naked, breathing, quivering, bronze bodies. I steamed up a bit, then swung downstream, and two thousand eyes followed the evolutions of the splashing, thumping, fierce river-demon beating the water with its terrible tail and breathing black smoke into the air. In front of the first rank, along the river, three men, plastered with bright red earth from head to foot, strutted to and fro restlessly. When we came abreast again, they faced the river, stamped their feet, nodded their horned heads, swayed their scarlet bodies; they shook towards the fierce river-demon a bunch of black feathers, a mangy skin with a pendent tail—something that looked like a dried gourd; they shouted periodically together strings of amazing words that resembled no sounds of human language; and the deep murmurs of the crowd, interrupted suddenly, were like the responses of some satanic litany.

"We had carried Kurtz into the pilot-house: there was more air there. Lying on the couch, he stared through the open shutter. There was an eddy in the mass of human bodies, and the woman with helmeted head and tawny cheeks rushed out to the very brink of the stream. She put out her hands, shouted something, and all that wild mob took up the shout in a roaring chorus of articulated, rapid, breathless utterance.

"'Do you understand this?' I asked.

"He kept on looking out past me with fiery, longing eyes, with a mingled expression of wistfulness and hate. He made no answer, but I saw a smile, a smile of indefinable meaning, appear on his colourless lips that a moment after twitched convulsively. 'Do I not?' he said slowly, gasping, as if the words had been torn out of him by a supernatural power.

"I pulled the string of the whistle, and I did this because I saw the pilgrims on deck getting out their rifles with an air of anticipating a jolly lark. At the sudden screech there was a movement of abject terror through that wedged mass of bodies. 'Don't! don't you frighten them away,' cried some one on deck disconsolately. I pulled the string time after time. They broke and ran, they leaped, they crouched, they swerved, they dodged the flying terror of the sound. The three red chaps had fallen flat, face down on the shore, as though they had been shot dead. Only the barbarous and superb woman did not so much as flinch, and stretched tragically her bare arms after us over the sombre and glittering river.

"And then that imbecile crowd down on the deck started their little fun, and I could see nothing more for smoke.

"The brown current ran swiftly out of the heart of darkness, bearing us down towards the sea with twice the speed of our upward progress; and Kurtz's life was running swiftly too, ebbing, ebbing out of his heart into the sea of inexorable time. The manager was very placid, he had no vital anxieties now, he took us both in with a comprehensive and satisfied glance: the 'affair' had come off as well as could be wished. I saw the time approaching when I would be left alone of the party of 'unsound method.' The pilgrims looked upon me with disfavour. I was, so to speak, numbered with the dead. It is strange how I accepted this unforeseen partnership, this choice of nightmares forced upon me in the tenebrous land invaded by these mean and greedy phantoms.

"Kurtz discoursed. A voice! a voice! It rang deep to the very last. It survived his strength to hide in the magnificent folds of eloquence the barren darkness of his heart. Oh, he struggled! he struggled! The wastes of his weary brain were haunted by shadowy images now—images of wealth and fame revolving obsequiously round his unextinguishable gift of noble and lofty expression. My Intended, my station, my career, my ideas—these were the subjects for the occasional utterances of elevated sentiments. The shade of the original Kurtz frequented the bedside of the hollow sham, whose fate it was to be buried presently in the mould of primeval earth. But both the diabolic love and the unearthly hate of the mysteries it had penetrated fought for the possession of that soul satiated with primitive emotions, avid of lying fame, of sham distinction, of all the appearances of success and power.

"Sometimes he was contemptibly childish. He desired to have kings meet him at railway stations on his return from some ghastly Nowhere, where he intended to accomplish great things. 'You show them you have in you something that is really profitable, and then there will be no limits to the recognition of your ability,' he would say. 'Of course you must take care of the motives—right motives—always.' The long reaches that were like one and the same reach, monotonous bends that were exactly alike, slipped past the steamer with their multitude of secular[8] trees looking patiently after this grimy fragment of another world, the forerunner of change, of conquest, of

8. Centuries old (from *séculaire*, French).

trade, of massacres, of blessings. I looked ahead—piloting. 'Close the shutter,' said Kurtz suddenly one day; 'I can't bear to look at this.' I did so. There was a silence. 'Oh, but I will wring your heart yet!' he cried at the invisible wilderness.

"We broke down—as I had expected—and had to lie up for repairs at the head of an island. This delay was the first thing that shook Kurtz's confidence. One morning he gave me a packet of papers and a photograph—the lot tied together with a shoe-string. 'Keep this for me,' he said. 'This noxious fool' (meaning the manager) 'is capable of prying into my boxes when I am not looking.' In the afternoon I saw him. He was lying on his back with closed eyes, and I withdrew quietly, but I heard him mutter, 'Live rightly, die, die . . .' I listened. There was nothing more. Was he rehearsing some speech in his sleep, or was it a fragment of a phrase from some newspaper article? He had been writing for the papers and meant to do so again, 'for the furthering of my ideas. It's a duty.'

"His was an impenetrable darkness. I looked at him as you peer down at a man who is lying at the bottom of a precipice where the sun never shines. But I had not much time to give him, because I was helping the engine-driver to take to pieces the leaky cylinders, to straighten a bent connecting-rod, and in other such matters. I lived in an infernal mess of rust, filings, nuts, bolts, spanners, hammers, ratchet-drills—things I abominate, because I don't get on with them. I tended the little forge we fortunately had aboard; I toiled wearily in a wretched scrap-heap—unless I had the shakes too bad to stand.

"One evening coming in with a candle I was startled to hear him say a little tremulously, 'I am lying here in the dark waiting for death.' The light was within a foot of his eyes. I forced myself to murmur, 'Oh, nonsense!' and stood over him as if transfixed.

"Anything approaching the change that came over his features I have never seen before, and hope never to see again. Oh, I wasn't touched. I was fascinated. It was as though a veil had been rent. I saw on that ivory face the expression of sombre pride, of ruthless power, of craven terror—of an intense and hopeless despair. Did he live his life again in every detail of desire, temptation, and surrender during that supreme moment of complete knowledge? He cried in a whisper at some image, at some vision—he cried out twice, a cry that was no more than a breath:

" 'The horror! The horror!'

"I blew the candle out and left the cabin. The pilgrims were dining in the mess-room, and I took my place opposite the manager, who lifted his eyes to give me a questioning glance, which I successfully ignored. He leaned back, serene, with that peculiar smile of his sealing the unexpressed depths of his meanness. A continuous shower of small flies streamed upon the lamp, upon the cloth, upon our hands and faces. Suddenly the manager's boy put his insolent black head in the doorway, and said in a tone of scathing contempt:

" 'Mistah Kurtz—he dead.'

"All the pilgrims rushed out to see. I remained, and went on with my dinner. I believe I was considered brutally callous. However, I did not eat much. There was a lamp in there—light, don't you know—and outside it was so beastly, beastly dark. I went no more near the remarkable man who had pronounced a judgement upon the adventures of his soul on this earth. The voice was gone. What else had been there? But I am of course aware that next day the pilgrims buried something in a muddy hole.

"And then they very nearly buried me.

"However, as you see, I did not go to join Kurtz there and then. I did not. I remained to dream the nightmare out to the end, and to show my loyalty to Kurtz once more. Destiny. My destiny! Droll thing life is—that mysterious arrangement of merciless logic for a futile purpose. The most you can hope from it is some knowledge of yourself—that comes too late—a crop of unextinguishable regrets. I have wrestled with death. It is the most unexciting contest you can imagine. It takes place in an impalpable greyness, with nothing underfoot, with nothing around, without spectators, without clamour, without glory, without the great desire of victory, without the great fear of defeat, in a sickly atmosphere of tepid scepticism, without much belief in your own right, and still less in that of your adversary. If such is the form of ultimate wisdom, then life is a greater riddle than some of us think it to be. I was within a hair's-breadth of the last opportunity for pronouncement, and I found with humiliation that probably I would have nothing to say. This is the reason why I affirm that Kurtz was a remarkable man. He had something to say. He said it. Since I had peeped over the edge myself, I understand better the meaning of his stare, that could not see the flame of the candle, but was wide enough to embrace the whole universe, piercing enough to penetrate all the hearts that beat in the darkness. He had summed up—he had judged. 'The horror!' He was a remarkable man. After all, this was the expression of some sort of belief; it had candour, it had conviction, it had a vibrating note of revolt in its whisper, it had the appalling face of a glimpsed truth—the strange commingling of desire and hate. And it is not my own extremity I remember best—a vision of greyness without form filled with physical pain, and a careless contempt for the evanescence of all things—even of this pain itself. No! It is his extremity that I seem to have lived through. True, he had made that last stride, he had stepped over the edge, while I had been permitted to draw back my hesitating foot. And perhaps in this is the whole difference; perhaps all the wisdom, and all truth, and all sincerity, are just compressed into that inappreciable moment of time in which we step over the threshold of the invisible. Perhaps! I like to think my summing-up would not have been a word of careless contempt. Better his cry—much better. It was an affirmation, a moral victory paid for by innumerable defeats, by abominable terrors, by abominable satisfactions. But it was a victory! That is why I have remained loyal to Kurtz to the last, and even beyond, when a long time after I heard once more, not his own voice, but the echo of his magnificent eloquence thrown to me from a soul as translucently pure as a cliff of crystal.

"No, they did not bury me, though there is a period of time which I remember mistily, with a shuddering wonder, like a passage through some inconceivable world that had no hope in it and no desire. I found myself back in the sepulchral city resenting the sight of people hurrying through the streets to filch a little money from each other, to devour their infamous cookery, to gulp their unwholesome beer, to dream their insignificant and silly dreams. They trespassed upon my thoughts. They were intruders whose knowledge of life was to me an irritating pretence, because I felt so sure they could not possibly know the things I knew. Their bearing, which was simply the bearing of commonplace individuals going about their business in the assurance of perfect safety, was offensive to me like the outrageous flauntings of folly in the face of a danger it is unable to comprehend. I had no particular desire to enlighten them, but I had some difficulty in restraining myself from laughing in their faces, so full of stupid importance. I daresay I was not very well at that time. I tottered about the streets—there were various affairs to settle—grinning bitterly at perfectly respectable persons. I admit my behaviour was inexcusable, but then my temperature was seldom normal in these days. My dear aunt's endeavours to 'nurse up my strength' seemed altogether beside the mark. It was not my strength that wanted nursing, it was my imagination that wanted soothing. I kept the bundle of papers given me by Kurtz, not knowing exactly what to do with it. His mother had died lately, watched over, as I was told, by his Intended. A clean-shaven man, with an official manner and wearing gold-rimmed spectacles, called on me one day and made inquiries, at first circuitous, afterwards suavely pressing, about what he was pleased to denominate certain 'documents.' I was not surprised, because I had had two rows with the manager on the subject out there. I had refused to give up the smallest scrap out of that package, and I took the same attitude with the spectacled man. He became darkly menacing at last, and with much heat argued that the Company had the right to every bit of information about its 'territories.' And, said he, 'Mr Kurtz's knowledge of unexplored regions must have been necessarily extensive and peculiar—owing to his great abilities and to the deplorable circumstances in which he had been placed: therefore—' I assured him Mr Kurtz's knowledge, however extensive, did not bear upon the problems of commerce or administration. He invoked then the name of science. 'It would be an incalculable loss if,' etc. etc. I offered him the report on the 'Suppression of Savage Customs,' with the postscriptum torn off. He took it up eagerly, but ended by sniffing at it with an air of contempt. 'This is not what we had a right to expect,' he remarked. 'Expect nothing else,' I said. 'There are only private letters.' He withdrew upon some threat of legal proceedings, and I saw him no more; but another fellow, calling himself Kurtz's cousin, appeared two days later, and was anxious to hear all the details about his dear relative's last moments. Incidentally he gave me to understand that Kurtz had been essentially a great musician. 'There was the making of an immense success,' said the man, who was an organist, I believe, with lank grey hair flowing over a greasy coat-collar. I had no reason to doubt his statement; and to this day I am unable to say what was Kurtz's profession, whether he ever had any—which was the greatest of his talents. I had taken him for a painter who wrote for the papers, or else for a journalist who could paint—but even the cousin (who took snuff during the interview) could not tell me what he had been—exactly. He was a universal genius—on that point I agreed with the old chap, who thereupon blew his nose noisily into a large cotton handkerchief and withdrew in senile agitation, bearing off some family letters and memoranda without importance. Ultimately a journalist anxious to know something of the fate of his 'dear colleague' turned up. This visitor informed me Kurtz's proper sphere ought to have been politics 'on the popular side.' He had furry straight eyebrows, bristly hair cropped short, an eyeglass on a broad ribbon, and, becoming expansive, confessed his opinion that Kurtz really couldn't write a bit—'but heavens! how that man could talk!

He electrified large meetings. He had faith—don't you see?—he had the faith. He could get himself to believe anything—anything. He would have been a splendid leader of an extreme party.' 'What party?' I asked. 'Any party,' answered the other. 'He was an—an—extremist.' Did I not think so? I assented. Did I know, he asked, with a sudden flash of curiosity, 'what it was that had induced him to go out there?' 'Yes,' said I, and forthwith handed him the famous Report for publication, if he thought fit. He glanced through it hurriedly, mumbling all the time, judged 'it would do,' and took himself off with this plunder.

"Thus I was left at last with a slim packet of letters and the girl's portrait. She struck me as beautiful—I mean she had a beautiful expression. I know that the sunlight can be made to lie too, yet one felt that no manipulation of light and pose could have conveyed the delicate shade of truthfulness upon those features. She seemed ready to listen without mental reservation, without suspicion, without a thought for herself. I concluded I would go and give her back her portrait and those letters myself. Curiosity? Yes; and also some other feeling perhaps. All that had been Kurtz's had passed out of my hands: his soul, his body, his station, his plans, his ivory, his career. There remained only his memory and his Intended—and I wanted to give that up too to the past, in a way—to surrender personally all that remained of him with me to that oblivion which is the last word of our common fate. I don't defend myself. I had no clear perception of what it was I really wanted. Perhaps it was an impulse of unconscious loyalty, or the fulfilment of one of those ironic necessities that lurk in the facts of human existence. I don't know. I can't tell. But I went.

"I thought his memory was like the other memories of the dead that accumulate in every man's life—a vague impress on the brain of shadows that had fallen on it in their swift and final passage; but before the high and ponderous door, between the tall houses of a street as still and decorous as a well-kept alley in a cemetery, I had a vision of him on the stretcher, opening his mouth voraciously, as if to devour all the earth with all its mankind. He lived then before me; he lived as much as he had ever lived—a shadow insatiable of splendid appearances, of frightful realities; a shadow darker than the shadow of the night, and draped nobly in the folds of a gorgeous eloquence. The vision seemed to enter the house with me—the stretcher, the phantom-bearers, the wild crowd of obedient worshippers, the gloom of the forests, the glitter of the reach between the murky bends, the beat of the drum, regular and muffled like the beating of a heart—the heart of a conquering darkness. It was a moment of triumph for the wilderness, an invading and vengeful rush which, it seemed to me, I would have to keep back alone for the salvation of another soul. And the memory of what I had heard him say afar there, with the horned shapes stirring at my back, in the glow of fires, within the patient woods, those broken phrases came back to me, were heard again in their ominous and terrifying simplicity. I remembered his abject pleading, his abject threats, the colossal scale of his vile desires, the meanness, the torment, the tempestuous anguish of his soul. And later on I seemed to see his collected languid manner, when he said one day, 'This lot of ivory now is really mine. The Company did not pay for it. I collected it myself at a very great personal risk. I am afraid they will try to claim it as theirs though. H'm. It is a difficult case. What do you think I ought to do—

resist? Eh? I want no more than justice.' . . . He wanted no more than justice—no more than justice. I rang the bell before a mahogany door on the first floor, and while I waited he seemed to stare at me out of the glossy panel—stare with that wide and immense stare embracing, condemning, loathing all the universe. I seemed to hear the whispered cry, 'The horror! The horror!'

"The dusk was falling. I had to wait in a lofty drawing-room with three long windows from floor to ceiling that were like three luminous and be-draped columns. The bent gilt legs and backs of the furniture shone in indistinct curves. The tall marble fireplace had a cold and monumental whiteness. A grand piano stood massively in a corner; with dark gleams on the flat surfaces like a sombre and polished sarcophagus. A high door opened—closed. I rose.

"She came forward, all in black, with a pale head, floating towards me in the dusk. She was in mourning. It was more than a year since his death, more than a year since the news came; she seemed as though she would remember and mourn for ever. She took both my hands in hers and murmured, 'I had heard you were coming.' I noticed she was not very young—I mean not girl-ish. She had a mature capacity for fidelity, for belief, for suffering. The room seemed to have grown darker, as if all the sad light of the cloudy evening had taken refuge on her forehead. This fair hair, this pale visage, this pure brow, seemed surrounded by an ashy halo from which the dark eyes looked out at me. Their glance was guileless, profound, confident, and trustful. She carried her sorrowful head as though she were proud of that sorrow, as though she would say, I—I alone know how to mourn for him as he deserves. But while we were still shaking hands, such a look of awful desolation came upon her face that I perceived she was one of those creatures that are not the play-things of Time. For her he had died only yesterday. And, by Jove! the impression was so powerful that for me too he seemed to have died only yesterday—nay, this very minute. I saw her and him in the same instant of time—his death and her sorrow—I saw her sorrow in the very moment of his death. Do you understand? I saw them together—I heard them together. She had said, with a deep catch of the breath, 'I have survived'; while my strained ears seemed to hear distinctly, mingled with her tone of despairing regret, the summing-up whisper of his eternal condemnation. I asked myself what I was doing there, with a sensation of panic in my heart as though I had blundered into a place of cruel and absurd mysteries not fit for a human being to behold. She motioned me to a chair. We sat down. I laid the packet gently on the little table, and she put her hand over it. . . . 'You knew him well,' she murmured, after a moment of mourning silence.

"'Intimacy grows quickly out there,' I said. 'I knew him as well as it is possible for one man to know another.'

"'And you admired him,' she said. 'It was impossible to know him and not to admire him. Was it?'

"'He was a remarkable man,' I said unsteadily. Then before the appealing fixity of her gaze, that seemed to watch for more words on my lips, I went on, 'It was impossible not to—'

"'Love him,' she finished eagerly, silencing me into an appalled dumbness. 'How true! how true! But when you think that no one knew him so well as I! I had all his noble confidence. I knew him best.'

"'You knew him best,' I repeated. And perhaps she did. But with every word spoken the room was growing darker, and only her forehead, smooth and white, remained illumined by the unextinguishable light of belief and love.

"'You were his friend,' she went on. 'His friend,' she repeated, a little louder. 'You must have been, if he had given you this, and sent you to me. I feel I can speak to you—and oh! I must speak. I want you—you who have heard his last words—to know I have been worthy of him. . . . It is not pride. . . . Yes! I am proud to know I understood him better than any one on earth—he told me so himself. And since his mother died I have had no one—no one—to—to—'

"I listened. The darkness deepened. I was not even sure whether he had given me the right bundle. I rather suspect he wanted me to take care of another batch of his papers which, after his death, I saw the manager examining under the lamp. And the girl talked, easing her pain in the certitude of my sympathy; she talked as thirsty men drink. I had heard that her engagement with Kurtz had been disapproved by her people. He wasn't rich enough or something. And indeed I don't know whether he had not been a pauper all his life. He had given me some reason to infer that it was his impatience of comparative poverty that drove him out there.

"'. . . Who was not his friend who had heard him speak once?' she was saying. 'He drew men towards him by what was best in them.' She looked at me with intensity. 'It is the gift of the great,' she went on, and the sound of her low voice seemed to have the accompaniment of all the other sounds, full of mystery, desolation, and sorrow, I had ever heard—the ripple of the river, the soughing of the trees swayed by the wind, the murmurs of the crowds, the faint ring of incomprehensible words cried from afar, the whisper of a voice speaking from beyond the threshold of an eternal darkness. 'But you have heard him! You know!' she cried.

"'Yes, I know,' I said with something like despair in my heart, but bowing my head before the faith that was in her, before that great and saving illusion that shone with an unearthly glow in the darkness, in the triumphant darkness from which I could not have defended her—from which I could not even defend myself.

"'What a loss to me—to us!'—she corrected herself with beautiful generosity; then added in a murmur, 'To the world.' By the last gleams of twilight I could see the glitter of her eyes, full of tears—of tears that would not fall.

"'I have been very happy—very fortunate—very proud,' she went on. 'Too fortunate. Too happy for a little while. And now I am unhappy for—for life.'

"She stood up; her fair hair seemed to catch all the remaining light in a glimmer of gold. I rose too.

"'And of all this,' she went on mournfully, 'of all his promise, and of all his greatness, of his generous mind, of his noble heart, nothing remains—nothing but a memory. You and I—'

"'We shall always remember him,' I said hastily.

"'No!' she cried. 'It is impossible that all this should be lost—that such a life should be sacrificed to leave nothing—but sorrow. You know what vast plans he had. I knew of them too—I could not perhaps understand—but others knew of them. Something must remain. His words, at least, have not died.'

"'His words will remain,' I said.

"'And his example,' she whispered to herself. 'Men looked up to him—his goodness shone in every act. His example—'

"'True,' I said; 'his example too. Yes, his example. I forgot that.'

"'But I do not. I cannot—I cannot believe—not yet. I cannot believe that I shall never see him again, that nobody will see him again, never, never, never.'

"She put out her arms as if after a retreating figure, stretching them black and with clasped pale hands across the fading and narrow sheen of the window. Never see him! I saw him clearly enough then. I shall see this eloquent phantom as long as I live, and I shall see her too, a tragic and familiar Shade, resembling in this gesture another one, tragic also, and bedecked with powerless charms, stretching bare brown arms over the glitter of the infernal stream, the stream of darkness. She said suddenly very low, 'He died as he lived.'

"'His end,' said I, with dull anger stirring in me, 'was in every way worthy of his life.'

"'And I was not with him,' she murmured. My anger subsided before a feeling of infinite pity.

"'Everything that could be done—' I mumbled.

"'Ah, but I believed in him more than any one on earth—more than his own mother, more than—himself. He needed me! Me! I would have treasured every sigh, every word, every sign, every glance.'

"I felt like a chill grip on my chest. 'Don't,' I said, in a muffled voice.

"'Forgive me. I—I—have mourned so long in silence—in silence. . . . You were with him—to the last? I think of his loneliness. Nobody near to understand him as I would have understood. Perhaps no one to hear. . . .'

"'To the very end,' I said shakily. 'I heard his very last words. . . .' I stopped in a fright.

"'Repeat them,' she murmured in a heart-broken tone. 'I want—I want—something—something—to—to live with.'

"I was on the point of crying at her, 'Don't you hear them?' The dusk was repeating them in a persistent whisper all around us, in a whisper that seemed to swell menacingly like the first whisper of a rising wind. 'The horror! The horror!'

"'His last word—to live with,' she insisted. 'Don't you understand I loved him—I loved him—I loved him!'

"I pulled myself together and spoke slowly.

"'The last word he pronounced was—your name.'

"I heard a light sigh and then my heart stood still, stopped dead short by an exulting and terrible cry, by the cry of inconceivable triumph and of unspeakable pain. 'I knew it—I was sure!' . . . She knew. She was sure. I heard her weeping; she had hidden her face in her hands. It seemed to me that the house would collapse before I could escape, that the heavens would fall upon my head. But nothing happened. The heavens do not fall for such a trifle. Would they have fallen, I wonder, if I had rendered Kurtz that justice which was his due? Hadn't he said he wanted only justice? But I couldn't. I could not tell her. It would have been too dark—too dark altogether. . . ."

Marlow ceased, and sat apart, indistinct and silent, in the pose of a meditating Buddha. Nobody moved for a time. "We have lost the first of the ebb," said the Director suddenly. I raised my head. The offing was barred by a black bank of clouds, and the tranquil waterway leading to the uttermost ends of the earth flowed sombre under an overcast sky—seemed to lead into the heart of an immense darkness.

RABINDRANATH TAGORE
1861–1941

The preeminent figure in the history of modern literature in Bengali (the language of the state of West Bengal in eastern India, and of the neighboring nation of Bangladesh), poet and novelist Rabindranath Tagore has deeply influenced writers in the other Indian languages as well. Winner of the Nobel Prize for literature in 1913, Tagore is also perhaps the Indian writer whose name is likely to be familiar to most readers in the West. No less a poet than W. B. Yeats was responsible for Tagore's fame in European and American literary circles, but Tagore did not wear well in translation. He was mistakenly perceived as a mystical poet, Western tastes in poetry changed rather rapidly, and, in spite of the many translations of his poetry and fiction that appeared in English and other European languages after 1913, few outside of Bengal have been aware of Tagore's achievement as a writer or of his substantial contributions to the history of ideas in the modern age.

Tagore was born in Calcutta, the capital of British India in the nineteenth century, into an illustrious Hindu family. The Tagores were pioneers of the Bengal Renaissance, a movement led by Bengali intellectuals who were in many ways shaped by English education, which had been introduced in Bengal by the British government, but who at the same time reacted with profound ambivalence to colonial rule and the imposition of Western cultural norms on Indians. Through their writings, and through the institutions they founded, the leaders of the Renaissance sought to refashion Indian society to meet the challenges of the modern world, but to do so without losing its moorings in the highest values and ideals of traditional Indian culture. Tagore's father, Debendranath Tagore, was among the first leaders of the Brahmo Samaj, a major Hindu social reform organization that was founded on just such a blend of Western and Indian ideas.

Each of Debendranath Tagore's fourteen children (including his daughter, Swarnakumari) made significant contributions to Bengali literature and culture. None of them, however, equaled Rabindranath, the youngest, in breadth and importance of achievement. In the course of a life that spanned the period during which India emerged from colonial domination to independent nationhood, Tagore wrote poems, novels, short stories, plays, and essays, transforming extant Bengali literary forms and creating new ones. *Gitanjali* (Song offering), an anthology of lyric poems that the poet himself translated from the Bengali into English, brought him international recognition in the form of the Nobel Prize. Tagore's own translations of the *Gitanjali* poems, and Yeats's praise of them in his preface to the first edition of the anthology, contributed to the misleading stereotyping of the poems as a combination of romantic lyricism and vague Eastern mysticism. The truth is that the *Gitanjali* poems reflect only one facet of Tagore's poetic sensibility, and that not accurately. On the one hand, he drew on earlier lyric traditions in Sanskrit and Bengali with great sensitivity; on the other, he nearly single-handedly brought the Bengali language and Bengali poetry into the domain of the modern. Tagore continued to write poetry to the end of his life, experimenting with language and with a variety of poetic forms, combining a spare, direct style with vivid yet deeply suggestive images in ways that are difficult to convey in translation. In addition to the lyric poems in *Gitanjali* and other collections (these are not true songs), Tagore composed and set to music nearly two thousand songs, which continue to dominate the Bengali song repertoire in the twentieth century. Included in these songs are the national anthems of India and Bangladesh.

Among Tagore's lasting contributions are Shantiniketan and Viswabharati, the school and the international university he founded near Calcutta as alternatives to colonial education and as arenas and training grounds for international cooperation. He used the international attention he gained as a result of the Nobel Prize to travel widely in Europe, Asia, and America, speaking out against the evils of colonialism, wars based on narrow nationalism, and abuses of human rights all over the world. When Mahatma Gandhi led the Indian people in their nonviolent (and ultimately successful) struggle for freedom from British colonial rule in the period between the two world wars, Tagore stood by Gandhi and his movement but pointed out the dangers of focusing on exclusively nationalistic goals, arguing instead for a new world order based on transnational values and ideals. A true "renaissance" figure, Tagore left no aspect of human experience untouched in his life and writings. The universalistic humanism that informs all his writings makes him one of the towering figures of the twentieth century.

Although the Bengali language had a rich tradition of medieval lyric and narrative poetry, Bengali prose fiction emerged in the late nineteenth century as a result of the impact of English education and Western literary forms. The novels of Tagore's elder contemporary Bankim Chandra Chatterjee (1838–1894) were mainly historical romances modeled on the novels of Sir Walter Scott, though Chatterjee also used the novel as a vehicle for social critique and nationalist propaganda. Concern about social issues, especially the need for the emancipation of Bengali women from oppressive cultural practices, dominates Tagore's major novels, beginning with *Cokher bali* (Speck in the eye) and *Nastanir* (The broken nest), published serially in 1901. Here, as well as in his more than one hundred short stories, his preoccupation with the emotional and psychological lives of his characters and his passionate championship of the integrity of the individual strike a new note in Bengali literature.

Tagore's short stories are the first major examples of the genre in any Indian language. Between 1891 and 1895 forty-four of his stories appeared in Bengali periodicals, the majority of them in the monthly journal *Sadhana* (Endeavor), edited by members of the Tagore family. The rest were written in the 1920s. "Punishment" ("*Sasti*," 1893) belongs to the earlier stories, which were inspired by Tagore's experience of rural Bengal during the decade he spent there as manager of the family estates in Shelidah. Shelidah is in what was formerly the British province of East Bengal, which became East Pakistan following the partition of India in 1947 and is now the independent nation of Bangladesh. The characters in Tagore's major fiction tend to be drawn from the Bengali middle class, which he knew well; but a number of these early stories are about the peasants and villagers with whom he came in contact during the Shelidah years. Here the great Padma River and the agricultural landscape of eastern Bengal become the focus of the love of nature and the lyrical, romantic sensibility that are characteristic of all the writer's works.

The stories of this period are by no means idyllic pictures of village life. In "Punishment," Tagore's sensitive portrayal of the complex relationships among the members of the low-caste Rui family and between them and the upper-class rural society that exploits them suggests both realism and a sense of tragedy. The transactions among Chandara, the proud and beautiful young woman; her husband, the farm-laborer Chidam; and landlord Ramlochan Chakravarti, "pillar of the village," reveal Tagore's intimate understanding both of the ways in which economic, social, and patriarchal oppression are intrinsically linked and of the ability of the oppressed to resist even the most powerful forms of oppression. However, as in his other stories and novels, his real interest in "Punishment" is in delineating the psychological ramifications of social and familial relationships. Chandara is a typical Tagore protagonist, representing the power and dignity of the human will in the face of societal degradation. And yet Tagore's world is a tragic one, populated by individuals who, trapped in what he called the "dreary desert sand of dead habit," are ultimately unable to transcend the tyranny of institutions.

PRONOUNCING GLOSSARY

The following list uses common English syllables and stress accents to provide rough equivalents of selected words whose pronunciation may be unfamiliar to the general reader.

Barobau: *baroh'-bau*

Chandara: *chuhn'-duh-rah*

Chidam Rui: *chee'-duhm roo'-yee*

Dukhiram Rui: *doo-khee'-rahm roo'-yee*

Kashi Majumdar: *kah'-shee muh'-joom-dahr*

koel: *koh'-yuhl*

Rabindranath Tagore: *ruh-beend'-run-naht tuh-gohr'*

Ram: *rahm*

Ramlochan Chakravarti: *rahm'-loh-chuhn chuhk'-ruh-vuhr-tee*

Thākur: *thah'-koor*

zamindar: *zuh-meen'-dahr*

Punishment[1]

I

When the brothers Dukhiram Rui and Chidam Rui went out in the morning with their heavy farm-knives, to work in the fields, their wives would quarrel and shout. But the people near by were as used to the uproar as they were to other customary, natural sounds. When they heard the shrill screams of the women, they would say, "They're at it again"—that is, what was happening was only to be expected: it was not a violation of Nature's rules. When the sun rises at dawn, no one asks why; and whenever the two wives in this *kuri*-caste[2] household let fly at each other, no one was at all curious to investigate the cause.

Of course this wrangling and disturbance affected the husbands more than the neighbours, but they did not count it a major nuisance. It was as if they were riding together along life's road in a cart whose rattling, clattering, unsprung wheels were inseparable from the journey. Indeed, days when there was no noise, when everything was uncannily silent, carried a greater threat of unpredictable doom.

The day on which our story begins was like this. When the brothers returned home at dusk, exhausted by their work, they found the house eerily quiet. Outside, too, it was extremely sultry. There had been a sharp shower in the afternoon, and clouds were still massing. There was not a breath of wind. Weeds and scrub round the house had shot up after the rain: the heavy scent of damp vegetation, from these and from the waterlogged jute-

---

1. Translated by William Radice.   2. In Bengal, a low caste originally of bird catchers, but by the 19th century, general laborers.

fields, formed a solid wall all around. Frogs croaked from the milkman's pond behind the house, and the buzz of crickets filled the leaden sky.

Not far off the swollen Padma[3] looked flat and sinister under the mounting clouds. It had flooded most of the grain-fields, and had come close to the houses. Here and there, roots of mango and jackfruit trees on the slipping bank stuck up out of the water, like helpless hands clawing at the air for a last fingerhold.

That day, Dukhiram and Chidam had been working near the zamindar's[4] office. On a sandbank opposite, paddy[5] had ripened. The paddy needed to be cut before the sandbank was washed away, but the village people were busy either in their own fields or in cutting jute: so a messenger came from the office and forcibly engaged the two brothers. As the office roof was leaking in places, they also had to mend that and make some new wickerwork panels: it had taken them all day. They couldn't come home for lunch; they just had a snack from the office. At times they were soaked by the rain; they were not paid normal labourers' wages; indeed, they were paid mainly in insults and sneers.

When the two brothers returned at dusk, wading through mud and water, they found the younger wife, Chandara, stretched on the ground with her sari[6] spread out. Like the sky, she had wept buckets in the afternoon, but had now given way to sultry exhaustion. The elder wife, Radha, sat on the verandah sullenly: her eighteen-month son had been crying, but when the brothers came in they saw him lying naked in a corner of the yard, asleep.

Dukhiram, famished, said gruffly, "Give me my food."

Like a spark on a sack of gunpowder, the elder wife exploded, shrieking out, "Where is there food? Did you give me anything to cook? Must I earn money myself to buy it?"

After a whole day of toil and humiliation, to return—raging with hunger—to a dark, joyless, foodless house, to be met by Radha's sarcasm, especially her final jibe, was suddenly unendurable. "What?" he roared, like a furious tiger, and then, without thinking, plunged his knife into her head. Radha collapsed into her sister-in-law's lap, and in minutes she was dead.

"What have you done?" screamed Chandara, her clothes soaked with blood. Chidam pressed his hand over her mouth. Dukhiram, throwing aside the knife, fell to his knees with his head in his hands, stunned. The little boy woke up and started to wail in terror.

Outside there was complete quiet. The herd-boys were returning with the cattle. Those who had been cutting paddy on the far sandbanks were crossing back in groups in a small boat—with a couple of bundles of paddy on their heads as payment. Everyone was heading for home.

Ramlochan Chakravarti, pillar of the village, had been to the post office with a letter, and was now back in his house, placidly smoking. Suddenly he remembered that his sub-tenant Dukhiram was very behind with his rent: he had promised to pay some today. Deciding that the brothers must be home by now, he threw his chadar[7] over his shoulders, took his umbrella, and stepped out.

---

3. A major river in what is now Bangladesh.   4. Landlord.   5. The rice crop.   6. A long strip of cloth draped around the body, Indian women's traditional clothing.   7. In Bengal, a sheet of cloth draped around the shoulders, usually worn by men but sometimes by women.

As he entered the Ruis' house, he felt uneasy. There was no lamp alight. On the dark verandah, the dim shapes of three or four people could be seen. In a corner of the verandah there were fitful, muffled sobs: the little boy was trying to cry for his mother, but was stopped each time by Chidam.

"Dukhi," said Ramlochan nervously, "are you there?"

Dukhiram had been sitting like a statue for a long time; now, on hearing his name, he burst into tears like a helpless child.

Chidam quickly came down from the verandah into the yard, to meet Ramlochan. "Have the women been quarelling again?" Ramlochan asked. "I heard them yelling all day."

Chidam, all this time, had been unable to think what to do. Various impossible stories occurred to him. All he had decided was that later that night he would move the body somewhere. He had never expected Ramlochan to come. He could think of no swift reply. "Yes," he stumbled, "today they were quarrelling terribly."

"But why is Dukhi crying so?" asked Ramlochan, stepping towards the verandah.

Seeing no way out now, Chidam blurted, "In their quarrel, *Chotobau* struck at *Barobau's*[8] head with a farm-knife."

When immediate danger threatens, it is hard to think of other dangers. Chidam's only thought was to escape from the terrible truth—he forgot that a lie can be even more terrible. A reply to Ramlochan's question had come instantly to mind, and he had blurted it out.

"Good grief," said Ramlochan in horror. "What are you saying? Is she dead?"

"She's dead," said Chidam, clasping Ramlochan's feet.

Ramlochan was trapped. *"Rām, Rām,"*[9] he thought, "what a mess I've got into this evening. What if I have to be a witness in court?" Chidam was still clinging to his feet, saying, "*Thākur*,[1] how can I save my wife?"

Ramlochan was the village's chief source of advice on legal matters. Reflecting further he said, "I think I know a way. Run to the police station: say that your brother Dukhi returned in the evening wanting his food, and because it wasn't ready he struck his wife on the head with his knife. I'm sure that if you say that, she'll get off."

Chidam felt a sickening dryness in his throat. He stood up and said, "*Thākur*, if I lose my wife I can get another, but if my brother is hanged, how can I replace him?" In laying the blame on his wife, he had not seen it that way. He had spoken without thought; now, imperceptibly, logic and awareness were returning to his mind.

Ramlochan appreciated his logic. "Then say what actually happened," he said. "You can't protect yourself on all sides."

He had soon, after leaving, spread it round the village that Chandara Rui had, in a quarrel with her sister-in-law, split her head open with a farm-knife. Police charged into the village like a river in flood. Both the guilty and the innocent were equally afraid.

---

8. Elder Daughter-in-Law; members of a family address each other by kinship terms. "*Chotobau*": Younger Daughter-in-Law.   9. God's name, repeated to express great emotion.   1. Master or lord, term of address for gods and upper-class (Brahmin) men. *Tagore* is an anglicized form of *Thākur*.

II

Chidam decided he would have to stick to the path he had chalked out for himself. The story he had given to Ramlochan Chakravarti had gone all round the village; who knew what would happen if another story was circulated? But he realized that if he kept to the story he would have to wrap it in five more stories if his wife was to be saved.

Chidam asked Chandara to take the blame on to herself. She was dumbfounded. He reassured her: "Don't worry—if you do what I tell you, you'll be quite safe." But whatever his words, his throat was dry and his face was pale.

Chandara was not more than seventeen or eighteen. She was buxom, well-rounded, compact and sturdy—so trim in her movements that in walking, turning, bending or climbing there was no awkwardness at all. She was like a brand-new boat: neat and shapely, gliding with ease, not a loose joint anywhere. Everything amused and intrigued her; she loved to gossip; her bright, restless, deep black eyes missed nothing as she walked to the *ghāṭ*,[2] pitcher on her hip, parting her veil slightly with her finger.

The elder wife had been her exact opposite: unkempt, sloppy and slovenly. She was utterly disorganized in her dress, housework, and the care of her child. She never had any proper work in hand, yet never seemed to have time for anything. The younger wife usually refrained from comment, for at the mildest barb Radha would rage and stamp and let fly at her, disturbing everyone around.

Each wife was matched by her husband to an extraordinary degree. Dukhiram was a huge man—his bones were immense, his nose was squat, in his eyes and expression he seemed not to understand the world very well, yet he never questioned it either. He was innocent yet fearsome: a rare combination of power and helplessness. Chidam, however, seemed to have been carefully carved from shiny black rock. There was not an inch of excess fat on him, not a wrinkle or dimple anywhere. Each limb was a perfect blend of strength and finesse. Whether jumping from a riverbank, or punting a boat, or climbing up bamboo-shoots for sticks, he showed complete dexterity, effortless grace. His long black hair was combed with oil back from his brow and down to his shoulders—he took great care over his dress and appearance. Although he was not unresponsive to the beauty of other women in the village, and was keen to make himself charming in their eyes, his real love was for his young wife. They quarrelled sometimes, but there was mutual respect too: neither could defeat the other. There was a further reason why the bond between them was firm: Chidam felt that a wife as nimble and sharp as Chandara could not be wholly trusted, and Chandara felt that all eyes were on her husband—that if she didn't bind him tightly to her she might one day lose him.

A little before the events in this story, however, they had a major row. Chandara had noticed that when her husband's work took him away for two days or more, he brought no extra earnings. Finding this ominous, she also began to overstep the mark. She would hang around by the *ghāṭ*, or wander about talking rather too much about Kashi Majumdar's middle son.

2. Steps leading down to a pond or river; meeting place, especially for women, who go there to get water or to wash clothes.

Something now seemed to poison Chidam's life. He could not settle his attention on his work. One day his sister-in-law rounded on him: she shook her finger and said in the name of her dead father, "That girl runs before the storm. How can I restrain her? Who knows what ruin she will bring?"

Chandara came out of the next room and said sweetly, "What's the matter, *Didi?*"[3] and a fierce quarrel broke out between them.

Chidam glared at his wife and said, "If I ever hear that you've been to the *ghāṭ* on your own, I'll break every bone in your body."

"The bones will mend again," said Chandara, starting to leave. Chidam sprang at her, grabbed her by the hair, dragged her back to the room and locked her in.

When he returned from work that evening he found that the room was empty. Chandara had fled three villages away, to her maternal uncle's house. With great difficulty Chidam persuaded her to return, but he had to surrender to her. It was as hard to restrain his wife as to hold a handful of mercury; she always slipped through his fingers. He did not have to use force any more, but there was no peace in the house. Ever-fearful love for his elusive young wife wracked him with intense pain. He even once or twice wondered if it would be better if she were dead: at least he would get some peace then. Human beings can hate each other more than death.

It was at this time that the crisis hit the house.

When her husband asked her to admit to the murder, Chandara stared at him, stunned; her black eyes burnt him like fire. Then she shrank back, as if to escape his devilish clutches. She turned her heart and soul away from him. "You've nothing to fear," said Chidam. He taught her repeatedly what she should say to the police and the magistrate. Chandara paid no attention—sat like a wooden statue whenever he spoke.

Dukhiram relied on Chidam for everything. When he told him to lay the blame on Chandara, Dukhiram said, "But what will happen to her?" "I'll save her," said Chidam. His burly brother was content with that.

III

This was what he instructed his wife to say: "The elder wife was about to attack me with the vegetable-slicer. I picked up a farm-knife to stop her, and it somehow cut into her." This was all Ramlochan's invention. He had generously supplied Chidam with the proofs and embroidery that the story would require.

The police came to investigate. The villagers were sure now that Chandara had murdered her sister-in-law, and all the witnesses confirmed this. When the police questioned Chandara, she said, "Yes, I killed her."

"Why did you kill her?"

"I couldn't stand her any more."

"Was there a brawl between you?"

"No."

"Did she attack you first?"

"No."

"Did she ill-treat you?"

---

3. Elder Sister, respectful form of address for Bengali women.

"No."

Everyone was amazed at these replies, and Chidam was completely thrown off balance. "She's not telling the truth," he said. "The elder wife first—"

The inspector silenced him sharply. He continued according to the rules of cross-examination and repeatedly received the same reply: Chandara would not accept that she had been attacked in any way by her sister-in-law. Such an obstinate girl was never seen! She seemed absolutely bent on going to the gallows; nothing would stop her. Such fierce, passionate pride! In her thoughts, Chandara was saying to her husband, "I shall give my youth to the gallows instead of to you. My final ties in this life will be with them."

Chandara was arrested, and left her home for ever, by the paths she knew so well, past the festival carriage, the market-place, the *ghāt*, the Majumdars' house, the post office, the school—an ordinary, harmless, flirtatious, fun-loving village wife; leaving a shameful impression on all the people she knew. A bevy of boys followed her, and the women of the village, her friends and companions—some of them peering through their veils, some from their doorsteps, some from behind trees—watched the police leading her away and shuddered with embarrassment, fear and contempt.

To the Deputy Magistrate, Chandara again confessed her guilt, claiming no ill-treatment from her sister-in-law at the time of the murder. But when Chidam was called to the witness-box he broke down completely, weeping, clasping his hands and saying, "I swear to you, sir, my wife is innocent." The magistrate sternly told him to control himself, and began to question him. Bit by bit the true story came out.

The magistrate did not believe him, because the chief, most trustworthy, most educated witness—Ramlochan Chakravarti—said: "I appeared on the scene a little after the murder. Chidam confessed everything to me and clung to my feet saying, 'Tell me how I can save my wife.' I did not say anything one way or the other. Then Chidam said, 'If I say that my elder brother killed his wife in a fit of fury because his food wasn't ready, then she'll get off.' I said, 'Be careful, you rogue: don't say a single false word in court—there's no worse offence than that.'" Ramlochan had previously prepared lots of stories that would save Chandara, but when he found that she herself was bending her neck to receive the noose, he decided, "Why take the risk of giving false evidence now? I'd better say what little I know." So Ramlochan said what he knew—or rather said a little more than he knew.

The Deputy Magistrate committed the case to a sessions trial.[4] Meanwhile in fields, houses, markets and bazaars, the sad or happy affairs of the world carried on; and just as in previous years, torrential monsoon rains fell on to the new rice-crop.

Police, defendant and witnesses were all in court. In the civil court opposite hordes of people were waiting for their cases. A Calcutta lawyer had come on a suit about the sharing of a pond behind a kitchen; the plaintiff had thirty-nine witnesses. Hundreds of people were anxiously waiting for

4. A trial that is settled through a special court *sessions* in one continuous sitting.

hair-splitting judgements, certain that nothing, at present, was more important. Chidam stared out of the window at the constant throng, and it seemed
like a dream. A *koel*-bird[5] was hooting from a huge banyan tree in the compound: no courts or cases in *his* world!

Chandara said to the judge, "Sir, how many times must I go on saying the
same thing?"

The judge explained, "Do you know the penalty for the crime you have
confessed?"

"No," said Chandara.

"It is death by the hanging."

"Then please give it to me, sir," said Chandara. "Do what you like—I can't
take any more."

When her husband was called to the court, she turned away. "Look at the
witness," said the judge, "and say who he is."

"He is my husband," said Chandara, covering her face with her hands.

"Does he not love you?"

"He loves me greatly."

"Do you not love him?"

"I love him greatly."

When Chidam was questioned, he said, "I killed her."

"Why?"

"I wanted my food and my sister-in-law didn't give it to me."

When Dukhiram came to give evidence, he fainted. When he had come
round again, he answered, "Sir, I killed her."

"Why?"

"I wanted a meal and she didn't give it to me."

After extensive cross-examination of various other witnesses, the judge
concluded that the brothers had confessed to the crime in order to save the
younger wife from the shame of the noose. But Chandara had, from the
police investigation right through to the sessions trial, said the same thing
repeatedly—she had not budged an inch from her story. Two barristers did
their utmost to save her from the death-sentence, but in the end were
defeated by her.

Who, on that auspicious night when, at a very young age, a dusky, diminutive, round-faced girl had left her childhood dolls in her father's house and
come to her in-laws' house, could have imagined these events? Her father,
on his deathbed, had happily reflected that at least he had made proper
arrangements for his daughter's future.

In gaol,[6] just before the hanging, a kindly Civil Surgeon asked Chandara,
"Do you want to see anyone?"

"I'd like to see my mother," she replied.

"Your husband wants to see you," said the doctor. "Shall I call him?"

"To hell with him,"[7] said Chandara.

---

5. Common Indian songbird.   6. Jail   7. Death to him (literal trans.); an expression usually uttered
in jest.

WILLIAM BUTLER YEATS
1865–1939

William Butler Yeats is not only the main figure in the Irish literary renaissance but also the twentieth century's greatest poet in the English language. His sensuously evocative descriptions and his fusion of concrete historical examples with an urgent metaphysical vision stir readers around the world. Years after the poet's death, the Nigerian Chinua Achebe borrowed three words from one of his lines as the title of a novel, *Things Fall Apart*—confident that his audience would immediately recognize the source. If the English language has a Symbolist poet, it is once again Yeats for his constant use of allusive imagery and large symbolic structures. Yeats's symbolism is not that of Baudelaire, Mallarmé, or other continental predecessors, however, for the European Symbolists did not share the Irish poet's fascination with occult wisdom and large historical patterns. Yeats adopted a cyclical model of history for which the rise and fall of civilizations are predetermined inside a series of interweaving evolutionary spirals. With this cyclical model, he created a private mythology that allowed him to come to terms with both personal and cultural pain and helped explain—as symptoms of Western civilization's declining spiral—the plight of contemporary Irish society and the chaos of European culture around World War I. Yeats shares with writers like Rilke and T. S. Eliot the quest for larger meaning in a time of trouble and the use of symbolic language to give verbal form to that quest.

Yeats was born in a Dublin suburb on June 13, 1865, the oldest of four children born to John Butler and Susan Pollexfen Yeats. His father, a cosmopolitan Anglo-Irishman who had turned from law to painting, took over Yeats's education when he found that, at age nine, the boy could not read. J. B. Yeats was a highly argumentative religious skeptic who alternately terrorized his son and awakened his interest in poetry and the visual arts, inspiring at one and the same time both rebellion against scientific rationalism and belief in the higher knowledge of art. His mother's strong ties to her home in County Sligo (where Yeats spent many summers and school holidays) introduced him to the beauties of the Irish countryside and the Irish folklore and supernatural legends that appear throughout his work. Living alternately in Ireland and England for much of his youth, Yeats became part of literary society in both countries and—though an Irish nationalist—was unable to adopt a narrowly patriotic point of view. Even the failed Easter Rebellion of 1916, which he celebrated in "Easter 1916," and the revolutionary figures who were beloved friends took their place in a larger mythic historical framework. By the end of his life, he had abandoned all practical politics and devoted himself to the reality of personal experience inside a mystic view of history.

For many, it is Yeats's mastery of images that defines his work. From his early use of symbols as private keys, or dramatic metaphors for complex personal emotions, to the immense cosmology of his last work, he continued to create a highly visual poetry whose power derives from the dramatic interweaving of specific images. Symbols such as the Tower, Byzantium, Helen of Troy, the opposition of sun and moon, birds of prey, the blind man, and the fool recur frequently and draw their meaning not from inner connections established inside the poem (as for the French Symbolists) but from an underlying myth based on occult tradition, Irish folklore, history, and Yeats's own personal experience. Symbols as Yeats used them, however, make sense in and among themselves: the "gyre," or spiral unfolding of history, is simultaneously the falcon's spiral flight; and the sphinxlike beast slouching blank-eyed toward Bethlehem in "The Second Coming" is a comprehensible horror capable of many explicit interpretations but resistant to all and, therefore, the more terrifying. Even readers unacquainted with Yeats's mythic system will respond to images precisely expressing a situation or state of mind (for example, golden Byzantium for intellect, art, wisdom—all that "body" cannot supply) and to a visionary organization that proposes shape and context for twentieth-century anxieties.

The nine poems included here cover the range of Yeats's career, which embraced several periods and styles. Yeats had attended art school and planned to be an artist before he turned fully to literature in 1886, and his early works show the influence of the Pre-Raphaelite school in art and literature. Pre-Raphaelitism called for a return to the sensuous representation and concrete particulars found in Italian painting before Raphael (1483–1520), and Pre-Raphaelite poetry evoked a poetic realm of luminous supernatural beauty described in allusive and erotically sensuous detail. Rossetti's "Blessed Damozel," yearning for her beloved "from the gold bar of heaven," has eyes "deeper than the depth / Of waters stilled at even; / She had three lilies in her hand, / And the stars in her hair were seven." The Pre-Raphaelite fascination with the medieval past (William Morris wrote a *Defense of Guenevere*, King Arthur's adulterous wife) combined with Yeats's own interest in Irish legend, and in 1889 a long poem describing a traveler in fairyland (*The Wanderings of Oisin*) established his reputation and won Morris's praise. The musical, evocative style of Yeats's Pre-Raphaelite period is well shown in "The Lake Isle of Innisfree" (1890), with its hidden "bee-loud glade" where "peace comes dropping slow" and evening, after the "purple glow" of noon, is "full of the linnet's wings." Another poem from the same period, "When You Are Old," pleads his love for the beautiful actress and Irish nationalist Maud Gonne, whom he met in 1889 and who repeatedly refused to marry him. From the love poems of his youth to his old age, when "The Circus Animals' Desertion" described her as prey to fanaticism and hate, Yeats returned again and again to examine his feelings for this woman, who personified love, beauty, and Irish nationalism along with hope, frustration, and despair.

Yeats's family moved to London in 1887, where he continued an earlier interest in mystical philosophy by taking up theosophy under its Russian interpreter Madame Blavatsky. Madame Blavatsky claimed mystic knowledge from Tibetan monks and preached a doctrine of the Universal Oversoul, individual spiritual evolution through cycles of incarnation, and the world as a conflict of opposites. Yeats was taken with her grandiose cosmology, although he inconveniently wished to test it by experiment and analysis and was ultimately expelled from the society in 1890. He found a more congenial literary model in the works of William Blake, which he co-edited in 1893 with F. J. Ellis. Yeats's interest in large mystical systems later waned but never altogether disappeared, and traces may be seen in the introduction that he wrote in 1916 for *Gitanjali*, a collection of poems by the Indian author Rabindranath Tagore.

Several collections of Irish folk and fairy tales and a book describing Irish traditions (*The Celtic Twilight*, 1893) demonstrated a corresponding interest in Irish national identity. In 1896 he had met Lady Gregory, an Irish nationalist who invited him to spend summers at Coole Park, her country house in Galway, and who worked closely with him (and later J. M. Synge) in founding the Irish National Theatre (later the Abbey Theatre). Along with other participants in what was once called the Irish literary renaissance, he aimed to create "a national literature that made Ireland beautiful in the memory . . . freed from provincialism by an exacting criticism." To this end, he wrote *Cathleen ni Houlihan* (1902), a play in which the title character personifies Ireland, which became immensely popular with Irish nationalists. He also established Irish literary societies in Dublin and Ireland, promoted and reviewed Irish books, and lectured and wrote about the need for Irish community. In 1922 he was elected senator of the Irish Free State, serving until 1928.

Gradually, Yeats became embittered by the split between narrow Irish nationalism and the free expression of Irish culture. He was outraged at the attacks on Synge's *Playboy of the Western World* (1907) for its supposed derogatory picture of Irish culture, and he commented scathingly in *Poems Written in Discouragement* (1913, reprinted in *Responsibilities*, 1914) on the inability of the Irish middle class to appreciate art or literature. When he celebrates the abortive Easter uprisings of 1916, it is with a more universal, aesthetic view; "A terrible beauty is born" in the self-sacrifice that leads even a "drunken, vainglorious lout" to be "transformed utterly" by political martyrdom. Except for summers at Coole Park, Yeats in his middle age was spending more time in England than in Ireland. He began his *Autobiographies* in 1914, and wrote symbolic plays intended for small audiences on the model of the Japanese *nō* theater. There is a change in the tone of his works at this time, a new precision and epigrammatic quality that is partly owing to his disappointment with Irish nationalism and partly to the new tastes in poetry promulgated by his friend Ezra Pound and by T. S. Eliot after the example of John Donne and the metaphysical poets.

Yeats's marriage in 1917 to Georgie Hyde-Lees provided him with much-needed stability and also an impetus to work out a larger symbolic scheme. He interpreted his wife's experiments with automatic writing (writing whatever comes to mind, without correction or rational intent) as glimpses into a hidden cosmic order and gradually evolved a total system, which he explained in *A Vision* (1925). The wheel of history takes twenty-six thousand years to turn; and inside that wheel civilizations evolve in roughly two-thousand-year *gyres*, spirals expanding outward until they collapse at the beginning of a new gyre, which will reverse the direction of the old. Human personalities fall into different types within the system, and both gyres and types are related to the different phases of the moon. Yeats's later poems in *The Tower* (1928), *The Winding Stair* (1933), and *Last Poems* (1939) are set in the context of this system. Even when it is not literally present, it suggests an organizing pattern that resolves contraries inside an immense historical perspective. "Leda and the Swan," on one level an erotic retelling of a mythic rape, also foreshadows the Trojan War—brute force mirroring brute force. In the two poems on the legendary city of Byzantium, Yeats admired an artistic civilization that "could answer all my questions" but that was also only a moment in history. Byzantine art, with its stylized perspectives and mosaics made by arranging tiny colored pieces of stone, was the exact opposite of the Western tendency to imitate nature, and it provided a kind of escape, or healing distance, for the poet. The idea of an inhuman, metallic, abstract beauty separated "out of nature" by art expresses a mystic and Symbolist quest for an invulnerable world distinct from the ravages of time. This world was to be found in an idealized Byzantium, where the poet's body would be transmuted into "such a form as Grecian goldsmiths make / Of hammered gold and gold enamelling / To keep a drowsy Emperor awake; / Or set upon a golden bough to sing / To lords and ladies of Byzantium / Of what is past, or passing, or to come." At the end of "Among School Children," the sixty-year-old "public man" compensates for the passing of youth by dreaming of pure "Presences" that never fade. Yeats had often adopted the persona of the old man for whom the perspectives of age, idealized beauty, or history were ways to keep human agony at a distance. In "Lapis Lazuli," the tragic figures of history transcend their roles by the calm "gaiety" with which they accept their fate; the ancient Chinamen carved in the poem's damaged blue stone climb toward a vantage point where they stare detachedly down on the world's tragedies: "Their eyes mid many wrinkles, their eyes, / Their ancient, glittering eyes, are gay."

But the world is still there, its tragedies still take place, and Yeats's poetry is always aware of the physical and emotional roots from which it sprang. Whatever the wished-for distance, his poems are full of passionate feelings, erotic desire and disappointment, delight in sensuous beauty, horror at civil war and anarchy, dismay at degradation and change. By the time of his death on January 28, 1939, Yeats had rejected his Byzantine identity as the golden songbird and sought out "the brutality, the ill breeding, the barbarism of truth." "The Wild Old Wicked Man" replaced earlier druids or ancient Chinamen as spokesman, and in "The Circus Animals' Desertion" Yeats described his former themes as so many circus animals put on display. No matter how much these themes embodied "pure mind," they were based in "a mound of refuse or the sweepings of a street . . . the foul rag-and-bone shop of the heart"— the rose springing from the dunghill. Yeats's poetry, which draws its initial power from the mastery of images and verbal rhythm, continues to resonate in the reader's mind for this attempt to come to terms with reality, to grasp and make sense of human experience in the transfiguring language of art.

PRONOUNCING GLOSSARY

The following list uses common English syllables and stress accents to provide rough equivalents of selected words whose pronunciation may be unfamiliar to the general reader.

Callimachus: *ca-li'-mah-cus*   gyre: *jai-er*

Cuchulain: *coo-hu'-lin*   Quattrocento: *kwah-troh-chen'-toh*

When You Are Old[1]

When you are old and gray and full of sleep,
And nodding by the fire, take down this book,
And slowly read, and dream of the soft look
Your eyes had once, and of their shadows deep;

How many loved your moments of glad grace,   5
And loved your beauty with love false or true,
But one man loved the pilgrim soul in you,
And loved the sorrows of your changing face;

And bending down beside the glowing bars,
Murmur, a little sadly, how Love fled   10
And paced upon the mountains overhead
And hid his face amid a crowd of stars.

Easter 1916[1]

I have met them at close of day
Coming with vivid faces
From counter or desk among grey
Eighteenth-century houses.
I have passed with a nod of the head   5
Or polite meaningless words,
Or have lingered awhile and said
Polite meaningless words,
And thought before I had done
Of a mocking tale or a gibe   10
To please a companion
Around the fire at the club,
Being certain that they and I
But lived where motley is worn:

1. An adaptation of a love sonnet by the French Renaissance poet Pierre de Ronsard (1524–1585), which begins similarly (*"Quand vous serez bien vieille"*) but ends by asking the beloved to "pluck the roses of life today."   1. On Easter Sunday 1916, Irish nationalists began an unsuccessful rebellion against British rule, which lasted throughout the week and ended in the surrender and execution of its leaders.

All changed, changed utterly: 15
A terrible beauty is born.

That woman's[2] days were spent
In ignorant good-will,
Her nights in argument
Until her voice grew shrill.   20
What voice more sweet than hers
When, young and beautiful,
She rode to harriers?
This man had kept a school
And rode our wingèd horse;   25
This other his helper and friend[3]
Was coming into his force;
He might have won fame in the end,
So sensitive his nature seemed,
So daring and sweet his thought.   30
This other man[4] I had dreamed
A drunken, vainglorious lout.
He had done most bitter wrong
To some who are near my heart,
Yet I number him in the song;   35
He, too, has resigned his part
In the casual comedy;
He, too, has been changed in his turn,
Transformed utterly:
A terrible beauty is born.   40

Hearts with one purpose alone
Through summer and winter seem
Enchanted to a stone
To trouble the living stream.
The horse that comes from the road,   45
The rider, the birds that range
From cloud to tumbling cloud,
Minute by minute they change;
A shadow of cloud on the stream
Changes minute by minute;   50
A horse-hoof slides on the brim,
And a horse plashes within it;
The long-legged moor-hens dive,
And hens to moor-cocks call;
Minute by minute they live: 55
The stone's in the midst of all.

Too long a sacrifice
Can make a stone of the heart.

2. Constance Gore-Booth (1868–1927), later Countess Markiewicz, an ardent nationalist.   3. Patrick
Pearse (1879–1916) and his friend Thomas MacDonagh (1878–1916), both schoolmasters and leaders of
the rebellion and both executed by the British. As a Gaelic poet, Pearse symbolically rode the winged horse
of the Muses, Pegasus.   4. Major John MacBride (1865–1916), who had married and separated from
Maud Gonne (1866–1953), Yeats's great love.

O when may it suffice?
That is Heaven's part, our part   60
To murmur name upon name,
As a mother names her child
When sleep at last has come
On limbs that had run wild.
What is it but nightfall?   65
No, no, not night but death;
Was it needless death after all?
For England may keep faith
For all that is done and said.
We know their dream; enough   70
To know they dreamed and are dead;
And what if excess of love
Bewildered them till they died?
I write it out in a verse—
MacDonagh and MacBride   75
And Connolly[5] and Pearse
Now and in time to be,
Wherever green is worn,
Are changed, changed utterly:
A terrible beauty is born.   80

The Second Coming[1]

Turning and turning in the widening gyre[2]
The falcon cannot hear the falconer;
Things fall apart; the centre cannot hold;
Mere anarchy is loosed upon the world,
The blood-dimmed tide is loosed, and everywhere   5
The ceremony of innocence is drowned;
The best lack all conviction, while the worst
Are full of passionate intensity.

Surely some revelation is at hand;
Surely the Second Coming is at hand.   10
The Second Coming! Hardly are those words out
When a vast image out of *Spiritus Mundi*[3]
Troubles my sight: somewhere in sands of the desert
A shape with lion body and the head of a man
A gaze blank and pitiless as the sun,   15
Is moving its slow thighs, while all about it
Reel shadows of the indignant desert birds.
The darkness drops again; but now I know

5. James Connolly (1870–1916), labor leader and nationalist executed by the British.   1. The Second Coming of Christ, believed by Christians to herald the end of the world, is transformed here into the prediction of a new birth initiating a new era and terminating the two-thousand-year cycle of Christianity. 2. The cone pattern of the falcon's flight and of historical cycles, in Yeats's vision.   3. World-soul (Latin) or, as *Anima Mundi* in Yeats's "Per Amica Silentia Lunae," a "great memory" containing archetypal images; recalls C. G. Jung's collective unconscious.

That twenty centuries of stony sleep
Were vexed to nightmare by a rocking cradle,   20
And what rough beast, its hour come round at last,
Slouches towards Bethlehem to be born?

Leda and the Swan[1]

A sudden blow: the great wings beating still
Above the staggering girl, her thighs caressed
By the dark webs, her nape caught in his bill,
He holds her helpless breast upon his breast.
How can those terrified vague fingers push   5
The feathered glory from her loosening thighs?
And how can body, laid in that white rush,
But feel the strange heart beating where it lies?

A shudder in the loins engenders there
The broken wall, the burning roof and tower   10
And Agamemnon dead.[2]
                          Being so caught up,
So mastered by the brute blood of the air,
Did she put on his knowledge with his power
Before the indifferent beak could let her drop?

Sailing to Byzantium[1]

I

That is no country for old men. The young
In one another's arms, birds in the trees
—Those dying generations—at their song,
The salmon-falls, the mackerel-crowded seas,
Fish, flesh, or fowl, commend all summer long   5
Whatever is begotten, born, and dies.
Caught in the sensual music all neglect
Monuments of unageing intellect.

2

An aged man is but a paltry thing,
A tattered coat upon a stick, unless   10
Soul clap its hands and sing, and louder sing
For every tatter in its mortal dress,
Nor is there singing school but studying

1. Zeus, ruler of the Greek gods, took the form of a swan to rape the mortal Leda; she gave birth to Helen of Troy, whose beauty caused the Trojan War.   2. The ruins of Troy and the death of Agamemnon, the Greek leader, whose sacrifice of his daughter Iphigenia to win the gods' favor caused his wife, Clytemnestra (also a daughter of Leda), to assassinate him on his return.   1. The ancient name for modern Istanbul, the capital of the Eastern Roman empire, which represented for Yeats (who had seen Byzantine mosaics in Italy) a highly stylized and perfectly integrated artistic world where "religious, aesthetic, and practical life were one."

Monuments of its own magnificence;
And therefore I have sailed the seas and come   15
To the holy city of Byzantium.

3

O sages standing in God's holy fire
As in the gold mosaic of a wall,
Come from the holy fire, perne in a gyre,[2]
And be the singing-masters of my soul.   20
Consume my heart away; sick with desire
And fastened to a dying animal
It knows not what it is; and gather me
Into the artifice of eternity.

4

Once out of nature I shall never take   25
My bodily form from any natural thing,
But such a form as Grecian goldsmiths make
Of hammered gold and gold enamelling
To keep a drowsy Emperor awake;
Or set upon a golden bough to sing   30
To lords and ladies of Byzantium
Of what is past, or passing, or to come.

Among School Children

I

I walk through the long schoolroom questioning;
A kind old nun in a white hood replies;
The children learn to cipher and to sing,
To study reading-books and history,
To cut and sew, be neat in everything   5
In the best modern way—the children's eyes
In momentary wonder stare upon
A sixty-year-old smiling public man.[1]

2

I dream of a Ledaean[2] body, bent
Above a sinking fire, a tale that she   10
Told of a harsh reproof, or trivial event
That changed some childish day to tragedy—
Told, and it seemed that our two natures blent
Into a sphere from youthful sympathy,

---

2. That is, come spinning down in a spiral. "Perne": a spool or bobbin. "Gyre": the cone pattern of the falcon's flight and of historical cycles, in Yeats's vision.   1. Yeats was elected senator of the Irish Free State in 1922.   2. Beautiful as Leda or as her daughter Helen of Troy.

Or else, to alter Plato's parable,   15
Into the yolk and white of the one shell.[3]

3

And thinking of that fit of grief or rage
I look upon one child or t'other there
And wonder if she stood so at that age—
For even daughters of the swan can share   20
Something of every paddler's heritage—
And had that color upon cheek or hair,
And thereupon my heart is driven wild:
She stands before me as a living child.

4

Her present image floats into the mind—   25
Did Quattrocento finger fashion it
Hollow of cheek[4] as though it drank the wind
And took a mess of shadows for its meat?
And I though never of Ledaean kind
Had pretty plumage once—enough of that,   30
Better to smile on all that smile, and show
There is a comfortable kind of old scarecrow.

5

What youthful mother, a shape upon her lap
Honey of generation had betrayed,
And that must sleep, shriek, struggle to escape   35
As recollection or the drug decide,[5]
Would think her son, did she but see that shape
With sixty or more winters on its head,
A compensation for the pang of his birth,
Or the uncertainty of his setting forth?   40

6

Plato thought nature but a spume that plays
Upon a ghostly paradigm of things;
Solider Aristotle played the taws
Upon the bottom of a king of kings;
World-famous golden-thighed Pythagoras[6]   45
Fingered upon a fiddle-stick or strings
What a star sang and careless Muses heard:
Old clothes upon old sticks to scare a bird.

---

3. In Plato's *Symposium*, Socrates explains love by telling how the gods split human beings into two halves—like halves of an egg—so that each half seeks its opposite throughout life. Yeats compares the two parts to the yolk and white of an egg.   4. Italian painters of the 15th century (the "Quattrocento"), such as Botticelli (1444–1510), were known for their delicate figures.   5. Yeats's note to this poem recalls the Greek scholar Porphyry (ca. 234–ca. 305), who associates "honey" with "the pleasure arising from copulation" that engenders children; the poet further describes honey as a drug that destroys the child's "'recollection' of pre-natal freedom."   6. Three Greek philosophers. Plato (427–337 B.C.E.) believed that nature was only a series of illusionistic reflections or appearances cast by abstract "forms" that were the only true realities. Aristotle (384–322 B.C.E.), more pragmatic, was Alexander the Great's tutor and spanked him with the "taws" (leather straps). Pythagoras (582–407 B.C.E.), a demigod to his disciples and thought to have a golden thigh bone, pondered the relationship of music, mathematics, and the stars.

7

Both nuns and mothers worship images,
But those the candles light are not as those   50
That animate a mother's reveries,
But keep a marble or a bronze repose.
And yet they too break hearts—O Presences
That passion, piety, or affection knows,
And that all heavenly glory symbolize—   55
O self-born mockers of man's enterprise;

8

Labor is blossoming or dancing where
The body is not bruised to pleasure soul,
Nor beauty born out of its own despair,
Nor blear-eyed wisdom out of midnight oil.   60
O chestnut tree, great-rooted blossomer,
Are you the leaf, the blossom, or the bole?
O body swayed to music, O brightening glance,
How can we know the dancer from the dance?

Byzantium[1]

The unpurged images of day recede;
The Emperor's drunken soldiery are abed;
Night resonance recedes, night-walkers' song
After great cathedral gong;
A starlit or a moonlit dome[2] disdains   5
All that man is,
All mere complexities,
The fury and the mire of human veins.

Before me floats an image, man or shade,
Shade more than man, more image than a shade;   10
For Hades' bobbin bound in mummy-cloth
May unwind the winding path;[3]
A mouth that has no moisture and no breath
Breathless mouths may summon;
I hail the superhuman;   15
I call it death-in-life and life-in-death.

Miracle, bird or golden handiwork,
More miracle than bird or handiwork,
Planted on the starlit golden bough,
Can like the cocks of Hades crow,[4]   20

1. The holy city of "Sailing to Byzantium" (p. 1139), seen here as it resists and transforms the blood and mire of human life into its own transcendent world of art.   2. According to Yeat's system in "A Vision" (1925), the first "starlit" phase in which the moon does not shine and the fifteenth, opposing phase of the full moon represent complete objectivity (potential being) and complete subjectivity (the achievement of complete beauty). In between these absolute phases lie the evolving "mere complexities" of human life.
3. Unwinding the spool of fate that leads from mortal death to the superhuman. Hades is the realm of the dead in Greek mythology.   4. To mark the transition from death to the dawn of new life.

Or, by the moon embittered, scorn aloud
In glory of changeless metal
Common bird or petal
And all complexities of mire or blood.

At midnight on the Emperor's pavement flit   25
Flames that no faggot feeds, nor steel has lit,
Nor storm disturbs, flames begotten of flame,
Where blood-begotten spirits come
And all complexities of fury leave,
Dying into a dance,   30
An agony of trance,
An agony of flame that cannot singe a sleeve.
Astraddle on the dolphin's[5] mire and blood,
Spirit after spirit! The smithies break the flood,
The golden smithies of the Emperor!   35
Marbles of the dancing floor
Break bitter furies of complexity,
Those images that yet
Fresh images beget,
That dolphin-torn, that gong-tormented sea.   40

Lapis Lazuli[1]

For Harry Clifton

I have heard that hysterical women say
They are sick of the palette and fiddle-bow,
Of poets that are always gay,
For everybody knows or else should know
That if nothing drastic is done   5
Aeroplane and Zeppelin will come out,
Pitch like King Billy bomb-balls in[2]
Until the town lie beaten flat.

All perform their tragic play,
There struts Hamlet, there is Lear,   10
That's Ophelia, that Cordelia;[3]
Yet they, should the last scene be there,
The great stage curtain about to drop,
If worthy their prominent part in the play,

5. A dolphin rescued the famous singer Arion by carrying him on his back over the sea. Dolphins were associated with Apollo, Greek god of music and prophecy, and in ancient art they are often shown escorting the souls of the dead to the Isles of the Blessed. Here, the dolphin is also flesh and blood, a part of life. 1. A deep blue semiprecious stone. One of Yeats's letters (to Dorothy Wellesley, July 6, 1935) describes a Chinese carving in lapis lazuli that depicts an ascetic and pupil about to climb a mountain:"Ascetic, pupil, hard stone, eternal theme of the sensual east . . . the east has its solutions always and therefore knows nothing of tragedy." 2. A linkage of past and present. According to an Irish ballad, King William III of England "threw his bomb-balls in" and set fire to the tents of the deposed James II at the Battle of the Boyne in 1690. Also a reference to Kaiser Wilhelm II (King William II) of Germany, who sent zeppelins to bomb London during World War I. "Zeppelin": a long, cylindrical airship, supported by internal gas chambers. 3. Tragic figures in Shakespeare's plays.

Do not break up their lines to weep. 15
They know that Hamlet and Lear are gay;
Gaiety transfiguring all that dread.
All men have aimed at, found and lost;
Black out; Heaven blazing into the head:[4]
Tragedy wrought to its uttermost. 20
Though Hamlet rambles and Lear rages,
And all the drop-scenes drop at once
Upon a hundred thousand stages,
It cannot grow by an inch or an ounce.

On their own feet they came, or on shipboard, 25
Camel-back, horse-back, ass-back, mule-back,
Old civilisations put to the sword.
Then they and their wisdom went to rack:

No handiwork of Callimachus[5]
Who handled marble as if it were bronze, 30
Made draperies that seemed to rise
When sea-wind swept the corner, stands;
His long lamp-chimney shaped like the stem
Of a slender palm, stood but a day;
All things fall and are built again, 35
And those that build them again are gay.

Two Chinamen, behind them a third,
Are carved in Lapis Lazuli,
Over them flies a long-legged bird,[6]
A symbol of longevity; 40
The third, doubtless a serving-man,
Carries a musical instrument.

Every discoloration of the stone,
Every accidental crack or dent,
Seems a water-course or an avalanche, 45
Or lofty slope where it still snows
Though doubtless plum or cherry-branch
Sweetens the little half-way house
Those Chinamen climb towards, and I
Delight to imagine them seated there; 50
There, on the mountain and the sky,
On all the tragic scene they stare.
One asks for mournful melodies;
Accomplished fingers begin to play.
Their eyes mid many wrinkles, their eyes, 55
Their ancient, glittering eyes, are gay.

---

4. The loss of rational consciousness making way for the blaze of inner revelation or "mad" tragic vision. Also suggests the final curtain and an air raid curfew.   5. Athenian sculptor (5th century B.C.E.), famous for a gold lamp in the Erechtheum (temple on the Acropolis) and for using drill lines in marble to give the effect of flowing drapery.   6. A crane.

The Circus Animals' Desertion

1

I sought a theme and sought for it in vain,
I sought it daily for six weeks or so.
Maybe at last, being but a broken man,
I must be satisfied with my heart, although
Winter and summer till old age began 5
My circus animals were all on show,
Those stilted boys, that burnished chariot,
Lion and woman[1] and the Lord knows what.

2

What can I but enumerate old themes?
First that sea-rider Oisin led by the nose 10
Through three enchanted islands, allegorical dreams,[2]
Vain gaiety, vain battle, vain repose,
Themes of the embittered heart, or so it seems,
That might adorn old songs or courtly shows;
But what cared I that set him on to ride, 15
I, starved for the bosom of his faery bride?

And then a counter-truth filled out its play,
The Countess Cathleen[3] was the name I gave it;
She, pity-crazed, had given her soul away,
But masterful Heaven had intervened to save it. 20
I thought my dear must her own soul destroy,
So did fanaticism and hate enslave it,
And this brought forth a dream and soon enough
This dream itself had all my thought and love.

And when the Fool and Blind Man stole the bread 25
Cuchulain[4] fought the ungovernable sea;
Heart-mysteries there, and yet when all is said
It was the dream itself enchanted me:
Character isolated by a deed
To engross the present and dominate memory. 30
Players and painted stage took all my love,
And not those things that they were emblems of.

3

Those masterful images because complete
Grew in pure mind, but out of what began?

1. Yeats enumerates images and themes from his earlier work; here, the sphinx of "The Double Vision of Michael Robartes." 2. In "The Wanderings of Oisin" (1889), an early poem in which Yeats describes a legendary Irish hero who wandered in fairyland for 150 years. 3. A play (1892), dedicated to Maud Gonne, in which the countess is saved by heaven after having sold her soul to the Devil in exchange for food for the poor. The figure of Cathleen comes up frequently in Yeats's work and is often taken as a personification of nationalist Ireland. 4. A legendary Irish hero. Yeats is referring to the play *On Baile's Strand* (1904).

A mound of refuse or the sweepings of a street,   35
Old kettles, old bottles, and a broken can,
Old iron, old bones, old rags, that raving slut
Who keeps the till. Now that my ladder's gone,
I must lie down where all the ladders start,
In the foul rag-and-bone shop of the heart.   40

LUIGI PIRANDELLO
1867–1936

"Who am I?" and "What is real?" are the persistent and even agonized questions that underlie Luigi Pirandello's novels, short stories, and plays. The term *Pirandellismo* or "Pirandellism"—coined from the author's name—suggests that there are as many truths as there are points of view. Here are already the basic issues of later existential philosophy as seen in writers like Jean-Paul Sartre and Albert Camus: the difficulty of achieving a sense of identity, the impossibility of authentic communication between people, and the overlapping frontiers of appearance and reality. These dilemmas are dramatic crises in self-knowledge and as such are particularly suited for demonstration in the theater. Indeed, Pirandello is best known as an innovative dramatist who revolutionized European stage techniques to break down comfortable illusions of compartmentalized, stable reality. Instead of the late nineteenth century's "well-made play"—with its neatly constructed plot that packaged real life into a conventional beginning, middle, and end, and its consistent characters remaining safely inaccessible on the other side of the footlights—he offers unpredictable plots and characters whose ambiguity puts into question the solidity of identities assumed in everyday life. It is not easy to know the truth, he suggests, or to make oneself known behind the face or "naked mask" that each of us wears in society. Pirandello's theater readily displays its nature as dramatic illusion: plays exist within plays until one is not sure where the "real" play begins or ends, and characters question their own reality and that of the audience. In their manipulation of ambiguous appearances and tragicomic effects, these plays foreshadow the absurdist theater of Samuel Beckett, Eugène Ionesco, and Harold Pinter, the cosmic irony of Antonin Artaud's "theater of cruelty," and the emphasis on spectacle and illusion in works by Jean Genet. Above all, they insist that the most "real" life is that which changes from moment to moment, exhibiting a fluidity that renders difficult and perhaps impossible any single formulation of either character or situation. This fluidity is a cause of existential anguish because it implies perpetual loss.

Pirandello was born in Girgenti (now Agrigento), Sicily, on June 28, 1867. His father was a sulfur merchant who intended his son to go into business like himself, but Pirandello preferred language and literature. After studying in Palermo and the University of Rome, he traveled to the University of Bonn in 1888, and in 1891 he received a doctorate in romance philology with a thesis on the dialect of his hometown. In 1894, Pirandello made an arranged marriage with the daughter of a rich sulfur merchant. They lived for ten years in Rome, where he wrote poetry and short stories, until the collapse of the sulfur mines destroyed the fortunes of both families, and he was suddenly forced to earn a living. To add to his misfortunes, his wife became insane with a jealous paranoia that lasted until her death in 1918. The author himself died on December 1, 1936.

Pirandello's early work shows a number of different influences. His poetry was indebted to nineteenth-century Italian predecessors like Giosuè Carducci (1835–1907), and in 1896 he translated Goethe's *Roman Elegies*. Soon, however, he turned to short stories or *novelle* under the influence of a narrative style called *verismo* (realism) exemplified in the work of the Sicilian writer Giovanni Verga (1840–1922). Pirandello wrote hundreds of stories of all lengths and—in his clarity, realism, and psychological acuteness (often including a taste for the grotesque)—is recognized as an Italian master of the story much as was Guy de Maupassant in France. Collections include the 1894 *Love without Love* and an anthology in 1922 titled *A Year's Worth of Stories*.

In such stories, and in his early novels, Pirandello begins to develop his characteristic themes: the questioning of appearance and reality, and problems of identity. In *The Outcast* (1901), an irate husband drives his innocent wife out of the house only to take her back when—without his knowing it—the supposed adultery has actually occurred. The hero of Pirandello's best-known novel, *The Late Mattia Pascal*, tries to create a fresh identity for himself and leave behind the old Mattia Pascal. When things become too difficult he returns to his "late" self and begins to write his life story, an early example of the tendency in Pirandello's works to comment on their own composition. The protagonists in these and other works are visibly commonplace, middle-class citizens, neither heroic nor villainous, but prototypes of the twentieth-century antihero who remains aggressively average while taking the center of the stage.

The questions of identity that obsessed Pirandello (he speaks of them as reflecting the "pangs of my spirit") are explored on social, psychological, and metaphysical levels. He was acquainted with the experimental psychology of his day, and learned from works such as Alfred Binet's *Personality Alterations* (1892) about the existence of a subconscious personality beneath our everyday awareness (a theme Pirandello shares with Proust and Freud). Successive layers of personality, conflicts among the various parts, and the simultaneous existence of multiple perspectives shape an identity that is never fixed but always fluid and changing. This identity escapes the grasp of onlookers and subject alike, and expresses a basic incongruity in human existence that challenges the most earnest attempts to create a unified self. The protagonist of a later novel, *One, None, and a Hundred Thousand* (1925–26), finds that what "he" is depends on the viewpoint of a great number of people. Such incongruity can be tragic or comic—or both at once—according to one's attitude, a topic that Pirandello explored in a 1908 essay, "On Humor," and that is echoed in the double-edged humor of his plays. The "Pirandellian" themes of ambiguous identity, lack of communication, and deceptive appearance reappear in all the genres, however, reaching a particular intensity in his first dramatic success, *It Is So [If You Think So]* (1917), and in the play included here, *Six Characters in Search of an Author*.

Six Characters in Search of an Author and *Henry IV* established Pirandello's stature as a major dramatist. He directed his own company (the Teatro d'Arte di Roma) from 1924 to 1928 and received the Nobel Prize for literature in 1934. His later plays, featuring fantastic and grotesque elements, did not achieve the wide popularity of their predecessors. In 1936, he published a collection of forty-three plays as *Naked Masks*, a title conceived in 1918 after Luigi Chiarelli's "grotesque theater." Pirandello's characters are "naked" and vulnerable inside the social roles or masks they put on to survive: Henry IV, trapped for life inside a pretense of insanity, or the Father in *Six Characters*, forced to play out a demeaning role in which, he insists, only part of his true nature is revealed. The term *naked mask* also suggests Pirandello's superb manipulation of theatrical ambiguity—the confusion between the actor and the character portrayed—that ultimately prolongs the confusion of appearance and reality, which is one of his chief themes. Pirandello was famous in twentieth-century theater for his use of the play within a play, a technique of embedded dramatic episodes that maintain a life of their own while serving as foil to the overall or governing plot. Dividing lines are sometimes hard to draw when stage dialogue can be taken as referring to either context—a situation that allows for double meanings at the same time that it reiterates the impossibility of real communication. *Six Characters in Search of an Author* combines all these elements in an extraordinarily self-reflexive style. At the very beginning, the Stage Hand's interrupted hammering suggests that the audience has chanced on a rehearsal—of still another play by Pirandello—instead of coming to a finished performance; concurrently, Pirandello's stage dialogue pokes fun at his own reputation for obscurity. Just as the Actors are apparently set to rehearse *The Rules of the Game,* six unexpected persons come down the aisle seeking the Producer: they are Characters out of an unwritten novel who demand to be given dramatic existence. The play *Six Characters* is continually in the process of being composed: composed as the interwoven double plot we see on stage, written down in shorthand by the Prompter for the Actors to reproduce, and potentially composed as the Characters' inner drama finally achieves its rightful existence as a work of art. The conflicts between the different levels of the play finally prevent the completion of any but the first work, but it has created a convincing dramatic illusion in the meantime that incorporates the psychological drama of the "six characters" as well as a discussion of the relationship of life and art.

The initial absurdity of the play appears when the six admittedly fictional characters arrive with their claim to be "truer and more real" than the "real" characters they confront. (Of course, to the audience all the actors on stage are equally unreal.) Their greater "truth" is the truth of art with its profound but formally fixed glimpses into human nature. Each Character represents, specifically and in depth, a particular identity created by the author, who later suggested that the Characters should wear masks to distinguish them from the Actors. These masks are not the conventional masks of ancient Greek drama or the Japanese *nō* theater, nor do they function as the ceremonial masks representing spirits in African ritual, masks that temporarily invest the wearer with the spirit's identity and authority. Instead, they are a theatrical device, a symbol and visual reminder of each character's unchanging essence. The Six Characters are incapable of developing outside their roles and are condemned, in their search for existence, painfully to reenact their essential selves.

Conversely, the fictional characters have a more stable personality than "real" people who are still "nobody," incomplete, open to change and misinterpretation. Characters are "somebody" because their nature has been decided once and for all. Yet there is a further complication to this contrast between real and fictional characters: the Characters have real anxieties in that they want to play their own roles and are disturbed at the prospect of having Actors represent them incorrectly. All human beings, suggests Pirandello, whether fictional or real, are subject to misunderstanding. We even misunderstand ourselves when we think we are the same person in all situations. "We always have the illusion of being the same person for everybody," says the Father, "but it's not true!" When he explains himself as a very human philosopher driven by the Demon of Experiment, his self-image is quite different from the picture held by his vengeful Stepdaughter or the passive Mother who blames him for her expulsion from the house. The Stepdaughter, in turn, appears to love an innocent little sister because she reminds her of an earlier self. It is an entanglement of motives and deceit of mutual understanding that goes beyond the tabloid level of a sordid family scandal and claims a broader scope. Pirandello, in fact, does not intend merely to describe a particular setting or situation; that is the concern of what he calls "historical writers." He belongs to the opposite category of "philosophical writers" whose characters and situations embody "a particular sense of life and acquire from it a universal value."

Six Characters in Search of an Author underwent an interesting evolution to become the play that we see today. First performed in Rome in 1921, where its unsettling plot and characters already scandalized a traditionalist audience, it was reshaped in more radical theatrical form after the remarkable performance produced by Georges Pitoëff in Paris in 1923. Pirandello, who came to Paris somewhat wary of Pitoëff's innovations (he brought on the Characters in a green-lit stage elevator), was soon convinced that the Russian director's stagecraft suggested changes that would enhance the original text. Pitoëff had used his knowledge of technical effects to accentuate the interrelationships of appearance and reality: he extended the stage with several steps leading down into the auditorium (a break in the conventional stage's "fourth wall" that Pirandello was quick to exploit); he underscored the play within a play with rehearsal effects, showing the Stage Hand hammering and the Director arranging suitable props and lighting; he emphasized the division between Characters and Actors by separating groups on stage and dressing the Characters (all except the Little Girl) in black. Pirandello welcomed and expanded on many of these changes. To distinguish even further the Characters from the Actors, he proposed stylized masks as well as black clothes for the former and light-colored summery clothing for the latter. To bring out Madame Pace's grotesque fictionality, he changed her costume from a sober black gown to a garish red silk dress and carrot-colored wool wig. Most striking, however, is the dramatist's development of Pitoëff's steps into a real bridge between the world of the stage and the auditorium, a strategy that allows his Actors (and Characters) to come and go in the "real world" of the audience. Pirandello's revised ending to *Six Characters in Search of an Author* makes a final break with theatrical illusion: with the other characters immobilized on stage, the Stepdaughter races down the steps, through the auditorium, and out into the foyer from which the audience can still hear her distraught laughter.

Pirandello does not hold his audience by uttering grand philosophical truths. There is constant suspense and a process of discovery in *Six Characters,* from the moment that the rehearsal with its complaining Actors and Manager is interrupted and the initial hints of melodrama and family scandal catch our attention in the Stepdaughter's and Mother's complaints. It is a story that could be found in the most sensational papers: an adulterous wife thrust out of her home and supporting herself and her children after her lover's death by sewing, the daughter's turn to prostitution to support the family, the Father's unknowing attempt to seduce his Stepdaughter (interpreted by the latter as the continuation of an old and perverse impulse), and the final drowning and suicide of the two youngest children. Pirandello plays with the sensational aspect of his story by focusing the play on the characters' repeated attempts to portray the seduction scene; Actors and Manager perceive the salable quality of such "human-interest" events and are eager to let the story unfold. The Stepdaughter's protective fondness for her doomed baby sister and her enigmatic reproach to the little Boy ("instead of killing myself, I'd have killed one of those two") hint at the inner plot that is revealed only as the action continues. The interplay of illusion and reality persists to the very end, when the Actors argue about whether the Boy is dead or not, the Producer is terrified as the lights change eerily around the surviving Characters, and the Stepdaughter breaks away from the ending tableau to escape into the audience.

The translation by John Linstrum has been selected on the one hand for its accuracy to the Italian text and its fluent use of contemporary English idiom and on the other for its quality as a performance-oriented script, staged in London in 1979. Readers are encouraged to test the continued liveliness of Pirandello's dialogue by rehearsing their own selection of scenes—or perhaps by relocating them in a contemporary setting. According to director Robert Brustein, whose 1988 production of *Six Characters in Search of an Author* set the action in New York and replaced Madame Pace with a pimp, "Pirandello both encourages and stimulates a pluralism in theater because there can be dozens, hundreds, thousands of productions of *Six Characters,* and every one of them is going to be different."

PRONOUNCING GLOSSARY

The following list uses common English syllables and stress accents to provide rough equivalents of selected words whose pronunciation may be unfamiliar to the general reader.

commedia dell'arte: *com-may'-dee-ah del ar'-tay*

Luigi Pirandello: *loo-ee'-jee pee-ran-del'-oh*

Pace: *pah'-chay*

Pitoëff: *pee'-toh-eff*

Six Characters in Search of an Author[1]

A Comedy in the Making

THE CHARACTERS	THE COMPANY
FATHER	THE PRODUCER
MOTHER	THE STAGE STAFF
STEPDAUGHTER	THE ACTORS
SON	
LITTLE BOY	
LITTLE GIRL	
MADAME PACE	

Act 1

When the audience enters, the curtain is already up and the stage is just as it would be during the day. There is no set; it is empty, in almost total darkness. This is so that from the beginning the audience will have the feeling of being present, not at a performance of a properly rehearsed play, but at a performance of a play that happens spontaneously. Two small sets of steps, one on the right and one on the left, lead up to the stage from the auditorium. On the stage, the top is off the PROMPTER'S *box and is lying next to it. Downstage, there is a small table and a chair with arms for the* PRODUCER: *it is turned with its back to the audience.*

Also downstage there are two small tables, one a little bigger than the other, and several chairs, ready for the rehearsal if needed. There are more chairs scattered on both left and right for the ACTORS *to one side at the back and nearly hidden is a piano.*

When the houselights go down the STAGE HAND *comes on through the back door. He is in blue overalls and carries a tool bag. He brings some pieces of wood on, comes to the front, kneels down and starts to nail them together.*

The STAGE MANAGER *rushes on from the wings.*

STAGE MANAGER   Hey! What are you doing?

STAGE HAND   What do you think I'm doing? I'm banging nails in.

STAGE MANAGER   Now? [*He looks at his watch.*]   It's half-past ten already. The Producer will be here in a moment to rehearse.

STAGE HAND   I've got to do my work some time, you know.

STAGE MANAGER   Right—but not now.

---

1. Translated by John Linstrum. In the Italian editions, Pirandello notes that he did not divide the play into formal acts or scenes. The translator has marked the divisions for clarity, however, according to the stage directions.

STAGE HAND   When?

STAGE MANAGER   When the rehearsal's finished. Come on, get all this out
of the way and let me set for the second act of *The Rules of the Game*.[2]

[*The* STAGE HAND *picks up his tools and wood and goes off, grumbling
and muttering. The* ACTORS *of the company come in through the door,
men and women, first one then another, then two together and so on:
there will be nine or ten, enough for the parts for the rehearsal of a play
by Pirandello,* The Rules of the Game, *today's rehearsal. They come in,
say their "Good-mornings" to the* STAGE MANAGER *and each other. Some
go off to the dressing-rooms; others, among them the* PROMPTER *with the
text rolled up under his arm, scatter about the stage waiting for the* PRO-
DUCER *to start the rehearsal. Meanwhile, sitting or standing in groups,
they chat together; some smoke, one complains about his part, another
one loudly reads something from "The Stage." It would be as well if the*
ACTORS *and* ACTRESSES *were dressed in colourful clothes, and this first
scene should be improvised naturally and vivaciously. After a while
somebody might sit down at the piano and play a song; the younger*
ACTORS *and* ACTRESSES *start dancing.*]

STAGE MANAGER   [*Clapping his hands to call their attention.*]   Come on,
everybody! Quiet please. The Producer's here.

[*The piano and the dancing both stop. The* ACTORS *turn to look out into
the theatre and through the door at the back comes the* PRODUCER; *he
walks down the gangway between the seats and, calling "Good-morning"
to the* ACTORS, *climbs up one of the sets of stairs onto the stage. The* SEC-
RETARY *gives him the post, a few magazines, a script. The* ACTORS *move
to one side of the stage.*]

PRODUCER   Any letters?

SECRETARY   No. That's all the post there is. [*Giving him the script.*]

PRODUCER   Put it in the office. [*Then looking round and turning to the*
STAGE MANAGER.]   I can't see a thing here. Let's have some lights please.

STAGE MANAGER   Right. [*Calling.*]   Workers please!

[*In a few seconds the side of the stage where the* ACTORS *are standing is brilliantly lit with white light. The* PROMPTER *has gone into his box and spread
out his script.*]

PRODUCER   Good. [*Clapping hands.*]   Well then, let's get started. Anybody
missing?

STAGE MANAGER   [*Heavily ironic.*]   Our leading lady.

PRODUCER   Not again! [*Looking at his watch.*]   We're ten minutes late
already. Send her a note to come and see me. It might teach her to be on
time for rehearsals. [*Almost before he has finished, the* LEADING ACTRESS'S
voice is heard from the auditorium.]

LEADING ACTRESS   Morning everybody. Sorry I'm late. [*She is very expensively dressed and is carrying a lap-dog. She comes down the aisle and goes
up on to the stage.*]

---

2. *Il giuoco delle parti*, written in 1918. The hero, Leone Gala, pretends to ignore his wife Silia's infidelity
until the end, when he takes revenge by tricking her lover Guido Venanzi into taking his place in a fatal
duel she had engineered to get rid of her husband.

PRODUCER You're determined to keep us waiting, aren't you?

LEADING ACTRESS I'm sorry. I just couldn't find a taxi anywhere. But you haven't started yet and I'm not on at the opening anyhow. [*Calling the* STAGE MANAGER, *she gives him the dog.*] Put him in my dressing-room for me will you?

PRODUCER And she's even brought her lap-dog with her! As if we haven't enough lap-dogs here already. [*Clapping his hands and turning to the* PROMPTER.] Right then, the second act of *The Rules of the Game*. [*Sits in his arm-chair.*] Quiet please! Who's on?

[*The* ACTORS *clear from the front of the stage and sit to one side, except for three who are ready to start the scene—and the* LEADING ACTRESS. *She has ignored the* PRODUCER *and is sitting at one of the little tables.*]

PRODUCER Are you in this scene, then?

LEADING ACTRESS No—I've just told you.

PRODUCER [*Annoyed.*] Then get off, for God's sake. [*The* LEADING ACTRESS *goes and sits with the others. To the* PROMPTER.] Come on then, let's get going.

PROMPTER [*Reading his script.*] "The house of Leone Gala. A peculiar room, both dining-room and study."

PRODUCER [*To the* STAGE MANAGER.] We'll use the red set.

STAGE MANAGER [*Making a note.*] The red set—right.

PROMPTER [*Still reading.*] "The table is laid and there is a desk with books and papers. Bookcases full of books and china cabinets full of valuable china. An exit at the back leads to Leone's bedroom. An exit to the left leads to the kitchen. The main entrance is on the right."

PRODUCER Right. Listen carefully everybody: there, the main entrance, there, the kitchen. [*To the* LEADING ACTOR *who plays Socrates.*[3]] Your entrances and exits will be from there. [*To the* STAGE MANAGER.] We'll have the French windows there and put the curtains on them.

STAGE MANAGER [*Making a note.*] Right.

PROMPTER [*Reading.*] "Scene One. Leone Gala, Guido Venanzi, and Filippo, who is called Socrates." [*To* PRODUCER.] Have I to read the directions as well?

PRODUCER Yes, you have! I've told you a hundred times.

PROMPTER [*Reading.*] "When the curtain rises, Leone Gala, in a cook's hat and apron, is beating an egg in a dish with a little wooden spoon. Filippo is beating another and he is dressed as a cook too. Guido Venanzi is sitting listening."

LEADING ACTOR Look, do I really have to wear a cook's hat?

PRODUCER [*Annoyed by the question.*] I expect so! That's what it says in the script. [*Pointing to the script.*]

LEADING ACTOR If you ask me it's ridiculous.

PRODUCER [*Leaping to his feet furiously.*] Ridiculous? It's ridiculous, is it? What do you expect me to do if nobody writes good plays any more[4] and we're reduced to putting on plays by Pirandello? And if you can understand them you must be very clever. He writes them on purpose so nobody

---

3. Nickname given to Gala's servant, Philip, in *The Rules of the Game*, the play they are rehearsing. 4. The producer refers to the realistic, tightly constructed plays (often French) that were internationally popular in the late 19th century and a staple of Italian theaters at the beginning of the 20th century.

enjoys them, neither actors nor critics nor audience. [*The* ACTORS *laugh. Then crosses to* LEADING ACTOR *and shouts at him.*] A cook's hat and you beat eggs. But don't run away with the idea that that's all you are doing— beating eggs. You must be joking! You have to be symbolic of the shells of the eggs you are beating. [*The* ACTORS *laugh again and start making ironical comments to each other.*] Be quiet! Listen carefully while I explain. [*Turns back to* LEADING ACTOR.] Yes, the shells, because they are symbolic of the empty form of reason, without its content, blind instinct! You are reason and your wife is instinct: you are playing a game where you have been given parts and in which you are not just yourself but the puppet of yourself.[5] Do you see?

LEADING ACTOR [*Spreading his hands.*]   Me? No.

PRODUCER [*Going back to his chair.*]   Neither do I! Come on, let's get going; you wait till you see the end! You haven't seen anything yet! [*Confidentially.*] By the way, I should turn almost to face the audience if I were you, about three-quarters face. Well, what with the obscure dialogue and the audience not being able to hear you properly in any case, the whole lot'll go to hell. [*Clapping hands again.*] Come on. Let's get going!

PROMPTER   Excuse me, can I put the top back on the prompt-box? There's a bit of a draught.

PRODUCER   Yes, yes, of course. Get on with it.

[*The* STAGE DOORKEEPER, *in a braided cap, has come into the auditorium, and he comes all the way down the aisle to the stage to tell the* PRODUCER *the* SIX CHARACTERS *have come, who, having come in after him, look about them a little puzzled and dismayed. Every effort must be made to create the effect that the* SIX CHARACTERS *are very different from the* ACTORS *of the company. The placings of the two groups, indicated in the directions, once the* CHARACTERS *are on the stage, will help this: so will using different coloured lights. But the most effective idea is to use masks for the* CHARACTERS, *masks specially made of a material that will not go limp with perspiration and light enough not to worry the actors who wear them: they should be made so that the eyes, the nose and the mouth are all free. This is the way to bring out the deep significance of the play. The* CHARACTERS *should not appear as ghosts, but as created realities, timeless creations of the imagination, and so more real and consistent than the changeable realities of the* ACTORS. *The masks are designed to give the impression of figures constructed by art, each one fixed forever in its own fundamental emotion; that is, Remorse for the* FATHER, *Revenge for the* STEPDAUGHTER, *Scorn for the* SON, *Sorrow for the* MOTHER. *Her mask should have wax tears in the corners of the eyes and down the cheeks like the sculptured or painted weeping Madonna in a church. Her dress should be of a plain material, in stiff folds, looking almost as if it were carved and not of an ordinary material you can buy in a shop and have made up by a dressmaker.*

The FATHER *is about fifty: his reddish hair is thinning at the temples, but he is not bald: he has a full moustache that almost covers his*

5. Leone Gala is a rationalist and an aesthete—the opposite of his impulsive, passionate wife, Silia. By masking his feelings and constantly playing the role of gourmet cook, he chooses his own role and thus becomes his own "puppet."

young-looking mouth, which often opens in an uncertain and empty smile. He is pale, with a high forehead: he has blue oval eyes, clear and sharp: he is dressed in light trousers and a dark jacket: his voice is sometimes rich, at other times harsh and loud.

The MOTHER *appears crushed by an intolerable weight of shame and humiliation. She is wearing a thick black veil and is dressed simply in black; when she raises her veil she shows a face like wax, but not suffering, with her eyes turned down humbly.*

The STEPDAUGHTER, *who is eighteen years old, is defiant, even insolent. She is very beautiful, dressed in mourning as well, but with striking elegance. She is scornful of the timid, suffering, dejected air of her young brother, a grubby* LITTLE BOY *of fourteen, also dressed in black; she is full of a warm tenderness, on the other hand, for the* LITTLE SISTER (GIRL), *a girl of about four, dressed in white with a black silk sash round her waist.*

The SON *is twenty-two, tall, almost frozen in an air of scorn for the* FATHER *and indifference to the* MOTHER: *he is wearing a mauve overcoat and a long green scarf round his neck.*]

DOORMAN Excuse me, sir.

PRODUCER [*Angrily.*] What the hell is it now?

DOORMAN There are some people here—they say they want to see you, sir. [*The* PRODUCER *and the* ACTORS *are astonished and turn to look out into the auditorium.*]

PRODUCER But I'm rehearsing! You know perfectly well that no-one's allowed in during rehearsals. [*Turning to face out front.*] Who are you? What do you want?

FATHER [*Coming forward, followed by the others, to the foot of one of the sets of steps.*] We're looking for an author.

PRODUCER [*Angry and astonished.*] An author? Which author?

FATHER Any author will do, sir.

PRODUCER But there isn't an author here because we're not rehearsing a new play.

STEPDAUGHTER [*Excitedly as she rushes up the steps.*] That's better still, better still! We can be your new play.

ACTORS [*Lively comments and laughter from the* ACTORS.] Oh, listen to that, etc.

FATHER [*Going up on the stage after the* STEPDAUGHTER.] Maybe, but if there isn't an author here . . . [*To the* PRODUCER.] Unless you'd like to be . . .
[*Hand in hand, the* MOTHER *and the* LITTLE GIRL, *followed by the* LITTLE BOY, *go up on the stage and wait. The* SON *stays sullenly behind.*]

PRODUCER Is this some kind of joke?

FATHER Now, how can you think that? On the contrary, we are bringing you a story of anguish.

STEPDAUGHTER We might make your fortune for you!

PRODUCER Do me a favour, will you? Go away. We haven't time to waste on idiots.

FATHER [*Hurt but answering gently.*] You know very well, as a man of the theatre, that life is full of all sorts of odd things which have no need at all to pretend to be real because they are actually true.

PRODUCER What the devil are you talking about?

FATHER What I'm saying is that you really must be mad to do things the opposite way round: to create situations that obviously aren't true and try to make them seem to be really happening. But then I suppose that sort of madness is the only reason for your profession.

[*The* ACTORS *are indignant.*]

PRODUCER [*Getting up and glaring at him.*] Oh, yes? So ours is a profession of madmen, is it?

FATHER Well, if you try to make something look true when it obviously isn't, especially if you're not forced to do it, but do it for a game . . . Isn't it your job to give life on the stage to imaginary people?

PRODUCER [*Quickly answering him and speaking for the* ACTORS *who are growing more indignant.*] I should like you to know, sir, that the actor's profession is one of great distinction. Even if nowadays the new writers only give us dull plays to act and puppets to present instead of men, I'd have you know that it is our boast that we have given life, here on this stage, to immortal works.

[*The* ACTORS, *satisfied, agree with and applaud the* PRODUCER].

FATHER [*Cutting in and following hard on his argument.*] There! You see? Good! You've given life! You've created living beings with more genuine life than people have who breathe and wear clothes! Less real, perhaps, but nearer the truth. We are both saying the same thing.

[*The* ACTORS *look at each other, astonished.*]

PRODUCER But just a moment! You said before . . .

FATHER I'm sorry, but I said that before, about acting for fun, because you shouted at us and said you'd no time to waste on idiots, but you must know better than anyone that Nature uses human imagination to lift her work of creation to even higher levels.

PRODUCER All right then: but where does all this get us?

FATHER Nowhere. I want to try to show that one can be thrust into life in many ways, in many forms: as a tree or a stone, as water or a butterfly— or as a woman. It might even be as a character in a play.

PRODUCER [*Ironic, pretending to be annoyed.*] And you, and these other people here, were thrust into life, as you put it, as characters in a play?

FATHER Exactly! And alive, as you can see.

[*The* PRODUCER *and the* ACTORS *burst into laughter as if at a joke.*]

FATHER I'm sorry you laugh like that, because we carry in us, as I said before, a story of terrible anguish as you can guess from this woman dressed in black.

[*Saying this, he offers his hand to the* MOTHER *and helps her up the last steps and, holding her still by the hand, leads her with a sense of tragic solemnity across the stage which is suddenly lit by a fantastic light.*

The LITTLE GIRL *and the* (LITTLE) BOY *follow the* MOTHER: *then the* SON *comes up and stands to one side in the background: then the* STEPDAUGH-TER *follows and leans against the proscenium arch: the* ACTORS *are astonished at first, but then, full of admiration for the "entrance," they burst into applause—just as if it were a performance specially for them.*]

PRODUCER [*At first astonished and then indignant.*] My God! Be quiet all of you. [*Turns to the* CHARACTERS.] And you lot get out! Clear off! [*Turns to the* STAGE MANAGER.] Jesus! Get them out of here.

STAGE MANAGER [*Comes forward but stops short as if held back by something strange.*]   Go on out! Get out!

FATHER [*To* PRODUCER.]   Oh no, please, you see, we . . .

PRODUCER [*Shouting.*]   We came here to work, you know.

LEADING ACTOR   We really can't be messed about like this.

FATHER [*Resolutely, coming forward.*]   I'm astonished! Why don't you believe me? Perhaps you are not used to seeing the characters created by an author spring into life up here on the stage face to face with each other. Perhaps it's because we're not in a script? [*He points to the* PROMPTER's *box.*]

STEPDAUGHTER [*Coming down to the* PRODUCER, *smiling and persuasive.*] Believe me, sir, we really are six of the most fascinating characters. But we've been neglected.

FATHER   Yes, that's right, we've been neglected. In the sense that the author who created us, living in his mind, wouldn't or couldn't make us live in a written play for the world of art.[6] And that really is a crime sir, because whoever has the luck to be born a character can laugh even at death. Because a character will never die! A man will die, a writer, the instrument of creation: but what he has created will never die! And to be able to live for ever you don't need to have extraordinary gifts or be able to do miracles. Who was Sancho Panza? Who was Prospero?[7] But they will live for ever because—living seeds—they had the luck to find a fruitful soil, an imagination which knew how to grow them and feed them, so that they will live for ever.

PRODUCER   This is all very well! But what do you want here?

FATHER   We want to live, sir.

PRODUCER [*Ironically.*]   For ever!

FATHER   No, no: only for a few moments—in you.

AN ACTOR   Listen to that!

LEADING ACTRESS   They want to live in us!

YOUNG ACTOR [*Pointing to the* STEPDAUGHTER.]   I don't mind . . . so long as I get her.

FATHER   Listen, listen: the play is all ready to be put together and if you and your actors would like to, we can work it out now between us.

PRODUCER [*Annoyed.*]   But what exactly do you want to do? We don't make up plays like that here! We present comedies and tragedies here.

FATHER   That's right, we know that of course. That's why we've come.

PRODUCER   And where's the script?

FATHER   It's in us, sir. [*The* ACTORS *laugh.*]   The play is in us: we are the play and we are impatient to show it to you: the passion inside us is driving us on.

STEPDAUGHTER [*Scornfully, with the tantalising charm of deliberate impudence.*]   My passion, if only you knew! My passion for him! [*She points at the* FATHER *and suggests that she is going to embrace him: but stops and bursts into a screeching laugh.*]

---

6. In the 1925 preface to *Six Characters*, Pirandello explains that these characters came to him first as characters for a novel that he later abandoned. Haunted by their half-realized personalities, he decided to use the situation in a play.   7. The magician and exiled Duke of Milan in Shakespeare's *The Tempest.* Sancho Panza was Don Quixote's servant in Cervantes's novel *Don Quixote* (1605–15).

FATHER [*With sudden anger.*]   You keep out of this for the moment! And stop laughing like that!

STEPDAUGHTER   Really? Then with your permission, ladies and gentlemen; even though it's only two months since I became an orphan, just watch how I can sing and dance.

[*The* ACTORS, *especially the younger, seem strangely attracted to her while she sings and dances and they edge closer and reach out their hands to catch hold of her.*[8] *She eludes them, and when the* ACTORS *applaud her and the* PRODUCER *speaks sharply to her she stays still quite removed from them all.*]

FIRST ACTOR   Very good! etc.

PRODUCER [*Angrily.*]   Be quiet! Do you think this is a nightclub? [*Turns to* FATHER *and asks with some concern.*] Is she a bit mad?

FATHER   Mad? Oh no—it's worse than that.

STEPDAUGHTER [*Suddenly running to the* PRODUCER.]   Yes. It's worse, much worse! Listen please! Let's put this play on at once, because you'll see that at a particular point I—when this darling little girl here— [*Taking the* LITTLE GIRL *by the hand from next to the* MOTHER *and crossing with her to the* PRODUCER.] Isn't she pretty? [*Takes her in her arms.*] Darling! Darling! [*Puts her down again and adds, moved very deeply but almost without wanting to.*] Well, this lovely little girl here, when God suddenly takes her from this poor Mother: and this little idiot here [*Turning to the* LITTLE BOY *and seizing him roughly by the sleeve.*] does the most stupid thing, like the half-wit he is,—then you will see me run away! Yes, you'll see me rush away! But not yet, not yet! Because, after all the intimate things there have been between him and me [*In the direction of the* FATHER, *with a horrible vulgar wink.*] I can't stay with them any longer, to watch the insult to this mother through that supercilious cretin over there. [*Pointing to the* SON.] Look at him! Look at him! Condescending, stand-offish, because he's the legitimate son, him! Full of contempt for me, for the boy and for the little girl: because we are bastards. Do you understand? Bastards. [*Running to the* MOTHER *and embracing her.*] And this poor mother— she—who is the mother of all of us—he doesn't want to recognise her as his own mother—and he looks down on her, he does, as if she were only the mother of the three of us who are bastards—the traitor. [*She says all this quickly, with great excitement, and after having raised her voice on the word "bastards" she speaks quietly, half-spitting the word "traitor."*]

MOTHER [*With deep anguish to the* PRODUCER.]   Sir, in the name of these two little ones, I beg you . . . [*Feels herself grow faint and sways.*] Oh, my God.

FATHER [*Rushing to support her with almost all the* ACTORS *bewildered and concerned.*]   Get a chair someone . . . quick, get a chair for this poor widow.

[*One of the* ACTORS *offers a chair: the others press urgently around. The* MOTHER, *seated now, tries to stop the* FATHER *lifting her veil.*]

ACTORS   Is it real? Has she really fainted? etc.

FATHER   Look at her, everybody, look at her.

MOTHER   No, for God's sake, stop it.

8. Pirandello uses a contemporary popular song, "Chu-Chin-Chow" from the Ziegfeld Follies of 1917, for the Stepdaughter to display her talents.

FATHER   Let them look?

MOTHER [*Lifting her hands and covering her face, desperately.*]   Oh, please, I beg you, stop him from doing what he is trying to do; it's hateful.

PRODUCER [*Overwhelmed, astounded.*]   It's no use, I don't understand this any more. [*To the* FATHER.] Is this woman your wife?

FATHER [*At once.*]   That's right, she is my wife.

PRODUCER   How is she a widow, then, if you're still alive?

[*The* ACTORS *are bewildered too and find relief in a loud laugh.*]

FATHER [*Wounded, with rising resentment.*]   Don't laugh! Please don't laugh like that! That's just the point, that's her own drama. You see, she had another man. Another man who ought to be here.

MOTHER   No, no! [*Crying out.*]

STEPDAUGHTER   Luckily for him he died. Two months ago, as I told you: we are in mourning for him, as you can see.

FATHER   Yes, he's dead: but that's not the reason he isn't here. He isn't here because—well just look at her, please, and you'll understand at once—hers is not a passionate drama of the love of two men, because she was incapable of love, she could feel nothing—except, perhaps a little gratitude (but not to me, to him). She's not a woman; she's a mother. And her drama—and, believe me, it's a powerful one—her drama is focused completely on these four children of the two men she had.

MOTHER   I had them? How dare you say that I had them, as if I wanted them myself? It was him, sir! He forced the other man on me. He made me go away with him!

STEPDAUGHTER [*Leaping up, indignantly.*]   It isn't true!

MOTHER [*Bewildered.*]   How isn't it true?

STEPDAUGHTER   It isn't true, it just isn't true.

MOTHER   What do you know about it?

STEPDAUGHTER   It isn't true. [*To the* PRODUCER.] Don't believe it! Do you know why she said that? She said it because of him, over there. [*Pointing to the* SON.] She tortures herself, she exhausts herself with worry and all because of the indifference of that son of hers. She wants to make him believe that she abandoned him when he was two years old because the Father made her do it.

MOTHER [*Passionately.*]   He did! He made me! God's my witness. [*To the* PRODUCER.] Ask him if it isn't true. [*Pointing to the* FATHER.] Make him tell our son it's true. [*Turning to the* STEPDAUGHTER.] You don't know anything about it.

STEPDAUGHTER   I know that when my father was alive you were always happy and contented. You can't deny it.

MOTHER   No, I can't deny it.

STEPDAUGHTER   He was always full of love and care for you. [*Turning to the* LITTLE BOY *with anger.*] Isn't it true? Admit it. Why don't you say something, you little idiot?

MOTHER   Leave the poor boy alone! Why do you want to make me appear ungrateful? You're my daughter. I don't in the least want to offend your father's memory. I've already told him that it wasn't my fault or even to please myself that I left his house and my son.

FATHER   It's quite true. It was my fault.

LEADING ACTOR [*To other actors.*]   Look at this. What a show!

LEADING ACTRESS   And we're the audience.

YOUNG ACTOR   For a change.

PRODUCER [*Beginning to be very interested.*]   Let's listen to them! Quiet! Listen!

[*He goes down the steps into the auditorium and stands there as if to get an idea of what the scene will look like from the audience's viewpoint.*]

SON [*Without moving, coldly, quietly, ironically.*]   Yes, listen to his little scrap of philosophy. He's going to tell you all about the Daemon of Experiment.

FATHER   You're a cynical idiot, and I've told you so a hundred times. [*To the* PRODUCER *who is now in the stalls.*] He sneers at me because of this expression I've found to defend myself.

SON   Words, words.

FATHER   Yes words, words! When we're faced by something we don't understand, by a sense of evil that seems as if it's going to swallow us, don't we all find comfort in a word that tells us nothing but that calms us?

STEPDAUGHTER   And dulls your sense of remorse, too. That more than anything.

FATHER   Remorse? No, that's not true. It'd take more than words to dull the sense of remorse in me.

STEPDAUGHTER   It's taken a little money too, just a little money. The money that he was going to offer as payment, gentlemen.

[*The* ACTORS *are horrified.*]

SON [*Contemptuously to his stepsister.*]   That's a filthy trick.

STEPDAUGHTER   A filthy trick? There it was in a pale blue envelope on the little mahogany table in the room behind the shop at Madame Pace's. You know Madame Pace, don't you? One of those Madames who sell "Robes et Manteaux" so that they can attract poor girls like me from decent families into their workroom.[9]

SON   And she's bought the right to tyrannise over the whole lot of us with that money—with what he was going to pay her: and luckily—now listen carefully—he had no reason to pay it to her.

STEPDAUGHTER   But it was close!

MOTHER [*Rising up angrily.*]   Shame on you, daughter! Shame!

STEPDAUGHTER   Shame? Not shame, revenge! I'm desperate, desperate to live that scene! The room . . . over here the showcase of coats, there the divan, there the mirror, and the screen, and over there in front of the window, that little mahogany table with the pale blue envelope and the money in it. I can see it all quite clearly. I could pick it up! But you should turn your faces away, gentlemen: because I'm nearly naked! I'm not blushing any longer—I leave that to him. [*Pointing at the* FATHER.] But I tell you he was very pale, very pale then. [*To the* PRODUCER.] Believe me.

PRODUCER   I don't understand any more.

FATHER   I'm not surprised when you're attacked like that! Why don't you put your foot down and let me have my say before you believe all these horrible slanders she's so viciously telling about me.

9. The implication is that Madame Pace (Italian for "peace") runs a call-girl operation under the guise of selling fashionable "dresses and coats."

STEPDAUGHTER We don't want to hear any of your long winded fairy-stories.

FATHER I'm not going to tell any fairy-stories! I want to explain things to him.

STEPDAUGHTER I'm sure you do. Oh, yes! In your own special way.

[*The* PRODUCER *comes back up on stage to take control.*]

FATHER But isn't that the cause of all the trouble? Words! We all have a world of things inside ourselves and each one of us has his own private world. How can we understand each other if the words I use have the sense and the value that I expect them to have, but whoever is listening to me inevitably thinks that those same words have a different sense and value, because of the private world he has inside himself too. We think we understand each other: but we never do. Look! All my pity, all my compassion for this woman [*Pointing to the* MOTHER.] she sees as ferocious cruelty.

MOTHER But he turned me out of the house!

FATHER There, do you hear? I turned her out! She really believed that I had turned her out.

MOTHER You know how to talk. I don't . . . But believe me, sir, [*Turning to the* PRODUCER.] after he married me . . . I can't think why! I was a poor, simple woman.

FATHER But that was the reason! I married you for your simplicity, that's what I loved in you, believing— [*He stops because she is making gestures of contradiction. Then, seeing the impossibility of making her understand, he throws his arms wide in a gesture of desperation and turns back to the* PRODUCER.] No, do you see? She says no! It's terrifying, sir, believe me, terrifying, her deafness, her mental deafness. [*He taps his forehead.*] Affection for her children, oh yes. But deaf, mentally deaf, deaf, sir, to the point of desperation.

STEPDAUGHTER Yes, but make him tell you what good all his cleverness has brought us.

FATHER If only we could see in advance all the harm that can come from the good we think we are doing.

[*The* LEADING ACTRESS, *who has been growing angry watching the* LEADING ACTOR *flirting with the* STEPDAUGHTER, *comes forward and snaps at the* PRODUCER.]

LEADING ACTRESS Excuse me, are we going to go on with our rehearsal?

PRODUCER Yes, of course. But I want to listen to this first.

YOUNG ACTOR It's such a new idea.

YOUNG ACTRESS It's fascinating.

LEADING ACTRESS For those who are interested. [*She looks meaningfully at the* LEADING ACTOR.]

PRODUCER [*To the* FATHER.] Look here, you must explain yourself more clearly. [*He sits down.*]

FATHER Listen then. You see, there was a rather poor fellow working for me as my assistant and secretary, very loyal: he understood her in everything. [*Pointing to the* MOTHER.] But without a hint of deceit, you must believe that: he was good and simple, like her: neither of them was capable even of thinking anything wrong, let alone doing it.

STEPDAUGHTER So instead he thought of it for them and did it too!

FATHER   It's not true! What I did was for their good—oh yes and mine too, I admit it! The time had come when I couldn't say a word to either of them without there immediately flashing between them a sympathetic look: each one caught the other's eye for advice, about how to take what I had said, how not to make me angry. Well, that was enough, as I'm sure you'll understand, to put me in a bad temper all the time, in a state of intolerable exasperation.

PRODUCER   Then why didn't you sack this secretary of yours?

FATHER   Right! In the end I did sack him! But then I had to watch this poor woman wandering about in the house on her own, forlorn, like a stray animal you take in out of pity.

MOTHER   It's quite true.

FATHER [*Suddenly, turning to her, as if to stop her.*]   And what about the boy? Is that true as well?

MOTHER   But first he tore my son from me, sir.

FATHER   But not out of cruelty! It was so that he could grow up healthy and strong, in touch with the earth.

STEPDAUGHTER [*Pointing to the* SON *jeeringly.*]   And look at the result!

FATHER [*Quickly.*]   And is it my fault, too, that he's grown up like this? I took him to a nurse in the country, a peasant, because his mother didn't seem strong enough to me, although she is from a humble family herself. In fact that was what made me marry her. Perhaps it was superstitious of me; but what was I to do? I've always had this dreadful longing for a kind of sound moral healthiness.

[*The* STEPDAUGHTER *breaks out again into noisy laughter.*]
Make her stop that! It's unbearable.

PRODUCER   Stop it will you? Let me listen, for God's sake.

[*When the* PRODUCER *has spoken to her, she resumes her previous position . . . absorbed and distant, a half-smile on her lips. The* PRODUCER *comes down into the auditorium again to see how it looks from there.*]

FATHER   I couldn't bear the sight of this woman near me. [*Pointing to the* MOTHER.] Not so much because of the annoyance she caused me, you see, or even the feeling of being stifled, being suffocated that I got from her, as for the sorrow, the painful sorrow that I felt for her.

MOTHER   And he sent me away.

FATHER   With everything you needed, to the other man, to set her free from me.

MOTHER   And to set yourself free!

FATHER   Oh, yes, I admit it. And what terrible things came out of it. But I did it for the best, and more for her than for me: I swear it! [*Folds his arms: then turns suddenly to the* MOTHER.] I never lost sight of you did I? Until that fellow, without my knowing it, suddenly took you off to another town one day. He was idiotically suspicious of my interest in them, a genuine interest, I assure you, without any ulterior motive at all. I watched the new little family growing up round her with unbelievable tenderness, she'll confirm that. [*He points to the* STEPDAUGHTER.]

STEPDAUGHTER   Oh yes, I can indeed. I was a pretty little girl, you know, with plaits down to my shoulders and my little frilly knickers showing under my dress—so pretty—he used to watch me coming out of school. He came to see how I was maturing.

FATHER That's shameful! It's monstrous.

STEPDAUGHTER No it isn't! Why do you say it is?

FATHER It's monstrous! Monstrous. [*He turns excitedly to the* PRODUCER *and goes on in explanation.*] After she'd gone away [*Pointing to the* MOTHER.] my house seemed empty. She'd been like a weight on my spirit but she'd filled the house with her presence. Alone in the empty rooms I wandered about like a lost soul. This boy here, [*Indicating the* SON.] growing up away from home—whenever he came back to the home—I don't know—but he didn't seem to be mine any more. We needed the mother between us, to link us together, and so he grew up by himself, apart, with no connection to me either through intellect or love. And then—it must seem odd, but it's true—first I was curious about and then strongly attracted to the little family that had come about because of what I'd done. And the thought of them began to fill all the emptiness that I felt around me. I needed, I really needed to believe that she was happy, wrapped up in the simple cares of her life, lucky because she was better off away from the complicated torments of a soul like mine. And to prove it, I used to watch that child coming out of school.

STEPDAUGHTER Listen to him! He used to follow me along the street; he used to smile at me and when we came near the house he'd wave his hand—like this! I watched him, wide-eyed, puzzled. I didn't know who he was. I told my mother about him and she knew at once who it must be. [MOTHER *nods agreement.*] At first, she didn't let me go to school again, at any rate for a few days. But when I did go back, I saw him standing near the door again—looking ridiculous—with a brown paper bag in his hand. He came close and petted me: then he opened the bag and took out a beautiful straw hat with a hoop of rosebuds round it—for me!

PRODUCER All this is off the point, you know.

SON [*Contemptuously.*] Yes . . . literature, literature.

FATHER What do you mean, literature? This is real life: real passions.

PRODUCER That may be! But you can't put it on the stage just like that.

FATHER That's right you can't. Because all this is only leading up to the main action. I'm not suggesting that this part should be put on the stage. In any case, you can see for yourself, [*Pointing at the* STEPDAUGHTER.] she isn't a pretty little girl any longer with plaits down to her shoulders.

STEPDAUGHTER —and with frilly knickers showing under her frock.

FATHER The drama begins now: and it's new and complex.

STEPDAUGHTER [*Coming forward, fierce and brooding.*] As soon as my father died . . .

FATHER [*Quickly, not giving her time to speak.*] They were so miserable. They came back here, but I didn't know about it because of the Mother's stubbornness. [*Pointing to the* MOTHER.] She can't really write you know; but she could have got her daughter to write, or the boy, or tell me that they needed help.

MOTHER But tell me, sir, how could I have known how he felt?

FATHER And hasn't that always been your fault? You've never known anything about how I felt.

MOTHER After all the years away from him and after all that had happened.

FATHER And was it my fault if that fellow took you so far away? [*Turning back to the* PRODUCER.] Suddenly, overnight, I tell you, he'd found a job away from here without my knowing anything about it. I couldn't possibly trace them; and then, naturally I suppose, my interest in them grew less over the years. The drama broke out, unexpected and violent, when they came back: when I was driven in misery by the needs of my flesh, still alive with desire . . . and it is misery, you know, unspeakable misery for the man who lives alone and who detests sordid, casual affairs; not old enough to do without women, but not young enough to be able to go and look for one without shame! Misery? Is that what I called it. It's horrible, it's revolting, because there isn't a woman who will give her love to him any more. And when he realises this, he should do without . . . It's easy to say though. Each of us, face to face with other men, is clothed with some sort of dignity, but we know only too well all the unspeakable things that go on in the heart. We surrender, we give in to temptation: but afterwards we rise up out of it very quickly, in a desperate hurry to rebuild our dignity, whole and firm as if it were a gravestone that would cover every sign and memory of our shame, and hide it from even our own eyes. Everyone's like that, only some of us haven't the courage to talk about it.

STEPDAUGHTER   But they've all got the courage to do it!

FATHER   Yes! But only in secret! That's why it takes more courage to talk about it! Because if a man does talk about it—what happens then?—everybody says he's a cynic. And it's simply not true; he's just like everybody else; only better perhaps, because he's not afraid to use his intelligence to point out the blushing shame of human bestiality, that man, the beast, shuts his eyes to, trying to pretend it doesn't exist. And what about woman—what is she like? She looks at you invitingly, teasingly. You take her in your arms. But as soon as she feels your arms round her she closes her eyes. It's the sign of her mission, the sign by which she says to a man, "Blind yourself—I'm blind!"

STEPDAUGHTER   And when she doesn't close her eyes any more? What then? When she doesn't feel the need to hide from herself any more, to shut her eyes and hide her own shame. When she can see instead, dispassionately and dry-eyed this blushing shame of a man who has blinded himself, who is without love. What then? Oh, then what disgust, what utter disgust she feels for all these intellectual complications, for all this philosophy that points to the bestiality of man and then tries to defend him, to excuse him . . . I can't listen to him, sir. Because when a man says he needs to "simplify" life like this—reducing it to bestiality—and throws away every human scrap of innocent desire, genuine feeling, idealism, duty, modesty, shame, then there's nothing more contemptible and nauseating than his remorse—crocodile tears!

PRODUCER   Let's get to the point, let's get to the point. This is all chat.

FATHER   Right then! But a fact is like a sack—it won't stand up if it's empty. To make it stand up, first you have to put in it all the reasons and feelings that caused it in the first place. I couldn't possibly have known that when that fellow died they'd come back here, that they were desperately poor and that the Mother had gone out to work as a dressmaker, nor that she'd gone to work for Madame Pace, of all people.

STEPDAUGHTER   She's a very high-class dressmaker—you must understand that. She apparently has only high-class customers, but she has arranged things carefully so that these high-class customers in fact serve her—they

give her a respectable front . . . without spoiling things for the other
ladies at the shop who are not quite so high-class at all.

MOTHER   Believe me, sir, the idea never entered my head that the old hag
gave me work because she had an eye on my daughter . . .

STEPDAUGHTER   Poor Mummy! Do you know what that woman would do
when I took back the work that my mother had been doing? She would
point out how the dress had been ruined by giving it to my mother to sew:
she bargained, she grumbled. So, you see, I paid for it, while this poor
woman here thought she was sacrificing herself for me and these two children, sewing dresses all night for Madame Pace.

[*The* ACTORS *make gestures and noises of disgust.*]

PRODUCER [*Quickly.*]   And there one day, you met . . .

STEPDAUGHTER [*Pointing at the* FATHER.]   Yes, him. Oh, he was an old customer of hers! What a scene that's going to be, superb!

FATHER   With her, the mother, arriving—

STEPDAUGHTER [*Quickly, viciously.*]   —Almost in time!

FATHER [*Crying out.*]   —No, just in time, just in time! Because, luckily, I
found out who she was in time. And I took them all back to my house, sir.
Can you imagine the situation now, for the two of us living in the same
house? She, just as you see her here: and I, not able to look her in the face.

STEPDAUGHTER   It's so absurd! Do you think it's possible for me, sir, after
what happened at Madame Pace's, to pretend that I'm a modest little
miss, well brought up and virtuous just so that I can fit in with his damned
pretensions to a "sound moral healthiness"?

FATHER   This is the real drama for me; the belief that we all, you see, think
of ourselves as one single person: but it's not true: each of us is several
different people, and all these people live inside us. With one person we
seem like this and with another we seem very different. But we always
have the illusion of being the same person for everybody and of always
being the same person in everything we do. But it's not true! It's not true!
We find this out for ourselves very clearly when by some terrible chance
we're suddenly stopped in the middle of doing something and we're left
dangling there, suspended. We realise then, that every part of us was not
involved in what we'd been doing and that it would be a dreadful injustice of other people to judge us only by this one action as we dangle there,
hanging in chains, fixed for all eternity, as if the whole of one's personality were summed up in that single, interrupted action. Now do you understand this girl's treachery? She accidentally found me somewhere I
shouldn't have been, doing something I shouldn't have been doing! She
discovered a part of me that shouldn't have existed for her: and now she
wants to fix on me a reality that I should never have had to assume for her:
it came from a single brief and shameful moment in my life. This is what
hurts me most of all. And you'll see that the play will make a tremendous
impact from this idea of mine. But then, there's the position of the others. His . . . [*Pointing to the* SON.]

SON [*Shrugging his shoulders scornfully.*]   Leave me out of it. I don't come
into this.

FATHER   Why don't you come into this?

SON   I don't come into it and I don't want to come into it, because you know
perfectly well that I wasn't intended to be mixed up with you lot.

STEPDAUGHTER   We're vulgar, common people, you see! He's a fine gentleman. But you've probably noticed that every now and then I look at him
contemptuously, and when I do, he lowers his eyes—he knows the harm
he's done me.

SON [*Not looking at her.*]   I have?

STEPDAUGHTER   Yes, you. It's your fault, dearie, that I went on the streets!
Your fault! [*Movement of horror from the* ACTORS.] Did you or didn't you,
with your attitude, deny us—I won't say the intimacy of your home—but
that simple hospitality that makes guests feel comfortable? We were
intruders who had come to invade the country of your "legitimacy"! [*Turning to the* PRODUCER.] I'd like you to have seen some of the little scenes
that went on between him and me, sir. He says that I tyrannised over
everyone. But don't you see? It was because of the way he treated us. He
called it "vile" that I should insist on the right we had to move into his
house with my mother—and she's his mother too. And I went into the
house as its mistress.

SON [*Slowly coming forward.*]   They're really enjoying themselves, aren't
they, sir? It's easy when they all gang up against me. But try to imagine
what happened: one fine day, there is a son sitting quietly at home and he
sees arrive as bold as brass, a young woman like this, who cheekily asks
for his father, and heaven knows what business she has with him. Then
he sees her come back with the same brazen look in her eye accompanied
by that little girl there: and he sees her treat his father—without knowing why—in a most ambiguous and insolent way—asking him for money
in a tone that leads one to suppose he really ought to give it, because he
is obliged to do so.

FATHER   But I was obliged to do so: I owed it to your mother.

SON   And how was I to know that? When had I ever seen her before? When
had I ever heard her mentioned? Then one day I see her come in with her,
[*Pointing at the* STEPDAUGHTER.] that boy and that little girl: they say to
me, "Oh, didn't you know? This is your mother, too." Little by little I
began to understand, mostly from her attitude. [*Points to* STEPDAUGHTER.]
Why they'd come to live in the house so suddenly. I can't and I won't say
what I feel, and what I think. I wouldn't even like to confess it to myself.
So I can't take any active part in this. Believe me, sir, I am a character who
has not been fully developed dramatically, and I feel uncomfortable, most
uncomfortable, in their company. So please leave me out of it.

FATHER   What! But it's precisely because you feel like this . . .

SON [*Violently exasperated.*]   How do you know what I feel?

FATHER   All right! I admit it! But isn't that a situation in itself? This withdrawing of yourself, it's cruel to me and to your mother: when she came
back to the house, seeing you almost for the first time, not recognising
you, but knowing that you're her own son . . . [*Turning to point out the*
MOTHER *to the* PRODUCER.] There, look at her: she's weeping.

STEPDAUGHTER [*Angrily, stamping her foot.*]   Like the fool she is!

FATHER [*Quickly pointing at the* STEPDAUGHTER *to the* PRODUCER.]   She
can't stand that young man, you know. [*Turning and referring to the* SON.]
He says that he doesn't come into it, but he's really the pivot of the action!
Look here at this little boy, who clings to his mother all the time, frightened, humiliated. And it's because of him over there! Perhaps this little

boy's problem is the worst of all: he feels an outsider, more than the others do; he feels so mortified, so humiliated just being in the house,—because it's charity, you see. [*Quietly.*] He's like his father: timid; he doesn't say anything . . .

PRODUCER   It's not a good idea at all, using him: you don't know what a nuisance children are on the stage.

FATHER   He won't need to be on the stage for long. Nor will the little girl—she's the first to go.

PRODUCER   That's good! Yes. I tell you all this interests me—it interests me very much. I'm sure we've the material here for a good play.

STEPDAUGHTER   [*Trying to push herself in.*]   With a character like me you have!

FATHER   [*Driving her off, wanting to hear what the* PRODUCER *has decided.*] You stay out of it!

PRODUCER   [*Going on, ignoring the interruption.*]   It's new, yes.

FATHER   Oh, it's absolutely new!

PRODUCER   You've got a nerve, though, haven't you, coming here and throwing it at me like this?

FATHER   I'm sure you understand. Born as we are for the *stage* . . .

PRODUCER   Are you amateur actors?

FATHER   No! I say we are born for the stage because . . .

PRODUCER   Come on now! You're an old hand at this, at acting!

FATHER   No I'm not. I only act, as everyone does, the part in life that he's chosen for himself, or that others have chosen for him. And you can see that sometimes my own passion gets a bit out of hand, a bit theatrical, as it does with all of us.

PRODUCER   Maybe, maybe . . . But you do see, don't you, that without an author . . . I could give you someone's address . . .

FATHER   Oh no! Look here! You do it.

PRODUCER   Me? What are you talking about?

FATHER   Yes, you. Why not?

PRODUCER   Because I've never written anything!

FATHER   Well, why not start now, if you don't mind my suggesting it? There's nothing to it. Everybody's doing it. And your job is even easier, because we're here, all of us, alive before you.

PRODUCER   That's not enough.

FATHER   Why isn't it enough? When you've seen us live our drama . . .

PRODUCER   Perhaps so. But we'll still need someone to write it.

FATHER   Only to write it down, perhaps, while it happens in front of him—live—scene by scene. It'll be enough to sketch it out simply first and then run through it.

PRODUCER   [*Coming back up, tempted by the idea.*]   Do you know I'm almost tempted . . . just for fun . . . it might work.

FATHER   Of course it will. You'll see what wonderful scenes will come right out of it! I could tell you what they will be!

PRODUCER   You tempt me . . . you tempt me! We'll give it a chance. Come with me to the office. [*Turning to the* ACTORS.] Take a break: but don't go far away. Be back in a quarter of an hour or twenty minutes. [*To the* FATHER.] Let's see, let's try it out. Something extraordinary might come out of this.

FATHER   Of course it will! Don't you think it'd be better if the others came
too? [*Indicating the other* CHARACTERS.]

PRODUCER   Yes, come on, come on. [*Going, then turning to speak to the*
ACTORS.] Don't forget: don't be late: back in a quarter of an hour.

[*The* PRODUCER *and the* SIX CHARACTERS *cross the stage and go. The*
ACTORS *look at each other in astonishment.*]

LEADING ACTOR   Is he serious? What's he going to do?

YOUNG ACTOR   I think he's gone round the bend.

ANOTHER ACTOR   Does he expect to make up a play in five minutes?

YOUNG ACTOR   Yes, like the old actors in the commedia dell'arte![1]

LEADING ACTRESS   Well if he thinks I'm going to appear in that sort of nonsense . . .

YOUNG ACTOR   Nor me!

FOURTH ACTOR   I should like to know who they are.

THIRD ACTOR   Who do you think? They're probably escaped lunatics—or
crooks.

YOUNG ACTOR   And is he taking them seriously?

YOUNG ACTRESS   It's vanity. The vanity of seeing himself as an author.

LEADING ACTOR   I've never heard of such a thing! If the theatre, ladies and
gentlemen, is reduced to this . . .

FIFTH ACTOR   I'm enjoying it!

THIRD ACTOR   Really! We shall have to wait and see what happens next I
suppose.

[*Talking, they leave the stage. Some go out through the back door, some
to the dressing-rooms.*
The curtain stays up.
The interval lasts twenty minutes.]

Act 2

The theatre warning-bell sounds to call the audience back. From the dressing-
rooms, the door at the back and even from the auditorium, the ACTORS, *the*
STAGE MANAGER, *the* STAGE HANDS, *the* PROMPTER, *the* PROPERTY MAN *and the*
PRODUCER, *accompanied by the* SIX CHARACTERS *all come back on to the stage.*
The house lights go out and the stage lights come on again.

PRODUCER   Come on, everybody! Are we all here? Quiet now! Listen! Let's
get started! Stage manager?

STAGE MANAGER   Yes, I'm here.

PRODUCER   Give me that little parlour setting, will you? A couple of plain
flats and a door flat will do. Hurry up with it!

[*The* STAGE MANAGER *runs off to order someone to do this immediately*
and at the same time the PRODUCER *is making arrangements with the*
PROPERTY MAN, *the* PROMPTER, *and the* ACTORS: *the two flats and the*
door flat are painted in pink and gold stripes.]

PRODUCER [*To* PROPERTY MAN.]   Go see if we have a sofa in stock.

PROPERTY MAN   Yes, there's that green one.

---

1. A form of popular theater beginning in 16th-century Italy; the actors improvised dialogue according to
basic comic or dramatic plots and in response to the audience's reaction.

STEPDAUGHTER   No, no, not a green one! It was yellow, yellow velvet with flowers on it: it was enormous! And so comfortable!

PROPERTY MAN   We haven't got one like that.

PRODUCER   It doesn't matter! Give me whatever there is.

STEPDAUGHTER   What do you mean, it doesn't matter? It was Mme. Pace's famous sofa.

PRODUCER   It's only for a rehearsal! Please, don't interfere. [*To the* STAGE MANAGER.] Oh, and see if there's a shop window, will you—preferably a long, low one.

STEPDAUGHTER   And a little table, a little mahogany table for the blue envelope.

STAGE MANAGER [*To the* PRODUCER.]   There's that little gold one.

PRODUCER   That'll do—bring it.

FATHER   A mirror!

STEPDAUGHTER   And a screen! A screen, please, or I won't be able to manage, will I?

STAGE MANAGER   All right. We've lots of big screens, don't you worry.

PRODUCER [*To* STEPDAUGHTER.]   Then don't you want some coat-hangers and some clothes racks?

STEPDAUGHTER   Yes, lots of them, lots of them.

PRODUCER [*To the* STAGE MANAGER.]   See how many there are and have them brought up.

STAGE MANAGER   Right, I'll see to it.

   [*The* STAGE MANAGER *goes off to do it: and while the* PRODUCER *is talking to the* PROMPTER, *the* CHARACTERS *and the* ACTORS, *the* STAGE MANAGER *is telling the* SCENE SHIFTERS *where to set up the furniture they have brought.*]

PRODUCER [*To the* PROMPTER.]   Now you, go sit down, will you? Look, this is an outline of the play, act by act. [*He hands him several sheets of paper.*] But you'll need to be on your toes.

PROMPTER   Shorthand?

PRODUCER [*Pleasantly surprised.*]   Oh, good! You know shorthand?

PROMPTER   I don't know much about prompting, but I do know about shorthand.

PRODUCER   Thank God for that anyway! [*He turns to a* STAGE HAND.] Go fetch me some paper from my office—lots of it—as much as you can find!

   [*The* STAGE HAND *goes running off and then comes back shortly with a bundle of paper that he gives to the* PROMPTER.]

PRODUCER [*Crossing to the* PROMPTER.]   Follow the scenes, one after another, as they are played and try to get the lines down . . . at least the most important ones. [*Then turning to the* ACTORS.] Get out of the way everybody! Here, go over to the prompt side [*Pointing to stage left.*] and pay attention.

LEADING ACTRESS   But, excuse me, we . . .

PRODUCER [*Anticipating her.*]   You won't be expected to improvise, don't worry!

LEADING ACTOR   Then what are we expected to do?

PRODUCER   Nothing! Just go over there, listen and watch. You'll all be given your parts later written out. Right now we're going to rehearse, as well as we can. And they will be doing the rehearsal. [*He points to the* CHARACTERS.]

FATHER [*Rather bewildered, as if he had fallen from the clouds into the middle of the confusion on the stage.*]   We are? Excuse me, but what do you mean, a rehearsal?

PRODUCER   I mean a rehearsal—a rehearsal for the benefit of the actors. [*Pointing to the* ACTORS.]

FATHER   But if we are the characters . . .

PRODUCER   That's right, you're "the characters": but characters don't act here, my dear chap. It's actors who act here. The characters are there in the script—[*Pointing to the* PROMPTER.] that's when there is a script.

FATHER   That's the point! Since there isn't one and you have the luck to have the characters alive in front of you . . .

PRODUCER   Great! You want to do everything yourselves, do you? To act your own play, to produce your own play!

FATHER   Well yes, just as we are.

PRODUCER   That would be an experience for us, I can tell you!

LEADING ACTOR   And what about us? What would we be doing then?

PRODUCER   Don't tell me you think you know how to act! Don't make me laugh! [*The* ACTORS *in fact laugh.*] There you are, you see, you've made them laugh. [*Then remembering.*] But let's get back to the point! We need to cast the play. Well, that's easy: it almost casts itself. [*To the* SECOND ACTRESS.] You, the mother. [*To the* FATHER.] You'll need to give her a name.

FATHER   Amalia.

PRODUCER   But that's the real name of your wife isn't it? We can't use her real name.

FATHER   But why not? That is her name . . . But perhaps if this lady is to play the part . . . [*Indicating the* ACTRESS *vaguely with a wave of his hand.*] I don't know what to say . . . I'm already starting to . . . how can I explain it . . . to sound false, my own words sound like someone else's.

PRODUCER   Now don't worry yourself about it, don't worry about it at all. We'll work out the right tone of voice. As for the name, if you want it to be Amalia, then Amalia it shall be: or we can find another. For the moment we'll refer to the characters like this: [*To the* YOUNG ACTOR, *the juvenile lead.*] you are The Son. [*To the* LEADING ACTRESS.] You, of course, are The Stepdaughter.

STEPDAUGHTER [*Excitedly.*]   What did you say? That woman is me? [*Bursts into laughter.*]

PRODUCER [*Angrily.*]   What are you laughing at?

LEADING ACTRESS [*Indignantly.*]   Nobody has ever dared to laugh at me before! Either you treat me with respect or I'm walking out! [*Starting to go.*]

STEPDAUGHTER   I'm sorry. I wasn't really laughing at you.

PRODUCER [*To the* STEPDAUGHTER.]   You should feel proud to be played by . . .

LEADING ACTRESS [*Quickly, scornfully.*]   . . . that woman!

STEPDAUGHTER   But I wasn't thinking about her, honestly. I was thinking about me: I can't see myself in you at all . . . you're not a bit like me!

FATHER   Yes, that's right: you see, our meaning . . .

PRODUCER   What are you talking about, "our meaning"? Do you think you have exclusive rights to what you represent? Do you think it can only exist inside you? Not a bit of it!

FATHER What? Don't we even have our own meaning?

PRODUCER Not a bit of it! Whatever you mean is only material here, to which the actors give form and body, voice and gesture, and who, through their art, have given expression to much better material than what you have to offer: yours is really very trivial and if it stands up on the stage, the credit, believe me, will all be due to my actors.

FATHER I don't dare to contradict you. But you for your part, must believe me—it doesn't seem trivial to us. We are suffering terribly now, with these bodies, these faces . . .

PRODUCER [*Interrupting impatiently.*] Yes, well, the make-up will change that, make-up will change that, at least as far as the faces are concerned.

FATHER Yes, but the voices, the gestures . . .

PRODUCER That's enough! You can't come on the stage here as yourselves. It is our actors who will represent you here: and let that be the end of it!

FATHER I understand that. But now I think I see why our author who saw us alive as we are here now, didn't want to put us on the stage. I don't want to offend your actors. God forbid that I should! But I think that if I saw myself represented . . . by I don't know whom . . .

LEADING ACTOR [*Rising majestically and coming forward, followed by a laughing group of* YOUNG ACTRESSES.] By me, if you don't object.

FATHER [*Respectfully, smoothly.*] I shall be honoured, sir. [*He bows.*] But I think, that no matter how hard this gentleman works with all his will and all his art to identify himself with me . . . [*He stops, confused.*]

LEADING ACTOR Yes, go on.

FATHER Well, I was saying the performance he will give, even if he is made up to look like me . . . I mean with the difference in our appearance . . . [*All the* ACTORS *laugh.*] it will be difficult for it to be a performance of me as I really am. It will be more like—well, not just because of his figure— it will be more an interpretation of what I am, what he believes me to be, and not how I know myself to be. And it seems to me that this should be taken into account by those who are going to comment on us.

PRODUCER So you are already worrying about what the critics will say, are you? And I'm still waiting to get this thing started! The critics can say what they like: and we'll worry about putting on the play. If we can! [*Stepping out of the group and looking around.*] Come on, come on! Is the scene set for us yet? [*To the* ACTORS *and* CHARACTERS.] Out of the way! Let's have a look at it. [*Climbing down off the stage.*] Don't let's waste any more time. [*To the* STEPDAUGHTER.] Does it look all right to you?

SON What! That? I don't recognise it at all.

PRODUCER Good God! Did you expect us to reconstruct the room at the back of Mme. Pace's shop here on the stage? [*To the* FATHER.] Did you say the room had flowered wallpaper?

FATHER White, yes.

PRODUCER Well it's not white: it's striped. That sort of thing doesn't matter at all! As for the furniture, it looks to me as if we have nearly everything we need. Move that little table a bit further downstage. [*A* STAGE HAND *does it. To the* PROPERTY MAN.] Go and fetch an envelope, pale blue if you can find one, and give it to that gentleman there. [*Pointing to the* FATHER.]

STAGE HAND An envelope for letters?

PRODUCER ⎫
FATHER   ⎬ Yes, an envelope for letters!

STAGE HAND   Right. [*He goes off.*]

PRODUCER   Now then, come on! The first scene is the young lady's. [*The* LEADING ACTRESS *comes to the centre.*] No, no, not yet. I said the young lady's. [*He points to the* STEPDAUGHTER.] You stay there and watch.

STEPDAUGHTER [*Adding quickly.*]   . . . how I bring it to life.

LEADING ACTRESS [*Resenting this.*]   I shall know how to bring it to life, don't you worry, when I am allowed to.

PRODUCER [*His head in his hands.*]   Ladies, please, no more arguments! Now then. The first scene is between the young lady and Mme. Pace. Oh! [*Worried, turning round and looking out into the auditorium.*] Where is Mme. Pace?

FATHER   She isn't here with us.

PRODUCER   So what do we do now?

FATHER   But she is real. She's real too!

PRODUCER   All right. So where is she?

FATHER   May I deal with this? [*Turns to the* ACTRESSES.] Would each of you ladies be kind enough to lend me a hat, a coat, a scarf or something?

ACTRESSES [*Some are surprised or amused.*]   What? My scarf? A coat? What's he want my hat for? What are you wanting to do with them? [*All the* ACTRESSES *are laughing.*]

FATHER   Oh, nothing much, just hang them up here on the racks for a minute or two. Perhaps someone would be kind enough to lend me a coat?

ACTORS   Just a coat? Come on, more! The man must be mad.

AN ACTRESS   What for? Only my coat?

FATHER   Yes, to hang up here, just for a moment. I'm very grateful to you. Do you mind?

ACTRESSES [*Taking off various hats, coats, scarves, laughing and going to hang them on the racks.*]   Why not? Here you are. I really think it's crazy. Is it to dress the set?

FATHER   Yes, exactly. It's to dress the set.

PRODUCER   Would you mind telling me what you are doing?

FATHER   Yes, of course: perhaps, if we dress the set better, she will be drawn by the articles of her trade and, who knows, she may even come to join us . . . [*He invites them to watch the door at the back of the set.*] Look! Look!

> [*The door at the back opens and* MME. PACE *takes a few steps downstage: she is a gross old harridan wearing a ludicrous carroty-coloured wig with a single red rose stuck in at one side, Spanish fashion: garishly made-up: in a vulgar but stylish red silk dress, holding an ostrich-feather fan in one hand and a cigarette between two fingers in the other. At the sight of this apparition, the* ACTORS *and the* PRODUCER *immediately jump off the stage with cries of fear, leaping down into the auditorium and up the aisles. The* STEPDAUGHTER, *however, runs across to* MME. PACE, *and greets her respectfully, as if she were the mistress.*]

STEPDAUGHTER [*Running across to her.*]   Here she is! Here she is!

FATHER [*Smiling broadly.*]   It's her! What did I tell you? Here she is!

PRODUCER [*Recovering from his shock, indignantly.*]   What sort of trick is this?

LEADING ACTOR [*Almost at the same time as the others.*]   What the hell is happening?

JUVENILE LEAD   Where on earth did they get that extra from?

YOUNG ACTRESS   They were keeping her hidden!

LEADING ACTRESS   It's a game, a conjuring trick!

FATHER   Wait a minute! Why do you want to spoil a miracle by being factual? Can't you see this is a miracle of reality, that is born, brought to life, lured here, reproduced, just for the sake of this scene, with more right to be alive here than you have? Perhaps it has more truth than you have yourselves. Which actress can improve on Mme. Pace there? Well? That is the real Mme. Pace. You must admit that the actress who plays her will be less true than she is herself—and there she is in person! Look! My daughter recognised her straight away and went to meet her. Now watch—just watch this scene.

> [*Hesitantly, the* PRODUCER *and the* ACTORS *move back to their original places on the stage.*
>
> *But the scene between the* STEPDAUGHTER *and* MME. PACE *had already begun while the* ACTORS *were protesting and the* FATHER *explaining: it is being played under their breaths, very quietly, very naturally, in a way that is obviously impossible on stage. So when the* ACTORS' *attention is recalled by the* FATHER *they turn and see that* MME. PACE *has just put her hand under the* STEPDAUGHTER's *chin to make her lift her head up: they also hear her speak in a way that is unintelligible to them. They watch and listen hard for a few moments, then they start to make fun of them.*]

PRODUCER   Well?

LEADING ACTOR   What's she saying?

LEADING ACTRESS   Can't hear a thing!

JUVENILE LEAD   Louder! Speak up!

STEPDAUGHTER [*Leaving* MME. PACE *who has an astonishing smile on her face, and coming down to the* ACTORS.]   Louder? What do you mean, "Louder"? What we're talking about you can't talk about loudly. I could shout about it a moment ago to embarrass him [*Pointing to the* FATHER.] to shame him and to get my own back on him! But it's a different matter for Mme. Pace. It would mean prison for her.

PRODUCER   What the hell are you on about? Here in the theatre you have to make yourself heard! Don't you see that? We can't hear you even from here, and we're on the stage with you! Imagine what it would be like with an audience out front! You need to make the scene go! And after all, you would speak normally to each other when you're alone, and you will be, because we shan't be here anyway. I mean we're only here because it's a rehearsal. So just imagine that there you are in the room at the back of the shop, and there's no one to hear you.

> [*The* STEPDAUGHTER, *with a knowing smile, wags her finger and her head rather elegantly, as if to say no.*]

PRODUCER   Why not?

STEPDAUGHTER [*Mysteriously, whispering loudly.*]   Because there is someone who will hear if she speaks normally. [*Pointing to* MME. PACE.]

PRODUCER [*Anxiously.*]   You're not going to make someone else appear are you?

> [*The* ACTORS *get ready to dive off the stage again.*]

FATHER No, no. She means me. I ought to be over there, waiting behind the door: and Mme. Pace knows I'm there, so excuse me will you: I'll go there now so that I shall be ready for my entrance.

[*He goes towards the back of the stage.*]

PRODUCER [*Stopping him.*] No, no wait a minute! You must remember the stage conventions! Before you can go on to that part . . .

STEPDAUGHTER [*Interrupts him.*] Oh yes, let's get on with that part. Now! Now! I'm dying to do that scene. If he wants to go through it now, I'm ready!

PRODUCER [*Shouting.*] But before that we must have, clearly stated, the scene between you and her. [*Pointing to* MME. PACE.] Do you see?

STEPDAUGHTER Oh God! She's only told me what you already know, that my mother's needlework is badly done again, the dress is spoilt and that I shall have to be patient if I want her to go on helping us out of our mess.

MME. PACE [*Coming forward, with a great air of importance.*] Ah, yes, sir, for that I do not wish to make a profit, to make advantage.

PRODUCER [*Half frightened.*] What? Does she really speak like that?

[*All the* ACTORS *burst out laughing.*]

STEPDAUGHTER [*Laughing too.*] Yes, she speaks like that, half in Spanish, in the silliest way imaginable!

MME. PACE Ah it is not good manners that you laugh at me when I make myself to speak, as I can, English, señor.

PRODUCER No, no, you're right! Speak like that, please speak like that, madam. It'll be marvelous. Couldn't be better! It'll add a little touch of comedy to a rather crude situation. Speak like that! It'll be great!

STEPDAUGHTER Great! Why not? When you hear a proposition made in that sort of accent, it'll almost seem like a joke, won't it? Perhaps you'll want to laugh when you hear that there's an "old señor"[2] who wants to "amuse himself with me"—isn't that right, Madame?

MME. PACE Not so old . . . but not quite young, no? But if he is not to your taste . . . he is, how you say, discreet!

[*The* MOTHER *leaps up, to the astonishment and dismay of the* ACTORS *who had not been paying any attention to her, so that when she shouts out they are startled and then smilingly restrain her: however she has already snatched off* MME. PACE's *wig and flung it on the floor.*]

MOTHER You witch! Witch! Murderess! Oh, my daughter!

STEPDAUGHTER [*Running across and taking hold of the* MOTHER.] No! No! Mother! Please!

FATHER [*Running across to her as well.*] Calm yourself, calm yourself! Come and sit down.

MOTHER Get her away from here!

STEPDAUGHTER [*To the* PRODUCER *who has also crossed to her.*] My mother can't bear to be in the same place with her.

FATHER [*Also speaking quietly to the* PRODUCER.] They can't possibly be in the same place! That's why she wasn't with us when we first came, do you see! If they meet, everything's given away from the very beginning.

PRODUCER It's not important, that's not important! This is only a first run-through at the moment! It's all useful stuff, even if it is confused. I'll sort

2. Old gentleman.

it all out later. [*Turning to the* MOTHER *and taking her to sit down on her chair.*] Come on, my dear, take it easy; take it easy: come and sit down again.

STEPDAUGHTER   Go on, Mme. Pace.

MME. PACE [*Offended.*]   Oh no, thank-you! I no longer do nothing here with your mother present.

STEPDAUGHTER   Get on with it, bring in this "old señor" who wants to "amuse himself with me"! [*Turning majestically to the others.*] You see, this next scene has got to be played out—we must do it now. [*To* MME. PACE.] Oh, you can go!

MME. PACE   Ah, I go, I go—I go! Most probably! I go!

> [*She leaves banging her wig back into place, glaring furiously at the* ACTORS *who applaud her exit, laughing loudly.*]

STEPDAUGHTER [*To the* FATHER.]   Now you come on! No, you don't need to go off again! Come back! Pretend you've just come in! Look, I'm standing here with my eyes on the ground, modestly—well, come on, speak up! Use that special sort of voice, like somebody who has just come in. "Good afternoon, my dear."

PRODUCER [*Off the stage by now.*]   Look here, who's the director here, you or me? [*To the* FATHER *who looks uncertain and bewildered.*] Go on, do as she says: go upstage—no, no don't bother to make an entrance. Then come down stage again.

> [*The* FATHER *does as he is told, half mesmerised. He is very pale but already involved in the reality of his re-created life, smiles as he draws near the back of the stage, almost as if he genuinely is not aware of the drama that is about to sweep over him. The* ACTORS *are immediately intent on the scene that is beginning now.*]

The Scene

FATHER [*Coming forward with a new note in his voice.*]   Good afternoon, my dear.

STEPDAUGHTER [*Her head down trying to hide her fright.*]   Good afternoon.

FATHER [*Studying her a little under the brim of her hat which partly hides her face from him and seeing that she is very young, he exclaims to himself a little complacently and a little guardedly because of the danger of being compromised in a risky adventure.*] Ah . . . but . . . tell me, this won't be the first time, will it? The first time you've been here?

STEPDAUGHTER   No, sir.

FATHER   You've been here before? [*And after the* STEPDAUGHTER *has nodded an answer.*] More than once? [*He waits for her reply: tries again to look at her under the brim of her hat: smiles: then says.*] Well then . . . it shouldn't be too . . . May I take off your hat?

STEPDAUGHTER [*Quickly, to stop him, unable to conceal her shudder of fear and disgust.*]   No, don't! I'll do it!

> [*She takes it off unsteadily.*
>
> The MOTHER *watches the scene intently with the* SON *and the two smaller children who cling close to her all the time: they make a group on one side of the stage opposite the* ACTORS: *She follows the words and actions of the* FATHER *and the* STEPDAUGHTER *in this scene with a variety*

of expressions on her face—sadness, dismay, anxiety, horror: sometimes she turns her face away and sobs.]

MOTHER   Oh God! Oh God!

FATHER [*He stops as if turned to stone by the sobbing: then he goes on in the same tone of voice.*]   Here, give it to me. I'll hang it up for you. [*He takes the hat in his hand.*] But such a pretty, dear little head like yours should have a much smarter hat than this! Would you like to help me choose one, then, from these hats of Madame's hanging up here? Would you?

YOUNG ACTRESS [*Interrupting.*]   Be careful! Those are our hats!

PRODUCER [*Quickly and angrily.*]   For God's sake, shut up! Don't try to be funny! We're rehearsing! [*Turns back to the* STEPDAUGHTER.] Please go on, will you, from where you were interrupted.

STEPDAUGHTER [*Going on.*]   No, thank you, sir.

FATHER   Oh, don't say no to me please! Say you'll have one—to please me. Isn't this a pretty one—look! And then it will please Madame too, you know. She's put them out here on purpose, of course.

STEPDAUGHTER   No, look, I could never wear it.

FATHER   Are you thinking of what they would say at home when you went in wearing a new hat? Goodness me! Don't you know what to do? Shall I tell you what to say at home?

STEPDAUGHTER [*Furiously, nearly exploding.*]   That's not why! I couldn't wear it because . . . as you can see: you should have noticed it before. [*Indicating her black dress.*]

FATHER   You're in mourning! Oh, forgive me. You're right, I see that now. Please forgive me. Believe me, I'm really very sorry.

STEPDAUGHTER [*Gathering all her strength and making herself overcome her contempt and revulsion.*]   That's enough. Don't go on, that's enough. I ought to be thanking you and not letting you blame yourself and get upset. Don't think any more about what I told you, please. And I should do the same. [*Forcing herself to smile and adding.*] I should try to forget that I'm dressed like this.

PRODUCER [*Interrupting, turning to the* PROMPTER *in the box and jumping up on the stage again.*]   Hold it, hold it! Don't put that last line down, leave it out. [*Turning to the* FATHER *and the* STEPDAUGHTER.] It's going well! It's going well! [*Then to the* FATHER *alone.*] Then we'll put in there the bit that we talked about. [*To the* ACTORS.] That scene with the hats is good, isn't it?

STEPDAUGHTER   But the best bit is coming now! Why can't we get on with it?

PRODUCER   Just be patient, wait a minute. [*Turning and moving across to the* ACTORS.] Of course, it'll all have to be made a lot more light-hearted.

LEADING ACTOR   We shall have to play it a lot quicker, I think.

LEADING ACTRESS   Of course: there's nothing particularly difficult in it. [*To the* LEADING ACTOR.] Shall we run through it now?

LEADING ACTOR   Yes right . . . Shall we take it from my entrance? [*He goes to his position behind the door upstage.*]

PRODUCER [*To the* LEADING ACTRESS.]   Now then, listen, imagine the scene between you and Mme. Pace is finished. I'll write it up myself properly later on. You ought to be over here I think—[*She goes the opposite way.*] Where are you going now?

LEADING ACTRESS   Just a minute, I want to get my hat—[*She crosses to take her hat from the stand.*]

PRODUCER   Right, good, ready now? You are standing here with your head down.

STEPDAUGHTER [*Very amused.*]   But she's not dressed in black!

LEADING ACTRESS   Oh, but I shall be, and I'll look a lot better than you do, darling.

PRODUCER [*To the* STEPDAUGHTER.]   Shut up, will you! Go over there and watch! You might learn something! [*Clapping his hands.*] Right! Come on! Quiet please! Take it from his entrance.

> [*He climbs off stage so that he can see better. The door opens at the back of the set and the* LEADING ACTOR *enters with the lively, knowing air of an ageing roué.*[3] *The playing of the following scene by the* ACTORS *must seem from the very beginning to be something quite different from the earlier scene, but without having the faintest air of parody in it.*
>
> *Naturally the* STEPDAUGHTER *and the* FATHER *unable to see themselves in the* LEADING ACTOR *and* LEADING ACTRESS, *hearing their words said by them, express their reactions in different ways, by gestures, or smiles or obvious protests so that we are aware of their suffering, their astonishment, their disbelief.*
>
> *The* PROMPTER's *voice is heard clearly between every line in the scene, telling the* ACTORS *what to say next.*]

LEADING ACTOR   Good afternoon, my dear.

FATHER [*Immediately, unable to restrain himself.*]   Oh, no!

> [*The* STEPDAUGHTER, *watching the* LEADING ACTOR *enter this way, bursts into laughter.*]

PRODUCER [*Furious.*]   Shut up, for God's sake! And don't you dare laugh like that! We're never going to get anywhere at this rate.

STEPDAUGHTER [*Coming to the front.*]   I'm sorry, I can't help it! The lady stands exactly where you told her to stand and she never moved. But if it were me and I heard someone say good afternoon to me in that way and with a voice like that I should burst out laughing—so I did.

FATHER [*Coming down a little too.*]   Yes, she's right, the whole manner, the voice . . .

PRODUCER   To hell with the manner and the voice! Get out of the way, will you, and let me watch the rehearsal!

LEADING ACTOR [*Coming down stage.*]   If I have to play an old man who has come to a knocking shop—

PRODUCER   Take no notice, ignore them. Go on please! It's going well, it's going well! [*He waits for the* ACTOR *to begin again.*] Right, again!

LEADING ACTOR   Good afternoon, my dear.

LEADING ACTRESS   Good afternoon.

LEADING ACTOR [*Copying the gestures of the* FATHER, *looking under the brim of the hat, but expressing distinctly the two emotions, first, complacent satisfaction and then anxiety.*]   Ah! But tell me . . . this won't be the first time I hope.

FATHER [*Instinctively correcting him.*]   Not "I hope"—"will it," "will it."

PRODUCER   Say "will it"—and it's a question.

---

3. Dissipated lover.

LEADING ACTOR [*Glaring at the* PROMPTER.] I distinctly heard him say "I hope."

PRODUCER So what? It's all the same, "I hope" or "isn't it." It doesn't make any difference. Carry on, carry on. But perhaps it should still be a little bit lighter; I'll show you—watch me! [*He climbs up on the stage again, and going back to the entrance, he does it himself.*] Good afternoon, my dear.

LEADING ACTRESS Good afternoon.

PRODUCER Ah, tell me . . . [*He turns to the* LEADING ACTOR *to make sure that he has seen the way he has demonstrated of looking under the brim of the hat.*] You see—surprise . . . anxiety and self-satisfaction. [*Then, starting again, he turns to the* LEADING ACTRESS.] This won't be the first time, will it? The first time you've been here? [*Again turns to the* LEADING ACTOR *questioningly.*] Right? [*To the* LEADING ACTRESS.] And then she says, "No, sir." [*Again to* LEADING ACTOR.] See what I mean? More subtlety. [*And he climbs off the stage.*]

LEADING ACTRESS No, sir.

LEADING ACTOR You've been here before? More than once?

PRODUCER No, no, no! Wait for it, wait for it. Let her answer first. "You've been here before?"

> [*The* LEADING ACTRESS *lifts her head a little, her eyes closed in pain and disgust, and when the* PRODUCER *says "Now" she nods her head twice.*]

STEPDAUGHTER [*Involuntarily.*] Oh, my God! [*And she immediately claps her hand over her mouth to stifle her laughter.*]

PRODUCER What now?

STEPDAUGHTER [*Quickly.*] Nothing, nothing!

PRODUCER [*To* LEADING ACTOR.] Come on, then, now it's you.

LEADING ACTOR More than once? Well then, it shouldn't be too . . . May I take off your hat?

> [*The* LEADING ACTOR *says this last line in such a way and adds to it such a gesture that the* STEPDAUGHTER, *even with her hand over her mouth trying to stop herself laughing, can't prevent a noisy burst of laughter.*]

LEADING ACTRESS [*Indignantly turning.*] I'm not staying any longer to be laughed at by that woman!

LEADING ACTOR Nor am I! That's the end—no more!

PRODUCER [*To* STEPDAUGHTER, *shouting.*] Once and for all, will you shut up! Shut up!

STEPDAUGHTER Yes, I'm sorry . . . I'm sorry.

PRODUCER You're an ill-mannered little bitch! That's what you are! And you've gone too far this time!

FATHER [*Trying to interrupt.*] Yes, you're right, she went too far, but please forgive her . . .

PRODUCER [*Jumping on the stage.*] Why should I forgive her? Her behaviour is intolerable!

FATHER Yes, it is, but the scene made such a peculiar impact on us . . .

PRODUCER Peculiar? What do you mean peculiar? Why peculiar?

FATHER I'm full of admiration for your actors, for this gentleman [*To the* LEADING ACTOR.] and this lady. [*To the* LEADING ACTRESS.] But, you see, well . . . they're not us!

PRODUCER Right! They're not! They're actors!

FATHER   That's just the point—they're actors. And they are acting our parts
very well, both of them. But that's what's different. However much they
want to be the same as us, they're not.

PRODUCER   But why aren't they? What is it now?

FATHER   It's something to do with . . . being themselves, I suppose, not
being us.

PRODUCER   Well we can't do anything about that! I've told you already. You
can't play the parts yourselves.

FATHER   Yes, I know, I know . . .

PRODUCER   Right then. That's enough of that. [*Turning back to the*
ACTORS.] We'll rehearse this later on our own, as we usually do. It's always
a bad idea to have rehearsals with authors there! They're never satisfied.
[*Turns back to the* FATHER *and the* STEPDAUGHTER.] Come on, let's get on
with it; and let's see if it's possible to do it without laughing.

STEPDAUGHTER   I won't laugh any more, I won't really. My best bit's coming up now, you wait and see!

PRODUCER   Right: when you say "Don't think any more about what I told
you, please. And I should do the same." [*Turning to the* FATHER.] Then you
come in immediately with the line "I understand, ah yes, I understand"
and then you ask . . .

STEPDAUGHTER [*Interrupting.*]   Ask what? What does he ask?

PRODUCER   Why you're in mourning.

STEPDAUGHTER   No! No! That's not right! Look: when I said that I should
try not to think abut the way I was dressed, do you know what he said?
"Well then, let's take it off, we'll take it off at once, shall we, your little
black dress."

PRODUCER   That's great! That'll be wonderful! That'll bring the house down!

STEPDAUGHTER   But it's the truth!

PRODUCER   The truth! Do me a favour will you? This is the theatre you
know! Truth's all very well up to a point but . . .

STEPDAUGHTER   What do you want to do then?

PRODUCER   You'll see! You'll see! Leave it all to me.

STEPDAUGHTER   No. No I won't. I know what you want to do! Out of my
feeling of revulsion, out of all the vile and sordid reasons why I am what
I am, you want to make a sugary little sentimental romance. You want him
to ask me why I'm in mourning and you want me to reply with the tears
running down my face that it is only two months since my father died. No.
No. I won't have it! He must say to me what he really did say. "Well then,
let's take it off, we'll take it off at once, shall we, your little black dress."
And I, with my heart still grieving for my father's death only two months
before, I went behind there, do you see? Behind that screen and with my
fingers trembling with shame and loathing I took off the dress, unfastened my bra . . .

PRODUCER [*His head in his hands.*]   For God's sake! What are you saying!

STEPDAUGHTER [*Shouting excitedly.*]   The truth! I'm telling you the truth!

PRODUCER   All right then, Now listen to me. I'm not denying it's the truth.
Right. And believe me I understand your horror, but you must see that we
can't really put a scene like that on the stage.

STEPDAUGHTER   You can't? Then thanks very much. I'm not stopping here.

PRODUCER   No, listen . . .

STEPDAUGHTER No, I'm going. I'm not stopping. The pair of you have worked it all out together, haven't you, what to put in the scene. Well, thank you very much! I understand everything now! He wants to get to the scene where he can talk about his spiritual torments but I want to show you my drama! Mine!

PRODUCER [*Shaking with anger.*] Now we're getting to the real truth of it, aren't we? Your drama—yours! But it's not only yours, you know. It's drama for the other people as well! For him [*Pointing to the* FATHER.] and for your mother! You can't have one character coming on like you're doing, trampling over the others, taking over the play. Everything needs to be balanced and in harmony so that we can show what has to be shown! I know perfectly well that we've all got a life inside us and that we all want to parade it in front of other people. But that's the difficulty, how to present only the bits that are necessary in relation to the other characters: and in the small amount we show, to hint at all the rest of the inner life of the character! I agree, it would be so much simpler, if each character, in a soliloquy or in a lecture could pour out to the audience what's bubbling away inside him. But that's not the way we work. [*In an indulgent, placating tone.*] You must restrain yourself, you see. And believe me, it's in your own interests: because you could so easily make a bad impression, with all this uncontrollable anger, this disgust and exasperation. That seems a bit odd, if you don't mind my saying so, when you've admitted that you'd been with other men at Mme. Pace's and more than once.

STEPDAUGHTER I suppose that's true. But you know, all the other men were all him as far as I was concerned.

PRODUCER [*Not understanding.*] Uum—? What? What are you talking about?

STEPDAUGHTER If someone falls into evil ways, isn't the responsibility for all the evil which follows to be laid at the door of the person who caused the first mistake? And in my case, it's him, from before I was even born. Look at him: see if it isn't true.

PRODUCER Right then! What about the weight of remorse he's carrying? Isn't that important? Then, give him the chance to show it to us.

STEPDAUGHTER But how? How on earth can he show all his long-suffering remorse, all his moral torments as he calls them, if you don't let him show his horror when he finds me in his arms one fine day, after he had asked me to take my dress off, a black dress for my father who had just died: and he finds that I'm the child he used to go and watch as she came out of school, me, a woman now, and a woman he could buy. [*She says these last words in a voice trembling with emotion.*]

[*The* MOTHER, *hearing her say this, is overcome and at first gives way to stifled sobs: but then she bursts out into uncontrollable crying. Everyone is deeply moved. There is a long pause.*]

STEPDAUGHTER [*As soon as the* MOTHER *has quietened herself she goes on, firmly and thoughtfully.*] At the moment we are here on our own and the public doesn't know about us. But tomorrow you will present us and our story in whatever way you choose, I suppose. But wouldn't you like to see the real drama? Wouldn't you like to see it explode into life, as it really did?

PRODUCER Of course, nothing I'd like better, then I can use as much of it as possible.

STEPDAUGHTER   Then persuade my mother to leave.

MOTHER [*Rising and her quiet weeping changing to a loud cry.*]   No! No! Don't let her! Don't let her do it!

PRODUCER   But they're only doing it for me to watch—only for me, do you see?

MOTHER   I can't bear it, I can't bear it!

PRODUCER   But if it's already happened, I can't see what's the objection.

MOTHER   No! It's happening now, as well: it's happening all the time. I'm not acting my suffering! Can't you understand that? I'm alive and here now but I can never forget that terrible moment of agony, that repeats itself endlessly and vividly in my mind. And these two little children here, you've never heard them speak have you? That's because they don't speak any more, not now. They just cling to me all the time: they help to keep my grief alive, but they don't really exist for themselves any more, not for themselves. And she [*Indicating the* STEPDAUGHTER.] . . . she has gone away, left me completely, she's lost to me, lost . . . you see her here for one reason only: to keep perpetually before me, always real, the anguish and the torment I've suffered on her account.

FATHER   The eternal moment, as I told you, sir. She is here [*Indicating the* STEPDAUGHTER.] to keep me too in that moment, trapped for all eternity, chained and suspended in that one fleeting shameful moment of my life. She can't give up her role and you cannot rescue me from it.

PRODUCER   But I'm not saying that we won't present that bit. Not at all! It will be the climax of the first act, when she [*He points to the* MOTHER.] surprises you.

FATHER   That's right, because that is the moment when I am sentenced: all our suffering should reach a climax in her cry. [*Again indicating the* MOTHER.]

STEPDAUGHTER   I can still hear it ringing in my ears! It was that cry that sent me mad! You can have me played just as you like: it doesn't matter! Dressed, too, if you want, so long as I can have at least an arm—only an arm—bare, because, you see, as I was standing like this [*She moves across to the* FATHER *and leans her head on his chest.*] with my head like this and my arms round his neck, I saw a vein, here in my arm, throbbing: and then it was almost as if that throbbing vein filled me with a shivering fear, and I shut my eyes tightly like this, like this and buried my head in his chest. [*Turning to the* MOTHER.] Scream, Mummy, scream. [*She buries her head in the* FATHER's *chest, and with her shoulders raised as if to try not to hear the scream, she speaks with a voice tense with suffering.*] Scream, as you screamed then!

MOTHER [*Coming forward to pull them apart.*]   No! She's my daughter! My daughter! [*Tearing her from him.*] You brute, you animal, she's my daughter! Can't you see she's my daughter?

PRODUCER [*Retreating as far as the footlights while the* ACTORS *are full of dismay.*]   Marvellous! Yes, that's great! And then curtain, curtain!

FATHER [*Running downstage to him, excitedly.*]   That's it, that's it! Because it really was like that!

PRODUCER [*Full of admiration and enthusiasm.*]   Yes, yes, that's got to be the curtain line! Curtain! Curtain!

[*At the repeated calls of the* PRODUCER, *the* STAGE MANAGER *lowers the curtain, leaving on the apron in front, the* PRODUCER *and the* FATHER.]

PRODUCER [*Looking up to heaven with his arms raised.*]   The idiots! I didn't mean now! The bloody idiots—dropping it in on us like that! [*To the* FATHER, *and lifting up a corner of the curtain.*] That's marvellous! Really marvellous! A terrific effect! We'll end the act like that! It's the best tag line I've heard for ages. What a First Act ending! I couldn't have done better if I'd written it myself!

[*They go through the curtain together.*]

Act 3

When the curtain goes up we see that the STAGE MANAGER *and* STAGE HANDS *have struck the first scene and have set another, a small garden fountain.*

From one side of the stage the ACTORS *come on and from the other the* CHARACTERS. *The* PRODUCER *is standing in the middle of the stage with his hand over his mouth, thinking.*

PRODUCER [*After a short pause, shrugging his shoulders.*]   Well, then: let's get on to the second act! Leave it all to me, and everything will work out properly.

STEPDAUGHTER   This is where we go to live at his house [*Pointing to the* FATHER.] In spite of the objections of him over there. [*Pointing to the* SON.]

PRODUCER [*Getting impatient.*] All right, all right! But leave it all to me, will you?

STEPDAUGHTER   Provided that you make it clear that he objected!

MOTHER [*From the corner, shaking her head.*]   That doesn't matter. The worse it was for us, the more he suffered from remorse.

PRODUCER [*Impatiently.*]   I know, I know! I'll take it all into account. Don't worry!

MOTHER [*Pleading.*]   To set my mind at rest, sir, please do make sure it's clear that I tried all I could—

STEPDAUGHTER [*Interrupting her scornfully and going on.*]   —to pacify me, to persuade me that this despicable creature wasn't worth making trouble about! [*To the* PRODUCER.] Go on, set her mind at rest, because it's true, she tried very hard. I'm having a whale of a time now! You can see, can't you, that the meeker she was and the more she tried to worm her way into his heart, the more lofty and distant he became! How's that for a dramatic situation!

PRODUCER   Do you think that we can actually begin the Second Act?

STEPDAUGHTER   I won't say another word! But you'll see that it won't be possible to play everything in the garden, like you want to do.

PRODUCER   Why not?

STEPDAUGHTER [*Pointing to the* SON.]   Because to start with, he stays shut up in his room in the house all the time! And then all the scenes for this poor little devil of a boy happen in the house. I've told you once.

PRODUCER   Yes, I know that! But on the other hand we can't put up a notice to tell the audience where the scene is taking place, or change the set three or four times in each Act.

LEADING ACTOR   That's what they used to do in the good old days.

PRODUCER   Yes, when the audience was about as bright as that little girl over there!

LEADING ACTRESS   And it makes it easier to create an illusion.

FATHER [*Leaping up.*]   An illusion? For pity's sake don't talk about illusions! Don't use that word, it's especially hurtful to us!

PRODUCER [*Astonished.*]   And why, for God's sake?

FATHER   It's so hurtful, so cruel! You ought to have realised that!

PRODUCER   What else should we call it? That's what we do here—create an illusion for the audience . . .

LEADING ACTOR   With our performance . . .

PRODUCER   A perfect illusion of reality!

FATHER   Yes, I know that, I understand. But on the other hand, perhaps you don't understand us yet. I'm sorry! But you see, for you and for your actors what goes on here on the stage is, quite rightly, well, it's only a game.

LEADING ACTRESS [*Interrupting indignantly.*]   A game! How dare you! We're not children! What happens here is serious!

FATHER   I'm not saying that it isn't serious. And I mean, really, not just a game but an art, that tries, as you've just said, to create the perfect illusion of reality.

PRODUCER   That's right!

FATHER   Now try to imagine that we, as you see us here, [*He indicates himself and the other* CHARACTERS.] that we have no other reality outside this illusion.

PRODUCER [*Astonished and looking at the* ACTORS *with the same sense of bewilderment as they feel themselves.*]   What the hell are you talking about now?

FATHER [*After a short pause as he looks at them, with a faint smile.*]   Isn't it obvious? What other reality is there for us? What for you is an illusion you create, for us is our only reality. [*Brief pause. He moves towards the* PRODUCER *and goes on.*] But it's not only true for us, it's true for others as well, you know. Just think about it. [*He looks intently into the* PRODUCER'*s eyes.*] Do you really know who you are? [*He stands pointing at the* PRODUCER.]

PRODUCER [*A little disturbed but with a half smile.*]   What? Who I am? I am me!

FATHER   What if I told you that that wasn't true: what if I told you that you were me?

PRODUCER   I would tell you that you were mad!

[*The* ACTORS *laugh.*]

FATHER   That's right, laugh! Because everything here is a game! [*To the* PRODUCER.] And yet you object when I say that it is only for a game that the gentleman there [*Pointing to the* LEADING ACTOR.] who is "himself" has to be "me," who, on the contrary, am "myself." You see, I've caught you in a trap.

[*The* ACTORS *start to laugh.*]

PRODUCER   Not again! We've heard all about this a little while ago.

FATHER   No, no. I didn't really want to talk about this. I'd like you to forget about your game. [*Looking at the* LEADING ACTRESS *as if to anticipate what she will say.*] I'm sorry—your artistry! Your art!—that you usually pursue here with your actors; and I am going to ask you again in all seriousness, who are you?

PRODUCER [*Turning with a mixture of amazement and annoyance, to the* ACTORS.] Of all the bloody nerve! A fellow who claims he is only a character comes and asks me who I am!

FATHER [*With dignity but without annoyance.*] A character, my dear sir, can always ask a man who he is, because a character really has a life of his own, a life full of his own specific qualities, and because of these he is always "someone." While a man—I'm not speaking about you personally, of course, but man in general—well, he can be an absolute "nobody."

PRODUCER All right, all right! Well, since you've asked me, I'm the Director, the Producer—I'm in charge! Do you understand?

FATHER [*Half smiling, but gently and politely.*] I'm only asking to try to find out if you really see yourself now in the same way that you saw yourself, for instance, once upon a time in the past, with all the illusions you had then, with everything inside and outside yourself as it seemed then—and not only seemed, but really was! Well then, look back on those illusions, those ideas that you don't have any more, on all those things that no longer seem the same to you. Don't you feel that not only this stage is falling away from under your feet but so is the earth itself, and that all these realities of today are going to seem tomorrow as if they had been an illusion?

PRODUCER So? What does that prove?

FATHER Oh, nothing much. I only want to make you see that if we [*Pointing to himself and the other* CHARACTERS.] have no other reality outside our own illusion, perhaps you ought to distrust your own sense of reality: because whatever is a reality today, whatever you touch and believe in and that seems real for you today, is going to be—like the reality of yesterday—an illusion tomorrow.

PRODUCER [*Deciding to make fun of him.*] Very good! So now you're saying that you as well as this play you're going to show me here, are more real than I am?

FATHER [*Very seriously.*] There's no doubt about that at all.

PRODUCER Is that so?

FATHER I thought you'd realised that from the beginning.

PRODUCER More real than I am?

FATHER If your reality can change between today and tomorrow—

PRODUCER But everybody knows that it can change, don't they? It's always changing! Just like everybody else's!

FATHER [*Crying out.*] But ours doesn't change! Do you see? That's the difference! Ours doesn't change, it can't change, it can never be different, never, because it is already determined, like this, for ever, that's what's so terrible! We are an eternal reality. That should make you shudder to come near us.

PRODUCER [*Jumping up, suddenly struck by an idea, and standing directly in front of the* FATHER.] Then I should like to know when anyone saw a character step out of his part and make a speech like you've done, proposing things, explaining things. Tell me when, will you? I've never seen it before.

FATHER You've never seen it because an author usually hides all the difficulties of creating. When the characters are alive, really alive and standing in front of their author, he has only to follow their words, the actions that they suggest to him: and he must want them to be what they want to

be: and it's his bad luck if he doesn't do what they want! When a character is born he immediately assumes such an independence even of his
own author that everyone can imagine him in scores of situations that his
author hadn't even thought of putting him in, and he sometimes acquires
a meaning that his author never dreamed of giving him.

PRODUCER   Of course I know all that.

FATHER   Well, then. Why are you surprised by us? Imagine what a disaster
it is for a character to be born in the imagination of an author who then
refuses to give him life in a written script. Tell me if a character, left like
this, suspended, created but without a final life, isn't right to do what we
are doing now, here in front of you. We spent such a long time, such a
very long time, believe me, urging our author, persuading him, first me,
then her, [*Pointing to the* STEPDAUGHTER.] then this poor Mother . . .

STEPDAUGHTER   [*Coming down the stage as if in a dream.*]   It's true, I would
go, would go and tempt him, time after time, in his gloomy study just as
it was growing dark, when he was sitting quietly in an armchair not even
bothering to switch a light on but leaving the shadows to fill the room: the
shadows were swarming with us, we had come to tempt him. [*As if she
could see herself there in the study and is annoyed by the presence of the*
ACTORS.] Go away will you! Leave us alone! Mother there, with that son
of hers—me with the little girl—that poor little kid always on his own—
and then me with him [*Pointing to the* FATHER.] and then at last, just me,
on my own, all on my own, in the shadows. [*She turns quickly as if she
wants to cling on to the vision she has of herself, in the shadows.*] Ah, what
scenes, what scenes we suggested to him! What a life I could have had! I
tempted him more than the others!

FATHER   Oh yes, you did! And it was probably all your fault that he did nothing about it! You were so insistent, you made too many demands.

STEPDAUGHTER   But he wanted me to be like that! [*She comes closer to the*
PRODUCER *to speak to him in confidence.*] I think it's more likely that he
felt discouraged about the theatre and even despised it because the public only wants to see . . .

PRODUCER   Let's go on, for God's sake, let's go on. Come to the point will
you?

STEPDAUGHTER   I'm sorry, but if you ask me, we've got too much happening
already, just with our entry into his house. [*Pointing to the* FATHER.] You
said that we couldn't put up a notice or change the set every five minutes.

PRODUCER   Right! Of course we can't! We must combine things, group
them together in one continuous flowing action: not the way you've been
wanting, first of all seeing your little brother come home from school and
wander about the house like a lost soul, hiding behind the doors and
brooding on some plan or other that would—what did you say it would do?

STEPDAUGHTER   Wither him . . . shrivel him up completely.

PRODUCER   That's good! That's a good expression. And then you "can see it
there in his eyes, getting stronger all the time"—isn't that what you said?

STEPDAUGHTER   Yes, that's right. Look at him! [*Pointing to him as he stands
next to his* MOTHER.]

PRODUCER   Yes, great! And then, at the same time, you want to show the little girl playing in the garden, all innocence. One in the house and the
other in the garden—we can't do it, don't you see that?

STEPDAUGHTER   Yes, playing in the sun, so happy! It's the only pleasure I have left, her happiness, her delight in playing in the garden: away from the misery, the squalor of that sordid flat where all four of us slept and where she slept with me—with me! Just think of it! My vile, contaminated body close to hers, with her little arms wrapped tightly round my neck, so lovingly, so innocently. In the garden, wherever she saw me, she would run and take my hand. She never wanted to show me the big flowers, she would run about looking for the "little weeny" ones, so that she could show them to me; she was so happy, so thrilled! [*As she says this, tortured by the memory, she breaks out into a long desperate cry, dropping her head on her arms that rest on a little table. Everybody is very affected by her. The* PRODUCER *comes to her almost paternally and speaks to her in a soothing voice.*]

PRODUCER   We'll have the garden scene, we'll have it, don't worry: and you'll see, you'll be very pleased with what we do! We'll play all the scenes in the garden! [*He calls out to a* STAGE HAND *by name.*] Hey . . . , let down a few bits of tree, will you? A couple of cypresses will do, in front of the fountain. [*Someone drops in the two cypresses and a* STAGE HAND *secures them with a couple of braces and weights.*]

PRODUCER   [*To the* STEPDAUGHTER.]   That'll do for now, won't it? It'll just give us an idea. [*Calling out to a* STAGE HAND *by name again.*] Hey, . . . give me something for the sky will you?

STAGE HAND   What's that?

PRODUCER   Something for the sky! A small cloth to come in behind the fountain. [*A white cloth is dropped from the flies.*] Not white! I asked for a sky! Never mind: leave it! I'll do something with it. [*Calling out.*] Hey lights! Kill everything will you? Give me a bit of moonlight—the blues in the batten and a blue spot on the cloth . . . [*They do.*] That's it! That'll do! [*Now on the scene there is the light he asked for, a mysterious blue light that makes the* ACTORS *speak and move as if in the garden in the evening under a moon. To the* STEPDAUGHTER.] Look here now: the little boy can come out here in the garden and hide among the trees instead of hiding behind the doors in the house. But it's going to be difficult to find a little girl to play the scene with you where she shows you the flowers. [*Turning to the* LITTLE BOY.] Come on, come on, son, come across here. Let's see what it'll look like. [*But the* (LITTLE) BOY *doesn't move.*] Come on will you, come on. [*Then he pulls him forward and tries to make him hold his head up, but every time it falls down again on his chest.*] There's something very odd about this lad . . . What's wrong with him? My God, he'll have to say something sometime! [*He comes over to him again, puts his hand on his shoulder and pushes him between the trees.*] Come a bit nearer: let's have a look. Can you hide a bit more? That's it. Now pop your head out and look round. [*He moves away to look at the effect and as the* BOY *does what he has been told to do, the* ACTORS *watch impressed and a little disturbed.*] Ahh, that's good, very good . . . [*He turns to the* STEPDAUGHTER.] How about having the little girl, surprised to see him there, run across. Wouldn't that make him say something?

STEPDAUGHTER   [*Getting up.*]   It's no use hoping he'll speak, not as long as that creature's there. [*Pointing to the* SON.] You'll have to get him out of the way first.

SON [*Moving determinedly to one of the sets of steps leading off the stage.*]
  With pleasure! I'll go now! Nothing will please me better!
PRODUCER [*Stopping him immediately.*]   Hey, no! Where are you going?
  Hang on!
      [*The* MOTHER *gets up, anxious at the idea that he is really going and
      instinctively raising her arms as if to hold him back, but without moving
      from where she is.*]
SON [*At the footlights, to the* PRODUCER *who is restraining him there.*]
  There's no reason why I should be here! Let me go will you? Let me go!
PRODUCER   What do you mean there's no reason for you to be here?
STEPDAUGHTER [*Calmly, ironically.*]   Don't bother to stop him. He won't go!
FATHER   You have to play that terrible scene in the garden with your
  mother.
SON [*Quickly, angry and determined.*]   I'm not going to play anything! I've
  said that all along! [*To the* PRODUCER.] Let me go will you?
STEPDAUGHTER [*Crossing to the* PRODUCER.]   It's all right. Let him go. [*She
  moves the* PRODUCER'*s hand from the* SON. *Then she turns to the* SON *and
  says.*] Well, go on then! Off you go!
      [*The* SON *stays near the steps but as if pulled by some strange force he is
      quite unable to go down them: then to the astonishment and even the
      dismay of the* ACTORS, *he moves along the front of the stage towards the
      other set of steps down into the auditorium: but having got there, he
      again stays near and doesn't actually go down them. The* STEPDAUGHTER
      who has watched him scornfully but very intently, bursts into laughter.]
STEPDAUGHTER   He can't, you see? He can't! He's got to stay here! He must.
  He's chained to us for ever! No, I'm the one who goes, when what must
  happen does happen, and I run away, because I hate him, because I can't
  bear the sight of him any longer. Do you think it's possible for him to run
  away? He has to stay here with that wonderful father of his and his
  mother there. She doesn't think she has any other son but him. [*She turns
  to the* MOTHER.] Come on, come on, Mummy, come on! [*Turning back to
  the* PRODUCER *to point her out to him.*] Look, she's going to try to stop
  him . . . [*To the* MOTHER, *half compelling her, as if by some magic power.*]
  Come on, come on. [*Then to the* PRODUCER *again.*] Imagine how she must
  feel at showing her affection for him in front of your actors! But her longing to be near him is so strong that—look! She's going to go through that
  scene with him again! [*The* MOTHER *has now actually come close to the
  SON as the* STEPDAUGHTER *says the last line: she gestures to show that she
  agrees to go on.*]
SON [*Quickly.*]   But I'm not! I'm not! If I can't get away then I suppose I
  shall have to stay here; but I repeat that I will not have any part in it.
FATHER [*To the* PRODUCER, *excitedly.*]   You must make him!
SON   Nobody's going to make me do anything!
FATHER   I'll make you!
STEPDAUGHTER   Wait! Just a minute! Before that, the little girl has to go to
  the fountain. [*She turns to take the* LITTLE GIRL, *drops on her knees in
  front of her and takes her face between her hands.*] My poor little darling,
  those beautiful eyes, they look so bewildered. You're wondering where
  you are, aren't you? Well, we're on a stage, my darling! What's a stage?
  Well, it's a place where you pretend to be serious. They put on plays here.

And now we're going to put on a play. Seriously! Oh, yes! Even you . . . [*She hugs her tightly and rocks her gently for a moment.*] Oh, my little one, my little darling, what a terrible play it is for you! What horrible things have been planned for you! The garden, the fountain . . . Oh, yes, it's only a pretend fountain, that's right. That's part of the game, my pretty darling: everything is pretends here. Perhaps you'll like a pretends fountain better than a real one: you can play here then. But it's only a game for the others; not for you, I'm afraid, it's real for you, my darling, and your game is in a real fountain, a big beautiful green fountain with bamboos casting shadows, looking at your own reflection, with lots of baby ducks paddling about, shattering the reflections. You want to stroke one! [*With a scream that electrifies and terrifies everybody.*] No, Rosetta, no! Your mummy isn't watching you, she's over there with that selfish bastard! Oh, God, I feel as if all the devils in hell were tearing me apart inside . . . And you . . . [*Leaving the* LITTLE GIRL *and turning to the* LIT-TLE BOY *in the usual way.*] What are you doing here, hanging about like a beggar? It'll be your fault too, if that little girl drowns; you're always like this, as if I wasn't paying the price for getting all of you into this house. [*Shaking his arm to make him take his hand out of his pocket.*] What have you got there? What are you hiding? Take it out, take your hand out! [*She drags his hand out of his pocket and to everyone's horror he is holding a revolver. She looks at him for a moment, almost with satisfaction: then she says, grimly.*] Where on earth did you get that? [*The* (LITTLE) BOY, *looking frightened, with his eyes wide and empty, doesn't answer.*] You idiot, if I'd been you, instead of killing myself, I'd have killed one of those two: either or both, the father and the son. [*She pushes him toward the cypress trees where he then stands watching: then she takes the* LITTLE GIRL *and helps her to climb in to the fountain, making her lie so that she is hidden: after that she kneels down and puts her head and arms on the rim of the fountain.*]

PRODUCER   That's good! It's good! [*Turning to the* STEPDAUGHTER.] And at the same time . . .

SON [*Scornfully.*]   What do you mean, at the same time? There was nothing at the same time! There wasn't any scene between her and me. [*Pointing to the* MOTHER.] She'll tell you the same thing herself, she'll tell you what happened.

     [*The* SECOND ACTRESS *and the* JUVENILE LEAD *have left the group of* ACTORS *and have come to stand nearer the* MOTHER *and the* SON *as if to study them so as to play their parts.*]

MOTHER   Yes, it's true. I'd gone to his room . . .

SON   Room, do you hear? Not the garden!

PRODUCER   It's not important! We've got to reorganize the events anyway. I've told you that already.

SON [*Glaring at the* JUVENILE LEAD *and the* SECOND ACTRESS.]   What do you want?

JUVENILE LEAD   Nothing. I'm just watching.

SON [*Turning to the* SECOND ACTRESS]   You as well! Getting ready to play her part are you? [*Pointing to the* MOTHER.]

PRODUCER   That's it. And I think you should be grateful—they're paying you a lot of attention.

SON Oh, yes, thank you! But haven't you realised yet that you'll never be able to do this play? There's nothing of us inside you and you actors are only looking at us from the outside. Do you think we could go on living with a mirror held up in front of us that didn't only freeze our reflection for ever, but froze us in a reflection that laughed back at us with an expression that we didn't even recognise as our own?

FATHER That's right! That's right!

PRODUCER [*To* JUVENILE LEAD *and* SECOND ACTRESS.] Okay. Go back to the others.

SON It's quite useless. I'm not prepared to do anything.

PRODUCER Oh, shut up, will you, and let me listen to your mother. [*To the* MOTHER.] Well, you'd gone to his room, you said.

MOTHER Yes, to his room. I couldn't bear it any longer. I wanted to empty my heart to him, tell him about all the agony that was crushing me. But as soon as he saw me come in . . .

SON Nothing happened. I got away! I wasn't going to get involved. I never have been involved. Do you understand?

MOTHER It's true! That's right!

PRODUCER But we must make up the scene between you, then. It's vital!

MOTHER I'm ready to do it! If only I had the chance to talk to him for a moment, to pour out all my troubles to him.

FATHER [*Going to the* SON *and speaking violently.*] You'll do it! For your Mother! For your Mother!

SON [*More than ever determined.*] I'm doing nothing!

FATHER [*Taking hold of his coat collar and shaking him.*] For God's sake, do as I tell you! Do as I tell you! Do you hear what she's saying? Haven't you any feelings for her?

SON [*Taking hold of his* FATHER.] No I haven't! I haven't! Let that be the end of it!

[*There is a general uproar. The* MOTHER *frightened out of her wits, tries to get between them and separate them.*]

MOTHER Please stop it! Please!

FATHER [*Hanging on.*] Do as I tell you! Do as I tell you!

SON [*Wrestling with him and finally throwing him to the ground near the steps. Everyone is horrified.*] What's come over you? Why are you so frantic? Do you want to parade our disgrace in front of everybody? Well, I'm having nothing to do with it! Nothing! And I'm doing what our author wanted as well—he never wanted to put us on the stage.

PRODUCER Then why the hell did you come here?

SON [*Pointing to the* FATHER.] He wanted to, I didn't.

PRODUCER But you're here now, aren't you?

SON He was the one who wanted to come and he dragged all of us here with him and agreed with you in there about what to put in the play: and that meant not only what had really happened, as if that wasn't bad enough, but what hadn't happened as well.

PRODUCER All right, then, you tell me what happened. You tell me! Did you rush out of your room without saying anything?

SON [*After a moment's hesitation.*] Without saying anything. I didn't want to make a scene.

PRODUCER [*Needling him.*] What then? What did you do then?

SON [*He is now the centre of everyone's agonised attention and he crosses the stage.*]   Nothing . . . I went across the garden . . . [*He breaks off gloomy and absorbed.*]

PRODUCER [*Urging him to say more, impressed by his reluctance to speak.*]   Well? What then? You crossed the garden?

SON [*Exasperated, putting his face into the crook of his arm.*]   Why do you want me to talk about it? It's horrible! [*The* MOTHER *is trembling with stifled sobs and looking towards the fountain.*]

PRODUCER [*Quietly, seeing where she is looking and turning to the* SON *with growing apprehension.*]   The little girl?

SON [*Looking straight in front, out to the audience.*]   There, in the fountain . . .

FATHER [*On the floor still, pointing with pity at the* MOTHER.]   She was trailing after him!

PRODUCER [*To the* SON, *anxiously.*]   What did you do then?

SON [*Still looking out front and speaking slowly.*]   I dashed across. I was going to jump in and pull her out . . . But something else caught my eye: I saw something behind the tree that made my blood run cold: the little boy, he was standing there with a mad look in his eyes: he was standing looking into the fountain at his little sister, floating there, drowned.

[*The* STEPDAUGHTER *is still bent at the fountain hiding the* LITTLE GIRL, *and she sobs pathetically, her sobs sounding like an echo. There is a pause.*]

SON [*Continued.*]   I made a move towards him: but then . . .

[*From behind the trees where the* LITTLE BOY *is standing there is the sound of a shot.*]

MOTHER [*With a terrible cry she runs along with the* SON *and all the* ACTORS *in the midst of a great general confusion.*]   My son! My son! [*And then from out of the confusion and crying her voice comes out.*] Help! Help me!

PRODUCER [*Amidst the shouting he tries to clear a space whilst the* LITTLE BOY *is carried by his feet and shoulders behind the white skycloth.*]   Is he wounded? Really wounded?

[*Everybody except the* PRODUCER *and the* FATHER *who is still on the floor by the steps, has gone behind the skycloth and stays there talking anxiously. Then independently the* ACTORS *start to come back into view.*]

LEADING ACTRESS [*Coming from the right, very upset.*]   He's dead! The poor boy! He's dead! What a terrible thing!

LEADING ACTOR [*Coming back from the left and smiling.*]   What do you mean, dead? It's all make-believe. It's a sham! He's not dead. Don't you believe it!

OTHER ACTORS FROM THE RIGHT   Make-believe? It's real! Real! He's dead!

OTHER ACTORS FROM THE LEFT   No, he isn't. He's pretending! It's all make-believe.

FATHER [*Running off and shouting at them as he goes.*]   What do you mean, make-believe? It's real! It's real, ladies and gentlemen! It's reality! [*And with desperation on his face he too goes behind the skycloth.*]

PRODUCER [*Not caring any more.*]   Make-believe?! Reality?! Oh, go to hell the lot of you! Lights! Lights! Lights!

[*At once all the stage and auditorium is flooded with light. The* PRODUCER *heaves a sigh of relief as if he has been relieved of a terrible weight and they all look at each other in distress and with uncertainty.*]

PRODUCER   God! I've never known anything like this! And we've lost a whole day's work! [*He looks at the clock.*] Get off with you, all of you! We can't do anything now! It's too late to start a rehearsal. [*When the* ACTORS *have gone, he calls out.*] Hey, lights! Kill everything! [*As soon as he has said this, all the lights go out completely and leave him in the pitch dark.*] For God's sake!! You might have left the workers![4] I can't see where I'm going!

> [*Suddenly, behind the skycloth, as if because of a bad connection, a green light comes up to throw on the cloth a huge sharp shadow of the* CHARACTERS, *but without the* LITTLE BOY *and the* LITTLE GIRL. *The* PRO-DUCER, *seeing this, jumps off the stage, terrified. At the same time the flood of light on them is switched off and the stage is again bathed in the same blue light as before. Slowly the* SON *comes on from the right, fol-lowed by the* MOTHER *with her arms raised towards him. Then from the left, the* FATHER *enters.*]

They come together in the middle of the stage and stand there as if transfixed. Finally from the left the STEPDAUGHTER *comes on and moves towards the steps at the front: on the top step she pauses for a moment to look back at the other three and then bursts out in a raucous laugh, dashes down the steps and turns to look at the three figures still on the stage. Then she runs out of the auditorium and we can still hear her manic laughter out into the foyer and beyond.*

After a pause the curtain falls slowly.]

---

4. Working lights.

RAINER MARIA RILKE
1875–1926

Rainer Maria Rilke's search for the "great mysteries" of the universe combines his own intensely personal awareness with a range of broad questions that are ordinarily called religious. Whether his gaze is turned toward the objects and creatures of Earth, which he describes with extraordinary clarity and affection, or toward a higher intuited realm whose enigma remains to be deciphered, he seeks throughout a comprehensive vision of cosmic unity. Rilke absorbs what he sees around him—objects, people, gestures—until they become part of his consciousness and are ready to emerge in the words of a poem. "Looking is such a wonderful thing, about which we as yet know so little," he wrote his wife, Clara; "we are turned completely out-ward, but just when we are most outward, things seem to happen inside us." The poet's role, he says, is to observe with a fresh sensitivity "this fleeting world, which in some strange way / keeps calling to us," and to bear witness, through language, to the transfiguration of its materiality in human emotions. Rilke writes at a transitional moment in modern European letters: inheritor of the Symbolists in his allusive imagery and intuitions of cosmic order, and modernist in the "thing-centered" con-creteness of individual descriptions, he also foreshadows existentialism as he strug-gles to comprehend the self's relation to the universe. The best-known and most influential German poet of the twentieth century, Rilke has been read and translated outside Europe in countries as far apart as the United States and Japan. He speaks to a variety of cultures and audiences even though he was perhaps the least socially oriented poet of his time.

Born in Prague on December 4, 1875, to German-speaking parents who separated when he was nine, Rilke had an unhappy childhood that included being dressed as a girl when he was young (thus his mother compensated for the earlier loss of a baby daughter) and being sent to military academies, where he was lonely and miserable, from 1886 to 1891. Illness caused his departure from the second academy; and after a year in business school, he worked in his uncle's law firm and studied at the University of Prague. Rilke hoped to persuade his family that he should devote himself to a literary career rather than business or law, and energetically wrote poetry (*Sacrifice to the Lares*, 1895, *Crowned by Dream*, 1896), plays, stories, and reviews. Moving to Munich in 1897, he met and fell in love with a fascinating and cultured older woman, Lou Andreas-Salomé, who would be a constant influence on him throughout his life. He accompanied Andreas-Salomé and her husband to Russia in 1899, where he met Leo Tolstoy and the painter Leonid Pasternak and—swayed by responding to Russian mysticism and the Russian landscape—wrote most of the poems later published as *The Book of Hours: The Book of Monastic Life* (1905) and a Romantic verse tale that became extremely popular, *The Tale of Love and Death of Cornet Christoph Rilke* (1906). After a second trip to Russia, Rilke spent some time at an artists' colony called Worpswede, where he met his future wife, the sculptor Clara Westhoff. They were married in March 1901 and settled in a cottage near the colony where Rilke wrote the second part of *The Book of Hours: The Book of Pilgrimage*. He and Clara separated in the following year, and Rilke moved to Paris where he embarked on a study of the French sculptor Auguste Rodin (1903).

Unhappy in Paris, where he felt lonely and isolated, he fled to Italy in 1903 to write the last section of *The Book of Hours: The Book of Poverty and Death*. Nonetheless, he had found in Paris a new kind of literary and artistic inspiration. He read French writers and especially Baudelaire, whose minutely realistic but strangely beautiful description of a rotting corpse ("A Carcass") initiated, he felt, "the entire development toward objective expression, which we now recognize in Cézanne." In Rodin, too, he recognized a workmanlike dedication to the technical demands of his craft; an intense concentration on visible, tangible objects; and above all, a belief in art as an essentially religious activity. Although he wrote in distress to his friend Andreas-Salomé, complaining of nightmares and a sense of failure, it is at this time (and with her encouragement) that Rilke began his major work. The anguished, semiautobiographical spiritual confessions of *The Notebooks of Malte Laurids Brigge* (1910) date to this period, as do a series of *New Poems* (1907–08) in which he abandoned his earlier, impressionistic and Romantic style and developed a more intense Symbolic vision focused on objects. The *New Poems* emphasized physical reality, the absolute otherness and "thing-like" nature of what was observed—be it fountain, panther, flower, human being, or the "Archaic Torso of Apollo." "Thing-poems" (*Dinggedichte*), in fact, is a term often used to describe Rilke's writing at this time, with its open emphasis on material description. In a letter to Andreas-Salomé, he described the way that ancient art objects took on a peculiar luster once they were detached from history and seen as "things" in and for themselves: "No subject matter is attached to them, no irrelevant voice interrupts the silence of their concentrated reality . . . no history casts a shadow over their naked clarity—: they *are*. That is all . . . one day one of them reveals itself to you, and shines like a first star."

Such "things" are not dead or inanimate but supremely alive, filled with a strange vitality before the poet's glance: the charged sexuality of the marble torso, the metamorphosis of the Spanish dance in which the dancer's flamelike dress "becomes a furnace / from which, like startled rattlesnakes, the long / naked arms uncoil, aroused and clicking" ("Spanish Dancer"), or the caged panther's circling "like a ritual dance around a center / in which a mighty will stands paralyzed" ("The Panther"). If things are not dead, neither is death unambiguous: when Rilke retells the ancient myth of Orpheus and his lost wife, Eurydice, the dead woman is seen as achieving a new and fuller existence in the underworld. "Deep within herself. Being dead / filled her beyond fulfillment. . . . She was already loosened like long hair, / poured out like fallen rain, / shared like a limitless supply. / She was already root." Themes of the interpenetration of life and death, the visible and invisible world, and creativity itself are taken up in Rilke's next major work, the sequence of ten elegies (mournful lyric poems, usually laments for loss, and generally of medium length) called the *Duino Elegies* (1923), which he was to begin in 1912 while spending the winter in Duino Castle near Trieste.

The composition of the *Duino Elegies* came in two bursts of inspiration separated by ten years. Despite Rilke's increasing reputation and the popularity of his earlier work, he felt frustrated and unhappy. It was not that he lacked friends or activity; back in Paris once more, he corresponded actively and traveled widely, visiting Italy, Flanders, Germany, Austria, Egypt, and Algeria. But social pressures and everyday anxieties kept him overly occupied, and when a patroness, Princess Marie von Thurn und Taxis-Hohenlohe, proposed that he stay by himself in her castle at Duino during the winter of 1911–12, he was delighted.

Completion did not come easily in the following years, however, with the beginning of World War I. After writing the third Duino elegy in Paris in 1913, Rilke left for Munich—never dreaming that his apartment and personal property would soon be confiscated as that of an enemy alien. In April 1915, everything was sold at public auction; that summer, Duino Castle was bombarded and reduced to ruins. Rilke wrote the somber fourth elegy in Munich on November 22 and 23, and the next day was called up for the draft. Three weeks later, at age forty, he was drafted and became a clerk in the War Archives Office in Vienna where he drew precise vertical and horizontal lines on paper until June 1916, when the intercession of friends released him from military service. Rilke composed little after this experience and feared that he would never be able to complete the Duino sequence. In 1922, however, a friend's purchase of the tiny Château de Muzot in Switzerland gave him a peaceful place to retire and write. He not only completed the *Duino Elegies* in Muzot but wrote in addition—as a memorial for the young daughter of a friend—a two-part sequence of fifty-five sonnets, the *Sonnets to Orpheus* (1923).

With the *Duino Elegies* and the *Sonnets to Orpheus*, Rilke's last great works were complete. The melancholy philosophic vision of the early elegies describes an angel of absolute reality, whose self-contained perfection is terrifyingly separate from mortal concerns. In the later elegies and the *Sonnets*, the idea of angelic perfection is balanced by a newly important human role for the human artist, who serves as a bridge between the worlds of Earth and of the angel. To the poet's initial sense of helplessness and alienation, the later poems respond that all creatures need the artist's transforming glance to reach full being. *Elegies* and the *Sonnets* together move toward a more positive celebration of simple things. A sequence of symbolic figures suggests this development from uncertainty to affirmation, as the dominant angel of the *Elegies* gives way to the human poet Orpheus, who in turn retires into the background of the later *Sonnets* before Eurydice, the woman whose passing into the realm of the dead brings her fuller being. With this major affirmation of the essential unity of life and death, Rilke closed his two complementary sequences ("the little rust-colored sail of the Sonnets and the Elegies' gigantic white canvas") and wrote little—chiefly poems in French—over the next few years. Increasingly ill with leukemia, he died on December 29, 1926, as the result of a sudden infection after pricking himself on roses he cut for a friend in his garden.

The four selections from the *New Poems* printed here demonstrate Rilke's acutely visual imagination and the ambivalent objectivity of his thing-poems. Whether a flamenco dancer, a caged panther, a swan entering the water, or the splendor of an ancient Greek statue, the subject is presented for itself—but it is also suffused with human emotions. These emotions are mixed and cannot be reduced to one meaning:

for example, there is a combined sense of relief and yet obscurely terrifying mortality as the swan glides through the water, and the panther's numbed consciousness, contained force, and momentary tension clearly evoke some kind of response from the reader—pity? horror? fear of entrapment? awe?—but Rilke does not define it for us. Steel bars are the only world known by the caged panther, who has so far forgotten his natural habitat as to react only for a moment when an unexpected (and unspecified) image briefly penetrates his consciousness. The Spanish dancer moves with complete mastery through the traditional flamenco dance steps with all the brilliance and triumph of the flame to which she is compared (*flamenco* is derived from *flamear*, to flame). Both the swan's awkward progress on land and its majestic glide upon entering the water are compared in the poem to the passage from life to death. Concurrently, the detailed physical description makes it easy for readers to identify with the frustrations of the initial laborious advance—and the subsequent letting go and release into a new state of indifference and ease. The "archaic torso of Apollo" is not a living being, but a fifth-century B.C.E. Greek sculpture on display in the Louvre Museum in Paris. This headless marble torso is truly a "thing," a lifeless, even defaced chunk of stone. Yet such is the perfection of its luminous sensuality—descended, the speaker suggests, from the brilliant gaze of its missing head and "ripening" eyes—that it seems impossibly alive, and an inner radiance bursts starlike from the marble. The *human* vitality of this marble torso, a vitality achieved through artistic vision, challenges and puts to shame the observer's own puny existence. Nor is there any place to escape from the lesson, once it is recognized; instead, "You must change your life."

Ultimately, Rilke is celebrating the power of human creativity to refashion the world in its own image. The poet observes reality and creates from it a new form, a new being. For the poet, however, it is a process of making the visible angelically "invisible," and a bridge between two worlds; he "delivers" things by absorbing them into his imagination's inner dimension, asking, as at the end of the ninth *Elegy*, "Earth, isn't this what you want: to arise within us, / *invisible*?" Rilke's poetic journey, from the *New Poems* to the *Elegies* and the *Sonnets to Orpheus*, was an inward journey that created a bridge between two worlds, preserving the most intense moments of human experience by subjecting them to the transfiguring perspective of art.

PRONOUNCING GLOSSARY

The following list uses common English syllables and stress accents to provide rough equivalents of selected words whose pronunciation may be unfamiliar to the general reader.

Dinggedichte: *ding'-ge-dikh-tuh*   Muzot: *moo-zoh'*

FROM NEW POEMS[1]

Archaic Torso of Apollo[2]

We cannot know his legendary head[3]
with eyes like ripening fruit. And yet his torso

---

1. All selections translated by Stephen Mitchell.   2. The first poem in the second volume of Rilke's *New Poems* (1908), which were dedicated "to my good friend, Auguste Rodin" (the French sculptor, 1840–1917, whose secretary Rilke was for a brief period and on whom he wrote two monographs, in 1903 and 1907). The poem itself was inspired by an ancient Greek statue discovered at Miletus (a Greek colony on the coast of Asia Minor) that was called simply the *Torso of a Youth from Miletus*; since the god Apollo was an ideal of youthful male beauty, his name was often associated with such statues.   3. In a torso, the head and limbs are missing.

is still suffused with brilliance from inside,
like a lamp, in which his gaze, now turned to low,

gleams in all its power. Otherwise   5
the curved breast could not dazzle you so, nor could
a smile run through the placid hips and thighs
to that dark center where procreation flared.

Otherwise this stone would seem defaced
beneath the translucent cascade of the shoulders   10
and would not glisten like a wild beast's fur:

would not, from all the borders of itself,
burst like a star: for here there is no place
that does not see you. You must change your life.

Archaïscher Torso Apollos

Wir kannten nicht sein unerhörtes Haupt,
darin die Augenäpfel reiften. Aber
sein Torso glüht noch wie ein Kandelaber,
in dem sein Schauen, nur zurückgeschraubt,

sich hält und glänzt. Sonst könnte nicht der Bug   5
der Brust dich blenden, und im leisen Drehen
der Lenden könnte nicht ein Lächeln gehen
zu jener Mitte, die die Zeugung trug.

Sonst stünde dieser Stein entstellt und kurz
unter der Schultern durchsichtigem Sturz   10
und flimmerte nicht so wie Raubtierfelle;

und bräche nicht aus allen seinen Rändern
aus wie ein Stern: denn da ist keine Stelle,
die dich nicht sieht. Du mußt dein Leben ändern.

The Panther

In the Jardin des Plantes,[1] Paris

His vision, from the constantly passing bars,
has grown so weary that it cannot hold
anything else. It seems to him there are
a thousand bars; and behind the bars, no world.

---

1. A zoo in Paris. Rilke also admired, at Rodin's studio, the plaster cast of an ancient statue of a panther.

As he paces in cramped circles, over and over,   5
the movement of his powerful soft strides
is like a ritual dance around a center
in which a mighty will stands paralyzed.

Only at times, the curtain of the pupils
lifts, quietly—. An image enters in,   10
rushes down through the tensed, arrested muscles,
plunges into the heart and is gone.

The Swan

This laboring through what is still undone,
as though, legs bound, we hobbled along the way,
is like the awkward walking of the swan.

And dying—to let go, no longer feel
the solid ground we stand on every day—   5
is like his anxious letting himself fall

into the water, which receives him gently
and which, as though with reverence and joy,
draws back past him in streams on either side;
while, infinitely silent and aware,   10
in his full majesty and ever more
indifferent, he condescends to glide.

Spanish Dancer[1]

As on all its sides a kitchen-match darts white
flickering tongues before it bursts into flame:
with the audience around her, quickened, hot,
her dance begins to flicker in the dark room.

And all at once it is completely fire.   5
One upward glance and she ignites her hair
and, whirling faster and faster, fans her dress
into passionate flames, till it becomes a furnace
from which, like startled rattlesnakes, the long
naked arms uncoil, aroused and clicking.[2]   10

And then: as if the fire were too tight
around her body, she takes and flings it out
haughtily, with an imperious gesture,
and watches: it lies raging on the floor,

1. A traditional Spanish dance, the *flamenco* (from *flamear*, "to flame").   2. The dancer accompanies herself with the rhythmic clicking of castanets (worn on the fingers).

> still blazing up, and the flames refuse to die—.   15
> Till, moving with total confidence and a sweet
> exultant smile, she looks up finally
> and stamps it out with powerful small feet.

LU XUN
1881–1936

No country in the world has had so long, continuous, and essentially autonomous a culture as China. For the past century Chinese intellectuals have struggled to free themselves from the oppressive weight of their past and to discover a Chinese cultural identity independent of the traditional civilization. This has, in fact, been a central concern throughout modern Chinese literature. The rapid importation of Western fiction, drama, and poetry in the early twentieth century provided a set of literary models quite distinct from those of the Chinese tradition. Rather than finding in the Western models new possibilities of art, however, many Chinese writers sought in them instruments by which to change the culture or a medium by which to analyze the problems posed by China's cultural legacy. Western writers have often had similar aims, but the marginal status of the writer in European civilization has been a helpful counterweight to such grand purposes. By contrast, the centrality of the writer and intellectual has proved to be one of the tenacious assumptions of traditional Chinese culture, and it is ironic that this assumption stands behind the continuing hope of modern Chinese writers to free China of the weight of its traditional civilization.

Modern China has produced many talented writers, on whom critical opinion is divided. There is, however, almost universal agreement on one authentic genius among them: Lu Xun (also romanized Lu Hsün), the pen name of Zhou Shuren. Few writers of fiction have gained so much fame for such a small oeuvre. His reputation rests entirely on twenty-five stories published between 1918 and 1926, gathered into two collections: *Cheering from the Sidelines* and *Wondering Where to Turn*. In addition to this fiction he published a collection of prose poems, *Wild Grass*, and a large number of literary and political essays. His small body of stories gives a ruthlessly bleak portrayal of an entire culture that has failed. Whether the culture had indeed failed is less important than the powerful representation he gives of it and the way in which his representations touched a deep chord of response in Chinese readers. Lu was a controlled ironist and a craftsman whose narrative skill far exceeded that of most of his contemporaries; yet underneath his mastery the reader senses the depth of his anger at traditional culture.

Lu was well prepared to engage traditional culture on its own terms. Born into a Shaoxing family of Confucian scholar-officials, he had a traditional education and became a classical scholar of considerable erudition and a writer of poetry in the classical language. Sometimes he displays this learning in his fiction, but there it is always undercut by irony. He grew up at a time when the traditional education system, based on the Confucian classics, was being supplanted by a modern one; and after the early death of his father in 1896, Lu, like so many young Chinese intellectuals of the period, went abroad to study—first at Tokyo and then in 1904 at Sendai, a remote Japanese university where he studied medicine. Because it was successfully modernizing a traditional culture, Japan attracted many young Chinese intellectuals. At the time, the Russians and Japanese were at war in the former Chinese territory of

Manchuria. In a famous anecdote describing his moment of decision to become a writer, Lu tells of seeing a slide of a Chinese prisoner about to be decapitated as a Russian spy. What shocked the young medical student was the apathetic crowd of Chinese onlookers, gathered around to watch the execution. At that moment he decided that it was their dulled spirits rather than their bodies that were in need of healing.

Returning to Tokyo, Lu founded a journal in which he published literary essays and set to work translating Western works of fiction. In 1909 financial difficulties drove him back to China, where he worked as a teacher in Hangzhou. When the Republican revolution came in 1911, he joined the ministry of education, moving north to Peking, where he also taught at various universities. The Republican government was soon at the mercy of the powerful armies competing for regional power, and during this period, perhaps for self-protection, Lu devoted himself to traditional scholarship. One might have expected the revolutionary writer of narrative to write the first history of Chinese fiction, as Lu did; but he also produced an erudite and painstaking textual study of the third-century writer Xi Kang that is still used.

On May 4, 1919, a massive student strike forced the Chinese government not to sign the Versailles Peace Treaty, which would have given Japan effective control over the Chinese province of Shandong. The date gave its name to the May Fourth Movement, a group of young intellectuals who advocated the use of vernacular Chinese in all writing and a repudiation of classical Chinese literature.* Though Lu himself kept out of the May Fourth Movement, it was during this period (1918–26) that he wrote all but one of his short stories. During the last decade of his life, he became a political activist and put his satirical talents at the service of the Left, becoming one of the favorite writers of the Communist leader Mao Zedong.

"Diary of a Madman," Lu's earliest story, takes its title from a work by the Russian novelist Gogol. On one level, it is a parable of the way in which Chinese society devours its members, told under the guise of the discovery of a continuing history of literal cannibalism. But the diarist who makes the "discovery" is indeed, as the title tells us, a madman, and his paranoid raving compels the reader to take the point of view of "sane" society, all the while uncomfortably recognizing that the diarist's claims are true in a figurative sense.

Lu's literary anger at Chinese culture was far from a new phenomenon in Chinese fiction. Traditional novels such as The Travels of Lao Can had often ruthlessly satirized the falseness and corruption of the social order. But in traditional Chinese satirical fiction, as in most premodern satire worldwide, the capacity to make moral judgments presumed a secure sense of what was right (whether or not such a sense agreed with conventional morality). In Lu's satire, however, the very capacity to judge evil is itself corrupted by that evil, a circularity perfectly embodied in the figure of a cannibalistic society that feeds on itself.

"Diary of a Madman" opens with a preface in mannered classical Chinese, giving an account of the discovery of the diary. Such ironic use of classical Chinese to suggest a falsely polite world of social appearances was quite common in traditional Chinese fiction; but its presence usually suggested the alternative possibility of immediate, direct, and genuine language, a language of the heart set against a language of society. The diary that follows the preface is indeed immediate, direct, and genuine, but it is also deluded and twisted. The diarist becomes increasingly convinced that everyone around him wants to eat him; from this growing circle of cannibals observed in the present, the diarist then turns to examine old texts, only to discover

---

*Written Chinese ranges between two extremes: the "classical" language, which is essentially that of the 4th to 3rd centuries B.C.E., and the "vernacular," which attempts to represent the spoken language. Poetry and essays tended to be in classical Chinese, while traditional fiction tended to use the vernacular (although there was also fiction in the classical language). In the modern period, poetry and essays also came to be written in vernacular Chinese. Traditional drama used a mixed style; modern drama, the vernacular.

that the entire history of the culture has been one of secret cannibalism. Beneath society's false politeness, represented by the voice in the preface, he detects a violent bestiality lurking, a hunger to assimilate others, to "eat men."

As the diary progresses, it becomes increasingly clear that the diarist, who sees himself as the potential victim, is no less the mirror of the society he describes, assimilating everyone around him into his own fixed view of the world. His reading of ancient texts to discover evidence of cannibalism is a parody of traditional Confucian scholarship, the distorting discovery of "secret meanings" that only serve to confirm beliefs already held. His is a world entirely closed in on itself, one that survives by feeding on itself and its young, a voracity that gives Lu his famous last line, "Save the children . . ."

PRONOUNCING GLOSSARY

The following list uses common English syllables to provide rough equivalents of selected words whose pronunciation may be unfamiliar to the general reader.

Lu Xun: *loo shoon*

Luosi: *lwoh-suh*

Mao Zedong: *mao dzuh-doong*

Shaoxing: *shao-shing*

Xu Xilin: *shoo shee-lin*

Zhao: *jao*

Zhou Shuren: *joe shoo-ren*

Diary of a Madman[1]

There was once a pair of male siblings whose actual names I beg your indulgence to withhold. Suffice it to say that we three were boon companions during our school years. Subsequently, circumstances contrived to rend us asunder so that we were gradually bereft of knowledge regarding each other's activities.

Not too long ago, however, I chanced to hear that one of them had been hard afflicted with a dread disease. I obtained this intelligence at a time when I happened to be returning to my native haunts and, hence, made so bold as to detour somewhat from my normal course in order to visit them. I encountered but one of the siblings. He apprised me that it had been his younger brother who had suffered the dire illness. By now, however, he had long since become sound and fit again; in fact he had already repaired to other parts to await a substantive official appointment.[2]

The elder brother apologized for having needlessly put me to the inconvenience of this visitation, and concluding his disquisition with a hearty smile, showed me two volumes of diaries which, he assured me, would reveal the nature of his brother's disorder during those fearful days.

As to the lapsus calami[3] *that occur in the course of the diaries, I have altered not a word. Nonetheless, I have changed all the names, despite the fact that their publication would be of no great consequence since they are all humble villagers unknown to the world at large.*

Recorded this 2nd day in the 7th year of the Republic.[4]

1. The first two selections translated by and with notes adapted from William A. Lyell.   2. When there were too many officials for the number of offices to be filled, a man might well be appointed to an office that already had an incumbent. The new appointee would proceed to his post and wait until said office was vacated. Sometimes there would be a number of such appointees waiting their turns.   3. "The fall of the reed [writing instrument]" (literal trans.); hence lapses in writing.   4. The Qing Dynasty was overthrown and the Republic of China was established in 1911; thus it is April 2, 1918. The introduction is written in classical Chinese, whereas the diary entries that follow are all in the colloquial language.

I

Moonlight's really nice tonight. Haven't seen it in over thirty years. Seeing it today, I feel like a new man. I know now that I've been completely out of things for the last three decades or more. But I've still got to be *very* careful. Otherwise, how do you explain those dirty looks the Zhao family's dog gave me?

I've got good reason for my fears.

2

No moonlight at all tonight—something's not quite right. When I made my way out the front gate this morning—ever so carefully—there was something funny about the way the Venerable Old Zhao looked at me: seemed as though he was afraid of me and yet, at the same time, looked as though he had it in for me. There were seven or eight other people who had their heads together whispering about me. They were afraid I'd see them too! All up and down the street people acted the same way. The meanest looking one of all spread his lips out wide and actually *smiled* at me! A shiver ran from the top of my head clear down to the tips of my toes, for I realized that meant they already had their henchmen well deployed, and were ready to strike.

But I wasn't going to let that intimidate *me*. I kept right on walking. There was a group of children up ahead and they were talking about me too. The expressions in their eyes were just like the Venerable Old Zhao's, and their faces were iron gray. I wondered what grudge the children had against me that they were acting this way too. I couldn't contain myself any longer and shouted, "Tell me, tell me!" But they just ran away.

Let's see now, what grudge can there be between me and the Venerable Old Zhao, or the people on the street for that matter? The only thing I can think of is that twenty years ago I trampled the account books kept by Mr. Antiquity, and he was hopping mad about it too. Though the Venerable Old Zhao doesn't know him, he must have gotten wind of it somehow. Probably decided to right the injustice I had done Mr. Antiquity by getting all those people on the street to gang up on me. But the children? Back then they hadn't even come into the world yet. Why should they have given me those funny looks today? Seemed as though they were afraid of me and yet, at the same time, looked as though they would like to do me some harm. That really frightens me. Bewilders me. Hurts me.

I have it! Their fathers and mothers have *taught* them to be like that!

3

I can never get to sleep at night. You really have to study something before you can understand it.

Take all those people: some have worn the cangue on the district magistrate's order, some have had their faces slapped by the gentry, some have had their wives ravished by *yamen*[5] clerks, some have had their dads and moms dunned to death by creditors; and yet, right at the time when all those terrible

---

5. Local government offices. The petty clerks who worked in them were notorious for relying on their proximity to power to bully and abuse the common people. "Cangue": a split board, hinged at one end and locked at the other; holes were cut out to accommodate the prisoner's neck and wrists.

things were taking place, the expressions on their faces were never as frightened, or as savage, as the ones they wore yesterday.

Strangest of all was that woman on the street. She slapped her son and said: "Damn it all, you've got me so riled up I could take a good bite right out of your hide!" She was talking to him, but she was looking at me! I tried, but couldn't conceal a shudder of fright. That's when that ghastly crew of people, with their green faces and protruding fangs, began to roar with laughter. Old Fifth Chen[6] ran up, took me firmly in tow, and dragged me away.

When we got back, the people at home all pretended not to know me. The expressions in their eyes were just like all the others too. After he got me into the study, Old Fifth Chen bolted the door from the outside—just the way you would pen up a chicken or a duck! That made figuring out what was at the bottom of it all harder than ever.

A few days back one of our tenant farmers came in from Wolf Cub Village to report a famine. Told my elder brother the villagers had all ganged up on a "bad" man and beaten him to death. Even gouged out his heart and liver. Fried them up and ate them to bolster their own courage! When I tried to horn in on the conversation, Elder Brother and the tenant farmer both gave me sinister looks. I realized for the first time today that the expression in their eyes was just the same as what I saw in those people on the street.

As I think of it now, a shiver's running from the top of my head clear down to the tips of my toes.

If they're capable of eating people, then who's to say they won't eat *me*?

Don't you see? That woman's words about "taking a good bite," and the laughter of that ghastly crew with their green faces and protruding fangs, and the words of our tenant farmer a few days back—it's perfectly clear to me now that all that talk and all that laughter were really a set of secret signals. Those words were poison! That laughter, a knife! Their teeth are bared and waiting—white and razor sharp! Those people are cannibals!

As I see it myself, though I'm not what you'd call an evil man, still, ever since I trampled the Antiquity family's account books, it's hard to say *what* they'll do. They seem to have something in mind, but I can't begin to guess what. What's more, as soon as they turn against someone, they'll *say* he's evil anyway. I can still remember how it was when Elder Brother was teaching me composition.[7] No matter how good a man was, if I could find a few things wrong with him he would approvingly underline my words; on the other hand, if I made a few allowances for a bad man, he'd say I was "an extraordinary student, an absolute genius." When all is said and done, how can I possibly guess what people like *that* have in mind, especially when they're getting ready for a cannibals' feast?

You have to *really* go into something before you can understand it. I seemed to remember, though not too clearly, that from ancient times on people have often been eaten, and so I started leafing through a history book to look it up. There were no dates in this history, but scrawled this way and that across every page were the words BENEVOLENCE, RIGHTEOUSNESS, and MORALITY. Since I couldn't get to sleep anyway, I read that

6. People were often referred to by their hierarchical position within their extended family.   7. That is, to compose essays in the classical style.

history very carefully for most of the night, and finally I began to make out what was written *between* the lines; the whole volume was filled with a single phrase: EAT PEOPLE!

The words written in the history book, the things the tenant farmer said—all of it began to stare at me with hideous eyes, began to snarl and growl at me from behind bared teeth!

Why sure, *I'm* a person too, and they want to eat *me!*

4

In the morning I sat in the study for a while, calm and collected. Old Fifth Chen brought in some food—vegetables and a steamed fish. The fish's eyes were white and hard. Its mouth was wide open, just like the mouths of those people who wanted to eat human flesh. After I'd taken a few bites, the meat felt so smooth and slippery in my mouth that I couldn't tell whether it was fish or human flesh. I vomited.

"Old Fifth," I said, "tell Elder Brother that it's absolutely stifling in here and that I'd like to take a walk in the garden." He left without answering, but sure enough, after a while the door opened. I didn't even budge—just sat there waiting to see what they'd do to me. I *knew* that they wouldn't be willing to set me loose.

Just as I expected! Elder Brother came in with an old man in tow and walked slowly toward me. There was a savage glint in the old man's eyes. He was afraid I'd see it and kept his head tilted toward the floor while stealing sidewise glances at me over the temples of his glasses. "You seem to be fine today," said Elder Brother.

"You bet!" I replied.

"I've asked Dr. He to come and examine your pulse today."

"He's welcome!" I said. But don't think for one moment that I didn't know the old geezer was an executioner in disguise! Taking my pulse was nothing but a ruse; he wanted to feel my flesh and decide if I was fat enough to butcher yet. He'd probably even get a share of the meat for his troubles. I wasn't a *bit* afraid. Even though I don't eat human flesh, I still have a lot more courage than those who do. I thrust both hands out to see how the old buzzard would make his move. Sitting down, he closed his eyes and felt my pulse[8] for a good long while. Then he froze. Just sat there without moving a muscle for another good long while. Finally he opened his spooky eyes and said: "Don't let your thoughts run away with you. Just convalesce in peace and quiet for a few days and you'll be all right."

Don't let my thoughts run away with me? Convalesce in peace and quiet? If I convalesce till I'm good and fat, they get more to eat, but what do *I* get out of it? How can I possibly be *all right?* What a bunch! All they think about is eating human flesh, and then they go sneaking around, thinking up every which way they can to camouflage their real intentions. They were comical enough to crack *anybody* up. I couldn't hold it in any longer and let out a good loud laugh. Now *that* really felt good. I knew in my heart of hearts that my laughter was *packed* with courage and righteousness. And do you know

8. In Chinese medicine the pulse is taken at both wrists.

what? They were so completely subdued by it that the old man and my elder brother both went pale!

But the more *courage* I had, the more that made them want to eat me so that they could get a little of it for free. The old man walked out. Before he had taken many steps, he lowered his head and told Elder Brother, "To be eaten as soon as possible!" He nodded understandingly. So, Elder Brother, you're in it too! Although that discovery seemed unforeseen, it really wasn't, either. My own elder brother had thrown in with the very people who wanted to eat me!

My elder brother is a cannibal!

I'm brother to a cannibal.

Even though I'm to be the victim of cannibalism, I'm *brother* to a cannibal all the same!

5

During the past few days I've taken a step back in my thinking. Supposing that old man wasn't an executioner in disguise but really was a doctor—well, he'd still be a cannibal just the same. In *Medicinal . . . something or other* by Li Shizhen,[9] the grandfather of the doctor's trade, it says quite clearly that human flesh can be eaten, so how can that old man say that *he's* not a cannibal too?

And as for my own elder brother, I'm not being the least bit unfair to him. When he was explaining the classics to me, he said with his very own tongue that it was all right to *exchange children and eat them*. And then there was another time when he happened to start in on an evil man and said that not only should the man be killed, but his *flesh should be eaten* and *his skin used as a sleeping mat*[1] as well.

When our tenant farmer came in from Wolf Cub Village a few days back and talked about eating a man's heart and liver, Elder Brother didn't seem to see anything out of the way in that either—just kept nodding his head. You can tell from that alone that his present way of thinking is every bit as malicious as it was when I was a child. If it's all right to exchange *children* and eat them, then *anyone* can be exchanged, anyone can be eaten. Back then I just took what he said as explanation of the classics and let it go at that, but now I realize that while he was explaining, the grease of human flesh was smeared all over his lips, and what's more, his mind was filled with plans for further cannibalism.

6

Pitch black out. Can't tell if it's day or night. The Zhao family's dog has started barking again.

Savage as a lion, timid as a rabbit, crafty as a fox . . .

---

9. Lived from 1518 to 1593. *Taxonomy of Medicinal Herbs*, a gigantic work, was the most important pharmacopoeia in traditional China.   1. Both italicized expressions are from the *Zuozhuan* (Zuo commentary to the *Spring and Summer Annals*, a historical work that dates from the 3rd century B.C.E.). In 448 B.C.E., an officer who was exhorting his own side not to surrender is recorded as having said, "When the army of Chu besieged the capital of Song [in 603 B.C.E.], the people exchanged their children and ate them, and used the bones for fuel; and still they would not submit to a covenant at the foot of their walls. For us who have sustained no great loss, to do so is to cast our state away" (trans. James Legge, 5.817). It is also recorded that in 551 B.C.E. an officer boasting of his own prowess before his ruler pointed to two men whom his ruler considered brave and said, "As to those two, they are like beasts, whose flesh I will eat, and then sleep upon their skins" (Legge 5.492).

7

I'm on to the way they operate. They'll never be willing to come straight out and kill me. Besides, they wouldn't dare. They'd be afraid of all the bad luck it might bring down on them if they did. And so, they've gotten everyone into cahoots with them and have set traps all over the place so that I'll do *myself* in. When I think back on the looks of those men and women on the streets a few days ago, coupled with the things my elder brother's been up to recently, I can figure out eight or nine tenths of it. From their point of view, the best thing of all would be for me to take off my belt, fasten it around a beam, and hang myself. They wouldn't be guilty of murder, and yet they'd still get everything they're after. Why, they'd be so beside themselves with joy, they'd sob with laughter. Or if they couldn't get me to do that, maybe they could torment me until I died of fright and worry. Even though I'd come out a bit leaner that way, they'd still nod their heads in approval.

Their kind only know how to eat dead meat. I remember reading in a book somewhere about something called the *hai-yi-na*.[2] Its general appearance is said to be hideous, and the expression in its eyes particularly ugly and malicious. Often eats carrion, too. Even chews the bones to a pulp and swallows them down. Just thinking about it's enough to frighten a man.

The *hai-yi-na* is kin to the wolf. The wolf's a relative of the dog, and just a few days ago the Zhao family dog gave me a funny look. It's easy to see that he's in on it too. How did that old man expect to fool *me* by staring at the floor?

My elder brother's the most pathetic of the whole lot. Since he's a human being too, how can he manage to be so totally without qualms, and what's more, even gang up with them to eat me? Could it be that he's been used to this sort of thing all along and sees nothing wrong with it? Or could it be that he's lost all conscience and just goes ahead and does it even though he knows it's wrong?

If I'm going to curse cannibals, I'll have to start with him. And if I'm going to *convert* cannibals, I'll have to start with him too.

8

Actually, by now even they should long since have understood the truth of this . . .

Someone came in. Couldn't have been more than twenty or so. I wasn't able to make out what he looked like too clearly, but he was all smiles. He nodded at me. His smile didn't look like the real thing either. And so I asked him, "Is this business of eating people right?"

He just kept right on smiling and said, "Except perhaps in a famine year, how could anyone get eaten?" I knew right off that he was one of them—one of those monsters who devour people!

At that point my own courage increased a hundredfold and I asked him, "Is it right?"

"Why are you talking about this kind of thing anyway? You really know how to . . . uh . . . how to pull a fellow's leg. Nice weather we're having."

2. Three Chinese characters are used here for phonetic value only; that is, *hai yi na* is a transliteration into Chinese of the English word *hyena*.

"The weather *is* nice. There's a nice moon out, too, but I *still* want to know if it's right."

He seemed quite put out with me and began to mumble, "It's not—"

"Not right? Then how come they're still eating people?"

"No one's eating anyone."

"No one's *eating* anyone? They're eating people in Wolf Cub Village this very minute. And it's written in all the books, too, written in bright red blood!"

His expression changed and his face went gray like a slab of iron. His eyes started out from their sockets as he said, "Maybe they are, but it's always been that way, it's—"

"Just because it's always been that way, does that make it *right?*"

"I'm not going to discuss such things with you. If you insist on talking about that, then *you're* the one who's in the wrong!"

I leaped from my chair, opened my eyes, and looked around—but the fellow was nowhere to be seen. He was far younger than my elder brother, and yet he was actually one of them. It must be because his mom and dad taught him to be that way. And he's probably already passed it on to his own son. No wonder that even the children give me murderous looks.

9

They want to eat others and at the same time they're afraid that other people are going to eat them. That's why they're always watching each other with such suspicious looks in their eyes.

But all they'd have to do is give up that way of thinking, and then they could travel about, work, eat, and sleep in perfect security. Think how happy they'd feel! It's only a threshold, a pass. But what do they do instead? What is it that these fathers, sons, brothers, husbands, wives, friends, teachers, students, enemies, and even people who don't know each other *really* do? Why they all join together to hold each other back, and talk each other out of it!

That's it! They'd rather *die* than take that one little step.

10

I went to see Elder Brother bright and early. He was standing in the courtyard looking at the sky. I went up behind him so as to cut him off from the door back into the house. In the calmest and friendliest of tones, I said, "Elder Brother, there's something I'd like to tell you."

"Go right ahead." He immediately turned and nodded his head.

"It's only a few words, really, but it's hard to get them out. Elder Brother, way back in the beginning, it's probably the case that primitive peoples *all* ate some human flesh. But later on, because their ways of thinking changed, some gave up the practice and tried their level best to improve themselves; they kept on changing until they became human beings, *real* human beings. But the others didn't; they just kept right on with their cannibalism and stayed at that primitive level.

"You have the same sort of thing with evolution[3] in the animal world. Some reptiles, for instance, changed into fish, and then they evolved into

---

3. Charles Darwin's (1809–1892) theory of evolution was immensely important to Chinese intellectuals during Lu's lifetime and the common coin of much discourse.

birds, then into apes, and then into human beings. But the others didn't want to improve themselves and just kept right on being reptiles down to this very day.

"Think how ashamed those primitive men who have remained cannibals must feel when they stand before *real* human beings. They must feel even more ashamed than reptiles do when confronted with their brethren who have evolved into apes.

"There's an old story from ancient times about Yi Ya boiling his son and serving him up to Jie Zhou.[4] But if the truth be known, people have *always* practiced cannibalism, all the way from the time when Pan Gu separated heaven and earth down to Yi Ya's son, down to Xu Xilin,[5] and on down to the man they killed in Wolf Cub Village. And just last year when they executed a criminal in town, there was even someone with T.B. who dunked a steamed bread roll in his blood and then licked it off.

"When they decided to eat me, by yourself, of course, you couldn't do much to prevent it, but why did you have to go and *join* them? Cannibals are capable of anything! If they're capable of eating me, then they're capable of eating *you* too! Even within their own group, they think nothing of devouring each other. And yet all they'd have to do is turn back—*change*—and then everything would be fine. Even though people may say, 'It's always been like this,' we can still do our best to improve. And we can start today!

"You're going to tell me it can't be done! Elder Brother, I think you're very likely to say that. When that tenant wanted to reduce his rent the day before yesterday, wasn't it you who said it couldn't be done?"

At first he just stood there with a cold smile, but then his eyes took on a murderous gleam. (I had exposed their innermost secrets.) His whole face had gone pale. Some people were standing outside the front gate. The Venerable Old Zhao and his dog were among them. Stealthily peering this way and that, they began to crowd through the open gate. Some I couldn't make out too well—their faces seemed covered with cloth. Some looked the same as ever—smiling green faces with protruding fangs. I could tell at a glance that they all belonged to the same gang, that they were all cannibals. But at the same time I also realized that they didn't all think the same way. Some thought *it's always been like this* and that they really should eat human flesh. Others knew they shouldn't but went right on doing it anyway, always on the lookout for fear someone might give them away. And since that's exactly what I had just done, I knew they must be furious. But they were all *smiling* at me—cold little smiles!

At this point Elder Brother suddenly took on an ugly look and barked, "Get out of here! All of you! What's so funny about a madman?"

4. An early philosophical text, *Guan Zi*, reports that the famous cook Yi Ya boiled his son and served him to his ruler, Duke Huan of Qi (685–643 B.C.E.), because the meat of a human infant was one of the few delicacies the duke had never tasted. Ji and Zhou were the last evil rulers of the Sang (1776–1122 B.C.E.) and Zhou (1122–221 B.C.E.) dynasties. The madman has mixed up some facts here.   5. From Lu's hometown, Shaoxing (1873–1907). After studies in Japan, he returned to China and served as head of the Anhui Police Academy. When a high Qing official, En Ming, participated in a graduation ceremony at the academy, Xu assassinated him, hoping that this would touch off the revolution. After the assassination, he and some of his students at the academy occupied the police armory and managed, for a while, to hold off En Ming's troops. When Xu was finally captured, En Ming's personal body guards dug out his heart and liver and ate them. Pan Gu (literally, "Coiled-up Antiquity") was born out of an egg. As he stood up, he separated heaven and earth. The world as we know it was formed from his body.

Now I'm on to *another* of their tricks: not only are they unwilling to change, but they're already setting me up for their next cannibalistic feast by labeling me a "madman." That way, they'll be able to eat me without getting into the slightest trouble. Some people will even be grateful to them. Wasn't that the very trick used in the case that the tenant reported? Everybody ganged up on a "bad" man and ate him. It's the same old thing.

Old Fifth Chen came in and made straight for me, looking mad as could be. But he wasn't going to shut *me* up! I was going to tell that bunch of cannibals off, and no two ways about it!

"You can change! You can change from the bottom of your hearts! You ought to know that in the future they're not going to allow cannibalism in the world anymore. If you don't change, you're going to devour each other anyway. And even if a lot of you *are* left, a real human being's going to come along and eradicate the lot of you, just like a hunter getting rid of wolves— or reptiles!"

Old Fifth Chen chased them all out. I don't know where Elder Brother disappeared to. Old Fifth talked me into going back to my room.

It was pitch black inside. The beams and rafters started trembling overhead. They shook for a bit, and then they started getting bigger and bigger. They piled themselves up into a great heap on top of my body!

The weight was incredibly heavy and I couldn't even budge—they were trying to kill me! But I knew their weight was an illusion, and I struggled out from under them, my body bathed in sweat. I was still going to have my say. "Change this minute! Change from the bottom of your hearts! You ought to know that in the future they're not going to allow cannibals in the world anymore . . ."

II

The sun doesn't come out. The door doesn't open. It's two meals a day.

I picked up my chopsticks and that got me thinking about Elder Brother. I realized that the reason for my younger sister's death lay entirely with him. I can see her now—such a lovable and helpless little thing, only five at the time. Mother couldn't stop crying, but *he* urged her to stop, probably because he'd eaten sister's flesh himself and hearing mother cry over her like that shamed him! But if he's still capable of feeling shame, then maybe . . .

Younger Sister was eaten by Elder Brother. I have no way of knowing whether Mother knew about it or not.

I think she *did* know, but while she was crying she didn't say anything about it. She probably thought it was all right, too. I can remember once when I was four or five, I was sitting out in the courtyard taking in a cool breeze when Elder Brother told me that when parents are ill, a son, in order to be counted as a really good person, should slice off a piece of his own flesh, boil it, and let them eat it.[6] At the time Mother didn't come out and say there was anything wrong with that. But if it was all right to eat one piece, then there certainly wouldn't be anything wrong with her eating the whole body. And yet when I think back to the way she cried and cried that day, it's enough to break my heart. It's all strange—very, very strange.

---

6. In traditional literature, stories about such gruesome acts of filial piety were not unusual.

12

Can't think about it anymore. I just realized today that I too have muddled around for a good many years in a place where they've been continually eating people for four thousand years. Younger Sister happened to die at just the time when Elder Brother was in charge of the house. Who's to say he didn't slip some of her meat into the food we ate?

Who's to say I didn't eat a few pieces of my younger sister's flesh without knowing it? And now it's my turn . . .

Although I wasn't aware of it in the beginning, now that I *know* I'm someone with four thousand years' experience of cannibalism behind me, how hard it is to look real human beings in the eye!

13

Maybe there are some children around who still haven't eaten human flesh. Save the children . . .

VIRGINIA WOOLF
1882–1941

Virginia Woolf did more than write innovative novels that stand on a par with those by her contemporaries, James Joyce and Marvel Proust; she also explained and exemplified a new kind of prose that she associated with feminine consciousness. Woolf is known for her precise evocations of states of mind—or of mind and body, since she refused to separate the two. She structures her novels according to her protagonists' moments of awareness, and in that way joins Proust and Joyce in their move away from the linear plots and objective descriptions of nineteenth-century realism. In novels like *Mrs. Dalloway* and *The Waves*, blocks of time are rearranged, different points of view juxtaposed, and incomplete perspectives set against each other to create a larger pattern. Alternating modes of narration prevent any single reference point and remind the reader that subjectivity is always at work, in literature and in everyday life. Woolf has an additional role in modernist literary history: she was an ardent feminist who explored—directly in her essays and indirectly in her novels and short stories—the situation of women in society, the construction of gender identity, and the predicament of the woman writer.

She was born Adeline Virginia Stephen on January 25, 1882, one of the four children of the eminent Victorian editor and historian Leslie Stephen and his wife, Julia. The family actively pursued intellectual and artistic interests, and Julia was admired and sketched by some of the most famous Pre-Raphaelite artists. Following the customs of the day, only the sons, Adrian and Thoby, were given formal and university education; Virginia and her sister, Vanessa (the painter Vanessa Bell), were instructed at home by their parents and depended for further education on their father's immense library. Virginia bitterly resented this unequal treatment and the systematic discouragement of women's intellectual development that it implied. Throughout her own work, themes of society's different attitudes toward men and women play a strong role, especially in *A Room of One's Own* (1929) and *Three Guineas* (1938). *A Room of One's Own* examines the history of literature written by women and contains also an impassioned plea that women writers be given conditions equal to those available for men: specifically, the privacy of a room in which to write and economic independence. (At the time Woolf wrote, it was unusual for women to have any money of their own or to be able to devote themselves to a career.) After her mother's death in 1895, Woolf was expected to take over the supervision of the family household, which she did until her father's death in 1904. Of fragile physical health after an attack of whooping cough when she was six, she suffered in addition a nervous breakdown after the death of each parent.

Woolf moved to central London with her sister and brother Adrian after their father's death and took a house in the Bloomsbury district. They soon became the focus of what was later called the Bloomsbury Group, a gathering of writers, artists, and intellectuals impatient with conservative Edwardian society who met regularly to discuss new ideas. It was an eclectic group and included the novelist E. M. Forster, the historian Lytton Strachey, the economist John Maynard Keynes, and the art critics Clive Bell (who married Vanessa) and Roger Fry (who introduced the group to the French painters Édouard Manet and Paul Cézanne). Woolf was not yet writing fiction but contributed reviews to the *Times Literary Supplement,* taught literature and composition at Morley College (an institution with a volunteer faculty that provided educational opportunities for workers), and worked for the adult suffrage movement and a feminist group. In 1912 she married Leonard Woolf, who encouraged her to write and with whom she founded the Hogarth Press in 1917. The press became one of the most respected of the small literary presses and published works by such major authors as T. S. Eliot, Katherine Mansfield, Strachey, Forster, Maxim Gorky, and John Middleton Murry as well as Woolf's own novels and translations of Freud. Over the next two decades she produced her best-known work while coping with frequent bouts of physical and mental illness. Already depressed during World War II and exhausted after the completion of her last novel, *Between the Acts* (1941), she sensed the approach of a serious attack of insanity and the confinement it would entail: in such situations, she was obliged to "rest" and forbidden to read or write. In March 1941, she drowned herself in a river close to her Sussex home.

As a fiction writer, Woolf is best known for her poetic evocations of the way we think and feel. Like Proust and Joyce, she is superbly capable of evoking all the concrete, sensuous details of everyday experience; like them, she explores the structures of consciousness. Her rejection of nineteenth-century realism was not a criticism of the great realist novels like *Madame Bovary;* she turned her attention to more recent and derivative writers. What she really deplored was the microscopic, documentary realism that contemporaries like Arnold Bennett and John Galsworthy drew from the nineteenth-century masters. Their contemporary attitude of scientific objectivity was false, she felt: they claimed to stand outside the scene they described but refused to take into account the fact that there are no neutral observers. Worse, their goal of scientific objectivity often resulted in a mere chronological accumulation of details, the "appalling narrative business of . . . getting from lunch to dinner." Woolf had an explanation for this documentary style: she attributed it to a consciously masculine (or patriarchal) perspective that found security only in logic, order, and the accumulation of knowledge. She proposed, in contrast, a more subjective and, therefore, a more accurate account of experience. Her focus was not so much the object under observation as the way the observer perceived that object: "Let us record the atoms as they fall upon the mind in the order in which they fall, let us trace the pattern, however disconnected and incoherent in appearance, which each sight or incident scores upon the consciousness." Such writing, underwritten by a feminine creative consciousness, would open new avenues for modern literature.

Woolf's writing has been compared with postimpressionist art in the way that it emphasizes the abstract arrangement of perspectives to suggest additional networks of meaning. After two relatively traditional novels, she began to develop a more flexible approach that openly manipulated fictional structure. The continuously developing plot gave way to an organization by juxtaposed points of view; the experience of "real" or chronological time was displaced (although not completely) by a mind ranging ambiguously among its memories; and an intricate pattern of symbolic themes connected otherwise unrelated characters in the same story. All these techniques made new demands on the reader's ability to synthesize and re-create a whole picture. In *Jacob's Room* (1922), a picture of the hero must be assembled from a series of partial points of view. In *The Waves* (1931), the multiple perspective of different characters soliloquizing on their relationship to the dead Percival is broken by ten interludes that together construct an additional, interacting perspective when they describe the passage of a single day from dawn to dusk. Her novels may expand or telescope the sense of time: *Mrs. Dalloway* (1925) focuses apparently on Clarissa Dalloway's preparations for a party that evening but at the same time calls up—at different times, and according to different contexts—her whole life from childhood to her present age of fifty. Problems of identity are a constant concern in these shifting perspectives, and Woolf often portrays the search of unfulfilled personalities for whatever will complete them. Her work is studded with moments of heightened awareness (comparable to Joyce's epiphanies) in which a character suddenly *sees into* a person or situation. With Woolf, this moment is less a matter of mystical insight (as it is with Joyce) than a creation of the mind using all its faculties.

No one can read Woolf without being struck by the importance she gives to the creative imagination. Her major characters display a sensitivity beyond rational logic, and her narrative style celebrates the aesthetic impulse to coordinate many dimensions inside one harmoniously significant whole. Human beings are not complete, Woolf suggests, without exercising their intuitive and imaginative faculties. Like other modernist writers, she is fascinated by the creative process and often makes reference to it in her work. Whether describing the struggles of a painter in *To the Lighthouse* (1927) or of a writer in the story *An Unwritten Novel,* she illustrates the exploratory and the creative work of human imagination. Not all this work is visible in the finished painting or novel: observing, sifting, coordinating, projecting different interpretations and relationships, the mind performs an enormous labor of coordinating consciousness that cannot be captured entirely in any fixed form.

A Room of One's Own itself does not conform to any one fixed form. At once lecture and essay, autobiography and fiction, it originated in a pair of lectures on women and fiction given at Newnham and Girton Colleges (for women) at Cambridge University in 1928. Woolf warns her audience that, instead of defining either women or fiction, she will use "all the liberties and licenses of a novelist" to get at the matter obliquely and leave her auditors to sort out the truth from the "lies [that] will flow from my lips." She will, she claims, retrace the days (that is, the narrator's days) preceding her visit, and lay bare the thought processes leading up to the lecture itself. The lecture, which is now identical with the thought processes leading up to it, is cast in the form of a meditative ramble through various parts of Oxbridge (a compound of Oxford and Cambridge Universities) and London. It includes the famous (and apparently true) anecdote in which she is warned off the university lawn and forbidden entrance to the library because she is a woman; a vivid contrast of the food and living quarters of women and men at Oxbridge; a literary history of English women writers and their socioeconomic situations; a concluding speculation on the androgynous nature of creativity with an exhortation to her young audience to write about the rich yet unrecorded experience of women; and, of course, the central chapters, printed here, that describe her research into definitions of women and offer the celebrated portrait of Judith Shakespeare.

In chapter 2, the narrator heads for the British Museum to locate a comprehensive definition of femininity. To her surprise and mounting anger, she discovers that the thousands of books on the subject written by fascinated men all define women as inferior animals, useful but somewhat alien in nature. Moreover, these same definitions have become prescriptions for generations of young women who learn to see themselves and their place in life accordingly. Raised in poverty and dependence, such women have neither the means nor the self-confidence to write seriously or to become anything other than the Victorian "Angel of the House." What they require, asserts the narrator, is the self-sufficiency brought by an annual income of five hundred pounds. (Woolf had recently inherited such an income.) Chapter 3 pursues similar themes, adding to the five hundred pounds the need for "a room of one's own" and the privacy necessary to follow out an idea. Moving to history, and focusing on the Elizabethan age after a discouraging inspection of Professor Trevelyan's *History of England,* it evokes the career of the "terribly gifted" Judith Shakespeare, William's imaginary sister. Judith has the same literary and dramatic ambitions as her brother, and she too finds her way to London, but she is blocked at each turn by her identity as a woman. Woolf does not belittle William Shakespeare with this contrast; instead, her narrator remarks meaningfully that his work reveals an "incandescent, unimpeded mind."

The bleak portrayals in these chapters are lightened by a great deal of satirical wit and humor, often conveyed by calculated fictional distortion. Woolf uses her novelist's license to subvert and criticize the patriarchal message she describes. The Reading Room of the British Museum, august repository of masculine knowledge about women, is seen as a (bald-foreheaded) dome crowned with the names of famous men. The narrator's scholarly seeming list of feminine characteristics is not only amusingly biased but contradictory and incoherent; it implies that the "masculine" passion for lists and documentation is not the best way to learn about human nature. Professor von X.'s portrait is an open caricature linked to suggestions that his scientific disdain hides repressed fear and anger. *A Room of One's Own* is still famous for its vivid, scathing, and occasionally humorous portrayal of women as objects of male definition and disapproval. Its model of a feminine literary history and its hypothesis of a separate feminine consciousness and manner of writing had substantial influence on writers and literary theory in the latter half of the twentieth century and will continue to do so into the twenty-first.

From A Room of One's Own

CHAPTER 2

The scene, if I may ask you to follow me, was now changed. The leaves were still falling, but in London now, not Oxbridge;[1] and I must ask you to imagine a room, like many thousands, with a window looking across people's hats and vans and motor-cars to other windows, and on the table inside the room a blank sheet of paper on which was written in large letters WOMEN AND FICTION, but no more. The inevitable sequel to lunching and dining at Oxbridge seemed, unfortunately, to be a visit to the British Museum. One must strain off what was personal and accidental in all these impressions and so reach the pure fluid, the essential oil of truth. For that visit to Oxbridge and the luncheon and the dinner had started a swarm of questions. Why did men drink wine and women water? Why was one sex so prosperous and the other so poor? What effect has poverty on fiction? What conditions are necessary for the creation of works of art?—a thousand questions at once suggested themselves. But one needed answers, not questions; and an answer was only

1. A fictional university combining the names of Oxford and Cambridge Universities in England. It was at Cambridge University in October 1928 that Woolf delivered the talks titled "Women and Fiction" that later became *A Room of One's Own.*

to be had by consulting the learned and the unprejudiced, who have removed themselves above the strife of tongue and the confusion of body and issued the result of their reasoning and research in books which are to be found in the British Museum. If truth is not to be found on the shelves of the British Museum, where, I asked myself, picking up a notebook and a pencil, is truth?

Thus provided, thus confident and enquiring, I set out in the pursuit of truth. The day, though not actually wet, was dismal, and the streets in the neighborhood of the Museum were full of open coal-holes, down which sacks were showering; four-wheeled cabs were drawing up and depositing on the pavement corded boxes containing, presumably, the entire wardrobe of some Swiss or Italian family seeking fortune or refuge or some other desirable commodity which is to be found in the boarding-houses of Bloomsbury[2] in the winter. The usual hoarse-voiced men paraded the streets with plants on barrows. Some shouted; others sang. London was like a workshop. London was like a machine. We were all being shot backwards and forwards on this plain foundation to make some pattern. The British Museum was another department of the factory. The swing-doors swung open; and there one stood under the vast dome, as if one were a thought in the huge bald forehead which is so splendidly encircled by a band of famous names.[3] One went to the counter; one took a slip of paper; one opened a volume of the catalogue, and . . . . . the five dots here indicate five separate minutes of stupefaction, wonder and bewilderment. Have you any notion how many books are written about women in the course of one year? Have you any notion how many are written by men? Are you aware that you are, perhaps, the most discussed animal in the universe? Here had I come with a notebook and a pencil proposing to spend a morning reading, supposing that at the end of the morning I should have transferred the truth to my notebook. But I should need to be a herd of elephants, I thought, and a wilderness of spiders, desperately referring to the animals that are reputed longest lived and most multitudinously eyed, to cope with all this. I should need claws of steel and beak of brass even to penetrate the husk. How shall I ever find the grains of truth embedded in all this mass of paper, I asked myself, and in despair began running my eye up and down the long list of titles. Even the names of the books gave me food for thought. Sex and its nature might well attract doctors and biologists; but what was surprising and difficult of explanation was the fact that sex—woman, that is to say—also attracts agreeable essayists, light-fingered novelists, young men who have taken the M.A. degree; men who have taken no degree; men who have no apparent qualification save that they are not women. Some of these books were, on the face of it, frivolous and facetious; but many, on the other hand, were serious and prophetic, moral and hortatory. Merely to read the titles suggested innumerable schoolmasters, innumerable clergymen mounting their platforms and pulpits and holding forth with a loquacity which far exceeded the hour usually allotted to such discourse on this one subject. It was a most strange phenomenon; and apparently—here I consulted the letter M—one confined to

2. A residential and academic borough in London, site of the British Museum and various educational institutions.   3. The names of famous men, including Chaucer, Spenser, Shakespeare, Milton, Pope, Wordsworth, Byron, Carlyle, and Tennyson, are painted in a circle around the dome of the Reading Room at the British Museum.

male sex. Women do not write books about men—a fact that I could not help welcoming with relief, for if I had first to read all that men have written about women, then all that women have written about men, the aloe that flowers once in a hundred years would flower twice before I could set pen to paper. So, making a perfectly arbitrary choice of a dozen volumes or so, I sent my slips of paper to lie in the wire tray, and waited in my stall, among the other seekers for the essential oil of truth.

What could be the reason, then, of this curious disparity, I wondered, drawing cart-wheels on the slips of paper provided by the British taxpayer for other purposes. Why are women, judging from this catalogue, so much more interesting to men than men are to women? A very curious fact it seemed, and my mind wandered to picture the lives of men who spend their time in writing books about women; whether they were old or young, married or unmarried, red-nosed or humpbacked—anyhow, it was flattering, vaguely, to feel oneself the object of such attention, provided that it was not entirely bestowed by the crippled and the infirm—so I pondered until all such frivolous thoughts were ended by an avalanche of books sliding down on to the desk in front of me. Now the trouble began. The student who has been trained in research at Oxbridge has no doubt some method of shepherding his question past all distractions till it runs into its answer as a sheep runs into its pen. The student by my side, for instance, who was copying assiduously from a scientific manual was, I felt sure, extracting pure nuggets of the essential ore every ten minutes or so. His little grunts of satisfaction indicated so much. But if, unfortunately, one has had no training in a university, the question far from being shepherded to its pen flies like a frightened flock hither and thither, helter-skelter, pursued by a whole pack of hounds. Professors, schoolmasters, sociologists, clergymen, novelists, essayists, journalists, men who had no qualification save that they were not women, chased my simple and single question—Why are women poor?—until it became fifty questions; until the fifty questions leapt frantically into midstream and were carried away. Every page in my notebook was scribbled over with notes. To show the state of mind I was in, I will read you a few of them, explaining that the page was headed quite simply, WOMEN AND POVERTY, in block letters; but what followed was something like this:

> *Condition in Middle Ages of,*
> *Habits in the Fiji Islands of,*
> *Worshipped as goddesses by,*
> *Weaker in moral sense than,*
> *Idealism of,*
> *Greater conscientiousness of,*
> *South Sea Islanders, age of puberty among,*
> *Attractiveness of,*
> *Offered as sacrifice to,*
> *Small size of brain of,*
> *Profounder sub-consciousness of,*
> *Less hair on the body of,*
> *Mental, moral and physical inferiority of,*
> *Love of children of,*
> *Greater length of life of,*
> *Weaker muscles of,*

Strength of affections of,
Vanity of,
Higher education of,
Shakespeare's opinion of,
Lord Birkenhead's opinion of,
Dean Inge's opinion of,
La Bruyère's opinion of,
Dr. Johnson's opinion of,
Mr. Oscar Browning's[4] opinion of, . . .

Here I drew breath and added, indeed, in the margin, Why does Samuel Butler[5] say, "Wise men never say what they think of women"? Wise men never say anything else apparently. But, I continued, leaning back in my chair and looking at the vast dome in which I was a single but by now somewhat harassed thought, what is so unfortunate is that wise men never think the same thing about women. Here is Pope:[6]

Most women have no character at all.

And here is La Bruyère:

Les femmes sont extrêmes; elles sont meilleures ou pires que les hommes[7]—

a direct contradiction by keen observers who were contemporary. Are they capable of education or incapable? Napoleon thought them incapable.[8] Dr. Johnson thought the opposite.[9] Have they souls or have they not souls? Some savages say they have none. Others, on the contrary, maintain that women are half divine and worship them on that account.[1] Some sages hold that they are shallower in the brain; others that they are deeper in the consciousness. Goethe honoured them; Mussolini[2] despises them. Wherever one looked men thought about women and thought differently. It was impossible to make head or tail of it all, I decided, glancing with envy at the reader next door who was making the neatest abstracts, headed often with an A or a B or a C, while my own notebook rioted with the wildest scribble of contradictory jottings. It was distressing, it was bewildering, it was humiliating. Truth had run through my fingers. Every drop had escaped.

4. A schoolmaster and later fellow of King's College. Cambridge (1837–1923); anecdotes about his strong opinions (see p. 1227) were published in a 1927 biography. The first Earl of Birkenhead, F. E. Smith (1872–1930), a conservative politician who opposed women's suffrage and praised the domestic "true functions of womanhood." William Ralph Inge (1860–1954), dean of St. Paul's Cathedral in London and a religious writer. Jean de La Bruyère (1645–1696), French moralist and author of satirical *Characters* (1688), imitating the Greek writer Theophrastus. Samuel Johnson (1709–1784), author of moral essays and of the famous *A Dictionary of the English Language* (1747).   5. Satirical author (1835–1902) who wrote *Erewhon* (1872) and *The Way of All Flesh* (1903); his *Notebooks* are the source of this statement. 6. Alexander Pope (1688–1744), translator of Homer and author of "An Essay on Man" (1733–34) and the satirical "The Rape of the Lock" (1712–14).   7. Women are extreme; they are better or worse than men (French).   8. Napoleon wrote: "What we ask of education is not that girls should think, but that they should believe. The weakness of women's brains, the instability of their ideas, the place they will fill in society, their need for perpetual resignation, and for an easy and generous type of charity—all this can only be met by religion" (notes written on May 15, 1807, concerning the establishment of a girl's school at Écouen).   9. " 'Men know that women are an overmatch for them, and therefore they choose the weakest or the most ignorant. If they did not think so, they never could be afraid of women knowing as much as themselves.' . . . Injustice to the sex, I think it but candid to acknowledge that, in a subsequent conversation, he told me that he was serious in what he said."—Boswell, *The Journal of a Tour to the Hebrides* [Woolf's note].   1. "The ancient Germans believed that there was something holy in women, and accordingly consulted them as oracles."—Frazer, *Golden Bough* [Woolf's note].   2. Benito Mussolini (1883–1945), Fascist dictator of Italy between 1922 and 1943. Johann Wolfgang von Goethe (1749–1832), German author of *Faust*. "The eternal feminine draws us along" is the last line of *Faust*, Part 2.

I could not possibly go home, I reflected, and add as a serious contribution to the study of women and fiction that women have less hair on their bodies than men, or that the age of puberty among the South Sea Islanders[3] is nine—or is it ninety?—even the handwriting had become in its distraction indecipherable. It was disgraceful to have nothing more weighty or respectable to show after a whole morning's work. And if I could not grasp the truth about W. (as for brevity's sake I had come to call her) in the past, why bother about W. in the future? It seemed pure waste of time to consult all those gentlemen who specialise in woman and her effect on whatever it may be—politics, children, wages, morality—numerous and learned as they are. One might as well leave their books unopened.

But while I pondered I had unconsciously, in my listlessness, in my desperation, been drawing a picture where I should, like my neighbour, have been writing a conclusion. I had been drawing a face, a figure. It was the face and the figure of Professor von X. engaged in writing his monumental work entitled *The Mental, Moral, and Physical Inferiority of the Female Sex*.[4] He was not in my picture a man attractive to women. He was heavily built; he had a great jowl; to balance that he had very small eyes; he was very red in the face. His expression suggested that he was labouring under some emotion that made him jab his pen on the paper as if he were killing some noxious insect as he wrote, but even when he had killed it that did not satisfy him; he must go on killing it; and even so, some cause for anger and irritation remained. Could it be his wife, I asked, looking at my picture. Was she in love with a cavalry officer? Was the cavalry officer slim and elegant and dressed in astrachan?[5] Had he been laughed at, to adopt the Freudian theory, in his cradle by a pretty girl? For even in his cradle the professor, I thought, could not have been an attractive child. Whatever the reason, the professor was made to look very angry and very ugly in my sketch, as he wrote his great book upon the mental, moral and physical inferiority of women. Drawing pictures was an idle way of finishing an unprofitable morning's work. Yet it is in our idleness, in our dreams, that the submerged truth sometimes comes to the top. A very elementary exercise in psychology, not to be dignified by the name of psycho-analysis, showed me, on looking at my notebook, that the sketch of the angry professor had been made in anger. Anger had snatched my pencil while I dreamt. But what was anger doing there? Interest, confusion, amusement, boredom—all these emotions I could trace and name as they succeeded each other throughout the morning. Had anger, the black snake, been lurking among them? Yes, said the sketch, anger had. It referred me unmistakably to the one book, to the one phrase, which had roused the demon; it was the professor's statement about the mental, moral and physical inferiority of women. My heart had leapt. My cheeks had burnt. I had flushed with anger. There was nothing specially remarkable, however foolish, in that. One does not like to be told that one is naturally the inferior of a little man—I looked at the student next me—who breathes hard, wears a ready-made tie, and has not shaved this fortnight.

3. The native peoples of the islands in the south-central Pacific Ocean were the subject of several anthropological studies in the early 20th century, including Margaret Mead's widely read *Coming of Age in Samoa* (1928). 4. A fictional portrait, probably based on Otto Weininger's *Sex and Character* (1906), that distinguished between male (productive and moral) and female (negative and amoral) characteristics. 5. Curly lambskin.

One has certain foolish vanities. It is only human nature, I reflected, and began drawing cart-wheels and circles over the angry professor's face till he looked like a burning bush or a flaming comet—anyhow, an apparition without human semblance or significance. The professor was nothing now but a faggot burning on the top of Hampstead Heath.[6] Soon my own anger was explained and done with; but curiosity remained. How explain the anger of the professors? Why were they angry? For when it came to analysing the impression left by these books there was always an element of heat. This heat took many forms; it showed itself in satire, in sentiment, in curiosity, in reprobation. But there was another element which was often present and could not immediately be identified. Anger, I called it. But it was anger that had gone underground and mixed itself with all kinds of other emotions. To judge from its odd effects, it was anger disguised and complex, not anger simple and open.

Whatever the reason, all these books,[7] I thought, surveying the pile on the desk, are worthless for my purposes. They were worthless scientifically, that is to say, though humanly they were full of instruction, interest, boredom, and very queer facts about the habits of the Fiji Islanders. They had been written in the red light of emotion and not in the white light of truth. Therefore they must be returned to the central desk and restored each to his own cell in the enormous honeycomb. All that I had retrieved from that morning's work had been the one fact of anger. The professors—I lumped them together thus—were angry. But why, I asked myself, having returned the books, why, I repeated, standing under the colonnade among the pigeons and the prehistoric canoes, why are they angry? And, asking myself this question, I strolled off to find a place for luncheon. What is the real nature of what I call for the moment their anger? I asked. Here was a puzzle that would last all the time that it takes to be served with food in a small restaurant somewhere near the British Museum. Some previous luncher had left the lunch edition of the evening paper on a chair, and, waiting to be served, I began idly reading the headlines. A ribbon of very large letters ran across the page. Somebody had made a big score in South Africa. Lesser ribbons announced that Sir Austen Chamberlain was at Geneva.[8] A meat axe with human hair on it had been found in a cellar. Mr. Justice———commented in the Divorce Courts upon the Shamelessness of Women. Sprinkled about the paper were other pieces of news. A film actress had been lowered from a peak in California and hung suspended in mid-air. The weather was going to be foggy. The most transient visitor to this planet, I thought, who picked up this paper could not fail to be aware, even from this scattered testimony, that England is under the rule of a patriarchy. Nobody in their senses could fail to detect the dominance of the professor. His was the power and the money and the influence. He was the proprietor of the paper and its editor and sub-editor. He was the Foreign Secretary and the Judge. He was the cricketer; he owned the race-horses and the yachts. He was the director of the company that pays two hundred per cent to its shareholders. He left millions

6. A public open space in the village of Hampstead, in London. 7. For example, *Fijian Society, or the Sociology and Psychology of the Fijians* (1921), by Reverend W. Deane, principal of a teachers' training college in Ndávuilévu, Fiji; and *The Hill Tribes of Fiji* (1922), by A. B. Brewster, a colonial functionary, mixed facts with interpretation. The Reverend Deane remarks that "the amount of sexual immorality and promiscuous intercourse during the past forty years is appalling." Fiji is an island in the South Pacific. 8. The site of the League of Nations. Chamberlain was the British Foreign Secretary between 1924 and 1929.

to charities and colleges that were ruled by himself. He suspended the film actress in mid-air. He will decide if the hair on the meat axe is human; he it is who will acquit or convict the murderer, and hang him, or let him go free. With the exception of the fog he seemed to control everything. Yet he was angry. I knew that he was angry by this token. When I read what he wrote about women I thought, not of what he was saying, but of himself. When an arguer argues dispassionately he thinks only of the argument; and the reader cannot help thinking of the argument too. If he had written dispassionately about women, had used indisputable proofs to establish his argument and had shown no trace of wishing that the result should be one thing rather than another, one would not have been angry either. One would have accepted the fact, as one accepts the fact that a pea is green or a canary yellow. So be it, I should have said. But I had been angry because he was angry. Yet it seemed absurd, I thought, turning over the evening paper, that a man with all this power should be angry. Or is anger, I wondered, somehow, the familiar, the attendant sprite on power? Rich people, for example, are often angry because they suspect that the poor want to seize their wealth. The professors, or patriarchs, as it might be more accurate to call them, might be angry for that reason partly, but partly for one that lies a little less obviously on the surface. Possibly they were not "angry" at all; often, indeed, they were admiring, devoted, exemplary in the relations of private life. Possibly when the professor insisted a little too emphatically upon the inferiority of women, he was concerned not with their inferiority, but with his own superiority. That was what he was protecting rather hotheadedly and with too much emphasis, because it was a jewel to him of the rarest price. Life for both sexes—and I looked at them, shouldering their way along the pavement—is arduous, difficult, a perpetual struggle. It calls for gigantic courage and strength. More than anything, perhaps, creatures of illusion as we are, it calls for confidence in oneself. Without self-confidence we are as babes in the cradle. And how can we generate this imponderable quality, which is yet so invaluable, most quickly? By thinking that other people are inferior to oneself. By feeling that one has some innate superiority—it may be wealth, or rank, a straight nose, or the portrait of a grandfather by Romney[9]—for there is no end to the pathetic devices of the human imagination—over other people. Hence the enormous importance to a patriarch who has to conquer, who has to rule, of feeling that great numbers of people, half the human race indeed, are by nature inferior to himself. It must indeed be one of the chief sources of his power. But let me turn the light of this observation on to real life, I thought. Does it help to explain some of those psychological puzzles that one notes in the margin of daily life? Does it explain my astonishment the other day when Z, most humane, most modest of men, taking up some book by Rebecca West[1] and reading a passage in it, exclaimed, "The arrant feminist! She says that men are snobs!" The exclamation, to me so surprising—for why was Miss West an arrant feminist for making a possibly true if uncomplimentary statement about the other sex?—was not merely the cry of wounded vanity; it was a protest against some infringement of his power to believe in himself. Women have

9. George Romney (1734–1802), portrait painter of 18th-century British society.   1. Pseudonym of Cicily Isabel Andrews (1892–1983), British novelist and journalist.

served all these centuries as looking-glasses possessing the magic and delicious power of reflecting the figure of man at twice its natural size. Without that power probably the earth would still be swamp and jungle. The glories of all our wars would be unknown. We should still be scratching the outlines of deer on the remains of mutton bones and bartering flints for sheepskins or whatever simple ornament took our unsophisticated taste. Supermen[2] and Fingers of Destiny would never have existed. The Czar and the Kaiser would never have worn their crowns or lost them. Whatever may be their use in civilized societies, mirrors are essential to all violent and heroic action. That is why Napoleon and Mussolini both insist so emphatically upon the inferiority of women, for if they were not inferior, they would cease to enlarge. That serves to explain in part the necessity that women so often are to men. And it serves to explain how restless they are under her criticism; how impossible it is for her to say to them this book is bad, this picture is feeble, or whatever it may be, without giving far more pain and rousing far more anger than a man would do who gave the same criticism. For if she begins to tell the truth, the figure in the looking-glass shrinks; his fitness for life is diminished. How is he to go on giving judgment, civilising natives, making laws, writing books, dressing up and speechifying at banquets, unless he can see himself at breakfast and at dinner at least twice the size he really is? So I reflected, crumbling my bread and stirring my coffee and now and again looking at the people in the street. The looking-glass vision is of supreme importance because it charges the vitality; it stimulates the nervous system. Take it away and man may die, like the drug fiend deprived of his cocaine. Under the spell of that illusion, I thought, looking out of the window, half the people on the pavement are striding to work. They put on their hats and coats in the morning under its agreeable rays. They start the day confident, braced, believing themselves desired at Miss Smith's tea party; they say to themselves as they go into the room, I am the superior of half the people here, and it is thus that they speak with that self-confidence, that self-assurance, which have had such profound consequences in public life and lead to such curious notes in the margin of the private mind.

But these contributions to the dangerous and fascinating subject of the psychology of the other sex—it is one, I hope, that you will investigate when you have five hundred a year of your own—were interrupted by the necessity of paying the bill. It came to five shillings and ninepence. I gave the waiter a ten-shilling note and he went to bring me change. There was another ten-shilling note in my purse; I noticed it, because it is a fact that still takes my breath away—the power of my purse to breed ten-shilling notes automatically. I open it and there they are. Society gives me chicken and coffee, bed and lodging, in return for a certain number of pieces of paper which were left me by an aunt, for no other reason than that I share her name.

My aunt, Mary Beton, I must tell you, died by a fall from her horse when she was riding out to take the air in Bombay. The news of my legacy reached me one night about the same time that the act was passed that gave votes to women.[3] A solicitor's letter fell into the post-box and when I opened it I

2. Fascist politicians, such as Adolf Hitler (1889–1945) in Germany and Mussolini (1883–1945) in Italy, rationalized their aggressive policies by exploiting and distorting Friedrich Nietzsche's (1844–1900) concept of the *Übermensch*, or superior being (in *Thus Spake Zarathustra*, 1883–85).   3. Women were given the vote in 1918; the voting age was lowered from thirty to twenty-one in 1928.

found that she had left me five hundred pounds[4] a year for ever. Of the two—the vote and the money—the money, I own, seemed infinitely the more important. Before that I had made my living by cadging odd jobs from newspapers, by reporting a donkey show here or a wedding there; I had earned a few pounds by addressing envelopes, reading to old ladies, making artificial flowers, teaching the alphabet to small children in a kindergarten. Such were the chief occupations that were open to women before 1918. I need not, I am afraid, describe in any detail the hardness of the work, for you know perhaps women who have done it; nor the difficulty of living on the money when it was earned, for you may have tried. But what still remains with me as a worse infliction than either was the poison of fear and bitterness which those days bred in me. To begin with, always to be doing work that one did not wish to do, and to do it like a slave, flattering and fawning, not always necessarily perhaps, but it seemed necessary and the stakes were too great to run risks; and then the thought of that one gift which it was death to hide[5]—a small one but dear to the possessor—perishing and with it myself, my soul—all this became like a rust eating away the bloom of the spring, destroying the tree at its hearts. However, as I say, my aunt died; and whenever I change a ten-shilling note a little of that rust and corrosion is rubbed off; fear and bitterness go. Indeed, I thought, slipping the silver into my purse, it is remarkable, remembering the bitterness of those days, what a change of temper a fixed income will bring about. No force in the world can take from me my five hundred pounds. Food, house and clothing are mine for ever. Therefore not merely do effort and labour cease, but also hatred and bitterness. I need not hate any man; he cannot hurt me. I need not flatter any man; he has nothing to give me. So imperceptibly I found myself adopting a new attitude towards the other half of the human race. It was absurd to blame any class or any sex, as a whole. Great bodies of people are never responsible for what they do. They are driven by instincts which are not within their control. They too, the patriarchs, the professors, had endless difficulties, terrible drawbacks to contend with. Their education had been in some ways as faulty as my own. It had bred in them defects as great. True, they had money and power, but only at the cost of harbouring in their breasts an eagle, a vulture, for ever tearing the liver out and plucking at the lungs—the instinct for possession, the rage for acquisition which drives them to desire other people's fields and goods perpetually; to make frontiers and flags; battleships and poison gas; to offer up their own lives and their children's lives. Walk through the Admiralty Arch[6] (I had reached that monument), or any other avenue given up to trophies and cannon, and reflect upon the kind of glory celebrated there. Or watch in the spring sunshine the stockbroker and the great barrister going indoors to make money and more money and more money when it is a fact that five hundred pounds a year will keep one alive in the sunshine. These are unpleasant instincts to harbour, I reflected. They are bred of the conditions of life; of the lack of civilisation, I thought, looking at the statue of the

---

4. Roughly twenty-four thousand dollars today, calculating inflation and exchange rates between the pound and the dollar in 1928 and 2008. Such calculations are ultimately unreliable, however, since the relative cost of specific items (such as bread or rent) varies.   5. From "When I Consider How My Light Is Spent" by John Milton (1608–1673): "And that one talent which is death to hide, / Lodged with me useless."   6. A triple arch in Trafalgar Square (London) at the entrance to the Mall, erected in 1910.

Duke of Cambridge,[7] and in particular at the feathers in his cocked hat, with a fixity that they have scarcely ever received before. And, as I realised these drawbacks, by degrees fear and bitterness modified themselves into pity and toleration; and then in a year or two, pity and toleration went, and the greatest release of all came, which is freedom to think of things in themselves. That building, for example, do I like it or not? Is that picture beautiful or not? Is that in my opinion a good book or a bad? Indeed my aunt's legacy unveiled the sky to me, and substituted for the large and imposing figure of a gentleman, which Milton recommended for my perpetual adoration, a view of the open sky.

So thinking, so speculating, I found my way back to my house by the river. Lamps were being lit and an indescribable change had come over London since the morning hour. It was as if the great machine after labouring all day had made with our help a few yards of something very exciting and beautiful—a fiery fabric flashing with red eyes, a tawny monster roaring with hot breath. Even the wind seemed flung like a flag as it lashed the houses and rattled the hoardings.

In my little street, however, domesticity prevailed. The house painter was descending his ladder; the nursemaid was wheeling the perambulator carefully in and out back to nursery tea; the coal-heaver was folding his empty sacks on top of each other; the woman who keeps the green-grocer's shop was adding up the day's takings with her hands in red mittens. But so engrossed was I with the problem you have laid upon my shoulders that I could not see even these usual sights without referring them to one centre. I thought how much harder it is now than it must have been even a century ago to say which of these employments is the higher, the more necessary. Is it better to be a coal-heaver or a nursemaid; is the charwoman who has brought up eight children of less value to the world than the barrister who has made a hundred thousand pounds? It is useless to ask such questions; for nobody can answer them. Not only do the comparative values of charwoman and lawyers rise and fall from decade to decade, but we have no rods with which to measure them even as they are at the moment. I had been foolish to ask my professor to furnish me with "indisputable proofs" of this or that in his argument about women. Even if one could state the value of any one gift at the moment, those values will change; in a century's time very possibly they will have changed completely. Moreover, in a hundred years, I thought, reaching my own doorstep, women will have ceased to be the protected sex. Logically they will take part in all the activities and exertions that were once denied them. The nursemaid will heave coal. The shop-woman will drive an engine. All assumptions founded on the facts observed when women were the protected sex will have disappeared—as, for example (here a squad of soldiers marched down the street), that women and clergymen and gardeners live longer than other people. Remove that protection, expose them to the same exertions and activities, make them soldiers and sailors and engine-drivers and dock labourers, and will not women die off so much younger, so much quicker, than men that one will say, "I saw a woman today," as one used to say, "I saw an aeroplane." Anything may happen when

7. An equestrian statue of the second Duke of Cambridge (1819–1904), cousin of Queen Victoria, in the full dress uniform of a field marshal.

womanhood has ceased to be a protected occupation, I thought, opening the door. But what bearing has all this upon the subject of my paper, Women and Fiction? I asked, going indoors.

CHAPTER 3

It was disappointing not to have brought back in the evening some important statement, some authentic fact. Women are poorer than men because—this or that. Perhaps now it would be better to give up seeking for the truth, and receiving on one's head an avalanche of opinion hot as lava, discoloured as dish-water. It would be better to draw the curtains; to shut out distractions; to light the lamp; to narrow the enquiry and to ask the historian, who records not opinions but facts, to describe under what conditions women lived, not throughout the ages, but in England, say in the time of Elizabeth.[8]

For it is a perennial puzzle why no woman wrote a word of that extraordinary literature when every other man, it seemed, was capable of song or sonnet. What were the conditions in which women lived, I asked myself; for fiction, imaginative work that is, is not dropped like a pebble upon the ground, as science may be; fiction is like a spider's web, attached ever so lightly perhaps, but still attached to life at all four corners. Often the attachment is scarcely perceptible; Shakespeare's plays, for instance, seem to hang there complete by themselves. But when the web is pulled askew, hooked up at the edge, torn in the middle, one remembers that these webs are not spun in mid-air by incorporeal creatures, but are the work of suffering human beings, and are attached to grossly material things, like health and money and the houses we live in.

I went, therefore, to the shelf where the histories stand and took down one of the latest, Professor Trevelyan's *History of England*.[9] Once more I looked up Women, found "position of," and turned to the pages indicated. "Wife-beating," I read, "was a recognised right of man, and was practised without shame by high as well as low. . . . Similarly," the historian goes on, "the daughter who refused to marry the gentleman of her parents' choice was liable to be locked up, beaten and flung about the room, without any shock being inflicted on public opinion. Marriage was not an affair of personal affection, but of family avarice, particularly in the 'chivalrous' upper classes. . . . Betrothal often took place while one or both of the parties was in the cradle, and marriage when they were scarcely out of the nurses' charge." That was about 1470, soon after Chaucer's[1] time. The next reference to the position of women is some two hundred years later, in the time of the Stuarts.[2] "It was still the exception for women of the upper and middle class to choose their own husbands, and when the husband had been assigned, he was lord and master, so far at least as law and custom could make him. Yet even so," Professor Trevelyan concludes, "neither Shakespeare's women nor those of authentic seventeenth-century memoirs, like the Verneys and the Hutchinsons,[3] seem wanting in personality and charac-

8. Queen of England from 1558 to 1603.   9. Published in London in 1926. References are to pages 260–61 and, later, to pages 436–37.   1. Geoffrey Chaucer (1340?–1400), author of *The Canterbury Tales* (1390–1400).   2. The British royal house from 1603 to 1714 (except for the Commonwealth interregnum of 1649–60).   3. Lucy Hutchinson recounted her husband's life in *Memoirs of the Life of Colonel Hutchinson* (1806). F. P. Verney compiled *The Memoirs of the Verney Family during the Seventeenth Century* (1892–99).

ter." Certainly, if we consider it, Cleopatra must have had a way with her; Lady Macbeth,[4] one would suppose, had a will of her own; Rosalind, one might conclude, was an attractive girl. Professor Trevelyan is speaking no more than the truth when he remarks that Shakespeare's women do not seem wanting in personality and character. Not being a historian, one might go even further and say that women have burnt like beacons in all the works of all the poets from the beginning of time—Clytemnestra, Antigone, Cleopatra, Lady Macbeth, Phèdre, Cressida, Rosalind, Desdemona, the Duchess of Malfi,[5] among the dramatists; then among the prose writers: Millamant, Clarissa, Becky Sharp, Anna Karenina, Emma Bovary, Madame de Guermantes[6]—the names flock to mind, nor do they recall women "lacking in personality and character." Indeed, if woman had no existence save in the fiction written by men, one would imagine her a person of the utmost importance; very various; heroic and mean; splendid and sordid; infinitely beautiful and hideous in the extreme; as great as a man, some think even greater.[7] But this is woman in fiction. In fact, as Professor Trevelyan points out, she was locked up, beaten and flung about the room.

A very queer, composite being thus emerges. Imaginatively she is of the highest importance; practically she is completely insignificant. She pervades poetry from cover to cover; she is all but absent from history. She dominates the lives of kings and conquerors in fiction; in fact she was the slave of any boy whose parents forced a ring upon her finger. Some of the most inspired words, some of the most profound thoughts in literature fall from her lips; in real life she could hardly read, could scarcely spell, and was the property of her husband.

It was certainly an odd monster that one made up by reading the historians first and the poets afterwards—a worm winged like an eagle; the spirit of life and beauty in a kitchen chopping up suet. But these monsters, however amusing to the imagination, have no existence in fact. What one must do to bring her to life was to think poetically and prosaically at one and the same moment, thus keeping in touch with fact—that she is Mrs. Martin, aged thirty-six, dressed in blue, wearing a black hat and brown shoes; but not losing sight of fiction either—that she is a vessel in which all sorts of spirits and forces are coursing and flashing perpetually. The moment, however, that

4. Heroine of Shakespeare's *Macbeth*. Cleopatra (69–30 B.C.E.), queen of Egypt and heroine of Shakespeare's *Antony and Cleopatra*. 5. Doomed heroine of John Webster's *The Duchess of Malfi* (ca. 1613). Clytemnestra is the heroine of Aeschylus's *Agamemnon* (458 B.C.E.). Antigone is the eponymous heroine of a 442 B.C.E. play by Sophocles. Phèdre is the heroine of Jean Racine's *Phèdre* (1677). Cressida, Rosalind, and Desdemona are heroines of Shakespeare's *Troilus and Cressida, As You Like It*, and *Othello*, respectively. 6. A character in Marcel Proust's *Remembrance of Things Past (The Guermantes Way*, 1920–21). Millamant is the heroine of William Congreve's satirical comedy *The Way of the World* (1700). Clarissa is the eponymous heroine of Samuel Richardson's seven-volume epistolary novel (1747–48). Becky Sharp appears in William Thackeray's *Vanity Fair* (1847–48). Anna Karenina is the title character in a Leo Tolstoy novel (1875–77). Emma Bovary is the heroine of Gustave Flaubert's *Madame Bovary* (1856). 7. "It remains a strange and almost inexplicable fact that in Athena's city, where women were kept in almost Oriental suppression as odalisques or drudges, the stage should yet have produced figures like Clytemnestra and Cassandra, Atossa and Antigone, Phèdre and Medea, and all the other heroines who dominate play after play of the 'misogynist' Euripides. But the paradox of this world where in real life a respectable woman could hardly show her face alone in the street, and yet on the stage woman equals or surpasses man, has never been satisfactorily explained. In modern tragedy the same predominance exists. At all events, a very cursory survey of Shakespeare's work (similarly with Webster, though not with Marlowe or Jonson) suffices to reveal how this dominance, this initiative of women, persists from Rosalind to Lady Macbeth. So too in Racine; six of his tragedies bear their heroines' names; and what male characters of his shall we set against Hermione and Andromaque, Bérénice and Roxane, Phèdre and Athalie? So again with Ibsen; what men shall we match with Solveig and Nora, Hedda and Hilda Wangel and Rebecca West?"—F. L. Lucas, *Tragedy*, pp. 114–15 [Woolf's note].

one tries this method with the Elizabethan woman, one branch of illumination fails; one is held up by the scarcity of facts. One knows nothing detailed, nothing perfectly true and substantial about her. History scarcely mentions her. And I turned to Professor Trevelyan again to see what history meant to him. I found by looking at his chapter headings that it meant—

"The Manor Court and the Methods of Open-field Agriculture . . . The Cistercians and Sheep-farming . . . The Crusades . . . The University . . . The House of Commons . . . The Hundred Years' War . . . The Wars of the Roses . . . The Renaissance Scholars . . . The Dissolution of the Monasteries . . . Agrarian and Religious Strife . . . The Origin of English Sea-power . . . The Armada . . ." and so on. Occasionally an individual woman is mentioned, an Elizabeth, or a Mary; a queen or a great lady. But by no possible means could middle-class women with nothing but brains and character at their command have taken part in any one of the great movements which, brought together, constitute the historian's view of the past. Nor shall we find her in any collection of anecdotes. Aubrey[8] hardly mentions her. She never writes her own life and scarcely keeps a diary; there are only a handful of her letters in existence. She left no plays or poems by which we can judge her. What one wants, I thought—and why does not some brilliant student at Newnham or Girton[9] supply it?—is a mass of information; at what age did she marry; how many children had she as a rule; what was her house like; had she a room to herself; did she do the cooking; would she be likely to have a servant? All these facts lie somewhere, presumably, in parish registers and account books; the life of the average Elizabethan woman must be scattered about somewhere, could one collect it and make a book of it. It would be ambitious beyond my daring, I thought, looking about the shelves for books that were not there, to suggest to the students of those famous colleges that they should re-write history, though I own that it often seems a little queer as it is, unreal, lop-sided; but why should they not add a supplement to history? calling it, of course, by some inconspicuous name so that women might figure there without impropriety? For one often catches a glimpse of them in the lives of the great, whisking away into the background, concealing, I sometimes think, a wink, a laugh, perhaps a tear. And, after all, we have lives enough of Jane Austen; it scarcely seems necessary to consider again the influence of the tragedies of Joanna Baillie upon the poetry of Edgar Allan Poe; as for myself, I should not mind if the homes and haunts of Mary Russell Mitford[1] were closed to the public for a century at least. But what I find deplorable, I continued, looking about the bookshelves again, is that nothing is known about women before the eighteenth century. I have no model in my mind to turn about this way and that. Here am I asking why women did not write poetry in the Elizabethan age, and I am not sure how they were educated; whether they were taught to write; whether they had sitting-rooms to themselves; how many women had children before they were twenty-one; what, in short, they did from eight in the morning till eight at night. They had no money evidently;

8. John Aubrey (1626–1697), author of *Brief Lives*, which includes sketches of his famous contemporaries. 9. Woolf delivered her lectures at Newnham and Girton Colleges for women, which had become part of Cambridge University in 1880 and 1873, respectively. 1. Dramatist, poet, and essayist (1787–1855), author of *Rienzi*, a tragedy in blank verse (1828), and *Our Village* (1832), sketches of country life. Austen (1775–1817), author of *Pride and Prejudice* (1813) and other novels. Baillie (1762–1851), poet and dramatist whose *Plays on the Passions* (1798–1812) were famous in her day.

according to Professor Trevelyan they were married whether they liked it or not before they were out of the nursery, at fifteen or sixteen very likely. It would have been extremely odd, even upon this showing, had one of them suddenly written the plays of Shakespeare, I concluded, and I thought of that old gentleman, who is dead now, but was a bishop, I think, who declared that it was impossible for any woman, past, present, or to come, to have the genius of Shakespeare. He wrote to the papers about it. He also told a lady who applied to him for information that cats do not as a matter of fact go to heaven, though they have, he added, souls of a sort. How much thinking those old gentlemen used to save one! How the borders of ignorance shrank back at their approach! Cats do not go to heaven. Women cannot write the plays of Shakespeare.

Be that as it may, I could not help thinking, as I looked at the works of Shakespeare on the shelf, that the bishop was right at least in this; it would have been impossible, completely and entirely, for any woman to have written the plays of Shakespeare in the age of Shakespeare. Let me imagine, since facts are so hard to come by, what would have happened had Shakespeare had a wonderfully gifted sister, called Judith,[2] let us say. Shakespeare himself went, very probably—his mother was an heiress—to the grammar school, where he may have learnt Latin—Ovid, Virgil and Horace[3]—and the elements of grammar and logic. He was, it is well known, a wild boy who poached rabbits, perhaps shot a deer, and had, rather sooner than he should have done, to marry a woman in the neighbourhood, who bore him a child rather quicker than was right. That escapade sent him to seek his fortune in London. He had, it seemed, a taste for the theatre; he began by holding horses at the stage door. Very soon he got work in the theatre, became a successful actor, and lived at the hub of the universe, meeting everybody, knowing everybody, practising his art on the boards, exercising his wits in the streets, and even getting access to the palace of the queen. Meanwhile his extraordinarily gifted sister, let us suppose, remained at home. She was as adventurous, as imaginative, as agog to see the world as he was. But she was not sent to school. She had no chance of learning grammar and logic, let alone of reading Horace and Virgil. She picked up a book now and then, one of her brother's perhaps, and read a few pages. But then her parents came in and told her to mend the stockings or mind the stew and not moon about with books and papers. They would have spoken sharply but kindly, for they were substantial people who knew the conditions of life for a woman and loved their daughter—indeed, more likely than not she was the apple of her father's eye. Perhaps she scribbled some pages up in an apple loft on the sly, but was careful to hide them or set fire to them. Soon, however, before she was out of her teens, she was to be betrothed to the son of a neighbouring wool-stapler. She cried out that marriage was hateful to her, and for that she was severely beaten by her father. Then he ceased to scold her. He begged her instead not to hurt him, not to shame him in this matter of her marriage. He would give her a chain of beads or a fine petticoat, he said; and there were tears in his eyes. How could she disobey him? How could she break his

2. The name of Shakespeare's younger daughter.   3. Roman authors. Publius Ovidius Naso (43 B.C.E.– 17 C.E.), author of the *Metamorphoses*. Publius Vergilius Maro (70–19 B.C.E.), author of the *Aeneid*. Quintus Horatius Flaccus (65–8 B.C.E.), author of *Odes* and satires.

heart? The force of her own gift alone drove her to it. She made up a small parcel of her belongings, let herself down by a rope one summer's night and took the road to London. She was not seventeen. The birds that sang in the hedge were not more musical than she was. She had the quickest fancy, a gift like her brother's, for the tune of words. Like him, she had a taste for the theatre. She stood at the stage door; she wanted to act, she said. Men laughed in her face. The manager—a fat, loose-lipped man—guffawed. He bellowed something about poodles dancing and women acting—no woman, he said, could possibly be an actress. He hinted—you can imagine what. She could get no training in her craft. Could she even seek her dinner in a tavern or roam the streets at midnight? Yet her genius was for fiction and lusted to feed abundantly upon the lives of men and women and the study of their ways. At last—for she was very young, oddly like Shakespeare the poet in her face, with the same grey eyes and rounded brows—at last Nick Greene[4] the actor-manager took pity on her; she found herself with child by that gentleman and so—who shall measure the heat and violence of the poet's heart when caught and tangled in a woman's body?—killed herself one winter's night and lies buried at some cross-roads where the omnibuses now stop outside the Elephant and Castle.[5]

That, more or less, is how the story would run, I think, if a woman in Shakespeare's day had had Shakespeare's genius. But for my part, I agree with the deceased bishop, if such he was—it is unthinkable that any woman in Shakespeare's day should have had Shakespeare's genius. For genius like Shakespeare's is not born among labouring, uneducated, servile people. It was not born in England among the Saxons and the Britons. It is not born today among the working classes. How, then, could it have been born among women whose work began, according to Professor Trevelyan, almost before they were out of the nursery, who were forced to it by their parents and held to it by all the power of law and custom? Yet genius of a sort must have existed among women as it must have existed among the working classes. Now and again an Emily Brontë or a Robert Burns[6] blazes out and proves its presence. But certainly it never got itself on to paper. When, however, one reads of a witch being ducked, of a woman possessed by devils, of a wise woman selling herbs, or even of a very remarkable man who had a mother, then I think we are on the track of a lost novelist, a suppressed poet, of some mute and inglorious[7] Jane Austen, some Emily Brontë who dashed her brains out on the moor or mopped and mowed about the highways crazed with the torture that her gift had put her to. Indeed, I would venture to guess that Anon, who wrote so many poems without signing them, was often a woman. It was a woman Edward Fitzgerald,[8] I think, suggested who made the ballads and the folk-songs, crooning them to her children, beguiling her spinning with them, or the length of the winter's night.

This may be true or it may be false—who can say?—but what is true in it, so it seemed to me, reviewing the story of Shakespeare's sister as I had made it, is that any woman born with a great gift in the sixteenth century would

4. A fictional character based on Shakespeare's contemporary Robert Greene (1558–1592) and appearing in Woolf's *Orlando*.   5. A popular London pub.   6. Scottish poet (1759–1796). Brontë (1818–1848), author of *Wuthering Heights*.   7. A reference to Thomas Grey's line in "Elegy Written in a Country Churchyard" (1751): "Some mute inglorious Milton here may rest."   8. British author (1809–1883), known for his translation from the Persian of the *Rubáiyát of Omar Khayyám* (1859).

certainly have gone crazed, shot herself, or ended her days in some lonely cottage outside the village, half witch, half wizard, feared and mocked at. For it needs little skill in psychology to be sure that a highly gifted girl who had tried to use her gift for poetry would have been so thwarted and hindered by other people, so tortured and pulled asunder by her own contrary instincts, that she must have lost her health and sanity to a certainty. No girl could have walked to London and stood at a stage door and forced her way into the presence of actor-managers without doing herself a violence and suffering an anguish which may have been irrational—for chastity may be a fetish invented by certain societies for unknown reasons—but were none the less inevitable. Chastity had then, it has even now, a religious importance in a woman's life, and has so wrapped itself round with nerves and instincts that to cut it free and bring it to the light of day demands courage of the rarest. To have lived a free life in London in the sixteenth century would have meant for a woman who was poet and playwright a nervous stress and dilemma which might well have killed her. Had she survived, whatever she had written would have been twisted and deformed, issuing from a strained and morbid imagination. And undoubtedly, I thought, looking at the shelf where there are no plays by women, her work would have gone unsigned. That refuge she would have sought certainly. It was the relic of the sense of chastity that dictated anonymity to women even so late as the nineteenth century. Currer Bell, George Eliot, George Sand,[9] all the victims of inner strife as their writings prove, sought ineffectively to veil themselves by using the name of a man. Thus they did homage to the convention, which if not implanted by the other sex was liberally encouraged by them (the chief glory of a woman is not to be talked of, said Pericles,[1] himself a much-talked-of man), that publicity in women is detestable. Anonymity runs in their blood. The desire to be veiled still possesses them. They are not even now as concerned about the health of their fame as men are, and, speaking generally, will pass a tombstone or a signpost without feeling an irresistible desire to cut their names on it, as Alf, Bert or Chas. must do in obedience to their instinct, which murmurs if it sees a fine woman go by, or even a dog, Ce chien est à moi.[2] And, of course, it may not be a dog, I thought, remembering Parliament Square, the Sièges Allée[3] and other avenues; it may be a piece of land or a man with curly black hair. It is one of the great advantages of being a woman that one can pass even a very fine negress without wishing to make an Englishwoman of her.

That woman, then, who was born with a gift of poetry in the sixteenth century, was an unhappy woman, a woman at strife against herself. All the conditions of her life, all her own instincts, were hostile to the state of mind which is needed to set free whatever is in the brain. But what is the state of mind that is most propitious to the act of creation, I asked. Can one come by any notion of the state that furthers and makes possible that strange activity? Here I opened the volume containing the Tragedies of Shakespeare. What

9. Pseudonyms of Charlotte Brontë; Mary Ann Evans (1819–1880), author of *Middlemarch* (1871–72); and Lucile-Aurore Dupin (1804–1876), author of *Lélia* (1833), respectively.   1. From the Greek leader Pericles' funeral oration (431 B.C.E.), as reported in Thucydides' history of the Peloponnesian War (2.35–46).   2. This dog is mine (French); from the philosopher Blaise Pascal's *Thoughts* (1657–58). He uses an anecdote about poor children to illustrate a universal impulse to assert property claims.   3. An avenue in Berlin containing statues of Hohenzollern rulers. Parliament Square is in London next to the Houses of Parliament and Westminster Abbey.

was Shakespeare's state of mind, for instance, when he wrote *Lear* and *Antony and Cleopatra*? It was certainly the state of mind most favourable to poetry that there has ever existed. But Shakespeare himself said nothing about it. We only know casually and by chance that he "never blotted a line."[4] Nothing indeed was ever said by the artist himself about his state of mind until the eighteenth century perhaps. Rousseau[5] perhaps began it. At any rate, by the nineteenth century self-consciousness had developed so far that it was the habit for men of letters to describe their minds in confessions and autobiographies. Their lives also were written, and their letters were printed after their deaths. Thus, though we do not know what Shakespeare went through when he wrote *Lear*, we do know what Carlyle went through when he wrote the *French Revolution*; what Flaubert went through when he wrote *Madame Bovary*; what Keats[6] was going through when he tried to write poetry against the coming of death and the indifference of the world.

And one gathers from this enormous modern literature of confession and self-analysis that to write a work of genius is almost always a feat of prodigious difficulty. Everything is against the likelihood that it will come from the writer's mind whole and entire. Generally material circumstances are against it. Dogs will bark; people will interrupt; money must be made; health will break down. Further, accentuating all these difficulties and making them harder to bear is the world's notorious indifference. It does not ask people to write poems and novels and histories; it does not need them. It does not care whether Flaubert finds the right word or whether Carlyle scrupulously verifies this or that fact. Naturally, it will not pay for what it does not want. And so the writer, Keats, Flaubert, Carlyle, suffers, especially in the creative years of youth, every form of distraction and discouragement. A curse, a cry of agony, rises from those books of analysis and confession. "Mighty poets in their misery dead"—that is the burden of their song. If anything comes through in spite of all this, it is a miracle, and probably no book is born entire and uncrippled as it was conceived.

But for women, I thought, looking at the empty shelves, these difficulties were infinitely more formidable. In the first place, to have a room of her own, let alone a quiet room or a sound-proof room, was out of the question, unless her parents were exceptionally rich or very noble, even up to the beginning of the nineteenth century. Since her pin money, which depended on the good will of her father, was only enough to keep her clothed, she was debarred from such alleviations as came even to Keats or Tennyson[7] or Carlyle, all poor men, from a walking tour, a little journey to France, from the separate lodging which, even if it were miserable enough, sheltered them from the claims and tyrannies of their families. Such material difficulties were formidable; but much worse were the immaterial. The indifference of the world which Keats and Flaubert and other men of genius have found so hard to bear was in her case not indifference but hostility. The world did not say to her as it said to them, Write if you choose; it makes no difference to me. The world said with a guffaw, Write? What's the good of your writing?

---

4. Ben Jonson's (1572–1637) description of Shakespeare.   5. Jean-Jacques Rousseau (1712–1778), French author of the *Confessions* (1781).   6. John Keats (1795–1821), British poet. Thomas Carlyle (1795–1881), essayist and historian, translator of Goethe and author of *The French Revolution* (1837). 7. Alfred, Lord Tennyson (1809–1892), British poet.

Here the psychologists of Newnham and Girton might come to our help, I thought, looking again at the blank spaces on the shelves. For surely it is time that the effect of discouragement upon the mind of the artist should be measured, as I have seen a dairy company measure the effect of ordinary milk and Grade A milk upon the body of the rat. They set two rats in cages side by side, and of the two one was furtive, timid and small, and the other was glossy, bold and big. Now what food do we feed women as artists upon? I asked, remembering, I suppose, that dinner of prunes and custard. To answer that question I had only to open the evening paper and to read that Lord Birkenhead is of opinion—but really I am not going to trouble to copy out Lord Birkenhead's opinion upon the writing of women. What Dean Inge says I will leave in peace. The Harley Street specialist may be allowed to rouse the echoes of Harley Street with his vociferations without raising a hair on my head. I will quote, however, Mr. Oscar Browning, because Mr. Oscar Browning was a great figure in Cambridge at one time, and used to examine the students at Girton and Newnham. Mr. Oscar Browning was wont to declare "that the impression left on his mind, after looking over any set of examination papers, was that, irrespective of the marks he might give, the best woman was intellectually the inferior of the worst man." After saying that Mr. Browning went back to his rooms—and it is this sequel that endears him and makes him a human figure of some bulk and majesty—he went back to his rooms and found a stable-boy lying on the sofa—"a mere skeleton, his cheeks were cavernous and sallow, his teeth were black, and he did not appear to have the full use of his limbs. . . . 'That's Arthur' [said Mr. Browning]. 'He's a dear boy really and most high-minded.'" The two pictures always seem to me to complete each other. And happily in this age of biography the two pictures often do complete each other, so that we are able to interpret the opinions of great men not only by what they say, but by what they do.

But though this is possible now, such opinions coming from the lips of important people must have been formidable enough even fifty years ago. Let us suppose that a father from the highest motives did not wish his daughter to leave home and become writer, painter or scholar. "See what Mr. Oscar Browning says," he would say; and there was not only Mr. Oscar Browning; there was the *Saturday Review*; there was Mr. Greg[8]—the "essentials of a woman's being," said Mr. Greg emphatically, "are that *they are supported by, and they minister to, men*"—there was an enormous body of masculine opinion to the effect that nothing could be expected of women intellectually. Even if her father did not read out loud these opinions, any girl could read them for herself; and the reading, even in the nineteenth century, must have lowered her vitality, and told profoundly upon her work. There would always have been that assertion—you cannot do this, you are incapable of doing that—to protest against, to overcome. Probably for a novelist this germ is no longer of much effect; for there have been women novelists of merit. But for painters it must still have some sting in it; and for musicians, I imagine, is even now active and poisonous in the extreme. The woman composer stands where the actress stood in the time of Shakespeare. Nick Greene, I thought, remembering the story I had made about

---

8. William Rathbone Greg (1809–1891), cited from a *Saturday Review* essay titled "Why Are Women Redundant?"

Shakespeare's sister, said that a woman acting put him in mind of a dog dancing. Johnson repeated the phrase two hundred years later of women preaching. And here, I said, opening a book about music, we have the very words used again in this year of grace, 1928, of women who try to write music. "Of Mlle. Germaine Tailleferre one can only repeat Dr. Johnson's dictum concerning a woman preacher, transposed into terms of music. 'Sir, a woman's composing is like a dog's walking on his hind legs. It is not done well, but you are surprised to find it done at all.' "[9] So accurately does history repeat itself.

Thus, I concluded, shutting Mr. Oscar Browning's life and pushing away the rest, it is fairly evident that even in the nineteenth century a woman was not encouraged to be an artist. On the contrary, she was snubbed, slapped, lectured and exhorted. Her mind must have been strained and her vitality lowered by the need of opposing this, of disproving that. For here again we come within range of that very interesting and obscure masculine complex which has had so much influence upon the woman's movement; that deep-seated desire, not so much that *she* shall be inferior as that *he* shall be superior, which plants him wherever one looks, not only in front of the arts, but barring the way to politics too, even when the risk to himself seems infinitesimal and the suppliant humble and devoted. Even Lady Bessborough,[1] I remembered, with all her passion for politics, must humbly bow herself and write to Lord Granville Leveson-Gower: ". . . notwithstanding all my violence in politics and talking so much on that subject, I perfectly agree with you that no woman has any business to meddle with that or any other serious business, farther than giving her opinion (if she is ask'd)." And so she goes on to spend her enthusiasm where it meets with no obstacle whatsoever upon that immensely important subject, Lord Granville's maiden speech in the House of Commons. The spectacle is certainly a strange one, I thought. The history of men's opposition to women's emancipation is more interesting perhaps than the story of that emancipation itself. An amusing book might be made of it if some young student at Girton or Newnham would collect examples and deduce a theory—but she would need thick gloves on her hands, and bars to protect her of solid gold.

But what is amusing now, I recollected, shutting Lady Bessborough, had to be taken in desperate earnest once. Opinions that one now pastes in a book labelled cock-a-doodle-dum and keeps for reading to select audiences on summer nights once drew tears, I can assure you. Among your grandmothers and great-grandmothers there were many that wept their eyes out. Florence Nightingale shrieked aloud in her agony.[2] Moreover, it is all very well for you, who have got yourselves to college and enjoy sitting-rooms—or is it only bed-sitting-rooms?—of your own to say that genius should disregard such opinions; that genius should be above caring what is said of it. Unfortunately, it is precisely the men or women of genius who mind most what is said of them. Remember Keats. Remember the words he had cut on

9. "*A Survey of Contemporary Music*, Cecil Gray, p. 246" [Woolf's note]. The statement is originally found in James Boswell's *Life of Johnson* (1791).   1. Henrietta, Countess of Bessborough, who corresponded with Lord Granville George Leveson-Gower (1815–1891), British foreign secretary in William Gladstone's administrations and after him the leader of the Liberal Party.   2. "See *Cassandra*, by Florence Nightingale, printed in *The Cause*, by R. Strachey" [Woolf's note]. Nightingale (1820–1910), English nurse and founder of nursing as a profession for women.

his tombstone.[3] Think of Tennyson; think—but I need hardly multiply instances of the undeniable, if very, unfortunate, fact that it is the nature of the artist to mind excessively what is said about him. Literature is strewn with the wreckage of men who have minded beyond reason the opinions of others.

And this susceptibility of theirs is doubly unfortunate, I thought, returning again to my original enquiry into what state of mind is most propitious for creative work, because the mind of an artist, in order to achieve the prodigious effort of freeing whole and entire the work that is in him, must be incandescent, like Shakespeare's mind, I conjectured, looking at the book which lay open at *Antony and Cleopatra*. There must be no obstacle in it, no foreign matter unconsumed.

For though we say that we know nothing about Shakespeare's state of mind, even as we say that, we are saying something about Shakespeare's state of mind. The reason perhaps why we know so little of Shakespeare—compared with Donne or Ben Jonson or Milton—is that his grudges and spites and antipathies are hidden from us. We are not held up by some "revelation" which reminds us of the writer. All desire to protest, to preach, to proclaim an injury, to pay off a score, to make the world the witness of some hardship or grievance was fired out of him and consumed. Therefore his poetry flows from him free and unimpeded. If ever a human being got his work expressed completely, it was Shakespeare. If ever a mind was incandescent, unimpeded, I thought, turning again to the bookcase, it was Shakespeare's mind.

3. "Here lies one whose name was writ in water."

FRANZ KAFKA
1883–1924

The predicament of Franz Kafka's writing is, for many, the predicament of modern civilization. Nowhere is the anxiety and alienation of twentieth-century society more visible than in his stories of individuals struggling to prevail against a vast, meaningless, and apparently hostile system. Identifying that system as bureaucracy, family, religion, language, or the invisible network of social habit is less important than recognizing the protagonists' bewilderment at being placed in impossible situations. Kafka's heroes are driven to find answers in an unresponsive world, and they are required to act according to incomprehensible rules administered by an inaccessible authority; small wonder that they fluctuate between fear, hope, anger, resignation, and despair. Kafka's fictional world has long fascinated contemporary writers, who find in it an extraordinary blend of prosaic realism and nightmarish, infinitely interpretable symbolism. Whether evoking the multilayered bureaucracy of the modern state, the sense of guilt felt by those facing the accusations of authority, or the vulnerability of characters who cannot make themselves understood, Kafka's descriptions are believable because of their scrupulous attention to detail: the flea on a fur collar, the dust under an unmade bed, the creases and yellowing of an old newspaper, or the helplessness of a cockroach turned upside down. The sheer *ordinariness* of these details grounds the entire narrative, giving the reader a continuing expectation of reality even when events escape all logic and the situation is at its most hallucinatory. This paradoxical combination has appealed to a range of contemporary writers— each quite different from the other—who have read and absorbed Kafka's lesson: Samuel Beckett, Harold Pinter, Alain Robbe-Grillet, Gabriel García Márquez.

Kafka was born into cultural alienation: Jewish (though not truly part of the Jewish community) in Catholic Bohemia, son of a German-speaking shopkeeper when German was the language of the imposed Austro-Hungarian government, and drawn to literature when his father—a domineering, self-made man—pushed him toward success in business. Nor was he happier at home. Resenting his father's overbearing nature and feeling deprived of maternal love, he nonetheless lived with his parents for most of his life and complained in long letters about his coldness and inability to love (despite numerous liaisons). Kafka took a degree in law to qualify himself for a position in a large accident-insurance corporation, where he worked until illness forced his retirement in 1922. By the time of his death from tuberculosis two years later, he had published a number of short stories and two novellas (*The Metamorphosis*, 1915; *In the Penal Colony*, 1919), but left behind him the manuscripts of three near-complete novels that—considering himself a failure—he asked to have burned. Instead, Kafka's executor, Max Brod, published the novels (*The Trial*, 1925; *The Castle*, 1926; *Amerika*, 1927) and a biography celebrating the genius of his tormented, guilt-ridden friend.

Despite the indubitable fact that Franz Kafka became a respected senior executive, handling claims, litigations, public relations, and his institute's annual reports, and was one of the few top German executives retained when Czechoslovakia came into existence in 1918, his image in the modern imagination is derived from the portraits of inner anguish given in his fiction, diaries, and letters. This "Kafka" is a tormented and sensitive soul, guiltily resentful of his job in a giant bureaucracy, unable to free himself from his family or to cope with the demands of love, physically feeble, and constantly beset by feelings of inferiority and doom in an existence whose laws he can never quite understand. "Before the Law," a parable published in Kafka's lifetime and included in *The Trial*, recounts the archetypal setting of the "Kafka" character: a countryman waits and waits throughout his lifetime for permission to enter a crucial Gate, where the doorkeeper (the first of many) repeatedly refuses him entrance. He tries everything from good behavior to bribes without success. Finally, as the now-aged countryman dies in frustration, he is told that the gate existed only for him, and that it is now being closed. For the countryman, there is no response. The Law that governs our existence is all-powerful but irrational; at least it is not to be understood by its human suppliants, a lesson that Kafka could have derived equally well from his readings in the Danish philosopher Søren Kierkegaard, in Friedrich Nietzsche, or in the Jewish Talmud.

The combination of down-to-earth, matter-of-fact setting and unreal or nightmarish events is the hallmark of Kafka's style. His characters speak prosaically and react in a commonsense way when such a response (given the situation) is utterly grotesque. A young businessman is changed overnight into a giant cockroach (*The Metamorphosis*) or charged with undefined crimes and finally executed (*The Trial*); a would-be land surveyor is unable to communicate with the castle that employs him and that keeps sending incomprehensible messages (*The Castle*); a visitor to a penal colony observes a gigantic machine whose function is to execute condemned criminals by inscribing their sentence deeper and deeper into their flesh (*In the Penal Colony*). The term *surrealist* is often attached to this blend of everyday reality and dream configuration, with its implication of psychic undercurrents and cosmic significance stirring beneath the most ordinary-seeming existence. Kafka, however, had no connection with the Surrealists, whose vision of a miraculous level of existence hidden behind everyday life is the obverse of his heroes' vain attempts to maintain control over the impossible and the absurd.

Kafka's stories are not allegories, although many readers have been tempted to find in them an underlying message. A political reading sees them as indictments of faceless bureaucracy controlling individual lives in the modern totalitarian state. The sense of being found guilty by an entire society recalls the traditional theme of the Wandering Jew and predicts for many the Holocaust of World War II (in fact, Kafka's three sisters died in concentration camps). His heroes' self-conscious quest to fit into some meaningful structure, their ceaseless attempts to do the right thing when there is no rational way of knowing what that is, is the very picture of absurdity and alienation that existentialist philosophers and writers examined during and after World War II. The assumption that there is a Law and the presence of protagonists who die in search for purity ("The Hunger Artist") or in a humble admission of guilt (*The Trial*) allow the stories to be taken as religious metaphors. Kafka's desperately lucid analysis of the way his parents' influence shaped an impressionable child into an unhappy adult ("Letter to My Father") articulates emotional tangles and parent-child rivalry with an openness and detail that recalls decades of psychoanalytical criticism following Freud. The picture of a sick society where individual rights and sensitivity no longer count and unreasoning torment is visited on the ignorant has been read as an indictment of disintegrating modern culture. Yet no one allegorical interpretation is finally possible, for all these potential meanings overlap as they expand toward social, familial, political, philosophical, and religious dimensions and constitute the richly allusive texture of separate tales by a master storyteller.

The Metamorphosis, Kafka's longest complete work published in his lifetime, is first of all a consummate narrative: the question "What happens next?" never disappears from the moment that Gregor Samsa wakes up to find himself transformed. "It was no dream," no nightmarish fantasy in which Gregor temporarily identified himself with other downtrodden vermin of society. Instead, this grotesque transformation is permanent, a single unshakable fact that renders almost comic his family's calculations and attempts to adjust. "The terror of art," said Kafka in a conversation about *The Metamorphosis,* is that "the dream reveals the reality." This artistic dream, become Gregor's reality, sheds light on the intolerable nature of his former daily existence. The other side of his job is its mechanical rigidity, personal rivalries, and threatening suspicion of any deviation from the norm. Gregor himself is part of this world, as he shows when he fawns on the manager and tries to manipulate him by criticizing their boss.

More disturbing is the transformation that takes place in Gregor's family, where the expected love and support turns into shamed acceptance and animal resentment now that Gregor has let the family down. Mother and sister are ineffectual, and their sympathy is slowly replaced by disgust. Gregor's father quickly reassumes his position of authority and beats the cockroach back into his room: first with the businesslike newspaper and manager's cane, and later with a barrage of apples from the family table. Gregor has become an "it" whose death is warmly wished by the whole family—and perhaps they are right, in one of Kafka's ironies.

The Metamorphosis[1]

I

When Gregor Samsa awoke one morning from troubled dreams, he found himself changed into a monstrous cockroach in his bed. He lay on his tough, armoured back, and, raising his head a little, managed to see—sectioned off by little crescent-shaped ridges into segments—the expanse of his arched,

---

1. Translated by Michael Hofmann.

brown belly, atop which the coverlet perched, forever on the point of slipping off entirely. His numerous legs, pathetically frail by contrast to the rest of him, waved feebly before his eyes.

'What's the matter with me?' he thought. It was no dream. There, quietly between the four familiar walls, was his room, a normal human room, if always a little on the small side. Over the table, on which an array of cloth samples was spread out—Samsa was a travelling salesman—hung the picture he had only recently clipped from a magazine, and set in an attractive gilt frame. It was a picture of a lady in a fur hat and stole, sitting bolt upright, holding in the direction of the onlooker a heavy fur muff into which she had thrust the whole of her forearm.

From there, Gregor's gaze directed itself towards the window, and the drab weather outside—raindrops could be heard plinking against the tin window-ledges—made him quite melancholy. 'What if I went back to sleep for a while, and forgot about all this nonsense?' he thought, but that proved quite impossible, because he was accustomed to sleeping on his right side, and in his present state he was unable to find that position. However vigorously he flung himself to his right, he kept rocking on to his back. He must have tried it a hundred times, closing his eyes so as not to have to watch his wriggling legs, and only stopped when he felt a slight ache in his side which he didn't recall having felt before.

'Oh, my Lord!' he thought. 'If only I didn't have to follow such an exhausting profession! On the road, day in, day out. The work is so much more strenuous than it would be in head office, and then there's the additional ordeal of travelling, worries about train connections, the irregular, bad meals, new people all the time, no continuity, no affection. Devil take it!' He felt a light itch at the top of his belly; slid a little closer to the bedpost, so as to be able to raise his head a little more effectively; found the itchy place, which was covered with a sprinkling of white dots the significance of which he was unable to interpret; assayed the place with one of his legs, but hurriedly withdrew it, because the touch caused him to shudder involuntarily.

He slid back to his previous position. 'All this getting up early,' he thought, 'is bound to take its effect. A man needs proper bed rest. There are some other travelling salesmen I could mention who live like harem women. Sometimes, for instance, when I return to the *pension* in the course of the morning, to make a note of that morning's orders, some of those gents are just sitting down to breakfast. I'd like to see what happened if I tried that out with my director some time; it would be the order of the boot just like that. That said, it might be just the thing for me. If I didn't have to exercise restraint for the sake of my parents, then I would have quit a long time ago; I would have gone up to the director and told him exactly what I thought of him. He would have fallen off his desk in surprise! That's a peculiar way he has of sitting anyway, up on his desk, and talking down to his staff from on high, making them step up to him very close because he's so hard of hearing. Well, I haven't quite given up hope; once I've got the money together to pay back what my parents owe him—it may take me another five or six years—then I'll do it, no question. Then we'll have the parting of the ways. But for the time being, I'd better look sharp, because my train leaves at five.'

And he looked across at the alarm clock, ticking away on the bedside table. 'Great heavenly Father!' he thought. It was half past six, and the clock hands were moving smoothly forward—in fact it was after half past, it was more like a quarter to seven. Had the alarm not gone off? He could see from the bed that it had been quite correctly set for four o'clock; it must have gone off. But how was it possible to sleep calmly through its ringing, which caused even the furniture to shake? Well, his sleep hadn't exactly been calm, but maybe it had been all the more profound. What to do now? The next train left at seven; to catch it meant hurrying like a madman, and his samples weren't yet packed, and he himself didn't feel exactly agile or vigorous. And even if he caught that train, he would still get a carpeting from the director, because the office boy would be on the platform at five o'clock, and would certainly have reported long since that Gregor hadn't been on the train. That boy was a real piece of work, so utterly beholden to the director, without any backbone or nous. Then what if he called in sick? That would be rather embarrassing and a little suspicious too, because in the course of the past five years, Gregor hadn't once been ill. The director was bound to retaliate by calling in the company doctor, would upbraid the parents for their idle son, and refute all objections by referring to the doctor, for whom there were only perfectly healthy but workshy patients. And who could say he was wrong, in this instance anyway? Aside from a continuing feeling of sleepiness that was quite unreasonable after such a long sleep, Gregor felt perfectly well, and even felt the stirrings of a healthy appetite.

As he was hurriedly thinking this, still no nearer to getting out of bed—the alarm clock was just striking a quarter to seven—there was a cautious knock on the door behind him. 'Gregor,' came the call—it was his mother—'it's a quarter to seven. Shouldn't you ought to be gone by now?' The mild voice. Gregor was dismayed when he heard his own in response. It was still without doubt his own voice from before, but with a little admixture of an irrepressible squeaking that left the words only briefly recognizable at the first instant of their sounding, only to set about them afterwards so destructively that one couldn't be at all sure what one had heard. Gregor had wanted to offer a full explanation of everything but, in these circumstances, kept himself to: 'All right, thank you, Mother, I'm getting up!' The wooden door must have muted the change in Gregor's voice, because his mother seemed content with his reply, and shuffled away. But the brief exchange had alerted other members of the family to the surprising fact that Gregor was still at home, and already there was his father, knocking on the door at the side of the room, feebly, but with his fist. 'Gregor, Gregor?' he shouted, 'what's the matter?' And after a little while, he came again, in a lower octave: 'Gregor! Gregor!' On the door on the other side of the room, meanwhile, he heard his sister lamenting softly: 'Oh, Gregor? Are you not well? Can I bring you anything?' To both sides equally Gregor replied, 'Just coming', and tried by careful enunciation and long pauses between the words to take any unusual quality from his voice. His father soon returned to his breakfast, but his sister whispered: 'Gregor, please, will you open the door.' Gregor entertained no thought of doing so; instead he gave silent thanks for the precaution, picked up on his travels, of locking every door at night, even at home.

His immediate intention was to get up calmly and leisurely, to get dressed and, above all, to have breakfast before deciding what to do next, because he was quite convinced he wouldn't arrive at any sensible conclusions as long as he remained in bed. There were many times, he remembered, when he had lain in bed with a sense of some dim pain somewhere in his body, perhaps from lying awkwardly, which then turned out, as he got up, to be mere imagining, and he looked forward to his present fanciful state gradually falling from him. He had not the least doubt that the alteration in his voice was just the first sign of a head-cold, always an occupational malady with travelling salesmen.

Casting off the blanket proved to be straightforward indeed; all he needed to do was to inflate himself a little, and it fell off by itself. But further tasks were more problematical, not least because of his great breadth. He would have needed arms and hands with which to get up; instead of which all he had were those numerous little legs, forever in varied movement, and evidently not under his control. If he wanted to bend one of them, then it was certain that that was the one that was next fully extended; and once he finally succeeded in performing whatever task he had set himself with that leg, then all its neglected fellows would be in a turmoil of painful agitation. 'Whatever I do, I mustn't loaf around in bed,' Gregor said to himself.

At first he thought he would get out of bed bottom half first, but this bottom half of himself, which he had yet to see, and as to whose specifications he was perfectly ignorant, turned out to be not very manoeuvrable; progress was slow; and when at last, almost in fury, he pushed down with all his strength, he misjudged the direction, and collided with the lower bedpost, the burning pain he felt teaching him that this lower end of himself might well be, for the moment, the most sensitive to pain.

He therefore tried to lever his top half out of bed first, and cautiously turned his head towards the edge of the bed. This was easily done, and, in spite of its breadth and bulk, the rest of his body slowly followed the direction of the head. But, now craning his neck in empty space well away from the bed, he was afraid to move any further, because if he were to fall in that position, it would take a miracle if he didn't injure his head. And he mustn't lose consciousness at any price; it were better then to stay in bed.

But as he sighed and lay there at the end of his endeavours, and once again beheld his legs struggling, if anything, harder than before, and saw no possibility of bringing any order or calm to their randomness, he told himself once more that he couldn't possibly stay in bed and that the most sensible solution was to try anything that offered even the smallest chance of getting free of his bed. At the same time, he didn't forget to remind himself periodically that clarity and calm were better than counsels of despair. At such moments, he levelled his gaze as sharply as possible at the window, but unfortunately there was little solace or encouragement to be drawn from the sight of the morning fog, which was thick enough to obscure even the opposite side of the street. 'Seven o'clock already,' he said to himself as his alarm clock struck another quarter, 'seven o'clock already, and still such dense fog.' And he lay there for a while longer, panting gently, as though perhaps expecting that silence would restore the natural order of things.

But then he said to himself: 'By quarter past seven, I must certainly have got out of bed completely. In any case, somebody will have come from work by then to ask after me, because the business opens before seven o'clock.' And he set about rhythmically rocking his body clear of the bed. If he dropped out of bed in that way, then he would try to raise his head sharply at the last moment, so that it remained uninjured. His back seemed to be tough; a fall on to the carpet would surely not do it any harm. What most concerned him was the prospect of the loud crash he would surely cause, which would presumably provoke anxiety, if not consternation, behind all the doors. But that was a risk he had to take.

As Gregor was already half-clear of the bed—this latest method felt more like play than serious exertion, requiring him only to rock himself from side to side—he thought how simple everything would be if he had some help. Two strong people—he thought of his father and the servant-girl—would easily suffice; they needed only to push their arms under his curved back, peel him out of bed, bend down under his weight, and then just pay attention while they flipped him over on to the floor, where his legs would hopefully come into their own. But then, even if the doors hadn't been locked, could he have really contemplated calling for help? Even in his extremity, he couldn't repress a smile at the thought.

He had already reached the point where his rocking was almost enough to send him off balance, and he would soon have to make up his mind once and for all what he was going to do, because it was ten past seven—when the doorbell rang. 'It must be someone from work,' he said to himself and went almost rigid, while his little legs, if anything, increased their agitation. For a moment there was silence. 'They won't open the door,' Gregor said to himself, from within some mad hope. But then of course, as always, the servant-girl walked with firm stride to the door and opened it. Gregor needed only to hear the first word from the visitor to know that it was the chief clerk in person. Why only was Gregor condemned to work for a company where the smallest lapse was greeted with the gravest suspicion? Were all the employees without exception scoundrels, were there really no loyal and dependable individuals among them, who, if once a couple of morning hours were not exploited for work, were driven so demented by pangs of conscience that they were unable to get out of bed? Was it really not enough to send a trainee to inquire—if inquiries were necessary at all—and did the chief clerk need to come in person, thereby demonstrating to the whole blameless family that the investigation of Gregor's delinquency could only be entrusted to the seniority and trained intelligence of a chief clerk? And more on account of the excitement that came over Gregor with these reflections, than as the result of any proper decision on his part, he powerfully swung himself right out of bed. There was a loud impact, though not a crash as such. The fall was somewhat muffled by the carpet; moreover, his back was suppler than Gregor had expected, and therefore the result was a dull thump that did not draw such immediate attention to itself. Only he had been a little careless of his head, and had bumped it; frantic with rage and pain, he turned and rubbed it against the carpet.

'Something's fallen down in there,' said the chief clerk in the hallway on the left. Gregor tried to imagine whether the chief clerk had ever experienced something similar to what had happened to himself today; surely it was within the bounds of possibility. But as if in blunt reply to this question, the chief clerk now took a few decisive steps next door, his patent-leather boots creaking. From the room on the right, his sister now whispered to Gregor: 'Gregor, the chief clerk's here.' 'I know,' Gregor replied to himself; but he didn't dare say it sufficiently loudly for his sister to hear him.

'Gregor,' his father now said from the left-hand room, 'the chief clerk has come, and wants to know why you weren't on the early train. We don't know what to tell him. He wants a word with you too. So kindly open the door. I'm sure he'll turn a blind eye to the untidiness in your room.' 'Good morning, Mr Samsa,' called the cheery voice of the chief clerk. 'He's not feeling well,' Gregor's mother interjected to the chief clerk, while his father was still talking by the door, 'he's not feeling well, believe me, Chief Clerk. How otherwise could Gregor miss his train! You know that boy has nothing but work in his head! It almost worries me that he never goes out on his evenings off; he's been in the city now for the past week, but he's spent every evening at home. He sits at the table quietly reading the newspaper, or studying the railway timetable. His only hobby is a little occasional woodwork. In the past two or three evenings, he's carved a little picture-frame; I think you'll be surprised by the workmanship; he's got it up on the wall in his room; you'll see it the instant Gregor opens the door. You've no idea how happy I am to see you, Chief Clerk; by ourselves we would never have been able to induce Gregor to open the door, he's so obstinate; and I'm sure he's not feeling well, even though he told us he was fine.' 'I'm just coming,' Gregor said slowly and deliberately, not stirring, so as not to miss a single word of the conversation outside. 'I'm sure you're right, madam,' said the chief clerk, 'I only hope it's nothing serious. Though again I have to say that—unhappily or otherwise—we businesspeople often find ourselves in the position of having to set aside some minor ailment, in the greater interest of our work.' 'So can we admit the chief clerk now?' asked his impatient father, knocking on the door again. 'No,' said Gregor. In the left-hand room there was now an awkward silence, while on the right his sister began to sob.

Why didn't his sister go and join the others? She had presumably only just got up, and hadn't started getting dressed yet. And then why was she crying? Because he wouldn't get up and admit the chief clerk, because he was in danger of losing his job, and because the director would then pursue his parents with the old claims? Surely those anxieties were still premature at this stage. Gregor was still here, and wasn't thinking at all about leaving the family. For now he was sprawled on the carpet, and no one who was aware of his condition could have seriously expected that he would allow the chief clerk into his room. But this minor breach of courtesy, for which he could easily find an explanation later, hardly constituted reason enough for Gregor to be sent packing. Gregor thought it was much more sensible for them to leave him alone now, rather than bother him with tears and appeals. It was just the uncertainty that afflicted the others and accounted for their behaviour.

'Mr Samsa,' the chief clerk now called out loudly, 'what's the matter? You've barricaded yourself into your room, you give us one-word answers, you cause your parents grave and needless anxiety and—this just by the by—you're neglecting your official duties in a quite unconscionable way. I am talking to you on behalf of your parents and the director, and I now ask you in all seriousness for a prompt and full explanation. I must say, I'm astonished, I'm astonished. I had taken you for a quiet and sensible individual, but you seem set on indulging a bizarre array of moods. This morning the director suggested a possible reason for your missing your train—it was to do with the authority to collect payments recently entrusted to you—but I practically gave him my word of honour that that couldn't be the explanation.

Now, though, in view of your baffling obstinacy, I'm losing all inclination to speak up on your behalf. And your position is hardly the most secure. I had originally come with the intention of telling you as much in confidence, but as you seem to see fit to waste my time, I really don't know why your parents shouldn't get to hear about it as well. Your performances of late have been extremely unsatisfactory; it's admittedly not the time of year for the best results, we freely concede that; but a time of year for no sales, that doesn't exist in our calendars, Mr Samsa, and it mustn't exist.'

'But Chief Clerk,' Gregor exclaimed, in his excitement forgetting everything else, 'I'll let you in right away. A light indisposition, a fit of giddiness, have prevented me from getting up. I'm still lying in bed. But I feel almost restored. I'm even now getting out of bed. Just one moment's patience! It seems I'm not as much improved as I'd hoped. But I feel better just the same. How is it something like this can befall a person! Only last night I felt fine, my parents will confirm it to you, or rather, last night I had a little inkling already of what lay ahead. It probably showed in my appearance somewhere. Why did I not think to inform work! It's just that one always imagines that one will get over an illness without having to take time off. Chief Clerk, sir! Spare my parents! All those complaints you bring against me, they're all of them groundless; it's the first I've heard of any of them. Perhaps you haven't yet perused the last batch of orders I sent in. By the way, I mean to set out on the eight o'clock train—the couple of hours rest have done me the world of good. Chief Clerk, don't detain yourself any longer; I'll be at work myself presently. Kindly be so good as to let them know, and pass on my regards to the director!'

While Gregor blurted all this out, almost unaware of what he was saying, he had moved fairly effortlessly—no doubt aided by the practice he had had in bed—up to the bedside table, and now attempted to haul himself into an upright position against it. He truly had it in mind to open the door, to show himself and to speak to the chief clerk; he was eager to learn what the others, who were all clamouring for him, would say when they got to see him. If they were shocked, then Gregor would have no more responsibility, and could relax. Whereas if they took it all calmly, then he wouldn't have any cause for agitation either, and if he hurried, he might still get to the station by eight o'clock. To begin with he could get no purchase on the smooth bedside table, but at last he gave himself one more swing, and stood there upright; he barely noticed the pain in his lower belly, though it did burn badly. Then he let himself drop against the back of a nearby chair, whose edges he clasped with some of his legs. With that he had attained mastery over himself, and was silent, because now he could listen to the chief clerk.

'Did you understand a single word of that?' the chief clerk asked Gregor's parents, 'you don't suppose he's pulling our legs, do you?' 'In the name of God,' his mother cried, her voice already choked with tears, 'perhaps he's gravely ill, and we're tormenting him. Grete! Grete!' she called out. 'Mother?' his sister called back from the opposite side. They were communicating with one another through Gregor's room. 'Go to the doctor right away. Gregor's ill. Hurry and fetch the doctor. Were you able to hear him just now?' 'That was the voice of an animal,' said the chief clerk, strikingly much more quietly than his mother and her screaming. 'Anna! Anna!' his father shouted through the hallway, in the direction of the kitchen, and clapped his hands, 'get the locksmith right away!' And already two girls in rustling skirts were hurrying through the hallway—however had his sister managed to dress so quickly?—and out through the front door. There wasn't the bang of it closing either; probably they had left it open, as happens at times when a great misfortune has taken place.

Meanwhile, Gregor had become much calmer. It appeared his words were no longer comprehensible, though to his own hearing they seemed clear enough, clearer than before, perhaps because his ear had become attuned to the sound. But the family already had the sense of all not being well with him, and were ready to come to his assistance. The clarity and resolve with which the first instructions had been issued did him good. He felt himself back within the human ambit, and from both parties, doctor and locksmith, without treating them really in any way as distinct one from the other, he hoped for magnificent and surprising feats. In order to strengthen his voice for the decisive conversations that surely lay ahead, he cleared his throat a few times, as quietly as possible, as it appeared that even this sound was something other than a human cough, and he no longer trusted himself to tell the difference. Next door, things had become very quiet. Perhaps his parents were sitting at the table holding whispered consultations with the chief clerk, or perhaps they were all pressing their ears to the door, and listening.

Gregor slowly pushed himself across to the door with the chair, there let go of it and dropped against the door, holding himself in an upright position against it—the pads on his little legs secreted some sort of sticky substance—and there rested a moment from his exertions. And then he set himself with his mouth to turn the key in the lock. Unfortunately, it appeared that he had no teeth as such—what was he going to grip the key with?—but luckily his jaws were very powerful; with their help, he got the key to move, and he didn't stop to consider that he was certainly damaging himself in some way, because a brown liquid came out of his mouth, ran over the key, and dribbled on to the floor. 'Listen,' the chief clerk was saying next door, 'he's turning the key.' This was a great encouragement for Gregor; but they all of them should have called out to him, his father and mother too: 'Go, Gregor,' they should have shouted, 'keep at it, work at the lock!' And with the idea that they were all following his efforts with tense concentration, he bit fast on to the key with all the strength he possessed, to the point when he was ready to black out. The more the key moved in the door, the more he danced around the lock; now he was holding himself upright with just his mouth, and, depending on the position, he either hung from the key, or was pressing against it with the full weight of his body. The light click of the snapping lock brought Gregor round, as from a spell of unconsciousness. Sighing with relief, he said to himself: 'Well, I didn't need the locksmith after all,' and he rested his head on the door handle to open the door fully.

As he had had to open the door in this way, it was already fairly ajar while he himself was still out of sight. He first had to twist round one half of the door, and very cautiously at that, if he wasn't to fall flat on his back just at the point of making his entry into the room. He was still taken up with the difficult manoeuvre, and didn't have time to think about anything else, when he heard the chief clerk emit a sharp 'Oh!'—it actually sounded like the rushing wind—and then he saw him as well, standing nearest to the door, his hand pressed against his open mouth, and slowly retreating, as if being pushed back by an invisible but irresistible force. Gregor's mother—in spite of the chief clerk's arrival, she was standing there with her hair loose, though now it was standing up stiffly in the air—first looked at his father with folded hands, then took two steps towards Gregor and collapsed in the midst of her skirts spreading out around her, her face irretrievably sunk against her bosom. His father clenched his fist with a pugnacious expression, as if ready to push Gregor back into his room, then looked uncertainly round the living room, covered his eyes with his hands and cried, his mighty chest shaking with sobs.

Now Gregor didn't even set foot in the room, but leaned against the inside of the fixed half of the door, so that only half his body could be seen, and the head with which he was peering across at the others cocked on its side a little. It was much brighter now; a little section of the endless grey-black frontage of the building opposite—it was a hospital—could clearly be seen, with its rhythmically recurring windows; it was still raining, but now only in single large drops, individually fashioned and flung to the ground. The breakfast things were out on the table in profusion, because for his father breakfast was the most important meal of the day, which he liked to draw out for hours over the perusal of several newspapers. Just opposite, on the facing wall, was a photograph of Gregor from his period in the army, as a lieutenant, his hand on his sabre, smiling confidently, the posture and uniform demanding respect. The door to the hallway was open, and as the front door was open too one could see out to the landing, and the top of the flight of stairs down.

'Now,' said Gregor, in the knowledge that he was the only one present to have maintained his equanimity, 'I'm just going to get dressed, pack up my samples, and then I'll set off. Do you want to let me set out, do you? You see, Chief Clerk, you see, I'm not stubborn, I like my work; the travel is arduous, but I couldn't live without it. Where are you off to, Chief Clerk? To work? Is that right? Will you accurately report everything you've seen here? It is possible to be momentarily unfit for work, but that is precisely the time to remind oneself of one's former achievements, and to reflect that, once the present obstacle has been surmounted, one's future work will be all the more diligent and focused. As you know all too well, I am under a very great obligation to the director. In addition, I have responsibilities for my parents and my sister. I am in a jam, but I will work my way out of it. Only don't make it any harder for me than it is already! Give me your backing at head office! I know the travelling salesman is not held in the highest regard there. People imagine he earns a packet, and has a nice life on top of it. These and similar assumptions remain unexamined. But you, Chief Clerk, you have a greater understanding of the circumstances than the rest of the staff, you even, if I may say this to you in confidence, have an understanding superior to that of the director himself, who, as an entrepreneur, is perhaps too easily swayed against an employee. You are also very well aware that the travelling salesman, spending, as he does, the best part of the year away from head office, may all too easily fall victim to tittle-tattle, to mischance, and to baseless allegations, against which he has no way of defending himself—mostly even does not get to hear of—and when he returns exhausted from his travels, it is to find himself confronted directly by practical consequences of whose causes he is ignorant. Chief Clerk, don't leave without showing me by a word or two of your own that you at least partly agree with me!'

But the chief clerk had turned his back on Gregor the moment he had begun speaking, and only stared back at him with mouth agape, over his trembling shoulder. All the while Gregor was speaking, he wasn't still for a moment, but, without taking his eyes off Gregor, moved towards the door, but terribly gradually, as though in breach of some secret injunction not to leave the room. Already he was in the hallway, and to judge by the sudden movement with which he snatched his foot back out of the living room for the last time, one might have supposed he had burned his sole. Once in the hallway, he extended his right hand fervently in the direction of the stairs, as though some supernatural salvation there awaited him.

Gregor understood that he must on no account allow the chief clerk to leave in his present frame of mind, not if he wasn't to risk damage to his place in the company. His parents didn't seem to grasp this issue with the same clarity; over the course of many years, they had acquired the conviction that in this business Gregor had a job for life and, besides, they were so consumed by their anxieties of the present moment, that they had lost any premonitory sense they might have had. Gregor, though, had his. The chief clerk had to be stopped, calmed, convinced, and finally won over; the future of Gregor and his family depended on that! If only his sister were back already! There was a shrewd person; she had begun to cry even as Gregor was still lying calmly on his back. And no doubt the chief clerk, notorious skirt-chaser that he was, would have allowed himself to be influenced by her; she would have closed the front door, and in the hallway talked him out of his panic. But his sister wasn't there. Gregor would have to act on his own behalf. Without stopping to think that he didn't understand his given loco-motive powers, without even thinking that this latest speech of his had possibly—no, probably—not been understood either, he left the shelter of the half-door and pushed through the opening, making for the chief clerk, who was laughably holding on to the balustrade on the landing with both hands. But straightaway, looking for a grip, Gregor dropped with a short cry on to his many little legs. No sooner had this happened, than for the first time that morning he felt a sense of physical well-being; the little legs had solid ground under them; they obeyed perfectly, as he noticed to his satis-faction, even seeking to carry him where he wanted to go; and he was on the point of believing a final improvement in his condition was imminent. But at that very moment, while he was still swaying from his initial impetus, not far from his mother and just in front of her on the ground, she, who had seemed so utterly immersed in herself, suddenly leaped into the air, arms wide, fingers spread, and screamed: 'Help, oh please God, help me!', inclined her head as though for a better view of Gregor, but then, quite at variance with that, ran senselessly away from him; she forgot the breakfast table was behind her; on reaching it, she hurriedly, in her distractedness, sat down on it, seeming oblivious to the fact that coffee was gushing all over the carpet from the large upset coffee pot.

'Mother, mother,' Gregor said softly, looking up at her. For the moment, he forgot all about the chief clerk; on the other hand, he couldn't help but move his jaws several times at the sight of the flowing coffee. At that his mother screamed again and fled from the table into the arms of Gregor's father who was rushing towards her. But now Gregor had no time for his parents; the chief clerk was already on the stairs; his chin on the balustrade, he stared behind him one last time. Gregor moved sharply to be sure of catching him up; the chief clerk must have sensed something, because he took the last few steps at a single bound and disappeared. 'Oof!' he managed to cry, the sound echoing through the stairwell. Regrettably, the consequence of the chief clerk's flight was finally to turn the senses of his father, who to that point had remained relatively calm, because, instead of himself taking off after the man, or at least not getting in the way of Gregor as he attempted to do just that, he seized in his right hand the chief clerk's cane, which he had left behind on a chair along with his hat and coat, with his left grabbed a large newspaper from the table, and, by stamping his feet, and brandishing stick and newspaper, attempted to drive Gregor back into his room. No pleas on Gregor's part were any use, no pleas were even understood. However imploringly he might turn his head, his father only stamped harder with his feet. Meanwhile, in spite of the cool temperature, his mother had thrown open a window on the other side of the room and, leaning out of it, plunged her face in her hands. A powerful draught was created between the stairwell and the street outside, the window curtains flew up, the newspapers rustled on the table, some individual pages fluttered across the floor. His father was moving forward implacably, emitting hissing sounds like a savage. Gregor had no practice in moving backwards, and he was moving, it had to be said, extremely slowly. If he had been able to turn round, he would have been back in his room in little or no time, but he was afraid lest the delay incurred in turning around would make his father impatient, and at any moment the stick in his father's hand threatened to strike him a fatal blow to the back of the head. Finally, Gregor had no alternative, because he noticed to his consternation that in his reversing he was unable to keep to a given course; and so, with continual fearful sidelong looks to his father, he started as quickly as possible, but in effect only very slowly, to turn round. It was possible that his father was aware of his good intentions, because he didn't obstruct him, but even directed the turning manoeuvre from a distance with gestures from his cane. If only there hadn't been those unbearable hissing sounds issuing from his father! They caused Gregor to lose all orientation. He had turned almost completely round, when, distracted by the hissing, he lost his way, and moved a little in the wrong direction. Then, when he found himself with his head successfully in the doorway, it became apparent that his body was too wide to slip through it. To his father, in his present frame of mind, it didn't remotely occur to open the other wing of the door, and so make enough space for Gregor. He was, rather, obsessed with the notion of getting Gregor back in his room post-haste. He could not possibly have countenanced the cumbersome preparations Gregor would have required to get up and perhaps so get around the door. Rather, as though there were no hindrance at all, he drove Gregor forward with even greater din; the sound to Gregor's ears was not that of one father alone; now it was really no laughing matter, and Gregor drove himself—happen what might—against the door. One side of his body was canted up, he found himself lifted at an angle in the doorway, his flank was rubbed raw, and some ugly stains appeared on the white door. Before long he was caught fast and could not have moved any more unaided, his little legs on one side were trembling in mid-air while those on the other found themselves painfully pressed against the ground—when from behind his father now gave him a truly liberating kick, and he was thrown, bleeding profusely, far into his room. The door was battered shut with the cane, and then at last there was quiet.

II

Not until dusk did Gregor awake from his heavy, almost comatose sleep. Probably he would have awoken around that time anyway, even if he hadn't been roused, because he felt sufficiently rested and restored. Still, it seemed to him as though a hurried footfall and a cautious shutting of the door to the hallway had awoken him. The pale gleam of the electric street-lighting outside showed on the ceiling and on the upper parts of the furniture, but down on the floor, where Gregor lay, it was dark. Slowly he rose and, groping clumsily with his feelers, whose function he only now began to understand, he made for the door, to see what had happened there. His whole left side was one long, unpleasantly stretched scab, and he was positively limping on his two rows of legs. One of his little legs had been badly hurt in the course of the morning's incidents—it was a wonder that it was only one—and it dragged after the rest inertly.

Not until he reached the door did he realize what had tempted him there; it was the smell of food. There stood a dish full of sweetened milk, with little slices of white bread floating in it. He felt like laughing for joy, because he was even hungrier now than he had been that morning, and straightaway he dunked his head into the milk past his eyes. But before long he withdrew it again in disappointment; it wasn't just that he found eating difficult on account of his damaged left flank—it seemed he could only eat if the whole of his body, panting, participated—more that he disliked the taste of milk, which otherwise was a favourite drink, and which his sister had certainly put out for him for that reason. In fact, he pulled his head away from the dish almost with revulsion, and crawled back into the middle of the room.

In the living room the gas-jet had been lit, as Gregor saw by looking through the crack in the door, but whereas usually at this time his father would be reading aloud to Gregor's mother or sometimes to his sister from the afternoon edition of the newspaper, there was now silence. Well, it was possible that this reading aloud, of which his sister had written and spoken to him many times, had been discontinued of late. But it was equally quiet to either side, even though it was hardly possible that there was no one home. 'What a quiet life the family used to lead,' Gregor said to himself, and, staring into the blackness, he felt considerable pride that he had made such a life possible for his parents and his sister, and in such a lovely flat. But what if all peace, all prosperity, all contentment, were to come to a sudden and terrible end? So as not to fall into such thoughts, Gregor thought he would take some exercise instead, and he crawled back and forth in the room.

Once in the course of the long evening one of the side-doors was opened a crack, and once the other, and then hurriedly closed again; someone seemed to feel a desire to step inside, but then again had too many cavils about so doing. Gregor took up position right against the living-room door, resolved to bring in the reluctant visitor in some way if he could, or, if nothing more, at least discover his identity; but then the door wasn't opened again, and Gregor waited in vain. Previously, when the doors were locked, everyone had tried to come in and see him, but now that he had opened one door himself, and the others had apparently been opened in the course of the day, no visitors came, and the keys were all on the outside too.

The light in the living room was left on far into the night, and that made it easy to verify that his parents and his sister had stayed up till then, because, as he could very well hear, that was when the three of them left on tiptoed feet. Now it was certain that no one would come in to Gregor's room until morning; so he had a long time ahead of him to reflect undisturbed on how he could reorder his life. But the empty high-ceilinged room where he was forced to lie flat on the floor disquieted him, without him being able to find a reason for his disquiet, because after all this was the room he had lived in these past five years—and with a half unconscious turn, and not without a little shame, he hurried under the sofa, where, even though his back was pressed down a little, and he was unable to raise his head, he straightaway felt very much at home, and only lamented the fact that his body was too broad to be entirely concealed under the sofa.

He stayed there all night, either half asleep, albeit woken by hunger at regular intervals, or kept half awake by anxieties and unclear hopes, which all seemed to lead to the point that he would comport himself quietly for the moment, and by patience and the utmost consideration for the family make the inconveniences he was putting them through in his present state a little bearable for them.

Early the next morning, while it was almost still night, Gregor had an opportunity to put his resolutions to the test, because the door from the hallway opened, and his sister, almost completely dressed, looked in on him with some agitation. It took her a while to find him, but when she spotted him under the sofa—my God, he had to be somewhere, he couldn't have flown off into space—she was so terrified that in an uncontrollable revulsion she slammed the door shut. But then, as if sorry for her behaviour, she straightaway opened the door again, and tiptoed in, as if calling on a grave invalid, or even a stranger. Gregor had pushed his head forward to the edge of the sofa, and observed her. Would she notice that he had left his milk, and then not by any means because he wasn't hungry, and would she bring in some different food that would suit him better? If she failed to do so of her own accord, then he preferred to die rather than tell her, even though he did feel an incredible urge to shoot out from under the sofa, hurl himself at his sister's feet, and ask her for some nice titbit to eat. But his sister was promptly startled by the sight of the full dish, from which only a little milk had been spilled round the edges. She picked it up right away, not with her bare hands but with a rag, and carried it out. Gregor was dying to see what she would bring him instead, and he entertained all sorts of conjectures on the subject. But never would he have been able to guess what in the goodness of her heart his sister did. She brought him, evidently to get a sense of his likes and dislikes, a whole array of things, all spread out on an old newspaper. There were some half-rotten vegetables; bones left over from dinner with a little congealed white sauce; a handful of raisins and almonds; a cheese that a couple of days ago Gregor had declared to be unfit for human consumption; a piece of dry bread, a piece of bread and butter, and a piece of bread and butter sprinkled with salt. In addition she set down a dish that was probably to be given over to Gregor's personal use, into which she had poured some water. Then, out of sheer delicacy, knowing that Gregor wouldn't be able to eat in front of her, she hurriedly left the room, even turning the key, just as a sign to Gregor that he could settle down and take his time over everything. Gregor's legs trembled as he addressed his meal. His wounds too must have completely healed over, for he didn't feel any hindrance, he was astonished to realize, and remembered how a little more than a month ago he had cut his finger with a knife, and only the day before yesterday the place still had hurt. 'I wonder if I have less sensitivity now?' he thought, as he sucked avidly on the cheese, which of all the proffered foodstuffs had most spontaneously and powerfully attracted him. Then, in rapid succession, and with eyes watering with satisfaction, he ate up the cheese, the vegetables and the sauce; the fresh foods, on the other hand, were not to his liking—he couldn't even bear the smell of them, and dragged such things as he wanted to eat a little way away from them. He was long done with everything, and was just lounging lazily where he had eaten, when his sister, to signal that he was to withdraw, slowly turned the key in the lock. That immediately stung him out of his drowsiness, and he dashed back under the sofa. But it cost him a great effort to remain there, even for the short time his sister was in the room, because his big meal had filled out his belly, and he was scarcely able to breathe in his little space. Amidst little fits of panic suffocation, he watched with slightly bulging eyes, as his sister, all unawares, swept everything together with a broom— not only the leftovers, but also those elements of food that Gregor hadn't touched, as though they too were now not good for anything—and as she hastily tipped everything into a bucket, on which she set a wooden lid, whereupon she carried everything back out. No sooner had she turned her back than Gregor came out from under the sofa, stretched and puffed himself up.

This was how Gregor was now fed every day, once in the morning, while his parents and the maid were still asleep, and a second time after lunch, when his parents had their little lie-down, and his sister sent the maid out on some errand or other. For sure, none of them wanted Gregor to starve, but maybe they didn't want to confront in so much material detail the idea of him eating anything. Perhaps also his sister wanted to spare them a little grief, because certainly they were suffering enough as it was.

With what excuses the doctor and locksmith were got rid of on that first morning was something Gregor never learned, because as he was not able to make himself understood, it didn't occur to anyone, not even his sister, that he could understand others, and so, when his sister was in his room, he had to content himself with hearing her occasional sighs and appeals to various saints. Only later, once she had got adjusted to everything a little—of course there could be no question of becoming fully used to it—Gregor sometimes caught a well-intentioned remark, or one that was capable of being interpreted as such. 'He had a good appetite today,' she said, when Gregor had dealt with his food in determined fashion, whereas, in the opposite case, which came to be the rule, she would sometimes say, almost sorrowfully: 'Oh, it's hardly been touched today.'

While Gregor was not given any news directly he was sometimes able to glean developments from the adjoining rooms, and whenever he heard anyone speaking, he would rush to the door in question, and press his whole body against it. Especially in the early days, there was no conversation that did not somehow, in some oblique way, deal with him. For two days, at each meal, there were debates as to how one ought to behave; and in between meals, the same subject was also discussed, because there were always at least two members of the household at home, probably as no one wanted to be alone at home, and couldn't in any case wholly leave it. On the very first day the cook had begged on her knees—it was unclear what and how much she knew about what had happened—to be let go right away, and when she took her leave a quarter of an hour later, she said thank-you for her dismissal, as if it was the greatest kindness she had experienced here, and, without anyone demanding it of her, gave the most solemn oath never to betray the least thing to anyone.

Now his sister had to do the cooking in harness with his mother; admittedly, it didn't create much extra work for her, because no one ate anything. Gregor kept hearing them vainly exhorting one another to eat, and receiving no reply, other than: 'Thank you, I've enough,' or words to that effect. Perhaps they didn't drink anything either. Often, his sister asked his father whether he would like a beer, and offered to fetch it herself, and when her father made no reply, she said, to get over his hesitation, that she could equally well send the janitor woman out for it, but in the end his father said a loud 'No', and there was an end of the matter.

Already in the course of that first day his father set out the fortunes and prospects of the family to his mother and sister. From time to time, he got up from the table and produced some certificate or savings book from his little home safe, which he had managed to rescue from the collapse of his business five years ago. One could hear him opening the complicated lock, and shutting it again after taking out the desired item. These explanations from his father constituted the first good news that had reached Gregor's ears since his incarceration. He had been of the view that the winding-up of the business had left his father with nothing—at any rate his father had never said anything to the contrary, and Gregor hadn't questioned him either. At the time Gregor had bent all his endeavours to helping the family to get over the commercial catastrophe, which had plunged them all into complete despair, as quickly as possible. And so he had begun working with an especial zeal and almost overnight had moved from being a little junior clerk to a travelling salesman, who of course had earning power of an entirely different order, and whose successes in the form of percentages were instantly turned into money, which could be laid out on the table of the surprised and delighted family. They had been good times, and they had never returned, at least not in that magnificence, even though Gregor went on to earn so much money that he was able to bear, and indeed bore, the expenses of the whole family. They had just become used to it, both the family and Gregor; they gratefully took receipt of his money, which he willingly handed over, but there was no longer any particular warmth about it. Only his sister had remained close to Gregor, and it was his secret project to send her, who unlike himself loved music and played the violin with great feeling, to the conservatory next year, without regard to the great expense that was surely involved, and that needed to be earned, most probably in some other fashion. In the course of Gregor's brief stays in the city, the conservatory often came up in conversations with his sister, but always as a beautiful dream, not conceivably to be realized, and their parents disliked even such innocent references; but Gregor thought about it quite purposefully, and meant to make a formal announcement about it at Christmas.

Such—in his present predicament—perfectly useless thoughts crowded his head, while he stuck to the door in an upright position, listening. Sometimes, from a general fatigue, he was unable to listen, and carelessly let his head drop against the door, before holding it upright again, because even the little noise he had made had been heard next door, and had caused them all to fall silent. 'Wonder what he's doing now,' said his father after a while, evidently turning towards the door, and only then was the interrupted conversation gradually resumed.

Because his father tended to repeat himself in his statements—partly because he had long disregarded these matters, and partly because Gregor's mother often didn't understand when they were first put to her—Gregor now had plenty of occasion to hear that, in spite of the calamity, an admittedly small nest egg had survived from the old days, and had grown a little over the intervening years through the compounding of interest. In addition to this, the money that Gregor had brought home every month—he kept back no more than a couple of guilder for himself—had not been used up completely, and had accrued to another small lump sum. Behind his door, Gregor nodded enthusiastically, delighted by this unexpected caution and prudence. The surplus funds might have been used to pay down his father's debt to the director, thereby bringing closer the day when he might quit this job, but now it seemed to him better done the way his father had done it.

Of course, the money was nowhere near enough for the family to live off the interest, say; it might be enough to feed them all for a year or two, at most, but no more. Really it was a sum that mustn't be touched, that ought to be set aside for an emergency; money for day-to-day living expenses needed to be earned. His father was a healthy, but now elderly man, who hadn't worked for five years now, and who surely shouldn't expect too much of himself; in those five years, which were the first holidays of a strenuous and broadly unsuccessful life, he had put on a lot of fat, and had slowed down considerably. And was his old mother to go out and earn money, who suffered from asthma, to whom merely going from one end of the flat to the other was a strain, and who spent every other day on the sofa struggling for breath in front of the open window? Or was his sister to make money, still a child with her seventeen years, and who so deserved to be left in the manner of her life heretofore, which had consisted of wearing pretty frocks, sleeping in late, helping out at the pub, taking part in a few modest celebrations and, above all, playing the violin. Whenever the conversation turned to the necessity of earning money, Gregor would let go of the door, and throw himself on to the cool leather sofa beside it, because he was burning with sorrow and shame.

Often he would lie there all night, not sleeping a wink, and just scraping against the leather for hours. Nor did he shun the great effort of pushing a chair over to the window, creeping up to the window-sill, and, propped against the armchair, leaning in the window, clearly in some vague recollection of the liberation he had once used to feel, gazing out of the window. For it was true to say that with each passing day his view of distant things grew fuzzier; the hospital across the road, whose ubiquitous aspect he had once cursed, he now no longer even saw, and if he hadn't known for a fact that he lived in the leafy, but perfectly urban Charlottenstrasse, he might have thought that his window gave on to a wasteland where grey sky merged indistinguishably with grey earth. His alert sister needed only to spot that the armchair had been moved across to the window once or twice, before she took to pushing the chair over there herself after tidying Gregor's room, and even leaving the inner window ajar.

Had Gregor been able to speak to his sister and to thank her for everything she had to do for him, he would have found it a little easier to submit to her ministrations; but, as it was, he suffered from them. His sister, for her part, clearly sought to blur the embarrassment of the whole thing, and the more time passed, the better able she was to do so, but Gregor was also able to see through everything more acutely. Even her entry was terrible for him. No sooner had she stepped into his room, than without even troubling to shut the door behind her—however much care she usually took to save anyone passing the sight of Gregor's room—she darted over to the window and flung it open with febrile hands, almost as if she were suffocating, and then, quite regardless of how cold it might be outside, she stood by the window for a while, taking deep breaths. She subjected Gregor to her scurrying and her din twice daily; for the duration of her presence, he trembled under the sofa, even though he knew full well that she would have been only too glad to spare him the awkwardness, had it been possible for her to remain in the same room as her brother with the window closed.

On one occasion—it must have been a month or so after Gregor's metamorphosis, and there was surely no more cause for his sister to get agitated about Gregor's appearance—she came in a little earlier than usual and saw Gregor staring out of the window, immobile, almost as though set up on purpose to give her a fright. Gregor would not have been surprised if she had stopped in her tracks, seeing as he impeded her from going over and opening the window, but not only did she not come in, she leaped back and locked the door; a stranger might have supposed that Gregor had been lying in wait for her, to bite her. Naturally, Gregor straightaway went and hid under the sofa, but he had to wait till noon for his sister to reappear, and then she seemed more agitated than usual. From that he understood that the sight of him was still unbearable to her and would continue to be unbearable to her, and that she probably had to control herself so as not to run away at the sight of that little portion of his body that peeped out from under the sofa. One day, in a bid to save her from that as well, he moved the tablecloth on to the sofa—the labour took him four hours—and arranged it in such a way that he was completely covered, and that his sister, even if she bent down, would be unable to see him. If this covering hadn't been required in her eyes, she could easily have removed it, because it was surely clear enough that it was no fun for Gregor to screen himself from sight so completely, but she left the cloth *in situ*, and once Gregor even thought he caught a grateful look from her, as he moved the cloth ever so slightly with his head to see how his sister was reacting to the new arrangement.

During the first fortnight, his parents would not be induced to come in and visit him, and he often heard their professions of respect for what his sister was now doing, whereas previously they had frequently been annoyed with her for being a somewhat useless girl. Now, though, both of them, father and mother, often stood outside Gregor's room while his sister was cleaning up inside, and no sooner had she come out than she had to tell them in precise detail how things looked in the room, what Gregor had eaten, how he had behaved this time, and whether there wasn't some sign of an improvement in his condition. His mother, by the way, quite soon wanted to visit Gregor herself, but his father and sister kept her from doing so with their common-sense arguments, to which Gregor listened attentively, and which met with his wholehearted approval. Later on, it took force to hold her back, and when she cried, 'Let me see Gregor, after all he is my unhappy son! Won't you understand that I have to see him?' then Gregor thought it might after all be a good thing if his mother saw him, not every day of course, but perhaps as often as once a week; she did have a much better grasp of everything than his sister, who, for all her pluck, was still a child, and ultimately had perhaps taken on such a difficult task purely out of child-ish high spirits.

Before very long, Gregor's desire to see his mother was granted. Gregor didn't care to sit in the window in the daytime out of regard for his parents, nor was he able to crawl around very much on the few square yards of floor; even at night he was scarcely able to lie quietly, his food soon stopped affording him the least pleasure, and so, to divert himself, he got into the habit of crawling all over the walls and ceiling. He was particularly given to hanging off the ceiling; it felt very different from lying on the floor; he could breathe more easily; a gentle thrumming vibration went through his body; and in the almost blissful distraction Gregor felt up there, it could even hap-pen that to his own surprise he let himself go, and smacked down on the floor. Of course his physical mastery of his body was of a different order from what it had been previously, and so now he didn't hurt himself, even after a fall from a considerable height. His sister observed the new amuse-ment Gregor had found for himself—as he crept here and there he couldn't avoid leaving some traces of his adhesive secretion—and she got it into her head to maximize the amount of crawling Gregor could do, by removing those pieces of furniture that got in his way, in particular the wardrobe and the desk. But it was not possible for her to do so unaided; she didn't dare ask her father for help; the maid would certainly not have helped, because while this girl of about sixteen had bravely stayed on after the cook's departure, she had also asked in return that she might keep the kitchen locked, and only have to open it when particularly required to do so; so Gregor's sister had no alternative but to ask her mother on an occasion when her father was away. Gregor's mother duly came along with cries of joy and excitement, only to lapse into silence outside Gregor's door. First, his sister checked to see that everything in the room was tidy; only then did she allow her mother to step inside. In a very great rush, Gregor had pulled the tablecloth down lower, with more pleats, and the whole thing really had the appearance of a cloth draped casually over the sofa. He also refrained from peeping out from underneath it; he declined to try to see his mother on this first visit, he was just happy she had come. 'It's all right, you won't see him,' said his sister, who was evidently taking her mother by the hand. Now Gregor heard the two weak women shifting the heavy old wardrobe from its place, and how his sister always did the bulk of the work, ignoring the warnings of his mother, who kept fearing she might overstrain herself. It took a very long time. It was probably after fifteen minutes of toil that his mother said it would be better to leave the wardrobe where it was, because firstly it was too heavy, they would never manage to get it moved before father's return, and by leaving it in the middle of the room they would only succeed in leaving an irritating obstruction for Gregor, and secondly it was by no means certain that they were doing Gregor a favour by removing that piece of furniture anyway. She rather thought the opposite; the sight of the empty stretch of wall clutched at her heart; and why shouldn't Gregor have a similar sensation too, seeing as he was long accustomed to his bedroom furniture, and was therefore bound to feel abandoned in the empty room. 'And isn't it the case as well,' his mother concluded very quietly—indeed she was barely talking above a whisper throughout, as though to prevent Gregor, whose whereabouts she didn't know, from even hearing the sound of her voice, seeing as she felt certain that he wasn't capable of understanding her words anyway—'isn't it the case as well, that by taking away his furniture, we would be showing him we were abandoning all hope of an improvement in his condition, and leaving him utterly to his own devices? I think it would be best if we try to leave the room in exactly the condition it was before, so that, if Gregor is returned to us, he will find everything unaltered, and will thereby be able to forget the intervening period almost as if it hadn't happened.'

As he listened to these words of his mother, Gregor understood that the want of any direct human address, in combination with his monotonous life at the heart of the family over the past couple of months, must have confused his understanding, because otherwise he would not have been able to account for the fact that he seriously wanted to have his room emptied out. Was it really his wish to have his cosy room, comfortably furnished with old heirlooms, transformed into a sort of cave, merely so that he would be able to crawl around in it freely, without hindrance in any direction—even at the expense of rapidly and utterly forgetting his human past? He was near enough to forgetting it now, and only the voice of his mother, which he hadn't heard for a long time, had reawakened the memory in him. Nothing was to be taken out; everything was to stay as it was; the positive influence of the furniture on his condition was indispensable; and if the furniture prevented him from crawling around without rhyme or reason, then that was no drawback either, but a great advantage.

But his sister was unfortunately of a different mind; she had become accustomed, not without some justification either, to cast herself in the role of a sort of expert when Gregor's affairs were discussed with her parents, and so her mother's urgings now had the effect on his sister of causing her to insist on the removal not merely of the wardrobe and the desk, which was all she had originally proposed, but of all the furniture, with the sole exception of the indispensable sofa. It wasn't merely childish stubbornness and a surge of unexpected and hard-won self-confidence that prompted her to take this view; she had observed that Gregor needed a lot of space for his crawling, and in the course of it, so far as she had seen, made no use whatever of the furniture. Perhaps the natural enthusiasm of a girl of her age played a certain role too, a quality that seeks its own satisfaction in any matter, and this now caused Grete to present Gregor's situation in even starker terms, so that she might do even more for him than she had thus far. For it was unthinkable that anyone else would dare to set foot in a room where Gregor all alone made free with the bare walls.

And so she refused to abandon her resolution in the face of the arguments of her mother, who seemed to have been overwhelmed by uncertainty in this room, and who, falling silent, to the best of her ability helped his sister to remove the wardrobe from the room. Well, Gregor could do without the wardrobe if need be, but the writing-desk had to stay. And no sooner had the two women left with the wardrobe, against which they pressed themselves groaning with effort, than Gregor thrust his head out from under the sofa, to see how best, with due care and respect, he might intervene on his own behalf. It was unfortunate that it was his mother who came back in first, while Grete was still clasping the wardrobe in the next-door room, hefting it this way and that, without of course being able to budge it from the spot. His mother was not accustomed to the sight of Gregor, it could have made her ill, and so Gregor reversed hurriedly to the far end of the sofa, but was unable to prevent the cloth from swaying slightly. That was enough to catch his mother's attention. She paused, stood still for a moment, and then went back to Grete.

Even though Gregor kept telling himself there was nothing particular going on, just a few sticks of furniture being moved around, he soon had to admit to himself that the to-ing and fro-ing of the two women, their little exhortations to one another, the scraping of the furniture on the floor, did have the effect on him of a great turmoil nourished on all sides, and he was compelled to admit that, however he drew in his head and his legs and pressed his belly to the floor, he would be unable to tolerate much more of it. They were clearing his room out; taking away everything that was dear to him; they had already taken the wardrobe that contained his jigsaw and his other tools; now they were prising away the desk that seemed to have taken root in the floor, where he had done his homework at trade school, at secondary, even at elementary school—he really had no more time to consider the good intentions of the two women, whose existence he had practically forgotten, because they were now so exhausted they were doing their work in near silence, all that could be heard of them being their heavy footfalls.

And so he erupted forth—the women were just resting on the desk next door, to catch their breath—and four times changed his direction for he really didn't know what he should rescue first, when he saw the picture of the fur-clad woman all the more prominent now, because the wall on which it hung had now been cleared, crawled hurriedly up to it and pressed himself against the glass, which stuck to him and imparted a pleasant coolness to his hot belly. At least no one would now take away this picture, which Gregor now completely covered. He turned his head in the direction of the living-room door, to see the women as they returned.

They hadn't taken much of a break, and here they came again; Grete had laid her arm around her mother, and was practically carrying her. 'Well, what shall we take next?' Grete said, looking around. Then her eyes encountered those of Gregor, up on the wall. She kept her calm, probably only on account of the presence of her mother, inclined her face towards her, to keep her from looking around, and said, with a voice admittedly trembling and uncontrolled: 'Oh, let's just go back to the living room for a moment, shall we?' Grete's purpose was clear enough to Gregor; she wanted to get her mother to safety, and then chase him off the wall. Well, just let her try! He would perch on his picture, and never surrender it. He would rather fly in Grete's face.

But Grete's words served only to disquiet her mother, who stepped to one side, spotted the giant brown stain on the flowered wallpaper, and, before she had time to understand what she saw, she cried in a hoarse, screaming voice, 'Oh my God, oh my God!' and with arms outspread, as though abandoning everything she had, fell across the sofa, and didn't stir. 'Ooh, Gregor!' cried his sister, brandishing her fist and glowering at him. Since his metamorphosis, they were the first words she had directly addressed to him. She ran next door to find some smelling-salts to rouse her mother from her faint; Gregor wanted to help too—he could always go back and rescue the picture later on—but he was stuck fast to the glass, and had to break free of it by force; then he trotted next door as though he could give his sister some advice, as in earlier times; was forced to stand around idly behind her while she examined various different flasks; and gave her such a shock, finally, when she spun round, that a bottle crashed to the ground and broke. One splinter cut Gregor in the face, the fumes of some harshly corrosive medicine causing him to choke; Grete ended up by grabbing as many little flasks as she could hold, and ran with them to her mother; she slammed the door shut with her foot. Gregor was now shut off from his mother, who, through his fault, was possibly close to death; there was nothing he could do but wait; and assailed by reproach and dread, he began to crawl. He crawled over everything, the walls, the furniture, the ceiling, and finally in his despair, with the whole room already spinning round him, he dropped on to the middle of the dining table.

Some time passed, Gregor lay there dully, there was silence all round, perhaps it was a good sign. Then the bell rang. The maid, of course, was locked away in her kitchen, and so Grete had to go to the door. His father was back. 'What happened?' were his first words; Grete's appearance must have given everything away. She answered in muffled tones; clearly she must be pressing her face to her father's chest: 'Mother had a faint, but she's feeling better now. Gregor's got loose.' 'I knew it,' said his father. 'Wasn't I always telling you, but you women never listen.' Gregor understood that his father must have put the worst possible construction on Grete's all too brief account, and supposed that Gregor had perpetrated some act of violence. Therefore Gregor must try to mollify his father, because for an explanation there was neither time nor means. And so he fled to the door of his room, and pressed himself against it, so that his father, on stepping in from the hallway, might see right away that Gregor had every intention of going back promptly into his room, and there was no necessity to use force, he had only to open the door for him, and he would disappear through it right away.

But his father wasn't in the mood to observe such details; 'Ah!' he roared, the moment he entered, in a tone equally enraged and delighted. Gregor withdrew his head from the door, and turned to look at his father. He really hadn't imagined him the way he was; admittedly, he had been distracted of late by the novel sensation of crawling, and had neglected to pay attention to goings-on in the rest of the flat, as he had previously, and so really he should have been prepared to come upon some alterations. But really, really, was that still his father? The same man who had lain feebly buried in bed, when Gregor had set out formerly on a business trip; who had welcomed him back at night, in his nightshirt and rocking-chair; not even properly able to get to his feet any more, but merely raising both arms in token of his pleasure; and who on his infrequent walks on one or two Sundays per year, and on the most solemn holidays, walked between Gregor and his wife slowly enough anyway, but still slower than them, bundled into his old overcoat, feeling his way forward with his carefully jabbing stick, and each time he wanted to speak, stopping to gather his listeners about him? And now here he was fairly erect; wearing a smart blue uniform with gold buttons, like the door-man of a bank; over the stiff collar of his coat, the bulge of a powerful double-chin; under the bushy eyebrows an alert and vigorous expression in his black eyes; his habitually unkempt white hair now briskly parted and combed into a shining tidy arrangement. He threw his cap, which had on it a gold monogram, presumably that of the bank, across the whole room in an arc on to the sofa, and, hands in his pockets, with the skirts of his long coat trailing behind him, he walked up to Gregor with an expression of grim resolve. He probably didn't know himself what he would do next; but even so, he raised his feet to an uncommon height, and Gregor was startled by the enormous size of his bootsoles. But he didn't allow himself the leisure to stop and remark on it; he had understood from the first day of his new life that his father thought the only policy to adopt was one of the utmost sever-ity towards him. And so he scurried along in front of his father, pausing when he stopped, and hurrying on the moment he made another movement. In this way, they circled the room several times, without anything decisive taking place, yes, even without the whole process having the appearance of a chase, because of its slow tempo. It was for that reason too that Gregor remained on the floor for the time being, because he was afraid that if he took to the walls or ceiling, his father might interpret that as a sign of partic-ular wickedness on his part. Admittedly, Gregor had to tell himself he couldn't keep up even this slow pace for very long, because in the time his father took a single step, he needed to perform a whole multiplicity of move-ments. He was already beginning to get out of breath—even in earlier times his lungs hadn't been altogether reliable. As he teetered along, barely keep-ing his eyes open, in order to concentrate all his resources on his movement—in his dull-wittedness not even thinking of any other form of salvation beyond merely keeping going; and had almost forgotten that the walls were available to him, albeit obstructed by carefully carved items of furniture, full of spikes and obstructions—something whizzed past him, something had been hurled at him, something now rolling around on the floor in front of him. It was an apple; straightaway it was followed by another; Gregor in ter-ror was rooted to the spot; there was no sense in keeping moving, not if his father had decided to have recourse to artillery. He had filled his pockets from the fruit bowl on the sideboard, and was hurling one apple after another, barely pausing to take aim. These little red apples rolled around on the floor as though electrified, often caroming into one another. A feebly tossed apple brushed against Gregor's back, only to bounce off it harmlessly. One thrown a moment later, however, seemed to pierce it; Gregor tried to drag himself away, as though the bewildering and scarcely credible pain might pass if he changed position; but he felt as though nailed to the spot, and in complete disorientation, he stretched out. With one last look he saw how the door to his room was flung open, and his mother ran out in front of his howling sister, in her chemise—his sister must have undressed her to make it easier for her to breathe after her fainting fit—how his mother ran towards his father, and as she ran her loosened skirts successively slipped to the floor, and how, stumbling over them she threw herself at his father, and embracing him, in complete union with him—but now Gregor's eyesight was failing him—with her hands clasping the back of his head, begged him to spare Gregor's life.

III

The grave wound to Gregor, from whose effects he suffered for over a month—as no one dared to remove the apple, it remained embedded in his flesh, as a visible memento—seemed to have reminded even his father that in spite of his current sorry and loathsome form, Gregor remained a member of the family, and must not be treated like an enemy, but as someone whom—all revulsion to the contrary—family duty compelled one to choke down, and who must be tolerated, simply tolerated.

Even if Gregor had lost his mobility, and presumably for good, so that now like an old invalid he took an age to cross his room—there could be no more question of crawling up out of the horizontal—this deterioration of his condition acquired a compensation, perfectly adequate in his view, in the fact that each evening now, the door to the living room, which he kept under sharp observation for an hour or two before it happened, was opened, so that, lying in his darkened room, invisible from the living room, he was permitted to see the family at their lit-up table, and, with universal sanction, as it were, though now in a completely different way than before, to listen to them talk together.

Admittedly, these were not now the lively conversations of earlier times, which Gregor had once called to mind with some avidity as he lay down exhausted in the damp sheets of some poky hotel room. Generally, things were very quiet. His father fell asleep in his armchair not long after supper was over; his mother and sister enjoined one another to be quiet; his mother, sitting well forward under the lamp, sewed fine linen for some haberdashery; his sister, who had taken a job as salesgirl, studied stenography and French in the evenings, in the hope of perhaps one day getting a better job. Sometimes his father would wake up, and as though unaware that he had been asleep, would say to his mother: 'Oh, you've been sewing all this time!' and promptly fall asleep again, while mother and sister exchanged tired smiles.

With an odd stubbornness, his father now refused to take off his uniform coat when he was at home; and while his dressing-gown hung uselessly on its hook, his fully dressed father dozed in his chair, as though ready at all times to be of service, waiting, even here, for the voice of his superior. As a result, the uniform, which even to begin with had not been new, in spite of all the precautions of mother and sister, rapidly lost its cleanliness, and Gregor often spent whole evenings staring at this comprehensively stained suit, with its invariably gleaming gold buttons, in which the old man slept so calmly and uncomfortably.

As soon as the clock struck ten, his mother would softly wake his father, and talk him into going to bed, because he couldn't sleep properly where he was, and proper sleep was precisely what he needed, given that he had to be back on duty at six in the morning. But with the obstinacy that characterized him ever since he had become a commissionaire, he would always insist on staying at table longer, even though he quite regularly fell asleep there, and it was only with the greatest difficulty that he was then persuaded to exchange his chair for bed. However Gregor's mother and sister pleaded and remonstrated with him, he would slowly shake his head for a whole quarter of an hour at a time, keep his eyes shut, and refuse to get up. Gregor's mother would tug at his sleeve, whisper blandishments in his ear, his sister would leave her work to support her mother, but all in vain. His father would only slump deeper into his chair. Only when the women took him under the arms did he open his eyes, look alternately at them both, and then usually say: 'What sort of life is this? What sort of peace and dignity in my old days?' And propped up by the women, he would cumbersomely get to his feet, as though he was a great weight on himself, let them conduct him as far as the door, then gesture to them, and go on himself, while Gregor's mother hurriedly threw down her sewing, and his sister her pen, to run behind him and continue to be of assistance.

Who in this exhausted and overworked family had the time to pay any more attention to Gregor than was absolutely necessary? The household seemed to shrink; the maid was now allowed to leave after all; a vast bony charwoman with a great mane of white hair came in the morning and evening to do the brunt of the work; everything else had to be done by mother, in addition to her copious needlework. Things even came to such a pass that various family jewels, in which mother and sister had once on special occasions decked themselves, were sold off, as Gregor learned one evening, from a general discussion of the prices that had been achieved. The bitterest complaint, however, concerned the impossibility of leaving this now far too large apartment, as there was no conceivable way of moving Gregor. Gregor understood perfectly well that it wasn't any regard for him that stood in the way of a move, because all it would have taken was a suitably sized shipping crate, with a few holes drilled in it for him to breathe through; no, what principally kept the family from moving to another flat was their complete and utter despair—the thought that they in all the circle of relatives and acquaintances had been singled out for such a calamity. The things the world requires of poor people, they performed to the utmost, his father running out to get breakfast for the little bank officials, his mother hurling herself at the personal linen of strangers, his sister trotting back and forth behind the desk, doing the bidding of the customers, but that was as far as the strength of the family reached. The wound in Gregor's back would start to play up again, when mother and sister came back, having taken his father to bed, and neglected their work to sit pressed together, almost cheek to cheek; when his mother pointed to Gregor's room and said, 'Will you shut the door now, Grete'; and when Gregor found himself once more in the dark, while next door the women were mingling their tears, or perhaps sitting staring dry-eyed at the table.

Gregor spent his days and nights almost without sleeping. Sometimes he thought that the next time they opened the door he would take the business of the family in hand, just exactly as he had done before; after a long time the director figured in his thoughts again, and the chief clerk, the junior clerk and the trainees, the dim-witted factotum, a couple of friends he had in other companies, a chambermaid in a hotel out in the provinces somewhere, a sweet, fleeting memory, a cashier in a hat shop whom he had courted assiduously, but far too slowly—all these appeared to him, together with others he never knew or had already forgotten, but instead of helping him and his family, they were all inaccessible to him, and he was glad when they went away again. And then he wasn't in the mood to worry about the family, but instead was filled with rage at how they neglected him, and even though he couldn't imagine anything for which he had an appetite, he made schemes as to how to inveigle himself into the pantry, to take there what was rightfully his, even if he didn't feel the least bit hungry now. No longer bothering to think what might please Gregor, his sister before going to work in the morning and afternoon now hurriedly shoved some food or other into Gregor's room with her foot, and in the evening reached in with the broom to hook it back out again, indifferent as to whether it had been only tasted or even—as most regularly happened—had remained quite untouched. The tidying of the room, which she now did always in the evening, really could not have been done more cursorily. The walls were streaked with grime, and here and there lay little tangled balls of dust and filth. At first, Gregor liked to take up position, for her coming, in the worst affected corners, as if to reproach her for their condition. But he could probably have stayed there for weeks without his sister doing anything better; after all, she could see the dirt as clearly as he could, she had simply taken it into her head to ignore it. And at the same time, with a completely new pernicketiness that seemed to have come over her, as it had indeed the whole family, she jealously guarded her monopoly on the tidying of Gregor's room. On one occasion, his mother had subjected Gregor's room to a great cleaning, involving several buckets full of water—the humidity was upsetting to Gregor, who lay miserably and motionlessly stretched out on the sofa—but his mother didn't get away with it either. Because no sooner had his sister noticed the change in Gregor's room that evening than, mortally offended, she ran into the sitting room, and ignoring her mother's imploringly raised hands, burst into a crying fit that her parents—her father had of course been shaken from his slumbers in his armchair—witnessed first with helpless surprise, and then they too were touched by it; his father on the one side blaming Gregor's mother for not leaving the cleaning of the room to his sister; while on the other yelling at the sister that she would never be allowed to clean Gregor's room again; while the mother tried to drag the father, who was quite beside himself with excitement, into the bedroom; his sister, shaken with sobs, pummelled at the table with her little fists; and Gregor hissed loudly in impotent fury that no one thought to shut the door, and save him from such a noise and spectacle.

But even if his sister, exhausted by office work, no longer had it in her to care for Gregor as she had done earlier, that still didn't mean that his mother had to take a hand to save Gregor from being utterly neglected. Because now there was the old charwoman. This old widow, who with her strong frame had survived everything that life had had to throw at her, was evidently quite undismayed by Gregor. It wasn't that she was nosy, but she had by chance once opened the door to Gregor's room, and at the sight of Gregor, who, caught out, started to scurry hither and thither, even though no one was chasing him, merely stood there with her hands folded and watched in astonishment. Since then, she let no morning or evening slip without opening the door a crack and looking in on Gregor. To begin with, she called to him as well, in terms she probably thought were friendly, such things as: 'Come here, you old dung-beetle!' or 'Will you take a look at that old dung-beetle!' Gregor of course didn't reply, but ignored the fact that the door had been opened, and stayed just exactly where he was. If only this old char-woman, instead of being allowed to stand and gawp at him whenever she felt like it, had been instructed to clean his room every day! Early one morning—a heavy rain battered against the windowpanes, a sign already, perhaps, of the approaching spring—Gregor felt such irritation when the charwoman came along with her words that, albeit slowly and ponderously, he made as if to attack her. The charwoman, far from being frightened, seized a chair that was standing near the door, and as she stood there with mouth agape it was clear that she would only close it when she had brought the chair crashing down on Gregor's back. 'So is that as far as it goes then?' she asked, as Gregor turned away, and she calmly put the chair back in a corner.

Gregor was now eating almost nothing at all. Only sometimes, happening to pass the food that had been put out for him, he would desultorily take a morsel in his mouth, and keep it there for hours, before usually spitting it out again. At first he thought it was grief about the condition of his room that was keeping him from eating, but in fact the alterations to his room were the things he came to terms with most easily. They had started pushing things into his room that would otherwise have been in the way, and there were now a good many such items, since one room in the flat had been let out to a trio of bachelors. These serious-looking gentlemen—all three wore full beards, as Gregor happened to see once, peering through a crack in the door—were insistent on hygiene, not just where their own room was con-cerned, but throughout the flat where they were now tenants, and therefore most especially in the kitchen. Useless or dirty junk was something for which they had no tolerance. Besides, they had largely brought their own furnishings with them. For that reason, many things had now become super-fluous that couldn't be sold, and that one didn't want to simply throw away either. All these things came into Gregor's room. And also the ashcan and the rubbish-bin from the kitchen. Anything that seemed even temporarily surplus to requirements was simply slung into Gregor's room by the char-woman, who was always in a tearing rush; it was fortunate that Gregor rarely saw more than the hand and the object in question, whatever it was. It might be that the charwoman had it in mind to reclaim the things at some future time, or to go in and get them all out one day, but what happened was that they simply lay where they had been thrown, unless Gregor, crawling about among the junk, happened to displace some of it, at first perforce, because there was simply no more room in which to move, but later on with increasing pleasure, even though, after such peregrinations he would find himself heartsore and weary to death, and wouldn't move for many hours.

Since the tenants sometimes took their supper at home in the shared liv-ing room, the door to it remained closed on some evenings, but Gregor hardly missed the opening of the door. After all, there were enough evenings when it had been open, and he had not profited from it, but, instead, without the family noticing at all, had merely lain still in the darkest corner of his room. On one occasion, however, the charwoman had left the door to the living room slightly ajar, and it remained ajar, even when the tenants walked in that evening, and the lights were turned on. They took their places at the table, where previously father, mother and Gregor had sat, unfurled their napkins and took up their eating irons. Straightaway his mother appeared in the doorway carrying a dish of meat, and hard behind her came his sister with a bowl heaped with potatoes. The food steamed mightily. The tenants inclined themselves to the dishes in front of them, as though to examine them before eating, and the one who was sitting at the head of the table, and who seemed to have some authority over the other two flanking him, cut into a piece of meat in the dish, as though to check whether it was sufficiently done, and didn't have to be sent back to the kitchen. He seemed content with what he found, and mother and sister, who had been watching in some trepidation, broke into relieved smiles.

The family were taking their meal in the kitchen. Even so, before going in there, the father came in and with a single reverence, cap in hand, walked once round the table. All the tenants got up and muttered something into their beards. Once they were on their own again, they ate in near silence. It struck Gregor that out of all the various sounds one could hear, it was that of their grinding teeth that stood out, as though to demonstrate to Gregor that teeth were needed to eat with, and the best toothless gums were no use. 'But I do have an appetite,' Gregor said to himself earnestly, 'only not for those things. The way those tenants fill their boots, while I'm left to starve!'

On that same evening—Gregor couldn't recall having heard the violin once in all this time—it sounded from the kitchen. The tenants had finished their supper, the one in the middle had produced a newspaper, and given the other two a page apiece, and now they were leaning back, reading and smoking. When the violin sounded, they pricked up their ears, got up and tiptoed to the door of the hallway where they stayed pressed together. They must have been heard from the kitchen, because father called: 'Do the gentlemen have any objection to the music? It can be stopped right away.' 'On the contrary,' said the middle gentleman, 'mightn't the young lady like to come in to us and play here, where it's more cosy and convenient?' 'Only too happy to oblige,' called the father, as if he were the violin player. The gentlemen withdrew to their dining room and waited. Before long up stepped the father with the music stand, the mother with the score, and the sister with the violin. Calmly the sister set everything up in readiness; the parents, who had never let rooms before, and therefore overdid politeness towards the tenants, didn't even dare to sit in their own chairs; Gregor's father leaned in the doorway, his right hand pushed between two buttons of his closed coat; Gregor's mother was offered a seat by one of the gentlemen, and, not presuming to move, remained sitting just where the gentleman had put her, off in a corner.

The sister began to play; father and mother, each on their respective side, attentively followed the movements of her hands. Gregor, drawn by the music, had slowly inched forward, and his head was already in the living room. He was no longer particularly surprised at his lack of discretion, where previously this discretion had been his entire pride. Even though now he would have had additional cause to remain hidden, because as a result of the dust that lay everywhere in his room, and flew up at the merest movement, he himself was covered with dust; on his back and along his sides he dragged around an assortment of threads, hairs and bits of food; his indifference to everything was far too great for him to lie down on his back, as he had done several times a day before, and rub himself clean on the carpet. And, in spite of his condition, he felt no shame at moving out on to the pristine floor of the living room.

Admittedly, no one paid him any regard. The family was completely absorbed by the violin playing; the tenants, on the other hand, hands in pockets, had initially taken up position far too close behind the music stand, so that they all could see the music, which must surely be annoying to his sister, but before long, heads lowered in half-loud conversation, they retreated to the window, where they remained, nervously observed by the father. It really did look all too evident that they were disappointed in their expectation of hearing some fine or entertaining playing, were fed up with the whole performance, and only suffered themselves to be disturbed out of politeness. The way they all blew their cigar smoke upwards from their noses and mouths indicated in particular a great nervousness on their part. And yet his sister was playing so beautifully. Her face was inclined to the side, and sadly and searchingly her eyes followed the columns of notes. Gregor crept a little closer and held his head close to the ground, so as to be prepared to meet her gaze. Could he be an animal, to be so moved by music? It was as though he sensed a way to the unknown sustenance he longed for. He was determined to go right up to his sister, to pluck at her skirt, and so let her know she was to come into his room with her violin, because no one rewarded music here as much as he wanted to reward it. He would not let her out of his room, at least not as long as he lived; for the first time his frightening form would come in useful for him; he would appear at all doors to his room at once, and hiss in the faces of attackers; but his sister wasn't to be forced, she was to remain with him of her own free will; she was to sit by his side on the sofa, and he would tell her he was resolved to send her to the conservatory, and that, if the calamity hadn't struck, he would have told everyone so last Christmas—was Christmas past? surely it was—without brooking any objections. After this declaration, his sister would burst into tears of emotion, and Gregor would draw himself up to her oxter and kiss her on the throat, which, since she'd started going to the office, she wore exposed, without a ribbon or collar.

'Mr Samsa!' cried the middle of the gentlemen, and not bothering to say another word, pointed with his index finger at the slowly advancing Gregor. The violin stopped, the middle gentleman first smiled, shaking his head, at his two friends, and then looked at Gregor once more. His father seemed to think it his first priority, even before driving Gregor away, to calm the tenants, though they were not at all agitated, and in fact seemed to find Gregor more entertaining than they had the violin playing. He hurried over to them, and with outspread arms tried simultaneously to push them back into their room, and with his body to block their sight of Gregor. At this point, they seemed to lose their temper. It wasn't easy to tell whether it was the father's behaviour or the understanding now dawning on them that they had been living next door to someone like Gregor. They called on the father for explanations, they too started waving their arms around, plucked nervously at their beards, and were slow to retreat into their room. In the meantime,

Gregor's sister had overcome the confusion that had befallen her after the sudden interruption in her playing, had, after holding her violin and bow in her slackly hanging hands a while and continuing to read the score as if still playing, suddenly got a grip on herself, deposited the instrument in the lap of her mother who was still sitting on her chair struggling for breath, and ran into the next room, which the tenants, yielding now to pressure from her father, were finally more rapidly nearing. Gregor could see how, under the practised hands of his sister, the blankets and pillows on the beds flew up in the air and were plumped and pulled straight. Even before the gentlemen had reached their room, she was finished with making the beds, and had slipped out. Father seemed once more so much in the grip of his stubbornness that he quite forgot himself towards the tenants. He merely pushed and pushed, till the middle gentleman stamped thunderously on the floor, and so brought him to a stop. 'I hereby declare,' he said, raising his hand and with his glare taking in also mother and sister, 'that as a result of the vile conditions prevailing in this flat and in this family'—here, he spat emphatically on the floor—'I am giving notice with immediate effect. I of course will not pay one cent for the days I have lived here, in fact I will think very carefully whether or not to proceed with—believe me—very easily substantiated claims against you.' He stopped and looked straight ahead of him, as though waiting for something else. And in fact his two friends chimed in with the words: 'We too are giving in our notice, with immediate effect.' Thereupon he seized the doorknob, and slammed the door with a mighty crash.

Gregor's father, with shaking hands, tottered to his chair, and slumped down into it; it looked as though he were settling to his regular evening snooze, but the powerful nodding of his somehow disconnected head showed that he was very far from sleeping. All this time, Gregor lay just exactly where he had been when the tenants espied him. Disappointment at the failure of his plan, perhaps also a slight faintness from his long fasting kept him from being able to move. With a certain fixed dread he awaited the calamity about to fall upon his head. Even the violin failed to startle him, when it slipped through the trembling fingers of his mother, and with a jangling echo fell to the floor.

'Dear parents,' said his sister, and brought her hand down on the table top to obtain silence, 'things cannot go on like this. You might not be able to see it, but I do. I don't want to speak the name of my brother within the hearing of that monster, and so I will merely say: we have to try to get rid of it. We did as much as humanly possible to try and look after it and tolerate it. I don't think anyone can reproach us for any measure we have taken or failed to take.'

'She's right, a thousand times right,' his father muttered to himself. His mother, who—with an expression of derangement in her eyes—was still experiencing difficulty breathing, started coughing softly into her cupped hand.

His sister ran over to her mother, and held her by the head. The sister's words seemed to have prompted some more precise form of thought in the father's mind, and he sat up and was toying with his doorman's cap among the plates, which still hadn't been cleared after the tenants' meal, from time to time shooting a look at the silent Gregor.

'We must try and get rid of it,' the sister now said, to her father alone, as her mother was caught up in her coughing and could hear nothing else, 'otherwise it'll be the death of you. I can see it coming. If we have to work as hard as we are all at present doing, it's not possible to stand this permanent torture at home as well. I can't do it any more either.' And she burst into such a flood of tears that they flowed down on to her mother's face, from which she wiped them away, with mechanical movements of her hand.

'My child,' said her father compassionately and with striking comprehension, 'but what shall we do?'

Grete merely shrugged her shoulders as a sign of the uncertainty into which—in striking contrast to her previous conviction—she had now fallen in her weeping.

'If only he understood us,' said the father, with rising intonation; the sister, still weeping, waved her hand violently to indicate that such a thing was out of the question.

'If only he understood us,' the father repeated, by closing his eyes accepting the sister's conviction of the impossibility of it, 'then we might come to some sort of settlement with him. But as it is . . .'

'We must get rid of it,' cried the sister again, 'that's the only thing for it, Father. You just have to put from your mind any thought that it's Gregor. Our continuing to think that it was, for such a long time, therein lies the source of our misfortune. But how can it be Gregor? If it was Gregor, he would long ago have seen that it's impossible for human beings to live together with an animal like that, and he would have left of his own free will. That would have meant I didn't have a brother, but we at least could go on with our lives, and honour his memory. But as it is, this animal hounds us, drives away the tenants, evidently wants to take over the whole flat, and throw us out on to the street. Look, Father,' she suddenly broke into a scream, 'he's coming again!' And in an access of terror wholly incomprehensible to Gregor, his sister even quit her mother, actually pushing herself away from her chair, as though she would rather sacrifice her mother than remain anywhere near Gregor, and dashed behind her father, who, purely on the basis of her agitation, got to his feet and half-raised his arms to shield the sister.

Meanwhile, Gregor of course didn't have the least intention of frightening anyone, and certainly not his sister. He had merely begun to turn around, to make his way back to his room, which was a somewhat laborious and eye-catching process, as, in consequence of his debility he needed his head to help with such difficult manoeuvres, raising it many times and bashing it against the floor. He stopped and looked around. His good intentions seemed to have been acknowledged; it had just been a momentary fright he had given them. Now they all looked at him sadly and silently. There lay his mother in her armchair, with her legs stretched out and pressed together, her eyes almost falling shut with fatigue; his father and sister were sitting side by side, his sister having placed her hand on her father's neck.

'Well, maybe they'll let me turn around now,' thought Gregor, and recommenced the manoeuvre. He was unable to suppress the odd grunt of effort, and needed to take periodic rests as well. But nobody interfered with him, and he was allowed to get on with it by himself. Once he had finished his turn, he straightaway set off wandering back. He was struck by the great distance that seemed to separate him from his room, and was unable to understand how, in his enfeebled condition, he had just a little while ago covered the same distance, almost without noticing. Intent on making the most rapid progress he could, he barely noticed that no word, no exclamation from his family distracted him. Only when he was in the doorway did he turn his head, not all the way, as his neck felt a little stiff, but even so he was able to see that behind him nothing had changed, only that his sister had got up. His last look lingered upon his mother, who was fast asleep.

No sooner was he in his room than the door was pushed shut behind him, and locked and bolted. The sudden noise so alarmed Gregor that his little legs gave way beneath him. It was his sister who had been in such a hurry. She had been already standing on tiptoe, waiting, and had then light-footedly leaped forward. Gregor hadn't even heard her until she cried 'At last!' as she turned the key in the lock.

'What now?' wondered Gregor, and looked around in the dark. He soon made the discovery that he could no longer move. It came as no surprise to him; if anything, it seemed inexplicable that he had been able to get as far as he had on his frail little legs. Otherwise, he felt as well as could be expected. He did have pains all over his body, but he felt they were gradually abating, and would finally cease altogether. The rotten apple in his back and the inflammation all round it, which was entirely coated with a soft dust, he barely felt any more. He thought back on his family with devotion and love. His conviction that he needed to disappear was, if anything, still firmer than his sister's. He remained in this condition of empty and peaceful reflection until the church clock struck three a.m. The last thing he saw was the sky gradually lightening outside his window. Then his head involuntarily dropped, and his final breath passed feebly from his nostrils.

When the charwoman came early in the morning—so powerful was she, and in such a hurry, that, even though she had repeatedly been asked not to, she slammed all the doors so hard that sleep was impossible after her coming—she at first found nothing out of the ordinary when she paid her customary brief call on Gregor. She thought he was lying there immobile on purpose, and was playing at being offended; in her opinion, he was capable of all sorts of understanding. Because she happened to be holding the long broom, she tried to tickle Gregor away from the doorway. When that bore no fruit, she grew irritable, and jabbed Gregor with the broom, and only when she had moved him from the spot without any resistance on his part did she take notice. When she understood what the situation was, her eyes went large and round, she gave a half-involuntary whistle, didn't stay longer, but tore open the door of the bedroom and loudly called into the darkness: 'Have a look, it's gone and perished; it's lying there, and it's perished!'

The Samsas sat up in bed, and had trouble overcoming their shock at the charwoman's appearance in their room, before even beginning to register the import of what she was saying. But then Mr and Mrs Samsa hurriedly climbed out of bed, each on his or her respective side, Mr Samsa flinging a blanket over his shoulders, Mrs Samsa coming along just in her nightdress; and so they stepped into Gregor's room. By now the door from the living room had been opened as well, where Grete had slept ever since the tenants had come; she was fully dressed, as if she hadn't slept at all, and her pale face seemed to confirm that. 'Dead?' said Mrs Samsa, and looked question-ingly up at the charwoman, even though she was in a position to check it all herself, and in fact could have seen it without needing to check. 'I should say so,' said the charwoman and, by way of proof, with her broom pushed Gregor's body across the floor a ways. Mrs Samsa moved as though to restrain the broom, but did not do so. 'Ah,' said Mr Samsa, 'now we can give thanks to God.' He crossed himself, and the three women followed his example. Grete, not taking her eye off the body, said: 'Look how thin he had become. He stopped eating such a long time ago. I brought food in and took it out, and it was always untouched.' Indeed, Gregor's body was utterly flat and desiccated—only so apparent now that he was no longer up on his little legs, and there was nothing else to distract the eye.

'Come in with us a bit, Grete,' said Mrs Samsa with a melancholy smile, and, not without turning back to look at the corpse, Grete followed her parents into the bedroom. The charwoman shut the door and opened the window as far as it would go. In spite of the early hour, there was already something sultry in the morning air. It was, after all, the end of March.

The three tenants emerged from their room and looked around for their breakfast in outrage; they had been forgotten about. 'Where's our breakfast?' the middle gentleman sulkily asked the charwoman. She replied by setting her finger to her lips, and then quickly and silently beckoning the gentlemen into Gregor's room. They followed and with their hands in the pockets of their somewhat shiny little jackets stood around Gregor's body in the bright sunny room.

The door from the bedroom opened, and Mr Samsa appeared in his uniform, with his wife on one arm and his daughter on the other. All were a little teary; from time to time Grete pressed her face against her father's arm.

'Leave my house at once!' said Mr Samsa, and pointed to the door, without relinquishing the women. 'How do you mean?' said the middle gentleman, with a little consternation, and smiled a saccharine smile. The other two kept their hands behind their backs and rubbed them together incessantly, as if in the happy expectation of a great scene, which was sure to end well for them. 'I mean just exactly what I said,' replied Mr Samsa, and with his two companions, walked straight towards the tenant. To begin with the tenant stood his ground, and looked at the floor, as if the things in his head were recombining in some new arrangement. 'Well, I suppose we'd better go then,' he said, and looked up at Mr Samsa, as if he required authority for this novel humility. Mr Samsa merely nodded curtly at him with wide eyes. Thereupon the gentleman did indeed swing into the hallway with long strides; his two friends had been listening for a little while, their hands laid to rest, and now skipped after him, as if afraid Mr Samsa might get to the hallway before them, and cut them off from their leader. In the hallway all three took their hats off the hatstand, pulled their canes out of the umbrella holder, bowed silently, and left the flat. Informed by what turned out to be a wholly unjustified suspicion, Mr Samsa and his womenfolk stepped out on to the landing; leaning against the balustrade, they watched the three gentlemen proceeding slowly but evenly down the long flight of stairs, disappearing on each level into a certain twist of the stairwell and emerging a couple of seconds later; the further they descended, the less interest the Samsa family took in their progress, and when a butcher's apprentice passed them and eventually climbed up much higher with his tray on his head, Mr Samsa and the women left the balustrade altogether, and all turned back, with relief, into their flat.

They decided to use the day to rest and to go for a walk; not only had they earned a break from work, but they stood in dire need of one. And so they all sat down at the table, and wrote three separate letters of apology—Mr Samsa to the board of his bank, Mrs Samsa to her haberdasher, and Grete to her manager. While they were so engaged, the charwoman came in to say she was leaving, because her morning's tasks were done. The three writers at first merely nodded without looking up, and only when the charwoman made no move to leave did they look up in some irritation. 'Well?' asked Mr Samsa. The charwoman stood smiling in the doorway, as though she had some wonderful surprise to tell the family about, but would only do so if asked expressly about it. The almost vertical ostrich feather in her hat, which had annoyed Mr Samsa the whole time she had been working for them, teetered in every direction. 'So what is it you want?' asked Mrs Samsa, who was the person most likely to command respect from the charwoman. 'Well,' replied the charwoman, and her happy laughter kept her from speaking, 'well, just to say, you don't have to worry about how to get rid of the thing next door. I'll take care of it.' Mrs Samsa and Grete inclined their heads over their letters, as if to go on writing; Mr Samsa, who noticed that the woman was about to embark on a more detailed description of everything, put up a hand to cut her off. Being thus debarred from speaking, she remembered the great rush she was in, and, evidently piqued, called out, 'Well, so long everyone', spun round and left the apartment with a terrible slamming of doors.

'I'm letting her go this evening,' said Mr Samsa, but got no reply from wife or daughter, because the reference to the charwoman seemed to have disturbed their concentration, no sooner than it had returned. The two women rose, went over to the window, and stayed there, holding one another in an embrace. Mr Samsa turned towards them in his chair, and watched them in silence for a while. Then he called: 'Well now, come over here. Leave that old business. And pay a little attention to me.' The women came straightaway, caressed him, and finished their letters.

Then the three of them all together left the flat, which was something they hadn't done for months, and took the tram to the park at the edge of the city. The carriage in which they sat was flooded with warm sunshine. Sitting back comfortably in their seats, they discussed the prospects for the future; it turned out that on closer inspection these were not at all bad, because the work of all of them, which they had yet to talk about properly, was proceeding in a very encouraging way, particularly in regard to future prospects. The greatest alleviation of the situation must be produced by moving house; they would take a smaller, cheaper, but also better situated and more practical apartment than their present one, which Gregor had found for them. While they were talking in these terms, almost at one and the same time Mr and Mrs Samsa noticed their increasingly lively daughter, the way that of late, in spite of the trouble that had made her cheeks pale, she had bloomed into an attractive and well-built girl. Falling silent, and communicating almost unconsciously through glances, they thought it was about time to find a suitable husband for her. And it felt like a confirmation of their new dreams and their fond intentions when, as they reached their destination, their daughter was the first to get up, and stretched her nubile young body.

T. S. ELIOT
1888–1965

In poetry and in literary criticism, Thomas Stearns Eliot has a unique position as a writer who not only expressed but helped define modernist taste and style. He rejected the narrative, moralizing, and frequently "noble" style of late Victorian poetry, employing instead precisely focused and often startling images and an elliptical, allusive, and ironic voice that had enormous influence on modern American poetry. His early essays on literature and literary history helped bring about not only a new appreciation of seventeenth-century "metaphysical" poetry but also a different understanding of the text, no longer seen as the inspired overflow of spontaneous emotion but as a carefully made aesthetic object. Yet much of Eliot's immediate impact was not merely formal but spiritual or philosophical. The search for meaning that pervades his work created a famous picture of the barrenness of modern culture in *The Waste Land* (1922), which juxtaposed images of past nobility and present decay, civilizations near and far, and biblical, mythical, and Buddhist allusions to evoke the dilemma of a composite, anxious, and infinitely vulnerable modern soul. Readers in different countries who know nothing of Eliot's other works are often familiar with *The Waste Land* as a literary-historical landmark representing the cultural crisis in European society after World War I. In many ways, Eliot's combination of spiritual insight and technical innovation carries on the tradition of the Symbolist poet who was both visionary artist and consummate craftsman.

Two countries, England and the United States, claim Eliot as part of their national literature. Born September 26, 1888, to a prosperous and educated family in St. Louis, Eliot went to Harvard University for his undergraduate and graduate education and moved to England only in 1915, where he became a British citizen in 1927. While at Harvard, Eliot was influenced by the anti-Romantic humanist Irving Babbitt and the philosopher and aesthetician George Santayana. He later wrote a doctoral dissertation on the philosophy of F. H. Bradley, whose examination of private consciousness (*Appearance and Reality*) appears in Eliot's own later essays and poems. Eliot also found literary examples that would be important for him in future years: the poetry of Dante and John Donne, and the Elizabethan and Jacobean dramatists. In 1908 he read Arthur Symons's *The Symbolist Movement in Literature* and became acquainted with the French Symbolist poets whose richly allusive images—as well as highly self-conscious, ironic, and craftsmanlike technique—he would adopt for his own. Eliot began writing poetry while in college, and published his first major poem, "The Love Song of J. Alfred Prufrock," in Chicago's *Poetry* magazine in 1915. When he moved to England, however, he began a many-sided career as poet, reviewer, essayist, editor, and later playwright. By the time he received the Nobel Prize for literature in 1948, Eliot was recognized as one of the most influential twentieth-century writers in English.

Eliot's first poems, in 1915, already displayed the evocative yet startling images, abrupt shifts in focus, and combination of human sympathy and ironic wit that would attract and puzzle his readers. The "Preludes" linked the "notion of some infinitely gentle / Infinitely suffering thing" with a harsh fatalism in which "The worlds revolve like ancient women / Gathering fuel in vacant lots." Prufrock's dramatic monologue openly tried to startle readers by asking them to imagine the evening spread out "like a patient etherised upon a table" and by changing focus abruptly between imaginary landscapes, metaphysical questions, drawing-room chatter, literary and biblical allusions, and tones of high seriousness set against the most banal and even sing-song speech. "I grow old . . . I grow old. . . . / I shall wear the bottoms of my trousers rolled." The individual stanzas of "Prufrock" are individual scenes, each with its own coherence (for example, the third stanza's yellow fog as a cat). Together, they compose a symbolic landscape sketched in the narrator's mind as a combination of factual observation and subjective feelings: the delicately stated eroticism of the arm "downed with light brown hair," and the frustrated aggression in "I should have been a pair of ragged claws / Scuttling across the floors of silent seas." In its discontinuity, precise yet evocative imagery, mixture of romantic and everyday reference, formal and conversational speech, and in the complex and ironic self-consciousness of its most unheroic hero, "The Love Song of J. Alfred Prufrock" already displays many of the modernist traits typical of Eliot's entire work. Also typical is the theme of spiritual void and of a disoriented protagonist who—at least at this point—does not know how to cope with a crisis that is as much that of modern Western culture as it is his own personal tragedy.

Once established in London, Eliot married, taught briefly before taking a job in the foreign department of Lloyd's Bank (1917–25), and in 1925 joined the publishing firm of Faber & Faber. He wrote a number of essays and book reviews that were published in *The Sacred Wood* (1920) and *Homage to Dryden* (1924) and enjoyed a great deal of influence as assistant editor of the *Egoist* (1917–19) and founding editor of the quarterly *Criterion* from 1922 until it folded in 1939. Eliot helped shape changing literary tastes as much by his essays and literary criticism as by his poetry. Influenced himself by T. E. Hulme's proposal that the time had come for a classical literature of "hard, dry wit" after Romantic vagueness and religiosity and following Imagism's goal of clear, precise physical images phrased in everyday language, he outlined his own definitions of literature and literary history and contributed to a theoretical approach later known as the *New Criticism*. In his essay "Tradition and the Individual Talent" (1919), Eliot proclaimed that there existed a special level of great works—"masterpieces"—that formed among themselves an "ideal order" of quality even though, as individual works, they expressed the characteristic sensibility of their age. The best poets were aware of fitting into the cumulative "mind of Europe" (for Eliot, the humanistic tradition of Homer, Dante, and Shakespeare) and thus of being to some extent depersonalized in their works. Eliot's "impersonal theory of poetry" emphasizes the medium in which a writer works, rather than his or her inner state; craft and control rather than the Romantic ideal of a spontaneous overflow of private emotion. In a famous passage that compares the creative mind to the untouched catalyst of a chemistry experiment, he insists that the writer makes the art object out of language and the experience of any number of people. "The poet's mind is in fact a receptacle for seizing and storing up numberless feelings, phrases, images, which remain there until all the particles which can unite to form a new compound are present together." Poetry can and should express the whole being—intellectual and emotional, conscious and unconscious. In a review of Herbert Grierson's edition of the seventeenth-century Metaphysical poets (1921), Eliot praised the complex mixture of intellect and passion that characterized John Donne and the other Metaphysicals (and that characterized Eliot himself) and criticized the tendency of English literature after the seventeenth century to separate the language of analysis from that of feeling. His criticism of this "dissociation of sensibility" implied a change in literary tastes: from Milton to Donne, from Tennyson to Gerard Manley Hopkins, from Romanticism to classicism, from simplicity to complexity.

The great poetic example of this change came with *The Waste Land* in 1922. Eliot dedicated the poem to Ezra Pound, who had helped him revise the first draft, with a quotation from Dante praising the "better craftsman." Quotations from, or allusions to, a wide range of sources, including Shakespeare, Dante, Charles Baudelaire, Richard Wagner, Ovid, Saint Augustine, Buddhist sermons, folk songs, and the anthropologists Jessie Weston and James Frazer, punctuate this lengthy poem, to which Eliot actually added explanatory notes when it was first published in book form. *The Waste Land* describes modern society in a time of cultural and spiritual crisis and sets off the fragmentation of modern experience against references (some in foreign languages) to a more stable cultural heritage. The ancient Greek prophet Tiresias is juxtaposed with the contemporary charlatan Madame Sosostris; celebrated lovers like Antony and Cleopatra with a house-agent's clerk who mechanically seduces an uninterested typist at the end of her day; the religious vision of Saint Augustine and Buddhist sermons with a sterile world of rock and dry sand where "one can neither stand nor lie nor sit." The modern wasteland could be redeemed if it learned to answer (or perhaps, to ask) the right questions: a situation Eliot symbolized by oblique references to the legend of a knight passing an evening of trial in a Chapel Perilous, and healing a Fisher King by asking the right questions about the Holy Grail and its lance. The series of references (many from literary masterworks) that Eliot integrated into his poem were so many "fragments I have shored against my ruins," pieces of a puzzle whose resolution would bring "shantih," or the peace that passes understanding, but that is still out of reach as the poem's final lines in a foreign language suggest.

The most influential technical innovation in *The Waste Land* was the deliberate use of fragmentation and discontinuity. Eliot pointedly refused to supply any transitional passages or narrative thread and expected the reader to construct a pattern whose implications would make sense as a whole. This was a direct attack on linear habits of reading, which are here broken up with sudden introductions of a different scene or unexplained literary references, shifts in perspective, interpolation of a foreign language, changes from elegant description to barroom gossip, from Elizabethan to modern scenes, from formal to colloquial language. Eliot's rupture of traditional expectations served several functions. It contributed to the general picture of cultural disintegration that the poem expressed, it allowed him to exploit the Symbolist or allusive powers of language inasmuch as they now carried the burden of meaning, and finally—by drawing attention to its own technique—it exemplified modernist "self-reflexive" or self-conscious style. It is impossible to read a triple shift such as "I remember / Those are pearls that were his eyes. / 'Are you alive, or not? Is there nothing in your head?'"—moving from the narrator's meditative recall to a quotation from Shakespeare and the woman's blunt attack—without noticing the abrupt changes in style and tone. Eliot's "heap of broken images" and "fragments shored against my ruins" also took the shape of fragments of thought and speech, and as such embodied a new tradition of literary language.

The spiritual search of "Prufrock", "Gerontion" (1919), and *The Waste Land* entered a new phase for Eliot in 1927, when he became a member of the Anglican Church. *Ash Wednesday* (1930) and a verse play on the death of the English Saint Thomas à Becket (*Murder in the Cathedral*, 1935) display the same distress over the human condition but now within a framework of hope for those who have accepted religious discipline. Eliot began writing plays to reach a larger audience, of which the best known are *The Family Reunion* (1939), which recasts the Orestes story from Greek tragedy, and *The Cocktail Party* (1949), a drawing room comedy that also explored its characters' search for salvation. He is still best known for his poetry, however, and his last major work in that genre is the *Four Quartets*, begun in 1934 and published in its entirety in 1943.

The Love Song of J. Alfred Prufrock

S'io credesse che mia risposta fosse
A persona che mai tornasse al mondo,
Questa fiamma staria senza piu scosse.
Ma percioccche giammai di questo fondo
Non torno vivo alcun, s'i'odo il vero,
Senza tema d'infamia ti rispondo.[1]

Let us go then, you and I,
When the evening is spread out against the sky
Like a patient etherised upon a table;
Let us go, through certain half-deserted streets,
The muttering retreats   5
Of restless nights in one-night cheap hotels
And sawdust restaurants with oyster-shells:
Streets that follow like a tedious argument
Of insidious intent
To lead you to an overwhelming question   10
Oh, do not ask, "What is it?"
Let us go and make our visit.

In the room the women come and go
Talking of Michelangelo.[2]

The yellow fog that rubs its back upon the window-panes,   15
The yellow smoke that rubs its muzzle on the window-panes
Licked its tongue into the corners of the evening,
Lingered upon the pools that stand in drains,
Let fall upon its back the soot that falls from chimneys,
Slipped by the terrace, made a sudden leap,   20
And seeing that it was a soft October night,
Curled once about the house, and fell asleep.

And indeed there will be time[3]
For the yellow smoke that slides along the street,
Rubbing its back upon the window-panes;   25
There will be time, there will be time
To prepare a face to meet the faces that you meet;
There will be time to murder and create,
And time for all the works and days of hands[4]
That lift and drop a question on your plate;   30
Time for you and time for me,
And time yet for a hundred indecisions,
And for a hundred visions and revisions,
Before the taking of a toast and tea.

---

1. From Dante's *Inferno* 27.61–66, where the false counselor Guido da Montefeltro, enveloped in flame, explains that he would never reveal his past if he thought the traveler could report it: "If I thought that my reply would be to one who would ever return to the world, this flame would stay without further movement. But since none has ever returned alive from this depth, if what I hear is true, I answer you without fear of infamy."   2. Michelangelo Buonarroti (1475–1564), famous Italian Renaissance sculptor, painter, architect, and poet; here, merely a topic of fashionable conversation.   3. Echo of a love poem by Andrew Marvell (1621–1678), "To His Coy Mistress": "Had we but world enough and time."   4. An implied contrast with the more productive agricultural labor of hands in the *Works and Days* of the Greek poet Hesiod (8th century B.C.E.).

In the room the women come and go   35
Talking of Michelangelo.

    And indeed there will be time
To wonder, "Do I dare?" and, "Do I dare?"
Time to turn back and descend the stair,
With a bald spot in the middle of my hair—   40
(They will say: "How his hair is growing thin!")
My morning coat, my collar mounting firmly to the chin,
My necktie rich and modest, but asserted by a simple pin—
(They will say: "But how his arms and legs are thin!")
Do I dare   45
Disturb the universe?
In a minute there is time
For decisions and revisions which a minute will reverse.

    For I have known them all already, known them all—
Have known the evenings, mornings, afternoons,   50
I have measured out my life with coffee spoons;
I know the voices dying with a dying fall[5]
Beneath the music from a farther room.
    So how should I presume?

    And I have known the eyes already, known them all—   55
The eyes that fix you in a formulated phrase,
And when I am formulated, sprawling on a pin,
When I am pinned and wriggling on the wall,
Then how should I begin
To spit out all the butt-ends of my days and ways?   60
    And how should I presume?

    And I have known the arms already, known them all—
Arms that are braceleted and white and bare
(But in the lamplight, downed with light brown hair!)
Is it perfume from a dress   65
That makes me so digress?
Arms that lie along a table, or wrap about a shawl.
    And should I then presume?
    And how should I begin?

    Shall I say, I have gone at dusk through narrow streets   70
And watched the smoke that rises from the pipes
Of lonely men in shirt-sleeves, leaning out of windows? . . .

    I should have been a pair of ragged claws
Scuttling across the floors of silent seas.

        And the afternoon, the evening, sleeps so peacefully!   75
Smoothed by long fingers,

---

5. Recalls Duke Orsino's description of a musical phrase in Shakespeare's *Twelfth Night* (1.1.4): "It has a
dying fall."

Asleep . . . tired . . . or it malingers,
Stretched on the floor, here beside you and me.
Should I, after tea and cakes and ices,
Have the strength to force the moment to its crisis?   80
But though I have wept and fasted, wept and prayed,
Though I have seen my head (grown slightly bald) brought in upon a
      platter,
I am no prophet[6]—and here's no great matter;
I have seen the moment of my greatness flicker,
And I have seen the eternal Footman hold my coat, and snicker,   85
And in short, I was afraid.

    And would it have been worth it, after all,
After the cups, the marmalade, the tea,
Among the porcelain, among some talk of you and me,
Would it have been worth while,   90
To have bitten off the matter with a smile,
To have squeezed the universe into a ball
To roll it toward some overwhelming question,[7]
To say: "I am Lazarus, come from the dead,[8]
Come back to tell you all, I shall tell you all"—   95
If one, settling a pillow by her head,
      Should say: "That is not what I meant at all.
      That is not it, at all."

    And would it have been worth it, after all,
Would it have been worth while,   100
After the sunsets and the dooryards and the sprinkled streets,
After the novels, after the teacups, after the skirts that trail along the
      floor—
And this, and so much more?—
It is impossible to say just what I mean!
But as if a magic lantern[9] threw the nerves in patterns on a screen: 105
Would it have been worth while
If one, settling a pillow or throwing off a shawl,
And turning toward the window, should say:
      "That is not it at all,
      That is not what I meant, at all."   110

            No! I am not Prince Hamlet, nor was meant to be;
Am an attendant lord, one that will do
To swell a progress,[1] start a scene or two,
Advise the prince; no doubt, an easy tool,
Deferential, glad to be of use,   115
Politic, cautious, and meticulous;
Full of high sentence, but a bit obtuse;
At times, indeed, almost ridiculous—
Almost, at times, the Fool.

6. Salome obtained the head of the prophet John the Baptist on a platter as a reward for dancing before
the tetrarch Herod (Matthew 14.3–11).   7. Another echo of "To His Coy Mistress," when the lover suggests rolling "all our strength and all / our sweetness up into one ball" to send against the "iron gates of
life."   8. The story of Lazarus, raised from the dead, is told in John 11.1–44.   9. A slide projector.
1. A procession of attendants accompanying a king or nobleman across the stage, as in Elizabethan drama.

I grow old . . . I grow old . . .   120
I shall wear the bottoms of my trousers rolled.

Shall I part my hair behind? Do I dare to eat a peach?
I shall wear white flannel trousers, and walk upon the beach.
I have heard the mermaids singing, each to each.

I do not think that they will sing to me.   125

I have seen them riding seaward on the waves
Combing the white hair of the waves blown back
When the wind blows the water white and black.

We have lingered in the chambers of the sea
By sea-girls wreathed with seaweed red and brown   130
Till human voices wake us, and we drown.

The Waste Land[1]

"Nam Sibyllam quidem Cumis ego ipse oculis meis vidi in ampulla
pendere, et cum illi pueri dicerent: Σίβυλλα τί θέλεισ; responde-
bat illa: αποθανεῖν θέλω."[2]

For Ezra Pound
il miglior fabbro.[3]

I. THE BURIAL OF THE DEAD[4]

April is the cruellest month, breeding
Lilacs out of the dead land, mixing
Memory and desire, stirring
Dull roots with spring rain.
Winter kept us warm, covering   5
Earth in forgetful snow, feeding
A little life with dried tubers.
Summer surprised us, coming over the Starnbergersee[5]
With a shower of rain; we stopped in the colonnade,
And went on in sunlight, into the Hofgarten,[6]   10
And drank coffee, and talked for an hour.
Bin gar keine Russin, stamm' aus Litauen, echt deutsch.[7]
And when we were children, staying at the archduke's,

---

1. Eliot provided footnotes for *The Waste Land* when it was first published in book form; these notes are included here. A general note at the beginning referred readers to the religious symbolism described in Jessie L. Weston's study of the Grail legend, *From Ritual to Romance* (1920), and to fertility myths and vegetation ceremonies (especially those involving Adonis, Attis, and Osiris) as described in the *The Golden Bough* (1890–1918) by the anthropologist Sir James Frazer.   2. Lines from Petronius's *Satyricon* (ca. 60 C.E.) describing the Sibyl, a prophetess shriveled with age and suspended in a bottle. "For indeed I myself have seen with my own eyes the Sibyl at Cumae, hanging in a bottle, and when those boys would say to her: 'Sibyl, what do you want?' she would reply: 'I want to die.'"   3. The dedication to Ezra Pound, who suggested cuts and changes in the first manuscript of *The Waste Land*, borrows words used by Guido Guinizelli to describe his predecessor, the Provençal poet Arnaut Daniel, in Dante's *Purgatorio* (26.117): he is "the better craftsman."   4. From the burial service of the Anglican Church.   5. A lake near Munich. Lines 8–16 recall *My Past*, the memoirs of Countess Marie Larisch.   6. A public park.   7. I am certainly no Russian, I come from Lithuania and am pure German(Germen). German settlers in Lithuania considered themselves superior to the Slavic natives.

My cousin's, he took me out on a sled,
And I was frightened. He said, Marie, 15
Marie, hold on tight. And down we went.
In the mountains, there you feel free.
I read, much of the night, and go south in the winter.

    What are the roots that clutch, what branches grow
Out of this stony rubbish? Son of man,[8] 20
You cannot say, or guess, for you know only
A heap of broken images, where the sun beats,
And the dead tree gives no shelter, the cricket no relief,[9]
And the dry stone no sound of water. Only
There is shadow under this red rock, 25
(Come in under the shadow of this red rock),
And I will show you something different from either
Your shadow at morning striding behind you
Or your shadow at evening rising to meet you;
I will show you fear in a handful of dust. 30
                    Frisch weht der Wind
                    Der Heimat zu
                    Mein Irisch Kind,
                    Wo weilest du?[1]
"You gave me hyacinths first a year ago; 35
"They called me the hyacinth girl."
—Yet when we came back, late, from the Hyacinth garden,
Your arms full, and your hair wet, I could not
Speak, and my eyes failed, I was neither
Living nor dead, and I knew nothing, 40
Looking into the heart of light, the silence.
Oed' und leer das Meer.[2]

    Madame Sosostris, famous clairvoyante,[3]
Had a bad cold, nevertheless
Is known to be the wisest woman in Europe, 45
With a wicked pack of cards.[4] Here, said she,

---

8. "Cf. Ezekiel II,i" [Eliot's note]. The passage reads "Son of man, stand upon thy feet, and I will speak unto thee." 9. "Cf. Ecclesiastes XII,v" [Eliot's note]. "Also when they shall be afraid of that which is high, and fears shall be in the way . . . the grasshopper shall be a burden, and desire shall fail." 1. "V. *Tristan und Isolde*, I, verses 5–8" [Eliot's note]. A sailor in Richard Wagner's opera sings "The wind blows fresh / Towards the homeland / My Irish child / Where are you waiting?" 2. "Id. III, verse 24" [Eliot's note]. "Barren and empty is the sea" is the erroneous report the dying Tristan hears as he waits for Isolde's ship in the third act of Wagner's opera. 3. A fortune-teller with an assumed Egyptian name, possibly suggested by a similar figure in a novel by Aldous Huxley (*Crome Yellow*, 1921). 4. "I am not familiar with the exact constitution of the Tarot pack of cards, from which I have obviously departed to suit my own convenience. The Hanged Man, a member of the traditional pack, fits my purpose in two ways: because he is associated in my mind with the Hanged God of Frazer, and because I associate him with the hooded figure in the passage of the disciples to Emmaus in Part V. The Phoenician Sailor and the Merchant appear later; also the 'crowds of people,' and Death by Water is executed in Part IV. The Man with Three Staves (an authentic member of the Tarot pack) I associate, quite arbitrarily, with the Fisher King himself" [Eliot's note]. Tarot cards are used for telling fortunes; the four suits (cup, lance, sword, and dish) are life symbols related to the Grail legend and, as Eliot suggests, various figures on the cards are associated with different characters and situations in *The Waste Land*. For example: the "drowned Phoenician Sailor" recurs in the merchant from Smyrna (III) and Phlebas the Phoenician (IV); Belladonna (a poison, hallucinogen, medicine, and cosmetic; in Italian, "beautiful lady"; also an echo of Leonardo da Vinci's painting of the Virgin *Madonna of the Rocks*) heralds the neurotic society woman amid her jewels and perfumes (II); the Wheel is the wheel of fortune; the Hanged Man becomes the sacrificed fertility god whose death ensures resurrection and new life for his people.

Is your card, the drowned Phoenician Sailor,
(Those are pearls that were his eyes.[5] Look!)
Here is Belladonna, the Lady of the Rocks,
The lady of situations. 50
Here is the man with three staves, and here the Wheel,
And here is the one-eyed merchant, and this card,
Which is blank, is something he carries on his back,
Which I am forbidden to see. I do not find
The Hanged Man. Fear death by water. 55
I see crowds of people, walking round in a ring.
Thank you. If you see dear Mrs. Equitone,
Tell her I bring the horoscope myself:
One must be so careful these days.

    Unreal City,[6] 60
Under the brown fog of a winter dawn,
A crowd flowed over London Bridge, so many,
I had not thought death had undone so many.[7]
Sighs, short and infrequent, were exhaled,[8]
And each man fixed his eyes before his feet. 65
Flowed up the hill and down King William Street,
To where Saint Mary Woolnoth kept the hours
With a dead sound on the final stroke of nine.[9]
There I saw one I knew, and stopped him, crying: "Stetson!
"You who were with me in the ships at Mylae![1] 70
"That corpse you planted last year in your garden,
"Has it begun to sprout? Will it bloom this year?
"Or has the sudden frost disturbed its bed?
"Oh keep the Dog far hence, that's friend to men,[2]
"Or with his nails he'll dig it up again! 75
"You! hypocrite lecteur!—mon semblable,—mon frère!"[3]

---

5. A line from Ariel's song in Shakespeare's *The Tempest* (1.2.398), which describes the transformation of a drowned man.   **6.** "Cf. Baudelaire: 'Fourmillante cité, cité pleine de rêves, / Où le spectre en plein jour raccroche le passant'"[Eliot's note]. "Swarming city, city full of dreams, / Where the specter in broad daylight accosts the passerby"; a description of Paris from "The Seven Old Men" in *The Flowers of Evil* (1857).   **7.** "Cf. *Inferno* III, 55–57: 'si lunga tratta / di gente, ch'io non avrei mai creduto / che morte tanta n'avesse disfatta'"[Eliot's note]. "So long a train / of people, that I would never have believed / death had undone so many"; not only is Dante amazed at the number of people who have died but he is also describing a crowd of people who were neither good nor bad—nonentities denied even the entrance to Hell.   **8.** "Cf. *Inferno* IV, 25–27: 'Quivi, secondo che per ascoltare, / non avea pianto, ma' che di sospiri, / che l'aura eterna facevan tremare'"[Eliot's note]. "Here, so far as I could tell by listening, there was no weeping but so many sighs that they caused the everlasting air to tremble"; the first circle of Hell, or Limbo, contained the souls of virtuous people who lived before Christ or had not been baptized.   **9.** "A phenomenon which I have often noticed" [Eliot's note]. The church is in the financial district of London, where King William Street is also located.   **1.** An "average" modern name (with business associations) linked to the ancient battle of Mylae (260 B.C.E.), where Rome was victorious over its commercial rival, Carthage.   **2.** "Cf. the Dirge in Webster's *White Devil*" [Eliot's note]. The dirge, or song of lamentation, sung by Cornelia in John Webster's play (1625), asks to "keep the wolf far thence, that's foe to men," so that the wolf's nails may not dig up the bodies of her murdered relatives. Eliot's reversal of dog for wolf, and friend for foe, domesticates the grotesque scene; it may also foreshadow rebirth since (according to Weston's book), the rise of the Dog Star Sirius announced the flooding of the Nile and the consequent return of fertility to Egyptian soil.   **3.** "V. Baudelaire, Preface to *Fleurs du Mal*" [Eliot's note]. Baudelaire's poem preface, titled "To the Reader," ended "Hypocritical reader!—my likeness!—my brother!" The poet challenges the reader to recognize that both are caught up in the worst sin of all—the moral wasteland of *ennui* ("boredom") as lack of will, the refusal to care one way or the other.

II.—A GAME OF CHESS[4]

The Chair she sat in, like a burnished throne,[5]
Glowed on the marble, where the glass
Held up by standards wrought with fruited vines
From which a golden Cupidon peeped out   80
(Another hid his eyes behind his wing)
Doubled the flames of sevenbranched candelabra
Reflecting light upon the table as
The glitter of her jewels rose to meet it,
From satin cases poured in rich profusion.   85
In vials of ivory and coloured glass
Unstoppered, lurked her strange synthetic perfumes,
Unguent, powdered, or liquid—troubled, confused
And drowned the sense in odours; stirred by the air
That freshened from the window, these ascended   90
In fattening the prolonged candle-flames,
Flung their smoke into the laquearia,[6]
Stirring the pattern on the coffered ceiling.
Huge sea-wood fed with copper
Burned green and orange, framed by the coloured stone,   95
In which sad light a carvèd dolphin swam.
Above the antique mantel was displayed
As though a window gave upon the sylvan scene[7]
The change of Philomel,[8] by the barbarous king
So rudely forced; yet there the nightingale[9]   100
Filled all the desert with inviolable voice
And still she cried, and still the world pursues,
"Jug Jug"[1] to dirty ears.
And other withered stumps of time
Were told upon the walls; staring forms   105
Leaned out, leaning, hushing the room enclosed.
Footsteps shuffled on the stair.
Under the firelight, under the brush, her hair
Spread out in fiery points
Glowed into words, then would be savagely still.   110
    "My nerves are bad to-night. Yes, bad. Stay with me.
Speak to me. Why do you never speak. Speak.
    What are you thinking of? What thinking? What?
I never know what you are thinking. Think."

---

4. Reference to a play, *A Game of Chess* (1627) by Thomas Middleton (1580–1627); see n. 4, p. 1274. Part II juxtaposes two scenes of modern sterility: an initial setting of wealthy boredom, neurosis, and lack of communication, and a pub scene where similar concerns of appearance, sexual attraction, and thwarted childbirth are brought out more visibly, and in more vulgar language.   5. "Cf. *Antony and Cleopatra*, II, ii, l. 190" [Eliot's note]. A paler version of Cleopatra's splendor as she met her future lover Antony: "The barge she sat in, like a burnished throne, / Burned on the water."   6. "Laquearia. V. *Aeneid*, I, 726: dependent lychni laquearibus aureis incensi, et noctem flammis funalia vincunt" [Eliot's note]. "Glowing lamps hang from the gold-paneled ceiling, and the torches conquer night with their flames"; the banquet setting of another classical love scene, where Dido is inspired with a fatal passion for Aeneas.   7. "Sylvan scene. V. Milton, *Paradise Lost*, IV, 140" [Eliot's note]. Eden as first seen by Satan.   8. "V. Ovid, *Metamorphoses*, VI, Philomela" [Eliot's note]. Philomela was raped by her brother-in-law, King Tereus, who cut out her tongue so that she could not tell her sister, Procne. Later Procne is changed into a swallow, and Philomela into a nightingale, to save them from the king's rage after they have revenged themselves by killing his son.   9. "Cf. Part III, l. 204" [Eliot's note].   1. Represents the nightingale's song in Elizabethan poetry.

I think we are in rats' alley[2]   115
Where the dead men lost their bones.

"What is that noise?"
            The wind under the door.[3]
"What is that noise now? What is the wind doing?"
            Nothing again nothing.   120
                  "Do
"You know nothing? Do you see nothing? Do you remember
"Nothing?"

    I remember
Those are pearls that were his eyes.   125
"Are you alive, or not? Is there nothing in your head?"
                        But

O O O O that Shakespeherian Rag—
It's so elegant
So intelligent   130
"What shall I do now? What shall I do?"
"I shall rush out as I am, and walk the street
"With my hair down, so. What shall we do to-morrow?
"What shall we ever do?"
            The hot water at ten.   135
And if it rains, a closed car at four.
And we shall play a game of chess,[4]
Pressing lidless eyes and waiting for a knock upon the door.

    When Lil's husband got demobbed,[5] I said—
I didn't mince my words, I said to her myself,   140
HURRY UP PLEASE ITS TIME[6]
Now Albert's coming back, make yourself a bit smart.
He'll want to know what you done with that money he gave you
To get yourself some teeth. He did, I was there.
You have them all out, Lil, and get a nice set,   145
He said, I swear, I can't bear to look at you.
And no more can't I, I said, and think of poor Albert,
He's been in the army four years, he wants a good time,
And if you don't give it him, there's others will, I said.
Oh is there, she said. Something o' that, I said.   150
Then I'll know who to thank, she said, and give me a straight look.
HURRY UP PLEASE ITS TIME
If you don't like it you can get on with it, I said.
Others can pick and choose if you can't.
But if Albert makes off, it won't be for lack of telling.   155

---

2. "Cf. Part III, 1. 195" [Eliot's note].   **3.** "Cf. Webster: 'Is the wind in that door still?'"[Eliot's note]. From *The Devil's Law Case* (1623), 3.2.162, with the implied meaning "is there still breath in him?" **4.** "Cf. the game of chess in Middleton's *Women Beware Women*" [Eliot's note]. In this scene, a woman is seduced in a series of strategic steps that parallel the moves of a chess game occupying her mother-in-law at the same time.   **5.** Demobilized, discharged from the army.   **6.** The British bartender's warning that the pub is about to close.

You ought to be ashamed, I said, to look so antique.
(And her only thirty-one.)
I can't help it, she said, pulling a long face,
It's them pills I took, to bring it off, she said.
(She's had five already, and nearly died of young George.)   160
The chemist[7] said it would be all right, but I've never been the same.
You are a proper fool, I said.
Well, if Albert won't leave you alone, there it is, I said,
What you get married for if you don't want children?
HURRY UP PLEASE ITS TIME   165
Well, that Sunday Albert was home, they had a hot gammon,[8]
And they asked me in to dinner, to get the beauty of it hot—
HURRY UP PLEASE ITS TIME
HURRY UP PLEASE ITS TIME
Goonight Bill. Goonight Lou. Goonight May. Goonight.   170
Ta ta. Goonight. Goonight.
Good night, ladies, good night, sweet ladies, good night, good night.[9]

III. THE FIRE SERMON[1]

The river's tent is broken: the last fingers of leaf
Clutch and sink into the wet bank. The wind
Crosses the brown land, unheard. The nymphs are departed.   175
Sweet Thames, run softly, till I end my song.[2]
The river bears no empty bottles, sandwich papers,
Silk handkerchiefs, cardboard boxes, cigarette ends
Or other testimony of summer nights. The nymphs are departed.
And their friends, the loitering heirs of city directors;   180
Departed, have left no addresses.
By the waters of Leman[3] I sat down and wept . . .
Sweet Thames, run softly till I end my song,
Sweet Thames, run softly, for I speak not loud or long.
But at my back in a cold blast I hear[4]   185
The rattle of the bones, and chuckle spread from ear to ear.

A rat crept softly through the vegetation
Dragging its slimy belly on the bank
While I was fishing in the dull canal
On a winter evening round behind the gashouse   190
Musing upon the king my brother's wreck
And on the king my father's death before him.[5]
White bodies naked on the low damp ground

7. The druggist, who gave her pills to cause a miscarriage.   8. Ham.   9. The popular song for a party's end ("Good Night, Ladies") shifts into Ophelia's last words in *Hamlet* (4.5.72) as she goes off to drown herself.   1. Reference to the Buddha's Fire Sermon (see n. 1, p. 1279) in which he denounced the fiery lusts and passions of earthly experience. "All things are on fire . . . with the fire of passion . . . of hatred . . . of infatuation." Part III describes the degeneration of even these passions in the sterile decadence of the modern Waste Land.   2. "V. Spenser, *Prothalamion*" [Eliot's note]. The line is the refrain of a marriage song by the Elizabethan poet Edmund Spenser (1552?–1599) and evokes a river of unpolluted pastoral beauty.   3. Lake Geneva (where Eliot wrote much of *The Waste Land*). "Leman": a mistress or lover. In Psalm 137.1, the exiled Hebrews sit by the rivers of Babylon and weep for their lost homeland.   4. Distorted echo of Andrew Marvell's (1621–1678) poem "To His Coy Mistress": "But at my back I always hear / Time's wingèd chariot hurrying near."   5. "Cf. *The Tempest* I.ii" [Eliot's note]. Ferdinand, the king's son, believing his father drowned and mourning his death, hears in the air a song containing the line that Eliot quotes earlier at lines 48 and 126.

And bones cast in a little low dry garret,
Rattled by the rat's foot only, year to year.   195
But at my back from time to time I hear[6]
The sound of horns and motors, which shall bring[7]
Sweeney to Mrs. Porter in the spring.
O the moon shone bright on Mrs. Porter[8]
And on her daughter   200
They wash their feet in soda water
Et O ces voix d'enfants, chantant dans la coupole![9]

Twit twit twit
Jug jug jug jug jug jug
So rudely forc'd.   205
Tereu[1]

   Unreal City
Under the brown fog of a winter noon
Mr. Eugenides, the Smyrna merchant
Unshaven, with a pocket full of currants   210
C.i.f. London: documents at sight,[2]
Asked me in demotic French
To luncheon at the Cannon Street Hotel
Followed by a weekend at the Metropole.[3]

   At the violet hour, when the eyes and back   215
Turn upward from the desk, when the human engine waits
Like a taxi throbbing waiting,
I Tiresias,[4] though blind, throbbing between two lives,
Old man with wrinkled female breasts, can see
At the violet hour, the evening hour that strives   220
Homeward, and brings the sailor home from sea,[5]
The typist home at teatime, clears her breakfast, lights

---

6. "Cf. Marvell, 'To His Coy Mistress'"[Eliot's note].   **7.** "Cf. Day, *Parliament of Bees*: 'When of the sudden, listening, you shall hear, / A noise of horns and hunting, which shall bring / Actaeon to Diana in the spring, / Where all shall see her naked skin.'"[Eliot's note]. The young hunter Actaeon was changed into a stag, hunted down, and killed when he came upon the goddess Diana bathing. Sweeney is in no such danger from his visit to Mrs. Porter.   **8.** "I do not know the origin of the ballad from which these lines are taken: it was reported to me from Sydney, Australia" [Eliot's note]. A song popular among Allied troops during World War I. One version continues lines 199–201 as follows: "And so they oughter / To keep them clean."   **9.** "V. Verlaine, *Parsifal*" [Eliot's note]. "And O these children's voices, singing in the dome!"; the last lines of a sonnet by Paul Verlaine (1844–1896), which ambiguously celebrates the Grail hero's chaste restraint. In Richard Wagner's opera, Parsifal's feet are washed to purify him before entering the presence of the Grail.   **1.** Tereus, who raped Philomela (see line 99); also the nightingale's song.   **2.** "The currants were quoted at a price 'carriage and insurance free to London'; and the Bill of Lading etc. were to be handed to the buyer upon payment of the sight draft" [Eliot's note].   **3.** Smyrna is an ancient Phoenician seaport, and early Smyrna merchants spread the Eastern fertility cults. In contrast, their descendant Mr. Eugenides ("Well-born") invites the poet to lunch in a large commercial hotel and a weekend at a seaside resort in Brighton.   **4.** "Tiresias, although a mere spectator and not indeed a 'character,' is yet the most important personage in the poem, uniting all the rest. Just as the one-eyed merchant, seller of currants, melts into the Phoenician Sailor, and the latter is not wholly distinct from Ferdinand Prince of Naples, so all the women are one woman, and the two sexes meet in Tiresias. What Tiresias *sees*, in fact, is the substance of the poem. The whole passage from Ovid is one of great anthropological interest" [Eliot's note]. The passage then quoted from Ovid's *Metamorphoses* (3.320–38) describes how Tiresias spent seven years of his life as a woman and thus experienced love from the point of view of both sexes. Blinded by Juno, he was recompensed by Jove with the gift of prophecy.   **5.** "This may or may not appear as exact as Sappho's lines, but I had in mind the 'longshore' or 'dory' fisherman, who returns at nightfall" [Eliot's note]. The Greek poet Sappho's poem describes how the evening star brings home those whom dawn has sent abroad; there is also an echo of Robert Louis Stevenson's (1850–1894) "Requiem," 1.221: "Home is the sailor, home from the sea."

Her stove, and lays out food in tins.
Out of the window perilously spread
Her drying combinations touched by the sun's last rays,   225
On the divan are piled (at night her bed)
Stockings, slippers, camisoles, and stays.
I Tiresias, old man with wrinkled dugs
Perceived the scene, and foretold the rest—
I too awaited the expected guest.   230
He, the young man carbuncular, arrives,
A small house agent's clerk, with one bold stare,
One of the low on whom assurance sits
As a silk hat on a Bradford⁶ millionaire.
The time is now propitious, as he guesses,   235
The meal is ended, she is bored and tired,
Endeavours to engage her in caresses
Which still are unreproved, if undesired.
Flushed and decided, he assaults at once;
Exploring hands encounter no defence;   240
His vanity requires no response,
And makes a welcome of indifference.
(And I Tiresias have foresuffered all
Enacted on this same divan or bed;
I who have sat by Thebes below the wall   245
And walked among the lowest of the dead.)⁷
Bestows one final patronising kiss,
And gropes his way, finding the stairs unlit . . .

　　She turns and looks a moment in the glass,
Hardly aware of her departed lover;   250
Her brain allows one half-formed thought to pass:
"Well now that's done: and I'm glad it's over."
When lovely woman stoops to folly and⁸
Paces about her room again, alone,
She smoothes her hair with automatic hand,   255
And puts a record on the gramophone.

　　"This music crept by me upon the waters"⁹
And along the Strand, up Queen Victoria Street.
O City city,¹ I can sometimes hear
Beside a public bar in Lower Thames Street,   260
The pleasant whining of a mandoline
And a clatter and a chatter from within
Where fishmen lounge at noon: where the walls

---

6. A manufacturing town in Yorkshire, which prospered greatly during World War I.　7. Tiresias prophesied in the marketplace at Thebes for many years before dying and continuing to prophesy in Hades.
8. "V. Goldsmith, the song in *The Vicar of Wakefield*" [Eliot's note]. "When lovely woman stoops to folly /
And finds too late that men betray / What charm can soothe her melancholy, / What art can wash her guilt
away?" Oliver Goldsmith (ca. 1730–1774), *The Vicar of Wakefield* (1766).　9. "V. *The Tempest*, as
above" [Eliot's note, referring to line 191]. Spoken by Ferdinand as he hears Ariel sing of his father's transformation by the sea, his eyes turning to pearls, his bones to coral, and everything else he formerly was into
"something rich and strange."　1. A double invocation: the city of London and the City as London's central financial district (see lines 60 and 207). See also lines 375–6, the great cities of Western civilization.

Of Magnus Martyr hold[2]
Inexplicable splendour of Ionian white and gold.   265
        The river sweats[3]
        Oil and tar
        The barges drift
        With the turning tide
        Red sails   270
        Wide
        To leeward, swing on the heavy spar.
        The barges wash
        Drifting logs
        Down Greenwich reach   275
        Past the Isle of Dogs.[4]
           Weialala leia
           Wallala leialala

        Elizabeth and Leicester[5]
        Beating oars   280
        The stern was formed
        A gilded shell
        Red and gold
        The brisk swell
        Rippled both shores   285
        Southwest wind
        Carried down stream
        The peal of bells
        White towers
           Weialala leia   290
           Wallala leialala

"Trams and dusty trees.
Highbury bore me. Richmond and Kew
Undid me.[6] By Richmond I raised my knees
Supine on the floor of a narrow canoe."   295

"My feet are at Moorgate,[7] and my heart
Under my feet. After the event
He wept. He promised 'a new start.'
I made no comment. What should I resent?"

---

2. "The interior of St. Magnus Martyr is to my mind one of the finest among Wren's interiors. See *The Proposed Demolition of Nineteen City Churches*: (P. S. King & Son, Ltd)" [Eliot's note]. The architect was Christopher Wren (1632–1723), and the church is located just below London Bridge on Lower Thames Street.   3. "The Song of the (three) Thames-daughters begins here. From line 292 to 306 inclusive they speak in turn. V. *Götterdämmerung* III.i: the Rhine-daughters" [Eliot's note]. In Wagner's opera *The Twilight of the Gods* (1876), the three Rhine-maidens mourn the loss of their gold, which gave the river its sparkling beauty; lines 177–8 here echo the Rhine-maidens' refrain.   4. A peninsula opposite Greenwich on the Thames.   5. "V. Froude, *Elizabeth*, vol. I, ch. iv, letter of De Quadra to Philip of Spain: 'In the afternoon we were in a barge, watching the games on the river. (The queen) was alone with Lord Robert and myself on the poop, when they began to talk nonsense, and went so far that Lord Robert at last said, as I was on the spot there was no reason why they should not be married if the queen pleased" [Eliot's note]. Sir Robert Dudley (1532–1588) was the Earl of Leicester, a favorite of Queen Elizabeth who at one point hoped to marry her.   6. "Cf. *Purgatorio*, V, 133: 'Ricorditi di me, che son la Pia; / Siena mi fe', disfecemi Maremma' "[Eliot's note]. La Pia, in Purgatory, recalls her seduction: "Remember me, who am La Pia. / Siena made me, Maremma undid me." Eliot's parody substitutes Highbury (a London suburb) and Richmond and Kew, popular excursion points on the Thames.   7. A London slum.

"On Margate Sands.[8]   300
I can connect
Nothing with nothing.
The broken fingernails of dirty hands.
My people humble people who expect
Nothing."   305
Nothing."
                    la la
To Carthage then I came[9]

Burning burning burning burning[1]
O Lord Thou pluckest me out[2]
O Lord Thou pluckest   310

burning

IV. DEATH BY WATER

Phlebas the Phoenician, a fortnight dead,
Forgot the cry of gulls, and the deep sea swell
And the profit and loss.
                    A current under sea   315
Picked his bones in whispers. As he rose and fell
He passed the stages of his age and youth
Entering the whirlpool.
                    Gentile or Jew
O you who turn the wheel and look to windward,   320
Consider Phlebas, who was once handsome and tall as you.

V. WHAT THE THUNDER SAID[3]

After the torchlight red on sweaty faces
After the frosty silence in the gardens
After the agony in stony places
The shouting and the crying   325
Prison and palace and reverberation
Of thunder of spring over distant mountains
He who was living is now dead[4]
We who were living are now dying
With a little patience   330

---

8. A seaside resort on the Thames. 9. "V. St. Augustine's *Confessions:* 'to Carthage then I came, where a cauldron of unholy loves sang all about mine ears'"[Eliot's note]. The youthful Augustine is described. Carthage is also the scene of Dido's faithful love for Aeneas, referred to in line 92. 1. "The complete text of the Buddha's Fire Sermon (which corresponds in importance to the Sermon on the Mount) from which these words are taken, will be found translated in the late Henry Clarke Warren's *Buddhism in Translation* (Harvard Oriental Studies). Mr. Warren was one of the great pioneers of Buddhist studies in the Occident" [Eliot's note]. The Sermon on the Mount is in Matthew 5–7. 2. "From St. Augustine's *Confessions* again. The collocation of these two representatives of eastern and western asceticism, as the culmination of this part of the poem is not an accident" [Eliot's note]. See also Zechariah 3.2, where the high priest Joshua is described as a "brand plucked out of the fire." 3. "In the first part of Part V three themes are employed: the journey to Emmaus, the approach to the Chapel Perilous (see Miss Weston's book) and the present decay of eastern Europe" [Eliot's note]. On their journey to Emmaus (Luke 24.13–34), Jesus' disciples were joined by a stranger who later revealed himself to be the crucified and resurrected Christ. The Thunder of the title is a divine voice in the Hindu *Upanishads* (see n. 2, p. 1281). 4. Allusions to stages in Christ's Passion: the betrayal, prayer in the garden of Gethsemane, imprisonment, trial, crucifixion, and burial. Despair reigns, for this is death before the resurrection.

Here is no water but only rock
Rock and no water and the sandy road
The road winding above among the mountains
Which are mountains of rock without water
If there were water we should stop and drink   335
Amongst the rock one cannot stop or think
Sweat is dry and feet are in the sand
If there were only water amongst the rock
Dead mountain mouth of carious teeth that cannot spit
Here one can neither stand nor lie nor sit   340
There is not even silence in the mountains
But dry sterile thunder without rain
There is not even solitude in the mountains
But red sullen faces sneer and snarl
From doors of mudcracked houses   345
                        If there were water

And no rock
If there were rock
And also water
And water   350
A spring
A pool among the rock
If there were the sound of water only
Not the cicada[5]
And dry grass singing   355
But sound of water over a rock
Where the hermit-thrush[6] sings in the pine trees
Drip drop drip drop drop drop drop
But there is no water

Who is the third who walks always beside you?   360
When I count, there are only you and I together[7]
But when I look ahead up the white road
There is always another one walking beside you
Gliding wrapt in a brown mantle, hooded
I do not know whether a man or a woman   365
—But who is that on the other side of you?

What is that sound high in the air[8]
Murmur of maternal lamentation
Who are those hooded hordes swarming
Over endless plains, stumbling in cracked earth   370

5. Grasshopper or cricket; see line 23.   6. "The hermit-thrush which I have heard in Quebec Province. . . . Its 'water-dripping song' is justly celebrated" [Eliot's note].   7. "The following lines were stimulated by the account of one of the Antarctic expeditions (I forget which, but I think one of Shackleton's): it was related that the party of explorers, at the extremity of their strength, had the constant delusion that there was *one more member* than could actually be counted" [Eliot's note]. See also n. 3, p. 1279.
8. Eliot's note to lines 367–77 refers to Hermann Hesse's *Blick ins Chaos* (Glimpse into chaos), and a passage that reads, translated, "Already half of Europe, already at least half of Eastern Europe is on the way to Chaos, drives drunk in holy madness on the edge of the abyss and sings at the same time, sings drunk and hymn-like, as Dimitri Karamazov sang [in Dostoevsky's *The Brothers Karamazov*]. The offended bourgeois laughs at the songs; the saint and the seer hear them with tears."

Ringed by the flat horizon only
What is the city over the mountains
Cracks and reforms and bursts in the violet air
Falling towers
Jerusalem Athens Alexandria 375
Vienna London
Unreal

    A woman drew her long black hair out tight
And fiddled whisper music on those strings
And bats with baby faces in the violet light 380
Whistled, and beat their wings
And crawled head downward down a blackened wall
And upside down in air were towers
Tolling reminiscent bells, that kept the hours
And voices singing out of empty cisterns and exhausted wells. 385

    In this decayed hole among the mountains
In the faint moonlight, the grass is singing
Over the tumbled graves, about the chapel
There is the empty chapel, only the wind's home.
It has no windows, and the door swings, 390
Dry bones can harm no one.
Only a cock stood on the rooftree
Co co rico co co rico[9]
In a flash of lightning. Then a damp gust
Bringing rain 395

    Ganga was sunken, and the limp leaves
Waited for rain, while the black clouds
Gathered far distant, over Himavant.[1]
The jungle crouched, humped in silence.
Then spoke the thunder 400
DA
Datta: what have we given?[2]
My friend, blood shaking my heart
The awful daring of a moment's surrender
Which an age of prudence can never retract 405
By this, and this only, we have existed
Which is not to be found in our obituaries
Or in memories draped by the beneficent spider[3]
Or under seals broken by the lean solicitor
In our empty rooms 410

---

9. European version of the cock's crow: *cock-a-doodle-doo*. The cock crowed in Matthew 26.34, 74, after Peter had denied Jesus three times.   1. A mountain in the Himalayas. The Ganga is the river Ganges in India.   2. "'Datta, dayadhvam, damyata' (Give, sympathise, control). The fable of the meaning of the Thunder is found in the *Brihadaranyaka*—Upanishad 5,1" [Eliot's note]. In the fable, the word *DA*, spoken by the supreme being Prajapati, is interpreted as *Datta* (to give alms), *Dayadhvam* (to sympathize or have compassion), and *Damyata* (to have self-control) by gods, human beings, and demons respectively. The conclusion is that when the thunder booms DA DA DA, Prajapati is commanding that all three virtues be practiced simultaneously.   3. "Cf. Webster, *The White Devil*, V, vi: . . . they'll remarry / Ere the worm pierce your winding-sheet, ere the spider / Make a thin curtain for your epitaphs" [Eliot's note].

DA
Dayadhvam:[4] I have heard the key
Turn in the door once and turn once only
We think of the key, each in his prison
Thinking of the key, each confirms a prison   415
Only at nightfall, aethereal rumours
Revive for a moment a broken Coriolanus[5]
DA
Damyata: The boat responded
Gaily, to the hand expert with sail and oar   420
The sea was calm, your heart would have responded
Gaily, when invited, beating obedient
To controlling hands
                                   I sat upon the shore
Fishing,[6] with the arid plain behind me   425
Shall I at least set my lands in order?
London Bridge is falling down falling down falling down
Poi s'ascose nel foco che gli affina[7]
Quando fiam uti chelidon[8]—O swallow swallow
Le Prince d'Aquitaine à la tour abolie[9]   430
These fragments I have shored against my ruins
Why then Ile fit you. Hieronymo's mad againe.[1]
Datta. Dayadhvam. Damyata.
            Shantih   shantih   shantih[2]

---

4. Eliot's note on the command to "sympathize" or reach outside the self cites two descriptions of helpless isolation. The first comes from Dante's *Inferno* 33:46: as Ugolino, imprisoned in a tower with his children to die of starvation, says "And I heard below the door of the horrible tower being locked up"). The second is a modern description by the English philosopher F. H. Bradley (1846–1924) of the inevitably self-enclosed or private nature of consciousness: "My external sensations are no less private to myself than are my thoughts or my feelings. In either case my experience falls within my own circle, a circle closed on the outside; and, with all its elements alike, every sphere is opaque to the others which surround it. . . . In brief, regarded as an existence which appears in a soul, the whole world for each is peculiar and private to that soul" (*Appearance and Reality*).   **5.** A proud Roman patrician who was exiled and led an army against his homeland. In Shakespeare's play, both his grandeur and his downfall come from a desire to be ruled only by himself.   **6.** "V. Weston: *From Ritual to Romance*; chapter on the Fisher King" [Eliot's note].   **7.** Eliot's note quotes a passage in the *Purgatorio* in which Arnaut Daniel (see n. 3, p. 1270) asks Dante to remember his pain. The line cited here, "then he hid himself in the fire which refines them" (*Purgatorio* 26.148), shows Daniel departing in fire which—in Purgatory—exists as a purifying rather than a destructive element.   **8.** "V. *Pervigilium Veneris*. Cf. Philomela in Parts II and III [Eliot's note]. "When shall I be as a swallow?" A line from the *Vigil of Venus*, an anonymous late Latin poem, that asks for the gift of song; here associated with Philomela as a swallow, not the nightingale of lines 99–103 and 203–6. **9.** "V. Gerard de Nerval, Sonnet *El Desdichado*" [Eliot's note]. The Spanish title means "The Disinherited One," and the sonnet is a monologue describing the speaker as a melancholy, ill-starred dreamer: "the Prince of Aquitaine in his ruined tower." Another line recalls the scene at the end of "Love Song of J. Alfred Prufrock": "I dreamed in the grotto where sirens swim."   **1.** "V. Kyd's *Spanish Tragedy*" [Eliot's note]. Thomas Kyd's revenge play (1594) is subtitled "Hieronymo's Mad Againe." The protagonist "fits" his son's murderers into appropriate roles in a court entertainment so that they may all be killed.   **2.** "Shantih. Repeated as here, a formal ending to an Upanishad. 'The Peace which passeth understanding' is our equivalent to this word' "[Eliot's note]. The *Upanishads* comment on the sacred Hindu scriptures, the *Vedas*.

ANNA AKHMATOVA
1889–1966

The voice of Anna Akhmatova is intensely personal, whether she speaks as lover, wife, and mother or as a national poet commemorating the mute agony of millions. From the subjective love lyrics of her earliest work to the communal mourning of *Requiem* and the many-layered drama of *Poem without a Hero,* she expresses universal themes in terms of individual experience, and historical events through the filter of basic emotions like fear, love, hope, and pain. Akhmatova is one of the great Russian poets of the twentieth century, but she retains a broad sense of European culture, both past and present, and fills her later works with references to Western music, literature, and art that give a startling breadth and scope to her very personalized poetry. Too cosmopolitan and too independent to be tolerated by the authorities, Akhmatova was viciously attacked and her books suppressed (1922–40) because they did not fit the government-approved model of literature: they were too "individualistic" and were not "socially useful." Although she was rehabilitated in the 1960s and eventually achieved recognized status as national poet, Akhmatova was read in secret for a long time, chiefly for the perfection of her early love lyrics. After the death of Joseph Stalin in 1953, however, her collected poems—including poems of the war years and unknown texts written during the periods of enforced silence—brought the full range of her work to public attention.

She was born Anna Andreevna Gorenko on June 11, 1889, in a suburb of the Black Sea port of Odessa and in a traditional society that she described as "Dostoevsky's Russia." Her father was a maritime engineer and her mother an independent woman of populist sympathies who belonged to an early revolutionary group called People's Will. The poet took the pen name of Akhmatova (accented on the second syllable) from her maternal great-grandmother, who was of Tatar descent. Her family soon moved to Tsarskoe Selo ("the Czar's Village"), a small town outside St. Petersburg that had been for centuries the site of the summer palace of the czars, and also— perhaps more important for Akhmatova—a place where the great Romantic poet Alexandr Pushkin wrote his youthful works. She attended the local school at Tsarskoe Selo, but completed her degree in Kiev; in 1907, she briefly studied law at the Kiev College for Women before moving to St. Petersburg to study literature.

In Tsarskoe Selo, Akhmatova met Nikolai Gumilyov, whom she married in April 1910. After their marriage, the couple visited Paris during the spring of 1910 and in 1911, meeting many writers and artists, including Amedeo Modigliani, who sketched Akhmatova several times and with whom she recalled wandering around Paris and reading aloud the poetry of Paul Verlaine. It was a time of change in the arts, and when the couple returned to St. Petersburg Gumilyov helped organize a Poets' Guild that became the core of a new small literary movement, Acmeism, which rejected the romantic, quasi-religious aims of Russian Symbolism and (like Imagism) valued clarity and concreteness and a closeness to things of this Earth. The Symbolist–Acmeist debate went on inside a lively literary and social life, while the three main figures of Acmeism—Akhmatova, Gumilyov, and Osip Mandelstam—gained a reputation as important poets.

Akhmatova's first collection of poems, *Evening,* was published in the spring of 1912; it is an intensely personal collection of lyrics in which the poet describes evening as a time of awakening to love—and grief. There is a new clarity and directness to these traditionally romantic subjects, however, as for the first time in Russian poetry a woman in love expresses and analyzes her own emotions. In October of the same year, her son, Lev Gumilyov, was born; it was his arrest and imprisonment in 1935 that inspired the first poems of the cycle that would become *Requiem.* Lev was ultimately imprisoned for a total of fourteen years as the government sought a way to punish his mother, who would not or could not write according to the approved socialist realist style praising the government. Even after she had become a national poet known for her patriotic poetry during World War II, Akhmatova was still criticized by the Stalinist regime as a reactionary "half-harlot, half-nun" who wrote subjective love lyrics without social significance: the love poetry of *Evening, Rosary* (1914), and *The White Flock* (1917, published a month before the start of the Russian Revolution).

The White Flock was published during World War I, the destruction of which so shocked Akhmatova that she wrote, "This untimely death is so terrible / I cannot look at God's world." Yet more bloodshed was to follow in the civil war following the Revolution of 1917. Akhmatova refused to flee abroad, as many Russians were doing. Her marriage with Gumilyov was breaking up, and they divorced in 1918; she remarried an Assyriologist, Vladimir Shileiko, who did not approve of his wife's writing poetry and burned some of her poems (she divorced him in 1928). Akhmatova's political difficulties began in 1922. Although she and Gumilyov were divorced, his arrest and execution for counterrevolutionary activities in 1921 put her own status into question. After 1922 and the publication of *Anno Domini*, she was no longer allowed to publish, and was forced into the unwilling withdrawal from public activity that Russians call "internal emigration." Officially forgotten, she was not forgotten in fact; in the schools, her poems were copied out by hand and circulated among students who would never hear her name mentioned in a literature class.

Depending on a meager and irregular pension, Akhmatova prepared essays on the life and works of Pushkin, and wrote poems that would not appear until much later. Stalin's "Great Purge" of 1935–38 sent millions of people to prison camps, and made the 1930s a time of terror and uncertainty for everyone. It is this fear and misery that is expressed in *Requiem,* as the poet blends references to her own life with an awareness of the common plight. The art critic Nikolai Punin, with whom she lived from 1926 to 1940, was arrested briefly in 1935; Osip Mandelstam, her great friend, was exiled to Voronezh in May 1934, and then sent to a prison camp in 1938 where he died the same year; her son, Lev, was arrested briefly in 1935 and again in 1938, remaining imprisoned until 1941 when he was allowed to enlist in military. Composing *Requiem* itself was a risky act carried out over several years, and Akhmatova and her friend Lidia Chukovskaya memorized the stanzas to preserve the poem in the absence of written copy. Akhmatova wrote of Mandelstam (but perhaps of them all) that "in the room of the poet in disgrace / Fear and the Muse keep watch by turns / And the night comes on / That knows no dawn." A temporary lifting of the ban against her works in 1940 did not last; although she was allowed to publish a new collection, *From Six Books,* the edition was recalled by officials after six months.

It was in 1940 that Akhmatova became interested in larger musical forms and began thinking in terms of cycles of poems instead of her accustomed separate lyrics. She envisaged a larger framework for the core poems of *Requiem* in this year, and wrote the "Dedication" and two epilogues. She also began work on the *Poem without a Hero,* a long and complex verse narrative in three parts that sums up many of her earlier themes: love, death, creativity, the unity of European culture, and the suffering of her people. During World War II the poet was allowed a partial return to public life, addressing women on the radio during the siege of Leningrad (St. Petersburg) in 1941, and writing patriotic lyrics such as the famous "Courage" (published in *Pravda* in 1942) which rallied the Russian people to defend their homeland (and national language) from enslavement. In spite of her patriotic activities, she was subject to vicious official attacks after the war. Stalin's minister of Culture, Andrei Zhdanov, in the famous Report of 1946 proclaimed the doctrine of socialist realism as the official style, and attacked Akhmatova's "individualistic" writing as the "poetry of an overwrought upper-class lady who frantically races back and forth between boudoir and chapel." Akhmatova was immediately expelled from the Writer's Union, which meant that she was not officially recognized as a professional writer (and hence could not earn her living in that career).

Unable once more to publish her work, she supported herself between 1946 and 1958 by translating poetry from a number of foreign languages. Her son was arrested again in 1949; hoping to obtain his release, she wrote the kind of adulatory poetry in praise of Stalin that the regime required. The attempt was unsuccessful, and her son remained in prison until 1956. The Stalinist cycle, *In Praise of Peace* (1950), contains such clumsy imitations of socialist-realist poetry that it has been considered a parody: "Where a tank rumbled, there is now a peaceful tractor." Akhmatova later directed that it be omitted from her collected works.

During the slow thaw that followed Stalin's death in 1953, Akhmatova was rehabilitated. Gradually her poems were allowed back into print; an edition of selected poems with added texts was published in 1958, and in the same year she was even elected to an honorary position on the executive council of the Writer's Union. In 1965 a larger collection appeared, *The Flight of Time,* which contained a new series called *The Seventh Book* as well as part of the still-unfinished *Poem without a Hero.* She took an interest in the young writers who flocked to her and supported those who—like Josif Brodsky—were accused by the new order of being a "parasite on the state." Akhmatova's work was already recognized internationally: Robert Frost visited her on his trip to the Soviet Union in 1962, *Requiem* was first published "without her consent" in Munich in 1963 (not until 1987 was the full text published in the Soviet Union), and in 1964 she traveled to Italy to receive the Taormina poetry prize. She was surrounded by admirers when she visited England in 1965 to receive an honorary degree from Oxford University. Her death in 1966 signaled the end of an era in modern Russian poetry, for she was the last of the famous "quartet" that also included Mandelstam, Tsvetaeva, and Pasternak.

Requiem is a lyrical cycle, a series of poems written on a common theme, but it is also a short epic narrative. The story it tells is acutely personal, even autobiographical, but like an epic it also transcends personal significance and describes (as in *The Song of Roland*) a moment in the history of a nation. Akhmatova, who had seen her husband and son arrested and her friends die in prison camps, was only one of millions who had suffered similar losses in the purges of the 1930s. The "Preface," "Dedication," and two epilogues to *Requiem* constitute a framework examining this image of a common fate, while the core of numbered poems develops a more subjective picture and the stages of an individual drama. In the inner poems, Akhmatova blends her separate personal losses—husband, son, and friends—to create a single focus, the figure of a mother grieving for her condemned son. In the frame, the poet identifies herself with the crowd of women with whom she waited for seventeen months outside the Leningrad prison—women who, in turn, represent bereaved women throughout the Soviet Union. The "I" of the speaker throughout remains anonymous, in spite of the fact that she describes her personal emotions in the central poems; her identity is that of a sorrowing mother, and she is distinguished from her fellow-suffers only by the poetic gift which makes her the "exhausted mouth, / Through which a hundred million scream." *Requiem* is at once a public and a private poem, a picture of individual grief simultaneously linked to a national disaster, and a vision of community suffering that extends past even national disaster into medieval Russian history and Greek mythology. The martyrdom of the Soviet people is consistently pictured in religious terms, from the recurrent mention of crosses and crucifixion to the culminating image of maternal suffering in Mary, the mother of Christ.

The "Dedication" and "Prologue" establish the context for the poem as a whole: the mass arrests in the 1930s after the assassination on December 1, 1934, of Sergei Kirov, the top Communist Party official in Leningrad. The women waiting outside the Kresty ("Crosses") prison of Leningrad arrive at dawn in the coldest of weather, waiting for news of their loved ones, hoping to be allowed to pass them a parcel or a letter, and fearing the sentence of death or exile to the prison camps of frozen Siberia.

Instead of living a natural life where "for someone the sunset luxuriates," these women and the prisoners are forced into a suspended existence of separation and uncertainty in which all values are inverted and the city itself has become only the setting for its prisons. It is a situation before which the great forces of nature bow in silent horror.

With the numbered poems, Akhmatova recounts the growing anguish of a bereaved mother as her son is arrested and sentenced to death. The speaker describes her husband's arrest at dawn, in the midst of the family. Her son was arrested later, and in the rest of the poem she relives her numbed incomprehension as she struggles against the increasing likelihood that he will be condemned to death. Recalling her own carefree adolescence in contrast to her current situation as she weeps outside the prison walls, or pleads with Stalin to relent, the mother has a premonition of her son's fate that pushes her into the temporary relief of insanity and forgetting, and to a desire for her own arrest and death. After sentence is passed, the traumatized mother can speak of his execution only in oblique terms that are at once universal and potentially consoling: by shifting the image of death onto the plane of the crucifixion and God's will. It is a tragedy that cannot be comprehended or looked at directly just as, she suggests, at the crucifixion "No one glanced and no one would have dared" to look at the grieving Mary. In the two epilogues, the grieving speaker returns from religious transcendence to Earth and current history. Here she takes on a newly composite identity, seeing herself not as an isolated sufferer but as reciprocally identified with the women whose fate she has shared. It is their memory she perpetuates by writing *Requiem* and it is in their memory that she herself lives on. No longer the victim of purely personal tragedy, she has become a bronze statue commemorating a community of suffering, a figure shaped by circumstances into a monument of public and private grief.

Requiem[1]

1935–1940

No, not under the vault of alien skies,[2]
And not under the shelter of alien wings—
I was with my people then,
There, where my people, unfortunately, were.

1961

Instead of a Preface

In the terrible years of the Yezhov terror,[3] I spent seventeen months in the prison lines of Leningrad. Once, someone "recognized" me. Then a woman with bluish lips standing behind me, who, of course, had never heard me called by name before, woke up from the stupor to which every one had succumbed and whispered in my ear (everyone spoke in whispers there):

"Can you describe this?"

And I answered: "Yes, I can."

---

1. Translated by Judith Hemschemeyer.   2. A phrase borrowed from "Message to Siberia" by the Russian poet Pushkin (1799–1837).   3. In 1937–38, mass arrests were carried out by the secret police, headed by Nikolai Yezhov.

Then something that looked like a smile passed over what had once been her face.

April 1, 1957
Leningrad[4]

Dedication

Mountains bow down to this grief,
Mighty rivers cease to flow,
But the prison gates hold firm,
And behind them are the "prisoners' burrows"
And mortal woe.   5
For someone a fresh breeze blows,
For someone the sunset luxuriates—
We[5] wouldn't know, we are those who everywhere
Hear only the rasp of the hateful key
And the soldiers' heavy tread.   10
We rose as if for an early service,
Trudged through the savaged capital
And met there, more lifeless than the dead;
The sun is lower and the Neva[6] mistier,
But hope keeps singing from afar.   15
The verdict . . . And her tears gush forth,
Already she is cut off from the rest,
As if they painfully wrenched life from her heart,
As if they brutally knocked her flat,
But she goes on . . . Staggering . . . Alone . . .   20
Where now are my chance friends
Of those two diabolical years?
What do they imagine is in Siberia's storms,[7]
What appears to them dimly in the circle of the moon?
I am sending my farewell greeting to them.   25

March 1940

Prologue

That was when the ones who smiled
Were the dead, glad to be at rest.
And like a useless appendage, Leningrad
Swung from its prisons.
And when, senseless from torment,   5
Regiments of convicts marched,
And the short songs of farewell
Were sung by locomotive whistles.
The stars of death stood above us

---

4. The prose preface was written after her son had been released from prison and it was possible to think of editing the poem for publication.   5. The women waiting in line before the prison gates.   6. The large river that flows through St. Petersburg.   7. Victims of the purges who were not executed were condemned to prison camps in Siberia. Their wives were allowed to accompany them into exile, although they had to live in towns at a distance from the camps.

And innocent Russia writhed   10
Under bloody boots
And under the tires of the Black Marias.[8]

I

They led you away at dawn,
I followed you, like a mourner,
In the dark front room the children were crying,[9]
By the icon shelf the candle was dying.
On your lips was the icon's chill.[1]   5
The deathly sweat on your brow . . . Unforgettable!—
I will be like the wives of the Streltsy,[2]
Howling under the Kremlin towers.

1935

II

Quietly flows the quiet Don,[3]
Yellow moon slips into a home.

He slips in with cap askew,
He sees a shadow, yellow moon.

This woman is ill,   5
This woman is alone,

Husband in the grave,[4] son in prison,
Say a prayer for me.

III

No, it is not I, it is somebody else who is suffering.
I would not have been able to bear what happened,
Let them shroud it in black,
And let them carry off the lanterns . . .
                              Night.   5

1940

IV

You should have been shown, you mocker,
Minion of all your friends,

---

8. Police cars for conveying those arrested.   9. Akhmatova's third husband, the art historian Nikolai Punin, was arrested at dawn while the children (his daughter and her cousin) cried.   1. The icon—a small religious painting—was set on a shelf before which a candle was kept lit. Punin had kissed the icon before being taken away.   2. Elite troops organized by Ivan the Terrible around 1550, rebelled and were executed by Peter the Great in 1698. Pleading in vain, their wives and mothers saw the men killed under the towers of the Kremlin.   3. The great Russian river, often celebrated in folk songs. This poem is modeled on a simple, rhythmic short folk song known as a *chastuska*.   4. Akhmatova's first husband, the poet Nikolai Gumilyov, was shot in 1921.

Gay little sinner of Tsarskoye Selo,[5]
What would happen in your life—
How three-hundredth in line, with a parcel,   5
You would stand by the Kresty prison,
Your tempestuous tears
Burning through the New Year's ice.
Over there the prison poplar bends,
And there's no sound—and over there how many 10
Innocent lives are ending now . . .

V

For seventeen months I've been crying out,
Calling you home.
I flung myself at the hangman's[6] feet,
You are my son and my horror.
Everything is confused forever,   5
And it's not clear to me
Who is a beast now, who is a man,
And how long before the execution.
And there are only dusty flowers,
And the chinking of the censer, and tracks 10
From somewhere to nowhere.
And staring me straight in the eyes,
And threatening impending death,
Is an enormous star.[7]

1939

VI

The light weeks will take flight,
I won't comprehend what happened.
Just as the white nights[8]
Stared at you, dear son, in prison

So they are staring again,   5
With the burning eyes of a hawk,
Talking about your lofty cross,
And about death.

1939

---

5. Akhmatova recalls her early, carefree, and privileged life in Tsarskoe Selo outside St. Petersburg.
6. Stalin. Akhmatova wrote a letter to him pleading for the release of her son. 7. The "star," the "censer," the foliage, and the confusion between beast and man recall apocalyptic passages in the book of Revelation (8.5, 7, 10–11 and 9:7–10). 8. In St. Petersburg, because it is so far north, the nights around the summer solstice are never totally dark.

VII

THE SENTENCE

And the stone word fell
On my still-living breast.
Never mind, I was ready.
I will manage somehow.
Today I have so much to do: 5
I must kill memory once and for all,
I must turn my soul to stone,
I must learn to live again—

Unless . . . Summer's ardent rustling
Is like a festival outside my window.   10
For a long time I've foreseen this
Brilliant day, deserted house.

June 22, 1939[9]
Fountain House

VIII

TO DEATH

You will come in any case—so why not now?
I am waiting for you—I can't stand much more.
I've put out the light and opened the door
For you, so simple and miraculous.
So come in any form you please,   5
Burst in as a gas shell
Or, like a gangster, steal in with a length of pipe,
Or poison me with typhus fumes.
Or be that fairy tale you've dreamed up,[1]
So sickeningly familiar to everyone—   10
In which I glimpse the top of a pale blue cap[2]
And the house attendant white with fear.
Now it doesn't matter anymore. The Yenisey[3] swirls,
The North Star shines.
And the final horror dims   15
The blue luster of beloved eyes.

August 19, 1939
Fountain House

IX

Now madness half shadows
My soul with its wing,

---

9. The date that her son was sentenced to labor camp.   **1.** A denunciation to the police for imaginary crimes, common during the purges as people hastened to protect themselves by accusing their neighbor. **2.** The NKVD (secret police) wore blue caps.   **3.** A river in Siberia along which there were many prison camps.

And makes it drunk with fiery wine
And beckons toward the black ravine.

And I've finally realized   5
That I must give in,
Overhearing myself
Raving as if it were somebody else.

And it does not allow me to take
Anything of mine with me   10
(No matter how I plead with it,
No matter how I supplicate):

Not the terrible eyes of my son—
Suffering turned to stone,
Not the day of the terror,   15
Not the hour I met with him in prison,

Not the sweet coolness of his hands,
Not the trembling shadow of the lindens,
Not the far-off, fragile sound—
Of the final words of consolation.   20

May 4, 1940
Fountain House

X

CRUCIFIXION

"Do not weep for Me, Mother,
I am in the grave."

I

A choir of angels sang the praises of that momentous hour,
And the heavens dissolved in fire.
To his Father He said: "Why hast Thou forsaken me!"[4]
And to his Mother: "Oh, do not weep for Me . . ."[5]

1940
Fountain House

2

Mary Magdalene beat her breast and sobbed,
The beloved disciple[6] turned to stone,

---

4. Jesus' last words from the cross (Matthew 27.46).   **5.** These words and the epigraph refer to a line from the Russian Orthodox prayer sung at services on Easter Saturday: "Weep not for Me, Mother, when you look upon the grave." Jesus is comforting Mary with the promise of his resurrection.   **6.** The apostle John.

But where the silent Mother stood, there
No one glanced and no one would have dared.

1943
Tashkent

Epilogue I

I learned how faces fall,
How terror darts from under eyelids,
How suffering traces lines
Of stiff cuneiform on cheeks,
How locks of ashen-blonde or black   5
Turn silver suddenly,
Smiles fade on submissive lips
And fear trembles in a dry laugh.
And I pray not for myself alone;
But for all those who stood there with me   10
In cruel cold, and in July's heat,
At that blind, red wall.

Epilogue II

Once more the day of remembrance[7] draws near.
I see, I hear, I feel you:

The one they almost had to drag at the end,
And the one who tramps her native land no more,

And the one who, tossing her beautiful head,   5
Said: "Coming here's like coming home."

I'd like to name them all by name,
But the list[8] has been confiscated and is nowhere to be found.

I have woven a wide mantle for them
From their meager, overheard words.   10

I will remember them always and everywhere,
I will never forget them no matter what comes.

And if they gag my exhausted mouth
Through which a hundred million scream,

Then may the people remember me   15
On the eve of my remembrance day.

And if ever in this country
They decide to erect a monument to me,

---

7. In the Russian Orthodox Church, a memorial service is held on the anniversary of a death.   8. Of prisoners.

I consent to that honor
Under these conditions—that it stand   20

Neither by the sea, where I was born:
My last tie with the sea is broken,

Nor in the tsar's garden near the cherished pine stump,[9]
Where an inconsolable shade[1] looks for me,

But here, where I stood for three hundred hours,   25
And where they never unbolted the doors for me.

This, lest in blissful death
I forget the rumbling of the Black Marias,

Forget how that detested door slammed shut
And an old woman howled like a wounded animal.   30

And may the melting snow stream like tears
From my motionless lids of bronze,

And a prison dove coo in the distance,
And the ships of the Neva sail calmly on.

March 1940

9. The gardens and park surrounding the summer palace in Tsarskoe Selo. Akhmatova writes elsewhere of the stump of a favorite tree in the gardens and of the poet Pushkin, whom she describes as walking in the park.   1. A ghost; probably the restless spirit of Akhmatova's executed husband, Gumilyov, who had courted her in Tsarskoe Selo.

FEDERICO GARCÍA LORCA
1898–1936

Although he died young, the poet and playwright Federico García Lorca is the best-known writer of modern Spain and perhaps the most famous Spanish writer since Cervantes. A member of the brilliant "Generation of 1927" (along with Jorgé Guillen, Vicente Aleixandre, Pedro Salinas, and Rafael Alberti), known for the striking imagery and lyric musicality of his work, Lorca is both classical and modern, traditional and innovative, difficult and popular, a voice combining regional and universal themes. The poetry and plays that began as (and always were) personal statements took on larger significance first as the expression of tragic conflicts in Spanish culture and then as poignant laments for humanity—seen especially in the plight of those who are deprived, by society or simply by death, of the fulfillment that could have been theirs. When Lorca was dragged from a friend's house and executed by a Fascist squad on August 19, 1936, his murder outraged the whole European and American literary and artistic community and seemed to symbolize in addition the mindless destruction of humane and cultural values that loomed with the approach of World War II.

Lorca (despite the Spanish practice of using both paternal and maternal last names—correctly "García Lorca"—the author is generally called "Lorca") was born on June 5, 1898, in the small village of Fuentevaqueros, near the Andalusian city of Granada. His father was a prosperous farmer, and his mother, who had been a schoolteacher, encouraged him to read widely and develop his musical talent. The composer Manuel de Falla befriended the young musician, who became an expert pianist and guitar player. Lorca began law studies at the University of Granada, where—after several years' absence—he received a degree in 1923. He published a book called *Impressions and Landscapes* (1918) after a trip through Spain but left Granada in 1919 for Madrid, where he entered the Residencia de Estudiantes, a modern college established to provide a cosmopolitan education for Spanish youth. Madrid was not only the capital of Spain but also the center of intellectual and artistic ferment, and the Residencia attracted many of those who would become the most influential writers and artists of their generation (among the latter the artist Salvador Dalí and the film director Luis Buñuel). Lorca soon gained the reputation of a rising young poet from poetry readings and the publication of a few poems in magazines, even before the appearance of his first collection of verse, the *Book of Poems* of 1921. Although he lived at the Residencia almost continuously until 1928, he never seriously pursued a degree but spent his time reading, writing, improvising music and poetry in company with his friends, and producing his first plays.

In these early years, before his departure for New York in 1929, Lorca concentrated on writing poetry, although he was clearly interested in the theater as well. *The Butterfly's Evil Spell* (1920), a fantasy about a cockroach that is hopelessly enchanted by the beauty of a butterfly, was staged in Barcelona; in 1923 Lorca wrote, designed sets for, and directed a puppet play on a theme from Andalusian folklore, *The Girl Who Waters the Sweet Basil Flower and the Inquisitive Prince*, for which de Falla himself arranged the music. Yet the major achievement of this period is the composition of several books of poetry, not all of which were published at the time: the *Book of Poems*; most of the *Songs* (1927); early versions of the poems in the *Poem of the Deep Song*, which was not published as a book until 1931, although several poems were recited at a 1922 Andalusian festival; and the *Gypsy Ballads* (1928), which was an immediate popular success.

From 1930 to his death in 1936, Lorca was extremely active in the theater both as writer and as director (after 1931) of a traveling theatrical group (La Barraca) subsidized by the Spanish Republic. After a series of farces that mixed romantically tragic and comic themes, he presented the tragedies for which he is best known: *Blood Wedding* (1933) and *Yerma* (1934). In 1936 he wrote the posthumously published *The House of Bernarda Alba* (1945). All Lorca's theater, from the early fantasy of *The Butterfly's Evil Spell* to the puppet plays, farces, and last tragedies, rejects the conventionally realistic nineteenth-century drama and employs an openly poetic form that suggests musical patterns, includes choruses, songs, and stylized movement, and may even (as in the fragmentary surrealist drama, *The Audience*) attack the audience itself. The tragic themes of Lorca's poetry emerge here in dramatic form, usually centering on the suffering of individual women whose instinctual fulfillment (through love or children) is denied by fate or social circumstance.

In 1936, the year of his death, Lorca was revising a series of short lyric poems based on the Arabic forms of *casida* and the *gacela*, a collection eventually published in 1940 as *The Divan at Tamarit* (a "divan" is a poetic collection, and Lorca wrote the poems at a country house called after the ancient place-name of Tamarit). In the previous year, he had published a long elegiac poem on the death of his good friend the famous bullfighter Ignacio Sánchez Mejías, who had been fatally gored by a bull on August 11, 1934, in Manzanares and died two days later in Madrid. Sánchez Mejías was a cultured man, well known in literary circles and himself the author of a play, and Lorca's "Lament for Ignacio Sánchez Mejías" celebrates both his friend and the value of human grace and courage in a world where everything ends in death.

Lorca's "Lament" not only is cast as an elegy (a medium-length poem that mourns a death) but also recalls one of the most famous poems of Spanish literature: the "Verses on the Death of His Father" written by the medieval poet Jorge Manrique (1440–1479). Manrique's catalog of his father's noble qualities ("What a friend to his friends!") and his description of individual lives as flowing into the sea of death are echoed by passages in the modern elegy. Yet there is a fundamental difference between the two: while Manrique's elegy stresses religious themes and the prospect of eternal life, Lorca—in grim contrast—rejects such consolation and insists that his friend's death is permanent.

The four parts of the "Lament" incorporate a variety of forms and perspectives, all working together to suggest a progression from the report of death in the precise first line—"At five in the afternoon"—to the end where the dead man's nobility and elegance survive in "a sad breeze through the olive trees." The "deep song" technique of an insistent refrain coloring the whole organizes the first section, "Cogida [the bull's toss] and Death," with its throbbing return to the moment of death. The scene in the arena wavers between an objective report—the boy with the shroud, the coffin on wheels—and the shared agony of the bull's bellowing and wounds burning like suns. Lorca moves in the next ballad section to a personal refusal of Sánchez Mejías's death ("I will not see it!") and a request that images of whiteness cover up this spilled blood; instead, he imagines Ignacio climbing steps to seek dawn and a mystic meeting with his true self but encountering, bewildered, only his broken body. After a tribute to his princely friend, the poet finally admits what he cannot force himself to see: the finality of physical dissolution as moss and grass invade the buried bullfighter's skull.

In "The Laid Out Body," a series of somber quatrains in regular meter recognizes the inevitability of death and dissolution (Ignacio's "pure shape which had nightingales" is now "filled with depthless holes"), and the fact that the bullfighter will be entombed in unyielding, lifeless stone. In this and the final section, with its rhythmic free verse, Lorca accepts physical death ("even the sea dies!") but preserves, in his poetry, a vision of his noble countryman that surpasses such obliteration. For those who exist only on the unthinking, physical level (the bull, fig tree, household ants, the black satin of his funeral suit), Ignacio has indeed "died for ever." Yet human beings recognize other qualities beyond the physical and in fact shape their estimate of an individual according to these qualities. In life, Sánchez Mejías was known to his friends for "the signal maturity of your understanding . . . your appetite for death and the taste of its mouth." These qualities survive, for a while, in memory. Lorca, echoing the pride with which the Latin poet Horace claimed to perpetuate his subjects in a "monument of lasting bronze," sings of his friend "for posterity" and captures the life and death of Sánchez Mejías in his "Lament."

Lament for Ignacio Sánchez Mejías[1]

1. Cogida[2] and Death

At five in the afternoon.
It was exactly five in the afternoon.
A boy brought the white sheet
at five in the afternoon.
A frail of lime[3] ready prepared

5

---

1. Translated by Stephen Spender and J. L. Gili.   2. Harvesting (Spanish, literal trans.); the toss when the bull catches the bullfighter.   3. A disinfectant that was sprinkled on the body after death. "Frail": a basket.

at five in the afternoon.
The rest was death, and death; alone
at five in the afternoon.

The wind carried away the cottonwool[4]
at five in the afternoon.   10
And the oxide scattered crystal and nickel
at five in the afternoon.
Now the dove and the leopard[5] wrestle
at five in the afternoon.
And a thigh with a desolate horn   15
at five in the afternoon.
The bass-string[6] struck up
at five in the afternoon.
Arsenic bells[7] and smoke
at five in the afternoon.   20
Groups of silence in the corners
at five in the afternoon.
And the bull alone with a high heart!
At five in the afternoon.
When the sweat of snow was coming   25
at five in the afternoon,
when the bull ring was covered in iodine
at five in the afternoon,
death laid eggs in the wound
at five in the afternoon.   30
At five in the afternoon.
Exactly at five o'clock in the afternoon.

A coffin on wheels is his bed
at five in the afternoon.
Bones and flutes resound in his ears[8]   35
at five in the afternoon.
Now the bull was bellowing through his forehead
at five in the afternoon.
The room[9] was iridescent with agony
at five in the afternoon.   40
In the distance the gangrene now comes
at five in the afternoon.
Horn of the lily through green[1] groins
at five in the afternoon.
The wounds were burning like suns   45
at five in the afternoon,
and the crowd was breaking the windows[2]
at five in the afternoon.
At five in the afternoon.

---

4. To stop the blood; the beginning of a series of medicinal, chemical, and inhuman images that empha-size the presence of death.   5. Traditional symbols for peace and violence; they wrestle with one another as the bullfighter's thigh struggles with the bull's horn.   6. That is, of a guitar, which plays a lament. 7. Rung to announce a death.   8. A suggestion of the medieval dance of death.   9. Adjoining the arena where wounded bullfighters are taken for treatment.   1. Gangrene turns flesh a greenish color. "Lily": the shape of the wound resembles this flower.   2. A Spanish idiom for the crowd's loud roar.

Ah, that fatal five in the afternoon!   50
It was five by all the clocks!
It was five in the shade of the afternoon!

2. The Spilled Blood

I will not see it!

Tell the moon to come
for I do not want to see the blood
of Ignacio on the sand.   55
I will not see it!

The moon wide open.
Horse of still clouds,
and the grey bull ring of dreams   60
with willows in the barreras.[3]
I will not see it!

Let my memory kindle![4]
Warn the jasmines[5]
of such minute whiteness!   65
I will not see it!

The cow of the ancient world
passed her sad tongue
over a snout of blood
spilled on the sand,   70
and the bulls of Guisando,[6]
partly death and partly stone,
bellowed like two centuries
sated with treading the earth.
No.   75
I do not want to see it!
I will not see it!

Ignacio goes up the tiers[7]
with all his death on his shoulders.
He sought for the dawn   80
but the dawn was no more.
He seeks for his confident profile
and the dream bewilders him.
He sought for his beautiful body
and encountered his opened blood.   85
Do not ask me to see it!
I do not want to hear it spurt
each time with less strength:

3. The barriers around the ring within which the fight takes place and over which a fighter may escape the bull's charge. "Willows": symbols of mourning. 4. My memory burns within me (literal trans.). 5. The poet calls on ("warn," as notify) the small white jasmine flowers to come and cover the blood. 6. Carved stone bulls from the Celtic past, a tourist attraction in the province of Madrid. 7. An imaginary scene in which the bullfighter mounts the stairs of the arena.

that spurt that illuminates
the tiers of seats, and spills   90
over the corduroy and the leather
of a thirsty multitude.
Who shouts that I should come near!
Do not ask me to see it!

His eyes did not close   95
when he saw the horns near,
but the terrible mothers
lifted their heads.[8]
And across the ranches,[9]
an air of secret voices rose,   100
shouting to celestial bulls,
herdsmen of pale mist.

There was no prince in Seville[1]
who could compare with him,
nor sword like his sword   105
nor heart so true.
Like a river of lions
was his marvellous strength,
and like a marble torso
his firm drawn moderation.   110
The air of Andalusian Rome
gilded his head[2]
where his smile was a spikenard[3]
of wit and intelligence.
What a great torero[4] in the ring!   115
What a good peasant in the sierra![5]
How gentle with the sheaves!
How hard with the spurs!
How tender with the dew!
How dazzling in the fiesta!   120
How tremendous with the final
banderillas[6] of darkness!

But now he sleeps without end.
Now the moss and the grass
open with sure fingers   125
the flower of his skull.
And now his blood comes out singing;
singing along marshes and meadows,
sliding on frozen horns,
faltering soulless in the mist,   130
stumbling over a thousand hoofs

---

8. The three Fates traditionally raised their heads when the thread of life was cut.   9. Fighting bulls are raised on the ranches of Lorca's home province of Andalusia.   1. Leading city of Andalusia.   2. The image suggests a statue from Roman times, when Andalusia was part of the Roman empire.   3. A small, white, fragrant flower common in Andalusia; by extension, the bullfighter's white teeth.   4. Bullfighter. 5. Mountainous country. Sánchez Mejías is seen as a good *serrano* ("man of the hills").   6. The multi-colored short spears that are thrust in the bull's shoulders to provoke him to attack.

like a long, dark, sad tongue,
to form a pool of agony
close to the starry Guadalquivir.[7]
Oh, white wall of Spain!   135
Oh, black bull of sorrow!
Oh, hard blood of Ignacio!
Oh, nightingale of his veins!
No.
I will not see it!   140
No chalice can contain it,
no swallows[8] can drink it,
no frost of light can cool it,
nor song nor deluge of white lilies,
no glass can cover it with silver.   145
No.
I will not see it!

3. The Laid Out Body[9]

Stone is a forehead where dreams grieve
without curving waters and frozen cypresses.
Stone is a shoulder on which to bear Time   150
with trees formed of tears and ribbons and planets.[1]

I have seen grey showers move towards the waves
raising their tender riddled arms,
to avoid being caught by the lying stone
which loosens their limbs without soaking the blood.   155

For stone gathers seed and clouds,
skeleton larks and wolves of penumbra:
but yields not sounds nor crystals nor fire,
only bull rings and bull rings and more bull rings without walls.

Now Ignacio the well born lies on the stone.   160
All is finished. What is happening? Contemplate his face:
death has covered him with pale sulphur
and has placed on him the head of a dark minotaur.[2]

All is finished. The rain penetrates his mouth.
The air, as if mad, leaves his sunken chest,   165
and Love, soaked through with tears of snow,
warms itself on the peak of the herd.[3]

What are they saying? A stenching silence settles down.
We are here with a body laid out which fades away,

---

7. A great river that passes through all the major cities of Andalusia. The singing stream of the bullfighter's blood suggests both the river and a nightingale.   8. According to a Spanish legend of the crucifixion, swallows—a symbol of innocence—drank the blood of Christ on the cross. The poet is seeking ways of concealing the dead man's blood.   9. Present body (literal trans.); the Spanish expression for a funeral wake, when the body is laid out for public mourning. The title contrasts with that of the next section: "Absent Soul."   1. Traditional funeral imagery carved on gravestones.   2. A monster from Greek myth: half man, half bull.   3. Of the ranch (literal trans.).

with a pure shape which had nightingales 170
and we see it being filled with depthless holes.

Who creases the shroud? What he says is not true![4]
Nobody sings here, nobody weeps in the corner,
nobody pricks the spurs, nor terrifies the serpent.
Here I want nothing else but the round eyes 175
to see this body without a chance of rest.

Here I want to see those men of hard voice.
Those that break horses and dominate rivers;
those men of sonorous skeleton who sing
with a mouth full of sun and flint. 180

Here I want to see them. Before the stone.
Before this body with broken reins.
I want to know from them the way out
for this captain strapped down by death.

I want them to show me a lament like a river 185
which will have sweet mists and deep shores,
to take the body of Ignacio where it loses itself
without hearing the double panting of the bulls.

Loses itself in the round bull ring of the moon
which feigns in its youth a sad quiet bull: 190
loses itself in the night without song of fishes
and in the white thicket of frozen smoke.

I don't want them to cover his face with handkerchiefs
that he may get used to the death he carries.
Go, Ignacio; feel not the hot bellowing. 195
Sleep, fly, rest: even the sea dies!

4. Absent Soul

The bull does not know you, nor the fig tree,
nor the horses, nor the ants in your own house.
The child and the afternoon do not know you
because you have died for ever. 200

The back of the stone does not know you,
nor the black satin in which you crumble.
Your silent memory does not know you
because you have died for ever.

The autumn will come with small white snails,[5] 205
misty grapes and with clustered hills,

---

4. Lorca criticizes the conventional pieties voiced by someone standing close to the shrouded body; the poet prefers a clear-eyed, realistic view of death.   **5.** Actually, conch shell–shaped horns; the shepherds' horns that sound in the hills each fall as the sheep are driven to new pastures.

but no one will look into your eyes
because you have died for ever.

Because you have died for ever,
like all the death of the Earth,   210
like all the dead who are forgotten
in a heap of lifeless dogs.[6]

Nobody knows you. No. But I sing of you.
For posterity I sing of your profile and grace.
Of the signal maturity of your understanding.   215
Of your appetite for death and the taste of its mouth.
Of the sadness of your once valiant gaiety.

It will be a long time, if ever, before there is born
an Andalusian so true, so rich in adventure.
I sing of his elegance with words that groan,   220
and I remember a sad breeze through the olive trees.

From Llanto por Ignacio Sánchez Mejías

4. Alma Ausente

No te conoce el toro ni la higuera,
ni caballos ni hormigas de tu casa.
No te conoce el niño ni la tarde
porque te has muerto para siempre.   200

No te conoce el lomo de la piedra,
ni el raso negro donde te destrozas.
No te conoce tu recuerdo mudo
porque te has muerto para siempre.

El otoño vendrá con caracolas,   205
uva de niebla y montes agrupados,
pero nadie querrá mirar tus ojos
porque te has muerto para siempre.

Porque te has muerto para siempre,
como todos los muertos de la Tierra,   210
como todos los muertos que se olvidan
en un montón de perros apagados.

No te conoce nadie. No. Pero yo te canto.
Yo canto para luego tu perfil y tu gracia.
La madurez insigne de tu conocimiento.   215
Tu apetencia de muerte y el gusto de su boca.
La tristeza que tuvo tu valiente alegría.

6. Dogs as a (typically continental) image for undignified, inferior creatures.

Tardará mucho tiempo en nacer, si es que nace,
un andaluz tan claro, tan rico de aventura.
Yo canto su elegancia con palabras que gimen   220
y recuerdo una brisa triste por los olivos.

JORGE LUIS BORGES
1899–1986

Although other modernist writers are known for their formal innovations, it is the Argentinian Jorge Luis Borges who represents, above all, the gamelike or playful aspect of literary creation. The "real world" is only one of the possible realities in Borges's multiple universe, which treats history, fantasy, and science fiction as having equal claim on our attention: since they all can be imagined, they all are perhaps equally real. His is a world of pure thought, in which abstract fictional games are played out when an initial situation or concept is pushed to its elegantly logical extreme. If everything is possible, there is no need for the artificial constraints imposed by conventional artistic attempts to represent reality: no need for psychological consistency, for a realistic setting, or for a story that unfolds in ordinary time and space. The voice telling the story becomes lost inside the setting it creates, just as a drawing by Saul Steinberg or Maurits Escher depicts a pen drawing the rest of the landscape in which it appears. Not unexpectedly, this thorough immersion in the play of subjective imagination appealed to writers such as the French "new novelists," who were experimenting with shifting perspectives and a refusal of objective reality. For a long time, Borges's European reputation outstripped his prestige in his native land.

Borges was born in Buenos Aires, Argentina, on August 24, 1899, to a prosperous family whose ancestors were distinguished in Argentinian history. The family moved early to a large house whose library and garden were to form an essential part of his literary imagination. His paternal grandmother being English, the young Borges knew English as soon as Spanish and was educated by an English tutor until he was nine. Traveling in Europe, the family was caught in Geneva at the outbreak of World War I; Borges attended secondary school in Switzerland and throughout the war, at which time he learned French and German. After the war they moved to Spain, where he associated with a group of young experimental poets known as the Ultraists. When Borges returned home in 1921, he founded his own group of Argentinian Ultraists (their mural review, *Prisma*, was printed on sign paper and plastered on walls); became close friends with the philosopher Macedonio Fernandez, whose dedication to pure thought and linguistic intricacies greatly influenced his own attitudes; and contributed regularly to the avant-garde review *Martín Fierro*, at that time associated with an apolitical art for art's sake attitude quite at odds with that of the Boedo group of politically committed writers. Although devoted to pure art, Borges also consistently opposed the military dictatorship of Juan Perón and made his political views plain in speeches and nonliterary writings even though they were not included in his fiction. His attitude did not go unnoticed: in 1946, the Perón regime removed him from the librarian's post that he had held since 1938 and offered him a job as a chicken inspector.

During the 1930s, Borges turned to short narrative pieces and in 1935 published a collection of sketches titled *Universal History of Infamy*. His more mature stories—brief, metaphysical fictions whose density and elegance at times approach poetry—

came as an experiment after a head injury and operation in 1938. *The Garden of Forking Paths* (1941), his first major collection, introduced him to a wider public as an intellectual and idealist writer, whose short stories subordinated familiar techniques of character, scene, plot, and narrative voice to a central idea, which was often a philosophical concept. This concept was used not as a lesson or dogma but as the starting point of fantastic elaborations to entertain readers within the game of literature.

Borges's imaginative world is an immense labyrinth, a "garden of forking paths" in which images of mazes and infinite mirroring, cyclical repetition and recall, illustrate the effort of an elusive narrative voice to understand its own significance and that of the world. In "Borges and I," he comments on the parallel existence of two Borgeses: the one who exists in his work (the one his readers know) and the living, fleshly identity felt by the man who sets pen to paper. "Little by little, I am giving over everything to him . . . I do not know which one of us has written this page." Borges has written on the idea (derived from the British philosophers David Hume and George Berkeley) of the individual self as a cluster of different perceptions, and he further elaborates this notion in his fictional proliferation of identities and alternate realities. Disdaining the "psychological fakery" of realistic novels (the "draggy novel of characters"), he prefers writing that is openly artful, concerned with technique for its own sake, and invents its own multidimensional reality.

Stories in *The Garden of Forking Paths*, *Fictions* (1944), and *The Aleph* (1949) develop these themes in a variety of styles. Borges is fond of detective stories (and has written a number of them) in which the search for an elusive explanation, given carefully planted clues, matters more than how recognizable the characters may be. In "Death and the Compass," a mysterious murderer leaves tantalizing traces that refer to points of the compass and lead the detective into a fatal trap that closes on him at a fourth compass point, symbolized by the architectural lozenges of the house in which he dies. The author composes an art of puzzles and discovery, a grand code that treats our universe as a giant library where meaning is locked away in endless hexagonal galleries ("The Library of Babel"), as an enormous lottery whose results are all the events of our lives ("The Lottery in Babylon"), as a series of dreams within dreams ("The Circular Ruins"), or as a small iridescent sphere containing all of the points in space ("The Aleph"). In "Pierre Menard, Author of the 'Quixote,'" the narrator is a scholarly reviewer of a certain fictitious Menard, whose masterwork has been to rewrite *Don Quixote* as if it were created today: not revise it or transcribe it, but actually *reinvent* it word for word. He has succeeded; the two texts are "verbally identical" although Menard's modern version is "more ambiguous" than Cervantes's and thus "infinitely richer."

The imaginary universe of "Tlön, Uqbar, Orbis Tertius" exemplifies the mixture of fact and fiction with which Borges invites us to speculate on the solidity of our own world. The narrator is engaged in tracking down mysterious references to a country called Tlön, whose language, science, and literature are exactly opposite (and perhaps related to) our own. For example, the Tlönians use verbs or adjectives instead of nouns, since they have no concept of objects in space, and their science consists of an association of ideas in which the most astounding theory becomes the truth. In a postscript, the narrator reveals that the encyclopedia has turned out to be an immense scholarly hoax, yet also mentions that strange and unearthly objects— recognizably from Tlön—have recently been found.

The intricate, riddling, mazelike ambiguity of Borges's stories earned him international reputation and influence, to the point that a "style like Borges" has become a recognized term. In Argentina, he was given the prestigious post of director of the National Library after the fall of Perón in 1955, and in 1961 he shared the International Publishers' Prize with Samuel Beckett. Always nearsighted, he grew increasingly blind in the mid-1950s and was forced to dictate his work. Nonetheless, he continued to travel, teach, and lecture in the company of his wife, Else Astete Milan, whom he married in 1967. Until his death Borges lived in his beloved Buenos Aires, the city he celebrated in his first volume of poetry.

"The Garden of Forking Paths" begins as a simple spy story purporting to reveal the hidden truth about a German bombing raid during World War I. Borges alludes to documented facts: the geographic setting of the town of Albert and the Ancre River; a famous Chinese novel as Ts'ui Pên's proposed model; the *History of the World War (1914–1918)* published by B. H. Liddell Hart in 1934. Official history is undermined on the first page, however, both by the newly discovered confession of Dr. Yu Tsun and by his editor's suspiciously defensive footnote. Ultimately, Yu Tsun will learn from his ancestor's novel that history is a labyrinth of alternate possibilities (much like the "alternate worlds" of science fiction).

Borges executes his detective story with the traditional carefully planted clues. We know from the beginning that Yu Tsun—even though arrested—has successfully outwitted his rival, Captain Richard Madden; that his problem was to convey the name of a bombing target to his chief in Berlin; that he went to the telephone book to locate someone capable of transmitting his message; and that he had one bullet in his revolver. The cut-off phone call, the chase at the railroad station, and Madden's hasty arrival at Dr. Albert's house provide the excitement and pressure expected in a straightforward detective plot. Quite different spatial and temporal horizons open up halfway through, however. Coincidences—those chance relationships that might well have happened differently—introduce the idea of forking paths or alternate possible routes for history. Both Yu Tsun and Richard Madden are aliens trying to prove their worth inside their respective bureaucracies; the road to Stephen Albert's house turns mazelike always to the left; the only suitable name in the phone book—the man Yu Tsun must kill—is a Sinologist who has reconstructed the labyrinthine text written long ago by Yu Tsun's ancestor. This text, Ts'ui Pên's "The Garden of Forking Paths," describes the universe as an infinite series of alternative versions of experience. In different versions of the story (taking place at different times), Albert and Yu Tsun are enemies or friends or not even there. The war and Richard Madden appear diminished (although no less real) in such a kaleidoscopic perspective, for they exist in only one of many possible dimensions. Yet Madden hurries up the walk, and current reality returns to demand Albert's death. It may seem as though the vision of other worlds in which Albert continues to exist (or is Yu Tsun's enemy) would soften the murderer's remorse for his deed. Instead, it makes more poignant the narrator's realization that in this dimension no other way could be found.

PRONOUNCING GLOSSARY

The following list uses common English syllables and stress accents to provide rough equivalents of selected words whose pronunciation may be unfamiliar to the general reader.

Borges: *bore'-hess*

Hsi P'êng: *shee pung*

Hung Lu Meng: *hoong low mung*

Ts'ui Pên: *tsoo-ay pun*

Yu Tsun: *yew tsoo-en*

The Garden of Forking Paths[1]

On page 22 of Liddell Hart's *History of World War I* you will read that an attack against the Serre-Montauban line by thirteen British divisions (supported by 1,400 artillery pieces), planned for the 24th of July, 1916, had to

---

1. Translated by Donald A. Yates.

be postponed until the morning of the 29th. The torrential rains, Captain Liddell Hart comments, caused this delay, an insignificant one, to be sure.

The following statement, dictated, reread and signed by Dr. Yu Tsun, former professor of English at the *Hochschule* at Tsingtao,[2] throws an unsuspected light over the whole affair. The first two pages of the document are missing.

". . . and I hung up the receiver. Immediately afterwards, I recognized the voice that had answered in German. It was that of Captain Richard Madden. Madden's presence in Viktor Runeberg's apartment meant the end of our anxieties and—but this seemed, *or should have seemed,* very secondary to me—also the end of our lives. It meant that Runeberg had been arrested or murdered.[3] Before the sun set on that day, I would encounter the same fate. Madden was implacable. Or rather, he was obliged to be so. An Irishman at the service of England, a man accused of laxity and perhaps of treason, how could he fail to seize and be thankful for such a miraculous opportunity: the discovery, capture, maybe even the death of two agents of the German Reich?[4] I went up to my room; absurdly I locked the door and threw myself on my back on the narrow iron cot. Through the window I saw the familiar roofs and the cloud-shaded six o'clock sun. It seemed incredible to me that that day without premonitions or symbols should be the one of my inexorable death. In spite of my dead father, in spite of having been a child in a symmetrical garden of Hai Feng, was I—now—going to die? Then I reflected that everything happens to a man precisely, precisely *now.* Centuries of centuries and only in the present do things happen; countless men in the air, on the face of the earth and the sea, and all that really is happening is happening to me . . . The almost intolerable recollection of Madden's horselike face banished these wanderings. In the midst of my hatred and terror (it means nothing to me now to speak of terror, now that I have mocked Richard Madden, now that my throat yearns for the noose) it occurred to me that that tumultuous and doubtless happy warrior did not suspect that I possessed the Secret. The name of the exact location of the new British artillery park on the River Ancre. A bird streaked across the gray sky and blindly I translated it into an airplane and that airplane into many (against the French sky) annihilating the artillery station with vertical bombs. If only my mouth, before a bullet shattered it, could cry out that secret name so it could be heard in Germany . . . My human voice was very weak. How might I make it carry to the ear of the Chief? To the ear of that sick and hateful man who knew nothing of Runeberg and me save that we were in Stafford shire[5] and who was waiting in vain for our report in his arid office in Berlin, endlessly examining newspapers . . . I said out loud: *I must flee.* I sat up noiselessly, in a useless perfection of silence, as if Madden were already lying in wait for me. Something—perhaps the mere vain ostentation of proving my resources were nil—made me look through my pockets. I found what I knew I would find. The American watch, the nickel chain and the square coin, the

---

2. Or Ch'ing-tao; a major port in east China, part of territory leased to (and developed by) Germany in 1898. *"Hochschule"*: university (German).   3. "A hypothesis both hateful and odd. The Prussian spy Hans Rabener, alias Viktor Runeberg, attacked with drawn automatic the bearer of the warrant for his arrest, Captain Richard Madden. The latter, in self-defense, inflicted the wound which brought about Runeberg's death [Editor's note]." This entire note is by Borges as "editor."   4. Empire (German).   5. County in west-central England.

key ring with the incriminating useless keys to Runeberg's apartment, the notebook, a letter which I resolved to destroy immediately (and which I did not destroy), a crown, two shillings and a few pence, the red and blue pencil, the handkerchief, the revolver with one bullet. Absurdly, I took it in my hand and weighed it in order to inspire courage within myself. Vaguely I thought that a pistol report can be heard at a great distance. In ten minutes my plan was perfected. The telephone book listed the name of the only person capable of transmitting the message; he lived in a suburb of Fenton,[6] less than a half hour's train ride away.

I am a cowardly man. I say it now, now that I have carried to its end a plan whose perilous nature no one can deny. I know its execution was terrible. I didn't do it for Germany, no. I care nothing for a barbarous country which imposed upon me the abjection of being a spy. Besides, I know of a man from England—a modest man—who for me is no less great than Goethe.[7] I talked with him for scarcely an hour, but during that hour he was Goethe . . . I did it because I sensed that the Chief somehow feared people of my race—for the innumerable ancestors who merge within me. I wanted to prove to him that a yellow man could save his armies. Besides, I had to flee from Captain Madden. His hands and his voice could call at my door at any moment. I dressed silently, bade farewell to myself in the mirror, went downstairs, scrutinized the peaceful street and went out. The station was not far from my home, but I judged it wise to take a cab. I argued that in this way I ran less risk of being recognized; the fact is that in the deserted street I felt myself visible and vulnerable, infinitely so. I remember that I told the cab driver to stop a short distance before the main entrance. I got out with voluntary, almost painful slowness; I was going to the village of Ashgrove but I bought a ticket for a more distant station. The train left within a very few minutes, at eight-fifty. I hurried; the next one would leave at nine-thirty. There was hardly a soul on the platform. I went through the coaches; I remember a few farmers, a woman dressed in mourning, a young boy who was reading with fervor the *Annals* of Tacitus,[8] a wounded and happy soldier. The coaches jerked forward at last. A man whom I recognized ran in vain to the end of the platform. It was Captain Richard Madden. Shattered, trembling, I shrank into the far corner of the seat, away from the dreaded window.

From this broken state I passed into an almost abject felicity. I told myself that the duel had already begun and that I had won the first encounter by frustrating, even if for forty minutes, even if by a stroke of fate, the attack of my adversary. I argued that this slightest of victories foreshadowed a total victory. I argued (no less fallaciously) that my cowardly felicity proved that I was a man capable of carrying out the adventure successfully. From this weakness I took strength that did not abandon me. I foresee that man will resign himself each day to more atrocious undertakings; soon there will be no one but warriors and brigands; I give them this counsel: *The author of an atrocious undertaking ought to imagine that he has already accomplished it,*

---

6. In Lincolnshire, a county in east England.   7. Johann Wolfgang von Goethe (1749–1832), German poet, novelist, and dramatist; author of *Faust*; often taken as representing the peak of German cultural achievement.   8. Cornelius Tacitus (55–117), Roman historian whose *Annals* give a vivid picture of the decadence and corruption of the Roman empire under Tiberius, Claudius, and Nero.

ought to impose upon himself a future as irrevocable as the past. Thus I proceeded as my eyes of a man already dead registered the elapsing of that day, which was perhaps the last, and the diffusion of the night. The train ran gently along, amid ash trees. It stopped, almost in the middle of the fields. No one announced the name of the station. "Ashgrove?" I asked a few lads on the platform. "Ashgrove," they replied. I got off.

A lamp enlightened the platform but the faces of the boys were in shadow. One questioned me, "Are you going to Dr. Stephen Albert's house?" Without waiting for my answer, another said, "The house is a long way from here, but you won't get lost if you take this road to the left and at every crossroads turn again to your left." I tossed them a coin (my last), descended a few stone steps and started down the solitary road. It went downhill, slowly. It was of elemental earth; overhead the branches were tangled; the low, full moon seemed to accompany me.

For an instant, I thought that Richard Madden in some way had penetrated my desperate plan. Very quickly, I understood that that was impossible. The instructions to turn always to the left reminded me that such was the common procedure for discovering the central point of certain labyrinths. I have some understanding of labyrinths: not for nothing am I the great grandson of that Ts'ui Pên who was governor of Yunnan and who renounced worldly power in order to write a novel that might be even more populous than the *Hung Lu Meng*[9] and to construct a labyrinth in which all men would become lost. Thirteen years he dedicated to these heterogeneous tasks, but the hand of a stranger murdered him—and his novel was incoherent and no one found the labyrinth. Beneath English trees I meditated on that lost maze: I imagined it inviolate and perfect at the secret crest of a mountain; I imagined it erased by rice fields or beneath the water; I imagined it infinite, no longer composed of octagonal kiosks and returning paths, but of rivers and provinces and kingdoms . . . I thought of a labyrinth of labyrinths, of one sinuous spreading labyrinth that would encompass the past and the future and in some way involve the stars. Absorbed in these illusory images, I forgot my destiny of one pursued. I felt myself to be, for an unknown period of time, an abstract perceiver of the world. The vague, living countryside, the moon, the remains of the day worked on me, as well as the slope of the road which eliminated any possibility of weariness. The afternoon was intimate, infinite. The road descended and forked among the now confused meadows. A high-pitched, almost syllabic music approached and receded in the shifting of the wind, dimmed by leaves and distance. I thought that a man can be an enemy of other men, of the moments of other men, but not of a country: not of fireflies, words, gardens, streams of water, sunsets. Thus I arrived before a tall, rusty gate. Between the iron bars I made out a poplar grove and a pavilion. I understood suddenly two things, the first trivial, the second almost unbelievable: the music came from the pavilion, and the music was Chinese. For precisely that reason I had openly accepted it without paying it any heed. I do not remember whether there was a bell or whether I knocked with my hand. The sparkling of the music continued.

9. *The Dream of the Red Chamber* (1791) by Ts'ao Hsüeh-ch'in; the most famous Chinese novel, a love story and panorama of Chinese family life involving more than 430 characters.

From the rear of the house within a lantern approached: a lantern that the trees sometimes striped and sometimes eclipsed, a paper lantern that had the form of a drum and the color of the moon. A tall man bore it. I didn't see his face for the light blinded me. He opened the door and said slowly, in my own language: "I see that the pious Hsi P'êng persists in correcting my solitude. You no doubt wish to see the garden?"

I recognized the name of one of our consuls and I replied, disconcerted, "The garden?"

"The garden of forking paths."

Something stirred in my memory and I uttered with incomprehensible certainty, "The garden of my ancestor Ts'ui Pên."

"Your ancestor? Your illustrious ancestor? Come in."

The damp path zigzagged like those of my childhood. We came to a library of Eastern and Western books. I recognized bound in yellow silk several volumes of the Lost Encyclopedia, edited by the Third Emperor of the Luminous Dynasty but never printed.[1] The record on the phonograph revolved next to a bronze phoenix. I also recall a *famille rose*[2] vase and another, many centuries older, of that shade of blue which our craftsmen copied from the potters of Persia . . .

Stephen Albert observed me with a smile. He was, as I have said, very tall, sharp-featured, with gray eyes and a gray beard. He told me that he had been a missionary in Tientsin "before aspiring to become a Sinologist."

We sat down—I on a long, low divan, he with his back to the window and a tall circular clock. I calculated that my pursuer, Richard Madden, could not arrive for at least an hour. My irrevocable determination could wait.

"An astounding fate, that of Ts'ui Pên," Stephen Albert said. "Governor of his native province, learned in astronomy, in astrology and in the tireless interpretation of the canonical books, chess player, famous poet and calligrapher—he abandoned all this in order to compose a book and a maze. He renounced the pleasures of both tyranny and justice, of his populous couch, of his banquets and even of erudition—all to close himself up for thirteen years in the Pavilion of the Limpid Solitude. When he died, his heirs found nothing save chaotic manuscripts. His family, as you may be aware, wished to condemn them to the fire; but his executor—a Taoist or Buddhist monk—insisted on their publication."

"We descendants of Ts'ui Pên," I replied, "continue to curse that monk. Their publication was senseless. The book is an indeterminate heap of contradictory drafts. I examined it once: in the third chapter the hero dies, in the fourth he is alive. As for the other undertaking of Ts'ui Pên, his labyrinth . . ."

"Here is Ts'ui Pên's labyrinth," he said, indicating a tall lacquered desk.

"An ivory labyrinth!" I exclaimed. "A minimum labyrinth."

"A labyrinth of symbols," he corrected. "An invisible labyrinth of time. To me, a barbarous Englishman, has been entrusted the revelation of this diaphanous mystery. After more than a hundred years, the details are irre-

1. The Yung-lo emperor of the Ming ("bright") Dynasty commissioned a massive encyclopedia between 1403 and 1408. A single copy of the 11,095 manuscript volumes was made in the mid-1500s; the original was later destroyed, and only 370 volumes of the copy remain today. 2. Pink family (French); refers to a Chinese decorative enamel ranging in color from an opaque pink to purplish rose. *Famille rose* pottery was at its best during the reign of Yung Chên (1723–1735).

trievable; but it is not hard to conjecture what happened. Ts'ui Pên must have said once: *I am withdrawing to write a book.* And another time: *I am withdrawing to construct a labyrinth.* Every one imagined two works; to no one did it occur that the book and the maze were one and the same thing. The Pavilion of the Limpid Solitude stood in the center of a garden that was perhaps intricate; that circumstance could have suggested to the heirs a physical labyrinth. Ts'ui Pên died; no one in the vast territories that were his came upon the labyrinth; the confusion of the novel suggested to me that *it* was the maze. Two circumstances gave me the correct solution of the problem. One: the curious legend that Ts'ui Pên had planned to create a labyrinth which would be strictly infinite. The other: a fragment of a letter I discovered."

Albert rose. He turned his back on me for a moment; he opened a drawer of the black and gold desk. He faced me and in his hands he held a sheet of paper that had once been crimson, but was now pink and tenuous and cross-sectioned. The fame of Ts'ui Pên as a calligrapher had been justly won. I read, uncomprehendingly and with fervor, these words written with a minute brush by a man of my blood: *I leave to the various futures (not to all) my garden of forking paths.* Wordlessly, I returned the sheet. Albert continued:

"Before unearthing this letter, I had questioned myself about the ways in which a book can be infinite. I could think of nothing other than a cyclic volume, a circular one. A book whose last page was identical with the first, a book which had the possibility of continuing indefinitely. I remembered too that night which is at the middle of the Thousand and One Nights when Scheherazade[3] (through a magical oversight of the copyist) begins to relate word for word the story of the Thousand and One Nights, establishing the risk of coming once again to the night when she must repeat it, and thus on to infinity. I imagined as well a Platonic, hereditary work, transmitted from father to son, in which each new individual adds a chapter or corrects with pious care the pages of his elders. These conjectures diverted me; but none seemed to correspond, not even remotely, to the contradictory chapters of Ts'ui Pên. In the midst of this perplexity, I received from Oxford the manuscript you have examined. I lingered, naturally, on the sentence: *I leave to the various futures (not to all) my garden of forking paths.* Almost instantly, I understood: 'The garden of forking paths' was the chaotic novel; the phrase 'the various futures (not to all)' suggested to me the forking in time, not in space. A broad rereading of the work confirmed the theory. In all fictional works, each time a man is confronted with several alternatives, he chooses one and eliminates the others; in the fiction of Ts'ui Pên, he chooses—simultaneously—all of them. *He creates,* in this way, diverse futures, diverse times which themselves also proliferate and fork. Here, then, is the explanation of the novel's contradictions. Fang, let us say, has a secret; a stranger calls at his door; Fang resolves to kill him. Naturally, there are several possible outcomes: Fang can kill the intruder, the intruder can kill Fang, they both can escape, they both can die, and so forth. In the work of Ts'ui Pên, all possible outcomes occur; each one is the point of departure for other forkings. Sometimes, the paths of this labyrinth converge: for example, you

---

3. The narrator of the collection also known as the *Arabian Nights*, 1,001 tales supposedly told by Scheherazade to her husband, Shahrayar, king of Samarkand, to postpone her execution.

arrive at this house, but in one of the possible pasts you are my enemy, in another, my friend. If you will resign yourself to my incurable pronunciation, we shall read a few pages."

His face, within the vivid circle of the lamplight, was unquestionably that of an old man, but with something unalterable about it, even immortal. He read with slow precision two versions of the same epic chapter. In the first, an army marches to a battle across a lonely mountain; the horror of the rocks and shadows makes the men undervalue their lives and they gain an easy victory. In the second, the same army traverses a palace where a great festival is taking place; the resplendent battle seems to them a continuation of the celebration and they win the victory. I listened with proper veneration to these ancient narratives, perhaps less admirable in themselves than the fact that they had been created by my blood and were being restored to me by a man of a remote empire, in the course of a desperate adventure, on a Western isle. I remember the last words, repeated in each version like a secret commandment: *Thus fought the heroes, tranquil their admirable hearts, violent their swords, resigned to kill and to die.*

From that moment on, I felt about me and within my dark body an invisible, intangible swarming. Not the swarming of the divergent, parallel and finally coalescent armies, but a more inaccessible, more intimate agitation that they in some manner prefigured. Stephen Albert continued:

"I don't believe that your illustrious ancestor played idly with these variations. I don't consider it credible that he would sacrifice thirteen years to the infinite execution of a rhetorical experiment. In your country, the novel is a subsidiary form of literature; in Ts'ui Pên's time it was a despicable form. Ts'ui Pên was a brilliant novelist, but he was also a man of letters who doubtless did not consider himself a mere novelist. The testimony of his contemporaries proclaims—and his life fully confirms—his metaphysical and mystical interests. Philosophic controversy usurps a good part of the novel. I know that of all problems, none disturbed him so greatly nor worked upon him so much as the abysmal problem of time. Now then, the latter is the only problem that does not figure in the pages of the *Garden.* He does not even use the word that signifies *time.* How do you explain this voluntary omission?"

I proposed several solutions—all unsatisfactory. We discussed them. Finally, Stephen Albert said to me:

"In a riddle whose answer is chess, what is the only prohibited word?"

I thought a moment and replied, "The word *chess.*"

"Precisely," said Albert. *"The Garden of Forking Paths* is an enormous riddle, or parable, whose theme is time; this recondite cause prohibits its mention. To omit a word always, to resort to inept metaphors and obvious periphrases, is perhaps the most emphatic way of stressing it. That is the tortuous method preferred, in each of the meanderings of his indefatigable novel, by the oblique Ts'ui Pên. I have compared hundreds of manuscripts, I have corrected the errors that the negligence of the copyists has introduced, I have guessed the plan of this chaos, I have re-established—I believe I have re-established—the primordial organization, I have translated the entire work: it is clear to me that not once does he employ the word 'time.' The explanation is obvious: *The Garden of Forking Paths* is an incomplete, but not false, image of the universe as Ts'ui Pên conceived it. In contrast to

Newton and Schopenhauer,[4] your ancestor did not believe in a uniform, absolute time. He believed in an infinite series of times, in a growing, dizzying net of divergent, convergent and parallel times. This network of times which approached one another, forked, broke off, or were unaware of one another for centuries, embraces *all* possibilities of time. We do not exist in the majority of these times; in some you exist, and not I; in others I, and not you; in others, both of us. In the present one, which a favorable fate has granted me, you have arrived at my house; in another, while crossing the garden, you found me dead; in still another, I utter these same words, but I am a mistake, a ghost."

"In every one," I pronounced, not without a tremble to my voice, "I am grateful to you and revere you for your re-creation of the garden of Ts'ui Pên."

"Not in all," he murmured with a smile. "Time forks perpetually toward innumerable futures. In one of them I am your enemy."

Once again I felt the swarming sensation of which I have spoken. It seemed to me that the humid garden that surrounded the house was infinitely saturated with invisible persons. Those persons were Albert and I, secret, busy and multiform in other dimensions of time. I raised my eyes and the tenuous nightmare dissolved. In the yellow and black garden there was only one man; but this man was as strong as a statue . . . this man was approaching along the path and he was Captain Richard Madden.

"The future already exists," I replied, "but I am your friend. Could I see the letter again?"

Albert rose. Standing tall, he opened the drawer of the tall desk; for the moment his back was to me. I had readied the revolver. I fired with extreme caution. Albert fell uncomplainingly, immediately. I swear his death was instantaneous—a lightning stroke.

The rest is unreal, insignificant. Madden broke in, arrested me. I have been condemned to the gallows. I have won out abominably; I have communicated to Berlin the secret name of the city they must attack. They bombed it yesterday; I read it in the same papers that offered to England the mystery of the learned Sinologist Stephen Albert who was murdered by a stranger, one Yu Tsun. The Chief had deciphered this mystery. He knew my problem was to indicate (through the uproar of the war) the city called Albert, and that I had found no other means to do so than to kill a man of that name. He does not know (no one can know) my innumerable contrition and weariness.

For Victoria Ocampo

---

4. Arthur Schopenhauer (1788-1860), German philosopher whose concept of will proceeded from a concept of the self as enduring through time. In *Seven Conversations with Jorge Luis Borges,* Borges also comments on Schopenhauer's interest in the "oneiric [dreamlike] essence of life." Sir Isaac Newton (1642–1727), English mathematician and philosopher best known for his formulation of laws of gravitation and motion.

NAGUIB MAHFOUZ
1911–2006

The foremost novelist writing in Arabic during the late twentieth century, Naguib Mahfouz traced his roots to the civilization of the ancient Egyptians, over five thousand years ago. Past and present combine for Naguib Mahfouz as he interrogates the destiny of his people and their often-traumatic adjustment to modern industrial society. Without Mahfouz, it is said, the turbulent history of twentieth-century Egypt would never have been known. His fictional families and frustrated middle-class clerks documented the successive stages of Egyptian social and political life from the time the country cast off foreign rule and became a "postcolonial" society. Time, in fact, is the real protagonist of his novels: the time in which individuals live and die, governments come and go, and social values are transformed—time, ultimately, as the conqueror that reduces human endeavor to nothing and forces attention on spiritual truth. Mahfouz's novels and short stories have millions of readers throughout the Arab world, and a growing audience in the West, because they deal with basic human issues in a realistic social context. Generations of Arabs have read his works or have seen them adapted to film and television, and his characters have become household words. Mahfouz the craftsman also wrought a change in Arabic prose, synthesizing traditional literary style and modern speech to create a new literary language understood by Arabs everywhere.

Readers of his best-known works, however, will find many similarities with the nineteenth-century realist novel in Europe. Mahfouz has been called the "Balzac of Egypt"—a comparison to the great French novelist and panoramic chronicler of society Honoré de Balzac (1799–1850)—and he was well acquainted with the works of Gustave Flaubert, Leo Tolstoy, and other nineteenth-century novelists. Traditional Arabic literature has many forms of narrative, but the novel is not one of them; and, like his contemporaries, Mahfouz adapted the Western form to his own needs. Readers will find familiar nineteenth-century strategies such as a chronological plot, unified characters, the inclusion of documentary information and realistic details, a panoramic view of society including a strong moral and humanistic perspective, and—typically if not necessarily—a picture of urban middle-class life. Mahfouz employed allegory much more than do traditionally realist authors, however; and his latest work made use of fragmented and absurdist techniques as well as a variety of classical Arabic forms. He continued to be preoccupied with individual experience inside what he called the "tragedies of society," although his focus was not restricted to the individualized existentialism of Jean-Paul Sartre or Albert Camus and embraced a complex of social relationships. Like the nineteenth-century novelists he followed, Mahfouz believed in the social function of art and the concomitant responsibility of the writer. His books have been censored and banned in many Arab countries, and he was blacklisted for several years for supporting Egypt's 1979 peace treaty with Israel.

Mahfouz was born in Cairo on December 11, 1911, the youngest of seven children in the family of a civil servant. The family moved from their home in the old Jamaliya district to the suburbs of Cairo when the boy was young. He attended government schools and entered the University of Cairo in 1930, graduating in 1934 with a degree in philosophy. These were not quiet years: Egypt, officially under Ottoman rule, had been occupied by the British since 1883 and was declared a British protectorate at the start of World War I in 1914. Mahfouz grew up in the midst of an ongoing struggle for national independence that culminated in a violent uprising against the British in 1919 and the negotiation of a constitutional monarchy in 1923. The consistent focus on Egyptian cultural identity that permeates his work may well have its roots in this early turbulent period. The difficulty of disentangling cultural traditions, however, is indicated by the fact that Mahfouz's first published book was a 1932 translation of an English work on ancient Egypt.

While at the university, Mahfouz made friends with the socialist and Darwinian thinker Salama Musa and began to write articles for Musa's journal, *Al-Majalla al-Jadida* (The modern magazine). In 1938, he published his first collection of stories, *Whispers of Madness*, and in 1939 the first of three historical novels set in ancient Egypt. He planned at that time to write a set of forty books on the model of the historical romance written by the British novelist Sir Walter Scott (1771–1832). These first novels already included modern references, and few missed the criticism of King Farouk in *Radubis* (1943) or the analogy in *The Struggle for Thebes* (1944) between the ancient Egyptian battle to expel Hyksos usurpers and twentieth-century rebellions against foreign rule. In 1945 Mahfouz shifted decisively to the realistic novel and a portrayal of modern society. He focused on the social and spiritual dilemmas of the middle class in Cairo, documenting in vivid detail the life of an urban society that represented modern Egypt.

The major work of this period, and Mahfouz's masterwork in many eyes, is *The Cairo Trilogy* (1956–57), three volumes depicting the experience of three generations of a Cairo family between 1918 and 1944. Into this story, whose main protagonist Mahfouz called Time, is woven a social history of Egypt after World War I. Mahfouz's achievement was recognized in the State Prize for literature in 1956, but he himself temporarily ceased to write after finishing the *Trilogy* in 1952. In that year, an officers' coup headed by Gamal Abdel Nasser overthrew the monarchy and instituted a republic that promised democratic reforms, and there was a change in the panorama of Egyptian society that Mahfouz described. Although the author was at first optimistic about the new order, he soon recognized that not much had changed for the general populace. When he started publishing again in 1959, his works included much open criticism of the Nasser regime.

Although he had become the best-known writer in the Arab world, his works read by millions, Mahfouz like other Arab authors could not make a living from his books. Copyright protection was minimal, and without copyright protection even best-selling authors received only small sums for their books. Until he began writing for motion pictures in the 1960s, he supported himself and his family through various positions in governmental ministries and as a contributing editor for the leading newspaper, *Al-Ahram*. Attached to the Ministry of Culture in 1954, he adapted novels for film and television and later became director-general of the governmental Cinema Organization. (Cinema, radio, and television are nationalized industries in Egypt.) After his retirement from the civil service in 1971, Mahfouz continued to publish articles and short stories in *Al-Ahram*, where most of his novels appeared in serialized form before being issued as paperbacks. When he received the Nobel Prize in 1988, at the age of seventy-seven, he was still publishing a weekly column, "Point of View," in *Al-Ahram*.

Three years after *The Cairo Trilogy* brought him international praise, Mahfouz shocked many readers with a new book, *Children of Gebelawi*. Serialized in *Al-Ahram*, *Children of Gebelawi* is on the surface another description of a patriarchal family evolving in modern times. The story of the patriarch Gebelawi and his disobedient or ambitious children, however, is also an allegory of religious history. Its personification of God, Adam, and the prophets—among whom science is included as the youngest and most destructive son—and its simultaneous portrayal of the prophets as primarily social reformers rather than religious figures, scandalized orthodox believers. The book was banned throughout the Arab world except in Lebanon, and the Jordan League of Writers attacked Mahfouz as a "delinquent man" whose novels were "plagued with sex and drugs." *Children of Gebelawi* remains unpublished in Egypt to this day.

Mahfouz took up writing short stories again in the early 1960s after concentrating on novels for two decades. His second collection, *God's World* (1963), combined social realism and metaphysical speculation. He also began to move away from an "objective," realistic style toward one that emphasized subjective and mystic awareness, drawing on an Islamic mystical tradition whose comprehensive tolerance is far from (and often opposed by) the rigid beliefs of contemporary Muslim fundamentalists. The perceptions of individual characters govern works such as "The Thief and the Dogs" (1962), the story of a released prisoner who—seeking revenge on his unfaithful wife and the man who betrayed him—is trapped by police dogs and shot; and "Miramar" (1967), in which different points of view describe the disappointed love of a young servant girl, her determination to shape her own career, and the death of a lodger. Mahfouz did not abandon social commentary in his new mode. Individual characters represent particular classes or even (with the servant girl in Miramar) Egypt itself, and the film made from "Miramar" attracted large audiences for its sharp criticism of the dominant political party, the Arab Socialist Union. In "Mirrors" (1972), brief accounts of fifty-four different characters "mirror" various aspects of contemporary Egyptian society.

Mahfouz's approach changed again in the late 1960s; social commentary in the novels became even more direct, while individual stories grew more fragmented and even absurdist in style. Egypt's defeat by Israel in the June 1967 war had a shattering effect on the nation's self-confidence, and Mahfouz responded to what he saw as the country's spiritual dilemma. Stories written between October and December 1967 and collected in *Under the Bus Shelter* repeatedly show contradictory and incomprehensible events happening to perplexed and frustrated people. An almost cinematic style emerged, emphasizing dialogue over interpretation; some pieces in later collections resemble one-act plays. In the title story of "Under the Bus Shelter," people waiting for a bus observe beatings, a car crash with several deaths, a couple making love on a corpse, dancing, the rapid construction of a monumental grave in which both corpses and lovers are buried, inaudible speeches, a man who may possibly be the director of the film (if it *is* a film) but may also be a thug, a decapitation, and finally "a group of official-looking men wandering around" whose appearance frightens off the others—until the puzzled observers are shot by a previously apathetic policeman when they ask questions. Several novels in the 1970s and 1980s reveal a similar bleak perspective in a more didactic style; *There Only Remains One Hour* (1982), for example, portrays current events as a sequence of failed efforts to achieve peace and prosperity.

Mahfouz's style continued to evolve in new directions. Among his latest works are adaptations of classical Arabic narrative forms such as the *maqama* (elaborate rhymed trickster tales) or folk narratives like the *Arabian Nights* into imaginative sequences such as *The Nights of "The Thousand and One Nights"* or *The Epic of the Riff-Raff*. While these works disconcerted some adherents of his earlier, realistic style, they were an integral part of the Egyptian writer's attempt to find new ways to express Arabic culture and to comment from a broader, often prophetic perspective on the contemporary scene. That Mahfouz was impelled by a sense of moral purpose is evident throughout his works, and perhaps no more so than in his Nobel Prize acceptance speech in 1988. Speaking first for Arabic letters but also as a representative of the third world, he addressed the leaders of a Western civilization that allowed science and technology to outweigh basic human values. "The developed world and the third world are but one family. Each human being bears responsibility towards it by the degree of what he has obtained of knowledge, wisdom, and civilization. . . . In the name of the third world: Be not spectators to our miseries." The "able ones, the civilized ones," he added, perhaps ironically, must be guided by the collective needs of humanity. He continued to defend humanitarian values in Egypt as well. After Islamic fundamentalists pressured the Ministry of Culture into establishing precensorship for books in 1994, Mahfouz attacked this "intellectual terrorism" against the arts; he was later stabbed in the neck and lost the use of his writing hand.

"Zaabalawi," a story included in *God's World*, contains many of Mahfouz's predominant themes. Written two years after "Children of Gebelawi," it echoes the earlier work's religious symbolism in the mysterious character of Zaabalawi himself. It is also a social document: the narrator's quest for Zaabalawi brings him before various representatives of modern Egyptian society inside a realistically described Cairo. "Zaabalawi," therefore, takes on the character of a social and metaphysical allegory. Its terminally ill narrator seeks to be cured in a quest that implies not only physical healing but also religious salvation. He has already exhausted the resources of medical science and, in desperation, he decides to seek out a holy man whose name he recalls from childhood tales.

In the initial stage of his search, the protagonist is coldly received by a lawyer and a district officer, former acquaintances of Zaabalawi who have become worldly, materialistic, and highly successful. Moreover, these bureaucrats who depend on reason, technology, and businesslike efficiency can do no more than send him to old addresses or draw him city maps. Zaabalawi is still alive, they say, but he is unpredictable and hard to find now that he no longer inhabits his old home—a now-dilapidated mansion in front of which an old bookseller sells used books on mysticism and theology. In contrast, the calligrapher and composer to whom the narrator next turns welcome him as a person. Indeed, the composer reproves him for thinking only of his errand and overlooking the value of getting to know another human being. The relationship among art, human sympathy, and spiritual values is made clear, for Zaabalawi is close to both artists and has provided inspiration for their best works. In the last scene, at the Negma Bar, Mahfouz fused the realistic description of a hardened drinker with a dream vision of another, peaceful world. At this stage of the quest, the narrator is not even allowed to state his errand but must place himself on a level with his drunken host before being allowed to speak. When he does sink into oblivion (in stages that suggest a mystic stripping-away of rational faculties), he is rewarded in his dreams by a glimpse of paradise and wakes to find that Zaabalawi has been beside him as he slept. "Zaabalawi" ends as it began—"I have to find Zaabalawi"—but the seeker is now more confident, and the route more clearly marked.

PRONOUNCING GLOSSARY

The following list uses common English syllables and stress accents to provide rough equivalents of selected words whose pronunciation may be unfamiliar to the general reader.

Hassanein: *hassan-ayn'*

Naguib Mahfouz: *nah-geeb' mah-fooz'*

Qamar: *ka'-mar*

Umm al-Ghulam: *oom' al–ghol-am'*

Wanas al-Damanhouri: *wah-nas' al–daman-hoo'-ree*

Zaabalawi: *zah-bah-lah'-wee*

Zaabalawi[1]

Finally I became convinced that I had to find Sheikh[2] Zaabalawi.

The first time I had heard of his name had been in a song:

> Oh what's become of the world, Zaabalawi?
> They've turned it upside down and taken away its taste.

---

1. Translated by Denys Johnson-Davies. 2. A title of respect (originally "old man"), often indicating rulership.

It had been a popular song in my childhood, and one day it had occurred to me to demand of my father, in the way children have of asking endless questions:

"Who is Zaabalawi?"

He had looked at me hesitantly as though doubting my ability to understand the answer. However, he had replied, "May his blessing descend upon you, he's a true saint of God, a remover of worries and troubles. Were it not for him I would have died miserably—"

In the years that followed, I heard my father many a time sing the praises of this good saint and speak of the miracles he performed. The days passed and brought with them many illnesses, for each one of which I was able, without too much trouble and at a cost I could afford, to find a cure, until I became afflicted with that illness for which no one possesses a remedy. When I had tried everything in vain and was overcome by despair, I remembered by chance what I had heard in my childhood: Why, I asked myself, should I not seek out Sheikh Zaabalawi? I recollected my father saying that he had made his acquaintance in Khan Gaafar[3] at the house of Sheikh Qamar, one of those sheikhs who practiced law in the religious courts, and so I took myself off to his house. Wishing to make sure that he was still living there, I made inquiries of a vendor of beans whom I found in the lower part of the house.

"Sheikh Qamar!" he said, looking at me in amazement. "He left the quarter ages ago. They say he's now living in Garden City and has his office in al-Azhar Square."[4]

I looked up the office address in the telephone book and immediately set off to the Chamber of Commerce Building, where it was located. On asking to see Sheikh Qamar, I was ushered into a room just as a beautiful woman with a most intoxicating perfume was leaving it. The man received me with a smile and motioned me toward a fine leather-upholstered chair. Despite the thick soles of my shoes, my feet were conscious of the lushness of the costly carpet. The man wore a lounge suit and was smoking a cigar; his manner of sitting was that of someone well satisfied both with himself and with his worldly possessions. The look of warm welcome he gave me left no doubt in my mind that he thought me a prospective client, and I felt acutely embarrassed at encroaching upon his valuable time.

"Welcome!" he said, prompting me to speak.

"I am the son of your old friend Sheikh Ali al-Tatawi," I answered so as to put an end to my equivocal position.

A certain languor was apparent in the glance he cast at me; the languor was not total in that he had not as yet lost all hope in me.

"God rest his soul," he said. "He was a fine man."

The very pain that had driven me to go there now prevailed upon me to stay.

"He told me," I continued, "of a devout saint named Zaabalawi whom he met at Your Honor's. I am in need of him, sir, if he be still in the land of the living."

---

3. Gaafar Market, an area of shops.   **4.** An area of Cairo close to the famous mosque and university of al-Azhar.

The languor became firmly entrenched in his eyes, and it would have come as no surprise if he had shown the door to both me and my father's memory.

"That," he said in the tone of one who has made up his mind to terminate the conversation, "was a very long time ago and I scarcely recall him now."

Rising to my feet so as to put his mind at rest regarding my intention of going, I asked, "Was he really a saint?"

"We used to regard him as a man of miracles."

"And where could I find him today?" I asked, making another move toward the door.

"To the best of my knowledge he was living in the Birgawi Residence in al-Azhar," and he applied himself to some papers on his desk with a resolute movement that indicated he would not open his mouth again. I bowed my head in thanks, apologized several times for disturbing him, and left the office, my head so buzzing with embarrassment that I was oblivious to all sounds around me.

I went to the Birgawi Residence, which was situated in a thickly populated quarter. I found that time had so eaten at the building that nothing was left of it save an antiquated façade and a courtyard that, despite being supposedly in the charge of a caretaker, was being used as a rubbish dump. A small, insignificant fellow, a mere prologue to a man, was using the covered entrance as a place for the sale of old books on theology and mysticism.

When I asked him about Zaabalawi, he peered at me through narrow, inflamed eyes and said in amazement, "Zaabalawi! Good heavens, what a time ago that was! Certainly he used to live in this house when it was habitable. Many were the times he would sit with me talking of bygone days, and I would be blessed by his holy presence. Where, though, is Zaabalawi today?"

He shrugged his shoulders sorrowfully and soon left me, to attend to an approaching customer. I proceeded to make inquiries of many shopkeepers in the district. While I found that a large number of them had never even heard of Zaabalawi, some, though recalling nostalgically the pleasant times they had spent with him, were ignorant of his present whereabouts, while others openly made fun of him, labeled him a charlatan, and advised me to put myself in the hands of a doctor—as though I had not already done so. I therefore had no alternative but to return disconsolately home.

With the passing of days like motes in the air, my pains grew so severe that I was sure I would not be able to hold out much longer. Once again I fell to wondering about Zaabalawi and clutching at the hope his venerable name stirred within me. Then it occurred to me to seek the help of the local sheikh of the district; in fact, I was surprised I had not thought of this to begin with. His office was in the nature of a small shop, except that it contained a desk and a telephone, and I found him sitting at his desk, wearing a jacket over his striped galabeya.[5] As he did not interrupt his conversation with a man sitting beside him, I stood waiting till the man had gone. The sheikh then looked up at me coldly. I told myself that I should win him over by the usual methods, and it was not long before I had him cheerfully inviting me to sit down.

---

5. The traditional Arabic robe, over which this modernized district officer wears a European jacket.

"I'm in need of Sheikh Zaabalawi," I answered his inquiry as to the purpose of my visit.

He gazed at me with the same astonishment as that shown by those I had previously encountered.

"At least," he said, giving me a smile that revealed his gold teeth, "he is still alive. The devil of it is, though, he has no fixed abode. You might well bump into him as you go out of here, on the other hand you might spend days and months in fruitless searching."

"Even you can't find him!"

"Even I! He's a baffling man, but I thank the Lord that he's still alive!"

He gazed at me intently, and murmured, "It seems your condition is serious."

"Very."

"May God come to your aid! But why don't you go about it systematically?" He spread out a sheet of paper on the desk and drew on it with unexpected speed and skill until he had made a full plan of the district, showing all the various quarters, lanes, alleyways, and squares. He looked at it admiringly and said, "These are dwelling-houses, here is the Quarter of the Perfumers, here the Quarter of the Coppersmiths, the Mouski,[6] the police and fire stations. The drawing is your best guide. Look carefully in the cafés, the places where the dervishes perform their rites, the mosques and prayer-rooms, and the Green Gate,[7] for he may well be concealed among the beggars and be indistinguishable from them. Actually, I myself haven't seen him for years, having been somewhat preoccupied with the cares of the world, and was only brought back by your inquiry to those most exquisite times of my youth."

I gazed at the map in bewilderment. The telephone rang, and he took up the receiver.

"Take it," he told me, generously. "We're at your service."

Folding up the map, I left and wandered off through the quarter, from square to street to alleyway, making inquiries of everyone I felt was familiar with the place. At last the owner of a small establishment for ironing clothes told me, "Go to the calligrapher[8] Hassanein in Umm al-Ghulam—they were friends."

I went to Umm al-Ghulam,[9] where I found old Hassanein working in a deep, narrow shop full of signboards and jars of color. A strange smell, a mixture of glue and perfume, permeated its every corner. Old Hassanein was squatting on a sheepskin rug in front of a board propped against the wall; in the middle of it he had inscribed the word "Allah"[1] in silver lettering. He was engrossed in embellishing the letters with prodigious care. I stood behind him, fearful of disturbing him or breaking the inspiration that flowed to his masterly hand. When my concern at not interrupting him had lasted some time, he suddenly inquired with unaffected gentleness, "Yes?"

Realizing that he was aware of my presence, I introduced myself. "I've been told that Sheikh Zaabalawi is your friend; I'm looking for him," I said.

His hand came to a stop. He scrutinized me in astonishment. "Zaabalawi! God be praised!" he said with a sigh.

6. The central bazaar.   7. A medieval gate in Cairo.   8. One who practices the art of decorative lettering (literally "beautiful writing"), which is respected as a fine art in Arabic and Asian cultures.   9. A street in Cairo.   1. God (Arabic).

"He *is* a friend of yours, isn't he?" I asked eagerly.

"He was, once upon a time. A real man of mystery: he'd visit you so often that people would imagine he was your nearest and dearest, then would disappear as though he'd never existed. Yet saints are not to be blamed."

The spark of hope went out with the suddenness of a lamp snuffed by a power-cut.

"He was so constantly with me," said the man, "that I felt him to be a part of everything I drew. But where is he today?"

"Perhaps he is still alive?"

"He's alive, without a doubt. . . . He had impeccable taste, and it was due to him that I made my most beautiful drawings."

"God knows," I said, in a voice almost stifled by the dead ashes of hope, "how dire my need for him is, and no one knows better than you[2] of the ailments in respect of which he is sought."

"Yes, yes. May God restore you to health. He is, in truth, as is said of him, a man, and more. . . ."

Smiling broadly, he added, "And his face possesses an unforgettable beauty. But where is he?"

Reluctantly I rose to my feet, shook hands, and left. I continued wandering eastward and westward through the quarter, inquiring about Zaabalawi from everyone who, by reason of age or experience, I felt might be likely to help me. Eventually I was informed by a vendor of lupine[3] that he had met him a short while ago at the house of Sheikh Gad, the well-known composer. I went to the musician's house in Tabakshiyya,[4] where I found him in a room tastefully furnished in the old style, its walls redolent with history. He was seated on a divan, his famous lute beside him, concealing within itself the most beautiful melodies of our age, while somewhere from within the house came the sound of pestle and mortar and the clamor of children. I immediately greeted him and introduced myself, and was put at my ease by the unaffected way in which he received me. He did not ask, either in words or gesture, what had brought me, and I did not feel that he even harbored any such curiosity. Amazed at his understanding and kindness, which boded well, I said, "O Sheikh Gad, I am an admirer of yours, having long been enchanted by the renderings of your songs."

"Thank you," he said with a smile.

"Please excuse my disturbing you," I continued timidly, "but I was told that Zaabalawi was your friend, and I am in urgent need of him."

"Zaabalawi!" he said, frowning in concentration. "You need him? God be with you, for who knows, O Zaabalawi, where you are."

"Doesn't he visit you?" I asked eagerly.

"He visited me some time ago. He might well come right now; on the other hand I mightn't see him till death!"

I gave an audible sigh and asked, "What made him like that?"

The musician took up his lute. "Such are saints or they would not be saints," he said, laughing.

"Do those who need him suffer as I do?"

"Such suffering is part of the cure!"

---

2. One of the calligrapher's major tasks is to write religious documents and prayers to Allah.   3. Beans.
4. A quarter named for the straw trays made and sold there.

He took up the plectrum and began plucking soft strains from the strings. Lost in thought, I followed his movements. Then, as though addressing myself, I said, "So my visit has been in vain."

He smiled, laying his cheek against the side of the lute. "God forgive you," he said, "for saying such a thing of a visit that has caused me to know you and you me!"

I was much embarrassed and said apologetically, "Please forgive me; my feelings of defeat made me forget my manners."

"Do not give in to defeat. This extraordinary man brings fatigue to all who seek him. It was easy enough with him in the old days when his place of abode was known. Today, though, the world has changed, and after having enjoyed a position attained only by potentates, he is now pursued by the police on a charge of false pretenses. It is therefore no longer an easy matter to reach him, but have patience and be sure that you will do so."

He raised his head from the lute and skillfully fingered the opening bars of a melody. Then he sang:

> I make lavish mention, even though I blame myself, of those I love,
> For the stories of the beloved are my wine.[5]

With a heart that was weary and listless, I followed the beauty of the melody and the singing.

"I composed the music to this poem in a single night," he told me when he had finished. "I remember that it was the eve of the Lesser Bairam.[6] Zaabalawi was my guest for the whole of that night, and the poem was of his choosing. He would sit for a while just where you are, then would get up and play with my children as though he were one of them. Whenever I was overcome by weariness or my inspiration failed me, he would punch me playfully in the chest and joke with me, and I would bubble over with melodies, and thus I continued working till I finished the most beautiful piece I have ever composed."

"Does he know anything about music?"

"He is the epitome of things musical. He has an extremely beautiful speaking voice, and you have only to hear him to want to burst into song and to be inspired to creativity. . . ."

"How was it that he cured those diseases before which men are powerless?"

"That is his secret. Maybe you will learn it when you meet him."

But when would that meeting occur? We relapsed into silence, and the hubbub of children once more filled the room.

Again the sheikh began to sing. He went on repeating the words "and I have a memory of her" in different and beautiful variations until the very walls danced in ecstasy. I expressed my wholehearted admiration, and he gave me a smile of thanks. I then got up and asked permission to leave, and he accompanied me to the front door. As I shook him by the hand, he said, "I hear that nowadays he frequents the house of Hagg Wanas al-Damanhouri. Do you know him?"

---

5. From a poem by the medieval mystic poet Ibn al-Farid, who represents spiritual ecstasy as a kind of drunkenness.   6. A major Islamic holiday, celebrated for three days to end the month's fasting during Ramadan.

I shook my head, though a modicum of renewed hope crept into my heart.

"He is a man of private means," the sheikh told me, "who from time to time visits Cairo, putting up at some hotel or other. Every evening, though, he spends at the Negma Bar in Alfi Street."

I waited for nightfall and went to the Negma Bar. I asked a waiter about Hagg Wanas, and he pointed to a corner that was semisecluded because of its position behind a large pillar with mirrors on all four sides. There I saw a man seated alone at a table with two bottles in front of him, one empty, the other two-thirds empty. There were no snacks or food to be seen, and I was sure that I was in the presence of a hardened drinker. He was wearing a loosely flowing silk galabeya and a carefully wound turban; his legs were stretched out toward the base of the pillar, and as he gazed into the mirror in rapt contentment, the sides of his face, rounded and handsome despite the fact that he was approaching old age, were flushed with wine. I approached quietly till I stood but a few feet away from him. He did not turn toward me or give any indication that he was aware of my presence.

"Good evening, Mr. Wanas," I greeted him cordially.

He turned toward me abruptly, as though my voice had roused him from slumber, and glared at me in disapproval. I was about to explain what had brought me to him when he interrupted in an almost imperative tone of voice that was none the less not devoid of an extraordinary gentleness, "First, please sit down, and, second, please get drunk!"

I opened my mouth to make my excuses but, stopping up his ears with his fingers, he said, "Not a word till you do what I say."

I realized I was in the presence of a capricious drunkard and told myself that I should at least humor him a bit. "Would you permit me to ask one question?" I said with a smile, sitting down.

Without removing his hands from his ears he indicated the bottle. "When engaged in a drinking bout like this, I do not allow any conversation between myself and another unless, like me, he is drunk, otherwise all propriety is lost and mutual comprehension is rendered impossible."

I made a sign indicating that I did not drink.

"That's your lookout," he said offhandedly. "And that's my condition!"

He filled me a glass, which I meekly took and drank. No sooner had the wine settled in my stomach than it seemed to ignite. I waited patiently till I had grown used to its ferocity, and said, "It's very strong, and I think the time has come for me to ask you about—"

Once again, however, he put his fingers in his ears. "I shan't listen to you until you're drunk!"

He filled up my glass for the second time. I glanced at it in trepidation; then, overcoming my inherent objection, I drank it down at a gulp. No sooner had the wine come to rest inside me than I lost all willpower. With the third glass, I lost my memory, and with the fourth the future vanished. The world turned round about me and I forgot why I had gone there. The man leaned toward me attentively, but I saw him—saw everything—as a mere meaningless series of colored planes. I don't know how long it was before my head sank down onto the arm of the chair and I plunged into deep sleep. During it, I had a beautiful dream the like of which I had never experienced. I dreamed that I was in an immense garden surrounded on all sides by luxuriant trees, and the sky was nothing but stars seen between the entwined branches, all enfolded in an atmosphere like that of sunset or a sky overcast with cloud. I was lying on a small hummock of jasmine petals, more of which fell upon me like rain, while the lucent spray of a fountain unceasingly sprinkled the crown of my head and my temples. I was in a state of deep contentedness, of ecstatic serenity. An orchestra of warbling and cooing played in my ear. There was an extraordinary sense of harmony between me and my inner self, and between the two of us and the world, everything being in its rightful place, without discord or distortion. In the whole world there was no single reason for speech or movement, for the universe moved in a rapture of ecstasy. This lasted but a short while. When I opened my eyes, consciousness struck at me like a policeman's fist and I saw Wanas al-Damanhouri regarding me with concern. Only a few drowsy customers were left in the bar.

"You have slept deeply," said my companion. "You were obviously hungry for sleep."

I rested my heavy head in the palms of my hands. When I took them away in astonishment and looked down at them, I found that they glistened with drops of water.

"My head's wet," I protested.

"Yes, my friend tried to rouse you," he answered quietly.

"Somebody saw me in this state?"

"Don't worry, he is a good man. Have you not heard of Sheikh Zaabalawi?"

"Zaabalawi!" I exclaimed, jumping to my feet.

"Yes," he answered in surprise. "What's wrong?"

"Where is he?"

"I don't know where he is now. He was here and then he left."

I was about to run off in pursuit but found I was more exhausted than I had imagined. Collapsed over the table, I cried out in despair, "My sole reason for coming to you was to meet him! Help me to catch up with him or send someone after him."

The man called a vendor of prawns and asked him to seek out the sheikh and bring him back. Then he turned to me. "I didn't realize you were afflicted. I'm very sorry. . . ."

"You wouldn't let me speak," I said irritably.

"What a pity! He was sitting on this chair beside you the whole time. He was playing with a string of jasmine petals he had around his neck, a gift from one of his admirers, then, taking pity on you, he began to sprinkle some water on your head to bring you around."

"Does he meet you here every night?" I asked, my eyes not leaving the doorway through which the vendor of prawns had left.

"He was with me tonight, last night and the night before that, but before that I hadn't seen him for a month."

"Perhaps he will come tomorrow," I answered with a sigh.

"Perhaps."

"I am willing to give him any money he wants."

Wanas answered sympathetically, "The strange thing is that he is not open to such temptations, yet he will cure you if you meet him."

"Without charge?"

"Merely on sensing that you love him."

The vendor of prawns returned, having failed in his mission.

I recovered some of my energy and left the bar, albeit unsteadily. At every street corner I called out "Zaabalawi!" in the vague hope that I would be rewarded with an answering shout. The street boys turned contemptuous eyes on me till I sought refuge in the first available taxi.

The following evening I stayed up with Wanas al-Damanhouri till dawn, but the sheikh did not put in an appearance. Wanas informed me that he would be going away to the country and would not be returning to Cairo until he had sold the cotton crop.

I must wait, I told myself; I must train myself to be patient. Let me content myself with having made certain of the existence of Zaabalawi, and even of his affection for me, which encourages me to think that he will be prepared to cure me if a meeting takes place between us.

Sometimes, however, the long delay wearied me. I would become beset by despair and would try to persuade myself to dismiss him from my mind completely. How many weary people in this life know him not or regard him as a mere myth! Why, then, should I torture myself about him in this way?

No sooner, however, did my pains force themselves upon me than I would again begin to think about him, asking myself when I would be fortunate enough to meet him. The fact that I ceased to have any news of Wanas and was told he had gone to live abroad did not deflect me from my purpose; the truth of the matter was that I had become fully convinced that I had to find Zaabalawi.

Yes, I have to find Zaabalawi.

ALBERT CAMUS
1913–1960

Albert Camus is often linked with the twentieth-century philosopher Jean-Paul Sartre as an "existentialist" writer, and indeed—as novelist, playwright, and essayist—he is widely known for his analysis of two concerns basic to existentialism: its distinctive assessment of the human condition and its search for authentic values. Yet Camus rejected doctrinaire labels, and Sartre himself suggested that the author was better placed in the tradition of French "moralist" writers such as Michel de Montaigne and René Pascal, who analyzed human behavior inside an implied ethical context with its own standards of good and evil. For Camus, liberty, justice, brotherhood, and happiness were some of these standards, along with the terms *revolt* and *absurd* that described human nonacceptance of a world without meaning or value. From his childhood among the very poor in Algiers to his later roles as journalist, Resistance fighter, internationally famous literary figure, and winner of the Nobel Prize in 1957, Camus never strayed from an intense awareness of the most basic levels of human existence or from a sympathy with those—often poor and oppressed—who lived at that level. "I can understand only in human terms. I understand the things I touch, things that offer me resistance." He describes the raw experience of life as it is shared by all human beings, and provides a bond between them. Camus's reaction to the "absurd," the human condition stripped bare, is, therefore, quite different from Samuel Beckett's retreat into agonized subjectivity; where Beckett is haunted by the fictionality of experience, Camus asserts human consciousness and human solidarity as the only values there are.

Camus was born on November 7, 1913, into a "world of poverty and light" in Mondavi, Algeria (then a colony of France). He was the second son in a poor family of mixed Alsatian-Spanish descent, and his father died in one of the first battles of World War I. The two boys lived together with their mother, uncle, and grandmother in a two-room apartment in the working-class section of the capital city, Algiers. Camus and his brother, Lucien, were raised by their strict grandmother while their mother worked as a cleaning woman to support the family. Images of the Mediterranean landscape, with its overwhelming, sensual closeness of sea and blazing sun, recur throughout his work, as does a profound compassion for those who—like his mother—labor unrecognized and in silence. (Camus's mother was illiterate and was left deaf and with a speech impediment by an untreated childhood illness.)

A passionate athlete as well as scholarship student, Camus completed his secondary education and enrolled as a philosophy student at the University of Algiers before contracting, at seventeen, the tuberculosis that undermined his health and shocked him with its demonstration of the human body's vulnerability to disease and death. Camus later finished his degree, but in the meantime he had gained from his illness a metaphor for everything that opposes and puts limits to human fulfillment and happiness: something he was later to term (after Antonin Artaud) the "plague" that infects bodies, minds, cities, and society. (*The Plague* is the title of his second novel.)

Camus lived and worked as a journalist in Algeria until 1940. He then moved to France when his political commentary (including a famous report on administrative mismanagement during a famine of Berber tribesmen) so embroiled him with the local government that his paper was suspended and he himself refused a work permit. Then as later, however, his work extended far beyond journalism. He published two collections of essays, *The Wrong Side and the Right Side* (1937) and *Nuptials* (1939), started a novel (*A Happy Death*), and founded a collective theater, Le Théâtre du Travail (The labor theater), for which he wrote and adapted a number of plays. The theater always fascinated Camus, possibly because it involved groups of people and live interaction between actors and audience. He not only continued to write plays after leaving Algeria (*Cross Purposes*, 1944; *The Just Assassins*, 1950) but was considering directing a new theater shortly before his death. The Labor Theater was a popular theater with performances on the docks in Algiers and was sponsored by the Communist Party, which Camus had joined in 1934. Like many intellectuals of his day, Camus found in the party a promising vehicle for social protest; he was unwilling to abandon either his independence or his convictions, however, and resigned in 1935 when the party line changed and he was asked to give up his support for Algerian nationalism. He left the Labor Theater in 1937 and, with a group of young Algerian intellectuals associated with the publishing house of Charlot, founded a similar but politically independent Team Theater (Théâtre de l'Equipe). During this decade, Camus also began work on his most famous novel, *The Stranger* (1942), the play *Caligula* (1944), and a lengthy essay defining his concept of the "absurd" hero, *The Myth of Sisyphus* (1942).

These three works established Camus's reputation as a philosopher of the absurd: the absurdly grotesque discrepancy between human beings' brief, material existence and their urge to believe in larger meanings—to "make sense" of a world that has no discernible sense. In *The Stranger,* Camus described a thirty-year-old clerk named Meursault who lives a series of "real" events: he attends his mother's funeral, makes love to his mistress, goes swimming, shoots an Arab on the beach, and is tried for murder. These events are described through Meursault's mind, and yet they appear without any connection, as if each one began a new world. They are simply a series of concrete, sensuous *facts* separated from each other and from any kind of human or social meaning. Meursault is finally condemned to death not for murder but for this alienation and for its failure to respond to society's expectations of proper behavior. Just before his execution, when he is infuriated by the prison chaplain's attempt to console him with thoughts of an afterlife, he rises to a new level of existential awareness and an ardent affirmation of life in the here-and-now, the only truly human field of action. Stylistically, much of *The Stranger*'s impact comes from the contrast between the immediacy of the physical experience described and the objective meaninglessness of that experience. On all levels, the novel reaffirms the importance of life lived moment by moment, in a total awareness that creates whatever meaning exists: the same awareness of his own activity that brings the mythological Sisyphus happiness when eternally pushing uphill the rock that will only roll down again, or the same search for an absolute honesty free of human pretenses that characterizes the mad emperor Caligula.

During World War II, Camus worked in Paris as a reader for the publishing firm of Gallimard, a post that he kept until his death in 1960. At the same time, he was part of the French Resistance and helped edit the underground journal *Combat*. His friendship with the existentialist philosopher Jean-Paul Sartre began in 1944, and after the war he and Sartre were internationally known as uncompromising analysts of the modern conscience. Camus's second novel, *The Plague* (1947), used a description of plague in a quarantined city, the Algerian Oran, to symbolize the spread of evil during World War II ("the feeling of suffocation from which we all suffered, and the atmosphere of threat and exile") and also to show the human struggle against physical and spiritual death in all its forms. Not content merely to symbolize his views in fiction, Camus also spoke out in philosophical essays and political statements, and his independent mind and refusal of doctrinaire positions brought him attacks from all sides. In the bitter struggle that brought independence to Algeria in 1962, Camus recognized the claims of both French and Arab Algerians to the land in which they were born. In the quest for social reform, he rejected any ideology that subordinated individual freedom and singled out Communism—the doctrine most reformist intellectuals saw as the only active hope—as a particular danger with its emphasis on the deindividualized and inevitable march of history. Camus's open anti-Communism led to a spectacular break with Sartre, whose review *Les Temps Modernes* (Modern times) condemned *The Rebel* (1951) in bitter personal attacks. The concept of revolt that Camus outlined in *The Rebel* was more ethical than political: he defined revolt as a basic nonacceptance of preestablished limits (whether by death or by oppression) that was shared by all human beings and, therefore, required a reciprocal acceptance and balancing of each person's rights. Such "revolt" was directly opposed to revolutionary nihilism in that it made the rebellious impulse a basis for social tolerance inside the individual's self-assertion; it had no patience for master plans that prescribed patterns of thought or action.

Five years after *The Rebel* was published, Camus produced a very different book in *The Fall* (1956). This novel is a rhetorical tour de force spoken by a fallen lawyer who uses all the tricks of language to confess his weaknesses and yet emerge triumphant, the omniscient judge of his fellow creatures. If Camus's *Notebooks* reveal in his early works a cycle of Sisyphus or the absurd, and his middle ones a Promethean cycle of revolt, *The Fall* inaugurates a third cycle, that of Nemesis, or judgment. It offers a complex, ironic picture that combines a yearning toward purity with a cynical debunking of all such attempts. The narrator, Clamence, is a composite personality including (among other things) satirized aspects of both Sartre and Camus, but it is impossible to get to the bottom of his character behind the layers of self-consciously manipulated language. The style itself challenges and disorients the reader, who is both included and excluded from a narration that presents Clamence's half of a dialogue in which "you," the reader, are presumed to be present as the other half.

Camus was a consummate artist as well as moralist, well aware of the opportunities as well as the illusions of his craft. When he received the Nobel Prize in 1957, his acceptance speech emphasized the artificial but necessary "human" order imposed by art on the chaos of immediate experience. The artist is important as *creator* because he or she shapes a human perspective, allows understanding in human terms, and therefore provides a basis for action. By stressing the gap between art and reality, Camus in effect provides a bridge between them as two poles of human understanding. His own works illustrate this act of bridging through their juxtaposition of realistic detail and almost mythic allegorization of human destiny. The symbolism of his titles, from *The Stranger* to the last collection of stories, *Exile and the Kingdom* (1957), repeatedly interprets human destiny in terms of a thematic opposition between the individual's sense of alienation and exile in the world, and simultaneous search for the true realm of human happiness and action.

With "The Guest," taken from *Exile and the Kingdom,* Camus returns to the landscape of his native Algeria. The colonial context is crucial in this story, not only to explain the real threat of guerrilla reprisal at the end (Camus may be recalling the actual killing of rural schoolteachers in 1954) but to establish the dimensions of a political situation in which the government, police, educational system, and economic welfare of Algeria are all controlled by France. A similar colonial (or newly post-colonial) setting is used to indicate a charged political atmosphere in works by Doris Lessing, Naguib Mahfouz, Chinua Achebe, and Wole Soyinka. The beginning of Camus's story illustrates how French colonial education reproduces French, not local concerns: the schoolteacher's geography lesson outlines the four main rivers of France. The Arab is led along like an animal behind the gendarme Balducci, who rides a horse (here too, Camus may be recalling a humiliation reported two decades before and used to inspire Algerian nationalists). Within this political context, however, he concentrates on quite different issues: freedom, brotherhood, responsibility, and the ambiguity of actions along with the inevitability of choice.

The remote desert landscape establishes a total physical and moral isolation for events in the story. "No one, in this desert . . . mattered," and the schoolteacher and his guest must each decide on his own what to do. When Balducci invades Daru's monastic solitude and tells him that he must deliver the Arab to prison, Daru is outraged to be involved and, indeed, to have responsibility for another's fate. Cursing both the system that tries to force him into complicity and the Arab who has not had enough sense to get away, Daru tries in every way possible to avoid taking a stand. In the morning, however, when the Arab has not in fact run away, the schoolteacher makes up a package of food and money and passes on to the Arab his own freedom of choice. We cannot underestimate the quiet heroism of this act, by which Daru alienates himself from his own people and—unexpectedly—from the Arab's compatriots too; he is, he believes, conveying to a fellow human being the freedom of action, which all people require. This level of common humanity is strongly underlined throughout the whole story as a "sort of brotherhood" and "strange alliance" that comes from having shared food and drink, and slept as equals under the same roof. Such hospitality is also the nomadic "law of the desert" that establishes fellowship between guest and host (a law that Daru refers to when he points out the second road at the end). The host's humane hospitality has placed a new burden and reciprocal responsibility on his guest, one that may explain why the Arab chooses—in apparent freedom—the road to prison. Camus considered "Cain" and "The Law" as titles for this story before settling on "The Guest" (and the title word *l'hôte,* is identical for "guest" and "host" in French). Both guest and host are obliged to shoulder the ambiguous, and potentially fatal, burden of freedom.

The Guest[1]

The schoolmaster was watching the two men climb toward him. One was on horseback, the other on foot. They had not yet tackled the abrupt rise leading to the schoolhouse built on the hillside. They were toiling onward, making slow progress in the snow, among the stones, on the vast expanse of the high, deserted plateau. From time to time the horse stumbled. Without hearing anything yet, he could see the breath issuing from the horse's nostrils. One of the men, at least, knew the region. They were following the trail although it had disappeared days ago under a layer of dirty white snow. The schoolmaster calculated that it would take them half an hour to get onto the hill. It was cold; he went back into the school to get a sweater.

He crossed the empty, frigid classroom. On the blackboard the four rivers of France,[2] drawn with four different colored chalks, had been flowing toward their estuaries for the past three days. Snow had suddenly fallen in mid-October after eight months of drought without the transition of rain, and the twenty pupils, more or less, who lived in the villages scattered over the plateau had stopped coming. With fair weather they would return. Daru now heated only the single room that was his lodging, adjoining the classroom and giving also onto the plateau to the east. Like the class windows, his window looked to the south too. On that side the school was a few kilometers from the point where the plateau began to slope toward the south. In clear weather could be seen the purple mass of the mountain range where the gap opened onto the desert.

Somewhat warmed, Daru returned to the window from which he had first seen the two men. They were no longer visible. Hence they must have tackled the rise. The sky was not so dark, for the snow had stopped falling during the night. The morning had opened with a dirty light which had scarcely become brighter as the ceiling of clouds lifted. At two in the afternoon it seemed as if the day were merely beginning. But still this was better than those three days when the thick snow was falling amidst unbroken darkness with little gusts of wind that rattled the double door of the classroom. Then Daru had spent long hours in his room, leaving it only to go to the shed and feed the chickens or get some coal. Fortunately the delivery truck from Tadjid, the nearest village to the north, had brought his supplies two days before the blizzard. It would return in forty-eight hours.

Besides, he had enough to resist a siege, for the little room was cluttered with bags of wheat that the administration left as a stock to distribute to those of his pupils whose families had suffered from the drought. Actually they had all been victims because they were all poor. Every day Daru would distribute a ration to the children. They had missed it, he knew, during these bad days. Possibly one of the fathers or big brothers would come this afternoon and he could supply them with grain. It was just a matter of carrying them over to the next harvest. Now shiploads of wheat were arriving from France and the worst was over. But it would be hard to forget that poverty, that army of ragged ghosts wandering in the sunlight, the plateaus burned to

---

1. Translated by Justin O'Brien.　　2. The Seine, Loire, Rhône, and Gironde rivers. French geography was taught in the French colonies.

a cinder month after month, the earth shriveled up little by little, literally scorched, every stone bursting into dust under one's foot. The sheep had died then by thousands and even a few men, here and there, sometimes without anyone's knowing.

In contrast with such poverty, he who lived almost like a monk in his remote schoolhouse, nonetheless satisfied with the little he had and with the rough life, had felt like a lord with his whitewashed walls, his narrow couch, his unpainted shelves, his well, and his weekly provision of water and food. And suddenly this snow, without warning, without the foretaste of rain. This is the way the region was, cruel to live in, even without men—who didn't help matters either. But Daru had been born here. Everywhere else, he felt exiled.

He stepped out onto the terrace in front of the schoolhouse. The two men were now halfway up the slope. He recognized the horseman as Balducci, the old gendarme he had known for a long time. Balducci was holding on the end of a rope an Arab who was walking behind him with hands bound and head lowered. The gendarme waved a greeting to which Daru did not reply, lost as he was in contemplation of the Arab dressed in a faded blue jellaba, his feet in sandals but covered with socks of heavy raw wool, his head surmounted by a narrow, short chèche.[3] They were approaching. Balducci was holding back his horse in order not to hurt the Arab, and the group was advancing slowly.

Within earshot, Balducci shouted: "One hour to do the three kilometers from El Ameur!" Daru did not answer. Short and square in his thick sweater, he watched them climb. Not once had the Arab raised his head. "Hello," said Daru when they got up onto the terrace. "Come in and warm up." Balducci painfully got down from his horse without letting go the rope. From under his bristling mustache he smiled at the schoolmaster. His little dark eyes, deep-set under a tanned forehead, and his mouth surrounded with wrinkles made him look attentive and studious. Daru took the bridle, led the horse to the shed, and came back to the two men, who were now waiting for him in the school. He led them into his room. "I am going to heat up the classroom," he said. "We'll be more comfortable there." When he entered the room again, Balducci was on the couch. He had undone the rope tying him to the Arab, who had squatted near the stove. His hands still bound, the chèche pushed back on his head, he was looking toward the window. At first Daru noticed only his huge lips, fat, smooth, almost Negroid; yet his nose was straight, his eyes were dark and full of fever. The chèche revealed an obstinate forehead and, under the weathered skin now rather discolored by the cold, the whole face had a restless and rebellious look that struck Daru when the Arab, turning his face toward him, looked him straight in the eyes. "Go into the other room," said the schoolmaster, "and I'll make you some mint tea." "Thanks," Balducci said. "What a chore! How I long for retirement." And addressing his prisoner in Arabic: "Come on, you." The Arab got up and, slowly, holding his bound wrists in front of him, went into the classroom.

---

3. Scarf; here, wound as a turban around the head. "Jellaba": a long hooded robe worn by Arabs in North Africa.

With the tea, Daru brought a chair. But Balducci was already enthroned on the nearest pupil's desk and the Arab had squatted against the teacher's platform facing the stove, which stood between the desk and the window. When he held out the glass of tea to the prisoner, Daru hesitated at the sight of his bound hands. "He might perhaps be untied." "Sure," said Balducci. "That was for the trip." He started to get to his feet. But Daru, setting the glass on the floor, had knelt beside the Arab. Without saying anything, the Arab watched him with his feverish eyes. Once his hands were free, he rubbed his swollen wrists against each other, took the glass of tea, and sucked up the burning liquid in swift little sips.

"Good," said Daru. "And where are you headed?"

Balducci withdrew his mustache from the tea. "Here, son."

"Odd pupils! And you're spending the night?"

"No. I'm going back to El Ameur. And you will deliver this fellow to Tinguit. He is expected at police headquarters."

Balducci was looking at Daru with a friendly little smile.

"What's this story?" asked the schoolmaster. "Are you pulling my leg?"

"No, son. Those are the orders."

"The orders? I'm not . . ." Daru hesitated, not wanting to hurt the old Corsican.[4] "I mean, that's not my job."

"What! What's the meaning of that? In wartime people do all kinds of jobs."

"Then I'll wait for the declaration of war!"

Balducci nodded.

"O.K. But the orders exist and they concern you too. Things are brewing, it appears. There is talk of a forthcoming revolt. We are mobilized, in a way."

Daru still had his obstinate look.

"Listen, son," Balducci said. "I like you and you must understand. There's only a dozen of us at El Ameur to patrol throughout the whole territory of a small department[5] and I must get back in a hurry. I was told to hand this guy over to you and return without delay. He couldn't be kept there. His village was beginning to stir; they wanted to take him back. You must take him to Tinguit tomorrow before the day is over. Twenty kilometers shouldn't faze a husky fellow like you. After that, all will be over. You'll come back to your pupils and your comfortable life."

Behind the wall the horse could be heard snorting and pawing the earth. Daru was looking out the window. Decidedly, the weather was clearing and the light was increasing over the snowy plateau. When all the snow was melted, the sun would take over again and once more would burn the fields of stone. For days, still, the unchanging sky would shed its dry light on the solitary expanse where nothing had any connection with man.

"After all," he said, turning around toward Balducci, "what did he do?" And, before the gendarme had opened his mouth, he asked: "Does he speak French?"

"No, not a word. We had been looking for him for a month, but they were hiding him. He killed his cousin."

"Is he against us?"[6]

"I don't think so. But you can never be sure."

---

4. Balducci is a native of Corsica, a French island north of Sardinia.   5. French administrative and territorial division; like a country.   6. That is, against the French colonial government.

"Why did he kill?"

"A family squabble, I think. One owed the other grain, it seems. It's not at all clear. In short, he killed his cousin with a billhook. You know, like a sheep, *kreezk!*"

Balducci made the gesture of drawing a blade across his throat and the Arab, his attention attracted, watched him with a sort of anxiety. Daru felt a sudden wrath against the man, against all men with their rotten spite, their tireless hates, their blood lust.

But the kettle was singing on the stove. He served Balducci more tea, hesitated, then served the Arab again, who, a second time, drank avidly. His raised arms made the jellaba fall open and the schoolmaster saw his thin, muscular chest.

"Thanks, kid," Balducci said. "And now, I'm off."

He got up and went toward the Arab, taking a small rope from his pocket.

"What are you doing?" Daru asked dryly.

Balducci, disconcerted, showed him the rope.

"Don't bother."

The old gendarme hesitated. "It's up to you. Of course, you are armed?"

"I have my shotgun."

"Where?"

"In the trunk."

"You ought to have it near your bed."

"Why? I have nothing to fear."

"You're crazy, son. If there's an uprising, no one is safe, we're all in the same boat."

"I'll defend myself. I'll have time to see them coming."

Balducci began to laugh, then suddenly the mustache covered the white teeth.

"You'll have time? O.K. That's just what I was saying. You have always been a little cracked. That's why I like you, my son was like that."

At the same time he took out his revolver and put it on the desk.

"Keep it; I don't need two weapons from here to El Ameur."

The revolver shone against the black paint of the table. When the gendarme turned toward him, the schoolmaster caught the smell of leather and horseflesh.

"Listen, Balducci," Daru said suddenly, "every bit of this disgusts me, and first of all your fellow here. But I won't hand him over. Fight, yes, if I have to. But not that."

The old gendarme stood in front of him and looked at him severely.

"You're being a fool," he said slowly. "I don't like it either. You don't get used to putting a rope on a man even after years of it, and you're even ashamed—yes, ashamed. But you can't let them have their way."

"I won't hand him over," Daru said again.

"It's an order, son, and I repeat it."

"That's right. Repeat to them what I've said to you: I won't hand him over."

Balducci made a visible effort to reflect. He looked at the Arab and at Daru. At last he decided.

"No, I won't tell them anything. If you want to drop us, go ahead; I'll not denounce you. I have an order to deliver the prisoner and I'm doing so. And now you'll just sign this paper for me."

"There's no need. I'll not deny that you left him with me."

"Don't be mean with me. I know you'll tell the truth. You're from here-abouts and you are a man. But you must sign, that's the rule."

Daru opened his drawer, took out a little square bottle of purple ink, the red wooden penholder with the "sergeant-major" pen he used for making models of penmanship, and signed. The gendarme carefully folded the paper and put it into his wallet. Then he moved toward the door.

"I'll see you off," Daru said.

"No," said Balducci. "There's no use being polite. You insulted me."

He looked at the Arab, motionless in the same spot, sniffed peevishly, and turned away toward the door. "Good-by, son," he said. The door shut behind him. Balducci appeared suddenly outside the window and then disappeared. His footsteps were muffled by the snow. The horse stirred on the other side of the wall and several chickens fluttered in fright. A moment later Balducci reappeared outside the window leading the horse by the bridle. He walked toward the little rise without turning around and disappeared from sight with the horse following him. A big stone could be heard bouncing down. Daru walked back toward the prisoner, who, without stirring, never took his eyes off him. "Wait," the schoolmaster said in Arabic and went toward the bedroom. As he was going through the door, he had a second thought, went to the desk, took the revolver, and stuck it in his pocket. Then, without looking back, he went into his room.

For some time he lay on his couch watching the sky gradually close over, listening to the silence. It was this silence that had seemed painful to him during the first days here, after the war. He had requested a post in the little town at the base of the foothills separating the upper plateaus from the desert. There, rocky walls, green and black to the north, pink and lavender to the south, marked the frontier of eternal summer. He had been named to a post farther north, on the plateau itself. In the beginning, the solitude and the silence had been hard for him on these wastelands peopled only by stones. Occasionally, furrows suggested cultivation, but they had been dug to uncover a certain kind of stone good for building. The only plowing here was to harvest rocks. Elsewhere a thin layer of soil accumulated in the hollows would be scraped out to enrich paltry village gardens. This is the way it was: bare rock covered three quarters of the region. Towns sprang up, flourished, then disappeared; men came by, loved one another or fought bitterly, then died. No one in this desert, neither he nor his guest, mattered. And yet, outside this desert neither of them, Daru knew, could have really lived.

When he got up, no noise came from the classroom. He was amazed at the unmixed joy he derived from the mere thought that the Arab might have fled and that he would be alone with no decision to make. But the prisoner was there. He had merely stretched out between the stove and the desk. With eyes open, he was staring at the ceiling. In that position, his thick lips were particularly noticeable, giving him a pouting look. "Come," said Daru. The Arab got up and followed him. In the bedroom, the schoolmaster pointed to a chair near the table under the window. The Arab sat down without taking his eyes off Daru.

"Are you hungry?"

"Yes," the prisoner said.

Daru set the table for two. He took flour and oil, shaped a cake in a frying-pan, and lighted the little stove that functioned on bottled gas. While the cake was cooking, he went out to the shed to get cheese, eggs, dates, and condensed milk. When the cake was done he set it on the window sill to cool, heated some condensed milk diluted with water, and beat up the eggs into an omelette. In one of his motions he knocked against the revolver stuck in his right pocket. He set the bowl down, went into the classroom, and put the revolver in his desk drawer. When he came back to the room, night was falling. He put on the light and served the Arab. "Eat," he said. The Arab took a piece of the cake, lifted it eagerly to his mouth, and stopped short.

"And you?" he asked.

"After you. I'll eat too."

The thick lips opened slightly. The Arab hesitated, then bit into the cake determinedly.

The meal over, the Arab looked at the schoolmaster. "Are you the judge?"

"No, I'm simply keeping you until tomorrow."

"Why do you eat with me?"

"I'm hungry."

The Arab fell silent. Daru got up and went out. He brought back a folding bed from the shed, set it up between the table and the stove, perpendicular to his own bed. From a large suitcase which, upright in a corner, served as a shelf for papers, he took two blankets and arranged them on the camp bed. Then he stopped, felt useless, and sat down on his bed. There was nothing more to do or to get ready. He had to look at this man. He looked at him, therefore, trying to imagine his face bursting with rage. He couldn't do so. He could see nothing but the dark yet shining eyes and the animal mouth.

"Why did you kill him?" he asked in a voice whose hostile tone surprised him.

The Arab looked away.

"He ran away. I ran after him."

He raised his eyes to Daru again and they were full of a sort of woeful interrogation. "Now what will they do to me?"

"Are you afraid?"

He stiffened, turning his eyes away.

"Are you sorry?"

The Arab stared at him openmouthed. Obviously he did not understand. Daru's annoyance was growing. At the same time he felt awkward and self-conscious with his big body wedged between the two beds.

"Lie down there," he said impatiently. "That's your bed."

The Arab didn't move. He called to Daru:

"Tell me!"

The schoolmaster looked at him.

"Is the gendarme coming back tomorrow?"

"I don't know."

"Are you coming with us?"

"I don't know. Why?"

The prisoner got up and stretched out on top of the blankets, his feet toward the window. The light from the electric bulb shone straight into his eyes and he closed them at once.

"Why?" Daru repeated, standing beside the bed.

The Arab opened his eyes under the blinding light and looked at him, trying not to blink.

"Come with us," he said.

In the middle of the night, Daru was still not asleep. He had gone to bed after undressing completely; he generally slept naked. But when he suddenly realized that he had nothing on, he hesitated. He felt vulnerable and the temptation came to him to put his clothes back on. Then he shrugged his shoulders; after all, he wasn't a child and, if need be, he could break his adversary in two. From his bed he could observe him, lying on his back, still motionless with his eyes closed under the harsh light. When Daru turned out the light, the darkness seemed to coagulate all of a sudden. Little by little, the night came back to life in the window where the starless sky was stirring gently. The schoolmaster soon made out the body lying at his feet. The Arab still did not move, but his eyes seemed open. A faint wind was prowling around the schoolhouse. Perhaps it would drive away the clouds and the sun would reappear.

During the night the wind increased. The hens fluttered a little and then were silent. The Arab turned over on his side with his back to Daru, who thought he heard him moan. Then he listened for his guest's breathing, become heavier and more regular. He listened to that breath so close to him and mused without being able to go to sleep. In this room where he had been sleeping alone for a year, this presence bothered him. But it bothered him also by imposing on him a sort of brotherhood he knew well but refused to accept in the present circumstances. Men who share the same rooms, soldiers or prisoners, develop a strange alliance as if, having cast off their armor with their clothing, they fraternized every evening, over and above their differences, in the ancient community of dream and fatigue. But Daru shook himself; he didn't like such musings, and it was essential to sleep.

A little later, however, when the Arab stirred slightly, the schoolmaster was still not asleep. When the prisoner made a second move, he stiffened, on the alert. The Arab was lifting himself slowly on his arms with almost the motion of a sleepwalker. Seated upright in bed, he waited motionless without turning his head toward Daru, as if he were listening attentively. Daru did not stir; it had just occurred to him that the revolver was still in the drawer of his desk. It was better to act at once. Yet he continued to observe the prisoner, who, with the same slithery motion, put his feet on the ground, waited again, then began to stand up slowly. Daru was about to call out to him when the Arab began to walk, in a quite natural but extraordinarily silent way. He was heading toward the door at the end of the room that opened into the shed. He lifted the latch with precaution and went out, pushing the door behind him but without shutting it. Daru had not stirred. "He is running away," he merely thought. "Good riddance!" Yet he listened attentively. The hens were not fluttering; the guest must be on the plateau. A faint sound of water reached him, and he didn't know what it was until the Arab again stood framed in the doorway, closed the door carefully, and came back to bed without a sound. Then Daru turned his back on him and fell asleep. Still later he seemed, from the depths of his sleep, to hear furtive steps around the schoolhouse. "I'm dreaming! I'm dreaming!" he repeated to himself. And he went on sleeping.

When he awoke, the sky was clear; the loose window let in a cold, pure air. The Arab was asleep, hunched up under the blankets now, his mouth open, utterly relaxed. But when Daru shook him, he started dreadfully, staring at Daru with wild eyes as if he had never seen him and such a frightened expression that the schoolmaster stepped back. "Don't be afraid. It's me. You must eat." The Arab nodded his head and said yes. Calm had returned to his face, but his expression was vacant and listless.

The coffee was ready. They drank it seated together on the folding bed as they munched their pieces of the cake. Then Daru led the Arab under the shed and showed him the faucet where he washed. He went back into the room, folded the blankets and the bed, made his own bed and put the room in order. Then he went through the classroom and out onto the terrace. The sun was already rising in the blue sky; a soft, bright light was bathing the deserted plateau. On the ridge the snow was melting in spots. The stones were about to reappear. Crouched on the edge of the plateau, the schoolmaster looked at the deserted expanse. He thought of Balducci. He had hurt him, for he had sent him off in a way as if he didn't want to be associated with him. He could still hear the gendarme's farewell and, without knowing why, he felt strangely empty and vulnerable. At that moment, from the other side of the schoolhouse, the prisoner coughed. Daru listened to him almost despite himself and then, furious, threw a pebble that whistled through the air before sinking into the snow. That man's stupid crime revolted him, but to hand him over was contrary to honor. Merely thinking of it made him smart with humiliation. And he cursed at one and the same time his own people who had sent him this Arab and the Arab too who had dared to kill and not managed to get away. Daru got up, walked in a circle on the terrace, waited motionless, and then went back into the schoolhouse.

The Arab, leaning over the cement floor of the shed, was washing his teeth with two fingers. Daru looked at him and said: "Come." He went back into the room ahead of the prisoner. He slipped a hunting-jacket on over his sweater and put on walking-shoes. Standing, he waited until the Arab had put on his *chèche* and sandals. They went into the classroom and the schoolmaster pointed to the exit, saying: "Go ahead." The fellow didn't budge. "I'm coming," said Daru. The Arab went out. Daru went back into the room and made a package of pieces of rusk, dates, and sugar. In the classroom, before going out, he hesitated a second in front of his desk, then crossed the threshold and locked the door. "That's the way," he said. He started toward the east, followed by the prisoner. But, a short distance from the schoolhouse, he thought he heard a slight sound behind them. He retraced his steps and examined the surroundings of the house, there was no one there. The Arab watched him without seeming to understand. "Come on," said Daru.

They walked for an hour and rested beside a sharp peak of limestone. The snow was melting faster and faster and the sun was drinking up the puddles at once, rapidly cleaning the plateau, which gradually dried and vibrated like the air itself. When they resumed walking, the ground rang under their feet. From time to time a bird rent the space in front of them with a joyful cry. Daru breathed in deeply the fresh morning light. He felt a sort of rapture before the vast familiar expanse, now almost entirely yellow under its dome of blue sky. They walked an hour more, descending toward the south. They reached a level height made up of crumbly rocks. From there on, the plateau sloped down, eastward, toward a low plain where there were a few spindly trees and, to the south, toward outcroppings of rock that gave the landscape a chaotic look.

Daru surveyed the two directions. There was nothing but the sky on the horizon. Not a man could be seen. He turned toward the Arab, who was looking at him blankly. Daru held out the package to him. "Take it," he said. "There are dates, bread, and sugar. You can hold out for two days. Here are a thousand francs too." The Arab took the package and the money but kept his full hands at chest level as if he didn't know what to do with what was being given him. "Now look," the schoolmaster said as he pointed in the direction of the east, "there's the way to Tinguit. You have a two-hour walk. At Tinguit you'll find the administration and the police. They are expecting you." The Arab looked toward the east, still holding the package and the money against his chest. Daru took his elbow and turned him rather roughly toward the south. At the foot of the height on which they stood could be seen a faint path. "That's the trail across the plateau. In a day's walk from here you'll find pasturelands and the first nomads. They'll take you in and shelter you according to their law." The Arab had now turned toward Daru and a sort of panic was visible in his expression. "Listen," he said. Daru shook his head: "No, be quiet. Now I'm leaving you." He turned his back on him, took two long steps in the direction of the school, looked hesitantly at the motionless Arab, and started off again. For a few minutes he heard nothing but his own step resounding on the cold ground and did not turn his head. A moment later, however, he turned around. The Arab was still there on the edge of the hill, his arms hanging now, and he was looking at the schoolmaster. Daru felt something rise in his throat. But he swore with impatience, waved vaguely, and started off again. He had already gone some distance when he again stopped and looked. There was no longer anyone on the hill.

Daru hesitated. The sun was now rather high in the sky and was beginning to beat down on his head. The schoolmaster retraced his steps, at first somewhat uncertainly, then with decision. When he reached the little hill, he was bathed in sweat. He climbed it as fast as he could and stopped, out of breath, at the top. The rock-fields to the south stood out sharply against the blue sky, but on the plain to the east a steamy heat was already rising. And in that slight haze, Daru, with heavy heart, made out the Arab walking slowly on the road to prison.

A little later, standing before the window of the classroom, the schoolmaster was watching the clear light bathing the whole surface of the plateau, but he hardly saw it. Behind him on the blackboard, among the winding French rivers, sprawled the clumsily chalked-up words he had just read: "You handed over our brother. You will pay for this." Daru looked at the sky, the plateau, and, beyond, the invisible lands stretching all the way to the sea. In this vast landscape he had loved so much, he was alone.

TADEUSZ BOROWSKI
1922–1951

Incarcerated in the extermination camps of Auschwitz-Birkenau, and Dachau from the age of twenty to the age of twenty-two, a tormented suicide by gas at twenty-nine, Tadeusz Borowski wrote stories of life in the camps that have made him the foremost writer of the "literature of atrocity." The stories' brutal realism and matter-of-fact tone convey, as passionate declamations could never do, the mind-numbing horror of a situation in which systematic slaughter was the background for everyday life. The narrator of these stories, modeled on Borowski but also a composite figure, has become part of the concentration camp system, to survive. He assists the Kapos, or senior prisoners who organize the camp; has a job in the system; and carries a burden of guilt that cannot quite be suppressed by his adopted impersonal attitude. Borowski's stories shocked their postwar audience by their uncompromising honesty: here were no saintly victims and demoniacally evil executioners, but human beings going about the business of extermination or, reduced to near-animal level, cooperating in their own and others' destruction. Any belief in civilization, in common humanity, or in divine Providence is sorely tested; Borowski's bleak picture questions everything and does not pretend to offer encouragement. His fiction is still read for its powerful evocation of the death camps, for its analysis of human relationships under pressure, and for an agonizing portrayal of individuals forced to choose between physical or spiritual survival.

Tadeusz Borowski was born on November 12, 1922, in the Polish city of Żytomierz, part of the then-Soviet Ukraine. When he was three years old, his father was sent to a labor camp in Siberia as a suspected dissident; four years later, his mother was deported as well, and Tadeusz and his twelve-year-old brother were separated. He was raised by an aunt and educated in a Soviet school until a prisoner exchange in 1932 brought his father home; his mother's release in 1934 reunited the family. Money was scarce, however, and the young boy was sent away to a Franciscan boarding school, where he could be educated inexpensively. Much later, he commented that he had never had a family life: "either my father was sitting in Murmansk or my mother was in Siberia, or I was in a boarding school, on my own or in a camp." World War II began when he was still sixteen, and—since the Nazis did not permit higher education for Poles—Borowski continued his studies at Warsaw University via illegal underground classes. Unlike his fellow students, he refused to join political groups and did not become involved in the resistance; he wanted merely to write poetry, continue his literary studies, and write a master's thesis on the poetry of Leopold Staff. Polish publications were illegal, however, and his first poetry collection, *Wherever the Earth* (1942)—run off in 165 copies on a clandestine mimeograph machine—was enough to condemn him. *Wherever the Earth* prefigures the bleak perspective of the concentration camp stories: prophesying the end of the human race, it sees the world as a gigantic labor camp and the sky as a "low, steel lid" or "a factory ceiling" (an oppressive image he may have adapted from Baudelaire's "Spleen LXXXI"). Borowski and his fiancée, Maria Rundo, were arrested in late February 1943 and sent to Auschwitz two months later. In the meantime, he was able to see from his cell window both the Jewish uprising in the Warsaw ghetto and the ghetto's fiery destruction by Nazi soldiers.

Borowski's camp experiences are reproduced in the 1948 story collection *Farewell to Maria*, from which "Ladies and Gentlemen, to the Gas Chamber" is taken. Arriving in Auschwitz, he was put to hard labor with the other prisoners; but after a bout with pneumonia, he learned to survive by taking a position as an orderly in the Auschwitz hospital—which was not just a clinic but a place where prisoners were used as experimental subjects. Maria had been sent to the women's barracks at the same camp, and he wrote her daily letters that were smuggled in. The story "Auschwitz, Our Home" contains a series of such letters and conveys, in addition to reassurances of his love, the writer's succeeding moods of hope, anger, cynicism, and despair ("We remain as numb as trees when they are being cut down"). Love lyrics written to Maria in 1942, published by his friends in 1944, display the sensuous softness of dream and contrast sharply with the camp stories' harsh illumination.

> I'm dreamy today. Noise from the street,
> the sky-curtain's rustlings, every
> sound comes in like the horizon's smoke
> through a mist.
> . . . It's how at night
> I take your hair in my hand, let its
> waves flow through my palm and
> stay quiet, full of you,
> as sleep is quiet now in me.
> (trans. Addison Bross)

The narrator's dispassionate tone in the stories, as he describes senseless cruelty and mass murder, individual scenes of desperation, or the eccentric emotions of people about to die, continue to shock many readers. Borowski is certainly describing a world of antiheroes, those who survive by accommodating themselves to things as they are and avoiding acts of heroism. His second collection of stories, *World of Stone* (1948), uses the same tone to describe life in the repatriation camps (he spent two years in such camps before being sent home) and the writer's disgust at the false normalcy of postwar society. Yet his impersonality is chiefly a shield; vulnerable, he finds a way to cope with overwhelming events by holding them at a distance. Borowski is recording events for future testimony, and he writes to his fiancée, "I do not know whether we shall survive, but I like to think that one day we shall have the courage to tell the world the whole truth and call it by its proper name." At the end of *The World of Stone*, his ambition is "to grasp the true significance of the events, things, and people I have seen. For I intend to write."

Upon his return to Poland after the war, Borowski's searing talent was recognized; the stories "Ladies and Gentlemen, to the Gas Chamber" and "A Day at Harmensee" (a subcamp of Auschwitz) had been published, and he became a prominent writer. He married Maria and was courted by Poland's Stalinist government. At the government's urging, he wrote journalism and weekly stories that followed political lines and employed a newly strident tone. The Cold War had begun, and Borowski was persuaded that he had joined a popular revolution that would prevent any more horrors like Auschwitz. He went so far as to do intelligence work in Berlin for the Polish secret police in 1949. The revelation of Soviet prison camps, however, and political purges in Poland, gradually disillusioned him: once more, he was part of a concentration-camp system and complicit with the oppressors. He committed suicide by gas on July 3, 1951.

"Ladies and Gentlemen, to the Gas Chamber" was written in Munich, at a repatriation camp where Borowski was sent after his release from Dachau (many Birkenau prisoners were transferred as the Allied armies moved farther into Germany.) Narrated in an impersonal tone by one of the prisoners, the story describes the extermination camp of Birkenau, the second and largest of three concentration camps at Auschwitz (Polish: Oświęcim), an enclosed world of hierarchical authority and desperate struggles to survive. Food, shoes, shirts, underwear: this vital currency of the camp is obtained when new prisoners are stripped of their belongings as they arrive in railway cattle cars. The story could equally well have been titled "A Day with Canada," for it follows the narrator's first trip to the railroad station with the labor battalion

"Canada." The trip will salvage goods from a train bringing fifteen thousand Polish Jews, former inhabitants of the cities Sosnowiec and Będzin. By the end of the day, most of the travelers will be burning in the crematorium, and the camp will live for a few more days on the loot from "a good, rich transport."

Borowski suggests the systematic dehumanization of the camps from the beginning: people are equated with lice, and they mill around by naked thousands in blocked-off sections. Lice and people are poisoned with the same gas, sealed tightly into the camp or expelled from a section by the delousing process. People will later be equated with sick horses (the converted stables retain their old signs), lumber and concrete trucked in from the railroad station, and insects whose jaws work away on moldy pieces of bread. Constantly supervised, subject to arbitrary rules and punishment, malnourished and pushed to exhaustion, their identities reduced to numbers tattooed on the arm, the prisoners live in the shadow of a hierarchical authority that is to be feared and placated. Paradoxically, their common vulnerability leads to alienation and rage at their fellow victims rather than at the executioners. The Nazis have foreseen everything, explains his friend Henri, including the fact that helplessness needs to vent itself on someone weaker. The only way to cope is to distance oneself from what is happening, to become a cog in the machine so that one does not really experience what is happening—to suspend, for the moment, one's humanity.

Borowski emphasizes the range of cultures and languages brought together in Birkenau, and that variety is contrasted with the rigid narrowness of their jailers. French, Russian, and German phrases appear in this Polish-language story, as well as the camp "Esperanto" spoken by the Greeks. Separate scenes focus on the suffering of individual men, women, and children; and the narrator mentions the chaotic, multicolored appearance of the crowds in their rags and variously striped uniforms. Over and against this cultural multiplicity is set the narrowly homogeneous model of the Nazi authorities: a lock-step "one mass, one will," bred from "Aryan" genes and trained in obedience to the Führer. The soldier with his blond hair and blue eyes, or the blonde woman commandant who wears her hair in a "Nordic" knot, offer images of the proposed master race. The SS officers are sleek, clean-shaven, and well-fed; they dress in identical uniforms with silver insignia, shiny boots, whips and revolvers, and briefcases to keep records in order. It is a picture of prosperity and efficient organization, all the more chilling in its pretense of normalcy and civilized behavior. The same officer who urges prisoners ("Gentlemen") to be orderly and show goodwill suddenly whips a woman stooping to pick up a handbag. Sharp contrasts emphasize the hollowness of their civilized image: a group of officers shake hands and share news from home and family pictures while the train of deportees rolls into the station; an officer fumbles with a balky cigarette lighter as he orders the labor detail to remove infants' corpses from the cattle car; another officer superciliously refers to a desperate woman who tries to escape being condemned with her child as an "unnatural mother."

It is the narrator's first experience with the Canada salvage team, and he expects that his carefully cultivated impersonality will work as well here as it has in the camp. This day will test his defenses, however, and his ability to survive through willful alienation. For a while, he registers events intellectually, noting the dimensions of the camp and crematoria. Soon, however, unforeseen emotional challenges arise and his control becomes shaky.

Words of sympathy from a condemned woman strike home: his vision blurs, and he asks Henri, "Are we good people?" It is only the first in a series of shocks, however, culminating when an apparently dead body grasps his hand. Vomiting from the cumulative horror, the narrator finds that the two dimensions he has tried to keep apart have temporarily fused—and he retreats once more to a dream of alienation. The narrator's utter defeat and despair are underlined when the returning labor battalion moves aside for an SS detachment singing lustily about conquering the world. Borowski's story was written after the Nazi downfall, but for the moment the picture is one of a spiritual desolation that not only illustrates a shameful moment in modern history but raises questions about what it means to be civilized, or even "human."

PRONOUNCING GLOSSARY

The following list uses common English syllables and stress accents to provide rough equivalents of selected words whose pronunciation may be unfamiliar to the general reader.

Auschwitz: *ow'-shvits*

Birkenau: *beer'-ken-ow*

Katowice: *kah-toh-veet'-seh*

Sosnowiec-Będzin: *sos-navv–yets ben–' jeen*

Tadeusz Borowski: *tah-day'-oosh baw-raw-skee*

Ladies and Gentlemen, to the Gas Chamber[1]

The whole camp[2] went about naked. True, we had already passed through the delousing process and received our clothing back from the tanks filled with a dilution of cyclone[3] in water which so excellently poisoned lice in clothing and people in gas chambers—and only the blocks separated from us by trestles had not yet been issued clothing, nonetheless both the former and the latter went about naked: the heat was terrific. The camp was sealed up tight. Not a prisoner, not a louse could venture beyond its gates. The work of the commandos[4] had stopped. Thousands of naked people milled about all day on the roads and roll-call grounds; they siestaed under walls and on the roofs. People slept on bare boards, for the straw mattresses and blankets were being disinfected. The FKL[5] could be seen from the last blocks; delousing was going on there, too. Twenty-eight thousand women had been stripped and turned out of the blocks; they could be seen right now scrambling on the meadows, roads and roll-call grounds.

The morning is spent in waiting for dinner, contents of food parcels are being eaten, friends visited. The hours pass slowly as they do in extreme heat. Even the usual recreation is lacking: the wide roads to the crematoria are empty. There have been no transports for some days. Part of "Canada"[6] has been liquidated and assigned to a commando. Being well-fed and rested they chanced on the hardest one: the Harmensee.[7] For envious justice rules in the camp: when a mighty one falls, his friends make every effort that he may fall as low as possible. Canada, our Canada, is not like Fiedler's,[8] fragrant with resin, only with French perfume, but fewer tall pines probably

1. Translated by Jadwiga Zwolska.   2. Auschwitz II, or Birkenau, the largest of the Nazi extermination camps, established in October 1941 near the town of Birkenau, Poland. Its death toll is usually estimated between 1 million and 2.5 million people.   3. Cyclone-B, the extermination gas.   4. Labor battalions. 5. Frauen Konzentration Lager, "women's concentration camp" (German).   6. The name given to the camp stores (as well as prisoners working there) where valuables and clothing taken from prisoners were sorted for dispatch to Germany. Like the nation of Canada, the store symbolized wealth and prosperity to the camp inmates.   7. One of the subcamps outside Birkenau itself.   8. Arkady Fiedler, Polish writer of travel books, one of which was about Canada.

grow there than the number of diamonds and coins—collected from all Europe—cached here.

Several of us are sitting right now on a top bunk swinging our legs in a carefree manner. We take out white, extravagantly baked bread: crumbly, falling to pieces, a little provoking in taste, but, for all that, bread that had not been moulding for weeks. Bread sent from Warsaw.[9] Barely a week ago, my mother had it in her hands. Good God . . .

We get out bacon and onions, open a tin of condensed milk. Huge, dripping with sweat, Henri yearns aloud for French wine brought by the transports from Strasbourg, from the vicinities of Paris, from Marseilles[1] . . .

"Listen, *mon ami*,[2] when we go on the loading platform again, I'll bring you real champagne. You've never drunk it, have you?"

"No. But you won't be able to smuggle it across the gate, so don't string me along. You'd better 'organize' a pair of shoes—you know, perforated leather, with a double sole.[3] And I'm not mentioning a sports shirt, you've promised me one long ago."

"Patience, patience. When the transports come I'll bring you everything. We'll go on the loading platform again."

"What if there won't be any more transports for the smokestack?"[4] I threw in maliciously. "You see how things eased up in the camp: unlimited food parcels, flogging not allowed. You've written home, haven't you? . . . People say all sorts of things about the regulations, you yourself do a lot of gabbing. Anyhow, damn it, they'll run out of people."

"Don't talk nonsense," says the plump Marseillaise, his face spiritual like a Cosway[5] miniature (he's my friend, and yet I don't know his name). His mouth filled with a sardine sandwich, he repeated, "don't talk nonsense," swallowing with difficulty ('it went down, damn it,') "don't talk nonsense, they can't run out of people or we'd all be finished in the camp. We all live on what they bring."

"Well, not all. We have food parcels . . ."

"You have, and a pal of yours has, and tens of your pals have them. You Poles have them, and not all of you at that. But we, the Jews, the Russkis? and what then? If we, the transport 'organization,' had nothing to eat, would you be eating these food parcels of yours so calmly? We wouldn't let you."

"You'd let us, or you'd die of starvation like the Greeks. Whoever in the camp has food, has power."

"You've got them and we've got them, so why quarrel?"

That is true, no use quarreling. You have them and I have them, we eat together, sleep in one bunk. Henri cuts the bread, makes a tomato salad. It has a marvellous taste with the mustard from the camp canteen.

Under us, in the block, naked, sweating people mill about. They move here and there in the passages between the bunks, alongside the huge, ingeniously built stove, amidst the improvements which change the stables (there is still a sign on the door saying that *verseuchte Pferde*[6]—infected horses, should be sent to such and such a place) into a cozy home for more

9. Capital of Poland; most of its Jewish residents were executed by the Nazis.   1. A large French port on the Mediterranean Sea. Strasbourg is a city in northeast France.   2. My friend (French).   3. A Hungarian style.   4. The crematorium.   5. Richard Cosway (1740–1821), an English miniaturist, or painter of miniature portraits that could be kept in a locket.   6. Infected horses (German).

than half a thousand men. They nest on the lower bunks by eights and nines: stinking of sweat and excrement, their cheeks emaciated, they lie naked and bony. Under me, on the very bottom bunk—a rabbi; he has covered his head[7] with a bit of rag torn from the blanket and is reading a Hebrew prayer book (there's plenty of that kind of reading here . . .) in a loud and monotonous lament.

"Maybe we could shut him up? He yells as though he had caught God by the feet."

"I don't feel like getting down from the bunk. Let him yell; he'll go all the quicker to the smokestack."

"Religion is the opium of the people.[8] I like to smoke opium," the Marseillaise to my left, who is a communist and a *rentier*,[9] adds sententiously.

"If they did not believe in God and in a life beyond they'd have wrecked the crematorium long ago."

"And why don't you do it?"

The sense of the question is metaphoric, however, the Marseillaise replies, "Idiot," stuffs his mouth with a tomato and gestures as though he would say something, but he munches and keeps silent. We just finished stuffing ourselves when a bigger hubbub started near the door of the block: the Mussulmen[1] jumped back and scurried off among the bunks. A messenger ran into the block leader's cubbyhole. After a moment the block leader emerged[2] majestically.

"Canada! Fall in! Snappy now! A transport's coming!"

"Good God," shouted Henri, leaping down from the bunk.

The Marseillaise choked on the tomato, grabbed his coat, shouted *"raus"*[3] to those who sat below him, and in a moment they were already in the doorway. Everything seethed on the other bunks. Canada was going to the loading platform.

"Henri, shoes!" I shouted as a farewell. *"Keine Angst,"*[4] he shouted back, already outside.

I packed up the food and tied the satchel with string. In it, cheek by jowl with Portuguese sardines, lay onions and tomatoes from my father's garden in Warsaw, and the bacon from the "Bacutil" in Lublin (from my brother) mingled with genuine candied fruit from Salonika.[5] I tied it all up, pulled my trousers on and climbed down from the bunk.

"Platz!"[6] I shouted, shouldering my way through the Greeks. They drew aside. In the door I came upon Henri.

"Allez, allez, vite, vite!"[7]

"Was ist los?"[8]

"Do you want to go to the loading platform with us?"

"Can do."

"Then hurry, take your coat. They're a few men short, I spoke to the kapo," and he pushed me out of the block.

7. Jews are expected to keep their heads covered while at prayer.   8. A quotation from the German political philosopher Karl Marx (1818–1883).   9. Someone with unearned income, a stockholder (French). 1. Or Muslim; people who had given up, considered the camp pariahs.   2. A Kapo, or senior prisoner in charge of a group of prisoners.   3. Outside (German).   4. Don't panic (German).   5. Major port city in northeast Greece. Bacutil was a meat-products company with branches in many Polish cities. Lublin is a city in eastern Poland.   6. Make room (German).   7. Come on, come on, quickly, quickly! (French).   8. What's the matter? (German).

We lined up, someone wrote down our numbers, someone at the head shouted: "march, march" and we ran up to the gates accompanied by the babel of the multitude already being driven back to the block with thongs. It was not everyone that could go to the loading platform . . . Good-byes said, we are already at the gate.

"*Links, zwei, drei, vier! Mützen ab!*"[9] Straightened up, with arms held stiffy at hips, we pass through the gate with a brisk, springy step—almost gracefully. Holding a huge tablet in his hand, a sleepy SS[1]-man counts drowsily, separating with his finger in the air every five men.

"*Hundert!*"[2] he shouted when the last five had passed him.

"*Stimmt!*"[3] a hoarse voice calls back from the head.

We march rapidly, almost at a run. Many outposts: youngsters with automatics. We pass all the sectors of Camp II B: the untenanted *Lager*[4] C, Czech and quarantine, and plunge deep among the apple and pear trees of the military hospital; amidst the exotic verdure, as though out of the moon, strangely exuberant these few sunny days, we pass in an arc some sort of wooden sheds, pass the big *Postenkette* lines and in a run reach the highway—we are there. A few score metres more, and among the trees—the loading platform.

It was an idyllic platform, as is usual with rural stations lost in remote areas. A square, bordered with the green of tall trees, was strewn with gravel. A tiny wooden shack squatted down at one side of the road, uglier and more jerry-built than the ugliest and flimsiest station shack. Farther away lay great stacks of rails, railway sleepers, piles of deal boards, parts of wooden sheds, bricks, stones and concrete well-rings. It is here that goods are unloaded for Birkenau: material for the expansion of the camp and people for the gas chambers. An ordinary work day: trucks drive up, take lumber, cement, people . . .

Guards take their places on the rails, on the lumber, under the green shade of the Silesian[5] chestnuts, they surround the loading platform with a tight circle. They wipe perspiration from their foreheads and drink from their canteens. The heat is terrific, the sun stands motionless in the zenith. "Fall out!" We sit in patches of shade under the stacked rails. The hungry Greeks (a few of them have managed, the devil knows how, to slip out with us) ferret among the rails; someone finds a tin of food, mouldy buns, an unfinished tin of sardines. They eat.

"*Schweinedreck,*"[6] a tall, young guard with abundant blond hair and dreamy blue eyes, spits at them. "After all, you'll have so much grub in a moment that you won't be able to gobble it all. You'll have your fill for a long time." He adjusts his automatic and wipes his face with a handkerchief.

"Swine," we confirm in unison.

---

9. Left, two, three, four! Caps off! (German).   1. Abbreviation for *Schutzstaffel* (Protective echelon, German), the Nazi police system that began as Hitler's private guard and grew, by 1939, to a powerful 250,000-member military and political organization that administered all state security functions. The SS was divided into many bureaucratic units, one of which, the Death's Head Battalions, managed the concentration camps. Selected for physical perfection and (Aryan) racial purity, SS members wore black or gray-green uniforms decorated with silver insignia.   2. A hundred! (German).   3. Right! (German). 4. Camp (German).   5. Probably local chestnuts. Silesia, in central Europe, was partitioned between Poland, Czechoslovakia, and Germany after World War I; Germany occupied Polish Silesia in 1939. 6. Dirty pigs (German).

"Hey you, fatty," the guard's shoe touches lightly the back of Henri's neck. "*Pass mal auf*,[7] want a drink?"

"I'm thirsty, but I've no marks," the Frenchman replies in a business-like manner.

"Too bad."

"But, *Herr*[8] Guard, doesn't my word mean anything any more? Hasn't *Herr* Guard done business with me? How much?"

"A hundred. A deal?"

"A deal."

We drink the insipid and tasteless water on tick against the money and people not yet here.

"Look here, you," the Frenchman says throwing away the empty bottle which crashes somewhere away on the rails, "take no money, for there may be a search. And, anyway, what the hell d'you need money for, you've got enough to eat. Don't take a suit either, for that's suspicious, and might look like a get-away. Take a shirt, but only a silk one and with a collar. Underneath, a gym vest. And if you find anything to drink, don't call me. I can take care of myself. And look out you don't get walloped."

"Do they whip you?"

"That's normal. One has to have eyes in the back. *Arschaugen*."[9]

All around us sit the Greeks; like huge, inhuman insects they move their jaws greedily and voraciously devour mouldy chunks of bread. They are uneasy because they do not know what they're going to do. They are alarmed by the lumber and the rails. They don't like lifting heavy loads.

"*Was wir arbeiten?*"[1] they ask.

"*Nix. Transport kommen, alles Krematorium, compris?*"[2]

"*Alles verstehen*," they reply in the crematorium Esperanto.[3] They calm down; they won't have to load the rails on trucks or carry the lumber.

In the meantime the loading platform has become more and more noisy and crowded. The foremen are dividing up the groups, assigning some to opening and unloading the railway cars that are to arrive; others they assign to the wooden steps and explain to them how to work properly. These were wide, portable steps like those to mount a rostrum. Roaring motorcycles arrived bringing non-commissioned SS officers, hefty, well fed men in glossy top-boots, with bespangled silver insignia, their faces churly and shiny. Some arrived with brief cases, others had flexible reed canes. This gave them an official and efficient air. They entered the canteen—for that miserable shack was their canteen where in summer they drank mineral water, *Sudetenquelle*,[4] and in winter warmed themselves with hot wine.

They greeted one another in stately fashion: the arm stretched out in the Roman manner[5] and then, cordially shaking hands, they smiled warmly at

---

7. See here (German).   8. Mister (German).   9. Eyes in your ass (German, literal trans.). 1. What are we working on? (German).   2. Nothing. Transport coming, everything crematorium, understood? (German; *compris* is French).   3. An artificial language created in 1887 by L. L. Zamenhof to simplify communication between different nationalities. "Alles verstehen": Everything understood. 4. Water from the Sudetenland or Sudeten Mountains; a narrow strip of land on the northern and western borders of the Czech Republic. The Sudeten was annexed by Hitler in 1938.   5. The official "Heil Hitler!" (Hail Hitler!) salute, with the straight right arm abruptly raised in imitation of ancient Roman military salutes. Adolf Hitler was chancellor of Germany under Nazism (1933–45).

one another, talked about letters, news from home, their children; they showed one another photographs. Some of them promenaded in the square with dignity, the gravel crunched, the boots crunched, the silver distinctions gleamed on the collars and the bamboo canes swished impatiently.

The throng in vari-coloured camp stripes lay in the narrow strips of shade under the rails, breathed heavily and unevenly, chattered in their own tongue, gazed lazily and indifferently at the majestic people in the green uniforms, at the green of the trees—near and unattainable, at the spires of a distant church from which a belated Angelus[6] was just being rung.

"The transport's coming," said someone, and all of them rose expectantly. The freight cars were coming around the bend, the locomotive driving from behind. The brakeman standing on the tender, leaned out, waved his arm and whistled. The locomotive whistled screechingly in reply, panted, and the train chugged slowly along the station. In the small, barred windows could be seen human faces, pale and crumpled, dishevelled as though they had not had enough sleep; terrified women, and men who, strange to say, had hair. They passed slowly and looked at the station in silence. And then, inside the cars there began a seething and a pounding on the wooden walls.

"Water! Air!" rose dull, despairing shrieks.

Human faces leaned out of windows, mouths desperately gasped for air. Having drawn a few gulps of air the people left the windows and others stormed their places and then also disappeared. The screams and the rattling grew louder and louder.

A man in a green uniform more bespangled with silver than that of the others, frowned with disgust. He puffed on his cigarette, then threw it away with a sudden motion, transferred his brief case from his right to his left hand and beckoned to a guard. The latter slowly removed his automatic from his shoulder, took aim and fired a round at the railway cars. Silence fell. In the meantime trucks backed up to the train, stools were placed at the back of each, and the camp workers took positions expertly at the cars. The giant with the brief case made a sign with his hand.

"Whoever takes gold or anything else but food will be shot as a thief of *Reich* property. Understood? *Verstanden?*"[7]

"*Jawohl!*"[8] came the shout, discordant but expressing good will.

"*Also loos!*[9] To work!"

The bolts clattered, the freight cars were opened. A wave of fresh air rushed inside, stunning people as though with monoxide gas. Packed to the limit, overwhelmed by a fantastic amount of luggage: suitcases, satchels, gladstone bags, rucksacks and bundles of every description (for they were bringing everything that had constituted their former life and was to start their future) they were squeezed into terribly cramped quarters, fainting from the heat, being suffocated and smothering others. Now they had clustered around the open door, panting like fish thrown on sand.

"Attention! Get down with your luggage. Take everything. Place all your duds in a pile near the car. Hand over your coats. It's summer. March to the left. Understand?"

---

6. A call to prayer, rung three times a day in the Catholic Church. "Green uniforms": that is, the regular gray-green army uniforms.   7. Understand? (German).   8. Yes! (German).   9. Then get going!

"Sir, what's going to happen to us?"—uneasy, nerves quivering, they are already jumping down onto the gravel.

"Where are you from?"

"Sosnowiec, Będzin.[1] Sir, what'll happen?" They stubbornly repeat the questions, gazing fervently into strange, tired eyes.

"I don't know, I don't understand Polish."

There is the law of the camp that people going to their death must be deceived to the last moment. It is the only permissible form of pity. The heat is sweltering. The sun has reached its zenith, the burnished sky trembles, the air shimmers; the wind, which blows through us intermittently, is merely hot, moist air. Lips are already cracked, the mouth savours the salty taste of blood. The body is weak and stiff from lying long in the sun. To drink, oh, to drink!

Like a stupefied, blind river that seeks a new bed, the motley throng, heavily laden, pours out of the car. But before they regain consciousness after being stunned by the fresh air and the smell of verdure, their baggage is torn from their hands, coats pulled off them, handbags snatched from the women's hands, sunshades taken away.

"But, mister, that's my sunshade, I can't . . ."

"*Verboten*,"[2] a guard barks through his teeth, hissing loud. In the back stands an SS-man: calm, self-possessed, expert.

"*Meine Herrschaften*,[3] don't throw your things about like that. You must show a little good will." He speaks kindly, and the thin cane bends with the nervous movement of his hands.

"Yes, sir, yes, sir," they reply in unison passing by, and walk at a brisker pace alongside the train cars. A woman bends down and quickly picks up a handbag. The cane swished, the woman cried out, stumbled and fell under the feet of the crowd. A child running behind her squeaked: "*Mamele!*"— just a tousled little girl . . .

The heap of things grows: suitcases, bundles, rucksacks, travel rugs, clothes, and handbags which open in falling and spill rainbow-coloured banknotes, gold, watches; in front of the car doors there rise piles of bread, collections of jars with multi-coloured jams and marmalades; pyramids of hams and sausages swell out, sugar spills on the gravel. Trucks packed with people drive away with an infernal racket amidst the lamentations and the shrieks of women wailing for their children separated from them, while the men, in stupefied silence, suddenly remain alone. They are the ones who went to the right: the young and healthy, they will go to the camp. They will not escape gassing, but first they will be put to work.

The trucks drive away and return continuously like some monstrous assembly line. The Red-Cross[4] ambulance goes back and forth ceaselessly. The huge, blood-red cross on the radiator cover melts in the sun. The Red-Cross ambulance travels tirelessly: it is precisely this car that carries that gas, the gas which will poison these people.

---

1. Two cities in Katowice province (southern Poland). Będzin was also the site of a concentration camp, and more than ten thousand of its inhabitants were exterminated.   2. Forbidden (German).   3. Gentlemen (German).   4. Ordinary trucks were painted with Red Cross insignia to quiet incoming prisoners by suggesting that they would receive humane treatment and medical care.

Those from "Canada" who are near the steps have not a moment's rest: they separate the people for gassing from those who go to the camp; they push the former on to the steps and pack them in the trucks: sixty, more or less, to a truck.

A young, clean-shaven gentleman, an SS-man, stands at the side with a notebook in his hand; each truck means a check mark—when sixteen trucks pass, it means a thousand, more or less. The gentleman is poised and accurate. No truck will leave without his knowledge and his check mark. *Ordnung muss sein.*[5] The check marks swell into thousands, the thousands swell into whole transports of which brief mention is made: "From Salonika," "from Strasbourg," "from Rotterdam."[6] Today's transport will be referred to as "from Będzin." But it will receive the permanent name of "Będzin–Sosnowiec." Those who will go to the work camp from this transport will receive numbers 131–132. Thousands, of course, but abbreviated they will be referred to just like that: 131–132.

The transports grow with the passing of weeks, months, years. When the war is over, the cremated will be counted. There will be four and a half million of them. The bloodiest battle of the war, the greatest victory of Germany united in solidarity. *Ein Reich, ein Volk, ein Führer*[7] and—four crematoria. But in Oświęcim there will be sixteen crematoria capable of incinerating fifty thousand bodies daily. The camp is being expanded until its electrified wire fence will reach the Vistula;[8] it will be inhabited by 300,000 people in camp stripes, it will be called *Verbrecher-Stadt*—the City of Criminals. No, they will not run short of people. Jews will be cremated, Poles will be cremated, Russians will be cremated; people will come from the West and from the South, from the continent and from islands. People in prison stripes will come, they will rebuild ruined German towns, plough the fallow soil and when they weaken from pitiless toil, from an eternal *Bewegung!*[9] *Bewegung!* the doors of the gas chambers will open. The chambers will be improved, more economical, more cleverly camouflaged. They will be like those in Dresden about which legends were already rife.

The cars are already empty. A thin, pock-marked SS-man calmly glances inside, nods his head with disgust, encompasses us with his glance and points inside:

"*Rein.*[1] Clean it out!"

We jump inside. Babies, naked monsters with huge heads and bloated bellies, lie scattered about in corners amidst human excrement and lost watches. They are carried out like chickens: a few of them making a handful.

"Don't take them to the truck. Let the women have them," says the SS-man lighting a cigarette. His lighter has stuck, he is extremely busy with it.

"For God's sake, take these babies," I burst out, for the women run away from me in terror, drawing in their heads between lifted shoulders.

The name of God is strangely unnecessary, for the women with the children go to the trucks, all of them—there is no exception. We all know what that means and look at one another with hate and horror.

---

5. Order in everything (German).   6. Large port city in the Netherlands.   7. One State, One People, One Leader! (the slogan of Nazi Germany).   8. A river running through central Poland.   9. Hurry up! (German).   1. Clean it (German).

"What's that, you don't want them?" The pock-marked SS-man asked as though surprised and reproachful, and starts to ready his revolver.

"No need to shoot, I'll take them."

A grey-haired, tall lady took the infants from me and for a while looked straight into my eyes.

"You poor child," she whispered smiling. Stumbling on the gravel she walked away.

I leaned on the side of a railway car. I was extremely tired. Someone is tugging my arm.

"*En avant*,[2] under the rails, come on!"

I gaze: the face flickers before my eyes, it melts—it is huge and transparent—it becomes confused with the trees, immobile and strangely black, with the pouring throngs . . . I blink my eyes sharply: Henri.

"Look here, Henri, are we good people?"

"Why ask stupid questions?"

"You see, my friend, an unreasonable rage at these people wells up in me that I must be here on their account. I am not in the least sorry for them, that they're going to the gas chambers. May the ground open under them all. I'd throw myself on them with my fists. This must be pathological, I can't understand it."

"Oh, no, quite the contrary, it's normal, foreseen and taken into account. You are tired with this unloading business, you're rebellious, and rage can best be vented on someone weaker. It's even desirable that you should vent it. That's common sense, *compris?*" says the Frenchman somewhat ironically, placing himself comfortably under the rails. "Look at the Greeks, they know how to make the best of it. They gobble up everything they lay their hands on; I saw one of them finish a whole jar of jam."

"Cattle. Half of them will die tomorrow of the trots."

"Cattle? You, too, were hungry."

"Cattle," I repeat obstinately. I close my eyes, hear the shrieks, feel the trembling of the ground and the humid air on my lips. My throat is completely dry.

The flow of people is endless, the trucks growl like enraged dogs. Corpses are brought out of the cars before my eyes; trampled children, cripples laid out with the corpses, and crowds, crowds . . . Railway cars are brought alongside the loading platform, the piles of rags, suitcases and rucksacks grow, people get out, look at the sun, breathe, beg for water, enter the trucks, drive away. Again cars are rolled up, again people . . . I feel the pictures become confused within me, I don't know if all this is really happening, or if I'm dreaming. I suddenly see the green of trees rocking with an entire street, with a motley crowd: but yes, it's the Avenue![3] My head is whirring. I feel that in a moment I will vomit.

Henri tugs at my arm.

"Don't sleep, we're going to load the stuff."

There are no more people. Stirring up huge clouds of dust, the last trucks move along the highway in the distance, the train has left, the SS-men walk stiff-necked on the emptied loading platform, the silver on their collars

2. Forward (French). 3. A famous boulevard in the center of Warsaw that used to be the Polish king's route from the current Old Town to outside the city.

sparkling. Their boots gleam, their bloated red faces shine. There is a woman among them. Only now do I realize that she been here all the time, this dried-up, bosomless, bony woman. Sparse, colourless hair combed smoothly back and tied in a "Nordic"[4] knot, her hands in the pockets of her wide trouser-skirt. She strides from one end of the loading platform to the other, a rat-like, rancorous smile on her dry lips. She hates feminine beauty with the hatred of a repulsive woman aware of her repulsiveness. Yes, I have seen her many times and well remember her; she's the commandant of the FKL; she has come to look over her acquisitions, for some of the women have been stood aside and will walk to the camp. Our boys, hairdressers from Zaune,[5] will shave their heads completely and will have no end of fun at the sight of their humiliation, so alien to camp life.

So we load the stuff. We drag the heavy valises, spacious, well stocked, and with an effort throw them on the truck. There they are stacked, rammed down, crammed; anything that can be cut is carved up with a knife for the pleasure of it and in search of alcohol and perfume; the latter is poured right over oneself. One of the valises opens up: clothing, shirts, books tumble out . . . I grab a bundle, it is heavy, I open it: gold, two good handfuls— watch cases, bracelets, rings, necklaces, diamonds . . .

"*Gib her*,"[6]—an SS-man says calmly, holding up an open brief case full of gold and coloured foreign banknotes. He closes it, gives it to an officer, takes another empty one and stands on guard at another truck. The gold will go to the *Reich*.[7]

Heat, sweltering heat. The air stands like an immobile, white-hot column. Throats are parched, every spoken word causes pain. Oh, for a drink! We work feverishly: faster and faster, if only to get into shade, if only to rest. We finish loading, the last trucks leave; we pick up every bit of paper lying on the railway track, dig out of the fine gravel the alien rubbish of the transport, "so that no trace of that filth is left," and at the moment when the last truck disappears beyond the trees and we finally go towards the rails to rest and drink (maybe the Frenchman will again buy it from the guard?), the whistle of the railway man is heard from beyond the bend. Slowly, extremely slowly cars roll up, the locomotive whistles back screechingly, from the windows human faces look out, pale and crumpled and flattened like paper cut-outs, their eyes huge and feverish. The trucks are here already, and the calm gentleman with his notebook; the SS-men with brief cases for the gold and money come out of the canteen. We open the cars.

No, self-control is no longer possible. Valises are brutally jerked out of people's hands, overcoats torn off. "Go on, go on, move on!" They go, they pass on. Men, women, children. Some of them know . . .

Here is a woman walking quickly, hurrying imperceptibly but feverishly. A small child only a few years old, with the rosy, chubby face of a cherub, runs after her; it cannot catch up with her and holds out its little arms crying: "Mummy, mummy!"

"You, woman, pick up the child!"

---

4. A northern (especially Scandinavian) style, encouraged by the Nazis to establish an image of Teutonic racial purity.   **5.** The "sauna" barracks, in front of Canada, where prisoners were bathed, shaved, and deloused.   **6.** Give it to me (German).   **7.** The German state.

"It isn't mine, sir, it isn't mine!" the woman shouts hysterically and, covering her face with her hands, runs away. She wants to hide, she wants to catch up with the other women who will not go by truck, who will walk, who will live. She is young, healthy and pretty, she wants to live.

But the child follows her, complaining loudly:

"Mummy, mummy, don't run away!"

"It isn't mine, no, it isn't!"

Finally, Andrei, a sailor from Sevastopol,[8] caught up with her. His eyes were bleary from vodka and the heat. He caught up with her, knocked her off her feet with one wide swing of his arm, grabbed her by the hair when she was falling and put her on her feet her again. His face is livid with rage.

"Oh, you, *yebi tvoyu mat' blad' jevreyskaya!*[9] So you'd run away from your child! I'll fix you, you whore!" He caught her round her waist, choked down her shriek with a huge paw and with a swing threw her like a heavy sack of grain on the truck.

"That's for you! Take it, you bitch!" and threw the child at her feet.

"*Gut gemacht,*[1] that's how unnatural mothers should be punished," said the SS-man who stood at the truck. "*Gut, gut Russki.*"[2]

"Shut up!" Andrei growled through his teeth and walked up to the railway cars. He drew out a canteen hidden under a pile of rags, unscrewed it, put it to his mouth and then to mine. Raw alcohol. It burns the throat. A roar in the head, my legs wobble under me, my gorge rises.

Suddenly, from this tide of humanity which, like a river driven by an invisible force, blindly pushes on toward the trucks, a girl emerged, jumped lightly from the car onto the gravel, and looked about her with a searching glance like one surprised at something.

Thick blond hair has spilled in a soft wave on her shoulders; she tossed it back impatiently. She instinctively passed her hands over her blouse, furtively adjusted her skirt. She stood like that for a moment. Finally, she tore her eyes away from the crowd and her gaze moved over our faces as though searching for someone. Unconsciously I sought to catch her glance, until our eyes met.

"Listen, tell me, where are they taking us?"

I looked at her. Here, before me, stood a girl with beautiful blond hair, wonderful breasts in an organdy summer blouse, her look wise and mature. Here she stood looking straight into my face and waited. Here, the gas chamber: mass death, loathsome and revolting. Here, the camp: a shaved head, quilted Soviet trousers in all that heat, the obnoxious, sickly odour of dirty, overheated feminine body; the animal hunger, inhuman toil, and the same gas chamber, only the death still more disgusting, more revolting, more horrible. Whoever has once entered here will never again pass the sentry post, not even as a handful of ashes, will never return to his former life.

"Why did she ever bring it here, they'll take it away from her," I thought automatically, seeing on her wrist a wonderful watch on a fine, gold bracelet. Tuśka had one like it, but hers was on a narrow, black ribbon.

"Listen, answer me."

8. A Soviet (now Russian) port on the Black Sea.   9. An untranslatable, extremely vulgar Russian expression.   1. Well done (German).   2. Good, good, Russky (German).

I remained silent. She set her mouth.

"I already know," she said with a shade of haughty contempt in her voice, throwing her head back; boldly she walked up to the trucks. Someone wanted to stop her, but she boldly moved him aside and ran up the steps into the nearly filled truck. In the distance I saw only the thick, blond hair tousled by the speed.

I went into cars, carried out the infants, threw out the luggage. I touched corpses but could not overcome the wild terror welling up within me. I ran away from them but they lay everywhere: placed side by side on the gravel, on the edge of the concrete platform, in the cars. Babies, repulsive, naked women, men twisted by convulsions. I ran away as far as I could. Someone caned me across the back, out of the corner of my eye I notice a cursing SS-man, I slip away from him and mix with the stripe-clad "Canada." Finally, I again crawl under the rails. The sun has gone down over the horizon and bathes the loading platform with its bloody, waning light. The shadows of the trees grow monstrously long; in the silence that settles on nature with the coming of evening, human cries soar skywards ever louder, ever more insistently.

It was only from here, from under the rails, that the entire inferno seething on the platform can be seen. Here is a couple fallen on the ground, locked in a desperate embrace. He has dug his fingers convulsively into her flesh and caught her dress in his teeth. She is shrieking hysterically, swearing, blaspheming until, trampled down by a boot, she gurgles and is still. Torn apart like pieces of wood, they are driven like animals into a truck. Here, four men from "Canada" strain under the weight of a corpse: a huge, swollen old woman: they swear and sweat with the effort, kick out of the way stray children who get underfoot all over the platform and howl horribly like dogs. They catch the children by the neck, by the head and arms and throw them in a pile on the trucks. Those four cannot manage to lift the woman to the truck, they call others and with a collective heave push the mountain of flesh on the floor of the truck. Huge, bloated, swollen corpses are carried from the whole ramp. Thrown among these are cripples, paralyzed, smothered and unconscious people. The mountain of corpses seethes, whines and howls. The driver starts the motor and drives away.

"*Halt, halt!*" the SS-man shrieks from a distance. "Stop, stop, damn you!"

They are dragging an old man in a full dress suit with an armband on his sleeve. His head is knocked about on the gravel and the stones, he groans and laments incessantly and monotonously: "*Ich will mit dem Herrn Kommendanten sprechen,* I want to speak to the commandant." He repeats this with senile doggedness all the way. Thrown into the truck, trampled down by someone's foot, smothered, he continues to rattle: "*Ich will mit dem . . . .*"

"Calm down, man!" calls out a young SS-man to him, laughing boisterously, "in half an hour you will speak to the supreme commandant! Only don't forget to say '*Heil Hitler*' to him."

Others carry a little girl who has only one leg, they hold her by the arms and that leg. Tears stream down her cheeks, and she whimpers pitifully: "Gentlemen, it hurts, it hurts . . ." They throw her on the truck with the corpses. She will be cremated alive with them.

Night falls, cool and starlit. We lie on the rails. It is immensely quiet. On tall posts anemic lamps throw out circles of light into the impenetrable darkness. A step into it and a man disappears irretrievably. But the eyes of the guards watch carefully. The automatics are ready to fire.

"Have you changed your shoes?" Henri asks me.

"No."

"Why not?"

"Man, I've had enough, completely enough."

"So soon, after the first transport? Just think, I . . . since Christmas, probably a million people have passed through my hands. The transports from around Paris are the worst ones, a man always comes upon acquaintances."

"And what do you tell them?"

"That they're going to have a bath and then we'll meet in the camp, And what would you say?"

I remain silent. We drink coffee spiked with alcohol; someone opens a tin of cocoa, mixes it with sugar. This is ladled up with the hand; the cocoa pastes up the mouth. Again coffee, again alcohol.

"What are we waiting for, Henri?"

"There'll be another transport. But no one knows."

"If there's another, I'm not going to unload it. I can't do it."

"It's got hold of you, yes? A fine 'Canada!' " Henri smiles benevolently and disappears in the dark. He returns shortly.

"Very well. But be careful that the SS-man doesn't catch you. You'll stay here all the time. And I'll fix you up with a pair of shoes."

"Don't bother me with the shoes."

I am sleepy. It is deep night.

Again *antreten*,[3] again a transport. Cars emerge from the dark, pass the strip of light and again disappear in the gloom. The loading platform is small but the circle of light is still smaller. We will unload the cars as they come, one by one. Trucks growl somewhere, they back up to the steps, spectrally black, their reflectors light up the trees. *Wasser! Luft!*[4] The same all over again, a late showing of the same film: they discharge a volley from their automatics; the railway cars calm down. Only a little girl has leaned down to her waist from the little window of the car and losing her balance fell to the gravel. For a while she lay stunned, finally got up and started walking around in a circle, faster and faster, waving her arms stiffly as if at calisthenics, drawing her breath in noisily, and monotonously and howling shrilly. Suffocating—she has gone mad. She set the nerves on edge, so an SS-man ran up to her and kicked her with a hobbled boot in the small of the back; she fell. He pressed her down with his foot, took his revolver out and fired once and then again; she lay, kicking the ground with her feet until she stiffened. The cars begin to be opened.

I was again at the cars. A warm, sweetish odour gushed out. The car is filled to half its height with a mound of humanity: immobile, horribly tangled up but still steaming.

"*Ausladen!*"[5] sounded the voice of the SS-man who emerged out of the dark. On his breast hung a portable reflector. He lighted up the inside of the car.

"Why are you standing so stupidly? Unload!" and he swished his cane across my back. I grabbed the arm of a corpse, his hand closed convulsively

3. In formation (German).   4. Water! Air! (German).   5. Unload! (German).

around mine. I jerked away with a shriek and ran off. My heart pounded, my gorge rose. Nausea suddenly doubled me up. Crouching under the car I vomited. Staggering, I stole away under the stack of rails.

I lay on the kind, cool iron and dreamed of returning to the camp, about my bunk on which there is no straw mattress, about a bit of sleep among comrades who will not go to the gas chambers in the night. All at once the camp seemed like some haven of quiet; others are constantly dying and somehow one is still alive, has something to eat, strength to work, has a fatherland, a home, a girl . . .

The lights twinkle spectrally, the wave of humanity flows endlessly—turbid, feverish, stupefied. It seems to these people that they are beginning a new life in the camp and they prepare themselves psychologically for a hard struggle for existence. They do not know that they will immediately die and that the gold, the money, the diamonds which they providently conceal in the folds and seams of their clothing, in the heels of their shoes, in recesses of their bodies, will no longer be needed by them. Efficient, business-like people will rummage in their intestines, pull gold from under the tongue, diamonds from the placenta and the rectum. They will pull out their gold teeth and send them in tightly nailed-up cases to Berlin.[6]

The black figures of the SS-men walk about calm and proficient. The gentleman with the notebook in hand puts down the last check marks, adds up the figures; fifteen thousand.

Many, many trucks have driven off to the crematorium.

They are finishing up. The corpses spread on the ramp will be taken by the last truck, the luggage is all loaded. "Canada," loaded with bread, jams, sugar, smelling of perfume and clean underwear, lines up to march away. The "kapo" finishes packing the tea cauldron with gold, silk, and coffee. That's for the guards at the gates, they will let the commando pass without a search. For a few days the camp will live off that transport: eat its hams and its sausages, its preserved and fresh fruit, drink its brandies and liqueurs, wear its underwear, trade in its gold and luggage. Much will be taken out of the camp by civilians to Silesia, to Cracow and points beyond. They will bring cigarettes, eggs, vodka and letters from home.

For a few days the camp will speak about the "Sosnowiec-Będzin" transport. It was a good, rich transport.

When we return to the camp, the stars begin to pale, the sky becomes more and more transparent, rises higher up above us: the night clears. It foretells a fine, hot day.

Mighty columns of smoke rise up from the crematoria and merge into a huge, black river which rolls very slowly across the sky over Birkenau and disappears beyond the forests in the direction of Trzebinia.[7] The Sosnowiec transport is already being cremated.

We pass an SS detachment marching with machine guns to change the guard. They walk in step, shoulder to shoulder, one mass, one will.

"*Und morgen die ganze Welt* . . ."[8] they sing lustily.

"*Rechts ran!*[9] To the right march!" comes the order from up front. We move out of their way.

---

6. The capital of Germany.   7. A town west of Auschwitz, near Krakow.   8. And tomorrow the whole world (German); the last line of the Nazi song "The Rotten Bones Are Shaking," written by Hans Baumann. The previous line reads "for today Germany belongs to us."   9. To the right, get going! (German).

MAHASWETA DEVI
born 1926

Author of more than a hundred books, including novels, plays, and collections of short stories, Mahasweta Devi is the leading contemporary writer in Bengali, the language of the state of West Bengal in eastern India, and of neighboring Bangladesh as well. Translations of her work into other Indian languages and into English have brought her national and international recognition. One of several modern Bengali writers committed to social and political critique from a leftist perspective, Mahasweta (the *Devi* in her name is a term of respect attached to a woman's name in Bengali) writes about peasants, outcastes, women, tribal peoples who live in the forest regions of India, and other marginalized groups struggling to survive and resisting their exploitation by dominant groups. Her fiction and plays are distinguished by a powerful, direct, unsentimental style and by the subtlety and sensitivity with which she approaches the themes of struggle, resistance, and empowerment.

Bengali fiction from the 1930s onward reflects the growing radicalization of various segments of Bengali society, including the rapidly growing middle class and the urban poor. Since the 1920s, when sharecroppers revolted against landlords and the British colonial government, Bengal has been the arena of a series of peasant uprisings and unrest among the masses. The region was devastated by a man-made famine in 1943. When India was partitioned in 1947, the eastern portion of Bengal (the former East Bengal) became East Pakistan, a part of the newly formed nation of Pakistan, which had been conceived as a homeland for the Muslim populations of the Indian subcontinent. As a result, the whole of Bengal was torn apart by Hindu-Muslim communal riots and the massive displacement of populations. Exploited as much in independent India as in the colonial era, the Munda and other tribal peoples in Bengal and the neighboring state of Bihar rose in revolt, and in the 1960s urban students participated in peasant and tribal struggles in a movement known as the Naxalbari movement (after the village where it began), only to be brutally suppressed by the Bengal state government. Yet another upheaval was caused by East Pakistan's proclamation of independence from Pakistan as the new nation of Bangladesh in 1970. Mahasweta and other major Bengali writers, such as Manik Bandyopadhyay (1908–1956), and Hasan Azizul Huq (born 1938), have responded to these events with fiction that shifted the focus of modern Bengali literature from the lives of the educated, urban middle class to the politics of the exploitation of the underclasses.

Mahasweta Devi was born into a family of distinguished and politically engaged artists and intellectuals in Dhaka (Dacca) in the former East Bengal (now Bangladesh). After graduating in 1946 from Santiniketan, the famous alternative school established by Rabindranath Tagore, she devoted several years to political activism in rural Bengal, in collaboration with her first husband. During this time she held a variety of jobs, including teaching. Throughout, Mahasweta wrote mainly fiction but also columns and articles for journals. In 1963, after receiving a master's degree in English literature at Calcutta University, she became a professor of English at a Calcutta college.

Although Mahasweta's early work was motivated by a concern for social justice, it was not until the Naxalbari student-peasant uprisings of the 1960s that the lives of tribal peoples and peasants became the primary focus of her fiction. At this time she adopted a pattern of activism that she still maintains, participating in, observing, and recording the struggles of oppressed groups in Bengal. Her experience with the Naxalbari movement resulted in *Hajar Churasir Ma* (Number 1084's mother, 1973), a nationally acclaimed novel indicting organized violence on the part of the state. In *Aranyer Adhikar* (Rights over the forest, 1977), perhaps the most famous of her novels, she turned to the history of the Munda tribal revolt in Bengal and Bihar in the nineteenth century. Since 1984, when she gave up her academic position, she has devoted her time entirely to grassroots work among tribals and outcastes in rural Bengal and Bihar and also edits a quarterly journal, the main contributors to which are people from these marginalized communities.

In "Breast-Giver" ("Stanadayini," 1980) Mahasweta focuses not so much on the resistance of the oppressed as on the dynamics of oppression itself. Theoretically a member of the highest of the Hindu castes, the brahmin Kangalicharan is a helpless victim of the rich patriarch Haldarbabu's clan. Forced to become the wage earner of the household, Kangalicharan's wife, Jashoda, becomes a wet-nurse for the Haldar family, who retain her services until she becomes useless to them. Mahasweta's narrative is aimed at exposing the relentless collusion of patriarchal and capitalist ideologies in the exploitation of the disadvantaged. Themselves victims, the women of the Haldar household are Jashoda's chief exploiters. The status of wage earner not only fails to release Jashoda from the expectations of wifehood and motherhood but saddles her with the ultimately self-destructive task of being "mother of the world." Nevertheless, neither victimization nor its awareness fully robs Jashoda and Kangalicharan of their sense of agency and power.

Like the funeral wailer and the medicine woman in Mahasweta's short story "Dhowli" or the landless tribal laborer in "Draupadi," Jashoda, the principal character in "Breast-Giver," is a working woman or, as the narrator puts it, *"professional mother."* As translator Gayatri Spivak has pointed out, in the story's title the author deliberately foregrounds the centrality of the female body in Jashoda's transactions with her clients—she is not just a "wet-nurse," a provider of milk, but a "breast-giver," a distinction further underscored by the grim ironies that unfold in the narrative of her career. The story offers new avenues for examining the points at which gender and class oppression intersect.

"Breast-Giver" is representative of Mahasweta's fiction, in which the deceptive surface of linear, seemingly realistic narrative is constantly undercut by mythic and satirical inflections. Not only is Jashoda the breast-giver named for Yashoda, the mother of the beloved cowherd-child-god Krishna, but in the course of the narrative the professional mother merges with other Indian icons of motherhood—sacred cows, the Lion-seated goddess, "mother India" herself. The story is open to competing, yet not mutually exclusive, analyses, in terms of Marxist and feminist economic and social theory, myth, or political allegory. While the many layers of meaning in "Breast-Giver" are accessible even in translation, much of the power of the original derives from Mahasweta's distinctive style and voice. In this story, as in the author's other works, classical Hindu myths connect with quotations from Shakespeare and Marx, and slang, dialect, literary Bengali, and English blend together. The result is a powerful language that in many respects resembles modern Bengali usage, yet remains a unique creation of the author.

PRONOUNCING GLOSSARY

The following list uses common English syllables and stress accents to provide rough equivalents of selected words whose pronunciation may be unfamiliar to the general reader.

Arun: *o-roon'*

Basini: *bah'-shee-nee*

Basanti: *bah'-shon-tee*

Beleghata: *bay'-lay-gah'-tah*

Dakshineswar: *dok'-khi-naysh'-wuhr*

Haldarkartha: *huhl'-duhr-kuhr-tah*

Harisal: *ho-ree'-shahl*

Jagaddhatri: *jo-god-dah'-tree*

Jashoda: *jo'-shoh-dah*

Kangalicharan Patitundo: *kahn-gah'-lee-chuh-ruhn po'-tee-toon'-do*

Kayastha: *kah-yuhs'-tuh*

Mahasweta Devi: *muh-hah'-shway-tah day'-vee*

Maniktala-Bagmari: *mah-neek'-to-lah—bahg'-mah-ree*

Nabin: *no'-been*

Naxalbari: *nuhk'-shuhl-bah'-ree*

Neno: *nay'-noh*

Padmarani: *puhd'-mah-rah-nee*

Sarala: *suh'-ro-lah*

Saratchandra: *shuh-ruht-chuhnd'-ruh*

Savitri: *shah-beet'-ree*

stanadayini: *sto'-no-dah'-ye-nee*

Tarakeswar: *tah'-ruh-kaysh-shor*

Breast-Giver[1]

I

> My aunties they lived in the woods, in the forest their home
> they did make.
> Never did Aunt say here's a sweet dear, eat, sweetie,
> here's a piece of cake.

Jashoda doesn't remember if her aunt was kind or unkind. It is as if she were Kangalicharan's wife from birth, the mother of twenty children, living or dead, counted on her fingers. Jashoda doesn't remember at all when there was no child in her womb, when she didn't feel faint in the morning, when Kangali's body didn't *drill* her body like a geologist in a darkness lit only by an oil-lamp. She never had the time to calculate if she could or could not bear motherhood. Motherhood was always her way of living and keeping alive her world of countless beings. Jashoda was a mother by profession, *professional mother.* Jashoda was not an *amateur* mama like the daughters and wives of the master's house. The world belongs to the professional. In this city, this kingdom, the amateur beggar-pickpocket-hooker has no place. Even the mongrel on the path or sidewalk, the greedy crow at the garbage don't make room for the upstart *amateur.* Jashoda had taken motherhood as her profession.

The responsibility was Mr. Haldar's new son-in-law's Studebaker and the sudden desire of the youngest son of the Haldar-house to be a driver. When the boy suddenly got a whim in mind or body, he could not rest unless he had satisfied it instantly. These sudden whims reared up in the loneliness of the afternoon and kept him at slave labor like the khalifa of Bagdad.[2] What he had done so far on that account did not oblige Jashoda to choose motherhood as a profession.

One afternoon the boy, driven by lust, attacked the cook and the cook, since her body was heavy with rice, stolen fishheads, and turnip greens, and her body languid with sloth, lay back, saying, "Yah, do what you like." Thus did the incubus of Bagdad get off the boy's shoulders and he wept repentant tears, mumbling, "Auntie, don't tell." The cook—saying, "What's there to tell?"—went quickly to sleep. She never told anything. She was sufficiently proud that her body had attracted the boy. But the thief thinks of the loot.

---

1. Translated by Gayatri Chakravorty Spivak. Spivak has italicized English words that appeared in the original Bengali text.   2. Or caliph ("ruler") of Baghdad; according to legend, he kept a djinn ("spirit") who would do his bidding.

The boy got worried at the improper supply of fish and fries in his dish. He considered that he'd be fucked if the cook gave him away. Therefore on another afternoon, driven by the Bagdad djinn, he stole his mother's ring, slipped it into the cook's pillowcase, raised a hue and cry, and got the cook kicked out. Another afternoon he lifted the radio set from his father's room and sold it. It was difficult for his parents to find the connection between the hour of the afternoon and the boy's behavior, since his father had created him in the deepest night by the astrological calendar[3] and the tradition of the Haldars of Harisal. In fact you enter the sixteenth century as you enter the gates of this house. To this day you take your wife by the astrological almanac. But these matters are mere blind alleys. Motherhood did not become Jashoda's profession for these afternoon-whims.

One afternoon, leaving the owner of the shop, Kangalicharan was returning home with a handful of stolen samosas and sweets under his dhoti.[4] Thus he returns daily. He and Jashoda eat rice. Their three offspring return before dark and eat stale samosas and sweets. Kangalicharan stirs the seething vat of milk in the sweet shop and cooks and feeds "food cooked by a good Brahmin"[5] to those pilgrims at the Lionseated goddess's[6] temple who are proud that they are not themselves "fake Brahmins by sleight of hand." Daily he lifts a bit of flour and such and makes life easier. When he puts food in his belly in the afternoon he feels a filial inclination toward Jashoda, and he goes to sleep after handling her capacious bosom. Coming home in the afternoon, Kangalicharan was thinking of his imminent pleasure and tasting paradise at the thought of his wife's large round breasts. He was picturing himself as a farsighted son of man as he thought that marrying a fresh young thing, not working her overmuch, and feeding her well led to pleasure in the afternoon. At such a moment the Haldar son, complete with Studebaker, swerving by Kangalicharan, ran over his feet and shins.

Instantly a crowd gathered. It was an accident in front of the house after all, "otherwise I'd have drawn blood," screamed Nabin, the pilgrim-guide. He guides the pilgrims to the Mother goddess of Shakti-power,[7] his temper is hot in the afternoon sun. Hearing him roar, all the Haldars who were at home came out. The Haldar chief started thrashing his son, roaring, "You'll kill a Brahmin,[8] you bastard, you unthinking bull?" The youngest son-in-law breathed relief as he saw that his Studebaker was not much damaged and, to prove that he was better human material than the money-rich, *culture*-poor in-laws, he said in a voice as fine as the finest muslin, "Shall we let the man die? Shouldn't we take him to the hospital?"—Kangali's boss was also in the crowd at the temple and, seeing the samosas and sweets flung on the roadway was about to say, "Eh Brahmin!! Stealing food?" Now he held his tongue and said, "Do that *sir*." The youngest son-in-law and the Haldar-chief took Kangalicharan quickly to the hospital. The master felt deeply grieved. Dur-

---

3. In traditional Indian belief, the position of the stars and planets at the time of conception and birth is one of the forces that shape the individual's personality and life.   4. Untailored cloth worn as a garment for the lower body by Indian men. "Samosas": savory, hot snacks.   5. In Hindu communities, food cooked by brahmins, who are highest in the caste hierarchy because of their ritually pure status, is considered to be beneficial.   6. Durga, a martial goddess who rides a lion; her worship is popular throughout Bengal.   7. The goddess, worshiped as the mother of the universe, is said to be a personification of Shakti, the energy of the cosmos.   8. A member of the priestly elite castes. Killing a brahmin is the worst offence a Hindu can commit.

ing the Second War, when he helped the anti-Fascist struggle of the Allies by buying and selling scrap iron—then Kangali was a mere lad. Reverence for Brahmins crawled in Mr. Haldar's veins. If he couldn't get chatterjee-babu in the morning he would touch the feet of Kangali, young enough to be his son, and put a pinch of dust from his chapped feet on his own tongue.[9] Kangali and Jashoda came to his house on feast days and Jashoda was sent a gift of cloth and vermillion when his daughters-in-law were pregnant.[1] Now he said to Kangali—"Kangali! don't worry son. You won't suffer as long as I'm around." Now it was that he thought that Kangali's feet, being turned to ground meat, he would not be able to taste their dust. He was most unhappy at the thought and he started weeping as he said, "What has the son of a bitch done." He said to the doctor at the hospital, "Do what you can! Don't worry about cash."

But the doctors could not bring the feet back. Kangali returned as a lame Brahmin. Haldarbabu had a pair of crutches made. The very day Kangali returned home on crutches, he learned that food had come to Jashoda from the Haldar house every day. Nabin was third in rank among the pilgrim-guides. He could only claim thirteen percent of the goddess's food[2] and so had an inferiority complex. Inspired by seeing Rama-Krishna[3] in the movies a couple of times, he called the goddess "my crazy one" and by the book of the Kali-worshippers kept his consciousness immersed in local spirits. He said to Kangali, "I put flowers on the crazy one's feet in your name. She said I have a share in Kangali's house, he will get out of the hospital by that fact." Speaking of this to Jashoda, Kangali said, "What? When I wasn't there, you were getting it off with Nabin?" Jashoda then grabbed Kangali's suspicious head between the two hemispheres of the globe and said, "Two maid servants from the big house slept here every day to guard me. Would I look at Nabin? Am I not your faithful wife?"

In fact Kangali heard of his wife's flaming devotion at the big house as well. Jashoda had fasted at the mother's temple, had gone through a female ritual, and had travelled to the outskirts to pray at the feet of the local guru.[4] Finally the Lionseated came to her in a dream as a midwife carrying a *bag* and said, "Don't worry. Your man will return." Kangali was most over-whelmed by this. Haldarbabu said, "See, Kangali? The bastard unbelievers say, the Mother gives a dream, why togged as a midwife? I say, she creates as mother, and preserves as midwife."

Then Kangali said, "Sir! How shall I work at the sweetshop any longer. I can't stir the vat with my kerutches.[5] You are god. You are feeding so many people in so many ways. I am not begging. Find me a job."

Haldarbabu said, "Yes Kangali! I've kept you a spot. I'll make you a shop in the corner of my porch. The Lionseated is across the way! Pilgrims come

<hr>

9. Younger men and women show respect to older persons and to those of higher social rank by touching their feet and (symbolically) placing dust from the feet on their own heads or lips. "*Chatterjeebabu*," or Chatterjee, is a brahmin family name; *babu* is a term of respect used for men of high castes or rank. 1. Married brahmin women are given gifts of cloth and vermilion (red cosmetic) powder, symbols of good luck, in return for the blessings that they are thought to be capable of giving pregnant women. 2. Temple priests divide up the food offerings pilgrims and devotees bring to the temple. 3. A renowned Bengali mystic and spiritual teacher (1836–1886), who was a priest and worshiper of the fierce and enigmatic goddess Kali, to whom goats are sacrificed. Some Kali worshipers engage in esoteric ritual practices, including breaking the Hindu ritual taboo against consuming alcohol. 4. Chaste women are thought to be capable of saving their husband's lives by the power they accumulate through fasting and performing other rituals of austerity and devotion. 5. Crutches.

and go. Put up a shop of dry sweets.[6] Now there's a wedding in the house. It's my bastard seventh son's wedding. As long as there's no shop, I'll send you food."

Hearing this, Kangali's mind took wing like a rainbug in the rainy season. He came home and told Jashoda, "Remember Kalidasa's pome? You eat because there isn't, wouldn't have got if there was? That's my lot, chuck. Master says he'll put up a shop after his son's wedding. Until then he'll send us food. Would this have happened if I had legs? All is Mother's will, dear!"[7]

Everyone is properly amazed that in this fallen age[8] the wishes and wills of the Lionseated, herself found by a dream-command a hundred and fifty years ago, are circulating around Kangalicharan Patitundo. Haldarbabu's change of heart is also Mother's will. He lives in independent India, the India that makes no distinctions among people, kingdoms, languages, varieties of Brahmins, varieties of Kayasthas[9] and so on. But he made his cash in the British era, when *Divide and Rule*[1] was the policy. Haldarbabu's mentality was constructed then. Therefore he doesn't trust anyone—not a Panjabi-Oriya-Bihari-Gujarati-Marathi-Muslim.[2] At the sight of an unfortunate Bihari child or a starvation-ridden Oriya beggar his flab-protected heart, located under a forty-two inch Gopal brand vest, does not itch with the rash of kindness. He is a successful son of Harisal. When he sees a West Bengali fly he says, "Tchah! at home even the flies were fat—in the bloody West[3] everything is pinched-skinny." All the temple people are struck that such a man is filling with the milk of humankindness toward the West Bengali Kangalicharan. For some time this news is the general talk. Haldarbabu is such a patriot that, if his nephews or grandsons read the lives of the nation's leaders in their schoolbook, he says to his employees, "Nonsense! why do they make 'em read the lives of characters from Dhaka, Mymansingh, Jashore?[4] Harisal is made of the bone of the martyr god. One day it will emerge that the *Vedas* and the *Upanishads* were also written in Harisal."[5] Now his employees tell him, "You have had a *change of heart*, so much kindness for a West Bengali, you'll see there is divine *purpose* behind this." The Boss is delighted. He laughs loudly and says, "There's no East or West for a Brahmin. If there's a sacred thread[6] around his neck you have to give him respect even when he's taking a shit."

Thus all around blow the sweet winds of sympathy-compassion-kindness. For a few days, whenever Nabin tries to think of the Lionseated, the heavy-breasted, languid-hipped body of Jashoda floats in his mind's eye. A slow rise

6. That is, not dipped in syrup, used as offerings for the goddess.   7. Kangali misquotes a Sanskrit verse attributed to Kālidāsa (ca. 4th century C.E.), the eminent classical poet of the Gupta era.   8. Hindus believe that the current era is one of deterioration, the fourth and last phase in the pattern of fourfold cosmic era cycles (*yuga*), by means of which time is measured in the Hindu tradition.   9. A high-ranking north Indian caste of administrators and educators.   1. Refers to the British colonial government's policy of dealing with Hindu and Muslim communities as separate constituencies. Mahasweta satirizes the rhetoric of politicians who claim that the independent nation of India has achieved equality for all its members, regardless of differences in language, regional affiliation, economic class, or caste.   2. Parody of a line in the Indian national anthem (written by the Bengali author Rabindranath Tagore), in which various regions of (preindependence) India are named: "Punjab-Sindh-Gujarat-Maratha-Dravida-Utkala-Vanga."   3. Harisal is in the eastern part of Bengal, in what was formerly East Bengal, later East Pakistan, and now Bangladesh. The British colonial government partitioned the older state of Bengal into a western and an eastern section in 1905.   4. In eastern Bengal.   5. Haldar asserts the superiority of Harisal, revealing the extent of his provincialism in the claim that the Vedas and the *Upanisads*, the oldest Sanskrit sacred texts of the Hindus, were probably written in Harisal (contrary to the scholarly opinion that the *Vedas* were composed by the Indo-Aryans who lived in northwestern India).   6. A symbol of brahmin caste identity, received at the time of religious initiation.

spreads in his body at the thought that perhaps she is appearing in his dream as Jashoda just as she appeared in Jashoda's as a midwife. The fifty percent pilgrim-guide says to him, "Male and female both get this disease. Bind the root of a white forget-me-not in your ear when you take a piss."

Nabin doesn't agree. One day he tells Kangali, "As the Mother's[7] son I won't make a racket with Shakti-power. But I've thought of a plan. There's no problem with making a Hare Krishna racket.[8] I tell you, get a Gopal in your dream. My Aunt brought a stony Gopal from Puri.[9] I give it to you. You announce that you got it in a dream. You'll see there'll be a to-do in no time, money will roll in. Start for money, later you'll get devoted to Gopal."

Kangali says, "Shame, brother! Should one joke with gods?"

"Ah get lost," Nabin scolds. Later it appears that Kangali would have done well to listen to Nabin. For Haldarbabu suddenly dies of heart failure. Shakespeare's *welkin*[1] breaks on Kangali and Jashoda's head.

2

Haldarbabu truly left Kangali in the lurch. Those wishes of the Lionseated that were manifesting themselves around Kangali *via-media* Haldarbabu disappeared into the blue like the burning promises given by a political party before the elections and became magically invisible like the heroine of a fantasy. A European witch's *bodkin* pricks the colored balloon of Kangali and Jashoda's dreams and the pair falls in deep trouble. At home, Gopal, Nepal, and Radharani whine interminably for food and abuse their mother. It is very natural for children to cry so for grub. Ever since Kangalicharan's loss of feet they'd eaten the fancy food of the Haldar household. Kangali also longs for food and is shouted at for trying to put his head in Jashoda's chest in the way of Gopal, the Divine Son.[2] Jashoda is fully an Indian woman, whose unreasonable, unreasoning, and unintelligent devotion to her husband and love for her children, whose unnatural renunciation and forgiveness have been kept alive in the popular consciousness by all Indian women from Sati-Savitri-Sita through Nirupa Roy and Chand Osmani.[3] The creeps of the world understand by seeing such women that the old Indian tradition is still flowing free—they understand that it was with such women in mind that the following aphorisms have been composed—"a female's life hangs on like a turtle's"—"her heart breaks but no word is uttered"—"the woman will burn, her ashes will fly[4] / Only then will we sing her / praise on high." Frankly, Jashoda never once wants to blame her husband for the present misfortune. Her mother-love wells up for Kangali as much as for the children. She wants to become the earth and feed her crippled husband and helpless children with a fulsome harvest. Sages did not write of this motherly feeling

---

7. That is, the mother goddess. 8. A reference to the worldwide Hare Krishna cult, an offshoot of the traditional worship of the Hindu god Krishna in India. 9. A pilgrimage center and the site of the great temple of Jagannath, a form of Krishna. "Stony Gopal": an image of Krishna made of stone. 1. Sky (archaic). 2. In the manner of the infant Krishna sucking at his mother Jashoda's breast. 3. Actresses in popular Hindi films made in Bombay in the 1940s and 1950s. Sita, or Sati ("the chaste wife"), the goddess Parvati, who sacrificed her life for the sake of her husband Siva's honor; thus her name is a word denoting all chaste wives. In the *Mahābhārata* epic, the devoted effort of Savitri saves her husband, Satyavan, from death. Sita is the devoted, self-sacrificing wife of Rama, the hero of the *Rāmāyana* epic. 4. A reference to the custom of Sati, in which virtuous widows were encouraged to burn themselves on the funeral pyres of their husbands (Hindus cremate their dead). Sati was officially banned in 1829 under British rule.

of Jashoda's for her husband. They explained female and male as Nature and the Human Principle.[5] But this they did in the days of yore—when they entered this *peninsula* from another land.[6] Such is the power of the Indian soil that all women turn into mothers here and all men remain immersed in the spirit of holy childhood. Each man the Holy Child and each woman the Divine Mother. Even those who deny this and wish to slap *current posters* to the effect of the *"eternal she"*—"Mona Lisa"—"La passionaria"—"Simone de Beauvoir," et cetera, over the old ones and look at women that way are, after all, Indian cubs. It is notable that the educated Babus desire all this from women outside the home. When they cross the threshold they want the Divine Mother in the words and conduct of the revolutionary ladies. The *process* is most complicated. Because he understood this the heroines of Saratchandra[7] always fed the hero an extra mouthful of rice. The apparent simplicity of Saratchandra's and other similar writers' writings is actually very complex and to be thought of in the evening, peacefully after a glass of wood-apple[8] juice. There is too much influence of fun and games in the lives of the people who traffic in studies and intellectualism in West Bengal and therefore they should stress the wood-apple correspondingly. We have no idea of the loss we are sustaining because we do not stress the wood-apple-type-herbal remedies correspondingly.

However, it's incorrect to cultivate the habit of repeated incursions into *byelanes* as we tell Jashoda's life story. The reader's patience, unlike the cracks in Calcutta[9] streets, will not widen by the decade. The real thing is that Jashoda was in a cleft stick. Of course they ate their fill during the Master's funeral days, but after everything was over Jashoda clasped Radharani to her bosom and went over to the big house. Her aim was to speak to the Mistress and ask for the cook's job in the vegetarian kitchen.[1]

The Mistress really grieved for the Master. But the lawyer let her know that the Master had left her the proprietorship of this house and the right to the rice warehouse. Girding herself with those assurances, she has once again taken the rudder of the family empire. She had really felt the loss of fish and fish-head.[2] Now she sees that the best butter, the best milk sweets from the best shops, heavy cream, and the best variety of bananas can also keep the body going somehow. The Mistress lights up her easychair. A six-months' babe in her lap, her grandson. So far six sons have married. Since the almanac approves of the taking of a wife almost every month of the year, the birth rooms in a row on the ground floor of the Mistress's house are hardly ever empty. The *lady doctor* and Sarala the midwife never leave the house. The Mistress has six daughters. They too breed every year and a half. So there is a constant *epidemic* of blanket-quilt-feeding spoon-bottle-oilcloth-*Johnson's baby powder*-bathing basin.

---

5. In several major schools of Indian philosophy Nature and the Human Principle are conceived as female and male in sexual relationship.   6. Reference to the coming of the Indo-Aryan tribes into India from west and central Asia, a theory advanced by Western scholars in the 19th and 20th centuries. 7. Saratchandra Chatterjee (1876—1938), the master of the sentimental middle-class novel in Bengali fiction.   8. A fruit that is used for its medicinal properties, especially as a laxative.   9. Established by the British East India Company in the 17th century, it was the capital of British India. It is now the capital of the state of West Bengal and the center of Bengali culture.   1. In Bengal, traditional Hindu women become strict vegetarians after the death of their husbands as a sign of austerity.   2. Fish is an important part of the Bengali diet.

The Mistress was out of her mind trying to feed the boy. As if relieved to see Jashoda she said, "You come like a god! Give her some milk, dear, I beg you. His mother's sick—such a brat, he won't touch a bottle." Jashoda immediately suckled the boy and pacified him. At the Mistress's special request Jashoda stayed in the house until nine p.m. and suckled the Mistress's grandson again and again. The Cook filled a big bowl with rice and curry for her own household. Jashoda said as she suckled the boy, "Mother! The Master said many things. He is gone, so I don't think of them. But Mother! Your Brahmin-son does not have his two feet. I don't think for myself. But thinking of my husband and sons I say, give me any kind of job. Perhaps you'll let me cook in your household?"

"Let me see dear! Let me think and see." The Mistress is not as sold on Brahmins as the Master was. She does not accept fully that Kangali lost his feet because of her son's afternoon whims. It was written for Kangali as well, otherwise why was he walking down the road in the blazing sun grinning from ear to ear? She looks in charmed envy at Jashoda's *mammal projections* and says, "The good lord sent you down as the legendary Cow of Fulfillment.[3] Pull the teat and milk flows! The ones I've brought to my house, haven't a quarter of this milk in their nipples!"

Jashoda says, "How true Mother! Gopal was weaned when he was three. This one hadn't come to my belly yet. Still it was like a flood of milk. Where does it come from, Mother? I have no good food, no pampering!"

This produced a lot of talk among the women at night and the menfolk got to hear it too at night. The second son, whose wife was sick and whose son drank Jashoda's milk, was particularly uxorious. The difference between him and his brothers was that the brothers created progeny as soon as the almanac gave a good day, with love or lack of love, with irritation or thinking of the accounts at the works. The second son impregnates his wife at the same *frequency,* but behind it lies deep love. The wife is often pregnant, that is an act of God. But the second son is also interested in that the wife remains beautiful at the same time. He thinks a lot about how to *combine* multiple pregnancies and beauty, but he cannot fathom it. But today, hearing from his wife about Jashoda's surplus milk, the second son said all of a sudden, "Way found."

"Way to what?"

"Uh, the way to save you pain."

"How? I'll be out of pain when you burn me. Can a year-breeder's[4] health mend?"

"It will, it will, I've got a divine engine in my hands! You'll breed yearly *and* keep your body."

The couple discussed. The husband entered his Mother's room in the morning and spoke in heavy whispers. At first the Mistress hemmed and hawed, but then she thought to herself and realized that the proposal was worth a million rupees. Daughters-in-law *will* be mothers. When they are mothers, they will suckle their children. Since they will be mothers as long as it's possible—progressive suckling will ruin their shape. Then if the sons look outside, or harass the maidservants, she won't have a voice to object.

---

3. The magical cow of Hindu legend, said to be able to fulfill all wishes.   4. A woman who gets pregnant every year.

Going out because they can't get it at home—this is just. If Jashoda becomes the infants' suckling-mother, her daily meals, clothes on feast days, and some monthly pay will be enough. The Mistress is constantly occupied with women's rituals. There Jashoda can act as the fruitful Brahmin wife.[5] Since Jashoda's misfortune is due to her son, that sin too will be lightened.

Jashoda received a portfolio when she heard her proposal. She thought of her breasts as most precious objects. At night when Kangalicharan started to give her a feel she said, "Look. I'm going to pull our weight with these. Take good care how you use them." Kangalicharan hemmed and hawed that night, of course, but his Gopal frame of mind disappeared instantly when he saw the amount of grains—oil—vegetables coming from the big house. He was illuminated by the spirit of Brahma the Creator[6] and explained to Jashoda, "You'll have milk in your breasts only if you have a child in your belly. Now you'll have to think of that and suffer. You are a faithful wife, a goddess. You will yourself be pregnant, be filled with a child, rear it at your breast, isn't this why Mother came to you as a midwife?"

Jashoda realized the justice of these words and said, with tears in her eyes, "You are husband, you are guru. If I forget and say no, correct me. Where after all is the pain? Didn't Mistress-Mother breed thirteen? Does it hurt a tree to bear fruit?"

So this rule held. Kangalicharan became a professional father. Jashoda was by *profession* Mother. In fact to look at Jashoda now even the skeptic is convinced of the profundity of that song of the path of devotion.[7] The song is as follows:

> Is a Mother so cheaply made?
> Not just by dropping a babe!

Around the paved courtyard on the ground floor of the Haldar house over a dozen auspicious milch cows live in some state in large rooms. Two Biharis look after them as Mother Cows.[8] There are mountains of rind-bran-hay-grass-molasses. Mrs. Haldar believes that the more the cow eats, the more milk she gives. Jashoda's place in the house is now above the Mother Cows. The Mistress's sons become incarnate Brahma and create progeny. Jashoda preserves the progeny.

Mrs. Haldar kept a strict watch on the free flow of her supply of milk. She called Kangalicharan to her presence and said, "Now then, my Brahmin son? You used to stir the vat at the shop, now take up the cooking at home and give her a rest. Two of her own, three here, how can she cook at day's end after suckling five?"

Kangalicharan's intellectual eye was thus opened. Downstairs the two Biharis gave him a bit of chewing tobacco and said, "Mistress Mother said right. We serve the Cow Mother as well—your woman is the Mother of the World."

From now on Kangalicharan took charge of the cooking at home. Made the children his assistants. Gradually he became an expert in cooking plantain curry, lentil soup, and pickled fish, and by constantly feeding Nabin a

<hr>

5. Brahmin women are important participants in Hindu women's rites of fertility and auspiciousness (see n. 1, p. 1357).   6. In the Hindu triad of gods.   7. Songs of devotion (*bhakti*) to particular gods are popular at all levels of Hindu society.   8. Cows that were tended but allowed to roam freely as sacred milch (milk) cows. Biharis are people of the state of Bihar, which borders West Bengal.

head-curry with the head of the goat dedicated to the Lionseated he tamed that ferocious cannabis-artist and drunkard.[9] As a result Nabin inserted Kangali into the temple of Shiva the King.[1] Jashoda, eating well-prepared rice and curry every day, became as inflated as the *bank account* of a Public Works Department *officer*. In addition, Mistress-Mother gave her milk gratis. When Jashoda became pregnant, she would send her preserves, conserves, hot and sweet balls.

Thus even the skeptics were persuaded that the Lionseated had appeared to Jashoda as a midwife for this very reason. Otherwise who has ever heard or seen such things as constant pregnancies, giving birth, giving milk like a cow, without a thought, to others' children? Nabin too lost his bad thoughts. Devotional feelings came to him by themselves. Whenever he saw Jashoda he called out "Mother! Mother! Dear Mother!" Faith in the greatness of the Lionseated was rekindled in the area and in the air of the neighborhood blew the *electrifying* influence of goddess-glory.

Everyone's devotion to Jashoda became so strong that at weddings, showers, namings, and sacred-threadings they invited her and gave her the position of chief fruitful woman. They looked with a comparable eye on Nepal-Gopal-Neno-Boncha-Patal etc. because they were Jashoda's children, and as each grew up, he got a sacred thread and started catching pilgrims for the temple. Kangali did not have to find husbands for Radharani, Altarani, Padmarani and such daughters. Nabin found them husbands with exemplary dispatch and the faithful mother's faithful daughters went off each to run the household of her own Shiva! Jashoda's worth went up in the Haldar house. The husbands are pleased because the wives' knees no longer knock when they riffle the almanac. Since their children are being reared on Jashoda's milk, they can be the Holy Child in bed at will. The wives no longer have an excuse to say "no." The wives are happy. They can keep their figures. They can wear blouses and bras of "European cut." After keeping the fast of Shiva's night by watching all-night picture shows they are no longer obliged to breast-feed their babies. All this was possible because of Jashoda. As a result Jashoda became vocal and, constantly suckling the infants, she opined as she sat in the Mistress's room, "A woman breeds, so here medicine, there bloodpeshur,[2] here doctor's visits. Showoffs! Look at me! I've become a year-breeder! So is my body failing, or is my milk drying? Makes your skin crawl? I hear they are drying their milk with injishuns.[3] Never heard of such things!"

The fathers and uncles of the current young men of the Haldar house used to whistle at the maidservants as soon as hair grew on their upper lips. The young ones were reared by the Milk-Mother's milk, so they looked upon the maid and the cook, their Milk-Mother's friends, as mothers too and started walking around the girls' school. The maids said, "Joshi! You came as The Goddess! You made the air of this house change!" So one day as the youngest son was squatting to watch Jashoda's milking, she said, "There dear, my Lucky! All this because you swiped him in the leg! Whose wish was it then?" "The Lionseated's," said Haldar junior.

9. That is, he tamed Nabin with the power of the goddess inherent in the flesh of the goat that was ritually sacrificed to her. Nabin's consumption of alcohol and cannabis (marijuana) is part of his esoteric regimen of Kali worship.   1. One of the three great gods of the Hindu pantheon; he is also said to be the spouse of Kali.   2. Blood pressure.   3. Injections.

He wanted to know how Kangalicharan could be Brahma without feet?[4] This encroached on divine area, and he forgot the question.

All is the Lionseated's will!

3

Kangali's shins were cut in the fifties, and our narrative has reached the present. In twenty-five years, sorry in thirty, Jashoda has been confined twenty times. The maternities toward the end were profitless, for a new wind entered the Haldar house somehow. Let's finish the business of the twenty-five or thirty years. At the beginning of the narrative Jashoda was the mother of three sons. Then she became gravid[5] seventeen times. Mrs. Haldar died. She dearly wished that one of her daughters-in-law should have the same good fortune as her mother-in-law. In the family the custom was to have a second wedding if a couple could produce twenty children. But the daughters-in-law called a halt at twelve-thirteen-fourteen. By evil counsel they were able to explain to their husbands and make arrangements at the hospital. All this was the bad result of the new wind. Wise men have never allowed a new wind to enter the house. I've heard from my grandmother that a certain gentleman would come to her house to read the liberal journal *Saturday Letter*. He would never let the tome enter his home. "The moment wife, or mother, or sister reads that paper," he would say, "she'll say 'I'm a woman! Not a mother, not a sister, not a wife.'" If asked what the result would be, he'd say, "They would wear shoes while they cooked." It is a perennial rule that the power of the new wind disturbs the peace of the women's quarter.

It was always the sixteenth century in the Haldar household. But at the sudden significant rise in the *membership* of the house the sons started building new houses and splitting. The most objectionable thing was that in the matter of motherhood, the old lady's granddaughters-in-law had breathed a completely different air before they crossed her threshold. In vain did the Mistress say that there was plenty of money, plenty to eat. The old man had dreamed of filling half Calcutta with Haldars. The granddaughters-in-law were unwilling. Defying the old lady's tongue, they took off to their husbands' places of work. At about this time, the pilgrim-guides of the Lionseated had a tremendous fight and some unknown person or persons turned the image of the goddess around. The Mistress's heart broke at the thought that the Mother had turned her back. In pain she ate an unreasonable quantity of jackfruit in full summer and died shitting and vomiting.

4

Death liberated the Mistress, but the sting of staying alive is worse than death. Jashoda was genuinely sorry at the Mistress's death. When an elderly person dies in the neighborhood, it's Basini who can weep most elaborately. She is an old maidservant of the house. But Jashoda's meal ticket was offered up with the Mistress. She astounded everyone by weeping even more elaborately.

---

4. Haldar junior's curiosity is in regard to Kangali's sexual and procreative capabilities.   5. Pregnant.

"Oh blessed Mother!.," Basini wept. "Widowed, when you lost your crown, you became the Master and protected everyone! Whose sins sent you away Mother! Ma, when I said, don't eat so much jackfruit, you didn't listen to me at all Mother!"

Jashoda let Basini get her breath and lamented in that pause, "Why should you stay, Mother! You are blessed, why should you stay in this sinful world! The daughters-in-law have moved the throne! When the tree says I won't bear, alas it's a sin! Could you bear so much sin, Mother! Then did the Lion-seated turn her back, Mother! You knew the abode of good works had become the abode of sin, it was not for you Mother! Your heart left when the Master left Mother! You held your body only because you thought of the family. O mistresses, o daughters-in-law! take a vermillion print of her foot-step! Fortune will be tied to the door if you keep that print! If you touch your forehead to it every morning, pain and disease will stay out!"[6]

Jashoda walked weeping behind the corpse to the burning ghat[7] and said on return, "I saw with my own eyes a chariot descend from heaven, take Mistress-Mother from the pyre, and go on up."

After the funeral days were over, the eldest daughter-in-law said to Jashoda, "Brahmin sister! the family is breaking up. Second and Third are moving to the house in Beleghata. Fourth and Fifth are departing to Maniktala-Bagmari. Youngest will depart to our Dakshineswar house."[8]

"Who stays here?"

"I will. But I'll let the downstairs. Now must the family be folded up. You reared everyone on your milk, food was sent every day. The last child was weaned, still Mother sent you food for eight years. She did what pleased her. Her children said nothing. But it's no longer possible."

"What'll happen to me, elder daughter-in-law-sister?"

"If you cook for my household, your board is taken care of. But what'll you do with yours?"

"What?"

"It's for you to say. You are the mother of twelve living children! The daughters are married. I hear the sons call pilgrims, eat temple food, stretch out in the courtyard. Your Brahmin-husband has set himself up in the Shiva temple, I hear. What do you need?"

Jashoda wiped her eyes. "Well! Let me speak to the Brahmin."

Kangalicharan's temple had really caught on. "What will you do in my temple?" he asked.

"What does Naren's niece do?"

"She looks after the temple household and cooks. You haven't been cooking at home for a long time. Will you be able to push the temple traffic?"

"No meals from the big house. Did that enter your thieving head? What'll you eat?"

"You don't have to worry," said Nabin.

"Why did I have to worry for so long? You're bringing it in at the temple, aren't you? You've saved everything and eaten the food that sucked my body."

"Who sat and cooked?"

6. Jashoda invokes the power of a Sati.   7. The cremation ground, usually situated near a river or other body of water.   8. Areas in the city of Calcutta.

"The man brings, the woman cooks and serves. My lot is inside out. Then you ate my food, now you'll give me food. Fair's fair."

Kangali said on the beat, "Where did you bring in the food? Could you have gotten the Haldar house? Their door opened for *you* because *my* legs were cut off. The Master had wanted to set *me* up in business. Forgotten everything, you cunt?"

"Who's the cunt, you or me? Living off a wife's carcass, you call that a man?"

The two fought tooth and nail and cursed each other to the death. Finally Kangali said, "I don't want to see your face again. Buzz off!"

"All right."

Jashoda too left angry. In the meantime the various pilgrim-guide factions conspired to turn the image's face forward, otherwise disaster was imminent. As a result, penance rituals were being celebrated with great ceremony at the temple. Jashoda went to throw herself at the goddess's feet. Her aging, milkless, capacious breasts are breaking in pain. Let the Lionseated understand her pain and tell her the way.

Jashoda lay three days in the courtyard. Perhaps the Lionseated has also breathed the new wind. She did not appear in a dream. Moreover, when, after her three days' fast, Jashoda went back shaking to her place, her youngest came by. "Dad will stay at the temple. He's told Naba and I to ring the bells. We'll get money and holy food every day."

"I see! Where's dad?"

"Lying down. Golapi-auntie is scratching the prickly heat on his back. Asked us to buy candy with some money. So we came to tell you."

Jashoda understood that her usefulness had ended not only in the Haldar house but also for Kangali. She broke her fast in name and went to Nabin to complain. It was Nabin who had dragged the Lionseated's image the other way. After he had settled the dispute with the other pilgrim-guides re the overhead income from the goddess Basanti ritual, the goddess Jagaddhatri ritual, and the autumn Durgapuja,[9] it was he who had once again pushed and pulled the image the right way. He'd poured some liquor into his aching throat, had smoked a bit of cannabis, and was now addressing the local electoral candidate: "No offerings for the Mother from you! Her glory is back. Now we'll see how you win!"

Nabin is the proof of all the miracles that can happen if, even in this decade, one stays under the temple's power. He had turned the goddess's head himself and had himself believed that the Mother was averse because the pilgrim-guides were not organizing like all the want-votes groups. Now, after he had turned the goddess's head he had the idea that the Mother had turned on her own.

Jashoda said, "What are you babbling?"

Nabin said, "I'm speaking of Mother's glory."

Jashoda said, "You think I don't know that you turned the image's head yourself?"

Nabin said, "Shut up, Joshi. God gave me ability, and intelligence, and only then could the thing be done through me."

9. Goddesses, who are also seen as aspects or forms of the great mother goddess.

"Mother's glory has disappeared when you put your hands on her."

"Glory disappeared! If so, how come, the fan is turning, and you are sitting under the fan? Was there ever an elettiri[1] fan on the porch ceiling?"

"I accept. But tell me, why did you burn my luck? What did I ever do to you?"

"Why? Kangali isn't dead."

"Why wait for death? He's more than dead to me."

"What's up?"

Jashoda wiped her eyes and said in a heavy voice, "I've carried so many, I was the regular milk-mother at the Master's house. You know everything. I've never left the straight and narrow."

"But of course. You are a portion of the Mother."

"But Mother remains in divine fulfillment. Her 'portion' is about to die for want of food. Haldar-house has lifted its hand from me."

"Why did you have to fight with Kangali? Can a man bear to be insulted on grounds of being supported?"

"Why did you have to plant your niece there?"

"That was divine play. Golapi used to throw herself in the temple. Little by little Kangali came to understand that he was the god's companion-incarnate and she *his* companion."

"Companion indeed! I can get my husband from her clutches with one blow of a broom!"

Nabin said, "No! that can't be any more. Kangali is a man in his prime, how can he be pleased with you any more? Besides, Golapi's brother is a real hoodlum, and he is guarding her. Asked *me* to *get out*. If I smoke ten pipes, he smokes twenty. Kicked me in the midriff. I went to speak for you. Kangali said, don't talk to me about her. Doesn't know her man, knows her master's house. The master's house is her household god, let her go there."

"I will."

Then Jashoda returned home, half-crazed by the injustice of the world. But her heart couldn't abide the empty room. Whether it suckled or not, it's hard to sleep without a child at the breast. Motherhood is a great addiction. The addiction doesn't break even when the milk is dry. Forlorn Jashoda went to the Haldaress. She said, "I'll cook and serve, if you want to pay me, if not, not. You must let me stay here. That sonofabitch is living at the temple. What disloyal sons! They are stuck there too. For whom shall I hold my room?"

"So stay. You suckled the children, *and* you're a Brahmin. So stay. But sister, it'll be hard for you. You'll stay in Basini's room with the others. You mustn't fight with anyone. The master is not in a good mood. His temper is rotten because his third son went to Bombay and married a local girl. He'll be angry if there's noise."

Jashoda's good fortune was her ability to bear children. All this misfortune happened to her as soon as that vanished. Now is the downward time for Jashoda, the milk-filled faithful wife who was the object of the reverence of the local houses devoted to the Holy Mother. It is human nature to feel an inappropriate vanity as one rises, yet not to feel the *surrender* of "let me learn to bite the dust since I'm down" as one falls. As a result one makes demands for worthless things in the old way and gets kicked by the weak.

1. Electric.

The same thing happened to Jashoda. Basini's crowd used to wash her feet and drink the water. Now Basini said easily, "You'll wash your own dishes. Are you my master, that I'll wash your dishes. You are the master's servant as much as I am."

As Jashoda roared, "Do you know who I am?" she heard the eldest daughter-in-law scold, "This is what I feared. Mother gave her a swelled head. Look here, Brahmin sister! I didn't call you, you begged to stay, don't break the peace."

Jashoda understood that now no one would attend to a word she said. She cooked and served in silence and in the late afternoon she went to the temple porch and started to weep. She couldn't even have a good cry. She heard the music for the evening worship at the temple of Shiva. She wiped her eyes and got up. She said to herself, "Now save me, Mother! Must I finally sit by the roadside with a tin cup? Is that what you want?"

The days would have passed in cooking at the Haldar-house and complaining to the Mother. But that was not enough for Jashoda. Jashoda's body seemed to keel over. Jashoda doesn't understand why nothing pleases her. Everything seems confused inside her head. When she sits down to cook she thinks she's the milk-mother of this house. She is going home in a showy sari with a free meal in her hand. Her breasts feel empty, as if wasted. She had never thought she wouldn't have a child's mouth at her nipple.

Joshi became bemused. She serves nearly all the rice and curry, but forgets to eat. Sometimes she speaks to Shiva the King, "If Mother can't do it, you take me away. I can't pull any more."

Finally it was the sons of the eldest daughter-in-law who said, "Mother! Is the milk-mother sick? She acts strange."

The eldest daughter-in-law said, "Let's see."

The eldest son said, "Look here? She's a Brahmin's daughter, if anything happens to her, it'll be a sin for us."

The eldest daughter-in-law went to ask. Jashoda had started the rice and then lain down in the kitchen on the spread edge of her sari.[2] The eldest daughter-in-law, looking at her bare body, said, "Brahmin sister! Why does the top of your left tit look so red? God! flaming red!"

"Who knows? It's like a stone pushing inside. Very hard, like a rock."

"What is it?"

"Who knows? I suckled so many, perhaps that's why?"

"Nonsense! One gets breast-stones or pus-in-the-tit if there's milk. Your youngest is ten."

"That one is gone. The one before survived. That one died at birth. Just as well. This sinful world!"

"Well the doctor comes tomorrow to look at my grandson. I'll ask. Doesn't look good to me."

Jashoda said with her eyes closed, "Like a stone tit, with a stone inside. At first the hard ball moved about, now it doesn't move, doesn't budge."

"Let's show the doctor."

"No, sister daughter-in-law, I can't show my body to a male doctor."

2. Indian woman's garment made of a long unconstructed length of fabric. It is draped around the body, with one end hanging free over the shoulder.

At night when the doctor came the eldest daughter-in-law asked him in her son's presence. She said, "No pain, no burning, but she is keeling over."

The doctor said, "Go ask if the *nipple* has shrunk, if the armpit is swollen like a seed."

Hearing "swollen like a seed," the eldest daughter-in-law thought, "How crude!" Then she did her field investigations and said, "She says all that you've said has been happening for some time."

"How old?"

"If you take the eldest son's age she'll be about about fifty-five."

The doctor said, "I'll give medicine."

Going out, he said to the eldest son, "I hear your *Cook* has a problem with her *breast*. I think you should take her to the *cancer hospital*. I didn't see her. But from what I heard it could be *cancer* of the *mammary gland*."

Only the other day the eldest son lived in the sixteenth century. He has arrived at the twentieth century very recently. Of his thirteen offspring he has arranged the marriages of the daughters, and the sons have grown up and are growing up at their own speed and in their own way. But even now his grey cells are covered in the darkness of the eighteenth- and the pre-Bengal-Renaissance[3] nineteenth centuries. He still does not take smallpox vaccination and says, "Only the lower classes get smallpox. I don't need to be vaccinated. An upper-caste family, respectful of gods and Brahmins, does not contract that disease."

He pooh-poohed the idea of cancer and said, "Yah! Cancer indeed! That easy! You misheard, all she needs is an ointment. I can't send a Brahmin's daughter to a hospital just on your word."

Jashoda herself also said, "I can't go to hospital. Ask me to croak instead. I didn't go to hospital to breed, and I'll go now? That corpse-burning devil returned a cripple because he went to hospital!"

The elder daughter-in-law said, "I'll get you a herbal ointment. This ointment will surely soothe. The hidden boil will show its tip and burst."

The herbal ointment was a complete failure. Slowly Jashoda gave up eating and lost her strength. She couldn't keep her sari on the left side. Sometimes she felt burning, sometimes pain. Finally the skin broke in many places and sores appeared. Jashoda took to her bed.

Seeing the hang of it, the eldest son was afraid, if at his house a Brahmin died! He called Jashoda's sons and spoke to them harshly, "It's your mother, she fed you so long, and now she is about to die! Take her with you! She has everyone and she should die in a Kayastha[4] household?"

Kangali cried a lot when he heard this story. He came to Jashoda's almost-dark room and said, "Wife! You are a blessed auspicious faithful woman! After I spurned you, within two years the temple dishes were stolen, I suffered from boils in my back, and that snake Golapi tricked Napla, broke the safe, stole everything and opened a shop in Tarakeswar. Come, I'll keep you in state."

Jashoda said, "Light the lamp."

Kangali lit the lamp.

---

3. The great flowering of cultural activity in Bengal (late 18th and the 19th centuries).   4. An elite caste, second only to brahmins.

Jashoda showed him her bare left breast, thick with running sores and said, "See these sores? Do you know how these sores smell? What will you do with me now? Why did you come to take me?"

"The Master called."

"Then the Master doesn't want to keep me."—Jashoda sighed and said, "There is no solution about me. What can you do with me?"

"Whatever, I'll take you tomorrow. Today I clean the room. Tomorrow for sure."

"Are the boys well? Noblay and Gaur used to come, they too have stopped."

"All the bastards are selfish. Sons of my spunk after all. As inhuman as I."

"You'll come tomorrow?"

"Yes—yes—yes."

Jashoda smiled suddenly. A heart-splitting nostalgia-provoking smile.

Jashoda said, "Dear, remember?"

"What, wife?"

"How you played with these tits? You couldn't sleep otherwise? My lap was never empty, if this one left my nipple, there was that one, and then the boys of the Master's house. How I could, I wonder now!"

"I remember everything, wife!"

In this instant Kangali's words are true. Seeing Jashoda's broken, thin, suffering form even Kangali's selfish body and instincts and belly-centered consciousness remembered the past and suffered some empathy. He held Jashoda's hand and said, "You have fever?"

"I get feverish all the time. I think by the strength of the sores."

"Where does this rotten stink come from?"

"From these sores."

Jashoda spoke with her eyes closed. Then she said, "Bring the holy doctor. He cured Gopal's *typhoid* with *homeopathy*."

"I'll call him. I'll take you tomorrow."

Kangali left. That he went out, the tapping of his crutches, Jashoda couldn't hear. With her eyes shut, with the idea that Kangali was in the room, she said spiritlessly, "If you suckle you're a mother, all lies! Nepal and Gopal don't look at me, and the Master's boys don't spare a peek to ask how I'm doing." The sores on her breast kept mocking her with a hundred mouths, a hundred eyes. Jashoda opened her eyes and said, "Do you hear?"

Then she realized that Kangali had left.

In the night she sent Basini for *Lifebuoy* soap[5] and at dawn she went to take a bath with the soap. Stink, what a stink! If the body of a dead cat or dog rots in the garbage can you get a smell like this. Jashoda had forever scrubbed her breasts carefully with soap and oil, for the master's sons had put the nipples in their mouth. Why did those breasts betray her in the end? Her skin burns with the sting of soap. Still Jashoda washed herself with soap. Her head was ringing, everything seemed dark. There was fire in Jashoda's body, in her head. The black floor was very cool. Jashoda spread her sari and lay down. She could not bear the weight of her breast standing up.

As Jashoda lay down, she lost sense and consciousness with fever. Kangali came at the proper time: but seeing Jashoda he lost his grip. Finally Nabin

---

5. A brand of antibacterial soap.

came and rasped, "Are these people human? She reared all the boys with her milk and they don't call a doctor? I'll call Hari the doctor."

Haribabu took one look at her and said, "Hospital."

Hospitals don't admit people who are so sick. At the efforts and recommendations of the eldest son, Jashoda was admitted.

"What's the matter? O Doctorbabu, what's the problem?"—Kangali asked, weeping like a boy.

"Cancer."

"You can get cancer in a tit?"

"Otherwise how did she get it?"

"Her own twenty, thirty boys at the Master's house—she had a lot of milk—"

"What did you say? How many did she *feed*?"

"About fifty for sure."

"Fif-ty!"

"Yes sir."

"She had twenty children?"

"Yes sir."

"*God!*"

"Sir!"

"What?"

"Is it because she suckled so many—?"

"One can't say why someone gets cancer, one can't say. But when people breast-feed too much—didn't you realize earlier? It didn't get to this in a day?"

"She wasn't with me, sir. We quarreled—"

"I see."

"How do you see her? Will she get well?"

"Get well! See how long she lasts. You've brought her in the last stages. No one survives this stage."

Kangali left weeping. In the late afternoon, harassed by Kangali's lamentations, the eldest son's second son went to the doctor. He was minimally anxious about Jashoda—but his father nagged him and he was financially dependent on his father.

The doctor explained everything to him. It happened not in a day, but over a long time. Why? No one could tell. How does one perceive breast cancer? A hard lump inside the breast toward the top can be removed. Then gradually the lump inside becomes large, hard, and like a congealed pressure. The skin is expected to turn orange, as is expected a shrinking of the nipple. The gland in the armpit can be inflamed. When there is *ulceration*, that is to say sores, one can call it the final stages. Fever? From the point of view of seriousness it falls in the second or third category. If there is something like a sore in the body, there can be fever. That is *secondary*.

The second son was confused with all this specialist talk. He said, "Will she live?"

"No."

"How long will she suffer?"

"I don't think too long."

"When there's nothing to be done, how will you treat her?"

"*Painkiller, sedative, antibiotic* for the fever. Her body is very, very *down*."

"She stopped eating."

"You didn't take her to a doctor?"

"Yes."

"Didn't he tell you?"

"Yes."

"What did he say?"

"That it might be cancer. Asked us to take her to the hospital. She didn't agree."

"Why would she? She'd die!"

The second son came home and said, "When Arun-doctor said she had *cancer,* she might have survived if treated then."

His mother said, "If you know that much then why didn't you take her? Did I stop you?"

Somewhere in the minds of the second son and his mother an unknown sense of guilt and remorse came up like bubbles in dirty and stagnant water and vanished instantly.

Guilt said—she lived with us, we never took a look at her, when did the disease catch her, we didn't take it seriously at all. She was a silly person, reared so many of us, we didn't look after her. Now, with everyone around her she's dying in hospital, so many children, husband living, when she clung to us, then we had ————! What an alive body she had, milk leaped out of her, we never thought she would have this disease.

The disappearance of guilt said—who can undo Fate? It was written that she'd die of *cancer*—who'd stop it? It would have been wrong if she had died here—her husband and sons would have asked, how did she die? We have been saved from that wrongdoing. No one can say anything.

The eldest son assured them, "Now Arun-doctor says no one survives *cancer.* The cancer that Brahmin-sister has can lead to cutting of the tit, removing the uterus, even after that people die of *cancer.* See, Father gave us a lot of reverence toward Brahmins—we are alive by father's grace. If Brahmin-sister had died in our house, we would have had to perform the penance-ritual."

Patients much less sick than Jashoda die much sooner. Jashoda astonished the doctors by hanging on for about a month in hospital. At first Kangali, Nabin, and the boys did indeed come and go, but Jashoda remained the same, comatose, cooking with fever, spellbound. The sores on her breast gaped more and more and the breast now looks like an open wound. It is covered by a piece of thin *gauze* soaked in *antiseptic lotion,* but the sharp smell of putrefying flesh is circulating silently in the room's air like incense-smoke. This brought an ebb in the enthusiasm of Kangali and the other visitors. The doctor said as well, "Is she not responding? All for the better. It's hard to bear without consciousness, can anyone bear such death-throes consciously?"

"Does she know that we come and go?"

"Hard to say."

"Does she eat."

"Through tubes."

"Do people live this way?"

"Now you're very ————"

The doctor understood that he was unreasonably angry because Jashoda was in this condition. He was angry with Jashoda, with Kangali, with women who don't take the signs of breast-cancer *seriously* enough and finally die in this dreadful and hellish pain. Cancer constantly defeats patient and doctor. One patient's cancer means the patient's death and the defeat of science, and of course of the doctor. One can medicate against the secondary symptom, if eating stops one can *drip glucose* and feed the body, if the lungs become incapable of breathing there is *oxygen*—but the advance of *cancer*, its expansion, spread, and killing, remain unchecked. The word *cancer* is a general signifier, by which in the different parts of the body is meant different *malignant growths*. Its characteristic properties are to destroy the infected area of the body, to spread by *metastasis*, to return after *removal*, to create *toximeia*.

Kangali came out without a proper answer to his question. Returning to the temple, he said to Nabin and his sons, "There's no use going any more. She doesn't know us, doesn't open her eyes, doesn't realize anything. The doctor is doing what he can."

Nabin said, "If she dies?"

"They have the *telephone number* of the old Master's eldest son, they'll call."

"Suppose she wants to see you. Kangali, your wife is a blessed auspicious faithful woman! Who would say the mother of so many. To see her body— but she didn't bend, didn't look elsewhere."

Talking thus, Nabin became gloomily silent. In fact, since he'd seen Jashoda's infested breasts, many a philosophic thought and sexological argument have been slowly circling Nabin's drug-and-booze-addled dim head like great rutting snakes emptied of venom. For example, I lusted after her? This is the end of that intoxicating bosom? Ho! Man's body's a zero. To be crazy for that is to be crazy.

Kangali didn't like all this talk. His mind had already *rejected* Jashoda. When he saw Jashoda in the Haldar-house he was truly affected and even after her admission into hospital he was passionately anxious. But now that feeling is growing cold. The moment the doctor said Jashoda wouldn't last, he put her out of mind almost painlessly. His sons are his sons. Their mother had become a distant person for a long time. Mother meant hair in a huge topknot, blindingly white clothes, a strong personality. The person lying in the hospital is someone else, not Mother.

Breast *cancer* makes the *brain comatose*, this was a solution for Jashoda.

Jashoda understood that she had come to hospital, she was in the hospital, and that this desensitizing sleep was a medicated sleep. In her weak, infected, dazed brain she thought, has some son of the Haldar-house become a doctor? No doubt he sucked her milk and is now repaying the milk-debt? But those boys entered the family business as soon as they left high school! However, why don't the people who are helping her so much free her from the stinking presence of her chest? What a smell, what treachery? Knowing these breasts to be the rice-winner, she had constantly conceived to keep them filled with milk. The breast's job is to hold milk. She kept her breast clean with perfumed soap, she never wore a top, even in youth, because her breasts were so heavy.

When the *sedation* lessens, Jashoda screams, "Ah! Ah! Ah!"—and looks for the *nurse* and the doctor with passionate bloodshot eyes. When the doctor comes, she mutters with hurt feelings, "You grew so big on my milk, and now you're hurting me so?"

The doctor says, "She sees her milk-sons all over the world."

Again injection and sleepy numbness. Pain, tremendous pain, the cancer is spreading *at the expense of the human host*. Gradually Jashoda's left breast bursts and becomes like the *crater* of a volcano. The smell of putrefaction makes approach difficult.

Finally one night, Jashoda understood that her feet and hands were getting cold. She understood that death was coming. Jashoda couldn't open her eyes, but she understood that some people were looking at her hand. A needle pricked her arm. Painful breathing inside. Has to be. Who is looking? Are these her own people? The people whom she suckled because she carried them, or those she suckled for a living? Jashoda thought, after all, she had suckled the world, could she then die alone? The doctor who sees her every day, the person who will cover her face with a sheet, will put her on a cart, will lower her at the burning ghat, the untouchable[6] who will put her in the furnace, are all her milk-sons. One must become Jashoda[7] if one suckles the world. One has to die friendless, with no one left to put a bit of water in the mouth. Yet someone was supposed to be there at the end. Who was it? It was who? Who was it?

Jashoda died at 11 p.m.

The Haldar-house was called on the phone. The phone didn't ring. The Haldars *disconnected* their phone at night.

Jashoda Devi, Hindu female, lay in the hospital morgue in the usual way, went to the burning ghat in a van, and was burnt. She was cremated by an untouchable.

Jashoda was God manifest, others do and did whatever she thought. Jashoda's death was also the death of God. When a mortal masquerades as God here below, she is forsaken by all and she must always die alone.

---

6. Outcastes who handle corpses at the cremation ground. They are considered untouchable because of their contact with ritually polluting objects and substances.   7. Here mother of the divine child Krishna and hence mother of the world.

GABRIEL GARCÍA MÁRQUEZ
born 1928

One of the great novelists and prose stylists for more than four decades, Gabriel García Márquez possesses both the technical virtuosity of the French "new novelists" and the breadth and historical scope of the traditional realistic writer. His most famous work, *One Hundred Years of Solitude* (1967), is also the best-known novel from the amazing literary explosion of the 1960s and 1970s called the Latin American "Boom," and embodies the mixture of fantasy and realism called "magical realism." In this novel and related stories, he follows the rise and fall of the Buendía family fortunes in a mythical town called Macondo, and sketches at the same time an echoing, intricate pattern of social, cultural, and psychological themes that become a symbolic picture of Latin American society. Not all of García Márquez's works are about Macondo, but the same themes and images reappear throughout: the contrast of dreamlike and everyday reality and the "magical" aspect of fictional creation, mythic overtones often rooted in local folklore, the representation of broader social and psychological conflicts through regional tales, the essential solitude of individuals facing love and death in a society of which they never quite seem a part. García Márquez is a political novelist in that many of his fictional situations are openly drawn from conditions in Latin American history, so that local readers will recognize current history in the change from prosperity to misery in Macondo that accompanies the presence and withdrawal of the banana company, the massacre of striking banana workers by government forces in 1928, the extreme separation of rich and poor, and the grotesquely oppressive power of political dictators pictured most recently in *The Autumn of the Patriarch* (1975). Yet his fiction achieves its impact not because of its base in real events but because these events are transformed and interpreted inside an artistic vision that—experimenting with many forms—creates a fictional universe all its own.

García Márquez was born in the small town of Aracataca in the "banana zone" of Colombia on March 6, 1928, to Gabriel Eligio García and Maria Márquez Iguarán. The first of twelve children, he was raised by his maternal grandparents until his grandfather died in 1936. He attributes his love of fantasy to his grandmother, who would tell him fantastic tales whenever she did not want to answer his questions. The recurring image of an old military man battered by circumstances (the grandfather of *Leaf Storm*, 1955; the protagonist of *No One Writes to the Colonel*, 1958; and in his younger days, Colonel Aureliano Buendía of *One Hundred Years of Solitude*) likewise recalls his grandfather, a retired colonel who had served on the Liberal side of a civil war at the beginning of the century. A scholarship student at the National Colegio in Zipaquirá, García Márquez received his bachelor's degree in 1946 and studied law at universities in Bogotá and Cartagena from 1947 to 1950. In 1947 he published his first story, "The Third Resignation," a Kafkaesque tale of a man who continued to grow and retain consciousness in his coffin for seventeen years after his death. García Márquez had worked as a journalist while studying law, and in 1950 he abandoned his legal studies for journalism in order to have more time as a writer. His first novel, *Leaf Storm*, was published in 1955 and—in its use of interior monologue and juxtaposition of different perspectives—shows the strong influence of Faulkner. He would soon abandon the more subjective Faulknerian style for an objective manner derived both from his experience in journalism and from Ernest Hemingway. In *Leaf Storm*, we may perceive reality through the mind of a ten-year-old boy: "The heat won't let you breathe in the closed room. You can hear the sun buzzing in the streets, but that's all. The air is stagnant, like concrete; you get the feeling that it could get all twisted like a sheet of steel." In his next novel, *No One Writes to the Colonel*, an impersonal narrator catalogs the actions of the colonel about to make coffee: "He removed the pot from the fire, poured half the water onto the earthen floor, and scraped the inside of the can with a knife until the last scrapings of the ground coffee, mixed with bits of rust, fell into the pot."

In 1954 García Márquez had joined the newspaper *El Espectador* (The spectator) in Bogotá; a report he wrote in 1955 that indirectly revealed corruption in the navy irritated the Rojas Pinilla dictatorship, and the paper was shut down. Working in Paris as *El Espectador*'s foreign correspondent when he learned that his job had been abolished, he lived in extreme poverty for the next year while beginning *The Evil Hour* (1962) and *No One Writes to the Colonel*. In 1957, after traveling in Eastern Europe, he returned to Latin America. Here he worked for several different newspapers in Venezuela, and later for the international press agency, Prensa Latina, in Cuba and New York, and for the Mexican periodicals *La Familia* and *Sucesos* (a sensationalist magazine) before beginning to write film scripts in 1963. A collection of short stories, *Big Mama's Funeral*, was published in 1962, along with the first edition of *The Evil Hour*, which, printed in Spain, was later repudiated by the author because of tampering by proofreaders. In 1965 the various themes and characters he had been developing throughout his earlier novels and short stories came together as the fully developed concept of a new book, and García Márquez shut himself up in his study for a year and a half to write *One Hundred Years of Solitude*. Published in 1967, the novel was a best-seller, immediately translated into numerous (now twenty-five) languages; it received prizes in Italy and France in 1969, and—when published in English in 1970—was chosen by American critics as one of the dozen best books of the year.

After *One Hundred Years of Solitude*, García Márquez found new ways to combine magical-realist techniques and social commentary. In 1972, he published a collection of seven stories, *The Incredible and Sad Story of Innocent Eréndira and Her Heartless Grandmother*, which contains the story printed here, "Death Constant beyond Love." From the title story, in which Eréndira's monstrously fat, tattooed, green-blooded grandmother is finally murdered after prostituting her grandchild to the entire countryside to repay a debt, to symbolic fantasies such as "A Very Old Man with Enormous Wings" (in which a castaway angel is exhibited in a chicken coop until his feathers grow back and he can fly away), the author presents tales in which the substance is incredible but the details themselves are highly realistic. The winged man smells bad and his wings are infested with parasites; the farm truck in which Eréndira tries to escape with her lover has an old motor and cannot outrun the military patrol summoned by her grandmother. The mixture of fantasy and realism is not easily interpretable in a single symbolic sense: Eréndira's prostitution may be political and cultural as well as personal, and larger social relationships may be symbolized in the town's attitude toward the angel. Throughout, the narrative line can easily be followed but also interpreted in several ways.

In recent years—questioning the effectiveness of literature to remedy the social ills he so often describes—García Márquez has been more and more active politically, speaking out for revolutionary governments in Latin America and organizing assistance for political prisoners. Living in Mexico City, he continues to write, including a number of stories that are still unpublished and an account of Cuba under the U.S. blockade. He received the Nobel Prize in literature in 1982.

"Death Constant beyond Love" (1970), also has a political background although its protagonist, Senator Onésimo Sánchez, is seen chiefly as he struggles with his elemental problem of death. He is no hero: in "Innocent Eréndira" he writes a letter vouching for the grandmother's morality, and in this story he is clearly a corrupt politician who accepts bribes and stays in power by helping the local property owners avoid reform. His electoral train is a traveling circus with carnival wagons, fireworks, a ready-made audience of hired Indians, and a cardboard village with imitation brick houses and a painted ocean liner to offer the illusion of future prosperity; he uses carefully placed gifts to encourage support and a feeling of dependence.

Yet the background of poverty and corruption, the entertaining spectacle of the senator's "fictional world," and the political campaign itself fade into insignificance before broader themes of life and death. Forty-two, happily married, in full control of his own and others' lives as a successful politician in midcareer, he is made to feel suddenly helpless, vulnerable, and alone when told that all this will stop and he will be dead "forever" by next Christmas. Theoretically, he knows that death is inevitable and nature cannot be defeated. He has read the Stoic philosopher Marcus Aurelius (121–180 C.E.) and even refers to the *Meditations*, which recommends the cheerful acceptance of natural order (including death and oblivion), criticizes the delusions of those "who have tenaciously stuck to life," and stresses both the tranquil "ordering of the mind" and the idea that human beings are all "fellow-citizens" of a shared "political community." The example of the philosopher is not mere chance: Marcus Aurelius was also a political figure, a Roman emperor who wrote his *Meditations* as personal guidelines in a time of plague and political unrest.

The senator does gain some Stoic insight into the illusions of his career: he notices how similar are the dusty village and the worn cardboard facade that represents its hopes, and he is fed up with what he recognizes to be background maneuverings that keep him in power by prolonging the exploitation of the poor. But he also loses sympathy for the barefoot Indians standing in the square, and his newly alienated perspective is not accompanied by the Stoic injunction to maintain a just and ordered mind and to accept everything that happens as necessary and good. In this crisis, the senator is reduced to a basic and instinctual existence, expressed in García Márquez's recurrent themes of solitude, love, and death. The beautiful Laura provides an opportunity for him to sublimate his fear of death in erotic passion (inextricably intertwined, according to Freud). His choice means scandal and the destruction of his political career, but by now Onésimo Sánchez has felt the emptiness of his earlier activities and is engaged in a struggle to cheat death.

He does not succeed, of course, and dies weeping with rage that death separates him from Laura Farina. "Death Constant beyond Love" has reversed the ambitious claim of a famous sonnet by the Spanish Golden Age writer Quevedo (1580–1645), according to which there is "Love Constant beyond Death." Such love is an illusion, for it is death that awaits us beyond everything else. García Márquez repeatedly plays on these oppositions and inversions when he describes the real village and the cardboard version created by false political promises, the paper birds that magically take on life and fly out to sea, the paper butterfly that seems to fly and lands on the wall, the bribery money that flaps around like butterflies, the grotesquely padlocked chastity belt that Laura Farina wears, and even the initial opposition between the senator's living rose (symbol of womanhood and love) and the roseless town (named "The Viceroy's Rosebush") where he encounters his destiny. His destiny is to be liberated from some illusions but not all: his final delusion is to try to hide from death in erotic love. The senator's defeat at the end, which is clearly emphasized as a defeat, suggests that his response was a futile retreat, and—at the same time that it evokes pity for his loneliness, terror, and rage—puts in question what that response should be.

Death Constant Beyond Love[1]

Senator Onésimo Sánchez had six months and eleven days to go before his death when he found the woman of his life. He met her in Rosal del Virrey,[2] an illusory village which by night was the furtive wharf for smugglers' ships, and on the other hand, in broad daylight looked like the most useless inlet on the desert, facing a sea that was arid and without direction and so far from everything no one would have suspected that someone capable of changing the destiny of anyone lived there. Even its name was a kind of joke, because the only rose in that village was being worn by Senator Onésimo Sánchez himself on the same afternoon when he met Laura Farina.

It was an unavoidable stop in the electoral campaign he made every four years. The carnival wagons had arrived in the morning. Then came the trucks with the rented Indians[3] who were carried into the towns in order to enlarge the crowds at public ceremonies. A short time before eleven o'clock, along with the music and rockets and jeeps of the retinue, the ministerial automobile, the color of strawberry soda, arrived. Senator Onésimo Sánchez was placid and weatherless inside the air-conditioned car, but as soon as he

1. Translated by Gregory Rabassa.   2. The Rosebush of the Viceroy (governor).   3. People descended from the original inhabitants of the continent; generally poorer and less privileged than those descended from Spanish or Portuguese colonists.

opened the door he was shaken by a gust of fire and his shirt of pure silk was soaked in a kind of light-colored soup and he felt many years older and more alone than ever. In real life he had just turned forty-two, had been graduated from Göttingen[4] with honors as a metallurgical engineer, and was an avid reader, although without much reward, of badly translated Latin classics. He was married to a radiant German woman who had given him five children and they were all happy in their home, he the happiest of all until they told him, three months before, that he would be dead forever by next Christmas.

While the preparations for the public rally were being completed, the senator managed to have an hour alone in the house they had set aside for him to rest in. Before he lay down he put in a glass of drinking water the rose he had kept alive all across the desert, lunched on the diet cereals that he took with him so as to avoid the repeated portions of fried goat that were waiting for him during the rest of the day, and he took several analgesic pills before the time prescribed so that he would have the remedy ahead of the pain. Then he put the electric fan close to the hammock and stretched out naked for fifteen minutes in the shadow of the rose, making a great effort at mental distraction so as not to think about death while he dozed. Except for the doctors, no one knew that he had been sentenced to a fixed term, for he had decided to endure his secret all alone, with no change in his life, not because of pride but out of shame.[5]

He felt in full control of his will when he appeared in public again at three in the afternoon, rested and clean, wearing a pair of coarse linen slacks and a floral shirt, and with his soul sustained by the anti-pain pills. Nevertheless, the erosion of death was much more pernicious than he had supposed, for as he went up onto the platform he felt a strange disdain for those who were fighting for the good luck to shake his hand, and he didn't feel sorry as he had at other times for the groups of barefoot Indians who could scarcely bear the hot saltpeter coals of the sterile little square. He silenced the applause with a wave of his hand, almost with rage, and he began to speak without gestures, his eyes fixed on the sea, which was sighing with heat. His measured, deep voice had the quality of calm water, but the speech that had been memorized and ground out so many times had not occurred to him in the nature of telling the truth, but, rather, as the opposite of a fatalistic pronouncement by Marcus Aurelius in the fourth book of his *Meditations*.

"We are here for the purpose of defeating nature," he began, against all his convictions. "We will no longer be foundlings in our own country, orphans of God in a realm of thirst and bad climate, exiles in our own land. We will be different people, ladies and gentlemen, we will be a great and happy people."

There was a pattern to his circus. As he spoke his aides threw clusters of paper birds into the air and the artificial creatures took on life, flew about the platform of planks, and went out to sea. At the same time, other men took some prop trees with felt leaves out of the wagons and planted them in the saltpeter soil behind the crowd. They finished by setting up a cardboard façade with make-believe houses of red brick that had glass windows, and with it they covered the miserable real-life shacks.

---

4. A well-known German university.   5. "Death is such as generation is, a mystery of nature . . . altogether not a thing of which any man should be ashamed" (Marcus Aurelius, *Meditations* 4.5).

The senator prolonged his speech with two quotations in Latin in order to give the farce more time. He promised rainmaking machines, portable breeders for table animals, the oils of happiness which would make vegetables grow in the saltpeter and clumps of pansies in the window boxes. When he saw that his fictional world was all set up, he pointed to it. "That's the way it will be for us, ladies and gentlemen," he shouted. "Look! That's the way it will be for us."

The audience turned around. An ocean liner made of painted paper was passing behind the houses and it was taller than the tallest houses in the artificial city. Only the senator himself noticed that since it had been set up and taken down and carried from one place to another the superimposed cardboard town had been eaten away by the terrible climate and that it was almost as poor and dusty as Rosal del Virrey.

For the first time in twelve years, Nelson Farina didn't go to greet the senator. He listened to the speech from his hammock amidst the remains of his siesta, under the cool bower of a house of unplaned boards which he had built with the same pharmacist's hands with which he had drawn and quartered his first wife. He had escaped from Devil's Island and appeared in Rosal del Virrey on a ship loaded with innocent macaws, with a beautiful and blasphemous black woman he had found in Paramaribo[6] and by whom he had a daughter. The woman died of natural causes a short while later and she didn't suffer the fate of the other, whose pieces had fertilized her own cauliflower patch, but was buried whole and with her Dutch name in the local cemetery. The daughter had inherited her color and her figure along with her father's yellow and astonished eyes, and he had good reason to imagine that he was rearing the most beautiful woman in the world.

Ever since he had met Senator Onésimo Sánchez during his first electoral campaign, Nelson Farina had begged for his help in getting a false identity card which would place him beyond the reach of the law. The senator, in a friendly but firm way, had refused. Nelson Farina never gave up, and for several years, every time he found the chance, he would repeat his request with a different recourse. But this time he stayed in his hammock, condemned to rot alive in that burning den of buccaneers. When he heard the final applause, he lifted his head, and looking over the boards of the fence, he saw the back side of the farce: the props for the buildings, the framework of the trees, the hidden illusionists who were pushing the ocean liner along. He spat without rancor.

"Merde," he said. "C'est le Blacamán de la politique."[7]

After the speech, as was customary, the senator took a walk through the streets of the town in the midst of the music and the rockets and was besieged by the townspeople, who told him their troubles. The senator listened to them good-naturedly and he always found some way to console everybody without having to do them any difficult favors. A woman up on the roof of a house with her six youngest children managed to make herself heard over the uproar and the fireworks.

---

6. Capital of Suriname (formerly Dutch Guiana) and a large port. Devil's Island is a former French penal colony off the coast of French Guiana in northern South America.   7. Shit. He's the Blacamán of politics (French). Blacamán is a charlatan and huckster who appears in several stories, including "Blacamán the Good, Vendor of Miracles."

"I'm not asking for much, Senator," she said. "Just a donkey to haul water from Hanged Man's Well."

The senator noticed the six thin children. "What became of your husband?" he asked.

"He went to find his fortune on the island of Aruba,"[8] the woman answered good-humoredly, "and what he found was a foreign woman, the kind that put diamonds on their teeth."

The answer brought on a roar of laughter.

"All right," the senator decided, "you'll get your donkey."

A short while later an aide of his brought a good pack donkey to the woman's house and on the rump it had a campaign slogan written in indelible paint so that no one would ever forget that it was a gift from the senator.

Along the short stretch of street he made other, smaller gestures, and he even gave a spoonful of medicine to a sick man who had had his bed brought to the door of his house so he could see him pass. At the last corner, through the boards of the fence, he saw Nelson Farina in his hammock, looking ashen and gloomy, but nonetheless the senator greeted him, with no show of affection.

"Hello, how are you?"

Nelson Farina turned in his hammock and soaked him in the sad amber of his look.

"*Moi, vous savez,*"[9] he said.

His daughter came out into the yard when she heard the greeting. She was wearing a cheap, faded Guajiro Indian[1] robe, her head was decorated with colored bows, and her face was painted as protection against the sun, but even in that state of disrepair it was possible to imagine that there had never been another so beautiful in the whole world. The senator was left breathless. "I'll be damned!" he breathed in surprise. "The Lord does the craziest things!"

That night Nelson Farina dressed his daughter up in her best clothes and sent her to the senator. Two guards armed with rifles who were nodding from the heat in the borrowed house ordered her to wait on the only chair in the vestibule.

The senator was in the next room meeting with the important people of Rosal del Virrey, whom he had gathered together in order to sing for them the truths he had left out of his speeches. They looked so much like all the ones he always met in all the towns in the desert that even the senator himself was sick and tired of that perpetual nightly session. His shirt was soaked with sweat and he was trying to dry it on his body with the hot breeze from an electric fan that was buzzing like a horse fly in the heavy heat of the room.

"We, of course, can't eat paper birds," he said. "You and I know that the day there are trees and flowers in this heap of goat dung, the day there are shad instead of worms in the water holes, that day neither you nor I will have anything to do here, do I make myself clear?"

---

8. Off the coast of Venezuela, famous as a tourist resort.   9. Oh well, as for me, you know (French).
1. Inhabitant of the rural Guajira Peninsula of northern Colombia. The figure of Laura Farina is thus connected with the rustic poor, with earthy reality (*farina* means "flour"), and with erotic inspiration. (*Laura* was the beloved celebrated by the Italian Renaissance poet Francis Petrarch, 1304–1374.)

No one answered. While he was speaking, the senator had torn a sheet off the calendar and fashioned a paper butterfly out of it with his hands. He tossed it with no particular aim into the air current coming from the fan and the butterfly flew about the room and then went out through the half-open door. The senator went on speaking with a control aided by the complicity of death.

"Therefore," he said, "I don't have to repeat to you what you already know too well: that my reelection is a better piece of business for you than it is for me, because I'm fed up with stagnant water and Indian sweat, while you people, on the other hand, make your living from it."

Laura Farina saw the paper butterfly come out. Only she saw it because the guards in the vestibule had fallen asleep on the steps, hugging their rifles. After a few turns, the large lithographed butterfly unfolded completely, flattened against the wall, and remained stuck there. Laura Farina tried to pull it off with her nails. One of the guards, who woke up with the applause from the next room, noticed her vain attempt.

"It won't come off," he said sleepily. "It's painted on the wall."

Laura Farina sat down again when the men began to come out of the meeting. The senator stood in the doorway of the room with his hand on the latch, and he only noticed Laura Farina when the vestibule was empty.

"What are you doing here?"

"*C'est de la part de mon père,*"[2] she said.

The senator understood. He scrutinized the sleeping guards, then he scrutinized Laura Farina, whose unusual beauty was even more demanding than his pain, and he resolved then that death had made his decision for him.

"Come in," he told her.

Laura Farina was struck dumb standing in the doorway to the room: thousands of bank notes were floating in the air, flapping like the butterfly. But the senator turned off the fan and the bills were left without air and alighted on the objects in the room.

"You see," he said, smiling, "even shit can fly."

Laura Farina sat down on a schoolboy's stool. Her skin was smooth and firm, with the same color and the same solar density as crude oil, her hair was the mane of a young mare, and her huge eyes were brighter than the light. The senator followed the thread of her look and finally found the rose, which had been tarnished by the saltpeter.

"It's a rose," he said.

"Yes," she said with a trace of perplexity. "I learned what they were in Riohacha."[3]

The senator sat down on an army cot, talking about roses as he unbuttoned his shirt. On the side where he imagined his heart to be inside his chest he had a corsair's tattoo of a heart pierced by an arrow. He threw the soaked shirt to the floor and asked Laura Farina to help him off with his boots.

She knelt down facing the cot. The senator continued to scrutinize her, thoughtfully, and while he was untying the laces he wondered which one of them would end up with the bad luck of that encounter.

---

2. My father sent me (French).   3. A port on the Guajira Peninsula.

"You're just a child," he said.

"Don't you believe it," she said. "I'll be nineteen in April."

The senator became interested.

"What day?"

"The eleventh," she said.

The senator felt better. "We're both Aries,"[4] he said. And smiling, he added:

"It's the sign of solitude."

Laura Farina wasn't paying attention because she didn't know what to do with the boots. The senator, for his part, didn't know what to do with Laura Farina, because he wasn't used to sudden love affairs and, besides, he knew that the one at hand had its origins in indignity. Just to have some time to think, he held Laura Farina tightly between his knees, embraced her about the waist, and lay down on his back on the cot. Then he realized that she was naked under her dress, for her body gave off the dark fragrance of an animal of the woods, but her heart was frightened and her skin disturbed by a glacial sweat.

"No one loves us," he sighed.

Laura Farina tried to say something, but there was only enough air for her to breathe. He laid her down beside him to help her, he put out the light and the room was in the shadow of the rose. She abandoned herself to the mercies of her fate. The senator caressed her slowly, seeking her with his hand, barely touching her, but where he expected to find her, he came across something iron that was in the way.

"What have you got there?"

"A padlock,"[5] she said.

"What in hell!" the senator said furiously and asked what he knew only too well. "Where's the key?"

Laura Farina gave a breath of relief.

"My papa has it," she answered. "He told me to tell you to send one of your people to get it and to send along with him a written promise that you'll straighten out his situation."

The senator grew tense. "Frog[6] bastard," he murmured indignantly. Then he closed his eyes in order to relax and he met himself in the darkness. *Remember,* he remembered, *that whether it's you or someone else, it won't be long before you'll be dead and it won't be long before your name won't even be left.*[7]

He waited for the shudder to pass.

"Tell me one thing," he asked then. "What have you heard about me?"

"Do you want the honest-to-God truth?"

"The honest-to-God truth."

"Well," Laura Farina ventured, "they say you're worse than the rest because you're different."

The senator didn't get upset. He remained silent for a long time with his eyes closed, and when he opened them again he seemed to have returned from his most hidden instincts.

---

4. The first sign in the zodiac; people born between March 21 and April 19 are said to be under the sign of Aries. 5. She is wearing a chastity belt, a medieval device worn by women to prevent sexual intercourse. 6. Epithet for "French." 7. A direct translation of a sentence from Marcus Aurelius's *Meditations* (4.6).

"Oh, what the hell," he decided. "Tell your son of a bitch of a father that I'll straighten out his situation."

"If you want, I can go get the key myself," Laura Farina said.

The senator held her back.

"Forget about the key," he said, "and sleep awhile with me. It's good to be with someone when you're so alone."

Then she laid his head on her shoulder with her eyes fixed on the rose. The senator held her about the waist, sank his face into woods-animal armpit, and gave in to terror. Six months and eleven days later he would die in that same position, debased and repudiated because of the public scandal with Laura Farina and weeping with rage at dying without her.

CHINUA ACHEBE
born 1930

The best-known African writer today is the Nigerian Chinua Achebe, whose first novel, *Things Fall Apart*, exploded the colonialist image of Africans as childlike people living in a primitive society. Achebe's novels, stories, poetry, and essays have made him a respected and prophetic figure in Africa. In Western countries, where he has traveled, taught, and lectured widely, he is admired as a major writer who has given an entirely new direction to the English-language novel. Achebe has created not only the African postcolonial novel with its new themes and characters but also a complex narrative point of view that questions cultural images—including its own—with a subtle irony and compassion born from bicultural experience. His vantage point is different from that of Doris Lessing or Albert Camus, two authors whose work is also concerned with African experience: Achebe writes, as he says, "from the inside." For him as for many other writers in this volume, literature is important because it liberates the human imagination; it "begins as an adventure in self-discovery and ends in wisdom and human conscience."

Chinua Achebe was born in the town of Ogidi, an Igbo-speaking town of Eastern Nigeria, on November 16, 1930. He was the fifth of six children in the family of Isaiah Okafor Achebe, a teacher for the Church Missionary Society, and his wife, Janet. Achebe's parents christened him Albert after Prince Albert, husband of Queen Victoria. When he entered the university the author rejected his British name in favor of his indigenous name Chinua, which abbreviates Chinualumogu, or "My spirit come fight for me." Achebe's novels offer a picture of Igbo society with its fierce egalitarianism and "town meeting" debates. Two cultures co-existed in Ogidi: on the one hand, African social customs and traditional religion, and on the other, British colonial authority and Christianity. Instead of being torn between the two, Achebe found himself curious about both ways of life and fascinated with the dual perspective that came from living "at the crossroads of cultures."

He attended church schools in Ogidi where instruction was carried out in English after the first two years. Achebe read the various books in his father's library, most of them primers or church related, but he also listened eagerly to his mother and sister when they told traditional Igbo stories. Entering a prestigious government college (secondary school) in Umuahia, he immediately took advantage of its well-stocked library. Achebe later commented on the crucial importance of books in creating writers and committed readers, noting that private secondary schools had few if any books and that almost all the first generation of Nigerian writers—including himself and Wole Soyinka (born 1934)—had gone to a government college.

After graduating in 1948, Achebe entered University College, Ibadan, on a scholarship to study medicine. In the following year he changed to a program in liberal arts that combined English, history, and religious studies. Research in the last two fields deepened his knowledge of Nigerian history and culture; the assigned literary texts, however, brought into sharp focus the distorted image of African culture offered by British colonial literature. Reading Joyce Cary's *Mister Johnson* (1939), a novel recommended for its depiction of life in Nigeria, he was shocked to find Nigerians described as violent savages with passionate instincts and simple minds: "and so I thought if this was famous, then perhaps someone ought to try and look at this from the inside." He began writing while at the university, contributing articles and sketches to several campus papers and publishing four stories in the *University Herald,* a magazine whose editor he became in his third year.

Upon receiving his B.A. in 1953, Achebe joined the Nigerian Broadcasting Service, working in the Talks Section and traveling to London in 1956 to attend the British Broadcasting Corporation Staff School. Promotions came quickly; he was named head of the Talks Section in 1957, controller of the Eastern Region Stations in 1959, and in 1961 director of External Services in charge of the Voice of Nigeria. The radio position was more than a merely administrative post, for Achebe and his colleagues were working to create a sense of shared national identity through broadcasting national news and information about Nigerian culture. Ever since the end of World War II, Nigeria had been torn by intellectual and political rivalries that overlaid the common struggle for independence (achieved in 1960). The three major ethnolinguistic groups—Yoruba, Hausa-Fulani, and Igbo (once spelled Ibo)—were increasingly locked in economic and political rivalry at the same time they were fighting to erase the vestiges of British colonial rule. These problems eventually boiled over in the Nigerian Civil War (1967–70). The persistence of political corruption is depicted in *A Man of the People* (1966) and *Anthills of the Savannah* (1987).

Achebe is convinced of the writer's social responsibility, and he draws frequent contrasts between the European "art for art's sake" tradition and an African belief in the indivisibility of art and society. His favorite example is the Owerri Igbo custom of *mbari,* a communal art project in which villagers selected by the priest of the earth goddess Ala live in a forest clearing for a year or more, working under the direction of master artists to prepare a temple of images in the goddess's honor. This creative communal enterprise and its culminating festival are diametrically opposed, he says, to the European custom of secluding art objects in museums or private collections. Instead, *mbari* celebrates art as a cultural process, affirming that "art belongs to all and is a 'function' of society." Achebe's own practice as novelist, poet, essayist, founder and editor of two journals, lecturer, and active representative of African letters exemplifies this commitment to the community.

His first novel, *Things Fall Apart* (1958), was a conscious attempt to counteract the distortions of Cary's *Mister Johnson* by describing the richness and complexity of traditional African society before the colonial and missionary invasion. It was important, Achebe said, to "teach my readers that their past—with all its imperfections—was not one long night of savagery from which the first Europeans acting on God's behalf delivered them." The novel was recognized immediately as an extraordinary work of literature in English. It also became the first classic work of modern African fiction, translated into nine languages, and Achebe became for many readers and writers the teacher of a whole generation. In 1959 he received the Margaret Wrong Memorial Prize, and in 1960—after the publication of a sequel, *No Longer at Ease*— he received the Nigerian National Trophy for literature. His later novels continue to examine the individual and cultural dilemmas of Nigerian society, although their background varies from the traditional religious society of *Arrow of God* (1964) to thinly disguised accounts of contemporary political strife.

Achebe's reputation as the "father of the African novel in English" does not depend solely on his accounts of Nigerian society. In contrast with writers such as

Ngugi wa Thiong'o (born 1938), who insist that the contemporary African writer has a moral obligation to write in one of the tribal languages, Achebe maintains his right to compose in the English he has used since his school days. His literary language is an English skillfully blended with Igbo vocabulary, proverbs, images, and speech patterns to create a new voice embodying the linguistic pluralism of modern African experience. By including standard English, Igbo, and pidgin in different contexts, Achebe demonstrates the existence of a diverse society that is otherwise concealed behind language barriers—a culture, he suggests, that escaped colonial officials who wrote about African character without ever understanding the language. He also thereby acknowledges that his primary African audience is composed of younger, schooled readers who are relatively fluent in English.

It is hard to overestimate the influence of Nigerian politics on Achebe's life after 1966. In January, a military coup d'état led by young Igbo officers overthrew the government; six months later, a second coup led by non-Igbo officers took power. Ethnic rivalries intensified: thousands of Igbos were killed and driven out of the north. Achebe and his family fled the capital of Lagos when soldiers were sent to find him, and the novelist became a senior research fellow at the University of Nigeria, Nsukka (in Eastern Nigeria). In May 1967 the eastern region, mainly populated by Igbo-speakers, seceded as the new nation of Biafra. From then on until the defeat of Biafra in January 1970, a bloody civil war was waged with high civilian casualties and widespread starvation. Achebe traveled in Europe, North America, and Africa to win support for Biafra, proclaiming that "no government, black or white, has the right to stigmatize and destroy groups of its own citizens without undermining the basis of its own existence." A group of his poems about the war won the Commonwealth Poetry Prize in 1972, the same year that he published a volume of short stories, *Girls at War,* and left Nigeria to take up a three-year position at the University of Massachusetts at Amherst. Returning to Nsukka as professor of literature in 1976, Achebe continued to participate in his country's political life. He published an attack on the corrupt leadership in *The Trouble with Nigeria* (1983) and—drawing on circumstances surrounding a fifth military coup in 1985—produced his fifth novel, *Anthills of the Savannah,* in 1987. Although it reiterates Achebe's familiar indictment of ruthless politicians, alienated intellectuals, and those who accept dictatorship as a route to reform, this novel offers hope for the future through a return to the people and a symbolic child born at the end: a girl child with a boy's name, "May the Path Never Close." Badly hurt in a car accident the year after *Anthills* was published, Achebe slowly recovered and returned to writing and teaching at Bard College. By the end of the century, he had published three more volumes, including interviews collected as *Conversations with Chinua Achebe* (1997) and another book of essays, *Home and Exile* (2000).

A predominant theme in Achebe's novels and essays is the notion of balance or interdependence: balance between earth and sky, individual and community, man and woman, or different perspectives on the same situation. Igbo thought is fundamentally dualistic, the novelist explains: "Wherever Something stands, Something Else will stand beside it. Nothing is absolute." Extremes carry the seeds of destruction. Indeed, destruction follows in Achebe's novels whenever balance is disturbed: when Okonkwo in *Things Fall Apart* represses any signs of "female" softness; when the priest Ezeulu in *Arrow of God* is imprisoned and refuses to authorize the feast of the New Yam, without which his people cannot plant their crops; and when, in later books, the lust for power and possessions blinds Nigerian leaders to the needs of the people.

The fundamental image of this balance is contained in the Igbo concept of *chi,* which recurs throughout Achebe's work. *Chi* is a personal deity, a fragment of the supreme being unique for each individual. A person's *chi,* says Achebe, may be visualized "as his other identity in spirit land—his *spirit being* complementing his terrestrial *human being.*" It is both all-powerful and subject to persuasion: "When a man says yes his *chi* says yes also," but at the same time "a man does not challenge his *chi* to a wrestling match." *Chi* is simultaneously destiny and an internal commitment that cannot be denied, a religious concept and also a picture of psychic harmony. Both aspects are linked throughout Achebe's novels, beginning with *Things Fall Apart*. In killing Ikemefuna, whom he loves and who calls him father, Okonkwo sins not only against the earth goddess, protector of family relations, but also against his inmost feelings and thus against his *chi*. If Okonkwo's destiny (*chi*) is marked by bad luck, one reason may be that—driven by fear of resembling his father—he struggles to repress part of his personality (*chi*), with predictably ill results. In the final assessment, no one can fully explain *chi*: it is mysteriously uncertain, the element of fate over which we have no real control.

Things Fall Apart is both Okonkwo's tragedy and that of his society. The title (taken from William Butler Yeats's "The Second Coming") introduces a narrative in which a complex and dignified traditional society disintegrates before foreign invaders who assault its political, economic, and religious institutions. The setting is eastern Nigeria around the turn of the century in the clan of Umuofia, which is composed of nine interrelated villages. One of these villages, Iguedo, is the home of the protagonist Okonkwo, an ambitious and powerful man who is driven by the memory of his father's failure and weakness.

During the first two-thirds of the book, Achebe paints the picture of a rich and coherent society, establishing an image of traditional African culture into which the final chapters' missionaries, court messengers, and district commissioner intrude as alien and disruptive elements. In sharp contrast to the simplified vision of African life given by European novelists Joyce Cary, Joseph Conrad, or Graham Greene, he explores the complex feelings and interpersonal relationships of diverse villagers seen as men, women, parents, children, friends, neighbors, or priests of the local deities. The intricate patterns of Umuofia's economic and social customs also emerge, belying European images of African "primitive" simplicity. No one who has read about Obierika's intricate marriage negotiations, the etiquette of *kola* hospitality, the religious "week of peace," Ezeudu's elaborate funeral rites, the domestic arbitration conducted by the *egwugwu* court, the female kinship customs linking families and villages, or indeed Umuofia's entire set of taboos and punishments will find this a simple society. The title system itself, which plays such a large part in the novel, is an ingenious social strategy for redistributing wealth throughout the community. The four honorific *ozo* titles (*Ozo, Idemili, Omalo,* and *Erulu*), through which a man enters the spiritual community of his ancestors and achieves increasing levels of prestige, are acquired in festivities during which the candidate divests himself of excess material wealth. There is a dignity and purpose to this society despite inner tensions that—as Achebe shows—create pain as well as vulnerability to attack from outside. The moderate Obierika disapproves of killing Ikemefuna and begins to question the practice of throwing away twins; one of the first converts to Christianity is a woman who gave birth to several sets of twins, all of whom were exposed (left in the wild) at birth. The general subordination of women is another source of tensions that have taken longer to surface. Whatever its cultural differences from European society, however, this is a highly organized and complex society that offers a great deal of continuity and coherence to its members.

Igbo names, like names throughout black Africa, consist of whole phrases or sentences. Some names are dictated by circumstance (referring to the day of birth, for example) and some (the "given" name selected by the child's father, for example) reflect the family situation or a child's expected destiny. Adults may earn additional titles of honor. Achebe uses the connotations of personal names to reinforce important themes in *Things Fall Apart*. Okonkwo's father's character as a lazy, artistic, and improvident man is suggested by the name Unoka, signifying "the home is supreme." Okonkwo's son Nwoye, who has inherited his grandfather's peace-loving nature and artistic qualities, is named after the second day of the Igbo week (*Oye*); unlike

Okonkwo, Nwoye lacks a prefix specifying adulthood or even gender, for *Nwa* means "child." Ikemefuna, who is condemned to death by the Oracle and will be killed by his adoptive father, is named "My strength should not be dissipated." Although all names have significance, only those with some relevance to the story will be annotated in this edition.

Okonkwo's character and career suggest epic dimensions. He is on the one hand a hero of enormous energy and determination, "one of the greatest men in Umuofia" as his friend Obierika says, but his particular mode of greatness also causes his downfall. Like Achilles in Homer's *Iliad*, Okonkwo clings to traditionally respected values of pride and warlike aggression, and he will die to preserve those values. His unwillingness to change sets him apart from the community and eventually isolates him from the clan with its emphasis on group decisions. Okonkwo is a passionate man who counts on physical strength, hard work, and courage to make his way. Humiliated by his father's laziness, shameful death, and lack of title, compelled early to support the entire family, he struggles desperately to root out any sign of inherited "feminine" weakness in himself or his son Nwoye. By cultivating strength and valor, he finds a way to surpass his father and become one of the village leaders. Okonkwo is not without tender feelings: he loves his wife Ekwefi; his daughter, Ezinma; and the youth Ikemefuna who is given to him to foster. When he cuts down Ikemefuna so as not to appear weak, he is shattered for days thereafter. Nonetheless, his obsession with fierce masculinity and his open disrespect for "womanly" qualities of gentleness, compassion, and peace separate him not only from other members of his clan such as the more balanced Obierika but also from the earth goddess herself. This imbalance leads to disaster.

PRONOUNCING GLOSSARY

The following list uses common English syllables and stress accents to provide rough equivalents of selected words whose pronunciation may be unfamiliar to the general reader. Most of the names in *Things Fall Apart* are pronounced basically as they would be in English (for example, Okonkwo as *oh-kon'-*kwo), except that Igbo (like other African languages and Chinese) is a tonal language and also uses high or low tones for individual syllables.

Chielo: *chee-e'-loh*

Chinua Achebe: *chin'-oo-ah ah-chay'-be*

egwugwu: *e'-gwoo-gwoo*

Erulu: *air-oo'-loo*

Ezeani: *ez-ah'-nee*

Ezeugo: *e-zoo'-goh*

Idemili: *ee-da'y-mee-lee*

Igbo: *ee'-boh*

Ikemefuna: *ee-kay-may'-foo-na*

mbari: *mbah'-ree*

Ndulue: *n'-doo-le*

Nwakibie: *nwa'-kee-byeh'*

Nwayieke: *nwah-ye'-ke*

Umuofia: *oo'-moo-off'-yah*

Things Fall Apart

Turning and turning in the widening gyre
The falcon cannot hear the falconer;
Things fall apart; the centre cannot hold;
Mere anarchy is loosed upon the world . . .
—W. B. Yeats, "The Second Coming"

Part One

I

Okonkwo[1] was well known throughout the nine villages and even beyond. His fame rested on solid personal achievements. As a young man of eighteen he had brought honor to his village by throwing Amalinze the Cat. Amalinze was the great wrestler who for seven years was unbeaten, from Umuofia to Mbaino.[2] He was called the Cat because his back would never touch the earth. It was this man that Okonkwo threw in a fight which the old men agreed was one of the fiercest since the founder of their town engaged a spirit of the wild for seven days and seven nights.

The drums beat and the flutes sang and the spectators held their breath. Amalinze was a wily craftsman, but Okonkwo was as slippery as a fish in water. Every nerve and every muscle stood out on their arms, on their backs and their thighs, and one almost heard them stretching to breaking point. In the end Okonkwo threw the Cat.

That was many years ago, twenty years or more, and during this time Okonkwo's fame had grown like a bush-fire in the harmattan.[3] He was tall and huge, and his bushy eyebrows and wide nose gave him a very severe look. He breathed heavily, and it was said that, when he slept, his wives and children in their houses could hear him breathe. When he walked, his heels hardly touched the ground and he seemed to walk on springs, as if he was going to pounce on somebody. And he did pounce on people quite often. He had a slight stammer and whenever he was angry and could not get his words out quickly enough, he would use his fists. He had no patience with unsuccessful men. He had had no patience with his father.

Unoka,[4] for that was his father's name, had died ten years ago. In his day he was lazy and improvident and was quite incapable of thinking about tomorrow. If any money came his way, and it seldom did, he immediately bought gourds of palm-wine, called round his neighbors and made merry. He always said that whenever he saw a dead man's mouth he saw the folly of not eating what one had in one's lifetime. Unoka was, of course, a debtor, and he owed every neighbor some money, from a few cowries[5] to quite substantial amounts.

He was tall but very thin and had a slight stoop. He wore a haggard and mournful look except when he was drinking or playing on his flute. He was very good on his flute, and his happiest moments were the two or three

---

1. Man (*oko*) Born on Nkwo Day. The name also suggests stubborn male pride.   2. Four settlements. Umuofia means children of the forest (literal trans.); but *ofia* ("forest") also means "bush" or land untouched by European influence.   3. A dusty wind from the Sahara.   4. Home is supreme. 5. Glossy half-inch-long tan-and-white shells, collected in strings and used as money. A bag of twenty-four thousand cowries weighed about sixty pounds and, at the time of the story, was worth approximately one British pound.

moons after the harvest when the village musicians brought down their instruments, hung above the fireplace. Unoka would play with them, his face beaming with blessedness and peace. Sometimes another village would ask Unoka's band and their dancing *egwugwu*[6] to come and stay with them and teach them their tunes. They would go to such hosts for as long as three or four markets,[7] making music and feasting. Unoka loved the good fare and the good fellowship, and he loved this season of the year, when the rains had stopped and the sun rose every morning with dazzling beauty. And it was not too hot either, because the cold and dry harmattan wind was blowing down from the north. Some years the harmattan was very severe and a dense haze hung on the atmosphere. Old men and children would then sit round log fires, warming their bodies. Unoka loved it all, and he loved the first kites[8] that returned with the dry season, and the children who sang songs of welcome to them. He would remember his own childhood, how he had often wandered around looking for a kite sailing leisurely against the blue sky. As soon as he found one he would sing with his whole being, welcoming it back from its long, long journey, and asking it if it had brought home any lengths of cloth.

That was years ago, when he was young. Unoka, the grown-up, was a failure. He was poor and his wife and children had barely enough to eat. People laughed at him because he was a loafer, and they swore never to lend him any more money because he never paid back. But Unoka was such a man that he always succeeded in borrowing more, and piling up his debts.

One day a neighbor called Okoye[9] came in to see him. He was reclining on a mud bed in his hut playing on the flute. He immediately rose and shook hands with Okoye, who then unrolled the goatskin which he carried under his arm, and sat down. Unoka went into an inner room and soon returned with a small wooden disc containing a kola nut, some alligator pepper and a lump of white chalk.[1]

"I have kola," he announced when he sat down, and passed the disc over to his guest.

"Thank you. He who brings kola brings life. But I think you ought to break it," replied Okoye, passing back the disc.

"No, it is for you, I think," and they argued like this for a few moments before Unoka accepted the honor of breaking the kola. Okoye, meanwhile, took the lump of chalk, drew some lines on the floor, and then painted his big toe.[2]

As he broke the kola, Unoka prayed to their ancestors for life and health, and for protection against their enemies. When they had eaten they talked about many things: about the heavy rains which were drowning the yams, about the next ancestral feast and about the impending war with the village of Mbaino. Unoka was never happy when it came to wars. He was in fact a coward and could not bear the sight of blood. And so he changed the subject

---

6. Here, masked performers as part of musical entertainment.   7. Counting one important market day a week, roughly two English weeks. The Igbo week has four days: Eke, Oye, Afo, and Nkwo. Eke is a rest day and the main market day; Afo, a half day on the farm; and Oye and Nkwo, full workdays.   8. A kind of hawk.   9. Man Born on Oye Day; a generic "Everyman" name.   1. Signifies coolness and peace, and is offered in rituals of hospitality so that the guest may draw his personal emblem on the floor. "Kola nut:" a bitter, caffeine-rich nut that is broken and eaten ceremonially; it indicates life or vitality. "Alligator pepper:" black pepper, known as the "pepper for kola" to distinguish it from cooking pepper, or chilies.   2. If the guest has taken the first title, he marks his big toe. Higher titles require different facial markings.

and talked about music, and his face beamed. He could hear in his mind's ear the blood-stirring and intricate rhythms of the *ekwe* and the *udu* and the *ogene*,[3] and he could hear his own flute weaving in and out of them, decorating them with a colorful and plaintive tune. The total effect was gay and brisk, but if one picked out the flute as it went up and down and then broke up into short snatches, one saw that there was sorrow and grief there.

Okoye was also a musician. He played on the *ogene*. But he was not a failure like Unoka. He had a large barn full of yams and he had three wives. And now he was going to take the Idemili title,[4] the third highest in the land. It was a very expensive ceremony and he was gathering all his resources together. That was in fact the reason why he had come to see Unoka. He cleared his throat and began:

"Thank you for the kola. You may have heard of the title I intend to take shortly."

Having spoken plainly so far, Okoye said the next half a dozen sentences in proverbs. Among the Ibo the art of conversation is regarded very highly, and proverbs are the palm-oil with which words are eaten. Okoye was a great talker and he spoke for a long time, skirting round the subject and then hitting it finally. In short, he was asking Unoka to return the two hundred cowries he had borrowed from him more than two years before. As soon as Unoka understood what his friend was driving at, he burst out laughing. He laughed loud and long and his voice rang out clear as the *ogene*, and tears stood in his eyes. His visitor was amazed, and sat speechless. At the end, Unoka was able to give an answer between fresh outbursts of mirth.

"Look at that wall," he said, pointing at the far wall of his hut, which was rubbed with red earth so that it shone. "Look at those lines of chalk;" and Okoye saw groups of short perpendicular lines drawn in chalk. There were five groups, and the smallest group had ten lines. Unoka had a sense of the dramatic and so he allowed a pause, in which he took a pinch of snuff and sneezed noisily, and then he continued: "Each group there represents a debt to someone, and each stroke is one hundred cowries. You see, I owe that man a thousand cowries. But he has not come to wake me up in the morning for it. I shall pay you, but not today. Our elders say that the sun will shine on those who stand before it shines on those who kneel under them. I shall pay my big debts first." And he took another pinch of snuff, as if that was paying the big debts first. Okoye rolled his goatskin and departed.

When Unoka died he had taken no title at all and he was heavily in debt. Any wonder then that his son Okonkwo was ashamed of him? Fortunately, among these people a man was judged according to his worth and not according to the worth of his father. Okonkwo was clearly cut out for great things. He was still young but he had won fame as the greatest wrestler in the nine villages. He was a wealthy farmer and had two barns full of yams, and had just married his third wife. To crown it all he had taken two titles and had shown incredible prowess in two inter-tribal wars. And so although

---

3. A bell-shaped gong made from two pieces of sheet iron. "*Ekwe*" a wooden drum, about three feet long, that produces high and low tones (as does the Igbo language). "*Udu*" a clay pot with a hole to one side of the neck opening; various resonant tones are produced when the hole is struck with one hand while the other hand covers or uncovers the top.   4. A title of honor named after the river god Idemili, to whom the python is sacred. "Barn": not a building, but a walled enclosure for the yam stacks (frames on which individual yams are tied, shaded with palm leaves, and exposed to circulating air).

Okonkwo was still young, he was already one of the greatest men of his time. Age was respected among his people, but achievement was revered. As the elders said, if a child washed his hands he could eat with kings. Okonkwo had clearly washed his hands and so he ate with kings and elders. And that was how he came to look after the doomed lad who was sacrificed to the village of Umuofia by their neighbors to avoid war and bloodshed. The ill-fated lad was called Ikemefuna.[5]

2

Okonkwo had just blown out the palm-oil lamp and stretched himself on his bamboo bed when he heard the *ogene* of the town crier piercing the still night air. *Gome, gome, gome, gome,* boomed the hollow metal. Then the crier gave his message, and at the end of it beat his instrument again. And this was the message. Every man of Umuofia was asked to gather at the market place tomorrow morning. Okonkwo wondered what was amiss, for he knew certainly that something was amiss. He had discerned a clear overtone of tragedy in the crier's voice, and even now he could still hear it as it grew dimmer and dimmer in the distance.

The night was very quiet. It was always quiet except on moonlight nights. Darkness held a vague terror for these people, even the bravest among them. Children were warned not to whistle at night for fear of evil spirits. Dangerous animals became even more sinister and uncanny in the dark. A snake was never called by its name at night, because it would hear. It was called a string. And so on this particular night as the crier's voice was gradually swallowed up in the distance, silence returned to the world, a vibrant silence made more intense by the universal trill of a million million forest insects.

On a moonlight night it would be different. The happy voices of children playing in open fields would then be heard. And perhaps those not so young would be playing in pairs in less open places, and old men and women would remember their youth. As the Ibo say: "When the moon is shining the cripple becomes hungry for a walk."

But this particular night was dark and silent. And in all the nine villages of Umuofia a town crier with his *ogene* asked every man to be present tomorrow morning. Okonkwo on his bamboo bed tried to figure out the nature of the emergency—war with a neighboring clan? That seemed the most likely reason, and he was not afraid of war. He was a man of action, a man of war. Unlike his father he could stand the look of blood. In Umuofia's latest war he was the first to bring home a human head. That was his fifth head; and he was not an old man yet. On great occasions such as the funeral of a village celebrity he drank his palm-wine from his first human head.

In the morning the market place was full. There must have been about ten thousand men there, all talking in low voices. At last Ogbuefi Ezeugo stood up in the midst of them and bellowed four times, *"Umuofia kwenu,"*[6] and on each occasion he faced a different direction and seemed to push the air with a clenched fist. And ten thousand men answered *"Yaa!"* each time. Then

---

5. My Strength Should Not Be Dissipated.   6. United Umuofia! An orator's call on the audience to respond as a group. "Ogbuefi:" cow killer (literal trans.); indicates someone who has taken a high title (for example the Idemili title) for which the celebration ceremony requires the slaughter of a cow. "Ezeugo:" a name denoting a priest or high initiate, someone who wears the eagle feather.

there was perfect silence. Ogbuefi Ezeugo was a powerful orator and was always chosen to speak on such occasions. He moved his hand over his white head and stroked his white beard. He then adjusted his cloth, which was passed under his right armpit and tied above his left shoulder.

"*Umuofia kwenu,*" he bellowed a fifth time, and the crowd yelled in answer. And then suddenly like one possessed he shot out his left hand and pointed in the direction of Mbaino, and said through gleaming white teeth firmly clenched: "Those sons of wild animals have dared to murder a daughter of Umuofia." He threw his head down and gnashed his teeth, and allowed a murmur of suppressed anger to sweep the crowd. When he began again, the anger on his face was gone and in its place a sort of smile hovered, more terrible and more sinister than the anger. And in a clear unemotional voice he told Umuofia how their daughter had gone to market at Mbaino and had been killed. That woman, said Ezeugo, was the wife of Ogbuefi Udo,[7] and he pointed to a man who sat near him with a bowed head. The crowd then shouted with anger and thirst for blood.

Many others spoke, and at the end it was decided to follow the normal course of action. An ultimatum was immediately dispatched to Mbaino asking them to choose between war on the one hand, and on the other the offer of a young man and a virgin as compensation.

Umuofia was feared by all its neighbors. It was powerful in war and in magic, and its priests and medicine men were feared in all the surrounding country. Its most potent war-medicine was as old as the clan itself. Nobody knew how old. But on one point there was general agreement—the active principle in that medicine had been an old woman with one leg. In fact, the medicine itself was called *agadi-nwayi,* or old woman. It had its shrine in the center of Umuofia, in a cleared spot. And if anybody was so foolhardy as to pass by the shrine after dusk he was sure to see the old woman hopping about.

And so the neighboring clans who naturally knew of these things feared Umuofia, and would not go to war against it without first trying a peaceful settlement. And in fairness to Umuofia it should be recorded that it never went to war unless its case was clear and just and was accepted as such by its Oracle—the Oracle of the Hills and the Caves. And there were indeed occasions when the Oracle had forbidden Umuofia to wage a war. If the clan had disobeyed the Oracle they would surely have been beaten, because their dreaded *agadi-nwayi* would never fight what the Ibo call *a fight of blame.*

But the war that now threatened was a just war. Even the enemy clan knew that. And so when Okonkwo of Umuofia arrived at Mbaino as the proud and imperious emissary of war, he was treated with great honor and respect, and two days later he returned home with a lad of fifteen and a young virgin. The lad's name was Ikemefuna, whose sad story is still told in Umuofia unto this day.

The elders, or *ndichie,* met to hear a report of Okonkwo's mission. At the end they decided, as everybody knew they would, that the girl should go to Ogbuefi Udo to replace his murdered wife. As for the boy, he belonged to the clan as a whole, and there was no hurry to decide his fate. Okonkwo was,

7. Peace.

therefore, asked on behalf of the clan to look after him in the interim. And so for three years Ikemefuna lived in Okonkwo's household.

Okonkwo ruled his houschold with a heavy hand. Ilis wives, especially the youngest, lived in perpetual fear of his fiery temper, and so did his little children. Perhaps down in his heart Okonkwo was not a cruel man. But his whole life was dominated by fear, the fear of failure and of weakness. It was deeper and more intimate than the fear of evil and capricious gods and of magic, the fear of the forest, and of the forces of nature, malevolent, red in tooth and claw. Okonkwo's fear was greater than these. It was not external but lay deep within himself. It was the fear of himself, lest he should be found to resemble his father. Even as a little boy he had resented his father's failure and weakness, and even now he still remembered how he had suffered when a playmate had told him that his father was *agbala*. That was how Okonkwo first came to know that *agbala* was not only another name for a woman, it could also mean a man who had taken no title. And so Okonkwo was ruled by one passion—to hate everything that his father Unoka had loved. One of those things was gentleness and another was idleness.

During the planting season Okonkwo worked daily on his farms from cock-crow until the chickens went to roost. He was a very strong man and rarely felt fatigue. But his wives and young children were not as strong, and so they suffered. But they dared not complain openly. Okonkwo's first son, Nwoye,[8] was then twelve years old but was already causing his father great anxiety for his incipient laziness. At any rate, that was how it looked to his father, and he sought to correct him by constant nagging and beating. And so Nwoye was developing into a sad-faced youth.

Okonkwo's prosperity was visible in his household. He had a large compound enclosed by a thick wall of red earth. His own hut, or *obi*, stood immediately behind the only gate in the red walls. Each of his three wives had her own hut, which together formed a half moon behind the *obi*. The barn was built against one end of the red walls, and long stacks of yam stood out prosperously in it. At the opposite end of the compound was a shed for the goats, and each wife built a small attachment to her hut for the hens. Near the barn was a small house, the "medicine house" or shrine where Okonkwo kept the wooden symbols of his personal god and of his ancestral spirits. He worshiped them with sacrifices of kola nut, food and palm-wine, and offered prayers to them on behalf of himself, his three wives and eight children.

So when the daughter of Umuofia was killed in Mbaino, Ikemefuna came into Okonkwo's household. When Okonkwo brought him home that day he called his most senior wife and handed him over to her.

"He belongs to the clan," he told her. "So look after him."

"Is he staying long with us?" she asked.

"Do what you are told, woman," Okonkwo thundered, and stammered. "When did you become one of the *ndichie* of Umuofia?"

And so Nwoye's mother took Ikemefuna to her hut and asked no more questions.

8. Child Born on Oye day.

As for the boy himself, he was terribly afraid. He could not understand what was happening to him or what he had done. How could he know that his father had taken a hand in killing a daughter of Umuofia? All he knew was that a few men had arrived at their house, conversing with his father in low tones, and at the end he had been taken out and handed over to a stranger. His mother had wept bitterly, but he had been too surprised to weep. And so the stranger had brought him, and a girl, a long, long way from home, through lonely forest paths. He did not know who the girl was, and he never saw her again.

3

Okonkwo did not have the start in life which many young men usually had. He did not inherit a barn from his father. There was no barn to inherit. The story was told in Umuofia, of how his father, Unoka, had gone to consult the Oracle of the Hills and the Caves to find out why he always had a miserable harvest.

The Oracle was called Agbala,[9] and people came from far and near to consult it. They came when misfortune dogged their steps or when they had a dispute with their neighbors. They came to discover what the future held for them or to consult the spirits of their departed fathers.

The way into the shrine was a round hole at the side of a hill, just a little bigger than the round opening into a henhouse. Worshipers and those who came to seek knowledge from the god crawled on their belly through the hole and found themselves in a dark, endless space in the presence of Agbala. No one had ever beheld Agbala, except his priestess. But no one who had ever crawled into his awful shrine had come out without the fear of his power. His priestess stood by the sacred fire which she built in the heart of the cave and proclaimed the will of the god. The fire did not burn with a flame. The glowing logs only served to light up vaguely the dark figure of the priestess.

Sometimes a man came to consult the spirit of his dead father or relative. It was said that when such a spirit appeared, the man saw it vaguely in the darkness, but never heard its voice. Some people even said that they had heard the spirits flying and flapping their wings against the roof of the cave.

Many years ago when Okonkwo was still a boy his father, Unoka, had gone to consult Agbala. The priestess in those days was a woman called Chika.[1] She was full of the power of her god, and she was greatly feared. Unoka stood before her and began his story.

"Every year," he said sadly, "before I put any crop in the earth, I sacrifice a cock to Ani, the owner of all land. It is the law of our fathers. I also kill a cock at the shrine of Ifejioku, the god of yams. I clear the bush and set fire to it when it is dry. I sow the yams when the first rain has fallen, and stake them when the young tendrils appear. I weed—"

"Hold your peace!" screamed the priestess, her voice terrible as it echoed through the dark void. "You have offended neither the gods nor your fathers. And when a man is at peace with his gods and his ancestors, his harvest will be good or bad according to the strength of his arm. You, Unoka, are known

---

9. The Oracle is masculine, but his priestess, or Voice, is feminine.   1. Sky Is Supreme.

in all the clan for the weakness of your machete and your hoe. When your neighbors go out with their ax to cut down virgin forests, you sow your yams on exhausted farms that take no labor to clear. They cross seven rivers to make their farms; you stay at home and offer sacrifices to a reluctant soil. Go home and work like a man."

Unoka was an ill-fated man. He had a bad *chi* or personal god, and evil fortune followed him to the grave, or rather to his death, for he had no grave. He died of the swelling which was an abomination to the earth goddess. When a man was afflicted with swelling in the stomach and the limbs he was not allowed to die in the house. He was carried to the Evil Forest and left there to die. There was the story of a very stubborn man who staggered back to his house and had to be carried again to the forest and tied to a tree. The sickness was an abomination to the earth, and so the victim could not be buried in her bowels. He died and rotted away above the earth, and was not given the first or the second burial. Such was Unoka's fate. When they carried him away, he took with him his flute.

With a father like Unoka, Okonkwo did not have the start in life which many young men had. He neither inherited a barn nor a title, nor even a young wife. But in spite of these disadvantages, he had begun even in his father's lifetime to lay the foundations of a prosperous future. It was slow and painful. But he threw himself into it like one possessed. And indeed he was possessed by the fear of his father's contemptible life and shameful death.

There was a wealthy man in Okonkwo's village who had three huge barns, nine wives and thirty children. His name was Nwakibie[2] and he had taken the highest but one title which a man could take in the clan. It was for this man that Okonkwo worked to earn his first seed yams.

He took a pot of palm-wine and a cock to Nwakibie. Two elderly neighbors were sent for, and Nwakibie's two grown-up sons were also present in his *obi*. He presented a kola nut and an alligator pepper, which were passed round for all to see and then returned to him. He broke the nut saying: "We shall all live. We pray for life, children, a good harvest and happiness. You will have what is good for you and I will have what is good for me. Let the kite perch and let the eagle perch too. If one says no to the other, let his wing break."

After the kola nut had been eaten Okonkwo brought his palm-wine from the corner of the hut where it had been placed and stood it in the center of the group. He addressed Nwakibie, calling him "Our father."

"*Nna ayi,*" he said. "I have brought you this little kola. As our people say, a man who pays respect to the great paves the way for his own greatness. I have come to pay you my respects and also to ask a favor. But let us drink the wine first."

Everybody thanked Okonkwo and the neighbors brought out their drinking horns from the goatskin bags they carried. Nwakibie brought down his own horn, which was fastened to the rafters. The younger of his sons, who was also the youngest man in the group, moved to the center, raised the pot on his left knee and began to pour out the wine. The first cup went to

2. The Child Surpasses His Neighbors.

Okonkwo, who must taste his wine before anyone else.[3] Then the group drank, beginning with the eldest man. When everyone had drunk two or three horns, Nwakibie sent for his wives. Some of them were not at home and only four came in.

"Is Anasi not in?" he asked them. They said she was coming. Anasi[4] was the first wife and the others could not drink before her, and so they stood waiting.

Anasi was a middle-aged woman, tall and strongly built. There was authority in her bearing and she looked every inch the ruler of the women-folk in a large and prosperous family. She wore the anklet of her husband's titles, which the first wife alone could wear.

She walked up to her husband and accepted the horn from him. She then went down on one knee, drank a little and handed back the horn. She rose, called him by his name and went back to her hut. The other wives drank in the same way, in their proper order, and went away.

The men then continued their drinking and talking. Ogbuefi Idigo was talking about the palm-wine tapper, Obiako, who suddenly gave up his trade.

"There must be something behind it," he said, wiping the foam of wine from his mustache with the back of his left hand. "There must be a reason for it. A toad does not run in the daytime for nothing."

"Some people say the Oracle warned him that he would fall off a palm tree and kill himself," said Akukalia.

"Obiako has always been a strange one," said Nwakibie. "I have heard that many years ago, when his father had not been dead very long, he had gone to consult the Oracle. The Oracle said to him, 'Your dead father wants you to sacrifice a goat to him.' Do you know what he told the Oracle? He said, 'Ask my dead father if he ever had a fowl when he was alive.'" Everybody laughed heartily except Okonkwo, who laughed uneasily because, as the saying goes, an old woman is always uneasy when dry bones are mentioned in a proverb. Okonkwo remembered his own father.

At last the young man who was pouring out the wine held up half a horn of the thick, white dregs and said, "What we are eating is finished." "We have seen it," the others replied. "Who will drink the dregs?" he asked. "Whoever has a job in hand," said Idigo, looking at Nwakibie's elder son Igwelo with a malicious twinkle in his eye.

Everyone agreed that Igwelo should drink the dregs. He accepted the half-full horn from his brother and drank it. As Idigo had said, Igwelo had a job in hand because he had married his first wife a month or two before. The thick dregs of palm-wine were supposed to be good for men who were going in to their wives.

After the wine had been drunk Okonkwo laid his difficulties before Nwakibie.

"I have come to you for help," he said. "Perhaps you can already guess what it is. I have cleared a farm but have no yams to sow. I know what it is to ask a man to trust another with his yams, especially these days when young men are afraid of hard work. I am not afraid of work. The lizard that jumped from the high iroko tree to the ground said he would praise himself

---

3. A ceremonial gesture; one who gives wine tastes it first to show that it is not poisoned. 4. First or favorite wife—not always the same.

if no one else did. I began to fend for myself at an age when most people still suck at their mothers' breasts. If you give me some yam seeds I shall not fail you."

Nwakibie cleared his throat. "It pleases me to see a young man like you these days when our youth has gone so soft. Many young men have come to me to ask for yams but I have refused because I knew they would just dump them in the earth and leave them to be choked by weeds. When I say no to them they think I am hard-hearted. But it is not so. Eneke the bird[5] says that since men have learned to shoot without missing, he has learned to fly without perching. I have learned to be stingy with my yams. But I can trust you. I know it as I look at you. As our fathers said, you can tell a ripe corn by its look. I shall give you twice four hundred yams. Go ahead and prepare your farm."

Okonkwo thanked him again and again and went home feeling happy. He knew that Nwakibie would not refuse him, but he had not expected he would be so generous. He had not hoped to get more than four hundred seeds. He would now have to make a bigger farm. He hoped to get another four hundred yams from one of his father's friends at Isiuzo.[6]

Sharecropping was a very slow way of building up a barn of one's own. After all the toil one only got a third of the harvest. But for a young man whose father had no yams, there was no other way. And what made it worse in Okonkwo's case was that he had to support his mother and two sisters from his meager harvest. And supporting his mother also meant supporting his father. She could not be expected to cook and eat while her husband starved. And so at a very early age when he was striving desperately to build a barn through sharecropping Okonkwo was also fending for his father's house. It was like pouring grains of corn into a bag full of holes. His mother and sisters worked hard enough, but they grew women's crops, like coco-yams, beans and cassava. Yam, the king of crops, was a man's crop.[7]

The year that Okonkwo took eight hundred seed-yams from Nwakibie was the worst year in living memory. Nothing happened at its proper time; it was either too early or too late. It seemed as if the world had gone mad. The first rains were late, and, when they came, lasted only a brief moment. The blazing sun returned, more fierce than it had ever been known, and scorched all the green that had appeared with the rains. The earth burned like hot coals and roasted all the yams that had been sown. Like all good farmers, Okonkwo had begun to sow with the first rains. He had sown four hundred seeds when the rains dried up and the heat returned. He watched the sky all day for signs of rain clouds and lay awake all night. In the morning he went back to his farm and saw the withering tendrils. He had tried to protect them from the smoldering earth by making rings of thick sisal leaves around them. But by the end of the day the sisal rings were burned dry and gray. He changed them every day, and prayed that the rain might fall in the night. But the drought continued for eight market weeks and the yams were killed.

---

5. Proverbial.   6. Head of the road; a small town.   7. Yams, a staple food in western Africa, were a sacred crop generally cultivated only by men, and eaten either roasted or boiled. "Coco-yams" (a brown root also called taro) and "cassava" (or manioc, which is refined in various ways to remove natural arsenic) were low-status root vegetables prepared for eating by boiling and pounding.

Some farmers had not planted their yams yet. They were the lazy easygoing ones who always put off clearing their farms as long as they could. This year they were the wise ones. They sympathized with their neighbors with much shaking of the head, but inwardly they were happy for what they took to be their own foresight.

Okonkwo planted what was left of his seed-yams when the rains finally returned. He had one consolation. The yams he had sown before the drought were his own, the harvest of the previous year. He still had the eight hundred from Nwakibie and the four hundred from his father's friend. So he would make a fresh start.

But the year had gone mad. Rain fell as it had never fallen before. For days and nights together it poured down in violent torrents, and washed away the yam heaps. Trees were uprooted and deep gorges appeared everywhere. Then the rain became less violent. But it went from day to day without a pause. The spell of sunshine which always came in the middle of the wet season did not appear. The yams put on luxuriant green leaves, but every farmer knew that without sunshine the tubers would not grow.

That year the harvest was sad, like a funeral, and many farmers wept as they dug up the miserable and rotting yams. One man tied his cloth to a tree branch and hanged himself.

Okonkwo remembered that tragic year with a cold shiver throughout the rest of his life. It always surprised him when he thought of it later that he did not sink under the load of despair. He knew that he was a fierce fighter, but that year had been enough to break the heart of a lion.

"Since I survived that year," he always said, "I shall survive anything." He put it down to his inflexible will.

His father, Unoka, who was then an ailing man, had said to him during that terrible harvest month: "Do not despair. I know you will not despair. You have a manly and a proud heart. A proud heart can survive a general failure because such a failure does not prick its pride. It is more difficult and more bitter when a man fails *alone*."

Unoka was like that in his last days. His love of talk had grown with age and sickness. It tried Okonkwo's patience beyond words.

4

"Looking at a king's mouth," said an old man, "one would think he never sucked at his mother's breast." He was talking about Okonkwo, who had risen so suddenly from great poverty and misfortune to be one of the lords of the clan. The old man bore no ill will towards Okonkwo. Indeed he respected him for his industry and success. But he was struck, as most people were, by Okonkwo's brusqueness in dealing with less successful men. Only a week ago a man had contradicted him at a kindred meeting which they held to discuss the next ancestral feast. Without looking at the man Okonkwo had said: "This meeting is for men." The man who had contradicted him had no titles. That was why he had called him a woman. Okonkwo knew how to kill a man's spirit.

Everybody at the kindred meeting took sides with Osugo[8] when Okonkwo called him a woman. The oldest man present said sternly that those whose

8. Low-Status (*osu*) Person.

palm-kernels were cracked for them by a benevolent spirit should not forget to be humble. Okonkwo said he was sorry for what he had said, and the meeting continued.

But it was really not true that Okonkwo's palm-kernels had been cracked for him by a benevolent spirit. He had cracked them himself. Anyone who knew his grim struggle against poverty and misfortune could not say he had been lucky. If ever a man deserved his success, that man was Okonkwo. At an early age he had achieved fame as the greatest wrestler in all the land. That was not luck. At the most one could say that his *chi* or personal god was good. But the Ibo people have a proverb that when a man says yes his *chi* says yes also. Okonkwo said yes very strongly; so his *chi* agreed. And not only his *chi* but his clan too, because it judged a man by the work of his hands. That was why Okonkwo had been chosen by the nine villages to carry a message of war to their enemies unless they agreed to give up a young man and a virgin to atone for the murder of Udo's wife. And such was the deep fear that their enemies had for Umuofia that they treated Okonkwo like a king and brought him a virgin who was given to Udo as wife, and the lad Ikemefuna.

The elders of the clan had decided that Ikemefuna should be in Okonkwo's care for a while. But no one thought it would be as long as three years. They seemed to forget all about him as soon as they had taken the decision.

At first Ikemefuna was very much afraid. Once or twice he tried to run away, but he did not know where to begin. He thought of his mother and his three-year-old sister and wept bitterly. Nwoye's mother was very kind to him and treated him as one of her own children. But all he said was: "When shall I go home?" When Okonkwo heard that he would not eat any food he came into the hut with a big stick in his hand and stood over him while he swallowed his yams, trembling. A few moments later he went behind the hut and began to vomit painfully. Nwoye's mother went to him and placed her hands on his chest and on his back. He was ill for three market weeks, and when he recovered he seemed to have overcome his great fear and sadness.

He was by nature a very lively boy and he gradually became popular in Okonkwo's household, especially with the children. Okonkwo's son, Nwoye, who was two years younger, became quite inseparable from him because he seemed to know everything. He could fashion out flutes from bamboo stems and even from the elephant grass. He knew the names of all the birds and could set clever traps for the little bush rodents. And he knew which trees made the strongest bows.

Even Okonkwo himself became very fond of the boy—inwardly of course. Okonkwo never showed any emotion openly, unless it be the emotion of anger. To show affection was a sign of weakness; the only thing worth demonstrating was strength. He therefore treated Ikemefuna as he treated everybody else—with a heavy hand. But there was no doubt that he liked the boy. Sometimes when he went to big village meetings or communal ancestral feasts he allowed Ikemefuna to accompany him, like a son, carrying his stool and his goatskin bag. And, indeed, Ikemefuna called him father.

Ikemefuna came to Umuofia at the end of the carefree season between harvest and planting. In fact he recovered from his illness only a few days before the Week of Peace began. And that was also the year Okonkwo broke the peace, and was punished, as was the custom, by Ezeani, the priest of the earth goddess.

Okonkwo was provoked to justifiable anger by his youngest wife, who went to plait her hair at her friend's house and did not return early enough to cook the afternoon meal. Okonkwo did not know at first that she was not at home. After waiting in vain for her dish he went to her hut to see what she was doing. There was nobody in the hut and the fireplace was cold.

"Where is Ojiugo?" he asked his second wife, who came out of her hut to draw water from a gigantic pot in the shade of a small tree in the middle of the compound.

"She has gone to plait her hair."

Okonkwo bit his lips as anger welled up within him.

"Where are her children? Did she take them?" he asked with unusual coolness and restraint.

"They are here," answered his first wife, Nwoye's mother. Okonkwo bent down and looked into her hut. Ojiugo's children were eating with the children of his first wife.

"Did she ask you to feed them before she went?"

"Yes," lied Nwoye's mother, trying to minimize Ojiugo's thoughtlessness.

Okonkwo knew she was not speaking the truth. He walked back to his *obi* to await Ojiugo's return. And when she returned he beat her very heavily. In his anger he had forgotten that it was the Week of Peace. His first two wives ran out in great alarm pleading with him that it was the sacred week. But Okonkwo was not the man to stop beating somebody half-way through, not even for fear of a goddess.

Okonkwo's neighbors heard his wife crying and sent their voices over the compound walls to ask what was the matter. Some of them came over to see for themselves. It was unheard of to beat somebody during the sacred week.

Before it was dusk Ezeani, who was the priest of the earth goddess, Ani, called on Okonkwo in his *obi*. Okonkwo brought out kola nut and placed it before the priest.

"Take away your kola nut. I shall not eat in the house of a man who has no respect for our gods and ancestors."

Okonkwo tried to explain to him what his wife had done, but Ezeani seemed to pay no attention. He held a short staff in his hand which he brought down on the floor to emphasize his points.

"Listen to me," he said when Okonkwo had spoken. "You are not a stranger in Umuofia. You know as well as I do that our forefathers ordained that before we plant any crops in the earth we should observe a week in which a man does not say a harsh word to his neighbor. We live in peace with our fellows to honor our great goddess of the earth without whose blessing our crops will not grow. You have committed a great evil." He brought down his staff heavily on the floor. "Your wife was at fault, but even if you came into your *obi* and found her lover on top of her, you would still have committed a great evil to beat her." His staff came down again. "The evil you have done can ruin the whole clan. The earth goddess whom you have insulted may refuse to give us her increase, and we shall all perish." His tone now changed from anger to command. "You will bring to the shrine of

Ani tomorrow one she-goat, one hen, a length of cloth and a hundred cowries." He rose and left the hut.

Okonkwo did as the priest said. He also took with him a pot of palm-wine. Inwardly, he was repentant. But he was not the man to go about telling his neighbors that he was in error. And so people said he had no respect for the gods of the clan. His enemies said his good fortune had gone to his head. They called him the little bird *nza*[9] who so far forgot himself after a heavy meal that he challenged his *chi*.

No work was done during the Week of Peace. People called on their neighbors and drank palm-wine. This year they talked of nothing else but the *nso-ani*[1] which Okonkwo had committed. It was the first time for many years that a man had broken the sacred peace. Even the oldest men could only remember one or two other occasions somewhere in the dim past.

Ogbuefi Ezeudu, who was the oldest man in the village, was telling two other men who came to visit him that the punishment for breaking the Peace of Ani had become very mild in their clan.

"It has not always been so," he said. "My father told me that he had been told that in the past a man who broke the peace was dragged on the ground through the village until he died. But after a while this custom was stopped because it spoiled the peace which it was meant to preserve."

"Somebody told me yesterday," said one of the younger men, "that in some clans it is an abomination for a man to die during the Week of Peace."

"It is indeed true," said Ogbuefi Ezeudu. "They have that custom in Obodoani.[2] If a man dies at this time he is not buried but cast into the Evil Forest. It is a bad custom which these people observe because they lack understanding. They throw away large numbers of men and women without burial. And what is the result? Their clan is full of the evil spirits of these unburied dead, hungry to do harm to the living."

After the Week of Peace every man and his family began to clear the bush to make new farms. The cut bush was left to dry and fire was then set to it. As the smoke rose into the sky kites appeared from different directions and hovered over the burning field in silent valediction. The rainy season was approaching when they would go away until the dry season returned.

Okonkwo spent the next few days preparing his seed-yams. He looked at each yam carefully to see whether it was good for sowing. Sometimes he decided that a yam was too big to be sown as one seed and he split it deftly along its length with his sharp knife. His eldest son, Nwoye, and Ikemefuna helped him by fetching the yams in long baskets from the barn and in counting the prepared seeds in groups of four hundred. Sometimes Okonkwo gave them a few yams each to prepare. But he always found fault with their effort, and he said so with much threatening.

"Do you think you are cutting up yams for cooking?" he asked Nwoye. "If you split another yam of this size, I shall break your jaw. You think you are still a child. I began to own a farm at your age. And you," he said to Ikemefuna, "do you not grow yams where you come from?"

9. The one that talks back (literal trans.); a small aggressive bird. In the story, it is easily defeated (alternatively, caught by a hawk) when it becomes foolish enough to challenge its personal god.   1. Sin, abomination against the earth goddess Ani.   2. The town of the land (literal trans.); that is, Anytown, Nigeria.

Inwardly Okonkwo knew that the boys were still too young to understand fully the difficult art of preparing seed-yams. But he thought that one could not begin too early. Yam stood for manliness, and he who could feed his family on yams from one harvest to another was a very great man indeed. Okonkwo wanted his son to be a great farmer and a great man. He would stamp out the disquieting signs of laziness which he thought he already saw in him.

"I will not have a son who cannot hold up his head in the gathering of the clan. I would sooner strangle him with my own hands. And if you stand staring at me like that," he swore, "Amadiora[3] will break your head for you!"

Some days later, when the land had been moistened by two or three heavy rains, Okonkwo and his family went to the farm with baskets of seed-yams, their hoes and machetes, and the planting began. They made single mounds of earth in straight lines all over the field and sowed the yams in them.

Yam, the king of crops, was a very exacting king. For three or four moons it demanded hard work and constant attention from cock-crow till the chickens went back to roost. The young tendrils were protected from earth-heat with rings of sisal leaves. As the rains became heavier the women planted maize, melons and beans between the yam mounds. The yams were then staked, first with little sticks and later with tall and big tree branches. The women weeded the farm three times at definite periods in the life of the yams, neither early nor late.

And now the rains had really come, so heavy and persistent that even the village rain-maker no longer claimed to be able to intervene. He could not stop the rain now, just as he would not attempt to start it in the heart of the dry season, without serious danger to his own health. The personal dynamism required to counter the forces of these extremes of weather would be far too great for the human frame.

And so nature was not interfered with in the middle of the rainy season. Sometimes it poured down in such thick sheets of water that earth and sky seemed merged in one gray wetness. It was then uncertain whether the low rumbling of Amadiora's thunder came from above or below. At such times, in each of the countless thatched huts of Umuofia, children sat around their mother's cooking fire telling stories, or with their father in his *obi* warming themselves from a log fire, roasting and eating maize. It was a brief resting period between the exacting and arduous planting season and the equally exacting but light-hearted month of harvests.

Ikemefuna had begun to feel like a member of Okonkwo's family. He still thought about his mother and his three-year-old sister, and he had moments of sadness and depression. But he and Nwoye had become so deeply attached to each other that such moments became less frequent and less poignant. Ikemefuna had an endless stock of folk tales. Even those which Nwoye knew already were told with a new freshness and the local flavor of a different clan. Nwoye remembered this period very vividly till the end of his life. He even remembered how he had laughed when Ikemefuna told him that the proper name for a corn cob with only a few scattered grains was *eze-*

---

3. God of thunder and lightning.

agadi-nwayi, or the teeth of an old woman. Nwoye's mind had gone immediately to Nwayieke, who lived near the udala[4] tree. She had about three teeth and was always smoking her pipe.

Gradually the rains became lighter and less frequent, and earth and sky once again became separate. The rain fell in thin, slanting showers through sunshine and quiet breeze. Children no longer stayed indoors but ran about singing:

> The rain is falling, the sun is shining,
> Alone Nnadi[5] is cooking and eating.

Nwoye always wondered who Nnadi was and why he should live all by himself, cooking and eating. In the end he decided that Nnadi must live in that land of Ikemefuna's favorite story where the ant holds his court in splendor and the sands dance forever.

5

The Feast of the New Yam was approaching and Umuofia was in a festival mood. It was an occasion for giving thanks to Ani, the earth goddess and the source of all fertility. Ani played a greater part in the life of the people than any other deity. She was the ultimate judge of morality and conduct. And what was more, she was in close communion with the departed fathers of the clan whose bodies had been committed to earth.

The Feast of the New Yam was held every year before the harvest began, to honor the earth goddess and the ancestral spirits of the clan. New yams could not be eaten until some had first been offered to these powers. Men and women, young and old, looked forward to the New Yam Festival because it began the season of plenty—the new year. On the last night before the festival, yams of the old year were all disposed of by those who still had them. The new year must begin with tasty, fresh yams and not the shriveled and fibrous crops of the previous year. All cooking pots, calabashes and wooden bowls were thoroughly washed, especially the wooden mortar in which yam was pounded. Yam foo-foo[6] and vegetable soup was the chief food in the celebration. So much of it was cooked that, no matter how heavily the family ate or how many friends and relatives they invited from neighboring villages, there was always a large quantity of food left over at the end of the day. The story was always told of a wealthy man who set before his guests a mound of foo-foo so high that those who sat on one side could not see what was happening on the other, and it was not until late in the evening that one of them saw for the first time his in-law who had arrived during the course of the meal and had fallen to on the opposite side. It was only then that they exchanged greetings and shook hands over what was left of the food.

The New Yam Festival was thus an occasion for joy throughout Umuofia. And every man whose arm was strong, as the Ibo people say, was expected to invite large numbers of guests from far and wide. Okonkwo always asked his wives' relations, and since he now had three wives his guests would make a fairly big crowd.

---

4. African star apple tree. Nwayieke means Woman Born on Eke Day.   5. Father Is There, or Father Exists.   6. A mashed, edible base that is shaped into balls with the fingers and then indented for cupping and eating soup.

But somehow Okonkwo could never become as enthusiastic over feasts as most people. He was a good eater and he could drink one or two fairly big gourds of palm-wine. But he was always uncomfortable sitting around for days waiting for a feast or getting over it. He would be very much happier working on his farm.

The festival was now only three days away. Okonkwo's wives had scrubbed the walls and the huts with red earth until they reflected light. They had then drawn patterns on them in white, yellow and dark green. They then set about painting themselves with cam wood and drawing beautiful black patterns on their stomachs and on their backs. The children were also decorated, especially their hair, which was shaved in beautiful patterns. The three women talked excitedly about the relations who had been invited, and the children reveled in the thought of being spoiled by these visitors from the motherland. Ikemefuna was equally excited. The New Yam Festival seemed to him to be a much bigger event here than in his own village, a place which was already becoming remote and vague in his imagination.

And then the storm burst. Okonkwo, who had been walking about aimlessly in his compound in suppressed anger, suddenly found an outlet.

"Who killed this banana tree?" he asked.

A hush fell on the compound immediately.

"Who killed this tree? Or are you all deaf and dumb?"

As a matter of fact the tree was very much alive. Okonkwo's second wife had merely cut a few leaves off it to wrap some food, and she said so. Without further argument Okonkwo gave her a sound beating and left her and her only daughter weeping. Neither of the other wives dared to interfere beyond an occasional and tentative, "It is enough, Okonkwo," pleaded from a reasonable distance.

His anger thus satisfied, Okonkwo decided to go out hunting. He had an old rusty gun made by a clever blacksmith who had come to live in Umuofia long ago. But although Okonkwo was a great man whose prowess was universally acknowledged, he was not a hunter. In fact he had not killed a rat with his gun. And so when he called Ikemefuna to fetch his gun, the wife who had just been beaten murmured something about guns that never shot. Unfortunately for her, Okonkwo heard it and ran madly into his room for the loaded gun, ran out again and aimed at her as she clambered over the dwarf wall of the barn. He pressed the trigger and there was a loud report accompanied by the wail of his wives and children. He threw down the gun and jumped into the barn, and there lay the woman, very much shaken and frightened but quite unhurt. He heaved a heavy sigh and went away with the gun.

In spite of this incident the New Yam Festival was celebrated with great joy in Okonkwo's household. Early that morning as he offered a sacrifice of new yam and palm-oil to his ancestors he asked them to protect him, his children and their mothers in the new year.

As the day wore on his in-laws arrived from three surrounding villages, and each party brought with them a huge pot of palm-wine. And there was eating and drinking till night, when Okonkwo's in-laws began to leave for their homes.

The second day of the new year was the day of the great wrestling match between Okonkwo's village and their neighbors. It was difficult to say which the people enjoyed more—the feasting and fellowship of the first day or the wrestling contest of the second. But there was one woman who had no doubt whatever in her mind. She was Okonkwo's second wife, Ekwefi, whom he nearly shot. There was no festival in all the seasons of the year which gave her as much pleasure as the wrestling match. Many years ago when she was the village beauty Okonkwo had won her heart by throwing the Cat in the greatest contest within living memory. She did not marry him then because he was too poor to pay her bride-price. But a few years later she ran away from her husband and came to live with Okonkwo. All this happened many years ago. Now Ekwefi[7] was a woman of forty-five who had suffered a great deal in her time. But her love of wrestling contests was still as strong as it was thirty years ago.

It was not yet noon on the second day of the New Yam Festival. Ekwefi and her only daughter, Ezinma,[8] sat near the fireplace waiting for the water in the pot to boil. The fowl Ekwefi had just killed was in the wooden mortar. The water began to boil, and in one deft movement she lifted the pot from the fire and poured the boiling water over the fowl. She put back the empty pot on the circular pad in the corner, and looked at her palms, which were black with soot. Ezinma was always surprised that her mother could lift a pot from the fire with her bare hands.

"Ekwefi," she said, "is it true that when people are grown up, fire does not burn them?" Ezinma, unlike most children, called her mother by her name.

"Yes," replied Ekwefi, too busy to argue. Her daughter was only ten years old but she was wiser than her years.

"But Nwoye's mother dropped her pot of hot soup the other day and it broke on the floor."

Ekwefi turned the hen over in the mortar and began to pluck the feathers.

"Ekwefi," said Ezinma, who had joined in plucking the feathers, "my eyelid is twitching."

"It means you are going to cry," said her mother.

"No," Ezinma said, "it is this eyelid, the top one."

"That means you will see something."

"What will I see?" she asked.

"How can I know?" Ekwefi wanted her to work it out herself.

"Oho," said Ezinma at last. "I know what it is—the wrestling match."

At last the hen was plucked clean. Ekwefi tried to pull out the horny beak but it was too hard. She turned round on her low stool and put the beak in the fire for a few moments. She pulled again and it came off.

"Ekwefi!" a voice called from one of the other huts. It was Nwoye's mother, Okonkwo's first wife.

"Is that me?" Ekwefi called back. That was the way people answered calls from outside. They never answered yes for fear it might be an evil spirit calling.

"Will you give Ezinma some fire to bring to me?" Her own children and Ikemefuna had gone to the stream.

Ekwefi put a few live coals into a piece of broken pot and Ezinma carried it across the clean swept compound to Nwoye's mother.

7. An abbreviation of "Do You Have a Cow?"; the cow being a symbol of wealth. Okonkwo would presumably have repaid Ekwefi's bride-price to her first husband.   8. True Beauty (literal trans.), or Goodness.

"Thank you, Nma," she said. She was peeling new yams, and in a basket beside her were green vegetables and beans.

"Let me make the fire for you," Ezinma offered.

"Thank you, Ezigbo," she said. She often called her Ezigbo, which means "the good one."

Ezinma went outside and brought some sticks from a huge bundle of firewood. She broke them into little pieces across the sole of her foot and began to build a fire, blowing it with her breath.

"You will blow your eyes out," said Nwoye's mother, looking up from the yams she was peeling. "Use the fan." She stood up and pulled out the fan which was fastened into one of the rafters. As soon as she got up, the troublesome nanny goat, which had been dutifully eating yam peelings, dug her teeth into the real thing, scooped out two mouthfuls and fled from the hut to chew the cud in the goats' shed. Nwoye's mother swore at her and settled down again to her peeling. Ezinma's fire was now sending up thick clouds of smoke. She went on fanning it until it burst into flames. Nwoye's mother thanked her and she went back to her mother's hut.

Just then the distant beating of drums began to reach them. It came from the direction of the *ilo*, the village playground. Every village had its own *ilo* which was as old as the village itself and where all the great ceremonies and dances took place. The drums beat the unmistakable wrestling dance— quick, light and gay, and it came floating on the wind.

Okonkwo cleared his throat and moved his feet to the beat of the drums. It filled him with fire as it had always done from his youth. He trembled with the desire to conquer and subdue. It was like the desire for a woman.

"We shall be late for the wrestling," said Ezinma to her mother.

"They will not begin until the sun goes down."

"But they are beating the drums."

"Yes. The drums begin at noon but the wrestling waits until the sun begins to sink. Go and see if your father has brought out yams for the afternoon."

"He has. Nwoye's mother is already cooking."

"Go and bring our own, then. We must cook quickly or we shall be late for the wrestling."

Ezinma ran in the direction of the barn and brought back two yams from the dwarf wall.

Ekwefi peeled the yams quickly. The troublesome nanny goat sniffed about, eating the peelings. She cut the yams into small pieces and began to prepare a pottage, using some of the chicken.

At that moment they heard someone crying just outside their compound. It was very much like Obiageli,[9] Nwoye's sister.

"Is that not Obiageli weeping?" Ekwefi called across the yard to Nwoye's mother.

"Yes," she replied. "She must have broken her waterpot."

The weeping was now quite close and soon the children filed in, carrying on their heads various sizes of pots suitable to their years. Ikemefuna came first with the biggest pot, closely followed by Nwoye and his two younger brothers. Obiageli brought up the rear, her face streaming with tears. In her hand was the cloth pad on which the pot should have rested on her head.

---

9. Born to Eat (Born into Prosperity).

"What happened?" her mother asked, and Obiageli told her mournful story. Her mother consoled her and promised to buy her another pot.

Nwoye's younger brothers were about to tell their mother the true story of the accident when Ikemefuna looked at them sternly and they held their peace. The fact was that Obiageli had been making *inyanga*[1] with her pot. She had balanced it on her head, folded her arms in front of her and began to sway her waist like a grown-up young lady. When the pot fell down and broke she burst out laughing. She only began to weep when they got near the iroko tree outside their compound.

The drums were still beating, persistent and unchanging. Their sound was no longer a separate thing from the living village. It was like the pulsation of its heart. It throbbed in the air, in the sunshine, and even in the trees, and filled the village with excitement.

Ekwefi ladled her husband's share of the pottage into a bowl and covered it. Ezinma took it to him in his *obi*.

Okonkwo was sitting on a goatskin already eating his first wife's meal. Obiageli, who had brought it from her mother's hut, sat on the floor waiting for him to finish. Ezinma placed her mother's dish before him and sat with Obiageli.

"Sit like a woman!" Okonkwo shouted at her. Ezinma brought her two legs together and stretched them in front of her.

"Father, will you go to see the wrestling?" Ezinma asked after a suitable interval.

"Yes," he answered. "Will you go?"

"Yes." And after a pause she said: "Can I bring your chair for you?"

"No, that is a boy's job." Okonkwo was specially fond of Ezinma. She looked very much like her mother, who was once the village beauty. But his fondness only showed on very rare occasions.

"Obiageli broke her pot today," Ezinma said.

"Yes, she has told me about it," Okonkwo said between mouthfuls.

"Father," said Obiageli, "people should not talk when they are eating or pepper may go down the wrong way."

"That is very true. Do you hear that, Ezinma? You are older than Obiageli but she has more sense."

He uncovered his second wife's dish and began to eat from it. Obiageli took the first dish and returned to her mother's hut. And then Nkechi came in, bringing the third dish. Nkechi was the daughter of Okonkwo's third wife.

In the distance the drums continued to beat.

6

The whole village turned out on the *ilo,* men, women and children. They stood round in a huge circle leaving the center of the playground free. The elders and grandees of the village sat on their own stools brought there by their young sons or slaves. Okonkwo was among them. All others stood except those who came early enough to secure places on the few stands which had been built by placing smooth logs on forked pillars.

1. Showing off.

The wrestlers were not there yet and the drummers held the field. They too sat just in front of the huge circle of spectators, facing the elders. Behind them was the big and ancient silk-cotton tree which was sacred. Spirits of good children lived in that tree waiting to be born. On ordinary days young women who desired children came to sit under its shade.

There were seven drums and they were arranged according to their sizes in a long wooden basket. Three men beat them with sticks, working feverishly from one drum to another. They were possessed by the spirit of the drums.

The young men who kept order on these occasions dashed about, consulting among themselves and with the leaders of the two wrestling teams, who were still outside the circle, behind the crowd. Once in a while two young men carrying palm fronds ran round the circle and kept the crowd back by beating the ground in front of them or, if they were stubborn, their legs and feet.

At last the two teams danced into the circle and the crowd roared and clapped. The drums rose to a frenzy. The people surged forward. The young men who kept order flew around, waving their palm fronds. Old men nodded to the beat of the drums and remembered the days when they wrestled to its intoxicating rhythm.

The contest began with boys of fifteen or sixteen. There were only three such boys in each team. They were not the real wrestlers; they merely set the scene. Within a short time the first two bouts were over. But the third created a big sensation even among the elders who did not usually show their excitement so openly. It was as quick as the other two, perhaps even quicker. But very few people had ever seen that kind of wrestling before. As soon as the two boys closed in, one of them did something which no one could describe because it had been as quick as a flash. And the other boy was flat on his back. The crowd roared and clapped and for a while drowned the frenzied drums. Okonkwo sprang to his feet and quickly sat down again. Three young men from the victorious boy's team ran forward, carried him shoulder high and danced through the cheering crowd. Everybody soon knew who the boy was. His name was Maduka, the son of Obierika.[2]

The drummers stopped for a brief rest before the real matches. Their bodies shone with sweat, and they took up fans and began to fan themselves. They also drank water from small pots and ate kola nuts. They became ordinary human beings again, talking and laughing among themselves and with others who stood near them. The air, which had been stretched taut with excitement, relaxed again. It was as if water had been poured on the tightened skin of a drum. Many people looked around, perhaps for the first time, and saw those who stood or sat next to them.

"I did not know it was you," Ekwefi said to the woman who had stood shoulder to shoulder with her since the beginning of the matches.

"I do not blame you," said the woman. "I have never seen such a large crowd of people. Is it true that Okonkwo nearly killed you with his gun?"

"It is true indeed, my dear friend. I cannot yet find a mouth with which to tell the story."

2. The Heart Eats [Enjoys] More.

"Your *chi* is very much awake, my friend. And how is my daughter, Ezinma?"

"She has been very well for some time now. Perhaps she has come to stay."

"I think she has. How old is she now?"

"She is about ten years old."

"I think she will stay. They usually stay if they do not die before the age of six."

"I pray she stays," said Ekwefi with a heavy sigh.

The woman with whom she talked was called Chielo.[3] She was the priestess of Agbala, the Oracle of the Hills and the Caves. In ordinary life Chielo was a widow with two children. She was very friendly with Ekwefi and they shared a common shed in the market. She was particularly fond of Ekwefi's only daughter, Ezinma, whom she called "my daughter." Quite often she bought beancakes and gave Ekwefi some to take home to Ezinma. Anyone seeing Chielo in ordinary life would hardly believe she was the same person who prophesied when the spirit of Agbala was upon her. The drummers took up their sticks and the air shivered and grew tense like a tightened bow.

The two teams were ranged facing each other across the clear space. A young man from one team danced across the center to the other side and pointed at whomever he wanted to fight. They danced back to the center together and then closed in.

There were twelve men on each side and the challenge went from one side to the other. Two judges walked around the wrestlers and when they thought they were equally matched, stopped them. Five matches ended in this way. But the really exciting moments were when a man was thrown. The huge voice of the crowd then rose to the sky and in every direction. It was even heard in the surrounding villages.

The last match was between the leaders of the teams. They were among the best wrestlers in all the nine villages. The crowd wondered who would throw the other this year. Some said Okafo was the better man; others said he was not the equal of Ikezue.[4] Last year neither of them had thrown the other even though the judges had allowed the contest to go on longer than was the custom. They had the same style and one saw the other's plans beforehand. It might happen again this year.

Dusk was already approaching when their contest began. The drums went mad and the crowds also. They surged forward as the two young men danced into the circle. The palm fronds were helpless in keeping them back.

Ikezue held out his right hand. Okafo seized it, and they closed in. It was a fierce contest. Ikezue strove to dig in his right heel behind Okafo so as to pitch him backwards in the clever *ege* style. But the one knew what the other was thinking. The crowd had surrounded and swallowed up the drummers, whose frantic rhythm was no longer a mere disembodied sound but the very heartbeat of the people.

The wrestlers were now almost still in each other's grip. The muscles on their arms and their thighs and on their backs stood out and twitched. It looked like an equal match. The two judges were already moving forward to separate them when Ikezue, now desperate, went down quickly on one knee

---

3. Chi Who Plants.   4. Strength Is Complete (a boastful name).

in an attempt to fling his man backwards over his head. It was a sad miscalculation. Quick as the lightning of Amadiora, Okafo raised his right leg and swung it over his rival's head. The crowd burst into a thunderous roar. Okafo was swept off his feet by his supporters and carried home shoulder high. They sang his praise and the young women clapped their hands:

> Who will wrestle for our village?
>   Okafo will wrestle for our village.
> Has he thrown a hundred men?
>   He has thrown four hundred men.
> Has he thrown a hundred Cats?
>   He has thrown four hundred Cats.
> Then send him word to fight for us.

7

For three years Ikemefuna lived in Okonkwo's household and the elders of Umuofia seemed to have forgotten about him. He grew rapidly like a yam tendril in the rainy season, and was full of the sap of life. He had become wholly absorbed into his new family. He was like an elder brother to Nwoye, and from the very first seemed to have kindled a new fire in the younger boy. He made him feel grown-up; and they no longer spent the evenings in mother's hut while she cooked, but now sat with Okonkwo in his *obi*, or watched him as he tapped his palm tree for the evening wine. Nothing pleased Nwoye now more than to be sent for by his mother or another of his father's wives to do one of those difficult and masculine tasks in the home, like splitting wood, or pounding food. On receiving such a message through a younger brother or sister, Nwoye would feign annoyance and grumble aloud about women and their troubles.

Okonkwo was inwardly pleased at his son's development, and he knew it was due to Ikemefuna. He wanted Nwoye to grow into a tough young man capable of ruling his father's household when he was dead and gone to join the ancestors. He wanted him to be a prosperous man, having enough in his barn to feed the ancestors with regular sacrifices. And so he was always happy when he heard him grumbling about women. That showed that in time he would be able to control his women-folk. No matter how prosperous a man was, if he was unable to rule his women and his children (and especially his women) he was not really a man. He was like the man in the song who had ten and one wives and not enough soup for his foo-foo.

So Okonkwo encouraged the boys to sit with him in his *obi*, and he told them stories of the land—masculine stories of violence and bloodshed. Nwoye knew that it was right to be masculine and to be violent, but somehow he still preferred the stories that his mother used to tell, and which she no doubt still told to her younger children—stories of the tortoise and his wily ways, and of the bird *eneke-nti-oba*[5] who challenged the whole world to a wrestling contest and was finally thrown by the cat. He remembered the story she often told of the quarrel between Earth and Sky long ago, and how Sky withheld rain for seven years, until crops withered and the dead could

---

5. The swallow with the ear of a crocodile [who is deaf] (literal trans.); a bird who proverbially flies without perching.

not be buried because the hoes broke on the stony Earth. At last Vulture was sent to plead with Sky, and to soften his heart with a song of the suffering of the sons of men. Whenever Nwoye's mother sang this song he felt carried away to the distant scene in the sky where Vulture, Earth's emissary, sang for mercy. At last Sky was moved to pity, and he gave to Vulture rain wrapped in leaves of coco-yam. But as he flew home his long talon pierced the leaves and the rain fell as it had never fallen before. And so heavily did it rain on Vulture that he did not return to deliver his message but flew to a distant land, from where he had espied a fire. And when he got there he found it was a man making a sacrifice. He warmed himself in the fire and ate the entrails.

That was the kind of story that Nwoye loved. But he now knew that they were for foolish women and children, and he knew that his father wanted him to be a man. And so he feigned that he no longer cared for women's stories. And when he did this he saw that his father was pleased, and no longer rebuked him or beat him. So Nwoye and Ikemefuna would listen to Okonkwo's stories about tribal wars, or how, years ago, he had stalked his victim, overpowered him and obtained his first human head. And as he told them of the past they sat in darkness or the dim glow of logs, waiting for the women to finish their cooking. When they finished, each brought her bowl of foo-foo and bowl of soup to her husband. An oil lamp was lit and Okonkwo tasted from each bowl, and then passed two shares to Nwoye and Ikemefuna.

In this way the moons and the seasons passed. And then the locusts came. It had not happened for many a long year. The elders said locusts came once in a generation, reappeared every year for seven years and then disappeared for another lifetime. They went back to their caves in a distant land, where they were guarded by a race of stunted men. And then after another lifetime these men opened the caves again and the locusts came to Umuofia.

They came in the cold harmattan season after the harvests had been gathered, and ate up all the wild grass in the fields.

Okonkwo and the two boys were working on the red outer walls of the compound. This was one of the lighter tasks of the after-harvest season. A new cover of thick palm branches and palm leaves was set on the walls to protect them from the next rainy season. Okonkwo worked on the outside of the wall and the boys worked from within. There were little holes from one side to the other in the upper levels of the wall, and through these Okonkwo passed the rope, or *tie-tie*,[6] to the boys and they passed it round the wooden stays and then back to him; and in this way the cover was strengthened on the wall.

The women had gone to the bush to collect firewood, and the little children to visit their playmates in the neighboring compounds. The harmattan was in the air and seemed to distill a hazy feeling of sleep on the world. Okonkwo and the boys worked in complete silence, which was only broken when a new palm frond was lifted on to the wall or when a busy hen moved dry leaves about in her ceaseless search for food.

And then quite suddenly a shadow fell on the world, and the sun seemed hidden behind a thick cloud. Okonkwo looked up from his work and wondered

---

6. A creeper used as a rope to lash sections in building (pidgin English from "to tie").

if it was going to rain at such an unlikely time of the year. But almost immediately a shout of joy broke out in all directions, and Umuofia, which had dozed in the noon-day haze, broke into life and activity.

"Locusts are descending," was joyfully chanted everywhere, and men, women and children left their work or their play and ran into the open to see the unfamiliar sight. The locusts had not come for many, many years, and only the old people had seen them before.

At first, a fairly small swarm came. They were the harbingers sent to survey the land. And then appeared on the horizon a slowly moving mass like a boundless sheet of black cloud drifting towards Umuofia. Soon it covered half the sky, and the solid mass was now broken by tiny eyes of light like shining star dust. It was a tremendous sight, full of power and beauty.

Everyone was now about, talking excitedly and praying that the locusts should camp in Umuofia for the night. For although locusts had not visited Umuofia for many years, everybody knew by instinct that they were very good to eat. And at last the locusts did descend. They settled on every tree and on every blade of grass; they settled on the roofs and covered the bare ground. Mighty tree branches broke away under them, and the whole country became the brown-earth color of the vast, hungry swarm.

Many people went out with baskets trying to catch them, but the elders counseled patience till nightfall. And they were right. The locusts settled in the bushes for the night and their wings became wet with dew. Then all Umuofia turned out in spite of the cold harmattan, and everyone filled his bags and pots with locusts. The next morning they were roasted in clay pots and then spread in the sun until they became dry and brittle. And for many days this rare food was eaten with solid palm-oil.

Okonkwo sat in his *obi* crunching happily with Ikemefuna and Nwoye, and drinking palm-wine copiously, when Ogbuefi Ezeudu came in. Ezeudu was the oldest man in this quarter of Umuofia. He had been a great and fearless warrior in his time, and was now accorded great respect in all the clan. He refused to join in the meal, and asked Okonkwo to have a word with him outside. And so they walked out together, the old man supporting himself with his stick. When they were out of earshot, he said to Okonkwo:

"That boy calls you father. Do not bear a hand in his death." Okonkwo was surprised, and was about to say something when the old man continued:

"Yes, Umuofia has decided to kill him. The Oracle of the Hills and the Caves has pronounced it. They will take him outside Umuofia as is the custom, and kill him there. But I want you to have nothing to do with it. He calls you his father."

The next day a group of elders from all the nine villages of Umuofia came to Okonkwo's house early in the morning, and before they began to speak in low tones Nwoye and Ikemefuna were sent out. They did not stay very long, but when they went away Okonkwo sat still for a very long time supporting his chin in his palms. Later in the day he called Ikemefuna and told him that he was to be taken home the next day. Nwoye overheard it and burst into tears, whereupon his father beat him heavily. As for Ikemefuna, he was at a loss. His own home had gradually become very faint and distant. He still missed his mother and his sister and would be very glad to see them. But somehow he knew he was not going to see them. He remembered once when men had talked in low tones with his father; and it seemed now as if it was happening all over again.

Later, Nwoye went to his mother's hut and told her that Ikemefuna was going home. She immediately dropped her pestle with which she was grinding pepper, folded her arms across her breast and sighed, "Poor child."

The next day, the men returned with a pot of wine. They were all fully dressed as if they were going to a big clan meeting or to pay a visit to a neighboring village. They passed their cloths under the right arm-pit, and hung their goatskin bags and sheathed machetes over their left shoulders. Okonkwo got ready quickly and the party set out with Ikemefuna carrying the pot of wine. A deathly silence descended on Okonkwo's compound. Even the very little children seemed to know. Throughout that day Nwoye sat in his mother's hut and tears stood in his eyes.

At the beginning of their journey the men of Umuofia talked and laughed about the locusts, about their women, and about some effeminate men who had refused to come with them. But as they drew near to the outskirts of Umuofia silence fell upon them too.

The sun rose slowly to the center of the sky, and the dry, sandy footway began to throw up the heat that lay buried in it. Some birds chirruped in the forests around. The men trod dry leaves on the sand. All else was silent. Then from the distance came the faint beating of the *ekwe*. It rose and faded with the wind—a peaceful dance from a distant clan.

"It is an *ozo* dance,"[7] the men said among themselves. But no one was sure where it was coming from. Some said Ezimili, others Abame or Aninta. They argued for a short while and fell into silence again, and the elusive dance rose and fell with the wind. Somewhere a man was taking one of the titles of his clan, with music and dancing and a great feast.

The footway had now become a narrow line in the heart of the forest. The short trees and sparse undergrowth which surrounded the men's village began to give way to giant trees and climbers which perhaps had stood from the beginning of things, untouched by the ax and the bush-fire. The sun breaking through their leaves and branches threw a pattern of light and shade on the sandy footway.

Ikemefuna heard a whisper close behind him and turned round sharply. The man who had whispered now called out aloud, urging the others to hurry up.

"We still have a long way to go," he said. Then he and another man went before Ikemefuna and set a faster pace.

Thus the men of Umuofia pursued their way, armed with sheathed machetes, and Ikemefuna, carrying a pot of palm-wine on his head, walked in their midst. Although he had felt uneasy at first, he was not afraid now. Okonkwo walked behind him. He could hardly imagine that Okonkwo was not his real father. He had never been fond of his real father, and at the end of three years he had become very distant indeed. But his mother and his three-year-old sister . . . of course she would not be three now, but six. Would he recognize her now? She must have grown quite big. How his mother would weep for joy, and thank Okonkwo for having looked after him so well and for bringing him back. She would want to hear everything that

---

7. Part of the *ozo* rituals, the spiritual ceremonies that accompanied the taking of titles.

had happened to him in all these years. Could he remember them all? He would tell her about Nwoye and his mother, and about the locusts. . . . Then quite suddenly a thought came upon him. His mother might be dead. He tried in vain to force the thought out of his mind. Then he tried to settle the matter the way he used to settle such matters when he was a little boy. He still remembered the song:

> Eze elina, elina!
> > Sala
> Eze ilikwa ya
> Ikwaba akwa oligholi
> Ebe Danda nechi eze
> Ebe Uzuzu nete egwu
> > Sala[8]

He sang it in his mind, and walked to its beat. If the song ended on his right foot, his mother was alive. If it ended on his left, she was dead. No, not dead, but ill. It ended on the right. She was alive and well. He sang the song again, and it ended on the left. But the second time did not count. The first voice gets to Chukwu, or God's house. That was a favorite saying of children. Ikemefuna felt like a child once more. It must be the thought of going home to his mother.

One of the men behind him cleared his throat. Ikemefuna looked back, and the man growled at him to go on and not stand looking back. The way he said it sent cold fear down Ikemefuna's back. His hands trembled vaguely on the black pot he carried. Why had Okonkwo withdrawn to the rear? Ikemefuna felt his legs melting under him. And he was afraid to look back.

As the man who had cleared his throat drew up and raised his machete, Okonkwo looked away. He heard the blow. The pot fell and broke in the sand. He heard Ikemefuna cry, "My father, they have killed me!" as he ran towards him. Dazed with fear, Okonkwo drew his machete and cut him down. He was afraid of being thought weak.

As soon as his father walked in, that night, Nwoye knew that Ikemefuna had been killed, and something seemed to give way inside him, like the snapping of a tightened bow. He did not cry. He just hung limp. He had had the same kind of feeling not long ago, during the last harvest season. Every child loved the harvest season. Those who were big enough to carry even a few yams in a tiny basket went with grown-ups to the farm. And if they could not help in digging up the yams, they could gather firewood together for roasting the ones that would be eaten there on the farm. This roasted yam soaked in red palm-oil and eaten in the open farm was sweeter than any meal at home. It was after such a day at the farm during the last harvest that Nwoye had felt for the first time a snapping inside him like the one he now felt. They were returning home with baskets of yams from a distant farm across the stream when they heard the voice of an infant crying in the thick forest. A sudden hush had fallen on the women, who had been talking, and they had quickened their steps. Nwoye had heard that twins were put in earthenware

---

8. King don't eat, don't eat / Sala / King if you eat it / You will weep for the abomination / Where Danda installs a king / Where Uzuzu dances / Sala. "Sala": meaningless refrain. "Danda": the ant. "Uzuzu": sand. Ikemefuna reassures himself by singing his favorite song about the country where the "sands dance forever."

pots and thrown away in the forest, but he had never yet come across them. A vague chill had descended on him and his head had seemed to swell, like a solitary walker at night who passes an evil spirit on the way. Then something had given way inside him. It descended on him again, this feeling, when his father walked in, that night after killing Ikemefuna.

8

Okonkwo did not taste any food for two days after the death of Ikemefuna. He drank palm-wine from morning till night, and his eyes were red and fierce like the eyes of a rat when it was caught by the tail and dashed against the floor. He called his son, Nwoye, to sit with him in his *obi*. But the boy was afraid of him and slipped out of the hut as soon as he noticed him dozing.

He did not sleep at night. He tried not to think about Ikemefuna, but the more he tried the more he thought about him. Once he got up from bed and walked about his compound. But he was so weak that his legs could hardly carry him. He felt like a drunken giant walking with the limbs of a mosquito. Now and then a cold shiver descended on his head and spread down his body.

On the third day he asked his second wife, Ekwefi, to roast plantains for him. She prepared it the way he liked—with slices of oil-bean and fish.

"You have not eaten for two days," said his daughter Ezinma when she brought the food to him. "So you must finish this." She sat down and stretched her legs in front of her. Okonkwo ate the food absent-mindedly. 'She should have been a boy,' he thought as he looked at his ten-year-old daughter. He passed her a piece of fish.

"Go and bring me some cold water," he said. Ezinma rushed out of the hut, chewing the fish, and soon returned with a bowl of cool water from the earthen pot in her mother's hut.

Okonkwo took the bowl from her and gulped the water down. He ate a few more pieces of plantain and pushed the dish aside.

"Bring me my bag," he asked, and Ezinma brought his goatskin bag from the far end of the hut. He searched in it for his snuff-bottle. It was a deep bag and took almost the whole length of his arm. It contained other things apart from his snuff-bottle. There was a drinking horn in it, and also a drinking gourd, and they knocked against each other as he searched. When he brought out the snuff-bottle he tapped it a few times against his knee-cap before taking out some snuff on the palm of his left hand. Then he remembered that he had not taken out his snuff-spoon. He searched his bag again and brought out a small, flat, ivory spoon, with which he carried the brown snuff to his nostrils.

Ezinma took the dish in one hand and the empty water bowl in the other and went back to her mother's hut. "She should have been a boy," Okonkwo said to himself again. His mind went back to Ikemefuna and he shivered. If only he could find some work to do he would be able to forget. But it was the season of rest between the harvest and the next planting season. The only work that men did at this time was covering the walls of their compound with new palm fronds. And Okonkwo had already done that. He had finished it on the very day the locusts came, when he had worked on one side of the wall and Ikemefuna and Nwoye on the other.

"When did you become a shivering old woman," Okonkwo asked himself, "you, who are known in all the nine villages for your valor in war? How can a man who has killed five men in battle fall to pieces because he has added a boy to their number? Okonkwo, you have become a woman indeed."

He sprang to his feet, hung his goatskin bag on his shoulder and went to visit his friend, Obierika.

Obierika was sitting outside under the shade of an orange tree making thatches from leaves of the raffia-palm. He exchanged greetings with Okonkwo and led the way into his *obi*.

"I was coming over to see you as soon as I finished that thatch," he said, rubbing off the grains of sand that clung to his thighs.

"Is it well?" Okonkwo asked.

"Yes," replied Obierika. "My daughter's suitor is coming today and I hope we will clinch the matter of the bride-price. I want you to be there."

Just then Obierika's son, Maduka, came into the *obi* from outside, greeted Okonkwo and turned towards the compound.

"Come and shake hands with me," Okonkwo said to the lad. "Your wrestling the other day gave me much happiness." The boy smiled, shook hands with Okonkwo and went into the compound.

"He will do great things," Okonkwo said. "If I had a son like him I should be happy. I am worried about Nwoye. A bowl of pounded yams can throw him in a wrestling match. His two younger brothers are more promising. But I can tell you, Obierika, that my children do not resemble me. Where are the young suckers that will grow when the old banana tree dies? If Ezinma had been a boy I would have been happier. She has the right spirit."

"You worry yourself for nothing," said Obierika. "The children are still very young."

"Nwoye is old enough to impregnate a woman. At his age I was already fending for myself. No, my friend, he is not too young. A chick that will grow into a cock can be spotted the very day it hatches. I have done my best to make Nwoye grow into a man, but there is too much of his mother in him."

"Too much of his grandfather," Obierika thought, but he did not say it. The same thought also came to Okonkwo's mind. But he had long learned how to lay that ghost. Whenever the thought of his father's weakness and failure troubled him he expelled it by thinking about his own strength and success. And so he did now. His mind went to his latest show of manliness.

"I cannot understand why you refused to come with us to kill that boy," he asked Obierika.

"Because I did not want to," Obierika replied sharply. "I had something better to do."

"You sound as if you question the authority and the decision of the Oracle, who said he should die."

"I do not. Why should I? But the Oracle did not ask me to carry out its decision."

"But someone had to do it. If we were all afraid of blood, it would not be done. And what do you think the Oracle would do then?"

"You know very well, Okonkwo, that I am not afraid of blood; and if any-one tells you that I am, he is telling a lie. And let me tell you one thing, my friend. If I were you I would have stayed at home. What you have done will not please the Earth. It is the kind of action for which the goddess wipes out whole families."

"The Earth cannot punish me for obeying her messenger," Okonkwo said. "A child's fingers are not scalded by a piece of hot yam which its mother puts into its palm."

"That is true," Obierika agreed. "But if the Oracle said that my son should be killed I would neither dispute it nor be the one to do it."

They would have gone on arguing had Ofoedu[9] not come in just then. It was clear from his twinkling eyes that he had important news. But it would be impolite to rush him. Obierika offered him a lobe of the kola nut he had broken with Okonkwo. Ofoedu ate slowly and talked about the locusts. When he finished his kola nut he said:

"The things that happen these days are very strange."

"What has happened?" asked Okonkwo.

"Do you know Ogbuefi Ndulue?"[1] Ofoedu asked.

"Ogbuefi Ndulue of Ire village," Okonkwo and Obierika said together.

"He died this morning," said Ofoedu.

"That is not strange. He was the oldest man in Ire," said Obierika.

"You are right," Ofoedu agreed. "But you ought to ask why the drum has not beaten to tell Umuofia of his death."

"Why?" asked Obierika and Okonkwo together.

"That is the strange part of it. You know his first wife who walks with a stick?"

"Yes. She is called Ozoemena."[2]

"That is so," said Ofoedu. "Ozoemena was, as you know, too old to attend Ndulue during his illness. His younger wives did that. When he died this morning, one of these women went to Ozoemena's hut and told her. She rose from her mat, took her stick and walked over to the *obi*. She knelt on her knees and hands at the threshold and called her husband, who was laid on a mat. 'Ogbuefi Ndulue,' she called, three times, and went back to her hut. When the youngest wife went to call her again to be present at the washing of the body, she found her lying on the mat, dead."

"That is very strange, indeed," said Okonkwo. "They will put off Ndulue's funeral until his wife has been buried."[3]

"That is why the drum has not been beaten to tell Umuofia."

"It was always said that Ndulue and Ozoemena had one mind," said Obierika. "I remember when I was a young boy there was a song about them. He could not do anything without telling her."

"I did not know that," said Okonkwo. "I thought he was a strong man in his youth."

"He was indeed," said Ofoedu.

Okonkwo shook his head doubtfully.

"He led Umuofia to war in those days," said Obierika.

Okonkwo was beginning to feel like his old self again. All that he required was something to occupy his mind. If he had killed Ikemefuna during the

---

9. The Ancestors Are Our Guide.   1. Life Has Arrived.   2. Another Bad Thing Will Not Happen.
3. A wife dying shortly after her husband was sometimes considered guilty of his death, so the village preserves appearances by burying Ozoemena before announcing Ogbuefi Ndule's death.

busy planting season or harvesting it would not have been so bad; his mind would have been centered on his work. Okonkwo was not a man of thought but of action. But in absence of work, talking was the next best.

Soon after Ofoedu left, Okonkwo took up his goatskin bag to go.

"I must go home to tap my palm trees for the afternoon," he said.

"Who taps your tall trees for you?" asked Obierika.

"Umezulike," replied Okonkwo.

"Sometimes I wish I had not taken the *ozo* title," said Obierika. "It wounds my heart to see these young men killing palm trees in the name of tapping."

"It is so indeed," Okonkwo agreed. "But the law of the land must be obeyed."

"I don't know how we got that law," said Obierika. "In many other clans a man of title is not forbidden to climb the palm tree. Here we say he cannot climb the tall tree but he can tap the short ones standing on the ground. It is like Dimaragana, who would not lend his knife for cutting up dogmeat because the dog was taboo to him, but offered to use his teeth."

"I think it is good that our clan holds the *ozo* title in high esteem," said Okonkwo. "In those other clans you speak of, *ozo* is so low that every beggar takes it."

"I was only speaking in jest," said Obierika. "In Abame and Aninta the title is worth less than two cowries. Every man wears the thread of title on his ankle, and does not lose it even if he steals."

"They have indeed soiled the name of *ozo*," said Okonkwo as he rose to go.

"It will not be very long now before my in-laws come," said Obierika.

"I shall return very soon," said Okonkwo, looking at the position of the sun.

There were seven men in Obierika's hut when Okonkwo returned. The suitor was a young man of about twenty-five, and with him were his father and uncle. On Obierika's side were his two elder brothers and Maduka, his sixteen-year-old son.

"Ask Akueke's mother to send us some kola nuts," said Obierika to his son. Maduka vanished into the compound like lightning. The conversation at once centered on him, and everybody agreed that he was as sharp as a razor.

"I sometimes think he is too sharp," said Obierika, somewhat indulgently. "He hardly ever walks. He is always in a hurry. If you are sending him on an errand he flies away before he has heard half of the message."

"You were very much like that yourself," said his eldest brother. "As our people say, 'When mother-cow is chewing grass its young ones watch its mouth.' Maduka has been watching your mouth."

As he was speaking the boy returned, followed by Akueke,[4] his half-sister, carrying a wooden dish with three kola nuts and alligator pepper. She gave the dish to her father's eldest brother and then shook hands, very shyly, with her suitor and his relatives. She was about sixteen and just ripe for marriage. Her suitor and his relatives surveyed her young body with expert eyes as if to assure themselves that she was beautiful and ripe.

---

4. Wealth of Eke (a divinity). Similar names built on *ako* ("wealth") connote riches and are associated with the idea of women as a form of exchangeable material wealth.

She wore a coiffure which was done up into a crest in the middle of the head. Cam wood was rubbed lightly into her skin, and all over her body were black patterns drawn with *uli*.[5] She wore a black necklace which hung down in three coils just above her full, succulent breasts. On her arms were red and yellow bangles, and on her waist four or five rows of *jigida*, or waist beads.

When she had shaken hands, or rather held out her hand to be shaken, she returned to her mother's hut to help with the cooking.

"Remove your *jigida* first," her mother warned as she moved near the fireplace to bring the pestle resting against the wall. "Every day I tell you that *jigida* and fire are not friends. But you will never hear. You grew your ears for decoration, not for hearing. One of these days your *jigida* will catch fire on your waist, and then you will know."

Akueke moved to the other end of the hut and began to remove the waistbeads. It had to be done slowly and carefully, taking each string separately, else it would break and the thousand tiny rings would have to be strung together again. She rubbed each string downwards with her palms until it passed the buttocks and slipped down to the floor around her feet.

The men in the *obi* had already begun to drink the palm-wine which Akueke's suitor had brought. It was a very good wine and powerful, for in spite of the palm fruit hung across the mouth of the pot to restrain the lively liquor, white foam rose and spilled over.

"That wine is the work of a good tapper," said Okonkwo.

The young suitor, whose name was Ibe, smiled broadly and said to his father: "Do you hear that?" He then said to the others: "He will never admit that I am a good tapper."

"He tapped three of my best palm trees to death," said his father, Ukegbu.

"That was about five years ago," said Ibe, who had begun to pour out the wine, "before I learned how to tap." He filled the first horn and gave to his father. Then he poured out for the others. Okonkwo brought out his big horn from the goatskin bag, blew into it to remove any dust that might be there, and gave it to Ibe to fill.

As the men drank, they talked about everything except the thing for which they had gathered. It was only after the pot had been emptied that the suitor's father cleared his voice and announced the object of their visit.

Obierika then presented to him a small bundle of short broomsticks. Ukegbu counted them.

"They are thirty?" he asked.

Obierika nodded in agreement.

"We are at last getting somewhere," Ukegbu said, and then turning to his brother and his son he said: "Let us go out and whisper together." The three rose and went outside. When they returned Ukegbu handed the bundle of sticks back to Obierika. He counted them; instead of thirty there were now only fifteen. He passed them over to his eldest brother, Machi, who also counted them and said:

---

5. A liquid made from crushed seeds, which caused the skin to pucker temporarily. It was used to create black tattoolike decorations. "Cam wood": a shrub. The powdered red heartwood of the shrub was used as a cosmetic and dye.

"We had not thought to go below thirty. But as the dog said, 'If I fall down for you and you fall down for me, it is play.' Marriage should be a play and not a fight; so we are falling down again." He then added ten sticks to the fifteen and gave the bundle to Ukegbu.

In this way Akuke's bride-price was finally settled at twenty bags of cowries. It was already dusk when the two parties came to this agreement.

"Go and tell Akueke's mother that we have finished," Obierika said to his son, Maduka. Almost immediately the women came in with a big bowl of foo-foo. Obierika's second wife followed with a pot of soup, and Maduka brought in a pot of palm-wine.

As the men ate and drank palm-wine they talked about the customs of their neighbors.

"It was only this morning," said Obierika, "that Okonkwo and I were talking about Abame and Aninta, where titled men climb trees and pound foo-foo for their wives."

"All their customs are upside-down. They do not decide bride-price as we do, with sticks. They haggle and bargain as if they were buying a goat or a cow in the market."

"That is very bad," said Obierika's eldest brother. "But what is good in one place is bad in another place. In Umunso they do not bargain at all, not even with broomsticks. The suitor just goes on bringing bags of cowries until his in-laws tell him to stop. It is a bad custom because it always leads to a quarrel."

"The world is large," said Okonkwo. "I have even heard that in some tribes a man's children belong to his wife and her family."

"That cannot be," said Machi. "You might as well say that the woman lies on top of the man when they are making the children."

"It is like the story of white men who, they say, are white like this piece of chalk," said Obierika. He held up a piece of chalk, which every man kept in his *obi* and with which his guests drew lines on the floor before they ate kola nuts. "And these white men, they say, have no toes."[6]

"And have you never seen them?" asked Machi.

"Have you?" asked Obierika.

"One of them passes here frequently," said Machi. "His name is Amadi."

Those who knew Amadi laughed. He was a leper, and the polite name for leprosy was "the white skin."

9

For the first time in three nights, Okonkwo slept. He woke up once in the middle of the night and his mind went back to the past three days without making him feel uneasy. He began to wonder why he had felt uneasy at all. It was like a man wondering in broad daylight why a dream had appeared so terrible to him at night. He stretched himself and scratched his thigh where a mosquito had bitten him as he slept. Another one was wailing near his right ear. He slapped the ear and hoped he had killed it. Why do they always go for one's ears? When he was a child his mother had told him a story about it. But it was as silly as all women's stories. Mosquito, she had said, had asked Ear to marry him, whereupon Ear fell on the floor in uncontrollable laughter. "How much longer do you think you will live?" she asked. "You are already a skeleton." Mosquito went away humiliated, and any time he passed her way he told Ear that he was still alive.

Okonkwo turned on his side and went back to sleep. He was roused in the morning by someone banging on his door.

"Who is that?" he growled. He knew it must be Ekwefi. Of his three wives Ekwefi was the only one who would have the audacity to bang on his door.

"Ezinma is dying," came her voice, and all the tragedy and sorrow of her life were packed in those words.

Okonkwo sprang from his bed, pushed back the bolt on his door and ran into Ekwefi's hut.

Ezinma lay shivering on a mat beside a huge fire that her mother had kept burning all night.

"It is *iba*,"[7] said Okonkwo as he took his machete and went into the bush to collect the leaves and grasses and barks of trees that went into making the medicine for *iba*.

Ekwefi knelt beside the sick child, occasionally feeling with her palm the wet, burning forehead.

Ezinma was an only child and the center of her mother's world. Very often it was Ezinma who decided what food her mother should prepare. Ekwefi even gave her such delicacies as eggs, which children were rarely allowed to eat because such food tempted them to steal. One day as Ezinma was eating an egg Okonkwo had come in unexpectedly from his hut. He was greatly shocked and swore to beat Ekwefi if she dared to give the child eggs again. But it was impossible to refuse Ezinma anything. After her father's rebuke she developed an even keener appetite for eggs. And she enjoyed above all the secrecy in which she now ate them. Her mother always took her into their bedroom and shut the door.

Ezinma did not call her mother *Nne* like all children. She called her by her name, Ekwefi, as her father and other grown-up people did. The relationship between them was not only that of mother and child. There was something in it like the companionship of equals, which was strengthened by such little conspiracies as eating eggs in the bedroom.

Ekwefi had suffered a good deal in her life. She had borne ten children and nine of them had died in infancy, usually before the age of three. As she buried one child after another her sorrow gave way to despair and then to grim resignation. The birth of her children, which should be a woman's crowning glory, became for Ekwefi mere physical agony devoid of promise. The naming ceremony after seven market weeks became an empty ritual. Her deepening despair found expression in the names she gave her children. One of them was a pathetic cry, Onwumbiko—"Death, I implore you." But Death took no notice; Onwumbiko died in his fifteenth month. The next child was a girl, Ozoemena—"May it not happen again." She died in her eleventh month, and two others after her. Ekwefi then became defiant and called her next child Onwuma—"Death may please himself." And he did.

7. A fever accompanied by jaundice, probably caused by malaria.

After the death of Ekwefi's second child, Okonkwo had gone to a medicine man, who was also a diviner of the Afa Oracle,[8] to inquire what was amiss. This man told him that the child was an *ogbanje*, one of those wicked children who, when they died, entered their mothers' wombs to be born again.

"When your wife becomes pregnant again," he said, "let her not sleep in her hut. Let her go and stay with her people. In that way she will elude her wicked tormentor and break its evil cycle of birth and death."

Ekwefi did as she was asked. As soon as she became pregnant she went to live with her old mother in another village. It was there that her third child was born and circumcised on the eighth day. She did not return to Okonkwo's compound until three days before the naming ceremony. The child was called Onwumbiko.

Onwumbiko was not given proper burial when he died. Okonkwo had called on another medicine man who was famous in the clan for his great knowledge about *ogbanje* children. His name was Okagbue Uyanwa. Okagbue was a very striking figure, tall, with a full beard and a bald head. He was light in complexion and his eyes were red and fiery. He always gnashed his teeth as he listened to those who came to consult him. He asked Okonkwo a few questions about the dead child. All the neighbors and relations who had come to mourn gathered round them.

"On what market-day was it born?" he asked.

"*Oye*," replied Okonkwo.

"And it died this morning?"

Okonkwo said yes, and only then realized for the first time that the child had died on the same market-day as it had been born. The neighbors and relations also saw the coincidence and said among themselves that it was very significant.

"Where do you sleep with your wife, in your *obi* or in her own hut?" asked the medicine man.

"In her hut."

"In future call her into your *obi*."

The medicine man then ordered that there should be no mourning for the dead child. He brought out a sharp razor from the goatskin bag slung from his left shoulder and began to mutilate the child. Then he took it away to bury in the Evil Forest, holding it by the ankle and dragging it on the ground behind him. After such treatment it would think twice before coming again, unless it was one of the stubborn ones who returned, carrying the stamp of their mutilation—a missing finger or perhaps a dark line where the medicine man's razor had cut them.

By the time Onwumbiko died Ekwefi had become a very bitter woman. Her husband's first wife had already had three sons, all strong and healthy. When she had borne her third son in succession, Okonkwo had gathered a goat for her, as was the custom. Ekwefi had nothing but good wishes for her. But she had grown so bitter about her own *chi* that she could not rejoice with others over their good fortune. And so, on the day that Nwoye's mother

8. One who comunicates with the clients' ancestors by reading patterns made by objects (for example, seeds, teeth, shells) thrown on a flat surface.

celebrated the birth of her three sons with feasting and music, Ekwefi was the only person in the happy company who went about with a cloud on her brow. Her husband's wife took this for malevolence, as husbands' wives were wont to. How could she know that Ekwefi's bitterness did not flow outwards to others but inwards into her own soul; that she did not blame others for their good fortune but her own evil *chi* who denied her any?

At last Ezinma was born, and although ailing she seemed determined to live. At first Ekwefi accepted her, as she had accepted others—with listless resignation. But when she lived on to her fourth, fifth and sixth years, love returned once more to her mother, and, with love, anxiety. She determined to nurse her child to health, and she put all her being into it. She was rewarded by occasional spells of health during which Ezinma bubbled with energy like fresh palm-wine. At such times she seemed beyond danger. But all of a sudden she would go down again. Everybody knew she was an *ogbanje*. These sudden bouts of sickness and health were typical of her kind. But she had lived so long that perhaps she had decided to stay. Some of them did become tired of their evil rounds of birth and death, or took pity on their mothers, and stayed. Ekwefi believed deep inside her that Ezinma had come to stay. She believed because it was that faith alone that gave her own life any kind of meaning. And this faith had been strengthened when a year or so ago a medicine man had dug up Ezinma's *iyi-uwa*. Everyone knew then that she would live because her bond with the world of *ogbanje* had been broken. Ekwefi was reassured. But such was her anxiety for her daughter that she could not rid herself completely of her fear. And although she believed that the *iyi-uwa* which had been dug up was genuine, she could not ignore the fact that some really evil children sometimes misled people into digging up a specious one.

But Ezinma's *iyi-uwa* had looked real enough. It was a smooth pebble wrapped in a dirty rag. The man who dug it up was the same Okagbue who was famous in all the clan for his knowledge in these matters. Ezinma had not wanted to cooperate with him at first. But that was only to be expected. No *ogbanje* would yield her secrets easily, and most of them never did because they died too young—before they could be asked questions.

"Where did you bury your *iyi-uwa*?" Okagbue had asked Ezinma. She was nine then and was just recovering from a serious illness.

"What is *iyi-uwa*?" she asked in return.

"You know what it is. You buried it in the ground somewhere so that you can die and return again to torment your mother."

Ezinma looked at her mother, whose eyes, sad and pleading, were fixed on her.

"Answer the question at once," roared Okonkwo, who stood beside her. All the family were there and some of the neighbors too.

"Leave her to me," the medicine man told Okonkwo in a cool, confident voice. He turned again to Ezinma. "Where did you bury your *iyi-uwa*?"

"Where they bury children," she replied, and the quiet spectators murmured to themselves.

"Come along then and show me the spot," said the medicine man.

The crowd set out with Ezinma leading the way and Okagbue following closely behind her. Okonkwo came next and Ekwefi followed him. When she came to the main road, Ezinma turned left as if she was going to the stream.

"But you said it was where they bury children?" asked the medicine man.

"No," said Ezinma, whose feeling of importance was manifest in her sprightly walk. She sometimes broke into a run and stopped again suddenly. The crowd followed her silently. Women and children returning from the stream with pots of water on their heads wondered what was happening until they saw Okagbue and guessed that it must be something to do with *ogbanje*. And they all knew Ekwefi and her daughter very well.

When she got to the big udala tree Ezinma turned left into the bush, and the crowd followed her. Because of her size she made her way through trees and creepers more quickly than her followers. The bush was alive with the tread of feet on dry leaves and sticks and the moving aside of tree branches. Ezinma went deeper and deeper and the crowd went with her. Then she suddenly turned round and began to walk back to the road. Everybody stood to let her pass and then filed after her.

"If you bring us all this way for nothing I shall beat sense into you," Okonkwo threatened.

"I have told you to let her alone. I know how to deal with them," said Okagbue.

Ezinma led the way back to the road, looked left and right and turned right. And so they arrived home again.

"Where did you bury your *iyi-uwa*?" asked Okagbue when Ezinma finally stopped outside her father's *obi*. Okagbue's voice was unchanged. It was quiet and confident.

"It is near that orange tree," Ezinma said.

"And why did you not say so, you wicked daughter of Akalogoli?" Okonkwo swore furiously. The medicine man ignored him.

"Come and show me the exact spot," he said quietly to Ezinma.

"It is here," she said when they got to the tree.

"Point at the spot with your finger," said Okagbue.

"It is here," said Ezinma touching the ground with her finger. Okonkwo stood by, rumbling like thunder in the rainy season.

"Bring me a hoe," said Okagbue.

When Ekwefi brought the hoe, he had already put aside his goatskin bag and his big cloth and was in his underwear, a long and thin strip of cloth wound round the waist like a belt and then passed between the legs to be fastened to the belt behind. He immediately set to work digging a pit where Ezinma had indicated. The neighbors sat around watching the pit becoming deeper and deeper. The dark top soil soon gave way to the bright red earth with which women scrubbed the floors and walls of huts. Okagbue worked tirelessly and in silence, his back shining with perspiration. Okonkwo stood by the pit. He asked Okagbue to come up and rest while he took a hand. But Okagbue said he was not tired yet.

Ekwefi went into her hut to cook yams. Her husband had brought out more yams than usual because the medicine man had to be fed. Ezinma went with her and helped in preparing the vegetables.

"There is too much green vegetable," she said.

"Don't you see the pot is full of yams?" Ekwefi asked. "And you know how leaves become smaller after cooking."

"Yes," said Ezinma, "that was why the snake-lizard killed his mother."

"Very true," said Ekwefi.

"He gave his mother seven baskets of vegetables to cook and in the end there were only three. And so he killed her," said Ezinma.

"That is not the end of the story."

"Oho," said Ezinma. "I remember now. He brought another seven baskets and cooked them himself. And there were again only three. So he killed himself too."

Outside the *obi* Okagbue and Okonkwo were digging the pit to find where Ezinma had buried her *iyi-uwa*. Neighbors sat around, watching. The pit was now so deep that they no longer saw the digger. They only saw the red earth he threw up mounting higher and higher. Okonkwo's son, Nwoye, stood near the edge of the pit because he wanted to take in all that happened.

Okagbue had again taken over the digging from Okonkwo. He worked, as usual, in silence. The neighbors and Okonkwo's wives were now talking. The children had lost interest and were playing.

Suddenly Okagbue sprang to the surface with the agility of a leopard.

"It is very near now," he said. "I have felt it."

There was immediate excitement and those who were sitting jumped to their feet.

"Call your wife and child," he said to Okonkwo. But Ekwefi and Ezinma had heard the noise and run out to see what it was.

Okagbue went back into the pit, which was now surrounded by spectators. After a few more hoe-fuls of earth he struck the *iyi-uwa*. He raised it carefully with the hoe and threw it to the surface. Some women ran away in fear when it was thrown. But they soon returned and everyone was gazing at the rag from a reasonable distance. Okagbue emerged and without saying a word or even looking at the spectators he went to his goatskin bag, took out two leaves and began to chew them. When he had swallowed them, he took up the rag with his left hand and began to untie it. And then the smooth, shiny pebble fell out. He picked it up.

"Is this yours?" he asked Ezinma.

"Yes," she replied. All the women shouted with joy because Ekwefi's troubles were at last ended.

All this had happened more than a year ago and Ezinma had not been ill since. And then suddenly she had begun to shiver in the night. Ekwefi brought her to the fireplace, spread her mat on the floor and built a fire. But she had got worse and worse. As she knelt by her, feeling with her palm the wet, burning forehead, she prayed a thousand times. Although her husband's wives were saying that it was nothing more than *iba*, she did not hear them.

Okonkwo returned from the bush carrying on his left shoulder a large bundle of grasses and leaves, roots and barks of medicinal trees and shrubs. He went into Ekwefi's hut, put down his load and sat down.

"Get me a pot," he said, "and leave the child alone."

Ekwefi went to bring the pot and Okonkwo selected the best from his bundle, in their due proportions, and cut them up. He put them in the pot and Ekwefi poured in some water.

"Is that enough?" she asked when she had poured in about half of the water in the bowl.

"A little more . . . I said a *little*. Are you deaf?" Okonkwo roared at her.

She set the pot on the fire and Okonkwo took up his machete to return to his *obi*.

"You must watch the pot carefully," he said as he went, "and don't allow it to boil over. If it does its power will be gone." He went away to his hut and Ekwefi began to tend the medicine pot almost as if it was itself a sick child. Her eyes went constantly from Ezinma to the boiling pot and back to Ezinma.

Okonkwo returned when he felt the medicine had cooked long enough. He looked it over and said it was done.

"Bring me a low stool for Ezinma," he said, "and a thick mat."

He took down the pot from the fire and placed it in front of the stool. He then roused Ezinma and placed her on the stool, astride the steaming pot. The thick mat was thrown over both. Ezinma struggled to escape from the choking and overpowering steam, but she was held down. She started to cry.

When the mat was at last removed she was drenched in perspiration. Ekwefi mopped her with a piece of cloth and she lay down on a dry mat and was soon asleep.

10

Large crowds began to gather on the village *ilo* as soon as the edge had worn off the sun's heat and it was no longer painful on the body. Most communal ceremonies took place at that time of the day, so that even when it was said that a ceremony would begin "after the midday meal" everyone understood that it would begin a long time later, when the sun's heat had softened.

It was clear from the way the crowd stood or sat that the ceremony was for men. There were many women, but they looked on from the fringe like outsiders. The titled men and elders sat on their stools waiting for the trials to begin. In front of them was a row of stools on which nobody sat. There were nine of them. Two little groups of people stood at a respectable distance beyond the stools. They faced the elders. There were three men in one group and three men and one woman in the other. The woman was Mgbafo and the three men with her were her brothers. In the other group were her husband, Uzowulu, and his relatives. Mgbafo and her brothers were as still as statues into whose faces the artist has molded defiance. Uzowulu and his relatives, on the other hand, were whispering together. It looked like whispering, but they were really talking at the top of their voices. Everybody in the crowd was talking. It was like the market. From a distance the noise was a deep rumble carried by the wind.

An iron gong sounded, setting up a wave of expectation in the crowd. Everyone looked in the direction of the *egwugwu*[9] house. *Gome, gome, gome* went the gong, and a powerful flute blew a high-pitched blast. Then came the voices of the *egwugwu*, guttural and awesome. The wave struck the women and children and there was a backward stampede. But it was momentary. They were already far enough where they stood and there was room for running away if any of the *egwugwu* should go towards them.

9. Here the term refers to the village's highest spiritual and judicial authority, prominent men who, after putting on elaborate ceremonial costumes, embody the village's ancestral spirits.

The drum sounded again and the flute blew. The *egwugwu* house was now a pandemonium of quavering voices: *Aru oyim de de de dei!*[1] filled the air as the spirits of the ancestors, just emerged from the earth, greeted themselves in their esoteric language. The *egwugwu* house into which they emerged faced the forest, away from the crowd, who saw only its back with the many-colored patterns and drawings done by specially chosen women at regular intervals. These women never saw the inside of the hut. No woman ever did. They scrubbed and painted the outside walls under the supervision of men. If they imagined what was inside, they kept their imagination to themselves. No woman ever asked questions about the most powerful and the most secret cult in the clan.

Aru oyim de de de dei! flew around the dark, closed hut like tongues of fire. The ancestral spirits of the clan were abroad. The metal gong beat continuously now and the flute, shrill and powerful, floated on the chaos.

And then the *egwugwu* appeared. The women and children sent up a great shout and took to their heels. It was instinctive. A woman fled as soon as an *egwugwu* came in sight. And when, as on that day, nine of the greatest masked spirits in the clan came out together it was a terrifying spectacle. Even Mgbafo took to her heels and had to be restrained by her brothers.

Each of the nine *egwugwu* represented a village of the clan. Their leader was called Evil Forest. Smoke poured out of his head.

The nine villages of Umuofia had grown out of the nine sons of the first father of the clan. Evil Forest represented the village of Umueru, or the children of Eru, who was the eldest of the nine sons.

"*Umuofia kwenu!*" shouted the leading *egwugwu*, pushing the air with his raffia arms. The elders of the clan replied, "*Yaa!*"

"*Umuofia kwenu!*"

"*Yaa!*"

"*Umuofia kwenu!*"

"*Yaa!*"

Evil Forest then thrust the pointed end of his rattling staff into the earth. And it began to shake and rattle, like something agitating with a metallic life. He took the first of the empty stools and the eight other *egwugwu* began to sit in order of seniority after him.

Okonkwo's wives, and perhaps other women as well, might have noticed that the second *egwugwu* had the springy walk of Okonkwo. And they might also have noticed that Okonkwo was not among the titled men and elders who sat behind the row of *egwugwu*. But if they thought these things they kept them within themselves. The *egwugwu* with the springy walk was one of the dead fathers of the clan. He looked terrible with the smoked raffia body, a huge wooden face painted white except for the round hollow eyes and the charred teeth that were as big as a man's fingers. On his head were two powerful horns.

When all the *egwugwu* had sat down and the sound of the many tiny bells and rattles on their bodies had subsided, Evil Forest addressed the two groups of people facing them.

1. Body of my friend, greetings!

"Uzowulu's body, I salute you," he said. Spirits always addressed humans as "bodies." Uzowulu bent down and touched the earth with his right hand as a sign of submission.

"Our father, my hand has touched the ground," he said.

"Uzowulu's body, do you know me?" asked the spirit.

"How can I know you, father? You are beyond our knowledge."

Evil Forest then turned to the other group and addressed the eldest of the three brothers.

"The body of Odukwe, I greet you," he said, and Odukwe bent down and touched the earth. The hearing then began.

Uzowulu stepped forward and presented his case.

"That woman standing there is my wife, Mgbafo. I married her with my money and my yams. I do not owe my in-laws anything. I owe them no yams. I owe them no coco-yams. One morning three of them came to my house, beat me up and took my wife and children away. This happened in the rainy season. I have waited in vain for my wife to return. At last I went to my in-laws and said to them, 'You have taken back your sister. I did not send her away. You yourselves took her. The law of the clan is that you should return her bride-price.' But my wife's brothers said they had nothing to tell me. So I have brought the matter to the fathers of the clan. My case is finished. I salute you."

"Your words are good," said the leader of the *egwugwu*. "Let us hear Odukwe. His words may also be good."

Odukwe was short and thickset. He stepped forward, saluted the spirits and began his story.

"My in-law has told you that we went to his house, beat him up and took our sister and her children away. All that is true. He told you that he came to take back her bride-price and we refused to give it him. That also is true. My in-law, Uzowulu, is a beast. My sister lived with him for nine years. During those years no single day passed in the sky without his beating the woman. We have tried to settle their quarrels time without number and on each occasion Uzowulu was guilty—"

"It is a lie!" Uzowulu shouted.

"Two years ago," continued Odukwe, "when she was pregnant, he beat her until she miscarried."

"It is a lie. She miscarried after she had gone to sleep with her lover."

"Uzowulu's body, I salute you," said Evil Forest, silencing him. "What kind of lover sleeps with a pregnant woman?" There was a loud murmur of approbation from the crowd. Odukwe continued:

"Last year when my sister was recovering from an illness, he beat her again so that if the neighbors had not gone in to save her she would have been killed. We heard of it, and did as you have been told. The law of Umuofia is that if a woman runs away from her husband her bride-price is returned. But in this case she ran away to save her life. Her two children belong to Uzowulu. We do not dispute it, but they are too young to leave their mother. If, in the other hand, Uzowulu should recover from his madness and come in the proper way to beg his wife to return she will do so on the understanding that if he ever beats her again we shall cut off his genitals for him."

The crowd roared with laughter. Evil Forest rose to his feet and order was immediately restored. A steady cloud of smoke rose from his head. He sat down again and called two witnesses. They were both Uzowulu's neighbors, and they agreed about the beating. Evil Forest then stood up, pulled out his staff and thrust it into the earth again. He ran a few steps in the direction of the women; they all fled in terror, only to return to their places almost immediately. The nine *egwugwu* then went away to consult together in their house. They were silent for a long time. Then the metal gong sounded and the flute was blown. The *egwugwu* had emerged once again from their underground home. They saluted one another and then reappeared on the *ilo*.

"*Umuofia kwenu!*" roared Evil Forest, facing the elders and grandees of the clan.

"*Yaa!*" replied the thunderous crowd; then silence descended from the sky and swallowed the noise.

Evil Forest began to speak and all the while he spoke everyone was silent. The eight other *egwugwu* were as still as statues.

"We have heard both sides of the case," said Evil Forest. "Our duty is not to blame this man or to praise that, but to settle the dispute." He turned to Uzowulu's group and allowed a short pause.

"Uzowulu's body, I salute you," he said.

"Our father, my hand has touched the ground," replied Uzowulu, touching the earth.

"Uzowulu's body, do you know me?"

"How can I know you, father? You are beyond our knowledge," Uzowulu replied.

"I am Evil Forest. I kill a man on the day that his life is sweetest to him."

"That is true," replied Uzowulu.

"Go to your in-laws with a pot of wine and beg your wife to return to you. It is not bravery when a man fights with a woman." He turned to Odukwe, and allowed a brief pause.

"Odukwe's body, I greet you," he said.

"My hand is on the ground," replied Odukwe.

"Do you know me?"

"No man can know you," replied Odukwe.

"I am Evil Forest, I am Dry-meat-that-fills-the-mouth, I am Fire-that-burns-without-faggots. If your in-law brings wine to you, let your sister go with him. I salute you." He pulled his staff from the hard earth and thrust it back.

"*Umuofia kwenu!*" he roared, and the crowd answered.

"I don't know why such a trifle should come before the *egwugwu*," said one elder to another.

"Don't you know what kind of man Uzowulu is? He will not listen to any other decision," replied the other.

As they spoke two other groups of people had replaced the first before the *egwugwu*, and a great land case began.

11

The night was impenetrably dark. The moon had been rising later and later every night until now it was seen only at dawn. And whenever the moon forsook evening and rose at cock-crow the nights were as black as charcoal.

Ezinma and her mother sat on a mat on the floor after their supper of yam foo-foo and bitter-leaf soup. A palm-oil lamp gave out yellowish light. Without it, it would have been impossible to eat; one could not have known where one's mouth was in the darkness of that night. There was an oil lamp in all the four huts on Okonkwo's compound, and each hut seen from the others looked like a soft eye of yellow half-light set in the solid massiveness of night.

The world was silent except for the shrill cry of insects, which was part of the night, and the sound of wooden mortar and pestle as Nwayieke pounded her foo-foo. Nwayieke lived four compounds away, and she was notorious for her late cooking. Every woman in the neighborhood knew the sound of Nwayieke's mortar and pestle. It was also part of the night.

Okonkwo had eaten from his wives' dishes and was now reclining with his back against the wall. He searched his bag and brought out his snuff-bottle. He turned it on to his left palm, but nothing came out. He hit the bottle against his knee to shake up the tobacco. That was always the trouble with Okeke's snuff. It very quickly went damp, and there was too much saltpeter in it. Okonkwo had not bought snuff from him for a long time. Idigo was the man who knew how to grind good snuff. But he had recently fallen ill.

Low voices, broken now and again by singing, reached Okonkwo from his wives' huts as each woman and her children told folk stories. Ekwefi and her daughter, Ezinma, sat on a mat on the floor. It was Ekwefi's turn to tell a story.

"Once upon a time," she began, "all the birds were invited to a feast in the sky. They were very happy and began to prepare themselves for the great day. They painted their bodies with red cam wood and drew beautiful patterns on them with *uli*.

"Tortoise saw all these preparations and soon discovered what it all meant. Nothing that happened in the world of the animals ever escaped his notice; he was full of cunning. As soon as he heard of the great feast in the sky his throat began to itch at the very thought. There was a famine in those days and Tortoise had not eaten a good meal for two moons. His body rattled like a piece of dry stick in his empty shell. So he began to plan how he would go to the sky."

"But he had no wings," said Ezinma.

"Be patient," replied her mother. "That is the story. Tortoise had no wings, but he went to the birds and asked to be allowed to go with them.

" 'We know you too well,' said the birds when they had heard him. 'You are full of cunning and you are ungrateful. If we allow you to come with us you will soon begin your mischief.'

" 'You do not know me,' said Tortoise. 'I am a changed man. I have learned that a man who makes trouble for others is also making it for himself.'

"Tortoise had a sweet tongue, and within a short time all the birds agreed that he was a changed man, and they each gave him a feather, with which he made two wings.

"At last the great day came and Tortoise was the first to arrive at the meeting place. When all the birds had gathered together, they set off in a body. Tortoise was very happy and voluble as he flew among the birds, and he was soon chosen as the man to speak for the party because he was a great orator.

" 'There is one important thing which we must not forget,' he said as they flew on their way. 'When people are invited to a great feast like this, they take new names for the occasion. Our hosts in the sky will expect us to honor this age-old custom.'

"None of the birds had heard of this custom but they knew that Tortoise, in spite of his failings in other directions, was a widely traveled man who knew the customs of different peoples. And so they each took a new name. When they had all taken, Tortoise also took one. He was to be called *All of you*.

"At last the party arrived in the sky and their hosts were very happy to see them. Tortoise stood up in his many-colored plumage and thanked them for their invitation. His speech was so eloquent that all the birds were glad they had brought him, and nodded their heads in approval of all he said. Their hosts took him as the king of the birds, especially as he looked somewhat different from the others.

"After kola nuts had been presented and eaten, the people of the sky set before their guests the most delectable dishes Tortoise had ever seen or dreamed of. The soup was brought out hot from the fire and in the very pot in which it had been cooked. It was full of meat and fish. Tortoise began to sniff aloud. There was pounded yam and also yam pottage cooked with palm-oil and fresh fish. There were also pots of palm-wine. When everything had been set before the guests, one of the people of the sky came forward and tasted a little from each pot. He then invited the birds to eat. But Tortoise jumped to his feet and asked: 'For whom have you prepared this feast?'

" 'For all of you,' replied the man.

"Tortoise turned to the birds and said: 'You remember that my name is *All of you*. The custom here is to serve the spokesman first and the others later. They will serve you when I have eaten.'

"He began to eat and the birds grumbled angrily. The people of the sky thought it must be their custom to leave all the food for their king. And so Tortoise ate the best part of the food and then drank two pots of palm-wine, so that he was full of food and drink and his body filled out in his shell.

"The birds gathered round to eat what was left and to peck at the bones he had thrown all about the floor. Some of them were too angry to eat. They chose to fly home on an empty stomach. But before they left each took back the feather he had lent to Tortoise. And there he stood in his hard shell full of food and wine but without any wings to fly home. He asked the birds to take a message for his wife, but they all refused. In the end Parrot, who had felt more angry than the others, suddenly changed his mind and agreed to take the message.

" 'Tell my wife,' said Tortoise, 'to bring out all the soft things in my house and cover the compound with them so that I can jump down from the sky without very great danger.'

"Parrot promised to deliver the message, and then flew away. But when he reached Tortoise's house he told his wife to bring out all the hard things in the house. And so she brought out her husband's hoes, machetes, spears, guns and even his cannon. Tortoise looked down from the sky and saw his wife bringing things out, but it was too far to see what they were. When all seemed ready he let himself go. He fell and fell and fell until he began to fear that he would never stop falling. And then like the sound of his cannon he crashed on the compound."

"Did he die?" asked Ezinma.

"No," replied Ekwefi. "His shell broke into pieces. But there was a great medicine man in the neighborhood. Tortoise's wife sent for him and he gathered all the bits of shell and stuck them together. That is why Tortoise's shell is not smooth."

"There is no song in the story," Ezinma pointed out.

"No," said Ekwefi. "I shall think of another one with a song. But it is your turn now."

"Once upon a time," Ezinma began, "Tortoise and Cat went to wrestle against Yams—no, that is not the beginning. Once upon a time there was a great famine in the land of animals. Everybody was lean except Cat, who was fat and whose body shone as if oil was rubbed on it . . ."

She broke off because at that very moment a loud and high-pitched voice broke the outer silence of the night. It was Chielo, the priestess of Agbala, prophesying. There was nothing new in that. Once in a while Chielo was possessed by the spirit of her god and she began to prophesy. But tonight she was addressing her prophecy and greetings to Okonkwo, and so everyone in his family listened. The folk stories stopped.

"*Agbala do-o-o-o! Agbala ekeneo-o-o-o,*"[2] came the voice like a sharp knife cutting through the night. "*Okonkwo! Agbala ekene gio-o-o-o! Agbala cholu ifu ada ya Ezinmao-o-o-o!*"[3]

At the mention of Ezinma's name Ekwefi jerked her head sharply like an animal that had sniffed death in the air. Her heart jumped painfully within her.

The priestess had now reached Okonkwo's compound and was talking with him outside his hut. She was saying again and again that Agbala wanted to see his daughter, Ezinma. Okonkwo pleaded with her to come back in the morning because Ezinma was now asleep. But Chielo ignored what he was trying to say and went on shouting that Agbala wanted to see his daughter. Her voice was as clear as metal, and Okonkwo's women and children heard from their huts all that she said. Okonkwo was still pleading that the girl had been ill of late and was asleep. Ekwefi quickly took her to their bedroom and placed her on their high bamboo bed.

The priestess screamed. "Beware, Okonkwo!" she warned. "Beware of exchanging words with Agbala. Does a man speak when a god speaks? Beware!"

She walked through Okonkwo's hut into the circular compound and went straight toward Ekwefi's hut. Okonkwo came after her.

"Ekwefi," she called, "Agbala greets you. Where is my daughter, Ezinma? Agbala wants to see her."

Ekwefi came out from her hut carrying her oil lamp in her left hand. There was a light wind blowing, so she cupped her right hand to shelter the flame. Nwoye's mother, also carrying an oil lamp, emerged from her hut. The children stood in the darkness outside their hut watching the strange event. Okonkwo's youngest wife also came out and joined the others.

"Where does Agbala want to see her?" Ekwefi asked.

"Where else but in his house in the hills and the caves?" replied the priestess.

"I will come with you, too," Ekwefi said firmly.

---

2. Agbala wants something! Agbala greets.   3. Agbala greets you! Agbala wants to see his daughter Ezinma!

"Tufia-a!"[4] the priestess cursed, her voice cracking like the angry bark of thunder in the dry season. "How dare you, woman, to go before the mighty Agbala of your own accord? Beware, woman, lest he strike you in his anger. Bring me my daughter."

Ekwefi went into her hut and came out again with Ezinma.

"Come, my daughter," said the priestess. "I shall carry you on my back. A baby on its mother's back does not know that the way is long."

Ezinma began to cry. She was used to Chielo calling her "my daughter." But it was a different Chielo she now saw in the yellow half-light.

"Don't cry, my daughter," said the priestess, "lest Agbala be angry with you."

"Don't cry," said Ekwefi, "she will bring you back very soon. I shall give you some fish to eat." She went into the hut again and brought down the smoke-black basket in which she kept her dried fish and other ingredients for cooking soup. She broke a piece in two and gave it to Ezinma, who clung to her.

"Don't be afraid," said Ekwefi, stroking her head, which was shaved in places, leaving a regular pattern of hair. They went outside again. The priestess bent down on one knee and Ezinma climbed on her back, her left palm closed on her fish and her eyes gleaming with tears.

"Agbala do-o-o-o! Agbala ekeneo-o-o-o! . . ." Chielo began once again to chant greetings to her god. She turned round sharply and walked through Okonkwo's hut, bending very low at the eaves. Ezinma was crying loudly now, calling on her mother. The two voices disappeared into the thick darkness.

A strange and sudden weakness descended on Ekwefi as she stood gazing in the direction of the voices like a hen whose only chick has been carried away by a kite. Ezinma's voice soon faded away and only Chielo was heard moving farther and farther into the distance.

"Why do you stand there as though she had been kidnapped?" asked Okonkwo as he went back to his hut.

"She will bring her back soon," Nwoye's mother said.

But Ekwefi did not hear these consolations. She stood for a while, and then, all of a sudden, made up her mind. She hurried through Okonkwo's hut and went outside. "Where are you going?" he asked.

"I am following Chielo," she replied and disappeared in the darkness. Okonkwo cleared his throat, and brought out his snuff-bottle from the goatskin bag by his side.

The priestess's voice was already growing faint in the distance. Ekwefi hurried to the main footpath and turned left in the direction of the voice. Her eyes were useless to her in the darkness. But she picked her way easily on the sandy footpath hedged on either side by branches and damp leaves. She began to run, holding her breasts with her hands to stop them flapping noisily against her body. She hit her left foot against an outcropped root, and terror seized her. It was an ill omen. She ran faster. But Chielo's voice was still a long way away. Had she been running too? How could she go so fast with Ezinma on her back? Although the night was cool, Ekwefi was beginning to

---

4. A curse in words meaning "spitting" or "clearing out," often accompanied by spitting.

feel hot from her running. She continually ran into the luxuriant weeds and creepers that walled in the path. Once she tripped up and fell. Only then did she realize, with a start, that Chielo had stopped her chanting. Her heart beat violently and she stood still. Then Chielo's renewed outburst came from only a few paces ahead. But Ekwefi could not see her. She shut her eyes for a while and opened them again in an effort to see. But it was useless. She could not see beyond her nose.

There were no stars in the sky because there was a rain-cloud. Fireflies went about with their tiny green lamps, which only made the darkness more profound. Between Chielo's outbursts the night was alive with the shrill tremor of forest insects woven into the darkness.

"Agbala do-o-o-o! . . . Agbala ekeneo-o-o-o! . . ." Ekwefi trudged behind, neither getting too near nor keeping too far back. She thought they must be going towards the sacred cave. Now that she walked slowly she had time to think. What would she do when they got to the cave? She would not dare to enter. She would wait at the mouth, all alone in that fearful place. She thought of all the terrors of the night. She remembered that night, long ago, when she had seen Ogbu-agali-odu, one of those evil essences loosed upon the world by the potent "medicines" which the tribe had made in the distant past against its enemies but had now forgotten how to control. Ekwefi had been returning from the stream with her mother on a dark night like this when they saw its glow as it flew in their direction. They had thrown down their water-pots and lain by the roadside expecting the sinister light to descend on them and kill them. That was the only time Ekwefi ever saw Ogbu-agali-odu. But although it had happened so long ago, her blood still ran cold whenever she remembered that night.

The priestess's voice came at longer intervals now, but its vigor was undiminished. The air was cool and damp with dew. Ezinma sneezed. Ekwefi muttered, "Life to you." At the same time the priestess also said, "Life to you, my daughter." Ezinma's voice from the darkness warmed her mother's heart. She trudged slowly along.

And then the priestess screamed. "Somebody is walking behind me!" she said. "Whether you are spirit or man, may Agbala shave your head with a blunt razor! May he twist your neck until you see your heels!"

Elkwefi stood rooted to the spot. One mind said to her: "Woman, go home before Agbala does you harm." But she could not. She stood until Chielo had increased the distance between them and she began to follow again. She had already walked so long that she began to feel a slight numbness in the limbs and in the head. Then it occurred to her that they could not have been heading for the cave. They must have by-passed it long ago; they must be going towards Umuachi, the farthest village in the clan. Chielo's voice now came after long intervals.

It seemed to Ekwefi that the night had become a little lighter. The cloud had lifted and a few stars were out. The moon must be preparing to rise, its sullenness over. When the moon rose late in the night, people said it was refusing food, as a sullen husband refuses his wife's food when they have quarrelled.

"Agbala do-o-o-o! Umuachi! Agbala ekene unuo-o-o!" It was just as Ekwefi had thought. The priestess was now saluting the village of Umuachi. It was unbelievable, the distance they had covered. As they emerged into the open village from the narrow forest track the darkness was softened and it became possible to see the vague shape of trees. Ekwefi screwed her eyes up in an effort to see her daughter and the priestess, but whenever she thought she saw their shape it immediately dissolved like a melting lump of darkness. She walked numbly along.

Chielo's voice was now rising continuously, as when she first set out. Ekwefi had a feeling of spacious openness, and she guessed they must be on the village *ilo,* or playground. And she realized too with something like a jerk that Chielo was no longer moving forward. She was, in fact, returning. Ekwefi quickly moved away from her line of retreat. Chielo passed by, and they began to go back the way they had come.

It was a long and weary journey and Ekwefi felt like a sleepwalker most of the way. The moon was definitely rising, and although it had not yet appeared on the sky its light had already melted down the darkness. Ekwefi could now discern the figure of the priestess and her burden. She slowed down her pace so as to increase the distance between them. She was afraid of what might happen if Chielo suddenly turned round and saw her.

She had prayed for the moon to rise. But now she found the half-light of the incipient moon more terrifying than darkness. The world was now peopled with vague, fantastic figures that dissolved under her steady gaze and then formed again in new shapes. At one stage Ekwefi was so afraid that she nearly called out to Chielo for companionship and human sympathy. What she had seen was the shape of a man climbing a palm tree, his head pointing to the earth and his legs skywards. But at that very moment Chielo's voice rose again in her possessed chanting, and Ekwefi recoiled, because there was no humanity there. It was not the same Chielo who sat with her in the market and sometimes bought bean-cakes for Ezinma, whom she called her daughter. It was a different woman—the priestess of Agbala, the Oracle of the Hills and Caves. Ekwefi trudged along between two fears. The sound of her benumbed steps seemed to come from some other person walking behind her. Her arms were folded across her bare breasts. Dew fell heavily and the air was cold. She could no longer think, not even about the terrors of night. She just jogged along in a half-sleep, only waking to full life when Chielo sang.

At last they took a turning and began to head for the caves. From then on, Chielo never ceased in her chanting. She greeted her god in a multitude of names—the owner of the future, the messenger of earth, the god who cut a man down when his life was sweetest to him. Ekwefi was also awakened and her benumbed fears revived.

The moon was now up and she could see Chielo and Ezinma clearly. How a woman could carry a child of that size so easily and for so long was a miracle. But Ekwefi was not thinking about that. Chielo was not a woman that night.

"*Agbala do-o-o-o! Agbala ekeneo-o-o-o! Chi negbu madu ubosi ndu ya nato ya uto daluo-o-o!* . . ."[5]

Ekwefi could already see the hills looming in the moonlight. They formed a circular ring with a break at one point through which the foot-track led to the center of the circle.

5. Agbala wants something! Agbala greets . . . God who kills a man on the day his life is so pleasant he give thanks!

As soon as the priestess stepped into this ring of hills her voice was not only doubled in strength but was thrown back on all sides. It was indeed the shrine of a great god. Ekwefi picked her way carefully and quietly. She was already beginning to doubt the wisdom of her coming. Nothing would happen to Ezinma, she thought. And if anything happened to her could she stop it? She would not dare to enter the underground caves. Her coming was quite useless, she thought.

As these things went through her mind she did not realize how close they were to the cave mouth. And so when the priestess with Ezinma on her back disappeared through a hole hardly big enough to pass a hen, Ekwefi broke into a run as though to stop them. As she stood gazing at the circular darkness which had swallowed them, tears gushed from her eyes, and she swore within her that if she heard Ezinma cry she would rush into the cave to defend her against all the gods in the world. She would die with her.

Having sworn that oath, she sat down on a stony ledge and waited. Her fear had vanished. She could hear the priestess's voice, all its metal taken out of it by the vast emptiness of the cave. She buried her face in her lap and waited.

She did not know how long she waited. It must have been a very long time. Her back was turned on the footpath that led out of the hills. She must have heard a noise behind her and turned round sharply. A man stood there with a machete in his hand. Ekwefi uttered a scream and sprang to her feet.

"Don't be foolish," said Okonkwo's voice. "I thought you were going into the shrine with Chielo," he mocked.

Ekwefi did not answer. Tears of gratitude filled her eyes. She knew her daughter was safe.

"Go home and sleep," said Okonkwo. "I shall wait here."

"I shall wait too. It is almost dawn. The first cock has crowed."

As they stood there together, Ekwefi's mind went back to the days when they were young. She had married Anene because Okonkwo was too poor then to marry. Two years after her marriage to Anene she could bear it no longer and she ran away to Okonkwo. It had been early in the morning. The moon was shining. She was going to the stream to fetch water. Okonkwo's house was on the way to the stream. She went in and knocked at his door and he came out. Even in those days he was not a man of many words. He just carried her into his bed and in the darkness began to feel around her waist for the loose end of her cloth.

12

On the following morning the entire neighborhood wore a festive air because Okonkwo's friend, Obierika, was celebrating his daughter's *uri*. It was the day on which her suitor (having already paid the greater part of her bride-price) would bring palm-wine not only to her parents and immediate relatives but to the wide and extensive group of kinsmen called *umunna*. Everybody had been invited—men, women and children. But it was really a woman's ceremony and the central figures were the bride and her mother.

As soon as day broke, breakfast was hastily eaten and women and children began to gather at Obierika's compound to help the bride's mother in her difficult but happy task of cooking for a whole village.

Okonkwo's family was astir like any other family in the neighborhood. Nwoye's mother and Okonkwo's youngest wife were ready to set out for Obierika's compound with all their children. Nwoye's mother carried a basket of coco-yams, a cake of salt and smoked fish which she would present to Obierika's wife. Okonkwo's youngest wife, Ojiugo, also had a basket of plantains and coco-yams and a small pot of palm-oil. Their children carried pots of water.

Ekwefi was tired and sleepy from the exhausting experiences of the previous night. It was not very long since they had returned. The priestess, with Ezinma sleeping on her back, had crawled out of the shrine on her belly like a snake. She had not as much as looked at Okonkwo and Ekwefi or shown any surprise at finding them at the mouth of the cave. She looked straight ahead of her and walked back to the village. Okonkwo and his wife followed at a respectful distance. They thought the priestess might be going to her house, but she went to Okonkwo's compound, passed through his *obi* and into Ekwefi's hut and walked into her bedroom. She placed Ezinma carefully on the bed and went away without saying a word to anybody.

Ezinma was still sleeping when everyone else was astir, and Ekwefi asked Nwoye's mother and Ojiugo to explain to Obierika's wife that she would be late. She had got ready her basket of coco-yams and fish, but she must wait for Ezinma to wake.

"You need some sleep yourself," said Nwoye's mother. "You look very tired."

As they spoke Ezinma emerged from the hut, rubbing her eyes and stretching her spare frame. She saw the other children with their water-pots and remembered that they were going to fetch water for Obierika's wife. She went back to the hut and brought her pot.

"Have you slept enough?" asked her mother.

"Yes," she replied, "Let us go."

"Not before you have had your breakfast," said Ekwefi. And she went into her hut to warm the vegetable soup she had cooked last night.

"We shall be going," said Nwoye's mother. "I will tell Obierika's wife that you are coming later." And so they all went to help Obierika's wife—Nwoye's mother with her four children and Ojiugo with her two.

As they trooped through Okonkwo's *obi* he asked: "Who will prepare my afternoon meal?"

"I shall return to do it," said Ojiugo.

Okonkwo was also feeling tired, and sleepy, for although nobody else knew it, he had not slept at all last night. He had felt very anxious but did not show it. When Ekwefi had followed the priestess, he had allowed what he regarded as a reasonable and manly interval to pass and then gone with his machete to the shrine, where he thought they must be. It was only when he had got there that it had occurred to him that the priestess might have chosen to go round the villages first. Okonkwo had returned home and sat waiting. When he thought he had waited long enough he again returned to the shrine. But the Hills and the Caves were as silent as death. It was only on his fourth trip that he had found Ekwefi, and by then he had become gravely worried.

Obierika's compound was as busy as an anthill. Temporary cooking tripods were erected on every available space by bringing together three blocks of sun-dried earth and making a fire in their midst. Cooking pots went up and down the tripods, and foo-foo was pounded in a hundred wooden mortars. Some of the women cooked the yams and the cassava, and others prepared vegetable soup. Young men pounded the foo-foo or split firewood. The children made endless trips to the stream.

Three young men helped Obierika to slaughter the two goats with which the soup was made. They were very fat goats, but the fattest of all was tethered to a peg near the wall of the compound. It was as big as a small cow. Obierika had sent one of his relatives all the way to Umuike to buy that goat. It was the one he would present alive to his in-laws.

"The market of Umuike is a wonderful place," said the young man who had been sent by Obierika to buy the giant goat. "There are so many people on it that if you threw up a grain of sand it would not find a way to fall to earth again."

"It is the result of a great medicine," said Obierika. "The people of Umuike wanted their market to grow and swallow up the markets of their neighbors. So they made a powerful medicine. Every market day, before the first cockcrow, this medicine stands on the market ground in the shape of an old woman with a fan. With this magic fan she beckons to the market all the neighboring clans. She beckons in front of her and behind her, to her right and to her left."

"And so everybody comes," said another man, "honest men and thieves. They can steal your cloth from off your waist in that market."

"Yes," said Obierika. "I warned Nwankwo to keep a sharp eye and a sharp ear. There was once a man who went to sell a goat. He led it on a thick rope which he tied round his wrist. But as he walked through the market he realized that people were pointing at him as they do to a madman. He could not understand it until he looked back and saw that what he led at the end of the tether was not a goat but a heavy log of wood."

"Do you think a thief can do that kind of thing single-handed?" asked Nwankwo.

"No," said Obierika. "They use medicine."

When they had cut the goats' throats and collected the blood in a bowl, they held them over an open fire to burn off the hair, and the smell of burning hair blended with the smell of cooking. Then they washed them and cut them up for the women who prepared the soup.

All this anthill activity was going smoothly when a sudden interruption came. It was a cry in the distance: *Oji odu achu ijiji-o-o!* (*The one that uses its tail to drive flies away!*) Every woman immediately abandoned whatever she was doing and rushed out in the direction of the cry.

"We cannot all rush out like that, leaving what we are cooking to burn in the fire," shouted Chielo, the priestess. "Three or four of us should stay behind."

"It is true," said another woman. "We will allow three or four women to stay behind."

Five women stayed behind to look after the cooking-pots, and all the rest rushed away to see the cow that had been let loose. When they saw it they drove it back to its owner, who at once paid the heavy fine which the village imposed on anyone whose cow was let loose on his neighbors' crops. When the women had exacted the penalty they checked among themselves to see if any woman had failed to come out when the cry had been raised.

"Where is Mgbogo?" asked one of them.

"She is ill in bed," said Mgbogo's next-door neighbor. "She has *iba*."

"The only other person is Udenkwo," said another woman, "and her child is not twenty-eight days yet."

Those women whom Obierika's wife had not asked to help her with the cooking returned to their homes, and the rest went back, in a body, to Obierika's compound.

"Whose cow was it?" asked the women who had been allowed to stay behind.

"It was my husband's," said Ezelagbo. "One of the young children had opened the gate of the cowshed."

Early in the afternoon the first two pots of palm-wine arrived from Obierika's in-laws. They were duly presented to the women, who drank a cup or two each, to help them in their cooking. Some of it also went to the bride and her attendant maidens, who were putting the last delicate touches of razor to her coiffure and cam wood on her smooth skin.

When the heat of the sun began to soften, Obierika's son, Maduka, took a long broom and swept the ground in front of his father's *obi*. And as if they had been waiting for that, Obierika's relatives and friends began to arrive, every man with his goatskin bag hung on one shoulder and a rolled goatskin mat under his arm. Some of them were accompanied by their sons bearing carved wooden stools. Okonkwo was one of them. They sat in a half-circle and began to talk of many things. It would not be long before the suitors came.

Okonkwo brought out his snuff-bottle and offered it to Ogbuefi Ezenwa, who sat next to him. Ezenwa[6] took it, tapped it on his kneecap, rubbed his left palm on his body to dry it before tipping a little snuff into it. His actions were deliberate, and he spoke as he performed them:

"I hope our in-laws will bring many pots of wine. Although they come from a village that is known for being closefisted, they ought to know that Akueke is the bride for a king."

"They dare not bring fewer than thirty pots," said Okonkwo. "I shall tell them my mind if they do."

At that moment Obierika's son, Maduka, led out the giant goat from the inner compound, for his father's relatives to see. They all admired it and said that that was the way things should be done. The goat was then led back to the inner compound.

Very soon after, the in-laws began to arrive. Young men and boys in single file, each carrying a pot of wine, came first. Obierika's relatives counted the pots as they came. Twenty, twenty-five. There was a long break, and the hosts looked at each other as if to say, "I told you." Then more pots came. Thirty, thirty-five, forty, forty-five. The hosts nodded in approval and seemed to say, "Now they are behaving like men." Altogether there were fifty pots of wine. After the pot-bearers came Ibe, the suitor, and the elders of his family. They sat in a half-moon, thus completing a circle with their hosts. The pots of wine stood in their midst. Then the bride, her mother and a half a dozen other women and girls emerged from the inner compound, and went round

6. King From Childhood (strong praise).

the circle shaking hands with all. The bride's mother led the way, followed by the bride and the other women. The married women wore their best cloths and the girls wore red and black waist-beads and anklets of brass.

When the women retired, Obierika presented kola nuts to his in-laws. His eldest brother broke the first one. "Life to all of us," he said as he broke it. "And let there be friendship between your family and ours."

The crowd answered: *"Ee-e-e!"*

"We are giving you our daughter today. She will be a good wife to you. She will bear you nine sons like the mother of our town."

"Ee-e-e!"

The oldest man in the camp of the visitors replied: "It will be good for you and it will be good for us."

"Ee-e-e!"

"This is not the first time my people have come to marry your daughter. My mother was one of you."

"Ee-e-e!"

"And this will not be the last, because you understand us and we understand you. You are a great family."

"Ee-e-e!"

"Prosperous men and great warriors." He looked in the direction of Okonkwo. "Your daughter will bear us sons like you."

"Ee-e-e!"

The kola was eaten and the drinking of palm-wine began. Groups of four or five men sat round with a pot in their midst. As the evening wore on, food was presented to the guests. There were huge bowls of foo-foo and steaming pots of soup. There were also pots of yam pottage. It was a great feast.

As night fell, burning torches were set on wooden tripods and the young men raised a song. The elders sat in a big circle and the singers went round singing each man's praise as they came before him. They had something to say for every man. Some were great farmers, some were orators who spoke for the clan; Okonkwo was the greatest wrestler and warrior alive. When they had gone round the circle they settled down in the center, and girls came from the inner compound to dance. At first the bride was not among them. But when she finally appeared holding a cock in her right hand, a loud cheer rose from the crowd. All the other dancers made way for her. She presented the cock to the musicians and began to dance. Her brass anklets rattled as she danced and her body gleamed with cam wood in the soft yellow light. The musicians with their wood, clay and metal instruments went from song to song. And they were all gay. They sang the latest song in the village:

> If I hold her hand
>> She says, "Don't touch!"
> If I hold her foot
>> She says, "Don't touch!"
> But when I hold her waist-beads
>> She pretends not to know.

The night was already far spent when the guests rose to go, taking their bride home to spend seven market weeks with her suitor's family. They sang songs as they went, and on their way they paid short courtesy visits to prominent men like Okonkwo, before they finally left for their village. Okonkwo made a present of two cocks to them.

13

Go-di-di-go-go-di-go. Di-go-go-di-go. It was the *ekwe* talking to the clan. One of the things every man learned was the language of the hollowed-out wooden instrument. Diim! Diim! Diim! boomed the cannon at intervals. The first cock had not crowed, and Umuofia was still swallowed up in sleep and silence when the *ekwe* began to talk, and the cannon shattered the silence. Men stirred on their bamboo beds and listened anxiously. Somebody was dead. The cannon seemed to rend the sky. Di-go-go-di-go-di-di-go-go floated in the message-laden night air. The faint and distant wailing of women settled like a sediment of sorrow on the earth. Now and again a full-chested lamentation rose above the wailing whenever a man came into the place of death. He raised his voice once or twice in manly sorrow and then sat down with the other men listening to the endless wailing of the women and the esoteric language of the *ekwe*. Now and again the cannon boomed. The wailing of the women would not be heard beyond the village, but the *ekwe* carried the news to all the nine villages and even beyond. It began by naming the clan: *Umuofia obodo dike*, "the land of the brave." *Umuofia obodo dike! Umuofia obodo dike!* It said this over and over again, and as it dwelt on it, anxiety mounted in every heart that heaved on a bamboo bed that night. Then it went nearer and named the village: *Iguedo*[7] of the yellow grinding-stone!"[7] It was Okonkwo's village. Again and again Iguedo was called and men waited breathlessly in all the nine villages. At last the man was named and people sighed "E-u-u, Ezeudu is dead." A cold shiver ran down Okonkwo's back as he remembered the last time the old man had visited him. "That boy calls you father," he had said. "Bear no hand in his death."

Ezeudu was a great man, and so all the clan was at his funeral. The ancient drums of death beat, guns and cannon were fired, and men dashed about in frenzy, cutting down every tree or animal they saw, jumping over walls and dancing on the roof. It was a warrior's funeral, and from morning till night warriors came and went in their age groups. They all wore smoked raffia skirts and their bodies were painted with chalk and charcoal. Now and again an ancestral spirit or *egwugwu* appeared from the underworld, speaking in a tremulous, unearthly voice and completely covered in raffia. Some of them were very violent, and there had been a mad rush for shelter earlier in the day when one appeared with a sharp machete and was only prevented from doing serious harm by two men who restrained him with the help of a strong rope tied round his waist. Sometimes he turned round and chased those men, and they ran for their lives. But they always returned to the long rope he trailed behind. He sang, in a terrifying voice, that Ekwensu, or Evil Spirit, had entered his eye.

But the most dreaded of all was yet to come. He was always alone and was shaped like a coffin. A sickly odor hung in the air wherever he went, and

---

7. The yellow grindstone.

flies went with him. Even the greatest medicine men took shelter when he was near. Many years ago another *egwugwu* had dared to stand his ground before him and had been transfixed to the spot for two days. This one had only one hand and it carried a basket full of water.

But some of the *egwugwu* were quite harmless. One of them was so old and infirm that he leaned heavily on a stick. He walked unsteadily to the place where the corpse was laid, gazed at it a while and went away again—to the underworld.

The land of the living was not far removed from the domain of the ancestors. There was coming and going between them, especially at festivals and also when an old man died, because an old man was very close to the ancestors. A man's life from birth to death was a series of transition rites which brought him nearer and nearer to his ancestors.

Ezeudu had been the oldest man in his village, and at his death there were only three men in the whole clan who were older, and four or five others in his own age group. Whenever one of these ancient men appeared in the crowd to dance unsteadily the funeral steps of the tribe, younger men gave way and the tumult subsided.

It was a great funeral, such as befitted a noble warrior. As the evening drew near, the shouting and the firing of guns, the beating of drums and the brandishing and clanging of machetes increased.

Ezeudu had taken three titles in his life. It was a rare achievement. There were only four titles in the clan, and only one or two men in any generation ever achieved the fourth and highest. When they did, they became the lords of the land. Because he had taken titles, Ezeudu was to be buried after dark with only a glowing brand to light the sacred ceremony.

But before this quiet and final rite, the tumult increased tenfold. Drums beat violently and men leaped up and down in frenzy. Guns were fired on all sides and sparks flew out as machetes clanged together in warriors' salutes. The air was full of dust and the smell of gunpowder. It was then that the one-handed spirit came, carrying a basket full of water. People made way for him on all sides and the noise subsided. Even the smell of gunpowder was swallowed in the sickly smell that now filled the air. He danced a few steps to the funeral drums and then went to see the corpse.

"Ezeudu!" he called in his guttural voice. "If you had been poor in your last life I would have asked you to be rich when you come again. But you were rich. If you had been a coward, I would have asked you to bring courage. But you were a fearless warrior. If you had died young, I would have asked you to get life. But you lived long. So I shall ask you to come again the way you came before. If your death was the death of nature, go in peace. But if a man caused it, do not allow him a moment's rest." He danced a few more steps and went away.

The drums and the dancing began again and reached fever-heat. Darkness was around the corner, and the burial was near. Guns fired the last salute and the cannon rent the sky. And then from the center of the delirious fury came a cry of agony and shouts of horror. It was as if a spell had been cast. All was silent. In the center of the crowd a boy lay in a pool of blood. It was the dead man's sixteen-year-old son, who with his brothers and half-brothers had been dancing the traditional farewell to their father. Okonkwo's gun had exploded and a piece of iron had pierced the boy's heart.

The confusion that followed was without parallel in the tradition of Umuofia. Violent deaths were frequent, but nothing like this had ever happened.

The only course open to Okonkwo was to flee from the clan. It was a crime against the earth goddess to kill a clansman, and a man who committed it must flee from the land. The crime was of two kinds, male and female. Okonkwo had committed the female, because it had been inadvertent. He could return to the clan after seven years.

That night he collected his most valuable belongings into head-loads. His wives wept bitterly and their children wept with them without knowing why. Obierika and half a dozen other friends came to help and to console him. They each made nine or ten trips carrying Okonkwo's yams to store in Obierika's barn. And before the cock crowed Okonkwo and his family were fleeing to his motherland. It was a little village called Mbanta,[8] just beyond the borders of Mbaino.

As soon as the day broke, a large crowd of men from Ezeudu's quarter stormed Okonkwo's compound, dressed in garbs of war. They set fire to his houses, demolished his red walls, killed his animals and destroyed his barn. It was the justice of the earth goddess, and they were merely her messengers. They had no hatred in their hearts against Okonkwo. His greatest friend, Obierika, was among them. They were merely cleansing the land which Okonkwo had polluted with the blood of a clansman.

Obierika was a man who thought about things. When the will of the goddess had been done, he sat down in his *obi* and mourned his friend's calamity. Why should a man suffer so grievously for an offense he had committed inadvertently? But although he thought for a long time he found no answer. He was merely led into greater complexities. He remembered his wife's twin children, whom he had thrown away. What crime had they committed? The Earth had decreed that they were an offense on the land and must be destroyed. And if the clan did not exact punishment for an offense against the great goddess, her wrath was loosed on all the land and not just on the offender. As the elders said, if one finger brought oil it soiled the others.

Part Two

14

Okonkwo was well received by his mother's kinsmen in Mbanta. The old man who received him was his mother's younger brother, who was now the eldest surviving member of that family. His name was Uchendu,[9] and it was he who had received Okonkwo's mother twenty and ten years before when she had been brought home from Umuofia to be buried with her people. Okonkwo was only a boy then and Uchendu still remembered him crying the traditional farewell: "Mother, mother, mother is going."

That was many years ago. Today Okonkwo was not bringing his mother home to be buried with her people. He was taking his family of three wives

---

8. Small Town. 9. The Thought Created by Life.

and their children to seek refuge in his motherland. As soon as Uchendu saw him with his sad and weary company he guessed what had happened, and asked no questions. It was not until the following day that Okonkwo told him the full story. The old man listened silently to the end and then said with some relief: "It is a female *ochu*."[1] And he arranged the requisite rites and sacrifices.

Okonkwo was given a plot of ground on which to build his compound, and two or three pieces of land on which to farm during the coming planting season. With the help of his mother's kinsmen he built himself an *obi* and three huts for his wives. He then installed his personal god and the symbols of his departed fathers. Each of Uchendu's five sons contributed three hundred seed-yams to enable their cousin to plant a farm, for as soon as the first rain came farming would begin.

At last the rain came. It was sudden and tremendous. For two or three moons the sun had been gathering strength till it seemed to breathe a breath of fire on the earth. All the grass had long been scorched brown, and the sands felt like live coals to the feet. Evergreen trees wore a dusty coat of brown. The birds were silenced in the forests, and the world lay panting under the live, vibrating heat. And then came the clap of thunder. It was an angry, metallic and thirsty clap, unlike the deep and liquid rumbling of the rainy season. A mighty wind arose and filled the air with dust. Palm trees swayed as the wind combed their leaves into flying crests like strange and fantastic coiffure.

When the rain finally came, it was in large, solid drops of frozen water which the people called "the nuts of the water of heaven." They were hard and painful on the body as they fell, yet young people ran about happily picking up the cold nuts and throwing them into their mouths to melt.

The earth quickly came to life and the birds in the forests fluttered around and chirped merrily. A vague scent of life and green vegetation was diffused in the air. As the rain began to fall more soberly and in smaller liquid drops, children sought for shelter, and all were happy, refreshed and thankful.

Okonkwo and his family worked very hard to plant a new farm. But it was like beginning life anew without the vigor and enthusiasm of youth, like learning to become left-handed in old age. Work no longer had for him the pleasure it used to have, and when there was no work to do he sat in a silent half-sleep.

His life had been ruled by a great passion—to become one of the lords of the clan. That had been his life-spring. And he had all but achieved it. Then everything had been broken. He had been cast out of his clan like a fish onto a dry, sandy beach, panting. Clearly his personal god or *chi* was not made for great things. A man could not rise beyond the destiny of his *chi*. The saying of the elders was not true—that if a man said yea his *chi* also affirmed. Here was a man whose *chi* said nay despite his own affirmation.

The old man, Uchendu, saw clearly that Okonkwo had yielded to despair and he was greatly troubled. He would speak to him after the *isa-ifi*[2] ceremony.

---

1. Murder, manslaughter.   2. A ceremony to ascertain that a wife (here, a promised bride) had been faithful to her husband during a separation.

The youngest of Uchendu's five sons, Amikwu, was marrying a new wife. The bride-price had been paid and all but the last ceremony had been performed. Amikwu and his people had taken palm-wine to the bride's kinsmen about two moons before Okonkwo's arrival in Mbanta. And so it was time for the final ceremony of confession.

The daughters of the family were all there, some of them having come a long way from their homes in distant villages. Uchendu's eldest daughter had come from Obodo, nearly half a day's journey away. The daughters of Uchendu's brothers were also there. It was a full gathering of *umuada*,[3] in the same way as they would meet if a death occurred in the family. There were twenty-two of them.

They sat in a big circle on the ground and the bride sat in the center with a hen in her right hand. Uchendu sat by her, holding the ancestral staff of the family. All the other men stood outside the circle, watching. Their wives watched also. It was evening and the sun was setting.

Uchendu's eldest daughter, Njide, asked the questions.

"Remember that if you do not answer truthfully you will suffer or even die at childbirth," she began. "How many men have lain with you since my brother first expressed the desire to marry you?"

"None," she answered simply.

"Answer truthfully," urged the other women.

"None?" asked Njide.

"None," she answered.

"Swear on this staff of my fathers," said Uchendu.

"I swear," said the bride.

Uchendu took the hen from her, slit its throat with a sharp knife and allowed some of the blood to fall on his ancestral staff.

From that day Amikwu took the young bride to his hut and she became his wife. The daughters of the family did not return to their homes immediately but spent two or three days with their kinsmen.

On the second day Uchendu called together his sons and daughters and his nephew, Okonkwo. The men brought their goatskin mats, with which they sat on the floor, and the women sat on a sisal mat spread on a raised bank of earth. Uchendu pulled gently at his gray beard and gnashed his teeth. Then he began to speak, quietly and deliberately, picking his words with great care:

"It is Okonkwo that I primarily wish to speak to," he began. "But I want all of you to note what I am going to say. I am an old man and you are all children. I know more about the world than any of you. If there is any one among you who thinks he knows more let him speak up." He paused, but no one spoke.

"Why is Okonkwo with us today? This is not his clan. We are only his mother's kinsmen. He does not belong here. He is an exile, condemned for seven years to live in a strange land. And so he is bowed with grief. But there is just one question I would like to ask him. Can you tell me, Okonkwo, why it is that one of the commonest names we give our children is Nneka, or

---

3. The daughters, who, according to Igbo custom, married outside the clan, perform a special initiation upon returning home for important gatherings.

"Mother is Supreme?" We all know that a man is the head of the family and his wives do his bidding. A child belongs to its father and his family and not to its mother and her family. A man belongs to his fatherland and not to his motherland. And yet we say Nneka—'Mother is Supreme.' Why is that?"

There was silence. "I want Okonkwo to answer me," said Uchendu.

"I do not know the answer," Okonkwo replied.

"You do not know the answer? So you see that you are a child. You have many wives and many children—more children than I have. You are a great man in your clan. But you are still a child, *my* child. Listen to me and I shall tell you. But there is one more question I shall ask you. Why is it that when a woman dies she is taken home to be buried with her own kinsmen? She is not buried with her husband's kinsmen. Why is that? Your mother was brought home to me and buried with my people. Why was that?"

Okonkwo shook his head.

"He does not know that either," said Uchendu, "and yet he is full of sorrow because he has come to live in his motherland for a few years." He laughed a mirthless laughter, and turned to his sons and daughters. "What about you? Can you answer my question?"

They all shook their heads.

"Then listen to me," he said and cleared his throat. "It's true that a child belongs to its father. But when a father beats his child, it seeks sympathy in its mother's hut. A man belongs to his fatherland when things are good and life is sweet. But when there is sorrow and bitterness he finds refuge in his motherland. Your mother is there to protect you. She is buried there. And that is why we say that mother is supreme. Is it right that you, Okonkwo, should bring to your mother a heavy face and refuse to be comforted? Be careful or you may displease the dead. Your duty is to comfort your wives and children and take them back to your fatherland after seven years. But if you allow sorrow to weigh you down and kill you, they will all die in exile." He paused for a long while. "These are now your kinsmen." He waved at his sons and daughters. "You think you are the greatest sufferer in the world? Do you know that men are sometimes banished for life? Do you know that men sometimes lose all their yams and even their children? I had six wives once. I have none now except that young girl who knows not her right from her left. Do you know how many children I have buried—children I begot in my youth and strength? Twenty-two. I did not hang myself, and I am still alive. If you think you are the greatest sufferer in the world ask my daughter, Akueni, how many twins she has borne and thrown away. Have you not heard the song they sing when a woman dies?

> For whom is it well, for whom is it well?
> There is no one for whom it is well.

"I have no more to say to you."

15

It was in the second year of Okonkwo's exile that his friend, Obierika, came to visit him. He brought with him two young men, each of them carrying a heavy bag on his head. Okonkwo helped them put down their loads. It was clear that the bags were full of cowries.

Okonkwo was very happy to receive his friend. His wives and children were very happy too, and so were his cousins and their wives when he sent for them and told them who his guest was.

"You must take him to salute our father," said one of the cousins.

"Yes," replied Okonkwo. "We are going directly." But before they went he whispered something to his first wife. She nodded, and soon the children were chasing one of their cocks.

Uchendu had been told by one of his grandchildren that three strangers had come to Okonkwo's house. He was therefore waiting to receive them. He held out his hands to them when they came into his *obi*, and after they had shaken hands he asked Okonkwo who they were.

"This is Obierika, my great friend. I have already spoken to you about him."

"Yes," said the old man, turning to Obierika. "My son has told me about you, and I am happy you have come to see us. I knew your father, Iweka. He was a great man. He had many friends here and came to see them quite often. Those were good days when a man had friends in distant clans. Your generation does not know that. You stay at home, afraid of your next-door neighbor. Even a man's motherland is strange to him nowadays." He looked at Okonkwo. "I am an old man and I like to talk. That is all I am good for now." He got up painfully, went into an inner room and came back with a kola nut.

"Who are the young men with you?" he asked as he sat down again on his goatskin. Okonkwo told him.

"Ah," he said. "Welcome, my sons." He presented the kola nut to them, and when they had seen it and thanked him, he broke it and they ate.

"Go into that room," he said to Okonkwo, pointing with his finger. "You will find a pot of wine there."

Okonkwo brought the wine and they began to drink. It was a day old, and very strong.

"Yes," said Uchendu after a long silence. "People traveled more in those days. There is not a single clan in these parts that I do not know very well. Aninta, Umuazu, Ikeocha, Elumelu, Abame—I know them all."

"Have you heard," asked Obierika, "that Abame is no more?"

"How is that?" asked Uchendu and Okonkwo together.

"Abame has been wiped out," said Obierika. "It is a strange and terrible story. If I had not seen the few survivors with my own eyes and heard their story with my own ears, I would not have believed. Was it not on an Eke day that they fled into Umuofia?" he asked his two companions, and they nodded their heads.

"Three moons ago," said Obierika, "on an Eke market day a little band of fugitives came into our town. Most of them were sons of our land whose mothers had been buried with us. But there were some too who came because they had friends in our town, and others who could think of nowhere else open to escape. And so they fled into Umuofia with a woeful story." He drank his palm-wine, and Okonkwo filled his horn again. He continued:

"During the last planting season a white man had appeared in their clan."

"An albino," suggested Okonkwo.

"He was not an albino. He was quite different." He sipped his wine. "And he was riding an iron horse.[4] The first people who saw him ran away, but he

4. Bicycle.

stood beckoning to them. In the end the fearless ones went near and even touched him. The elders consulted their Oracle and it told them that the strange man would break their clan and spread destruction among them." Obierika again drank a little of his wine. "And so they killed the white man and tied his iron horse to their sacred tree because it looked as if it would run away to call the man's friends. I forgot to tell you another thing which the Oracle said. It said that other white men were on their way. They were locusts, it said, and that first man was their harbinger sent to explore the terrain. And so they killed him."

"What did the white man say before they killed him?" asked Uchendu.

"He said nothing," answered one of Obierika's companions.

"He said something, only they did not understand him," said Obierika. "He seemed to speak through his nose."

"One of the men told me," said Obierika's other companion, "that he repeated over and over again a word that resembled Mbaino. Perhaps he had been going to Mbaino and had lost his way."

"Anyway," resumed Obierika, "they killed him and tied up his iron horse. This was before the planting season began. For a long time nothing happened. The rains had come and yams had been sown. The iron horse was still tied to the sacred silk-cotton tree. And then one morning three white men led by a band of ordinary men like us came to the clan. They saw the iron horse and went away again. Most of the men and women of Abame had gone to their farms. Only a few of them saw these white men and their followers. For many market weeks nothing else happened. They have a big market in Abame on every other Afo day and, as you know, the whole clan gathers there. That was the day it happened. The three white men and a very large number of other men surrounded the market. They must have used a powerful medicine to make themselves invisible until the market was full. And they began to shoot. Everybody was killed, except the old and the sick who were at home and a handful of men and women whose *chi* were wide awake and brought them out of that market."[5] He paused.

"Their clan is now completely empty. Even the sacred fish in their mysterious lake have fled and the lake has turned the color of blood. A great evil has come upon their land as the Oracle had warned."

There was a long silence. Uchendu ground his teeth together audibly. Then he burst out:

"Never kill a man who says nothing. Those men of Abame were fools. What did they know about the man?" He ground his teeth again and told a story to illustrate his point. "Mother Kite once sent her daughter to bring food. She went, and brought back a duckling. 'You have done very well,' said Mother Kite to her daughter, 'but tell me, what did the mother of this duckling say when you swooped and carried its child away?' 'It said nothing,' replied the young kite. It just walked away.' 'You must return the duckling,' said Mother Kite. 'There is something ominous behind the silence.' And so Daughter Kite returned the duckling and took a chick instead. 'What did the mother of this chick do?' asked the old kite. 'It cried and raved and cursed me,' said the young kite. 'Then we can eat the chick,' said her mother. 'There

---

5. Achebe bases his account on a similar incident in 1905 when British troops massacred the town of Ahiara in reprisal for the death of a missionary.

is nothing to fear from someone who shouts.' Those men of Abame were fools."

"They were fools," said Okonkwo after a pause. "They had been warned that danger was ahead. They should have armed themselves with their guns and their machetes even when they went to market."

"They have paid for their foolishness," said Obierika. "But I am greatly afraid. We have heard stories about white men who made the powerful guns and the strong drinks and took slaves away across the seas, but no one thought the stories were true."

"There is no story that is not true," said Uchendu. "The world has no end, and what is good among one people is an abomination with others. We have albinos among us. Do you not think that they came to our clan by mistake, that they have strayed from their way to a land where everybody is like them?"

Okonkwo's first wife soon finished her cooking and set before their guests a big meal of pounded yams and bitter-leaf soup. Okonkwo's son, Nwoye, brought in a pot of sweet wine tapped from the raffia palm.

"You are a big man now," Obierika said to Nwoye. "Your friend Anene asked me to greet you."

"Is he well?" asked Nwoye.

"We are all well," said Obierika.

Ezinma brought them a bowl of water with which to wash their hands. After that they began to eat and to drink the wine.

"When did you set out from home?" asked Okonkwo.

"We had meant to set out from my house before cock-crow," said Obierika. "But Nweke did not appear until it was quite light. Never make an early morning appointment with a man who has just married a new wife." They all laughed.

"Has Nweke married a wife?" asked Okonkwo.

"He has married Okadigbo's second daughter," said Obierika.

"That is very good," said Okonkwo. "I do not blame you for not hearing the cock crow."

When they had eaten, Obierika pointed at the two heavy bags.

"That is the money from your yams," he said. "I sold the big ones as soon as you left. Later on I sold some of the seed-yams and gave out others to sharecroppers. I shall do that every year until you return. But I thought you would need the money now and so I brought it. Who knows what may happen tomorrow? Perhaps green men will come to our clan and shoot us."

"God will not permit it," said Okonkwo. "I do not know how to thank you."

"I can tell you," said Obierika. "Kill one of your sons for me."

"That will not be enough," said Okonkwo.

"Then kill yourself," said Obierika.

"Forgive me," said Okonkwo, smiling. "I shall not talk about thanking you any more."

16

When nearly two years later Obierika paid another visit to his friend in exile the circumstances were less happy. The missionaries had come to Umuofia. They had built their church there, won a handful of converts and were already sending evangelists to the surrounding towns and villages. That was a source of great sorrow to the leaders of the clan; but many of them believed that the strange faith and the white man's god would not last. None of his converts was a man whose word was heeded in the assembly of the people. None of them was a man of title. They were mostly the kind of people that were called *efulefu,* worthless, empty men. The imagery of an *efulefu* in the language of the clan was a man who sold his machete and wore the sheath to battle. Chielo, the priestess of Agbala, called the converts the excrement of the clan, and the new faith was a mad dog that had come to eat it up.

What moved Obierika to visit Okonkwo was the sudden appearance of the latter's son, Nwoye, among the missionaries in Umuofia.

"What are you doing here?" Obierika had asked when after many difficulties the missionaries had allowed him to speak to the boy.

"I am one of them," replied Nwoye.

"How is your father?" Obierika asked, not knowing what else to say.

"I don't know. He is not my father," said Nwoye, unhappily.

And so Obierika went to Mbanta to see his friend. And he found that Okonkwo did not wish to speak about Nwoye. It was only from Nwoye's mother that he heard scraps of the story.

The arrival of the missionaries had caused a considerable stir in the village of Mbanta. There were six of them and one was a white man. Every man and woman came out to see the white man. Stories about these strange men had grown since one of them had been killed in Abame and his iron horse tied to the sacred silk-cotton tree. And so everybody came to see the white man. It was the time of the year when everybody was at home. The harvest was over.

When they had all gathered, the white man began to speak to them. He spoke through an interpreter who was an Ibo man, though his dialect was different and harsh to the ears of Mbanta. Many people laughed at his dialect and the way he used words strangely. Instead of saying "myself" he always said "my buttocks."[6] But he was a man of commanding presence and the clansmen listened to him. He said he was one of them, as they could see from his color and his language. The other four black men were also their brothers, although one of them did not speak Ibo. The white man was also their brother because they were all sons of God. And he told them about this new God, the Creator of all the world and all the men and women. He told them that they worshipped false gods, gods of wood and stone. A deep murmur went through the crowd when he said this. He told them that the true God lived on high and that all men when they died went before Him for judgment. Evil men and all the heathen who in their blindness bowed to wood and stone were thrown into a fire that burned like palm-oil. But good men who worshipped the true God lived forever in His happy kingdom. "We have been sent by this great God to ask you to leave your wicked ways and false gods and turn to Him so that you may be saved when you die," he said.

6. The Igbo language has high and low tones so that the same word may have different meanings according to its pronunciation. Here, Achebe is probably referring to a famous pair of near-homonyms: *íké* ("strength") and *íkè* ("buttocks").

"Your buttocks understand our language," said someone light-heartedly and the crowd laughed.

"What did he say?" the white man asked his interpreter. But before he could answer, another man asked a question: "Where is the white man's horse?" he asked. The Ibo evangelists consulted among themselves and decided that the man probably meant bicycle. They told the white man and he smiled benevolently.

"Tell them," he said, "that I shall bring many iron horses when we have settled down among them. Some of them will even ride the iron horse themselves." This was interpreted to them but very few of them heard. They were talking excitedly among themselves because the white man had said he was going to live among them. They had not thought about that.

At this point an old man said he had a question. "Which is this god of yours," he asked, "the goddess of the earth, the god of the sky, Amadiora of the thunderbolt, or what?"

The interpreter spoke to the white man and he immediately gave his answer. "All the gods you have named are not gods at all. They are gods of deceit who tell you to kill your fellows and destroy innocent children. There is only one true God and He has the earth, the sky, you and me and all of us."

"If we leave our gods and follow your god," asked another man, "who will protect us from the anger of our neglected gods and ancestors?"

"Your gods are not alive and cannot do you any harm," replied the white man. "They are pieces of wood and stone."

When this was interpreted to the men of Mbanta they broke into derisive laughter. These men must be mad, they said to themselves. How else could they say that Ani and Amadiora were harmless? And Idemili and Ogwugwu too? And some of them began to go away.

Then the missionaries burst into song. It was one of those gay and rollicking tunes of evangelism which had the power of plucking at silent and dusty chords in the heart of an Ibo man. The interpreter explained each verse to the audience, some of whom now stood enthralled. It was a story of brothers who lived in darkness and in fear, ignorant of the love of God. It told of one sheep out on the hills, away from the gates of God and from the tender shepherd's care.

After the singing the interpreter spoke about the Son of God whose name was Jesu Kristi. Okonkwo, who only stayed in the hope that it might come to chasing the men out of the village or whipping them, now said:

"You told us with your own mouth that there was only one god. Now you talk about his son. He must have a wife, then." The crowd agreed.

"I did not say He had a wife," said the interpreter, somewhat lamely.

"Your buttocks said he had a son," said the joker. "So he must have a wife and all of them must have buttocks."

The missionary ignored him and went on to talk about the Holy Trinity. At the end of it Okonkwo was fully convinced that the man was mad. He shrugged his shoulders and went away to tap his afternoon palm-wine.

But there was a young lad who had been captivated. His name was Nwoye, Okonkwo's first son. It was not the mad logic of the Trinity that captivated him. He did not understand it. It was the poetry of the new religion, something felt in the marrow. The hymn about brothers who sat in darkness and in fear seemed to answer a vague and persistent question that haunted his young soul—the question of the twins crying in the bush and the question of Ikemefuna who was killed. He felt a relief within as the hymn poured into his parched soul. The words of the hymn were like the drops of frozen rain melting on the dry palate of the panting earth. Nwoye's callow mind was greatly puzzled.

17

The missionaries spent their first four or five nights in the marketplace, and went into the village in the morning to preach the gospel. They asked who the king of the village was, but the villagers told them that there was no king. "We have men of high title and the chief priests and the elders," they said.

It was not very easy getting the men of high title and the elders together after the excitement of the first day. But the missionaries persevered, and in the end they were received by the rulers of Mbanta. They asked for a plot of land to build their church.

Every clan and village had its "evil forest." In it were buried all those who died of the really evil diseases, like leprosy and smallpox. It was also the dumping ground for the potent fetishes of great medicine men when they died. An "evil forest" was, therefore, alive with sinister forces and powers of darkness. It was such a forest that the rulers of Mbanta gave to the missionaries. They did not really want them in their clan, and so they made them that offer which nobody in his right senses would accept.

"They want a piece of land to build their shrine," said Uchendu to his peers when they consulted among themselves. "We shall give them a piece of land." He paused, and there was a murmur of surprise and disagreement. "Let us give them a portion of the Evil Forest. They boast about victory over death. Let us give them a real battlefield in which to show their victory." They laughed and agreed, and sent for the missionaries, whom they had asked to leave them for a while so that they might "whisper together." They offered them as much of the Evil Forest as they cared to take. And to their greatest amazement the missionaries thanked them and burst into song.

"They do not understand," said some of the elders. "But they will understand when they go to their plot of land tomorrow morning." And they dispersed.

The next morning the crazy men actually began to clear a part of the forest and to build their house. The inhabitants of Mbanta expected them all to be dead within four days. The first day passed and the second and third and fourth, and none of them died. Everyone was puzzled. And then it became known that the white man's fetish had unbelievable power. It was said that he wore glasses on his eyes so that he could see and talk to evil spirits. Not long after, he won his first three converts.

Although Nwoye had been attracted to the new faith from the very first day, he kept it secret. He dared not go too near the missionaries for fear of his father. But whenever they came to preach in the open marketplace or the village playground, Nwoye was there. And he was already beginning to know some of the simple stories they told.

"We have now built a church," said Mr. Kiaga, the interpreter, who was now in charge of the infant congregation. The white man had gone back to

Umuofia, where he built his headquarters and from where he paid regular visits to Mr. Kiaga's congregation at Mbanta.

"We have now built a church," said Mr. Kiaga, "and we want you all to come in every seventh day to worship the true God."

On the following Sunday, Nwoye passed and repassed the little red-earth and thatch building without summoning enough courage to enter. He heard the voice of singing and although it came from a handful of men it was loud and confident. Their church stood on a circular clearing that looked like the open mouth of the Evil Forest. Was it waiting to snap its teeth together? After passing and repassing by the church, Nwoye returned home.

It was well known among the people of Mbanta that their gods and ancestors were sometimes long-suffering and would deliberately allow a man to go on defying them. But even in such cases they set their limit at seven market weeks or twenty-eight days. Beyond that limit no man was suffered to go. And so excitement mounted in the village as the seventh week approached since the impudent missionaries built their church in the Evil Forest. The villagers were so certain about the doom that awaited these men that one or two converts thought it wise to suspend their allegiance to the new faith.

At last the day came by which all the missionaries should have died. But they were still alive, building a new red-earth and thatch house for their teacher, Mr. Kiaga. That week they won a handful more converts. And for the first time they had a woman. Her name was Nneka, the wife of Amadi, who was a prosperous farmer. She was very heavy with child.

Nneka had had four previous pregnancies and childbirths. But each time she had borne twins, and they had been immediately thrown away. Her husband and his family were already becoming highly critical of such a woman and were not unduly perturbed when they found she had fled to join the Christians. It was a good riddance.

One morning Okonkwo's cousin, Amikwu, was passing by the church on his way from the neighboring village, when he saw Nwoye among the Christians. He was greatly surprised, and when he got home he went straight to Okonkwo's hut and told him what he had seen. The women began to talk excitedly, but Okonkwo sat unmoved.

It was late afternoon before Nwoye returned. He went into the *obi* and saluted his father, but he did not answer. Nwoye turned round to walk into the inner compound when his father, suddenly overcome with fury, sprang to his feet and gripped him by the neck.

"Where have you been?" he stammered.

Nwoye struggled to free himself from the choking grip.

"Answer me," roared Okonkwo, "before I kill you!" He seized a heavy stick that lay on the dwarf wall and hit him two or three savage blows.

"Answer me!" he roared again. Nwoye stood looking at him and did not say a word. The women were screaming outside, afraid to go in.

"Leave that boy at once!" said a voice in the outer compound. It was Okonkwo's uncle, Uchendu. "Are you mad?"

Okonkwo did not answer. But he left hold of Nwoye, who walked away and never returned.

He went back to the church and told Mr. Kiaga that he had decided to go to Umuofia where the white missionary had set up a school to teach young Christians to read and write.

Mr. Kiaga's joy was very great. "Blessed is he who forsakes his father and his mother for my sake," he intoned. "Those that hear my words are my father and my mother."

Nwoye did not fully understand. But he was happy to leave his father. He would return later to his mother and his brothers and sisters and convert them to the new faith.

As Okonkwo sat in his hut that night, gazing into a log fire, he thought over the matter. A sudden fury rose within him and he felt a strong desire to take up his machete, go to the church and wipe out the entire vile and miscreant gang. But on further thought he told himself that Nwoye was not worth fighting for. Why, he cried in his heart, should he, Okonkwo, of all people, be cursed with such a son? He saw clearly in it the finger of his personal god or *chi*. For how else could he explain his great misfortune and exile and now his despicable son's behavior? Now that he had time to think of it, his son's crime stood out in its stark enormity. To abandon the gods of one's father and go about with a lot of effeminate men clucking like old hens was the very depth of abomination. Suppose when he died all his male children decided to follow Nwoye's steps and abandon their ancestors? Okonkwo felt a cold shudder run through him at the terrible prospects, like the prospect of annihilation. He saw himself and his fathers crowding round their ancestral shrine waiting in vain for worship and sacrifice and finding nothing but ashes of bygone days, and his children the while praying to the white man's god. If such a thing were ever to happen, he, Okonkwo, would wipe them off the face of the earth.

Okonkwo was popularly called the "Roaring Flame." As he looked into the log fire he recalled the name. He was a flaming fire. How then could he have begotten a son like Nwoye, degenerate and effeminate? Perhaps he was not his son. No! he could not be. His wife had played him false. He would teach her! But Nwoye resembled his grandfather, Unoka, who was Okonkwo's father. He pushed the thought out of his mind. He, Okonkwo, was called a flaming fire. How could he have begotten a woman for a son? At Nwoye's age Okonkwo had already become famous throughout Umuofia for his wrestling and his fearlessness.

He sighed heavily, and as if in sympathy the smoldering log also sighed. And immediately Okonkwo's eyes were opened and he saw the whole matter clearly. Living fire begets cold, impotent ash. He sighed again, deeply.

18

The young church in Mbanta had a few crises early in its life. At first the clan had assumed that it would not survive. But it had gone on living and gradually becoming stronger. The clan was worried, but not overmuch. If a gang of *efulefu* decided to live in the Evil Forest it was their own affair. When one came to think of it, the Evil Forest was a fit home for such undesirable people. It was true they were rescuing twins from the bush, but they never brought them into the village. As far as the villagers were concerned, the twins still remained where they had been thrown away. Surely the earth goddess would not visit the sins of the missionaries on the innocent villagers?

But on one occasion the missionaries had tried to overstep the bounds. Three converts had gone into the village and boasted openly that all the gods were dead and impotent and that they were prepared to defy them by burning all their shrines.

"Go and burn your mothers' genitals," said one of the priests. The men were seized and beaten until they streamed with blood. After that nothing happened for a long time between the church and the clan.

But stories were already gaining ground that the white man had not only brought a religion but also a government. It was said that they had built a place of judgment in Umuofia to protect the followers of their religion. It was even said that they had hanged one man who killed a missionary.

Although such stories were now often told they looked like fairy-tales in Mbanta and did not as yet affect the relationship between the new church and the clan. There was no question of killing a missionary here, for Mr. Kiaga, despite his madness, was quite harmless. As for his converts, no one could kill them without having to flee from the clan, for in spite of their worthlessness they still belonged to the clan. And so nobody gave serious thought to the stories about the white man's government or the consequences of killing the Christians. If they became more troublesome than they already were they would simply be driven out of the clan.

And the little church was at that moment too deeply absorbed in its own troubles to annoy the clan. It all began over the question of admitting outcasts.

These outcasts, or *osu*, seeing that the new religion welcomed twins and such abominations, thought that it was possible that they would also be received. And so one Sunday two of them went into the church. There was an immediate stir; but so great was the work the new religion had done among the converts that they did not immediately leave the church when the outcasts came in. Those who found themselves nearest to them merely moved to another seat. It was a miracle. But it only lasted till the end of the service. The whole church raised a protest and was about to drive these people out, when Mr. Kiaga stopped them and began to explain.

"Before God," he said, "there is no slave or free. We are all children of God and we must receive these our brothers."

"You do not understand," said one of the converts. "What will the heathen say of us when they hear that we receive *osu* into our midst? They will laugh."

"Let them laugh," said Mr. Kiaga. "God will laugh at them on the judgment day. Why do the nations rage and the peoples imagine a vain thing? He that sitteth in the heavens shall laugh. The Lord shall have them in derision."

"You do not understand," the convert maintained. "You are our teacher, and you can teach us the things of the new faith. But this is a matter which we know." And he told him what an *osu* was.

He was a person dedicated to a god, a thing set apart—a taboo for ever, and his children after him. He could neither marry nor be married by the free-born. He was in fact an outcast, living in a special area of the village, close to the Great Shrine. Wherever he went he carried with him the mark of his forbidden caste—long, tangled and dirty hair. A razor was taboo to him. An *osu* could not attend an assembly of the free-born, and they, in turn, could not shelter under his roof. He could not take any of the four titles of the clan, and when he died he was buried by his kind in the Evil Forest. How could such a man be a follower of Christ?

"He needs Christ more than you and I," said Mr. Kiaga.

"Then I shall go back to the clan," said the convert. And he went. Mr. Kiaga stood firm, and it was his firmness that saved the young church. The wavering converts drew inspiration and confidence from his unshakable faith. He ordered the outcasts to shave off their long, tangled hair. At first they were afraid they might die.

"Unless you shave off the mark of your heathen belief I will not admit you into the church," said Mr. Kiaga. "You fear that you will die. Why should that be? How are you different from other men who shave their hair? The same God created you and them. But they have cast you out like lepers. It is against the will of God, who has promised everlasting life to all who believe in His holy name. The heathen say you will die if you do this or that, and you are afraid. They also said I would die if I built my church on this ground. Am I dead? They said I would die if I took care of twins. I am still alive. The heathen speak nothing but falsehood. Only the word of our God is true."

The two outcasts shaved off their hair, and soon they were the strongest adherents of the new faith. And what was more, nearly all the *osu* in Mbanta followed their example. It was in fact one of them who in his zeal brought the church into serious conflict with the clan a year later by killing the sacred python, the emanation of the god of water.

The royal python was the most revered animal in Mbanta and all the surrounding clans. It was addressed as "Our Father," and was allowed to go wherever it chose, even into people's beds. It ate rats in the house and sometimes swallowed hens' eggs. If a clansman killed a royal python accidentally, he made sacrifices of atonement and performed an expensive burial ceremony such as was done for a great man. No punishment was prescribed for a man who killed the python knowingly. Nobody thought that such a thing could ever happen.

Perhaps it never did happen. That was the way the clan at first looked at it. No one had actually seen the man do it. The story had arisen among the Christians themselves.

But, all the same, the rulers and elders of Mbanta assembled to decide on their action. Many of them spoke at great length and in fury. The spirit of wars was upon them. Okonkwo, who had begun to play a part in the affairs of his motherland, said that until the abominable gang was chased out of the village with whips there would be no peace.

But there were many others who saw the situation differently, and it was their counsel that prevailed in the end.

"It is not our custom to fight for our gods," said one of them. "Let us not presume to do so now. If a man kills the sacred python in the secrecy of his hut, the matter lies between him and the god. We did not see it. If we put ourselves between the god and his victim we may receive blows intended for the offender. When a man blasphemes, what do we do? Do we go and stop his mouth? No. We put our fingers into our ears to stop us hearing. That is a wise action."

"Let us not reason like cowards," said Okonkwo. "If a man comes into my hut and defecates on the floor, what do I do? Do I shut my eyes? No! I take a stick and break his head. That is what a man does. These people are daily pouring filth over us, and Okeke says we should pretend not to see." Okonkwo made a sound full of disgust. This was a womanly clan, he thought. Such a thing could never happen in his fatherland, Umuofia.

"Okonkwo has spoken the truth," said another man. "We should do something. But let us ostracize these men. We would then not be held accountable for their abominations."

Everybody in the assembly spoke, and in the end it was decided to ostracize the Christians. Okonkwo ground his teeth in disgust.

That night a bell-man went through the length and breadth of Mbanta proclaiming that the adherents of the new faith were thenceforth excluded from the life and privileges of the clan.

The Christians had grown in number and were now a small community of men, women and children, self-assured and confident. Mr. Brown, the white missionary, paid regular visits to them. "When I think that it is only eighteen months since the Seed was first sown among you," he said, "I marvel at what the Lord hath wrought."

It was Wednesday in Holy Week and Mr. Kiaga had asked the women to bring red earth and white chalk and water to scrub the church for Easter; and the women had formed themselves into three groups for this purpose. They set out early that morning, some of them with their water-pots to the stream, another group with hoes and baskets to the village red-earth pit, and the others to the chalk quarry.

Mr. Kiaga was praying in the church when he heard the women talking excitedly. He rounded off his prayer and went to see what it was all about. The women had come to the church with empty water-pots. They said that some young men had chased them away from the stream with whips. Soon after, the women who had gone for red earth returned with empty baskets. Some of them had been heavily whipped. The chalk women also returned to tell a similar story.

"What does it all mean?" asked Mr. Kiaga, who was greatly perplexed.

"The village has outlawed us," said one of the women. "The bellman announced it last night. But it is not our custom to debar anyone from the stream or the quarry."

Another woman said, "They want to ruin us. They will not allow us into the markets. They have said so."

Mr. Kiaga was going to send into the village for his men-converts when he saw them coming on their own. Of course they had all heard the bell-man, but they had never in all their lives heard of women being debarred from the stream.

"Come along," they said to the women. "We will go with you to meet those cowards." Some of them had big sticks and some even machetes.

But Mr. Kiaga restrained them. He wanted first to know why they had been outlawed.

"They say that Okoli killed the sacred python," said one man.

"It is false," said another. "Okoli told me himself that it was false."

Okoli was not there to answer. He had fallen ill on the previous night. Before the day was over he was dead. His death showed that the gods were still able to fight their own battles. The clan saw no reason then for molesting the Christians.

19

The last big rains of the year were falling. It was the time for treading red earth with which to build walls. It was not done earlier because the rains were too heavy and would have washed away the heap of trodden earth; and it could not be done later because harvesting would soon set in, and after that the dry season.

It was going to be Okonkwo's last harvest in Mbanta. The seven wasted and weary years were at last dragging to a close. Although he had prospered in his motherland Okonkwo knew that he would have prospered even more in Umuofia, in the land of his fathers where men were bold and warlike. In these seven years he would have climbed to the utmost heights. And so he regretted every day of his exile. His mother's kinsmen had been very kind to him, and he was grateful. But that did not alter the facts. He had called the first child born to him in exile Nneka—"Mother is Supreme"—out of politeness to his mother's kinsmen. But two years later when a son was born he called him Nwofia—"Begotten in the Wilderness."

As soon as he entered his last year in exile Okonkwo sent money to Obierika to build him two huts in his old compound where he and his family would live until he built more huts and the outside wall of his compound. He could not ask another man to build his own *obi* for him, nor the walls of his compound. Those things a man built for himself or inherited from his father.

As the last heavy rains of the year began to fall, Obierika sent word that the two huts had been built and Okonkwo began to prepare for his return, after the rains. He would have liked to return earlier and build his compound that year before the rains stopped, but in doing so he would have taken something from the full penalty of seven years. And that could not be. So he waited impatiently for the dry season to come.

It came slowly. The rain became lighter and lighter until it fell in slanting showers. Sometimes the sun shone through the rain and a light breeze blew. It was a gay and airy kind of rain. The rainbow began to appear, and sometimes two rainbows, like a mother and her daughter, the one young and beautiful, and the other an old and faint shadow. The rainbow was called the python of the sky.

Okonkwo called his three wives and told them to get things together for a great feast. "I must thank my mother's kinsmen before I go," he said.

Ekwefi still had some cassava left on her farm from the previous year. Neither of the other wives had. It was not that they had been lazy, but that they had many children to feed. It was therefore understood that Ekwefi would provide cassava for the feast. Nwoye's mother and Ojiugo would provide the other things like smoked fish, palm-oil and pepper for the soup. Okonkwo would take care of meat and yams.

Ekwefi rose early on the following morning and went to her farm with her daughter, Ezinma, and Ojiugo's daughter, Obiageli, to harvest cassava tubers. Each of them carried a long cane basket, a machete for cutting down the soft cassava stem, and a little hoe for digging out the tuber. Fortunately, a light rain had fallen during the night and the soil would not be very hard.

"It will not take us long to harvest as much as we like," said Ekwefi.

"But the leaves will be wet," said Ezinma. Her basket was balanced on her head, and her arms folded across her breasts. She felt cold. "I dislike cold water dropping on my back. We should have waited for the sun to rise and dry the leaves."

Obiageli called her "Salt" because she said that she disliked water. "Are you afraid you may dissolve?"

The harvesting was easy, as Ekwefi had said. Ezinma shook every tree violently with a long stick before she bent down to cut the stem and dig out the tuber. Sometimes it was not necessary to dig. They just pulled the stump, and earth rose, roots snapped below, and the tuber was pulled out.

When they had harvested a sizable heap they carried it down in two trips to the stream, where every woman had a shallow well for fermenting her cassava.

"It should be ready in four days or even three," said Obiageli. "They are young tubers."

"They are not all that young," said Ekwefi. "I planted the farm nearly two years ago. It is a poor soil and that is why the tubers are so small."

Okonkwo never did things by halves. When his wife Ekwefi protested that two goats were sufficient for the feast he told her that it was not her affair.

"I am calling a feast because I have the wherewithal. I cannot live on the bank of a river and wash my hands with spittle. My mother's people have been good to me and I must show my gratitude."

And so three goats were slaughtered and a number of fowls. It was like a wedding feast. There was foo-foo and yam pottage, egusi[7] soup and bitter-leaf soup and pots and pots of palm-wine.

All the umunna[8] were invited to the feast, all the descendants of Okolo, who had lived about two hundred years before. The oldest member of this extensive family was Okonkwo's uncle, Uchendu. The kola nut was given him to break, and he prayed to the ancestors. He asked them for health and children. "We do not ask for wealth because he that has health and children will also have wealth. We do not pray to have more money but to have more kinsmen. We are better than animals because we have kinsmen. An animal rubs its itching flank against a tree, a man asks his kinsman to scratch him." He prayed especially for Okonkwo and his family. He then broke the kola nut and threw one of the lobes on the ground for the ancestors.

As the broken kola nuts were passed round, Okonkwo's wives and children and those who came to help them with the cooking began to bring out the food. His sons brought out the pots of palm-wine. There was so much food and drink that many kinsmen whistled in surprise. When all was laid out, Okonkwo rose to speak.

"I beg you to accept this little kola," he said. "It is not to pay you back for all you did for me in these seven years. A child cannot pay for its mother's milk. I have only called you together because it is good for kinsmen to meet."

---

7. Melon seed, which is roasted, ground, and cooked in soup. 8. Children of the father (literal trans.); the clan (male).

Yam pottage was served first because it was lighter than foo-foo and because yam always came first. Then the foo-foo was served. Some kinsmen ate it with egusi soup and others with bitter-leaf soup. The meat was then shared so that every member of the *umunna* had a portion. Every man rose in order of years and took a share. Even the few kinsmen who had not been able to come had their shares taken out for them in due term.

As the palm-wine was drunk one of the oldest members of the *umunna* rose to thank Okonkwo:

"If I say that we did not expect such a big feast I will be suggesting that we did not know how open-handed our son, Okonkwo, is. We all know him, and we expected a big feast. But it turned out to be even bigger than we expected. Thank you. May all you took out return again tenfold. It is good in these days when the younger generation consider themselves wiser than their sires to see a man doing things in the grand, old way. A man who calls his kinsmen to a feast does not do so to save them from starving. They all have food in their own homes. When we gather together in the moonlit village ground it is not because of the moon. Every man can see it in his own compound. We come together because it is good for kinsmen to do so. You may ask why I am saying all this. I say it because I fear for the younger generation, for you people." He waved his arm where most of the young men sat. "As for me, I have only a short while to live, and so have Uchendu and Unachukwu and Emefo. But I fear for you young people because you do not understand how strong is the bond of kinship. You do not know what it is to speak with one voice. And what is the result? An abominable religion has settled among you. A man can now leave his father and his brothers. He can curse the gods of his fathers and his ancestors, like a hunter's dog that suddenly goes mad and turns on his master. I fear for you; I fear for the clan." He turned again to Okonkwo and said, "Thank you for calling us together."

Part Three

20

Seven years was a long time to be away from one's clan. A man's place was not always there, waiting for him. As soon as he left, someone else rose and filled it. The clan was like a lizard; if it lost its tail it soon grew another.

Okonkwo knew these things. He knew that he had lost his place among the nine masked spirits who administered justice in the clan. He had lost the chance to lead his warlike clan against the new religion, which, he was told, had gained ground. He had lost the years in which he might have taken the highest titles in the clan. But some of these losses were not irreparable. He was determined that his return should be marked by his people. He would return with a flourish, and regain the seven wasted years.

Even in his first year in exile he had begun to plan for his return. The first thing he would do would be to rebuild his compound on a more magnificent scale. He would build a bigger barn than he had had before and he would build huts for two new wives. Then he would show his wealth by initiating his sons into the *ozo* society. Only the really great men in the clan were able to do this. Okonkwo saw clearly the high esteem in which he would be held, and he saw himself taking the highest title in the land.

As the years of exile passed one by one it seemed to him that his *chi* might now be making amends for the past disaster. His yams grew abundantly, not only in his motherland but also in Umuofia, where his friend gave them out year by year to sharecroppers.

Then the tragedy of his first son had occurred. At first it appeared as if it might prove too great for his spirit. But it was a resilient spirit, and in the end Okonkwo overcame his sorrow. He had five other sons and he would bring them up in the way of the clan.

He sent for the five sons and they came and sat in his *obi*. The youngest of them was four years old.

"You have all seen the great abomination of your brother. Now he is no longer my son or your brother. I will only have a son who is a man, who will hold his head up among my people. If any one of you prefers to be a woman, let him follow Nwoye now while I am alive so that I can curse him. If you turn against me when I am dead I will visit you and break your neck."

Okonkwo was very lucky in his daughters. He never stopped regretting that Ezinma was a girl. Of all his children she alone understood his every mood. A bond of sympathy had grown between them as the years had passed.

Ezinma grew up in her father's exile and became one of the most beautiful girls in Mbanta. She was called Crystal of Beauty, as her mother had been called in her youth. The young ailing girl who had caused her mother so much heartache had been transformed, almost overnight, into a healthy, buoyant maiden. She had, it was true, her moments of depression when she would snap at everybody like an angry dog. These moods descended on her suddenly and for no apparent reason. But they were very rare and short-lived. As long as they lasted, she could bear no other person but her father.

Many young men and prosperous middle-aged men of Mbanta came to marry her. But she refused them all, because her father had called her one evening and said to her: "There are many good and prosperous people here, but I shall be happy if you marry in Umuofia when we return home."

That was all he had said. But Ezinma had seen clearly all the thought and hidden meaning behind the few words. And she had agreed.

"Your half-sister, Obiageli, will not understand me," Okonkwo said. "But you can explain to her."

Although they were almost the same age, Ezinma wielded a strong influence over her half-sister. She explained to her why they should not marry yet, and she agreed also. And so the two of them refused every offer of marriage in Mbanta.

"I wish she were a boy," Okonkwo thought within himself. She understood things so perfectly. Who else among his children could have read his thoughts so well? With two beautiful grown-up daughters his return to Umuofia would attract considerable attention. His future sons-in-law would be men of authority in the clan. The poor and unknown would not dare to come forth.

Umuofia had indeed changed during the seven years Okonkwo had been in exile. The church had come and led many astray. Not only the low-born and the outcast but sometimes a worthy man had joined it. Such a man was

Ogbuefi Ugonna,[9] who had taken two titles, and who like a madman had cut the anklet of his titles and cast it away to join the Christians. The white missionary was very proud of him and he was one of the first men in Umuofia to receive the sacrament of Holy Communion, or Holy Feast as it was called in Ibo. Ogbuefi Ugonna had thought of the Feast in terms of eating and drinking, only more holy than the village variety. He had therefore put his drinking-horn into his goatskin bag for the occasion.

But apart from the church, the white men had also brought a government. They had built a court where the District Commissioner judged cases in ignorance. He had court messengers who brought men to him for trial. Many of these messengers came from Umuru on the bank of the Great River, where the white men first came many years before and where they had built the center of their religion and trade and government. These court messengers were greatly hated in Umuofia because they were foreigners and also arrogant and high-handed. They were called *kotma*,[1] and because of their ash-colored shorts they earned the additional name of Ashy-Buttocks. They guarded the prison, which was full of men who had offended against the white man's law. Some of these prisoners had thrown away their twins and some had molested the Christians. They were beaten in the prison by the *kotma* and made to work every morning clearing the government compound and fetching wood for the white Commissioner and the court messengers. Some of these prisoners were men of title who should be above such mean occupation. They were grieved by the indignity and mourned for their neglected farms. As they cut grass in the morning the younger men sang in time with the strokes of their machetes:

> *Kotma* of the ash buttocks,
> He is fit to be a slave.
> The white man has no sense,
> He is fit to be a slave.

The court messengers did not like to be called Ashy-Buttocks, and they beat the men. But the song spread in Umuofia.

Okonkwo's head was bowed in sadness as Obierika told him these things.

"Perhaps I have been away too long," Okonkwo said, almost to himself. "But I cannot understand these things you tell me. What is it that has happened to our people? Why have they lost the power to fight?"

"Have you not heard how the white man wiped out Abame?" asked Obierika.

"I have heard," said Okonkwo. "But I have also heard that Abame people were weak and foolish. Why did they not fight back? Had they no guns and machetes? We would be cowards to compare ourselves with the men of Abame. Their fathers had never dared to stand before our ancestors. We must fight these men and drive them from the land."

"It is already too late," said Obierika sadly. "Our own men and our sons have joined the ranks of the stranger. They have joined his religion and they help to uphold his government. If we should try to drive out the white men in Umuofia we should find it easy. There are only two of them. But what of

---

9. Father's Honor (with the Eagle Feather). **1.** Court messenger (pidgin English).

our own people who are following their way and have been given power? They would go to Umuru and bring the soldiers, and we would be like Abame." He paused for a long time and then said: "I told you on my last visit to Mbanta how they hanged Aneto."

"What has happened to that piece of land in dispute?" asked Okonkwo.

"The white man's court has decided that it should belong to Nnama's family, who had given much money to the white man's messengers and interpreter."

"Does the white man understand our custom about land?"

"How can he when he does not even speak our tongue? But he says that our customs are bad; and our own brothers who have taken up his religion also say that our customs are bad. How do you think we can fight when our own brothers have turned against us? The white man is very clever. He came quietly and peaceably with his religion. We were amused at his foolishness and allowed him to stay. Now he has won our brothers, and our clan can no longer act like one. He has put a knife on the things that held us together and we have fallen apart."

"How did they get hold of Aneto to hang him?" asked Okonkwo.

"When he killed Oduche in the fight over the land, he fled to Aninta to escape the wrath of the earth. This was about eight days after the fight, because Oduche had not died immediately from his wounds. It was on the seventh day that he died. But everybody knew that he was going to die and Aneto got his belongings together in readiness to flee. But the Christians had told the white man about the accident, and he sent his *kotma* to catch Aneto. He was imprisoned with all the leaders of his family. In the end Oduche died and Aneto was taken to Umuru and hanged. The other people were released, but even now they have not found the mouth with which to tell of their suffering."

The two men sat in silence for a long while afterwards.

21

There were many men and women in Umuofia who did not feel as strongly as Okonkwo about the new dispensation. The white man had indeed brought a lunatic religion, but he had also built a trading store and for the first time palm-oil and kernel[2] became things of great price, and much money flowed into Umuofia.

And even in the matter of religion there was a growing feeling that there might be something in it after all, something vaguely akin to method in the overwhelming madness.

This growing feeling was due to Mr. Brown, the white missionary, who was very firm in restraining his flock from provoking the wrath of the clan. One member in particular was very difficult to restrain. His name was Enoch and his father was the priest of the snake cult. The story went around that Enoch had killed and eaten the sacred python, and that his father had cursed him.

---

2. The red fleshy husk of the palm nut is crushed manually to produce cooking oil, leaving a fibrous residue along with hard kernels. The Europeans bought both the red oil and the kernels, from which they could extract a very fine oil by using machines.

Mr. Brown preached against such excess of zeal. Everything was possible, he told his energetic flock, but everything was not expedient. And so Mr. Brown came to be respected even by the clan, because he trod softly on its faith. He made friends with some of the great men of the clan and on one of his frequent visits to the neighboring villages he had been presented with a carved elephant tusk, which was a sign of dignity and rank. One of the great men in that village was called Akunna[3] and he had given one of his sons to be taught the white man's knowledge in Mr. Brown's school.

Whenever Mr. Brown went to that village he spent long hours with Akunna in his *obi* talking through an interpreter about religion. Neither of them succeeded in converting the other but they learned more about their different beliefs.

"You say that there is one supreme God who made heaven and earth," said Akunna on one of Mr. Brown's visits. "We also believe in Him and call Him Chukwu. He made all the world and the other gods."

"There are no other gods," said Mr. Brown. "Chukwu is the only God and all others are false. You carve a piece of wood—like that one" (he pointed at the rafters from which Akunna's carved *Ikenga*[4] hung), "and you call it a god. But it is still a piece of wood."

"Yes," said Akunna. "It is indeed a piece of wood. The tree from which it came was made by Chukwu, as indeed all minor gods were. But He made them for His messengers so that we could approach Him through them. It is like yourself. You are the head of your church."

"No," protested Mr. Brown. "The head of my church is God Himself."

"I know," said Akunna, "but there must be a head in this world among men. Somebody like yourself must be the head here."

"The head of my church in that sense is in England."

"That is exactly what I am saying. The head of your church is in your country. He has sent you here as his messenger. And you have also appointed your own messengers and servants. Or let me take another example, the District Commissioner. He is sent by your king."

"They have a queen," said the interpreter on his own account.

"Your queen sends her messenger, the District Commissioner. He finds that he cannot do the work alone and so he appoints *kotma* to help him. It is the same with God, or Chukwu. He appoints the smaller gods to help Him because His work is too great for one person."

"You should not think of Him as a person," said Mr. Brown. "It is because you do so that you imagine He must need helpers. And the worst thing about it is that you give all the worship to the false gods you have created."

"That is not so. We make sacrifices to the little gods, but when they fail and there is no one else to turn to we go to Chukwu. It is right to do so. We approach a great man through his servants. But when his servants fail to help us, then we go to the last source of hope. We appear to pay greater attention to the little gods but that is not so. We worry them more because we are afraid to worry their Master. Our fathers knew that Chukwu was the Overlord and that is why many of them gave their children the name Chukwuka—"Chukwu is Supreme.""

---

3. Father's Wealth.   4. A carved wooden figure with the horns of a ram that symbolized the strength of a man's right hand. Every adult male kept an *Ikenga* in his personal shrine.

"You said one interesting thing," said Mr. Brown. "You are afraid of Chukwu. In my religion Chukwu is a loving Father and need not be feared by those who do His will."

"But we must fear Him when we are not doing His will," said Akunna. "And who is to tell His will? It is too great to be known."

In this way Mr. Brown learned a good deal about the religion of the clan and he came to the conclusion that a frontal attack on it would not succeed. And so he built a school and a little hospital in Umuofia. He went from family to family begging people to send their children to his school. But at first they only sent their slaves or sometimes their lazy children. Mr. Brown begged and argued and prophesied. He said that the leaders of the land in the future would be men and women who had learned to read and write. If Umuofia failed to send her children to the school, strangers would come from other places to rule them. They could already see that happening in the Native Court, where the D.C. was surrounded by strangers who spoke his tongue. Most of these strangers came from the distant town of Umuru on the bank of the Great River where the white man first went.

In the end Mr. Brown's arguments began to have an effect. More people came to learn in his school, and he encouraged them with gifts of singlets[5] and towels. They were not all young, these people who came to learn. Some of them were thirty years old or more. They worked on their farms in the morning and went to school in the afternoon. And it was not long before the people began to say that the white man's medicine was quick in working. Mr. Brown's school produced quick results. A few months in it were enough to make one a court messenger or even a court clerk. Those who stayed longer became teachers; and from Umuofia laborers went forth into the Lord's vineyard. New churches were established in the surrounding villages and a few schools with them. From the very beginning religion and education went hand in hand.

Mr. Brown's mission grew from strength to strength, and because of its link with the new administration it earned a new social prestige. But Mr. Brown himself was breaking down in health. At first he ignored the warning signs. But in the end he had to leave his flock, sad and broken.

It was in the first rainy season after Okonkwo's return to Umuofia that Mr. Brown left for home. As soon as he had learned of Okonkwo's return five months earlier, the missionary had immediately paid him a visit. He had just sent Okonkwo's son, Nwoye, who was now called Isaac,[6] to the new training college for teachers in Umuru. And he had hoped that Okonkwo would be happy to hear of it. But Okonkwo had driven him away with the threat that if he came into his compound again, he would be carried out of it.

Okonkwo's return to his native land was not as memorable as he had wished. It was true his two beautiful daughters aroused great interest among suitors and marriage negotiations were soon in progress, but, beyond that, Umuofia did not appear to have taken any special notice of the warrior's return. The clan had undergone such profound change during his exile that it was barely recognizable. The new religion and government and the trading

---

5. Undershirts, T-shirts.   6. Son of Abraham, offered to God as a sacrifice (Genesis 22).

stores were very much in the people's eyes and minds. There were still many who saw these new institutions as evil, but even they talked and thought about little else, and certainly not about Okonkwo's return.

And it was the wrong year too. If Okonkwo had immediately initiated his two sons into the *ozo* society as he had planned he would have caused a stir. But the initiation rite was performed once in three years in Umuofia, and he had to wait for nearly two years for the next round of ceremonies.

Okonkwo was deeply grieved. And it was not just a personal grief. He mourned for the clan, which he saw breaking up and falling apart, and he mourned for the warlike men of Umuofia, who had so unaccountably become soft like women.

22

Mr. Brown's successor was the Reverend James Smith, and he was a different kind of man. He condemned openly Mr. Brown's policy of compromise and accommodation. He saw things as black and white. And black was evil. He saw the world as a battlefield in which the children of light were locked in mortal conflict with the sons of darkness. He spoke in his sermons about sheep and goats and about wheat and tares. He believed in slaying the prophets of Baal.

Mr. Smith was greatly distressed by the ignorance which many of his flock showed even in such things as the Trinity and the Sacraments. It only showed that they were seeds sown on a rocky soil. Mr. Brown had thought of nothing but numbers. He should have known that the kingdom of God did not depend on large crowds. Our Lord Himself stressed the importance of fewness. Narrow is the way and few the number. To fill the Lord's holy temple with an idolatrous crowd clamoring for signs was a folly of everlasting consequence. Our Lord used the whip only once in His life—to drive the crowd away from His church.

Within a few weeks of his arrival in Umuofia Mr. Smith suspended a young woman from the church for pouring new wine into old bottles. This woman had allowed her heathen husband to mutilate her dead child. The child had been declared an *ogbanje*, plaguing its mother by dying and entering her womb to be born again. Four times this child had run its evil round. And so it was mutilated to discourage it from returning.

Mr. Smith was filled with wrath when he heard of this. He disbelieved the story which even some of the most faithful confirmed, the story of really evil children who were not deterred by mutilation, but came back with all the scars. He replied that such stories were spread in the world by the Devil to lead men astray. Those who believed such stories were unworthy of the Lord's table.

There was a saying in Umuofia that as a man danced so the drums were beaten for him. Mr. Smith danced a furious step and so the drums went mad. The over-zealous converts who had smarted under Mr. Brown's restraining hand now flourished in full favor. One of them was Enoch, the son of the snake-priest who was believed to have killed and eaten the sacred python. Enoch's devotion to the new faith had seemed so much greater than Mr. Brown's that the villagers called him the outsider who wept louder than the bereaved.

Enoch was short and slight of build, and always seemed in great haste. His feet were short and broad, and when he stood or walked his heels came together and his feet opened outwards as if they had quarreled and meant to go in different directions. Such was the excessive energy bottled up in Enoch's small body that it was always erupting in quarrels and fights. On Sundays he always imagined that the sermon was preached for the benefit of his enemies. And if he happened to sit near one of them he would occasionally turn to give him a meaningful look, as if to say, "I told you so." It was Enoch who touched off the great conflict between church and clan in Umuofia which had been gathering since Mr. Brown left.

It happened during the annual ceremony which was held in honor of the earth deity. At such times the ancestors of the clan who had been committed to Mother Earth at their death emerged again as *egwugwu* through tiny ant-holes.

One of the greatest crimes a man could commit was to unmask an *egwugwu* in public, or to say or do anything which might reduce its immortal prestige in the eyes of the uninitiated. And this was what Enoch did.

The annual worship of the earth goddess fell on a Sunday, and the masked spirits were abroad. The Christian women who had been to church could not therefore go home. Some of their men had gone out to beg the *egwugwu* to retire for a short while for the women to pass. They agreed and were already retiring, when Enoch boasted aloud that they would not dare to touch a Christian. Whereupon they all came back and one of them gave Enoch a good stroke of the cane, which was always carried. Enoch fell on him and tore off his mask. The other *egwugwu* immediately surrounded their desecrated companion, to shield him from the profane gaze of women and children, and led him away. Enoch had killed an ancestral spirit, and Umuofia was thrown into confusion.

That night the Mother of the Spirits walked the length and breadth of the clan, weeping for her murdered son. It was a terrible night. Not even the oldest man in Umuofia had ever heard such a strange and fearful sound, and it was never to be heard again. It seemed as if the very soul of the tribe wept for a great evil that was coming—its own death.

On the next day all the masked *egwugwu* of Umuofia assembled in the marketplace. They came from all the quarters of the clan and even from the neighboring villages. The dreaded Otakagu came from Imo, and Ekwensu, dangling a white cock, arrived from Uli. It was a terrible gathering. The eerie voices of countless spirits, the bells that clattered behind some of them, and the clash of machetes as they ran forwards and backwards and saluted one another, sent tremors of fear into every heart. For the first time in living memory the sacred bull-roarer was heard in broad daylight.

From the marketplace the furious band made for Enoch's compound. Some of the elders of the clan went with them, wearing heavy protections of charms and amulets. These were men whose arms were strong in *ogwu*, or medicine. As for the ordinary men and women, they listened from the safety of their huts.

The leaders of the Christians had met together at Mr. Smith's parsonage on the previous night. As they deliberated they could hear the Mother of Spirits wailing for her son. The chilling sound affected Mr. Smith, and for the first time he seemed to be afraid.

"What are they planning to do?" he asked. No one knew, because such a thing had never happened before. Mr. Smith would have sent for the District Commissioner and his court messengers, but they had gone on tour on the previous day.

"One thing is clear," said Mr. Smith. "We cannot offer physical resistance to them. Our strength lies in the Lord." They knelt down together and prayed to God for delivery.

"O Lord, save Thy people," cried Mr. Smith.

"And bless Thine inheritance," replied the men.

They decided that Enoch should be hidden in the parsonage for a day or two. Enoch himself was greatly disappointed when he heard this, for he had hoped that a holy war was imminent; and there were a few other Christians who thought like him. But wisdom prevailed in the camp of the faithful and many lives were thus saved.

The band of egwugwu moved like a furious whirlwind to Enoch's compound and with machete and fire reduced it to a desolate heap. And from there they made for the church, intoxicated with destruction.

Mr. Smith was in his church when he heard the masked spirits coming. He walked quietly to the door which commanded the approach to the church compound, and stood there. But when the first three or four egwugwu appeared on the church compound he nearly bolted. He overcame this impulse and instead of running away he went down the two steps that led up to the church and walked towards the approaching spirits.

They surged forward, and a long stretch of the bamboo fence with which the church compound was surrounded gave way before them. Discordant bells clanged, machetes clashed and the air was full of dust and weird sounds. Mr. Smith heard a sound of footsteps behind him. He turned round and saw Okeke, his interpreter. Okeke had not been on the best of terms with his master since he had strongly condemned Enoch's behavior at the meeting of the leaders of the church during the night. Okeke had gone as far as to say that Enoch should not be hidden in the parsonage, because he would only draw the wrath of the clan on the pastor. Mr. Smith had rebuked him in very strong language, and had not sought his advice that morning. But now, as he came up and stood by him confronting the angry spirits, Mr. Smith looked at him and smiled. It was a wan smile, but there was deep gratitude there.

For a brief moment the onrush of the egwugwu was checked by the unexpected composure of the two men. But it was only a momentary check, like the tense silence between blasts of thunder. The second onrush was greater than the first. It swallowed up the two men. Then an unmistakable voice rose above the tumult and there was immediate silence. Space was made around the two men, and Ajofia began to speak.

Ajofia was the leading egwugwu of Umuofia. He was the head and spokesman of the nine ancestors who administered justice in the clan. His voice was unmistakable and so he was able to bring immediate peace to the agitated spirits. He then addressed Mr. Smith, and as he spoke clouds of smoke rose from his head.

"The body of the white man, I salute you," he said, using the language in which immortals spoke to men.

"The body of the white man, do you know me?" he asked.

Mr. Smith looked at his interpreter, but Okeke, who was a native of distant Umuru, was also at a loss.

Ajofia laughed in his guttural voice. It was like the laugh of rusty metal. "They are strangers," he said, "and they are ignorant. But let that pass." He turned round to his comrades and saluted them, calling them the fathers of Umuofia. He dug his rattling spear into the ground and it shook with metallic life. Then he turned once more to the missionary and his interpreter.

"Tell the white man that we will not do him any harm," he said to the interpreter. "Tell him to go back to his house and leave us alone. We liked his brother who was with us before. He was foolish, but we liked him, and for his sake we shall not harm his brother. But this shrine which he built must be destroyed. We shall no longer allow it in our midst. It has bred untold abominations and we have come to put an end to it." He turned to his comrades. "Fathers of Umuofia, I salute you"; and they replied with one guttural voice. He turned again to the missionary. "You can stay with us if you like our ways. You can worship your own god. It is good that a man should worship the gods and the spirits of his fathers. Go back to your house so that you may not be hurt. Our anger is great but we have held it down so that we can talk to you."

Mr. Smith said to his interpreter: "Tell them to go away from here. This is the house of God and I will not live to see it desecrated."

Okeke interpreted wisely to the spirits and leaders of Umuofia: "The white man says he is happy you have come to him with your grievances, like friends. He will be happy if you leave the matter in his hands."

"We cannot leave the matter in his hands because he does not understand our customs, just as we do not understand his. We say he is foolish because he does not know our ways, and perhaps he says we are foolish because we do not know his. Let him go away."

Mr. Smith stood his ground. But he could not save his church. When the *egwugwu* went away the red-earth church which Mr. Brown had built was a pile of earth and ashes. And for the moment the spirit of the clan was pacified.

23

For the first time in many years Okonkwo had a feeling that was akin to happiness. The times which had altered so unaccountably during his exile seemed to be coming round again. The clan which had turned false on him appeared to be making amends.

He had spoken violently to his clansmen when they had met in the marketplace to decide on their action. And they had listened to him with respect. It was like the good old days again, when a warrior was a warrior. Although they had not agreed to kill the missionary or drive away the Christians, they had agreed to do something substantial. And they had done it. Okonkwo was almost happy again.

For two days after the destruction of the church, nothing happened. Every man in Umuofia went about armed with a gun or a machete. They would not be caught unawares, like the men of Abame.

Then the District Commissioner returned from his tour. Mr. Smith went immediately to him and they had a long discussion. The men of Umuofia did not take any notice of this, and if they did, they thought it was not important. The missionary often went to see his brother white man. There was nothing strange in that.

Three days later the District Commissioner sent his sweet-tongued messenger to the leaders of Umuofia asking them to meet him in his headquarters. That also was not strange. He often asked them to hold such palavers, as he called them. Okonkwo was among the six leaders he invited.

Okonkwo warned the others to be fully armed. "An Umuofia man does not refuse a call," he said. "He may refuse to do what he is asked; he does not refuse to be asked. But the times have changed, and we must be fully prepared."

And so the six men went to see the District Commissioner, armed with their machetes. They did not carry guns, for that would be unseemly. They were led into the courthouse where the District Commissioner sat. He received them politely. They unslung their goatskin bags and their sheathed machetes, put them on the floor, and sat down.

"I have asked you to come," began the Commissioner, "because of what happened during my absence. I have been told a few things but I cannot believe them until I have heard your own side. Let us talk about it like friends and find a way of ensuring that it does not happen again."

Ogbuefi Ekwueme[7] rose to his feet and began to tell the story.

"Wait a minute," said the Commissioner. "I want to bring in my men so that they too can hear your grievances and take warning. Many of them come from distant places and although they speak your tongue they are ignorant of your customs. James! Go and bring in the men." His interpreter left the courtroom and soon returned with twelve men. They sat together with the men of Umuofia, and Ogbuefi Ekwueme began to tell the story of how Enoch murdered an *egwugwu*.

It happened so quickly that the six men did not see it coming. There was only a brief scuffle, too brief even to allow the drawing of a sheathed machete. The six men were handcuffed and led into the guardroom.

"We shall not do you any harm," said the District Commissioner to them later, "if only you agree to cooperate with us. We have brought a peaceful administration to you and your people so that you may be happy. If any man ill-treats you we shall come to your rescue. But we will not allow you to ill-treat others. We have a court of law where we judge cases and administer justice just as it is done in my own country under a great queen. I have brought you here because you joined together to molest others, to burn people's houses and their place of worship. That must not happen in the dominion of our queen, the most powerful ruler in the world. I have decided that you will pay a fine of two hundred bags of cowries. You will be released as soon as you agree to this and undertake to collect that fine from your people. What do you say to that?"

The six men remained sullen and silent and the Commissioner left them for a while. He told the court messengers, when he left the guardroom, to treat the men with respect because they were the leaders of Umuofia. They said, "Yes, sir," and saluted.

---

7. A Person Who Does What He Says (a praise name).

As soon as the District Commissioner left, the head messenger, who was also the prisoners' barber, took down his razor and shaved off all the hair on the men's heads. They were still handcuffed, and they just sat and moped.

"Who is the chief among you?" the court messengers asked in jest. "We see that every pauper wears the anklet of title in Umuofia. Does it cost as much as ten cowries?"

The six men ate nothing throughout that day and the next. They were not even given any water to drink, and they could not go out to urinate or go into the bush when they were pressed. At night the messengers came in to taunt them and to knock their shaven heads together.

Even when the men were left alone they found no words to speak to one another. It was only on the third day, when they could no longer bear the hunger and the insults, that they began to talk about giving in.

"We should have killed the white man if you had listened to me," Okonkwo snarled.

"We could have been in Umuru now waiting to be hanged," someone said to him.

"Who wants to kill the white man?" asked a messenger who had just rushed in. Nobody spoke.

"You are not satisfied with your crime, but you must kill the white man on top of it." He carried a strong stick, and he hit each man a few blows on the head and back. Okonkwo was choked with hate.

As soon as the six men were locked up, court messengers went into Umuofia to tell the people that their leaders would not be released unless they paid a fine of two hundred and fifty bags of cowries.

"Unless you pay the fine immediately," said their head-man, "we will take your leaders to Umuru before the big white man, and hang them."

This story spread quickly through the villages, and was added to as it went. Some said that the men had already been taken to Umuru and would be hanged on the following day. Some said that their families would also be hanged. Others said that soldiers were already on their way to shoot the people of Umuofia as they had done in Abame.

It was the time of the full moon. But that night the voice of children was not heard. The village *ilo* where they always gathered for a moon-play was empty. The women of Iguedo did not meet in their secret enclosure to learn a new dance to be displayed later to the village. Young men who were always abroad in the moonlight kept to their huts that night. Their manly voices were not heard on the village paths as they went to visit their friends and lovers. Umuofia was like a startled animal with ears erect, sniffing the silent, ominous air and not knowing which way to run.

The silence was broken by the village crier beating his sonorous *ogene*. He called every man in Umuofia, from the Akakanma age group upwards, to a meeting in the marketplace after the morning meal. He went from one end of the village to the other and walked all its breadth. He did not leave out any of the main footpaths.

Okonkwo's compound was like a deserted homestead. It was as if cold water had been poured on it. His family was all there, but everyone spoke in whispers. His daughter Ezinma had broken her twenty-eight-day visit to the family of her future husband, and returned home when she heard that her father had been imprisoned, and was going to be hanged. As soon as she got home she went to Obierika to ask what the men of Umuofia were going to do about it. But Obierika had not been home since morning. His wives thought he had gone to a secret meeting. Ezinma was satisfied that something was being done.

On the morning after the village crier's appeal the men of Umuofia met in the marketplace and decided to collect without delay two hundred and fifty bags of cowries to appease the white man. They did not know that fifty bags would go to the court messengers, who had increased the fine for that purpose.

24

Okonkwo and his fellow prisoners were set free as soon as the fine was paid. The District Commissioner spoke to them again about the great queen, and about peace and good government. But the men did not listen. They just sat and looked at him and at his interpreter. In the end they were given back their bags and sheathed machetes and told to go home. They rose and left the courthouse. They neither spoke to anyone nor among themselves.

The courthouse, like the church, was built a little way outside the village. The footpath that linked them was a very busy one because it also led to the stream, beyond the court. It was open and sandy. Footpaths were open and sandy in the dry season. But when the rains came the bush grew thick on either side and closed in on the path. It was now dry season.

As they made their way to the village the six men met women and children going to the stream with their waterpots. But the men wore such heavy and fearsome looks that the women and children did not say "nno" or "welcome" to them, but edged out of the way to let them pass. In the village little groups of men joined them until they became a sizable company. They walked silently. As each of the six men got to his compound, he turned in, taking some of the crowd with him. The village was astir in a silent, suppressed way.

Ezinma had prepared some food for her father as soon as news spread that the six men would be released. She took it to him in his *obi*. He ate absentmindedly. He had no appetite; he only ate to please her. His male relations and friends had gathered in his *obi*, and Obierika was urging him to eat. Nobody else spoke, but they noticed the long stripes on Okonkwo's back where the warder's whip had cut into his flesh.

The village crier was abroad again in the night. He beat his iron gong and announced that another meeting would be held in the morning. Everyone knew that Umuofia was at last going to speak its mind about the things that were happening.

Okonkwo slept very little that night. The bitterness in his heart was now mixed with a kind of childlike excitement. Before he had gone to bed he had brought down his war dress, which he had not touched since his return from exile. He had shaken out his smoked raffia skirt and examined his tall feather head-gear and his shield. They were all satisfactory, he had thought.

As he lay on his bamboo bed he thought about the treatment he had received in the white man's court, and he swore vengeance. If Umuofia decided on war, all would be well. But if they chose to be cowards he would go out and avenge himself. He thought about wars in the past. The noblest, he thought, was the war against Isike. In those days Okudo[8] was still alive. Okudo sang a war song in a way that no other man could. He was not a fighter, but his voice turned every man into a lion.

"Worthy men are no more," Okonkwo sighed as he remembered those days. "Isike will never forget how we slaughtered them in that war. We killed twelve of their men and they killed only two of ours. Before the end of the fourth market week they were suing for peace. Those were days when men were men."

As he thought of these things he heard the sound of the iron gong in the distance. He listened carefully, and could just hear the crier's voice. But it was very faint. He turned on his bed and his back hurt him. He ground his teeth. The crier was drawing nearer and nearer until he passed by Okonkwo's compound.

"The greatest obstacle in Umuofia," Okonkwo thought bitterly, "is that coward, Egonwanne.[9] His sweet tongue can change fire into cold ash. When he speaks he moves our men to impotence. If they had ignored his womanish wisdom five years ago, we would not have come to this." He ground his teeth. "Tomorrow he will tell them that our fathers never fought a 'war of blame.' If they listen to him I shall leave them and plan my own revenge."

The crier's voice had once more become faint, and the distance had taken the harsh edge off his iron gong. Okonkwo turned from one side to the other and derived a kind of pleasure from the pain his back gave him. "Let Egonwanne talk about a 'war of blame' tomorrow and I shall show him my back and head." He ground his teeth.

The marketplace began to fill as soon as the sun rose. Obierika was waiting in his *obi* when Okonkwo came along and called him. He hung his goatskin bag and his sheathed machete on his shoulder and went out to join him. Obierika's hut was close to the road and he saw every man who passed to the marketplace. He had exchanged greetings with many who had already passed that morning.

When Okonkwo and Obierika got to the meeting place there were already so many people that if one threw up a grain of sand it would not find its way to the earth again. And many more people were coming from every quarter of the nine villages. It warmed Okonkwo's heart to see such strength of numbers. But he was looking for one man in particular, the man whose tongue he dreaded and despised so much.

"Can you see him?" he asked Obierika.

"Who?"

"Egonwanne," he said, his eyes roving from one corner of the huge marketplace to the other. Most of the men sat on wooden stools they had brought with them.

"No," said Obierika, casting his eyes over the crowd. "Yes, there he is, under the silk-cotton tree. Are you afraid he would convince us not to fight?"

"Afraid? I do not care what he does to *you*. I despise him and those who listen to him. I shall fight alone if I choose."

8. Great Eagle Feather (a praise name).　　9. Wealth of a Sibling.

They spoke at the top of their voices because everybody was talking, and it was like the sound of a great market.

"I shall wait till he has spoken," Okonkwo thought. "Then I shall speak."

"But how do you know he will speak against war?" Obierika asked after a while.

"Because I know he is a coward," said Okonkwo. Obierika did not hear the rest of what he said because at that moment somebody touched his shoulder from behind and he turned round to shake hands and exchange greetings with five or six friends. Okonkwo did not turn round even though he knew the voices. He was in no mood to exchange greetings. But one of the men touched him and asked about the people of his compound.

"They are well," he replied without interest.

The first man to speak to Umuofia that morning was Okika, one of the six who had been imprisoned. Okika was a great man and an orator. But he did not have the booming voice which a first speaker must use to establish silence in the assembly of the clan. Onyeka[1] had such a voice; and so he was asked to salute Umuofia before Okika began to speak.

"*Umuofia kwenu!*" he bellowed, raising his left arm and pushing the air with his open hand.

"*Yaa!*" roared Umuofia.

"*Umuofia kwenu!*" he bellowed again, and again and again, facing a new direction each time. And the crowd answered, "*Yaa!*"

There was immediate silence as though cold water had been poured on a roaring flame.

Okika sprang to his feet and also saluted his clansmen four times. Then he began to speak:

"You all know why we are here, when we ought to be building our barns or mending our huts, when we should be putting our compounds in order. My father used to say to me: 'Whenever you see a toad jumping in broad daylight, then know that something is after its life.' When I saw you all pouring into this meeting from all the quarters of our clan so early in the morning, I knew that something was after our life." He paused for a brief moment and then began again:

"All our gods are weeping. Idemili is weeping, Ogwugwu is weeping, Agbala is weeping, and all the others. Our dead fathers are weeping because of the shameful sacrilege they are suffering and the abomination we have all seen with our eyes." He stopped again to steady his trembling voice.

"This is a great gathering. No clan can boast of greater numbers or greater valor. But are we all here? I ask you: Are all the sons of Umuofia with us here?" A deep murmur swept through the crowd.

"They are not," he said. "They have broken the clan and gone their several ways. We who are here this morning have remained true to our fathers, but our brothers have deserted us and joined a stranger to soil their fatherland. If we fight the stranger we shall hit our brothers and perhaps shed the blood of a clansman. But we must do it. Our fathers never dreamed of such a thing, they never killed their brothers. But a white man never came to them. So we must do what our fathers would never have done. Eneke the bird was

---

1. "Who Surpasses [God]?" (a rhetorical question).

asked why he was always on the wing and he replied: 'Men have learned to shoot without missing their mark and I have learned to fly without perching on a twig.' We must root out this evil. And if our brothers take the side of evil we must root them out too. And we must do it *now*. We must bail this water now that it is only ankle-deep. . . ."

At this point there was a sudden stir in the crowd and every eye was turned in one direction. There was a sharp bend in the road that led from the marketplace to the white man's court, and to the stream beyond it. And so no one had seen the approach of the five court messengers until they had come round the bend, a few paces from the edge of the crowd. Okonkwo was sitting at the edge.

He sprang to his feet as soon as he saw who it was. He confronted the head messenger, trembling with hate, unable to utter a word. The man was fearless and stood his ground, his four men lined up behind him.

In that brief moment the world seemed to stand still, waiting. There was utter silence. The men of Umuofia were merged into the mute backcloth of trees and giant creepers, waiting.

The spell was broken by the head messenger. "Let me pass!" he ordered.

"What do you want here?"

"The white man whose power you know too well has ordered this meeting to stop."

In a flash Okonkwo drew his machete. The messenger crouched to avoid the blow. It was useless. Okonkwo's machete descended twice and the man's head lay beside his uniformed body.

The waiting backcloth jumped into tumultuous life and the meeting was stopped. Okonkwo stood looking at the dead man. He knew that Umuofia would not go to war. He knew because they had let the other messengers escape. They had broken into tumult instead of action. He discerned fright in that tumult. He heard voices asking: "Why did he do it?"

He wiped his machete on the sand and went away.

25

When the District Commissioner arrived at Okonkwo's compound at the head of an armed band of soldiers and court messengers he found a small crowd of men sitting wearily in the *obi*. He commanded them to come outside, and they obeyed without a murmur.

"Which among you is called Okonkwo?" he asked through his interpreter.

"He is not here," replied Obierika.

"Where is he?"

"He is not here!"

The Commissioner became angry and red in the face. He warned the men that unless they produced Okonkwo forthwith he would lock them all up. The men murmured among themselves, and Obierika spoke again.

"We can take you where he is, and perhaps your men will help us."

The Commissioner did not understand what Obierika meant when he said, "Perhaps your men will help us." One of the most infuriating habits of these people was their love of superfluous words, he thought.

Obierika with five or six others led the way. The Commissioner and his men followed, their firearms held at the ready. He had warned Obierika that if he and his men played any monkey tricks they would be shot. And so they went.

There was a small bush behind Okonkwo's compound. The only opening into this bush from the compound was a little round hole in the red-earth wall through which fowls went in and out in their endless search for food. The hole would not let a man through. It was to this bush that Obierika led the Commissioner and his men. They skirted round the compound, keeping close to the wall. The only sound they made was with their feet as they crushed dry leaves.

Then they came to the tree from which Okonkwo's body was dangling, and they stopped dead.

"Perhaps your men can help us bring him down and bury him," said Obierika. "We have sent for strangers from another village to do it for us, but they may be a long time coming."

The District Commissioner changed instantaneously. The resolute administrator in him gave way to the student of primitive customs.

"Why can't you take him down yourselves?" he asked.

"It is against our custom," said one of the men. "It is an abomination for a man to take his own life. It is an offense against the Earth, and a man who commits it will not be buried by his clansmen. His body is evil, and only strangers may touch it. That is why we ask your people to bring him down, because you are strangers."

"Will you bury him like any other man?" asked the Commissioner.

"We cannot bury him. Only strangers can. We shall pay your men to do it. When he has been buried we will then do our duty by him. We shall make sacrifices to cleanse the desecrated land."

Obierika, who had been gazing steadily at his friend's dangling body, turned suddenly to the District Commissioner and said ferociously: "That man was one of the greatest men in Umuofia. You drove him to kill himself; and now he will be buried like a dog. . . ." He could not say any more. His voice trembled and choked his words.

"Shut up!" shouted one of the messengers, quite unnecessarily.

"Take down the body," the Commissioner ordered his chief messenger, "and bring it and all these people to the court."

"Yes, sah," the messenger said, saluting.

The Commissioner went away, taking three or four of the soldiers with him. In the many years in which he had toiled to bring civilization to different parts of Africa he had learned a number of things. One of them was that a District Commissioner must never attend to such undignified details as cutting a hanged man from the tree. Such attention would give the natives a poor opinion of him. In the book which he planned to write he would stress that point. As he walked back to the court he thought about that book. Every day brought him some new material. The story of this man who had killed a messenger and hanged himself would make interesting reading. One could almost write a whole chapter on him. Perhaps not a whole chapter but a reasonable paragraph, at any rate. There was so much else to include, and one must be firm in cutting out details. He had already chosen the title of the book, after much thought: *The Pacification of the Primitive Tribes of the Lower Niger*.

NAWAL EL SAADAWI
born 1931

In her autobiography *A Daughter of Isis* (1999), Nawal El Saadawi states that she realized early in her life how the very fact of their gender constitutes for women in the Arab-Islamic world in which she grew up an almost insuperable limiting factor to their life chances. "I had been born a female in a world that wanted only males," she writes. Elsewhere in the same book, she sums up the essential predicament of women in this world, as determined by religion and social convention: "When I was six years old, I learnt these three words by heart and they were like one sentence: 'God, calamity, marriage.'" Her work challenges the patriarchal conception of the nature and role of women in the general culture of her world, a conception that governs attitudes and social practice, and imposes on women an immense burden of existence. It is her acute awareness of the damaging impact of this burden and her strong sense of solidarity with her fellow females that have sustained her abundant output—novels, short stories, autobiography, essays, and addresses as well as scientific treatises and sociological studies—in an active career that has spanned some fifty years.

Nawal El Saadawi was born in 1931 in Kafir Tahla, a village in the delta region of Egypt, into a well-to-do middle-class family with strong connections to the ruling elite of the country. Her father was a highly placed government functionary, her mother descended from the traditional aristocracy. They saw to it that all their nine children received an education all the way to university level. Nawal El Saadawi herself studied medicine at the University of Cairo and, after her graduation in 1955, practiced as a psychiatrist before being appointed in 1958 to the Ministry of Health, where she rose to become director of public health. However, she was dismissed from her post in 1972 after the publication of her book *Woman and Sex*, which aroused the displeasure of the Egyptian authorities for its frank treatment of a subject that was considered taboo. This was the beginning of her long struggle for her individual right of expression and of her crusade for female emancipation in Egypt specifically and the Arab world generally.

After losing her government position, she devoted herself to research on women; she also worked for a year with the United Nations. In 1981, she was imprisoned during the campaign of repression directed against intellectuals by the Sadat regime, an experience that inspired her novel *The Fall of the Imam*. Upon her release in 1982, she founded the Arab Women's Solidarity Association (AWSA), a nongovernmental organization dedicated to informed discussion of women's problems. The association was dissolved by the government in 1991 and its assets confiscated. Nawal El Saadawi sued the government, but, despite support from a distinguished panel of lawyers, she could not prevail against the forces ranged against her. Because she had also incurred the wrath of Islamic fundamentalists and ran a real risk of being assassinated, she went into exile in 1992. She was writer-in-residence at Duke University in North Carolina between 1993 and 1994.

Nawal El Saadawi is probably best known for her novel *Woman at Point Zero*, a reliving of the experience of a female prisoner condemned to death for killing a pimp who preys on her during her life as a prostitute in the city after her flight from the village in order to escape a forced marriage and the constricted existence it promised. The psychological and moral dilemmas highlighted by the novel and the arresting simplicity of its narrative style have ensured the continuing success of the work. In other novels such as *God Dies by the Nile* and *The Innocence of the Devil*, Nawal El Saadawi develops plot and situation while exploring customs and religious beliefs as they affect women in her society. The former novel is an uncompromising examination of the brutalization these women often have to endure, and the violent responses the depredations of the men are liable to engender even in the most unlikely of circumstances. The latter novel, in which the action takes place in a mental institution, dramatizes the psychic disruptions generated by Islamic orthodoxy, which is invoked to rationalize the unfeeling conduct of men toward women in her society. In their bleak depiction of the female predicament, both novels seek to document, albeit in fictional form, the vicissitudes in the lives of her women, denied fulfillment by forces beyond their control.

The short story "In Camera," taken from the collection entitled *Death of an Ex-Minister*, is a representative sample of her work. Its ironic title highlights the reversal of situations in which the public trial of the heroine is transformed into a closed session at which judge himself becomes the accused. The triviality of the legal discourse in the final episode of the story extends the critique of the entire ideological apparatus that underwrites the social system and state machinery in the fictional kingdom portrayed in the story. Its political theme is developed at the explicit level of its narrative of the trial and through the irreverence of the portrayal, notably the animal imagery employed to represent the king and the agents of the state in his service.

The story's emphasis, however, is placed firmly on the ordeal of the female protagonist, on trial for an act of defiance against the system. Her physical violation and mental agony are reconstructed through the series of flashbacks that constitute the frames by which the story's atmosphere is built up. The bonds between her and her parents, the values she shares with them as well as the gulf that also separates her from them, are interwoven with the vivid enactment of their anxieties as they all sit through her trial. The subtle modulations of narrative voice and alternating of points of view enable the reader to participate in the mental life of the characters in the closed world of a private tragedy that the story portrays, against the background of a desolate public order.

Nawal El Saadawi's focus on the female condition in the Arab-Islamic world is joined to a vision of artistic creativity as dissidence—the refusal of traditional patterns and the assertion of new possibilities. In a lecture delivered at Oxford in 1995, she emphasized the link between changing the world and changing perceptions:

> Every struggle has its own unique theory inseparable from action. Creativity means uniqueness: innovation. Discovering new ways of thinking and acting, of creating a system based on more and more justice, freedom, love, and compassion. If you are creative, you must be dissident.

This statement places her preoccupation with the oppression of women in her society within the broad human perspective that gives it resonance beyond its immediate reference to a particularized historical moment and sociocultural context. It also clarifies the essential relationship that she perceives between the imaginative function and the fabric of experience as it shapes the lives of individuals. For her, this relationship is necessarily defined by a determined and constant calling into question of an unacceptable destiny. The act of writing represents here a gesture of refusal, an effort to break the silence that surrounds the culture of abuse and repression of which her women are victims, by uncovering the inner spaces of female consciousness. Nawal El Saadawi's work thus illustrates in its concrete references and vindicates the claims of the imagination to represent a heightened awareness of experience as a mode of meeting its moral challenges.

PRONOUNCING GLOSSARY

The following list uses common English syllables and stress accents to provide rough equivalents of selected words whose pronunciation may be unfamiliar to the general reader.

Leila Al-Fargani: *lay'-ee-lah al–fahr'-gah-nee*

Nawal El Saadawi: *nah'-wahl el sah'-dah-wee*

In Camera[1]

The first thing she felt was a blinding light. She saw nothing. The light was painful, even though her eyes were still shut. The cold air hit her face and bare neck, crept down to her chest and stomach and then fell lower to the weeping wound, where it turned into a sharp blow. She put one hand over her eyes to protect them from the light, whilst with the other she covered her neck, clenching her thighs against the sudden pain. Her lips too were clenched tight against a pain the like of which her body had never known, like the sting of a needle in her eyes and breasts and armpits and lower abdomen. From sleeping so long while standing and standing so long while sleeping, she no longer knew what position her body was in, whether vertical or horizontal, dangling in the air by her feet or standing on her head in water.

The moment they sat her down and she felt the seat on which she was sitting with the palms of her hands, the muscles of her face relaxed and resumed their human form. A shudder of sudden and intense pleasure shook her from inside when her body took up a sitting position on the wooden seat and her lips curled into a feeble smile as she said to herself: Now I know what pleasure it is to sit!

The light was still strong and her eyes still could not see, but her eyes were beginning to catch the sound of voices and murmurings. She lifted her hand off her eyes and gradually began to open them. Blurred human silhouettes moved before her on some elevated construction. She suddenly felt frightened, for human forms frightened her more than any others. Those long, rapid and agile bodies, legs inside trousers and feet inside shoes. Everything had been done in the dark with the utmost speed and agility. She could not cry or scream. Her tongue, her eyes, her mouth, her nose, all the parts of her body, were constrained. Her body was no longer hers but was like that of a small calf struck by the heels of boots. A rough stick entered between her thighs to tear at her insides. Then she was kicked into a dark corner where she remained curled up until the following day. By the third day, she still had not returned to normal but remained like a small animal incapable of uttering the simple words: My God! She said to herself: Do animals, like humans, know of the existence of something called God?

Her eyes began to make out bodies sitting on that elevated place, above each head a body, smooth heads without hair, in the light as red as monkeys' rumps. They must all be males, for however old a woman grew, her head could never look like a monkey's rump. She strained to see more clearly. In the centre was a fat man wearing something like a black robe, his mouth open; in his hand something like a hammer. It reminded her of the village magician, when her eyes and those of all the other children had been mesmerized by the hand which turned a stick into a snake or into fire. The hammer squirmed in his hand like a viper and in her ears a sharp voice resounded: The Court! To herself she said: He must be the judge. It was the first time in her life she'd seen a judge or been inside a court. She'd heard the word 'court' for the first time as a child. She'd heard her aunt tell her mother: The judge did not believe me and told me to strip so he could see

---

1. Translated by Shirley Eber. "In camera": the judicial term for "closed session." The oppressive atmosphere of the trial scene is immediately conveyed by the title.

where I'd been beaten. I told him that I would not strip in front of a strange man, so he rejected my claim and ordered me to return to my husband. Her aunt had cried and at that time she had not understood why the judge had told her aunt to strip. I wonder if the judge will ask me to strip and what he will say when he sees that wound, she said to herself.

Gradually, her eyes were growing used to the light. She began to see the judge's face more clearly. His face was as red as his head, his eyes as round and bulging as a frog's, moving slowly here and there, his nose as curved as a hawk's beak, beneath it a yellow moustache as thick as a bundle of dry grass, which quivered above the opening of a mouth as taut as wire and permanently gaping like a mousetrap.

She did not understand why his mouth stayed open. Was he talking all the time or breathing through it? His shiny bald head moved continually with a nodding movement. It moved upwards a little and then backwards, entering into something pointed; then it moved downwards and forwards, so that his chin entered his neck opening. She could not yet see what was behind him, but when he raised his head and moved it backwards, she saw it enter something pointed which looked like the cap of a shoe. She focused her vision and saw that it really was a shoe, drawn on the wall above the judge's head. Above the shoe she saw taut legs inside a pair of trousers of expensive leather or leopard skin or snakeskin and a jacket, also taut, over a pair of shoulders. Above the shoulders appeared the face she'd seen thousands of times in the papers, eyes staring into space filled with more stupidity than simplicity, the nose as straight as though evened out by a hammer, the mouth pursed to betray that artificial sincerity which all rulers and kings master when they sit before a camera. Although his mouth was pinched in arrogance and sincerity, his cheeks were slack, beneath them a cynical and comical smile containing chronic corruption and childish petulance.

She had been a child in primary school the first time she saw a picture of the king. The face was fleshy, the eyes narrow, the lips thin and clenched in impudent arrogance. She recalled her father's voice saying: he was decadent and adulterous. But they were all the same. When they stood in front of a camera, they thought they were god.

Although she could still feel her body sitting on the wooden seat, she began to have doubts. How could they allow her to sit all this time? Sitting like this was so very relaxing. She could sit, leaving her body in a sitting position, and enjoy that astounding ability which humans have. For the first time she understood that the human body differed from that of an animal in one important way—sitting. No animal could sit the way she could. If it did, what would it do with its four legs? She remembered a scene that had made her laugh as a child, of a calf which had tried to sit on its backside and had ended up on its back. Her lips curled in a futile attempt to open her mouth and say something or smile. But her mouth remained stuck, like a horizontal line splitting the lower part of her face into two. Could she open her mouth a little to spit? But her throat, her mouth, her neck, her chest, everything, was dry, all except for that gaping wound between her thighs.

She pressed her legs together tighter to close off the wound and the pain and to enjoy the pleasure of sitting on a seat. She could have stayed in that position for ever, or until she died, had she not suddenly heard a voice calling her name: Leila Al-Fargani.

Her numbed senses awoke and her ears pricked up to the sound of that strange name: Leila Al-Fargani. As though it wasn't her name. She hadn't heard it for ages. It was the name of a young woman named Leila, a young woman who had worn young woman's clothes, had seen the sun and walked on two feet like other human beings. She had been that woman a very long time ago, but since then she hadn't worn a young woman's clothes nor seen the sun nor walked on two feet. For a long time she'd been a small animal inside a dark and remote cave and when they addressed her, they only used animal names.

Her eyes were still trying to see clearly. The judge's head had grown clearer and moved more, but it was still either inside the cap of the shoe whenever he raised it or was inside his collar whenever he lowered it. The picture hanging behind him had also become clearer. The shiny pointed shoes, the suit as tight as a horseman's, the face held taut on the outside by artificial muscles full of composure and stupidity, on the inside depraved and contentious.

The power of her sight was no longer as it had been, but she could still see ugliness clearly. She saw the deformed face and remembered her father's words: They only reach the seat of power, my girl, when they are morally deformed and internally corrupt.

And what inner corruption! She had seen their real corruption for herself. She wished at that moment they would give her pen and paper so that she could draw that corruption. But would her fingers still be capable of holding a pen or of moving it across a piece of paper? Would she still have at least two fingers which could hold a pen? What could she do if they cut off one of those two fingers? Could she hold a pen with one finger? Could a person walk on one leg? It was one of those questions her father used to repeat. But she hated the questions of the impotent and said to herself: I will split the finger and press the pen into it, just as Isis split the leg of Osiris.[2] She remembered that old story, still saw the split leg pouring with blood. What a long nightmare she was living! How she wanted her mother's hand to shake her so she could open her eyes and wake up. She used to be so happy when, as a child, she opened her eyes and realized that the monster which had tried to rip her body to pieces was nothing but a dream, or a nightmare as her mother used to call it. Each time she had opened her eyes, she was very happy to discover that the monster had vanished, that it was only a dream. But now she opened her eyes and the monster did not go away. She opened her eyes and the monster stayed on her body. Her terror was so great that she closed her eyes again to sleep, to make believe that it was a nightmare. But she opened her eyes and knew it was no dream. And she remembered everything.

The first thing she remembered was her mother's scream in the silence of the night. She was sleeping in her mother's arms, like a child of six even though she was an adult and in her twenties. But her mother had said: You'll

2. Isis and Osiris were a royal couple in Egyptian mythology. In the celebrated story of the couple, Isis wandered the land in search of the body of her murdered husband (who was also her brother), whose body had been thrown into the Nile in a golden casket. She recovered the body, into which she was able to breathe life and from which she conceived a son. However, the body was discovered by his murderer, who tore it into pieces, leaving Isis to collect the limbs and other parts, into which she again breathed life. Osiris soon died again and descended into the underworld, where he reigned over the dead.

sleep in my arms so that even if they come in the middle of the night, I will know it and I'll hold on to you with all my might and if they take you they'll have to take me as well.

Nothing was as painful to her as seeing her mother's face move further and further away until it disappeared. Her face, her eyes, her hair, were so pale. She would rather have died than see her mother's face so haggard. To herself she said: Can you forgive me, Mother, for causing you so much pain? Her mother always used to say to her: What's politics got to do with you? You're not a man. Girls of your age think only about marriage. She hadn't replied when her mother had said: Politics is a dirty game which only ineffectual men play.

The voices had now become clearer. The picture also looked clearer, even though the fog was still thick. Was it winter and the hall roofless, or was it summer and they were smoking in a windowless room? She could see another man sitting not far from the judge. His head, like the judge's, was smooth and red but, unlike the judge's, it was not completely under the shoe. He was sitting to one side and above his head hung another picture in which there was something like a flag or a small multicoloured banner. And for the first time, her ears made out some intelligible sentences:

Imagine, ladies and gentlemen. This student, who is not yet twenty years old, refers to Him, whom God protect to lead this noble nation all his life, as 'stupid'.

The word 'stupid' fell like a stone in a sea of awesome silence, making a sound like the crash of a rock in water or the blow of a hand against something solid, like a slap or the clap of one hand against another.

Was someone clapping? She pricked up her ears to catch the sound. Was it applause? Or a burst of laughter, like a cackle? Then that terrifying silence pervaded the courtroom once again, a long silence in which she could hear the beating of her heart. The sound of laughter or of applause echoed in her ears. She asked herself who could be applauding at so serious a moment as when the mighty one was being described as stupid, and aloud too.

Her body was still stuck to the wooden seat, clinging on to it, frightened it would suddenly be taken away. The wound in her lower abdomen was still weeping. But she was able to move her head and half opened her eyes to search for the source of that applause. Suddenly she discovered that the hall was full of heads crammed together in rows, all of them undoubtedly human. Some of the heads appeared to have a lot of hair, as if they were those of women or girls. Some of them were small, as if those of children. One head seemed to be like that of her younger sister. Her body trembled for a moment on the seat as her eyes searched around. Had she come alone or with her father and mother? Were they looking at her now? How did she look? Could they recognize her face or her body?

She turned her head to look. Although her vision had grown weak, she could just make out her mother. She could pick out her mother's face from among thousands of faces even with her eyes closed. Could her mother really be here in the hall? Her heartbeats grew audible and anxiety grew inside her. Anxiety often gripped her and she felt that something terrible had happened to her mother. One night, fear had overcome her when she was curled up like a small animal and she'd told herself: She must have died and I will not see her when I get out. But the following day, she had seen her mother when she came to visit. She'd come, safe and sound. She was happy and said: Don't die, Mother, before I get out and can make up for all the pain I've caused you.

The sound was now clear in her ears. It wasn't just one clap but a whole series of them. The heads in the hall were moving here and there. The judge was still sitting, his smooth head beneath the shoe. The hammer in his hand was moving impatiently, banging rapidly on the wooden table. But the clapping did not stop. The judge rose to his feet so that his head was in the centre of the stomach in the picture. His lower lip trembled as he shouted out words of rebuke which she couldn't hear in all the uproar.

Then silence descended for a period. She was still trying to see, her hands by her side holding on to the seat, clinging on to it, pressing it as if she wanted to confirm that it was really beneath her or that she was really sitting on it. She knew she was awake and not asleep with her eyes closed. Before, when she opened her eyes, the monster would disappear and she'd be happy that it was only a dream. But now she was no longer capable of being happy and had become frightened of opening her eyes.

The noise in the hall had died down and the heads moved as they had done before. All except one head. It was neither smooth nor red. It was covered in a thick mop of white hair and was fixed and immobile. The eyes also did not move and were open, dry and fixed on that small body piled on top of the wooden seat. Her hands were clasped over her chest, her heart under her hand beating fast, her breath panting as if she were running to the end of the track and could no longer breath. Her voice broke as she said to herself: My God! Her eyes turn in my direction but she doesn't see me. What have they done to her eyes? Or is she fighting sleep? God of Heaven and Earth, how could you let them do all that? How, my daughter, did you stand so much pain? How did I stand it together with you? I always felt that you, my daughter, were capable of anything, of moving mountains or of crumbling rocks, even though your body is small and weak like mine. But when your tiny feet used to kick the walls of my stomach, I'd say to myself: God, what strength and power there is inside my body? Your movements were strong while you were still a foetus and shook me from inside, like a volcano shakes the earth. And yet I knew that you were as small as I was, your bones as delicate as your father's, as tall and slim as your grandmother, your feet as large as the feet of prophets.[3] When I gave birth to you, your grandmother pursed her lips in sorrow and said: A girl and ugly too! A double catastrophe! I tensed my stomach muscles to close off my womb to the pain and the blood and, breathing with difficulty, for your birth had been hard and I suffered as though I'd given birth to a mountain, I said to her: She's more precious to me than the whole world! I held you to my breast and slept deeply. Can I, my daughter, again enjoy another moment of deep sleep whilst you are inside me or at least near to me so that I can reach out to touch you? Or whilst you are in your room next to mine so that I can tiptoe in to see you whilst you sleep? The blanket always used to fall off you as you slept, so I'd lift it and cover you. Anxiety would waken me every night and make me creep into your

3. The passage conjures up an image of devoted pupils sitting at the feet of the prophets.

room. What was that anxiety and at what moment did it happen? Was it the moment the cover fell off your body? I could always feel you, even if you had gone away and were out of my sight. Even if they were to bury you under the earth or build a solid wall of mud or iron around you, I would still feel a draught of air on your body as though it were on mine. I sometimes wonder whether I ever really gave birth to you or if you are still inside me. How else could I feel the air when it touches you and hunger when it grips you. Your pain is mine, like fire burning in my breast and stomach. God of Heaven and Earth, how did your body and mine stand it? But I couldn't have stood it were it not for the joy of you being my daughter, of having given birth to you. And you can raise your head high above the mountains of filth. For three thousand and twenty-five hours (I've counted them one by one), they left you with the vomit and pus and the weeping wound in your stomach. I remember the look in your eyes when you told me, the bars between us: If only the weeping were red blood. But it's not red. It's white and has the smell of death. What was it I said to you that day? I don't know, but I said something. I said that the smell becomes normal when we get used to it and live with it every day. I could not look into your emaciated face, but I heard you say: It's not a smell, mother, like other smells which enter through the nose or mouth. It's more like liquid air or steam turned to viscid[4] water or molten lead flowing into every opening of the body. I don't know, mother, if it is burning hot or icy cold. I clasped my hands to my breast, then grasped your slender hand through the bars, saying: When heat became like cold, my daughter, then everything is bearable. But as soon as I left you, I felt my heart swell and swell until it filled my chest and pressed on my lungs so I could no longer breathe. I felt I was choking and tilted my head skywards to force air into my lungs. But the sky that day was void of air and the sun over my head was molten lead like the fire of hell. The eyes of the guards stung me and their uncouth voices piled up inside me. If the earth had transformed into the face of one of them, I'd have spat and spat and spat on it until my throat and chest dried up. Yes, my daughter, brace the muscles of your back and raise your head and turn it in my direction, for I'm sitting near you. You may have heard them when they applauded you. Did you hear them? I saw you move your head towards us. Did you see us? Me and your father and little sister? We all applauded with them. Did you see us?

Her eyes were still trying to penetrate the thick fog. The judge was still standing, his head smooth and red, his lower lip trembling with rapid words. To his right and to his left, she saw smooth red heads begin to move away from that elevated table. The judge's head and the others vanished, although the picture on the wall remained where it was. The face and the eyes were the same as they had been, but now one eye appeared to her to be smaller, as though half-closed or winking at her, that common gesture that a man makes to a woman when he wants to flirt with her. Her body trembled in surprise. Was it possible that he was winking at her? Was it possible for his eyes in the picture to move? Could objects move? Or was she sick and hallucinating? She felt the seat under her palm and raised her hand to touch her body.

4. Sticky.

A fierce heat emanated from it, like a searing flame, a fire within her chest. She wanted to open her mouth and say: Please, a glass of water. But her lips were stuck together, a horizontal line as taut as wire. Her eyes too were stuck on the picture, while the eye in the picture continued to wink at her. Why was it winking at her? Was it flirting with her? She had only discovered that winking was a form of greeting when, two years previously, she'd seen a file of foreign tourists walking in the street. She'd been on her way to the university. Whenever she looked at the faces of one of the men or women, an eye would suddenly wink at her strangely. She had been shocked and hadn't understood how a woman could flirt with her in such a way. Only later had she understood that it was an American form of greeting.

The podium was still empty, without the judge and the smooth heads around him. Silence prevailed. The heads in the hall were still close together in rows and her eyes still roamed in search of a mop of white hair, a pair of black eyes which she could see with eyes closed. But there were so many heads close together she could only see a mound of black and white, circles or squares or oblongs. Her nose began to move as if she were sniffing, for she knew her mother's smell and could distinguish it from thousands of others. It was the smell of milk when she was a child at the breast or the smell of the morning when it rises or the night when it sleeps or the rain on wet earth or the sun above the bed or hot soup in a bowl. She said to herself: Is it possible that you're not here, Mother? And Father, have you come?

The fog before her eyes was still thick. Her head continued to move in the direction of the rows of crammed heads. The black and white circles were interlocked in tireless movement. Only one circle of black hair was immobile above a wide brown forehead, two firm eyes in a pale slender face and a small body piled on to a chair behind bars. His large gaunt hands gripped his knees, pressing on them from the pain. But the moment he heard the applause, he took his hands off his knees and brought them together to clap. His hands did not return to his knees, the pain in his legs no longer tangible. His heart beat loudly in time to his clapping which shook his slender body on the seat. His eyes began to scour the faces and eyes, and his lips parted a little as though he were about to shout: I'm her father, I'm Al-Fargani who fathered her and whose name she bears. My God, how all the pain in my body vanished in one go with the burst of applause. What if I were to stand up now and reveal my identity to them? This moment is unique and I must not lose it. Men like us live and die for one moment such as this, for others to recognize us, to applaud us, for us to become heroes with eyes looking at us and fingers pointing at us. I have suffered the pain and torture with her, day after day, hour after hour, and now I have the right to enjoy some of the reward and share in her heroism.

He shifted his body slightly on his seat as if he were about to stand up. But he remained seated, though his head still moved. His eyes glanced from face to face, as if he wanted someone to recognize him. The angry voice of the judge and the sharp rapid blows of his hammer on the table broke into the applause. Presently the judge and those with him withdrew to the conference chambers. Silence again descended on the hall, a long and awesome silence, during which some faint whispers reached his ears: They'll cook up the case in the conference chamber . . . That's common pratice . . . Justice and law don't exist here . . . In a while they'll declare the public hearing closed . . . She must be a heroine to have stayed alive until now . . . Imagine that young girl who is sitting in the dock causing the government so much alarm . . . Do you know how they tortured her? Ten men raped her, one after the other. They trampled on her honour and on her father's honour. Her poor father! Do you know him! They say he's ill in bed. Maybe he can't face people after his honour was violated!

At that moment he raised his hands to cover his ears so as not to hear, to press on his head so that it sunk into his chest, pushing it more and more to merge his body into the seat or underneath it or under the ground. He wanted to vanish so that no one would see or know him. His name was not Al-Fargani, not Assharqawi, not Azziftawi, not anything. He had neither name nor existence. What is left of a man whose honour is violated? He had told her bitterly: Politics, my girl, is not for women and girls. But she had not listened to him. If she had been a man, he would not be suffering now the way he was. None of those dogs would have been able to violate his honour and dignity. Death was preferable for him and for her now.[5]

Silence still reigned over the hall. The judge and his entourage had not yet reappeared. Her eyes kept trying to see, searching out one face amongst the faces, for eyes she recognized, for a mop of white hair the colour of children's milk. But all she could see were black and white circles and squares intermingled and constantly moving. Is it possible you're not here, Mother? Is Father still ill? Her nose too continued to move here and there, searching for a familiar smell, the smell of a warm breast full of milk, the smell of the sun and of drizzle on grass. But her nose was unable to pick up the smell. All it could pick up was the smell of her body crumpled on the seat and the weeping wound between her thighs. It was a smell of pus and blood and the putrid stench of the breath and sweat of ten men, the marks of whose nails were still on her body, with their uncouth voices, their saliva and the sound of their snorting. One of them, lying on top of her, had said: This is the way we torture you women—by depriving you of the most valuable thing you possess. Her body under him was as cold as a corpse but she had managed to open her mouth and say to him: You fool! The most valuable thing I possess is not between my legs. You're all stupid. And the most stupid among you is the one who leads you.

She craned her neck to raise her head and penetrate the fog with her weak eyes. The many heads were still crammed together and her eyes still strained. If only she could have seen her mother for a moment, or her father or little sister, she would have told them something strange. She would have told them that they had stopped using that method of torture when they discovered that it didn't torture her. They began to search for other methods.

In the conference chamber next to the hall, the judge and his aides were meeting, deliberating the case. What should they do now that the public had applauded the accused? The judge began to face accusations in his turn:

5. According to the Arab-Islamic code of honor, decreed and upheld by men.

—We're not accusing you, Your Honour, but you did embarrass us all. As the saying goes: 'The road to hell is paved with good intentions'! You did what you thought was right, but you only managed to make things worse. How could you say, Your Honour, about Him, whom God protect to lead this noble nation all his life, that he is stupid?

—God forbid, sir! I didn't say that, I said that *she* said he was stupid.

—Don't you know the saying, 'What the ear doesn't hear, the heart doesn't grieve over'? You declared in public that he's stupid.

—I didn't say it, sir. I merely repeated what the accused said to make the accusation stick. That's precisely what my job is.

—Yes, that's your job, Your Honour. We know that. But you should have been smarter and wiser than that.

—I don't understand.

—Didn't you hear how the people applauded her?

—Is that my fault?

—Don't you know why they applauded?

—No, I don't.

—Because you said in public what is said in private and it was more like confirming a fact than proving an accusation.

—What else could I have done, sir?

—You could have said that she cursed the mighty one without saying exactly *what* she said.

—And if I'd been asked what kind of curse it was?

—Nobody would have asked you. And besides, you volunteered the answer before anyone asked, as though you'd seized the opportunity to say aloud and in her words, what you yourself wanted to say or perhaps what you do say to yourself in secret.

—Me? How can you accuse me in this way? I was simply performing my duty as I should. Nobody can accuse me of anything. Perhaps I was foolish, but you cannot accuse me of bad faith.

—But foolishness can sometimes be worse than bad faith. You must know that foolishness is the worst label you can stick on a man. And as far as he's concerned, better that he be a swindler, a liar, a miser, a trickster, even a thief or a traitor, rather than foolish. Foolishness means that he doesn't think, that he's mindless, that he's an animal. That's the worst thing you can call an ordinary man. And all the more so if he's a ruler. You don't know rulers, Your Honour, but I know them well. Each of them fancies his brain to be better than any other man's. And it's not just a matter of fantasy, but of blind belief, like the belief in God. For the sake of this illusion, he can kill thousands.[6]

—I didn't know that, sir. How can I get out of this predicament?

—I don't know why you began with the description 'stupid', Your Honour. If you'd read everything she said, you'd have found that she used other less ugly terms to describe him.

—Such as what, sir? Please, use your experience to help me choose some of them. I don't want to leave here accused, after coming in this morning to raise an accusation.

---

6. An overt critique of the murderous inclinations fostered by religious fanaticism.

—Such descriptions cannot be voiced in public. The session must be closed. Even a less ugly description will find an echo in the heart of the people if openly declared. That's what closed sessions are for, Your Honour. Many matters escape you and it seems you have little experience in law.

A few minutes later, utter silence descended on the hall. The courtroom was completely emptied. As for her, they took her back to where she'd been before.

LESLIE MARMON SILKO
born 1948

Novelist, poet, memoirist, and writer of short fiction, Leslie Marmon Silko, within the confines of a single work, can comfortably alternate between prose and poetry in a manner reminiscent of the traditional Native American narrators from whom she descends. Among her primary concerns as an artist are the continuity of native tradition and the power of ancient forces to govern modern life. The people of whom she writes draw vitality from the mysterious personifications that represent the land; and reciprocally, the land maintains, or regains, its freshness through prescribed contact with its human tenants. Conflict, illness, and despair are traced to a disharmony between people and nature, sometimes recognizable in the form of witchcraft. Such trouble is as old as time itself and perhaps ineradicable. For healing to take place, at least temporarily, the disharmony and its perpetrators must be removed. It follows that modern evils are neither caused nor cured by Western civilization. The West simply does not have that power. Control, then, rests in the hands of those who harness the energies of native thought. The techniques involve ritual and, especially, storytelling. Because the latter implies a mixture of humor and detachment, it is understandable that Silko's work, for all its seriousness and its lyricism, is marked by a touch of irreverence. She is well acquainted with the proverbial trickster, Coyote, and has demonstrated that she herself is an accomplished live teller of Coyote tales. But storytelling holds more than amusement. "I will tell you something about stories," protests an unnamed voice in one of her novels. "They aren't just entertainment. Don't be fooled."

Storytelling has deep roots. But if a story is to be viable it must be constantly reshaped; and Silko is an unabashed reshaper. Her view of tradition as an ever-shifting body of knowledge, responsive to new influences even if deeply planted, is objectively correct, yet it may also be said to emerge from her personal background. She has written:

> My family are the Marmons at Old Laguna on the Laguna Pueblo Reservation where I grew up. We are mixed bloods—Laguna, Mexican, white—but the way we live is like Marmons, and if you are from Laguna Pueblo you will understand what I mean. All those languages, all those ways of living are combined, and we live somewhere on the fringes of all three. But I don't apologize for this any more—not to whites, not to full bloods—our origin is unlike any other. My poetry, my storytelling rise out of this source.

She has also written: "I grew up at Laguna Pueblo. I am of mixed-breed ancestry, but what I know is Laguna. This place I am from is everything I am as a writer and human being."

Situated on a knoll above the San José River, forty miles west of the Rio Grande, Laguna Pueblo, like its near neighbor Acoma, is one of the Keresan-speaking communities of northern New Mexico. In existence at its present site since the 1400s, it has absorbed migrants from other Keresan towns and from among the Zuni, Hopi, and Navajo. In the 1860s and 1870s, two surveyors from Ohio, first Walter Marmon and, a little later, his brother, Robert, both government employees, settled in Laguna and married Laguna women. The Marmons wrote a constitution for Laguna, modeled after the U.S. Constitution, and each served a term as governor of the pueblo, an office never before held by a nonnative. The second of the two Marmons to arrive in Laguna, Robert Gunn Marmon, was the great-grandfather of Leslie Marmon Silko.

Born in Albuquerque on March 5, 1948, Silko spent her early years at Laguna, attending Laguna Day School until fifth grade, when she was transferred to Manzano Day School, a small private school in Albuquerque. Between 1964 and 1969 she attended the University of New Mexico (where she earned a B.A. in English), married, and gave birth to the first of her two sons, Cazimir Silko. During these years she published her first story, "Tony's Story," a provocative tale of witchery and renewal that foreshadowed her masterwork, *Ceremony*, which would not appear for another decade.

Following graduation, she stayed on at the university and taught courses in creative writing and oral literature. After giving birth to her second son, Robert William Chapman, she studied for three semesters in the university's American Indian Law Program, with the intention of filing native land claims. In 1971 a National Endowment for the Arts Discovery Grant changed her mind about law school, and she quit to devote herself to writing. Seven of her stories, including "Yellow Woman," were published in 1974 in a collection edited by Kenneth Rosen—*The Man to Send Rain Clouds: Contemporary Stories by American Indians*. It was from this that her reputation began to build.

The novel *Ceremony*, her first large-scale work, appeared in 1977. Widely hailed, it propelled her into the front rank of a growing legion of indigenous writers in the United States whose combined activity would now be recognized as a Native American renaissance. This group's success in winning critical attention and a broad audience would be comparable to the earlier "boom" in Latin American letters that had brought acclaim to such writers as Jorge Luis Borges and Gabriel García Márquez. The Kiowa novelist N. Scott Momaday, whose *House Made of Dawn* had won the Pulitzer Prize in 1969, was already being viewed as the father of the new movement; and the prolific, talented Louise Erdrich, of Chippewa descent, would eventually be accorded its greatest commercial success. But it was Silko—and *Ceremony*—that enabled the movement to come of age.

Though of average length, *Ceremony* is an extremely complex novel; it has two casts of characters, one predominantly male and human, the other female-dominated and intimately connected to the landscape. It is a story of illness and healing, witchery and exorcism, drought and revivification, with political overtones that acknowledge the influence of nonnative society without permitting this to overwhelm or even direct the inner core of native experience. *Ceremony* is a love story but of a special Native American kind that connects the human and nonhuman worlds, transferring power from nature to culture. With a sure grasp of its material, the novel rolls to its conclusion, sweeping up smaller, parablelike stories along the way, creating a many-chambered vehicle that energizes subplots as well as the larger story.

On the strength of *Ceremony*, Silko in 1981 was awarded a MacArthur Fellowship. That same year she brought out a second large work, *Storyteller*, combining previously published poems and short stories (including "Yellow Woman") with new material in an arrangement one critic has called an autobiography. It is at least partly that, partly a tribute to Laguna, and partly a showcase in which her earlier work, contextualized, takes on a deeper significance.

Another result of *Ceremony* had been the opportunity to teach at the University of Arizona in Tucson. But with the MacArthur grant Silko was able to withdraw from teaching and (while continuing to live in Tucson) concentrate on an ambitious new writing project. Virtually silent for ten years, as rumors of a major new novel kept building, Silko in due course brought forth *The Almanac of the Dead* (1991). An ocean of story, spreading far beyond Laguna Pueblo to embrace all of North America, including Mexico, Silko's largest work documents the imagined history of an American apocalypse. Inspired by prophetic texts ranging from the Maya Books of Chilam Balam to the songs of the Plains Ghost Dance, native people in league with the spirits of their ancestors conspire to heal the American land and rid it of alien influence. As the various stories converge and the millennium draws near, an irresistible army led by twin heroes, newly emerged from ancient Native American tradition, marches northward out of Mexico to reclaim the continent. In the words of one critic the novel is a "wild, jarring, graphic, mordant, prodigious book" with "genius in the sheer, tireless variousness of its interconnecting tales."

Over the years, as Silko's work has expanded and deepened, one of her shortest and earliest pieces, "Yellow Woman," has continued to grow in esteem. Often reprinted, it became the subject of a volume of critical essays published in 1993. In traditional Laguna lore Yellow Woman is either the heroine or a minor character in a wide range of tales. Occasionally Yellow Woman is mentioned together with her three sisters, Blue Woman, Red Woman, and White Woman, thus completing the four colors of corn. But although she may originally have been a corn spirit, she eventually became a kind of Everywoman. In fact, a traditional Laguna prayer-song, recited at the naming ceremony for a newborn daughter, begins, "Yellow Woman is born, Yellow Woman is born." In narrative lore, however, Yellow Woman most frequently appears in tales of abduction, where she is said to have been captured by a strange man at a stream while she is fetching water. Her captor, who carries her off to another world, is sometimes a kachina, or ancestral spirit; and when at last she returns to her home she is imbued with new power that proves of value for her people. In Silko's version, these traditional elements are constantly in the foreground. Or are they merely in the background? The story's ambiguity, frequently commented on by critics, is the source of its fascination.

PRONOUNCING GLOSSARY

The following list uses common English syllables and stress accents to provide rough equivalents of selected words whose pronunciation may be unfamiliar to the general reader.

kachina: *kuh-chee'-nuh*   Keres: *kay'-ruhs*

ka'tsina: *kuht-see'-nuh*

Yellow Woman

My thigh clung to his with dampness, and I watched the sun rising up through the tamaracks and willows. The small brown water birds came to the river and hopped across the mud, leaving brown scratches in the alkali-white crust. They bathed in the river silently. I could hear the water, almost at our feet where the narrow fast channel bubbled and washed green ragged moss and fern leaves. I looked at him beside me, rolled in the red blanket on the white river sand. I cleaned the sand out of the cracks between my toes, squinting because the sun was above the willow trees. I looked at him for the last time, sleeping on the white river sand.

I felt hungry and followed the river south the way we had come the afternoon before, following our footprints that were already blurred by lizard tracks and bug trails. The horses were still lying down, and the black one whinnied when he saw me but he did not get up—maybe it was because the corral was made out of thick cedar branches and the horses had not yet felt the sun like I had. I tried to look beyond the pale red mesas to the pueblo. I knew it was there, even if I could not see it, on the sandrock hill above the river, the same river that moved past me now and had reflected the moon last night.

The horse felt warm underneath me. He shook his head and pawed the sand. The bay whinnied and leaned against the gate trying to follow, and I remembered him asleep in the red blanket beside the river. I slid off the horse and tied him close to the other horse, I walked north with the river again, and the white sand broke loose in footprints over footprints.

"Wake up."

He moved in the blanket and turned his face to me with his eyes still closed. I knelt down to touch him.

"I'm leaving."

He smiled now, eyes still closed. "You are coming with me, remember?" He sat up now with his bare dark chest and belly in the sun.

"Where?"

"To my place."

"And will I come back?"

He pulled his pants on. I walked away from him, feeling him behind me and smelling the willows.

"Yellow Woman," he said.

I turned to face him. "Who are you?" I asked.

He laughed and knelt on the low, sandy bank, washing his face in the river. "Last night you guessed my name, and you knew why I had come."

I stared past him at the shallow moving water and tried to remember the night, but I could only see the moon in the water and remember his warmth around me.

"But I only said that you were him and that I was Yellow Woman—I'm not really her—I have my own name and I come from the pueblo on the other side of the mesa. Your name is Silva and you are a stranger I met by the river yesterday afternoon."

He laughed softly. "What happened yesterday has nothing to do with what you will do today, Yellow Woman."

"I know—that's what I'm saying—the old stories about the ka'tsina[1] spirit and Yellow Woman can't mean us."

My old grandpa liked to tell those stories best. There is one about Badger and Coyote who went hunting and were gone all day, and when the sun was going down they found a house. There was a girl living there alone, and she had light hair and eyes and she told them that they could sleep with her. Coyote wanted to be with her all night so he sent Badger into a prairie-dog hole, telling him he thought he saw something in it. As soon as Badger crawled in, Coyote blocked up the entrance with rocks and hurried back to Yellow Woman.

"Come here," he said gently.

1. Kachina, an ancestral spirit.

He touched my neck and I moved close to him to feel his breathing and to hear his heart. I was wondering if Yellow Woman had known who she was—if she knew that she would become part of the stories. Maybe she'd had another name that her husband and relatives called her so that only the ka'tsina from the north and the storytellers would know her as Yellow Woman. But I didn't go on; I felt him all around me, pushing me down into the white river sand.

Yellow Woman went away with the spirit from the north and lived with him and his relatives. She was gone for a long time, but then one day she came back and she brought twin boys.

"Do you know the story?"

"What story?" He smiled and pulled me close to him as he said this. I was afraid lying there on the red blanket. All I could know was the way he felt, warm, damp, his body beside me. This is the way it happens in the stories, I was thinking, with no thought beyond the moment she meets the ka'tsina spirit and they go.

"I don't have to go. What they tell in stories was real only then, back in time immemorial, like they say."

He stood up and pointed at my clothes tangled in the blanket. "Let's go," he said.

I walked beside him, breathing hard because he walked fast, his hand around my wrist. I had stopped trying to pull away from him, because his hand felt cool and the sun was high, drying the river bed into alkali. I will see someone, eventually I will see someone, and then I will be certain that he is only a man—some man from nearby—and I will be sure that I am not Yellow Woman. Because she is from out of time past and I live now and I've been to school and there are highways and pickup trucks that Yellow Woman never saw.

It was an easy ride north on horseback. I watched the change from the cottonwood trees along the river to the junipers that brushed past us in the foothills, and finally there were only piñons, and when I looked up at the rim of the mountain plateau I could see pine trees growing on the edge. Once I stopped to look down, but the pale sandstone had disappeared and the river was gone and the dark lava hills were all around. He touched my hand, not speaking, but always singing softly a mountain song and looking into my eyes.

I felt hungry and wondered what they were doing at home now—my mother, my grandmother, my husband, and the baby. Cooking breakfast, saying, "Where did she go?—maybe kidnapped." And Al going to the tribal police with the details: "She went walking along the river."

The house was made with black lava rock and red mud. It was high above the spreading miles of arroyos and long mesas. I smelled a mountain smell of pitch and buck brush. I stood there beside the black horse, looking down on the small, dim country we had passed, and I shivered.

"Yellow Woman, come inside where it's warm."

He lit a fire in the stove. It was an old stove with a round belly and an enamel coffeepot on top. There was only the stove, some faded Navajo blankets, and a bedroll and cardboard box. The floor was made of smooth adobe plaster, and there was one small window facing east. He pointed at the box.

"There's some potatoes and the frying pan." He sat on the floor with his arms around his knees pulling them close to his chest and he watched me fry the potatoes. I didn't mind him watching me because he was always watching me—he had been watching me since I came upon him sitting on the river bank trimming leaves from a willow twig with his knife. We ate from the pan and he wiped the grease from his fingers on his Levi's.

"Have you brought women here before?" He smiled and kept chewing, so I said, "Do you always use the same tricks?"

"What tricks?" He looked at me like he didn't understand.

"The story about being a ka'tsina from the mountains. The story about Yellow Woman."

Silva was silent; his face was calm.

"I don't believe it. Those stories couldn't happen now," I said.

He shook his head and said softly, "But someday they will talk about us, and they will say, 'Those two lived long ago when things like that happened.'"

He stood up and went out. I ate the rest of the potatoes and thought about things—about the noise the stove was making and the sound of the mountain wind outside. I remembered yesterday and the day before, and then I went outside.

I walked past the corral to the edge where the narrow trail cut through the black rim rock. I was standing in the sky with nothing around me but the wind that came down from the blue mountain peak behind me. I could see faint mountain images in the distance miles across the vast spread of mesas and valleys and plains. I wondered who was over there to feel the mountain wind on those sheer blue edges—who walks on the pine needles in those blue mountains.

"Can you see the pueblo?" Silva was standing behind me.

I shook my head. "We're too far away."

"From here I can see the world." He stepped out on the edge. "The Navajo reservation begins over there." He pointed to the east. "The Pueblo boundaries are over here." He looked below us to the south, where the narrow trail seemed to come from. "The Texans have their ranches over there, starting with that valley, the Concho Valley. The Mexicans run some cattle over there too."

"Do you ever work for them?"

"I steal from them," Silva answered. The sun was dropping behind us and the shadows were filling the land below. I turned away from the edge that dropped forever into the valleys below.

"I'm cold," I said, "I'm going inside." I started wondering about this man who could speak the Pueblo language so well but who lived on a mountain and rustled cattle. I decided that this man Silva must be Navajo, because Pueblo men didn't do things like that.

"You must be a Navajo."

Silva shook his head gently. "Little Yellow Woman," he said, "you never give up, do you? I have told you who I am. The Navajo people know me, too." He knelt down and unrolled the bedroll and spread the extra blankets out on a piece of canvas. The sun was down, and the only light in the house came from outside—the dim orange light from sundown.

I stood there and waited for him to crawl under the blankets.

"What are you waiting for?" he said, and I lay down beside him. He undressed me slowly like the night before beside the river—kissing my face gently and running his hands up and down my belly and legs. He took off my pants and then he laughed.

"Why are you laughing?"

"You are breathing so hard."

I pulled away from him and turned my back to him.

He pulled me around and pinned me down with his arms and chest. "You don't understand, do you, little Yellow Woman? You will do what I want."

And again he was all around me with his skin slippery against mine, and I was afraid because I understood that his strength could hurt me. I lay underneath him and I knew that he could destroy me. But later, while he slept beside me, I touched his face and I had a feeling—the kind of feeling for him that overcame me that morning along the river. I kissed him on the forehead and he reached out for me.

When I woke up in the morning he was gone. It gave me a strange feeling because for a long time I sat there on the blankets and looked around the little house for some object of his—some proof that he had been there or maybe that he was coming back. Only the blankets and the cardboard box remained. The 30-30 that had been leaning in the corner was gone, and so was the knife I had used the night before. He was gone, and I had my chance to go now. But first I had to eat, because I knew it would be a long walk home.

I found some dried apricots in the cardboard box, and I sat down on a rock at the edge of the plateau rim. There was no wind and the sun warmed me. I was surrounded by silence. I drowsed with apricots in my mouth, and I didn't believe that there were highways or railroads or cattle to steal.

When I woke up, I stared down at my feet in the black mountain dirt. Little black ants were swarming over the pine needles around my foot. They must have smelled the apricots. I thought about my family far below me. They would be wondering about me, because this had never happened to me before. The tribal police would file a report. But if old Grandpa weren't dead he would tell them what happened—he would laugh and say, "Stolen by a ka'tsina, a mountain spirit. She'll come home—they usually do." There are enough of them to handle things. My mother and grandmother will raise the baby like they raised me. Al will find someone else, and they will go on like before, except that there will be a story about the day I disappeared while I was walking along the river. Silva had come for me; he said he had. I did not decide to go. I just went. Moonflowers blossom in the sand hills before dawn, just as I followed him. That's what I was thinking as I wandered along the trail through the pine trees.

It was noon when I got back. When I saw the stone house I remembered that I had meant to go home. But that didn't seem important any more, maybe because there were little blue flowers growing in the meadow behind the stone house and the gray squirrels were playing in the pines next to the house. The horses were standing in the corral, and there was a beef carcass hanging on the shady side of a big pine in front of the house. Flies buzzed around the clotted blood that hung from the carcass. Silva was washing his hands in a bucket full of water. He must have heard me coming because he spoke to me without turning to face me.

"I've been waiting for you."

"I went walking in the big pine trees."

I looked into the bucket full of bloody water with brown-and-white animal hairs floating in it. Silva stood there letting his hand drip, examining me intently.

"Are you coming with me?"

"Where?" I asked him.

"To sell the meat in Marquez."

"If you're sure it's O.K."

"I wouldn't ask you if it wasn't," he answered.

He sloshed the water around in the bucket before he dumped it out and set the bucket upside down near the door. I followed him to the corral and watched him saddle the horses. Even beside the horses he looked tall, and I asked him again if he wasn't Navajo. He didn't say anything; he just shook his head and kept cinching up the saddle.

"But Navajos are tall."

"Get on the horse," he said, "and let's go."

The last thing he did before we started down the steep trail was to grab the .30-30 from the corner. He slid the rifle into the scabbard that hung from his saddle.

"Do they ever try to catch you?" I asked.

"They don't know who I am."

"Then why did you bring the rifle?"

"Because we are going to Marquez where the Mexicans live."

The trail leveled out on a narrow ridge that was steep on both sides like an animal spine. On one side I could see where the trail went around the rocky gray hills and disappeared into the southeast where the pale sandrock mesas stood in the distance near my home. On the other side was a trail that went west, and as I looked far into the distance I thought I saw the little town. But Silva said no, that I was looking in the wrong place, that I just thought I saw houses. After that I quit looking off into the distance; it was hot and the wildflowers were closing up their deep-yellow petals. Only the waxy cactus flowers bloomed in the bright sun, and I saw every color that a cactus blossom can be; the white ones and the red ones were still buds, but the purple and the yellow were blossoms, open full and the most beautiful of all.

Silva saw him before I did. The white man was riding a big gray horse, coming up the trail towards us. He was traveling fast and the gray horse's feet sent rocks rolling off the trail into the dry tumbleweeds. Silva motioned for me to stop and we watched the white man. He didn't see us right away, but finally his horse whinnied at our horses and he stopped. He looked at us briefly before he lapped the gray horse across the three hundred yards that separated us. He stopped his horse in front of Silva, and his young fat face was shadowed by the brim of his hat. He didn't look mad, but his small, pale eyes moved from the blood-soaked gunny sacks hanging from my saddle to Silva's face and then back to my face.

"Where did you get the fresh meat?" the white man asked.

"I've been hunting," Silva said, and when he shifted his weight in the saddle the leather creaked.

"The hell you have, Indian. You've been rustling cattle. We've been looking for the thief for a long time."

The rancher was fat, and sweat began to soak through his white cowboy shirt and the wet cloth stuck to the thick rolls of belly fat. He almost seemed to be panting from the exertion of talking, and he smelled rancid, maybe because Silva scared him.

Silva turned to me and smiled. "Go back up the mountain, Yellow Woman."

The white man got angry when he heard Silva speak in a language he couldn't understand. "Don't try anything, Indian. Just keep riding to Marquez. We'll call the state police from there."

The rancher must have been unarmed because he was very frightened and if he had a gun he would have pulled it out then. I turned my horse around and the rancher yelled, "Stop!" I looked at Silva for an instant and there was something ancient and dark—something I could feel in my stomach—in his eyes, and when I glanced at his hand I saw his finger on the trigger of the .30-30 that was still in the saddle scabbard. I slapped my horse across the flank and the sacks of raw meat swung against my knees as the horse leaped up the trail. It was hard to keep my balance, and once I thought I felt the saddle slipping backward; it was because of this that I could not look back.

I didn't stop until I reached the ridge where the trail forked. The horse was breathing deep gasps and there was a dark film of sweat on its neck. I looked down in the direction I had come from, but I couldn't see the place. I waited. The wind came up and pushed warm air past me. I looked up at the sky, pale blue and full of thin clouds and fading vapor trails left by jets.

I think four shots were fired—I remember hearing four hollow explosions that reminded me of deer hunting. There could have been more shots after that, but I couldn't have heard them because my horse was running again and the loose rocks were making too much noise as they scattered around his feet.

Horses have a hard time running downhill, but I went that way instead of uphill to the mountain because I thought it was safer. I felt better with the horse running southeast past the round gray hills that were covered with cedar trees and black lava rock. When I got to the plain in the distance I could see the dark green patches of tamaracks that grew along the river; and beyond the river I could see the beginning of the pale sandrock mesas. I stopped the horse and looked back to see if anyone was coming; then I got off the horse and turned the horse around, wondering if it would go back to its corral under the pines on the mountain. It looked back at me for a moment and then plucked a mouthful of green tumbleweeds before it trotted back up the trail with its ears pointed forward, carrying its head daintily to one side to avoid stepping on the dragging reins. When the horse disappeared over the last hill, the gunny sacks full of meat were still swinging and bouncing.

I walked toward the river on a wood-hauler's road that I knew would eventually lead to the paved road. I was thinking about waiting beside the road for someone to drive by, but by the time I got to the pavement I had decided it wasn't very far to walk if I followed the river back the way Silva and I had come.

The river water tasted good, and I sat in the shade under a cluster of silvery willows. I thought about Silva, and I felt sad at leaving him; still, there was something strange about him, and I tried to figure it out all the way back home.

I came back to the place on the river bank where he had been sitting the first time I saw him. The green willow leaves that he had trimmed from the branch were still lying there, wilted in the sand. I saw the leaves and I wanted to go back to him—to kiss him and to touch him—but the mountains were too far away now. And I told myself, because I believe it, he will come back sometime and be waiting again by the river.

I followed the path up from the river into the village. The sun was getting low, and I could smell supper cooking when I got to the screen door of my house. I could hear their voices inside—my mother was telling my grandmother how to fix the Jell-O and my husband, Al, was playing with the baby. I decided to tell them that some Navajo had kidnaped me, but I was sorry that old Grandpa wasn't alive to hear my story because it was the Yellow Woman stories he liked to tell best.

Selected Bibliography

NATIVE AMERICA AND EUROPE IN THE NEW WORLD

Fernando Horcasitas, *The Aztecs Then and Now* (1979), offers a concise summary of Aztec history and culture from pre-Aztec times to the mid-twentieth century. The Maya are surveyed in Michael D. Coe, *The Maya* (1993). Harold E. Driver's comprehensive *Indians of North America* (1969) remains a standard work in its field. Diego Durán, *The Aztecs* (1964), is a readable, richly detailed sixteenth-century source on the history of Tenochtitlán. John Bierhorst's three-volume series—*The Mythology of North America* (1985), *The Mythology of South America* (1988), and *The Mythology of Mexico and Central America* (1990)—presents an overview of Native American narrative traditions. Munro S. Edmonson, ed., *Literatures* (1985), vol. 3 of *Supplement to the Handbook of Middle American Indians*, ed. Victoria Reifler Bricker, consists of survey articles on Nahuatl and four Maya literatures.

Cantares Mexicanos
The only complete edition of the Cantares Mexicanos is John Bierhorst, *Cantares Mexicanos: Songs of the Aztecs* (1985), which includes extensive commentary. Robert Stevenson, *Music in Aztec and Inca Territory* (1968), gives useful background on instrumentation and performance. Modern poetry inspired by the Cantares can be found in William Carlos Williams, *Pictures from Brueghel and Other Poems* (1949); Stephen Berg, *Nothing in the Word* (1972); and Ernesto Cardenal, *Los Ovnis de Oro/Golden UFOs* (1992).

Florentine Codex
Sahagún's *History* has been published in a thirteen-part English-Nahuatl edition, *Florentine Codex* (1950–82), ed. Arthur J. O. Anderson and Charles E. Dibble; the introductory volume (Part 1) includes background data and a subject guide; Part 7 (book 6) has the complete oratory. Articles on various aspects of Sahagún's *History*, including the oratory, are included in Munro S. Edmonson, ed., *Sixteenth-Century Mexico: The Work of Sahagún* (1974). More of the midwifery orations are in Thelma Sullivan, *A Scattering of Jades: Stories, Poems, and Prayers of the Aztecs* (1994), ed. T. J. Knab.

Popol Vuh
Dennis Tedlock's translation, satisfyingly annotated, is published as *Popol Vuh: The Mayan Book of the Dawn of Life* (1985; revised 1996). The text reprinted in this anthology is from the 1996 edition. Older translations with useful introductions are Adrián Recinos, Delia Goetz, and Sylvanus Morley, *Popol Vuh: The Sacred Book of the Ancient Quiché Maya* (1950); and Munro S. Edmonson, *The Book of Counsel: The Popol Vuh of the Quiche Maya of Guatemala* (1971). Edmonson's is the only Quiché-English edition. Essays on the Popol Vuh and related topics are in Tedlock, *The Spoken Word and the Work of Interpretation* (1983). Maya vase paintings related to Part 3 of the Popol Vuh are illustrated and discussed in Michael D. Coe, *Lords of the Underworld: Masterpieces of Classic Maya Ceramics* (1978).

VERNACULAR LITERATURE IN CHINA

A basic survey of the history of Chinese drama can be found in William Dolby, *A History of Chinese Drama* (1976). C. T. Hsia, *The Classic Chinese Novel: A Critical Introduction* (1968), remains one of the most readable introductions to the major novels. Patrick Hanan, *The Chinese Vernacular Story* (1981), provides an insightful study of the cultural background of vernacular fiction.

Cao Xueqin (Ts'ao Hsüeh-Ch'in)
There is a complete translation of *The Story of the Stone* in five volumes (1973–82), the first three volumes by David Hawkes and the last two by John Minford. Andrew Plaks, *Archetype and Allegory in the Dream of the Red Chamber* (1976), is a useful study.

Wu Ch'eng-en
Like most Chinese novels, *Monkey* is very long. Arthur Waley's translation (1943) is an abridged version of thirty chapters out of the original one hundred, but Waley's gifts as a translator and the nature of his abridgement make this version a delight to read. In addition to Waley's abridgement, there is a complete and accurate four-volume translation of the novel by Anthony Yu, *Journey to the West* (1977–83), with a long introduction. There is also an excellent chapter on the novel in C. T. Hsia, *The Classic Chinese Novel: A Critical Introduction* (1968).

THE ENLIGHTENMENT IN EUROPE

Useful books on the Enlightenment include, for English background, H. Nicolson, *The Age of Reason: The Eighteenth Century* (1960), and, for an opposed view, D. Greene, *The Age of Exuberance: Backgrounds to Eighteenth-Century English Literature* (1970). For the intellectual and social situation in France, L. G. Crocker, *An Age of Crisis: Man and World in Eighteenth-Century French Thought* (1959); L. Gossman, *French Society and Culture: Background for Eighteenth-Century Literature* (1972); and A. Adam, *Grandeur and Illusion: French Literature and Society, 1600–1715* (1972). Also useful are F. C. Beiser, *The Sovereignty of Reason: The Defense of Rationality in the Early English Enlightenment* (1996). S. Gearhart, *The Open Boundary of History and Fiction: A Critical Approach to the French Enlightenment* (1984); and J. C. Hayes, *Reading the French Enlightenment: System and Subversion* (1999). An excellent treatment of the period's literature in England is M. Price, *To the Palace of Wisdom: Studies in Order and Energy from Dryden to Blake* (1964). M. L. Williamson, *Raising Their Voices: British Women Writers 1650–1750* (1990), discusses women's contributions to the English Enlightenment. For the artistic situation of France, see T. M. Kavanaugh, *Esthetics of the Moment: Literature and Art in the French Enlightenment* (1996). For the philosophic background and its implications, see M. Losonsky, *Enlightenment and Action from Descartes to Kant: Passionate Thought* (2001). A good introduction to the intellectual situation of eighteenth-century England is J. Sambrook, *The Eighteenth Century: The Intellectual and Cultural Context of English Literature, 1700–1789* (1986). An unusual perspective on the meaning of the eighteenth century to our own time is provided by N. Postman, *Building a Bridge to the Eighteenth Century: How the Past Can Improve Our Future* (1999). R. A. Barney, *Plots of Enlightenment: Education and the Novel in Eighteenth-Century England* (1999), examines important issues of education (particularly relevant to the situation of women), especially as they are refracted through the novel.

Sor Juana Inés de la Cruz
A volume in the Twayne series by Gerard Flynn, *Sor Juana Inés de la Cruz* (1971), provides a biographical, critical, and bibliographical introduction to Sister Juana. She is also treated in histories of Latin American literature: for example, J. Franco, *An Introduction to Spanish-American Literature*, 3rd ed. (1994). An important critical work, belatedly translated into English, is Octavio Paz, *Sor Juana; or, The Traps of Faith* (1988). Other studies include Stephanie Merrim, ed., *Feminist Perspectives on Sor Juana Inés de la Cruz* (1991); F. Royer, *The Tenth Muse: Sor Juana Inés de la Cruz* (1952); P. Kirk, *Sor Juana Inés de la Cruz: Religion, Art, and Feminism* (1998); and S. Merrim, *Early Modern Women's Writing and Sor Juana Inés de la Cruz* (1999).

Molière (Jean-Baptiste Poquelin)
H. Walker, *Molière* (1990), provides a general biographical and critical introduction to the playwright. Useful critical studies include J. D. Hubert, *Molière and the Comedy of Intellect* (1962); L. Gossman, *Men and Masks: A Study of Molière* (1963); Jacques Guicharnaud, ed., *Molière: A Collection of Critical Essays* (1964); N. Gross, *From Gesture to Idea: Esthetics and Ethics in Molière's Comedy* (1982). J. F. Gaines, *Social Structures in Molière Theater* (1984); and L. F. Norman, *The Public Mirror: Molière and the Social Commerce of Depiction* (1999). An excellent treatment of Molière in his historical context is W. D. Howarth, *Molière: A Playwright and His Audience* (1984). Martin Turnell, *The Classical Moment: Studies of Corneille, Molière, and Racine* (1975), offers useful insight into French dramatic tradition. More specialized studies include R. D. Lalande, *Intruders in the Play World: The Dynamics of Gender in Molière's Comedies* (1996) and Harold G. Knutson, *The Triumph of Wit* (1988), which examines Molière in relation to Shakespeare and Ben Jonson. For stage history, see G. McCarthy, *The Theatres of Molière* (2002).

François-Marie Arouet de Voltaire
Biographies and critical studies of Voltaire include R. Aldington, *Voltaire* (1934); G. Brandes, *The Life of Voltaire* (undated); I. O. Wade, *Voltaire and "Candide": A Study in the Fusion of History, Art, and Philosophy* (1959); M. Hayden, *Voltaire: A Biography* (1981); and T. Besterman, *Voltaire*, 3rd ed. (1976). A good

general introduction is P. E. Richter and Ilona Ricardo, *Voltaire* (1980). A work placing Voltaire in a broad context is F. M. Keener, *The Chain of Becoming: The Philosophical Tale, the Novel, and a Neglected Realism of the Enlightenment—Swift, Montesquieu, Voltaire, Johnson, and Austen* (1983), on Voltaire and his English contemporaries. Two useful works specifically about *Candide* are William Bottiglia, *Voltaire's Candide: Analysis of a Classic*

(1964), and Haydn Mason, *Candide: Optimism Demolished* (1992). D. Williams, *Candide* (1997), a critical guide intended for inexperienced readers. *Candide*, ed. D. Gordon (1999), provides accompanying material that helps establish Voltaire's work in its cultural context. A useful survey of Voltaire's thought and writing is B. L. Knappe, *Voltaire Revisited* (2000). J. Gray, *Voltaire* (1999) focuses specifically on Voltaire's philosophical ideas.

THE RISE OF POPULAR ARTS IN PREMODERN JAPAN

Matsuo Bashō

For another, more colloquial rendering of *The Narrow Road of the Interior,* translated by the poet Cid Corman in collaboration with Kamaike Susumu, see *Back Roads to Far Towns* (1986). All five of Bashō's travel journals are found in *The Narrow Road to the Deep North and Other Travel Sketches* (1966), tran. Nobuyuki Yuasa, whose re-creation of *haiku* as four-line poems seems less successful. For examples of Bashō's linked poetry see Earl Miner and Hiroko Odagiri, trans., *The Monkey's Straw Raincoat* (1981). For more poems by Bashō and his followers see Steven D. Carter, *Traditional Japanese Poetry: An Anthology* (1991). Two excellent book-length introductions to Bashō, both by Makoto Ueda, are *Matsuo Bashō* (1982) and

Bashō and His Interpreters (1991). Shorter introductions are found in two literary histories by Donald Keene: *World within Walls* (1976) and *Travelers of a Hundred Ages* (1989). For a general study of *haiku* see Kenneth Yasuda, *The Japanese Haiku* (1957); Nippon Gakujutsu Shinkokai, ed., *Haikai and Haiku* (1958), is a basic reference; and for an anthology of *haiku* from Bashō to modern times see Harold G. Henderson, *An Introduction to Haiku* (1958). Haruo Shirane, *Traces of Dreams: Landscape, Cultural Memory, and the Poetry of Bashō* (1998), explores important themes. An interesting comparative study is Earl Miner, *Naming Properties: Nominal References in Travel Writings by Bashō and Sora, Johnson and Boswell* (1996).

THE NINETEENTH CENTURY: ROMANTICISM

Useful introductions to the Romantic period include L. R. Furst, *Romanticism in Perspective: A Comparative Study of Aspects of the Romantic Movements in England, France, and Germany,* 2nd ed. (1979); R. F. Gleckner and G. E. Enscoe, eds., *Romanticism: Points of View,* 2nd ed. (1970), a collection of essays by various contributors; Charles E. Larmore, *The Romantic Legacy* (1996); and M. Cranston, *The Romantic Movement* (1994). On French Romanticism, see P. T. Comeau, *Diehards and Innovators: The French Romantic Struggle, 1800–1830* (1988); on Germany, T. Ziolkowski, *German Romanticism and Its Institutions* (1990); on English and American developments, B. Taylor, R. Bain, and M. H. Abrams, *The Cast of Consciousness: Concepts of the Mind in British and American Romanticism* (1987); on the English and German situation, C. Jacobs, *Uncontainable Romanticism: Shelley, Brontë, and Kleist* (1989). A comparative study of European Romantic poetry appears in *Romantic Poetry* (2002), ed. A. Esterhammer. More specialized studies include M. Redfield, *The Politics of Aesthetics: Nationalism, Gender, Romanticism* (2003); R. M. Turley, *The Politics of Language in Romantic Literature* (2002); and H. Thomas, *Romanticism and Slave Narratives: Transatlantic Testimonies* (2000).

William Blake

Blake has provided material for an enormous outpouring of critical work. Particularly useful for the student are N. Frye, ed., *Blake: A Collection of Critical Essays* (1966), and H. Adams, ed., *Critical Essays on William Blake* (1991). Valuable longer studies include M. Schorer, *William Blake: The Politics of Vision* (1946); H. Adams, *William Blake: A Reading of the Shorter Poems* (1963); E. D. Hirsch, *Innocence and Experience: An Introduction to Blake,* 2nd. ed. (1975); D. G. Gillham, *William Blake* (1973); and S. Gardner, *Blake's Innocence and Experience Retraced* (1986). A useful recent volume is *The Cambridge Companion to William Blake,* ed. M. Eaves (2003). Two full-length studies explore special aspects of the poet: K. D. Hutchings, *Imagining Nature: Blake's Environmental Poetics* (2002), and S. Makdisi, *William Blake and the Impossible History of the 1790s* (2003), on the political implications of Blake's poetry.

Emily Dickinson

Emily Dickinson: An Interpretive Biography (1955), by T. H. Johnson, Dickinson's editor, is indispensable. Useful critical sources include C. Blake and C. F. Wells, eds., *The Recognition of Emily Dickinson: Selected Criticism since*

1890 (1964), Albert J. Gelpi, *Emily Dickinson: The Mind of the Poet* (1965); P. Bennett, *Emily Dickinson: Woman Poet* (1990); S. Juhasz, ed., *Feminist Critics Read Emily Dickinson* (1983), a collection with a specifically feminist orientation; and J. Dobson, *Dickinson and the Strategies of Reticence: The Woman Writer in Nineteenth-Century America* (1989). Other critical studies are K. Stocks, *Emily Dickinson and the Modern Consciousness: A Poet of Our Time* (1988), and M. N. Smith, *Rowing in Eden: Rereading Emily Dickinson* (1992). A study that emphasizes formal aspects of Dickinson's work is C. L. Cooley, *The Music of Emily Dickinson's Poems and Letters: A Study of Imagery and Form* (2003). Useful for providing multiple views is *The Cambridge Companion to Emily Dickinson*, ed. Wendy Martin (2002).

Johann Wolfgang von Goethe
E. Ludwig, *Goethe, The History of a Man, 1749–1832* (1928), is a solid biography. Also useful are V. Lange, ed., *Goethe: A Collection of Critical Essays* (1968); and the essays contained in the critical edition of W. Arndt, trans., and C. Hamlin, ed., *Faust* (1976). See also H. Hatfield, *Goethe: A Critical Introduction* (1963); M. Bidney, *Blake and Goethe: Psychology, Ontology, Imagination* (1988); and specifically for *Faust*, L. Dieckmann, *Goethe's Faust: A Critical Reading* (1972). A study relating Goethe's play to other versions of the Faust legend is A. Hoelzel, *The Paradoxical Quest: A Study of Faustian Vicissitudes* (1988). A varied group of essays appears in Reinhold Grimm and Jost Hermand, eds., *Our Faust? Roots and Ramifications of a Modern German Myth* (1987). An ongoing, ambitious study of Goethe's life and work in their historical context is N. Boyle, *Goethe: The Poet and the Age*, I: *The Poetry of Desire: 1749–1790*, II: *Revolution and Renunciation: 1790–1803* (1991). For a less complicated approach, see I. Wagner, *Goethe* (1999).

Heinrich Heine
Biographies of Heine include Philip Kossoff, *Valiant Heart: A Biography of Heinrich Heine* (1983). Valuable critical studies are Jeffrey L. Sammons, *Heinrich Heine, the Elusive Poet* (1969); Ursula Franklin, *Exiles and Ironists: Essays on the Kinship of Heine and Laforgue* (1988); G. F. Peters, *The Poet as Provocateur: Heinrich Heine and His Critics* (2000); and R. F. Cook, *By the Rivers of Babylon: Heinrich Heine's Late Songs and Reflections* (1998). See also R. F. Cook, ed., *A Companion to the Works of Heinrich Heine* (2002).

Friedrich Hölderlin
A valuable biographical and critical study is L. S. Salzberger, *Hölderlin* (1952). Also useful is E. L. Stahl, *Hölderlin's Symbolism, an Essay*

(1945). Interpretations by various critics are supplied in *The Solid Letter; Readings of Friedrich Hölderlin* (1999), ed. A. Fioretos.

Victor Hugo
A. Maurois, *Victor Hugo and His World* (1966), trans. O. Bernard, provides a useful introduction. S. Guerlac, *The Impersonal Sublime: Hugo, Baudelaire, Lautréamont* (1990), and the collection of critical essays edited by H. Bloom, *Victor Hugo* (1988), are also valuable. R. Graham, *Victor Hugo* (1997), supplies a biographical interpretation; L. M. Porter, *Victor Hugo* (1999), examines the life and work. J. C. Ireson, *Victor Hugo* (1997), offers a companion to the poetry.

John Keats
A first-rate critical biography is A. Ward, *John Keats: The Making of a Poet*, rev. ed. (1986). Also useful are W. J. Bate, *John Keats* (1963); S. Coote, *John Keats: A Life* (1995); T. Hilton, *Keats and His World* (1971); C. T. Watts, *A Preface to Keats* (1985); J. Barnard, *John Keats* (1987); H. Bloom, ed., *The Odes of Keats* (1987), a collection of essays; and H. de Almeida, *Critical Essays on John Keats* (1990). S. Hebron, *John Keats* (2002), and *The Cambridge Companion to Keats*, ed. S. Wolfson (2001), contain valuable material.

Giacomo Leopardi
The best biography of Leopardi is I. Origo, *Leopardi: A Biography* (1935), revised and enlarged as *Leopardi: A Study in Solitude* (1999). A study of Leopardi in relation to contemporaries from other countries is R. R. Fleming, *Keats, Leopardi, and Hölderlin: The Poet as Priest of the Absolute* (1976, 1987). For critical insight, see the commentary in O. M. Casale, ed. and trans., *A Leopardi Reader* (1981); J. P. Barricelli, *Giacomo Leopardi* (1986); and D. Bini, *A Fragrance from the Desert: Poetry and Philosophy in Giacomo Leopardi* (1983).

Alexander Sergeyevich Pushkin
Henri Troyat, *Pushkin* (1970), trans. N. Amphoux, is an excellent biography. For biography and criticism, the student might also consult Walter Arndt, *Pushkin Threefold: Narrative, Lyric, Polemic and Ribald Verse* (1972); John Bayley, *Pushkin: A Comparative Commentary* (1971); Paul Debreczeny, *The Other Pushkin: A Study of Alexander Pushkin's Prose Fiction* (1983); John Oliver Killens, *Great Black Russian: A Novel on the Life and Times of Alexander Pushkin* (1989); and D. M. Bethea, ed., *Puškin Today* (1993), an ambitious collection of essays. A useful biography is Stephanie Sandler, *Distant Pleasures: Alexander Pushkin and The Writing of Exile* (1989). See also Brett Cooke, *Pushkin and the Creative Process* (1998).

Jean-Jacques Rousseau

F. C. Green, *Jean-Jacques Rousseau: A Critical Study of His Life and Writings* (1955), provides biography and criticism. Thomas McFarland, *Romanticism and the Heritage of Rousseau* (1995), examines the relation of Rousseau's assumptions to those of the Romantic movement. A thorough evaluation of Rousseau's achievement is L. G. Crocker, *Jean-Jacques Rousseau: A New Interpretative Analysis of His Works* (1973). More directly focused on the *Confessions* is H. Williams, *Rousseau and Romantic Autobiography* (1983). More recent studies include T. M. Kavanagh, *Writing the Truth: Authority and Desire in Rousseau* (1987); M. Morgenstern, *Rousseau and the Politics of Ambiguity: Self, Culture, and Society* (1996); and C. Kelly, *Rousseau's Exemplary Life: The Confessions as Political Philosophy* (1987). Special perspectives are provided by E. L. Stelzig, *The Romantic Subject in Autobiography: Rousseau and Goethe* (2000), and L. Lange, ed., *Feminist Interpretations of Jean-Jacques Rousseau* (2002). A good starting point for understanding Rousseau is R. Wokler, *Rousseau: A Very Short Introduction*, 2nd ed. (2001).

Walt Whitman

G. W. Allen, *The Solitary Singer: A Critical Biography of Walt Whitman* (1985), provides both biography and criticism. An important recent study is D. S. Reynolds, *Walt Whitman's America: A Cultural Biography* (1995). M. Hindus, ed., *Walt Whitman: The Critical Heritage* (1971), contains nineteenth- and twentieth-century essays; J. E. Miller Jr., *A Critical Guide to Leaves of Grass* (1957), is helpful. Also valuable are R. V. Chase, *Walt Whitman Reconsidered* (1955); M. J. Killingsworth, *Whitman's Poetry of the Body: Sexuality, Politics, and the Text* (1989); B. Erkkila, *Whitman the Political Poet* (1989); M. W. Thomas, *The Lunar Light of Whitman's Poetry* (1987); and J. E. Miller Jr., *Leaves of Grass: America's Lyric-Epic of Self and Democracy* (1992). A general guide is G. W. Allen, *The New Walt Whitman Handbook* (1986). A recent exploration of Whitman's poetry in relation to his contemporaries is D. Wardrop, *Word, Birth, and Culture: The Poetry of Poe, Whitman, and Dickinson* (2002). Investigating the bearing of Whitman's sexuality on his poetry is M. Maslan, *Whitman Possessed: Poetry, Sexuality, and Popular Authority* (2001).

William Wordsworth

G. M. Harper, *Wordsworth: His Life, Works and Influence*, 3rd ed. (1929), remains the standard biography. A more recent biographical study is S. C. Gill, *William Wordsworth: A Life* (1989). Other important works (critical in emphasis) include R. D. Havens, *The Mind of a Poet* (1962), 2 vols.; G. Hartman, *Wordsworth's Poetry, 1787–1814* (1971); Thomas McFarland, *William Wordsworth: Intensity and Achievement* (1992); and J. H. Alexander, *Reading Wordsworth* (1987). A useful collection of critical essays is G. H. Gilpin, ed., *Critical Essays on William Wordsworth* (1990). Valuable contextualization is provided by P. Fletcher and J. Murphy, eds., *Wordsworth in Context* (1992). Recent years have seen the publication of several biographies, of which the best is K. R. Johnston, *The Hidden Wordsworth: Poet, Lover, Rebel, Spy* (1998). Also provocative is D. Wu, *Wordsworth: An Inner Life* (2002). A useful compendium is *The Cambridge Companion to Wordsworth* (2003), ed. S. Gill. Among the many works concerning Wordsworth and other Romantic poets, a valuable collection of essays is *Inventing the Individual: Romanticism and the Idea of individualism* (2002), ed. L. H. Peer, which includes essays on Keats and Goethe as well as Wordsworth.

THE NINETEENTH CENTURY: REALISM AND SYMBOLISM

E. Auerbach, *Mimesis: The Representation of Reality in Western Literature* (1953), is a wide-ranging book (from Homer to Proust) with chapters on nineteenth-century realism. G. J. Becker, ed., *Documents of Modern Literary Realism* (1963), surveys the development of modern realism and offers documents and essays from 1835 to 1955. H. Levin, *The Gates of Horn: A Study of Five French Realists* (1963), contains much on realism in general as well as specifically dealing with Stendhal, Balzac, Flaubert, Zola, and Proust. Linda Nochlin, *Realism* (1971), discusses realism in the visual arts. Naomi Schor, *Breaking the Chain: Women, Theory, and French Realists Fiction* (1985), discusses the realist fiction of Flaubert, Zola, Balzac, and others in terms of feminist and psy-choanalytic theory. Also helpful is R. Wellek, "The Concept of Realism in Literary Scholarship," in R. Wellek, *Concepts of Criticism: Essays* (1963). Nicholas Boyle and Martin Swales, eds., *Realism in European Literature: Essays in Honour of J. P. Stern* (1986), is a varied and useful collection that includes a discussion of realism as it relates to modernism and language consciousness. Elise Boulding, *The Underside of History: A View of Women through Time*, rev. ed. (1992), arranged by periods and sociological categories, contains much pertinent information about the role of women that is omitted from traditional histories. John Rignall, *Realist Fiction and the Strolling Spectator* (1992), indebted to Nietzsche and Walter Benjamin, analyzes realism's distanced point of view in eight nineteenth-century and three twentieth-century novelists.

Marcel Raymond, *From Baudelaire to Surrealism* (1933; trans. 1949, 1950), is a fundamental study of the evolution of the new poetry. Laurence M. Porter, *The Crisis of French Symbolism* (1990), situates the poetry of Baudelaire, Mallarmé, Verlaine, and Rimbaud between neoclassicism and the Symbolist school. An influential and still valuable presentation is found in *The Symbolist Movement in Literature* (1899; repr. 1980), by the English Symbolist Arthur Symons. P. Mansell Jones, *The Background of Modern French Poetry: Essays and Interviews* (1951; repr. 1968), describes the influence of Poe, Baudelaire, Mallarmé, and Whitman on modern free verse. Georges Poulet, *Exploding Poetry: Baudelaire/Rimbaud*, trans. Françoise Meltzer (1984), interprets the poetry of the two poets.

Charles Baudelaire

Lois Boe Hyslop, *Charles Baudelaire Revisited* (1992), is a useful introductory survey. F. W. Leakey, *Baudelaire, Les Fleurs du Mal* (1992), is a short guide to the poet's major work. Enid Starkie, *Baudelaire* (1957), is the fullest biography in English. Henri Peyre, ed., *Baudelaire: A Collection of Critical Essays* (1962), contains eleven essays on *The Flowers of Evil*, with selections by major writers. Harold Bloom, ed., *Charles Baudelaire* (1987), presents ten contemporary critics on Baudelaire's themes, literary and artistic criticism, selected texts, and relation to Poe. Patricia Clements, *Baudelaire and the English Tradition* (1985), is a penetrating analysis of Baudelaire's influence on English literature from Swinburne to T. S. Eliot; it includes comparisons and contrasts with late Symbolist tradition. Edward K. Kaplan, *Baudelaire's Prose Poems* (1990), studies the prose poems as a many-sided but coherent ensemble of "fables of modern life." Baudelaire's criticism of literature and art are discussed in Rosemary Lloyd, *Baudelaire's Literary Criticism* (1981), David Carrier, *High Art: Charles Baudelaire and the Origins of Modernist Painting* (1996). Lloyd's *Selected Letters of Charles Baudelaire: The Conquest of Solitude* (1986) contains personal and literary letters. Laurence M. Porter, *The Crisis of French Symbolism* (1990), has an interesting chapter on Baudelaire's relation to his imagined audience. Margery A. Evans, *Baudelaire and Intertextuality: Poetry at the Crossroads* (1993), analyzes the literary conventions manipulated in the prose poems. Rosemary Lloyd's *Selected Letters of Charles Baudelaire: The Conquest of Solitude* (1986). F. W. Leakey, *Baudelaire, Les Fleurs du Mal* (1992), is a short guide to the poet's major work.

Anton Chekhov

Donald Rayfield, *The Cherry Orchard: Catastrophe and Comedy* (1994), presents an extended discussion of the play; good chapters are also found in Beverly Hahn, *Chekhov: A Study of the Major Stories and Plays* (1977); Harvey Pitcher, *The Chekhov Play: A New Interpretation* (1973); and Richard Pearce, *Chekhov: A Study of the Four Major Plays* (1983). Francis Fergusson compares Ibsen and Chekhov in "*Ghosts* and *The Cherry Orchard*," in *The Idea of a Theater, a Study of Ten Plays: The Art of Drama in Changing Perspective* (1949). There is helpful critical analysis in R. L. Jackson, ed., *Chekhov: A Collection of Critical Essays* (1967), and *Reading Chekhov's Text* (1993); in Donald Rayfield, *Chekhov: The Evolution of His Art* (1975); and in René Wellek and N. D. Wellek, eds., *Chekhov: New Perspectives* (1984), which includes a sketch of Chekhov criticism in England and America. Laurence Senelick, *The Chekhov Theatre: A Century of the Plays in Performance* (1997), presents a different perspective. J. L. Styan discusses *The Cherry Orchard* from a different perspective in *Chekhov in Performance: A Commentary on the Major Plays* (1971); and Nicholas Worrall, *File on Chekhov* (1986), offers an introductory survey with useful cited passages and suggestions for further study. Ralph E. Matlaw, ed., *Anton Chekhov's Short Stories: Texts of the Stories, Backgrounds, Criticism* (1979), includes eight valuable essays on aspects of the short stories and selections from Chekhov's letters. Virginia Llewellyn Smith, *Anton Chekhov and the Lady with the Dog* (1973), argues for autobiographical elements in Gurov's portrayal. Nick Worrall, *Chekhov on File* (1986), offers an introductory survey with useful cited passages and suggestions for further study. Donald Rayfield, *Anton Chekhov: A Life* (1998), is a revisionary biography that evokes a more complex personality based on newly discovered evidence.

Fyodor Dostoevsky

Monroe C. Beardsley, "Dostoevsky's Metaphor of the 'Underground,'" *Journal of the History of Ideas* 3 (June 1942), is a subtle interpretation of the central metaphor of the *Notes*. Joseph Frank, "Nihilism and *Notes from Underground*," *Sewanee Review*, 69 (1961), interprets the *Notes* in the context of the history of the times. Robert L. Jackson, *Dostoevsky's Underground Man in Russian Literature* (1981), traces the impact of the *Notes* on Russian literature. Konstantin Mochulsky, *Dostoevsky: His Life and Work*, trans. Michael A. Minihan (1967), is the best general work translated from Russian, the work of an emigré in Paris. René Wellek, ed., *Dostoevsky: A Collection of Critical Essays* (1962), contains an essay by the editor on the history of Dostoevsky criticism. Alba della Fazia Amoia, *Feodor Dostoevsky* (1993), is a general introduction to Dostoevsky's work aimed at a student audience. Joseph Frank, *Dostoevsky* (1976–2002), is an impressive biographical study in five volumes. Frank's *Through the Russian Prism: Essays on Literature and Culture* (1990) includes review essays that examine various approaches to Dostoevsky. Louis Breger, *Dostoevsky: The Author as Psychoanalyst* (1989), takes a psychoanalytic approach in analyzing levels of meaning in Dostoevsky's work as a new sensibility that anticipates the modern novel; he includes a chapter on *Notes*. Malcolm V. Jones, *Dostoyevsky after Bakhtin: Readings in Dostoyevsky's Fantastic Realism* (1990), examines Dostoevsky's "higher realism" in various perspectives and includes a chapter on *Notes*. Nina Pelikan Straus, *Dostoevsky and the Woman Question: Rereadings at the End of a Century* (1994), examines the presence of women and Dostoevsky's construction of the feminine.

Gustave Flaubert

William J. Berg and Laurey K. Martin, *Gustave Flaubert* (1997), is a general introduction to Flaubert's life and work. Victor H. Brombert, *The Novels of Flaubert: A Study of Themes and Techniques* (1966), has an excellent chapter on *Madame Bovary;* Raymond D. Giraud, ed., *Flaubert: A Collection of Critical Essays* (1964), and Harold Bloom, ed., *Emma Bovary* (1994), provide a range of short studies. Jonathan Culler, *Flaubert; The Uses of Uncertainty* (1974), is a clear and carefully argued study that emphasizes the modernity of Flaubert's style. Aimée Israel-Pelletier, *Flaubert's Straight and Suspect Saints: The Unity of Trois Contes* (1991), contains a valuable chapter on *A Simple Heart* and also a bibliography. Paul de Man, ed., *Gustave Flaubert: Madame Bovary, Backgrounds and Sources: Essays in Criticism* (1965), will help the reader, as will Alison Fairlie, *Flaubert: Madame Bovary* (1962), a good discussion of problems, structures, people, and values addressed to students. The chapter on *Madame Bovary* in Anthony Thorlby, *Gustave Flaubert and the Art of Realism* (1957), is still to be recommended, as is Margaret Lowe, *Towards the Real Flaubert: A Study of Madame Bovary* (1984).

Henrik Ibsen

Michael Meyer, *Ibsen: A Biography* (1971), is a general work. J. W. McFarlane, ed., *Discussions of Henrik Ibsen* (1962), contains Henry James's "On the Occasion of 'Hedda Gabler.'"

Rolf Fjelde, ed., *Ibsen: A Collection of Critical Essays* (1965), has a good essay on *Hedda Gabler;* and James McFarlane, ed., *The Cambridge Companion to Ibsen* (1994), offers sixteen essays on a wide variety of topics. Joan Templeton, *Ibsen's Women* (2001), is an excellent study that includes a chapter on *Hedda Gabler* and a discussion of Ibsen's modernism. Michael Goldman, *Ibsen: The Dramaturgy of Fear* (1999), discusses the plays from a different perspective, and Frederick J. Marker and Lise-Lone Marker, *Ibsen's Lively Art: A Performance Study of the Major Plays* (1989), use descriptions of the various performances of *Hedda Gabler* to examine differing interpretations of the main characters.

Arthur Rimbaud

Frederic C. St. Aubyn, *Arthur Rimbaud* (1988), is a useful biography that also treats Rimbaud's work. Wallace Fowlie, *Rimbaud* (1965), discusses the *Illuminations* and the myth of childhood in Rimbaud. Harold Bloom, ed., *Arthur Rimbaud* (1988), collects eleven essays on various aspects of Rimbaud's work. Georges Poulet, *Exploding Poetry: Baudelaire/Rimbaud,* trans. Françoise Meltzer, (1984), examines poetic worldviews in the work of the two poets.

Leo Tolstoy

R. F. Christian, *Tolstoy: A Critical Introduction* (1969), is clear, instructive, and informative. E. B. Greenwood, *Tolstoy: The Comprehensive Vision* (1975), is helpful in placing *The Death of Ivan Ilyich* in the perspective of Tolstoy's work as a whole. Some good analysis is found in H. Gifford, ed., *Leo Tolstoy: A Critical Anthology* (1971). Ralph E. Matlaw, ed., *Tolstoy: A Collection of Critical Essays* (1967), and Philip Rahv, *Image and Idea: Fourteen Essays on Literary Themes* (1949), both present essays on *The Death of Ivan Ilyich.* Theodore Redpath, *Tolstoy,* 2nd ed. (1969), provides a brief introduction with good criticism of ideas. Ernest J. Simmons, *Leo Tolstoy* (1946), and A. N. Wilson, *Tolstoy* (1988), are both excellent biographies. Rimvydas Šilbajoris, *Tolstoy's Aesthetics and His Art* (1991), includes accounts of reactions to the author at home and abroad as well as many substantial quotations.

THE TWENTIETH CENTURY

The Modern Tradition: Backgrounds of Modern Literature (1965), ed. Richard Ellmann and Charles Feidelson Jr., is a valuable collection of statements by writers, artists, philosophers, and scientists, arranged by themes. Monique Chefdor, Ricardo Quinones, and Albert Wachtel, eds., *Modernism: Challenges and Perspectives* (1986), offers many valuable essays on international modernism, ranging from definitions to historical practice in art, music, literature, and politics.

David Hayman, *Re-forming the Narrative: Toward a Mechanics of Modernist Fiction* (1987), proposes five tactics that distinguish modernist narrative from earlier fiction; examples include Robbe-Grillet, Kafka, Rilke, Joyce, Beckett, and Borges. Cultural background is provided in Wilson H. Coates and Hayden V. White, *The Ordeal of Liberal Humanism: An Intellectual History of Western Europe* (1970), an excellent intellectual history of Western Europe after the French

Revolution, and David Harvey, *Paris: Capital of Modernity* (2003), a copiously documented and illustrated study of the rise of social, economic, and literary modernism in late nineteenth-century Paris. Harry Levin, "What Was Modernism?" (1962), in *Refractions: Essays in Comparative Literature* (1966), is an influential survey of modernist writers as humanists and inheritors of the Enlightenment. Renato Poggioli, *The Theory of the Avant-Garde*, trans. Gerald Fitzgerald (1968), locates basic categories of attitudes toward society inside the different arts of the twentieth-century American avant-garde. William S. Rubin, *Dada, Surrealism and Their Heritage* (1968), gives a detailed history of Surrealist art with many superb illustrations. John D. Erickson, *Dada: Performance, Poetry, and Art* (1984), and Herbert S. Gershman, *The Surrealist Revolution in France* (1974), are valuable surveys. Matei Călinescu, *Five Faces of Modernity: Modernism, Avant-Garde, Decadence, Kitsch, Postmodernism* (1987), is a subtly argued, informative collection of essays on the aesthetics of five modern movements. Morton P. Levitt, *Modernist Survivors: The Contemporary Novel in England, the United States, France, and Latin America* (1987), illustrates the impact of literary modernism and the continuity of humanist values. James F. Knapp, *Literary Modernism and the Transformation of Work* (1988), examines work-related themes in English and American modernist literature, and modernism's contradictory attitudes toward a changing economic order. Harry R. Garvin, ed., *Romanticism, Modernism, Postmodernism* (1980), is a useful collection of essays that attempts to define changing views of the artistic imagination and its place in society.

Daniel R. Schwarz, *Reconfiguring Modernism: Explorations in the Relationships between Modern Art and Modern Literature* (1997), is a comparative study. Ihab Hassan and Sally Hassan, eds., *Innovation/Renovation: New Perspectives on the Humanities* (1983), explores change in contemporary Western culture. H. H. Arnason, *History of Modern Art: Painting, Sculpture, Architecture* (1977, illustrated), follows the evolution of the arts in the West from the nineteenth century to the 1960s. Peter Nicholls, *Modernisms* (1995), offers an informative and analytic overview of twentieth-century modernisms. Marjorie Perloff, *The Poetics of Indeterminacy: Rimbaud to Cage* (1981), has significance beyond its primary focus on contemporary English and American poetry stemming from the French tradition. See also Perloff, ed., *Postmodern Genres* (1989), for a collection of essays on postmodernism in art and literature. Susan Rubin Suleiman, *Subversive Intent: Gender, Politics, and the Avant-Garde* (1990), analyzes the cultural implications of avant-garde artistic practices. Jean-Michel Rabaté, *The Ghosts of Modernity* (1996), uses poststructural methods to reread the history of modernity; it includes references to Symbolist writers. Nancy K. Miller, ed., *The Poetics of Gender* (1986), presents essays on various aspects of feminist criticism. Elise Boulding, *The Underside of History: A View of Women through Time*, rev. ed. (1992), complements traditional histories by drawing attention to the position and contributions of women. *Freedom Dreams: The Black Radical Imagination*, by Robin Kelley (2002), includes a discussion of modern African-American arts and Surrealism.

Chinua Achebe

A recent and full biography is Ezenwa-Ohaeto, *Chinua Achebe: A Biography* (1997). C. L. Innes, *Chinua Achebe* (1990), is a comprehensive study of Achebe's work through 1988 that emphasizes his literary techniques and Africanization of the novel. Simon Gikandi, *Reading Chinua Achebe: Language and Ideology in Fiction* (1991), is also recommended. Robert M. Wren, *Achebe's World: The Historical and Cultural Context of the Novels of Chinua Achebe* (1980), provides historical background and cultural context for Achebe's novels and includes glossary and bibliography. Studies of *Things Fall Apart* include Kate Turkington, *Chinua Achebe: Things Fall Apart* (1977), a concise introductory study; and the nine essays in Solomon Ogbede Iyasere, ed., *Understanding Things Fall Apart: Selected Essays and Criticism* (1998). C. L. Innes and Bernth Lindfors, eds., *Critical Perspectives on Chinua Achebe* (1978), collect twenty-one essays on Achebe's work (almost exclusively the novels) through 1973. G. D. Killam, *The Writings of Chinua Achebe*, rev. ed. (1977), is a commentary on Achebe's work through the mid-1970s, concentrating on the first four novels. Also of interest is *Conversations with Chinua Achebe* (1977), ed. Bernth Lindfors. Further information may be found in Ezenwa-Ohaeto, *Chinua Achebe: A Biography* (1997); *Conversations with Chinua Achebe*, ed. Bernth Lindfors (1997); and Robert M. Wren, *Achebe's World: The Historical and Cultural Context of the Novels of Chinua Achebe* (1980).

Anna Akhmatova

Sam N. Driver, *Anna Akhmatova* (1972), is an excellent introduction to Akhmatova's work and its historical context that stresses the years up to 1922, and Roberta Reeder, *Anna Akhmatova: Poet and Prophet* (1995), is a good recent biography. David Wells, *Anna Akhmatova: Her Poetry* (1996), is a readable, well-documented study that discusses works in chronological order. Amanda Haight, *Anna Akhmatova: A Poetic Pilgrimage* (1976, 1990), and Susan Amert, *In a Shattered Mirror: The Later Poetry of Anna Akhmatova* (1992), are perceptive book-length studies. Ronald Hingley, *Nightin-*

gale Fever: Russian Poets in Revolution (1981), discusses Akhmatova, Pasternak, Tsvetaeva, and Mandelstam in the context of Russian literary history and Soviet politics up to the early years of World War II. Wendy Rosslyn, ed., *The Speech of Unknown Eyes: Akhmatova's Readers on Her Poetry* (1990), collects a range of different responses. Sharon Leiter, *Akhmatova's Petersburg* (1983), examines the image of St. Petersburg as a focus for spiritual and historical themes in Akhmatova's poetry. Anna Akhmatova, *My Half Century: Selected Prose* (1992), ed. Ronald Meyer, includes autobiographical material, correspondence, short pieces on other writers, and an essay on Akhmatova's prose.

Jorge Luis Borges

Useful biographies are James Woodall, *The Man in the Mirror of the Book: A Life of Jorge Luis Borges* (1996), and his *Borges: A Life* (1996). Martin S. Stabb, *Borges Revisited* (1991), is a general introduction to the man and his work. Jaime Alazraki, ed., *Critical Essays on Jorge Luis Borges* (1987), assembles articles and reviews (including the 1970 *Autobiographical Essay*), four comparative essays, and a general introduction that offer valuable perspectives on Borges's writing as well as his impact on American writers and critics. Linda S. Maier, *Borges and the European Avant-garde* (1996), focuses on the European scene. Edna Aizenberg, ed., *Borges and His Successors: The Borgesian Impact on Literature and the Arts* (1990), is a wide-ranging collection of essays describing Borges as the precursor of postmodern fiction and criticism. Ana María Barrenechea, *Borges, the Labyrinth Maker* (1965), trans. Robert Lima, discusses Borges's intricate style, while Daniel Balderston, *Out of Context: Historical Reference and the Representation of Reality in Borges* (1993), focuses on the texts' manipulation of fictional and historical reality. Fernando Sorrentino, *Seven Conversations with Jorge Luis Borges* (1982), trans. Clark M. Zlotchew, is a series of informal, widely ranging interviews from 1972 with a prefaced list of the topics of each conversation. José Eduardo González, *Borges and the Politics of Form* (1998), examines the way Borges's style represents the aesthetic and political views of different cultural periods.

Tadeusz Borowski

Brief discussions of Borowski are found in Czesław Miłosz, *The History of Polish Literature* (1969); and from a different perspective, Sidra DeKoven Ezrahi, *By Words Alone: The Holocaust in Literature* (1980). Jan Kott, "Introduction" to *This Way for the Gas, Ladies and Gentlemen* (1967), and Jan Walc, "When the Earth Is No Longer a Dream and Cannot Be Dreamed through to the End," *Polish Review* (1987), combine biography and literary analysis. Selections from the poetry are available in *Selected Poems: Tadeusz Borowski* (1990), trans. Tadeusz Pióro with Larry Rafferty and Meryl Natchez, and "Five Poems by Tadeusz Borowski," trans. Addison Bross, *Polish Review* (1983). Also pertinent are the *Historical Atlas of the Holocaust* (1996) and psychiatrist Bruno Bettelheim's analysis of different responses to genocide in *Surviving the Holocaust* (1986).

Albert Camus

Germaine Brée, *Camus*, rev. ed. (1972), is an excellent general study; see also by Brée *Camus: A Collection of Critical Essays* (1962). Phillip Rhein, *Albert Camus*, rev. ed. (1989), is a brief introduction and biography. Herbert Lottman, *Albert Camus: A Biography* (1979; repr. 1997), and Olivier Todd, *Albert Camus: A Life*, trans. Benjamin Ivry (1997), are detailed biographies. English Showalter, *Exiles and Strangers: A Reading of Camus's Exile and the Kingdom* (1984), offers essays on the six stories of Camus's collection and separate comments on translations. Stephen E. Bronner, *Camus: Portrait of a Moralist* (1999), relates art, philosophy, and French and Algerian politics in a brief biographical study.

Joseph Conrad

Among the many sources of biographical information are Conrad's *The Mirror of the Sea* (1906) and *A Personal Record* (1912), and Jocelyn Baines, *Joseph Conrad: A Critical Biography* (1960). Albert J. Guérard's critical study *Conrad the Novelist* (1958) is also recommended, and Ian Watt, *Conrad in the Nineteenth Century* (1979), contains an interesting discussion of Impressionist techniques in Conrad. Chinua Achebe's essay "An Image of Africa: Racism in Conrad's *Heart of Darkness*" is published in his *Hopes and Impediments: Selected Essay, 1965–1987* (1988). Recent works focusing on *Heart of Darkness* include Peter Edgerly Firchow, *Envisioning Africa: Racism and Imperialism in Conrad's "Heart of Darkness"* (2000), and *Conrad in Africa: New Essays on "Heart of Darkness"* (2002), ed. Attie de Lange and Gail Fincham, with Wiesław Krajka (2002). Adam Hochschild, *King Leopold's Ghost: A Story of Greed, Terror, and Heroism in Colonial Africa* (1998), is a detailed and informative study of the Congo setting of Conrad's novella.

T. S. Eliot

Bernard Bergonzi, *T. S. Eliot*, 2nd ed. (1978), and Tony Sharpe, *T. S. Eliot: A Literary Life* (1991), are brief and readable introductions to the life and works. Martin Scofield, *T. S. Eliot: The Poems* (1988), offers a concise, balanced discussion of the evolution of Eliot's poetry. *The Waste Land* is discussed in Jay Martin, ed., *A Collection of Critical Essays on The Waste Land*

(1968); Lois A. Cuddy and David H. Hirsch, eds., *Critical Essays on T. S. Eliot's The Waste Land* (1991); and as part of John T. Mayer, *T. S. Eliot's Silent Voices* (1989), which analyzes themes of awareness and self-consciousness in the early poetry. *Little Gidding* is examined in Steve Ellis, *The English Eliot: Design, Language, and Landscape in Four Quartets* (1991), and Edward Lobb, ed., *Words in Time: New Essays on Eliot's Four Quartets* (1993). John Paul Riquelme, *Harmony of Dissonances: T. S. Eliot, Romanticism, and Imagination* (1991), links Eliot's response to Romanticism with postmodern views. Useful general collections are Linda W. Wagner, ed., *T. S. Eliot: A Collection of Criticism* (1974), and Ronald Bush, ed., *T. S. Eliot: The Modernist in History* (1991).

Franz Kafka
Anthony Thorlby, *Kafka: A Study* (1972), is a brief general introduction. Heinz Politzer, *Franz Kafka: Parable and Paradox* (1966), presents an interesting, readable study of symbolic relationships. Ernst Pawel, *The Nightmare of Reason: A Life of Franz Kafka* (1984), is an excellent contemporary biography with penetrating descriptions of his family and friends. Max Brod, *Franz Kafka: A Biography* (1960), is an early, admiring biography by a close friend and Kafka's executor. Ronald Gray, ed., *Kafka: A Collection of Critical Essays* (1962), is a useful early collection of essays on different works. Harold Bloom, ed., *Franz Kafka's The Metamorphosis* (1988), collects essays on spiritual, metaphorical, formal, social, and psychoanalytic aspects of *The Metamorphosis*. Jack Murray analyzes the sense of space in *The Landscapes of Alienation: Ideological Subversion in Kafka, Céline, and Onetti* (1991). Kurt Fickert, *End of a Mission: Kafka's Search for Truth in His Last Stories* (1993), interprets the stories as metaphors for an autobiographical quest to resolve personal problems. Walter H. Sokel, *The Myth of Power and the Self: Essays on Franz Kafka* (2002), collects penetrating essays written over four decades by a leading Kafka scholar.

Federico García Lorca
Ian Gibson, *Federico García Lorca: A Life* (1989), is an extensive and detailed biography. Carl W. Cobb, *Federico García Lorca* (1967), is a good general biography. Candelas Newton, *Understanding Federico García Lorca* (1995), is a brief general discussion of the work; Edwin Honig, *García Lorca* (1981), provides a critical introduction in literary historical context; and C. Brian Morris, *Son of Andalusia: The Lyrical Landscapes of Federico García Lorca* (1997), offers a more specialized view, with illustrations. Manuel Durán, ed., *Lorca: A Collection of Critical Essays* (1962), is a valuable collection of essays on the poet and his work (mainly

the poetry). Manuel Durán and Francesca Colecchia, eds., *Lorca's Legacy: Essays on Lorca's Life, Poetry, and Theatre* (1991), offer a range of essays and a recent bibliography.

Lu Xun
Leo Ou-fan Lee, *Voices from the Iron House: A Study of Lu Xun* (1987), is an excellent introduction to Lu Xun's work, placing it in the context of his life and Chinese cultural history, and Lee, *Lu Xun and His Legacy* (1985), is a collection of scholarly articles treating Lu's literary work, his politics, and his influence. William A. Lyell, *Lu Hsün's Vision of Reality* (1976), is also useful.

Gabriel García Márquez
Gabriel García Márquez, *Living to Tell the Tale*, trans. Edith Grossman (2003), is the first volume of a projected three-volume autobiography. Regina Janes, *Gabriel García Márquez: Revolutions in Wonderland* (1981), is an excellent general study on García Márquez in a Latin American context. Other useful introductions to the writer and his work are George R. McMurray, *Gabriel García Márquez* (1977), and Robin W. Fiddian, ed., *García Márquez* (1995). The summer 1972 issue of *Books Abroad* is dedicated to García Márquez. Harley D. Oberhelman, ed., *Gabriel García Márquez: A Study of the Short Fiction* (1991), includes a bibliography.

Mahasweta Devi
In addition to her excellent translations of *Breast-Giver* and *Draupadi*, Gayatri Chakravorty Spivak, *In Other Worlds: Essays in Cultural Politics* (1988), offers an analysis of Mahasweta Devi's stories from theoretical perspectives in gender and Third World studies. Compare Spivak's translation with that of Ella Dutta, *The Wet Nurse*, in Kali for Women, ed., *Truth Tales: Contemporary Stories Written by Women Writers of India* (1986). Several of Mahasweta's stories can be found in Kalpana Bardhan, *Of Women, Outcastes, Peasants, and Rebels* (1990), an anthology of translations of short fiction by the major modern Bengali writers on the themes of oppression and resistance, with reference to issues of gender and class.

Naguib Mahfouz
Roger M. A. Allen, *The Arabic Novel: An Historical and Critical Introduction* (1982), is an authoritative introduction that situates Mahfouz in the context of modern Arabic literature and includes a bibliography of works in Arabic and Western languages. The author's own perspective is given in Najib Mahfuz, *Echoes of an Autobiography* (1997), trans. Denys Johnson-Davies. Sasson Somekh, *"Za'balawi"—Author, Theme and Technique"* in *Journal of Arabic Literature* (1970), examines the story as a "double-layered" structure governed by references to Sufi mysti-

cism. Michael Beard and Adnan Haydar, eds., *Naguib Mahfouz: From Regional Fame to Global Recognition* (1993), assembles eleven original essays on themes, individual works, and cultural contexts in Mahfouz's work. Trevor le Gassick, ed., *Critical Perspectives on Naguib Mahfouz* (1991), reprints articles on Mahfouz's work up to the 1970s. Rasheed El-Enany, ed., *Naguib Mahfouz: The Pursuit of Meaning* (1993), is an excellent study that includes biography, analyses of novels, short stories, and plays and a guide for further reading. Comparative studies include Mona Mikhail, *Studies in the Short Fiction of Mahfouz and Idris* (1992), an introductory work juxtaposing themes in Hemingway, Idris, Mahfouz, and Camus; and Samia Mehrez, *Egyptian Writers Between History and Fiction: Essays on Naguib Mahfouz, Sonallah Ibrahim, and Gamal al-Ghitani* (1994). Rasheed El-Enany discusses the place of religion in Mahfouz's work in "The Dichotomy of Islam and Modernity in the Fiction of Naguib Mahfouz," in John C. Hawley, ed., *The Postcolonial Crescent: Islam's Impact on Contemporary Literature* (1998).

Luigi Pirandello
A good biography and general introduction is found in Susan Bassnett-McGuire, *Pirandello* (1983). Useful introductions are Fiora A. Bassanese, *Understanding Luigi Pirandello* (1997), and Walter Starkie, *Luigi Pirandello, 1867–1936*, 3rd ed. (1965). Glauco Cambon, comp., *Pirandello: A Collection of Critical Essays* (1967), emphasizes the plays. A. Richard Sogliuzzo, *Luigi Pirandello, Director: The Playwright in the Theatre* (1982), deals with Pirandello's dramatic theories and practices; it contains a discussion of *Six Characters*. John Louis DiGaetani, ed., *A Companion to Pirandello Studies* (1991), is an excellent collection of twenty-seven essays and four appendices on diverse aspects of Pirandello's thought and work; many essays take up *Six Characters*. Luigi Pirandello, *Pirandello's Love Letters to Marta Abba*, ed. and trans. Benito Ortonolani (1994), illuminates the author's personal life in 1925–36 and his plans to reform the Italian theater.

Rainer Maria Rilke
J. F. Hendry, *The Sacred Threshold: A Life of Rainer Maria Rilke* (1983), is a brief and readable biography with numerous citations from Rilke's letters and work. Heinz F. Peters, *Rainer Maria Rilke: Masks and the Man* (1977), is a biographical and thematic study of Rilke's work and influence. Romano Guardini examines the elegies in *Rilke's Duino Elegies: An Interpretation* (1961). Donald Prater, *A Ringing Glass: The Life of Rainer Maria Rilke* (1993), is an excellent account of the poet's life and the conditions in which his work developed; it includes extensive quotations from many unpublished

letters. *Rainer Maria Rilke: Aspects of His Mind and Poetry*, ed. William Rose and G. Craig Houston (1973), contains an excellent essay by C. M. Bowra on the *New Poems*. William H. Gass, *Reading Rilke: Reflections on the Problems of Translation* (1999), combines biography, philosophy, and reflections on specific translation problems in the *Duino Elegies*.

Nawal El Saadawi
Several articles in journals and collective volumes offer views and assessments of aspects of Nawal El Saadawi's work, but Fedwa Malti-Douglas, *Men, Women and God(s): Nawal El Saadawi and Arab Feminist Poetics* (1995), is the only study so far devoted to a systematic account and critical interpretation of the entire corpus in the light of its social and cultural background.

Leslie Marmon Silko
Gregory Salyer, *Leslie Marmon Silko* (1997), is a brief introduction to the author and her work; Helen Jaskoski, *Leslie Marmon Silko: A Study of the Short Fiction* (1998), focuses on the stories. Leslie Silko, *Sacred Water: Narratives and Pictures* (1993), is an autobiographical narrative. Melody Graulich, ed., *"Yellow Woman": Leslie Marmon Silko* (1993), is a collection of pertinent critical essays. The story itself is profitably read, or reread, in Silko's *Storyteller* (1981), where it appears in context with several of her other short pieces on the Yellow Woman theme. For traditional texts on Yellow Woman and other figures in Laguna mythology, the best source is Franz Boas, *Keresan Texts* (1928); the stories in Boas's volume were obtained in 1919–21 from several Laguna informants, including Leslie Silko's great-grandfather, Robert Marmon.

Rabindranath Tagore
Two histories of Bengali literature, Dushan Zbavitel, *Bengali Literature* (1976), and Asit Kumar Bandhyopadhyay, *Modern Bengali Literature* (1986), provide information about the context of Tagore's achievement. Humayun Kabir, *The Bengali Novel* (1968), discusses Tagore with reference to the development of the Bengali novel. William Radice, *Rabindranath Tagore: Selected Short Stories* (1991), offers faithful, readable translations of thirty of Tagore's early short stories, including some of his best known ones. For a comparison of Tagore's short stories with those of later Bengali writers on the themes of oppression and resistance, see Kalpana Bardhan, ed. and trans., *Of Women, Outcastes, Peasants, and Rebels* (1990). Krishna Kripalani, *Rabindranath Tagore* (1962), is the authoritative Tagore biography, and Amiya Chakravarty, ed., *A Tagore Reader* (1961), remains the best introduction to the full range of Tagore's writing.

Virginia Woolf
Phyllis Rose, *Woman of Letters: A Life of Virginia Woolf* (1978), is a valuable biography; Edward Bishop, *Virginia Woolf* (1991), is a recent brief introduction. Two valuable collections of essays on Woolf's writing and her position in the modernist/postmodernist tradition are Patricia Clements and Isobel Grundy, eds., *Virginia Woolf: New Critical Essays* (1983), and Margaret Homans, ed., *Virginia Woolf: A Collection of Critical Essays* (1993). Jane Marcus, *Virginia Woolf and the Languages of Patriarchy* (1987), and Rachel Bowlby, *Feminist Destinations and Further Essays on Virginia Woolf* (1997), offer perceptive feminist analyses that include discussion of *A Room of One's Own*. Mark Hussey and Vara Neverow, eds., *Virginia Woolf: Emerging Perspectives* (1994), contains several essays on *A Room of One's Own*. S. P. Rosenbaum, ed., *Women and Fiction: The Manuscript Versions of "A Room of One's Own"* (1992), transcribes and edits two draft manuscripts that are the basis for *A Room of One's Own*. Gillian Beer, *Virginia Woolf: The Common Ground* (1996), offers four useful general essays and four discussions of specific novels. Patricia Ondek Laurence situates Woolf in *The Reading of Silence: Virginia Woolf in the English Tradition* (1991); comparative studies include Richard Pearce, *The Politics of Narration: James Joyce, William Faulkner, and Virginia Woolf* (1991).

William Butler Yeats
Edward Malins presents a brief introduction with biography, illustrations, and maps in *A Preface to Yeats*, 2nd ed. (1994). Richard Ellmann, *The Identity of Yeats*, 2nd ed. (1970), is an excellent discussion of Yeats's work as a whole. A. Norman Jeffares has revised his major study, *A New Commentary on the Poems of W. B. Yeats* (1984); a useful reference work is Lester I. Conner, *A Yeats Dictionary: Persons and Places in the Poetry of William Butler Yeats* (1998). Jeffares's *W. B. Yeats: A New Biography* (1989) takes into account new information about the poet. Elizabeth Cullingford, *Gender and History in Yeats's Love Poetry* (1993), examines aesthetic form and cultural perspectives in the love lyrics; Deirdre Toomey, *Yeats and Women*, 2nd ed. (1997), discusses Yeats's relations with women and the women in his poetry; and Marjorie Elizabeth Howes, *Yeats's Nations: Gender, Class, and Irishness* (1996), stresses political and social views. Essay collections include Harold Bloom, ed., *William Butler Yeats* (1986), and Richard J. Finneran, ed., *Critical Essays on W. B. Yeats* (1986). Essays in Deborah Fleming, ed., *Learning the Trade: Essays on W. B. Yeats and Contemporary Poetry* (1993), discuss Yeats's imprint on various contemporary poets; and contributions to Leonard Orr, ed., *Yeats and Postmodernism* (1991), approach Yeats from different postmodernist perspectives.

A Note on Translation

Reading literature in translation is a pleasure on which it is fruitless to frown. The purist may insist that we ought always read in the original languages, and we know ideally that this is true. But it is a counsel of perfection, quite impractical even for the purist, because no one in a lifetime can master all the languages whose literatures it would be a joy to explore. Master languages as fast as we may, we shall always have to read to some extent in translation, and this means we must be alert to what we are about: if in reading a work of literature in translation we are not reading the "original," what precisely are we reading? This is a question of great complexity, to which justice cannot be done in a brief note, but the following sketch of some of the considerations may be helpful.

One of the memorable scenes of ancient literature is the meeting of Hector and Andromache in book VI of Homer's *Iliad*. Hector, leader and mainstay of the armies defending Troy, is implored by his wife, Andromache, to withdraw within the city walls and carry on the defense from there, where his life will not be constantly at hazard. In Homer's text her opening words to him are these: δαιμόνιε δθίσει σε τό σόν μένος (*daimonie, phthisei se to son menos*). How should they be translated into English?

Here is how they have actually been translated into English by capable translators, at various periods, in verse and prose:

1. George Chapman, 1598:

> O noblest in desire,
> Thy mind, inflamed with others' good, will set thy self on fire.

2. John Dryden, 1693:

> Thy dauntless heart (which I foresee too late),
> Too daring man, will urge thee to thy fate.

3. Alexander Pope, 1715:

> Too daring Prince! . . .
> For sure such courage length of life denies,
> And thou must fall, thy virtue's sacrifice.

4. William Cowper, 1791:

> Thy own great courage will cut short thy days,
> My noble Hector . . .

5. Lang, Leaf, and Myers, 1883 (prose):

Dear my lord, this thy hardihood will undo thee. . . .

6. A. T. Murray, 1924 (prose):

Ah, my husband, this prowess of thine will be thy doom. . . .

7. E. V. Rieu, 1950 (prose):

"Hector," she said, "you are possessed. This bravery of yours will be your end."

8. I. A. Richards, 1950 (prose):

"Strange man," she said, "your courage will be your destruction."

9. Richmond Lattimore, 1951:

Dearest,
Your own great strength will be your death. . . .

10. Robert Fitzgerald, 1979:

O my wild one, your bravery will be
Your own undoing!

11. Robert Fagles, 1990:

reckless one,
Your own fiery courage will destroy you!

From these strikingly different renderings of the same six words, certain facts about the nature of translation begin to emerge. We notice, for one thing, that Homer's word μένος (*menos*) is diversified by the translators into "mind," "dauntless heart," "such courage," "great courage," "hardihood," "prowess," "bravery," "courage," "great strength," "bravery," and "fiery courage." The word has in fact all these possibilities. Used of things, it normally means "force"; of animals, "fierceness" or "brute strength" or (in the case of horses) "mettle"; of men and women, "passion" or "spirit" or even "purpose." Homer's application of it in the present case points our attention equally—whatever particular sense we may imagine Andromache to have uppermost—to Hector's force, strength, fierceness in battle, spirited heart and mind. But because English has no matching term of like inclusiveness, the passage as the translators give it to us reflects this lack and we find one attribute singled out to the exclusion of the rest.

Here then is the first and most crucial fact about any work of literature read in translation. It cannot escape the linguistic characteristics of the language into which it is turned: the grammatical, syntactical, lexical, and phonetic boundaries that constitute collectively the individuality or "genius" of that language. A Greek play or a Russian novel in English will be governed first of all by the resources of the English language, resources that are certain to be in every instance very different, as the efforts with μένος show, from those of the original.

Turning from μένος to δαιμόνιε (*daimonie*) in Homer's clause, we encounter a second crucial fact about translations. Nobody knows exactly what shade of meaning δαιμονιε had for Homer. In later writers the word normally suggests divinity, something miraculous, wondrous; but in Homer it appears as a vocative of address for both chieftain and commoner, man and wife. The coloring one gives it must, therefore, be determined either by the way one thinks a Greek wife of Homer's era might actually address her husband (a subject on which we have no information whatever) or in the way one thinks it suitable for a hero's wife to address her husband in an epic poem, that is to say, a highly stylized and formal work. In general, the translators of our century have abandoned formality to stress the intimacy; the wifeliness; and, especially in Lattimore's case, a certain chiding tenderness, in Andromache's appeal: (6) "Ah, my husband," (7) "Hector" (with perhaps a hint, in "you are possessed," of the alarmed distaste with which wives have so often viewed their husbands' bellicose moods), (8) "Strange man," (9) "Dearest," (10) "O my wild one" (mixing an almost motherly admiration with reproach and concern), and (11) "reckless one." On the other hand, the older translators have obviously removed Andromache to an epic or heroic distance from her beloved, whence she sees and kindles to his selfless courage, acknowledging, even in the moment of pleading with him to be otherwise, his moral grandeur and the tragic destiny this too certainly implies: (1) "O noblest in desire, . . . inflamed by others' good"; (2) "Thy dauntless heart (which I foresee too late), / Too daring man"; (3) "Too daring Prince! . . . / And thou must fall, thy virtue's sacrifice"; (4) "My noble Hector." Even the less specific "Dear my lord" of Lang, Leaf, and Myers looks in the same direction because of its echo of the speech of countless Shakespearean men and women who have shared this powerful moral sense: "Dear my lord, make me acquainted with your cause of grief"; "Perseverance, dear my lord, keeps honor bright"; etc.

The fact about translation that emerges from all this is that just as the translated work reflects the individuality of the language it is turned into, so it reflects the individuality of the age in which it is made, and the age will permeate it everywhere like yeast in dough. We think of one kind of permeation when we think of the governing verse forms and attitudes toward verse at a given epoch. In Chapman's time, experiments seeking an "heroic" verse form for English were widespread, and accordingly he tries a "fourteener" couplet (two rhymed lines of seven stresses each) in his *Iliad* and a pentameter couplet in his *Odyssey*. When Dryden and Pope wrote, a closed pentameter couplet had become established as the heroic form par excellence. By Cowper's day, thanks largely to the prestige of *Paradise Lost*, the couplet had gone out of fashion for narrative poetry in favor of blank verse. Our age, inclining to prose and in verse to proselike informalities and relaxations, has, predictably, produced half a dozen excellent prose translations of the *Iliad* but only three in verse (by Fagles, Lattimore, and Fitzgerald), all relying on rhythms that are much of the time closer to the verse of William Carlos Williams and some of the prose of novelists like Faulkner than to the swift firm tread of Homer's Greek. For if it is true that what we translate from a given work is what, wearing the spectacles of our time, we see in it, it is also true that we see in it what we have the power to translate.

Of course, there are other effects of the translator's epoch on a translation besides those exercised by contemporary taste in verse and verse forms. Chapman writes in a great age of poetic metaphor and, therefore, almost instinctively translates his understanding of Homer's verb φθίσει (*phthisei*, "to cause to wane, consume, waste, pine") into metaphorical terms of flame, presenting his Hector to us as a man of burning generosity who will be consumed by his very ardor. This is a conception rooted in large part in the psychology of the Elizabethans, who had the habit of speaking of the soul as "fire," of one of the four temperaments as "fiery," of even the more material bodily processes, like digestion, as if they were carried on by the heat of fire ("concoction," "decoction"). It is rooted too in that characteristic Renaissance élan so unforgettably expressed in characters such as Tamburlaine and Dr. Faustus, the former of whom exclaims to the stars above:

> . . . I, the chiefest lamp of all the earth,
> First rising in the East with mild aspect,
> But fixèd now in the meridian line,
> Will send up fire to your turning spheres,
> And cause the sun to borrow light of you. . . .

Pope and Dryden, by contrast, write to audiences for whom strong metaphor has become suspect. They, therefore, reject the fire image (which we must recall is not present in the Greek) in favor of a form of speech more congenial to their age, the *sententia* or aphorism, and give it extra vitality by making it the scene of a miniature drama: in Dryden's case, the hero's dauntless heart "urges" him (in the double sense of physical as well as moral pressure) to his fate; in Pope's, the hero's courage, like a judge, "denies" continuance of life, with the consequence that he "falls"—and here Pope's second line suggests analogy to the sacrificial animal—the victim of his own essential nature, of what he is.

To pose even more graphically the pressures that a translator's period brings, consider the following lines from Hector's reply to Andromache's appeal that he withdraw, first in Chapman's Elizabethan version, then in Lattimore's twentieth-century one:

Chapman, 1598:

> The spirit I did first breathe
> Did never teach me that—much less since the contempt of death
> Was settled in me, and my mind knew what a Worthy was,
> Whose office is to lead in fight and give no danger pass
> Without improvement. In this fire must Hector's trial shine.
> Here must his country, father, friends be in him made divine.

Lattimore, 1951:

> and the spirit will not let me, since I have learned to be valiant
> and to fight always among the foremost ranks of the Trojans,
> winning for my own self great glory, and for my father.

If one may exaggerate to make a necessary point, the world of Henry V and Othello suddenly gives way here to our own, a world whose discomfort with any form of heroic self-assertion is remarkably mirrored in the burial of Homer's key terms (*spirit, valiant, fight, foremost, glory*)—five out of twenty-two words in the original, five out of thirty-six in the translation—in a cushioning huddle of harmless sounds.

Besides the two factors so far mentioned (language and period) as affecting the character of a translation, there is inevitably a third—the translator, with a particular degree of talent; a personal way of regarding the work to be translated; a special hierarchy of values, moral, aesthetic, metaphysical (which may or may not be summed up in a "worldview"); and a unique style or lack of it. But this influence all readers are likely to bear in mind, and it needs no laboring here. That, for example, two translators of Hamlet, one a Freudian, the other a Jungian, will produce impressively different translations is obvious from the fact that when Freudian and Jungian argue about the play in English they often seem to have different plays in mind.

We can now return to the question from which we started. After all allowances have been made for language, age, and individual translator, is anything of the original left? What, in short, does the reader of translations read? Let it be said at once that in utility prose—prose whose function is mainly referential—the reader who reads a translation reads everything that matters. "*Nicht Rauchen*," "*Défense de Fumer*," and "No Smoking," posted in a railway car, make their point, and the differences between them in sound and form have no significance for us in that context. Since the prose of a treatise and of most fiction is preponderantly referential, we rightly feel, when we have paid close attention to Cervantes or Montaigne or Machiavelli or Tolstoy in a good English translation, that we have had roughly the same experience as a native Spaniard, Frenchman, Italian, or Russian. But *roughly* is the correct word; for good prose points iconically *to* itself as well as referentially beyond itself, and everything that it points to in itself in the original (rhythms, sounds, idioms, wordplay, etc.) must alter radically in being translated. The best analogy is to imagine a van Gogh painting reproduced in the medium of tempera, etching, or engraving: the "picture" remains, but the intricate interanimation of volumes with colorings with brushstrokes has disappeared.

When we move on to poetry, even in its longer narrative and dramatic forms— plays like *Oedipus*, poems like the *Iliad* or *The Divine Comedy*—our situation as English readers worsens appreciably, as the many unlike versions of Andromache's appeal to Hector make very clear. But, again, only appreciably. True, this is the point at which the fact that a translation is *always* an interpretation explodes irresistibly on our attention; but if it is the best translation of its time, like Robert Fagles's translation of the *Odyssey* for our time, the result will be not only a sensitive interpretation but also a work with intrinsic interest in its own right—at very best, a true work of art, a new poem. In these longer works, moreover, even if the translation is uninspired, many distinctive structural features—plot, setting, characters, meetings, partings, confrontations, and specific episodes generally—survive virtually unchanged. It is only when the shorter, primarily lyrical forms of poetry are presented that the reader of translations faces insuperable disadvantage. In these forms, the referential aspect of language has a tendency to disappear into, or, more often, draw its real meaning and accreditation from, the iconic aspect. Let us look for just a moment at a brief poem by Federico García Lorca and its English translation (by Stephen Spender and J. L. Gili):

> ¡Alto pinar!
> Cuatro palomas por el aire van.
>
> Cuatro palomas
> vuelan y tornan.
> Llevan heridas
> sus cuatro sombras.
>
> ¡Bajo pinar!
> Cuatro palomas en la tierra están.

> the pine trees:
> Four pigeons go through the air.
>
> Four pigeons
> fly and turn round.
> They carry wounded
> their four shadows.
>
> Below the pine trees:
> Four pigeons lie on the earth.

In this translation the referential sense of the English words follows with remarkable exactness the referential sense of the Spanish words they replace. But the life of Lorca's poem does not lie in that sense. It lies in such matters as the abruptness, like an intake of breath at a sudden revelation, of the two exclamatory lines (1 and 7), which then exhale musically in images of flight and death; or as the echoings of *palomas* in *heridas* and *sombras*, bringing together (as in fact the hunter's gun has done) these unrelated nouns and the unrelated experiences they stand for in a sequence that seems, momentarily, to have all the logic of a tragic action, in which *doves* become *wounds* become *shadows*, or as the external and internal rhyming among the five verbs, as though all motion must (as in fact it must) end with *están*.

Because none of this can be brought over into another tongue (least of all Lorca's rhythms), the translator must decide between leaving a reader to wonder why Lorca is a poet to be bothered about at all and making a new but true poem, whose merit will almost certainly be in inverse ratio to its likeness to the original. Samuel Johnson made such a poem in translating Horace's famous *Diffugere nives*, and so did A. E. Housman. If we juxtapose the last two stanzas of each translation, and the corresponding Latin, we can see at a glance that each has the consistency and inner life of a genuine poem and that neither of them (even if we consider only what is obvious to the eye, the line-lengths) is very close to Horace:

> Cum semel occideris, et de te splendida Minos
>   fecerit arbitria,
> non, Torquate, genus, non te facundia, non te
>   restituet pietas.
> Infernis neque enim tenebris Diana pudicum
>   liberat Hippolytum

> *nec Lethaea valet Theseus abrumpere caro*
> *vincula Pirithoo.*

Johnson:

> Not you, Torquatus, boast of Rome,
> When Minos once has fixed your doom,
> Or eloquence, or splendid birth,
> Or virtue, shall restore to earth.
> Hippolytus, unjustly slain,
> Diana calls to life in vain;
> Nor can the might of Theseus rend
> The chains of hell that hold his friend.

Housman:

> When thou descendest once the shades among,
>   The stern assize and equal judgment o'er,
> Not thy long lineage nor thy golden tongue,
>   No, nor thy righteousness, shall friend thee more.
>
> Night holds Hippolytus the pure of stain,
>   Diana steads him nothing, he must stay;
> And Theseus leaves Pirithous in the chain
>   The love of comrades cannot take away.

The truth of the matter is that when the translator of short poems chooses to be literal, most or all of the poetry is lost; and when the translator succeeds in forging a new poetry, most or all of the original author is lost.

The best practical advice for those of us who must read poems in English translations is to focus intently on the images and dramatic scenes these poems evoke and ask ourselves what there is in them or in their effect on each other that produces each poem's particular electricity. To that extent, we can compensate for a part of our losses, learn something positive about the immense explosive powers of imagery, and rest easy in the secure knowledge that translation even in the mode of the short poem brings us (despite losses) closer to the work itself than not reading it at all. "To a thousand cavils," said Samuel Johnson, "one answer is sufficient; the purpose of a writer is to be read, and the criticism which would destroy the power of pleasing must be blown aside." Johnson was defending Pope's Homer for those marks of its own time and place that make it the great interpretation it is, but Johnson's exhilarating common sense applies equally to the problem we are considering here. Literature is to be read, and the criticism that would destroy the reader's power to make some form of contact with much of the world's great writing must indeed be blown aside.

MAYNARD MACK

Nawal El Saadawi: "In Camera" from DEATH OF AN EX-MINISTER by Nawal El Saadawi, trans. by Shirley Eber, published by Methuen. Copyright © 1987. Reprinted by permission of the author.

Gustave Flaubert: "A Simple Heart," from THREE TALES by Gustave Flaubert, trans. by Arthur McDowall, translation copyright 1924 by Alfred A. Knopf, a division of Random House, Inc. Used by permission of Alfred A. Knopf, a division of Random House, Inc.

Florentine Codex: "The Midwife Addresses the Woman Who Has Died in Childbirth" translated by John Bierhorst. Translation copyright © 1994 by John Bierhorst. Reprinted by permission of the translator. "The Midwife Addresses the Newly Delivered Woman" from A SCATTERING OF JADES, trans. by Thelma Sullivan. Copyright © 1994 by Rita Wilensky. Reprinted by permission of The Balkin Agency.

Federico García Lorca: *"Liento por Ignacio Sanchez Mejias*/Lament for Ignacio Sanchez Mejias" by Federico García Lorca © Herederos de Federico García Lorca. OBRAS COMPLETAS (Galaxia/Gutenberg, 1996 edition). English-language translation by Stephen Spender and J. L. Gili © Herederos de Federico García Lorca and Stephen Spender and J. L. Gili. All rights reserved. For information regarding rights and permission, please contact lorca@artslaw.co.uk or William Peter Kosmas, Esq., 6 Franklin Square, London W14 9UU.

Gabriel García Marquez: Entire story "Death Constant Beyond Love" from INNOCENT ERENDIRA AND OTHER STORIES by Gabriel García Marquez, translated from the Spanish by Gregory Rabassa. English translation copyright © 1978 by Harper & Row, Publishers, Inc. Reprinted by permission of HarperCollins Publishers.

Johann Wolfgang von Goethe: From FAUST: Part One, trans. by Martin Greenberg. Copyright © 1992 by Martin Greenberg. Used by permission of Yale University Press.

Heinrich Heine: From THE COMPLETE POEMS OF HEINRICH HEINE, trans. by Hal Draper, reprinted by permission of the Center for Socialist History, Alameda, CA.

Friedrich Hölderlin: From FRIEDRICH HÖLDERLIN/EDUARD MORIKE: SELECTED POEMS, trans. by Christopher Middleton. Copyright © 1972 by University of Chicago. Reprinted by permission of the University of Chicago Press.

Victor Hugo: "Et nox facta est" trans. by Mary Ann Caws. Copyright © 1990 by Mary Ann Caws. Reprinted by permission of the translator.

Henrik Ibsen: *Hedda Gabler* from FOUR MAJOR PLAYS, Vol. 1, by Henrik Ibsen, trans. by Rick Davis and Brian Johnston. Copyright © 1995 by Rick Davis and Brian Johnston. By permission of Smith and Kraus Publishers, Inc.

Franz Kafka: *Metamorphosis* from METAMORPHOSIS AND OTHER STORIES by Franz Kafka, trans. by Michael Hofmann, copyright © 2007 by Michael Hofmann. Used by permission of Penguin, a division of Penguin Group (USA), Inc.

Giacomo Leopardi: From A LEOPARDI READER, trans. and ed. by Ottavio M. Casale. Reprinted by permission of Linda L. Casale.

Lu Xun: From DIARY OF A MADMAN AND OTHER STORIES, trans. by William A. Lyell. Copyright © by University of Hawaii Press. Reprinted by permission of University of Hawaii Press.

Mahasweta Devi: "Breast-Giver" from IN OTHER WORLDS: ESSAYS IN CULTURAL POLITICS by Mahasweta Devi, trans. by Gayatri Spivak. Reprinted by permission of Routledge, a member of the Taylor & Francis Group.

Naguib Mahfouz: "Zaabalawi" from MODERN ARABIC SHORT STORIES, trans. by Denys Johnson-Davies. Translation copyright © 1967 by Denys Johnson-Davies. Reprinted by permission of the translator.

Molière: TARTUFFE BY MOLIÉRE, English translation copyright © 1963, 1962, 1961 and renewed 1991, 1990, and 1989 by Richard Wilbur, reprinted by permission of Houghton Mifflin Harcourt Publishing Company. CAUTION: Professionals and amateurs are hereby warned that this translation, being fully protected under the copyright laws of the United States of America, the British Empire, including the Dominion of Canada, and all other countries which are signatories to the Universal Copyright Convention and the International Copyright Union, are subject to royalty. All rights, including professional, amateur, motion picture, recitation, lecturing, public reading, radio broadcasting, and television, are strictly reserved. Particular emphasis is laid on the question of readings, permission for which must be secured from the author's agent in writing. Inquiries on professional rights (except for amateur rights) should be addressed to Peter Franklin, William Morris Agency, 1325 Avenue of the Americas, New York, NY 10019; inquiries on translation rights should be addressed to Houghton Mifflin Harcourt Publishing Company, Permissions Department, Orlando, FL 32887. The stock and amateur acting rights of TARTUFFE are controlled exclusively by the Dramatists Play Service, Inc., 440 Park Avenue South, New York, NY. No amateur performance of the play may be given without obtaining in advance the written permission of the Dramatists Play Service, Inc., and paying the requisite fee.

Luigi Pirandello: SIX CHARACTERS IN SEARCH OF AN AUTHOR, trans. by John Linstrum. We have made diligent efforts to contact the copyright holder to obtain permission to reprint this selection. If you have information that would help us, please write to W. W. Norton & Company, Inc., 500 Fifth Ave., New York, NY 10110.

Popol Vuh: Reprinted with the permission of Simon & Schuster Adult Publishing Group from POPOL VUH by Dennis Tedlock. Copyright © 1985, 1996 by Dennis Tedlock.

Alexander Sergeyevich Pushkin: "The Queen of Spades" by Gillon R. Aitken, trans., from THE COMPLETE PROSE TALES OF ALEXANDR SERGEYEVITCH PUSHKIN. Copyright © 1966 by Barrie & Rockliff (Barrie Books Ltd.). Revised translation published by Random House Group Ltd. 2008. Used by permission of W. W. Norton & Company, Inc., and the translator.

Rainer Maria Rilke: "Archaic Torso of Apollo," trans. by Stephen Mitchell, copyright © 1982 by Stephen Mitchell; "The Panther," copyright © 1982 by Stephen Mitchell; "The Swan," trans. by Stephen Mitchell, copyright © 1982 by Stephen Mitchell; "Spanish Dancer," trans. by Stephen Mitchell, copyright © 1982 by Stephen Mitchell, from THE SELECTED POETRY OF RAINER MARIA RILKE, trans. by Stephen Mitchell. Used by permission of Random House, Inc.

Arthur Rimbaud: From ARTHUR RIMBAUD: COMPLETE WORKS, pp. 101-03, trans. from the French by Paul Schmidt. Copyright © 1967, 1970, 1971, 1972, 1975 by Paul Schmidt. Reprinted by permission of HarperCollins Publishers. From A SEASON IN HELL: THE ILLUMINATIONS (1973) by Rimbaud, ed. by Rhodes Peschell (trans.). By permission of Oxford University Press. "The Drunken Boat" trans. by Stephen Stepanchev is reprinted by permission of the translator.

Jean-Jacques Rousseau: From THE CONFESSIONS OF JEAN-JACQUES ROUSSEAU, trans. with an introduction by J. M. Cohen (Penguin Classics, 1953). Copyright © 1953 J. M. Cohen. Reproduced by permission of Penguin Books Ltd.

Leslie Marmon Silko: Reprinted by permission from STORYTELLER by Leslie Marmon Silko, published by Seaver Books, New York, NY. Copyright © 1981 by Leslie Marmon Silko.

Rabindranath Tagore: "Punishment" from RABINDRANATH TAGORE: SELECTED SHORT STORIES, trans. by William Radice. Copyright © 1991 by William Radice. Reprinted by permission of John Johnson Ltd.

François-Marie Arouet de Voltaire: From CANDIDE: A NORTON CRITICAL EDITION, Second Edition, trans. by Robert M. Adams. Copyright © 1991, 1966 by W. W. Norton & Company, Inc. Used by permission of W. W. Norton & Company, Inc.

Virginia Woolf: Excerpts from A ROOM OF ONE'S OWN by Virginia Woolf, copyright 1929 by Houghton Mifflin Harcourt Publishing Company and renewed 1957 by Leonard Woolf. Reprinted by permission of the publisher.

Wu Ch'eng-En: From MONKEY by Ch'eng-en Wu, trans. by Arthur Waley. Copyright 1943 by John Day Company, Inc. Copyright © renewed 1970 by Alison Waley. Used by permission of Grove/Atlantic, Inc, and © copyright by permission of The Arthur Waley Estate.

W. B. Yeats: Reprinted with the permission of Scribner, a division of Simon & Schuster Adult Publishing Group, from THE COMPLETE WORKS OF W. B. YEATS, Volume 1: THE POEMS, ed. by Richard J. Finneran. Copyright © 1940 by Georgie Yeats. Copyright renewed © 1968 by Bertha Georgie Yeats, Michael Butler Yeats, and Anne Yeats. All rights reserved.

COLOR PLATES

Adouma mask. Musée National d'Art Moderne, Centre Georges Pompidou, Paris. Photo: CNAC / MNAM / Dist. Réunion des Musées Nationaux / Art Resource, NY.

Anonymous. *The Fish Pond of the Commune.* Photo: Snark / Art Resource, NY.

Anonymous. *Industrialization along the Yang-Tse-Kiang River.* Photo: Snark / Art Resource, NY.

Giuseppe Castiglione. *Inauguration Portraits of Emperor Qianlong, the Empress and Eleven Imperial Consorts,* 1736. The Cleveland Museum of Art. Photo: The Cleveland Museum of Art.

Honoré Victorin Daumier. *Third-Class Carriage,* 1863–65. The Metropolitan Museum of Art, H. O. Havemeyer Collection, Bequest of Mrs. H. O. Havemeyer. Photo: Burstein Collection / Corbis.

Jacques Louis David. *The Oath at the Tennis Court at Versailles, 20 June 1789,* 1791–92. Chateaux de Versailles et de Trianon, Versailles, France. Photo: Erich Lessing / Art Resource, NY.

Thomas Eakins. *The Agnew Clinic,* 1889. University of Pennsylvania, Philadelphia, PA. Photo: Geoffrey

Engraving of the Great Fire of London, 1666. Photo: Historical Picture Archive / Corbis.

Paul Gauguin. *Tahitian Women on the Beach,* 1891. Musée d'Orsay, Paris. Photo: Erich Lessing / Art Resource, NY.

Hall of Supreme Harmony in the Forbidden City, Beijing, China. Photo: Brian A. Vikander / Corbis

Illustration of the Founding of Tenochtitlán by the Aztecs. Photo: Michael D. Coe

Frida Kahlo. *Self Portrait with Monkey,* 1940. Private collection. Reproduced by courtesy of the I.N.B.A. and Banco de Mexico Trust. Photo: Art Resource, NY.

Godfrey Kneller. *Portrait of Sir Isaac Newton.* Trinity College, Cambridge, Great Britain. Photo: Erich Lessing / Art Resource, NY.

Käthe Kollwitz. *Woman with Dead Child.* Kunsthalle, Bremen, Germany. © 2003 Artists Rights Society (ARS), New York / VG Bild-Kunst, Bonn. Photo: Erich Lessing / Art Resource, NY.

Index